VANITY FAIR

WILLIAM MAKEPEACE THACKERAY was born in 1811 in Calcutta. In 1817 he was sent to England to be educated as a gentleman. From Charterhouse school, he went to Cambridge in 1829. His career at university was undistinguished, and led into an unsettled young-manhood. After false starts in the law, in art (which he studied in Paris) and journalism he compounded his misfortunes with an imprudent marriage in 1835. Tragically, his wife went mad five years later, leaving Thackeray with two young daughters to provide for. His first successes in authorship came with publications (of a largely satirical nature) in *Fraser's Magazine* and *Punch*. Triumph came with the publication of *Vanity Fair* (1847–8). This serialized novel promoted Thackeray to the rank of Dickens's principal rival in fiction. It was followed by the more autobiographical *Pendennis* (1848–50) and the historical *Henry Esmond* (1852), works which consolidated Thackeray's reputation without equalling the runaway popularity of his first full-length novel. Thackeray's energies flagged somewhat in the second half of his writing life. He lectured in America in 1852 and 1855; stood unsuccessfully for parliament as an Independent Liberal in 1857. His stature as a leading man of letters was confirmed in 1859, when he took over the editorship of the new *Cornhill Magazine* (a post he held until 1862). Thackeray's last years were his most prosperous. But since 1850, his health had never been good, and his writing suffered correspondingly. He died suddenly in December 1863.

JOHN SUTHERLAND is Lord Northcliffe Professor of Modern English Literature at University College London, and is the author of a number of books, including *Thackeray at Work*, *Victorian Novelists and Publishers*, and *Mrs Humphry Ward*. He has also edited *Pendennis*, *The Woman in White*, Trollope's *Early Short Stories*, *Late Short Stories*, and *The Way We Live Now* and written *Can Jane Eyre Be Happy?* in Oxford World's Classics.

OXFORD WORLD'S CLASSICS

*For over 100 years Oxford World's Classics have brought
readers closer to the world's great literature. Now with over 700
titles—from the 4,000-year-old myths of Mesopotamia to the
twentieth century's greatest novels—the series makes available
lesser-known as well as celebrated writing.*

*The pocket-sized hardbacks of the early years contained
introductions by Virginia Woolf, T. S. Eliot, Graham Greene,
and other literary figures which enriched the experience of reading.
Today the series is recognized for its fine scholarship and
reliability in texts that span world literature, drama and poetry,
religion, philosophy and politics. Each edition includes perceptive
commentary and essential background information to meet the
changing needs of readers.*

OXFORD WORLD'S CLASSICS

W. M. THACKERAY

Vanity Fair
A Novel without a Hero

Edited with an Introduction by
JOHN SUTHERLAND

With 193 Illustrations by the Author

OXFORD
UNIVERSITY PRESS

OXFORD
UNIVERSITY PRESS

Great Clarendon Street, Oxford OX2 6DP

Oxford University Press is a department of the University of Oxford.
It furthers the University's objective of excellence in research, scholarship,
and education by publishing worldwide in

Oxford   New York

Athens Auckland Bangkok Bogotá Buenos Aires Calcutta
Cape Town Chennai Dar es Salaam Delhi Florence Hong Kong Istanbul
Karachi Kuala Lumpur Madrid Melbourne Mexico City Mumbai
Nairobi Paris São Paulo Shanghai Singapore Taipei Tokyo Toronto Warsaw

with associated companies in Berlin Ibadan

Published in the United States
by Oxford University Press Inc., New York

Editorial matter © John Sutherland 1983

First published as a World's Classics paperback 1983
Reissued as an Oxford World's Classics paperback 1998

British Library Cataloguing in Publication Data

Data available

Library of Congress Cataloging in Publication Data

Data available

ISBN 0-19-283443-6

5

Printed in Great Britain by
Clays Ltd, St Ives plc

CONTENTS

Introduction   vii

The Composition and Publication of
Vanity Fair   xxxi

Note on the Text   xlii

Thackeray as Illustrator   xliv

Select Bibliography   xlvii

A Chronology of Thackeray's Life
and Works   xlviii

VANITY FAIR

Explanatory Notes   881

INTRODUCTION

By the best reckoning we can make, Thackeray began serious work on *Vanity Fair* (as the novel was eventually to be called) in late 1844–early 1845. Up to this point his career, in and out of writing, had been chequered. He was born a gentleman, so brought up and educated; Charterhouse, Trinity College Cambridge, European travel, Inns of Court—his youth followed a high road to Victorian success. Had he not gambled away part of his patrimony and lost the rest in a bank crash, not idled at college, not been bored by law, and above all not compounded everything with a horribly unlucky marriage, Thackeray might have entered the leisured, lettered, professional life for which birth and upbringing destined him. One can imagine him, in later years, a mellowly Fieldingesque magistrate; an MP regularly prosing away in the heavier journals; a subtle diplomat or—most likely of all—a historian. For of all literary men, it was the historians (Macaulay notably) that Thackeray most revered. Had he lived longer, in his late prosperity he would certainly have written the history of Queen Anne's reign that he promised himself. Failing all else, the young Thackeray could have married money; he was charming and personable enough. Instead he chose Isabella Shawe. She brought him no dowry, no connections (except those of an Irish mother-in-law, whom he punished relentlessly in fiction to the end of his life), gave him two surviving daughters but went incurably mad in 1842.

Thackeray finally achieved membership of the Athenaeum, in 1851. But he did it with a difficult instrument of entry—the bestselling novelist's pen. Nor was his path to sales success in fiction easy. Few authors can have had a tougher or more wide-ranging apprenticeship. From 1835 to 1845 he 'wrote for his life'. His output was prodigious, and bewilderingly various. To short order he turned in reviews and essays of a social, political or historical kind as the nature of the journal required. He produced reportage,

travel books, comic squibs and journalism (for a while in
the 1830s, he was even a newspaper proprietor), 'sketches',
social physiologies and short fiction. All that he wrote was
anonymous or pseudonymous. His pre-*Vanity Fair* pen-
names and assumed personae are legion: *inter alia*, Yellow-
plush the footman, 'Our Fat Contributor', Major Gahagan
the fiery Irish warrior, Barry Lyndon the picaro soldier of
fortune, Ikey Solomons Jr. the fence, Launcelot Wagstaff
and George Fitz-Boodle—bon bourgeois club gents, Mr.
Snob (for London), Mr. Squab (for Calcutta), and his
favourite cockneyfied Michaelangelo Titmarsh. Obscure
but versatile, Thackeray even put himself forward as an
illustrator to Harrison Ainsworth and Charles Dickens,
novelists of his generation who had made a faster and more
brilliant start. It is a curious speculation how literary
history would have been rewritten, had they commissioned
him rather than Phiz and Cruikshank.

By early 1845, Thackeray had a substantial body of
published work behind him. But he had published nothing
in itself substantial. *Vanity Fair*, when it finally appeared in
January 1847, took him with one jump to the top of the tree
with Dickens. It made his name (literally, being published
under the superscription 'W. M. Thackeray') and his
fortune. Riding *Vanity Fair*'s success he became, with
Dickens, the best paid novelist of the age. Not *quite* as well
paid, admittedly. (Bradbury and Evans came to reckon his
maximum price per monthly part at £250 and Dickens's an
astronomical £600.) But for many discriminating readers,
Thackeray was the more highly regarded of the two. (See,
for instance, Jane Carlyle's verdict on reading four of *Vanity
Fair*'s instalments: 'beats Dickens out of the world!')

The story of *Vanity Fair* is easily summarized and stripped
down into shapes and patterns. It follows, through their
turns of fortune, the careers of two women. One is good,
stupid, bourgeois and (initially) rich; the other is clever,
selfish, bohemian and (initially) poor. They leave their
school at Chiswick in the same coach, in 1813. Both have
vexed courtships and marry in 1815 to 'disoblige their
families' (as Jane Austen would say). A great historical

event, Waterloo, lies athwart their newly-wed lives. Amelia's husband dies on the battlefield; Becky's husband survives. Both wives give birth to a son in 1816. There follows a decade of mounting triumph for Becky culminating in presentation to her monarch; a decade of intensifying misery for Amelia culminating in separation from her child. Then, in 1827, there is a spin of the wheel; Becky is plunged into (deserved) ruin, Amelia comes into (deserved) good fortune. But with an ironic twist, Thackeray brings both heroines into final equilibrium. As we first met them, Regency girls, together in a coach, so we leave them, now two early-Victorian ladies, either side of the charity stall which declares their mutual respectability in the eyes of the world.

Before Waterloo, the business of the novel is marriage, family disfavour and disinheritance. After Waterloo, as the heroines' lives separate, the great issue is marital fidelity. Two triangular relationships develop. Becky is faithless to her increasingly worthy husband Rawdon with the lecherous Marquis of Steyne. Amelia is faithful to her dead husband, the worthless George, denying the steadfast love of Dobbin. In so doing, both women sin.

Around their see-sawing careers and the congruent geometry of the post-marital affairs, Thackeray creates a narrative of panoramic historical sweep and of subtle ironic effects. It was work designed to be meditated on by fellow novelists, as well as consumed by the paying reading public. Gordon Ray is surely right in his insistence that Thackeray labours in *Vanity Fair* to raise the tone of mid-nineteenth-century fiction and with it the status of the novelist. (This, incidentally, was in line with Carlyle's stern judgement that the novelists of England had hitherto shirked their God-given mission.) Thackeray, one might paraphrase, found the English novel sloppy romance; he left it solid realism.

This Thackerayan correction entailed the lash as well as good example. Among his many parts, he is a supreme parodist. Like that of his master, Fielding, Thackeray's fiction is founded on a repudiation of the fashionable falsity of the day. And like Fielding again, Thackeray does not

merely disdain, but on occasion scornfully recreates in all
its absurdity what he despises. Did he so choose, he could
do it better is the implication of the exercise. Most of the
currently popular novels shied at in *Vanity Fair* have since
died a death so complete that they will be unknown to the
modern reader. Thackeray, it might even be argued, did his
work rather too well, helping burlesque into extinction such
genres as the 'Newgate', 'silver fork', and Napoleonic
soldier of fortune novel.

It is instructive to look carefully at the beginning of
Chapter VI, 'Vauxhall', with its challenging opening: 'We
might have treated this subject in the genteel, or in the
romantic, or in the facetious manner.' Good as his word,
Thackeray proceeds to offer hilarious samples of these
alternative manners. The burlesque parade makes multiple
parody of Mrs. Gore, Bulwer Lytton, G. P. R. James,
Douglas Jerrold, Eugène Sue, Harrison Ainsworth, Victor
Hugo, Mrs. Trollope, G. W. M. Reynolds and even (though
Thackeray was chary of picking this particular fight)
Dickens himself. The satiric overture to Chapter VI was
shortened from the original manuscript version for the first
printed issue of *Vanity Fair*, and further reduced for the next
revised edition of the novel, in 1853, leaving the comparative stump which is printed in the text here (see note to
p. 60). But elsewhere, the project was expanded. In April
1847 (Chapter VI was first published in February) Thackeray launched in *Punch* a series of parodic novelettes,
'Novels by Eminent Hands' (the title hits at Ainsworth, see
the following note on the composition and publication of
Vanity Fair). These vastly extend the *Vanity Fair* burlesques,
and are agreed to be among the best things of their kind
ever written.

As Gordon Ray puts it, *Vanity Fair* signals clearly and
early the kind of novel Thackeray will not write; that is to
say, the kind of novel the majority of his writing and
reading contemporaries affect. Throughout *Vanity Fair*, and
explicitly in Chapter VI, Thackeray makes the pharisaical
assertion that he is not as other novelists are. But, as critics
have come round to noticing, this *censor morum literariorum*

would often seem to have a dangerously soft spot for his victims. *Vanity Fair*, for all its show of repudiation, frequently conforms to the fiction it purports to chastise. With its 'arsenical' ending (Becky poisoning Jos) *Vanity Fair* is as much of the Newgate genre as Lytton's sensational *Lucretia* (1846). K. J. Hollingsworth, the authority on this early shoot of crime fiction, goes so far as to claim that *Vanity Fair* is the Newgate novel to end Newgate novels. So too, Matthew Rosa sees Thackeray's novel as the *summum genus* of silver forkery. It has certainly survived as the greatest of Waterloo novels (who now remembers the multitudinous works of W. H. Maxwell, or Lever's *Charles O'Malley*, the bestselling novel of 1841 which Thackeray put down hilariously with his spoof, 'Phil Fogarty. A Tale of the Fighting Onety-Oneth'?). Thackeray was loftily contemptuous in his two reviews of *Coningsby*, affecting to find Disraeli's romance of power politics in the 'saloons of the mighty' obnoxious and absurd. (See also 'Codlingsby', by the dubiously eminent hand of 'B. de Shrewsbury, Esq.') But who is the arch villain of *Vanity Fair*? Why, Steyne, avowedly based on the Marquis of Hertford, the same aristocrat who modelled for the all-powerful Monmouth in *Coningsby*.

Thackeray, we may say, has a more complex and intimate relationship with the modes of fashionable fiction of the age than his apparently dismissive satirical manner would suggest. Neither is it easy to fix his feelings about the period in which *Vanity Fair* is principally set—the dissolute Regency and reign of George IV. Here, again, we detect in Thackeray mixed feelings of nostalgia and severe moral criticism. But at least we are on firm ground with the age's figurehead. Of all the historical figures whom Thackeray loathed, the bloated 'first gentleman of Europe' was the blackest of beasts. Even Marlborough in *Esmond* is treated with more tenderness than 'the great simulacrum'. Thackeray's ink boils whenever he describes Florizel. He often did describe him. More or less full-length portraits are found in *Punch* (see, particularly, *The Georges*, *Punch*, 11 October 1845), in *The Snobs of England* (see particularly Chapter II,

'The Snob Royal'), and—most vituperatively—in *The Four Georges* where the fourth lecture is devoted to an hour-long diatribe against the last Hanoverian. Thackeray's theme is simple. The Prince Regent represents the sink of corruption against which the present, Victorian, age is the wholesome reaction:

> He is dead but thirty years, and one asks how a great society could have tolerated him? Would we bear him now? In this quarter of a century, what a silent revolution has been working! how it has separated us from old times and manners! How it has changed men themselves!

In *Vanity Fair*, the fourth George is referred to frequently. He actually appears on stage twice (and speaks once) at the apogee of Becky's career; in the charade scene at Gaunt House and in the Drawing-room presentation in 1827— Becky's moment of glory. On neither occasion can Thackeray, with a satiric attack of commoner's humility, bring himself to describe, nor even name, the 'great personage':

> What were the circumstances of the interview between Rebecca Crawley, *née* Sharp, and her Imperial Master, it does not become such a feeble and inexperienced pen as mine to attempt to relate. The dazzled eyes close before that Magnificent Idea. Loyal respect and decency tell even the imagination not to look too keenly and audaciously about the sacred audience-chamber, but to back away rapidly, silently, and respectfully, making profound bows out of the August Presence. (p. 604)

But while miming loyal blindness at the incandescence of the Hanoverian sun god, Thackeray insinuates his derogatory view of the Prince Regent and his dandified parasites with the namesake Osborne, and George Osborne's very fat friend, Jos. ('William' Dobbin is significantly named for the decent, if maladroit, 'Silly Billy'. One of his first royal edicts on coming to power in 1830 was to restrict the extravagant military uniforms so beloved of the 'padded booby' George. Dobbin embodies that 'change' Thackeray eulogizes in *The Four Georges*.)

Vanity Fair, then, is an historical novel. In particular the middle-class social life of the Regency (i.e. 1811–20) is reconstructed with apparently personal familiarity. Thackeray, however, was born in the year George was declared Regent. He could scarcely have been conscious of Waterloo, four years later. But the victory remained for him, as for many Victorians, the age's great event. Indeed, with the English 'saving revolution' of 1688, the American Revolution of 1776 and the French Revolution of 1789, Waterloo could easily be conceived as the most monumental occurrence in modern history. The close-run thing in Belgium was the foundation of Britain's century of triumph and the spread of imperial red over the world's map. And had the battle been lost, history would probably have delivered a bloody English Revolution, rather than the Reform Bill of 1832. Nor was it just the European balance of power which was rearranged by Waterloo. The victory had profound social consequences; it marked a moment of regeneration for the British aristocracy. Dandyism fell; Brummell was disgraced in 1815—a fall 'as great as Napoleon's' it was said. The Duke of Wellington was himself a 'dandy general' and led an army whose fashionable regiments fought brilliantly. (Hence, of course, the famous 'won on the playing fields of Eton' proverb.) Thackeray's 'silent revolution' can more plausibly be dated from 1815 than from 1830, when George died. Despite his monarchic radiance in mid-1820s *Vanity Fair*, George's last ten years were spent in almost total social eclipse and public unpopularity.

But despite his fascination with Waterloo, and its profound effect on the novel's five main characters and the world they inhabit, Thackeray's treatment of the battle is tantalizing in the highest degree. The suspense builds from Dobbin's 'the regiment's called away' to the Duchess of Richmond's eve of battle ball, from which officers slip out one by one, some to death, some to glory. We arrive to within earshot of the cannonade at Quatre Bras. But then, at the most teasing moment, we are denied satisfaction (which as thrill-seeking and *paying* readers we legitimately demand) by Thackeray's mock-humble and maidenish retraction:

We do not claim to rank among the military novelists. Our place is with the non-combatants. When the decks are cleared for action we go below and wait meekly. We should only be in the way of the manoeuvres that the gallant fellows are performing overhead. We shall go no farther with the —th than to the city gate . . . (p. 361)

As a matter of literary record, the reader indignantly retorts that Thackeray is an excellent military novelist. Any number of examples could be given; but for the nearest turn to Chapters IV, V, VI of *Barry Lyndon*, which Thackeray was writing virtually up to the month when he began *Vanity Fair*. This rollicking autobiography of an eighteenth-century soldier of fortune demonstrates the skill which Thackeray disowns, with infuriating modesty, at the start of the ninth number of *Vanity Fair*.

The novelist teases at other similarly exciting moments in the novel's action. He will not, for instance, conduct us into the penetralium of Gaunt House, giving us, instead, serpentine, 'Tomeavesian' gossip. What we crave is reliable eye-witness report of what's going on at this climax of Becky's English campaign. 'Great personages' pop up momentarily on the edge of *Vanity Fair*'s narrative, only to pop down. Thus the Duke of Wellington himself rides past the novel's heroes and heroines in a Brussels public park. It is his sole appearance and what does Thackeray give us? Peggy O'Dowd's chauvinist Hibernian irrelevance: 'the Wellesleys and Moloneys are related; but, of course, poor *I* would never dream of introjuicing myself unless his Grace thought proper to remember our family tie.' The Duchess of Richmond's Brussels ball on 15 June—that conjunction of brilliant social glitter and carnage—is famous from at least two other literary presentations. But Thackeray's thinned account keeps off-stage Byron's 'fated Brunswick'; the glamorous hostess; the martial guest of honour and indeed all personages above field rank. *Charles O'Malley*, by contrast, has the hero on the most hob-nobbing terms with the ducal hostess and Commander-in-Chief. The 'great captain' in Lever's narrative actually 'introjuices' himself to the hero ('know your face well; how d'ye do?') with the lack of reserve which suggests that the brash Moloneys and the Wellesleys might indeed be related.

No more than with Thackeray's battlefield reticence can we put this omission down to authorial inadequacy. The depiction of Marlborough in *Esmond*, of Washington in *The Virginians* (and probably the imminent depiction of Paul Jones in the unfinished *Duval*) testify that Thackeray was as capable of rendering the portrait of a military chief as he was a military fight—when he chose to do so. *Vanity Fair*, then, is an historical novel in whose historical fabric there are gaping, but evidently carefully placed, holes. Thackeray gives us Regency London without Brummell, Byron or the Regent (how easy it would have been to send the Osborne–Sedley–Dobbin party to Vauxhall on the festive night of 13 July: see note to p. 63); the great Brussels ball without grandees; the frontline in 1815 without Waterloo, Wellington or Napoleon; and, later in the novel, Weimar without Goethe. An historical novel, we might call it, without everything conventionally historical.

The artful anticlimaxes in *Vanity Fair*, and particularly the frustrating vacancy around Waterloo, are partly explained by Thackeray's determination to avoid romantic stereotype. Other factors are his ambivalence about British imperial might, and his circumstances while actually composing *Vanity Fair*. To take this last (and probably least) consideration: the novelist was evidently very pressed for time and space during the writing of the middle sections of his narrative. He intended to get the action to the battle at least two numbers earlier than he actually managed. But what with the marriages and all the falling-out between relatives in the 'hundred days' between March and June, *Vanity Fair* was fairly bursting at the seams. Of course, with a narrator as deft as Thackeray, pressure could not have been the deciding factor. In fact, as the Tillotsons point out, Thackeray's gimmick of telling the story of Waterloo indirectly through its domestic repercussions had been aired as early as 1842, during a visit to Charles Lever's house near Dublin. As reported, Thackeray 'seemed much inclined to "laugh at martial might", although he still held to the idea that "something might be made out of Waterloo", even without the smoke and din of the action being introduced.' In Lever's *Charles O'Malley*, published in 1841, smoke and din is prominent and the hero observes the epic encounter at Napoleon's side.

Silence in the face of Waterloo was probably also encouraged by Thackeray's perplexity when he went to visit the battlefield, a few weeks before embarking on his novel. What he describes (in a 'Little Travels and Roadside Sketches' piece, published in *Fraser's Magazine*, January 1845) is strikingly like Orwell's painful sense of British greatness, lying underfoot in the mouldering carcasses of the expendable 'natives' whose sweat, suffering and hunger is empire's real foundation. Walking over the place where thousands of uncommemorated private soldiers were cut, blasted or bled to death, Thackeray felt pride—as what Englishman would not. But he also felt ashamed of a pride so paid for by others' sacrifice. Moreover, the strength of his mixed feelings induced a conviction that here was a place where one ought to be decently quiet, as in a church:

Let an Englishman go and see that field, and he *never forgets it*. The sight is an event in his life; and, though it has been seen by millions of peaceable *gents*—grocers from Bond Street, meek attorneys from Chancery Lane, and timid tailors from Piccadilly— I will wager that there is not one of them but feels a glow as he looks at the place, and remembers that he, too, is an Englishman.

It is a wrong, egotistical, savage, unchristian feeling, and that's the truth of it. A man of peace has no right to be dazzled by that red-coated glory, and to intoxicate his vanity with those remembrances of carnage and triumph. The same sentence which tells us that on earth there ought to be peace and good-will amongst men, tells us to whom GLORY belongs.

One cannot know for certain, but I suspect that until he actually came to writing it, Thackeray kept open the important question of how he should treat Waterloo. We know, for instance, that he ordered an early copy of G. R. Gleig's *Story of the Battle of Waterloo* in June 1847. He evidently devoured the book when it arrived (see notes to Chapters XXVII–XXXII). And he must have been struck by one feature in particular. Gleig, at one point, complains at the feeble powers of the 'pen and pencil' (a phrase Thackeray had used in his novel's title) when it comes to describing this battle of battles. Moreover, the most vivacious by far of Gleig's chapters are those dealing with the furious carnival in Brussels before Waterloo, and the stiltedly entitled chapter 'State of Feeling Where the War was not', which records, with lively detail, the wild currents of pessimism and rumour that swept over Brussels during the three days of fighting. Thackeray plundered these sections for *Vanity Fair*'s ninth number. With one notable exception (see note to p. 406), the stodgier battle chapters seem to have inspired him less. It is possible, too, that having read Gleig, the novelist felt disinclined to compete with the military historian on his own ground.

To summarize. There is no need to retract, nor even to modify the assertion that *Vanity Fair* is an historical novel. But the sense of historical period and the passage of world-shaking events around the characters is conveyed obliquely. Most obviously by the introduction of minor period detail such as seven shilling pieces and hessian boots. Thackeray inserts material of this kind very judiciously—but it is a simple device, equivalent to theatrical 'props'. More complex is the way in which he throws up a London subtly different from that familiar to his 1848 readers. Thus, in Chapter XXII, Dobbin meets George at the old Slaughter's Coffee House (it stood in St. Martin's Lane until 1843) before his furtive marriage cum elopement with Amelia:

It was about half an hour from twelve when this brief meeting and colloquy took place between the two captains. A coach, into which Captain Osborne's servant put his master's desk and dressing-case, had been in waiting for some time; and into this the two gentlemen hurried under an umbrella, and the valet mounted on the box, cursing the rain and the dampness of the coachman who was steaming beside him. 'We shall find a better trap than this at the chutch-door,' says he; 'that's a comfort.' And the carriage drove on, taking the road down Piccadilly; where Apsley House and St. George's Hospital wore red jackets still; where there

were oil-lamps; where Achilles was not yet born; nor the Pimlico
arch raised; nor the hideous equestrian monster which pervades it
and the neighbourhood;—and so they drove down by Brompton to
a certain chapel near the Fulham road there.(p. 262)

Misfortune is predicted in the proverbially unlucky rain
which falls on the bride and groom. Other predictions are
contained in the urban landscape. This is early 1815.
Apsley House, on Hyde Park Corner, was to become the
residence of the Duke of Wellington, victor of Waterloo.
Wyatt encased it in Bath stone in 1828 ('red coat' means
literally 'brick' but also has a military significance here, as
does St. George's Hospital, which is to care for Waterloo
wounded). Wyatt was also responsible for the heroic statue
of Wellington—weighing forty tons—erected at a cost of
£30,000 by public subscription, in 1846. This monstrosity,
as Thackeray and many of his contemporaries thought, also
stood at the south-eastern entrance to the Park. (It figures,
in caricature, on the serial cover—see notes.) The Achilles
statue was subscribed for (£10,000), and inscribed by 'the
women of England.' It was also dedicated as a tribute to
Wellington, and was raised in 1822. It was cast partly from
enemy cannon captured at Waterloo.

This elaboration of scenic detail serves a number of
purposes. It emphasizes how London has changed (omni-
buses in 1846 serve this part of London; oil-lighting gave
way to gas in 1828). More thematically, we feel the
marriage threatened by futurity, a futurity centred on
Waterloo. These monuments to victory are also, we sense,
George's gravestone. Amelia, although she does not know
it, will join the 'women of England' in making a widow's
sacrificial donation.

In the above example, Thackeray dwarfs a major
novelistic event (the marriage of two principal characters)
by throwing gigantic historical shadows across their bridal
path. Examples can be found where—for artistic effect—he
does just the opposite. In the following, the dizzying
European crisis of 1813–14 is shrunk by reflection in
Amelia's preoccupation about her engagement to George:

Meanwhile matters went on in Russell Square, Bloomsbury, just as if matters in Europe were not in the least disorganised. The retreat from Leipsic made no difference in the number of meals Mr. Sambo took in the servants' hall; the allies poured into France, and the dinner-bell rang at five o'clock just as usual. I don't think poor Amelia cared anything about Brienne and Montmirail, or was fairly interested in the war until the abdication of the Emperor; when she clapped her hands and said prayers,— oh, how grateful! and flung herself into George Osborne's arms with all her soul, to the astonishment of every body who witnessed the ebullition of sentiment. The fact is, peace was declared ... Lieutenant Osborne's regiment would not be ordered on service. That was the way in which Miss Amelia reasoned. The fate of Europe was Lieutenant George Osborne to her. His dangers being over, she sang Te Deum. He was her Europe; her emperor: her allied monarchs and august prince regent. He was her sun and moon; and I believe she thought the grand illumination and ball at the Mansion House, given to the sovereigns, were especially in honour of George Osborne. (p. 137)

There are ironies at work here. Amelia's naive perspective is both admirable and—in a very loaded word which Thackeray used about his 'Vanityfairians'—'selfish'. Soon she is to discover that the great convulsions of European history (which will ruin her father and slaughter her husband) are no respecters of girlish romance, however good and worthy the girl.

In the second half of the novel, after Waterloo, the historical background to *Vanity Fair* fades somewhat. As we follow the fortunes of Thackeray's characters over this most troubled of eras, one has the odd impression of social tranquillity. Perhaps, as he looked back in a spirit of 'De Juventute', that is how it seemed to Thackeray in 1847–8. *Vanity Fair* is blind to Peterloo, corn law riots, industrial revolution, reform agitation. Even the great Bill itself sneaks in only parenthetically with a reference to Sir Pitt's disappointed retirement from public life after 1832. From the 1820s onwards, things gradually melt into the Victorian present. The novel's last numbers feature many fewer historical markers than their early counterparts. Imperceptibly, the historical texture merges if not into the 'now' of 1847–8, then into the Victorian reader's well-remembered yesterday. It is a fine and very moving effect in the novel.

Students of literature are routinely told that Thackeray is an 'omniscient' novelist; indeed, that with Fielding he is probably the perfect specimen of the type. He himself tells us, repeatedly and with apparent complacency in *Vanity Fair*, that 'the novelist knows everything'. But just as with the historical backdrop, the front of stage drama has its holes. The reader is again teased by what this allegedly omniscient novelist would seem not to know, will not acquaint himself with, or declines to impart. Omniscient he may be; omnidictive he is not.

Most provoking of the text's silences is that concerning Jos's death. He dies in mysterious circumstances on the continent, sometime in the early 1830s, while in the dangerous company of Becky Crawley. From his first encounter with her, some twenty years before, Jos has been in danger from this fatal woman. In 1813, she almost netted him; but George, unwilling to have a governess in the family ('low enough without *her*!') frightened the fat man off. At Pumpernickel, despite Dobbin's efforts, she finally lands her prey. Becky cannot marry Jos (Rawdon, her estranged husband, is still staving off the fevers of Coventry Island). But she lives with her victim until he dies—prematurely. She is his insurance beneficiary; the rest of his nabob's wealth has mysteriously evaporated. And in later life, Becky is a *very* prosperous lady, we are told. When she first set her hat at Jos in Russell Square, she was netting a purse; now, at last it would seem, the purse is comfortably full.

How does Jos die? The insurance people are suspicious. Their solicitor swears it is 'the blackest case that ever came before him'. Thackerayan innuendo confirms our sense that Becky helped Jos out of the world. *Her* solicitors are ominously named Messrs. Burke, Thurtell and Hayes. Burke, with Hare, was the Edinburgh body snatcher who killed and sold the corpses. John Thurtell was a murderer, hanged in 1824. Catherine Hayes was a husband killer,

INTRODUCTION xxi

celebrated by Thackeray in his anti-Newgate satire, *Catherine* (1839).

There is another broad hint in the penultimate full-plate illustration to the novel, 'Becky's second appearance in the character of Clytemnestra'. Her first appearance as the Greek uxoricide was in the charade at Gaunt House, just before she betrayed Rawdon into the hands of the bailiffs. Here we feel she will use the knife that—somewhat melodramatically—Thackeray shows her holding. (An ironic, Hogarthian print of the good Samaritan is behind Jos, who vainly implores an implacable Dobbin to help him.)

It all points one way. But why does Thackeray not tell us straight out? It is a mote that he seems deliberately to have left to trouble generations of readers. And when asked in later life by just one such troubled reader 'did Becky kill Jos?' the novelist is reported to have merely smiled and answered, 'I don't know.' This paradox of a novelist who 'knows everything' but does not know if one principal character murders another may be partly explained by the way in which the narrator's implied social status and personality emerge in the closing pages. In the last double number the diplomat Tapeworm fills in Becky's unsalubrious background to a startled Dobbin, and, in an interesting aside, we are told that 'it was at that very table years ago that the present writer had the pleasure of hearing the tale' which, in his turn, he passes on to us as *Vanity Fair* (p. 849). Pumpernickel is transparently Weimar, and Thackeray, the young man, was there for his 'Lehrjahre' in 1830–31—the presumed date in which these chapters are set. It's an odd little play with the mask. But the important thing is that this 'I' who flits briefly into our view is definitely one of the Dobbin set (see p. 793). As a gentleman, Dobbin's behaviour towards Mrs. Crawley is exemplary in its averted gaze. He will not help Jos, in spite of that desperate man's pleas. He 'rigidly declines to hold any communication' with the tainted wife. In Thackeray's Christmas Book, *Our Street* (1848) there is a cameo portrait of 'A Woman whom Nobody Knows'. Of course, everyone in the street does know her in the literal sense of the verb

and everything about her circumstances as well. But since
she is a kept woman and 'fallen' no one may 'know' her
socially. At the end of *Vanity Fair*, it would seem that the
newly identified and gentlemanly narrator is similarly
disabled. He can no more 'know' Becky, or her sordid
doings, than gentlemanly Dobbin can.

'Was she guilty?' The narrative asks that question of
Becky (but gives no direct answers) at two crucial
junctures. First in the liaison with Steyne; secondly after
Jos's death. It is, of course, odds on that Becky was
thoroughly guilty of both these and many like offences.
Would the notoriously lecherous Steyne have given Becky a
cheque for over a thousand pounds, provided for her son
and companion, have given her diamonds (which she feels
obliged to hide from her husband) and have hung around
Curzon Street for *ten years* (see note to p. 693) were he not
enjoying with her what he more flagrantly enjoys with the
Countess of Belladonna? So too with Jos: any open-minded
reader concurs with the insurance office's suspicion.

But if we pass a verdict of guilty, we have on our hands
an extraordinary Victorian novel. English fiction of this
period was ruled by canons of poetic justice, quite Mosaic
in their severity. There is no adulteress I can think of who
escapes capital punishment in the pages of mid-Victorian
fiction and only one other murderer (Paul Ferroll, in Mrs.
Archer Clive's very eccentric 1855 romance). Yet at the end
of *Vanity Fair*, Becky and Amelia are found in what is
apparently a condition of perfect social equality—both
ladies of impeccable respectability. Becky may even be
happier in her mind than Amelia. For with that *amari aliquid*
that Thackeray liked to introduce at the end of his novels,
we find that the long-deferred marriage is not entirely
happy, and Mrs. Dobbin is troubled that, after all, her
husband does not love her. (I think, incidentally, Chesterton misreads when he sees in Becky's final victory over
society, 'the energy of a dead woman . . . like the rhythmic
kicking of some dead, bisected insect'. Better Becky's
kicking than the 'parasitic' green growth of Amelia round
Dobbin's oak.)

There are for this soi-disant omniscient narrator, mysteriously impenetrable parts of Amelia's life as well. When she
returns as a newly-married woman to Fulham, she goes up
to her bedroom and contemplates the 'little white bed' of
her maidenhood. She contrasts it in her mind with the
'great funereal damask pavilion' in the West End Hotel
which George has chosen for their honeymoon. He,
meanwhile, is off at the play and she is evidently very
unhappy. She prays: 'Have we a right to repeat or overhear
her prayers?' asks the narrator. Yes, we answer—Vanity
Fairian readers that we are. But Thackeray chides us:
'these, brothers, are secrets, and out of the domain of
Vanity Fair, in which our story lies.' We are not, after all, to
know.

Yet Thackeray knows that the reader, in his 'Tomeavesian' way will be impelled to put two and two together.
Amelia is miserable—but why? She has her George at last;
he has not yet taken to consorting with Mrs. Highflyer or
offering elopement to her best friend. A clue to her
unhappiness and what seems rather like guilt as she
contemplates the virginal white bed, may be found in her
mother's welcome:

All people have their ways of expressing kindness, and it seemed to
Mrs. Sedley that a muffin and a quantity of orange marmalade
spread out in a little cut-glass saucer would be peculiarly
agreeable refreshments to Amelia in her most interesting situation.
(p. 319)

What rings oddly here is the phrase, 'interesting situation'.
'Mrs. Dickens is in a very uninteresting situation again'
Dickens will tell a correspondent by way of announcing his
wife's tiresomely predictable pregnancy. Later in *Vanity
Fair*, Peggy O'Dowd informs the new regimental wife that
'Mrs. Bunny's in an interesting situation—faith, and she
always is.' And Mrs. Sedley's tender attention to her
daughter's possibly upset stomach confirms this sense that
Amelia is with child. But, we are told, Amelia has only been
married 'a few days' (nine, to be exact). Post-marital
pregnancy surely cannot be on the cards so soon after the

wedding night. So—the reader presumes—Amelia and George must have jumped the gun. (He would not be the only fornicator in *Vanity Fair*; see note to p. 125). This would explain her apparent remorse before the symbol of maidenly purity and such things as Dobbin's otherwise too urgent 'George, she's dying' in Chapter XVIII. It would also explain the oddly proleptic note that he sends up to her, by way of proposal: 'Dearest Emmy—dearest love—dearest wife, come to me.' She may be his Emmy and his love; but she is not yet George's wife, at least not in name.

Having raised this unworthy speculation, one has to pursue it. Becky marries some time in March, and we are told, quite precisely, that little Rawdon is born a year later on 23 March. Amelia is married 25 April, we are as precisely told. But we are never told the day or month that little George is delivered by the widow. Old Osborne visits Brussels 'towards the end of autumn' (September–October, presumably; soldiers are still sunning themselves in parks). Dobbin tells him that 'Amelia will be a mother soon'. What 'soon' means is unclear. 'A day came when she was a mother' is all we get. If Amelia were only four or five months gone, could Dobbin have said 'soon'?

In this question of Amelia's pregnancy I am, of course, pressing too hard on what is, at most, an enigmatic passage of narrative. But the fact is that Thackeray—the novelist who knows everything—does not choose to disclose the intimate post-marital thoughts of his good heroine and in the vacuum that he leaves, speculation breeds—as he knew it would. And if my speculation on this matter seems far-fetched, read Neal B. Houston's 'A Brief Inquiry into the Morality of Amelia in *Vanity Fair*' (*Victorian Newsletter*, 1966, pp. 23–4). This ingenious essay discovers an affair between Dobbin and Amelia in Brussels after George's death and postulates that little Georgy is, in fact, Dobbin's son.

In the apparatus which surrounds his text (i.e. the allegorical monthly cover, the frontispiece, the preface-cum-epilogue 'Before the Curtain') Thackeray splits his narrative persona into four parts. There is the 'manager of the performance'—narrator we may say. There is harlequin, the popular entertainer (looking ruefully, however, at his own visage in a cracked mirror). There is 'the man with a reflective turn of mind' wandering through the fair and observing his fellow men—Thackeray the worldly reporter of the Victorian social scene. And finally, there is 'the moralist who is holding forth on the cover'.

All commentators find *Vanity Fair* a powerfully moral novel. None more so than Charlotte Bronte, who used *her* preface to the second edition of *Jane Eyre* (1848) to salute Thackeray in terms appropriate to an old testament prophet:

There is a man in our own days whose words are not framed to tickle delicate ears: who, to my thinking, comes before the great ones of society, much as the son of Imlah came before the throned kings of Judah and Israel; and who speaks truth as deep, with a power as prophet-like and as vital—a mien as dauntless and as daring. Is the satirist of 'Vanity Fair' admired in high places? I cannot tell; but I think if some of those amongst whom he hurls the Greek fire of his sarcasm, and over whom he flashes the levinbrand of his denunciation, were to take his warnings in time, they or their seed might yet escape a fatal Ramoth-Gilead.

But what is the central moral contention of *Vanity Fair*? Gordon Ray is in no doubt. The novel is part of an ambitious programme to which, in the largest sense, all Thackeray's mature writing devotes itself: namely, 'redefining the gentlemanly ideal to fit a middle class rather than an aristocratic context'. *Vanity Fair* answers that perennial Thackerayan question 'What is it to be a gentleman?' It is not, of course, to resemble in any particular the 'first gentleman in Europe', Becky's adored monarch. Indeed rank—as bestowed by birth and ancient lineage—would seem a positive disqualification. None are so morally ignoble in *Vanity Fair* as the nobly born. Pitt and Steyne (pit and stain) are exactly what their dynastic names imply. Nor does hard work, rewarded by merited business success, make the gentleman. There is no less a gentleman (in the true Thackerayan meaning) than the self-made merchant,

John Osborne. This brute is trapped in the rank system by his slavish lordolatry, just as the aristocratic objects of his worship are trapped by their arrogant hauteur and self-regard:

The old gentleman pronounced . . . aristocratic names with the greatest gusto. Whenever he met a great man he grovelled before him, and my-lorded him as only a free-born Briton can do. He came home and looked out his history in the peerage: he introduced his name into his daily conversation: he bragged about his Lordship to his daughters. He fell down and basked in him as a Neapolitan beggar does in the sun. (p. 152)

So much for the City of London.

When the negative images and antitypes are withdrawn, what we are left with as the representative of Thackeray's 'ideal of gentlemanliness' is William Dobbin. This paragon, as we know, was a later arrival in the novel (see the following note on composition and publication). He is not physically prepossessing ('no Adonis' as George complacently says, thinking of a fellow officer who is rather handsome). Dobbin has a lisp, a gaunt yellow face and—what especially irritated contemporary reviewers— big clumsy feet. Are we then to admire above all others a clod who cannot see through George Osborne—who plays Man Friday to this simulacrum of the Great Simulacrum fully as blindly as old Osborne worships his lords? As a *cavaliere-servente* Dobbin wastes the best years of his life on a woman he finally (when it's too late) recognizes as 'unworthy of my love'. It is not an impressive record. As Chesterton put it: 'we may sum up Thackeray's view of life by saying that amid all the heroes and geniuses he saw only one thing worth being: a fool.'

Why, one may go on to ask, is Dobbin so much nobler than Fred Bullock? Bullock, of course, says things to Jane Osborne like: 'Gad . . . Eels will be sorry he cried off. You may be a fifty thousand pounder yet,' and we hate him for it. After his marriage to the Osborne daughter, he truckles to aristocracy, setting up his carriage (with bullocks *or* on the panels), toadying to the Castletoddys (already polluted by alliance with the mulatto heiress, Miss Swartz). But, when all is considered, is an ox generically more ignoble than Dobbin the carthorse? What was Dobbin senior? A greengrocer. And who, one may ask, finally ends up with a lion's share of Osborne's tallow-begotten wealth (sweated—if we wish to pursue the question, out of greasy hides imported from Russia)? None other than Colonel Dobbin, via his wife, eventual heiress to the bulk of Osborne's fortune.

The distinction between Bullock and Dobbin lies not in their comparable origins, or their rise in the world, but in the course of life they devote themselves to. In his maturity, Fred is a Lombard Street banker (rather a good one, it would appear). He works. In his maturity, Colonel Dobbin (retd.) lives the life of an eighteenth-century squire, with no other occupation than the writing of his 'History of the Punjaub' (a Shandyan project, we understand, like George Warrington's history of the Revolution in *The Virginians*). The Colonel has 'professional' status but is, in every sense, retired from active engagement with society. What, one wonders, would Dobbin do without the unearned income that supports his gentlemanly leisure?

This question of work (the great Carlylean imperative) is vexing when one applies it to Thackeray's 'ideal of gentlemanliness'. For what his 'true' gentleman and lady have in common with the abhorred drones of the peerage is necessary idleness. To work in *Vanity Fair* is, as Arnold Kettle observes, to take a terrible risk with one's identity. There is a graphic illustration when the well-meaning but naive Amelia resolves to earn her living so as to keep Georgy from his grandfather's clutches:

Amelia thinks, and thinks, and racks her brain, to find some means of increasing the small pittance upon which the household is starving. Can she give lessons in anything? paint card-racks? do fine work? She finds that women are working hard, and better than she can, for twopence a day. She buys a couple of begilt Bristol boards at the fancy stationer's, and paints her very best upon them—a shepherd with a red waistcoat on one, and a pink face smiling in the midst of a pencil landscape—a shepherdess on the other, crossing a little bridge, with a little dog, nicely shaded. The man of the Fancy Repository and Brompton Emporium of Fine Arts (of whom she bought the screens, vainly hoping that he would re-purchase them when ornamented by her hand) can hardly hide the sneer with which he examines these feeble works of art. He looks askance at the lady who waits in the shop, and ties up the cards again in their envelope of whity-brown paper, and hands them to the poor widow and Miss Clapp, who had never seen such beautiful things in her life, and had been quite confident that the man must give at least two guineas for the screens. They try at other shops in the interior of London, with faint sickening hopes. 'Don't want 'em,' says one. 'Be off,' says another, fiercely. Three and sixpence have been spent in vain—the screens retire to Miss Clapp's bedroom, who persists in thinking them lovely. (p. 622)

It's a terrifying, if momentary, glimpse of the world of the industrial base described in Charles Kingsley's *Alton Locke* (1850) and Hood's 'Song of the Shirt' (1843). The clothes on the backs of these characters (with whose genteel hardships we commiserate) are, we suddenly realize, sweated out of exploited seamstresses and tailors, working for wages that would not keep the Sedleys in tea. This passage reminds us that in *Vanity Fair* wealth always comes from wealth. We rarely if ever seen the source of exploitation or labour. By the time money reaches George and Amelia from old Osborne, or Dobbin from his father, or Becky from Jos, it has been washed clean of tallow grease, grocer's grime and Indian sweat.

As significant is the calculus implied in the above episode. If Amelia doesn't find work, she will lose Georgy. If she does find work, she will lose caste; she will no longer be a 'lady'. Which is the greater loss? It is a dilemma found elsewhere in *Vanity Fair*. George Osborne is odious, of course. But his question to Dobbin, on learning that he is cut off with a mere £2,000, is a good one:

What the deuce am I to do with two thousand pounds? Such a sum won't last two years ... Do you suppose a man of my habits can live on his pay and a hundred a year? ... You must be a fool to talk so, Dobbin. How the deuce am I to keep up my position in the world upon such a pitiful pittance? I can't change my habits. I *must* have my comforts. *I* wasn't brought up on porridge like MacWhirter, or on potatoes, like old O'Dowd. Do you expect my wife to take in soldiers' washing, or ride after the regiment in a baggage waggon? (p. 295).

What would he and Amelia have done, had he survived? He has neither the wit nor the skill at play to live on 'nothing a year' like the Crawleys. At best the Osbornes would have sunk to that most pathetic of conditions in Thackeray's world, 'shabby gentility'. More likely, George would have drunk, wasted and womanized his family into the gutter— his only remaining hope that the 'governor' would come round and pension his vices. One thing we may be sure of; George Osborne would never have soiled his hands with work.

The amount of work not done in *Vanity Fair* is prodigious. The Colonel, as we have seen, would seem to spend the second half of his life on a book which he is unlikely to finish, and which few will want to read. The other Colonel, Rawdon Crawley, passes the ten years after Waterloo in retirement, living on nothing a year and doing nothing. (Even his cardsharping is eventually given up.) Jos retires from the Indian service in 1827 (not a very onerous burden, we understand) and devotes the remainder of his life to wandering the continent. Pitt Crawley spends the years 1813–25 apparently occupied with polishing up his pamphlet on malt. On coming to his inheritance he enters parliament on one of his rotten borough's two seats. But he does not speak in the House nor hold any political office. And with the Reform Act, he retires to Queen's Crawley, to decay in gentlemanly style.

In these inactive lives, the passage of time ceases to have meaning. Jos and Dobbin return from India in 1827. Between then and 1831, when they relieve their ennui with a jaunt to Pumpernickel, these gentlemen do nothing, apparently, but escort Mrs. Osborne (who, in her turn, is doing nothing). When he breaks with Amelia over her taking up Becky again in Pumpernickel, Dobbin returns to active soldiering for a couple of months. But she promptly writes her letter, he comes back, resigns his commission and thereafter dedicates himself to a married life of doing nothing except his Indian history.

Dobbin's Newfoundland dog-like fidelity is an impressive measure of his virtue; he could well take Henry Esmond's motto 'je meurs où je m'attache'. But it is hard not to feel that a man of his evident talents is burying what God has lavishly given him. Surely, in the prime of his life he could be better occupied than in carrying Mrs. Osborne's shawls; arranging her travel tickets; chatting with her dinner guests; taking her son to the theatre? But Dobbin is caught in a peculiar contradiction, how to reconcile the stern Carlylean imperative 'Work and Despair Not' with the Ciceronian 'Otium cum dignitate'. It was a contradiction that Thackeray was to return to in his subsequent great panoramic novels of the nineteenth century, *Pendennis*, *The Newcomes*, *Philip*, all of which deal with the question of putting the gentleman to work.

THE COMPOSITION AND
PUBLICATION OF *VANITY FAIR*

THE composition and publication of *Vanity Fair* raises a
number of crucial and often controversial issues. It is not
established for certain when Thackeray first conceived the
novel. The Tillotsons surmise that he began writing it in
late 1844. Ray goes for February 1845 (I tend to agree with
him: see note to p. 36). But the Tillotsons are right to point
out that, whenever he actually put pen to paper, Thackeray
had the germ of the novel in his mind for some years (see,
for instance, the conversation with Lever, discussed in the
Introduction).

The manuscript of *Vanity Fair* which survives is incomplete and enigmatic as regards composition. It comprises
some 110 handwritten pages, taking the narrative up to the
end of Chapter XIII. It is generally agreed that the earliest
layer of composition is represented by Chapters I–IV,
substantially as we have them in the printed text, together
with an early version (A) of Chapter VI ('Vauxhall').
Chapter V which introduces Dobbin, was evidently afterthought. When Thackeray devised Dobbin, and inserted
Chapter V between the postponed and the actual Vauxhall
visits is not clear. But since the chapter contains no
reference to 'Vanity Fair', one assumes that it was some
time before October–November 1846, when he hit on the
novel's eventual title. At the same time as Dobbin was
introduced, Thackeray would seem to have written a new
Chapter VI (hereafter 'VIB') substantially cannibalizing
the old VIA, but accommodating Dobbin in place of his
morally neutral precursor, Captain Tawney. By this date,
Thackeray evidently knew that his novel was to be brought
out in monthly numbers, and he formulated the cunning
courtship of Jos by Becky as the climax of the first, and the
débâcle at Vauxhall as the nucleus of the second number.
This spreading out of material left some gaps. Chapter VII
does not exist in manuscript, and may have been written

late in the day, to plump out the second number. (It contains nothing in terms of narrative information that is not given, briefly, at the beginning of Chapter VIII.) Chapter VIII bears evidence of two stages of composition— one early, and one very late since it incorporates sententious allusions to 'Vanity Fair', and a reference to the novel's monthly cover illustration.

It is logical to assume that Thackeray made up the original I–IV, VIA group to show interested publishers. It could stand as the introduction to a three-volume novel, or of a serial either in magazine or monthly part form. That Thackeray intended this unit as a sample is borne out by the neatness with which he put these opening chapters on paper, in his 'sloping' hand. At this time, the work was entitled, provisionally, 'Novel without a Hero' and 'Pen and Pencil Sketches of English Society' (both survive as subtitles). It is known that Thackeray submitted the opening of 'Novel without a Hero' to the publisher Colburn, since a fragment of letter has survived, dated May 1845, asking for his 'Novel without a Hero' material back. Presumably, what Colburn had (and evidently gave an advance for) was I–IV, VIA. He was, on the face of things, an odd publisher for Thackeray to have had dealings with; certainly if the novelist foresaw the importance of *Vanity Fair* to his career. Colburn, at this period was legitimately regarded as a book trade rogue.

Nevertheless, Thackeray was clearly in with Colburn in 1844–5, and in that year contributed regularly to his *New Monthly Magazine*, with a string of Launcelot Wagstaff papers. Colburn himself edited his magazine from 1843 to June 1845, but it was not his proper line of work and he was apparently on the lookout for an editor to take over the task. It is conceivable that Thackeray may have had himself in mind for this post; he was keen for anything that paid at this time. If so, he was disappointed when, in June 1845, Colburn sold the *New Monthly Magazine*, lock, stock and barrel to Harrison Ainsworth, who took over as proprietor, editor and main contributor. One of Ainsworth's first acts, according to his biographer S. M. Ellis, was to mollify

Thackeray over the rejection of his 'Pencil Sketches of English Society'.

For whatever reason, Thackeray at this period suddenly turned angry and somewhat spiteful towards Colburn and Ainsworth. Ainsworth, for instance, put out an advertisement on taking over Colburn's journal, that henceforth the *New Monthly Magazine* would be notable not just for the quality of its contributions but the 'eminence' of its contributors. This provoked Thackeray to an immediate squib in *Punch* ('Immense Opportunity', 5 July 1845). Later, Thackeray was to expand his indignation into the full-blown parodic series, 'Novels by Eminent Hands' (April–October 1847). In *The Snobs of England*, he attacked the injudicious 'eminent hands' advertisement yet again (see Chapter XXXVIII) and was further sarcastic about Mrs. 'Wallop' and the 'Countess of L——.' (see Chapters III and XVI). Thackeray had been a regular, if not frequent, contributor to the *New Monthly Magazine* since 1838; after 1845 he never published in the magazine again. In *Pendennis* (1848–50) Colburn is lampooned as the publisher 'Bungay'—a portrait which implies no lost love. All of this suggests that Thackeray was piqued both with Colburn (whom he may have thought had let him down) and with Ainsworth (who may have turned him down). It is possible that he did not like the idea of his work being passed on to the new proprietor-editor like so much office-stock.

It is part of literary lore that as well as being rejected by (or withdrawn from) Colburn, the *Vanity Fair* proposal was turned down by a string of other imperceptive publishers. Thackeray himself testified to this, in a letter to an unknown correspondent in the early 1860s, claiming that he had 'tried 3 or 4 publishers' with the novel, before finding one who would take it. In America in 1855 Thackeray was evidently telling the same tale. A reporter in the *New York Daily Times* (19 December 1855) records:

I have seen Mr. Thackeray for the first time and a stately man he is and a kindly, as I have convincing reason to know. I learned to

my astonishment that his novel of 'Vanity Fair', the first of his
series of successful novels, was refused by the magazine editor to
whose order it had been written, price five dollars a page, by Mr.
Thackeray's own publisher and by sundry others, before he could
find any of 'the trade' willing to undertake it.

There is some mystery here. In 1845, Thackeray was far
from unknown, or struggling in his profession. He had
numerous contacts; had published with many of the great
houses and in the leading journals of the day. If he was
turned down so universally, it is likely that the reason was
that he was asking too much, or offering too little by way of
sample.

If it was the I–IV, VIA group that Colburn had, we can
be fairly sure that Thackeray did not foresee *Vanity Fair* as it
was to emerge in all its narrative complexity two years later.
There are some internal clues as to what he may originally
have had in mind. Without Dobbin, the whole conception
would have been more negative. Becky's epistolary narrative is extensively used in the earliest layer of composition,
and it is possible that Thackeray felt he might rest a
substantial part of the subsequent narrative on her outrageously amoral communications with Amelia. 'Novel
without a Hero' implies a Carlylean-corrective tone, and
something less morally sententious than what later emerged
in 1847. 'Pen and Pencil Sketches' promises fiction less
structured, something along the lines of the opportunistic
and panoramic *The Snobs of England* (which ran in *Punch*
from February 1846 to February 1847). Having just
finished a male rogue's progress, *Barry Lyndon* (published in
Fraser's Magazine, January–December 1844) there may have
been the intention to provide a female rogue's progress for
Colburn's magazine.

At this point, we encounter a major controversy. Gordon
Ray has deduced from late corrections which Thackeray
made to early stretches of *Vanity Fair*'s MS narrative
(especially in Chapters VIII and IX) that the writer
underwent a 'change of heart' in the period 1846–7. One
record of this change, he argues, is to be found in additions
to the *Vanity Fair* manuscript—particularly the long senten-

tious tailpiece which directly addresses the reader at the end of Chapter VIII. Ray points out that Thackeray's life was revolutionized during these two years. He had his first literary successes. He was reconciled with his daughters, and set up home at 13 Young Street. The shift from bohemian-club to domestic-familial lifestyle was radical. It resulted, according to Ray, in a new sense of 'responsibility' in the author. The unregenerate Thackeray of I–IV, VIA was savage, misanthropic, and typified by *Barry Lyndon*— that most bitter of fictions. The early sections of *Vanity Fair* shape the same way. A new Thackeray of 1846–7 is evident in the additions to the second and third numbers (they are, incidentally, written in Thackeray's later upright hand). A morally positive dimension is laid over the early narrative and substantially informs the later composition of the bulk of the novel.

This change of heart, and its allegedly critical impact on the composition of *Vanity Fair* is controversial. But it is undeniable that as well as settling down with his family, Thackeray in 1845–6 settled down for the first time with an employer. The proprietors of *Punch* were Bradbury and Evans. Good-natured and easy-going, they tended to let the journal run itself under the genial management of Mark Lemon. Bradbury and Evans, as it happened, were also Dickens's publishers, since his break with Chapman and Hall in 1845. For Dickens, they provided a form of publication specially tailored to his unique talents. This was the novel in monthly numbers, delivered to the reader in twenty instalments, each of 32 pages and illustrated, costing one shilling each.

Fortified by his growing reputation as the leading *Punch* man, Thackeray evidently tried his 'Novel without a Hero' sample on *Punch*'s proprietors. His encounter is recalled by Henry Vizetelly, who met Thackeray on the way to see Bradbury and Evans:

In little more than half an hour Mr. Thackeray again made his appearance and with a beaming face gleefully informed me that he had settled the business. 'B&E' said he, 'accepted so readily that I am deuced sorry I didn't ask them another tenner I am certain they would have given it.' He then explained to me that he had named fifty guineas per part, including the two sheets of letterpress a couple of etchings and the initials at the commencement of the chapters. He reckoned the text, I remember, at no more than five and twenty shillings a page, the two etchings at six guineas each, while, as for the few initials at the beginning of the chapters, he threw these in. Such was Mr. Thackeray's own estimate of his commercial value as an author and illustrator A.D. 1846.

(Thackeray eventually got £60 per monthly number.) In coming to terms with him, it was natural for Bradbury and Evans to offer the Dickensian serial form, just as a year earlier it had been logical for the magazine proprietor Colburn to offer serialization in the *New Monthly Magazine* at a pound (five dollars) a page.

The contract with Bradbury and Evans was a great step for Thackeray. But triumph was by no means guaranteed. Other writers pulled at the Dickensian bow, but found the novel in monthly numbers too much for them. (Charles Lever, for instance, was taken up by Chapman and Hall after Dickens's defection, but had a notable failure with the *Knight of Gwynne* in 1847. Harrison Ainsworth's *Mervyn Clitheroe*, in 1851, was so unsuccessful that serial publication was aborted after the fourth number.) Ominously, the contract which Bradbury and Evans made with Thackeray did not specify how many instalments *Vanity Fair* was to run to. There was, reportedly, some gloomy thought of closing down after the third number. And as late as the fifteenth, it was apparently unsure whether the novel was to go to eighteen or the full Dickensian twenty.

Thackeray was well used to magazine serialization. (*Barry Lyndon* and *Catherine*, for instance, had been serialized in *Fraser's Magazine*.) But he had done nothing in monthly numbers. Unlike portions for magazines, the length of the Dickensian instalment was inflexible; and chapters needed to be shorter and tighter. More than with magazine serialization it was necessary to devise suspenseful climaxes. (Thackeray entirely rewrote the fine ending to the first number, 'Mr. Joseph entangled', see note to p. 43.)

And there was the added problem of the intratextual illustrations, which for *Vanity Fair* Thackeray was himself to provide. But length and pace were probably Thackeray's main problem. Before 'Novel without a Hero' was renamed *Vanity Fair* (i.e. before October–November 1846) Thackeray had the group I–IV, VIA set up in galley and page proof. (We know this, since he cannibalistically used bits of the proof in putting together Chapter VIB). It over-ran to 35 or more pages—which may have been another reason for splitting up and dispersing his material, postponing Vaux-hall to the second number.

Thackeray was evidently pleased with his deal with Bradbury and Evans. The novel was to be advertised and published under his own name. Moreover, he was allowed some idiosyncratic variation from the Dickensian pattern. *Vanity Fair* would be published from the *Punch* Office which was now Thackeray's main literary base. The work was to have an appropriately jaunty *Punch* flavour to it with cartoons, capital vignette illustrations and a free and easy Charivari manner (see note to p. 8).

This *Punch*-flavoured 'Novel without a Hero' was orig-inally scheduled for publication in May 1846. But in the event, it had to wait until January 1847. The reason for the delay must be guessed at. Possibly Thackeray was too busy with 'Snobs'. But it is more likely that the publication of *Dombey and Son* (which began to come out in October 1846) pushed Thackeray's serial aside. Dickens was surefire, and Bradbury and Evans's main literary property. Whether or not Dickens's precedence were the cause, the delay allowed Thackeray leisure to work over his manuscript (he evident-ly had about three numbers in hand by the end of 1846). While at Brighton in the autumn of 1846, he is reported to have hit on the brilliant title, *Vanity Fair*. Allegedly, the Bunyanesque idea 'came upon him unawares in the middle of the night'. He 'jumped out of bed and ran three times round his room, uttering as he went, "Vanity Fair, Vanity Fair, Vanity Fair".' Less dramatically, Brighton would also seem to have inspired the names of principal characters—notably Steine and Crawley; doubtless the Prince Regent's favourite residence also heightened Thackeray's sense of the novel's period.

Thackeray by this stage had made two significant design changes to his original 'Novel without a Hero'. The innovation of Dobbin and the degradation of George Osborne into a despicable, underbred dandy (see note to p. 48) gave him the opposition required for his 'redefinition of the gentlemanly ideal' theme. And 'Vanity Fair' gave him the perfect moral perspective on the social world of the novel. In themselves, Bunyanesque denunciations of modern times were nothing new. In the May 1846 issue of *Blackwood's Magazine* there was, for instance, an article by George Moir, 'The Modern Pilgrim's Progress' which satirized the contemporary world as a new Vanity Fair. In 1843, Nathaniel Hawthorne brought out a short story, 'The Celestial Railroad', which employed the same extended literary allusion.

But Thackeray's use of the 'Vanity Fair' motif is more subtle than Moir's or Hawthorne's. This is a novel principally set in Mayfair—then as now the most fashionable area of residential London. Mayfair is so called, because the old May Fair used to be held there, just north of Piccadilly, from the middle ages up to the eighteenth century. As Timbs's *Curiosities of London* describes this annual orgy, the May Fair was:

not for trade . . . but for musicke, showes, drinking, gaming, raffling, lotteries, stage plays and drolls . . . with boothes for jugglers . . . prize fighters . . . mountebanks, fire-eaters, ass racing, sausage tables, dice tables, ups and downs, merry go rounds, bull baiting, grinning for a hat, running for a shift, hasty pudding eating, eel divers, etc.

Thackeray would have known about May Fair from his beloved *Tatler*, papers 4 and 20. And, of course, the fair inspires 'Before the Curtain'. Thackeray was probably tickled by the fact that the old May Fair actually took place on a site where the modern Curzon Street (Becky and Rawdon live at 201) and Hertford Street (named after Steyne's original) now stand.

Vanity Fair, the old May Fair and metropolitan Mayfair thus mingle in one, complex, saturnalian image. And once he had hit upon it, the 'fair' idea provided a theme which Thackeray could thread right through the novel: from riotous Vauxhall night in 1813, to Brussels *en fête* before Waterloo, to the junket at Gaunt House before Becky's Luciferian fall, to the Pumpernickel Grand-Ducal gala at which she bounces back, to the demure little charity 'fair'—or bazaar—where Amelia finally encounters a rehabilitated 'Lady' Crawley.

The novel which had been so usefully delayed began to appear in monthly instalments from January 1847 onwards (see Note on the Text). According to Thackeray's daughter, the opening numbers 'hung fire'. Not until the fourth, or so, did the work begin to catch on with the public. Sales built up Thackeray's determination to hook the reader—evident in the suspenseful endings to the early numbers (see particularly, that between 4 and 5, which keeps the subscriber waiting a month to find out whom Becky is 'already' married to). Later in the novel, when he is secure that he has the public firmly caught, Thackeray does just the opposite. George's death at the end of 9, for instance, is a magnificently conceived anticlimax: 'Darkness came down on the field and city: and Amelia was praying for George, who was lying on his face, dead, with a bullet through his heart.' A less secure writer would surely (on the 'make 'em laugh, make 'em cry, make 'em wait' principle) have put the full stop after 'George'.

Serialization in monthly numbers set up peculiar relationships and conditions. It encouraged, famously, intimacy with the reading-buying public, who could write in their opinions about the unfolding novel (see the opening to Chapter XII), or silently vote (dis)approval by (dis)continuing purchase. The serialist writing month by month, like Dickens or Thackeray, had a *Spitzgefühl* finer than his colleague writing in volumes. The serialist was also more of a performer—with all the risks entailed in performance art. It was, for example, quite possible to dry up, or say something injudicious in the press of month to month composition. Another aspect (more than with the magazine serials to which Thackeray was used) was the need of writing to 'two unities'. Each number had to be complete in itself, yet component with the larger whole of the novel. Thackeray's skill in this respect is not obtrusive. But Edgar F. Harden has shown convincingly a system of unifying patterning in *Vanity Fair*. John Lester, in another important article, has analysed the 'redoublings' of Thackeray's narrative manner. Apparently artless, Thackeray's movements forwards and backwards in time are found to be both logical and artistically coherent.

Reading and writing a novel intermittently, at monthly intervals, put strain on the reader's and author's memories of foregoing event. Thackeray was obliged to recapitulate, or flashback, from time to time in his narrative. There was a compensating advantage, however, in the fuzzied recollection which resulted from having to hold events in the mind for a year or so. For local effect liberties could be taken with what had been written months before. Thus, in number 17, when Amelia finally discovers who it was gave her the little square piano in 1815 (it changes from a Broadwood to a 'Stothard', by the way), Dobbin is encouraged at last to speak out his love:

'Amelia, Amelia . . . I did buy it for you. I loved you then as I do now. I must tell you. I think I loved you from the first minute that I saw you, when George brought me to your house, to show me the Amelia whom he was engaged to. You were but a girl in white, with large ringlets; you came down singing—do you remember?— and we went to Vauxhall . . . ' (p. 759)

It makes a powerfully poignant scene. But if we turn back to what was written fifteen months earlier, we discover that Dobbin knew Amelia when she was a little girl and had in fact ruined one of her juvenile birthday parties by breaking a punch bowl. This unromantic encounter took place years before the Vauxhall trip in 1813 (see p. 59).

A lot could happen to an author in eighteen months. *Vanity Fair* might 'make' him, Thackeray confided to his mother, a week before first publication day. Six months

later, he was indeed 'made'. As his friend, Edward
Fitzgerald put it, he was now a 'great man'. Quite possibly,
social and literary success had its inhibiting effect on the
later parts of the novel. Thackeray might have been more
direct in the Steyne-Hertford business, had he not been
meeting the Marquis's kind socially in late 1847. Lions,
paradoxically, may be less fierce than literary jackals. Early
critics were in no doubt that Thackeray, over 1847, grew
socially and artistically into the role of great novelist. This
was his first big enterprise, and he had 'to feel his way to a
method'. Such was the opinion of the *Athenaeum* reviewer,
who had the advantage of genuine first impressions of *Vanity
Fair*:

In the early numbers of that work he kept the secret at once of his
plans—if he had any—and of his power. So poor were the
beginnings of the tale that the subsequent numbers ran a great
chance of being thrown aside on the faith of the early ones . . . It
was interesting to see how the writer's power grew and accumu-
lated by its own exercise. Number after number of the work
seemed to present a new strength drawn out and nourished by the
strength of that which preceded. No reader could have pre-
pictured the final mastery of hand from the feeble workmanship
that laid the first inadequate foundations of that remarkable book.

Modern critics have been divided on this question. Most
recently and forcefully, Edgar F. Harden has argued for a
much more thoughtful, careful and painstaking Thackeray
than the hand-to-mouth novelist of legend.

NOTE ON THE TEXT

THIS edition reproduces with photographic fidelity George Saintsbury's 1908 text, prepared for the complete 'Oxford Thackeray'. Saintsbury's was the first attempt to establish the authoritative text of *Vanity Fair*. Although modern scholarship will no longer trust it as such, it has always been accepted as reliable, and the modern reader may confidently use it as a 'practical' edition (to use Fredson Bowers's distinction). Genetically, as Peter Shillingsburg has shown, Saintsbury drew eclectically on the first printing of 1847–8, the second printing of 1848 and the 'Revised Edition' of 1853 for his text. Hence Thackeray's revisions in 1853 (such as the short opening of Chapter VI) coexist with the full range of illustrations (which 1853 did not have). An authoritative *Vanity Fair* is forthcoming from the Tennessee University Press edition of Thackeray's works (this particular title is edited by Robert A. Colby). The student interested in the very technical matter of what the ideal text of *Vanity Fair* should be, is directed to Peter Shillingsburg, 'Thackeray Texts', *Costerus*, 1974, pp. 287–314.

In the first serial edition of *Vanity Fair*, the divisions in the narrative were as follows:

No.			
1.	January 1847	Chapters	I–IV
2.	February 1847		V–VII
3.	March 1847		VIII–XI
4.	April 1847		XII–XIV
5.	May 1847		XV–XVIII
6.	June 1847		XIX–XXII
7.	July 1847		XXIII–XXV
8.	August 1847		XXVI–XXIX
9.	September 1847		XXX–XXXII
10.	October 1847		XXXIII–XXXV
11.	November 1847		XXXVI–XXXVIII
12.	December 1847		XXXIX–XLII

13.	January 1848	XLIII–XLVI
14.	February 1848	XLVII–L
15.	March 1848	LI–LIII
16.	April 1848	LIV–LVI
17.	May 1848	LVII–LX
18.	June 1848	LXI–LXIII
19 and 20.	July 1848	LXIV–LXVII

THACKERAY AS ILLUSTRATOR

BY the terms of his January 1847 contract with Bradbury and Evans, Thackeray was to supply 'by the 15th of every month sufficient matter for at least two printed Sheets with two etchings on Steel, and as many drawings on wood as may be thought necessary'. All in all, Thackeray provides nearly 200 'candles' to his own performance. *Vanity Fair*'s illustrations fall into four categories. There are the two naturalistic full plates, etched on steel, for each of the twenty numbers. There are naturalistic woodcuts, dropped strategically mid-text. There are pictorial capitals. And there are incidental allegorical designs, placed as frontis- or end-pieces.

Thackeray regarded himself as a poor draughtsman (twentieth-rate was his self-deprecating estimate) and the etchings on steel are usually regarded as his weakest illustrative work. His figures tend to be stilted, his faces (especially Becky's, unfortunately) unnatural. Nor is it always easy to see the relevance of picture to text (see, for instance, p. 333, 'Mrs. Osborne's Carriage Stopping the Way'). Thackeray's naturalistic woodcuts (which he could throw off spontaneously in between writing) have been found both good and bad by critics. That of Amelia sitting woebegone in Russell Square pining for Georgy (p. 630) is universally deplored. On the other hand, the little sketch of the 'tainted' Gaunt girls, unconsciously reading with the Damoclean swords over their heads shows Thackeray at his finest and deftest (p. 596). Another example, indicative of the way in which he uses illustration for ironic undercutting is to be found at the beginning of Chapter VIII (p. 88); the false sentimentality of Becky's effusive letter to Amelia is juxtaposed with her very calculating examination of the first Lady Crawley's portrait.

The density of illustration varies according, presumably, to the time Thackeray had at his disposal (thus the first number has thirteen, the ninth only nine). But as Edgar F.

Harden shows, in *The Emergence of Thackeray's Serial Fiction*, the novelist took great pains to 'place' his woodcuts, and certainly did not regard them as mere space-fillers. Thus in the MS. he specified that the illustration of Dobbin's awkwardness on being introduced to Amelia (p. 58) should follow exactly on: 'one of the clumsiest bows that was ever performed by a mortal.' And on p. 122, he added to his MS. the comment that 'the Captain and poor little Rebecca had just performed a dance together' specifying again that this was precisely where the illustration was to be. As Harden notes, not even Thackeray's first printers, Bradbury and Evans, were always able to locate his illustrations as exactly in the text as he would have liked.

The allegorical frontis- and end-pieces to the novel are magnificent (see detailed note to p. liii). In the first, Harlequin ruefully regards his own face in a cracked mirror, to the background of the towers of the church at Ottery St. Mary, where Thackeray spent happy childhood holidays. The end-piece shows two children putting the novel's characters (reduced to puppets and dolls) away in a box—the wicked nobleman and Becky have fallen out, we notice. The faint allusion to the coffin reminds us, with a pang, that most of the characters in *Vanity Fair* will by now (i.e. 1848) be in the ground, their place assumed by the new generation: Vanitas Vanitatum. The wayside allegorical sketches found in the text are similarly felicitous; see, for instance, Thackeray's little self-portrait of himself glum and unmasked at the end of Chapter IX.

Thackeray's talent for incidental cartoon is probably best evident in the pictorial capitals with which he begins his chapters. These are invariably amusing, and often subtle. Some contain topical allusion (see the 'Daily News' allusion in Chapter V). More often, they make some moral point. See, for instance, the 'I' (p. 140) which is transmuted into an image of egotistic George Osborne preening himself in a mirror. His son on being 'made a gentleman' (p. 707) is pictured as the monarch, George IV, in his notoriously extravagant coronation robes. In Chapter LXIV, Becky's continental exile is given an ironic resonance by allusion to

Haydon's grand historical study of 'Napoleon musing at St. Helena'. As Joan Stevens has persuasively argued (*Costerus*, 1974, pp. 113–40), the pictorial capitals (which are missing from the Revised 1853 edition) are a necessary feature of any complete *Vanity Fair* and constitute much more than incidental embellishment. General discussion of Thackeray's illustrations will be found in J. R. Harvey, *Victorian Novelists and their Illustrators* (London, 1970). Joan Stevens argues the value of Thackeray's illustrations for a full understanding of the novel in the *Review of English Literature*, 1965, pp. 19–38.

SELECT BIBLIOGRAPHY

Two surveys of Thackeray criticism are valuable: Dudley Flamm, *Thackeray's Critics: An Annotated Bibliography of British and American Criticism, 1836–1900* (North Carolina, 1966); John C. Olmsted, *Thackeray and his Twentieth Century Critics* (New York, 1977). The authoritative biography.is by Gordon N. Ray, in two volumes: *Thackeray: The Uses of Adversity* (London, 1955); *Thackeray: The Age of Wisdom* (London, 1958). Ray is editor of the four volumes of *Letters and Private Papers of William Makepeace Thackeray* (London, 1945–6) and is also author of the study in biographical criticism, *The Buried Life* (Harvard, 1952).

The following book-length studies of Thackeray are recommended, though not all agree with each other on the question of how to read Thackeray:

Lionel Stevenson, *The Showman of Vanity Fair* (London, 1947)

J. Y. T. Greig, *Thackeray: A Reconsideration* (London, 1950)

Geoffrey Tillotson, *Thackeray the Novelist* (Cambridge, 1954)

John Loofbourow, *Thackeray and the Form of Fiction* (Princeton, 1963)

Juliet McMaster, *Thackeray: The Major Novels* (Manchester, 1971)

Barbara Hardy, *The Exposure of Luxury: Radical Themes in Thackeray's Fiction* (London, 1972)

John Sutherland, *Thackeray at Work* (London, 1974)

Robert A. Colby, *Thackeray's Canvass of Humanity* (Ohio, 1979)

Edgar F. Harden, *The Emergence of Thackeray's Serial Fiction* (Tennessee, 1979)

The following titles are relevant to matters discussed in the Introduction:

Matthew W. Rosa, *The Silver Fork School: Novels of Fashion preceding Vanity Fair* (New York, 1936)

K. J. Hollingsworth, *The Newgate Novel, 1830–47* (Detroit, 1963)

Robin Gilmour, *The Idea of the Gentleman in the Victorian Novel* (London, 1981)

A very useful set of *Annotations to Vanity Fair* is provided by Oscar Mandel (Washington, 1981).

A CHRONOLOGY OF THACKERAY'S LIFE AND WORKS

1811   18 July: Born in Calcutta, India

1817   Sent by his parents to England

1822–8   At Charterhouse School

1829–30   At Trinity College, Cambridge; leaves without a degree

1830–1   July–Mar.: In Weimar

1831   June: Enters Middle Temple, with view to a career in law

1832–6   From July 1832 largely resident in Paris; studies art and contributes to various journals

1834   May: First identified contribution to *Fraser's Magazine*

1835   Meets Isabella Shawe, whom he marries in Aug. 1836

1837   Settles in London (18 Albion Street); with the *Yellow-plush Correspondence* (*Fraser's*, Nov. 1837–Aug. 1838) enjoys his first notable literary success

1839   *Catherine* (*Fraser's*, May 1839–Feb. 1840)

1840   *A Shabby-Genteel Story* (*Fraser's*, June–Oct.); *Paris Sketch Book*, Thackeray's first book, published; beginning of his wife's madness

1841   *The Second Funeral of Napoleon*; *The Great Hoggarty Diamond* (*Fraser's*, Sept.–Dec.)

1843   *The Irish Sketch Book*

1844   *Barry Lyndon* (*Fraser's*, Jan.–Dec.); undertakes a trip to the East (22 Aug.–26 Nov.)

1845   Wife. now incurably insane, placed in care

1846   *Notes of a Journey from Cornhill to Grand Cairo*; *The Snobs of England* (*Punch*, Mar. 1846–Feb. 1847); moves with his daughters to 13 Young Street, Kensington; publishes his first Christmas book, *Mrs. Perkins's Ball*

1847–8   *Vanity Fair* published in monthly numbers (Jan. 1847–June 1848)

1848–50   *Pendennis* published in 24 monthly numbers (23—the last being a double instalment) from Nov. 1848–Nov. 1850, interrupted by severe illness Sept.–Nov. 1849

1851   Lectures on the English Humourists in London
            (May–July); resigns from *Punch*

1852   *Esmond* published in 3 volumes

1852–3   Lectures in America on the English Humourists
            (Nov.–April)

1853–5   *The Newcomes* published in 24 (as 23) monthly numbers
            (Oct.–Aug.)

1854   *The Rose and the Ring*

1855–6   Lecturing in America on *The Four Georges* (Oct.–April),
            not published in England until 1860

1856–7   Lectures in England (Nov.–May)

1857   July: Stands unsuccessfully as Independent Liberal for
            the city of Oxford

1857–9   *The Virginians* published in 24 (as 23) monthly numbers
            (Nov.–Oct.)

1858   The 'Garrick Club Affair', provoked by a malicious
            article by Edmund Yates in *Town Talk*, sets Thackeray
            against Dickens

1859   August: Accepts editorship of the *Cornhill Magazine*; the
            first issue put out Jan. 1860; Thackeray holds the post
            until Mar. 1862, when he resigns

1860   *Lovel the Widower* (*Cornhill*, Jan.–June); *The Four Georges*
            (*Cornhill*, July–Oct.); *Roundabout Papers* (*Cornhill*, Jan.
            1860–Nov. 1863)

1861–2   *Philip* published in *Cornhill* (Jan. 1861–Aug. 1862)

1862   March: Moves to 2 Palace Green, Kensington

1863   May: Begins writing *Denis Duval*, published post-
            humously and incomplete, *Cornhill*, Mar.–June 1864

            24 Dec.: Dies; buried Kensal Green Cemetery

More detailed chronologies may be found in *Letters* (vol. 1), and in
Colby, *Thackeray's Canvass of Humanity* (see Select Bibliography).
The fullest chronological bibliography of Thackeray's works is to
be found in Lewis Melville, *William Makepeace Thackeray* (vol. 2),
London, 1910. This last, however, should be supplemented by
reference to the *Cambridge Bibliography of English Literature* and the
Wellesley Index for publications of Thackeray's identified by
subsequent scholarship.

VANITY FAIR:

PEN AND PENCIL SKETCHES OF ENGLISH SOCIETY.

BY W. M. THACKERAY,

Author of " The Irish Sketch Book :" " Journey from Cornhill to Grand Cairo:" of " Jeames's Diary "
and the "Snob Papers" in Punch : &c. &c.

LONDON:
PUBLISHED AT THE PUNCH OFFICE, 85, FLEET STREET.
J. MENZIES, EDINBURGH ; J. M'LEOD, GLASGOW ; J. M'GLASHAN, DUBLIN.

1847.

[Bradbury 123 MOUNT 31 , Whitefriars.]

[*Facsimile of wrapper to one of the original monthly numbers.*]*

VANITY FAIR

A Novel without a Hero.

BY

WILLIAM MAKEPEACE THACKERAY

LONDON

BRADBURY & EVANS BOUVERIE STREET,

1848

*[Facsimile of title-page to the first edition.]**

CONTENTS

BEFORE THE CURTAIN - - - - - - - 1

I. CHISWICK MALL - - - - - - 3

II. IN WHICH MISS SHARP AND MISS SEDLEY PREPARE TO
OPEN THE CAMPAIGN - - - - - 13

III. REBECCA IS IN PRESENCE OF THE ENEMY - - 24

IV. THE GREEN SILK PURSE - - - - 32

V. DOBBIN OF OURS - - - - - 48

VI. VAUXHALL - - - - - - 60

VII. CRAWLEY OF QUEEN'S CRAWLEY - - - 76

VIII. PRIVATE AND CONFIDENTIAL - - - - 88

IX. FAMILY PORTRAITS - - - - - 97

X. MISS SHARP BEGINS TO MAKE FRIENDS - - 105

XI. ARCADIAN SIMPLICITY - - - - - 113

XII. QUITE A SENTIMENTAL CHAPTER - - - 131

XIII. SENTIMENTAL AND OTHERWISE - - - 140

XIV. MISS CRAWLEY AT HOME - - - - 158

XV. IN WHICH REBECCA'S HUSBAND APPEARS FOR A SHORT
TIME - - - - - - 179

XVI. THE LETTER ON THE PINCUSHION - - - 189

XVII. HOW CAPTAIN DOBBIN BOUGHT A PIANO - - 200

XVIII. WHO PLAYED ON THE PIANO CAPTAIN DOBBIN BOUGHT? 211

XIX. MISS CRAWLEY AT NURSE - - - - 224

XX. IN WHICH CAPTAIN DOBBIN ACTS AS THE MESSENGER
OF HYMEN - - - - - 235

XXI. A QUARREL ABOUT AN HEIRESS - - 248

XXII. A MARRIAGE AND PART OF A HONEYMOON - 260

XXIII. CAPTAIN DOBBIN PROCEEDS ON HIS CANVASS - 269

XXIV. IN WHICH MR. OSBORNE TAKES DOWN THE FAMILY
BIBLE - - - - - - 276

CONTENTS

XXV. In which all the Principal Personages think fit to leave Brighton - - - - 292

XXVI. Between London and Chatham - - - 315

XXVII. In which Amelia joins her Regiment - - 325

XXVIII. In which Amelia invades the Low Countries - 332

XXIX. Brussels - - - - - - 344

XXX. 'The Girl I left behind Me' - - - 361

XXXI. In which Jos Sedley takes Care of his Sister 373

XXXII. In which Jos takes Flight, and the War is brought to a Close - - - - 386

XXXIII. In which Miss Crawley's Relations are very anxious about her - - - - 406

XXXIV. James Crawley's Pipe is put out - - 418

XXXV. Widow and Mother - - - - 438

XXXVI. How to live well on Nothing a Year - - 452

XXXVII. The Subject continued - - - - 464

XXXVIII. A Family in a very Small Way - - - 482

XXXIX. A Cynical Chapter - - - - 498

XL. In which Becky is recognized by the Family - 510

XLI. In which Becky revisits the Halls of her Ancestors - - - - - 522

XLII. Which treats of the Osborne Family - - 535

XLIII. In which the Reader has to double the Cape 543

XLIV. A Roundabout Chapter between London and Hampshire - - - - - 555

XLV. Between Hampshire and London - - 568

XLVI. Struggles and Trials - - - 579

XLVII. Gaunt House - - - - - 588

XLVIII. In which the Reader is introduced to the very best of Company - - - - 598

XLIX. In which we enjoy Three Courses and a Dessert 612

L. Contains a Vulgar Incident - - - 621

LI. In which a Charade is acted which may or may not puzzle the Reader - - - - 633

LII. In which Lord Steyne shows himself in a most Amiable Light - - - - 657

LIII. A Rescue and a Catastrophe   -   -   -   668
LIV. Sunday after the Battle -   -   -   - 678
LV. In which the same Subject is pursued   -   690
LVI. Georgy is made a Gentleman   -   -   - 707
LVII. Eothen   -   -   -   -   -   -   723
LVIII. Our Friend the Major   -   -   -   - 733
LIX. The Old Piano   -   -   -   -   -   - 749
LX. Returns to the Genteel World   -   -   - 761
LXI. In which Two Lights are put out   -   - 768
LXII. Am Rhein   -   -   -   -   -   -   - 783
LXIII. In which we meet an Old Acquaintance   - 797
LXIV. A Vagabond Chapter   -   -   -   - 812
LXV. Full of Business and Pleasure   -   -   - 830
LXVI. Amantium Irae   -   -   -   -   - 839
LXVII. Which contains Births, Marriages, and Deaths 856

LIST OF PLATES

Facsimile of Wrapper to one of the original Monthly
    Numbers   -   -   -   -   -   -   -   li
Facsimile Title-page to the First Edition -   -   - liii
Rebecca's Farewell   -   -   -   -   -   -   - 11
Mr. Joseph entangled   -   -   -   -   -   - 45
Mr. Joseph in a State of Excitement   -   -   - 67
Rebecca makes Acquaintance with a Live Baronet   - 79
Miss Sharp in her Schoolroom   -   -   -   - 107
Miss Crawley's Affectionate Relatives   -   - 119
Lieutenant Osborne and his Ardent Love-Letters   - 141
Mr. Osborne's Welcome to Amelia   -   -   - 151
The Note on the Pincushion   -   -   -   - 194
An Elephant for Sale   -   -   -   -   -   - 203
Mr. Sedley at the Coffee-house   -   -   -   - 239
Miss Swartz rehearsing for the Drawing-room   - 253
Ensign Stubble practising the Art of War   -   - 289
A Family Party at Brighton   -   -   -   - 299
Mrs. Osborne's Carriage stopping the Way   -   - 333
Mrs. O'Dowd at the Flower Market   -   -   - 345
Venus preparing the Armour of Mars   -   -   - 363

MR. JOS SHAVES OFF HIS MOUSTACHIOS - - - - - 403
MR. JAMES'S PIPE IS PUT OUT - - - - - 433
MAJOR SUGARPLUMS - - - - - - 449
MRS. RAWDON'S DEPARTURE FROM PARIS - - - 459
GEORGY MAKES ACQUAINTANCE WITH A WATERLOO MAN - 480
THE RIBBONS DISCOVERED IN THE FACT - - - - 507
SIR PITT'S LAST STAGE - - - - - - 513
GLORVINA TRIES HER FASCINATION ON THE MAJOR - - 547
THE ARRIVAL AT QUEEN'S CRAWLEY - - - - 565
BECKY IN LOMBARD STREET - - - - - 610
GEORGY GOES TO CHURCH GENTEELLY - - - - 631
THE TRIUMPH OF CLYTEMNESTRA - - - - 647
COLONEL CRAWLEY IS WANTED - - - - - 655
SIR PITT'S STUDY-CHAIR - - - - - - 681
GEORGY A GENTLEMAN - - - - - - 714
MR. JOS'S HOOKAHBADAR - - - - - - 735
A MEETING - - - - - - - 743
A FINE SUMMER EVENING - - - - - - 789
JOS PERFORMS A POLONAISE - - - - - 801
THE LETTER BEFORE WATERLOO - - - - - 867
BECKY'S SECOND APPEARANCE IN THE CHARACTER OF CLYTE-
　　MNESTRA - - - - - - - 875
VIRTUE REWARDED: A BOOTH IN VANITY FAIR - - - 879

BEFORE THE CURTAIN

As the Manager of the Performance sits before the curtain on the boards, and looks into the Fair, a feeling of profound melancholy comes over him in his survey of the bustling place. There is a great quantity of eating and drinking, making love and jilting, laughing and the contrary, smoking, cheating, fighting, dancing, and fiddling : there are bullies pushing about, bucks ogling the women, knaves picking pockets, policemen on the look-out, quacks (*other* quacks, plague take them !) bawling in front of their booths, and yokels looking up at the tinselled dancers and poor old rouged tumblers, while the light-fingered folk are operating upon their pockets behind. Yes, this is VANITY FAIR ; not a moral place certainly ; nor a merry one, though very noisy: Look at the faces of the actors and buffoons when they come off from their business ; and Tom Fool washing the paint off his cheeks before he sits down to dinner with his wife and the little Jack Puddings behind the canvas. The curtain will be up presently, and he will be turning over head and heels, and crying ' How are you ? '

A man with a reflective turn of mind, walking through an exhibition of this sort, will not be oppressed, I take it, by his own or other people's hilarity. An episode of humour or kindness touches and amuses him here and there ;—a pretty child looking at a gingerbread stall ; a pretty girl blushing whilst her lover talks to her and chooses her fairing ;—poor Tom Fool, yonder behind the wagon, mumbling his bone with the honest family which lives by his tumbling ;—but the general impression is one more melancholy than mirthful. When you come home, you sit down, in a sober, contemplative, not uncharitable frame of mind, and apply yourself to your books or your business.

I have no other moral than this to tag to the present story of *Vanity Fair*. Some people consider Fairs immoral altogether, and eschew such, with their servants and families : very likely they are right. But persons who think otherwise, and are of a lazy, or a benevolent, or a sarcastic mood, may perhaps like to step in for half an hour, and look at the performances. There are scenes of all sorts ; some dreadful combats, some grand and lofty horse-riding, some scenes of high life, and some of very middling indeed ; some love-making for the sentimental, and some light comic business ; the whole accompanied by appropriate scenery, and brilliantly illuminated with the Author's own candles.

What more has the Manager of the Performance to say ?—To acknowledge the kindness with which it has been received in all the principal towns of England through which the Show has passed, and where it has been most favourably noticed by the respected conductors of the Public Press, and by the Nobility and Gentry. He is proud to think that his Puppets have given satisfaction to the very best company in this empire. The famous little Becky Puppet has been pronounced to be uncommonly flexible in the joints, and lively on the wire : the Amelia Doll, though it has had a smaller circle of admirers, has yet been carved and dressed with the greatest care by the artist : the Dobbin Figure, though apparently clumsy, yet dances in a very amusing and natural manner : the Little Boys' Dance has been liked by some ; and please to remark the richly-dressed figure of the Wicked Nobleman, on which no expense has been spared, and which Old Nick will fetch away at the end of this singular performance.

And with this, and a profound bow to his patrons, the Manager retires, and the curtain rises.

LONDON, June 28, 1848.*

VANITY FAIR.

A NOVEL WITHOUT A HERO

CHAPTER I

CHISWICK MALL

HILE the present century was in its teens, and on one sunshiny morning in June, there drove up to the great iron gate of Miss Pinkerton's academy*for young ladies, on Chiswick Mall, a large family coach, with two .fat horses in blazing harness, driven by a fat coachman in a three-cornered hat and wig, at the rate of four miles an hour. A black servant, who reposed on the box beside the fat coachman, uncurled his bandy legs as soon as the equipage drew up opposite Miss Pinkerton's shining brass plate, and as he pulled the bell, at least a score of young heads were seen peering out of the narrow windows of the stately old brick house. Nay, the acute observer might have recognized the little red nose of good-natured Miss Jemima Pinkerton herself, rising over some geranium-pots in the window of that lady's own drawing-room.

'It is Mrs. Sedley's coach, sister,' said Miss Jemima. 'Sambo, the black servant, has just rung the bell; and the coachman has a new red waistcoat.'

'Have you completed all the necessary preparations incident to Miss Sedley's departure, Miss Jemima?' asked Miss Pinkerton herself, that majestic lady; the Semiramis of Hammersmith, the friend of Doctor Johnson, the correspondent of Mrs. Chapone herself.*

'The girls were up at four this morning, packing her trunks, sister,' replied Miss Jemima; 'we have made her a bow-pot.'

'Say a bouquet, sister Jemima, 'tis more genteel.'

'Well, a booky as big almost as a haystack; I have

put up two bottles of the gillyflower-water for Mrs. Sedley, and the receipt for making it, in Amelia's box.'

'And I trust, Miss Jemima, you have made a copy of Miss Sedley's account. This is it, is it? Very good—. ninety-three pounds, four shillings. Be kind enough to address it to John Sedley, Esquire, and to seal this billet which I have written to his lady.'

In Miss Jemima's eyes an autograph letter of her sister, Miss Pinkerton, was an object of as deep veneration, as would have been a letter from a sovereign. Only when her pupils quitted the establishment, or when they were about to be married, and once, when poor Miss Birch died of the scarlet fever, was Miss Pinkerton known to write personally to the parents of her pupils; and it was Jemima's opinion that if anything *could* console Mrs. Birch for her daughter's loss, it would be that pious and eloquent composition in which Miss Pinkerton announced the event.

In the present instance, Miss Pinkerton's ' billet ' was to the following effect :—

THE MALL, CHISWICK, June 15, 18—.

MADAM,—After her six years' residence at the Mall, I have the honour and happiness of presenting Miss Amelia Sedley to her parents, as a young lady not unworthy to occupy a fitting position in their polished and refined circle.   Those virtues which characterize the young English gentlewoman, those accomplishments which become her birth and station, will not be found wanting in the amiable Miss Sedley, whose *industry* and *obedience* have endeared her to her instructors, and whose delightful sweetness of temper has charmed her *aged* and her *youthful* companions.

In music, in dancing, in orthography, in every variety of embroidery and needlework, she will be found to have realized her friends' *fondest wishes*.   In geography there is still much to be desired ; and a careful and undeviating use of the backboard, for four hours daily during the next three years, is recommended as necessary to the acquirement of that dignified *deportment and carriage*, so requisite for every young lady of *fashion*.

In the principles of religion and morality, Miss Sedley will be found worthy of an establishment which has been honoured by the presence of *The Great Lexicographer*, and the patronage of the admirable Mrs. Chapone.   In leaving the Mall, Miss Amelia carries with her the hearts of her companions, and the affectionate regards of her mistress, who has the honour to subscribe herself,

Madam,

Your most obliged humble servant,

BARBARA PINKERTON.

PS.—Miss Sharp accompanies Miss Sedley.   It is particularly requested that Miss Sharp's stay in Russell Square may not exceed ten days.   The family of distinction with whom she is engaged desire to avail themselves of her services as soon as possible.'

This letter completed, Miss Pinkerton proceeded to write her own name, and Miss Sedley's, in the fly-leaf of a Johnson's Dictionary—the interesting work which she invariably presented to her scholars, on their departure from the Mall.   On the cover was inserted a copy of ' Lines addressed to a young lady on quitting Miss Pinkerton's school, at the Mall ; by the late revered Doctor Samuel Johnson.'*   In fact, the lexicographer's name was always on the lips of this majestic woman, and a visit he had paid to her was the cause of her reputation and her fortune.

Being commanded by her elder sister to get ' the Dictionary ' from the cupboard, Miss Jemima had extracted

two copies of the book from the receptacle in question.
When Miss Pinkerton had finished the inscription in the
first, Jemima, with rather a dubious and timid air, handed
her the second.

'For whom is this, Miss Jemima?' said Miss Pinkerton,
with awful coldness.

'For Becky Sharp,' answered Jemima, trembling very
much, and blushing over her withered face and neck, as
she turned her back on her sister. 'For Becky Sharp:
she's going too.'

'MISS JEMIMA!' exclaimed Miss Pinkerton, in the
largest capitals. 'Are you in your senses? Replace the
Dixonary in the closet, and never venture to take such
a liberty in future.'

'Well, sister, it's only two-and-ninepence, and poor
Becky will be miserable if she don't get one.'

'Send Miss Sedley instantly to me,' said Miss Pinkerton.
And so venturing not to say another word, poor Jemima
trotted off, exceedingly flurried and nervous.

Miss Sedley's papa was a merchant in London, and
a man of some wealth; whereas Miss Sharp was an articled
pupil, for whom Miss Pinkerton had done, as she thought,
quite enough, without conferring upon her at parting the
high honour of the Dixonary.

Although schoolmistresses' letters are to be trusted no
more nor less than churchyard epitaphs; yet, as it sometimes happens that a person departs this life, who is really
deserving of all the praises the stone-cutter carves over
his bones; who *is* a good Christian, a good parent, child,
wife or husband; who actually *does* leave a disconsolate
family to mourn his loss; so in academies of the male
and female sex it occurs every now and then, that the
pupil is fully worthy of the praises bestowed by the disinterested instructor. Now, Miss Amelia Sedley was a
young lady of this singular species, and deserved not only
all that Miss Pinkerton said in her praise, but had many
charming qualities which that pompous old Minerva of
a woman could not see, from the differences of rank and
age between her pupil and herself.

For she could not only sing like a lark, or a Mrs. Billington, and dance like Hillisberg or Parisot;* and embroider
beautifully; and spell as well as the Dixonary itself; but
she had such a kindly, smiling, tender, gentle, generous

heart of her own, as won the love of everybody who came near her, from Minerva herself down to the poor girl in the scullery, and the one-eyed tartwoman's daughter, who was permitted to vend her wares once a week to the young ladies in the Mall. She had twelve intimate and bosom friends out of the twenty-four young ladies. Even envious Miss Briggs never spoke ill of her : high and mighty Miss Saltire (Lord Dexter's granddaughter) allowed that her figure was genteel : and as for Miss Swartz,* the rich woolly-haired mulatto from St. Kitts, on the day Amelia went away, she was in such a passion of tears, that they were obliged to send for Dr. Floss, and half tipsify her with sal volatile. Miss Pinkerton's attachment was, as may be supposed, from the high position and eminent virtues of that lady, calm and dignified ; but Miss Jemima had already whimpered several times at the idea of Amelia's departure ; and, but for fear of her sister, would have gone off in downright hysterics, like the heiress (who paid double) of St. Kitts. Such luxury of grief, however, is only allowed to parlour-boarders. Honest Jemima had all the bills, and the washing, and the mending, and the puddings, and the plate and crockery, and the servants to superintend. But why speak about her ? It is probable that we shall not hear of her again from this moment to the end of time, and that when the great filigree iron gates are once closed on her, she and her awful sister will never issue therefrom into this little world of history.*

But as we are to see a great deal of Amelia, there is no harm in saying, at the outset of our acquaintance, that she was a dear little creature ; and a great mercy it is, both in life and in novels, which (and the latter especially) abound in villains of the most sombre sort, that we are to have for a constant companion, so guileless and good-natured a person. As she is not a heroine, there is no need to describe her person ; indeed I am afraid that her nose was rather short than otherwise, and her cheeks a great deal too round and red for a heroine ; but her face blushed with rosy health, and her lips with the freshest of smiles, and she had a pair of eyes, which sparkled with the brightest and honestest good-humour, except indeed when they filled with tears, and that was a great deal too often ; for the silly thing would cry over a dead canary bird ; or over a mouse, that the cat haply had seized upon ;

or over the end of a novel, were it ever so stupid ; and as
for saying an unkind word to her, were any persons hard-
hearted enough to do so—why, so much the worse for them.
Even Miss Pinkerton, that austere and god-like woman,
ceased scolding her after the first time, and though she no
more comprehended sensibility than she did algebra, gave
all masters and teachers particular orders to treat Miss
Sedley with the utmost gentleness, as harsh treatment was
injurious to her.

So that when the day of departure came, between her
two customs of laughing and crying, Miss Sedley was
greatly puzzled how to act. She was glad to go home,
and yet most wofully sad at leaving school. For three
days before, little Laura Martin, the orphan, followed her
about, like a little dog. She had to make and receive at
least fourteen presents,—to make fourteen solemn promises
of writing every week : ' Send my letters under cover to
my grandpapa, the Earl of Dexter,' said Miss Saltire (who,
by the way, was rather shabby) : ' Never mind the postage,
but write every day, you dear darling,' said the impetuous
and woolly-headed, but generous and affectionate Miss
Swartz ; and the orphan, little Laura Martin (who was
just in round-hand), took her friend's hand and said,
looking up in her face wistfully, ' Amelia, when I write
to you I shall call you mamma.' All which details, I have
no doubt, Jones, who reads this book at his Club,* will
pronounce to be excessively foolish, trivial, twaddling, and
ultra-sentimental. Yes ; I can see Jones at this minute
(rather flushed with his joint of mutton and half-pint of
wine), taking out his pencil and scoring under the words
' foolish, twaddling,' &c., and adding to them his own
remark of ' quite true '. Well, he is a lofty man of genius,
and admires the great and heroic in life and novels ; and
so had better take warning and go elsewhere.

Well, then. The flowers, and the presents, and the
trunks, and bonnet-boxes of Miss Sedley having been
arranged by Mr. Sambo in the carriage, together with
a very small and weather-beaten old cow's-skin trunk with
Miss Sharp's card neatly nailed upon it, which was delivered
by Sambo with a grin, and packed by the coachman with
a corresponding sneer—the hour for parting came ; and
the grief of that moment was considerably lessened by the
admirable discourse which Miss Pinkerton addressed to her

pupil. Not that the parting speech caused Amelia to philosophize, or that it armed her in any way with a calmness, the result of argument; but it was intolerably dull, pompous, and tedious; and having the fear of her schoolmistress greatly before her eyes, Miss Sedley did not venture, in her presence, to give way to any ebullitions of private grief. A seed-cake and a bottle of wine were produced in the drawing-room, as on the solemn occasions of the visit

of parents, and these refreshments being partaken of, Miss Sedley was at liberty to depart.

You'll go in and say good-bye to Miss Pinkerton, Becky!' said Miss Jemima to a young lady of whom nobody took any notice, and who was coming downstairs with her own bandbox.

'I suppose I must,' said Miss Sharp calmly, and much to the wonder of Miss Jemima; and the latter having knocked at the door and receiving permission to come in, Miss Sharp advanced in a very unconcerned manner, and said in French, and with a perfect accent, ' *Mademoiselle, je viens vous faire mes adieux.*'

Miss Pinkerton did not understand French; she only directed those who did: but biting her lips and throwing up her venerable and Roman-nosed head (on the top of

which figured a large and solemn turban), she said, 'Miss
Sharp, I wish you a good morning.' As the Hammersmith
Semiramis spoke, she waved one hand, both by way of
adieu, and to give Miss Sharp an opportunity of shaking
one of the fingers of the hand which was left out for that
purpose.

Miss Sharp only folded her own hands with a very frigid
smile and bow, and quite declined to accept the proffered
honour ; on which Semiramis tossed up her turban more
indignantly than ever. In fact, it was a little battle
between the young lady and the old one, and the latter
was worsted. 'Heaven bless you, my child,' said she,
embracing Amelia, and scowling the while over the girl's
shoulder at Miss Sharp. 'Come away, Becky,' said Miss
Jemima, pulling the young woman away in great alarm,
and the drawing-room door closed upon them for ever.

Then came the struggle and parting below. Words refuse
to tell it. All the servants were there in the hall—all the
dear friends—all the young ladies—the dancing-master who
had just arrived ; and there was such a scuffling, and
hugging, and kissing, and crying, with the hysterical *yoops*
of Miss Swartz, the parlour-boarder, from her room, as no
pen can depict, and as the tender heart would fain pass
over. The embracing was over ; they parted—that is,
Miss Sedley parted from her friends. Miss Sharp had
demurely entered the carriage some minutes before. Nobody cried for leaving *her*.

Sambo of the bandy-legs slammed the carriage-door on
his young weeping mistress. He sprang up behind the
carriage. 'Stop !' cried Miss Jemima, rushing to the gate
with a parcel.

'It's some sandwiches, my dear,' said she to Amelia.
'You may be hungry, you know ; and Becky, Becky
Sharp, here's a book for you that my sister—that is,
I—Johnson's Dixonary, you know ; you mustn't leave us
without that. Good-bye. Drive on, coachman. God bless
you !'

And the kind creature retreated into the garden, overcome with emotions.

But, lo ! and just as the coach drove off, Miss Sharp
put her pale face out of the window, and actually flung
the book back into the garden.

This almost caused Jemima to faint with terror. 'Well,

REBECCA'S FAREWELL

I never,'—said she—'what an audacious——' Emotion
prevented her from completing either sentence. The
carriage rolled away; the great gates were closed; the
bell rang for the dancing lesson. The world is before the
two young ladies; and so, farewell to Chiswick Mall.

CHAPTER II

IN WHICH MISS SHARP AND MISS SEDLEY PREPARE TO OPEN
THE CAMPAIGN

WHEN Miss Sharp had performed the heroical
act mentioned in the last chapter, and had
seen the Dixonary flying over the pavement
of the little garden, fall at length at the
feet of the astonished Miss Jemima, the
young lady's countenance, which had before
worn an almost livid look of hatred, assumed a smile that perhaps was scarcely more agreeable,
and she sank back in the carriage in an easy frame of
mind, saying, 'So much for the Dixonary; and, thank God,
I'm out of Chiswick.'

Miss Sedley was almost as flurried at the act of defiance
as Miss Jemima had been;' for, consider, it was but one
minute that she had left school, and the impressions of
six years are not got over in that space of time. Nay,
with some persons those awes and terrors of youth last

for ever and ever. I know, for instance, an old gentleman
of sixty-eight, who said to me one morning at breakfast,
with a very agitated countenance, 'I dreamed last night
that I was flogged by Dr. Raine.'* Fancy had carried him
back five-and-fifty years in the course of that evening.
Dr. Raine and his rod were just as awful to him in his
heart, then, at sixty-eight, as they had been at thirteen.
If the Doctor, with a large birch, had appeared bodily to
him, even at the age of three score and eight, and had said
in awful voice, 'Boy, take down your pant——'? Well,
well, Miss Sedley was exceedingly alarmed at this act of
insubordination.

'How could you do so, Rebecca?' at last she said, after
a pause.

'Why, do you think Miss Pinkerton will come out and
order me back to the black-hole?' said Rebecca, laughing.

'No: but——'

'I hate the whole house,' continued Miss Sharp, in a
fury. 'I hope I may never set eyes on it again. I wish
it were in the bottom of the Thames, I do; and if Miss
Pinkerton were there, I wouldn't pick her out, that I
wouldn't. Oh, how I should like to see her floating in
the water yonder, turban and all, with her train streaming
after her, and her nose like the beak of a wherry.'

'Hush!' cried Miss Sedley.

'Why, will the black footman tell tales?' cried Miss
Rebecca, laughing. 'He may go back and tell Miss Pinkerton that I hate her with all my soul; and I wish he would;
and I wish I had a means of proving it, too. For two
years I have only had insults and outrage from her. I have
been treated worse than any servant in the kitchen. I
have never had a friend or a kind word, except from you.
I have been made to tend the little girls in the lower schoolroom, and to talk French to the misses until I grew sick
of my mother-tongue. But that talking French to Miss
Pinkerton was capital fun, wasn't it? She doesn't know
a word of French, and was too proud to confess it. I
believe it was that which made her part with me; and
so thank Heaven for French. *Vive la France! Vive
l'Empereur! Vive Bonaparte!*'

'O Rebecca, Rebecca, for shame!' cried Miss Sedley;
for this was the greatest blasphemy Rebecca had as yet
uttered; and in those days, in England, to say 'Long live

Bonaparte ! ' was as much as to say ' Long live Lucifer ! '
' How can you—how dare you have such wicked, revengeful thoughts ? '

'Revenge may be wicked, but it's natural,' answered
Miss Rebecca. 'I'm no angel.' And, to say the truth,
she certainly was not.

For it may be remarked in the course of this little conversation (which took place as the coach rolled along lazily
by the riverside) that though Miss Rebecca Sharp has
twice had occasion to thank Heaven, it has been, in the
first place, for ridding her of some person whom she hated,
and secondly, for enabling her to bring her enemies to
some sort of perplexity or confusion ; neither of which
are very amiable motives for religious gratitude, or such
as would be put forward by persons of a kind and placable
disposition. Miss Rebecca was not, then, in the least kind
or placable. All the world used her ill, said this young
misanthropist*, and we may be pretty certain that persons
whom all the world treats ill, deserve entirely the treatment they get. The world is a looking-glass, and gives
back to every man the reflection of his own face. Frown
at it, and it will in turn look sourly upon you ; laugh at it
and with it, and it is a jolly kind companion ; and so let
all young persons take their choice. This is certain, that
if the world neglected Miss Sharp, she never was known
to have done a good action in behalf of anybody ; nor
can it be expected that twenty-four young ladies should
all be as amiable as the heroine of this work, Miss Sedley
(whom we have selected for the very reason that she was
the best-natured of all, otherwise what on earth was to
have prevented us from putting up Miss Swartz, or Miss
Crump, or Miss Hopkins, as heroine in her place ?)—it
could not be expected that every one should be of the
humble and gentle temper of Miss Amelia Sedley ; should
take every opportunity to vanquish Rebecca's hard-heartedness and ill-humour ; and, by a thousand kind words and
offices, overcome, for once at least, her hostility to her kind.

Miss Sharp's father was an artist, and in that quality
had given lessons of drawing at Miss Pinkerton's school.
He was a clever man ; a pleasant companion ; a careless
student ; with a great propensity for running into debt,
and a partiality for the tavern. When he was drunk, he

used to beat his wife and daughter ; and the next morning,
with a headache, he would rail at the world for its neglect
of his genius, and abuse, with a good deal of cleverness,
and sometimes with perfect reason, the fools, his brother
painters. As it was with the utmost difficulty that he
could keep himself, and as he owed money for a mile
round Soho, where he lived, he thought to better his circumstances by marrying a young woman of the French
nation, who was by profession an opera-girl. The humble
calling of her female parent, Miss Sharp never alluded to,
but used to state subsequently that the Entrechats were
a noble family of Gascony, and took great pride in her
descent from them.* And curious it is, that as she advanced
in life this young lady's ancestors increased in rank and
splendour.

Rebecca's mother had had some education somewhere,
and her daughter spoke French with purity and a Parisian
accent. It was in those days rather a rare accomplishment,
and led to her engagement with the orthodox Miss Pinkerton. For her mother being dead, her father, finding himself
not likely to recover, after his third attack of *delirium
tremens*, wrote a manly and pathetic letter to Miss Pinkerton, recommending the orphan child to her protection,
and so descended to the grave, after two bailiffs had quarrelled over his corpse.* Rebecca was seventeen when she
came to Chiswick, and was bound over as an articled pupil;*
her duties being to talk French, as we have seen ; and
her privileges to live cost free, and, with a few guineas
a year, to gather scraps of knowledge from the professors
who attended the school.

She was small and slight in person ; pale, sandy-haired,
and with eyes habitually cast down : when they looked up
they were very large, odd, and attractive ; so attractive,
that the Reverend Mr. Crisp, fresh from Oxford, and curate
to the Vicar of Chiswick, the Reverend Mr. Flowerdew,
fell in love with Miss Sharp ; being shot dead by a glance
of her eyes, which was fired all the way across Chiswick
Church from the school-pew to the reading-desk. This
infatuated young man used sometimes to take tea with
Miss Pinkerton, to whom he had been presented by his
mamma, and actually proposed something like marriage
in an intercepted note, which the one-eyed applewoman
was charged to deliver. Mrs. Crisp was summoned from

Buxton, and abruptly carried off her darling boy ; but the idea, even, of such an eagle in the Chiswick dovecot caused a great flutter in the breast of Miss Pinkerton, who would have sent away Miss Sharp, but that she was bound to her under a forfeit, and who never could thoroughly believe the young lady's protestations that she had never exchanged a single word with Mr. Crisp, except under her own eyes on the two occasions when she had met him at tea.

By the side of many tall and bouncing young ladies in the establishment, Rebecca Sharp looked like a child. But she had the dismal precocity of poverty. Many a dun had she talked to, and turned away from her father's door ; many a tradesman had she coaxed and wheedled into good humour, and into the granting of one meal more. She sat commonly with her father, who. was very proud of her wit, and heard the talk of many of his wild companions —often but ill-suited for a girl to hear. But she never had been a girl, she said ; she had been a woman since she was eight years old. Oh, why did Miss Pinkerton let such a dangerous bird into her cage ?

The fact is, the old lady believed Rebecca to be the meekest creature in the world, so admirably, on the occasions when her father brought her to Chiswick, used Rebecca to perform the part of the *ingénue ;* and only a year before the arrangement by which Rebecca had been admitted into her house, and when Rebecca was sixteen years old, Miss Pinkerton majestically, and with a little speech, made her a present of a doll—which was, by the way, the confiscated property of Miss Swindle, discovered surreptitiously nursing it in school hours. How the father and daughter laughed as they trudged home together after the evening party (it was on the occasion of the speeches, when all the professors were invited), and how Miss Pinkerton would have raged had she seen the caricature of herself which the little mimic, Rebecca, managed to make out of her doll. Becky used to go through dialogues with it ; it formed the delight of Newman Street, Gerrard Street, and the artists' quarter : and the young painters, when they came to take their gin-and-water with their lazy, dissolute, clever, jovial senior, used regularly to ask Rebecca if Miss Pinkerton was at home : she was well known to them, poor soul ! ! as Mr. Lawrence or President West.* Once she had the honour to pass a few days at Chiswick ; after which

she brought back Jemima, and erected another doll as
Miss Jemmy; for though that honest creature had made
and given her jelly and cake enough for three children,
and a seven-shilling piece* at parting, the girl's sense of
ridicule was far stronger than her gratitude, and she
sacrificed Miss Jemmy quite as pitilessly as her sister.

The catastrophe came, and she was brought to the Mall

as to her home. The rigid formality of the place suffocated
her: the prayers and the meals, the lessons and the walks,
which were arranged with a conventual regularity, oppressed
her almost beyond endurance; and she looked back to
the freedom and the beggary of the old studio in Soho
with so much regret, that everybody, herself included,
fancied she was consumed with grief for her father. She
had a little room in the garret, where the maids heard her

walking and sobbing at night ; but it was with rage, and not with grief. She had not been much of a dissembler, until now her loneliness taught her to feign. She had never mingled in the society of women : her father, reprobate as he was, was a man of talent ; his conversation was a thousand times more agreeable to her than the talk of such of her own sex as she now encountered. The pompous vanity of the old schoolmistress, the foolish good humour of her sister, the silly chat and scandal of the elder girls, and the frigid correctness of the governesses equally annoyed her ; and she had no soft maternal heart, this unlucky girl, otherwise the prattle and talk of the younger children, with whose care she was chiefly entrusted, might have soothed and interested her ; but she lived among them two years, and not one was sorry that she went away. The gentle tender-hearted Amelia Sedley was the only person to whom she could attach herself in the least ; and who could help attaching herself to Amelia ?

The happiness—the superior advantages of the young women round about her, gave Rebecca inexpressible pangs of envy. ' What airs that girl gives herself, because she is an earl's granddaughter,' she said of one. ' How they cringe and bow to that Creole, because of her hundred thousand pounds ! I am a thousand times cleverer and more charming than that creature, for all her wealth. I am as well-bred as the earl's granddaughter, for all her fine pedigree ; and yet every one passes me by here. And yet, when I was at my father's, did not the men give up their gayest balls and parties in order to pass the evening with me ? ' She determined at any rate to get free from the prison in which she found herself, and now began to act for herself, and for the first time to make connected plans for the future.

She took advantage, therefore, of the means of study the place offered her ; and as she was already a musician and a good linguist, she speedily went through the little course of study which was considered necessary for ladies in those days. Her music she practised incessantly, and one day, when the girls were out, and she had remained at home, she was overheard to play a piece so well, that Minerva thought wisely, she could spare herself the expense of a master for the juniors, and intimated to Miss Sharp that she was to instruct them in music for the future.

The girl refused ; and for the first time, and to the astonishment of the majestic mistress of the school. ' I am here
to speak French with the children,' Rebecca said abruptly,
' not to teach them music, and save money for you. Give
me money, and I will teach them.'

Minerva was obliged to yield, and, of course, disliked her
from that day. · ' For five-and-thirty years,' she said, and
with great justice, ' I never have seen the individual who
has dared in my own house to question my authority.
I have nourished a viper in my bosom.'

' A viper—a fiddlestick,' said Miss Sharp to the old lady,
almost fainting with astonishment. ' You took me because
I was useful. There is no question of gratitude between
us. I hate this place, and want to leave it. I will do
nothing here but what I am obliged to do.'

It was in vain that the old lady asked her if she was
aware she was speaking to Miss Pinkerton ? Rebecca
laughed in her face, with a horrid sarcastic demoniacal
laughter, that almost sent the schoolmistress into fits.
' Give me a sum of money,' said the girl, ' and get rid of
me—or, if you like better, get me a good place as governess
in a nobleman's family—you can do so if you please.'
And in their further disputes she always returned to this
point, ' Get me a situation—we hate each other, and I am
ready to go.'

Worthy Miss Pinkerton, although she had a Roman nose
and a turban, and was as tall as a grenadier, and had been
up to this time an irresistible princess, had no will or strength
like that of her little apprentice, and in vain did battle
against her, and tried to overawe her. Attempting once
to scold her in public, Rebecca hit upon the before-mentioned
plan of answering her in French, which quite routed the
old woman. In order to maintain authority in her school,
it became necessary to remove this rebel, this monster,
this serpent, this firebrand ; and hearing about this time
that Sir Pitt Crawley's family was in want of a governess,
she actually recommended Miss Sharp for the situation,
firebrand and serpent as she was. ' I cannot, certainly,'
she said, ' find fault with Miss Sharp's conduct, except to
myself ; and must allow that her talents and accomplishments are of a high order. As far as the head goes, at
least, she does credit to the educational system pursued at
my establishment.'

And so the schoolmistress reconciled the recommendation to her conscience, and the indentures were cancelled,
and the apprentice was free. The battle here described
in a few lines, of course lasted for some months. And
as Miss Sedley, being now in her seventeenth year, was
about to leave school, and had a friendship for Miss
Sharp (' 'tis the only point in Amelia's behaviour,' said
Minerva, ' which has not been satisfactory to her mistress '),
Miss Sharp was invited by her friend to pass a week with her
at home, before she entered upon her duties as governess
in a private family.

Thus the world began for these two young ladies. For
Amelia it was quite a new, fresh, brilliant world, with all
the bloom upon it. It was not quite a new one for Rebecca
(indeed, if the truth must be told with respect to the
Crisp affair, the tart-woman hinted to somebody, who took
an affidavit of the fact to somebody else, that there was
a great deal more than was made public regarding Mr. Crisp
and Miss Sharp, and that his letter was *in answer* to another
letter). But who can tell you the real truth of the matter ?
At all events, if Rebecca was not beginning the world, she
was beginning it over again.

By the time the young ladies reached Kensington turnpike,*
Amelia had not forgotten her companions, but had dried
her tears, and had blushed very much and been delighted
at a young officer of the Life Guards, who spied her as he
was riding by, and said, ' A dem fine gal, egad ! ' and before
the carriage arrived in Russell Square, a great deal of
conversation had taken place about the Drawing-room,
and whether or not young ladies wore powder as well as
hoops when presented, and whether she was to have that
honour : to the Lord Mayor's ball she knew she was to
go. And when at length home was reached, Miss Amelia
Sedley skipped out on Sambo's arm, as happy and as handsome a girl as any in the whole big city of London. Both he
and coachman agreed on this point, and so did her father
and mother, and so did every one of the servants in the
house, as they stood bobbing, and curtsying, and smiling, in
the hall, to welcome their young mistress.

You may be sure that she showed Rebecca over every
room of the house, and everything in every one of her
drawers ; and her books, and her piano, and her dresses,
and all her necklaces, brooches, laces, and gimcracks.

She insisted upon Rebecca accepting the white cornelian and the turquoise rings, and a sweet sprigged muslin, which was too small for her now, though it would fit her friend to a nicety ; and she determined in her heart to ask her mother's permission to present her white Cashmere shawl to her friend. Could she not spare it ? and had not her brother Joseph just brought her two from India ?

When Rebecca saw the two magnificent Cashmere shawls which Joseph Sedley had brought home to his sister, she said, with perfect truth, ' that it must be delightful to have a brother,' and easily got the pity of the tender-hearted Amelia, for being alone in the world, an orphan without friends or kindred.

' Not alone,' said Amelia ; ' you know, Rebecca, I shall always be your friend, and love you as a sister—indeed I will.'

' Ah, but to have parents, as you have—kind, rich, affectionate parents, who give you everything you ask for ; and their love, which is more precious than all ! My poor papa could give me nothing, and I had but two frocks in all the world ! And then, to have a brother, a dear brother ! Oh, how you must love him ! '

Amelia laughed.

' What ! *don't* you love him ? you, who say you love everybody ? '

' Yes, of course, I do—only——'

' Only what ? '

' Only Joseph doesn't seem to care much whether I love him or not. He gave me two fingers to shake when he arrived after ten years' absence ! He is very kind and good, but he scarcely ever speaks to me ; I think he loves his pipe a great deal better than his——' but here Amelia checked herself, for why should she speak ill of her brother ? ' He was very kind to me as a child,' she added ; ' I was but five years old when he went away.'

' Isn't he very rich ? ' said Rebecca. ' They say all Indian nabobs are enormously rich.'

' I believe he has a very large income.'

' And is your sister-in-law a nice pretty woman ? '

' La ! Joseph is not married,' said Amelia, laughing again.

Perhaps she had mentioned the fact already to Rebecca, but that young lady did not appear to have remembered

it ; indeed, vowed and protested that she expected to
see a number of Amelia's nephews and nieces. She was
quite disappointed that Mr. Sedley was not married ; she
was sure Amelia had said he was, and she doted so on little
children.

' I think you must have had enough of them at Chiswick,'
said Amelia, rather wondering at the sudden tenderness
on her friend's part ; and indeed in later days Miss Sharp
would never have committed herself so far as to advance
opinions, the untruth of which would have been so easily
detected. But we must remember that she is but nineteen
as yet, unused to the art of deceiving, poor innocent creature!
and making her own experience in her own person. The
meaning of the above series of queries, as translated in the
heart of this ingenious young woman, was simply this :—
' If Mr. Joseph Sedley is rich and unmarried, why should
I not marry him ? I have only a fortnight, to be sure,
but there is no harm in trying.' And she determined
within herself to make this laudable attempt. She redoubled her caresses to Amelia ; she kissed the white
cornelian necklace as she put it on ; and vowed she would
never, never part with it. When the dinner-bell rang she
went downstairs with her arm round her friend's waist, as
is the habit of young ladies. She was so agitated at the
drawing-room door, that she could hardly find courage to
enter. ' Feel my heart, how it beats, dear ! ' said she to
her friend.

' No, it doesn't,' said Amelia. ' Come in, don't be
frightened. Papa won't do you any harm.'

CHAPTER III

 VERY stout, puffy man, in buckskins and hessian boots, with several immense neckcloths, that rose almost to his nose, with a red striped waistcoat and an apple-green coat with steel buttons almost as large as crown pieces (it was the morning costume of a dandy or blood of those days), was reading the paper by the fire when the two girls entered, and bounced off his arm-chair, and blushed excessively, and hid his entire face almost in his neckcloths at this apparition.*

'It's only your sister, Joseph,' said Amelia, laughing and shaking the two fingers which he held out. 'I've come home *for good*, you know; and this is my friend, Miss Sharp, whom you have heard me mention.'

'No, never, upon my word,' said the head under the neckcloth, shaking very much,—'that is, yes,—what abominably cold weather. miss;'—and herewith he fell to poking the fire with all his might, although it was in the middle of June.

'He's very handsome,' whispered Rebecca to Amelia, rather loud.

'Do you think so?' said the latter. 'I'll tell him.'

'Darling! not for worlds,' said Miss Sharp, starting back as timid as a fawn. She had previously made a respectful virgin-like curtsy to the gentleman, and her modest eyes gazed so perseveringly on the carpet that it was a wonder how she should have found an opportunity to see him.

'Thank you for the beautiful shawls, brother,' said Amelia to the fire-poker. 'Are they not beautiful, Rebecca?'

'Oh, heavenly!' said Miss Sharp, and her eyes went from the carpet straight to the chandelier.

Joseph still continued a huge clattering at the poker and tongs, puffing and blowing the while, and turning as red as his yellow face would allow him. 'I can't make you such handsome presents, Joseph,' continued his sister, 'but while I was at school, I have embroidered for you a very beautiful pair of braces.'

'Good Gad! Amelia,' cried the brother, in serious alarm, 'what do you mean?' and plunging with all his might at the bell-rope, that article of furniture came away in his hand, and increased the honest fellow's confusion. 'For heaven's sake see if my buggy's at the door. I *can't* wait. I must go. D—— that groom of mine. I must go.'

At this minute the father of the family walked in, rattling his seals like a true British merchant. 'What's the matter, Emmy?' says he.

'Joseph wants me to see if his—his *buggy** is at the door. What is a buggy, papa?'

'It is a one-horse palanquin,' said the old gentleman, who was a wag in his way.

Joseph at this burst out into a wild fit of laughter; in which, encountering the eye of Miss Sharp, he stopped all of a sudden, as if he had been shot.

'This young lady is your friend? Miss Sharp, I am very happy to see you. Have you and Emmy been quarrelling already with Joseph, that he wants to be off?'

'I promised Bonamy of our service, sir,' said Joseph, 'to dine with him.'

'Oh, fie! didn't you tell your mother you would dine here?'

'But in this dress it's impossible.'

'Look at him, isn't he handsome enough to dine anywhere, Miss Sharp?'

On which, of course, Miss Sharp looked at her friend, and they both set off in a fit of laughter, highly agreeable to the old gentleman.

'Did you ever see a pair of buckskins like those at Miss Pinkerton's?' continued he, following up his advantage.

'Gracious heavens! father,' cried Joseph.

'There now, I have hurt his feelings. Mrs. Sedley, my dear, I have hurt your son's feelings. I have alluded to his buckskins. Ask Miss Sharp if I haven't? Come, Joseph, be friends with Miss Sharp, and let us all go to dinner.'

'There's a pillau, Joseph, just as you like it, and papa has brought home the best turbot in Billingsgate.'

'Come, come, sir, walk downstairs with Miss Sharp, and I will follow with these two young women,' said the father,

and he took an arm of wife and daughter and walked
merrily off.

If Miss Rebecca Sharp had determined in her heart upon
making the conquest of this big beau, I don't think, ladies,
we have any right to blame her; for though the task of
husband-hunting is generally, and with becoming modesty,
entrusted by young persons to their mammas, recollect
that Miss Sharp had no kind parent to arrange these
delicate matters for her, and that if she did not get a husband for herself, there was no one else in the wide world
who would take the trouble off her hands. What causes
young people to 'come *out*', but the noble ambition of
matrimony? What sends them trooping to watering-
places? What keeps them dancing till five o'clock in the
morning through a whole mortal season? What causes
them to labour at pianoforte sonatas, and to learn four
songs from a fashionable master at a guinea a lesson, and
to play the harp if they have handsome arms and neat
elbows, and to wear Lincoln green toxopholite hats and
feathers, but that they may bring down some 'desirable'
young man with those killing bows and arrows of theirs?
What causes respectable parents to take up their carpets,
set their houses topsy-turvy, and spend a fifth of their
year's income in ball suppers and iced champagne? Is it
sheer love of their species, and an unadulterated wish to
see young people happy and dancing? Psha! they want
to marry their daughters; and, as honest Mrs. Sedley has,
in the depths of her kind heart, already arranged a score
of little schemes for the settlement of her Amelia, so also
had our beloved but unprotected Rebecca determined to
do her very best to secure the husband, who was even more
necessary for her than for her friend. She had a vivid
imagination; she had, besides, read the *Arabian Nights*
and *Guthrie's Geography;** and it is a fact, that while she
was dressing for dinner, and after she had asked Amelia
whether her brother was very rich, she had built for herself
a most magnificent castle in the air, of which she was mistress, with a husband somewhere in the background (she
had not seen him as yet, and his figure would not therefore
be very distinct); she had arrayed herself in an infinity of
shawls, turbans, and diamond necklaces, and had mounted
upon an elephant to the sound of the march in Bluebeard,

in order to pay a visit of ceremony to the Grand Mogul.
Charming Alnaschar visions !* it is the happy privilege of
youth to construct you, and many a fanciful young creature
besides Rebecca Sharp has indulged in these delightful
day-dreams ere now !

Joseph Sedley was twelve years older than his sister
Amelia. He was in the East India Company's Civil
Service, and his name appeared, at the period of which we
write, in the Bengal division of the East India Register,
as collector of Boggley Wollah,* an honourable and lucrative
post, as everybody knows : in order to know to what higher
posts Joseph rose in the service, the reader is referred to
the same periodical.

Boggley Wollah is situated in a fine, lonely, marshy,
jungly district, famous for snipe-shooting, and where not
unfrequently you may flush a tiger. Ramgunge, where
there is a magistrate, is only forty miles off, and there is
a cavalry station about thirty miles farther ; so Joseph
wrote home to his parents, when he took possession of his
collectorship. He had lived for about eight years of his
life, quite alone, at this charming place, scarcely seeing
a Christian face except twice a year, when the detachment
arrived to carry off the revenues which he had collected,
to Calcutta.

Luckily, at this time he caught a liver complaint, for the
cure of which he returned to Europe, and which was the
source of great comfort and amusement to him in his
native country. He did not live with his family while
in London, but had lodgings of his own, like a gay young
bachelor. Before he went to India he was too young to
partake of the delightful pleasures of a man about town,
and plunged into them, on his return, with considerable
assiduity. He drove his horses in the Park ; he dined
at the fashionable taverns (for the Oriental Club was not
as yet invented)*; he frequented the theatres, as the mode
was in those days, or made his appearance at the opera,
laboriously attired in tights and a cocked hat.

On returning to India, and ever after, he used to talk
of the pleasure of this period of his existence with great
enthusiasm, and give you to understand that he and Brummell were the leading bucks of the day. But he was as
lonely here as in his jungle at Boggley Wollah. He scarcely
knew a single soul in the metropolis : and were it not for

his doctor, and the society of his blue-pill, and his liver complaint, he must have died of loneliness. He was lazy, peevish, and a *bon-vivant;* the appearance of a lady frightened him beyond measure ; hence it was but seldom that he joined the paternal circle in Russell Square,* where there was plenty of gaiety, and where the jokes of his good-natured old father frightened his *amour-propre.* His bulk caused Joseph much anxious thought and alarm ; now and then he would make a desperate attempt to get rid of his superabundant fat ; but his indolence and love of good living speedily got the better of these endeavours at reform, and he found himself again at his three meals a day. He never was well dressed ; but he took the hugest pains to adorn his big person, and passed many hours daily in that occupation. His valet made a fortune out of his wardrobe : his toilet-table was covered with as many pomatums and essences as ever were employed by an old beauty : he had tried, in order to give himself a waist, every girth, stay, and waistband then invented. Like most fat men, he *would* have his clothes made too tight, and took care they should be of the most brilliant colours and youthful cut. When dressed at length, in the afternoon, he would issue forth to take a drive with nobody in the Park ; and then would come back in order to dress again and go and dine with nobody at the Piazza Coffee-house.* He was as vain as a girl ; and perhaps his extreme shyness was one of the results of his extreme vanity. If Miss Rebecca can get the better of *him,* and at her first entrance into life, she is a young person of no ordinary cleverness.

The first move showed considerable skill. When she called Sedley a very handsome man, she knew that Amelia would tell her mother, who would probably tell Joseph, or who, at any rate, would be pleased by the compliment paid to her son. All mothers are. If you had told Sycorax that her son Caliban was as handsome as Apollo, she would have been pleased, witch as she was. Perhaps, too, Joseph Sedley would overhear the compliment—Rebecca spoke loud enough—and he *did* hear, and (thinking in his heart that he was a very fine man) the praise thrilled through every fibre of his big body, and made it tingle with pleasure. Then, however, came a recoil. ' Is the girl making fun of me ? ' he thought, and straightway he bounced towards

the bell, and was for retreating, as we have seen, when his
father's jokes and his mother's entreaties caused him to
pause and stay where he was. He conducted the young
lady down to dinner in a dubious and agitated frame of
mind. ' Does she really think I am handsome ? ' thought
he, ' or is she only making game of me ? ' We have talked
of Joseph Sedley being as vain as a girl. Heaven help us !
the girls have only to turn the tables, and say of one of their
own sex, ' She is as vain as a man,' and they will have
perfect reason. The bearded creatures are quite as eager
for praise, quite as finikin over their toilets, quite as proud
of their personal advantages, quite as conscious of their
powers of fascination, as any coquette in the world.

Downstairs, then, they went, Joseph very red and
blushing, Rebecca very modest, and holding her green
eyes downwards. She was dressed in white, with bare
shoulders as white as snow—the picture of youth, unprotected innocence, and humble virgin simplicity. ' I
must be very quiet,' thought Rebecca, ' and very much
interested about India.'

Now we have heard how Mrs. Sedley had prepared a fine
curry for her son, just as he liked it, and in the course of
dinner a portion of this dish was offered to Rebecca. ' What
is it ? ' said she, turning an appealing look to Mr. Joseph.

' Capital,' said he. His mouth was full of it : his face
quite red with the delightful exercise of gobbling. ' Mother,
it's as good as my own curries in India. '

' Oh, I must try some, if it is an Indian dish,' said Miss
Rebecca. ' I am sure everything must be good that comes
from there.'

' Give Miss Sharp some curry, my dear,' said Mr. Sedley,
laughing.

Rebecca had never tasted the dish before.

' Do you find it as good as everything else from India ? '
said Mr. Sedley.

' Oh, excellent ! ' said Rebecca, who was suffering tortures with the cayenne pepper.

' Try a chili with it, Miss Sharp,' said Joseph, really
interested.

' A chili,' said Rebecca, gasping. ' Oh, yes ! ' She
thought a chili was something cool, as its name imported,
and was served with some. ' How fresh and green they
look,' she said, and put one into her mouth. It was hotter

than the curry; flesh and blood could bear it no longer.
She laid down her fork. ' Water, for Heaven's sake, water ! '
she cried.   Mr. Sedley burst out laughing (he was a coarse
man, from the Stock Exchange, where they love all sorts
of practical jokes). ' They are real Indian, I assure you,'
said he. ' Sambo, give Miss Sharp some water.'

The paternal laugh was echoed by Joseph, who thought
the joke capital. The ladies only smiled a little. They
thought poor Rebecca suffered too much. She would have
liked to choke old Sedley, but she swallowed her mortification as well as she had the abominable curry before it,
and as soon as she could speak, said, with a comical good-
humoured air, ' I ought to have remembered the pepper
which the Princess of Persia puts in the cream-tarts in
the *Arabian Nights*. Do you put cayenne into your cream-
tarts in India, sir ? '

Old Sedley began to laugh, and thought Rebecca was
a good-humoured girl. Joseph simply said, ' Cream-tarts,
miss ? Our cream is very bad in Bengal. We generally
use goats' milk; and, 'gad, do you know, I've got to
prefer it ? '

' You won't like *everything* from India now, Miss Sharp,'
said the old gentleman; but when the ladies had retired
after dinner, the wily old fellow said to his son, ' Have
a care, Joe; that girl is setting her cap at you.'

' Pooh ! nonsense ! ' said Joe, highly flattered. ' I recollect, sir, there was a girl at Dumdum, a daughter of Cutler
of the Artillery, and afterwards married to Lance, the
surgeon, who made a dead set at me in the year '4—at
me and Mulligatawney, whom I mentioned to you before
dinner—a devilish good fellow Mulligatawney—he's a magistrate at Budgebudge, and sure to be in council in five
years. Well, sir, the Artillery gave a ball, and Quintin,
of the King's 14th, said to me, " Sedley," said he, " I bet
you thirteen to ten that Sophy Cutler hooks either you
or Mulligatawney before the rains." " Done," says I ;
and egad, sir—this claret's very good. Adamson's or
Carbonell's ? *——'

A slight snore was the only reply : the honest stockbroker was asleep, and so the rest of Joseph's story was
lost for that day. But he was always exceedingly communicative in a man's party, and has told this delightful
tale many scores of times to his apothecary, Dr. Gollop,

when he came to inquire about the liver and the blue-pill.

Being an invalid, Joseph Sedley contented himself with a bottle of claret, besides his madeira at dinner, and he managed a couple of plates full of strawberries and cream, and twenty-four little rout cakes, that were lying neglected in a plate near him, and certainly (for novelists have the privilege of knowing everything), he thought a great deal about the girl upstairs. ' A nice, gay, merry young creature,' thought he to himself. ' How she looked at me when I picked up her handkerchief at dinner ! She dropped it twice. Who's that singing in the drawing-room ? ' 'Gad ! shall I go up and see ? '

But his modesty came rushing upon him with uncontrollable force. His father was asleep : his hat was in the hall : there was a hackney-coach stand hard by in Southampton Row. ' I'll go and see the *Forty Thieves*,' said he, ' and Miss Decamp's dance ;'* and he slipped away gently on the pointed toes of his boots, and disappeared, without waking his worthy parent.

' There goes Joseph,' said Amelia, who was looking from the open windows of the drawing-room, while Rebecca was singing at the piano.

' Miss Sharp has frightened him away,' said Mrs. Sedley. ' Poor Joe, why *will* he be so shy ? '

CHAPTER IV

THE GREEN SILK PURSE

OOR Joe's panic lasted for two or three days; during which he did not visit the house, nor during that period did Miss Rebecca ever mention his name. She was all respectful gratitude to Mrs. Sedley; delighted beyond measure at the bazaars; and in a whirl of wonder at the theatre, whither the good-natured lady took her. One day, Amelia had a headache, and could not go upon some party of pleasure to which the two young people were invited: nothing could induce her friend to go without her. 'What! you who have shown the poor orphan what happiness and love are for the first time in her life—quit *you?* never!' and the green eyes looked up to Heaven and filled with tears; and Mrs. Sedley could not but own that her daughter's friend had a charming kind heart of her own.

As for Mr. Sedley's jokes, Rebecca laughed at them with a cordiality and perseverance which not a little pleased and softened that good-natured gentleman. Nor was it with the chiefs of the family alone that Miss Sharp found favour. She interested Mrs. Blenkinsop by evincing the deepest sympathy in the raspberry-jam preserving, which operation was then going on in the housekeeper's room; she persisted in calling Sambo 'Sir', and 'Mr. Sambo', to the delight of that attendant; and she apologized to the lady's maid for giving her trouble in venturing to ring the bell, with such sweetness and humility that the Servants' Hall was almost as charmed with her as the Drawing-room.*

Once, in looking over some drawings which Amelia had sent from school, Rebecca suddenly came upon one which caused her to burst into tears and leave the room. It was on the day when Joe Sedley made his second appearance.

Amelia hastened after her friend to know the cause of this display of feeling, and the good-natured girl came back without her companion, rather affected too. 'You know, her father was our drawing-master, mamma, at Chiswick, and used to do all the best parts of our drawings.'

'My love! I'm sure I always heard Miss Pinkerton say that he did not touch them—he only *mounted* them.'

'It was called mounting, mamma. Rebecca remembers the drawing, and her father working at it, and the thought of it came upon her rather suddenly—and so, you know, she——'

'The poor child is all heart,' said Mrs. Sedley.

'I wish she could stay with us another week,' said Amelia.

'She's devilish like Miss Cutler that I used to meet at Dumdum, only fairer. She's married now to Lance, the Artillery surgeon. Do you know, ma'am, that once Quintin, of the 14th, bet me——'

'Oh, Joseph, we know that story,' said Amelia, laughing. 'Never mind about telling that; but persuade mamma to write to Sir Something Crawley, for leave of absence for poor dear Rebecca :—here she comes, her eyes red with weeping.'

'I'm better now,' said the girl, with the sweetest smile possible, taking good-natured Mrs. Sedley's extended hand and kissing it respectfully. 'How kind you all are to me! All,' she added with a laugh, 'except you, Mr. Joseph.'

'Me!' said Joseph, meditating an instant departure. 'Gracious Heavens! Good Gad! Miss Sharp!'

'Yes; how could you be so cruel as to make me eat that horrid pepper dish at dinner, the first day I ever saw you? You are not so good to me as dear Amelia.'

'He doesn't know you so well,' cried Amelia.

'I defy anybody not to be good to you, my dear,' said her mother.

'The curry was capital; indeed it was,' said Joe, quite gravely. 'Perhaps there was *not* enough citron juice in it ;—no, there was *not*.'

'And the chilis?'

'By Jove, how they made you cry out!' said Joe, caught by the ridicule of the circumstance, and exploding in a fit of laughter which ended quite suddenly, as usual.

'I shall take care how I let *you* choose for me another time,' said Rebecca, as they went down again to dinner. 'I didn't think men were fond of putting poor harmless girls to pain.'

' By Gad, Miss Rebecca, I wouldn't hurt you for the world.'

' No,' said she, ' I *know* you wouldn't ; ' and then she gave him ever so gentle a pressure with her little hand, and drew it back quite frightened, and looked first for one instant in his face, and then down at the carpet-rods ; and I am not prepared to say that Joe's heart did not thump at this little involuntary, timid, gentle motion of regard on the part of the simple girl.

It was an advance, and as such, perhaps, some ladies of indisputable correctness and gentility will condemn the action as immodest ; but, you see, poor dear Rebecca had all this work to do for herself. If a person is too poor to keep a servant, though ever so elegant, he must sweep his own rooms : if a dear girl has no dear mamma to settle matters with the young man, she must do it for herself. And oh, what a mercy it is that these women do not exercise their powers oftener ! We can't resist them, if they do. Let them show ever so little inclination, and men go down on their knees at once : old or ugly, it is all the same. And this I set down as a positive truth. A woman with fair opportunities, and without an absolute hump, may marry WHOM SHE LIKES. Only let us be thankful that the darlings are like the beasts of the field, and don't know their own power. They would overcome us entirely if they did.

' Egad ! ' thought Joseph, entering the dining-room, ' I exactly begin to feel as I did at Dumdum with Miss Cutler.' Many sweet little appeals, half tender, half jocular, did Miss Sharp make to him about the dishes at dinner ; for by this time she was on a footing of considerable familiarity with the family, and as for the girls, they loved each other like sisters. Young unmarried girls always do, if they are in a house together for ten days.

As if bent upon advancing Rebecca's plans in every way—what must Amelia do, but remind her brother of a promise made last Easter holidays. ' When I was a girl at school,' said she, laughing—a promise that he, Joseph, would take her to Vauxhall. ' Now,' she said, ' that Rebecca is with us, will be the very time.'

' Oh, delightful ! ' said Rebecca, going to clap her hands ; but she recollected herself, and paused, like a modest creature as she was.

' To-night is not the night,' said Joe.

' Well, to-morrow.'

' To-morrow your papa and I dine out,' said Mrs. Sedley.

' You don't suppose that *I*'m going, Mrs. Sed. ? ' said her husband, ' and that a woman of your years and size is to catch cold, in such an abominable damp place ? '

' The children must have some one with them,' cried Mrs. Sedley.

' Let Joe go,' said his father, laughing. ' He's *big* enough.' At which speech even Mr. Sambo at the side-board burst out laughing, and poor fat Joe felt inclined to become a parricide almost.

' Undo his stays ! ' continued the pitiless old gentleman. ' Fling some water in his face, Miss Sharp, or carry him upstairs : the dear creature's fainting. Poor victim ! carry him up ; he's as light as a feather ! '

' If he stand this, sir, I'm d—— ! ' roared Joseph.

' Order Mr. Jos's elephant, Sambo ! '* cried the father. ' Send to Exeter 'Change, Sambo ; ' but seeing Jos ready almost to cry with vexation, the old joker stopped his laughter, and said, holding out his hand to his son, ' It's all fair on the Stock Exchange, Jos,—and, Sambo, never mind the elephant, but give me and Mr. Jos a glass of champagne. Boney himself hasn't got such in his cellar, my boy ! '

A goblet of champagne restored Joseph's equanimity, and before the bottle was emptied, of which as an invalid he took two-thirds, he had agreed to take the young ladies to Vauxhall.

' The girls must have a gentleman apiece,' said the old gentleman. ' Jos will be sure to leave Emmy in the crowd, he will be so taken up with Miss Sharp here. Send to 96, and ask George Osborne if he'll come.'

At this, I don't know in the least for what reason, Mrs. Sedley looked at her husband and laughed. Mr. Sedley's eyes twinkled in a manner indescribably roguish, and he looked at Amelia ; and Amelia, hanging down her head, blushed as only young ladies of seventeen know how to blush, and as Miss Rebecca Sharp never blushed in her life—at least not since she was eight years old, and when she was caught stealing jam out of a cupboard by her god-mother. ' Amelia had better write a note,' said her father ; ' and let George Osborne see what a beautiful handwriting we have brought back from Miss Pinkerton's. Do you remember when you wrote to him to come on Twelfth Night, Emmy, and spelt twelfth without the f ? '

'That was years ago,' said Amelia.

'It seems like yesterday, don't it, John ? ' said Mrs. Sedley to her husband ; and that night in a conversation which took place in a front room in the second floor, in a sort of tent, hung round with chintz of a rich and fantastic India pattern, and *doublé* with calico of a tender rose-colour ; in the interior of which species of marquee was a feather-bed, on which were two pillows, on which were two round red faces, one in a laced nightcap, and one in a simple cotton one, ending in a tassel :—in *a curtain lecture,*[*] I say, Mrs. Sedley took her husband to task for his cruel conduct to poor Joe.

'It was quite wicked of you, Mr. Sedley,' said she, ' to torment the poor boy so.'

' My dear,' said the cotton-tassel in defence of his conduct, ' Jos is a great deal vainer than you ever were in your life, and that's saying a good deal. Though, some thirty years ago, in the year seventeen hundred and eighty—what was it ?—perhaps you had a right to be vain.— I don't say no. But I've no patience with Jos and his dandified modesty. It is out-Josephing Joseph, my dear, and all the while the boy is only thinking of himself, and what a fine fellow he is. I doubt, ma'am, we shall have some trouble with him yet. Here is Emmy's little friend making love to him as hard as she can ; that's quite clear ; and if she does not catch him some other will. That man is destined to be a prey to woman, as I am to go on 'Change every day. It's a mercy he did not bring us over a black daughter-in-law, my dear. But, mark my words, the first woman who fishes for him, hooks him.'

' She shall go off to-morrow, the little artful creature,' said Mrs. Sedley, with great energy.

' Why not she as well as another, Mrs. Sedley ? The girl's a white face at any rate. *I* don't care who marries him. Let Joe please himself.'

And presently the voices of the two speakers were hushed, or were replaced by the gentle but unromantic music of the nose ; and save when the church bells tolled the hour and the watchman called it, all was silent at the house of John Sedley, Esquire, of Russell Square, and the Stock Exchange.

When morning came, the good-natured Mrs. Sedley no longer thought of executing her threats with regard to Miss Sharp; for though nothing is more keen, nor more common, nor more justifiable, than maternal jealousy, yet she could not bring herself to suppose that the little, humble, grateful, gentle governess, would dare to look up to such a magnificent personage as the collector of Boggley Wollah. The petition, too, for an extension of the young lady's leave of absence had already been dispatched, and it would be difficult to find a pretext for abruptly dismissing her.

And as if all things conspired in favour of the gentle Rebecca, the very elements (although she was not inclined at first to acknowledge their action in her behalf) interposed to aid her. For on the evening appointed for the Vauxhall party, George Osborne having come to dinner, and the elders of the house having departed, according to invitation, to dine with Alderman Balls, at Highbury Barn, there came on such a thunder-storm as only happens on Vauxhall nights, and as obliged the young people, perforce, to remain at home. Mr. Osborne did not seem in the least disappointed at this occurrence. He and Joseph Sedley drank a fitting quantity of port wine, *tête à tête*, in the dining-room,—during the drinking of which Sedley told a number of his best Indian stories; for he was extremely talkative in man's society;—and afterwards Miss Amelia Sedley did the honours of the drawing-room; and these four young persons passed such a comfortable evening together, that they declared they were rather glad of the thunder-storm than otherwise, which had caused them to put off their visit to Vauxhall.

Osborne was Sedley's godson, and had been one of the family any time these three-and-twenty years. At six weeks old, he had received from John Sedley a present of a silver cup; at six months old, a coral with gold whistle and bells; from his youth, upwards, he was 'tipped' regularly by the old gentleman at Christmas: and on going back to school, he remembered perfectly well being thrashed by Joseph Sedley, when the latter was a big, swaggering hobbledehoy, and George an impudent urchin of ten years old. In a word, George was as familiar with the family as such daily acts of kindness and intercourse could make him.

'Do you remember, Sedley, what a fury you were in,
when I cut off the tassels of your Hessian boots, and how
Miss—hem!—how Amelia rescued me from a beating, by
falling down on her knees and crying out to her brother
Jos, not to beat little George?'

Jos remembered this remarkable circumstance perfectly
well, but vowed that he had totally forgotten it.

'Well, do you remember coming down in a gig to
Dr. Swishtail's to see me, before you went to India, and
giving me half a guinea and a pat on the head? I always
had an idea that you were at least seven feet high, and
was quite astonished at your return from India to find
you no taller than myself.'

'How good of Mr. Sedley to go to your school and give
you the money!' exclaimed Rebecca, in accents of extreme
delight.

'Yes, and after I had cut the tassels of his boots too.
Boys never forget those tips at school, nor the givers.'

'I delight in Hessian boots,' said Rebecca. Jos Sedley
who admired his own legs prodigiously, and always wore
his ornamental *chaussure*, was extremely pleased at this
remark, though he drew his legs under his chair as it was
made.

'Miss Sharp,' said George Osborne, 'you who are so
clever an artist, you must make a grand historical picture
of the scene of the boots. Sedley shall be represented in
buckskins, and holding one of the injured boots in one
hand; by the other he shall have hold of my shirt-frill.
Amelia shall be kneeling near him, with her little hands
up; and the picture shall have a grand allegorical title,
as the frontispieces have in the Medulla and the spelling-
book.'*

'I shan't have time to do it here,' said Rebecca. 'I'll
do it when—when I'm gone.' And she dropped her voice,
and looked so sad and piteous, that everybody felt how
cruel her lot was, and how sorry they would be to part
with her.

'Oh, that you could stay longer, dear Rebecca,' said
Amelia.

'Why?' answered the other, still more sadly. 'That
I may be only the more unhap—unwilling to lose you?'
And she turned away her head. Amelia began to give
way to that natural infirmity of tears which, we have said,

was one of the defects of this silly little thing. George Osborne looked at the two young women with a touched curiosity ; and Joseph Sedley heaved something very like a sigh out of his big chest, as he cast his eyes down towards his favourite Hessian boots.

'Let us have some music, Miss Sedley—Amelia,' said George, who felt at that moment an extraordinary, almost irresistible impulse to seize the above-mentioned young woman in his arms, and to kiss her in the face of the company ; and she looked at him for a moment, and if I should say that they fell in love with each other at that single instant of time, I should perhaps be telling an untruth, for the fact is, that these two young people had been bred up by their parents for this very purpose, and their banns had, as it were, been read in their respective families any time these ten years. They went off to the piano, which was situated, as pianos usually are, in the back drawing-room ; and as it was rather dark, Miss Amelia, in the most unaffected way in the world, put her hand into Mr. Osborne's, who, of course, could see the way among the chairs and ottomans a great deal better than she could. But this arrangement left Mr. Joseph Sedley *tête à tête* with Rebecca, at the drawing-room table, where the latter was occupied in netting a green silk purse.

'There is no need to ask family secrets,' said Miss Sharp. 'Those two have told theirs.'

'As soon as he gets his company,' said Joseph, 'I believe the affair is settled. George Osborne is a capital fellow.'*

'And your sister the dearest creature in the world,' said Rebecca. 'Happy the man who wins her !' With this, Miss Sharp gave a great sigh.

When two unmarried persons get together, and talk upon such delicate subjects as the present, a great deal of confidence and intimacy is presently established between them. There is no need of giving a special report of the conversation which now took place between Mr. Sedley and the young lady ; for the conversation, as may be judged from the foregoing specimen, was not especially witty or eloquent ; it seldom is in private societies, or anywhere except in very high-flown and ingenious novels. As there was music in the next room, the talk was carried on, of course, in a low and becoming tone, though, for the matter of that, the couple in the next apartment would not have been disturbed had the talking been ever so loud, so occupied were they with their own pursuits.

Almost for the first time in his life, Mr. Sedley found himself talking, without the least timidity or hesitation, to a person of the other sex. Miss Rebecca asked him a great number of questions about India, which gave him an opportunity of narrating many interesting anecdotes about that country and himself. He described the balls at Government House, and the manner in which they kept themselves cool in the hot weather, with punkahs, tatties, and other contrivances ; and he was very witty regarding the number of Scotchmen whom Lord Minto, the Governor-General,* patronized ; and then he described a tiger-hunt ; and the manner in which the mahout of his elephant had been pulled off his seat by one of the infuriated animals. How delighted Miss Rebecca was at the Government balls, and how she laughed at the stories of the Scotch aides de camp, and called Mr. Sedley a sad wicked satirical creature ; and how frightened she was at the story of the elephant ! ' For your mother's sake, dear Mr. Sedley,' she said, ' for the sake of all your friends, promise *never* to go on one of those horrid expeditions.'

' Pooh, pooh, Miss Sharp,' said he, pulling up his shirt-collars ; ' the danger makes the sport only the pleasanter.' He had never been but once at a tiger-hunt, when the accident in question occurred, and when he was half killed— not by the tiger, but by the fright. And as he talked on, he grew quite bold, and actually had the audacity to ask Miss Rebecca for whom she was knitting the green silk purse ? He was quite surprised and delighted at his own graceful familiar manner.

' For any one who wants a purse,' replied Miss Rebecca, looking at him in the most gentle winning way. Sedley was going to make one of the most eloquent speeches possible, and had begun, ' Oh, Miss Sharp, how——' when some song which was performed in the other room came to an end, and caused him to hear his own voice so distinctly that he stopped, blushed, and blew his nose in great agitation.

' Did you ever hear anything like your brother's eloquence ? ' whispered Mr. Osborne to Amelia. ' Why, your friend has worked miracles.'

' The more the better,' said Miss Amelia ; who, like

almost all women who are worth a pin, was a matchmaker
in her heart, and would have been delighted that Joseph
should carry back a wife to India. She had, too, in the
course of this few days' constant intercourse, warmed into
a most tender friendship for Rebecca, and discovered a
million of virtues and amiable qualities in her which she
had not perceived when they were at Chiswick together.
For the affection of young ladies is of as rapid growth
as Jack's beanstalk, and reaches up to the sky in a night.
It is no blame to them that after marriage this *Sehnsucht
nach der Liebe** subsides. It is what sentimentalists, who
deal in *very* big words, call a yearning after the Ideal, and
simply means that women are commonly not satisfied until
they have husbands and children on whom they may
centre affections, which are spent elsewhere, as it were, in
small change.

Having expended her little store of songs, or having
stayed long enough in the back drawing-room, it now
appeared proper to Miss Amelia to ask her friend to sing.
'You would not have listened to me,' she said to Mr.
Osborne (though she knew she was telling a fib), 'had you
heard Rebecca first.'

'I give Miss Sharp warning, though,' said Osborne, 'that,
right or wrong, I consider Miss Amelia Sedley the first
singer in the world.'

'You shall hear,' said Amelia ; and Joseph Sedley was
actually polite enough to carry the candles to the piano.
Osborne hinted that he should like quite as well to sit in
the dark ; but Miss Sedley, laughing, declined to bear him
company any farther, and the two accordingly followed
Mr. Joseph. Rebecca sang far better than her friend
(though of course Osborne was free to keep his opinion),
and exerted herself to the utmost, and, indeed, to the
wonder of Amelia, who had never known her perform so
well. She sang a French song, which Joseph did not understand in the least, and which George confessed he did not
understand, and then a number of those simple ballads
which were the fashion forty years ago, and in which
British tars, our King, poor Susan, blue-eyed Mary, and
the like, were the principal themes. They are not, it is
said, very brilliant, in a musical point of view, but contain
numberless good-natured, simple appeals to the affections,
which people understood better than the milk-and-water

lagrime, sospiri, and *felicità* of the eternal Donizettian
music with which we are favoured nowadays.*

Among these ditties was one, the last of the concert,
and to the following effect :—

> Ah, bleak and barren was the moor !
>   Ah, loud and piercing was the storm !
> The cottage roof was shelter'd sure,
>   The cottage hearth was bright and warm—
> An orphan boy the lattice pass'd,
>   And, as he mark'd its cheerful glow,
> Felt doubly keen the midnight blast,
>   And doubly cold the fallen snow.
>
> They mark'd him as he onward pressed,
>   With fainting heart and weary limb ;
> Kind voices bade him turn and rest,
>   And gentle faces welcomed him.
> The dawn is up—the guest is gone,
>   The cottage hearth is blazing still ;
> Heaven pity all poor wanderers lone !
>   Hark to the wind upon the hill ! *

It was the sentiment of the before-mentioned words,
'When I'm gone,' over again. As she came to the last
words, Miss Sharp's 'deep-toned voice faltered'.* Everybody felt the allusion to her departure, and to her hapless
orphan state. Joseph Sedley, who was fond of music, and
soft-hearted, was in a state of ravishment during the
performance of the song, and profoundly touched at its
conclusion. If he had had the courage ; if George and
Miss Sedley had remained, according to the former's proposal, in the farther room ; Joseph Sedley's bachelorhood
would have been at an end, and this work would never
have been written. But at the close of the ditty, Rebecca
quitted the piano, and giving her hand to Amelia, walked
away into the front drawing-room twilight ; and, at this
moment, Mr. Sambo made his appearance with a tray,
containing sandwiches, jellies, and some glittering glasses
and decanters, on which Joseph Sedley's attention was
immediately fixed. When the parents of the house of
Sedley returned from their dinner-party, they found the
young people so busy in talking, that they had not heard
the arrival of the carriage, and Mr. Joseph was in the act
of saying, 'My dear Miss Sharp, one little teaspoonful of

jelly to recruit you after your immense—your—your *delightful* exertions.'

'Bravo, Jos!' said Mr. Sedley; on hearing the bantering of which well-known voice, Jos instantly relapsed into an alarmed silence, and quickly took his departure. He did not lie awake all night thinking whether or not he was in love with Miss Sharp; the passion of love never interfered with the appetite or the slumber of Mr. Joseph Sedley; but he thought to himself how delightful it would be to hear such songs as those after Cutcherry*—what a *distinguée* girl she was—how she could speak French better than the Governor-General's lady herself—and what a sensation she would make at the Calcutta balls. 'It's evident the poor devil's in love with me,' thought he. 'She is just as rich as most of the girls who come out to India. I might go farther and fare worse, egad!' And in these meditations he fell asleep.

How Miss Sharp lay awake, thinking, will he come or not to-morrow? need not be told here. To-morrow came, and, as sure as fate, Mr. Joseph Sedley made his appearance before luncheon. He had never been known before to confer such an honour on Russell Square.* George Osborne was somehow there already (sadly 'putting out' Amelia, who was writing to her twelve dearest friends at Chiswick Mall), and Rebecca was employed upon her yesterday's work. As Joe's buggy drove up, and while, after his usual thundering knock and pompous bustle at the door, the ex-collector of Boggley Wollah laboured upstairs to the drawing-room, knowing glances were telegraphed between Osborne and Miss Sedley, and the pair, smiling archly, looked at Rebecca, who actually blushed as she bent her fair ringlets over her netting. How her heart beat as Joseph appeared,—Joseph, puffing from the staircase in shining creaking boots,—Joseph, in a new waistcoat, red with heat and nervousness, and blushing behind his wadded neckcloth. It was a nervous moment for all; and as for Amelia, I think she was more frightened than even the people most concerned.

Sambo, who flung open the door and announced Mr. Joseph, followed grinning, in the collector's rear, and bearing two handsome nosegays of flowers, which the monster had actually had the gallantry to purchase in Covent Garden market that morning—they were not as big as the haystacks which ladies carry about with them nowadays, in cones of filigree paper; but the young women were delighted with the gift, as Joseph presented one to each, with an exceedingly solemn bow.

'Bravo, Jos,' cried Osborne.

'Thank you, dear Joseph,' said Amelia, quite ready to kiss her brother, if he were so minded. (And I think for a kiss from such a dear creature as Amelia, I would purchase all Mr. Lee's conservatories* out of hand.)

'O heavenly, heavenly flowers!' exclaimed Miss Sharp, and smelt them delicately, and held them to her bosom, and cast up her eyes to the ceiling, in an ecstasy of admiration. Perhaps she just looked first into the bouquet, to see whether there was a *billet-doux* hidden among the flowers; but there was no letter.

'Do they talk the language of flowers at Boggley Wollah, Sedley?' asked Osborne, laughing.

'Pooh, nonsense!' replied the sentimental youth. 'Bought 'em at Nathan's; very glad you like 'em; and eh, Amelia, my dear, I bought a pineapple at the same time, which I gave to Sambo. Let's have it for tiffin; very cool and nice this hot weather.' Rebecca said she had never tasted a pine, and longed beyond everything to taste one.

So the conversation went on. I don't know on what pretext Osborne left the room, or why, presently, Amelia went away, perhaps to superintend the slicing of the pineapple; but Jos was left alone with Rebecca, who had resumed her work, and the green silk and the shining needles were quivering rapidly under her white slender fingers.

'What a beautiful, *byoo-ootiful* song that was you sang last night, dear Miss Sharp,' said the collector. 'It made me cry almost; 'pon my honour it did.'

'Because you have a kind heart, Mr. Joseph; all the Sedleys have, I think.'

'It kept me awake last night, and I was trying to hum it this morning in bed; I was, upon my honour. Gollop, my doctor, came in at eleven (for I'm a sad invalid, you know, and see Gollop every day), and, 'gad! there I was, singing away like—a robin.'

'Oh, you droll creature! Do let me hear you sing it.'

'Me? No, you, Miss Sharp; my dear Miss Sharp, do sing it.'

MR. JOSEPH ENTANGLED

'Not now, Mr. Sedley,' said Rebecca, with a sigh. 'My spirits are not equal to it : besides I must finish the purse. Will you help me, Mr. Sedley ? ' And before he had time to ask how, Mr. Joseph Sedley, of the East India Company's service, was actually seated *tête à tête* with a young lady, looking at her with a most killing expression ; his arms stretched out before her in an imploring attitude, and his hands bound in a web of green silk, which she was unwinding.

In this romantic position Osborne and Amelia found the interesting pair, when they entered to announce that tiffin was ready. The skein of silk was just wound round the card ; but Mr. Jos had never spoken.

'I am sure he will to-night, dear,' Amelia said, as she pressed Rebecca's hand ; and Sedley, too, had communed with his soul, and said to himself, ' 'Gad, I'll pop the question at Vauxhall.'

CHAPTER V

DOBBIN OF OURS*

UFF'S fight with Dobbin, and the unexpected issue of that contest, will long be remembered by every man who was educated at Dr. Swishtail's famous school. The latter youth (who used to be called Heigh-ho Dobbin, Gee-ho Dobbin, and by many other names indicative of puerile contempt) was the quietest, the clumsiest, and, as it seemed, the dullest of all Dr. Swishtail's young gentlemen. His parent was a grocer in the city : and it was bruited abroad that he was admitted into Dr. Swishtail's academy upon what are called ' mutual principles '—that is to say, the expenses of his board and schooling were defrayed by his father in goods, not money ; and he stood there—almost at the bottom of the school— in his scraggy corduroys and jacket, through the seams of which his great big bones were bursting—as the representative of so many pounds of tea, candles, sugar, mottled-soap, plums (of which a very mild proportion was supplied for the puddings of the establishment), and other commodities. A dreadful day it was for young Dobbin when one of the youngsters of the school, having run into the town upon a poaching excursion for hardbake and polonies. espied the cart of Dobbin & Rudge, Grocers and Oilmen, Thames Street, London, at the doctor's door, discharging a cargo of the wares in which the firm dealt.

Young Dobbin had no peace after that. The jokes were frightful, and merciless against him. ' Hullo, Dobbin,' one wag would say, ' here's good news in the paper. Sugars is ris', my boy.' Another would set a sum—' If a pound of mutton-candles cost sevenpence-halfpenny, how much must Dobbin cost ? ' and a roar would follow from all the circle of young knaves, usher and all, who rightly considered that the selling of goods by retail is a shameful

and infamous practice, meriting the contempt and scorn
of all real gentlemen.

'Your father's only a merchant,* Osborne,' Dobbin said
in private to the little boy who had brought down the storm
upon him. At which the latter replied haughtily, 'My
father's a gentleman, and keeps his carriage;' and Mr.
William Dobbin retreated to a remote out-house in the
playground, where he passed a half-holiday in the bitterest
sadness and woe. Who amongst us is there that does not
recollect similar hours of bitter, bitter childish grief?
Who feels injustice; who shrinks before a slight; who has
a sense of wrong so acute, and so glowing a gratitude for
kindness, as a generous boy? and how many of those
gentle souls do you degrade, estrange, torture, for the sake
of a little loose arithmetic, and miserable dog-Latin?

Now, William Dobbin, from an incapacity to acquire
the rudiments of the above language, as they are propounded
in that wonderful book the Eton Latin Grammar, was compelled to remain among the very last of Dr. Swishtail's
scholars, and was 'taken down' continually by little
fellows with pink faces and pinafores when he marched up
with the lower form, a giant amongst them, with his downcast stupefied look, his dog's-eared primer, and his tight
corduroys. High and low, all made fun of him. They
sewed up those corduroys, tight as they were. They cut
his bed-strings. They upset buckets and benches, so that
he might break his shins over them, which he never failed
to do. They sent him parcels, which, when opened, were
found to contain the paternal soap and candles. There
was no little fellow but had his jeer and joke at Dobbin;
and he bore everything quite patiently, and was entirely
dumb and miserable.

Cuff, on the contrary, was the great chief and dandy of
the Swishtail Seminary. He smuggled wine in. He fought
the town-boys. Ponies used to come for him to ride home
on Saturdays. He had his top-boots in his room, in which
he used to hunt in the holidays. He had a gold repeater:
and took snuff like the Doctor. He had been to the Opera,
and knew the merits of the principal actors, preferring
Mr. Kean to Mr. Kemble.* He could knock you off forty
Latin verses in an hour. He could make French poetry.
What else didn't he know, or couldn't he do? They said
even the Doctor himself was afraid of him.

Cuff, the unquestioned king of the school, ruled over his subjects and bullied them, with splendid superiority. This one blacked his shoes : that toasted his bread, others would fag out, and give him balls at cricket during whole summer afternoons. 'Figs' was the fellow whom he despised most, and with whom, though always abusing him, and sneering at him, he scarcely ever condescended to hold personal communication.

One day in private, the two young gentlemen had had a difference. Figs, alone in the schoolroom, was blundering over a home letter ; when Cuff, entering, bade him go upon some message, of which tarts were probably the subject.

'I can't,' says Dobbin ; 'I want to finish my letter.'

'You *can't* ?' says Mr. Cuff, laying hold of that document (in which many words were scratched out, many were misspelt, on which had been spent I don't know how much thought, and labour, and tears ; for the poor fellow was writing to his mother, who was fond of him, although she was a grocer's wife, and lived in a back-parlour in Thames Street). 'You *can't* ?' says Mr. Cuff : 'I should like to know why, pray ? Can't you write to old Mother Figs to-morrow ?'

'Don't call names,' Dobbin said, getting off the bench, very nervous.

'Well, sir, will you go ?' crowed the cock of the school.

'Put down the letter,' Dobbin replied ; 'no gentleman readth letterth.'

'Well, *now* will you go ?' says the other.

'No, I won't. Don't strike, or I'll *thmash* you,' roars out Dobbin, springing to a leaden inkstand, and looking so wicked, that Mr. Cuff paused, turned down his coat-sleeves again, put his hands into his pockets, and walked away with a sneer. But he never meddled personally with the grocer's boy after that ; though we must do him the justice to say he always spoke of Mr. Dobbin with contempt behind his back.

Some time after this interview, it happened that Mr. Cuff, on a sunshiny afternoon, was in the neighbourhood of poor William Dobbin, who was lying under a tree in the play-ground, spelling over a favourite copy of the *Arabian Nights* which he had—apart from the rest of the school, who were pursuing their various sports—quite lonely, and almost happy. If people would but leave children to themselves; if teachers would cease to bully them; if parents would not insist upon directing their thoughts, and dominating their feelings—those feelings and thoughts which are a mystery to all (for how much do you and I know of each other, of our children, of our fathers, of our neighbour, and how far more beautiful and sacred are the thoughts of the poor lad or girl whom you govern likely to be, than those of the dull and world-corrupted person who rules him?)—

if, I say, parents and masters would leave their children alone a little more,—small harm would accrue, although a less quantity of *as in praesenti** might be acquired.

Well, William Dobbin had for once forgotten the world, and was away with Sindbad the Sailor in the Valley of Diamonds, or with Prince Ahmed and the Fairy Peribanou in that delightful cavern where the prince found her, and whither we should all like to make a tour; when shrill cries, as of a little fellow weeping, woke up his pleasant reverie; and, looking up, he saw Cuff before him, belabouring a little boy,

It was the lad who had peached upon him about the
grocer's cart ; but he bore little malice, not at least towards
the young and small. 'How dare you, sir, break the
bottle ? ' says Cuff to the little urchin, swinging a yellow
cricket-stump over him.

The boy had been instructed to get over the playground
wall (at a selected spot where the broken-glass had been
removed from the top, and niches made convenient in the
brick) ; to run a quarter of a mile ; to purchase a pint
of rum-shrub* on credit; to brave all the Doctor's outlying
spies, and to clamber back into the playground again ;
during the performance of which feat his foot had slipped,
and the bottle was broken, and the shrub had been spilt, and
his pantaloons had been damaged, and he appeared before
his employer a perfectly guilty and trembling, though harmless, wretch.

'How dare you, sir, break it ? ' says Cuff ; 'you blundering little thief. You drank the shrub, and now you pretend
to have broken the bottle. Hold out your hand, sir.'

Down came the stump with a great heavy thump on the
child's hand. A moan followed. Dobbin looked up.
The Prince Peribanou had fled into the inmost cavern with
Prince Ahmed : the Roc had whisked away Sindbad the
Sailor out of the Valley of Diamonds out of sight, far into
the clouds : and there was everyday life before honest
William ; and a big boy beating a little one without cause.

'Hold out your other hand, sir,' roars Cuff to his little
schoolfellow, whose face was distorted with pain. Dobbin
quivered, and gathered himself up in his narrow old clothes.

'Take that, you little devil ! ' cried Mr. Cuff, and down
came the wicket again on the child's hand.—Don't be
horrified, ladies, every boy at a public school has done it.
Your children will so do and be done by, in all probability.
Down came the wicket again ; and Dobbin started up.

I can't tell what his motive was. Torture in a public
school is as much licensed as the knout in Russia. It
would be ungentlemanlike (in a manner) to resist it.
Perhaps Dobbin's foolish soul revolted against that exercise
of tyranny ; or perhaps he had a hankering feeling of
revenge in his mind, and longed to measure himself against
that splendid bully and tyrant, who had all the glory, pride,
pomp, circumstance, banners flying, drums beating, guards
saluting, in the place. Whatever may have been his

incentive, however, up he sprang, and screamed out,
' Hold off, Cuff ; don't bully that child any more ; or
I'll——'
' Or you'll what ? ' Cuff asked in amazement at this
interruption. ' Hold out your hand, you little beast.'
' I'll give you the worst thrashing you ever had in your
life,' Dobbin said, in reply to the first part of Cuff's sentence ;
and little Osborne, gasping and in tears, looked up with
wonder and incredulity at seeing this amazing champion
put up suddenly to defend him : while Cuff's astonishment
was scarcely less. Fancy our late monarch George III
when he heard of the revolt of the North American colonies :
fancy brazen Goliath when little David stepped forward
and claimed a meeting ; and you have the feelings of
Mr. Reginald Cuff when this rencontre was proposed to him.
' After school,' says he, of course ; after a pause and a
look, as much as to say, ' Make your will, and communicate
your best wishes to your friends between this time and that.'
' As you please,' Dobbin said. ' You must be my bottle-
holder, Osborne.'
' Well, if you like,' little Osborne replied ; for you see his
papa kept a carriage, and he was rather ashamed of his
champion.

Yes, when the hour of battle came, he was almost
ashamed to say ' Go it, Figs ' ; and not a single other boy
in the place uttered that cry for the first two or three
rounds of this famous combat ; at the commencement of
which the scientific Cuff, with a contemptuous smile on his
face, and as light and as gay as if he was at a ball, planted
his blows upon his adversary, and floored that unlucky
champion three times running. At each fall there was
a cheer ; and everybody was anxious to have the honour
of offering the conqueror a knee.
' What a licking I shall get when it's over,' young
Osborne thought, picking up his man. ' You'd best give
in,' he said to Dobbin ; ' it's only a thrashing, Figs, and
you know I'm used to it.' But Figs, all whose limbs were
in a quiver, and whose nostrils were breathing rage, put his
little bottle-holder aside, and went in for a fourth time.
As he did not in the least know how to parry the blows
that were aimed at himself, and Cuff had begun the attack
on the three preceding occasions, without ever allowing his

enemy to strike, Figs now determined that he would commence the engagement by a charge on his own part;
and accordingly, being a left-handed man, brought that
arm into action, and hit out a couple of times with all his
might—once at Mr. Cuff's left eye, and once on his beautiful
Roman nose.

Cuff went down this time, to the astonishment of the
assembly. 'Well hit, by Jove,' says little Osborne, with
the air of a connoisseur, clapping his man on the back.
'Give it him with the left, Figs, my boy.'

Figs's left made terrific play during all the rest of the
combat. Cuff went down every time. At the sixth round
there were almost as many fellows shouting out, 'Go it,
Figs,' as there were youths exclaiming, 'Go it, Cuff.'
At the twelfth round the latter champion was all abroad,
as the saying is, and had lost all presence of mind and power
of attack or defence. Figs, on the contrary, was as calm
as a quaker. His face being quite pale, his eyes shining
open, and a great cut on his under-lip bleeding profusely,
gave this young fellow a fierce and ghastly air, which perhaps
struck terror into many spectators. Nevertheless, his
intrepid adversary prepared to close for the thirteenth
time.

If I had the pen of a Napier, or a *Bell's Life*,* I should like
to describe this combat properly. It was the last charge
of the Guard (that is, *it would* have been, only Waterloo
had not yet taken place)—it was Ney's column breasting
the hill of La Haye Sainte, bristling with ten thousand
bayonets, and crowned with twenty eagles—it was the
shout of the beef-eating British, as leaping down the hill
they rushed to hug the enemy in the savage arms of battle
—in other words, Cuff coming up full of pluck, but quite
reeling and groggy, the Fig-merchant put in his left as
usual on his adversary's nose, and sent him down for the
last time.

'I think *that* will do for him,' Figs said, as his opponent
dropped as neatly on the green as I have seen Jack Spot's
ball plump into the pocket at billiards; and the fact is,
when time was called, Mr. Reginald Cuff was not able,
or did not choose, to stand up again.

And now all the boys set up such a shout for Figs as would
make you think he had been their darling champion
through the whole battle; and as absolutely brought

Dr. Swishtail out of his study, curious to know the cause of the uproar. He threatened to flog Figs violently, of course; but Cuff, who had come to himself by this time, and was washing his wounds, stood up and said, 'It's my fault, sir—not Figs's—not Dobbin's. I was bullying a little boy; and he served me right.' By which magnanimous speech he not only saved his conqueror a whipping, but got back all his ascendancy over the boys which his defeat had nearly cost him.

Young Osborne wrote home to his parents an account of the transaction.

SUGARCANE HOUSE, RICHMOND, March, 18—.

DEAR MAMA,—I hope you are quite well. I should be much obliged to you to send me a cake and five shillings. There has been a fight here between Cuff & Dobbin. Cuff, you know, was the Cock of the School. They fought thirteen rounds, and Dobbin Licked. So Cuff is now Only Second Cock. The fight was about me. Cuff was licking me for breaking a bottle of milk, and Figs wouldn't stand it. We call him Figs because his father is a Grocer. Figs & Rudge, Thames St., City—I think as he fought for me you ought to buy your Tea & Sugar at his father's. Cuff goes home every Saturday, but can't this, because he has 2 Black Eyes. He has a white Pony to come and fetch him, and a groom in livery on a bay mare. I wish my Papa would let me have a Pony, and I am,

Your dutiful Son,

GEORGE SEDLEY OSBORNE.

PS.—Give my love to little Emmy. I am cutting her out a Coach in cardboard. Please not a seed-cake, but a plum-cake.'

In consequence of Dobbin's victory, his character rose prodigiously in the estimation of all his schoolfellows, and the name of Figs, which had been a byword of reproach, became as respectable and popular a nickname as any other in use in the school. 'After all, it's not his fault that his father's a grocer,' George Osborne said, who, though a little chap, had a very high popularity among the Swishtail youth; and his opinion was received with great applause. It was voted low to sneer at Dobbin about this accident of birth. 'Old Figs' grew to be a name of kindness and endearment; and the sneak of an usher jeered at him no longer.

And Dobbin's spirit rose with his altered circumstances. He made wonderful advances in scholastic learning. The

superb Cuff himself, at whose condescension Dobbin could
only blush and wonder, helped him on with his Latin
verses; 'coached' him in play-hours; carried him
triumphantly out of the little-boy class into the middle-
sized form; and even there got a fair place for him. It
was discovered, that although dull at classical learning,
at mathematics he was uncommonly quick. To the
contentment of all, he passed third in algebra, and got
a French prize-book at the public midsummer examination.
You should have seen his mother's face when *Télémaque**
(that delicious romance) was presented to him by the Doctor
in the face of the whole school and the parents and company, with an inscription to Gulielmo Dobbin. All the
boys clapped hands in token of applause and sympathy.
His blushes, his stumbles, his awkwardness, and the number
of feet which he crushed as he went back to his place, who
shall describe or calculate? Old Dobbin, his father, who
now respected him for the first time, gave him two guineas
publicly; most of which he spent in a general tuck-out
for the school: and he came back in a tail-coat after the
holidays.

Dobbin was much too modest a young fellow to suppose
that this happy change in all his circumstances arose from
his own generous and manly disposition · he chose, from
some perverseness, to attribute his good fortune to the sole
agency and benevolence of little George Osborne, to whom
henceforth he vowed such a love and affection as is only felt
by children—such an affection as we read in the charming
fairy-book uncouth Orson had for splendid young Valentine
his conqueror. He flung himself down at little Osborne's
feet, and loved him. Even before they were acquainted,
he had admired Osborne in secret. Now he was his valet,
his dog, his man Friday.* He believed Osborne to be the
possessor of every perfection, to be the handsomest, the
bravest, the most active, the cleverest, the most generous
of created boys. He shared his money with him: bought
him uncountable presents of knives, pencil-cases, gold seals,
toffee, Little Warblers,* and romantic books, with large
coloured pictures of knights and robbers, in many of which
latter you might read inscriptions to George Sedley Osborne,
Esquire, from his attached friend William Dobbin—the
which tokens of homage George received very graciously,
as became his superior merit.

So that when Lieutenant Osborne, coming to Russell Square on the day of the Vauxhall party, said to the ladies, 'Mrs. Sedley, ma'am, I hope you have room; I've asked Dobbin of ours to come and dine here, and go with us to Vauxhall. He's almost as modest as Jos.'

'Modesty! pooh,' said the stout gentleman, casting a *vainqueur* look at Miss Sharp.

'He is—but you are incomparably more graceful, Sedley,' Osborne added, laughing. 'I met him at the Bedford, when I went to look for you; and I told him that Miss Amelia was come home, and that we were all bent on going out for a night's pleasuring; and that Mrs. Sedley had forgiven his breaking the punch-bowl at the child's party. Don't you remember the catastrophe, ma'am, seven years ago?'

'Over Mrs Flamingo's crimson silk gown,' said good-natured Mrs. Sedley. 'What a gawky it was! And his sisters are not much more graceful. Lady Dobbin was at Highbury last night with three of them. Such figures, my dears.'

'The Alderman's very rich, isn't he?' Osborne said archly. 'Don't you think one of the daughters would be a good spec for me, ma'am?'

'You foolish creature! Who would take *you*, I should like to know, with your yellow face?'*

'Mine a yellow face? Stop till you see Dobbin. Why, he had the yellow fever three times; twice at Nassau, and once at St. Kitts.'*

'Well, well; yours is quite yellow enough for us. Isn't it, Emmy?' Mrs. Sedley said: at which speech Miss Amelia only made a smile and a blush; and looking at Mr. George Osborne's pale interesting countenance, and those beautiful black, curling, shining whiskers, which the young gentleman himself regarded with no ordinary complacency, she thought, in her little heart, that in His Majesty's army, or in the wide world, there never was such a face or such a hero. 'I don't care about Captain Dobbin's complexion,' she said, 'or about his awkwardness. *I* shall always like him, I know;' her little reason being that he was the friend and champion of George.

'There's not a finer fellow in the service,' Osborne said, 'nor a better officer, though he is not an Adonis, certainly.' And he looked towards the glass himself with much *naïveté;* and in so doing, caught Miss Sharp's eye fixed keenly upon

him, at which he blushed a little, and, Rebecca thought
in her heart, ' *Ah, mon beau monsieur !* I think I have *your*
gauge '—the little artful minx !

That evening, when Amelia came tripping into the drawing-room in a white muslin frock, prepared for conquest
at Vauxhall, singing like a lark, and as fresh as a rose—
a very tall ungainly gentleman, with large hands and feet,
and large ears, set off by a closely cropped head of black
hair, and in the hideous military frogged coat and cocked

hat of those times, advanced to meet her, and made her
one of the clumsiest bows that was ever performed by
a mortal.

This was no other than Captain William Dobbin, of His
Majesty's ——— Regiment of Foot, returned from yellow
fever in the West Indies, to which the fortune of the service
had ordered his regiment, whilst so many of his gallant
comrades were reaping glory in the Peninsula.

He had arrived with a knock so very timid and quiet,
that it was inaudible to the ladies upstairs : otherwise,

you may be sure Miss Amelia would never have been so
bold as to come singing into the room. As it was, the
sweet fresh little voice went right into the captain's heart,
and nestled there. When she held out her hand for him
to shake, before he enveloped it in his own, he paused and
thought—'Well, is it possible—are you the little maid
I remember in the pink frock, such a short time ago—the
night I upset the punch-bowl, just after I was gazetted?
Are you the little girl that George Osborne said should
marry him ? What a blooming young creature you seem,
and what a prize the rogue has got ! ' All this he thought
before he took Amelia's hand into his own, and as he let his
cocked-hat fall.

His history since he left school, until the very moment
when we have the pleasure of meeting him again, although
not fully narrated, has yet, I think, been indicated sufficiently for an ingenious reader by the conversation in the
last page. Dobbin, the despised grocer, was Alderman
Dobbin—Alderman Dobbin was Colonel of the City Light
Horse, then burning with military ardour to resist the French
Invasion. Colonel Dobbin's corps, in which old Mr. Osborne
himself was but an indifferent corporal, had been reviewed
by the Sovereign and the Duke of York ;* and the colonel
and alderman had been knighted. His son had entered
the army : and young Osborne followed presently in the
same regiment. They had served in the West Indies and
in Canada. Their regiment had just come home, and the
attachment of Dobbin to George Osborne was as warm and
generous now, as it had been when the two were
schoolboys.

So these worthy people sat down to dinner presently.
They talked about war and glory, and Boney and Lord
Wellington, and the last *Gazette*. In those famous days
every gazette had a victory in it, and the two gallant
young men longed to see their own names in the glorious
list, and cursed their unlucky fate to belong to a regiment
which had been away from the chances of honour. Miss
Sharp kindled with this exciting talk, but Miss Sedley
trembled and grew quite faint as she heard it. Mr. Jos
told several of his tiger-hunting stories : finished the one
about Miss Cutler and Lance the surgeon ; helped Rebecca
to everything on the table, and himself gobbled and drank
a great deal.

He sprang to open the door for the ladies, when they
retired, with the most killing grace—and coming back to
the table, filled himself bumper after bumper of claret,
which he swallowed with nervous rapidity.

' He's priming himself,' Osborne whispered to Dobbin,
and at length the hour and the carriage arrived for Vauxhall.

CHAPTER VI

VAUXHALL

 KNOW that the tune I am piping is a very
mild one (although there are some terrific
chapters coming presently), and must beg
the good-natured reader to remember, that
we are only discoursing at present about a
stockbroker's family in Russell Square,
who are taking walks, or luncheon, or
dinner, or talking, and making love as
people do in common life, and without a
single passionate and wonderful incident to
mark the progress of their loves. The
argument stands thus—Osborne, in love
with Amelia, has asked an old friend to
dinner and to Vauxhall—Jos Sedley is in
love with Rebecca. Will he marry her ? That is the great
subject now in hand.

We might have treated this subject in the genteel, or in
the romantic, or in the facetious manner.* Suppose we had
laid the scene in Grosvenor Square, with the very same
adventures—would not some people have listened ? Suppose
we had shown how Lord Joseph Sedley fell in love, and the
Marquis of Osborne became attached to Lady Amelia, with
the full consent of the duke, her noble father : or instead
of the supremely genteel, suppose we had resorted to the
entirely low, and described what was going on in Mr. Sedley's
kitchen ;—how black Sambo was in love with the cook (as
indeed he was), and how he fought a battle with the coachman in her behalf ; how the knife-boy was caught stealing
a cold shoulder of mutton, and Miss Sedley's new *femme
de chambre* refused to go to bed without a wax candle ; such

incidents might be made to provoke much delightful laughter, and be supposed to represent scenes of ' life '. Or if, on the contrary, we had taken a fancy for the terrible, and made the lover of the new *femme de chambre* a professional burglar, who bursts into the house with his band, slaughters black Sambo at the feet of his master, and carries off Amelia in her night-dress, not to be let loose again till the third volume, we should easily have constructed a tale of thrilling interest, through the fiery chapters of which the readers should hurry, panting. But my readers must hope for no such romance, only a homely story, and must be content with a chapter about Vauxhall, which is so short that it scarce deserves to be called a chapter at all.* And yet it is a chapter, and a very important one too. Are not there little chapters in everybody's life, that seem to be nothing, and yet affect all the rest of the history ?

Let us then step into the coach with the Russell Square party, and be off to the Gardens. There is barely room between Jos and Miss Sharp, who are on the front seat. Mr. Osborne sitting bodkin opposite, between Captain Dobbin and Amelia.

Every soul in the coach agreed, that on that night Jos would propose to make Rebecca Sharp Mrs. Sedley. The parents at home had acquiesced in the arrangement, though, between ourselves, old Mr. Sedley had a feeling very much akin to contempt for his son. He said he was vain, selfish, lazy, and effeminate. He could not endure his airs as a man of fashion, and laughed heartily at his pompous braggadocio stories. 'I shall leave the fellow half my property,' he said ; ' and he will have, besides, plenty of his own ; but as I am perfectly sure that if you, and I, and his sister were to die to-morrow he would say " Good Gad ! " and eat his dinner just as well as usual, I am not going to make myself anxious about him. Let him marry whom he likes. It's no affair of mine.'

Amelia, on the other hand, as became a young woman of her prudence and temperament, was quite enthusiastic for the match. Once or twice Jos had been on the point of saying something very important to her, to which she was most willing to lend an ear, but the fat fellow could not be brought to unbosom himself of his great secret, and very much to his sister's disappointment he only rid himself of a large sigh and turned away.

This mystery served to keep Amelia's gentle bosom in a
perpetual flutter of excitement. If she did not speak with
Rebecca on the tender subject, she compensated herself
with long and intimate conversations with Mrs. Blenkinsop,
the housekeeper, who dropped some hints to the lady's-maid,
who may have cursorily mentioned the matter to the cook,
who carried the news, I have no doubt, to all the tradesmen,
so that Mr. Jos's marriage was now talked of by a very
considerable number of persons in the Russell Square world.

It was, of course, Mrs. Sedley's opinion that her son would
demean himself by a marriage with an artist's daughter.
'But, lor', ma'am,' ejaculated Mrs. Blenkinsop, 'we was
only grocers when we married Mr. S., who was a stockbroker's clerk, and we hadn't five hundred pounds among
us, and we're rich enough now.' And Amelia was entirely
of this opinion, to which, gradually, the good-natured
Mrs. Sedley was brought.

Mr. Sedley was neutral. 'Let Jos marry whom he likes,'
he said; 'it's no affair of mine. This girl has no fortune;
no more had Mrs. Sedley. She seems good-humoured and
clever, and will keep him in order, perhaps. Better she,
my dear, than a black Mrs. Sedley, and a dozen of mahogany
grandchildren.'

So that everything seemed to smile upon Rebecca's
fortunes. She took Jos's arm, as a matter of course, on
going to dinner; she had sat by him on the box of his
open carriage (a most tremendous 'buck' he was, as he sat
there, serene, in state, driving his greys), and though
nobody said a word on the subject of the marriage, everybody seemed to understand it. All she wanted was the
proposal, and ah! how Rebecca now felt the want of a
mother!—a dear, tender mother, who would have managed
the business in ten minutes, and, in the course of a little
delicate confidential conversation, would have extracted
the interesting avowal from the bashful lips of the young
man!

Such was the state of affairs as the carriage crossed Westminster Bridge.*

The party was landed at the Royal Gardens* in due time.
As the majestic Jos stepped out of the creaking vehicle the
crowd gave a cheer for the fat gentleman, who blushed and
looked very big and mighty, as he walked away with
Rebecca under his arm. George, of course, took charge

of Amelia. She looked as happy as a rose-tree in sun-shine.

'I say, Dobbin,' says George, 'just look to the shawls and things, there's a good fellow.' And so while he paired off with Miss Sedley, and Jos squeezed through the gate into the Gardens with Rebecca at his side, honest Dobbin contented himself by giving an arm to the shawls, and by paying at the door for the whole party.*

He walked very modestly behind them.* He was not willing to spoil sport. About Rebecca and Jos he did not care a fig. But he thought Amelia worthy even of the brilliant George Osborne, and as he saw that good-looking couple, threading the walks to the girl's delight and wonder, he watched her artless happiness with a sort of fatherly pleasure. Perhaps he felt that he would have liked to have something on his own arm besides a shawl (the people laughed at seeing the gawky young officer carrying this female burden) ; but William Dobbin was very little addicted to selfish calculation at all ; and so long as his friend was enjoying himself, how should he be discontented ? And the truth is, that of all the delights of the Gardens ; of the hundred thousand *extra* lamps,* which were always lighted ; the fiddlers, in cocked-hats,* who played ravishing melodies under the gilded cockle-shell in the midst of the Gardens ; the singers, both of comic and sentimental ballads, who charmed the ears there ; the country dances, formed by bouncing cockneys and cockneyesses, and exe-cuted amidst jumping, thumping, and laughter ; the signal which announced that Madame Saqui*was about to mount skyward on a slack-rope ascending to the stars ; the hermit that always sat in the illuminated hermitage ; the dark walks, so favourable to the interviews of young lovers ; the pots of stout handed about by the people in the shabby old liveries ; and the twinkling boxes, in which the happy feasters made believe to eat slices of almost invisible ham ;*— of all these things, and of the gentle Simpson, that kind smiling idiot, who, I dare say, presided even then*over the place—Captain William Dobbin did not take the slightest notice.

He carried about Amelia's white Cashmere shawl, and having attended under the gilt cockle-shell, while Mrs. Salmon performed the Battle of Borodino*(a savage Cantata against the Corsican upstart, who had lately met with his

Russian reverses)—Mr. Dobbin tried to hum it as he walked away, and found he was humming—the tune which Amelia Sedley sang on the stairs, as she came down to dinner.

He burst out laughing at himself; for the truth is, he could sing no better than an owl.*

It is to be understood, as a matter of course, that our young people being in parties of two and two, made the most solemn promises to keep together during the evening,

and separated in ten minutes afterwards. Parties at Vauxhall always did separate, but 'twas only to meet again at supper-time, when they could talk of their mutual adventures in the interval.

What were the adventures of Mr. Osborne and Miss Amelia? That is a secret. But be sure of this—they were perfectly happy, and correct in their behaviour; and as they had been in the habit of being together any time these fifteen years, their *tête-à-tête* offered no particular novelty.

But when Miss Rebecca Sharp and her stout companion lost themselves in a solitary walk, in which there were not

above five score more of couples similarly straying, they both
felt that the situation was extremely tender and critical,
and now or never was the moment, Miss Sharp thought, to
provoke that declaration which was trembling on the timid
lips of Mr. Sedley. They had previously been to the
panorama of Moscow, where a rude fellow, treading on Miss
Sharp's foot, caused her to fall back with a little shriek into
the arms of Mr. Sedley, and this little incident increased the
tenderness and confidence of that gentleman to such a degree,
that he told her several of his favourite Indian stories over
again for, at least, the sixth time.

'How I should like to see India!' said Rebecca.

'*Should* you?' said Joseph, with a most killing tenderness ; and was no doubt about to follow up this artful
interrogatory by a question still more tender (for he puffed
and panted a great deal, and Rebecca's hand, which was
placed near his heart, could count the feverish pulsations of
that organ), when, oh, provoking! the bell rang for the
fireworks, and, a great scuffling and running taking place,
these interesting lovers were obliged to follow in the stream
of people.

Captain Dobbin had some thoughts of joining the party
at supper : as, in truth, he found the Vauxhall amusement
not particularly lively—but he paraded twice before the
box where the now united couples were met, and nobody
took any notice of him. Covers were laid for four. The
mated pairs were prattling away quite happily, and Dobbin
knew he was as clean forgotten as if he had never existed
in this world.

'I should only be *de trop*,' said the captain, looking at
them rather wistfully. 'I'd best go and talk to the hermit,'
—and so he strolled off out of the hum of men, and noise, and
clatter of the banquet, into the dark walk, at the end of
which lived that well-known pasteboard Solitary. It wasn't
very good fun for Dobbin—and, indeed, to be alone at
Vauxhall, I have found, from my own experience, to be
one of the most dismal sports ever entered into by a bachelor.

The two couples were perfectly happy then in their box :
where the most delightful and intimate conversation took
place. Jos was in his glory, ordering about the waiters
with great majesty. He made the salad; and uncorked
the champagne; and carved the chickens; and ate and
drank the greater part of the refreshments on the tables.

Finally, he insisted upon having a bowl of rack punch ; everybody had rack punch at Vauxhall. 'Waiter, rack punch.'

That bowl of rack punch was the cause of all this history. And why not a bowl of rack punch as well as any other cause ? Was not a bowl of prussic acid the cause of Fair Rosamond's retiring from the world ? Was not a bowl of wine the cause of the demise of Alexander the Great, or at least, does not Dr. Lemprière* say so?—so did this bowl of rack punch influence the fates of all the principal characters in this ' Novel without a Hero ', which we are now relating. It influenced their life, although most of them did not taste a drop of it.

The young ladies did not drink it ; Osborne did not like it ; and the consequence was that Jos, that fat *gourmand*, drank up the whole contents of the bowl ; and the consequence of his drinking up the whole contents of the bowl was, a liveliness which at first was astonishing, and then became almost painful ; for he talked and laughed so loud as to bring scores of listeners round the box, much to the confusion of the innocent party within it ; and, volunteering to sing a song (which he did in that maudlin high key peculiar to gentlemen in an inebriated state), he almost drew away the audience who were gathered round the musicians in the gilt scallop-shell, and received from his hearers a great deal of applause.

' Brayvo, Fat un ! ' said one ; ' Angcore, Daniel Lambert ! '* said another ; ' What a figure for the tight-rope ! ' exclaimed another wag, to the inexpressible alarm of the ladies, and the great anger of Mr. Osborne.

' For Heaven's sake, Jos, let us get up and go,' cried that gentleman, and the young women rose.

' Stop, my dearest diddle-diddle-darling,' shouted Jos, now as bold as a lion, and clasping Miss Rebecca round the waist. Rebecca started, but she could not get away her hand. The laughter outside redoubled. Jos continued to drink, to make love, and to sing ; and, winking and waving his glass gracefully to his audience, challenged all or any to come in and take a share of his punch.

Mr. Osborne was just on the point of knocking down a gentleman in top-boots,* who proposed to take advantage of this invitation, and a commotion seemed to be inevitable, when by the greatest good luck a gentleman of the name of Dobbin, who had been walking about the Gardens, stepped

MR. JOSEPH IN A STATE OF EXCITEMENT

up to the box. ' Be off, you fools ! ' said this gentleman -- shouldering off a great number of the crowd, who vanished presently before his cocked-hat and fierce appearance—and he entered the box in a most agitated state.

' Good Heavens ! Dobbin, where *have* you been ? ' Osborne said, seizing the white Cashmere shawl from his friend's arm, and huddling up Amelia in it.—' Make yourself useful, and take charge of Jos here, whilst I take the ladies to the carriage.'

Jos was for rising to interfere—but a single push from Osborne's finger sent him puffing back into his seat again, and the lieutenant was enabled to remove the ladies in safety. Jos kissed his hand to them as they retreated, and hiccupped out, ' Bless you ! Bless you ! ' Then seizing Captain Dobbin's hand, and weeping in the most pitiful way, he confided to that gentleman the secret of his loves. He adored that girl who had just gone out ; he had broken her heart, he knew he had, by his conduct ; he would marry her next morning at St. George's, Hanover Square ; he'd knock up the Archbishop of Canterbury at Lambeth :* he would, by Jove ! and have him in readiness ; and, acting on this hint, Captain Dobbin shrewdly induced him to leave the Gardens and hasten to Lambeth Palace, and, when once out of the gates, easily conveyed Mr. Jos Sedley into a hackney-coach, which deposited him safely at his lodgings.

George Osborne conducted the girls home in safety, and when the door was closed upon them, and as he walked across Russell Square, laughed so as to astonish the watchman. Amelia looked very ruefully at her friend, as they went upstairs, and kissed her, and went to bed without any more talking.

' He must propose to-morrow,' thought Rebecca. ' He called me his soul's darling four times; he squeezed my hand in Amelia's presence. He must propose to-morrow.' And so thought Amelia, too. And I dare say she thought of the dress she was to wear as bride's-maid, and of the presents which she should make to her nice little sister-in-law, and of a subsequent ceremony in which she herself might play a principal part, &c., and &c., and &c., and &c.

O, ignorant young creatures ! How little do you know the effect of rack punch ! What is the rack in the punch, at

night, to the rack in the head of a morning ! To this truth
I can vouch as a man ; there is no headache in the world
like that caused by Vauxhall punch. Through the lapse
of twenty years, I can remember the consequence of two
glasses !—two wine-glasses !—but two, upon the honour of a
gentleman ; and Joseph Sedley, who had a liver complaint,
had swallowed at least a quart of the abominable mixture.

That next morning, which Rebecca thought was to dawn
upon her fortune, found Sedley groaning in agonies which
the pen refuses to describe. Soda-water was not invented
yet. Small beer—will it be believed !—was the only drink
with which unhappy gentlemen soothed the fever of their

previous night's potation. With this
mild beverage before him, George
Osborne found the ex-collector of
Boggley Wollah groaning on the sofa
at his lodgings. Dobbin was already
in the room, good-naturedly tending his
patient of the night before. The two
officers, looking at the prostrate Bacchanalian, and askance at each other,
exchanged the most frightful sympathetic grins. Even Sedley's valet, the
most solemn and correct of gentlemen,
with the muteness and gravity of an undertaker, could
hardly keep his countenance in order, as he looked at his
unfortunate master.

'Mr. Sedley was uncommon wild last night, sir,' he
whispered in confidence to Osborne, as the latter mounted
the stair. ' He wanted to fight the 'ackney-coachman, sir.
The capting was obliged to bring him upstairs in his harms
like a babby.' A momentary smile flickered over Mr.
Brush's features as he spoke ; instantly, however, they
relapsed into their usual unfathomable calm, as he flung
open the drawing-room door, and announced ' Mr. Hosbin '.

'How are you, Sedley ? ' that young wag began, after
surveying his victim. ' No bones broke ? There's a
hackney-coachman downstairs with a black eye, and a
tied up head, vowing he'll have the law of you.'

'What do you mean,—law ? ' Sedley faintly asked.

'For thrashing him last night—didn't he, Dobbin ? You
hit out, sir, like Molyneux.* The watchman says he never
saw a fellow go down so straight. Ask Dobbin.'

'You *did* have a round with the coachman,' Captain Dobbin said, ' and showed plenty of fight too.'

'And that fellow with the white coat at Vauxhall! How Jos drove at him! How the women screamed! By Jove, sir, it did my heart good to see you. I thought you civilians had no pluck; but *I'll* never get in your way when you are in your cups, Jos.'

'I believe I'm very terrible, when I'm roused,' ejaculated Jos from the sofa, and made a grimace so dreary and ludicrous, that the captain's politeness could restrain him no longer, and he and Osborne fired off a ringing volley of laughter.

Osborne pursued his advantage pitilessly.* He thought Jos a milksop. He had been revolving in his mind the marriage-question pending between Jos and Rebecca, and was not over-well pleased that a member of a family into which he, George Osborne, of the —th, was going to marry, should make a *mésalliance* with a little nobody—a little upstart governess. 'You hit, you poor old fellow?' said Osborne. 'You terrible? Why, man, you couldn't stand— you made everybody laugh in the Gardens, though you were crying yourself. You were maudlin, Jos. Don't you remember singing a song?'

'A what?' Jos asked.

'A sentimental song, and calling Rosa, Rebecca, what's her name, Amelia's little friend—your dearest diddle-diddle-darling?' And this ruthless young fellow, seizing hold of Dobbin's hand, acted over the scene, to the horror of the original performer, and in spite of Dobbin's good-natured entreaties to him to have mercy.

'Why should I spare him?' Osborne said to his friend's remonstrances, when they quitted the invalid, leaving him under the hands of Dr. Gollop. 'What the deuce right has he to give himself his patronizing airs, and make fools of us at Vauxhall? Who's this little schoolgirl that is ogling and making love to him? Hang it, the family's low enough already, without *her*. A governess is all very well, but I'd rather have a lady for my sister-in-law. I'm a liberal man; but I've proper pride, and know my own station: let her know hers. And I'll take down that great hectoring nabob, and prevent him from being made a greater fool than he is. That's why I told him to look out, lest she brought an action against him.'

' I suppose you know best,' Dobbin said, though rather dubiously. ' You always were a Tory, and your family's one of the oldest in England. But,——'

' Come and see the girls, and make love to Miss Sharp yourself,' the lieutenant here interrupted his friend; but Captain Dobbin declined to join Osborne in his daily visit to the young ladies in Russell Square.

As George walked down Southampton Row, from Holborn, he laughed as he saw, at the Sedley mansion, in two different stories, two heads on the look-out.

The fact is, Miss Amelia, in the drawing-room balcony, was looking very eagerly towards the opposite side of the Square, where Mr. Osborne dwelt, on the watch for the lieutenant himself; and Miss Sharp, from her little bedroom on the second floor, was in observation until Mr. Joseph's great form should heave in sight.

' Sister Anne is on the watch-tower,'* said he to Amelia, ' but there's nobody coming; ' and laughing and enjoying the joke hugely, he described in the most ludicrous terms to Miss Sedley the dismal condition of her brother.

' I think it's very cruel of you to laugh, George,' she said, looking particularly unhappy; but George only laughed the more at her piteous and discomfited mien, persisted in thinking the joke a most diverting one, and when Miss Sharp came downstairs, bantered her with a great deal of liveliness upon the effect of her charms on the fat civilian.

' Oh Miss Sharp! if you could but see him this morning,' he said,—' moaning in his flowered dressing-gown—writhing on his sofa; if you could but have seen him lolling out his tongue to Gollop the apothecary.'

' See whom ? ' said Miss Sharp.

' Whom ? Oh whom ? Captain Dobbin, of course, to whom we were all so attentive, by the way, last night.'

' We were very unkind to him,' Emmy said, blushing very much. ' I—I quite forgot him.'

' Of course you did,' cried Osborne, still on the laugh. ' One can't be *always* thinking about Dobbin, you know, Amelia. Can one, Miss Sharp ? '

' Except when he overset the glass of wine at dinner,' Miss Sharp said, with a haughty air and a toss of the head, ' I never gave the existence of Captain Dobbin one single moment's consideration.'

' Very good, Miss Sharp, I'll tell him,' Osborne said; and

as he spoke Miss Sharp began to have a feeling of distrust and hatred towards this young officer, which he was quite unconscious of having inspired. ' *He* is to make fun of me, is he ? ' thought Rebecca. ' Has he been laughing about me to Joseph ? Has he frightened him ? Perhaps he won't come.'—A film passed over her eyes, and her heart beat quite quick.

' You're always joking,' said she, smiling as innocently as she could. ' Joke away, Mr. George ; there's nobody to defend *me*.' And George Osborne, as she walked away— and Amelia looked reprovingly at him—felt some little manly compunction for having inflicted any unnecessary unkindness upon this helpless creature. ' My dearest Amelia,' said he, ' you are too good—too kind. You don't know the world. I do. And your little friend, Miss Sharp, must learn her station.'

' Don't you think Jos will——'

' Upon my word, my dear, I don't know. He may, or may not. I'm not his master. I only know he's a very foolish vain fellow, and put my dear little girl into a very painful and awkward position last night. My dearest diddle-diddle-darling ! ' He was off laughing again ; and he did it so drolly, that Emmy laughed too.

All that day Jos never came. But Amelia had no fear about this ; for the little schemer had actually sent away the page, Mr. Sambo's aide de camp, to Mr. Joseph's lodgings, to ask for some book he had promised, and how he was ; and the reply through Jos's man, Mr. Brush, was, that his master was ill in bed, and had just had the doctor with him. He must come to-morrow, she thought, but she never had the courage to speak a word on the subject to Rebecca ; nor did that young woman herself allude to it in any way during the whole evening after the night at Vauxhall.

The next day, however, as the two young ladies sat on the sofa, pretending to work, or to write letters, or to read novels, Sambo came into the room with his usual engaging grin, with a packet under his arm, and a note on a tray. ' Note from Mr. Jos, miss,' says Sambo.

How Amelia trembled as she opened it !

So it ran—

DEAR AMELIA,—I send you the *Orphan of the Forest.** I was too ill to come yesterday. I leave town to-day for Cheltenham. Pray

excuse me, if you can, to the amiable Miss Sharp, for my conduct at
Vauxhall, and entreat her to pardon and forget every word I may
have uttered when excited by that fatal supper. As soon as I
have recovered, for my health is very much shaken, I shall go to
Scotland for some months, and am

                              Truly yours,
                                    JOS SEDLEY.

It was the death-warrant. All was over. Amelia did
not dare to look at Rebecca's pale face and burning eyes,

but she dropped the letter into her friend's lap ; and got
up, and went upstairs to her room, and cried her little
heart out.

Blenkinsop, the housekeeper, there sought her presently
with consolation ; on whose shoulder Amelia wept confidentially, and relieved herself a good deal. 'Don't take on,
miss. I didn't like to tell you. But none of us in the house
have liked her except at fust. I sor her with my own eyes
reading your ma's letters. Pinner says she's always about
your trinket-box and drawers, and everybody's drawers,
and she's sure she's put your white ribbing into her box.'

'I gave it her, I gave it her,' Amelia said.

But this did not alter Mrs. Blenkinsop's opinion of Miss

Sharp. ' I don't trust them governesses, Pinner,' she remarked to the maid. ' They give themselves the hairs and hupstarts of ladies, and their wages is no better than you nor me.'

It now became clear to every soul in the house, except poor Amelia, that Rebecca should take her departure, and high and low (always with the one exception) agreed that that event should take place as speedily as possible. Our good child ransacked all her drawers, cupboards, reticules, and gimcrack boxes—passed in review all her gowns, fichus, tags, bobbins, laces, silk stockings, and fallals—selecting this thing and that and the other, to make a little heap for Rebecca. And going to her papa, that generous British merchant, who had promised to give her as many guineas as she was years old—she begged the old gentleman to give the money to dear Rebecca, who must want it, while she lacked for nothing.

She even made George Osborne contribute, and nothing loath (for he was as free-handed a young fellow as any in the army), he went to Bond Street, and bought the best hat and spencer that money could buy.

' That's George's present to you, Rebecca dear,' said Amelia, quite proud of the bandbox conveying these gifts.* ' What a taste he has ! There's nobody like him.'

' Nobody,' Rebecca answered. ' How thankful I am to him !' She was thinking in her heart, ' It was George Osborne who prevented my marriage.'—And she loved George Osborne accordingly.

She made her preparations for departure with great equanimity ; and accepted all the kind little Amelia's presents, after just the proper degree of hesitation and reluctance. She vowed eternal gratitude to Mrs. Sedley, of course ; but did not intrude herself upon that good lady too much, who was embarrassed, and evidently wishing to avoid her. She kissed Mr. Sedley's hand, when he presented her with the purse ; and asked permission to consider him for the future as her kind, kind friend and protector. Her behaviour was so affecting that he was going to write her a cheque for twenty pounds more ; but he restrained his feelings : the carriage was in waiting to take him to dinner : so he tripped away with a 'God bless you, my dear. Always come here when you come to town, you know.—Drive to the Mansion House, James.'

Finally came the parting with Miss Amelia, over which picture I intend to throw a veil. But after a scene in which one person was in earnest and the other a perfect performer —after the tenderest caresses, the most pathetic tears, the smelling-bottle, and some of the very best feelings of the heart, had been called into requisition—Rebecca and Amelia parted, the former vowing to love her friend for ever and ever and ever.

CHAPTER VII

CRAWLEY OF QUEEN'S CRAWLEY

MONG the most respected of the names beginning in C, which the Court-Guide contained, in the year 18—, was that of Crawley, Sir Pitt, Baronet, Great Gaunt Street, and Queen's Crawley, Hants. This honourable name had figured constantly also in the Parliamentary list for many years, in conjunction with that of a number of other worthy gentlemen who sat in turns for the borough.

It is related, with regard to the borough of Queen's Crawley, that Queen Elizabeth, in one of her progresses stopping at Crawley to breakfast, was so delighted with some remarkably fine Hampshire beer which was then presented to her by the Crawley of the day (a handsome gentleman with a trim beard and a good leg), that she forthwith erected Crawley into a borough to send two members to Parliament ; and the place, from the day of that illustrious visit, took the name of Queen's Crawley, which it holds up to the present moment. And though by the lapse of time, and those mutations which ages produce in empires, cities, and boroughs, Queen's Crawley was no longer so populous a place as it had been in Queen Bess's time—nay, was come down to that condition of borough which used to be denominated rotten—yet, as Sir Pitt Crawley would say with perfect justice in his elegant way, 'Rotten! be hanged—it produces me a good fifteen hundred a year.'

Sir Pitt Crawley. (named after the great Commoner), was the son of Walpole Crawley, first baronet, of the Tape and Sealing-Wax Office in the reign of George II, when he was impeached for peculation, as were a great number of other honest gentlemen of those days ; and Walpole Crawley was, as need scarcely be said, son of John Churchill Crawley, named after the celebrated military commander of the reign of Queen Anne. The family tree (which hangs up at Queen's Crawley) furthermore mentions Charles Stuart, afterwards called Barebones Crawley, son of the Crawley of James the First's time ; and finally, Queen Elizabeth's Crawley, who is represented as the foreground of the picture in his forked beard and armour. Out of his waistcoat, as usual, grows a tree, on the main branches of which the above illustrious names are inscribed. Close by the name of Sir Pitt Crawley, Baronet (the subject of the present memoir), are written that of his brother, the Reverend Bute Crawley (the great Commoner was in disgrace when the reverend gentleman was born), rector of Crawley-cum-Snailby, and of various other male and female members of the Crawley family.

Sir Pitt was first married to Grizzel, sixth daughter of Mungo Binkie, Lord Binkie, and cousin, in consequence, of Mr. Dundas. She brought him two sons : Pitt, named not so much after his father as after the heaven-born minister ; and Rawdon Crawley, from the Prince of Wales's friend, whom His Majesty George IV forgot so completely.* Many years after her ladyship's demise, Sir Pitt led to the altar Rosa, daughter of Mr. G. Dawson, of Mudbury, by whom he had two daughters, for whose benefit Miss Rebecca Sharp was now engaged as governess. It will be seen that the young lady was come into a family of very genteel connexions, and was about to move in a much more distinguished circle than that humble one which she had just quitted in Russell Square.

She had received her orders to join her pupils, in a note which was written upon an old envelope, and which contained the following words : —

Sir Pitt Crawley begs Miss Sharp and baggidge may be hear on Tuesday, as I leaf for Queen's Crawley to-morrow morning *erly.*

Great Gaunt Street.

Rebecca had never seen a baronet, as far as she knew, and as soon as she had taken leave of Amelia, and counted the guineas which good-natured Mr. Sedley had put into a purse for her, and as soon as she had done wiping her eyes with her handkerchief (which operation she concluded the very moment the carriage had turned the corner of the street), she began to depict in her own mind what a baronet must be. 'I wonder, does he wear a star?' thought she, 'or is it only lords that wear stars? But he will be very handsomely dressed in a court suit, with ruffles and his hair a little powdered, like Mr. Wroughton at Covent Garden.* I suppose he will be awfully proud, and that I shall be treated most contemptuously. Still I must bear my hard lot as well as I can—at least, I shall be amongst *gentlefolks*, and not with vulgar city people:' and she fell to thinking of her Russell Square friends with that very same philosophical bitterness with which, in a certain apologue, the fox is represented as speaking of the grapes.

Having passed through Gaunt Square* into Great Gaunt Street, the carriage at length stopped at a tall gloomy house between two other tall gloomy houses, each with a hatchment over the middle drawing-room window; as is the custom of houses in Great Gaunt Street, in which gloomy locality death seems to reign perpetual. The shutters of the first-floor windows of Sir Pitt's mansion were closed—those of the dining-room were partially open, and the blinds neatly covered up in old newspapers.

John, the groom, who had driven the carriage alone, did not care to descend to ring the bell; and so prayed a passing milk-boy to perform that office for him. When the bell was rung, a head appeared between the interstices of the dining-room shutters, and the door was opened by a man in drab breeches and gaiters, with a dirty old coat, a foul old neckcloth lashed round his bristly neck, a shining bald head, a leering red face, a pair of twinkling grey eyes, and a mouth perpetually on the grin.

'This Sir Pitt Crawley's?' says John, from the box.

'Ees,' says the man at the door with a nod.

'Hand down these 'ere trunks then,' said John.

'Hand 'n down yourself,' said the porter.

'Don't you see I can't leave my hosses? Come, bear a hand, my fine feller, and miss will give you some beer,'

REBECCA MAKES ACQUAINTANCE WITH A LIVE BARONET

said John, with a horse-laugh, for he was no longer respectful to Miss Sharp, as her connexion with the family was broken off, and as she had given nothing to the servants on coming away.

The bald-headed man, taking his hands out of his breeches-pockets, advanced on this summons, and throwing Miss Sharp's trunk over his shoulder, carried it into the house.

'Take this basket and shawl, if you please, and open the door,' said Miss Sharp, and descended from the carriage in much indignation. 'I shall write to Mr. Sedley, and inform him of your conduct,' said she to the groom.

'Don't,' replied that functionary. 'I hope you've forgot nothink? Miss 'Melia's gownds—have you got them—as the lady's maid was to have 'ad? I hope they'll fit you. Shut the door, Jim, you'll get no good out of '*er*,' continued John, pointing with his thumb towards Miss Sharp: 'a bad lot, I tell you, a bad lot,' and so saying, Mr. Sedley's groom drove away. The truth is, he was attached to the lady's maid in question, and indignant that she should have been robbed of her perquisites.

On entering the dining-room, by the orders of the individual in gaiters, Rebecca found that apartment not more cheerful than such rooms usually are, when genteel families are out of town. The faithful chambers seem, as it were, to mourn the absence of their masters. The Turkey carpet has rolled itself up, and retired sulkily under the sideboard: the pictures have hidden their faces behind old sheets of brown paper: the ceiling-lamp is muffled up in a dismal sack of brown holland: the window-curtains have disappeared under all sorts of shabby envelopes: the marble bust of Sir Walpole Crawley is looking from its black corner at the bare boards and the oiled fire-irons, and the empty card-racks over the mantelpiece: the cellaret* has lurked away behind the carpet: the chairs are turned up heads and tails along the walls; and in the dark corner opposite the statue, is an old-fashioned crabbed knife-box, locked and sitting on a dumb-waiter.

Two kitchen-chairs, and a round table, and an attenuated old poker and tongs were, however, gathered round the fireplace, as was a saucepan over a feeble sputtering fire. There was a bit of cheese and bread, and a tin candlestick on the table, and a little black porter in a pint-pot.

'Had your dinner, I suppose? It is not too warm for
you? Like a drop of beer?'

'Where is Sir Pitt Crawley?' said Miss Sharp, majestically.

'He, he! *I'm* Sir Pitt Crawley. Reklect you owe me
a pint for bringing down your luggage. He, he! Ask
Tinker if I aynt. Mrs. Tinker, Miss Sharp! Miss Governess,
Mrs. Charwoman. Ho, ho!'

The lady addressed as Mrs. Tinker at this moment made
her appearance with a pipe and a paper of tobacco, for
which she had been dispatched a minute before Miss
Sharp's arrival; and she handed the articles over to Sir
Pitt, who had taken his seat by the fire.

'Where's the farden?' said he. 'I gave you three
halfpence. Where's the change, old Tinker?'

'There!' replied Mrs. Tinker, flinging down the coin;
'it's only baronets as cares about farthings.'

'A farthing a day is seven shillings a year,' answered
the M.P.; 'seven shillings a year is the interest of seven
guineas. Take care of your farthings, old Tinker and your
guineas will come quite nat'ral.'

'You may be sure it's Sir Pitt Crawley, young woman,' said Mrs. Tinker, surlily ; 'because he looks to his farthings. You'll know him better afore long.'

'And like me none the worse, Miss Sharp,' said the old gentleman, with an air almost of politeness. 'I must be just before I'm generous.'

'He never gave away a farthing in his life,' growled Tinker.

'Never, and never will : it's against my principle. Go and get another chair from the kitchen, Tinker, if you want to sit down ; and then we'll have a bit of supper.'

Presently the baronet plunged a fork into the saucepan on the fire, and withdrew from the pot a piece of tripe and an onion, which he divided into pretty equal portions, and of which he partook with Mrs. Tinker. 'You see, Miss Sharp, when I'm not here Tinker's on board wages : when I'm in town she dines with the family. Haw! haw! I'm glad Miss Sharp's not hungry, ain't you, Tink ?' And they fell to upon their frugal supper.

After supper Sir Pitt Crawley began to smoke his pipe ; and when it became quite dark, he lighted the rushlight in the tin candlestick, and producing from an interminable pocket a huge mass of papers, began reading them, and putting them in order.

'I'm here on law business, my dear, and that's how it happens that I shall have the pleasure of such a pretty travelling companion to-morrow.'

'He's always at law business,' said Mrs. Tinker, taking up the pot of porter.

'Drink and drink about,' said the baronet. 'Yes, my dear, Tinker is quite right : I've lost and won more lawsuits than any man in England. Look here at Crawley, Bart. v. Snaffle. I'll throw him over, or my name's not Pitt Crawley. Podder and another versus Crawley, Bart. Overseers of Snaily parish against Crawley, Bart. They can't prove it's common : I'll defy 'em ; the land's mine. It no more belongs to the parish than it does to you or Tinker here. I'll beat 'em, if it cost me a thousand guineas. Look over the papers ; you may if you like, my dear. Do you write a good hand ? I'll make you useful when we're at Queen's Crawley, depend on it, Miss Sharp. Now the dowager's dead I want some one.'

'She was as bad as he,' said Tinker. 'She took the law

of every one of her tradesmen ; and turned away forty-
eight footmen in four year.'

'She was close—very close,' said the baronet, simply ;
' but she was a valyble woman to me, and saved me a
steward.'—And in this confidential strain, and much to the
amusement of the new-comer, the conversation continued
for a considerable time. Whatever Sir Pitt Crawley's
qualities might be, good or bad, he did not make the least
disguise of them. He talked of himself incessantly, sometimes in the coarsest and vulgarest Hampshire accent ;
sometimes adopting the tone of a man of the world. And
so, with injunctions to Miss Sharp to be ready at five in the
morning, he bade her good night. ' You'll sleep with
Tinker to-night,' he said. ' It's a big bed, and there's
room for two. Lady Crawley died in it. Good night.'

Sir Pitt went off after this benediction, and the solemn
Tinker, rushlight in hand, led the way up the great bleak
stone stairs, past the great dreary drawing-room doors,
with the handles muffled up in paper, into the great front
bedroom, where Lady Crawley had slept her last. The
bed and chamber were so funereal and gloomy, you might
have fancied, not only that Lady Crawley died in the room,
but that her ghost inhabited it. Rebecca sprang about the
apartment, however, with the greatest liveliness, and had
peeped into the huge wardrobes, and the closets, and the
cupboards, and tried the drawers which were locked, and
examined the dreary pictures and toilette appointments,
while the old charwoman was saying her prayers. ' I
shouldn't like to sleep in this yeer bed without a good
conscience, miss,' said the old woman. ' There's room for
us and a half-dozen of ghosts in it,' says Rebecca. ' Tell me
all about Lady Crawley and Sir Pitt Crawley, and everybody, my *dear* Mrs. Tinker.'

But old Tinker was not to be pumped by this little cross-
questioner ; and signifying to her that bed was a place
for sleeping, not conversation, set up in her corner of the
bed such a snore as only the nose of innocence can produce.
Rebecca lay awake for a long, long time, thinking of the
morrow, and of the new world into which she was going,
and of her chances of success there. The rushlight flickered
in the basin. The mantelpiece cast up a great black
shadow over half of a mouldy old sampler, which her
defunct ladyship had worked, no doubt, and over two little

family pictures of young lads, one in a college gown, and the other in a red jacket like a soldier. When she went to sleep, Rebecca chose that one to dream about.

At four o'clock, on such a roseate summer's morning as even made Great Gaunt Street look cheerful, the faithful Tinker, having wakened her bedfellow, and bid her prepare for departure, unbarred and unbolted the great hall-door (the clanging and clapping whereof startled the sleeping echoes in the street), and taking her way into Oxford Street, summoned a coach from a stand there. It is needless to particularize the number of the vehicle, or to state that the driver was stationed thus early in the neighbourhood of Swallow Street,* in hopes that some young buck, reeling homeward from the tavern, might need the aid of his vehicle, and pay him with the generosity of intoxication.

It is likewise needless to say that the driver, if he had any such hopes as those above stated, was grossly disappointed ; and that the worthy baronet whom he drove to the City did not give him one single penny more than his fare. It was in vain that Jehu* appealed and stormed ; that he flung down Miss Sharp's bandboxes in the gutter at the 'Necks,* and swore he would take the law of his fare.

' You'd better not,' said one of the ostlers ; ' it's Sir Pitt Crawley.'

' So it is, Joe,' cried the baronet, approvingly ; ' and I'd like to see the man can do me.'

' So should oi,' said Joe, grinning sulkily, and mounting the baronet's baggage on the roof of the coach.

' Keep the box for me, Leader,'* exclaims the Member of Parliament to the coachman ; who replied, ' Yes, Sir Pitt,' with a touch of his hat, and rage in his soul (for he had promised the box to a young gentleman from Cambridge, who would have given a crown to a certainty), and Miss Sharp was accommodated with a back seat inside the carriage, which may be said to be carrying her into the wide world.

How the young man from Cambridge sulkily put his five great coats in front ; but was reconciled when little Miss Sharp was made to quit the carriage, and mount up beside him—when he covered her up in one of his Benjamins,* and became perfectly good-humoured—how the asthmatic

gentleman, the prim lady, who declared upon her sacred
honour she had never travelled in a public carriage before
(there is always such a lady in a coach—Alas! was; for
the coaches, where are they?), and the fat widow with the
brandy-bottle, took their places inside—how the porter
asked them all for money, and got sixpence from the gentleman and five greasy halfpence from the fat widow—and
how the carriage at length drove away—now threading
the dark lanes of Aldersgate, anon clattering by the Blue

Cupola of Paul's, jingling rapidly by the strangers' entry
of Fleet Market, which, with Exeter 'Change, has now
departed to the world of shadows—how they passed the
' White Bear'* in Piccadilly, and saw the dew rising up from
the market-gardens of Knightsbridge—how Turnham
Green, Brentford, Bagshot, were passed—need not be told
here. But the writer of these pages, who has pursued in
former days, and in the same bright weather, the same
remarkable journey, cannot but think of it with a sweet
and tender regret. Where is the road now, and its merry
incidents of life? Is there no Chelsea or Greenwich for the
old honest pimple-nosed coachmen? I wonder where are
they, those good fellows? Is old Weller*alive or dead?

and the waiters, yea and the inns at which they waited,
and the cold rounds of beef inside, and the stunted ostler
with his blue nose and clinking pail, where is he, and where
is his generation ?   To those great geniuses now in petticoats, who shall write novels for the beloved reader's
children, these men and things will be as much legend and
history as Nineveh, or Cœur de Lion, or Jack Sheppard.*
For them stage-coaches will have become romances—a team
of four bays as fabulous as Bucephalus or Black Bess.
Ah, how their coats shone, as the stablemen pulled their
clothes off, and away they went—ah, how their tails shook,
as with smoking sides at the stage's end they demurely
walked away into the inn-yard.   Alas ! we shall never
hear the horn sing at midnight, or see the pike-gates fly
open any more.   Whither, however, is the light four-inside
'Trafalgar' coach carrying us ?   Let us be set down at
Queen's Crawley without further divagation, and see how
Miss Rebecca Sharp speeds there.

CHAPTER VIII

PRIVATE AND CONFIDENTIAL

*Miss Rebecca Sharp to Miss Amelia Sedley, Russell Square,
London.*

(Free.—Pitt Crawley.)*

MY DEAREST, SWEETEST AMELIA—With what mingled joy and
sorrow do I take up the pen to write to my dearest friend! Oh,
what a change between to-day and yesterday! *Now* I am friendless
and alone; yesterday I was at home, in the sweet company of a
sister, whom I shall ever, *ever* cherish!

I will not tell you in what tears and sadness I passed the fatal
night in which I separated from you. *You* went on Tuesday to joy
and happiness, with your mother and *your devoted young soldier*
by your side; and I thought of you all night, dancing at the Perkins's,* the prettiest, I am sure, of all the young ladies at the Ball.
I was brought by the groom in the old carriage to Sir Pitt Crawley's
town house, where, after John the groom had behaved most rudely
and insolently to me (alas! 'twas safe to insult poverty and misfortune!), I was given over to Sir P.'s care, and made to pass the
night in an old gloomy bed, and by the side of a horrid gloomy old
charwoman, who keeps the house. I did not sleep one single wink
the whole night.

Sir Pitt is not what we silly girls, when we used to read *Cecilia* at Chiswick, imagined a baronet must have been. Anything, indeed, less like Lord Orville cannot be imagined. Fancy an old, stumpy, short, vulgar, and very dirty man, in old clothes and shabby old gaiters, who smokes a horrid pipe, and cooks his own horrid supper in a saucepan. He speaks with a country accent, and swore a great deal at the old charwoman, at the hackney-coachman who drove us to the inn where the coach went from, and on which I made the journey *outside for the greater part of the way.*

I was wakened at daybreak by the charwoman, and having arrived at the inn, was at first placed inside the coach. But, when we got to a place called Leakington, where the rain began to fall very heavily—will you believe it ?—I was forced to come outside ; for Sir Pitt is a proprietor of the coach, and as a passenger came at Mudbury, who wanted an inside place, I was obliged to go outside in the rain, where, however, a young gentleman from Cambridge College sheltered me very kindly in one of his *several* great-coats.

This gentleman and the guard seemed to know Sir Pitt very well, and laughed at him a great deal. They both agreed in calling him an *old screw ;* which means a very stingy, avaricious person. He never gives any money to anybody, they said (and this meanness I hate) ; and the young gentleman made me remark that we drove very slow for the last two stages on the road, because Sir Pitt was on the box, and because he is proprietor of the horses for this part of the journey. ' But won't I flog 'em on to Squashmore, when I take thé ribbons ? ' said the young *Cantab.* ' And sarve 'em right, Master Jack,' said the guard. When I comprehended the meaning of this phrase, and that Master Jack intended to drive the rest of the way, and revenge himself on Sir Pitt's horses, of course I laughed too.*

A carriage and four splendid horses, covered with armorial bearings, however awaited us at Mudbury, four miles from Queen's Crawley, and we made our entrance to the baronet's park in state. There is a fine avenue of a mile long leading to the house, and the woman at the lodge-gate (over the pillars of which are a serpent and a dove, the supporters of the Crawley arms) made us a number of curtsies as she flung open the old iron carved doors, which are something like those at odious Chiswick.

' There's an avenue,' said Sir Pitt, ' a mile long. There's six thousand pound of timber in them there trees. Do you call that nothing ? ' He pronounced avenue—*evenue,* and nothing—*nothink,* so droll ; and he had a Mr. Hodson, his hind from Mudbury, into the carriage with him, and they talked about distraining and selling up, and draining and subsoiling, and a great deal about tenants and farming—much more than I could understand. Sam Miles had been caught poaching, and Peter Bailey had gone to the work-house at last. ' Serve him right,' said Sir Pitt ; ' him and his fam'ly has been cheating me on that farm these hundred and fifty years.' Some old tenant, I suppose, who could not pay his rent.

Sir Pitt might have said '*he* and his family', to be sure; but rich baronets do not need to be careful about grammar, as poor governesses must be.

As we passed, I remarked a beautiful church-spire rising above some old elms in the park; and before them, in the midst of a lawn, and some outhouses, an old red house with tall chimneys covered with ivy, and the windows shining in the sun. 'Is that your church, sir?' I said.

'Yes, hang it' (said Sir Pitt, only he used, dear, *a much wickeder word*); 'how's Buty, Hodson? Buty's my brother Bute, my dear —my brother the parson. Buty and the Beast I call him, ha, ha!'

Hodson laughed too, and then looking more grave and nodding his head, said, 'I'm afraid he's better, Sir Pitt. He was out on his pony yesterday, looking at our corn.'

'Looking after his tithes, hang 'un' (only he used the same wicked word). 'Will brandy-and-water never kill him? He's as tough as old whatdyecallum—old Methusalem.'

Mr. Hodson laughed again. 'The young men is home from college. They've whopped John Scroggins till he's wellnigh dead.'

'Whop my second keeper!' roared out Sir Pitt.

'He was on the parson's ground, sir,' replied Mr. Hodson; and Sir Pitt in a fury swore that if ever he caught 'em poaching on his ground, he'd transport 'em, by the lord he would. However, he said, 'I've sold the presentation of the living, Hodson; none of that breed shall get it I war'nt;' and Mr. Hodson said he was quite right: and I have no doubt from this that the two brothers are at variance— as brothers often are, and sisters too. Don't you remember the two Miss Scratchleys at Chiswick, how they used always to fight and quarrel—and Mary Box, how she was always thumping Louisa?

Presently, seeing two little boys gathering sticks in the wood, Mr. Hodson jumped out of the carriage, at Sir Pitt's order, and rushed upon them with his whip. 'Pitch into 'em, Hodson,' roared the baronet; 'flog their little souls out, and bring 'em up to the house, the vagabonds; I'll commit 'em as sure as my name's Pitt.' And presently we heard Mr. Hodson's whip clacking on the shoulders of the poor little blubbering wretches, and Sir Pitt, seeing that the malefactors were in custody, drove on to the hall.

All the servants were ready to meet us, and

.   .   .   .   .   .

Here, my dear, I was interrupted last night by a dreadful thumping at my door; and who do you think it was? Sir Pitt Crawley in his nightcap and dressing-gown, such a figure! As I shrank away from such a visitor, he came forward and seized my candle; 'no candles after eleven o'clock, Miss Becky,' said he. 'Go to bed in the dark, you pretty little hussy' (that is what he called me), 'and unless you wish me to come for the candle every night, mind and be in bed at eleven.' And with this, he and Mr. Horrocks the butler went off laughing. You may be sure I shall not encourage any more of their visits. They let loose two immense bloodhounds at night, which all last night were yelling and howling at the moon. ' I call the dog Gorer,' said Sir Pitt ; ' he's killed a man, that dog has, and is master of a bull, and the mother I used to call Flora ; but now I calls her Aroarer, for she's too old to bite.   Haw, haw ! '

Before the house of Queen's Crawley, which is an odious old-fashioned red-brick mansion, with tall chimneys and gables of the style of Queen Bess, there is a terrace flanked by the family dove and serpent, and on which the great hall-door opens.   And oh, my dear, the great hall, I am sure, is as big and as glum as the great hall in the dear castle of Udolpho.*   It has a large fire-place, in which we might put half Miss Pinkerton's school, and the grate is big enough to roast an ox at the very least.   Round the room hang I don't know how many generations of Crawleys, some with beards and ruffs, some with huge wigs and toes turned out ; some dressed in long straight stays and gowns that look as stiff as towers, and some with long ringlets, and, oh my dear ! scarcely any stays at all.   At one end of the hall is the great staircase all in black oak, as dismal as may be, and on either side are tall doors with stags' heads over them, leading to the billiard-room and the library, and the great yellow saloon and the morning-rooms.   I think there are at least twenty bedrooms on the first floor ; one of them has the bed in which Queen Elizabeth slept ; and I have been taken by my new pupils through all these fine apartments this morning. They are not rendered less gloomy, I promise you, by having the shutters always shut ; and there is scarce one of the apartments, but when the light was let into it, I expected to see a ghost in the room.   We have a schoolroom on the second floor, with my bed-room leading into it on one side, and that of the young ladies on the other.   Then there are Mr. Pitt's apartments—Mr. Crawley, he is called—the eldest son, and Mr. Rawdon Crawley's rooms— he is an officer like *somebody*, and away with his regiment.   There is no want of room, I assure you.   You might lodge all the people in Russell Square in the house, I think, and have space to spare.

Half an hour after our arrival, the great dinner-bell was rung, and I came down with my two pupils (they are very thin insignificant little chits of ten and eight years old).   I came down in your *dear* muslin gown (about which that odious Mrs. Pinner was so rude, because you gave it me) ; for I am to be treated as one of the family, except on company days, when the young ladies and I are to dine upstairs.*

Well, the great dinner-bell rang, and we all assembled in the little drawing-room where my Lady Crawley sits.   She is the second Lady Crawley, and mother of the young ladies.   She was an iron-monger's daughter, and her marriage was thought a great match. She looks as if she had been handsome once, and her eyes are always weeping for the loss of her beauty.   She is pale and meagre, and high-shouldered ; and has not a word to say for herself, evidently. Her step-son, Mr. Crawley, was likewise in the room.   He was in full dress, as pompous as an undertaker.   He is pale, thin, ugly,

silent; he has thin legs, no chest, hay-coloured whiskers, and straw-
coloured hair. He is the very picture of his sainted mother over the
mantelpiece—Griselda of the noble house of Binkie.

'This is the new governess, Mr. Crawley,' said Lady Crawley,
coming forward and taking my hand; 'Miss Sharp.'

'Oh!' said Mr. Crawley, and pushed his head once forward and
began again to read a great pamphlet with which he was busy.

'I hope you will be kind to my girls,' said Lady Crawley; with her
pink eyes always full of tears.

'Law, ma, of course she will,' said the eldest: and I saw at
a glance that I need not be afraid of *that* woman.

'My lady is served,' says the butler in black, in an immense white

shirt-frill, that looked as if it had been one of the Queen Elizabeth's
ruffs depicted in the hall; and so taking Mr. Crawley's arm, she led
the way to the dining-room, whither I followed with my little pupils
in each hand.

Sir Pitt was already in the room with a silver jug. He had just
been to the cellar, and was in full dress too; that is, he had taken his
gaiters off and showed his little dumpy legs in black worsted stockings. The sideboard was covered with glistening old plate—old
cups, both gold and silver; old salvers and cruet-stands, like
Rundell and Bridge's shop.* Everything on the table was in silver
too, and two footmen, with red hair and canary-coloured liveries,
stood on either side of the sideboard.

Mr. Crawley said a long grace, and Sir Pitt said amen, and the
great silver dish-covers were removed.

'What have we for dinner, Betsy?' said the baronet.

'Mutton broth, I believe, Sir Pitt,' answered Lady Crawley.*

'*Mouton aux navets*,' added the butler gravely (pronounce, if you please, moutongonavvy); and the soup is *potage de mouton à l'Écossaise*. The side dishes contain *pommes de terre au naturel* and *choufleur à l'eau*.'

'Mutton's mutton,' said the baronet, 'and a devilish good thing. What *ship* was it, Horrocks, and when did you kill?'

'One of the black-faced Scotch, Sir Pitt: we killed on Thursday.'

'Who took any?'

'Steel, of Mudbury, took the saddle and two legs, Sir Pitt; but he says the last was too young and confounded woolly, Sir Pitt.'

'Will you take some *potage*? Miss ah—Miss Blunt,' said Mr. Crawley.

'Capital Scotch broth, my dear,' said Sir Pitt, 'though they call it by a French name.'

'I believe it is the custom, sir, in decent society,' said Mr. Crawley, haughtily, 'to call the dish as I have called it;' and it was served to us on silver soup-plates by the footmen in the canary coats, with the *mouton aux navets*. Then 'ale and water' were brought and served to us young ladies in wine-glasses. I am not a judge of ale, but I can say with a clear conscience I prefer water.

While we were enjoying our repast, Sir Pitt took occasion to ask what had become of the shoulders of the mutton.

'I believe they were eaten in the servants' hall,' said my lady, humbly.

'They was, my lady,' said Horrocks, 'and precious little else we get there neither.'

Sir Pitt burst into a horse-laugh, and continued his conversation with Mr. Horrocks. 'That there little black pig of the Kent sow's breed must be uncommon fat now.'

'It's not quite busting, Sir Pitt,' said the butler with the gravest air, at which Sir Pitt, and with him the young ladies, this time, began to laugh violently.

'Miss Crawley, Miss Rose Crawley,' said Mr. Crawley, 'your laughter strikes me as being exceedingly out of place.'

'Never mind my lord,' said the baronet, 'we'll try the porker on Saturday. Kill 'un on Saturday morning, John Horrocks. Miss Sharp adores pork, don't you, Miss Sharp?'

And I think this is all the conversation that I remember at dinner. When the repast was concluded a jug of hot water was placed before Sir Pitt, with a case-bottle containing, I believe, rum. Mr. Horrocks served myself and my pupils with three little glasses of wine, and a bumper was poured out for my lady. When we retired, she took from her work-drawer an enormous interminable piece of knitting; the young ladies began to play at cribbage with a dirty pack of cards. We had but one candle lighted, but it was in a magnificent old silver candlestick, and after a very few questions from my lady, I had my choice of amusement between a volume of sermons, and a pamphlet on the corn-laws, which Mr. Crawley had been reading before dinner.

So we sat for an hour until steps were heard.

' Put away the cards, girls,' cried my lady, in a great tremor ; ' put down Mr. Crawley's books, Miss Sharp : ' and these orders had been scarcely obeyed, when Mr. Crawley entered the room.

' We will resume yesterday's discourse, young ladies,' said he, ' and you shall each read a page by turns ; so that Miss a—Miss Short may have an opportunity of hearing you ; ' and the poor girls began to spell a long dismal sermon delivered at Bethesda Chapel, Liverpool, on behalf of the mission for the Chickasaw Indians. Was it not a charming evening ?

At ten the servants were told to call Sir Pitt and the household to prayers. Sir Pitt came in first, very much flushed, and rather unsteady in his gait ;* and after him the butler, the canaries, Mr. Crawley's man, three other men, smelling very much of the stable, and four women, one of whom, I remarked, was very much over-dressed, and who flung me a look of great scorn as she plumped down on her knees.

After Mr. Crawley had done haranguing and expounding, we received our candles, and then we went to bed ; and then I was disturbed in my writing, as I have described to my dearest, sweetest Amelia.

Good night. A thousand thousand thousand kisses !

Saturday.—This morning, at five, I heard the shrieking of the little black pig. Rose and Violet introduced me to it yesterday ; and to the stables, and to the kennel, and to the gardener, who was picking fruit to send to market, and from whom they begged hard a bunch of hot-house grapes ; but he said that Sir Pitt had numbered every ' Man Jack ' of them, and it would be as much as his place was worth to give any away. The darling girls caught a colt in a paddock, and asked me if I would ride, and began to ride themselves, when the groom, coming with horrid oaths, drove them away.

Lady Crawley is always knitting the worsted. Sir Pitt is always tipsy, every night ; and, I believe, sits with Horrocks, the butler. Mr. Crawley always reads sermons in the evening; and in the morning is locked up in his study, or else rides to Mudbury, on county business, or to Squashmore, where he preaches, on Wednesdays and Fridays, to the tenants there.*

A hundred thousand grateful loves to your dear papa and mamma. Is your poor brother recovered of his rack-punch ? Oh, dear ! Oh, dear ! How men should beware of wicked punch !

Ever and ever thine own,

REBECCA.

Everything considered,* I think it is quite as well for our dear Amelia Sedley, in Russell Square, that Miss Sharp and she are parted. Rebecca is a droll funny creature, to be sure ; and those descriptions of the poor lady weeping for the loss of her beauty, and the gentleman ' with hay-coloured whiskers and straw-coloured hair', are very smart, doubtless, and show a great knowledge of the world. That she might, when on her knees, have been thinking of something better than Miss Horrocks's ribbons, has possibly struck both of us. But my kind reader will please to remember that this history* has ' Vanity Fair' for a title, and that Vanity Fair is a very vain, wicked, foolish place, full of all sorts of humbugs and falsenesses and pretensions. And while the moralist, who is holding forth on the cover (an accurate portrait of your humble servant), professes to wear neither gown nor bands, but only the very same long-eared livery in which his congregation is arrayed : yet, look you, one is bound to speak the truth as far as one knows it, whether one mounts a cap and bells or a shovel-hat ; and a deal of disagreeable matter must come out in the course of such an undertaking.

I have heard a brother of the story-telling trade, at Naples, preaching to a pack of good-for-nothing honest lazy fellows by the sea-shore, work himself up into such a rage and passion with some of the villains whose wicked deeds he was describing and inventing, that the audience could not resist it, and they and the poet together would burst out into a roar of oaths and execrations against the fictitious monster of the tale, so that the hat went round, and the bajocchi tumbled into it, in the midst of a perfect storm of sympathy.

At the little Paris theatres, on the other hand, you will not only hear the people yelling out ' Ah gredin ! Ah monstre !' and cursing the tyrant of the play from the boxes ; but the actors themselves positively refuse to play the wicked parts, such as those of infâmes Anglais, brutal Cossacks, and what not, and prefer to appear at a smaller salary, in their real characters as loyal Frenchmen. I set the two stories one against the other, so that you may see that it is not from mere mercenary motives that the present performer is desirous to show up and trounce his villains ; but because he has a sincere hatred of them, which he cannot keep down, and which must find a vent in suitable abuse and bad language.

I warn my ' kyind friends'* then, that I am going to tell a story of harrowing villany and complicated—but, as

I trust, intensely interesting—crime. My rascals are no milk-and-water rascals, I promise you. When we come to the proper places we won't spare fine language—No, no ! But when we are going over the quiet country we must perforce be calm. A tempest in a slop-basin is absurd. We will reserve that sort of thing for the mighty ocean and the lonely midnight. The present Number will be very mild. Others——but we will not anticipate *those*.

And, as we bring our characters forward, I will ask leave, as a man and a brother,* not only to introduce them, but occasionally to step down from the platform, and talk about them : if they are good and kindly, to love them and shake them by the hand ; if they are silly, to laugh at them confidentially in the reader's sleeve : if they are wicked and heartless, to abuse them in the strongest terms which politeness admits of.

Otherwise you might fancy it was I who was sneering at the practice of devotion, which Miss Sharp finds so ridiculous ; that it was I who laughed good-humouredly at the reeling old Silenus of a baronet—whereas the laughter comes from one who has no reverence except for prosperity, and no eye for anything beyond success. Such people there are living and flourishing in the world—Faithless, Hopeless, Charityless : let us have at them, dear friends, with might and main. Some there are, and very successful too, mere quacks and fools : and it was to combat and expose such as those, no doubt, that Laughter was made.

CHAPTER IX

FAMILY PORTRAITS

IR PITT CRAWLEY was a philosopher with a taste for what is called low life. His first marriage with the daughter of the noble Binkie had been made under the auspices of his parents ; and as he often told Lady Crawley in her lifetime she was such a confounded quarrelsome high-bred jade that when she died he was hanged if he would ever take another of her sort, at her ladyship's demise he kept his promise, and selected for a second wife Miss Rose Dawson, daughter of Mr. John Thomas Dawson, ironmonger,* of Mudbury. What a happy woman was Rose to be my Lady Crawley !

Let us set down the items of her happiness. In the first place, she gave up Peter Butt, a young man who kept company with her, and in consequence of his disappointment in love took to smuggling, poaching, and a thousand other bad courses. Then she quarrelled, as in duty bound, with all the friends and intimates of her youth, who, of course, could not be received by my lady at Queen's Crawley—nor did she find in her new rank and abode any persons who were willing to welcome her. Who ever did ? Sir Huddleston Fuddleston had three daughters who all hoped to be Lady Crawley. Sir Giles Wapshot's family were insulted that one of the Wapshot girls had not the preference in the marriage, and the remaining baronets of the county were indignant at their comrade's *mésalliance*. Never mind the commoners, whom we will leave to grumble anonymously.

Sir Pitt did not care, as he said, a brass farden for any one of them. He had his pretty Rose, and what more need a man require than to please himself ? So he used to get drunk every night : to beat his pretty Rose sometimes : to leave her in Hampshire when he went to London for the parliamentary session, without a single friend in the wide world. Even Mrs. Bute Crawley, the rector's wife,

refused to visit her, as she said she would never give the
pas to a tradesman's daughter.

As the only endowments with which Nature had gifted
Lady Crawley were those of pink cheeks and a white skin,
and as she had no sort of character, nor talents, nor opinions,
nor occupations, nor amusements, nor that vigour of soul
and ferocity of temper which often falls to the lot of entirely
foolish women, her hold upon Sir Pitt's affections was not
very great. Her roses faded out of her cheeks, and the
pretty freshness left her figure after the birth of a couple
of children, and she became a mere machine in her husband's
house, of no more use than the late Lady Crawley's grand
piano. Being a light-complexioned woman, she wore light
clothes, as most blondes will, and appeared, in preference,
in draggled sea-green, or slatternly sky-blue. She worked
that worsted day and night, or other pieces like it. She
had counterpanes in the course of a few years to all the
beds in Crawley. She had a small flower-garden, for which
she had rather an affection ; but beyond this no other like
or disliking. When her husband was rude to her she was
apathetic : whenever he struck her she cried. She had
not character enough to take to drinking, and moaned
about, slip-shod and in curl-papers, all day. Oh, Vanity
Fair—Vanity Fair ! This might have been, but for you,
a cheery lass ; Peter Butt and Rose a happy man and
wife, in a snug farm, with a hearty family, and an honest
portion of pleasures, cares, hopes, and struggles :—but
a title and a coach and four are toys more precious than
happiness in Vanity Fair : and if Harry the Eighth or
Bluebeard were alive now, and wanted a tenth wife, do you
suppose he could not get the prettiest girl that shall be
presented this season ?

The languid dullness of their mamma did not, as it may
be supposed, awaken much affection in her little daughters,
but they were very happy in the servants' hall and in the
stables ; and the Scotch gardener having luckily a good
wife and some good children, they got a little wholesome
society and instruction in his lodge, which was the only
education bestowed upon them until Miss Sharp came.

Her engagement was owing to the remonstrances of
Mr. Pitt Crawley, the only friend or protector Lady Crawley
ever had, and the only person, besides her children, for
whom she entertained a little feeble attachment. Mr. Pitt

took after the noble Binkies, from whom he was descended, and was a very polite and proper gentleman. When he grew to man's estate, and came back from Christchurch, he began to reform the slackened discipline of the hall, in spite of his father, who stood in awe of him. He was a man of such rigid refinement, that he would have starved rather than have dined without a white neckcloth. Once, when just from college, and when Horrocks the butler brought him a letter without placing it previously on a tray, he gave that domestic a look, and administered to him a speech so cutting, that Horrocks ever after trembled before him ; the whole household bowed to him : Lady Crawley's curl-papers came off earlier when he was at home : Sir Pitt's muddy gaiters disappeared ; and if that incorrigible old man still adhered to other old habits, he never fuddled himself with rum-and-water in his son's presence, and only talked to his servants in a very reserved and polite manner ; and those persons remarked that Sir Pitt never swore at Lady Crawley while his son was in the room.

It was he who taught the butler to say ' My lady is served,' and who insisted on handing her ladyship into dinner. He seldom spoke to her, but when he did it was with the most powerful respect ; and he never let her quit the apartment, without rising in the most stately manner to open the door, and making an elegant bow at her egress.

At Eton he was called Miss Crawley ; and there, I am sorry to say, his younger brother Rawdon used to lick him violently. But though his parts were not brilliant, he made up for his lack of talent by meritorious industry, and was never known, during eight years at school, to be subject to that punishment which it is generally thought none but a cherub can escape.

At college his career was of course highly creditable. And here he prepared himself for public life, into which he was to be introduced by the patronage of his grandfather, Lord Binkie, by studying the ancient and modern orators with great assiduity, and by speaking unceasingly at the debating societies. But though he had a fine flux of words, and delivered his little voice with great pomposity and pleasure to himself, and never advanced any sentiment or opinion which was not perfectly trite and stale, and supported by a Latin quotation : yet he failed somehow,

in spite of a mediocrity which ought to have insured any
man a success. He did not even get the prize poem, which
all his friends said he was sure of.

After leaving college he became Private Secretary to
Lord Binkie, and was then appointed Attaché to the
Legation at Pumpernickel, which post he filled with perfect
honour, and brought home dispatches, consisting of Strasburg pie,* to the Foreign Minister of the day. After remaining ten years Attaché (several years after the lamented
Lord Binkie's demise), and finding the advancement slow,
he at length gave up the diplomatic service in some disgust,
and began to turn country gentleman.

He wrote a pamphlet on Malt on returning to England
(for he was an ambitious man, and always liked to be before
the public), and took a strong part in the Negro Emancipation question. Then he became a friend of Mr. Wilberforce's,* whose politics he admired, and had that famous
correspondence with the Reverend Silas Hornblower, on
the Ashantee Mission. He was in London, if not for the
Parliament session, at least in May, for the religious
meetings. In the country he was a magistrate, and an
active visitor and speaker among those destitute of religious
instruction. He was said to be paying his addresses to
Lady Jane Sheepshanks, Lord Southdown's third daughter,
and whose sister, Lady Emily, wrote those sweet tracts,
The Sailor's True Binnacle, and *The Applewoman of
Finchley Common*.

Miss Sharp's accounts of his employment at Queen's
Crawley were not caricatures. He subjected the servants
there to the devotional exercises before mentioned, in
which (and so much the better) he brought his father to
join. He patronized an Independent meeting-house in
Crawley parish, much to the indignation of his uncle the
rector, and to the consequent delight of Sir Pitt, who was
induced to go himself once or twice, which occasioned
some violent sermons at Crawley parish church, directed
point-blank at the baronet's old gothic pew there. Honest
Sir Pitt, however, did not feel the force of these discourses,
as he always took his nap during sermon-time.

Mr. Crawley was very earnest, for the good of the nation
and of the Christian world, that the old gentleman should
yield him up his place in Parliament; but this the elder
constantly refused to do. Both were of course too prudent

to give up the fifteen hundred a year which was brought in by the second seat (at this period filled by Mr. Quadroon, with carte-blanche on the Slave question); indeed the family estate was much embarrassed, and the income drawn from the borough was of great use to the house of Queen's Crawley.

It had never recovered the heavy fine imposed upon Walpole Crawley, first baronet, for peculation in the Tape and Sealing-Wax Office. Sir Walpole was a jolly fellow, eager to seize and to spend money ('*alieni appetens, sui profusus*,'* as Mr. Crawley would remark with a sigh), and in his day beloved by all the county for the constant drunkenness and hospitality which was maintained at Queen's Crawley. The cellars were filled with burgundy then, the kennels with hounds, and the stables with gallant hunters; now, such horses as Queen's Crawley possessed went to plough, or ran in the 'Trafalgar' coach; and it was with a team of these very horses, on an off-day, that Miss Sharp was brought to the Hall; for, boor as he was, Sir Pitt was a stickler*for his dignity while at home, and seldom drove out but with four horses, and, though he dined off boiled mutton, had always three footmen to serve it.

If mere parsimony would have made a man rich, Sir Pitt Crawley might have become very wealthy—if he had been an attorney in a country town, with no capital but his brains, it is very possible that he would have turned them to good account, and might have achieved for himself a very considerable influence and competency. But he was unluckily endowed with a good name and a large though encumbered estate, both of which went rather to injure than to advance him. He had a taste for law, which cost him many thousands yearly; and being a great deal too clever to be robbed, as he said, by any single agent, allowed his affairs to be mismanaged by a dozen, whom he all equally mistrusted. He was such a sharp landlord, that he could hardly find any but bankrupt tenants; and such a close farmer, as to grudge almost the seed to the ground, whereupon revengeful Nature grudged him the crops which she granted to more liberal husbandmen. He speculated in every possible way; he worked mines; bought canal-shares; horsed coaches; took government contracts, and was the busiest man and magistrate of his county. As he would not pay honest agents at his granite-quarry,

he had the satisfaction of finding that four overseers ran
away, and took fortunes with them to America. For want
of proper precautions, his coal-mines filled with water :
the government flung his contract of damaged beef upon
his hands : and for his coach-horses, every mail proprietor
in the kingdom knew that he lost more horses than any
man in the country, from under-feeding and buying cheap.
In disposition he was sociable, and far from being proud ;
nay, he rather preferred the society of a farmer or a horse-
dealer to that of a gentleman, like my lord, his son : he
was fond of drink, of swearing, of joking with the farmers'
daughters : he was never known to give away a shilling
or to do a good action, but was of a pleasant, sly, laughing
mood, and would cut his joke, and drink his glass with
a tenant and sell him up the next day ; or have his laugh
with the poacher he was transporting with equal good
humour. His politeness for the fair sex has already been
hinted at by Miss Rebecca Sharp—in a word, the whole
baronetage, peerage, commonage of England did not contain
a more cunning, mean, selfish, foolish, disreputable old
man. That blood-red hand* of Sir Pitt Crawley's would
be in anybody's pocket except his own ; and it is with grief
and pain that, as admirers of the British aristocracy, we
find ourselves obliged to admit the existence of so many
ill qualities in a person whose name is in *Debrett*.

One great cause why Mr. Crawley had such a hold over
the affections of his father, resulted from money arrangements. The baronet owed his son a sum of money out of
the jointure of his mother, which he did not find it convenient to pay.; indeed he had an almost invincible repugnance to paying anybody, and could only be brought by
force to discharge his debts. Miss Sharp calculated (for
she became, as we shall hear speedily, inducted into most
of the secrets of the family), that the mere payment of
his creditors cost the honourable baronet several hundreds
yearly ; but this was a delight he could not forgo ; he had
a savage pleasure in making the poor wretches wait, and
in shifting from court to court and from term to term the
period of satisfaction. What's the good of being in Parliament, he said, if you must pay your debts ?* Hence,
indeed, his position as a senator was not a little useful to
him.

Vanity Fair—Vanity Fair !* Here was a man, who could

not spell, and did not care to read—who had the habits
and the cunning of a boor : whose aim in life was petti-
fogging : who never had a taste, or emotion, or enjoyment,
but what was sordid and foul ; and yet he had rank, and
honours, and power, somehow : and was a dignitary of the
land, and a pillar of the state. He was high sheriff, and
rode in a golden coach. Great ministers and statesmen
courted him ; and in Vanity Fair he had a higher place
than the most brilliant genius or spotless virtue.

Sir Pitt had an unmarried half-sister who inherited her
mother's large fortune, and though the baronet proposed
to borrow this money of her on mortgage, Miss Crawley
declined the offer, and preferred the security of the funds.
She had signified, however, her intention of leaving her
inheritance between Sir Pitt's second son and the family
at the rectory, and had once or twice paid the debts of
Rawdon Crawley in his career at college and in the army.
Miss Crawley was, in consequence, an object of great
respect when she came to Queen's Crawley, for she had
a balance at her banker's which would have made her
beloved anywhere.

What a dignity it gives an old lady, that balance at the
banker's ! How tenderly we look at her faults, if she is
a relative (and may every reader have a score of such),
what a kind, good-natured old creature we find her ! How
the junior partner of Hobbs and Dobbs leads her smiling
to the carriage with the lozenge upon it, and the fat wheezy
coachman ! How, when she comes to pay us a visit, we
generally find an opportunity to let our friends 'know her
station in the world ! We say (and with perfect truth)
I wish I had Miss MacWhirter's signature to a cheque for
five thousand pounds. She wouldn't miss it, says your
wife. She is my aunt, say you, in an easy careless way,
when your friend asks if Miss MacWhirter is any relative ?
Your wife is perpetually sending her little testimonies of
affection, your little girls work endless worsted baskets
cushions, and footstools for her. What a good fire there
is in her room when she comes to pay you a visit, although
your wife laces her stays without one ! The house during
her stay assumes a festive, neat, warm, jovial, snug appearance not visible at other seasons. You yourself, dear sir,
forget to go to sleep after dinner, and find yourself all of

a sudden (though you invariably lose) very fond of a rubber.
What good dinners you have—game every day, Malmsey-
Madeira, and no end of fish from London. Even the servants
in the kitchen share in the general prosperity ; and, somehow, during the stay of Miss MacWhirter's fat coachman,
the beer is grown much stronger, and the consumption
of tea and sugar in the nursery (where her maid takes her
meals) is not regarded in the least. Is it so, or is it not
so ? I appeal to the middle classes. Ah, gracious powers !
I wish you would send me an old aunt—a maiden aunt—an
aunt with a lozenge on her carriage, and a front of light
coffee-coloured hair—how my children should work work-
bags for her, and my Julia and I would make her comfortable ! Sweet, sweet vision ! Foolish, foolish dream !*

CHAPTER X

MISS SHARP BEGINS TO MAKE FRIENDS

ND now, being received as a member of the amiable family whose portraits we have sketched in the foregoing pages, it became naturally Rebecca's duty to make herself, as she said, agreeable to her benefactors, and to gain their confidence to the utmost of her power. Who could not admire this quality of gratitude in an unprotected orphan ; and if there entered some degree of selfishness into her calculations, who can say but that her prudence was perfectly justifiable ? ' I am alone in the world,' said the friendless girl. ' I have nothing to look for but what my own labour can bring me ; and while that little pink-faced chit Amelia, with not half my sense, has ten thousand pounds and an establishment secure, poor Rebecca (and my figure is far better than hers) has only herself and her own wits to trust to. Well, let us see if my wits cannot provide me with an honourable maintenance, and if some day or the other I cannot show Miss Amelia my real superiority over her. Not that I dislike poor Amelia : who can dislike such a harmless, good-natured creature ?—only it will be a fine day when I can take my place above her in the world, as why, indeed, should I not ? ' Thus it was that our little romantic friend formed visions of the future for herself—nor must we be scandalized that, in all her castles in the air, a husband was the principal inhabitant. Of what else have young ladies to think, but husbands ? Of what else do their dear mammas think ? ' I must be my own mamma,' said Rebecca ; not without a tingling consciousness of defeat, as she thought over her little misadventure with Jos Sedley.

So she wisely determined to render her position with the

Queen's Crawley family comfortable and secure, and to this
end resolved to make friends of every one around her who
could at all interfere with her comfort.

As my Lady Crawley was not one of these personages,
and a woman, moreover, so indolent and void of character
as not to be of the least consequence in her own house,
Rebecca soon found that it was not at all necessary to
cultivate her good will—indeed, impossible to gain it.
She used to talk to her pupils about their ' poor mamma ' ;
and, though she treated that lady with every demonstration
of cool respect, it was to the rest of the family that she
wisely directed the chief part of her attentions.

With the young people, whose applause she thoroughly
gained, her method was pretty simple. She did not pester
their young brains with too much learning, but, on the
contrary, let them have their own way in regard to educa-
ting themselves ; for what instruction is more effectual
than self-instruction ? The eldest was rather fond of
books, and as there was in the old library at Queen's
Crawley a considerable provision of works of light literature
of the last century, both in the French and English languages (they had been purchased by the Secretary of the
Tape and Sealing-Wax Office at the period of his disgrace),
and as nobody ever troubled the bookshelves but herself, Rebecca was enabled agreeably, and, as it were, in
playing, to impart a great deal of instruction to Miss Rose
Crawley.

She and Miss Rose thus read together many delightful
French and English works, among which may be mentioned
those of the learned Dr. Smollett, of the ingenious Mr. Henry
Fielding, of the graceful and fantastic Monsieur Crébillon
the younger, whom our immortal poet Gray so much
admired, and of the universal Monsieur de Voltaire. Once,
when Mr. Crawley asked what the young people were
reading, the governess replied 'Smollett'. 'Oh, Smollett,'
said Mr. Crawley, quite satisfied. 'His history is more
dull, but by no means so dangerous as that of Mr. Hume.
It is history you are reading ? ' ' Yes,' said Miss Rose ;
without, however, adding that it was the history of Mr.
Humphry Clinker.* On another occasion he was rather
scandalized at finding his sister with a book of French plays ;
but as the governess remarked that it was for the purpose
of acquiring the French idiom in conversation, he was fain

MISS SHARP IN HER SCHOOLROOM

to be content.   Mr. Crawley, as a diplomatist, was exceedingly proud of his own skill in speaking the French language
(for he was of the world still), and not a little pleased with
the compliments which the governess continually paid
him upon his proficiency.

Miss Violet's tastes were, on the contrary, more rude and
boisterous than those of her sister. She knew the seques-
tered spots where the hens laid their eggs. She could
climb a tree to rob the nests of the feathered songsters of
their speckled spoils. And her pleasure was to ride the
young colts, and to scour the plains like Camilla.* She was
the favourite of her father and of the stablemen. She
was the darling, and withal the terror, of the cook ; for she
discovered the haunts of the jampots, and would attack
them when they were within her reach. She and her
sister were engaged in constant battles. Any of which
peccadilloes if Miss Sharp discovered, she did not tell them
to Lady Crawley, who would have told them to the father,
or, worse, to Mr. Crawley ; but promised not to tell if Miss
Violet would be a good girl and love her governess.*

With Mr. Crawley Miss Sharp was respectful and obedient.
She used to consult him on passages of French which she
could not understand, though her mother was a Frenchwoman, and which he would construe to her satisfaction :
and, besides giving her his aid in profane literature, he was
kind enough to select for her books of a more serious
tendency, and address to her much of his conversation.
She admired, beyond measure, his speech at the Quashi-
maboo-Aid Society ; took an interest in his pamphlet on
malt ; was often affected, even to tears, by his discourses
of an evening, and would say—' Oh, thank you, sir,' with
a sigh, and a look up to heaven, that made him occasionally
condescend to shake hands with her.   ' Blood is everything,
after all,' would that aristocratic religionist say.   ' How
Miss Sharp is awakened by my words, when not one of the
people here is touched. I am too fine for them—too
delicate. I must familiarize my style—but she under-
stands it. Her mother was a Montmorency.'

Indeed it was from this famous family, as it appears,
that Miss Sharp, by the mother's side, was descended.
Of course she did not say that her mother had been on the
stage ; it would have shocked Mr. Crawley's religious
scruples. How many noble *emigrées* had this horrid

revolution plunged in poverty! She had several stories
about her ancestors ere she had been many months in
the house; some of which Mr. Crawley happened to find
in D'Hozier's dictionary, which was in the library, and
which strengthened his belief in their truth, and in the
high-breeding of Rebecca. Are we to suppose from this
curiosity and prying into dictionaries, could our heroine
suppose, that Mr. Crawley was interested in her?—no,
only in a friendly way. Have we not stated that he was
attached to Lady Jane Sheepshanks?

He took Rebecca to task once or twice about the propriety of playing at backgammon with Sir Pitt, saying that
it was a godless amusement, and that she would be much
better engaged in reading *Thrump's Legacy*, or *The Blind
Washerwoman of Moorfields*, or any work of a more serious
nature; but Miss Sharp said her dear mother used often
to play the same game with the old Count de Trictrac and
the venerable Abbé du Cornet, and so found an excuse for
this and other worldly amusement.

But it was not only by playing at backgammon with
the baronet that the little governess rendered herself
agreeable to her employer. She found many different ways
of being useful to him. She read over, with indefatigable
patience, all those law papers, with which, before she came
to Queen's Crawley, he had promised to entertain her.
She volunteered to copy many of his letters, and adroitly
altered the spelling of them so as to suit the usages of
the present day. She became interested in everything
appertaining to the estate, to the farm, the park, the
garden, and the stables; and so delightful a companion
was she, that the baronet would seldom take his after-
breakfast walk without her (and the children of course),
when she would give her advice as to the trees which were
to be lopped in the shrubberies, the garden-beds to be dug,
the crops which were to be cut, the horses which were to
go to cart or plough. Before she had been a year at
Queen's Crawley she had quite won the baronet's confidence; and the conversation at the dinner-table, which
before used to be held between him and Mr. Horrocks the
butler, was now almost exclusively between Sir Pitt and
Miss Sharp. She was almost mistress of the house when
Mr. Crawley was absent, but conducted herself in her new
and exalted situation with such circumspection and modesty

as not to offend the authorities of the kitchen and stable, among whom her behaviour was always exceedingly modest and affable. She was quite a different person from the haughty, shy, dissatisfied little girl whom we have known previously, and this change of temper proved great prudence, a sincere desire of amendment, or at any rate great moral courage on her part. Whether it was the heart which dictated this new system of complaisance and humility adopted by our Rebecca, is to be proved by her after-history. A system of hypocrisy, which lasts through whole years, is one seldom satisfactorily practised by a person of one-and-twenty; however, our readers will recollect, that, though young in years, our heroine was old in life and experience, and we have written to no purpose if they have not discovered that she was a very clever woman.

The elder and younger son of the house of Crawley were, like the gentleman and lady in the weather-box, never at home together—they hated each other cordially: indeed, Rawdon Crawley, the dragoon, had a great contempt for the establishment altogether, and seldom came thither except when his aunt paid her annual visit.

The great good quality of this old lady has been mentioned. She possessed seventy thousand pounds, and had almost adopted Rawdon. She disliked her elder nephew exceedingly, and despised him as a milksop. In return he did not hesitate to state that her soul was irretrievably lost, and was of opinion that his brother's chance in the next world was not a whit better. 'She is a godless woman of the world,' would Mr. Crawley say; 'she lives with atheists and Frenchmen. My mind shudders when I think of her awful, awful situation, and that, near as she is to the grave, she should be so given up to vanity, licentiousness, profaneness, and folly.' In fact, the old lady declined altogether to hear his hour's lecture of an evening; and when she came to Queen's Crawley alone, he was obliged to pretermit his usual devotional exercises.

'Shut up your sarmons, Pitt, when Miss Crawley comes down,' said his father; 'she has written to say that she won't stand the preachifying.'

'Oh, sir! consider the servants.'

'The servants be hanged,' said Sir Pitt; and his son thought even worse would happen were they deprived of the benefit of his instruction.

'Why, hang it, Pitt!' said the father to his remonstrance. 'You wouldn't be such a flat as to let three thousand a year go out of the family?'

'What is money compared to our souls, sir?' continued Crawley.

'You mean that the old lady won't leave the money to you?'*—and who knows but it *was* Mr. Crawley's meaning?

Old Miss Crawley was certainly one of the reprobate. She had a snug little house in Park Lane, and, as she ate and drank a great deal too much during the season in London, she went to Harrogate or Cheltenham for the summer. She was the most hospitable and jovial of old vestals, and had been a beauty in her day, she said. (All old women were beauties once, we very well know.) She was a *bel esprit*, and a dreadful Radical for those days. She had been in France (where St. Just,* they say, inspired her with an unfortunate passion), and loved, ever after, French novels, French cookery, and French wines. She read Voltaire, and had Rousseau by heart; talked very lightly about divorce, and most energetically of the rights of women. She had pictures' of Mr. Fox in every room in the house: when that statesman was in opposition, I am not sure that she had not flung a main with him; and when he came into office, she took great credit for bringing over to him Sir Pitt and his colleague for Queen's Crawley, although Sir Pitt would have come over himself, without any trouble on the honest lady's part. It is needless to say that Sir Pitt was brought to change his views after the death of the great Whig statesman.*

This worthy old lady took a fancy to Rawdon Crawley when a boy, sent him to Cambridge (in opposition to his brother at Oxford), and, when the young man was requested by the authorities of the first-named University to quit after a residence of two years, she bought him his commission in the Life Guards Green.

A perfect and celebrated 'blood', or dandy about town, was this young officer. Boxing, rat-hunting, the fives-court, and four-in-hand driving were then the fashion of our British aristocracy; and he was an adept in all these noble sciences. And though he belonged to the household troops, who, as it was their duty to rally round the Prince Regent,* had not shown their valour in foreign service yet, Rawdon Crawley had already (à propos of play, of which he was immoderately fond) fought three bloody duels in which he gave ample proofs of his contempt for death.*

'And for what follows after death,' would Mr. Crawley observe, throwing his gooseberry-coloured eyes up to the ceiling. He was always thinking of his brother's soul, or of the souls of those who differed with him in opinion : it is a sort of comfort which many of the serious give themselves.

Silly, romantic Miss Crawley, far from being horrified at the courage of her favourite, always used to pay his debts after his duels ; and would not listen to a word that was whispered against his morality. 'He will sow his wild oats,' she would say, 'and is worth far more than that puling hypocrite of a brother of his.'

CHAPTER XI

ARCADIAN SIMPLICITY

BESIDES these honest folks at the Hall (whose simplicity and sweet rural purity surely show the advantage of a country life over a town one), we must introduce the reader to their relatives and neighbours at the Rectory, Bute Crawley and his wife.*

The Reverend Bute Crawley was a tall, stately, jolly, shovel-hatted man, far more popular in his county than the baronet his brother. At college he pulled stroke-oar in the Christchurch boat, and had thrashed all the best bruisers of the 'town'. He carried his taste for boxing and athletic exercises into private life ; there was not a fight within twenty miles at which he was not present, nor a race, nor a coursing match, nor a regatta, nor a ball, nor an election, nor a visitation dinner, nor indeed a good dinner in the whole county, but he found means to attend it. You might see

his bay mare and gig-lamps* a score of miles away from
his rectory house, whenever there was any dinner-party
at Fuddleston, or at Roxby, or at Wapshot Hall, or at
the great lords of the county, with all of whom he was
intimate. He had a fine voice ; sang ' A southerly wind
and a cloudy sky ' ;* and gave the ' whoop ' in chorus with
general applause. He rode to hounds in a pepper-and-salt
frock, and was one of the best fishermen in the county.

Mrs. Crawley, the rector's wife, was a smart little body,
who wrote this worthy divine's sermons. Being of a
domestic turn, and keeping the house a great deal with
her daughters, she ruled absolutely within the Rectory,
wisely giving her husband full liberty without. He was
welcome to come and go, and dine abroad as many days
as his fancy dictated, for Mrs. Crawley was a saving woman
and knew the price of port wine. Ever since Mrs. Bute
carried off the young rector of Queen's Crawley (she was
of a good family, daughter of the late Lieut.-Colonel Hector
MacTavish, and she and her mother played for Bute and
won him at Harrogate),* she had been a prudent and
thrifty wife to him. In spite of her care, however, he was
always in debt. It took him at least ten years to pay off
his college bills contracted during his father's lifetime. In
the year 179—, when he was just clear of these incumbrances, he gave the odds of 100 to 1 (in twenties) against
Kangaroo, who won the Derby. The rector was obliged
to take up the money at a ruinous interest, and had been
struggling ever since. His sister helped him with a hundred
now and then, but of course his great hope was in her
death—when ' hang it ' (as he would say), ' Matilda *must*
leave me half her money.'

So that the baronet and his brother had every reason
which two brothers possibly can have for being by the
ears. Sir Pitt had had the better of Bute in innumerable
family transactions. Young Pitt not only did not hunt,
but set up a meeting-house under his uncle's very nose.
Rawdon, it was known, was to come in for the bulk of
Miss Crawley's property. These money transactions—
these speculations in life and death—these silent battles
for reversionary spoil—make brothers very loving towards
each other in Vanity Fair. I, for my part, have known
a five-pound note to interpose and knock up a half-
century's attachment between two brethren ; and can't

but admire, as I think what a fine and durable thing Love
is among worldly people.

It cannot be supposed that the arrival of such a personage
as Rebecca at Queen's Crawley, and her gradual establishment in the good graces of all people there, could be un-
remarked by Mrs. Bute Crawley. Mrs. Bute, who knew
how many days the sirloin of beef lasted at the Hall;
how much linen was got ready at the great wash; how
many peaches were on the south wall; how many doses
her ladyship took when she was ill—for such points are
matters of intense interest to certain persons in the country
—Mrs. Bute, I say, could not pass over the Hall governess
without making every inquiry respecting her history and
character. There was always the best understanding
between the servants at the Rectory and the Hall. There
was always a good glass of ale in the kitchen of the former
place for the Hall people, whose ordinary drink was very
small—and, indeed, the rector's lady knew exactly how
much malt went to every barrel of Hall beer—ties of relationship existed between the Hall and Rectory domestics,
as between their masters; and through these channels
each family was perfectly well acquainted with the doings
of the other. That, by the way, may be set down as
a general remark. When you and your brother are friends,
his doings are indifferent to you. When you have quarrelled, all his outgoings and incomings you know, as if you
were his spy.

Very soon then after her arrival, Rebecca began to take
a regular place in Mrs. Crawley's bulletin from the Hall.
It was to this effect :—' The black porker's killed—weighed
x stone—salted the sides—pig's pudding and leg of pork
for dinner. Mr. Cramp from Mudbury, over with Sir Pitt
about putting John Blackmore in gaol—Mr. Pitt at meeting
(with all the names of the people who attended)—my lady
as usual—the young ladies with the governess.'

Then the report would come—the new governess be
a rare manager—Sir Pitt be very sweet on her—Mr. Crawley
too—He be reading tracts to her—' What an abandoned
wretch ! ' said little, eager, active, black-faced Mrs. Bute
Crawley.

Finally, the reports were that the governess had ' come
round ' everybody, wrote Sir Pitt's letters, did his business,
managed his accounts—had the upper hand of the whole

house, my lady, Mr. Crawley, the girls and all—at which
Mrs. Crawley declared she was an artful hussy, and had
some dreadful designs in view. Thus the doings at the
Hall were the great food for conversation at the Rectory,
and Mrs. Bute's bright eyes spied out everything that took
place in the enemy's camp—everything and a great deal
besides.

Mrs. Bute Crawley to Miss Pinkerton, The Mall, Chiswick.

RECTORY, QUEEN'S CRAWLEY, December —.

MY DEAR MADAM,—Although it is so *many* years since I profited
by your *delightful* and *invaluable* instructions, yet I have *ever* retained
the *fondest* and *most reverential* regard for Miss Pinkerton, and *dear*
Chiswick. I hope your health is *good*. The world and *the cause of
education* cannot afford to lose Miss Pinkerton for *many many years*.
When my friend, Lady Fuddleston, mentioned that her dear girls
required an instructress (I am *too poor* to engage a governess for
mine, but was I not educated at Chiswick?)—'Who,' I exclaimed,
'can we consult but the excellent, the incomparable Miss Pinkerton?' In a word, have you, dear madam, any ladies on your list,
whose services might be made available to my kind friend and
neighbour? I assure you she will take no governess *but of your
choosing*.

My dear husband is pleased to say that he likes *everything which
comes from Miss Pinkerton's school*. How I wish I could present him
and my beloved girls to the friend of my youth, and the *admired* of
the great lexicographer of our country! If you ever travel into
Hampshire, Mr. Crawley begs me to say, he hopes you will adorn our
rural rectory with your presence. 'Tis the humble but happy home of
　　　　　　　　　Your affectionate
　　　　　　　　　MARTHA CRAWLEY.

PS.—Mr. Crawley's brother, the baronet, with whom we are not,
alas! upon those terms of *unity* in which it *becomes brethren to dwell*,
has a governess for his little girls, who, I am told, had the good
fortune to be educated at Chiswick. I hear various reports of her;
and as I have the tenderest interest in my dearest little nieces, whom
I wish, in spite of family differences, to see among my own children—
and as I long to be attentive to *any pupil of yours*—do, my dear
Miss Pinkerton, tell me *the history* of this young lady, whom, for
your sake, I am most anxious to befriend.—M. C.

Miss Pinkerton to Mrs. Bute Crawley.

JOHNSON HOUSE, CHISWICK, December, 18—.

DEAR MADAM,—I have the honour to acknowledge your polite
communication, to which I promptly reply. 'Tis most gratifying to
one in my most arduous position to find that my maternal cares

have elicited a responsive affection ; and to recognize in the amiable Mrs. Bute Crawley my excellent pupil of former years, *the sprightly and accomplished* Miss Martha MacTavish. I am happy to have under my charge now the daughters of many of those who were your contemporaries at my establishment—what pleasure it would give me if your own beloved young ladies had need of my instructive superintendence !

Presenting my respectful compliments to Lady Fuddleston, I have the honour (epistolarily) to introduce to her ladyship my two friends, Miss Tuffin and Miss Hawky.

Either of these young ladies is *perfectly qualified* to instruct in Greek, Latin, and the rudiments of Hebrew ; in mathematics and history ; in Spanish, French, Italian, and geography ; in music, vocal and instrumental ; in dancing, without the aid of a master ; and in the elements of natural sciences. In the use of the globes both are proficients. In addition to these, Miss Tuffin, who is daughter of the late Reverend Thomas Tuffin (Fellow of Corpus College, Cambridge), can instruct in the Syriac language, and the elements of Constitutional law. But as she is only eighteen years of age, and of exceedingly pleasing personal appearance, perhaps this young lady may be objectionable in Sir Huddleston Fuddleston's family.

Miss Letitia Hawky, on the other hand, is not personally well-favoured. She is twenty-nine ; her face is much pitted with the small-pox. She has a halt in her gait, red hair, and a trifling obliquity of vision. Both ladies are endowed with *every moral and religious virtue.* Their terms, of course, are such as their accomplishments merit. With my most grateful respects to the Reverend Bute Crawley, I have the honour to be, Dear Madam,

Your most faithful and obedient servant,
BARBARA PINKERTON.

PS.—The Miss Sharp, whom you mention as governess to Sir Pitt Crawley, Bart., M.P., was a pupil of mine, and I have nothing to say in her disfavour. Though her appearance is disagreeable, we cannot control the operations of nature : and though her parents were disreputable (her father being a painter, several times bankrupt ; and her mother, as I have since learned, with horror, a dancer at the Opera) ; yet her talents are considerable, and I cannot regret that I received her *out of charity.* My dread is, lest the principles of the mother—who was represented to me as a French countess, forced to emigrate in the late revolutionary horrors ; but who, as I have since found, was a person of the *very lowest order and morals*—should at any time prove to be *hereditary* in the unhappy young woman whom I took as *an outcast.* But her principles have *hitherto* been correct (I believe), and I am sure nothing will occur to injure them in the elegant and refined circle of the eminent Sir Pitt Crawley.

Miss Rebecca Sharp to Miss Amelia Sedley.

I have not written to my beloved Amelia for these many weeks*
past, for what news was there to tell of the sayings and doings at
Humdrum Hall, as I have christened it ; and what do you care
whether the turnip crop is good or bad ; whether the fat pig weighed
thirteen stone or fourteen ; and whether the beasts thrive well upon
mangel-wurzel ? Every day since I last wrote has been like its
neighbour. Before breakfast, a walk with Sir Pitt and his spud;*
after breakfast, studies (such as they are) in the schoolroom; reading
and writing about lawyers, leases, coal-mines, canals, with Sir Pitt
(whose secretary I am become) ; after dinner, Mr. Crawley's discourses or the baronet's backgammon ; during both of which
amusements my lady looks on with equal placidity. She has
become rather more interesting by being ailing of late, which has
brought a new visitor to the Hall, in the person of a young doctor.
Well, my dear, young women need never despair. The young doctor
gave a certain friend of yours to understand that, if she chose to
be Mrs. Glauber, she was welcome to ornament the surgery ! I told
his impudence that the gilt pestle and mortar was quite ornament
enough ; as if I was born, indeed, to be a country surgeon's wife !
Mr. Glauber went home seriously indisposed at his rebuff, took a cool-
ing draught, and is now quite cured. Sir Pitt applauded my resolution highly ; he would be sorry to lose his little secretary, I think ;
and I believe the old wretch likes me as much as it is in his nature
to like any one. Marry, indeed ! and with a country apothecary,
after——No, no, one cannot so soon forget old associations, about
which I will talk no more. Let us return to Humdrum Hall.

For some time past it is Humdrum Hall no longer. My dear, Miss
Crawley has arrived with her fat horses, fat servants, fat spaniel—the
great rich Miss Crawley, with seventy thousand pounds in the five
per cents., whom, or I had better say *which*, her two brothers adore.
She looks very apoplectic, the dear soul ; no wonder her brothers are
anxious about her. You should see them struggling to settle her
cushions, or to hand her coffee ! 'When I come into the country,'
she says (for she has a great deal of humour), 'I leave my toady,
Miss Briggs, at home. My brothers are my toadies here, my dear,
and a pretty pair they are !'*

When she comes into the country our Hall is thrown open, and for
a month, at least, you would fancy old Sir Walpole was come to life
again. We have dinner-parties, and drive out in the coach-and-
four—the footmen put on their newest canary-coloured liveries ;
we drink claret and champagne as if we were accustomed to it every
day. We have wax-candles in the schoolroom, and fires to warm
ourselves with. Lady Crawley is made to put on the brightest
pea-green in her wardrobe, and my pupils leave off their thick
shoes and tight old tartan pelisses, and wear silk stockings and
muslin frocks, as fashionable baronets' daughters should. Rose
came in yesterday in a sad plight—the Wiltshire sow (an enormous
pet of hers) ran her down, and destroyed a most lovely flowered lilac

MISS CRAWLEY'S AFFECTIONATE RELATIVES

silk dress by dancing over it—had this happened a week ago, Sir Pitt would have sworn frightfully, have boxed the poor wretch's ears, and put her upon bread and water for a month. All he said was, 'I'll serve you out, miss, when your aunt's gone,' and laughed off the accident as quite trivial. Let us hope his wrath will have passed away before Miss Crawley's departure. I hope so, for Miss Rose's sake, I am sure. What a charming reconciler and peacemaker money is !

Another admirable effect of Miss Crawley and her seventy thousand pounds is to be seen in the conduct of the two brothers Crawley. I mean the baronet and the rector, not *our* brothers—but the former, who hate each other all the year round become quite loving at Christmas. I wrote to you last year how the abominable horse-racing rector was in the habit of preaching clumsy sermons at us at church, and how Sir Pitt snored in answer. When Miss Crawley arrives there is no such thing as quarrelling heard of—the Hall visits the Rectory, and vice versa—the parson and the baronet talk about the pigs and the poachers, and the county business, in the most affable manner, and without quarrelling in their cups, I believe—indeed Miss Crawley won't hear of their quarrelling, and vows that she will leave her money to the Shropshire Crawleys if they offend her. If they were clever people, those Shropshire Crawleys, they might have it all, I think ; but the Shropshire Crawley is a clergyman like his Hampshire cousin, and mortally offended Miss Crawley (who had fled thither in a fit of rage against her impracticable brethren) by some strait-laced notions of morality. He would have prayers in the house, I believe.

Our sermon-books are shut up when Miss Crawley arrives, and Mr. Pitt, whom she abominates, finds it convenient to go to town. On the other hand, the young dandy—' blood,' I believe, is the term—Captain Crawley makes his appearance, and I suppose you would like to know what sort of a person he is.

Well, he is a very large young dandy.* He is six feet high, and speaks with a great voice ; and swears a great deal ; and orders about the servants, who all adore him nevertheless ; for he is very generous of his money, and the domestics will do anything for him. Last week the keepers almost killed a bailiff and his man who came down from London to arrest the captain, and who were found lurking about the park wall—they beat them, ducked them, and were going to shoot them for poachers, but the baronet interfered.

The captain has a hearty contempt for his father, I can see, and calls him an old *put*, an old *snob*, an old *chaw-bacon*,* and numberless other pretty names. He has a *dreadful reputation* among the ladies. He brings his hunters home with him, lives with the squires of the county, asks whom he pleases to dinner, and Sir Pitt dares not say no, for fear of offending Miss Crawley, and missing his legacy when she dies of her apoplexy. Shall I tell you a compliment the captain paid me ? I must, it is so pretty. One evening we actually had a dance ; there was Sir Huddleston Fuddleston and his family, Sir Giles Wapshot and his young ladies, and I don't know how many more. Well, I heard him say—' By Jove, she's a neat little filly!' meaning your humble servant; and he did me the honour to dance two country-dances with me. He gets on pretty gaily with the young squires, with whom he drinks, bets, rides, and talks about hunting and shooting; but he says the country girls are *bores*; indeed, I don't think he is far wrong. You should see the contempt

with which they look down on poor me! When they dance I sit and play the piano very demurely; but the other night coming in rather flushed from the dining-room, and seeing me employed in this way, he swore out loud that I was the best dancer in the room, and took a great oath that he would have the fiddlers from Mudbury.

' I'll go and play a country-dance,' said Mrs. Bute Crawley, very readily (she is a little, black-faced old woman in a turban, rather crooked, and with very twinkling eyes); and after the captain and your poor little Rebecca had performed a dance together, do you know she actually did me the honour to compliment me upon my steps! Such a thing was never heard of before; the proud Mrs. Bute Crawley, first cousin to the Earl of Tiptoff, who won't condescend to visit Lady Crawley, except when her sister is in the country. Poor Lady Crawley! during most part of these gaieties, she is upstairs taking pills.

Mrs. Bute has all of a sudden taken a great fancy to me. ' My

dear Miss Sharp,' she says, ' why not bring over your girls to the
Rectory ?—their cousins will be so happy to see them.'   I know what
she means.   Signor Clementi did not teach us the piano for nothing ;
at which price Mrs. Bute hopes to get a professor for her children.
I can see through her schemes, as though she told them to me; but I
shall go, as I am determined to make myself agreeable—is it not
a poor governess's duty, who has not a friend or protector in the
world ?   The rector's wife paid me a score of compliments about the
progress my pupils made, and thought, no doubt, to touch my heart
—poor, simple, country soul !—as if I cared a fig about my pupils !

Your India muslin and your pink silk, dearest Amelia, are said to
become me very well.   They are a good deal worn now ; but, you
know, we poor girls can't afford *des fraiches toilettes*.   Happy, happy
you ! who have but to drive to St. James's Street, and a dear mother
who will give you anything you ask.   Farewell, dearest girl.

Your affectionate
REBECCA.

PS.—I wish you could have seen the faces of the Miss Blackbrooks
(Admiral Blackbrook's daughters, my dear) : fine young ladies, with
dresses from London, when Captain Rawdon selected poor me for a
partner ! Here they are. 'Tis the very image of them. Adieu, adieu !*

When Mrs. Bute Crawley (whose artifices our ingenious
Rebecca had so soon discovered) had procured from Miss
Sharp the promise of a visit, she induced the all-powerful
Miss Crawley to make the necessary application to Sir Pitt,
and the good-natured old lady, who loved to be gay herself, and to see every one gay and happy round about her,
was quite charmed, and ready to establish a reconciliation
and intimacy between her two brothers. It was therefore
agreed that the young people of both families should visit
each other frequently for the future, and the friendship of
course lasted as long as the jovial old mediatrix was there
to keep the peace.

'Why did you ask that scoundrel, Rawdon Crawley, to
dine?' said the rector to his lady, as they were walking
home through the park. '*I* don't want the fellow. He
looks down upon us country people as so many blacka-
moors. He's never content unless he gets my yellow-sealed
wine, which costs me ten shillings a bottle, hang him!
Besides, he's such an infernal character—he's a gambler—
he's a drunkard—he's a profligate in every way. He's
shot a man in a duel—he's over head and ears in debt,
and he's robbed me and mine of the best part of Miss
Crawley's fortune. Waxy says she has him'—here the
rector shook his fist at the moon, with something very
like an oath, and added, in a melancholious tone—'——,
down in her will for fifty thousand; and there won't be
above thirty to divide.'

'I think she's going,' said the rector's wife. 'She was
very red in the face when we left dinner. I was obliged
to unlace her.'

'She drank seven glasses of champagne, said the reverend
gentleman, in a low voice; 'and filthy champagne it is,
too, that my brother poisons us with—but you women
never know what's what.'

'We know nothing,' said Mrs. Bute Crawley.

'She drank cherry-brandy after dinner,' continued his
reverence, 'and took curaçao with her coffee. *I* wouldn't
take a glass for a five-pound note: it kills me with heart-
burn. She can't stand it, Mrs. Crawley—she must go—
flesh and blood won't bear it! and I lay five to two, Matilda
drops in a year.'

Indulging in these solemn speculations, and thinking
about his debts, and his son Jim at college, and Frank

at Woolwich, and the four girls, who were no beauties, poor things, and would not have a penny but what they got from the aunt's expected legacy, the rector and his lady walked on for a while.

'Pitt can't be such an infernal villain as to sell the reversion of the living. And that Methodist milksop of an eldest son looks to Parliament,' continued Mr. Crawley, after a pause.

'Sir Pitt Crawley will do anything,' said the rector's wife. 'We must get Miss Crawley to make him promise it to James.'

'Pitt will promise anything,' replied the brother. 'He promised he'd pay my college bills, when my father died; he promised he'd build the new wing to the Rectory; he promised he'd let me have Jibb's field and the Six-acre Meadow—and much he executed his promises! And it's to this man's son—this scoundrel, gambler, swindler, murderer of a Rawdon Crawley, that Matilda leaves the bulk of her money. I say it's unchristian. By Jove, it is. The infamous dog has got every vice except hypocrisy, and that belongs to his brother.'

'Hush, my dearest love! we're in Sir Pitt's grounds,' interposed his wife.

'I say he *has* got every vice, Mrs. Crawley. Don't, ma'am, bully *me*. Didn't he shoot Captain Marker? Didn't he rob young Lord Dovedale at the "Cocoa-Tree"? Didn't he cross the fight between Bill Soames and the Cheshire Trump, by which I lost forty pound? You know he did; and as for the women, why, you heard that before me, in my own magistrate's room——'*

'For Heaven's sake, Mr. Crawley,' said the lady, 'spare me the details.'

'And you ask this villain into your house!' continued the exasperated rector. 'You, the mother of a young family—the wife of a clergyman of the Church of England. By Jove!'

'Bute Crawley, you are a fool,' said the rector's wife, scornfully.

'Well, ma'am, fool or not—and I don't say, Martha, I'm so clever as *you* are. I never did. But I won't meet Rawdon Crawley, that's flat. I'll go over to Huddleston, that I will, and see his black greyhound, Mrs. Crawley; and I'll run Lancelot against him for fifty. By Jove,

I will ; or against any dog in England.   But I won't meet that beast Rawdon Crawley.'

'Mr. Crawley, you are intoxicated, as usual,' replied his wife.   And the next morning, when the rector woke, and called for small beer, she put him in mind of his promise to visit Sir Huddleston Fuddleston, on Saturday, and as he knew he should have a *wet night*, it was agreed that he might gallop back again in time for church on Sunday morning.   Thus it will be seen that the parishioners of Crawley were equally happy in their squire and in their rector.

Miss Crawley had not long been established at the Hall before Rebecca's fascinations had won the heart of that good-natured London rake, as they had of the country innocents whom we have been describing.   Taking her accustomed drive, one day, she thought fit to order that 'that little governess' should accompany her to Mudbury. Before they had returned Rebecca had made a conquest of her ;   having made her laugh four times, and amused her during the whole of the little journey.

'Not let Miss Sharp dine at table ! ' said she to Sir Pitt, who had arranged a dinner of ceremony, and asked all the neighbouring baronets.   'My dear creature, do you sup-pose I can talk about the nursery with Lady Fuddleston, or discuss justices' business with that goose, old Sir Giles Wapshot ?   I insist upon Miss Sharp appearing.   Let Lady Crawley remain upstairs, if there is no room.   But little Miss Sharp !   Why, she's the only pe`son fit to talk to in the county ! '

Of course, after such a peremptory order as this, Miss Sharp, the governess, received commands to dine with the illustrious company below stairs.   And when Sir Huddleston had, with great pomp and ceremony, handed Miss Crawley into dinner, and was preparing to take his place by her side, the old lady cried out, in a shrill voice, ' Becky Sharp ! Miss Sharp !   Come you and sit by me and amuse me ; and let Sir Huddleston sit by Lady Wapshot.'

When the parties were over, and the carriages had rolled away, the insatiable Miss Crawley would say, ' Come to my dressing-room, Becky, and let us abuse the company,'— which, between them, this pair of friends did perfectly. Old Sir Huddleston wheezed a great deal at dinner ;   Sir

Giles Wapshot had a particularly noisy manner of imbibing his soup, and her ladyship a wink of the left eye ; all of which Becky caricatured to admiration ; as well as the particulars of the night's conversation ; the politics ; the war ; the quarter-sessions ; the famous run with the H. H.; and those heavy and dreary themes, about which country gentlemen converse. As for the Misses Wapshot's toilettes and Lady Fuddleston's famous yellow hat, Miss Sharp tore them to tatters, to the infinite amusement of her audience.

' My dear, you are a perfect *trouvaille*,' Miss Crawley would say. ' I wish you could come to me in London, but I couldn't make a butt of you as I do of poor Briggs— no, no, you little sly creature ; you are too clever—Isn't she, Firkin ? '

Mrs. Firkin (who was dressing the very small remnant of hair which remained on Miss Crawley's pate) flung up her head and said, ' I think miss *is* very clever,' with the most killing sarcastic air. In fact, Mrs. Firkin had that natural jealousy which is one of the main principles of every honest woman.

After rebuffing Sir Huddleston Fuddleston, Miss Crawley ordered that Rawdon Crawley should lead her in to dinner every day, and that Becky should follow with her cushion— or else she would have Becky's arm and Rawdon with the pillow. ' We must sit together,' she said. ' We're the only three Christians in the county, my love '—in which case, it must be confessed, that religion was at a very low ebb in the county of Hants.

Besides being such a fine religionist, Miss Crawley was, as we have said, an ultra-liberal in opinions and always took occasion to express these in the most candid manner.

' What is birth, my dear ? ' she would say to Rebecca— ' Look at my brother Pitt ; look at the Huddlestons, who have been here since Henry II ; look at poor Bute at the parsonage ;—are any one of them equal to you in intelligence or breeding ? Equal to *you*—they are not even equal to poor dear Briggs, my companion, or Bowls, my butler. You, my love, are a little paragon—positively a little jewel —You have more brains than half the shire—if merit had its reward, you ought to be a duchess—no, there ought to be no duchesses at all—but you ought to have no superior, and I consider you, my love, as my equal in every respect ;

and—will you put some coals on the fire, my dear ; and will
you pick this dress of mine, and alter it, you who can do it
so well ? ' So this old philanthropist used to make her
equal run of her errands, execute her millinery, and read
her to sleep with French novels, every night.

At this time, as some old readers may recollect, the genteel
world had been thrown into a considerable state of excitement, by two events, which, as the papers say, might give
employment to the gentlemen of the long robe. Ensign
Shafton had run away with Lady Barbara Fitzurse, the
Earl of Bruin's daughter and heiress ; and poor Vere
Vane, a gentleman who, up to forty, had maintained a most
respectable character and reared a numerous family, suddenly and outrageously left his home, for the sake of
Mrs. Rougemont, the actress, who was sixty-five years
of age.

' That was the most beautiful part of dear Lord Nelson's
character,' Miss Crawley said. ' He went to the deuce for
a woman. There *must* be good in a man who will do that.
I adore all imprudent matches.—What I like best, is for
a nobleman to marry a miller's daughter as Lord Flowerdale
did—it makes all the women so angry—I wish some great
man would run away with *you*, my dear ; I'm sure you're
pretty enough.'

' Two postboys !—Oh, it would be delightful ! ' Rebecca
owned.

' And what I like next best, is, for a poor fellow to run
away with a rich girl. I have set my heart on Rawdon
running away with some one.'

' A rich someone, or a poor someone ? '

' Why, you goose ! Rawdon has not a shilling but what
I give him. He is *criblé de dettes*—he must repair his
fortunes, and succeed in the world.'

' Is he very clever ? ' Rebecca asked.

' Clever, my love ?—not an idea in the world beyond his
horses, and his regiment, and his hunting, and his play ;
but he must succeed—he's so delightfully wicked. Don't
you know he has hit a man, and shot an injured father
through the hat only ? He's adored in his regiment ; and
all the young men at Wattier's and the " Cocoa-Tree "
swear by him.'*

When Miss Rebecca Sharp wrote to her beloved friend the
account of the little ball at Queen's Crawley, and the manner

in which, for the first time, Captain Crawley had distinguished her, she did not, strange to relate, give an altogether accurate account of the transaction. The captain had distinguished her a great number of times before. The captain had met her in a half-score of walks. The captain had lighted upon her in a half-hundred of corridors and passages. The captain had hung over her piano twenty times of an evening (my lady was now upstairs, being ill, and nobody heeded her), as Miss Sharp sang. The captain had written her notes (the best that the great blundering dragoon could devise and spell; but dullness gets on as well as any other quality with women). But when he put the first of the notes into the leaves of the song she was singing, the little governess, rising and looking him steadily in the face, took up the triangular missive daintily, and waved it about as if it were a cocked hat, and she, advancing to the enemy, popped the note into the fire, and made him a very low curtsy, and went back to her place, and began to sing away again more merrily than ever.

'What's that?' said Miss Crawley, interrupted in her after-dinner doze by the stoppage of the music.

'It's a false note,' Miss Sharp said, with a laugh; and Rawdon Crawley fumed with rage and mortification.

Seeing the evident partiality of Miss Crawley for the new governess, how good it was of Mrs. Bute Crawley not to be jealous, and to welcome the young lady to the Rectory, and not only her, but Rawdon Crawley, her husband's rival in the Old Maid's five per cents! They became very fond of each other's society, Mrs. Crawley and her nephew. He gave up hunting: he declined entertainments at Fuddleston: he would not dine with the mess of the dépôt at Mudbury: his great pleasure was to stroll over to Crawley parsonage—whither Miss Crawley came too; and as their mamma was ill, why not the children with Miss Sharp? So the children (little dears!) came with Miss Sharp; and of an evening some of the party would walk back together.* Not Miss Crawley—she preferred her carriage—but the walk over the Rectory fields, and in at the little park wicket, and through the dark plantation, and up the chequered avenue to Queen's Crawley, was charming in the moonlight to two such lovers of the picturesque as the captain and Miss Rebecca.

'Oh, those stars, those stars!' Miss Rebecca would say,

turning her twinkling green eyes up towards them. 'I feel
myself almost a spirit when I gaze upon them.'

'Oh—ah—Gad—yes, so do I exactly, Miss Sharp,' the
other enthusiast replied. 'You don't mind my cigar, do
you, Miss Sharp?' Miss Sharp loved the smell of a cigar
out of doors beyond everything in the world—and she just
tasted one too, in the prettiest way possible, and gave
a little puff, and a little scream, and a little giggle, and
restored the delicacy to the captain; who twirled his
moustache, and straightway puffed it into a blaze that
glowed quite red in the dark plantation, and swore—'Jove
—aw—Gad—aw—it's the finest segaw I ever smoked in the
world—aw,'—for his intellect and conversation were alike
brilliant and becoming to a heavy young dragoon.

Old Sir Pitt, who was taking his pipe and beer, and talking
to John Horrocks about a 'ship' that was to be killed,
espied the pair so occupied from his study-window, and
with dreadful oaths swore that if it wasn't for Miss Crawley,
he'd take Rawdon and bundle un out of doors, like a rogue
as he was.

'He *be* a bad 'n, sure enough,' Mr. Horrocks remarked;
'and his man Flethers is wuss, and have made such a row
in the housekeeper's room about the dinners and hale,
as no lord would make—but I think Miss Sharp's a match
for 'n, Sir Pitt,' he added, after a pause.

And so, in truth, she was—for father and son too.

CHAPTER XII

QUITE A SENTIMENTAL CHAPTER

E must now take leave of Arcadia, and those amiable people practising the rural virtues there, and travel back to London, to inquire what has become of Miss Amelia.

'We don't care a fig for her,' writes some unknown correspondent with a pretty little handwriting and a pink seal to her note. 'She is *fade* and insipid,' and adds some more kind remarks in this strain, which I should never have repeated at all, but that they are in truth prodigiously complimentary to the young lady whom they concern.

Has the beloved reader, in his experience of society, never heard similar remarks by good-natured female friends; who always wonder what you *can* see in Miss Smith that is so fascinating; or what *could* induce Major Jones to propose for that silly insignificant simpering Miss Thompson, who has nothing but her wax-doll face to recommend her? What is there in a pair of pink cheeks and blue eyes, forsooth? these dear moralists ask, and hint wisely that the gifts of genius, the accomplishments of the mind, the mastery of *Mangnall's Questions*, and a ladylike knowledge of botany and geology, the knack of making poetry, the power of rattling sonatas in the Herz-manner, and so forth, are far more valuable endowments for a female, than those fugitive charms which a few years will inevitably tarnish. It is quite edifying to hear women speculate upon the worthlessness and the duration of beauty.

But though virtue is a much finer thing, and those hapless creatures who suffer under the misfortune of good looks ought to be continually put in mind of the fate which awaits them; and though, very likely, the heroic female character which ladies admire is a more glorious and beautiful object than the kind, fresh, smiling, artless, tender little domestic

goddess, whom men are inclined to worship—yet the latter
and inferior sort of women must have this consolation—that
the men *do* admire them after all ; and that, in spite of all
our kind friends' warnings and protests, we go on in our
desperate error and folly, and shall to the end of the chapter.
Indeed, for my own part, though I have been repeatedly
told by persons for whom I have the greatest respect,
that Miss Brown is an insignificant chit, and Mrs. White
has nothing but her *petit minois chiffonné,** and Mrs. Black
has not a word tb say for herself ; yet I know that I have
had the most delightful conversations with Mrs. Black
(of course, my dear madam, they are inviolable) : I see all
the men in a cluster round Mrs. White's chair : all the
young fellows battling to dance with Miss Brown ; and so
I am tempted to think that to be despised by her sex
is a very great compliment to a woman.

The young ladies in Amelia's society did this for her very
satisfactorily.   For instance, there was scarcely any point
upon which the Miss Osbornes, George's sisters, and the
Mesdemoiselles Dobbin agreed so well as in their estimate
of her very trifling merits : and their wonder that their
brothers could find any charms in her.   ' We are kind to
her,' the Misses Osborne said, a pair of fine black-browed
young ladies who had had the best of governesses, masters,
and milliners ; and they treated her with such extreme
kindness and condescension, and patronized her so insufferably, that the poor little thing *was* in fact perfectly
dumb in their presence, and to all outward appearance as
stupid as they thought her.   She made efforts to like
them, as in duty bound, and as sisters of her future husband.
She passed ' long mornings ' with them—the most dreary
and serious of forenoons.   She drove out solemnly in their
great family coach with them, and Miss Wirt their governess,
that raw-boned Vestal.   They took her to the ancient
concerts by way of a treat, and to the oratorio, and to
St. Paul's to see the charity children, where in such terror
was she of her friends, she almost did not dare be affected
by the hymn the children sang.   Their house was comfortable ; their papa's table rich and handsome ; their
society solemn and genteel ; their self-respect prodigious ;
they had the best pew at the Foundling ;* all their habits
were pompous and orderly, and all their amusements
intolerably dull and decorous.   After every one of her visits

(and oh how glad she was when they were over !) Miss Osborne and Miss Maria Osborne, and Miss Wirt, the vestal governess, asked each other with increased wonder, ' What *could* George find in that creature ? '

How is this ? some carping reader exclaims. How is it that Amelia, who had such a number of friends at school, and was so beloved there, comes out into the world and is spurned by her discriminating sex ? My dear sir, there were no men at Miss Pinkerton's establishment except the old dancing-master ; and you would not have had the girls fall out about *him* ? When George, their handsome brother, ran off directly after breakfast, and dined from home half a dozen times a week ; no wonder the neglected sisters felt a little vexation. When young Bullock (of the firm of Hulker, Bullock & Co., Bankers, Lombard Street) who had been making up to Miss Maria the last two seasons, actually asked Amelia to dance the cotillon, could you expect that the former young lady should be pleased ? And yet she said she was, like an artless forgiving creature. ' I'm so delighted you like dear Amelia,' she said quite eagerly to Mr. Bullock after the dance. ' She's engaged to my brother George ; there's not much in her, but she's the best-natured and most unaffected young creature : at home we're all *so* fond of her.' Dear girl ! who can calculate the depth of affection expressed in that enthusiastic *so ?*

Miss Wirt and these two affectionate young women so earnestly and frequently impressed upon George Osborne's mind the enormity of the sacrifice he was making, and his romantic generosity in throwing himself away upon Amelia, that I'm not sure but that he really thought he was one of the most deserving characters in the British army, and gave himself up to be loved with a good deal of easy resignation.

Somehow, although he left home every morning, as was stated, and dined abroad six days in the week, when his sister believed the infatuated youth to be at Miss Sedley's apron-strings : he was *not* always with Amelia, whilst the world supposed him at her feet. Certain it is that on more occasions than one, when Captain Dobbin called to look for his friend, Miss Osborne (who was very attentive to the captain, and anxious to hear his military stories, and to know about the health of his dear mamma), Miss Osborne would laughingly point to the opposite side of the square, and say,

'Oh, you must go to the Sedleys' to ask for George; *we* never see him from morning till night.' At which kind of speech the captain would laugh in rather an absurd constrained manner, and turn off the conversation, like a consummate man of the world, to some topic of general interest, such as the opera, the prince's last ball at Carlton House,* or the weather—that blessing to society.

'What an innocent it is, that pet of yours,' Miss Maria would then say to Miss Jane, upon the captain's departure. 'Did you see how he blushed at the mention of poor George on duty?'

'It's a pity Frederick Bullock hadn't some of his modesty, Maria,' replies the elder sister, with a toss of her head.

'Modesty! Awkwardness you mean, Jane. I don't want Frederick to trample a hole in my muslin frock, as Captain Dobbin did in yours at Mrs. Perkins's.'

'In *your* frock, he, he! How could he? Wasn't he dancing with Amelia?'

The fact is, when Captain Dobbin blushed so, and looked so awkward, he remembered a circumstance of which he did not think it was necessary to inform the young ladies, viz., that he had been calling at Mr. Sedley's house already, on the pretence of seeing George, of course, and George wasn't there, only poor little Amelia, with rather a sad wistful face, seated near the drawing-room window, who, after some very trifling stupid talk, ventured to ask, was there any truth in the report that the regiment was soon to be ordered abroad; and had Captain Dobbin seen Mr. Osborne that day?

The regiment was not ordered abroad as yet; and Captain Dobbin had not seen George. 'He was with his sister, most likely,' the captain said. 'Should he go and fetch the truant?' So she gave him her hand kindly and gratefully: and he crossed the square; and she waited and waited, but George never came.

Poor little tender heart! and so it goes on hoping and beating, and longing and trusting. You see it is not much of a life to describe. There is not much of what you call incident in it. Only one feeling all day—when will he come? only one thought to sleep and wake upon. I believe George was playing billiards with Captain Cannon in Swallow Street at the time when Amelia was asking

Captain Dobbin about him ; for George was a jolly sociable
fellow, and excellent in all games of skill.*

Once, after three days of absence, Miss Amelia put on her
bonnet, and actually invaded the Osborne house. ' What !
leave our brother to come to us ? ' said the young ladies.
' Have you had a quarrel, Amelia ? Do tell us ! ' No,

indeed, there had been no quarrel. ' Who could quarrel
with him ? ' says she, with her eyes filled with tears. She
only came over to—to see her dear friends ; they had
not met for so long. And this day she was so perfectly
stupid and awkward, that the Miss Osbornes and their
governess, who stared after her as she went sadly away,
wondered more than ever what George could see in poor
little Amelia.

Of course they did.   How was she to bare that timid little
heart for the inspection of those young ladies with their
bold black eyes ?   It was best that it should shrink and hide
itself.   I know the Miss Osbornes were excellent critics
of a Cashmere shawl, or a pink satin slip ; and when
Miss Turner had hers dyed purple, and made into a spencer ;
and when Miss Pickford had her ermine tippet twisted
into a muff and trimmings, I warrant you the changes did
not escape the two intelligent young women before mentioned.   But there are things, look you, of a finer texture
than fur or satin, and all Solomon's glories, and all the
wardrobe of the Queen of Sheba ;—things whereof the
beauty escapes the eyes of many connoisseurs.   And there
are sweet modest little souls on which you light, fragrant
and blooming tenderly in quiet shady places ; and there are
garden-ornaments, as big as brass warming-pans, that are
fit to stare the sun itself out of countenance.   Miss Sedley
was not of the sunflower sort ; and I say it is out of the
rules of all proportion to draw a violet of the size of a double
dahlia.

No, indeed ; the life of a good young girl who is in the
paternal nest as yet, can't have many of those thrilling
incidents to which the heroine of romance commonly lays
claim.   Snares or shot may take off the old birds foraging
without—hawks may be abroad, from which they escape
or by whom they suffer ; but the young ones in the nest
have a pretty comfortable unromantic sort of existence in
the down and the straw, till it comes to their turn, too, to
get on the wing.   While Becky Sharp was on her own
wing in the country, hopping on all sorts of twigs, and
amid a multiplicity of traps, and pecking up her food quite
harmless and successful, Amelia lay snug in her home
of Russell Square ; if she went into the world, it was under
the guidance of the elders ; nor did it seem that any evil
could befall her or that opulent cheery comfortable home
in which she was affectionately sheltered.   Mamma had
her morning duties, and her daily drive, and that delightful
round of visits and shopping which forms the amusement,
or the profession as you may call it, of the rich London lady.
Papa conducted his mysterious operations in the city—
a stirring place in those days, when war was raging all over
Europe, and empires were being staked ; when the *Courier*
newspaper had tens of thousands of subscribers ; when

one day brought you a battle of Vittoria, another a burning
of Moscow, or a newsman's horn blowing down Russell
Square about dinner-time, announced such a fact as—
' Battle of Leipsic—*six hundred thousand men engaged—
total defeat of the French—two hundred thousand killed.'
Old Sedley once or twice came home with a very grave
face ; and no wonder, when such news as this was agitating
all the hearts and all the Stocks of Europe.

Meanwhile matters went on in Russell Square, Bloomsbury, just as if matters in Europe were not in the least
disorganized. The retreat from Leipsic made no difference
in the number of meals Mr. Sambo took in the servants'
hall ; the allies poured into France, and the dinner-bell
rang at five o'clock just as usual. I don't think poor
Amelia cared anything about Brienne and Montmirail, or
was fairly interested in the war until the abdication of the
Emperor ; when she clapped 'her hands and said prayers,—
oh, how grateful ! and flung herself into George Osborne's
arms with all her soul, to the astonishment of everybody
who witnessed that ebullition of sentiment. The fact
is, peace was declared, Europe was going to be at rest ; the
Corsican was overthrown, and Lieutenant Osborne's
regiment would not be ordered on service. That was the
way in which Miss Amelia reasoned. The fate of Europe
was Lieutenant George Osborne to her. His dangers
being over, she sang *Te Deum*. He was her Europe : her
emperor : her allied monarchs and august prince regent.
He was her sun and moon ; and I believe she thought the
grand illumination and ball at the Mansion House, given
to the sovereigns, were especially in honour of George
Osborne.

We have talked of shift, self, and poverty, as those dismal
instructors under whom poor Miss Becky Sharp got her
education. Now, love was Miss Amelia Sedley's last
tutoress, and it was amazing what progress our young
lady made under that popular teacher. In the course of
fifteen or eighteen months' daily and constant attention
to this eminent finishing governess, what a deal of secrets
Amelia learned, which Miss Wirt and the black-eyed young
ladies over the way, which old Miss Pinkerton of Chiswick
herself, had no cognizance of ! As, indeed, how should any
of those prim and reputable virgins ? With Misses P. and W.

the tender passion is out of the question : I would not
dare to breathe such an idea regarding them.   Miss Maria
Osborne, it is true, was 'attached' to Mr. Frederick Augustus
Bullock, of the firm of Hulker, Bullock & Bullock ; but
hers was a most respectable attachment, and she would
have taken Bullock Senior, just the same, her mind being
fixed as that of a well-bred young woman should be,—
upon a house in Park Lane, a country house at Wimbledon,
a handsome chariot, and two prodigious tall horses and
footmen, and a fourth of the annual profits of the eminent
firm of Hulker & Bullock, all of which advantages were
represented in the person of Frederick Augustus.   Had
orange blossoms been invented then* (those touching
emblems of female purity imported by us from France,
where people's daughters are universally sold in marriage),
Miss Maria, I say, would have assumed the spotless wreath,
and stepped into the travelling carriage by the side of
gouty, old, bald-headed, bottle-nosed Bullock Senior ; and
devoted her beautiful existence to his happiness with perfect
modesty,—only the old gentleman was married already ;
so she bestowed her young affections on the junior partner.
Sweet, blooming orange flowers !   The other day I saw
Miss Trotter (that was), arrayed in them, trip into the
travelling carriage at St. George's, Hanover Square, and
Lord Methuselah hobbled in after.   With what an engaging
modesty she pulled down the blinds of the chariot—the
dear innocent !   There were half the carriages of Vanity
Fair at the wedding.

This was not the sort of love that finished Amelia's
education ; and in the course of a year turned a good young
girl into a good young woman—to be a good wife presently,
when the happy time should come.   This young person
(perhaps it was very imprudent in her parents to encourage
her, and abet her in such idolatry and silly romantic ideas)
loved, with all her heart, the young officer in His Majesty's
service with whom we have made a brief acquaintance.
She thought about him the very first moment on waking ;
and his was the very last name mentioned in her prayers.
She never had seen a man so beautiful or so clever : such
a figure on horseback : such a dancer : such a hero in
general.   Talk of the prince's bow ! what was it to George's ?
She had seen Mr. Brummell* whom everybody praised so.
Compare such a person as that to her George !   Not

amongst all the beaux at the Opera (and there were beaux
in those days with actual opera hats) was there any one
to equal him. He was only good enough to be a fairy
prince ; and oh, what magnanimity to stoop to such a
humble Cinderella ! Miss Pinkerton would have tried to
check this blind devotion very likely, had she been Amelia's
confidante ; but not with much success, depend upon it.
It is in the nature and instinct of some women. Some
are made to scheme, and some to love ; and I wish any
respected bachelor that reads this may take the sort that
best likes him.

While under this overpowering impression, Miss Amelia
neglected her twelve dear friends at Chiswick most cruelly,
as such selfish people commonly will do. She had but this
subject, of course, to think about ; and Miss Saltire was too
cold for a confidante, and she couldn't bring her mind to
tell Miss Swartz, the woolly-haired young heiress from
St. Kitts. She had little Laura Martin home for the
holidays ; and my belief is, she made a confidante of her,
and promised that Laura should come and live with her
when she was married, and gave Laura a great deal of information regarding the passion of love, which must have
been singularly useful and novel to that little person. Alas,
alas ! I fear poor Emmy had not a well-regulated mind.

What were her parents doing, not to keep this little heart
from beating so fast ? Old Sedley did not seem much to
notice matters. He was graver of late, and his City affairs
absorbed him. Mrs. Sedley was of so easy and uninquisitive
a nature, that she wasn't even jealous. Mr. Jos was away,
being besieged by an Irish widow at Cheltenham. Amelia
had the house to herself—ah ! too much to herself sometimes—not that she ever doubted ; for, to be sure, George
must be at the Horse Guards ; and he can't always get leave
from Chatham ; and he must see his friends and sisters, and
mingle in society when in town (he, such an ornament to
every society !) ; and when he is with the regiment, he is
too tired to write long letters. I know where she kept that
packet she had—and can steal in and out of her chamber
like Iachimo—like Iachimo ? No—that is a bad part. I
will only act Moonshine, and peep harmless into the bed
where faith and beauty and innocence lie dreaming.

But if Osborne's were short and soldierlike letters, it
must be confessed, that were Miss Sedley's letters to Mr.

Osborne to be published, we should have to extend this
novel to such a multiplicity of volumes as not the most
sentimental reader could support ; that she not only filled
sheets of large paper, but crossed them with the most
astonishing perverseness ; that she wrote whole pages out
of poetry-books without the least pity ; that she underlined
words and passages with quite a frantic emphasis ; and, in
fine, gave the usual tokens of her condition. She wasn't
a heroine. Her letters *were* full of repetition. She wrote
rather doubtful grammar sometimes, and in her verses took
all sorts of liberties with the metre. But oh, mesdames, if
you are not allowed to touch the heart sometimes in spite of
syntax, and are not to be loved until you all know the difference between trimeter and tetrameter, may all Poetry go
to the deuce, and every schoolmaster perish miserably !

CHAPTER XIII

SENTIMENTAL AND OTHERWISE

 I FEAR the gentleman to whom Miss
Amelia's letters were addressed was
rather an obdurate critic. Such a
number of notes followed Lieutenant
Osborne about the country, that he
became almost ashamed of the jokes
of his mess-room companions regarding them, and ordered his servant
never to deliver them, except at his
private apartment. He was seen
lighting his cigar with one, to the
horror of Captain Dobbin, who, it is my belief, would have
given a bank-note for the document.

For some time George strove to keep the liaison a secret.
There *was* a woman in the case, that he admitted. ' And
not the first either,' said Ensign Spooney to Ensign Stubbles.
' That Osborne's a devil of a fellow. There was a judge's
daughter at Demerara went almost mad about him ; then
there was that beautiful quadroon girl, Miss Pye, at St.
Vincent's, you know ; and since he's been home, they say
he's a regular Don Giovanni, by Jove.'

LIEUTENANT OSBORNE AND HIS ARDENT LOVE-LETTERS

Stubbles and Spooney thought that to be a 'regular Don Giovanni, by Jove', was one of the finest qualities a man could possess ; and Osborne's reputation was prodigious amongst the young men of the regiment. He was famous in field-sports, famous at a song, famous on parade ; free with his money, which was bountifully supplied by his father. His coats were better made than any man's in the regiment, and he had more of them. He was adored by the men. He could drink more than any officer of the whole mess, including old Heavytop, the colonel. He could spar better than Knuckles, the private (who would have been a corporal but for his drunkenness, and who had been in the prize-ring) ; and was the best batter and bowler, out and out, of the regimental club. He rode his own horse, Greased Lightning, and won the Garrison cup at Quebec races. There were other people besides Amelia who worshipped him. Stubbles and Spooney thought him a sort of Apollo ; Dobbin took him to be an Admirable Crichton ; and Mrs. Major O'Dowd acknowledged he was an elegant young fellow, and put her in mind of Fitzjurld Fogarty, Lord Castlefogarty's second son.

Well, Stubbles and Spooney and the rest indulged in most romantic conjectures regarding this female correspondent of Osborne's,—opining that it was a duchess·in London, who was in love with him,—or that it was a general's daughter, who was engaged to somebody else, and madly attached to him,—or that it was a Member of Parliament's lady, who proposed four horses and an elopement,—or that it was some other victim of a passion delightfully exciting, romantic, and disgraceful to all parties, on none of which conjectures would Osborne throw the least light, leaving his young admirers and friends to invent and arrange their whole history.

And the real state of the case would never have been known at all in the regiment but for Captain Dobbin's indiscretion. The captain was eating his breakfast one day in the mess-room, while Cackle, the assistant-surgeon, and the two above-named worthies were speculating upon Osborne's intrigue—Stubbles holding out that the lady was a duchess about Queen Charlotte's court, and Cackle vowing she was an opera-singer of the worst reputation. At this idea Dobbin became so moved, that though his mouth was full of egg and bread-and-butter at the time, and though he

ought not to have spoken at all, yet he couldn't help blurting
out, ' Cackle, you're a stupid* fool. You're always talking
nonsense and scandal. Osborne is not going to run off with
a duchess or ruin a milliner. Miss Sedley is one of the
most charming young women that ever lived. He's been
engaged to her ever so long ; and the man who calls her
names had better not do so in my hearing.' With which,
turning exceedingly red, Dobbin ceased speaking, and
almost choked himself with a cup of tea. The story was
over the regiment in half an hour ; and that very evening
Mrs. Major O'Dowd wrote off to her sister Glorvina at
O'Dowdstown not to hurry from Dublin,—young Osborne
being prematurely engaged already.

She complimented the lieutenant in an appropriate
speech over a glass of whisky-toddy that evening, and he
went home perfectly furious to quarrel with Dobbin (who
had declined Mrs. Major O'Dowd's party, and sat in his own
room playing the flute, and, I believe, writing poetry in a
very melancholy manner)—to quarrel with Dobbin for
betraying his secret.

' Who the deuce asked you to talk about my affairs? '
Osborne shouted indignantly. ' Why the devil is all the
regiment to know that I am going to be married ? Why is
that tattling old harridan, Peggy O'Dowd, to make free
with my name at her d—d supper-table, and advertise my
engagement over the three kingdoms ? After all, what
right have you to say I *am* engaged, or to meddle in my
business at all, Dobbin ? '

' It seems to me—' Captain Dobbin began.

' Seems be hanged, Dobbin,' his junior interrupted him.
' I am under obligations to you, I know it, a d—d deal too
well too ; but I won't be always sermonized by you because
you're five years my senior. I'm hanged if I'll stand your
airs of superiority and infernal pity and patronage. Pity
and patronage ! I should like to know in what I'm your
inferior ? '

' Are you engaged ? ' Captain Dobbin interposed.

' What the devil's that to you or any one here if I am ? '

' Are you ashamed of it ? ' Dobbin resumed.

' What right have you to ask me that question, sir ?
I should like to know,' George said.

' Good God, you don't mean to say you want to break
off ? ' asked Dobbin, starting up.

'In other words, you ask me if I'm a man of honour,' said Osborne, fiercely; 'is that what you mean? You've adopted such a tone regarding me lately that I'm —— if I'll bear it any more.'

'What have I done? I've told you you were neglecting a sweet girl, George. I've told you that when you go to town you ought to go to her, and not to the gambling-houses about St. James's.'

'You want your money back, I suppose,' said George, with a sneer.

'Of course I do—I always did, didn't I?' says Dobbin. 'You speak like a generous fellow.'

'No, hang it, William, I beg your pardon'—here George interposed in a fit of remorse; 'you *have* been my friend in a hundred ways, Heaven knows. You've got me out of a score of scrapes. When Crawley of the Guards won that sum of money of me I should have been done but for you: I know I should. But you shouldn't deal so hardly with me; you shouldn't be always catechizing me. I *am* very fond of Amelia; I adore her, and that sort of thing. Don't look angry. She's faultless; I know she is. But you see there's no fun in winning a thing unless you play for it. Hang it: the regiment's just back from the West Indies, I must have a little fling, and then when I'm married I'll reform; I will upon my honour, now. And—I say—Dob —don't be angry with me, and I'll give you a hundred next month, when I know my father will stand something handsome; and I'll ask Heavytop for leave, and I'll go to town, and see Amelia to-morrow—there now, will *that* satisfy you?'

'It's impossible to be long angry with you, George,' said the good-natured captain; 'and as for the money, old boy, you know if I wanted it you'd share your last shilling with me.'

'That I would, by Jove, Dobbin,' George said, with the greatest generosity, though by the way he never had any money to spare.

'Only I wish you had sown those wild oats of yours, George. If you could have seen poor little Miss Emmy's face when she asked me about you the other day, you would have pitched those billiard-balls to the deuce. Go and comfort her, you rascal. Go and write her a long letter. Do something to make her happy; a very little will.'

'I believe she's d—d fond of me,' the lieutenant said,
with a self-satisfied air ; and went off to finish the evening
with some jolly fellows in the mess-room.

Amelia meanwhile, in Russell Square, was looking at the
moon, which was shining upon that peaceful spot, as well
as upon the square of the Chatham barracks, where Lieutenant Osborne was quartered, and thinking to herself how
her hero was employed.   Perhaps he is visiting the sentries,
thought she ;   perhaps he is bivouacking ;   perhaps he is

attending the couch of a wounded comrade, or studying
the art of war up in his own desolate chamber.   And her
kind thoughts sped away as if they were angels and had
wings, and flying down the river to Chatham and Rochester,
strove to peep into the barracks where George was. . . .
All things considered, I think it was as well the gates were
shut, and the sentry allowed no one to pass ; so that the
poor little white-robed angel could not hear the songs those
young fellows were roaring over the whisky-punch.

The day after the little conversation at Chatham barracks,
young Osborne, to show that he would be as good as his

word, prepared to go to town, thereby incurring Captain
Dobbin's applause. ' I should have liked to make her a
little present,' Osborne said to his friend in confidence,
' only I am quite out of cash until my father tips up.'   But
Dobbin would not allow this good nature and generosity
to be balked, and so accommodated Mr. Osborne with a few
pound notes, which the latter took after a little faint scruple.

And I dare say he would have bought something very
handsome for Amelia ; only, getting off the coach in Fleet
Street, he was attracted by a handsome shirt-pin in a
jeweller's window, which he could not resist ; and having
paid for that, had very little money to spare for indulging
in any further exercise of kindness.   Never mind : you may
be sure it was not his presents Amelia wanted.   When he
came to Russell Square, her face lighted up as if he had been
sunshine.   The little cares, fears, tears, timid misgivings,
sleepless fancies of I don't know how many days and nights,
were forgotten, under one moment's influence of that
familiar, irresistible smile.   He beamed on her from the
drawing-room door—magnificent with ambrosial whiskers,
like a god.   Sambo, whose face as he announced Captain
Osbin (having conferred a brevet rank on that young officer)
blazed with a sympathetic grin, saw the little girl start, and
flush, and jump up from her watching-place in the window ;
and Sambo retreated : and as soon as the door was shut,
she went fluttering to Lieutenant George Osborne's heart
as if it was the only natural home for her to nestle in.   Oh,
thou poor panting little soul ! The very finest tree in the
whole forest, with the straightest stem, and the strongest
arms, and the thickest foliage, wherein you choose to build
and coo, may be marked, for what you know, and may be
down with a crash ere long.   What an old, old simile that
is, between man and timber !

In the meanwhile, George kissed her very kindly on her
forehead and glistening eyes, and was very gracious and
good ; and she thought his diamond shirt-pin (which she
had not known him to wear before) the prettiest ornament
ever seen.

The observant reader, who has marked our young
lieutenant's previous behaviour, and has preserved our
report of the brief conversation which he has just had with
Captain Dobbin, has possibly come to certain conclusions

regarding the character of Mr. Osborne. Some cynical
Frenchman[*] has said that there are two parties to a love-
transaction : the one who loves and the other who condescends to be so treated. Perhaps the love is occasionally
on the man's side . perhaps on the lady's. Perhaps some
infatuated swain has ere this mistaken insensibility for
modesty, dullness for maiden-reserve, mere vacuity for
sweet bashfulness, and a goose, in a word, for a swan.
Perhaps some beloved female subscriber has arrayed an ass
in the splendour and glory of her imagination ; admired his
dullness as manly simplicity ; worshipped his selfishness
as manly superiority ; treated his stupidity as majestic
gravity, and used him as the brilliant fairy Titania did a
certain weaver at Athens. I think I have seen such
comedies of errors going on in the world. But this is certain,
that Amelia believed her lover to be one of the most gallant
and brilliant men in the empire : and it is possible Lieutenant Osborne thought so too.

He was a little wild : how many young men are ; and
don't girls like a rake better than a milksop ? He hadn't
sown his wild oats as yet, but he would soon : and quit the
army now that peace was proclaimed ; the Corsican monster
locked up at Elba ; promotion by consequence over ; and
no chance left for the display of his undoubted military
talents and valour : and his allowance, with Amelia's settlement, would enable them to take a snug place in the country
somewhere, in a good sporting neighbourhood ; and he
would hunt a little, and farm a little ; and they would be
very happy. As for remaining in the army as a married
man, that was impossible. Fancy Mrs. George Osborne in
lodgings in a county town ; or, worse still, in the East or
West Indies, with a society of officers, and patronized by
Mrs. Major O'Dowd! Amelia died with laughing at Osborne's
stories about Mrs. Major O'Dowd. He loved her much too
fondly to subject her to that horrid woman and her vulgari-
ties, and the rough treatment of a soldier's wife. He didn't
care for himself—not he ; but his dear little girl should
take the place in society to which, as his wife, she was
entitled · and to these proposals you may be sure she
acceded, as she would to any other from the same author.

Holding this kind of conversation, and building numberless castles in the air (which Amelia adorned with all sorts
of flower-gardens. rustic walks, country churches, Sunday

schools, and the like ; while George had his mind's eye
directed to the stables, the kennel, and the cellar), this
young pair passed away a couple of hours very pleasantly ;
and as the lieutenant had only that single day in town, and
a great deal of most important business to transact, it was
proposed that Miss Emmy should dine with her future
sisters-in-law. This invitation was accepted joyfully. He
conducted her to his sisters ; where he left her talking and
prattling in a way that astonished those ladies, who thought
that George might make something of her ; and he then
went off to transact his business.

In a word, he went out and ate ices at a pastrycook's
shop in Charing Cross ; tried a new coat in Pall Mall ;
dropped in at the Old Slaughters'*, and called for Captain
Cannon ; played eleven games at billiards with the captain,
of which he won eight, and returned to Russell Square half
an hour late for dinner, but in very good humour.

It was not so with old Mr. Osborne. When that gentleman came from the City, and was welcomed in the drawing-
room by his daughters and the elegant Miss Wirt, they saw
at once by his face—which was puffy, solemn, and yellow
at the best of times—and by the scowl and twitching of
his black eyebrows, that the heart within his large white
waistcoat was disturbed and uneasy. When Amelia stepped
forward to salute him, which she always did with great
trembling and timidity, he gave a surly grunt of recognition,
and dropped the little hand out of his great hirsute paw
without any attempt to hold it there. He looked round
gloomily at his eldest daughter ; who, comprehending the
meaning of his look, which asked unmistakably, ' Why
the devil is *she* here.? ' said at once :—

' George is in town, papa ; and has gone to the Horse
Guards, and will be back to dinner.'

'Oh, he is, is he? I won't have the dinner kept waiting for
him, Jane ; ' with which this worthy man lapsed into his
particular chair, and then the utter silence in his genteel,
well-furnished drawing-room was only interrupted by the
alarmed ticking of the great French clock.

When that chronometer, which was surmounted by a
cheerful brass group of the sacrifice of Iphigenia,* tolled five
in a heavy cathedral tone, Mr. Osborne pulled the bell at
his right hand violently, and the butler rushed up.

'Dinner !' roared Mr. Osborne.

'Mr. George isn't come in, sir,' interposed the man.

'Damn Mr. George, sir. Am I master of the house ? DINNER !' Mr. Osborne scowled. Amelia trembled. A telegraphic communication of eyes passed between the other three ladies. The obedient bell in the lower regions began ringing the announcement of the meal. The tolling over, the head of the family thrust his hands into the great tail-pockets of his great blue coat and brass buttons, and without waiting for a further announcement, strode downstairs alone, scowling over his shoulder at the four females.

'What's the matter now, my dear ?' asked one of the other, as they rose and tripped gingerly behind the sire.

'I suppose the funds are falling,' whispered Miss Wirt ; and so, trembling and in silence, this hushed female company followed their dark leader. They took their places in silence. He growled out a blessing, which sounded as gruffly as a curse. The great silver dish-covers were removed. Amelia trembled in her place, for she was next to the awful Osborne, and alone on her side of the table— the gap being occasioned by the absence of George.

'Soup ?' says Mr. Osborne, clutching the ladle, fixing his eyes on her, in a sepulchral tone ; and having helped her and the rest, did not speak for a while.

'Take Miss Sedley's plate away,' at last he said. 'She can't eat the soup—no more can I. It's beastly. Take away the soup, Hicks, and to-morrow turn the cook out of the house, Jane.'

Having concluded his observations upon the soup, Mr. Osborne made a few curt remarks respecting the fish, also of a savage and satirical tendency, and cursed Billings-gate with an emphasis quite worthy of the place Then he lapsed into silence, and swallowed sundry glasses of wine, looking more and more terrible, till a brisk knock at the door told of George's arrival, when everybody began to rally.

'He could not come before. General Daguilet had kept him waiting at the Horse Guards. Never mind soup or fish. Give him anything—he didn't care what. Capital mutton—capital everything.' His good humour contrasted with his father's severity ; and he rattled on unceasingly during dinner, to the delight of all—of one especially, who need not be mentioned.

MR. OSBORNE'S WELCOME TO AMELIA

As soon as the young ladies had discussed the orange and the glass of wine which formed the ordinary conclusion of the dismal banquets at Mr. Osborne's house, the signal to make sail for the drawing-room was given, and they all arose and departed. Amelia hoped George would soon join them there. She began playing some of his favourite waltzes (then newly imported)* at the great carved-legged, leather-cased grand piano in the drawing-room overhead. This little artifice did not bring him. He was deaf to the waltzes; they grew fainter and fainter; the discomfited performer left the huge instrument presently; and though her three friends performed some of the loudest and most brilliant new pieces of their répertoire, she did not hear a single note, but sat thinking, and boding evil. Old Osborne's scowl, terrific always, had never before looked so deadly to her. His eyes followed her out of the room, as if she had been guilty of something. When they brought her coffee, she started as though it were a cup of poison which Mr. Hicks, the butler, wished to propose to her. What mystery was there lurking? Oh, those women! They nurse and cuddle their presentiments, and make darlings of their ugliest thoughts, as they do of their deformed children.

The gloom on the paternal countenance had also impressed George Osborne with anxiety. With such eyebrows, and a look so decidedly bilious, how was he to extract that money from the governor, of which George was consumedly in want? He began praising his father's wine. That was generally a successful means of cajoling the old gentleman.

'We never got such madeira in the West Indies, sir, as yours. Colonel Heavytop took off three bottles of that you sent me down, under his belt the other day.'

'Did he?' said the old gentleman. 'It stands me in eight shillings a bottle.'

'Will you take six guineas a dozen for it, sir?' said George, with a laugh. 'There's one of the greatest men in the kingdom wants some.'

'Does he?' growled the senior. 'Wish he may get it.'

'When General Daguilet was at Chatham, sir, Heavytop gave him a breakfast, and asked me for some of the wine. The general liked it just as well—wanted a pipe for the commander-in-chief.* He's His Royal Highness's right-hand man.'

'It *is* devilish fine wine,' said the Eyebrows, and they looked more good-humoured ; and George was going to take advantage of this complacency, and bring the supply question on the mahogany ; when the father, relapsing into solemnity, though rather cordial in manner, bade him ring the bell for claret. 'And we'll see if that's as good as the madeira, George, to which His Royal Highness is welcome, I'm sure. And as we are drinking it, I'll talk to you about a matter of importance.'

Amelia heard the claret bell ringing as she sat nervously upstairs. She thought, somehow, it was a mysterious and presentimental bell. Of the presentiments which some people are always having, *some* surely must come right.

'What I want to know, George,' the old gentleman said, after slowly smacking his first bumper. 'What I want to know is, how you and—ah—that little thing upstairs, are carrying on ? '

'I think, sir, it's not hard to see,' George said, with a self-satisfied grin. 'Pretty clear, sir.—What capital wine ! '

'What d'you mean, pretty clear, sir ? '

'Why, hang it, sir, don't push me too hard. I'm a modest man. I—ah—I don't set up to be a lady-killer ; but I do own that she's as devilish fond of me as she can be. Anybody can see that with half an eye.'

'And you, yourself ? '

'Why, sir, didn't you order me to marry her, and ain't I a good boy ? Haven't our papas settled it ever so long ? '

'A pretty boy, indeed. Haven't I heard of your doings, sir, with Lord Tarquin, Captain Crawley of the Guards, the Honourable Mr. Deuceace and that set ? Have a care, sir, have a care.'

The old gentleman pronounced these aristocratic names with the greatest gusto. Whenever he met a great man he grovelled before him, and my-lorded him as only a freeborn Briton can do. He came home and looked out his history in the *Peerage :* he introduced his name into his daily conversation ; he bragged about his lordship to his daughters. He fell down prostrate and basked in him as a Neapolitan beggar does in the sun. George was alarmed when he heard the names. He feared his father might have been informed of certain transactions at play. But the old moralist eased him by saying serenely :—

'Well, well, young men will be young men. And the comfort to me is, George, that living in the best society in England, as I hope you do ; as I think you do ; as my means will allow you to do——'

'Thank you, sir,' says George, making his point at once. 'One can't live with these great folks for nothing ; and my purse, sir, look at it ; ' and he held up a little token which had been netted by Amelia, and contained the very last of Dobbin's pound notes.

'You shan't want, sir. The British merchant's son shan't want, sir. My guineas are as good as theirs, George, my boy ; and I don't grudge 'em. Call on Mr. Chopper as you go through the City to-morrow ; he'll have some-thing for you. I don't grudge money when I know you're in good society, because I know that good society can never go wrong. There's no pride in me. I was a humbly born man—but you have had advantages. Make a good use of 'em. Mix with the young nobility. There's many of 'em who can't spend a dollar to your guinea, my boy. And as for the pink bonnets ' (here from under the heavy eyebrows there came a knowing and not very pleasing leer)—'why, boys will be boys. Only there's one thing I order you to avoid, which, if you do not, I'll cut you off with a shilling, by Jove ; and that's gambling, sir.'

'Oh, of course, sir,' said George.

'But to return to the other business about Amelia : why shouldn't you marry higher than a stockbroker's daughter, George—that's what I want to know ? '

'It's a family business, sir,' says George, cracking filberts. 'You and Mr. Sedley made the match a hundred years ago.'

'I don't deny it ; but people's positions alter, sir. I don't deny that Sedley made my fortune, or rather put me in the way of acquiring, by my own talents and genius, that proud position, which, I may say, I occupy in the tallow trade and the City of London. I've shown my gratitude to Sedley ; and he's tried it of late, sir, as my cheque-book can show. George ! I tell you in confidence I don't like the looks of Mr. Sedley's affairs. My chief clerk, Mr. Chopper, does not like the looks of 'em, and he's an old file, and knows 'Change as well as any man in London.

Hulker & Bullock are looking shy at him. He's been
dabbling on his own account, I fear. They say the *Jeune
Amélie* was his, which was taken by the Yankee privateer
*Molasses.** And that's flat,—unless I see Amelia's ten
thousand down you don't marry her. I'll have no lame
duck's daughter in my family. Pass the wine, sir—or
ring for coffee.'

With which Mr. Osborne spread out the evening paper,
and George knew from this signal that the colloquy was
ended, and that his papa was about to take a nap.

He hurried upstairs to Amelia in the highest spirits.
What was it that made him more attentive to her on that
night than he had been for a long time—more eager to
amuse her, more tender, more brilliant in talk ? Was it
that his generous heart warmed to her at the prospect
of misfortune ; or that the idea of losing the dear little
prize made him value it more ?

She lived upon the recollections of that happy evening
for many days afterwards, remembering his words ; his
looks ; the song he sang ; his attitude, as he leant over her
or looked at her from a distance. As it seemed to her,
no night ever passed so quickly at Mr. Osborne's house
before ; and for once this young person was almost provoked to be angry by the premature arrival of Mr. Sambo
with her shawl.

George came and took a tender leave of her the next
morning ; and then hurried off to the City, where he visited
Mr. Chopper, his father's head man, and received from that
gentleman a document which he exchanged at Hulker's &
Bullock's for a whole pocketful of money. As George
entered the house, old John Sedley was passing out of the
banker's parlour, looking very dismal. But his godson
was much too elated to mark the worthy stockbroker's
depression, or the dreary eyes which the kind old gentleman cast upon him. Young Bullock did not come grinning
out of the parlour with him as had been his wont in former
years.

And as the swinging doors of Hulker, Bullock & Co. closed
upon Mr. Sedley, Mr. Quill, the cashier (whose benevolent
occupation it is to hand out crisp bank-notes from a
drawer and dispense sovereigns out of a copper shovel),
winked at Mr. Driver, the clerk at the desk on his right.
Mr. Driver winked again.

' No go,' Mr. D. whispered.

' Not at no price,' Mr. Q. said.   ' Mr. George Osborne, sir, how will you take it ? '   George crammed eagerly a quantity of notes into his pockets, and paid Dobbin fifty pounds that very evening at mess.*

That very evening Amelia wrote him the tenderest of long letters. Her heart was overflowing with tenderness, but it still foreboded evil. What was the cause of Mr. Osborne's dark looks ? she asked. Had any difference arisen between him and her papa ? Her poor papa returned so melancholy from the City, that all were alarmed about him at home—in fine, there were four pages of loves and fears and hopes and forebodings.

' Poor little Emmy—dear little Emmy. How fond she is of me,' George said, as he perused the missive—' and Gad, what a headache that mixed punch has given me !' Poor little Emmy, indeed.

CHAPTER XIV

MISS CRAWLEY AT HOME

BOUT this time there drove up to an exceedingly snug and well-appointed house in Park Lane, a travelling chariot with a lozenge on the panels, a discontented female in a green veil and crimped curls on the rumble, and a large and confidential man on the box. It was the equipage of our friend Miss Crawley, returning from Hants. The carriage-windows were shut ; the fat spaniel, whose head and tongue ordinarily lolled out of one of them, reposed on the lap of the discontented female. When the vehicle stopped, a large round bundle of shawls was taken out of the carriage by the aid of various domestics and a young lady who accompanied the heap of cloaks. That bundle contained Miss Crawley, who was conveyed upstairs forthwith, and put into a bed and chamber warmed properly as for the reception of an invalid. Messengers went off for her physician and medical man. They came, consulted, prescribed, vanished. The young companion of Miss Crawley, at the conclusion of their interview, came in to receive their instructions, and administered those antiphlogistic medicines which the eminent men ordered.

Captain Crawley of the Life Guards rode up from Knightsbridge Barracks the next day ; his black charger pawed the straw before his invalid aunt's door. He was most affectionate in his inquiries regarding that amiable relative. There seemed to be much source of apprehension. He found Miss Crawley's maid (the discontented female) unusually sulky and despondent ; he found Miss Briggs, her *dame de compagnie*, in tears alone in the drawing-room. She had hastened home, hearing of her beloved friend's illness. She wished to fly to her couch, that couch which she, Briggs, had so often smoothed in the hour of sickness. She was denied admission to Miss Crawley's apartment. A stranger was administering her medicines—a stranger from the country—an odious Miss . . .—tears choked the utterance of the *dame de compagnie*, and she buried her crushed affections and her poor old red nose in her pocket-handkerchief.

Rawdon Crawley sent up his name by the sulky *femme de chambre*, and Miss Crawley's new companion, coming tripping down from the sick-room, put a little hand into his as he stepped forward eagerly to meet her, gave a glance of great scorn at the bewildered Briggs, and, beckoning the young Guardsman out of the back drawing-room, led him downstairs into that now desolate dining-parlour, where so many a good dinner had been celebrated.

Here these two talked for ten minutes, discussing, no doubt, the symptoms of the old invalid above stairs ; at the end of which period the parlour-bell was rung briskly, and answered on that instant by Mr. Bowls, Miss Crawley's large confidential butler (who, indeed, happened to be at the keyhole during the most part of the interview) ; and the captain coming out, curling his moustachios, mounted the black charger pawing among the straw, to the admiration of the little blackguard boys collected in the street. He looked in at the dining-room window, managing his horse, which curveted and capered beautifully—for one instant the young person might be seen at the window, then her figure vanished, and, doubtless, she went upstairs again to resume the affecting duties of benevolence.

Who could this young woman be, I wonder ? That evening a little dinner for two persons was laid in the dining-room—when Mrs. Firkin, the lady's maid, pushed into her mistress's apartment, and bustled about there during the vacancy occasioned by the departure of the new nurse—and the latter and Miss Briggs sat down to the neat little meal.

Briggs was so much choked by emotion that she could hardly take a morsel of meat. The young person carved a fowl with the utmost delicacy, and asked so distinctly for egg-sauce, that poor Briggs, before whom that delicious condiment was placed, started, made a great clattering with the ladle, and once more fell back in the most gushing hysterical state.

' Had you not better give Miss Briggs a glass of wine ? ' said the person to Mr. Bowls, the large confidential man.

He did so. Briggs seized it mechanically, gasped it down convulsively, moaned a little, and began to play with the chicken on her plate.

'I think we shall be able to help each other,' said the person, with great suavity : 'and shall have no need of Mr. Bowls's kind services. Mr. Bowls, if you please, we will ring when we want you.' He went downstairs, where, by the way, he vented the most horrid curses upon the unoffending footman, his subordinate.

'It is a pity you take on so, Miss Briggs,' the young lady said, with a cool, slightly sarcastic air.

'My dearest friend is so ill, and wo—o—o—on't see me,' gurgled out Briggs in an agony of renewed grief.

'She's not very ill any more. Console yourself, dear Miss Briggs. She has only overeaten herself—that is all. She is greatly better. She will soon be quite restored again. She is weak from being cupped and from medical treatment, but she will rally immediately. Pray console yourself, and take a little more wine.'

'But why, why won't she see me again ?' Miss Briggs bleated out. 'Oh, Matilda, Matilda, after three-and-twenty years' tenderness ! is this the return to your poor, poor Arabella ? '

'Don't cry too much, poor Arabella,' the other said (with ever so little of a grin) ; 'she only won't see you, because she says you don't nurse her as well as I do. It's no pleasure to me to sit up all night. I wish you might do it instead.'

'Have I not tended that dear couch for years ? ' Arabella said, ' and now——'

'Now she prefers somebody else. Well, sick people have these fancies, and must be humoured. When she's well I shall go.'

'Never, never,' Arabella exclaimed, madly inhaling her salts-bottle.

'Never be well or never go, Miss Briggs ? ' the other said, with the same provoking good nature. 'Pooh—she will be well in a fortnight, when I shall go back to my little pupils at Queen's Crawley, and to their mother, who is a great deal more sick than our friend. You need not be jealous about me, my dear Miss Briggs. I am a poor little girl without any friends, or any harm in me. I don't want to supplant you in Miss Crawley's good graces. She

will forget me a week after I am gone : and her affection
for you has been the work of years. Give me a little
wine if you please, my dear Miss Briggs, and let us be
friends. I'm sure I want friends.'

The placable and soft-hearted Briggs speechlessly pushed
out her hand at this appeal ; but she felt the desertion
most keenly for all that, and bitterly, bitterly moaned the
fickleness of her Matilda. At the end of half an hour,
the meal over, Miss Rebecca Sharp (for such, astonishing
to state, is the name of her who has been described ingeniously as ' the person ' hitherto) went upstairs again to
her patient's rooms, from which, with the most engaging
politeness, she eliminated poor Firkin. 'Thank you,
Mrs. Firkin, that will quite do ; how nicely you make it !
I will ring when anything is wanted.' 'Thank you ; ' and
Firkin came downstairs in a tempest of jealousy, only the
more dangerous because she was forced to confine it in
her own bosom.

Could it be the tempest which, as she passed the landing
of the first floor, blew open the drawing-room door ? No ;
it was stealthily opened by the hand of Briggs. Briggs
had been on the watch. Briggs too well heard the creaking
Firkin descend the stairs, and the clink of the spoon and
gruel-basin the neglected female carried.

'Well, Firkin ?' says she, as the other entered the
apartment. 'Well, Jane ?'

'Wuss and wuss, Miss B.,' Firkin said, wagging her
head.

'Is she not better then ?'

'She never spoke but once, and I asked her if she felt
a little more easy, and she told me to hold my stupid
tongue. Oh, Miss B., I never thought to have seen *this*
day ! ' And the waterworks again began to play.

'What sort of a person is this Miss Sharp, Firkin ? I little
thought, while enjoying my Christmas revels in the elegant
home of my firm friends, the Reverend Lionel Delamere
and his amiable lady, to find a stranger had taken my
place in the affections of my dearest, my still dearest
Matilda ! ' Miss Briggs, it will be seen by her language,
was of a literary and sentimental turn, and had once
published a volume of poems—*Trills of the Nightingale*—
by subscription.

'Miss B., they are all infatuated about that young

woman,' Firkin replied. 'Sir Pitt wouldn't have let her
go, but he daredn't refuse Miss Crawley anything. Mrs.
Bute at the Rectory jist as bad—never happy out of her
sight. The capting quite wild about her. Mr. Crawley
mortial jealous. Since Miss C. was took ill, she won't
have nobody near her but Miss Sharp, I can't tell for
where nor for why ; and I think somethink has bewidged
everybody.'

Rebecca passed that night in constant watching upon
Miss Crawley ; the next night the old lady slept so comfortably, that Rebecca had time for several hours' comfortable repose herself on the sofa, at the foot of her
patroness's bed ; very soon, Miss Crawley was so well
that she sat up and laughed heartily at a perfect imitation
of Miss Briggs and her grief, which Rebecca described to
her. Briggs's weeping snuffle, and her manner of using the
handkerchief, were so completely rendered, that Miss
Crawley became quite cheerful, to the admiration of the
doctors when they visited her, who usually found this
worthy woman of the world, when the least sickness
attacked her, under the most abject depression and terror
of death.

Captain Crawley came every day, and received bulletins
from Miss Rebecca respecting his aunt's health. This
improved so rapidly, that poor Briggs was allowed to see
her patroness ; and persons with tender hearts may imagine
the smothered emotions of that sentimental female, and
the affecting nature of the interview.

Miss Crawley liked to have Briggs in a good deal soon.
Rebecca used to mimic her to her face with the most
admirable gravity, thereby rendering the imitation doubly
piquant to her worthy patroness.

The causes which had led to the deplorable illness of
Miss Crawley, and her departure from her brother's house
in the country, were of such an unromantic nature that
they are hardly fit to be explained in this genteel and
sentimental novel. For how is it possible to hint of a
delicate female, living in good society, that she ate and
drank too much, and that a hot supper of lobsters profusely enjoyed at the Rectory was the reason of an indis-
position which Miss Crawley herself persisted was solely
attributable to the dampness of the weather ? The attack

was so sharp that Matilda—as his reverence expressed it—
was very nearly 'off the hooks'; all the family was in
a fever of expectation regarding the will, and Rawdon
Crawley was making sure of at least forty thousand pounds
before the commencement of the London season. Mr. Crawley sent over a choice parcel of tracts, to prepare her for
the change from Vanity Fair and Park Lane for another
world; but a good doctor from Southampton being called
in in time, vanquished the lobster which was so nearly
fatal to her, and gave her sufficient strength to enable her
to return to London. The baronet did not disguise his
exceeding mortification at the turn which affairs took.

While everybody was attending on Miss Crawley, and
messengers every hour from the Rectory were carrying
news of her health to the affectionate folks there, there
was a lady in another part of the house being exceedingly
ill, of whom no one took any notice at all; and this was
the lady of Crawley herself. The good doctor shook his
head after seeing her; to which visit Sir Pitt consented,
as it could be paid without a fee;* and she was left fading
away in her lonely chamber, with no more heed paid to
her than to a weed in the park.

The young ladies, too, lost much of the inestimable
benefit of their governess's instruction. So affectionate
a nurse was Miss Sharp, that Miss Crawley would take
her medicines from no other hand. Firkin had been deposed
long before her mistress's departure from the country.
That faithful attendant found a gloomy consolation on
returning to London, in seeing Miss Briggs suffer the same
pangs of jealousy and undergo the same faithless treatment
to which she herself had been subject.

Captain Rawdon got an extension of leave on his aunt's
illness, and remained dutifully at home. He was always
in her antechamber. (She lay sick in the state bedroom,
into which you entered by the little blue saloon.) His
father was always meeting him there; or if he came down
the corridor ever so quietly, his father's door was sure to
open, and the hyena face of the old gentleman to glare
out. What was it set one to watch the other so? A
generous rivalry, no doubt, as to which should be most
attentive to the dear sufferer in the state bedroom.
Rebecca used to come out and comfort both of them; or
one or the other of them, rather. Both of these worthy

gentlemen were most anxious to have news of the invalid from her little confidential messenger.

At dinner—to which meal she descended for half an hour—she kept the peace between them, after which she disappeared for the night ; when Rawdon would ride over to the dépôt of the 150th at Mudbury, leaving his papa to the society of Mr. Horrocks and his rum-and-water. She passed as weary a fortnight as ever mortal spent in Miss Crawley's sick-room ; but her little nerves seemed to be of iron, and she was quite unshaken by the duty and the tedium of the sick-chamber.

She never told until long afterwards how painful that duty was ; how peevish a patient was the jovial old lady ; how angry ; how sleepless ; in what horrors of death ; during what long nights she lay moaning, and in almost delirious agonies respecting that future world which she quite ignored when she was in good health.—Picture to yourself, O fair young reader, a worldly, selfish, graceless, thankless, religionless old woman, writhing in pain and fear, and without her wig. Picture her to yourself, and ere you be old, learn to love and pray !

Sharp watched this graceless bedside with indomitable patience. Nothing escaped her ; and, like a prudent steward, she found a use for everything. She told many a good story about Miss Crawley's illness in after-days,— stories which made the lady blush through her artificial carnations. During the illness she was never out of temper ; always alert ; she slept light, having a perfectly clear conscience ; and could take that refreshment at almost any minute's warning. And so you saw few traces of fatigue in her appearance. Her face might be a trifle paler, and the circles round her eyes a little blacker than usual ; but whenever she came out from the sick-room she was always smiling, fresh, and neat, and looked as trim in her little dressing-gown and cap, as in her smartest evening suit.

The captain thought so, and raved about her in uncouth convulsions. The barbed shaft of love had penetrated his dull hide. Six weeks—appropinquity—opportunity—had victimized him completely. He made a confidant of his aunt at the Rectory, of all persons in the world. She rallied him about it ; she had perceived his folly ; she warned him ; she finished by owning that little Sharp was the most clever, droll, odd, good-natured, simple, kindly creature in England. Rawdon must not trifle with her affections, though—dear Miss Crawley would never pardon him for that; for she, too, was quite overcome by the little governess, and loved Sharp like a daughter. Rawdon must go away—go back to his regiment and naughty London, and not play with a poor artless girl's feelings.

Many and many a time this good-natured lady, compassionating the forlorn life-guardsman's condition, gave him an opportunity of seeing Miss Sharp at the Rectory, and of walking home with her, as we have seen. When men of a certain sort, ladies, are in love, though they see the hook and the string, and the whole apparatus with which they are to be taken, they gorge the bait nevertheless —they must come to it—they must swallow it—and are presently struck and landed gasping. Rawdon saw there was a manifest intention on Mrs. Bute's part to captivate him with Rebecca. He was not very wise; but he was a man about town, and had seen several seasons. A light dawned upon his dusky soul, as he thought, through a speech of Mrs. Bute's.

'Mark my words, Rawdon,' she said. 'You will have Miss Sharp one day for your relation.'

'What relation,—my cousin, hey, Mrs. Bute? Francis sweet on her, hey?' inquired the waggish officer.

'More than that,' Mrs. Bute said, with a flash from her black eyes.

'Not Pitt?—He sha'n't have her. The sneak a'n't worthy of her. He's booked to Lady Jane Sheepshanks.'

'You men perceive nothing. You silly, blind creature— if anything happens to Lady Crawley, Miss Sharp will be your mother-in-law; and *that's* what will happen.'

Rawdon Crawley, Esquire, gave vent to a prodigious whistle, in token of astonishment at this announcement. He couldn't deny it. His father's evident liking for Miss Sharp had not escaped him. He knew the old gentleman's character well; and a more unscrupulous old—whyou— he did not conclude the sentence, but walked home, curling his moustachios, and convinced he had found a clue to Mrs. Bute's mystery.

'By Jove, it's too bad,' thought Rawdon, 'too bad, by Jove! I do believe the woman wants the poor girl to be ruined, in order that she shouldn't come into the family as Lady Crawley.'

When he saw Rebecca alone, he rallied her about his
father's attachment in his graceful way. She flung up her
head scornfully, looked him full in the face, and said,—

'Well, suppose he *is* fond of me. I know he is, and
others too. You don't think I am afraid of him, Captain
Crawley? You don't suppose I can't defend my own
honour,' said the little woman, looking as stately as a
queen.

'Oh, ah, why—give you fair warning—look out, you
know—that's all,' said the moustachio-twiddler.

'You hint at something not honourable, then?' said
she, flashing out.

'Oh—Gad—really—Miss Rebecca,' the heavy dragoon
interposed.

'Do you suppose I have no feeling of self-respect, because
I am poor and friendless, and because rich people have
none? Do you think, because I am a governess, I have
not as much sense, and feeling, and good breeding as you
gentlefolks in Hampshire? I'm a Montmorency. Do you
suppose a Montmorency is not as good as a Crawley?'

When Miss Sharp was agitated, and alluded to her
maternal relatives, she spoke with ever so slight a foreign
accent, which gave a great charm to her clear ringing
voice. 'No,' she continued, kindling as she spoke to the
captain; 'I can endure poverty, but not shame—neglect,
but not insult; and insult from—from *you*.'

Her feelings gave way, and she burst into tears.

'Hang it, Miss Sharp—Rebecca—by Jove—upon my
soul, I wouldn't for a thousand pounds. Stop, Rebecca!'

She was gone. She drove out with Miss Crawley that
day. It was before the latter's illness. At dinner she was
unusually brilliant and lively; but she would take no
notice of the hints, or the nods, or the clumsy expostula-
tions of the humiliated, infatuated guardsman. Skirmishes
of this sort passed perpetually during the little campaign—
tedious to relate, and similar in result. The Crawley heavy
cavalry was maddened by defeat, and routed every day.

If the baronet of Queen's Crawley had not had the fear
of losing his sister's legacy before his eyes, he never would
have permitted his dear girls to lose the educational blessings
which their invaluable governess was conferring upon them.
The old house at home seemed a desert without her, so

useful and pleasant had Rebecca made herself there. Sir
Pitt's letters were not copied and corrected; his books
not made up; his household business and manifold schemes
neglected, now that his little secretary was away. And it
was easy to see how necessary such an amanuensis was to
him, by the tenor and spelling of the numerous letters
which he sent to her, entreating her and commanding her
to return. Almost every day brought a frank from the
baronet, enclosing the most urgent prayers to Becky for
her return, or conveying pathetic statements to Miss Crawley, regarding the neglected state of his daughters' education; of which documents Miss Crawley took very little
heed.

Miss Briggs was not formally dismissed, but her place
as companion was a sinecure and a derision; and her
company was the fat spaniel in the drawing-room, or
occasionally the discontented Firkin in the housekeeper's
closet. Nor though the old lady would by no means hear
of Rebecca's departure, was the latter regularly installed
in office in Park Lane. Like many wealthy people, it was
Miss Crawley's habit to accept as much service as she
could get from her inferiors; and good-naturedly to take
leave of them when she no longer found them useful.
Gratitude among certain rich folks is scarcely natural or
to be thought of. They take needy people's services as
their due. Nor have you, O poor parasite and humble
hanger-on, much reason to complain! Your friendship for
Dives is about as sincere as the return which it usually
gets. It is money you love, and not the man; and were
Croesus and his footman to change places, you know, you
poor rogue, who would have the benefit of your allegiance.

And I am not sure that, in spite of Rebecca's simplicity
and activity, and gentleness and untiring good humour,
the shrewd old London lady, upon whom these treasures
of friendship were lavished, had not a lurking suspicion
all the while of her affectionate nurse and friend. It must
have often crossed Miss Crawley's mind that nobody does
anything for nothing. If she measured her own feeling
towards the world, she must have been pretty well able
to gauge those of the world towards herself; and perhaps
she reflected, that it is the ordinary lot of people to have
no friends if they themselves care for nobody.

Well, meanwhile, Becky was the greatest comfort and

convenience to her, and she gave her a couple of new gowns,
and an old necklace and shawl, and showed her friendship
by abusing all her intimate acquaintances to her new
confidante (than which there can't be a more touching
proof of regard), and meditated vaguely some great future
benefit—to marry her perhaps to Clump, the apothecary,
or to settle her in some advantageous way of life ; or, at
any rate, to send her back to Queen's Crawley when she
had done with her, and the full London season had begun.

When Miss Crawley was convalescent and descended to
the drawing-room, Becky sang to her, and otherwise amused
her ; when she was well enough to drive out, Becky accompanied her. And amongst the drives which they took,
whither, of all places in the world, did Miss Crawley's
admirable good nature and friendship actually induce her
to penetrate, but to Russell Square, Bloomsbury, and the
house of John Sedley, Esquire.

Ere that event, many notes had passed, as may be
imagined, between the two dear friends. During the
months of Rebecca's stay in Hampshire, the eternal friendship had (must it be owned ?) suffered considerable diminu-
tion, and grown so decrepit and feeble with old age as to
threaten demise altogether. The fact is, both girls had
their own real affairs to think of : Rebecca her advance
with her employers—Amelia her own absorbing topic.
When the two girls met, and flew into each other's arms
with that impetuosity which distinguishes the behaviour of
young ladies towards each other, Rebecca performed her
part of the embrace with the most perfect briskness and
energy. Poor little Amelia blushed as she kissed her friend,
and thought she had been guilty of something very like coldness towards her.

Their first interview was but a very short one. Amelia
was just ready to go out for a walk. Miss Crawley was
waiting in her carriage below, her people wondering at the
locality in which they found themselves, and gazing upon
honest Sambo, the black footman of Bloomsbury, as one
of the queer natives of the place. But when Amelia came
down with her kind smiling looks (Rebecca must introduce
her to her friend, Miss Crawley was longing to see her,
and was too ill to leave her carriage)—when, I say, Amelia
came down, the Park Lane shoulder-knot aristocracy
wondered more and more that such a thing could come

out of Bloomsbury ; and Miss Crawley was fairly captivated by the sweet blushing face of the young lady who
came forward so timidly and so gracefully to pay her
respects to the protector of her friend.

'What a complexion, my dear. What a sweet voice ! '
Miss Crawley said, as they drove away westward after the
little interview. ' My dear Sharp, your young friend is
charming. Send for her to Park Lane, do you hear ? '
Miss Crawley had a good taste. She liked natural manners
—a little timidity only set them off. She liked pretty
faces near her ; as she liked pretty pictures and nice china.
She talked of Amelia with rapture half a dozen times that
day. She mentioned her to Rawdon Crawley, who came
dutifully to partake of his aunt's chicken.

Of course, on this Rebecca instantly stated, that Amelia
was engaged to be married—to a Lieutenant Osborne—
a very old flame.

' Is he a man in a line-regiment ? '* Captain Crawley
asked, remembering after an effort, as became a guardsman,
the number of the regiment, the —th.

Rebecca thought that was the regiment. ' The captain's
name,' she said, ' was Captain Dobbin.'

' A lanky gawky fellow,' said Crawley, ' tumbles over
everybody. I know him ; and Osborne's a goodish-looking
fellow, with large black whiskers ? '

' Enormous,' Miss Rebecca Sharp said, ' and enormously
proud of them, I assure you.'

Captain Rawdon Crawley burst into a hoarse laugh by
way of reply ; and being pressed by the ladies to explain,
did so when the explosion of hilarity was over. ' He
fancies he can play at billiards,' said he. ' I won two
hundred of him at the " Cocoa-Tree." *He* play, the young
flat !* He'd have played for anything that day, but his
friend Captain Dobbin carried him off, hang him ! '

' Rawdon, Rawdon, don't be so wicked,' Miss Crawley
remarked, highly pleased.

' Why, ma'am, of all the young fellows I've seen out of
the line. I think this fellow's the greenest. Tarquin and
Deuceace get what money they like out of him. He'd go
to the deuce to be seen with a lord. He pays their dinners
at Greenwich, and they invite the company.'

' And very pretty company too, I dare say.'

' Quite right, Miss Sharp. Right, as usual, Miss Sharp.

Uncommon pretty company,—haw, haw !' and the captain
laughed more and more, thinking he had made a good joke.

'Rawdon, don't be naughty !' his aunt exclaimed.

'Well, his father's a City man—immensely rich, they
say. Hang those City fellows, they must bleed ; and I've
not done with him yet, I can tell you. Haw, haw !'

'Fie, Captain Crawley ; I shall warn Amelia. A gambling
husband !'

'Horrid, ain't he, hey ?' the captain said with great
solemnity ; and then added, a sudden thought having
struck him :—' Gad, I say, ma'am, we'll have him here.'

'Is he a presentable sort of a person ?' the aunt inquired.

'Presentable ?—oh, very well. You wouldn't see any
difference,' Captain Crawley answered. 'Do let's have him,
when you begin to see a few people ; and his whatdye-
callem—his inamorato—eh, Miss Sharp ; that's what you
call it—comes. Gad, I'll write him a note, and have him ;
and I'll try if he can play piquet as well as billiards.
Where does he live, Miss Sharp ?'

Miss Sharp told Crawley the lieutenant's town address ;
and a few days after this conversation, Lieutenant Osborne
received a letter, in Captain Rawdon's schoolboy hand,
and enclosing a note of invitation from Miss Crawley.

Rebecca dispatched also an invitation to her darling
Amelia, who, you may be sure, was ready enough to accept
it when she heard that George was to be of the party.
It was arranged that Amelia was to spend the morning
with the ladies of Park Lane, where all were very kind to
her. Rebecca patronized her with calm superiority : she
was so much the cleverer of the two, and her friend
so gentle and unassuming, that she always yielded when
anybody chose to command, and so took Rebecca's orders
with perfect meekness and good humour. Miss Crawley's
graciousness was also remarkable. She continued her raptures about little Amelia, talked about her before her face
as if she were a doll, or a servant, or a picture, and admired
her with the most benevolent wonder possible. I admire
that admiration which the genteel world sometimes extends
to the commonalty. There is no more agreeable object in
life · than to see May Fair folks condescending. Miss
Crawley's prodigious benevolence rather fatigued poor little
Amelia, and I am not sure that of the three ladies in Park
Lane she did not find honest Miss Briggs the most agreeable.

She sympathized with Briggs as with all neglected or gentle people : she wasn't what you call a woman of spirit.

George came to dinner—a repast *en garçon* with Captain Crawley.

The great family coach of the Osbornes transported him to Park Lane from Russell Square ; where the young ladies, who were not themselves invited, and professed the greatest indifference at that slight, nevertheless looked at Sir Pitt Crawley's name in the *Baronetage ;* and learned everything which that work had to teach about the Crawley family and their pedigree, and the Binkies, their relatives, &c. &c. Rawdon Crawley received George Osborne with great frankness and graciousness : praised his play at billiards : asked him when he would have his revenge . was interested about Osborne's regiment : and would have proposed piquet to him that very evening, but Miss Crawley absolutely forbade any gambling in her house ; so that the young lieutenant's purse was not lightened by his gallant patron, for that day at least. However, they made an engagement for the next, somewhere : to look at a horse that Crawley had to sell, and to try him in the Park ; and to dine together, and to pass the evening with some jolly fellows. ' That is, if you're not on duty to that pretty Miss Sedley,' Crawley said, with a knowing wink. ' Monstrous nice girl, 'pon my honour, though, Osborne,' he was good enough to add. ' Lots of tin, I suppose, eh ? '

Osborne wasn't on duty ; he would join Crawley with pleasure : and the latter, when they met the next day, praised his new friend's horsemanship—as he might with perfect honesty—and introduced him to three or four young men of the first fashion, whose acquaintance immensely elated the simple young officer.

' How's little Miss Sharp, by the by,' Osborne inquired of his friend over their wine, with a dandified air. ' Good-natured little girl that. Does she suit you well at Queen's Crawley ? Miss Sedley liked her a good deal last year.'

Captain Crawley looked savagely at the lieutenant out of his little blue eyes, and watched him when he went up to resume his acquaintance with the fair governess. Her conduct must have relieved Crawley if there was any jealousy in the bosom of that life-guardsman.

When the young men went upstairs, and after Osborne's introduction to Miss Crawley, he walked up to Rebecca

with a patronizing, easy swagger. He was going to be
kind to her and protect her. He would even shake hands
with her, as a friend of Amelia's; and saying, 'Ah, Miss
Sharp! how-dy-doo?' held out his left hand towards her,
expecting that she would be quite confounded at the honour.

Miss Sharp put out her right forefinger,—

and gave him a little nod, so cool and killing, that
Rawdon Crawley, watching the operations from the other
room, could hardly restrain his laughter as he saw the
lieutenant's entire discomfiture; the start he gave, the
pause, and the perfect clumsiness with which he at length
condescended to take the finger which was offered for
his embrace.

'She'd beat the devil, by Jove!' the captain said, in
a rapture and the lieutenant, by way of beginning the

conversation, agreeably asked Rebecca how she liked her
new place.

'My place?' said Miss Sharp, coolly, 'how kind of you
to remind me of it! It's a tolerably good place: the
wages are pretty good—not so good as Miss Wirt's, I believe,
with your sisters in Russell Square. How are those young
ladies?—not that I ought to ask.'

'Why not?' Mr. Osborne said, amazed.

'Why, they never condescended to speak to me, or to
ask me into their house, whilst I was staying with Amelia;
but we poor governesses, you know, are used to slights of
this sort.'

'My dear Miss Sharp!' Osborne ejaculated.

'At least in some families,' Rebecca continued. 'You
can't think what a difference there is though. We are not
so wealthy in Hampshire as you lucky folks of the City.
But then I am in a gentleman's family—good old English
stock. I suppose you know Sir Pitt's father refused a
peerage. And you see how I am treated. I am pretty
comfortable. Indeed, it is rather a good place. But how
very good of you to inquire!'

Osborne was quite savage. The little governess patronized
him and *persiflé*'d him until this young British Lion felt
quite uneasy; nor could he muster sufficient presence of
mind to find a pretext for backing out of this most delectable conversation.

'I thought you liked the City families pretty well,' he
said, haughtily.

'Last year you mean, when I was fresh from that horrid
vulgar school? Of course I did. Doesn't every girl like
to come home for the holidays? And how was I to know
any better? But oh, Mr. Osborne, what a difference
eighteen months' experience makes!—eighteen months
spent, pardon me for saying so, with gentlemen. As for
dear Amelia, she, I grant you, is a pearl, and would be
charming anywhere. There now, I see you are beginning
to be in a good humour; but oh, these queer odd City
people! And Mr. Jos—how is that wonderful Mr.
Joseph?'

'It seems to me you didn't dislike that wonderful Mr.
Joseph last year,' Osborne said, kindly.

'How severe of you! Well, *entre nous*, I didn't break
my heart about him; yet if he had asked me to do what

you mean by your looks (and very expressive and kind
they are, too), I wouldn't have said no.'

Mr. Osborne gave a look as much as to say, ' Indeed, how
very obliging ! '

' What an honour to have had you for a brother-in-law,
you are thinking ?   To be sister-in-law to George Osborne,
Esquire, son of John Osborne, Esquire, son of—what was
your grandpapa, Mr. Osborne ?   Well, don't be angry.
You can't help your pedigree, and I quite agree with you
that I would have married Mr. Joe Sedley ; for could a poor
penniless girl do better ?   Now you know the whole secret.
I'm frank and open ; and, considering all things, it was
very kind of you to allude to the circumstance—very kind
and polite.   Amelia dear, Mr. Osborne and I were talking
about your poor brother Joseph.   How is he ? '

Thus was George utterly routed.   Not that Rebecca was
in the right ; but she had managed most successfully to
put him in the wrong.   And he now shamefully fled, feeling,
if he stayed another minute, that he would have been made
to look foolish in the presence of Amelia.

Though Rebecca had had the better of him, George was
above the meanness of tale-bearing or revenge upon a lady,
—only he could not help cleverly confiding to Captain
Crawley, next day, some notions of his regarding Miss
Rebecca—that she was a sharp one, a dangerous one, a
desperate flirt, &c. ; in all of which opinions Crawley
agreed laughingly, and with every one of which Miss
Rebecca was made acquainted before twenty-four hours
were over.   They added to her original regard for Mr.
Osborne.   Her woman's instinct had told her that it was
George who had interrupted the success of her first love-
passage, and she esteemed him accordingly.

' I only just warn you,' he said to Rawdon Crawley,
with a knowing look—he had bought the horse, and lost
some score of guineas after dinner, ' I just warn you—
I know women, and counsel you to be on the look-out.'

' Thank you, my boy,' said Crawley, with a look of
peculiar gratitude.   ' You're wide awake, I see.'   And
George went off, thinking Crawley was quite right.

He told Amelia of what he had done, and how he had
counselled Rawdon Crawley—a devilish good, straightforward fellow—to be on his guard against that little sly,
scheming Rebecca.

'Against *whom?*' Amelia cried.

'Your friend the governess.—Don't look so astonished.'

'Oh, George, what *have* you done?' Amelia said. For her woman's eyes, which Love had made sharp-sighted, had in one instant discovered a secret which was invisible to Miss Crawley, to poor virgin Briggs, and, above all, to the stupid peepers of that young whiskered prig, Lieutenant Osborne.

For as Rebecca was shawling her in an upper apartment, where these two friends had an opportunity for a little of that secret talking and conspiring which forms the delight of female life, Amelia, coming up to Rebecca, and taking her two little hands in hers, said, 'Rebecca, I see it all.'

Rebecca kissed her.

And regarding this delightful secret, not one syllable more was said by either of the young women. But it was destined to come out before long.

Some short period after the above events, and Miss Rebecca Sharp still remaining at her patroness's house in Park Lane, one more hatchment might have been seen in Great Gaunt Street, figuring amongst the many which usually ornament that dismal quarter. It was over Sir Pitt Crawley's house; but it did not indicate the worthy baronet's demise. It was a feminine hatchment,* and indeed a few years back had served as a funeral compliment to Sir Pitt's old mother, the late dowager Lady Crawley. Its period of service over, the hatchment had come down from the front of the house, and lived in retirement somewhere in the back premises of Sir Pitt's mansion. It reappeared now for poor Rose Dawson. Sir Pitt was a widower again. The arms quartered on the shield along with his own were not, to be sure, poor Rose's. She had no arms. But the cherubs painted on the scutcheon answered as well for her as for Sir Pitt's mother, and *Resurgam* was written under the coat, flanked by the Crawley Dove and Serpent. Arms and Hatchments, Resurgam.—Here is an opportunity for moralizing!

Mr. Crawley had tended that otherwise friendless bedside. She went out of the world strengthened by such words and comfort as he could give her. For many years his was the only kindness she ever knew; the only friendship that solaced in any way that feeble, lonely soul. Her heart was dead long before her body. She had sold it to become Sir Pitt Crawley's wife. Mothers and daughters are making the same bargain every day in Vanity Fair.

When the demise took place, her husband was in London attending to some of his innumerable schemes, and busy with his endless lawyers. He had found time, nevertheless, to call often in Park Lane, and to dispatch many notes to Rebecca, entreating her, enjoining her, commanding her to return to her young pupils in the country, who were now utterly without companionship during their mother's illness. But Miss Crawley would not hear of her departure; for though there was no lady of fashion in London who would desert her friends more complacently as soon as she was tired of their society, and though few tired of them sooner, yet as long as her *engouement* lasted her attachment was prodigious, and she clung still with the greatest energy to Rebecca.

The news of Lady Crawley's death provoked no more grief or comment than might have been expected in Miss Crawley's family circle. 'I suppose I must put off my party for the 3rd,' Miss Crawley said; and added, after a pause, ' I hope my brother will have the decency not to marry again.' ' What a confounded rage Pitt will be in if he does,' Rawdon remarked, with his usual regard for his elder brother. Rebecca said nothing. She seemed by far the gravest and most impressed of the family. She left the room before Rawdon went away that day; but they met by chance below, as he was going away after taking leave, and had a parley together.

On the morrow, as Rebecca was gazing from the window, she startled Miss Crawley, who was placidly occupied with a French novel, by crying out in an alarmed tone, ' Here's Sir Pitt, ma'am!' and the baronet's knock followed this announcement.

' My dear, I can't see him. I won't see him. Tell Bowls not at home, or go downstairs and say I'm too ill to receive any one. My nerves really won't bear my brother at this moment;' cried out Miss Crawley, and resumed the novel.

' She's too ill to see you, sir,' Rebecca said, tripping down to Sir Pitt, who was preparing to ascend.

' So much the better,' Sir Pitt answered. ' I want to

see *you*, Miss Becky. Come along a me into the parlour,' and they entered that apartment together.

'I wawnt you back at Queen's Crawley, miss,' the baronet said, fixing his eyes upon her, and taking off his black gloves and his hat with its great crape hatband. His eyes had such a strange look, and fixed upon her so steadfastly, that Rebecca Sharp began almost to tremble.

'I hope to come soon,' she said in a low voice, ' as soon as Miss Crawley is better—and return to—to the dear children.'

'You've said so these three months, Becky,' replied Sir Pitt, ' and still you go hanging on to my sister, who'll

fling you off like an old shoe, when she's wore you out. I tell you I *want* you. I'm going back to the Vuneral. Will you come back ? Yes or no.'

'I daren't—I don't think—it would be right—to be alone —with you, sir,' Becky said, seemingly in great agitation.

'I say agin, I want you,' Sir Pitt said, thumping the table. 'I can't git on without you. I didn't see what it was till you went away. The house all goes wrong. It's not the same place. All my accounts has got muddled agin. You *must* come back. Do come back. Dear Becky, do come.'

'Come—as what, sir?' Rebecca gasped out.

'Come as Lady Crawley, if you like,' the baronet said,
grasping his crape hat. 'There! will that zatusfy you?
Come back and be my wife. Your vit vor't. Birth be
hanged. Your as good a lady as ever I see. You've got
more brains in your little vinger than any baronet's wife
in the county. Will you come? Yes or no?'

'Oh, Sir Pitt!' Rebecca said, very much moved.

'Say yes, Becky,' Sir Pitt continued. 'I'm an old man,
but a good'n. I'm good for twenty years. I'll make you
happy, zee if I don't. You shall do what you like; spend
what you like; and 'av it all your own way. I'll make
you a zettlement. I'll do everything reglar. Look year!'
and the old man fell down on his knees and leered at her
like a satyr.

Rebecca started back a picture of consternation. In the
course of this history we have never seen her lose her presence of mind; but she did now, and wept some of the
most genuine tears that ever fell from her eyes.

'Oh, Sir Pitt!' she said. 'Oh, sir—I—I'm *married
already*.'

CHAPTER XV

IN WHICH REBECCA'S HUSBAND APPEARS FOR A SHORT TIME

 VERY reader of a sentimental turn (and we desire no other) must have been pleased with the tableau with which the last act of our little drama concluded ; for what can be prettier than an image of Love on his knees before Beauty ?

But when Love heard that awful confession from Beauty that she was married already, he bounced up from his attitude of humility on the carpet, uttering exclamations which caused poor little Beauty to be more frightened than she was when she made her avowal. ' Married ; you're joking,' the baronet cried, after the first explosion of rage and wonder. ' You're making vun of me, Becky. Who'd ever go to marry you without a shilling to your vortune ? '

' Married ! married ! ' Rebecca said, in an agony of tears—her voice choking with emotion, her handkerchief up to her ready eyes, fainting against the mantelpiece—a figure of woe fit to melt the most obdurate heart. ' Oh, Sir Pitt, dear Sir Pitt, do not think me ungrateful for all your goodness to me. It is only your generosity that has extorted my secret.'

' Generosity be hanged ! ' Sir Pitt roared out. ' Who is it tu, then, you're married ? Where was it ? '

' Let me come back with you to the country, sir ! Let me watch over you as faithfully as ever ! Don't, don't separate me from dear Queen's Crawley ! '

' The feller has left you, has he ? ' the baronet said, beginning, as he fancied, to comprehend. ' Well, Becky—come back if you like. You can't eat your cake and have it. Any ways I made you a vair offer. Coom back as governess—you shall have it all your own way.' She held out one hand. She cried fit to break her heart ; her

ringlets fell over her face, and over the marble mantelpiece where she laid it.

'So the rasca ran off, eh ?' Sir Pitt said, with a hideous
attempt at consolation. 'Never mind, Becky, *I'll* take
care of 'ee.'

'Oh, sir ! it would be the pride of my life to go back to
Queen's Crawley, and take care of the children, and of you
as formerly, when you said you were pleased with the
services of your little Rebecca. When I think of what

you have just offered me, my heart fills with gratitude—
indeed it does. I can't be your wife, sir ; let me—let me
be your daughter.'

Saying which, Rebecca went down on *her* knees in a most
tragical way, and taking Sir Pitt's horny black hand between
her own two (which were very pretty and white, and as
soft as satin), looked up in his face with an expression
of exquisite pathos and confidence, when—when the door
opened, and Miss Crawley sailed in.

Mrs. Firkin and Miss Briggs, who happened by chance

to be at the parlour-door soon after the baronet and Rebecca
entered the apartment, had also seen accidentally through
the keyhole the old gentleman prostrate before the
governess, and had heard the generous proposal which he
made her. It was scarcely out of his mouth, when Mrs.
Firkin and Miss Briggs had streamed up the stairs, had
rushed into the drawing-room where Miss Crawley was
reading the French novel, and had given that old lady the
astounding intelligence that Sir Pitt was on his knees,
proposing to Miss Sharp. And if you calculate the time
for the above dialogue to take place—the time for Briggs
and Firkin to fly to the drawing-room—the time for Miss
Crawley to be astonished, and to drop her volume of Pigault
le Brun—*—and the time for her to come downstairs—you
will see how exactly accurate this history is, and how Miss
Crawley *must* have appeared at the very instant when
Rebecca had assumed the attitude of humility.

' It is the lady on the ground, and not the gentleman,'
Miss Crawley said, with a look and voice of great scorn.
' They told me that *you* were on your knees, Sir Pitt : do
kneel once more, and let me see this pretty couple ! '

' I have thanked Sir Pitt Crawley, ma'am,' Rebecca said,
rising, ' and have told him that—that I never can become
Lady Crawley.'

' Refused him ! ' Miss Crawley said, more bewildered than
ever. Briggs and Firkin at the door opened the eyes of
astonishment and the lips of wonder.

' Yes—refused,' Rebecca continued, with a sad, tearful
voice.

' And am I to credit my ears that you absolutely proposed to her, Sir Pitt ? ' the old lady asked.

' Ees,' said the baronet, ' I did.'

' And she refused you as she says ? '

' Ees,' Sir Pitt said, his features on a broad grin.

' It does not seem to break your heart at any rate,' Miss
Crawley remarked.

' Nawt a bit,' answered Sir Pitt, with a coldness and
good humour which set Miss Crawley almost mad with
bewilderment. That an old gentleman of station should
fall on his knees to a penniless governess, and burst out
laughing because she refused to marry him—that a penniless
governess should refuse a baronet with four thousand a year,
—these were mysteries which Miss Crawley could never

comprehend. It surpassed any complications of intrigue in her favourite Pigault le Brun.

'I'm glad you think it good sport, brother,' she continued, groping wildly through this amazement.

'Vamous,' said Sir Pitt. 'Who'd ha' thought it! what a sly little devil! what a little fox it waws!' he muttered to himself, chuckling with pleasure.

'Who'd have thought what?' cries Miss Crawley, stamping with her foot. 'Pray, Miss Sharp, are you waiting for the Prince Regent's divorce,* that you don't think our family good enough for you?'

'My attitude,' Rebecca said, 'when you came in, ma'am, did not look as if I despised such an honour as this good —this noble man has deigned to offer me. Do you think I have no heart? Have you all loved me, and been so kind to the poor orphan—deserted—girl, and am *I* to feel nothing? O my friends! O my benefactors! may not my love, my life, my duty, try to repay the confidence you have shown me? Do you grudge me even gratitude, Miss Crawley? It is too much—my heart is too full;' and she sank down in a chair so pathetically, that most of the audience present were perfectly melted with her sadness.

'Whether you marry me or not, you're a good little girl, Becky, and I'm your vriend, mind,' said Sir Pitt, and putting on his crape-bound hat, he walked away—greatly to Rebecca's relief; for it was evident that her secret was unrevealed to Miss Crawley, and she had the advantage of a brief reprieve.

Putting her handkerchief to her eyes, and nodding away honest Briggs, who would have followed her upstairs, she went up to her apartment; while Briggs and Miss Crawley, in a high state of excitement, remained to discuss the strange event, and Firkin, not less moved, dived down into the kitchen regions, and talked of it with all the male and female company there. And so impressed was Mrs. Firkin with the news, that she thought proper to write off by that very night's post, 'with her humble duty to Mrs. Bute Crawley and the family at the Rectory, and Sir Pitt has been and proposed for to marry Miss Sharp, wherein she has refused him, to the wonder of all.'

The two ladies in the dining-room (where worthy Miss Briggs was delighted to be admitted once more to a confidential conversation with her patroness) wondered to their hearts' content at Sir Pitt's offer, and Rebecca's refusal;

Briggs very acutely suggesting that there must have been some obstacle in the shape of a previous attachment, otherwise no young woman in her senses would ever have refused so advantageous a proposal.

'You would have accepted it yourself, wouldn't you, Briggs ? ' Miss Crawley said, kindly.

'Would it not be a privilege to be Miss Crawley's sister ? ' Briggs replied, with meek evasion.

'Well, Becky would have made a good Lady Crawley, after all,' Miss Crawley remarked (who was mollified by the girl's refusal, and very liberal and generous now there was no call for her sacrifices). 'She has brains in plenty (much more wit in her little finger than you have, my poor dear Briggs, in all your head). Her manners are excellent, now I have formed her. She's a Montmorency, Briggs, and blood *is* something, though I despise it for my part ; and she would have held her own amongst those pompous stupid Hampshire people much better than that unfortunate ironmonger's daughter.'

Briggs coincided as usual, and the ' previous attachment ' was then discussed in conjectures. ' You poor friendless creatures are always having some foolish *tendre*,' Miss Crawley said. ' You yourself, you know, were in love with a writing-master (don't cry, Briggs—you're always crying, and it won't bring him to life again), and I suppose this unfortunate Becky has been silly and sentimental too—some apothecary, or house-steward, or painter, or young curate, or something of that sort.'

' Poor thing, poor thing ! ' says Briggs (who was thinking of twenty-four years back, and that hectic young writing-master, whose lock of yellow hair, and whose letters, beautiful in their illegibility, she cherished in her old desk upstairs). ' Poor thing, poor thing ! ' says Briggs. Once more she was a fresh-cheeked lass of eighteen ; she was at evening church, and the hectic writing-master and she were quavering out of the same psalm-book.

' After such conduct on Rebecca's part,' Miss Crawley said enthusiastically, ' our family should do something. Find out who is the *objet*, Briggs. I'll set him up in a shop ; or order my portrait of him, you know ; or speak to my cousin, the bishop—and I'll *doter* Becky,* and we'll have a wedding, Briggs, and you shall make the breakfast, and be a bridesmaid.'

Briggs declared that it would be delightful, and vowed
that her dear Miss Crawley was always kind and generous,
and went up to Rebecca's bedroom to console her and
prattle about the offer, and the refusal, and the cause
thereof ; and to hint at the generous intentions of Miss
Crawley, and to find out who was the gentleman that had
the mastery of Miss Sharp's heart.

Rebecca was very kind, very affectionate and affected—
responded to Briggs's offers of tenderness with grateful
fervour—owned there was a secret attachment—a delicious
mystery—what a pity Miss Briggs had not remained half
a minute longer at the keyhole ! Rebecca might perhaps,
have told more : but five minutes after Miss Briggs's arrival
in Rebecca's apartment, Miss Crawley actually made her
appearance there—an unheard-of honour ;—her impatience
had overcome her ; she could not wait for the tardy operations of her ambassadress : so she came in person, and
ordered Briggs out of the room. And expressing her
approval of Rebecca's conduct, she asked particulars of
the interview, and the previous transactions which had
brought about the astonishing offer of Sir Pitt.

Rebecca said she had long had some notion of the partiality with which Sir Pitt honoured her (for he was in the
habit of making his feelings known in a very frank and
unreserved manner), but, not to mention private reasons
with which she would not for the present trouble Miss
Crawley, Sir Pitt's age, station, and habits were such as to
render a marriage quite impossible ; and could a woman
with any feeling of self-respect and any decency listen to
proposals at such a moment, when the funeral of the lover's
deceased wife had not actually taken place ?

' Nonsense, my dear, you would never have refused him
had there not been some one else in the case,' Miss Crawley
said, coming to her point at once. ' Tell me the private
reasons : what are the private reasons ? There *is* some
one ; who is it that has touched your heart ? '

Rebecca cast down her eyes, and owned there was. ' You
have guessed right, dear lady,' she said, with a sweet simple
faltering voice. ' You wonder at one so poor and friendless
having an attachment, don't you ? I have never heard
that poverty was any safeguard against it. I wish it
were.'

' My poor dear child,' cried Miss Crawley. who was always

quite ready to be sentimental, ' is our passion unrequited, then ? Are we pining in secret ? Tell me all, and let me console you.'

' I wish you could, dear madam,' Rebecca said in the same tearful tone. ' Indeed, indeed, I need it.' And she laid her head upon Miss Crawley's shoulder and wept there so naturally that the old lady, surprised into sympathy, embraced her with an almost maternal kindness, uttered many soothing protests of regard and affection for her, vowed that she loved her as a daughter, and would do everything in her power to serve her. ' And now who is it, my dear ? Is it that pretty Miss Sedley's brother ? You said something about an affair with him. I'll ask him here, my dear. And you shall have him : indeed you shall.'

' Don't ask me now,' Rebecca said. ' You shall know all soon. Indeed you shall. Dear kind Miss Crawley—dear friend, may I say so ? '

' That you may, my child,' the old lady replied, kissing her.

' I can't tell you now,' sobbed out Rebecca, ' I am very miserable. But oh ! love me always—promise you will love me always.' And in the midst of mutual tears—for the emotions of the younger woman had awakened the sympathies of the elder—this promise was solemnly given by Miss Crawley, who left her little protégée, blessing and admiring her as a dear, artless, tender-hearted, affectionate, incomprehensible creature.

And now she was left alone to think over the sudden and wonderful events of the day, and of what had been and what might have been. What think you were the private feelings of Miss, no (begging her pardon), of Mrs. Rebecca ? If, a few pages back, the present writer claimed the privilege of peeping into Miss Amelia Sedley's bedroom, and understanding with the omniscience of the novelist all the gentle pains and passions which were tossing upon that innocent pillow, why should he not declare himself to be Rebecca's confidant too, master of her secrets, and seal-keeper of that young woman's conscience ?

Well then, in the first place, Rebecca gave way to some very sincere and touching regrets that a piece of marvellous good fortune should have been so near her, and she actually obliged to decline it. In this natural emotion every properly regulated mind will certainly share. What good mother is there that would not commiserate a penniless spinster, who might have been my lady, and have shared four thousand a year ? What well-bred young person is there in all Vanity Fair, who will not feel for a hard-working, ingenious, meritorious girl, who gets such an honourable, advantageous, provoking offer, just at the very moment when it is out of her power to accept it ? I am sure our friend Becky's disappointment deserves and will command every sympathy.

I remember one night being in the Fair myself, at an evening party. I observed old Miss Toady there also present, single out for her special attentions and flattery little Mrs. Briefless, the barrister's wife, who is of a good family certainly, but, as we all know, is as poor as poor can be.

What, I asked in my own mind, can cause this obsequious-ness on the part of Miss Toady ; has Briefless got a county court, or has his wife had a fortune left her ? Miss Toady explained presently, with that simplicity which distin-guishes all her conduct. ' You know,' she said, ' Mrs. Briefless is grand-daughter of Sir John Redhand, who is so ill at Cheltenham that he can't last six months. Mrs. Briefless's papa succeeds ; so you see she *will* be a baronet's daughter.' And Toady asked Briefless and his wife to dinner the very next week.

If the mere chance of becoming a baronet's daughter can procure a lady such homage in the world, surely, surely we may respect the agonies of a young woman who has lost the opportunity of becoming a baronet's wife. Who would have dreamed of Lady Crawley dying so soon ? She was one of those sickly women that might have lasted these ten years—Rebecca thought to herself, in all the woes of repentance—and I might have been my lady ! I might have led that old man whither I would. I might have thanked Mrs. Bute for her patronage, and Mr. Pitt for his insufferable condescension. I would have had the town-house newly furnished and decorated. I would have had the handsomest carriage in London, and a box at the opera ; and I would have been presented next season. All this *might* have been ; and now—now all was doubt and mystery.

But Rebecca was a young lady of too much resolution

and energy of character to permit herself much useless and
unseemly sorrow for the irrevocable past; so, having
devoted only the proper portion of regret to it, she wisely
turned her whole attention towards the future, which was
now vastly more important to her. And she surveyed her
position, and its hopes, doubts, and chances.

In the first place, she was *married ;*—that was a great
fact. Sir Pitt knew it. She was not so much surprised
into the avowal, as induced to make it by a sudden calculation. It must have come some day : and why not now
as at a later period ? He who would have married her
himself must at least be silent with regard to her marriage.
How Miss Crawley would bear the news—was the great
question. Misgivings Rebecca had ; but she remembered
all Miss Crawley had said ; the old lady's avowed contempt
for birth ; her daring liberal opinions ; her general
romantic propensities ; her almost doting attachment to
her nephew, and her repeatedly-expressed fondness for
Rebecca herself. She is so fond of him, Rebecca thought,
that she will forgive him anything : she is so used to me
that I don't think she could be comfortable without me :
when the *éclaircissement* comes there will be a scene, and
hysterics, and a great quarrel, and then a great reconciliation. At all events, what use was there in delaying ? the
die was thrown, and now or to-morrow the issue must be
the same. And so, resolved that Miss Crawley should have
the news, the young person debated in her mind as to the
best means of conveying it to her ; and whether she should
face the storm that must come, or fly and avoid it until
its first fury was blown over. In this state of meditation
she wrote the following letter :—

DEAREST FRIEND,—The great crisis which we have debated about
so often is *come.* Half of my secret is known, and I have thought
and thought, until I am quite sure that now is the time to reveal
the whole of the mystery. Sir Pitt came to me this morning, and
made—what do you think ?—*a declaration in form.* Think of that !
Poor little me ! I might have been Lady Crawley. How pleased
Mrs. Bute would have been ; and *ma tante* if I had taken precedence
of her ! I might have been somebody's mamma, instead of—Oh,
I tremble, I tremble, when I think how soon we must tell all !—

Sir Pitt knows I am married, and not knowing to whom, is not very
much displeased as yet. *Ma tante* is *actually angry* that I should
have refused him. But she is all kindness and graciousness. She
condescends to say I would have made him a good wife ; and vows

that she will be a mother to your little Rebecca. She will be shaken when she first hears the news. But need we fear anything beyond a momentary anger ? I think not : *I am sure* not. She dotes upon you so (you naughty, good-for-nothing man), that she would pardon you *anything :* and, indeed, I believe, the next place in her heart is mine : and that she would be miserable without me. Dearest ! something *tells me* we shall conquer. You shall leave that odious regiment : quit gaming, racing, and *be a good boy ;* and we shall all live in Park Lane, and *ma tante* shall leave us all her money.

I shall try and walk to-morrow at 3 in the usual place. If Miss B. accompanies me, you must come to dinner, and bring an answer, and put it in the third volume of Porteus's *Sermons*. But, at all events, come to your own   R.

    To Miss Eliza Styles,
       At Mr. Barnet's, Saddler, Knightsbridge.

And I trust there is no reader of this little story who has not discernment enough to perceive that the Miss Eliza Styles (an old schoolfellow, Rebecca said, with whom she had resumed an active correspondence of late), and who used to fetch these letters from the saddler's, wore brass spurs, and large curling moustachios, and was indeed no other than Captain Rawdon Crawley.

CHAPTER XVI

THE LETTER ON THE PINCUSHION

 OW they were married is not of the slightest consequence to anybody. What is to hinder a captain who is a major, and a young lady who is of age, from purchasing a licence, and uniting themselves at any church in this town? Who needs to be told, that if a woman has a will, she will assuredly find a way?—My belief is, that one day, when Miss Sharp had gone to pass the forenoon with her dear friend Miss Amelia Sedley in Russell Square, a lady very like her might have been seen entering a church in the city, in company with a gentleman with dyed moustachios, who, after a quarter of an hour's interval, escorted her back to the hackney-coach in waiting, and that this was a quiet bridal party.

And who on earth, after the daily experience we have, can question the probability of a gentleman marrying anybody? How many of the wise and learned have married their cooks? Did not Lord Eldon himself, the most prudent of men, make a runaway match?* Were not Achilles and Ajax both in love with their servant-maids? And are we to expect a heavy dragoon with strong desires and small brains, who had never controlled a passion in his life, to become prudent all of a sudden, and to refuse to pay any price for an indulgence to which he had a mind? If people only made prudent marriages, what a stop to population there would be!

It seems to me, for my part, that Mr. Rawdon's marriage was one of the honestest actions which we shall have to record in any portion of that gentleman's biography which has to do with the present history. No one will ‸y it

is unmanly to be captivated by a woman, or, being captivated, to marry her; and the admiration, the delight,
the passion, the wonder, the unbounded confidence, and
frantic adoration with which, by degrees, this big warrior
got to regard the little Rebecca, were feelings which the
ladies at least will pronounce were not altogether dis-
creditable to him. When she sang, every note thrilled in
his dull soul, and tingled through his huge frame. When
she spoke, he brought all the force of his brains to listen
and wonder. If she was jocular, he used to revolve her
jokes in his mind, and explode over them half an hour
afterwards in the street, to the surprise of the groom in
the tilbury by his side, or the comrade riding with him in
Rotten Row. Her words were oracles to him, her smallest
actions marked by an infallible grace and wisdom. 'How
she sings—how she paints,' thought he. 'How she rode
that kicking mare at Queen's Crawley!' And he would
say to her in confidential moments, 'By Jove, Beck, you're
fit to be Commander-in-Chief, or Archbishop of Canterbury,
by Jove.' Is his case a rare one? and don't we see every
day in the world many an honest Hercules at the apron-
strings of Omphale, and great whiskered Samsons prostrate in Delilah's lap?

When, then, Becky told him that the great crisis was
near, and the time for action had arrived, Rawdon expressed himself as ready to act under her orders, as he would
be to charge with his troop at the command of his colonel.
There was no need for him to put his letter into the third
volume of Porteus. Rebecca easily found a means to get
rid of Briggs, her companion, and met her faithful friend in
'the usual place' on the next day. She had thought over
matters at night, and communicated to Rawdon the result of
her determinations. He agreed, of course, to everything;
was quite sure that it was all right: that what she proposed
was best; that Miss Crawley would infallibly relent, or
'come round', as he said, after a time. Had Rebecca's
resolutions been entirely different, he would have followed
them as implicitly. 'You have head enough for both of us,
Beck,' said he. 'You're sure to get us out of the scrape.
I never saw your equal, and I've met with some clippers in
my time too.' And with this simple confession of faith,
the love-stricken dragoon left her to execute his part of
the project which she had formed for the pair.

It consisted simply in the hiring of quiet lodgings at Brompton, or in the neighbourhood of the barracks, for Captain and Mrs. Crawley. For Rebecca had determined, and very prudently, we think, to fly. Rawdon was only too happy at her resolve ; he had been entreating her to take this measure any time for weeks past. He pranced off to engage the lodgings with all the impetuosity of love. He agreed to pay two guineas a week so readily, that the landlady regretted she had asked him so little. He ordered in a piano ; and half a nursery-house full of flowers : and a heap of good things. As for shawls, kid gloves, silk stockings, gold French watches, bracelets and perfumery, he sent them in with the profusion of blind love and un-bounded credit. And having relieved his mind by this out-pouring of generosity, he went and dined nervously at the club, waiting until the great moment of his life should come.

The occurrences of the previous day ; the admirable con-duct of Rebecca in refusing an offer so advantageous to her, the secret unhappiness preying upon her, the sweetness and silence with which she bore her affliction, made Miss Crawley much more tender than usual. An event of this nature, a marriage, or a refusal, or a proposal, thrills through a whole houseful of women, and sets all their hysterical sympathies at work. As an observer of human nature, I regularly frequent St. George's, Hanover Square, during the genteel marriage season ; and though I have never seen the bride-groom's male friends give way to tears, or the beadles and officiating clergy any way affected, yet it is not at all uncom-mon to see women who are not in the least concerned in the operations going on—old ladies who are long past marrying, stout middle-aged females with plenty of sons and daughters, let alone pretty young creatures in pink bonnets, who are on their promotion, and may naturally take an interest in the ceremony,—I say it is quite common to see the women present piping, sobbing, sniffling ; hiding their little faces in their little useless pocket-handkerchiefs ; and heaving, old and young, with emotion. When my friend, the fashion-able John Pimlico, married the lovely Lady Belgravia Green Parker, the excitement was so general, that even the little snuffy old pew-opener who let me into the seat, was in tears. And wherefore ? I inquired of my own soul : *she* was not going to be married.

Miss Crawley and Briggs in a word, after the affair of Sir Pitt, indulged in the utmost luxury of sentiment, and Rebecca became an object of the most tender interest to them. In her absence Miss Crawley solaced herself with the most sentimental of the novels in her library. Little Sharp, with her secret griefs, was the heroine of the day.

That night Rebecca sang more sweetly and talked more pleasantly than she had ever been heard to do in Park Lane. She twined herself round the heart of Miss Crawley. She spoke lightly and laughingly of Sir Pitt's proposal, ridiculed it as the foolish fancy of an old man ; and her eyes filled with tears, and Briggs's heart with unutterable pangs of defeat, as she said she desired no other lot than to remain for ever with her dear benefactress. ' My dear little creature,' the old lady said, ' I don't intend to let you stir for years, that you may depend upon it. As for going back to that odious brother of mine after what has passed, it is out of the question. Here you stay with me and Briggs. Briggs wants to go to see her relations very often. Briggs, you may go when you like. But as for you, my dear, you must stay and take care of the old woman.'

If Rawdon Crawley had been then and there present, instead of being at the club nervously drinking claret, the pair might have gone down on their knees before the old spinster, avowed all, and been forgiven in a twinkling. But that good chance was denied to the young couple, doubtless in order that this story might be written, in which numbers of their wonderful adventures are narrated—adventures which could never have occurred to them if they had been housed and sheltered under the comfortable uninteresting forgiveness of Miss Crawley.

Under Mrs. Firkin's orders, in the Park Lane establishment, was a young woman from Hampshire, whose business it was, among other duties, to knock at Miss Sharp's door with that jug of hot water, which Firkin would rather have perished than have presented to the intruder. This girl, bred on the family estate, had a brother in Captain Crawley's troop, and if the truth were known, I dare say it would come out that she was aware of certain arrangements, which have a great deal to do with this history. At any rate she purchased a yellow shawl, a pair of green boots, and a light blue hat with a red feather, with three guineas which

THE NOTE ON THE PINCUSHION

Rebecca gave her, and as little Sharp was by no means too liberal with her money, no doubt it was for services rendered that Betty Martin was so bribed.

On the second day after Sir Pitt Crawley's offer to Miss Sharp, the sun rose as usual, and at the usual hour Betty Martin, the upstairs maid, knocked at the door of the governess's bed-chamber.

No answer was returned, and she knocked again. Silence was still uninterrupted; and Betty, with the hot water, opened the door and entered the chamber.

The little white dimity bed was as smooth and trim as on the day previous, when Betty's own hands had helped to make it. Two little trunks were corded in one end of the room; and on the table before the window—on the pincushion—the great fat pincushion lined with pink inside, and twilled like a lady's nightcap—lay a letter. It had been reposing there probably all night.

Betty advanced towards it on tiptoe, as if she were afraid to awake it—looked at it, and round the room, with an air of great wonder and satisfaction; took up the letter, and grinned intensely as she turned it round and over, and finally carried it in to Miss Briggs's room below.

How could Betty tell that the letter was for Miss Briggs, I should like to know? All the schooling Betty had was at Mrs. Bute Crawley's Sunday School, and she could no more read writing than Hebrew.

'La, Miss Briggs,' the girl exclaimed, 'oh, miss, something must have happened—there's nobody in Miss Sharp's room; the bed ain't been slep in, and she've run away, and left this letter for you, miss.'

'What!' cries Briggs, dropping her comb, the thin wisp of faded hair falling over her shoulders; 'an elopement! Miss Sharp a fugitive! What, what is this?' and she eagerly broke the neat seal, and, as they say, devoured the contents' of the letter addressed to her.

DEAR MISS BRIGGS (the refugee wrote), the kindest heart in the world as yours is, will pity and sympathize with me and excuse me. With tears, and prayers, and blessings, I leave the home where the poor orphan has ever met with kindness and affection. Claims even superior to those of my benefactress call me hence. I go to my duty — to my *husband*. Yes, I am married. My husband *commands* me to seek the *humble home* which we call ours. Dearest Miss Briggs, break the news as your delicate sympathy will know how to do it-

to my dear, my beloved friend and benefactress. Tell her, ere I went,
I shed tears on her dear pillow—that pillow that I have so often
soothed in sickness—that I long *again* to watch—Oh, with what
joy shall I return to dear Park Lane! How I tremble for the
answer which is to *seal my fate!* When Sir Pitt deigned to offer
me his hand, an honour of which my beloved Miss Crawley said I
was *deserving* (my blessings go with her for judging the poor orphan
worthy to be *her sister!*), I told Sir Pitt that I was *already a wife.*
Even he forgave me. But my courage failed me, when I should
have told him all—that I could not be his wife, for I *was his daughter!*
I am wedded to the best and most generous of men—Miss Crawley's
Rawdon is *my* Rawdon. At his *command* I open my lips, and
follow him to our humble home, as I would *through the world.* Oh,
my excellent and kind friend, intercede with my Rawdon's beloved
aunt for him and the poor girl to whom all *his noble race* have
shown such *unparalleled affection.* Ask Miss Crawley to receive *her
children.* I can say no more, but blessings, blessings on all in the
dear house I leave, prays

Your affectionate and *grateful,*
REBECCA CRAWLEY.

Midnight.

Just as Briggs had finished reading this affecting and
interesting document which reinstated her in her position
as first confidante of Miss Crawley, Mrs. Firkin entered the
room. 'Here's Mrs. Bute Crawley just arrived by the mail
from Hampshire, and wants some tea : will you come down
and make breakfast, miss ? '

And to the surprise of Firkin, clasping her dressing-gown
around her, the wisp of hair floating dishevelled behind her,
the little curl-papers still sticking in bunches round her
forehead, Briggs sailed down to Mrs. Bute with the letter in
her hand containing the wonderful news.

'Oh, Mrs. Firkin,' gasped Betty, 'sech a business. Miss
Sharp have a gone and run away with the capting, and
they're off to Gretny Green ! ' We would devote a chapter
to describe the emotions of Mrs. Firkin, did not the passions
of her mistresses occupy our genteeler muse.

When Mrs. Bute Crawley, numbed with midnight travelling, and warming herself at the newly-crackling parlour
fire, heard from Miss Briggs the intelligence of the clandestine
marriage, she declared it was quite providential that she
should have arrived at such a time to assist poor dear Miss
Crawley in supporting the shock—that Rebecca was an art
ful little hussy of whom she had always had her suspicions ;

and that as for Rawdon Crawley, she never could account for his aunt's infatuation regarding him, and had long considered him a profligate, lost, and abandoned being. And this awful conduct, Mrs. Bute said, will have at least *this* good effect, it will open poor dear Miss Crawley's eyes to the real character of this wicked man. Then Mrs. Bute had a comfortable hot toast and tea ; and as there was a vacant room in the house now, there was no need for her to remain at the 'Gloster'* Coffee-house where the Portsmouth mail had set her down, and whence she ordered Mr. Bowls's aide de camp, the footman, to bring away her trunks.

Miss Crawley, be it known, did not leave her room until near noon—taking chocolate in bed in the morning, while Becky Sharp read the *Morning Post* to her, or otherwise amusing herself or dawdling. The conspirators below agreed that they would spare the dear lady's feelings until she appeared in her drawing-room : meanwhile it was announced to her, that Mrs. Bute Crawley had come up from Hampshire by the mail, was staying at the 'Gloster ', sent her love to Miss Crawley, and asked for breakfast with Miss Briggs. The arrival of Mrs. Bute, which would not have caused any extreme delight at another period, was hailed with pleasure now ; Miss Crawley being pleased at the notion of a gossip with her sister-in-law regarding the late Lady Crawley, the funeral arrangements pending, and Sir Pitt's abrupt proposals to Rebecca.

It was not until the old lady was fairly ensconced in her usual arm-chair in the drawing-room, and the preliminary embraces and inquiries had taken place between the ladies, that the conspirators thought it advisable to submit her to the operation. Who has not admired the artifices and delicate approaches with which women ' prepare ' their friends for bad news ? Miss Crawley's two friends made such an apparatus of mystery before they broke the intelligence to her, that they worked her up to the necessary degree of doubt and alarm.

' And she refused Sir Pitt, my dear, dear Miss Crawley, prepare yourself for it,' Mrs. Bute said, ' because—because she couldn't help herself.'

' Of course there was a reason,' Miss Crawley answered. ' She liked somebody else. I told Briggs so yesterday.'

' *Likes* somebody else !' Briggs gasped. ' Oh, my dear friend, she is married already.'

'Married already,' Mrs. Bute chimed in ; and both sat
with clasped hands looking from each other at their victim.

'Send her to me, the instant she comes in.   The little
sly wretch : how dared she not tell me ? ' cried out Miss
Crawley.

'She won't come in soon.   Prepare yourself, dear friend—
she's gone out for a long time—she's—she's gone altogether.'

'Gracious goodness, and who's to make my chocolate ?
Send for her and have her back ; I desire that she come
back,' the old lady said.

'She decamped last night, ma'am,' cried Mrs. Bute.

'She left a letter for me,' Briggs exclaimed.   'She's
married to——'

'Prepare her, for heaven's sake.   Don't torture her, my
dear Miss Briggs.'

'She's married to whom ? ' cries the spinster in a nervous
fury.

'To—to a relation of——'

'She refused Sir Pitt,' cried the victim.   'Speak at once.
Don't drive me mad.'

'Oh, ma'am—prepare her, Miss Briggs—she's married to
Rawdon Crawley.'

'Rawdon married—Rebecca—governess—nobod—Get
out of my house, you fool, you idiot—you stupid old Briggs
—how dare you ? You're in the plot—you made him marry,
thinking that I'd leave my money from him—you did,
Martha,' the poor old lady screamed in hysteric sentences.

'I, ma'am, ask a member of this family to marry a
drawing-master's daughter ? '

'Her mother was a Montmorency,' cried out the old lady,
pulling at the bell with all her might.

'Her mother was an opera-girl, and she has been on the
stage or worse herself,' said Mrs. Bute.

Miss Crawley gave a final scream, and fell back in a faint.
They were forced to take her back to the room which she
had just quitted.   One fit of hysterics succeeded another.
The doctor was sent for—the apothecary arrived.   Mrs.
Bute took up the post of nurse by her bedside.   'Her
relations ought to be round about her,' that amiable woman
said.

She had scarcely been carried up to her room, when a new
person arrived to whom it was also necessary to break the
news.   This was Sir Pitt.   'Where's Becky ? ' he said,

coming in. ' Where's her traps ? She's coming with me to Queen's Crawley.'

' Have you not heard the astonishing intelligence regarding her surreptitious union ? ' Briggs asked.

' What's that to me ? ' Sir Pitt asked. ' I know she's married. That makes no odds. Tell her to come down at once, and not keep me.'

' Are you not aware, sir,' Miss Briggs asked, ' that she has left our roof, to the dismay of Miss Crawley, who is nearly killed by the intelligence of Captain Rawdon's union with her ? '

When Sir Pitt Crawley heard that Rebecca was married to his son, he broke out into a fury of language, which it would do no good to repeat in this place, as indeed it sent poor Briggs shuddering out of the room ; and with her we will shut the door upon the figure of the frenzied old man, wild with hatred and insane with baffled desire.

One day after he went to Queen's Crawley, he burst like a madman into the room she had used when there—dashed open her boxes with his foot, and flung about her papers, clothes, and other relics. Miss Horrocks, the butler's daughter, took some of them. The children dressed themselves and acted plays in the others. It was but a few days after the poor mother had gone to her lonely burying-place ; and was laid, unwept and disregarded, in a vault full of strangers.

' Suppose the old lady doesn't come to,' Rawdon said to his little wife, as they sat together in the snug little Brompton lodgings. She had been trying the new piano all the morning. The new gloves fitted her to a nicety ; the new shawls became her wonderfully ; the new rings glittered on her little hands, and the new watch ticked at her waist ; ' suppose she don't come round, eh, Becky ? '

' *I'll* make your fortune,' she said ; and Delilah patted Samson's cheek.

' You can do anything,' he said, kissing the little hand. ' By Jove, you can ; and we'll drive down to the ' Star and Garter '; and dine, by Jove.'

CHAPTER XVII

HOW CAPTAIN DOBBIN BOUGHT A PIANO

 F there is any exhibition in all Vanity
Fair which Satire and Sentiment can
visit arm-in-arm together; where you
light on the strangest contrasts laugh-
able and tearful: where you may be
gentle and pathetic, or savage and
cynical with perfect propriety: it is
at one of those public assemblies, a
crowd of which are advertised every
day in the last page of the *Times* newspaper, and over which the late Mr.
George Robins*used to preside with so
much dignity. There are very few London people, as I
fancy, who have not attended at these meetings, and all
with a taste for moralizing must have thought, with a
sensation and interest not a little startling and queer, of
the day when their turn shall come too, and Mr. Hammerdown will sell by the orders of Diogenes's assignees, or will
be instructed by the executors, to offer to public competition, the library, furniture, plate, wardrobe, and choice
cellar of wines of Epicurus deceased.

Even with the most selfish disposition, the Vanity-
Fairian, as he witnesses this sordid part of the obsequies of
a departed friend, can't but feel some sympathies and regret.
My Lord Dives's remains are in the family vault: the
statuaries are cutting an inscription veraciously commemo-
rating his virtues, and the sorrows of his heir, who is disposing of his goods. What guest at Dives's table can pass
the familiar house without a sigh ?—the familiar house of
which the lights used to shine so cheerfully at seven o'clock,
of which the hall-doors opened so readily, of which the
obsequious servants, as you passed up the comfortable
stair, sounded your name from landing to landing, until
it reached the apartment where jolly old Dives welcomed
his friends ! What a number of them he had; and what
a noble way of entertaining them. How witty people used
to be here, who were morose when they got out of the door ;

and how courteous and friendly men who slandered and
hated each other everywhere else ! He was pompous, but
with such a cook what would one not swallow ? he was
rather dull, perhaps, but would not such wine make any
conversation pleasant ? We must get some of his burgundy
at any price, the mourners cry at his club. ' I got this box
at old Dives's sale,' Pincher says, handing it round, ' one
of Louis XV's mistresses—pretty thing, is it not—sweet
miniature,' and they talked of the way in which young
Dives is dissipating his fortune.

How changed the house is, though ! The front is patched
over with bills, setting forth the particulars of the furniture
in staring capitals. They have hung a shred of carpet out
of an upstairs window—a half-dozen of porters are lounging
on the dirty steps—the hall swarms with dingy guests of
oriental countenance, who thrust printed cards into your
hand and offer to bid. Old women and amateurs have
invaded the upper apartments, pinching the bed-curtains,
poking into the feathers, shampooing*the mattresses, and
clapping the wardrobe drawers to and fro. Enterprising
young housekeepers are measuring the looking-glasses and
hangings to see if they will suit the new *ménage* (Snob
will brag for years that he has purchased this or that at
Dives's sale), and Mr. Hammerdown is sitting on the great
mahogany dining-tables, in the dining-room below, waving
the ivory hammer, and employing all the artifices of eloquence, enthusiasm, entreaty, reason, despair ; shouting
to his people ; satirizing Mr. Davids for his sluggishness ;
inspiriting Mrs. Moss into action ; imploring, commanding,
bellowing, until down comes the hammer like fate, and we
pass to the next lot. O Dives, who would ever have thought,
as we sat round the broad table sparkling with plate and
spotless linen, to have seen such a dish at the head of it as
that roaring auctioneer ?

It was rather late in the sale. The excellent drawing-
room furniture by the best makers ; the rare and famous
wines selected, regardless of cost, and with the well-known
taste of the purchaser ; the rich and complete set of family
plate had been sold on the previous days. Certain of the
best wines (which all had a great character among amateurs
in the neighbourhood) had been purchased for his master,
who knew them very well, by the butler of our friend John
Osborne, Esquire, of Russell Square. A small portion of

the most useful articles of the plate had been bought by
some young stockbrokers from the City. And now the
public being invited to the purchase of minor objects, it
happened that the orator on the table was expatiating on
the merits of a picture, which he sought to recommend to
his audience : it was by no means so select or numerous
a company as had attended the previous days of the auction.

'No. 369,' roared Mr. Hammerdown. 'Portrait of a
gentleman on an elephant. Who'll bid for the gentleman on
the elephant ? Lift up the picture, Blowman, and let the
company examine this lot.' A long, pale, military-looking
gentleman, seated demurely at the mahogany table, could
not help grinning as this valuable lot was shown by Mr.
Blowman. 'Turn the elephant to the captain, Blowman.
What shall we say, sir, for the elephant ? ' but the captain,
blushing in a very hurried and discomfited manner, turned
away his head, and the auctioneer respected his discomposure.

'Shall we say twenty guineas for this work of art ?—
fifteen, five, name your own price. The gentleman without
the elephant is worth five pound.'

'I wonder it ain't come down with him,' said a professional
wag, 'he's anyhow a precious big one ; ' at which (for the
elephant-rider was represented as of a very stout figure)
there was a general giggle in the room.

'Don't be trying to deprecate the value of the lot, Mr.
Moss,' Mr. Hammerdown said ; 'let the company examine
it as a work of art—the attitude of the gallant animal quite
according to natur' ; the gentleman in a nankeen jacket, his

gun in his hand, is going to the
chase ; in the distance a banyhann-
tree and a pagody, most likely re-
semblances of some interesting spot
in our famous Eastern possessions.
How much for this lot ? Come, gentlemen, don't keep me here all day.'

Some one bid five shillings, at
which the military gentleman looked
towards the quarter from which this
splendid offer had come, and there
saw another officer with a young lady
on his arm, who both appeared to
be highly amused with the scene, and to whom, finally, this
lot was knocked down for half a guinea. He at the table

AN ELEPHANT FOR SALE

looked more surprised and discomposed than ever when
he spied this pair, and his head sank into his military
collar, and he turned his back upon them, so as to avoid
them altogether.

Of all the other articles which Mr. Hammerdown had
the honour to offer for public competition that day it
is not our purpose to make mention, save of one only,
a little square piano, which came down from the upper
regions of the house (the state grand piano having been
disposed of previously) ; this the young lady tried with a
rapid and skilful hand (making the officer blush and start
again), and for it, when its turn came, her agent began to
bid.

But there was an opposition here. The Hebrew aide de
camp in the service of the officer at the table bid against the
Hebrew gentleman employed by the elephant purchasers,
and a brisk battle ensued over this little piano, the com-
batants being greatly encouraged by Mr. Hammerdown.

At last, when the competition had been prolonged for
some time, the elephant captain and lady desisted from
the race ; and the hammer coming down, the auctioneer
said :—' Mr. Lewis, twenty-five,' and Mr. Lewis's chief thus
became the proprietor of the little square piano. Having
effected the purchase, he sat up as if he was greatly relieved,
and the unsuccessful competitors catching a glimpse of him
at this moment, the lady said to her friend,

' Why, Rawdon, it's Captain Dobbin.'

I suppose Becky was discontented with the new piano
her husband had hired for her, or perhaps the proprietors of
that instrument had fetched it away, declining farther
credit, or perhaps she had a particular attachment for the
one which she had first tried to purchase, recollecting it in
old days, when she used to play upon it, in the little sitting-
room of our dear Amelia Sedley.

The sale was at the old house in Russell Square, where
we passed some evenings together at the beginning of this
story. Good old John Sedley was a ruined man. His
name had been proclaimed as a defaulter on the Stock
Exchange, and his bankruptcy and commercial extermination had followed. Mr. Osborne's butler came to buy
some of the famous port wine to transfer to the cellars over
the way. As for one dozen well-manufactured silver spoons

and forks at per oz., and one dozen dessert ditto ditto, there
were three young stockbrokers (Messrs. Dale, Spiggot, and
Dale, of Threadneedle Street, indeed), who, having had
dealings with the old man, and kindnesses from him in days
when he was kind to everybody with whom he dealt, sent
this little spar out of the wreck with their love to good
Mrs. Sedley ; and with respect to the piano, as it had been
Amelia's, and as she might miss it and want one now, and
as Captain William Dobbin could no more play upon it than
he could dance on the tight-rope, it is probable that he did
not purchase the instrument for his own use.

In a word, it arrived that evening, at a wonderful small
cottage in a street leading from the Fulham Road—one of
those streets which have the finest romantic names—(this
was called St. Adelaide Villas,* Anna-Maria Road, West),
where the houses look like baby-houses ; where the people,
looking out of the first-floor windows, must infallibly, as
you think, sit with their feet in the parlours ; where the
shrubs in the little gardens in front, bloom with a perennial
display of little children's pinafores, little red socks, caps,
&c. (polyandria polygynia)*; whence you hear the sound of
jingling spinets and women singing ; where little porter
pots hang on the railings sunning themselves ; whither of
evenings you see city clerks padding wearily : here it was
that Mr. Clapp, the clerk of Mr. Sedley, had his domicile, and
in this asylum the good old gentleman hid his head with
his wife and daughter when the crash came.

Jos Sedley had acted as a man of his disposition would,
when the announcement of the family-misfortune reached
him. He did not come to London, but he wrote to his
mother to draw upon his agents for whatever money was
wanted, so that his kind broken-spirited old parents had no
present poverty to fear. This done, Jos went on at the
boarding-house at Cheltenham pretty much as before. He
drove his curricle ; he drank his claret ; he played his
rubber ; he told his Indian stories, and the Irish widow
consoled and flattered him as usual. His present of money,
needful as it was, made little impression on his parents ; and
I have heard Amelia say, that the first day on which she
saw her father lift up his head after the failure, was on the
receipt of the packet of forks and spoons with the young
stockbrokers' love, over which he burst out crying like a
child, being greatly more affected than even his wife, to

whom the present was addressed.   Edward Dale, the
junior of the house, who purchased the spoons for the firm,
was, in fact, very sweet upon Amelia, and offered for her
in spite of all.   He married Miss Louisa Cutts (daughter of
Higham and Cutts, the eminent corn-factors), with a handsome fortune in 1820 ; and is now living in splendour, and
with a numerous family, at his elegant villa, Muswell Hill.
But we must not let the recollections of this good fellow
cause us to diverge from the principal history.

I hope the reader has much too good an opinion of Captain
and Mrs. Crawley to suppose that they ever would have
dreamed of paying a visit to so remote a district as Bloomsbury, if they thought the family whom they proposed to
honour with a visit were not merely out of fashion, but out
of money, and could be serviceable to them in no possible
manner.   Rebecca was entirely surprised at the sight of
the comfortable old house where she had met with no small
kindness, ransacked by brokers and bargainers, and its
quiet family treasures given up to public desecration and
plunder.   A month after her flight, she had bethought her
of Amelia, and Rawdon, with a horse laugh, had expressed
a perfect willingness to see young George Osborne again.
' He's a very agreeable acquaintance, Beck,' the wag added.
' I'd like to sell him another horse, Beck.   I'd like to play
a few more games at billiards with him.   He'd be what
I call *useful* just now, Mrs. C.—ha, ha !' by which sort of
speech it is not to be supposed that Rawdon Crawley had
a deliberate desire to cheat Mr. Osborne at play, but only
wished to take that fair advantage of him which almost
every sporting gentleman in Vanity Fair considers to be his
due from his neighbour.
The old aunt was long in ' coming-to'.   A month had
elapsed.   Rawdon was denied the door by Mr. Bowls ; his
servants could not get a lodgement in the house at Park
Lane ; his letters were sent back unopened.   Miss Crawley
never stirred out—she was unwell—and Mrs. Bute remained
still and never left her.   Crawley and his wife both of them
augured evil from the continued presence of Mrs. Bute.
' Gad, I begin to perceive now why she was always bringing us together at Queen's Crawley,' Rawdon said.
' What an artful little woman !' ejaculated Rebecca.
' Well, *I* don't regret it, if you don't,' the captain cried,

still in an amorous rapture with his wife, who rewarded
him with a kiss by way of reply, and was indeed not a little
gratified by the generous confidence of her husband.

' If he had but a little more brains,' she thought to herself,
' I might make something of him ; ' but she never let him
perceive the opinion she had of him ; listened with indefatigable complacency to his stories of the stable and the
mess ; laughed at all his jokes ; felt the greatest interest in
Jack Spatterdash, whose cab-horse had come down, and
Bob Martingale, who had been taken up in a gambling-
house, and Tom Cinqbars, who was going to ride the steeple-
chase.   When he came home she was alert and happy :
when he went out she pressed him to go : when he stayed
at home, she played and sang for him, made him good drinks,
superintended his dinner, warmed his slippers, and steeped
his soul in comfort.   The best of women (I have heard my
grandmother say) are hypocrites.   We don't know how
much they hide from us : how watchful they are when they
seem most artless and confidential : how often those frank
smiles which they wear so easily, are traps to cajole or elude
or disarm—I don't mean in your mere coquettes, but your
domestic models, and paragons of female virtue.   Who has
not seen a woman hide the dullness of a stupid husband, or
coax the fury of a savage one ?   We accept this amiable
slavishness, and praise a woman for it : we call this pretty
treachery truth.   A good housewife is of necessity a humbug; and Cornelia's husband was hoodwinked, as Potiphar*
was—only in a different way.

By these attentions that veteran rake, Rawdon Crawley,
found himself converted into a very happy and submissive
married man.   His former haunts knew him not.   They
asked about him once or twice at his clubs, but did not miss
him much : in those booths of Vanity Fair people seldom
do miss each other.   His secluded wife ever smiling and
cheerful, his little comfortable lodgings, snug meals, and
homely evenings, had all the charms of novelty and secrecy.
The marriage was not yet declared to the world, or published
in the *Morning Post*.   All his creditors would have come
rushing on him in a body, had they known that he was united
to a woman without fortune.   ' My relations won't cry fie
upon me,' Becky said, with rather a bitter laugh ; and she
was quite contented to wait until the old aunt should be
reconciled, before she claimed her place in society.   So she

lived at Brompton, and meanwhile saw no one, or only those
few of her husband's male companions who were admitted
into her little dining-room. These were all charmed with
her. The little dinners, the laughing and chatting, the
music afterwards, delighted all who participated in these
enjoyments. Major Martingale never thought about asking
to see the marriage licence. Captain Cinqbars was perfectly
enchanted with her skill in making punch. And young
Lieutenant Spatterdash (who was fond of piquet, and whom
Crawley would often invite) was evidently and quickly
smitten by Mrs. Crawley; but her own circumspection and
modesty never forsook her for a moment, and Crawley's
reputation as a fire-eating and jealous warrior, was a further
and complete defence to his little wife.

There are gentlemen of very good blood and fashion in this
city who never have entered a lady's drawing-room; so
that though Rawdon Crawley's marriage might be talked
about in his county, where, of course, Mrs. Bute had spread
the news, in London it was doubted, or not heeded, or not
talked about at all. He lived comfortably on credit. He
had a large capital of debts, which, laid out judiciously, will
carry a man along for many years, and on which certain
men about town contrive to live a hundred times better
than even men with ready money can do. Indeed who is
there that walks London streets, but can point out a half-
dozen of men riding by him splendidly, while he is on foot,
courted by fashion, bowed into their carriages by tradesmen,
denying themselves nothing, and living on who knows what?
We see Jack Thriftless prancing in the Park, or darting in his
brougham down Pall Mall: we eat his dinners served on his
miraculous plate. 'How did this begin,' we say, 'or where will
it end?' 'My dear fellow,' I heard Jack once say, 'I owe
money in every capital in Europe.' The end must come
some day, but in the mean time Jack thrives as much as
ever; people are glad enough to shake him by the hand,
ignore the little dark stories that are whispered every now
and then against him, and pronounce him a good-natured,
jovial, reckless fellow.

Truth obliges us to confess that Rebecca had married
a gentleman of this order. Everything was plentiful in his
house but ready money, of which their *ménage* pretty early
felt the want; and reading the *Gazette* one day, and
coming upon the announcement of ' Lieutenant G. Osborne

to be captain by purchase, vice Smith, who exchanges,'
Rawdon uttered that sentiment regarding Amelia's lover,
which ended in the visit to Russell Square.

When Rawdon and his wife wished to communicate with
Captain Dobbin at the sale, and to know particulars of the
catastrophe which had befallen Rebecca's old acquaintances,
the captain had vanished; and such information as they
got was from a stray porter or broker at the auction.

' Look at them with their hooked beaks,' Becky said,
getting into the buggy, her picture under her arm in great
glee.   ' They're like vultures after a battle.'

' Don't know.   Never was in action, my dear.   Ask
Martingale; he was in Spain, aide de camp to General
Blazes.'

' He was a very kind old man, Mr. Sedley,' Rebecca said;
' I'm really sorry he's gone wrong.'

' Oh, stockbrokers—bankrupts—used to it, you know.'
Rawdon replied, cutting a fly off the horse's ear.

' I wish we could have afforded some of the plate, Rawdon,'
the wife continued sentimentally.   ' Five-and-twenty
guineas was monstrously dear for that little piano.   We
chose it at Broadwood's* for Amelia, when she came from
school.   It only cost five-and-thirty then.'

' What-d'ye-call-'em—" Osborne "—will cry off now, I
suppose, since the family is smashed.   How cut up your
pretty little friend will be ; hey, Becky ? '

' I dare say she'll recover it,' Becky said, with a smile—
and they drove on and talked about something else.

CHAPTER XVIII

WHO PLAYED ON THE PIANO CAPTAIN DOBBIN BOUGHT?

UR surprised story now finds itself for a moment among very famous events and personages, and hanging on to the skirts of history. When the eagles of Napoleon Bonaparte, the Corsican upstart, were flying from Provence, where they had perched after a brief sojourn in Elba, and from steeple to steeple until they reached the towers of Notre Dame, I wonder whether the Imperial birds had any eye for a little corner of the parish of Bloomsbury, London, which you might have thought so quiet, that even the whirring and flapping of those mighty wings would pass unobserved there?

'Napoleon has landed at Cannes.' Such news might create a panic at Vienna, and cause Russia to drop his cards, and take Prussia into a corner, and Talleyrand and Metternich to wag their heads together, while Prince Hardenberg, and even the present Marquis of Londonderry,* were puzzled; but how was this intelligence to affect a young lady in Russell Square, before whose door the watchman sang the hours when she was asleep: who, if she strolled in the square, was guarded there by the railings and the beadle: who, if she walked ever so short a distance to buy a ribbon in Southampton Row, was followed by black Sambo with an enormous cane: who was always cared for, dressed, put to bed, and watched over by ever so many guardian angels, with and without wages. *Bon Dieu*, I say, is it not hard that the fateful rush of the great Imperial struggle can't take place without affecting a poor little harmless girl of eighteen, who is occupied in billing and cooing, or working muslin collars in Russell Square? You, too, kindly, homely flower!—is the great roaring war tempest coming to sweep you down, here,

although cowering under the shelter of Holborn? Yes;
Napoleon is flinging his last stake, and poor little Emmy
Sedley's happiness forms, somehow, part of it.

In the first place, her father's fortune was swept down
with that fatal news. All his speculations had of late gone
wrong with the luckless old gentleman. Ventures had
failed; merchants had broken; funds had risen when he
calculated they would fall. What need to particularize?
If success is rare and slow, everybody knows how quick
and easy ruin is. Old Sedley had kept his own sad counsel.
Everything seemed to go on as usual in the quiet, opulent
house; the good-natured mistress pursuing, quite unsuspiciously, her bustling idleness, and daily easy avocations; the daughter absorbed still in one selfish, tender
thought, and quite regardless of all the world besides,
when that final crash came, under which the worthy family
fell.

One night Mrs. Sedley was writing cards for a party; the
Osbornes had given one, and she must not be behindhand;
John Sedley, who had come home very late from the City,
sat silent at the chimney side, while his wife was prattling
to him; Emmy had gone up to her room ailing and low-
spirited. 'She's not happy,' the mother went on. 'George
Osborne neglects her. I've no patience with the airs of
those people. The girls have not been in the house these
three weeks; and George has been twice in town without
coming. Edward Dale saw him at the opera. Edward
would marry her, I'm sure: and there's Captain Dobbin
who, I think, would—only I hate all army men. Such
a dandy as George has become. With his military airs,
indeed! We must show some folks that we're as good as
they. Only give Edward Dale any encouragement, and
you'll see. We must have a party, Mr. S. Why don't
you speak, John? Shall I say Tuesday fortnight? Why
don't you answer? Good God, John, what has happened?'

John Sedley sprang up out of his chair to meet his wife,
who ran to him. He seized her in his arms, and said, with
a hasty voice, 'We're ruined, Mary. We've got the world
to begin over again, dear. It's best that you should know
all, and at once.' As he spoke, he trembled in every limb,
and almost fell. He thought the news would have overpowered his wife—his wife, to whom he had never said
a hard word. But it was he that was the most moved,

sudden as the shock was to her.   When he sank back into
his seat, it was the wife that took the office of consoler.
She took his trembling hand, and kissed it, and put it
round her neck : she called him her John—her dear John
—her old man—her kind old man; she poured out a hundred
words of incoherent love and tenderness ; her faithful voice
and simple caresses wrought this sad heart up to an inexpressible delight and anguish, and cheered and solaced
his overburdened soul.

Only once in the course of the long night as they sat
together, and poor Sedley opened his pent-up soul, and told
the story of his losses and embarrassments—the treason
of some of his oldest friends, the manly kindness of some,
from whom he never could have expected it—in a general
confession—only once did the faithful wife give way to
emotion.

' My God, my God, it will break Emmy's heart,' she said.

The father had forgotten the poor girl.   She was lying,
awake and unhappy, overhead.   In the midst of friends,
home, and kind parents, she was alone.   To how many
people can any one tell all ?   Who will be open where there
is no sympathy, or has call to speak to those who never can
understand ?   Our gentle Amelia was thus solitary.   She
had no confidante, so to speak, ever since she had anything
to confide.   She could not tell the old mother her doubts
and cares ; the would-be sisters seemed every day more
strange to her.   And she had misgivings and fears which
she dared not acknowledge to herself, though she was
always secretly brooding over them.

Her heart tried to persist in asserting that George Osborne
was worthy and faithful to her, though she knew otherwise.
How many a thing had she said, and got no echo from him.
How many suspicions of selfishness and indifference had she
to encounter and obstinately overcome.   To whom could
the poor little martyr tell these daily struggles and tortures ?
Her hero himself only half understood her.   She did not
dare to own that the man she loved was her inferior ; or
to feel that she had given her heart away too soon.   Given
once, the pure bashful maiden was too modest, too tender,
too trustful, too weak, too much woman to recall it.   We
are Turks with the affections of our women ; and have
made them subscribe to our doctrine too.   We let their
bodies go abroad liberally enough, with smiles and ringlets

and pink bonnets to disguise them instead of veils and
yakmaks. But their souls must be seen by only one man,
and they obey not unwillingly, and consent to remain at
home as our slaves—ministering to us and doing drudgery
for us.

So imprisoned and tortured was this gentle little heart,
when in the month of March, Anno Domini 1815, Napoleon
landed at Cannes, and Louis XVIII fled, and all Europe
was in alarm, and the funds fell, and old John Sedley
was ruined.

We are not going to follow the worthy old stockbroker
through those last pangs and agonies of ruin through which
he passed before his commercial demise befell. They
declared him at the Stock Exchange ; he was absent from
his house of business : his bills were protested : his act of
bankruptcy formal. The house and furniture of Russell
Square were seized and sold up, and he and his family
were thrust away, as we have seen, to hide their heads where
they might.

John Sedley had not the heart to review the domestic
establishment who have appeared now and anon in our
pages, and of whom he was now forced by poverty to take
leave. The wages of those worthy people were discharged
with that punctuality which men frequently show who
only owe in great sums—they were sorry to leave good
places—but they did not break their hearts at parting from
their adored master and mistress. Amelia's maid was profuse in condolences, but went off quite resigned to better
herself in a genteeler quarter of the town. Black Sambo,
with the infatuation of his profession, determined on setting
up a public-house. Honest old Mrs. Blenkinsop indeed,
who had seen the birth of Jos and Amelia, and the wooing
of John Sedley and his wife, was for staying by them without
wages, having amassed a considerable sum in their service :
and she accompanied the fallen people into their new and
humble place of refuge, where she tended them and grumbled
against them for a while.

Of all Sedley's opponents in his debates with his creditors
which now ensued, and harassed the feelings of the humiliated
old gentleman so severely, that in six weeks he oldened
more than he had done for fifteen years before—the most
determined and obstinate seemed to be John Osborne,

his old friend and neighbour—John Osborne, whom he had set up in life—who was under a hundred obligations to him—and whose son was to marry Sedley's daughter. Any one of these circumstances would account for the bitterness of Osborne's opposition.

When one man has been under very remarkable obligations to another, with whom he subsequently quarrels, a common sense of decency, as it were, makes of the former a much severer enemy than a mere stranger would be. To account for your own hard-heartedness and ingratitude in such a case, you are bound to prove the other party's crime. It is not that you are selfish, brutal, and angry at the failure of a speculation—no, no—it is that your partner has led you into it by the basest treachery and with the most sinister motives. From a mere sense of consistency, a persecutor is bound to show that the fallen man is a villain—otherwise he, the persecutor, is a wretch himself.

And as a general rule, which may make all creditors who are inclined to be severe, pretty comfortable in their minds, no men embarrassed are altogether honest, very likely. They conceal something; they exaggerate chances of good luck; hide away the real state of affairs; say that things are flourishing when they are hopeless; keep a smiling face (a dreary smile it is) upon the verge of bankruptcy—are ready to lay hold of any pretext for delay or of any money, so as to stave off the inevitable ruin a few days longer. 'Down with such dishonesty,' says the creditor in triumph, and reviles his sinking enemy. 'You fool, why do you catch at a straw?' calm good sense says to the man that is drowning. 'You villain, why do you shrink from plunging into the irretrievable *Gazette*?'* says prosperity to the poor devil battling in that black gulf. Who has not remarked the readiness with which the closest of friends and honestest of men suspect and accuse each other of cheating when they fall out on money matters? Everybody does it. Everybody is right, I suppose, and the world is a rogue.

Then Osborne had the intolerable sense of former benefits to goad and irritate him: these are always a cause of hostility aggravated. Finally, he had to break off the match between Sedley's daughter and his son; and as it had gone very far indeed, and as the poor girl's happiness

and perhaps character were compromised, it was necessary
to show the strongest reasons for the rupture, and for John
Osborne to prove John Sedley to be a very bad character
indeed.

At the meetings of creditors, then, he comported himself
with a savageness and scorn towards Sedley, which almost
succeeded in breaking the heart of that ruined bankrupt
man. On George's intercourse with Amelia he put an
instant veto—menacing the youth with maledictions if
he broke his commands, and vilipending the poor innocent
girl as the basest and most artful of vixens. One of the
great conditions of anger and hatred is, that you must tell
and believe lies against the hated object, in order, as we
said, to be consistent.

When the great crash came—the announcement of ruin,
and the departure from Russell Square, and the declaration
that all was over between her and George—all over between
her and love, her and happiness, her and faith in the world—
a brutal letter from John Osborne told her in a few curt lines
that her father's conduct had been of such a nature that
all engagements between the families were at an end—
when the final award came, it did not shock her so much
as her parents, as her mother rather expected (for John
Sedley himself was entirely prostrate in the ruins of his
own affairs and shattered honour). Amelia took the news
very palely and calmly. It was only the confirmation of
the dark presages which had long gone before. It was the
mere reading of the sentence—of the crime she had long ago
been guilty—the crime of loving wrongly, too violently,
against reason. She told no more of her thoughts now
than she had before. She seemed scarcely more unhappy
now when convinced all hope was over, than before when
she felt but dared not confess that it was gone. So she
changed from the large house to the small one without any
mark or difference ; remained in her little room for the most
part ; pined silently ; and died away day by day. I do not
mean to say that all females are so. My dear Miss Bullock,
I do not think *your* heart would break in this way. You
are a strong-minded young woman with proper principles.
I do not venture to say that mine would ; it has suffered,
and, it must be confessed, survived. But there are some
souls thus gently constituted, thus frail, and delicate, and
tender.

Whenever old John Sedley thought of the affair between
George and Amelia, or alluded to it, it was with bitterness
almost as great as Mr. Osborne himself had shown. He
cursed Osborne and his family as heartless, wicked, and
ungrateful. No power on earth, he swore, would induce
him to marry his daughter to the son of such a villain,
and he ordered Emmy to banish George from her mind,
and to return all the presents and letters which she had ever
had from him.

She promised acquiescence, and tried to obey. She put
up the two or three trinkets : and, as for the letters, she
drew them out of the place where she kept them ; and read
them over—as if she did not know them by heart already :
but she could not part with them. That effort was too
much for her ; she placed them back in her bosom again—
as you have seen a woman nurse a child that is dead.
Young Amelia felt that she would die or lose her senses
outright, if torn away from this last consolation. How
she used to blush and lighten up when those letters came !
How she used to trip away with a beating heart, so that she
might read unseen ! If they were cold, yet how perversely
this fond little soul interpreted them into warmth. If they
were short or selfish, what excuses she found for the
writer !

It was over these few worthless papers that she brooded
and brooded. She lived in her past life—every letter seemed
to recall some circumstance of it. How well she remembered
them all ! His looks and tones, his dress, what he said and
how—these relics and remembrances of dead affection
were all that were left her in the world. And the business
of her life was—to watch the corpse of Love.

To death she looked with inexpressible longing. Then,
she thought, I shall always be able to follow him. I am not
praising her conduct or setting her up as a model for
Miss Bullock to imitate. Miss B. knows how to regulate
her feelings better than this poor little creature. Miss
B. would never have committed herself as that imprudent
Amelia had done ; pledged her love irretrievably ; confessed her heart away, and got back nothing—only a brittle
promise which was snapped and worthless in a moment.
A long engagement is a partnership which one party is free
to keep or to break, but which involves all the capital of
the other.

Be cautious then, young ladies ; be wary how you engage.
Be shy of loving frankly ; never tell all you feel, or (a better
way still) feel very little. See the consequences of being
prematurely honest and confiding, and mistrust yourselves
and everybody. Get yourselves married as they do in
France, where the lawyers are the bridesmaids and con-
fidantes. At any rate, never have any feelings which may
make you uncomfortable, or make any promises which you
cannot at any required moment command and withdraw.
That is the way to get on, and be respected, and have a
virtuous character in Vanity Fair.

If Amelia could have heard the comments regarding her
which were made in the circle from which her father's ruin
had just driven her, she would have seen what her own crimes
were, and how entirely her character was jeopardied. Such
criminal imprudence Mrs. Smith never knew of ; such
horrid familiarities Mrs. Brown had always condemned,
and the end might be a warning to *her* daughters. ' Captain
Osborne, of course, could not marry a bankrupt's daughter,'
the Miss Dobbins said.   ' It was quite enough to have been
swindled by the father. As for that little Amelia, her
folly had really passed all—— '

' All what ? ' Captain Dobbin roared out. ' Haven't
they been engaged ever since they were children ?   Wasn't
it as good as a marriage ?   Dare any soul on earth breathe
a word against the sweetest, the purest, the tenderest, the
most angelical of young women ? '

' La, William, don't be so highty-tighty with *us*. We're
not men. We can't fight you,' Miss Jane said. ' We've
said nothing against Miss Sedley : but that her conduct
throughout was *most imprudent*, not to call it by any worse
name ; and that her parents are people who certainly merit
their misfortunes.'

' Hadn't you better, now that Miss Sedley is free, propose
for her yourself, William ? ' Miss Ann asked sarcastically.
' It would be a most eligible family connexion. He ! he ! '

' I marry her ! ' Dobbin said, blushing very much, and
talking quick. ' If you are so ready, young ladies, to chop
and change, do you suppose that *she* is ?   Laugh and sneer
at that angel. She can't hear it ; and she's miserable and
unfortunate, and deserves to be laughed at. Go on joking,
Ann. You're the wit of the family, and the others like to
hear it.'

' I must tell you again we're not in a barrack, William,'
. Miss Ann remarked.

' In a barrack, by Jove—I wish anybody in a barrack
would say what you do,' cried out this uproused British
lion. ' I should like to hear a man breathe a word against
her, by Jupiter. But men don't talk in this way, Ann :
it's only women, who get together and hiss, and shriek
and cackle. There, get away—don't begin to cry. I only
said you were a couple of geese,' Will Dobbin said, per-
ceiving Miss Ann's pink eyes were beginning to moisten
as usual. ' Well, you're not geese, you're swans—anything
you like, only do, do leave Miss Sedley alone.'

Anything like William's infatuation about that silly
little flirting, ogling thing was never known, the mamma
and sisters agreed together in thinking : and they trembled
lest, her engagement being off with Osborne, she should
take up immediately her other admirer and captain. In
which forebodings these worthy young women no doubt
judged according to the best of their experience ; or rather
(for as yet they had had no opportunities of marrying or
of jilting) according to their own notions of right and wrong.

' It is a mercy, mamma, that the regiment is ordered
abroad,' the girls said. ' *This* danger, at any rate, is spared
our brother.'

Such, indeed, was the fact ; and so it is that the French
Emperor comes in to perform a part in this domestic comedy
of Vanity Fair which we are now playing, and which would
never have been enacted without the intervention of this
august mute personage. It was he that ruined the Bourbons and Mr. John Sedley. It was he whose arrival in his
capital called up all France in arms to defend him there ;
and all Europe to oust him. While the French nation and
army were swearing fidelity round the eagles in the Champ
de Mai,* four mighty European hosts were getting in motion
for the great *chasse à l'aigle ;* and one of these was a British
army, of which two heroes of ours, Captain Dobbin and
Captain Osborne, formed a portion.

The news of Napoleon's escape and landing was received
by the gallant —th with a fiery delight and enthusiasm,
which everybody can understand who knows that famous
corps. From the colonel to the smallest drummer in the
regiment, all were filled with hope and ambition and
patriotic fury ; and thanked the French Emperor as for

a personal kindness in coming to disturb the peace of
Europe. Now was the time the —th had so long panted
for, to show their comrades in arms that they could fight
as well as the Peninsular veterans, and that all the pluck
and valour of the —th had not been killed by the West
Indies and the yellow fever. Stubble and Spooney looked
to get their companies without purchase. Before the end
of the campaign (which she resolved to share), Mrs. Major
O'Dowd hoped to write herself Mrs. Colonel O'Dowd, C.B.
Our two friends (Dobbin and Osborne) were quite as much
excited as the rest : and each in his way—Mr. Dobbin
very quietly, Mr. Osborne very loudly and energetically—
was bent upon doing his duty, and gaining his share of
honour and distinction.

The agitation thrilling through the country and army in
consequence of this news was so great, that private matters
were little heeded : and hence probably George Osborne,
just gazetted to his company, busy with preparations for the
march, which must come inevitably, and panting for further
promotion—was not so much affected by other incidents
which would have interested him at a more quiet period.
He was not, it must be confessed, very much cast down by
good old Mr. Sedley's catastrophe. He tried his new
uniform, which became him very handsomely, on the day
when the first meeting of the creditors of the unfortunate
gentleman took place. His father told him of the wicked,
rascally, shameful conduct of the bankrupt, reminded
him of what he had said about Amelia, and that their
connexion was broken off for ever ; and gave him that
evening a good sum of money to pay for the new clothes
and epaulets in which he looked so well. Money was always
useful to this free-handed young fellow, and he took it
without many words. The bills were up in the Sedley
house, where he had passed so many, many happy hours.
He could see them as he walked from home that night
(to the Old Slaughter's, where he put up when in town),
shining white in the moon. That comfortable home was
shut, then, upon Amelia and her parents : where had they
taken refuge ? The thought of their ruin affected him not
a little. He was very melancholy that night in the coffee-
room at the Slaughter's ; and drank a good deal, as his
comrades remarked there.

Dobbin came in presently, cautioned him about the drink,

which he only took, he said, because he was deuced low ;
but when his friend began to put to him clumsy inquiries,
and asked him for news in a significant manner, Osborne
declined entering into conversation with him ; avowing,
however, that he was devilish disturbed and unhappy.

Three days afterwards, Dobbin found Osborne in his
room at the barracks :—his head on the table, a number
of papers about, the young captain evidently in a state of
great despondency. ' She—she's sent me back some things
I gave her—some damned trinkets. Look here ! ' There
was a little packet directed in the well-known hand to
Captain George Osborne, and some things lying about—
a ring, a silver knife he had bought, as a boy, for her
at a fair ; a gold chain, and a locket with hair in it. ' It's
all over,' said he, with a groan of sickening remorse.
' Look, Will, you may read it if you like.'

There was a little letter of a few lines, to which he pointed,
which said :—

My papa has ordered me to return to you these presents, which you
made in happier days to me ; and I am to write to you for the last
time. I think, I know you feel as much as I do the blow which has
come upon us. It is I that absolve you from an engagement which
is impossible in our present misery. I am sure you had no share in
it, or in the cruel suspicions of Mr. Osborne, which are the hardest
of all our griefs to bear. Farewell. Farewell. I pray God to
strengthen me to bear this and other calamities, and to bless you
always.   A.

I shall often play upon the piano—your piano. It was like you to
send it.

Dobbin was very soft-hearted. The sight of women
and children in pain always used to melt him. The idea
of Amelia broken-hearted and lonely, tore that good-
natured soul with anguish. And he broke out into an
emotion, which anybody who likes may consider unmanly.
He swore that Amelia was an angel, to which Osborne
said aye with all his heart. He, too, had been reviewing the
history of their lives,—and had seen her from her childhood to her present age, so sweet, so innocent, so charmingly
simple, and artlessly fond and tender.

What a pang it was to lose all that : to have had it and not
prized it ! A thousand homely scenes and recollections
crowded on him—in which he always saw her good and
beautiful. And for himself, he blushed with remorse and

shame, as the remembrance of his own selfishness and indifference contrasted with that perfect purity. For a
while, glory, war, everything was forgotten, and the pair
of friends talked about her only.

' Where are they ? ' Osborne asked, after a long talk, and
a long pause,—and, in truth, with no little shame at
thinking that he had taken no steps to follow her. ' Where
are they ?   There's no address to the note.'

Dobbin knew.   He had not merely sent the piano ; but
had written a note to Mrs. Sedley, and asked permission
to come and see her,—and he had seen her, and Amelia too,
yesterday, before he came down to Chatham ; and, what
is more, he had brought that farewell letter and packet
which had so moved them.

The good-natured fellow had found Mrs. Sedley only too
willing to receive him, and greatly agitated by the arrival
of the piano, which, as she conjectured, *must* have come
from George, and was a signal of amity on his part. Captain
Dobbin did not correct this error of the worthy lady, but
listened to all her story of complaints and misfortunes
with great sympathy—condoled with her losses and
privations, and agreed in reprehending the cruel conduct
of Mr. Osborne towards his first benefactor. When she
had eased her overflowing bosom somewhat, and poured
forth many of her sorrows, he had the courage to ask
actually to see Amelia, who was above in her room as usual,
and whom her mother led trembling downstairs.

Her appearance was so ghastly, and her look of despair
so pathetic, that honest William Dobbin was frightened
as he beheld it ; and read the most rate ' forebodings in that
pale fixed face.   After sitting in his company a minute or
two, she put the packet into his hand, and said, ' Take this
to Captain Osborne, if you please, and—and I hope he's
quite well—and it was very kind of you to come and see us
—and we like our new house very much.   And I—I think
I'll go upstairs, mamma, for I'm not very strong.'   And
with this, and a curtsy and a smile, the poor child went her
way.   The mother, as she led her up, cast back looks of
anguish towards Dobbin.   The good fellow wanted no
such appeal.   He loved her himself too fondly for that.
Inexpressible grief, and pity, and terror pursued him, and
he came away as if he was a criminal after seeing her.

When Osborne heard that his friend had found her, he

made hot and anxious inquiries regarding the poor child. How was she ? How did she look ? What did she say ? His comrade took his hand, and looked him in the face.

' George, she's dying,' William Dobbin said,—and could speak no more.

There was a buxom Irish servant-girl, who performed all the duties of the little house where the Sedley family had found refuge ; and this girl had in vain, on many previous days, striven to give Amelia aid or consolation. Emmy was much too sad to answer, or even to be aware of the attempts the other was making in her favour.

Four hours after the talk between Dobbin and Osborne, this servant-maid came into Amelia's room, where she sat as usual, brooding silently over her letters—her little treasures. The girl, smiling, and looking arch and happy, made many trials to attract poor Emmy's attention, who, however, took no heed of her.

' Miss Emmy,' said the girl.

' I'm coming,' Emmy said, not looking round.

' There's a message,' the maid went on. ' There's something—somebody—sure, here's a new letter for you—don't be reading them old ones any more.' And she gave her a letter, which Emmy took, and read.

' I must see you,' the letter said. ' Dearest Emmy— dearest love—dearest wife, come to me.'

George and her mother were outside, waiting until she had read the letter.

CHAPTER XIX

MISS CRAWLEY AT NURSE

E have seen how Mrs. Firkin, the lady's-maid, as soon as any event of importance to the Crawley family came to her knowledge, felt bound to communicate it to Mrs. Bute Crawley, at the Rectory; and have before mentioned how particularly kind and attentive that good-natured lady was to Miss Crawley's confidential servant. She had been a gracious friend to Mrs. Briggs, the companion, also; and had secured the latter's goodwill by a number of those attentions and promises, which cost so little in the making, and are yet so valuable and agreeable to the recipient. Indeed, every good economist and manager of a household must know how cheap and yet how amiable these professions are, and what a flavour they give to the most homely dish in life. Who was the blundering idiot who said that ' fine words butter no parsnips ' ? Half the parsnips of society are served and rendered palatable with no other sauce. As the immortal Alexis Soyer* can make more delicious soup for a halfpenny than an ignorant cook can concoct with pounds of vegetables and meat, so a skilful artist will make a few simple and pleasing phrases go farther than ever so much substantial benefit-stock in the hands of a mere bungler. Nay, we know that substantial benefits often sicken some stomachs; whereas, most will digest any amount of fine words, and be always eager for more of the same food. Mrs. Bute had told Briggs and Firkin so often of the depth of her affection for them; and what *she* would do, if she had Miss Crawley's fortune, for friends so excellent and attached, that the ladies in question had the deepest regard for her; and felt as much gratitude and confidence as if Mrs. Bute had loaded them with the most expensive favours.

Rawdon Crawley, on the other hand, like a selfish heavy dragoon as he was, never took the least trouble to conciliate his aunt's aides de camp, showed his contempt for the pair with entire frankness—made Firkin pull off his boots on one occasion—sent her out in the rain on ignominious messages —and if he gave her a guinea, flung it to her as if it were a box on the ear. As his aunt, too, made a butt of Briggs, the captain followed the example, and levelled his jokes at her—jokes about as delicate as a kick from his charger. Whereas, Mrs. Bute consulted her in matters of taste or difficulty, admired her poetry, and by a thousand acts of kindness and politeness, showed her appreciation of Briggs ; and if she made Firkin a twopenny-halfpenny present, accompanied it with so many compliments, that the two-pence-halfpenny was transmuted into gold in the heart of the grateful waiting-maid, who, besides, was looking forwards quite contentedly to some prodigious benefit which must happen to her on the day when Mrs. Bute came into her fortune.

The different conduct of these two people is pointed out respectfully to the attention of persons commencing the world. Praise everybody, I say to such: never be squeam-ish, but speak out your compliment both point-blank in a man's face, and behind his back, when you know there is a reasonable chance of his hearing it again. Never lose a chance of saying a kind word. As Collingwood never saw a vacant place in his estate but he took an acorn* out of his pocket and popped it in ; so deal with your compliments through life. An acorn costs nothing ; but it may sprout into a prodigious bit of timber.

In a word, during Rawdon Crawley's prosperity, he was only obeyed with sulky acquiescence ; when his disgrace came, there was nobody to help or pity him. Whereas, when Mrs. Bute took the command at Miss Crawley's house, the garrison there were charmed to act under such a leader, expecting all sorts of promotion from her promises, her generosity, and her kind words.

That he would consider himself beaten, after one defeat, and make no attempt to regain the position he had lost, Mrs. Bute Crawley never allowed herself to suppose. She knew Rebecca to be too clever and spirited and desperate

a woman to submit without a struggle ; and felt that she
must prepare for that combat, and be incessantly watchful
against assault, or mine, or surprise.

In the first place, though she held the town, was she
sure of the principal inhabitant ? Would Miss Crawley
herself hold out ; and had she not a secret longing to welcome back the ousted adversary ? The old lady liked
Rawdon, and Rebecca, who amused her. Mrs. Bute could
not disguise from herself the fact that none of her party
could so contribute to the pleasures of the town-bred lady.
'My girls' singing, after that little odious governess's, I know
is unbearable,' the candid rector's wife owned to herself.
' She always used to go to sleep when Martha and Louisa
played their duets. Jim's stiff college manners and poor
dear Bute's talk about his dogs and horses always annoyed
her. If I took her to the Rectory, she would grow angry
with us all, and fly, I know she would ; and might fall into
that horrid Rawdon's clutches again, and be the victim of
that little viper of a Sharp.   Meanwhile, it is clear to me that
she is exceedingly unwell, and cannot move for some weeks,
at any rate ; during which we must think of some plan to
protect her from the arts of those unprincipled people.'

In the very best of moments, if anybody told Miss
Crawley that she was, or looked ill, the trembling old lady
sent off for her doctor ; and I daresay she *was* very unwell
after the sudden family event, which might serve to shake
stronger nerves than hers. At least, Mrs. Bute thought
it was her duty to inform the physician, and the apothecary,
and the *dame de compagnie*, and the domestics, that Miss
Crawley was in a most critical state, and that they were to
act accordingly. She had the street laid knee-deep with
straw ; and the knocker put by with Mr. Bowls's plate.
She insisted that the doctor should call twice a day ; and
deluged her patient with draughts every two hours. When
anybody entered the room, she uttered a *shshshsh* so
sibilant and ominous, that it frightened the poor old lady
in her bed, from which she could not look without seeing
Mrs. Bute's beady eyes eagerly fixed on her, as the latter
sat steadfast in the arm-chair by the bedside. They seemed
to lighten in the dark (for she kept the curtains closed)
as she moved about the room on velvet paws like a cat.
There Miss Crawley lay for days—ever so many days—
Mrs. Bute reading books of devotion to her : for nights,

long nights, during which she had to hear the watchman
sing, the night-light sputter ; visited at midnight, the
last thing, by the stealthy
apothecary ; and then left to
look at Mrs. Bute's twinkling
eyes, or the flicks of yellow that
the rushlight threw on the
dreary darkened ceiling. Hygeia
herself would háve fallen sick
under such a regimen ; and how
much more this poor old nervous
victim ? It has been said that
when she was in health and good
spirits, this venerable inhabitant
of VanityFair had as free notions
about religion and morals as
Monsieur de Voltaire himself
could desire, but when illness
overtook her, it was aggravated
by the most dreadful terrors of

death, and an utter cowardice took possession of the prostrate old sinner.

Sick-bed homilies and pious reflections are, to be sure,
out of place in mere story-books, and we are not going
(after the fashion of some novelists of the present day)
to cajole the public into a sermon, when it is only a comedy
that the reader pays his money to witness. But, without
preaching, the truth may surely be borne in mind, that
the bustle, and triumph, and laughter, and gaiety which
Vanity Fair exhibits in public, do not always pursue the
performer into private life, and that the most dreary
depression of spirits and dismal repentances sometimes
overcome him. Recollection of the best ordained banquets
will scarcely cheer sick epicures. Reminiscences of the
most becoming dresses and brilliant ball-triumphs will
go very little way to console faded beauties. Perhaps
statesmen, at a particular period of existence, are not much
gratified at thinking over the most triumphant divisions ;
and the success or the pleasure of yesterday become of
very small account when a certain (albeit uncertain) morrow
is in view, about which all of us must some day or other
be speculating. O brother wearers of motley ! Are there
not moments when one grows sick of grinning and tumbling,

and the jingling of cap and bells ? This, dear friends and
companions, is my amiable object—to walk with you
through the Fair, to examine the shops and the shows
there ; and that we should all come home after the flare,
and the noise, and the gaiety, and be perfectly miserable
in private.

' If that poor man of mine had a head on his shoulders,'
Mrs. Bute Crawley thought to herself, ' how useful he
might be, under present circumstances, to this unhappy
old lady ! He might make her repent of her shocking
free-thinking ways ; he might urge her to do her duty,
and cast off that odious reprobate who has disgraced himself
and his family ; and he might induce her to do justice to
my dear girls and the two boys, who require and deserve,
I am sure, every assistance which their relatives can give
them.'

And, as the hatred of vice is always a progress towards
virtue, Mrs. Bute Crawley endeavoured to instil into her
sister-in-law a proper abhorrence for all Rawdon Crawley's
manifold sins : of which his uncle's wife brought forward
such a catalogue as indeed would have served to condemn
a whole regiment of young officers. If a man has committed wrong in life, I don't know any moralist more anxious
to point his errors out to the world than his own relations ;
so Mrs. Bute showed a perfect family interest and knowledge of Rawdon's history. She had all the particulars
of that ugly quarrel with Captain Marker, in which Rawdon,
wrong from the beginning, ended in shooting the captain.
She knew how the unhappy Lord Dovedale, whose mamma
had taken a house at Oxford, so that he might be educated
there, and who had never touched a card in his life till he
came to London, was perverted by Rawdon at the ' Cocoa-
Tree,' made helplessly tipsy by this abominable seducer
and perverter of youth, and fleeced of four thousand
pounds. She described with the most vivid minuteness
the agonies of the country families whom he had ruined—
the sons whom he had plunged into dishonour and poverty—
the daughters whom he had inveigled into perdition. She
knew the poor tradesmen who were bankrupt by his
extravagance—the mean shifts and rogueries with which
he had ministered to it—the astounding falsehoods by
which he had imposed upon the most generous of aunts,

and the ingratitude and ridicule by which he had repaid
her sacrifices. She imparted these stories gradually to
Miss Crawley ; gave her the whole benefit of them ; felt
it to be her bounden duty as a Christian woman and mother
of a family to do so ; had not the smallest remorse or
compunction for the victim whom her tongue was im-
molating ; nay, very likely thought her act was quite
meritorious, and plumed herself upon her resolute manner
of performing it. Yes, if a man's character is to be abused,
say what you will, there's nobody like a relation to do the
business. And one is bound to own, regarding this unfortunate wretch of a Rawdon Crawley, that the mere truth
was enough to condemn him, and that all inventions of
scandal were quite superfluous pains on his friends' parts.

Rebecca, too, being now a relative, came in for the fullest
share of Mrs. Bute's kind inquiries. This indefatigable
pursuer of truth (having given strict orders that the door
was to be denied to all emissaries or letters from Rawdon),
took Miss Crawley's carriage, and drove to her old friend
Miss Pinkerton, at Minerva House, Chiswick Mall,
to whom she announced the dreadful intelligence of Captain
Rawdon's seduction by Miss Sharp, and from whom she got
sundry strange particulars regarding the ex-governess's
birth and early history. The friend of the Lexicographer
had plenty of information to give. Miss Jemima was made
to fetch the drawing-master's receipts and letters. This
one was from a spunging-house : that entreated an advance :
another was full of gratitude for Rebecca's reception by
the ladies of Chiswick : and the last document from the
unlucky artist's pen was that in which, from his dying
bed, he recommended his orphan child to Miss Pinkerton's
protection. There were juvenile letters and petitions
from Rebecca, too, in the collection, imploring aid for her
father, or declaring her own gratitude. Perhaps in Vanity
Fair there are no better satires than letters. Take a bundle
of your dear friend's of ten years back—your dear friend
whom you hate now. Look at a file of your sister's : how
you clung to each other till you quarrelled about the twenty-
pound legacy ! Get down the roundhand scrawls of your
son who has half broken your heart with selfish undutifulness since ; or a parcel of your own, breathing endless
ardour and love eternal, which were sent back by your
mistress when she married the nabob—your mistress for

whom you now care no more than for Queen Elizabeth.
Vows, love, promises, confidences, gratitude, how queerly
they read after a while ! There ought to be a law in Vanity
Fair ordering the destruction of every written document
(except receipted tradesmen's bills) after a certain brief
and proper interval. Those quacks and misanthropes
who advertise indelible Japan ink, should be made to perish
along with their wicked discoveries. The best ink for
Vanity Fair use would be one that faded utterly in a couple
of days, and left the paper clean and blank, so that you
might write on it to somebody else.

From Miss Pinkerton's the indefatigable Mrs. Bute
followed the track of Sharp and his daughter back to the
lodgings in Greek Street, which the defunct painter had
occupied ; and where portraits of the landlady in white
satin, and of the husband in brass buttons, done by Sharp
in lieu of a quarter's rent, still decorated the parlour walls.
Mrs. Stokes was a communicative person, and quickly
told all she knew about Mr. Sharp ; how dissolute and
poor he was ; how good-natured and amusing ; how he
was always hunted by bailiffs and duns ; how, to the
landlady's horror, though she never could abide the woman,
he did not marry his wife till a short time before her death ;
and what a queer little wild vixen his daughter was ; how
she kept them all laughing with her fun and mimicry ;
how she used to fetch the gin from the public-house, and
was known in all the studios in the quarter—in brief,
Mrs. Bute got such a full account of her new niece's parentage, education, and behaviour as would scarcely have
pleased Rebecca, had the latter known that such inquiries
were being made concerning her.

Of all these industrious researches Miss Crawley had the
full benefit. Mrs. Rawdon Crawley was the daughter
of an opera-girl. She had danced herself. She had been
a model to the painters. She was brought up as became
her mother's daughter. She drank gin with her father,
&c. &c. It was a lost woman who was married to a lost
man ; and the moral to be inferred from Mrs. Bute's tale
was, that the knavery of the pair was irremediable, and that
no properly-conducted person should ever notice them again.

These were the materials which prudent Mrs. Bute
gathered together in Park Lane, the provisions and ammunition as it were with which she fortified the house against

the siege which she knew that Rawdon and his wife would
lay to Miss Crawley.

But if a fault may be found with her arrangements, it is
this, that she was too eager : she managed rather too well ;
undoubtedly she made Miss Crawley more ill than was
necessary ; and though the old invalid succumbed to her
authority, it was so harassing and severe, that the victim
would be inclined to escape at the very first chance which
fell in her way. Managing women, the ornaments of their
sex—women who order everything for everybody, and
know so much better than any person concerned what is
good for their neighbours, don't sometimes speculate upon
the possibility of a domestic revolt, or upon other extreme
consequences resulting from their overstrained authority.

Thus, for instance, Mrs. Bute, with the best intentions
no doubt in the world, and wearing herself to death as she
did by forgoing sleep, dinner, fresh air, for the sake of
her invalid sister-in-law, carried her conviction of the old
lady's illness so far that she almost managed her into her
coffin. She pointed out her sacrifices and their results one
day to the constant apothecary, Mr. Clump.

'I am sure, my dear Mr. Clump,' she said, 'no efforts
of mine have been wanting to restore our dear invalid,
whom the ingratitude of her nephew has laid on the bed
of sickness. *I* never shrink from personal discomfort :
I never refuse to sacrifice myself.'

'Your devotion, it must be confessed, is admirable,'
Mr. Clump says, with a low bow ; 'but——'

'I have scarcely closed my eyes since my arrival : I give
up sleep, health, every comfort, to my sense of duty. When
my poor James was in the small-pox, did I allow any hire-
ling to nurse him ?   No.'

'You did what became an excellent mother, my dear
madam—the best of mothers ; but——'

'As the mother of a family and the wife of an English
clergyman, I humbly trust that my principles are good,'
Mrs. Bute said, with a happy solemnity of conviction ;
'and, as long as Nature supports me, never, never, Mr.
Clump, will I desert the post of duty. Others may bring
that grey head with sorrow to the bed of sickness' (here
Mrs. Bute, waving her hand, pointed to one of old Miss
Crawley's coffee-coloured fronts, which was perched on

a stand in the dressing-room), 'but *I* will never quit it.
Ah, Mr. Clump! I fear, I know, that that couch needs
spiritual as well as medical consolation.'

'What I was going to observe, my dear madam,'—here
the resolute Clump once more interposed with a bland air
—'what I was going to observe when you gave utterance
to sentiments which do you so much honour, was that I
think you alarm yourself needlessly about our kind friend,
and sacrifice your own health too prodigally in her favour.'

'I would lay down my life for my duty, or for any member
of my husband's family,' Mrs. Bute interposed.

'Yes, madam, if need were; but we don't want Mrs.
Bute Crawley to be a martyr,' Clump said gallantly. 'Dr.
Squills and myself*have both considered Miss Crawley's
case with every anxiety and care, as you may suppose.
We see her low-spirited and nervous; family events have
agitated her.'

'Her nephew will come to perdition,' Mrs. Crawley cried.

'Have agitated her: and you arrived like a guardian
angel, my dear madam, a positive guardian angel, I assure
you, to soothe her under the pressure of calamity. But
Dr. Squills and I were thinking that our amiable friend
is not in such a state as renders confinement to her bed
necessary. She is depressed, but this confinement perhaps
adds to her depression. She should have change, fresh
air, gaiety; the most delightful remedies in the phar-
macopoeia,' Mr. Clump said, grinning and showing his
handsome teeth. 'Persuade her to rise, dear madam;
drag her from her couch and her low spirits; insist upon
her taking little drives. They will restore the roses too
to *your* cheeks, if I may so speak to Mrs. Bute Crawley.'

'The sight of her horrid nephew casually in the Park,
where I am told the wretch drives with the brazen partner
of his crimes,' Mrs. Bute said (letting the cat of selfishness
out of the bag of secrecy), 'would cause her such a shock,
that we should have to bring her back to bed again. She
must not go out, Mr. Clump. She shall not go out as long
as I remain to watch over her. And as for *my* health, what
matters it? I give it cheerfully, sir. I sacrifice it at the
altar of my duty.'

'Upon my word, madam,' Mr. Clump now said bluntly,
'I won't answer for her life if she remains locked up in that
dark room. She is so nervous that we may lose her any

day ; and if you wish Captain Crawley to be her heir, I warn
you frankly, madam, that you are doing your very best to
serve him.'

'Gracious mercy! is her life in danger?' Mrs. Bute
cried. 'Why, why, Mr. Clump, did you not inform me
sooner?'

The night before, Mr. Clump and Dr. Squills had had
a consultation (over a bottle of wine at the house of Sir
Lapin Warren, whose lady was about to present him with
a thirteenth blessing), regarding Miss Crawley and her case.

'What a little harpy that woman from Hampshire is,
Clump,' Squills remarked, 'that has seized upon old Tilly
Crawley. Devilish good madeira.'

'What a fool Rawdon Crawley has been,' Clump replied,
'to go and marry a governess! There was something about
the girl, too.'

'Green eyes, fair skin, pretty figure, famous frontal
development,' Squills remarked. 'There is something
about her ; and Crawley *was* a fool, Squills.'

'A d—— fool—always was,' the apothecary replied.

'Of course the old girl will fling him over,' said the
physician, and after a pause added, 'She'll cut up well,
I suppose.'

'Cut up,' says Clump with a grin ; 'I wouldn't have her
cut up for two hundred a year.'

'That Hampshire woman will kill her in two months,
Clump, my boy, if she stops about her,' Dr. Squills said.
'Old woman ; full feeder ; nervous subject ; palpitation
of the heart ; pressure on the brain ; apoplexy ; off she
goes. Get her up, Clump ; get her out : or I wouldn't
give many weeks' purchase for your two hundred a year.'
And it was acting upon this hint that the worthy apothecary
spoke with so much candour to Mrs. Bute Crawley.

Having the old lady under her hand : in bed : with
nobody near, Mrs. Bute had made more than one assault
upon her, to induce her to alter her will.   But Miss Crawley's
usual terrors regarding death increased greatly when such
dismal propositions were made to her, and Mrs. Bute saw
that she must get her patient into cheerful spirits and
health before she could hope to attain the pious object
which she had in view.   Whither to take her was the next
puzzle.   The only place where she is not likely to meet
those odious Rawdons is at church, and that won't amuse

her, Mrs. Bute justly felt. ' We must go and visit our
beautiful suburbs of London,' she then thought. ' I hear
they are the most picturesque in the world ; ' and so she
had a sudden interest for Hampstead, and Hornsey, and
found that Dulwich had great charms for her, and getting
her victim into her carriage, drove her to those rustic spots,
beguiling the little journeys with conversations about
Rawdon and his wife, and telling every story to the old
lady which could add to her indignation against this pair
of reprobates.

Perhaps Mrs. Bute pulled the string unnecessarily tight.
For though she worked up Miss Crawley to a proper dislike
of her disobedient nephew, the invalid had a great hatred
and secret terror of her victimizer, and panted to escape
from her. After a brief space, she rebelled against Highgate
and Hornsey utterly. She would go into the Park. Mrs.
Bute knew they would meet the abominable Rawdon there,
and she was right. One day in the ring, Rawdon's stanhope
came in sight ; Rebecca was seated by him. In the
enemy's equipage Miss Crawley occupied her usual place,
with Mrs. Bute on her left, the poodle* and Miss Briggs on
the back seat. It was a nervous moment, and Rebecca's
heart beat quick as she recognized the carriage ; and as
the two vehicles crossed each other in the line, she clasped
her hands, and looked towards the spinster with a face
of agonized attachment and devotion. Rawdon himself
trembled, and his face grew purple behind his dyed moustachios. Only old Briggs was moved in the other carriage,
and cast her great eyes nervously towards her old friends.
Miss Crawley's bonnet was resolutely turned towards the
Serpentine. Mrs. Bute happened to be in ecstacies with the
poodle, and was calling him a little darling, and a sweet
little zoggy, and a pretty pet. The carriages moved on,
each in his line.

' Done, by Jove,' Rawdon said to his wife.

' Try once more, Rawdon,' Rebecca answered. ' Could
not you lock your wheels into theirs, dearest ? '

Rawdon had not the heart for that manœuvre. When
the carriages met again, he stood up in his stanhope ;* he
raised his hand ready to doff his hat ; he looked with all
his eyes. But this time Miss Crawley's face was not turned
away ; she and Mrs. Bute looked him full in the face, and
cut their nephew pitilessly. He sank back in his seat with

an oath, and striking out of the ring, dashed away desperately homewards.

It was a gallant and decided triumph for Mrs. Bute. But she felt the danger of many such meetings, as she saw the evident nervousness of Miss Crawley; and she determined that it was most necessary for her dear friend's health, that they should leave town for a while, and recommended Brighton very strongly.

CHAPTER XX

IN WHICH CAPTAIN DOBBIN ACTS AS THE MESSENGER OF HYMEN

 ITHOUT knowing how, Captain William Dobbin found himself the great promoter, arranger, and manager of the match between George Osborne and Amelia. But for him it never would have taken place : he could not but confess as much to himself, and smiled rather bitterly as he thought that he of all men in the world should be the person upon whom the care of this marriage had fallen. But though indeed the conducting of this negotiation was about as painful a task as could be set to him, yet when he had a duty to perform, Captain Dobbin was accustomed to go through it without many words or much hesitation : and, having made up his mind completely, that if Miss Sedley was balked of her husband she would die of the disappointment, he was determined to use all his best endeavours to keep her alive.

I forbear to enter into minute particulars of the interview between George and Amelia, when the former was brought back to the feet (or should we venture to say the arms ?) of his young mistress by the intervention of his friend honest William. A much harder heart than George's would have melted at the sight of that sweet face so sadly ravaged by grief and despair, and at the simple tender

accents in which she told her little broken-hearted story :
but as she did not faint when her mother, trembling,
brought Osborne to her ; and as she only gave relief to
her overcharged grief, by laying her head on her lover's
shoulder and there weeping for a while the most tender,
copious, and refreshing tears—old Mrs. Sedley, too greatly
relieved, thought it was best to leave the young persons
to themselves ; and so quitted Emmy crying over George's
hand, and kissing it humbly, as if he were her supreme
chief and master, and as if she were quite a guilty and
unworthy person needing every favour and grace from him.

This prostration and sweet unrepining obedience exquisitely touched and flattered George Osborne. He saw
a slave before him in that simple yielding faithful creature,
and his soul within him thrilled secretly somehow at the
knowledge of his power. He would be generous-minded,
Sultan as he was, and raise up this kneeling Esther and make
a queen of her : besides, her sadness and beauty touched
him as much as her submission, and so he cheered her,
and raised her up and forgave her, so to speak. All her
hopes and feelings, which were dying and withering, this
her sun having been removed from her, bloomed again
and at once, its light being restored. You would scarcely
have recognized the beaming little face upon Amelia's
pillow that night as the one that was laid there the night
before, so wan, so lifeless, so careless of all round about.
The honest Irish maid-servant, delighted with the change,
asked leave to kiss the face that had grown all of a sudden
so rosy. Amelia put her arms round the girl's neck and
kissed her with all her heart, like a child. She was little
more. She had that night a sweet refreshing sleep, like
one—and what a spring of inexpressible happiness as she
woke in the morning sunshine !

' He will be here again to-day,' Amelia thought. ' He is
the greatest and best of men.' And the fact is, that
George thought he was one of the generousest creatures
alive ; and that he was making a tremendous sacrifice in
marrying this young creature.

While she and Osborne were having their delightful
tête-à-tête above-stairs, old Mrs. Sedley and Captain Dobbin
were conversing below upon the state of the affairs, and
the chances and future arrangements of the young people.
Mrs. Sedley having brought the two lovers together and

left them embracing each other with all their might, like
a true woman, was of opinion that no power on earth would
induce Mr. Sedley to consent to the match between his
daughter and the son of a man who had so shamefully,
wickedly, and monstrously treated him. And she told a
long story about happier days and their earlier splendours,
when Osborne lived in a very humble way in the New Road,
and his wife was *too glad* to receive some of Jos's little baby
things, with which Mrs. Sedley accommodated her at the
birth of one of Osborne's own children. The fiendish
ingratitude of that man, she was sure, had broken Mr. S.'s
heart : and as for a marriage, he would never, never, never,
never consent.

'They must run away together, ma'am,' Dobbin said,
laughing, 'and follow the example of Captain Rawdon
Crawley, and Miss Emmy's friend the little governess.'
Was it possible ? Well she never ! Mrs. Sedley was all
excitement about this news. She wished that Blenkinsop
were here to hear it : Blenkinsop always mistrusted that Miss
Sharp.—What an escape Jos had had ! and she described
the already well-known love-passages between Rebecca and
the collector of Boggley Wollah.

It was not, however, Mr. Sedley's wrath which Dobbin
feared, so much as that of the other parent concerned, and
he owned that he had a very considerable doubt and anxiety
respecting the behaviour of the black-browed old tyrant
of a Russia merchant* in Russell Square. He has forbidden
the match peremptorily, Dobbin thought. He knew what
a savage determined man Osborne was, and how he stuck
by his word. 'The only chance George has of reconcilement,' argued his friend, 'is by distinguishing himself in
the coming campaign. If he dies they both go together.
If he fails in distinction—what then ? He has some
money from his mother, I have heard—enough to purchase
his majority—or he must sell out and go and dig in Canada,
or rough it in a cottage in the country.' With such a partner Dobbin thought he would not mind Siberia—and,
strange to say, this absurd and utterly imprudent young
fellow never for a moment considered that the want of
means to keep a nice carriage and horses, and of an income
which should enable its possessors to entertain their friends
genteelly, ought to operate as bars to the union of George
and Miss Sedley.

It was these weighty considerations which made him
think too that the marriage should take place as quickly
as possible. Was he anxious himself, I wonder, to have it
over ?—as people, when death has occurred, like to press
forward the funeral, or when a parting is resolved upon,
hasten it. It is certain that Mr. Dobbin, having taken the
matter in hand, was most extraordinarily eager in the
conduct of it. He urged on George the necessity of immediate action : he showed the chances of reconciliation with
his father, which a favourable mention of his name in the
Gazette must bring about. If need were he would go
himself and brave both the fathers in the business. At all
events, he besought George to go through with it before
the orders came, which everybody expected, for the departure of the regiment from England on foreign service.

Bent upon these hymeneal projects, and with the applause
and consent of Mrs. Sedley, who did not care to break the
matter personally to her husband, Mr. Dobbin went to seek
John Sedley at his house of call in the City, the ' Tapioca '
Coffee-house, where, since his own offices were shut up, and
fate had overtaken him, the poor broken-down old gentleman used to betake himself daily, and write letters and
receive them, and tie them up into mysterious bundles,
several of which he carried in the flaps of his coat. I don't
know anything more dismal than that business and bustle
and mystery of a ruined man : those letters from the
wealthy which he shows you : those worn greasy documents
promising support and offering condolence which he places
wistfully before you, and on which he builds his hopes
of restoration and future fortune. My beloved reader has
no doubt in the course of his experience been waylaid by
many such a luckless companion. He takes you into the
corner ; he has his bundle of papers out of his gaping coat
pocket ; and the tape off, and the string in his mouth, and
the favourite letters selected and laid before you ; and
who does not know the sad eager half-crazy look which he
fixes on you with his hopeless eyes ?

Changed into a man of this sort, Dobbin found the once
florid, jovial, and prosperous John Sedley. His coat,
that used to be so glossy and trim, was white at the seams,
and the buttons showed the copper. His face had fallen
in, and was unshorn ; his frill and neckcloth hung limp
under his bagging waistcoat. When he used to treat the

MR. SEDLEY AT THE COFFEE-HOUSE

boys in old days at a coffee-house, he would shout and laugh louder than anybody there, and have all the waiters skipping round him ; it was quite painful to see how humble and civil he was to John of the 'Tapioca', a blear-eyed old attendant in dingy stockings and cracked pumps, whose business it was to serve glasses of wafers, and bumpers of ink in pewter, and slices of paper to the frequenters of this dreary house of entertainment, where nothing else seemed to be consumed. As for William Dobbin, whom he had tipped repeatedly in his youth, and who had been the old gentleman's butt on a thousand occasions, old Sedley gave his hand to him in a very hesitating humble manner now, and called him ' sir '. A feeling of shame and remorse took possession of William Dobbin as the broken old man so received and addressed him, as if he himself had been somehow guilty of the misfortunes which had brought Sedley so low.

' I am very glad to see you, Captain Dobbin, sir,' says he, after a skulking look or two at his visitor (whose lanky figure and military appearance caused some excitement likewise to twinkle in the blear eyes of the waiter in the cracked dancing-pumps, and awakened the old lady in black, who dozed among the mouldy old coffee-cups in the bar). ' How is the worthy alderman, and my lady, your excellent mother, sir ? ' He looked round at the waiter as he said ' My lady ', as much as to say, ' Hark ye, John, I have friends still, and persons of rank and reputation, too.' ' Are you come to do anything in my way, sir ? My young friends, Dale and Spiggot, do all my business for me now, until my new offices are ready ; for I'm only here temporarily, you know, captain. What can we do for you, sir ? Will you like to take anything ? '

Dobbin, with a great deal of hesitation and stuttering, protested that he was not in the least hungry or thirsty ; that he had no business to transact ; that he only came to ask if Mr. Sedley was well, and to shake hands with an old friend ; and, he added, with a desperate perversion of truth, ' My mother is very well—that is, she's been very unwell, and is only waiting for the first fine day to go out and call upon Mrs. Sedley. How is Mrs. Sedley, sir ? I hope she's quite well.' And here he paused, reflecting on his own consummate hypocrisy : for the day was as fine, and the sunshine as bright as it ever is in Coffin Court, where the

'Tapioca' Coffee-house is situated : and Mr. Dobbin remembered that he had seen Mrs. Sedley himself only an hour
before, having driven Osborne down to Fulham in his gig,
and left him there *tête à tête* with Miss Amelia.

' My wife will be very happy to see her ladyship,' Sedley
replied, pulling out his papers. ' I've a very kind letter
here from your father, sir, and beg my respectful compliments to him. Lady D. will find us in rather a smaller
house than we were accustomed to receive our friends in ;
but it's snug, and the change of air does good to my daughter,
who was suffering in town rather—you remember little
Emmy, sir ?—yes, suffering a good deal.' The old gentleman's eyes were wandering as he spoke, and he was thinking
of something else, as he sat thrumming on his papers and
fumbling at the worn red tape.

' You're a military man,' he went on ; ' I ask you, Bill
Dobbin, could any man ever have speculated upon the
return of that Corsican scoundrel from Elba ? When the
allied sovereigns were here last year, and we gave 'em that
dinner in the City, sir, and we saw the Temple of Concord,
and the fireworks, and the Chinese bridge in St. James's
Park, could any sensible man suppose that peace wasn't
really concluded, after we'd actually sung *Te Deum* for it,
sir ? I ask you, William, could I suppose that the Emperor
of Austria was a damned traitor—a traitor, and nothing
more ? I don't mince words—a double-faced infernal traitor
and schemer, who meant to have his son-in-law back all
along. And I say that the escape of Boney from Elba was
a damned imposition and plot, sir, in which half the powers
of Europe were concerned, to bring the funds down, and to
ruin this country. That's why I'm here, William. That's
why my name is in the *Gazette*. Why, sir ?—because I
trusted the Emperor of Russia and the Prince Regent. Look
here. Look at my papers. Look what the funds were on
the 1st of March—what the French fives were when I bought
for the account. And what they're at now. There was
collusion, sir, or that villain never would have escaped.
Where was the English Commissioner who allowed him to
get away ? He ought to be shot,* sir—brought to a court
martial, and shot, by Jove.'

' We're going to hunt Boney out, sir,' Dobbin said, rather
alarmed at the fury of the old man, the veins of whose
forehead began to swell, and who sat drumming his papers

with his clenched fist. ' We are going to hunt him out,
sir—the Duke's in Belgium already, and we expect marching-
orders every day.'

' Give him no quarter. Bring back the villain's head, sir.
Shoot the coward down, sir,' Sedley roared. ' I'd enlist
myself, by —— ; but I'm a broken old man—ruined by
that damned scoundrel—and by a parcel of swindling thieves
in this country whom I made, sir, and who are rolling in their
carriages now,' he added, with a break in his voice.

Dobbin was not a little affected by the sight of this once
kind old friend, crazed almost with misfortune and raving
with senile anger. Pity the fallen gentleman : you to whom
money and fair repute are the chiefest good ; and so, surely,
are they in Vanity Fair.

' Yes,' he continued, ' there are some vipers that you warm,
and they sting you afterwards. There are some beggars
that you put on horseback, and they're the first to ride you
down. You know whom I mean, William Dobbin, my boy.
I mean a purse-proud villain in Russell Square, whom I knew
without a shilling, and whom I pray and hope to see a beggar
as he was when I befriended him.'

' I have heard something of this, sir, from my friend,
George,' Dobbin said, anxious to come to his point. ' The
quarrel between you and his father has cut him up a great
deal, sir. Indeed, I'm the bearer of a message from him.'

' Oh, *that's* your errand, is it ? ' cried the old man,
jumping up. ' What ! perhaps he condoles with me, does
he ? Very kind of him, the stiff-backed prig, with his dandified airs and West End swagger. He's hankering about my
house, is he still ? If my son had the courage of a man, he'd
shoot him. He's as big a villain as his father. I won't
have his name mentioned in my house. I curse the day
that ever I let him into it ; and I'd rather see my daughter
dead at my feet than married to him.'

' His father's harshness is not George's fault, sir. Your
daughter's love for him is as much your doing as his. Who
are you, that you are to play with two young people's affections and break their hearts at your will ? '

' Recollect it's not his father that breaks the match off,'
old Sedley cried out. ' It's I that forbid it. That family
and mine are separated for ever. I'm fallen low, but not
so low as that : no, no. And so you may tell the whole
race—son, and father, and sisters, and all.'

' It's my belief, sir, that you have not the power or the right to separate those two,' Dobbin answered in a low voice ; ' and that if you don't give your daughter your consent, it will be her duty to marry without it. There's no reason she should die or live miserably because you are wrong-headed. To my thinking she's just as much married as if the banns had been read in all the churches in London. And what better answer can there be to Osborne's charges against you, as charges there are, than that his son claims to enter your family and marry your daughter ? '

A light of something like satisfaction seemed to break over old Sedley as this point was put to him : but he still persisted that with his consent the marriage between Amelia and George should never take place.

' We must do it without,' Dobbin said, smiling, and told Mr. Sedley, as he had told Mrs. Sedley in the day, before, the story of Rebecca's elopement with Captain Crawley. It evidently amused the old gentleman. ' You're terrible fellows, you captains,' said he, tying up his papers ; and his face wore something like a smile upon it, to the astonishment of the blear-eyed waiter who now entered, and had never seen such an expression upon Sedley's countenance since he had used the dismal coffee-house.

The idea of hitting his enemy Osborne such a blow soothed, perhaps, the old gentleman : and, their colloquy presently ending, he and Dobbin parted pretty good friends.

' My sisters say she has diamonds as big as pigeons' eggs,' George said, laughing. ' How they must set off her com

plexion ! A perfect illumination it must be when her jewels
are on her neck. Her jet-black hair is as curly as Sambo's.
I dare say she wore a nose-ring when she went to Court ; and
with a plume of feathers in her top-knot she would look
a perfect Belle Sauvage.'*

George, in conversation with Amelia, was rallying the
appearance of a young lady of whom his father and sisters
had lately made the acquaintance, and who was an object of
vast respect to the Russell Square family. She was reported
to have I don't know how many plantations in the West
Indies ; a deal of money in the funds ; and three stars to
her name* in the East India stockholders' list. She had
a mansion in Surrey, and a house in Portland Place. The
name of the rich West India heiress had been mentioned
with applause in the *Morning Post.** Mrs. Haggistoun,
Colonel Haggistoun's widow, her relative, ' chaperoned '
her, and kept her house. She was just from school,
where she had completed her education, and George and
his sisters had met her at an evening party at old Hulker's
house, Devonshire Place (Hulker, Bullock, & Co. were
long the correspondents of her house in the West Indies),
and the girls had made the most cordial advances to her,
which the heiress had received with great good humour.
An orphan in her position—with her money—so interesting !
the Misses Osborne said. They were full of their new
friend when they returned from the Hulker ball to Miss
Wirt, their companion : they had made arrangements
for continually meeting, and had the carriage and drove
to see her the very next day. Mrs. Haggistoun, Colonel
Haggistoun's widow, a relation of Lord Binkie, and
always talking of him, struck the dear unsophisticated girls
as rather haughty, and too much inclined to talk about her
great relations : but Rhoda was everything they could wish
—the frankest, kindest, most agreeable creature—wanting
a little polish, but so good-natured. The girls Christian-
named each other at once.

' You should have seen her dress for court, Emmy,'
Osborne cried, laughing. ' She came to my sisters to show
it off, before she was presented in state by my Lady Binkie,
the Haggistoun's kinswoman. She's related to every one,
that Haggistoun. Her diamonds blazed out like Vauxhall
on the night we were there. (Do you remember Vauxhall,
Emmy, and Jos singing to his dearest diddle-iddle-darling ?)

Diamonds and mahogany, my dear ! think what an advantageous contrast—and the white feathers in her hair—
I mean in her wool. She had ear-rings like chandeliers ; you
might have lighted 'em up, by Jove—and a yellow satin
train that streeled after her like the tail of a comet.'
    ' How old is she ?' asked Emmy, to whom George was
rattling away regarding this dark paragon, on the morning
of their re-union—rattling away as no other man in the
world surely could.
    ' Why, the Black Princess, though she has only just left
school, must be two- or three-and-twenty. And you should
see the hand she writes ! Mrs. Colonel Haggistoun usually
writes her letters, but in a moment of confidence, she put
pen to paper for my sisters ; she spelt satin satting, and
Saint James's, Saint Jams.'
    ' Why, surely it must be Miss Swartz, the parlour
boarder,'* Emmy said, remembering that good-natured
young mulatto girl, who had been so hysterically affected
when Amelia left Miss Pinkerton's academy.
    ' The very name,' George said. ' Her father was a Ger-
man Jew—a slave-owner they say—connected with the
Cannibal Islands in some way or other. He died last year,
and Miss Pinkerton has finished her education. She can
play two pieces on the piano ; she knows three songs ; she
can write when Mrs. Haggistoun is by to spell for her ; and
Jane and Maria already have got to love her as a sister.'
    ' I wish they would have loved me,' said Emmy, wistfully.
' They were always very cold to me.'
    ' My dear child, they would have loved you if you had
had two hundred thousand pounds,' George replied. ' That
is the way in which they have been brought up. Ours is
a ready-money society. We live among bankers and city
big-wigs, and be hanged to them, and every man, as he
talks to you, is jingling his guineas in his pocket. There is
that jackass Fred Bullock, is going to marry Maria—there's
Goldmore, the East India Director, there's Dipley, in the
tallow trade—*our* trade,' George said, with an uneasy laugh
and a blush. ' Curse the whole pack of money-grubbing
vulgarians ! I fall asleep at their great heavy dinners. I
feel ashamed in my father's great stupid parties. I've been
accustomed to live with gentlemen, and men of the world
and fashion, Emmy, not with a parcel of turtle-fed tradesmen. Dear little woman, you are the only person of our set

who ever looked, or thought, or spoke like a lady : and you
do it because you're an angel and can't help it.   Don't
remonstrate.   You *are* the only lady.   Didn't Miss Crawley
remark it, who has lived in the best company in Europe ?
And as for Crawley, of the Life Guards, hang it, he's a fine
fellow : and I like him for marrying the girl he had chosen.'

Amelia admired Mr. Crawley very much, too, for this ;
and trusted Rebecca would be happy with him, and hoped
(with a laugh) Jos would be consoled.   And so the pair went
on prattling, as in quite early days.   Amelia's confidence
being perfectly restored to her, though she expressed a great
deal of pretty jealousy about Miss Swartz, and professed to
be dreadfully frightened—like a hypocrite as she was—lest
George should forget her for the heiress and her money and
her estates in St. Kitts.   But the fact is, she was a great
deal too happy to have fears or doubts or misgivings of any
sort : and having George at her side again, was not afraid
of any heiress or beauty, or indeed of any sort of danger.

When Captain Dobbin came back in the afternoon to
these people—which he did with a great deal of sympathy
for them—it did his heart good to see how Amelia had grown
young again—how she laughed, and chirped, and sang
familiar old songs at the piano, which were only interrupted
by the bell from without proclaiming Mr. Sedley's return
from the City, before whom George received a signal to
retreat.

Beyond the first smile of recognition—and even that was
an hypocrisy, for she thought his arrival rather provoking—
Miss Sedley did not once notice Dobbin during his visit.
But he was content, so that he saw her happy ; and thankful
to have been the means of making her so.

CHAPTER XXI

OVE may be felt for any young lady
endowed with such qualities as
Miss Swartz possessed ; and a
great dream of ambition entered
into old Mr. Osborne's soul, which
she was to realize. He encouraged,
with the utmost enthusiasm and
friendliness, his daughters' amiable
attachment to the young heiress,
and protested that it gave him the
sincerest pleasure as a father to see
the love of his girls so well disposed.

' You won't find,' he would say
to Miss Rhoda, ' that splendour
and rank to which you are accustomed at the West End,
my dear miss, at our humble mansion in Russell Square.
My daughters are plain, disinterested girls, but their hearts
are in the right place, and they've conceived an attachment
for you which does them honour—I say, which does them
honour. I'm a plain, simple, humble British merchant—
an honest one, as my respected friends Hulker & Bullock
will vouch, who were the correspondents of your late
lamented father. You'll find us a united, simple, happy,
and I think I may say respected, family—a plain table,
a plain people, but a warm welcome, my dear Miss Rhoda—
Rhoda, let me say, for my heart warms to you, it does
really. I'm a frank man, and I like you. A glass of
champagne ! Hicks, champagne to Miss Swartz.'

There is little doubt that old Osborne believed all he said,
and that the girls were quite earnest in their protestations of
affection for Miss Swartz. People in Vanity Fair fasten on
to rich folks quite naturally. If the simplest people are
disposed to look not a little kindly on great Prosperity (for
I defy any member of the British public to say that the
notion of Wealth has not something awful and pleasing to
him ; and you, if you are told that the man next you at
dinner has got half a million, not to look at him with a

certain interest)—if the simple look benevolently on
money, how much more do your old worldlings regard it !
Their affections rush out to meet and welcome money.
Their kind sentiments awaken spontaneously towards the
interesting possessors of it. I know some respectable
people who don't consider themselves at liberty to indulge
in friendship for any individual who has not a certain competency, or place in society. They give a loose to their
feelings on proper occasions. And the proof is, that the
major part of the Osborne family, who had not, in fifteen
years, been able to get up a hearty regard for Amelia Sedley,
became as fond of Miss Swartz in the course of a single
evening as the most romantic advocate of friendship at
first sight could desire.

What a match for George she'd be (the sister and Miss
Wirt agreed), and how much better than that insignificant
little Amelia ! Such a dashing young fellow as he is, with
his good looks, rank, and accomplishments, would be the
very husband for her. Visions of balls in Portland Place,
presentations at Court, and introductions to half the
peerage, filled the minds of the young ladies ; who talked
of nothing but George and his grand acquaintances to their
beloved new friend.

Old Osborne thought she would be a great match, too,
for his son. He should leave the army ; he should go into
Parliament ; he should cut a figure in the fashion and in
the state. His blood boiled with honest British exultation,
as he saw the name of Osborne ennobled in the person of
his son, and thought that he might be the progenitor of
a glorious line of baronets. He worked in the City and
on 'Change, until he knew everything relating to the fortune
of the heiress, how her money was placed, and where her
estates lay. Young Fred Bullock, one of his chief in-
formants, would have liked to make a bid for her himself (it
was so the young banker expressed it), only he was booked
to Maria Osborne. But not being able to secure her as
a wife, the disinterested Fred quite approved of her as a
sister-in-law. ' Let George cut in directly and win her,'
was his advice. ' Strike while the iron's hot, you know—
while she's fresh to the town : in a few weeks some d——
fellow from the West End will come in with a title and a
rotten rent-roll and cut all us City men out, as Lord Fitzrufus
did last year with Miss Grogram, who was actually engaged

to Podder, of Podder & Brown's. The sooner it is done
the better, Mr. Osborne; them's my sentiments,' the wag
said; though, when Osborne had left the bank parlour,
Mr. Bullock remembered Amelia, and what a pretty girl she
was, and how attached to George Osborne; and he gave
up at least ten seconds of his valuable time to regretting the
misfortune which had befallen that unlucky young woman.

While thus George Osborne's good feelings, and his good
friend and genius, Dobbin, were carrying back the truant
to Amelia's feet, George's parent and sisters were arranging
this splendid match for him, which they never dreamed he
would resist.

When the elder Osborne gave what he called ' a hint ',
there was no possibility for the most obtuse to mistake his
meaning. He called kicking a footman downstairs, a hint
to the latter to leave his service. With his usual frankness
and delicacy he told Mrs. Haggistoun that he would give
her a cheque for five thousand pounds* on the day his son
was married to her ward; and called that proposal a hint,
and considered it a very dexterous piece of diplomacy. He
gave George finally such another hint regarding the heiress;
and ordered him to marry her out of hand, as he would have
ordered his butler to draw a cork, or his clerk to write
a letter.

This imperative hint disturbed George a good deal. He
was in the very first enthusiasm and delight of his second
courtship of Amelia, which was inexpressibly sweet to him.
The contrast of her manners and appearance with those of
the heiress, made the idea of a union with the latter appear
doubly ludicrous and odious. Carriages and opera-boxes,
thought he; fancy being seen in them by the side of such
a mahogany charmer as that! Add to all, that the Junior
Osborne was quite as obstinate as the Senior: when he
wanted a thing, quite as firm in his resolution to get it;
and quite as violent when angered, as his father in his most
stern moments.

On the first day when his father formally gave him the
hint that he was to place his affections at Miss Swartz's
feet, George temporized with the old gentleman. ' You
should have thought of the matter sooner, sir,' he said. ' It
can't be done now, when we're expecting every day to go
on foreign service. Wait till my return, if I do return;'
and then he represented, that the time when the regiment

was daily expecting to quit England, was exceedingly ill-chosen : that the few days or weeks during which they were still to remain at home, must be devoted to business and not to love-making : time enough for that when he came home with his majority ; ' for, I promise you,' said he, with a satisfied air, ' that one way or other you shall read the name of George Osborne in the *Gazette*.'

The father's reply to this was founded upon the information which he had got in the City : that the West End chaps would infallibly catch hold of the heiress if any delay took place : that if he didn't marry Miss S., he might at least have an engagement in writing, to come into effect when he returned to England ; and that a man who could get ten thousand a year by staying at home, was a fool to risk his life abroad.

' So that you would have me shown up as a coward, sir, and our name dishonoured for the sake of Miss Swartz's money,' George interposed.

This remark staggered the old gentleman ; but as he had to reply to it, and as his mind was nevertheless made up, he said, ' You will dine here to-morrow, sir, and every day Miss Swartz comes, you will be here to pay your respects to her. If you want for money, call upon Mr. Chopper.' Thus a new obstacle was in George's way, to interfere with his plans regarding Amelia ; and about which he and Dobbin had more than one confidential consultation. His friend's opinion respecting the line of conduct which he ought to pursue, we know already. And as for Osborne, when he was once bent on a thing, a fresh obstacle or two only rendered him the more resolute.

The dark object of the conspiracy into which the chiefs of the Osborne family had entered, was quite ignorant of all their plans regarding her (which, strange to say, her friend and chaperon did not divulge), and, taking all the young ladies' flattery for genuine sentiment, and being, as we have before had occasion to show, of a very warm and impetuous nature, responded to their affection with quite a tropical ardour. And if the truth may be told, I dare say that she too had some selfish attraction in the Russell Square house ; and, in a word, thought George Osborne a very nice young man. His whiskers had made an impression upon her, on the very first-night she beheld them at the ball at Messrs.

Hulkers ; and, as we know, she was not the first woman
who had been charmed by them. George had an air at
once swaggering and melancholy, languid and fierce. He
looked like a man who had passions, secrets, and private
harrowing griefs and adventures. His voice was rich and
deep. He would say it was a warm evening, or ask his
partner to take an ice, with a tone as sad and confidential
as if he were breaking her mother's death to her, or preluding
a declaration of love. He trampled over all the young
bucks of his father's circle, and was the hero among those
third-rate men. Some few sneered at him and hated him.
Some, like Dobbin, fanatically admired him. And his
whiskers had began to do their work, and to curl themselves
round the affections of Miss Swartz.

Whenever there was a chance of meeting him in Russell
Square, that simple and good-natured young woman was
quite in a flurry to see her dear Miss Osbornes. She went
to great expenses in new gowns, and bracelets, and bonnets,
and in prodigious feathers. She adorned her person with
her utmost skill to please the Conqueror, and exhibited all
her simple accomplishments to win his favour. The girls
would ask her, with the greatest gravity, for a little music,
and she would sing her three songs and play her two little
pieces as often as ever they asked, and with an always
increasing pleasure to herself. During these delectable
entertainments, Miss Wirt and the chaperon sat by, and
conned over the *Peerage*, and talked about the nobility.

The day after George had his hint from his father, and
a short time before the hour of dinner, he was lolling upon
a sofa in the drawing-room in a very becoming and perfectly
natural attitude of melancholy. He had been, at his
father's request, to Mr. Chopper in the City (the old gentleman, though he gave great sums to his son, would never
specify any fixed allowance for him, and rewarded him
only as he was in the humour). He had then been to pass
three hours with Amelia, his dear little Amelia, at Fulham ;
and he came home to find his sisters spread in starched
muslin in the drawing-room, the dowagers cackling in the
background, and honest Swartz in her favourite amber-
coloured satin, with turquoise-bracelets, countless rings,
flowers, feathers, and all sorts of tags and gimcracks, about
as elegantly decorated as a she chimney-sweep on May-
Day.

MISS SWARTZ REHEARSING FOR THE DRAWING-ROOM

The girls, after vain attempts to engage him in conversation, talked about fashions and the last Drawing-room until he was perfectly sick of their chatter. He contrasted their behaviour with little Emmy's—their shrill voices with her tender ringing tones ; their attitudes and their elbows and their starch, with her humble soft movements and modest graces. Poor Swartz was seated in a place where Emmy had been accustomed to sit. Her bejewelled hands lay sprawling in her amber satin lap. Her tags and ear-rings twinkled, and her big eyes rolled about. She was doing nothing with perfect contentment, and thinking herself charming. Anything so becoming as the satin the sisters had never seen.

'Dammy,' George said to a confidential friend, 'she looked like a China doll, which has nothing to do all day but to grin and wag its head. By Jove, Will, it was all I could do to prevent myself from throwing the sofa-cushion at her.' He restrained that exhibition of sentiment, however.

The sisters began to play the Battle of Prague. 'Stop that d—— thing,' George howled out in a fury from the sofa. 'It makes me mad. *You* play us something, Miss Swartz, do. Sing something, anything but the Battle of Prague.'

'Shall I sing *Blue Eyed Mary*, or the air from the Cabinet ?' Miss Swartz asked.

'That sweet thing from the Cabinet,' the sisters said.

'We've had that,' replied the misanthrope on the sofa.

'I can sing *Fluvy du Tajy*,' Swartz said, in a meek voice, 'if I had the words.' It was the last of the worthy young woman's collection.

'Oh, *Fleuve du Tage*,* Miss Maria cried ; 'we have the song,' and went to fetch the book in which it was.

Now it happened that this song, then in the height of the fashion, had been given to the young ladies by a young friend of theirs, whose name was on the title, and Miss Swartz, having concluded the ditty with George's applause (for he remembered that it was a favourite of Amelia's), was hoping for an encore perhaps, and fiddling with the leaves of the music, when her eye fell upon the title, and she saw 'Amelia Sedley' written in the corner.

'Lor !' cried Miss Swartz, spinning swiftly round on the music-stool, 'is it *my* Amelia? Amelia that was at Miss P.'s

at Hammersmith ? I know it is. It's her, and—Tell me
about her—where is she ? '

'Don't mention her,' Miss Maria Osborne said hastily.
' Her family has disgraced itself. Her father cheated papa,
and as for her, she is never to be mentioned *here*.' This
was Miss Maria's return for George's rudeness about the
Battle of Prague.

'Are you a friend of Amelia's ? ' George said, bouncing

up. 'God bless you for it, Miss Swartz. Don't believe
what the girls say. *She's* not to blame at any rate. She's
the best——'

'You know you're not to speak about her, George,' cried
Jane. 'Papa forbids it.'

'Who's to prevent me ? ' George cried out. 'I *will*
speak of her. I say she's the best, the kindest, the gentlest,
the sweetest girl in England ; and that, bankrupt or no,
my sisters are not fit to hold candles to her. If you like
her, go and see her, Miss Swartz ; she wants friends now ;
and I say, God bless everybody who befriends her. Anybody who speaks kindly of her is my friend ; anybody who
speaks against her is my enemy. Thank you, Miss Swartz ; '
and he went up and wrung her hand.

'George! George!' one of the sisters cried imploringly.

'I say,' George said fiercely, 'I thank everybody who loves Amelia Sed——.' He stopped. Old Osborne was in the room with a face livid with rage, and eyes like hot coals.

Though George had stopped in his sentence, yet, his blood being up, he was not to be cowed by all the generations of Osborne; rallying instantly, he replied to the bullying look of his father, with another so indicative of resolution and defiance, that the elder man quailed in his turn, and looked away. He felt that the tussle was coming. 'Mrs. Haggistoun, let me take you down to dinner,' he said. 'Give your arm to Miss Swartz, George,' and they marched.

'Miss Swartz, I love Amelia, and we've been engaged almost all our lives,' Osborne said to his partner; and during all the dinner, George rattled on with a volubility which surprised himself, and made his father doubly nervous for the fight which was to take place as soon as the ladies were gone.

The difference between the pair was, that while the father was violent and a bully, the son had thrice the nerve and courage of the parent, and could not merely make an attack, but resist it; and finding that the moment was now come when the contest between him and his father was to be decided, he took his dinner with perfect coolness and appetite before the engagement began. Old Osborne, on the contrary, was nervous, and drank much. He floundered in his conversation with the ladies, his neighbours: George's coolness only rendering him more angry. It made him half mad to see the calm way in which George, flapping his napkin, and with a swaggering bow, opened the door for the ladies to leave the room; and filling himself a glass of wine, smacked it, and looked his father full in the face, as if to say, 'Gentlemen of the Guard, fire first.' The old man also took a supply of ammunition, but his decanter clinked against the glass as he tried to fill it.

After giving a great heave, and with a purple choking face, he then began. 'How dare you, sir, mention that person's name before Miss Swartz to-day, in my drawing-room? I ask you, sir, how dare you do it?'

'Stop, sir,' says George, 'don't say dare, sir. Dare isn't a word to be used to a captain in the British Army.'

'I shall say what I like to my son, sir. I can cut him off with a shilling if I like. I can make him a beggar if I like. I *will* say what I like,' the elder said.

'I'm a gentleman though I *am* your son, sir,' George answered haughtily. 'Any communications which you have to make to me, or any orders which you may please to give, I beg may be couched in that kind of language which I am accustomed to hear.'

Whenever the lad assumed his haughty manner, it always created either great awe or great irritation in the parent. Old Osborne stood in secret terror of his son as a better gentleman than himself; and perhaps my readers may have remarked in their experience of this Vanity Fair of ours, that there is no character which a low-minded man so much mistrusts, as that of a gentleman.

'My father didn't give me the education you have had, nor the advantages you have had, nor the money you have had. If I had kept the company *some folks* have had through *my means*, perhaps my son wouldn't have any reason to brag, of his *superiority* and *West End airs*' (these words were uttered in the elder Osborne's most sarcastic tones). 'But it wasn't considered the part of a gentleman, in *my* time, for a man to insult his father. If I'd done any such thing, mine would have kicked me downstairs, sir.'

'I never insulted you, sir. I said I begged you to remember your son was a gentleman as well as yourself. I know very well that you give me plenty of money,' said George (fingering a bundle of notes which he had got in the morning from Mr. Chopper). 'You tell it me often enough, sir. There's no fear of my forgetting it.'

'I wish you'd remember other things as well, sir,' the sire answered. 'I wish you'd remember that in this house —so long as you choose to *honour* it with your *company*, captain—I'm the master, and that name, and that that— that you—that I say——'

'That what, sir?' George asked, with scarcely a sneer, filling another glass of claret.

'——!' burst out his father with a screaming oath— 'that the name of those Sedleys never be mentioned here, sir—not one of the whole damned lot of 'em, sir.'

'It wasn't I, sir, that introduced Miss Sedley's name. It was my sisters who spoke ill of her to Miss Swartz; and by Jove I'll defend her wherever I go. Nobody shall speak

lightly of that name in my presence. Our family has done
her quite enough injury already, I think, and may leave
off reviling her now she's down. I'll shoot any man but
you who says a word against her.'

'Go on, sir, go on,' the old gentleman said, his eyes
starting out of his head.

'Go on about what, sir ? about the way in which we've
treated that angel of a girl ? Who told me to love her ?
It was your doing. I might have chosen elsewhere, and
looked higher, perhaps, than your society : but I obeyed
you. And now that her heart's mine you give me orders
to fling it away, and punish her, kill her perhaps—for the
faults of other people. It's a shame, by Heavens,' said
George, working himself up into passion and enthusiasm
as he proceeded, ' to play at fast and loose with a young
girl's affections—and with such an angel as that—one so
superior to the people amongst whom she lived that she
might have excited envy, only she was so good and gentle
that it's a wonder anybody dared to hate her. If I desert
her, sir, do you suppose she forgets me ? '

'I ain't going to have any of this dam sentimental
nonsense and humbug here, sir,' the father cried out.
' There shall be no beggar-marriages in my family. If you
choose to fling away eight thousand a year, which you may
have for the asking, you may do it : but by Jove you take
your pack and walk out of this house, sir. Will you do as
I tell you, once for all, sir, or will you not ? '

'Marry that mulatto woman ? ' George said, pulling up
his shirt-collars. ' I don't like the colour, sir. Ask the
black that sweeps opposite Fleet Market,* sir. I'm not
going to marry a Hottentot Venus.'

Mr. Osborne pulled frantically at the cord by which he
was accustomed to summon the butler when he wanted
wine—and, almost black in the face, ordered that functionary to call a coach for Captain Osborne.

'I've done it,' said George, coming into the Slaughter's
an hour afterwards, looking very pale.

'What, my boy ? ' says Dobbin.

George told what had passed between his father and
himself.

'I'll marry her to-morrow,' he said with an oath. ' I love
ner more every day, Dobbin.'

CHAPTER XXII

A MARRIAGE AND PART OF A HONEYMOON

NEMIES the most obstinate and courageous can't hold out against starva-
tion; so the elder Osborne felt himself
pretty easy about his adversary in
the encounter we have just described;
and as soon as George's supplies fell
short, confidently expected his un-
conditional submission. It was unlucky, to be sure, that the lad should
have secured a stock of provisions
on the very day when the first
encounter took place; but this
relief was only temporary, old Osborne thought, and would
but delay George's surrender. No communication passed
between father and son for some days. The former was
sulky at this silence, but not disquieted; for, as he said,
he knew where he could put the screw upon George, and
only waited the result of that operation. He told the
sisters the upshot of the dispute between them, but
ordered them to take no notice of the matter, and welcome
George on his return as if nothing had happened. His
cover was laid as usual every day, and perhaps the old
gentleman rather anxiously expected him; but he never
came. Some one inquired at the Slaughter's regarding
him, where it was said that he and his friend Captain
Dobbin had left town.

One gusty, raw day at the end of April,—the rain whipping
the pavement of that ancient street where the old Slaughter's
Coffee-house was once situated—George Osborne came
into the coffee-room, looking very haggard and pale;
although dressed rather smartly in a blue coat and brass
buttons, and a neat buff waistcoat of the fashion of those
days. Here was his friend Captain Dobbin, in blue and
brass too, having abandoned the military frock and French-
grey trousers, which were the usual coverings of his lanky
person.

Dobbin had been in the coffee-room for an hour or more. He had tried all the papers, but could not read them. He had looked at the clock many scores of times; and at the street, where the rain was pattering down, and the people as they clinked by in pattens, left long reflections on the shining stones : he tattooed at the table : he bit his nails most completely, and nearly to the quick (he was accustomed to ornament his great big hands in this way) : he balanced the teaspoon dexterously on the milk jug : upset it, &c. &c. ; and in fact showed those signs of disquietude, and practised those desperate attempts at amusement, which men are accustomed to employ when very anxious, and expectant, and perturbed in mind.

Some of his comrades, gentlemen who used the room, joked him about the splendour of his costume and his agitation of manner. One asked him if he was going to be married ? Dobbin laughed, and said he would send his acquaintance (Major Wagstaff, of the Engineers) a piece of cake when that event took place. At length Captain Osborne made his appearance, very smartly dressed, but very pale and agitated, as we have said. He wiped his pale face with a large yellow bandanna pocket-handkerchief that was prodigiously scented. He shook hands with Dobbin, looked at the clock, and told John, the waiter, to bring him some curaçoa. Of this cordial he swallowed off a couple of glasses with nervous eagerness. His friend asked with some interest about his health.

' Couldn't get a wink of sleep till daylight, Dob,' said he. ' Infernal headache and fever. Got up at nine, and went down to the Hummums* for a bath. I say, Dob, I feel just as I did on the morning I went out with Rocket at Quebec.'

' So do I,' William responded. ' I was a deuced deal more nervous than you were that morning. You made a famous breakfast, I remember. Eat something now.'

' You're a good old fellow, Will. I'll drink your health, old boy, and farewell to——'

' No, no ; two glasses are enough,' Dobbin interrupted him. ' Here, take away the liqueurs, John. Have some cayenne-pepper with your fowl. Make haste though, for it is time we were there.'

It was about half an hour from twelve when this brief meeting and colloquy took place between the two captains.

A coach, into which Captain Osborne's servant put his master's desk and dressing-case, had been in waiting for some time ; and into this the two gentlemen hurried under an umbrella, and the valet mounted on the box, cursing the rain and the dampness of the coachman who was steaming beside him. ' We shall find a better trap than this at the chutch-door,' says he ; ' that's a comfort.' And the carriage drove on, taking the road down Piccadilly ; where Apsley House and St. George's Hospital wore red jackets still ; where there were oil-lamps ; where Achilles was not yet born ; nor the Pimlico arch raised ; nor the hideous equestrian monster which pervades it and the neighbourhood ;—and so they drove down by Brompton to a certain chapel near the Fulham Road there.*

A chariot was in waiting with four horses ; likewise a coach of the kind called glass coaches. Only a very few idlers were collected on account of the dismal rain.

' Hang it ! ' said George, ' I said only a pair.'

' My master would have four,' said Mr. Joseph Sedley's servant, who was in waiting ; and he and Mr. Osborne's man agreed, as they followed George and William into the church, that it was a ' reg'lar shabby turn hout ; and with scarce so much as a breakfast or a wedding faviour.'

' Here you are,' said our old friend, Jos Sedley, coming forward. ' You're five minutes late, George, my boy. What a day, eh ? Demmy, it's like the commencement of the rainy season in Bengal. But you'll find my carriage is watertight. Come along, my mother and Emmy are in the vestry.'

Jos Sedley was splendid. He was fatter than ever. His shirt-collars were higher ; his face was redder ; his shirt-frill flaunted gorgeously out of his variegated waistcoat. Varnished boots were not invented as yet ; but the Hessians on his beautiful legs shone so, that they must have been the identical pair in which the gentleman in the old picture used to shave himself ;* and on his light-green coat there bloomed a fine wedding-favour, like a great white spreading magnolia.

In a word, George had thrown the great cast. He was going to be married. Hence his pallor and nervousness— his sleepless night and agitation in the morning. I have heard people who have gone through the same thing own to the same emotion. After three or four ceremonies, you get accustomed to it, no doubt; but the first dip, everybody allows, is awful.

The bride was dressed in a brown silk pelisse (as Captain Dobbin has since informed me), and wore a straw bonnet with a pink ribbon; over the bonnet she had a veil of white Chantilly lace, a gift from Mr. Joseph Sedley, her brother. Captain Dobbin himself had asked leave to present her with a gold chain and watch, which she sported on this occasion; and her mother gave her her diamond brooch—almost the only trinket which was left to the old lady. As the service went on, Mrs. Sedley sat and whimpered a great deal in a pew, consoled by the Irish maid-servant and Mrs. Clapp from the lodgings. Old Sedley would not be present. Jos acted for his father, giving away the bride, whilst Captain Dobbin stepped up as groomsman to his friend George.

There was nobody in the church besides the officiating persons and the small marriage party and their attendants. The two valets sat aloof superciliously. The rain came rattling down on the windows. In the intervals of the service you heard it, and the sobbing of old Mrs. Sedley in the pew. The parson's tones echoed sadly through the empty walls. Osborne's 'I will' was sounded in very deep bass. Emmy's response came fluttering up to her lips from her heart, but was scarcely heard by anybody except Captain Dobbin.

When the service was completed, Jos Sedley came forward and kissed his sister, the bride, for the first time for many months; George's look of gloom had gone, and he seemed quite proud and radiant. 'It's your turn, William,' says he, putting his hand fondly upon Dobbin's shoulder; and Dobbin went up and touched Amelia on the cheek.

Then they went into the vestry and signed the register. 'God bless you, Old Dobbin,' George said, grasping him by the hand, with something very like moisture glistening in his eyes. William replied only by nodding his head. His heart was too full to say much.

'Write directly, and come down as soon as you can, you know,' Osborne said. After Mrs. Sedley had taken an hysterical adieu of her daughter, the pair went off to the carriage. 'Get out of the way, you little devils,' George cried to a small crowd of damp urchins, that were hanging about the chapel-door. The rain drove into the bride and

bridegroom's faces as they passed to the chariot. The
postilions' favours draggled on their dripping jackets.
The few children made a dismal cheer, as the carriage,
splashing mud, drove away.

William Dobbin stood in the church-porch, looking at
it, a queer figure. The small crew of spectators jeered
him. He was not thinking about them or their laughter.

'Come home and have some tiffin, Dobbin,' a voice cried
behind him ; as a pudgy hand was laid on his shoulder,
and the honest fellow's reverie was interrupted. But the
captain had no heart to go a-feasting with Jos Sedley.
He put the weeping old lady and her attendants into the
carriage along with Jos, and left them without any farther
words passing. This carriage, too, drove away, and the
urchins gave another sarcastical cheer.

'Here, you little beggars,' Dobbin said, giving some
sixpences amongst them, and then went off by himself
through the rain. It was all over. They were married,
and happy, he prayed God. Never since he was a boy had
he felt so miserable and so lonely. He longed with a heart-
sick yearning for the first few days to be over, that he
might see her again.

Some ten days after the above ceremony, three young
men of our acquaintance were enjoying that beautiful prospect of bow-windows on the one side and blue sea on the
other, which Brighton affords to the traveller. Sometimes
it is towards the ocean—smiling with countless dimples,
speckled with white sails, with a hundred bathing-machines
kissing the skirt of his blue garment—that the Londoner
looks enraptured : sometimes, on the contrary, a lover
of human nature rather than of prospects of any kind, it is
towards the bow-windows that he turns, and that swarm
of human life which they exhibit. From one issue the
notes of a piano, which a young lady in ringlets practises
six hours daily, to the delight of the fellow lodgers : at
another, lovely Polly, the nursemaid, may be seen dandling
Master Omnium in her arms : whilst Jacob, his papa, is
beheld eating prawns, and devouring the *Times* for breakfast, at the window below. Yonder are the Misses Leery,
who are looking out for the young officers of the Heavies,
who are pretty sure to be pacing the cliff ; or again it is
a City man, with a nautical turn, and a telescope, the size

of a six-pounder, who has his instrument pointed seawards, so as to command every pleasure-boat, herring-boat, or bathing-machine that comes to, or quits, the shore, &c., &c.   But have we any leisure for a description of Brighton ? —for Brighton, a clean Naples with genteel lazzaroni—for Brighton, that always looks brisk, gay, and gaudy, like a harlequin's jacket—for Brighton, which used to be seven hours' distant from London at the time of our story ; which is now only a hundred minutes off ; and which may approach who knows how much nearer, unless Joinville comes and untimely bombards it ?*

'What a monstrous fine girl that is in the lodgings over the milliner's,' one of these three promenaders remarked to the other ; 'Gad, Crawley, did you see what a wink she gave me as I passed ? '

'Don't break her heart, Jos, you rascal,' said another. 'Don't trifle with her affections, you Don Juan ! '

'Get away,' said Jos Sedley, quite pleased, and leering up at the maidservant in question with a most killing ogle.   Jos was even more splendid at Brighton than he had been at his sister's marriage.   He had brilliant under-waistcoats, any one of which would have set up a moderate buck.   He sported a military frock-coat, ornamented with frogs, knobs, black buttons, and meandering embroidery. He had affected a military appearance and habits of late ; and he walked with his two friends, who were of that profession, clinking his boot-spurs, swaggering prodigiously, and shooting death-glances at all the servant girls who were worthy to be slain.

'What shall we do, boys, till the ladies return ? ' the buck asked.   The ladies were out to Rottingdean in his carriage on a drive.   'Let's have a game at billiards,' one of his friends said—the tall one, with lacquered moustachios.

'No, dammy ; no, captain,' Jos replied, rather alarmed. 'No billiards to-day, Crawley, my boy ; yesterday was enough.'

'You play very well,' said Crawley, laughing.   'Don't he, Osborne ?   How well he made that five stroke,* eh ? '

'Famous,' Osborne said.   'Jos is a devil of a fellow at billiards, and at everything else, too.   I wish there were any tiger-hunting about here ; we might go and kill a few before dinner. (There goes a fine girl ! what an ankle, eh,

Jos ?) Tell us that story about the tiger-hunt, and the
way you did for him in the jungle—it's a wonderful story
that, Crawley.' Here George Osborne gave a yawn. 'It's
rather slow work,' said he, 'down here; what *shall* we do ?'

'Shall we go and look at some horses that Snaffler's just
brought from Lewes fair ?' Crawley said.

'Suppose we go and have some jellies at Dutton's,' said
the rogue Jos, willing to kill two birds with one stone.
'Devilish fine gal at Dutton's.'*

'Suppose we go and see the "Lightning" come in, it's just
about time ?' George said. This advice prevailing over
the stables and the jelly, they turned towards the coach-
office to witness the 'Lightning's' arrival.*

As they passed, they met the carriage—Jos Sedley's
open carriage, with its magnificent armorial bearings—that
splendid conveyance in which he used to drive about at
Cheltenham, majestic and solitary, with his arms folded,
and his hat cocked; or, more happy, with ladies by his
side.

Two were in the carriage now : one a little person, with
light hair, and dressed in the height of the fashion; the
other in a brown silk pelisse, and a straw bonnet with pink
ribbons, with a rosy, round, happy face, that did you good
to behold. She checked the carriage as it neared the
three gentlemen, after which exercise of authority she
looked rather nervous, and then began to blush most
absurdly. 'We have had a delightful drive, George,' she
said, 'and—and we're so glad to come back; and Joseph,
don't let him be late.'

'Don't be leading our husbands into mischief, Mr. Sedley,
you wicked, wicked man you,' Rebecca said, shaking at
Jos a pretty little finger covered with the neatest French
kid glove. 'No billiards, no smoking, no naughtiness !'

'My dear Mrs. Crawley—Ah now ! upon my honour !'
was all Jos could ejaculate by way of reply ; but he managed
to fall into a tolerable attitude, with his head lying on his
shoulder, grinning upwards at his victim, with one hand
at his back, which he supported on his cane, and the other
hand (the one with the diamond ring) fumbling in his shirt-
frill and among his under-waistcoats. As the carriage
drove off he kissed the diamond hand to the fair ladies
within. He wished all Cheltenham, all Chowringhee, all
Calcutta, could see him in that position, waving his hand

to such a beauty, and in company with such a famous
buck as Rawdon Crawley of the Guards.

Our young bride and bridegroom had chosen Brighton
as the place where they would pass the first few days after
their marriage ; and having engaged apartments at the
'Ship' Inn,* enjoyed themselves there in great comfort and
quietude, until Jos presently joined them. Nor was he
the only companion they found there. As they were
coming into the hotel from a seaside walk one afternoon,
on whom should they light but Rebecca and her husband.
The recognition was immediate. Rebecca flew into the
arms of her dearest friend. Crawley and Osborne shook
hands together cordially enough : and Becky, in the
course of a very few hours, found means to make the latter
forget that little unpleasant passage of words which had
happened between them. 'Do you remember the last
time we met at Miss Crawley's, when I was so rude to you,
dear Captain Osborne ? I thought you seemed careless
about dear Amelia. It was that made me angry : and
so pert : and so unkind : and so ungrateful. Do forgive
me !' Rebecca said, and she held out her hand with so
frank and winning a grace, that Osborne could not but
take it. By humbly and frankly acknowledging yourself
to be in the wrong, there is no knowing, my son, what good
you may do. I knew once a gentleman, and very worthy
practitioner in Vanity Fair, who used to do little wrongs
to his neighbours on purpose, and in order to apologize
for them in an open and manly way afterwards—and
what ensued ? My friend Crocky Doyle was liked everywhere, and deemed to be rather impetuous—but the
honestest fellow. Becky's humility passed for sincerity
with George Osborne.

These two young couples had plenty of tales to relate
to each other. The marriages of either were discussed ;
and their prospects in life canvassed with the greatest
frankness and interest on both sides. George's marriage
was to be made known to his father by his friend Captain
Dobbin ; and young Osborne trembled rather for the
result of that communication. Miss Crawley, on whom
all Rawdon's hopes depended, still held out. Unable to
make an entry into her house in Park Lane, her affectionate
nephew and niece had followed her to Brighton, where they
had emissaries continually planted at her door.

'I wish you could see some of Rawdon's friends who
are always about *our* door,' Rebecca said, laughing. 'Did
you ever see a dun, my dear ; or a bailiff and his man ?
Two of the abominable wretches watched all last week at
the greengrocer's opposite, and we could not get away until
Sunday. If aunty does not relent, what *shall* we do ? '

Rawdon, with roars of laughter, related a dozen amusing
anecdotes of his duns, and Rebecca's adroit treatment of
them. He vowed with a great oath, that there was no
woman in Europe who could talk a creditor over as she
could. Almost immediately after their marriage, her
practice had begun, and her husband found the immense
value of such a wife. They had credit in plenty, but they
had bills also in abundance, and laboured under a scarcity
of ready money. Did these debt-difficulties affect Rawdon's
good spirits ? No. Everybody in Vanity Fair must have
remarked how well those live who are comfortably and
thoroughly in debt : how they deny themselves nothing ;
how jolly and easy they are in their minds. Rawdon and
his wife had the very best apartments at the inn at Brighton ;
the landlord, as he brought in the first dish, bowed before
them as to his greatest customers : and Rawdon abused
the dinners and wine with an audacity which no grandee
in the land could surpass. Long custom, a manly appearance, faultless boots and clothes, and a happy fierceness of
manner, will often help a man as much as a great balance
at the banker's.

The two wedding parties met constantly in each other's
apartments. After two or three nights the gentlemen of
an evening had a little piquet, as their wives sat and chatted
apart. This pastime, and the arrival of Jos Sedley, who
made his appearance in his grand open carriage, and who
played a few games at billiards with Captain Crawley,
replenished Rawdon's purse somewhat, and gave him the
benefit of that ready money for which the greatest spirits
are sometimes at a standstill.

So the three gentlemen walked down to see the 'Lightning'
coach come in. Punctual to the minute, the coach crowded
inside and out, the guard blowing his accustomed tune on
the horn—the ' Lightning ' came tearing down the street,
and pulled up at the coach-office.

' Hullo ! there's old Dobbin,' George cried, quite delighted
to see his old friend perched on the roof ; and whose pro-

mised visit to Brighton had been delayed until now. ' How
are you, old fellow ? Glad you're come down. Emmy 'll
be delighted to see you,' Osborne said, shaking his comrade
warmly by the hand as soon as his descent from the vehicle
was effected—and then he added, in a lower and agitated
voice, ' What's the news. Have you been in Russell
Square ? What does the governor say ? Tell me everything.'

Dobbin looked very pale and grave. ' I've seen your
father,' said he. ' How's Amelia—Mrs. George ? I'll
tell you all the news presently : but I've brought the great
news of all : and that is——'

' Out with it, old fellow,' George said.

' We're ordered to Belgium. All the army goes—Guards
and all. Heavytop's got the gout, and is mad at not being
able to move. O'Dowd goes in command, and we embark
from Chatham next week.'

This news of war could not but come with a shock upon
our lovers, and caused all these gentlemen to look very
serious.

CHAPTER XXIII

CAPTAIN DOBBIN PROCEEDS ON HIS CANVASS

HAT is the secret mesmerism
which friendship possesses,
and under the operation of
which a person ordinarily
sluggish, or cold, or timid,
becomes wise, active, and
resolute, in another's behalf ?
As Alexis, after a few passes
from Dr. Elliotson,* despises
pain, reads with the back of
his head, sees miles off, looks
into next week, and performs
other wonders, of which, in
his own private normal condition, he is quite incapable ;
so you see, in the affairs of the world, and under the mag-
netism of friendship, the modest man become bold, the

shy confident, the lazy active, or the impetuous prudent
and peaceful. What is it, on the other hand, that makes
the lawyer eschew his own cause, and call in his learned
brother as an adviser ? And what causes the doctor,
when ailing, to send for his rival, and not sit down and
examine his own tongue in the chimney-glass,* or write his
own prescription at his study-table ? I throw out these
queries for intelligent readers to answer, who know, at
once, how credulous we are, and how sceptical, how soft
and how obstinate, how firm for others and how diffident
about ourselves : meanwhile, it is certain that our friend
William Dobbin, who was personally of so complying
a disposition that if his parents had pressed him much,
it is probable he would have stepped down into the kitchen
and married the cook, and who, to further his own interests,
would have found the most insuperable difficulty in walking
across the street, found himself as busy and eager in the
conduct of George Osborne's affairs, as the most selfish
tactician could be in the pursuit of his own.

Whilst our friend George and his young wife were enjoying
the first blushing days of the honeymoon at Brighton,
honest William was left as George's plenipotentiary in
London, to transact all the business part of the marriage.
His duty it was to call upon old Sedley and his wife, and
to keep the former in good humour : to draw Jos and his
brother-in-law nearer together, so that Jos's position and
dignity, as collector of Boggley Wollah, might compensate
for his father's loss of station, and tend to reconcile old
Osborne to the alliance : and finally, to communicate it
to the latter in such a way as should least irritate the old
gentleman.

Now, before he faced the head of the Osborne house with
the news which it was his duty to tell, Dobbin bethought
him that it would be politic to make friends of the rest of
the family, and, if possible, have the ladies on his side.
They can't be angry in their hearts, thought he. No woman
ever was really angry at a romantic marriage. A little
crying out, and they must come round to their brother ;
when the three of us will lay siege to old Mr. Osborne.
So this Machiavellian captain of infantry cast about him
for some happy means or stratagem by which he could
gently and gradually bring the Miss Osbornes to a knowledge of their brother's secret.

By a little inquiry regarding his mother's engagements, he was pretty soon able to find out by whom of her ladyship's friends parties were given at that season ; where he would be likely to meet Osborne's sisters ; and, though he had that abhorrence of routs and evening parties, which many sensible men, alas ! entertain, he soon found one where the Miss Osbornes were to be present. Making his appearance at the ball, where he danced a couple of sets with both of them, and was prodigiously polite, he actually had the courage to ask Miss Osborne for a few minutes' conversation at an early hour the next day, when he had, he said, to communicate to her news of the very greatest interest.

What was it that made her start back, and gaze upon him for a moment, and then on the ground at her feet, and make as if she would faint on his arm, had he not by opportunely treading on her toes, brought the young lady back to self-control ? Why was she so violently agitated at Dobbin's request ? This can never be known. But when he came the next day, Maria was not in the drawing-room with her sister, and Miss Wirt went off for the purpose of fetching the latter, and the captain and Miss Osborne were left together. They were both so silent that the tick-tock of the Sacrifice of Iphigenia clock on the mantelpiece became quite rudely audible.

'What a nice party it was last night,' Miss Osborne at length began, encouragingly ; 'and—and how you're improved in your dancing, Captain Dobbin. Surely somebody has taught you,' she added, with amiable archness.

'You should see me dance a reel with Mrs. Major O'Dowd of ours ; and a jig—did you ever see a jig ? But I think anybody could dance with *you*, Miss Osborne, who dance so well.'

'Is the major's lady young and beautiful, captain ?' the fair questioner continued. 'Ah, what a terrible thing it must be to be a soldier's wife ! I wonder they have any spirits to dance, and in these dreadful times of war, too ! Oh, Captain Dobbin, I tremble sometimes when I think of our dearest George, and the dangers of the poor soldier. Are there many married officers of the —th, Captain Dobbin ?'

'Upon my word, she's playing her hand rather too openly,' Miss Wirt thought ; but this observation is merely

parenthetic, and was not heard through the crevice of the
door at which the governess uttered it.

'One of our young men is just married,' Dobbin said,
now coming to the point. 'It was a very old attachment,
and the young couple are as poor as church mice.'

'Oh, how delightful! Oh, how romantic!' Miss Osborne
cried, as the captain said 'old attachment' and 'poor'.
Her sympathy encouraged him.

'The finest young fellow in the regiment,' he continued.
'Not a braver or handsomer officer in the army; and such
a charming wife! How you would like her! how you
will like her when you know her, Miss Osborne.' The young
lady thought the actual moment had arrived, and that
Dobbin's nervousness which now came on and was visible
in many twitchings of his face, in his manner of beating
the ground with his great feet, in the rapid buttoning and
unbuttoning of his frock-coat, &c.—Miss Osborne, I say,
thought that when he had given himself a little air, he
would unbosom himself entirely, and prepared eagerly to
listen. And the clock, in the altar on which Iphigenia
was situated, beginning, after a preparatory convulsion,
to toll twelve, the mere tolling seemed as if it would last
until one—so prolonged was the knell to the anxious spinster.

'But it's not about marriage that I came to speak—that
is that marriage—that is—no, I mean—my dear Miss
Osborne, it's about our dear friend George,' Dobbin said.

'About George?' she said in a tone so discomfited that
Maria and Miss Wirt laughed at the other side of the door,
and even that abandoned wretch of a Dobbin felt inclined
to smile himself; for he was not altogether unconscious of
the state of affairs: George having often bantered him
gracefully and said 'Hang it, Will, why don't you take old
Polly? She'll have you if you ask her. I'll bet you five
to two she will.'

'Yes, about George, then,' he continued. 'There has
been a difference between him and Mr. Osborne. And
I regard him so much—for you know we have been like
brothers—that I hope and pray the quarrel may be settled.
We must go abroad, Miss Osborne. We may be ordered off
at a day's warning. Who knows what may happen in
the campaign? Don't be agitated, dear Miss Osborne;
and those two at least should part friends.'

'There has been no quarrel, Captain Dobbin, except

a little usual scene with papa,' the lady said. ' We are
expecting George back daily. What papa wanted was
only for his good. He has but to come back, and I'm
sure all will be well ; and dear Rhoda, who went away from
here in sad, sad anger, I know will forgive him. Woman
forgives but too readily, captain.'

' Such an angel as *you* I am sure would,' Mr. Dobbin said,
with atrocious astuteness. ' And no man can pardon
himself for giving a woman pain. What would you feel, if
a man were faithless to you ? '

' I should perish—I should throw myself out of window—
I should take poison—I should pine and die. I know
I should,' Miss cried, who had nevertheless gone through
one or two affairs of the heart without any idea of
suicide.

' And there are others,' Dobbin continued, ' as true and
as kind-hearted as yourself. I'm not speaking about the
West India heiress, Miss Osborne, but about a poor girl
whom George once loved, and who was bred from her childhood to think of nobody but him. I've seen her in her
poverty uncomplaining, broken-hearted, without a fault.
It is of Miss Sedley I speak. Dear Miss Osborne, can your
generous heart quarrel with your brother for being faithful
to her ?   Could his own conscience ever forgive him if he
deserted her ?   Be her friend—she always loved you—
and—and I am come here charged by George to tell you
that he holds his engagement to her as the most sacred duty
he has ; and to entreat *you*, at least, to be on his side.'

When any strong emotion took possession of Mr. Dobbin,
and after the first word or two of hesitation, he could speak
with perfect fluency, and it was evident that his eloquence
on this occasion made some impression upon the lady whom
he addressed.

' Well,' said she, ' this is—most surprising—most painful
—most extraordinary—what will papa say ?—that George
should fling away such a superb establishment as was
offered to him,—but at any rate he has found a very
brave champion in you, Captain Dobbin. It is of no
use, however,' she continued, after a pause ; ' I feel for
poor Miss Sedley, most certainly—most sincerely, you
know. We never thought the match a good one, though
we were always very kind to·her here—very. But papa
will never consent, I am sure. And a well-brought-up

young woman, you know,—with a well-regulated mind
must—George must give her up, dear Captain Dobbin,
indeed he must.'

'Ought a man to give up the woman he loved, just when
misfortune befell her?' Dobbin said, holding out his
hand. 'Dear Miss Osborne, is this the counsel I hear
from *you*? My dear young lady! you must befriend her.
He can't give her up. He must not give her up. Would
a man, think you, give *you* up if you were poor?'

This adroit question touched the heart of Miss Jane
Osborne not a little. 'I don't know whether we poor girls
ought to believe what you men say, captain,' she said.
'There is that in woman's tenderness which induces her to
believe too easily. I'm afraid you are cruel, cruel deceivers,'
—and Dobbin certainly thought he felt a pressure of the
hand which Miss Osborne had extended to him.

He dropped it in some alarm. 'Deceivers!' said he.
'No, dear Miss Osborne, all men are not; your brother
is not; George has loved Amelia Sedley ever since they
were children; no wealth would make him marry any
but her. Ought he to forsake her? Would you counsel
him to do so?'

What could Miss Jane say to such a question, and with
her own peculiar views? She could not answer it, so she
parried it by saying, 'Well, if you are not a deceiver,
at least you are *very* romantic;' and Captain William let
this observation pass without challenge.

At length when, by the help of further polite speeches,
he deemed that Miss Osborne was sufficiently prepared to
receive the whole news, he poured it into her ear. 'George
could not give up Amelia—George was married to her'—
and then he related the circumstances of the marriage as
we know them already: how the poor girl would have died
had not her lover kept his faith: how Old Sedley had
refused all consent to the match, and a licence had been got:
and Jos Sedley had come from Cheltenham to give away
the bride: how they had gone to Brighton in Jos's chariot-
and-four to pass the honeymoon: and how George counted
on his dear kind sisters to befriend him with their father, as
women—so true and tender as they were—assuredly would
do. And so, asking permission (readily granted) to see
her again, and rightly conjecturing that the news he had
brought would be told in the next five minutes to the other

ladies, Captain Dobbin made his bow and took his leave.

He was scarcely out of the house, when Miss Maria and Miss Wirt rushed in to Miss Osborne, and the whole wonderful secret was imparted to them by that lady. To do them justice, neither of the sisters were very much displeased. There is something about a runaway match with which few ladies can be seriously angry, and Amelia rather rose in their estimation, from the spirit which she had displayed in consenting to the union. As they debated the story, and prattled about it, and wondered what papa would do and say, came a loud knock, as of an avenging thunderclap at the door, which made these conspirators start. It must be papa, they thought. But it was not he. It was only Mr. Frederick Bullock, who had come from the City according to appointment, to conduct the ladies to a flower-show.

This gentleman, as may be imagined, was not kept long in ignorance of the secret. But his face, when he heard it, showed an amazement which was very different to that look of sentimental wonder which the countenances of the sisters wore. Mr. Bullock was a man of the world, and a junior partner of a wealthy firm. He knew what money was, and the value of it : and a delightful throb of expectation lighted up his little eyes, and caused him to smile on his Maria, as he thought that by this piece of folly of Mr. George's she might be worth thirty thousand pounds more than he had ever hoped to get with her.

' Gad! Jane,' said he, surveying even the elder sister with some interest, ' Eels will be sorry he cried off. You may be a fifty thousand pounder yet.'

The sisters had never thought of the money question up to that moment, but Fred Bullock bantered them with graceful gaiety about it during their forenoon's excursion ; and they had risen not a little in their own esteem by the time when, the morning amusement over, they drove back to dinner. And do not let my respected reader exclaim against this selfishness as unnatural. It was but this present morning, as he rode on the omnibus from Richmond;* while it changed horses, this present chronicler, being on the roof, marked three little children playing in a puddle below, very dirty and friendly and happy. To these three presently came another little one. ' *Polly*,' says she,

'*your sister's got a penny.*' At which the children got up
from the puddle instantly, and ran off to pay their court to
Peggy. And as the omnibus drove off I saw Peggy with
the infantine procession at her tail, marching with great
dignity towards the stall of a neighbouring lollipop-woman.

CHAPTER XXIV

IN WHICH MR. OSBORNE TAKES DOWN THE FAMILY BIBLE

 o having prepared the sisters, Dobbin
hastened away to the City to perform
the rest and more difficult part of the
task which he had undertaken. The
idea of facing old Osborne rendered
him not a little nervous, and more than
once he thought of leaving the young
ladies to communicate the secret,
which, as he was aware, they could not
long retain. But he had promised to
report to George upon the manner in
which the elder Osborne bore the in-
telligence; so going into the City to the paternal counting-
house in Thames Street, he dispatched thence a note
to Mr. Osborne begging for a half-hour's conversation
relative to the affairs of his son George. Dobbin's messenger
returned from Mr. Osborne's house of business, with the
compliments of the latter, who would be very happy to
see the captain immediately, and away accordingly Dobbin
went to confront him.

The captain, with a half-guilty secret to confess, and with
the prospect of a painful and stormy interview before
him, entered Mr. Osborne's offices with a most dismal
countenance and abashed gait, and, passing through the
outer room where Mr. Chopper presided, was greeted by
that functionary from his desk with a waggish air which
farther discomfited him. Mr. Chopper winked and nodded
and pointed his pen towards his patron's door, and said,
' You'll find the governor all right,' with the most provoking
good humour.

Osborne rose too, and shook him heartily by the hand,

and said, ' How do, my dear boy ? ' with a cordiality that
made poor George's ambassador feel doubly guilty.   His
hand lay as if dead in the old gentleman's grasp.   He felt
that he, Dobbin, was more or less the cause of all that had
happened.   It was he had brought back George to Amelia :
it was he had applauded, encouraged, transacted almost
the marriage which he was come to reveal to George's
father : and the latter was receiving him with smiles of
welcome ; patting him on the shoulder, and calling him
' Dobbin, my dear boy '.   The envoy had indeed good reason
to hang his head.

Osborne fully believed that Dobbin had come to announce
his son's surrender.   Mr. Chopper and his principal were
talking over the matter between George and his father,
at the very moment when Dobbin's messenger arrived.
Both agreed that George was sending in his submission.
Both had been expecting it for some days—and ' Lord !
Chopper, what a marriage we'll have ! ' Mr. Osborne said to
his clerk, snapping his big fingers, and jingling all the
guineas and shillings in his great pockets as he eyed his
subordinate with a look of triumph.

With similar operations conducted in both pockets, and a
knowing jolly air, Osborne from his chair regarded Dobbin
seated blank and silent opposite to him.   ' What a bumpkin
he is for a captain in the army,' old Osborne thought.
' I wonder George hasn't taught him better manners.'

At last Dobbin summoned courage to begin.   ' Sir,'
said he, ' I've brought you some very grave news.   I have
been at the Horse Guards* this morning, and there's no doubt
that our regiment will be ordered abroad, and on its way
to Belgium before the week is over.   And you know, sir,
that we shan't be home again before a tussle which may be
fatal to many of us.'

Osborne looked grave.   ' My s——, the regiment will
do its duty, sir, I dare say,' he said.

' The French are very strong, sir,' Dobbin went on.   ' The
Russians and Austrians will be a long time before they can
bring their troops down.   We shall have the first of the
fight, sir ; and depend on it Boney will take care that it shall
be a hard one.'

' What are you driving at, Dobbin ? ' his interlocutor said,
uneasy and with a scowl.   ' I suppose no Briton's afraid
of any d—— Frenchman, hay ? '

' I only mean, that before we go, and considering the great and certain risk that hangs over every one of us—if there are any differences between you and George—it would be as well, sir, that—that you should shake hands : wouldn't it ? Should anything happen to him, I think you would never forgive yourself if you hadn't parted in charity.'

As he said this, poor William Dobbin blushed crimson, and felt and owned that he himself was a traitor. But for him, perhaps, this severance need never have taken place. Why had not George's marriage been delayed ? What call was there to press it on so eagerly ? He felt that George would have parted from Amelia at any rate without a mortal pang. Amelia, too, *might* have recovered the shock of losing him. It was his counsel had brought about this marriage, and all that was to ensue from it. And why was it ? Because he loved her so much that he could not bear to see her unhappy : or because his own sufferings of suspense were so unendurable that he was glad to crush them at once—as we hasten a funeral after a death, or, when a separation from those we love is imminent, cannot rest until the parting be over.

' You are a good fellow, William,' said Mr. Osborne in a softened voice ; ' and me and George shouldn't part in anger, that is true. Look here. I've done for him as much as any father ever did. He's had three times as much money from me, as I warrant your father ever gave you. But I don't brag about that. How I've toiled for him, and worked and employed my talents and energy, *I* won't say. Ask Chopper. Ask himself. Ask the City of London. Well, I propose to him such a marriage as any nobleman in the land might be proud of—the only thing in life I ever asked him—and he refuses me. Am *I* wrong ? Is the quarrel of *my* making ? What do I seek but his good, for which I've been toiling like a convict ever since he was born ? Nobody can say there's anything selfish in *me*. Let him come back. I say, here's my hand. I say, forget and forgive. As for marrying now, it's out of the question. Let him and Miss S. make it up, and make out the marriage afterwards, when he comes back a colonel ; for he shall be a colonel, by G—— he shall, if money can do it. I'm glad you've brought him round. I know it's you, Dobbin. You've took him out of many a scrape before. Let him come. *I* shan't be hard. Come along, and dine in

Russell Square to-day : both of you.   The old shop, the old
hour.   You'll find a neck of venison, and no questions asked.'

This praise and confidence smote Dobbin's heart very
keenly.   Every moment the colloquy continued in this
tone, he felt more and more guilty.   ' Sir,' said he, ' I fear
you deceive yourself.   I am sure you do.   George is much
too high-minded a man ever to marry for money.   A threat
on your part that you would disinherit him in case of disobedience would only be followed by resistance on his.'

' Why, hang it, man, you don't call offering him eight
or ten thousand a year, threatening him ? '   Mr. Osborne
said, with still provoking good humour.   ' 'Gad, if Miss S.
will have me, I'm her man.   *I* ain't particular about
a shade or so of tawny.'   And the old gentleman gave
his knowing grin and coarse laugh.

' You forget, sir, previous engagements into which Captain
Osborne had entered,' the ambassador said, gravely.

' What engagements ?   What the devil do you mean ?
You don't mean,' Mr. Osborne continued, gathering wrath
and astonishment as the thought now first came upon him ;
' you don't mean that he's such a d—— fool as to be
still hankering after that swindling old bankrupt's daughter?
You've not come here for to make me suppose that he wants
to marry *her* ?   Marry *her*, that *is* a good one.   My son and
heir marry a beggar's girl out of a gutter.   D—— him, if he
does, let him buy a broom and sweep a crossing.   She was
always dangling and ogling after him, I recollect now ; and
I've no doubt she was put on by her old sharper of a father.'

' Mr. Sedley was your very good friend, sir,' Dobbin
interposed, almost pleased at finding himself growing angry.
' Time was you called him better names than rogue and
swindler.   The match was of your making.   George had
not right to play fast and loose —— '

' Fast and loose ! ' howled out old Osborne.   ' Fast and
loose !   Why, hang me, those are the very words my
gentleman used himself when he gave himself airs, last
Thursday was a fortnight, and talked about the British
army to his father who made him.   What, it's you who
have been a setting of him up—is it ?   and my service to you,
captain.   It's you who want to introduce beggars into my
family.   Thank you for nothing, captain.   Marry *her* indeed
—he, he !   why should he ?   I warrant you she'd go to him
fast enough without.'

' Sir,' said Dobbin, starting up in undisguised anger ;
' no man shall abuse that lady in my hearing, and you
least of all.'

' Oh, you're a going to call me out, are you ?   Stop, let
me ring the bell for pistols for two.   Mr. George sent you
here to insult his father, did he ? ' Osborne said, pulling
at the bell-cord.

' Mr. Osborne,' said Dobbin, with a faltering voice, ' it's
you who are insulting the best creature in the world.   You
had best spare her, sir, for she's your son's wife.'

And with this, feeling that he could say no more, Dobbin
went away, Osborne sinking back in his chair, and looking
wildly after him.   A clerk came in, obedient to the bell ;
and the captain was scarcely out of the court where Mr.
Osborne's offices were, when Mr. Chopper the chief clerk
came rushing hatless after him.

' For God's sake, what is it ? ' Mr. Chopper said, catching
the captain by the skirt.   ' The governor's in a fit.   What
has Mr. George been doing ? '

' He married Miss Sedley five days ago,' Dobbin replied.
' I was his groomsman, Mr. Chopper, and you must stand
his friend.'

The old clerk shook his head.   ' If that's your news,
captain, it's bad.   The governor will never forgive him.'

Dobbin begged Chopper to report progress to him at
the hotel where he was stopping, and walked off moodily
westwards, greatly perturbed as to the past and the future.

When the Russell Square family came to dinner that evening, they found the father of the house seated in his usual
place, but with that air of gloom on his face, which, whenever it appeared there, kept the whole circle silent.   The
ladies, and Mr. Bullock who dined with them, felt that the
news had been communicated to Mr. Osborne.   His dark
looks affected Mr. Bullock so far as to render him still and
quiet : but he was unusually bland and attentive to Miss
Maria, by whom he sat, and to her sister presiding at the
head of the table.

Miss Wirt, by consequence, was alone on her side of the
board, a gap being left between her and Miss Jane Osborne.
Now this was George's place when he dined at home ;
and his cover, as we said, was laid for him in expectation
of that truant's return.   Nothing occurred during dinner-
time except smiling Mr. Frederick's flagging confidential

whispers, and the clinking of plate and china, to interrupt
the silence of the repast. The servants went about stealthily
doing their duty. Mutes at funerals could not look more
glum than the domestics of Mr. Osborne. The neck of
venison of which he had invited Dobbin to partake, was
carved by him in perfect silence ; but his own share went
away almost untasted, though he drank much, and the
butler assiduously filled his glass.

At last, just at the end of the dinner, his eyes, which had
been staring at everybody in turn, fixed themselves for
a while upon the plate laid for George. He pointed to it
presently with his left hand. His daughters looked at him
and did not comprehend, or choose to comprehend, the
signal ; nor did the servants at first understand it.

'Take that plate away,' at last he said, getting up with
an oath—and with this pushing his chair back, he walked
into his own room.

Behind Mr. Osborne's dining-room was the usual apartment which went in his house by the name of the study ;
and was sacred to the master of the house. Hither Mr.
Osborne would retire of a Sunday forenoon when not minded
to go to church ; and here pass the morning in his crimson
leather chair, reading the paper. A couple of glazed
bookcases were here, containing standard works in stout gilt
bindings. The *Annual Register*, the *Gentleman's Magazine*,
Blair's *Sermons*, and Hume and Smollett.* From year's
end to year's end he never took one of these volumes from
the shelf ; but there was no member of the family that would
dare for his life to touch one of the books, except upon
those rare Sunday evenings when there was no dinner
party, and when the great scarlet Bible and Prayer-book
were taken out from the corner where they stood beside
his copy of the *Peerage*, and the servants being rung up
to the dining parlour, Osborne read the evening service
to his family in a loud grating pompous voice. No member
of the household, child or domestic, ever entered that room
without a certain terror. Here he checked the housekeeper's accounts, and overhauled the butler's cellar-book.
Hence he could command, across the clean gravel courtyard, the back entrance of the stables with which one of
his bells communicated, and into this yard the coachman
issued from his premises as into a dock, and Osborne swore
at him from the study window. Four times a year Miss

Wirt entered this apartment to get her salary; and his
daughters to receive their quarterly allowance. George
as a boy had been horsewhipped in this room many times;
his mother sitting sick on the stair listening to the cuts of
the whip. The boy was scarcely ever known to cry under
the punishment; the poor woman used to fondle and kiss
him secretly, and give him money to soothe him when he
came out.

There was a picture of the family over the mantelpiece,
removed thither from the front room after Mrs. Osborne's
death—George was on a pony, the elder sister holding him
up a bunch of flowers; the younger led by her mother's
hand; all with red cheeks and large red mouths, simpering
on each other in the approved family-portrait manner.
The mother lay under ground now, long since forgotten—
the sisters and brother had a hundred different interests of
their own, and, familiar still, were utterly estranged from
each other. Some few score of years afterwards, when all
the parties represented are grown old, what bitter satire
there is in those flaunting childish family-portraits, with
their farce of sentiment and smiling lies, and innocence
so self-conscious and self-satisfied. Osborne's own state
portrait, with that of his great silver inkstand and arm-
chair, had taken the place of honour in the dining-room,
vacated by the family-piece.

To this study old Osborne retired then, greatly to the
relief of the small party whom he left. When the servants
had withdrawn, they began to talk for a while volubly
but very low; then they went upstairs quietly, Mr. Bullock
accompanying them stealthily on his creaking shoes. He
had no heart to sit alone drinking wine, and so close to the
terrible old gentleman in the study hard at hand.

An hour at least after dark, the butler, not having
received any summons, ventured to tap at his door and
take him in wax candles and tea. The master of the house
sat in his chair, pretending to read the paper, and when
the servant, placing the lights and refreshment on the
table by him, retired, Mr. Osborne got up and locked the
door after him. This time there was no mistaking the
matter; all the household knew that some great catastrophe
was going to happen which was likely direly to affect
Master George.

In the large shining mahogany escritoire Mr. Osborne had

a drawer especially devoted to his son's affairs and papers.
Here he kept all the documents relating to him ever since
he had been a boy : here were his prize copy-books and
drawing-books, all bearing George's hand, and that of the
master : here were his first letters in large roundhand sending his love to papa and mamma, and conveying his petitions
for a cake. His dear godpapa Sedley was more than once
mentioned in them. Curses quivered on old Osborne's
livid lips, and horrid hatred and disappointment writhed
in his heart, as looking through some of these papers he
came on that name. They were all marked and docketed,
and tied with red tape. It was—'From Georgy, requesting
5s., April 23, 18— ; answered April 25,'—or 'Georgy about
a pony, October 13,'—and so forth. In another packet
were 'Dr. S.'s accounts '—'G.'s tailor's bills and outfits,
drafts on me by G. Osborne, jun.' &c.,—his letters from the
West Indies—his agent's letters, and the newspapers containing his commissions : here was a whip he had when
a boy, and in a paper a locket containing his hair, which his
mother used to wear.

Turning one over after another, and musing over these
memorials, the unhappy man passed many hours. His
dearest vanities, ambitious hopes, had all been here. What
pride he had in his boy ! He was the handsomest child
ever seen. Everybody said he was like a nobleman's son.
A royal princess had remarked him, and kissed him, and
asked his name in Kew Gardens. What City man could
show such another ? Could a prince have been better cared
for ? Anything that money could buy had been his son's.
He used to go down on speech-days with four horses and
new liveries, and scatter new shillings among the boys
at the school where George was : when he went with George
to the dépôt of his regiment, before the boy embarked for
Canada, he gave the officers such a dinner as the Duke of
York might have sat down to. Had he ever refused a bill
when George drew one ? There they were—paid without
a word. Many a general in the army couldn't ride the
horses he had ! He had the child before his eyes, on a hundred different days when he remembered George—after
dinner, when he used to come in as bold as a lord and drink
off his glass by his father's side, at the head of the table—
on the pony at Brighton, when he cleared the hedge and
kept up with the huntsman- on the day when he was

presented to the Prince Regent at the levée,* when all
St. James's couldn't produce a finer young fellow.
And this, this was the end of all !—to marry a bankrupt
and fly in the face of duty and fortune !   What humiliation
and fury :   what pangs of sickening rage, balked ambition
and love ; what wounds of outraged vanity, tenderness
even, had this old worldling now to suffer under !

Having examined these papers, and pondered over this
one and the other, in that bitterest of all helpless woe,
with which miserable men think of happy past times—
George's father took the whole of the documents out of the
drawer in which he had kept them so long, and locked
them into a writing-box, which he tied, and sealed with
his seal.   Then he opened the bookcase, and took down
the great red Bible we have spoken of—a pompous book,
seldom looked at, and shining all over with gold.   There
was a frontispiece to the volume, representing Abraham
sacrificing Isaac.   Here according to custom, Osborne had
recorded on the fly-leaf, and in his large clerk-like hand,
the dates of his marriage and his wife's death, and the
births and Christian names of his children.   Jane came first,
then George Sedley Osborne, then Maria Frances, and
the days of the christening of each.   Taking a pen, he carefully obliterated George's name from the page ;   and when
the leaf was quite dry, restored the volume to the place
from which he had moved it.   Then he took a document out
of another drawer, where his own private papers were kept ;
and having read it, crumpled it up and lighted it at one of
the candles, and saw it burn entirely away in the grate.
It was his will ;   which being burned, he sat down and wrote
off a letter, and rang for his servant, whom he charged to
deliver it in the morning.   It was morning already :   as
he went up to bed : the whole house was alight with the
sunshine ;   and the birds were singing among the fresh
green leaves in Russell Square.

Anxious to keep all Mr. Osborne's family and dependants
in good humour, and to make as many friends as possible
for George in his hour of adversity, William Dobbin, who
knew the effect which good dinners and good wines have upon
the soul of man, wrote off immediately on his return to his
inn the most hospitable of invitations to Thomas Chopper,
Esquire, begging that gentleman to dine with him at
the Slaughter's next day.   The note reached Mr. Chopper

before he left the City, and the instant reply was, that
' Mr. Chopper presents his respectful compliments, and will
have the honour and pleasure of waiting on Captain D.'
The invitation and the rough draft of the answer were
shown to Mrs. Chopper and her daughters on his return
to Somers Town that evening, and they talked about military
gents and West End men with great exultation as the family
sat and partook of tea. When the girls had gone to rest,
Mr. and Mrs. C. discoursed upon the strange events which
were occurring in the governor's family. Never had the
clerk seen his principal so moved. When he went in to
Mr. Osborne, after Captain Dobbin's departure, Mr. Chopper

found his chief black in the face,
and all but in a fit : some dreadful quarrel, he was certain, had
occurred between Mr. O. and the
young captain. Chopper had been
instructed to make out an account
of all sums paid to Captain Osborne within the last three years.
' And a precious lot of money he
has had too,' the chief clerk said,
and respected his old and young
master the more, for the liberal
way in which the guineas had been
flung about. The dispute was
something about Miss Sedley.
Mrs. Chopper vowed and declared she pitied that poor young
lady to lose such a handsome

young fellow as the capting. As the daughter of an
unlucky speculator, who had paid a very shabby dividend,
Mr. Chopper had no great regard for Miss Sedley. He
respected the house of Osborne before all others in the City
of London : and his hope and wish was that Captain George
should marry a nobleman's daughter. The clerk slept
a great deal sounder than his principal that night ; and,
cuddling his children after breakfast (of which he partook
with a very hearty appetite, though his modest cup of life
was only sweetened with brown sugar), he set off in his best
Sunday suit and frilled shirt for business, promising his
admiring wife not to punish Captain D.'s port too severely
that evening.

Mr. Osborne's countenance, when he arrived in the City at his usual time, struck those dependants who were accustomed, for good reasons, to watch its expression, as peculiarly ghastly and worn. At twelve o'clock Mr. Higgs (of the firm of Higgs & Blatherwick, solicitors, Bedford Row) called by appointment, and was ushered into the governor's private room, and closeted there for more than an hour. At about one Mr. Chopper received a note brought by Captain Dobbin's man, and containing an inclosure for Mr. Osborne, which the clerk went in and delivered. A short time afterwards Mr. Chopper and Mr. Birch, the next clerk, were summoned, and requested to witness a paper. 'I've been making a new will,' Mr. Osborne said, to which these gentlemen appended their names accordingly. No conversation passed. Mr. Higgs looked exceedingly grave as he came into the outer rooms, and very hard in Mr. Chopper's face; but there were not any explanations. It was remarked that Mr. Osborne was particularly quiet and gentle all day, to the surprise of those who had augured ill from his darkling demeanour. He called no man names that day, and was not heard to swear on... he left business early; and before going away, su... ed his chief clerk once more, and having given h... neral instructions, asked him, after some seeming he... on and reluctance to speak, if he knew whether Cap... Dobbin was in town?

Chopper said he... he was. Indeed both of them knew the fact per...

Osborne took a... rected to that officer, and, giving it to the clerk, requ... the latter to deliver it into Dobbin's own hands imme... ly.

'And now, C... er,' says he, taking his hat, and with strange look, ... my mind will be easy.' Exactly as the clock struck two (there was no doubt an appointment between the pair), Mr. Frederick Bullock called, and he and Mr. Osborne walked away together.

The colonel of the —th regiment, in which Messieurs Dobbin and Osborne had companies, was an old general who had made his first campaign under Wolfe at Quebec, and was long since quite too old and feeble for command; but he took some interest in the regiment of which he was the nominal head, and made certain of his young officers welcome at his table, a kind of hospitality which I believe is

not now common amongst his brethren. Captain Dobbin
was an especial favourite of this old general. Dobbin was
versed in the literature of his profession, and could talk
about the great Frederic, and the Empress Queen, and their
wars, almost as well as the general himself, who was indifferent to the triumphs of the present day, and whose heart
was with the tacticians of fifty years back. This officer
sent a summons to Dobbin to come and breakfast with him,
on the morning when Mr. Osborne altered his will, and
Mr. Chopper put on his best shirt-frill, and then informed
his young favourite, a couple of days in advance, of that
which they were all expecting—a marching order to go to
Belgium. The order for the regiment to hold itself in readiness would leave the Horse Guards in a day or two ; and as
transports were in plenty, they would get their route before
the week was over. Recruits had come in during the stay
of the regiment at Chatham ; and the old general hoped
that the regiment which had helped to beat Montcalm in
Canada, and to rout Mr. Washington on Long Island, would
prove itself worthy of its historical reputation on the oft-
trodden battle-grounds of the Low Countries. ' And so my
good friend, if you have any *affaire là*,' said the old general,
taking a pinch of snuff with his trembling white old hand,
and then pointing to the spot of his *robe de chambre* under
which his heart was still feebly beating, ' if you have any
Phillis to console, or to bid farewell to papa and mamma, or
any will to make, I recommend you to set about your
business without delay.' With which the general gave
his young friend a finger to shake, and a good-natured
nod of his powdered and pigtailed head ; and the door
being closed upon Dobbin, sat down to pen a *poulet* (he was
exceedingly vain of his French) to Mademoiselle Aménaide of His Majesty's Theatre.*

This news made Dobbin grave, and he thought of our
friends at Brighton, and then he was ashamed of himself
that Amelia was always the first thing in his thoughts
(always before anybody—before father and mother, sisters
and duty—always at waking and sleeping indeed, and all
day long) ; and returning to his hotel, he sent off a brief
note to Mr. Osborne acquainting him with the information
which he had received, and which might tend further, he
hoped, to bring about a reconciliation with George.

This note, dispatched by the same messenger who had

carried the invitation to Chopper on the previous day,
alarmed the worthy clerk not a little. It was enclosed to
him, and as he opened the letter he trembled lest the dinner
should be put off on which he was calculating. His mind
was inexpressibly relieved when he found that the envelope
was only a reminder for himself. (' I shall expect you at
half-past five,' Captain Dobbin wrote.) He was very much
interested about his employer's family; but, *que voulez-vous?*
a grand dinner was of more concern to him than the affairs
of any other mortal.

Dobbin was quite justified in repeating the general's
information to any officers of the regiment whom he should
see in the course of his peregrinations ; accordingly he
imparted it to Ensign Stubble, whom he met at the agent's,
and who—such was his military ardour—went off instantly
to purchase a new sword at the accoutrement-makers. Here
this young fellow, who, though only seventeen years of age,
and about sixty-five inches high, with a constitution
naturally rickety and much impaired by premature brandy-
and-water, had an undoubted courage and a lion's heart,
poised, tried, bent, and balanced a weapon such as he
thought would do execution amongst Frenchmen. Shouting ' Ha, ha ! ' and stamping his little feet with tremendous
energy, he delivered the point twice or thrice at Captain
Dobbin, who parried the thrust laughingly with his bamboo
walking-stick.

Mr. Stubble, as may be supposed from his size and slender-
ness, was of the Light Bobs. Ensign Spooney, on the contrary, was a tall youth and belonged to (Captain Dobbin's)
the Grenadier Company,* and he tried on a new bearskin
cap, under which he looked savage beyond his years. Then
these two lads went off to the Slaughter's, and having ordered
a famous dinner, sat down and wrote off letters to the kind
anxious parents at home—letters full of love and heartiness,
and pluck and bad spelling. Ah ! there were many anxious
hearts beating through England at that time ; and mothers'
prayers and tears flowing in many homesteads.

Seeing young Stubble engaged in composition at one of
the coffee-room tables at the Slaughter's, and the tears
trickling down his nose on to the paper (for the youngster
was thinking of his mamma, and that he might never
see her again), Dobbin, who was going to write off a letter
to George Osborne, relented, and locked up his desk.

ENSIGN STUBBLE PRACTISING THE ART OF WAR

'Why should I?' said he. 'Let her have this night happy. I'll go and see my parents early in the morning, and go down to Brighton myself to-morrow.'

So he went up and laid his big hand on young Stubble's shoulder, and backed up that young champion, and told him if he would leave off brandy-and-water he would be a good soldier, as he always was a gentlemanly good-hearted fellow. Young Stubble's eyes brightened up at this, for Dobbin was greatly respected in the regiment, as the best officer and the cleverest man in it.

'Thank you, Dobbin,' he said, rubbing his eyes with his knuckles, 'I was just—just telling her I would. And, oh, sir, she's so *dam* kind to me.' The water-pumps were at work again, and I am not sure that the soft-hearted captain's eyes did not also twinkle.

The two ensigns, the captain, and Mr. Chopper, dined together in the same box. Chopper brought the letter from Mr. Osborne, in which the latter briefly presented his compliments to Captain Dobbin, and requested him to forward the enclosed to Captain George Osborne. Chopper knew nothing further; he described Mr. Osborne's appearance, it is true, and his interview with his lawyer, wondered how the governor had sworn at nobody, and—especially as the wine circled round—abounded in speculations and conjectures. But these grew more vague with every glass, and at length became perfectly unintelligible. At a late hour Captain Dobbin put his guest into a hackney-coach, in a hiccupping state, and swearing that he would be the kick—the kick—captain's friend for ever and ever.

When Captain Dobbin took leave of Miss Osborne we have said that he asked leave to come and pay her another visit, and the spinster expected him for some hours the next day, when, perhaps, had he come, and had he asked her that question which she was prepared to answer, she would have declared herself as her brother's friend, and a reconciliation

might have been effected between George and his angry
father.   But though she waited at home the captain never
came.   He had his own affairs to pursue ; his own parents to
visit and console ; and at an early hour of the day to take his
place on the 'Lightning' coach, and go down to his friends
at Brighton.   In the course of the day Miss Osborne heard
her father give orders that that meddling scoundrel, Captain
Dobbin, should never be admitted within his doors again,
and any hopes in which she may have indulged privately
were thus abruptly brought to an end.   Mr. Frederick
Bullock came, and was particularly affectionate to Maria,
and attentive to the broken-spirited old gentleman.   For
though he said his mind would be easy, the means which he
had taken to secure quiet did not seem to have succeeded
as yet, and the events of the past two days had visibly
shattered him.

CHAPTER XXV

IN WHICH ALL THE PRINCIPAL PERSONAGES THINK FIT TO LEAVE BRIGHTON

ONDUCTED to the ladies, at the
Ship Inn, Dobbin assumed a
jovial and rattling manner,
which proved that this young
officer was becoming a more
consummate hypocrite every
day of his life.   He was trying
to hide his own private feelings,
first upon seeing Mrs. George
Osborne in her new condition,
and secondly to mask the apprehensions he entertained as to the
effect which the dismal news brought down by him would
certainly have upon her.

   ' It is my opinion, George,' he said, ' that the French
Emperor will be upon us, horse and foot, before three weeks
are over, and will give the duke such a dance as shall make
the Peninsula appear mere child's play.   But you need not
say that to Mrs. Osborne, you know.   There mayn't be any

fighting on our side after all, and our business in Belgium
may turn out to be a mere military occupation.   Many
persons think so ; and Brussels is full of fine people and
ladies of fashion.'   So it was agreed to represent the duty
of the British army in Belgium in this harmless light to
Amelia.

This plot being arranged, the hypocritical Dobbin saluted
Mrs. George Osborne quite gaily, tried to pay her one or two
compliments relative to her new position as a bride (which
compliments, it must be confessed, were exceedingly clumsy
and hung fire wofully), and then fell to talking about
Brighton, and the sea-air, and the gaieties of the place, and
the beauties of the road and the merits of the ' Lightning '
coach and horses,—all in a manner quite incomprehensible
to Amelia, and very amusing to Rebecca, who was watching
the captain, as indeed she watched every one near whom
she came.

Little Amelia, it must be owned, had rather a mean opinion
of her husband's friend, Captain Dobbin.   He lisped—he
was very plain and homely-looking : and exceedingly
awkward and ungainly.   She liked him for his attachment
to her husband (to be sure there was very little merit in that),
and she thought George was most generous and kind in
extending his friendship to his brother officer.   George had
mimicked Dobbin's lisp and queer manners many times to
her, though to do him justice, he always spoke most highly
of his friend's good qualities.   In her little day of triumph,
and not knowing him intimately as yet, she made light of
honest William—and he knew her opinions of him quite
well, and acquiesced in them very humbly.   A time came
when she knew him better, and changed her notions regarding him : but that was distant as yet.

As for Rebecca, Captain Dobbin had not been two hours
in the ladies' company before she understood his secret
perfectly.   She did not like him, and feared him privately ;
nor was he very much prepossessed in her favour.   He was
so honest, that her arts and cajoleries did not affect him,
and he shrank from her with instinctive repulsion.   And, as
she was by no means so far superior to her sex as to be
above jealousy, she disliked him the more for his adoration
of Amelia.   Nevertheless, she was very respectful and
cordial in her manner tôwards him.   A friend to the Osbornes ! a friend to her dearest benefactors ! She vowed

she should always love him sincerely : she remembered
him quite well on the Vauxhall night, as she told Amelia
archly, and she made a little fun of him when the two ladies
went to dress for dinner. Rawdon Crawley paid scarcely
any attention to Dobbin, looking upon him as a good-natured
nincompoop, and under-bred City man. Jos patronized
him with much dignity.

When George and Dobbin were alone in the latter's
room, to which George had followed him, Dobbin took from
his desk the letter which he had been charged by Mr.
Osborne to deliver to his son. ' It's not in my father's
handwriting,' said George, looking rather alarmed ; nor
was it : the letter was from Mr. Osborne's lawyer, and to the
following effect :—

BEDFORD ROW, May 7, 1815.

SIR,—I am commissioned by Mr. Osborne to inform you, that he
abides by the determination which he before expressed to you, and
that in consequence of the marriage which you have been pleased
to contract, he ceases to consider you henceforth as a member of
his family. This determination is final and irrevocable.

Although the moneys expended upon you in your minority, and the
bills which you have drawn upon him so unsparingly of late years,
far exceed in amount the sum to which you are entitled in your own
right (being the third part of the fortune of your mother, the late
Mrs. Osborne, and which reverted to you at her decease, and to
Miss Jane Osborne and Miss Maria Frances Osborne); yet I am
instructed by Mr. Osborne to say, that he waives all claim upon your
estate, and that the sum of 2,000l., 4 per cent annuities, at the value
of the day (being your one-third share of the sum of 6,000l.), shall
be paid over to yourself or your agents upon your receipt for the
same, by

Your obedient Servt., S. HIGGS.

PS.—Mr. Osborne desires me to say, once for all, that he declines
to receive any messages, letters, or communications from you on this
or any other subject.

' A pretty way you have managed the affair,' said George,
looking savagely at William Dobbin. ' Look there, Dobbin,'
and he flung over to the latter his parent's letter. ' A
beggar, by Jove, and all in consequence of my d—d sentimentality. Why couldn't we have waited ? A ball might
have done for me in the course of the war, and may still,
and how will Emmy be bettered by being left a beggar's

widow ? It was all your doing. You were never easy until you had got me married and ruined. What the deuce am I to do with two thousand pounds ? Such a sum won't last two years. I've lost a hundred and forty to Crawley at cards and billiards since I've been down here. A pretty manager of a man's matters *you* are, forsooth.'

' There's no denying that the position is a hard one,' Dobbin replied, after reading over the letter with a blank countenance ; ' and, as you say, it is partly of my making. There are some men that wouldn't mind changing with you,' he added, with a bitter smile. ' How many captains in the regiment have two thousand pounds to the fore, think you ? You must live on your pay till your father relents, and if you die, you leave your wife a hundred a year.'

' Do you suppose a man of my habits can live on his pay and a hundred a year ? ' George cried out in great anger. ' You must be a fool to talk so, Dobbin. How the deuce am I to keep up my position in the world upon such a pitiful pittance ? I can't change my habits. I *must* have my comforts. *I* wasn't brought up on porridge like MacWhirter, or on potatoes, like old O'Dowd. Do you expect my wife to take in soldiers' washing, or ride after the regiment in a baggage-wagon ? '

' Well, well,' said Dobbin, still good-naturedly, ' we'll get her a better conveyance. But try and remember that you are only a dethroned prince now, George, my boy ; and be quiet whilst the tempest lasts. It won't be for long. Let your name be mentioned in the *Gazette*, and I'll engage the old father relents towards you.'

' Mentioned in the *Gazette !* ' George answered. ' And in what part of it ? Among the killed and wounded returns, and at the top of the list, very likely.'

' Psha ! It will be time enough to cry out when we are hurt,' Dobbin said. ' And if anything happens, you know, George, I have got a little, and I am not a marrying man, and I shall not forget my godson in my will,' he added, with a smile. Whereupon the dispute ended,—as many scores of such conversations between Osborne and his friend had concluded previously—by the former declaring there was no possibility of being angry with Dobbin long, and forgiving him very generously after abusing him without cause.

' I say, Becky,' cried Rawdon Crawley out of his dressing-

room, to his lady, who was attiring herself for dinner in her
own chamber.

'What?' said Becky's shrill voice. She was looking
over her shoulder in the glass. She had put on the neatest
and freshest white frock imaginable, and with bare shoulders
and a little necklace, and a light-blue sash, she looked the
image of youthful innocence and girlish happiness.

'I say, what'll Mrs. O. do, when O. goes out with the
regiment?' Crawley said, coming into the room, performing
a duet on his head with two huge hair-brushes, and looking
out from under his hair with admiration on his pretty
little wife.

'I suppose she'll cry her eyes out,' Becky answered.
'She has been whimpering half a dozen of times at the very
notion of it, already to me.'

'You don't care, I suppose,' Rawdon said, half angry at
his wife's want of feeling.

'You wretch! don't you know that I intend to go with
you,' Becky replied. 'Besides, you're different. You go
as General Tufto's aide de camp. We don't belong to the
line,'* Mrs. Crawley said, throwing up her head with an air
that so enchanted her husband that he stooped down and
kissed it.

'Rawdon, dear—don't you think—you'd better get that
—money from Cupid, before he goes?' Becky continued,
fixing on a killing bow. She called George Osborne, Cupid.
She had flattered him about his good looks a score of times
already. She watched over him kindly at écarté of a night
when he would drop into Rawdon's quarters for a half-hour
before bedtime.

She had often called him a horrid dissipated wretch, and
threatened to tell Emmy of his wicked ways and naughty
extravagant habits. She brought his cigar and lighted it for
him; she knew the effect of that manœuvre, having practised it in former days upon Rawdon Crawley. He thought
her gay, brisk, arch, distinguée, delightful. In their little
drives and dinners, Becky, of course, quite outshone poor
Emmy, who remained very mute and timid while Mrs.
Crawley and her husband rattled away together, and
Captain Crawley (and Jos after he joined the young married
people) gobbled in silence.

Emmy's mind somehow misgave her about her friend.
Rebecca's wit, spirits, and accomplishments troubled her

with a rueful disquiet. They were only a week married, and
here was George already suffering ennui, and eager for
others' society! She trembled for the future. How shall
I be a companion for him, she thought,—so clever and so
brilliant, and I such a humble foolish creature? How noble
it was of him to marry me—to give up everything and stoop
down to me! I ought to have refused him, only I had not
the heart. I ought to have stopped at home and taken care
of poor papa. And her neglect of her parents (and indeed
there was some foundation for this charge which the poor

child's uneasy conscience brought against her) was now
remembered for the first time, and caused her to blush with
humiliation. Oh! thought she, I have been very wicked
and selfish—selfish in forgetting them in their sorrows—
selfish in forcing George to marry me. I know I'm not
worthy of him—I know he would have been happy without
me—and yet—I tried, I tried to give him up.

It is hard when, before seven days of marriage are over,
such thoughts and confessions as these force themselves on
a little bride's mind. But so it was, and the night before
Dobbin came to join these young people—on a fine brilliant

moonlight night of May—so warm and balmy that the windows were flung open to the balcony, from which George and Mrs. Crawley were gazing upon the calm ocean spread shining before them, while Rawdon and Jos were engaged at backgammon within—Amelia couched in a great chair quite neglected, and watching both these parties, felt a despair and remorse such as were bitter companions for that tender lonely soul. Scarce a week was past, and it was come to this! The future, had she regarded it, offered a dismal prospect; but Emmy was too shy, so to speak, to look to that, and embark alone on that wide sea, and unfit to navigate it without a guide and protector. I know Miss Smith has a mean opinion of her. But how many, my dear madam, are endowed with your prodigious strength of mind?

'Gad, what a fine night, and how bright the moon is!' George said, with a puff of his cigar, which went soaring up skywards.

'How delicious they smell in the open air! I adore them. Who'd think the moon was two hundred and thirty-six thousand eight hundred and forty-seven miles off?' Becky added, gazing at that orb with a smile. 'Isn't it clever of me to remember that? Pooh! we learned it all at Miss Pinkerton's! How calm the sea is, and how clear everything. I declare I can almost see the coast of France!' and her bright green eyes streamed out, and shot into the night as if they *could* see through it.

'Do you know what I intend to do one morning?' she said; 'I find I can swim beautifully, and some day, when my Aunt Crawley's companion—old Briggs, you know—you remember her—that hook-nosed woman, with the long wisps of hair—when Briggs goes out to bathe, I intend to dive under her awning, and insist on a reconciliation in the water. Isn't that a stratagem?'

George burst out laughing at the idea of this aquatic meeting. 'What's the row there, you two?' Rawdon shouted out, rattling the box. Amelia was making a fool of herself in an absurd hysterical manner, and retired to her own room to whimper in private.

Our history is destined in this chapter to go backwards and forwards in a very irresolute manner seemingly, and having conducted our story to to-morrow presently, we shall immediately again have occasion to step back to yester-

A FAMILY PARTY AT BRIGHTON

day, so that the whole of the tale may get a hearing.   As you behold at Her Majesty's drawing-room, the ambassadors' and high dignitaries' carriages whisk off from a private door, while Captain Jones's ladies are waiting for their fly : as you see in the Secretary of the Treasury's antechamber, a half-dozen of petitioners waiting patiently for their audience, and called out one by one, when suddenly an Irish member or some eminent personage enters the apartment, and instantly walks into Mr. Under-Secretary over the heads of all the people present : so in the conduct of a tale, the romancer is obliged to exercise this most partial sort of justice.   Although all the little incidents must be heard, yet they must be put off when the great events make their appearance ; and surely such a circumstance as that which brought Dobbin to Brighton, viz., the ordering out of the Guards and the line to Belgium, and the mustering of the allied armies in that country under the command of his Grace the Duke of Wellington—such a dignified circumstance as that, I say, was entitled to the *pas* over all minor occurrences whereof this history is composed mainly, and hence a little trifling disarrangement and disorder was excusable and becoming. We have only now advanced in time so far beyond Chapter XXII as to have got our various characters up into their dressing-rooms before the dinner, which took place as usual on the day of Dobbin's arrival.

George was too humane or too much occupied with the tie of his neckcloth to convey at once all the news to Amelia which his comrade had brought with him from London. He came into her room, however, holding the attorney's letter in his hand, and with so solemn and important an air that his wife, always ingeniously on the watch for calamity, thought the worst was about to befall, and running up to her husband, besought her dearest George to tell her every-thing—he was ordered abroad ; there would be a battle next week—she knew there would.

Dearest George parried the question about foreign service, and with a melancholy shake of the head said, ' No, Emmy ; it isn't that : it's not myself I care about : it's you.   I have had bad news from my father.   He refuses any communica-tion with me ; he has flung us off ; and leaves us to poverty. *I* can rough it well enough ; but you, my dear, how will you bear it ? read here.'   And he handed her over the letter.

Amelia, with a look of tender alarm in her eyes, listened

to her noble hero as he uttered the above generous sentiments, and sitting down on the bed, read the letter which
George gave her with such a pompous martyr-like air. Her
face cleared up as she read the document, however. The
idea of sharing poverty and privation in company with the
beloved object, is, as we have before said, far from being
disagreeable to a warm-hearted woman. The notion was
actually pleasant to little Amelia.   Then, as usual, she was
ashamed of herself for feeling happy at such an indecorous
moment, and checked her pleasure, saying demurely,
' Oh, George, how your poor heart must bleed at the idea
of being separated from your papa.'

' It does,' said George, with an agonized countenance.

' But he can't be angry with you long,' she continued.
' Nobody could, I'm sure. He must forgive you, my dearest,
kindest husband. Oh, I shall never forgive myself if he
does not.'

' What vexes me, my poor Emmy, is not *my* misfortune,
but yours,' George said.   ' I don't care for a little poverty ;
and I think, without vanity, I've talents enough to make
my own way.'

' That you have,' interposed his wife, who thought that
war should cease, and her husband should be made a general
instantly.

' Yes, I shall make my way as well as another,' Osborne
went on ; ' but you, my dear girl, how can I bear your being
deprived of the comforts and station in society which my
wife had a right to expect ? My dearest girl in barracks ;
the wife of a soldier in a marching regiment ; subject to all
sorts of annoyance and privation ! It makes me miserable.'

Emmy, quite at ease, as this was her husband's only cause
of disquiet, took his hand, and with a radiant face and smile
began to warble that stanza from the favourite song of
' Wapping Old Stairs ', in which the heroine after rebuking
her Tom for inattention, promises ' his trousers to mend,
and his grog too to make ', if he will be constant and kind,
and not forsake her. ' Besides,' she said, after a pause,
during which she looked as pretty and happy as any young
woman need, ' isn't two thousand pounds an immense deal
of money, George ? '

George laughed at her *naïveté ;* and finally they went
down to dinner, Amelia clinging on George's arm, still
warbling the tune of ' Wapping Old Stairs ',* and more

pleased and light of mind than she had been for some days past.

Thus the repast, which at length came off, instead of being dismal, was an exceedingly brisk and merry one. The excitement of the campaign counteracted in George's mind the depression occasioned by the disinheriting letter. Dobbin still kept up his character of rattle. He amused the company with accounts of the army in Belgium, where nothing but fêtes and gaiety and fashion were going on. Then, having a particular end in view, this dexterous captain proceeded to describe Mrs. Major O'Dowd, packing her own and her major's wardrobe, and how his best epaulets had been stowed into a tea canister, whilst her own famous yellow turban, with the bird of paradise wrapped in brown paper, was locked up in the major's tin cocked-hat case, and wondered what effect it would have at the French king's court at Ghent, or the great military balls at Brussels.

' Ghent ! Brussels ! ' cried out Amelia with a sudden shock and start. ' Is the regiment ordered away, George,—is it ordered away ? ' A look of terror came over the sweet smiling face, and she clung to George as by an instinct.

' Don't be afraid, dear,' he said good-naturedly ; ' it is but a twelve hours' passage. It won't hurt you. You shall go, too, Emmy.'

' I intend to go,' said Becky, ' I'm on the staff. General Tufto is a great flirt of mine. Isn't he, Rawdon ? '

Rawdon laughed out with his usual roar. William Dobbin flushed up quite red. ' She can't go,' he said ; ' think of the —of the danger,' he was going to add ; but had not all his conversation during dinner-time tended to prove there was none ? He became very confused and silent.

' I must and will go,'* Amelia cried with the greatest spirit ; and George, applauding her resolution, patted her under the chin, and asked all the persons present if they ever saw such a termagant of a wife, and agreed that the lady should bear him company. ' We'll have Mrs. O'Dowd to chaperon you,' he said. What cared she so long as her husband was near her ? Thus somehow the bitterness of a parting was juggled away. Though war and danger were in store, war and danger might not befall for months to come. There was a respite at any rate, which made the timid little Amelia almost as happy as a full reprieve would have done, and which even Dobbin owned in his heart was very welcome. For, to be permitted to see her was now the greatest privilege and hope of his life, and he thought with himself secretly how he would watch and protect her. I wouldn't have let her go if I had been married to her, he thought. But George was the master, and his friend did not think fit to remonstrate.

Putting her arm round her friend's waist, Rebecca at length carried Amelia off from the dinner-table where so much business of importance had been discussed, and left the gentlemen in a highly exhilarated state drinking and talking very gaily.

In the course of the evening Rawdon got a little family-note from his wife, which although he crumpled it up and burnt it instantly in the candle, we had the good luck to read over Rebecca's shoulder. ' Great news,' she wrote. ' Mrs. Bute is gone. Get the money from Cupid to-night, as he'll be off to-morrow most likely. Mind this.—R.' So when the little company was about adjourning to coffee in the women's apartment, Rawdon touched Osborne on the elbow, and said gracefully, 'I say, Osborne, my boy, if quite convenient, I'll trouble you for that 'ere small trifle.' It was not quite convenient, but nevertheless George gave him a considerable present instalment in bank-notes from his pocket-book, and a bill on his agents at a week's date, for the remaining sum.

This matter arranged, George, and Jos, and Dobbin, held a council of war over their cigars, and agreed that a general move should be made for London in Jos's open carriage the next day. Jos, I think, would have preferred staying until Rawdon Crawley quitted Brighton, but Dobbin and George overruled him, and he agreed to carry the party to town, and ordered four horses, as became his dignity. With these they set off in state, after breakfast, the next day. Amelia had risen very early in the morning, and packed her little trunks with the greatest alacrity, while Osborne lay in bed deploring that she had not a maid to help her. She was only too glad, however, to perform this office for herself. A dim uneasy sentiment about Rebecca filled her mind already ; and although they kissed each other most tenderly at parting, yet we know what jealousy is ; and Mrs. Amelia possessed that among other virtues of her sex.

Besides these characters who are coming and going away, we must remember that there were some other old friends

of ours at Brighton ; Miss Crawley, namely, and the suite
in attendance upon her.   Now, although Rebecca and her
husband were but at a few stones' throw of the lodgings
which the invalid Miss Crawley occupied, the old lady's door
remained as pitilessly closed to them as it had been heretofore in London.   As long as she remained by the side of her
sister-in-law, Mrs. Bute Crawley took care that her beloved
Matilda should not be agitated by a meeting with her nephew.
When the spinster took her drive, the faithful Mrs. Bute sat
beside her in the carriage.   When Miss Crawley took the
air in a chair, Mrs. Bute marched on one side of the vehicle,
whilst honest Briggs occupied the other wing.   And if

they met Rawdon and
his wife by chance—
although the former
constantly and obsequi-
ously took off his
hat, the Miss-Crawley
party passed him by
with such a frigid and
killing   indifference,
that Rawdon began to
despair.

' We might as well be
in London as here,'
Captain Rawdon often
said, with a downcast
air.

' A comfortable inn
in Brighton is better
than a spunging-house
in Chancery Lane,' his
wife answered, who was of a more cheerful temperament.
' Think of those two aides de camp of Mr. Moses, the
sheriff's officer,* who watched our lodging for a week.   Our
friends here are very stupid, but Mr. Jos and Captain
Cupid are better companions than Mr. Moses's men, Rawdon, my love.'

' I wonder the writs haven't followed me down here,'
Rawdon continued, still desponding.

' When they do, we'll find means to give them the
slip,' said dauntless little Becky, and further pointed out
to her husband the great comfort and advantage of meeting

Jos and Osborne, whose acquaintance had brought to Rawdon Crawley a most timely little supply of ready money.

' It will hardly be enough to pay the inn bill,' grumbled
the Guardsman.

' Why need we pay it ? ' said the lady, who had an answer
for everything.

Through Rawdon's valet, who still kept up a trifling
acquaintance with the male inhabitants of Miss Crawley's
servants' hall, and was instructed to treat the coachman
to drink whenever they met, old Miss Crawley's movements
were pretty well known by our young couple ; and Rebecca
luckily bethought herself of being unwell, and of calling in
the same apothecary who was in attendance upon the
spinster, so that their information was on the whole tolerably
complete. Nor was Miss Briggs, although forced to adopt
a hostile attitude, secretly inimical to Rawdon and his wife.
She was naturally of a kindly and forgiving disposition.
Now that the cause of jealousy was removed, her dislike for
Rebecca disappeared also, and she remembered the latter's
invariable good words and good humour. And, indeed, she
and Mrs. Firkin, the lady's-maid, and the whole of Miss
Crawley's household, groaned under the tyranny of the
triumphant Mrs. Bute.

As often will be the case, that good but imperious woman
pushed her advantages too far, and her successes quite
unmercifully. She had in the course of a few weeks brought
the invalid to such a state of helpless docility, that the poor
soul yielded herself entirely to her sister's orders, and did
not even dare to complain of her slavery to Briggs or
Firkin. Mrs. Bute measured out the glasses of wine which
Miss Crawley was daily allowed to take, with irresistible
accuracy, greatly to the annoyance of Firkin and the
butler, who found themselves deprived of control over
even the sherry-bottle. She apportioned the sweetbreads,
jellies, chickens ; their quantity and order. Night and
noon and morning she brought the abominable drinks
ordained by the doctor, and made her patient swallow
them with so affecting an obedience, that Firkin said my
poor missus du take her physic like a lamb. She prescribed
the drive in the carriage or the ride in the chair, and, in
a word, ground down the old lady in her convalescence
in such a way as only belongs to your proper-managing,
motherly, moral woman. If ever the patient faintly resisted,

and pleaded for a little bit more dinner or a little drop less medicine, the nurse threatened her with instantaneous death, when Miss Crawley instantly gave in. ' She's no spirit left in her,' Firkin remarked to Briggs ; ' she ain't 'ave called me a fool these three weeks.' Finally, Mrs. Bute had made up her mind to dismiss the aforesaid honest lady's-maid, Mr. Bowls the large confidential man, and Briggs herself, and to send for her daughters from the Rectory, previous to removing the dear invalid bodily to Queen's Crawley, when an odious accident happened which called her away from duties so pleasing. The Reverend Bute Crawley, her husband, riding home one night, fell with his horse and broke his collar-bone. Fever and inflammatory symptoms set in, and Mrs. Bute was forced to leave Sussex for Hampshire. As soon as ever Bute was restored, she promised to return to her dearest friend, and departed, leaving the strongest injunctions with the household regarding their behaviour to their mistress ; and as soon as she got into the Southampton coach, there was such a jubilee and sense of relief in all Miss Crawley's house, as the company of persons assembled there had not experienced for many a week before. That very day Miss Crawley left off her afternoon dose of medicine : that afternoon Bowls opened an independent bottle of sherry for himself and Mrs. Firkin : that night Miss Crawley and Miss Briggs indulged in a game of piquet instead of one of Porteus's sermons. It was as in the old nursery-story, when the stick forgot to beat the dog, and the whole course of events underwent a peaceful and happy revolution.

At a very early hour in the morning, twice or thrice a week, Miss Briggs used to betake herself to a bathing-machine, and disport in the water in a flannel gown and an oilskin cap. Rebecca, as we have seen, was aware of this circumstance, and though she did not attempt to storm Briggs as she had threatened, and actually dive into that lady's presence and surprise her under the sacredness of the awning, Mrs. Rawdon determined to attack Briggs as she came away from her bath, refreshed and invigorated by her dip, and likely to be in good humour.

So, getting up very early the next morning, Becky brought the telescope in their sitting-room, which faced the sea, to bear upon the bathing-machines on the beach ; saw Briggs arrive, enter her box, and put out to sea ; and

was on the shore just as the nymph of whom she came
in quest stepped out of the little caravan on to the shingles.
It was a pretty picture : the beach ; the bathing women's
faces ; the long line of rocks and building were blushing
and bright in the sunshine.   Rebecca wore a kind, tender
smile on her face, and was holding out her pretty white
hand as Briggs emerged from the box.   What could Briggs
do but accept the salutation ?

' Miss Sh—, Mrs. Crawley,' she said.

Mrs. Crawley seized her hand, pressed it to her heart,
and with a sudden impulse, flinging her arms round Briggs,
kissed her affectionately.   ' Dear, dear friend ! ' she said,
with a touch of such natural feeling, that Miss Briggs of
course at once began to melt, and even the bathing-woman
was mollified.

Rebecca found no difficulty in engaging Briggs in a long,
intimate, and delightful conversation.   Everything that
had passed since the morning of Becky's sudden departure
from Miss Crawley's house in Park Lane up to the present
day, and Mrs. Bute's happy retreat, was discussed and
described by Briggs.   All Miss Crawley's symptoms, and
the particulars of her illness and medical treatment, were
narrated by the confidante with that fullness and accuracy
which women delight in.   About their complaints and their
doctors do ladies ever tire of talking to each other ?   Briggs
did not on this occasion ; nor did Rebecca weary of listening.
She was thankful, truly thankful, that the dear kind Briggs,
that the faithful, the invaluable Firkin, had been permitted
to remain with their benefactress through her illness.
Heaven bless her ! though she, Rebecca, had seemed to
act undutifully towards Miss Crawley ; yet was not her
fault a natural and excusable one ?   Could she help giving
her hand to the man who had won her heart ?   Briggs, the
sentimental, could only turn up her eyes to heaven at this
appeal, and heave a sympathetic sigh,. and think that she,
too, had given away her affections long years ago, and own
that Rebecca was no very great criminal.

' Can I ever forget her who so befriended the friendless
orphan ?   No, though she has cast me off,' the latter said,
' I shall never cease to love her, and I would devote my
life to her service.   As my own benefactress, as my
beloved Rawdon's adored relative, I love and admire
Miss Crawley, dear Miss Briggs, beyond any woman in

the world, and next to her I love all those who are faithful
to her. *I* would never have treated Miss Crawley's faithful
friends as that odious designing Mrs. Bute had done.
Rawdon, who was all heart,' Rebecca continued, ' although
his outward manners might seem rough and careless, had
said a hundred times, with tears in his eyes, that he blessed
Heaven for sending his dearest aunty two such admirable
nurses as her attached Firkin and her admirable Miss
Briggs.   Should the machinations of the horrible Mrs. Bute
end, as she too much feared they would, in banishing
everybody that Miss Crawley loved from her side, and
leaving that poor lady a victim to those harpies at the
Rectory, Rebecca besought her (Miss Briggs) to remember
that her own home, humble as it was, was always open to
receive Briggs.   Dear friend,' she exclaimed, in a transport
of enthusiasm, ' *some* hearts can *never* forget benefits ;
all women are not Bute Crawleys ! Though why should
I complain of her,' Rebecca added ; ' though I have been
her tool and the victim to her arts, do I not owe my dearest
Rawdon to her ? '   And Rebecca unfolded to Briggs all
Mrs. Bute's conduct at Queen's Crawley, which, though
unintelligible to her then, was clearly enough explained
by the events now,—now that the attachment had sprung
up which Mrs. Bute had encouraged by a thousand artifices,
—now that two innocent people had fallen into the snares
which she had laid for them, and loved and married and
been ruined through her schemes.

It was all very true. Briggs saw the stratagems as
clearly as possible. Mrs. Bute had made the match between
Rawdon and Rebecca. Yet, though the latter was a perfectly innocent victim, Miss Briggs could not disguise from
her friend her fear that Miss Crawley's affections were
hopelessly estranged from Rebecca, and that the old lady
would never forgive her nephew for making so imprudent
a marriage.

On this point Rebecca had her own opinion, and still
kept up a good heart. If Miss Crawley did not forgive
them at present, she might at least relent on a future day.
Even now, there was only that puling, sickly Pitt Crawley
between Rawdon and a baronetcy ; and should anything
happen to the former, all would be well. At all events,
to have Mrs. Bute's designs exposed, and herself well abused,
was a satisfaction, and might be advantageous to Rawdon's

interest; and Rebecca, after an hour's chat with her
recovered friend, left her with the most tender demonstrations of regard, and quite assured that the conversation
they had had together would be reported to Miss Crawley
before many hours were over.

This interview ended, it became full time for Rebecca
to return to her inn, where all the party of the previous day
were assembled at a farewell breakfast. Rebecca took
such a tender leave of Amelia as became two women who
loved each other as sisters; and having used her handkerchief plentifully, and hung on her friend's neck as if
they were parting for ever, and waved the handkerchief
(which was quite dry, by the way) out of the window, as
the carriage drove off; she came back to the breakfast-
table, and ate some prawns with a good deal of appetite,
considering her emotion; and while she was munching
these delicacies, explained to Rawdon what had occurred
in her morning walk between herself and Briggs. Her
hopes were very high: she made her husband share them.
She generally succeeded in making her husband share all
her opinions, whether melancholy or cheerful.

'You will now, if you please, my dear, sit down at the
writing-table and pen me a pretty little letter to Miss
Crawley, in which you'll say that you are a good boy, and
that sort of thing.' So Rawdon sat down, and wrote off,
'Brighton, Thursday,' and 'My dear Aunt,' with great
rapidity: but there the gallant officer's imagination failed
him. He mumbled the end of his pen, and looked up in
his wife's face. She could not help laughing at his rueful
countenance, and, marching up and down the room with
her hands behind her, the little woman began to dictate
a letter, which he took down.

'Before quitting the country and commencing a campaign, which very possibly may be fatal—'

'What?' said Rawdon, rather surprised, but took the
humour of the phrase, and presently wrote it down with
a grin.

'Which very possibly may be fatal, I have come hither—'

'Why not say come here, Becky; come here's grammar,'
the dragoon interposed.

'I have come hither,' Rebecca insisted, with a stamp
of her foot, 'to say farewell to my dearest and earliest
friend. I beseech you before I go, not perhaps to return,

once more to let me press the hand from which I have received nothing but kindnesses all my life.'

' Kindnesses all my life,' echoed Rawdon, scratching down the words, and quite amazed at his own facility of composition.

' I ask nothing from you but that we should part not in anger.   I have the pride of my family on some points, though not on all.   I married a painter's daughter, and am not ashamed of the union.'

' No, run me through the body if I am ! ' Rawdon ejaculated.

' You old booby,' Rebecca said, pinching his ear, and looking over to see that he made no mistakes in spelling —' beseech is not spelt with an *a*, and earliest is.'   So he altered these words, bowing to the superior knowledge of his little missis.

' I thought that you were aware of the progress of my attachment,' Rebecca continued :   ' I knew that Mrs. Bute Crawley confirmed and encouraged it.   But I make no reproaches.   I married a poor woman, and am content to abide by what I have done.   Leave your property, dear aunt, as you will.   *I* shall never complain of the way in which you dispose of it.   I would have you believe that I love you for yourself, and not for money's sake.   I want to be reconciled to you ere I leave England.   Let me, let me see you before I go.   A few weeks or months hence it may be too late, and I cannot bear the notion of quitting the country without a kind word of farewell from you.'

' She won't recognize my style in *that*,' said Becky. ' I made the sentences short and brisk on purpose.'   And this authentic missive was dispatched under cover to Miss Briggs.

Old Miss Crawley laughed when Briggs, with great mystery, handed her over this candid and simple statement. ' We may read it now Mrs. Bute is away,' she said.   ' Read it to me, Briggs.'

When Briggs had read the epistle out, her patroness laughed more.   ' Don't you see, you goose,' she said to Briggs, who professed to be much touched by the honest affection which pervaded the composition—' don't you see that Rawdon never wrote a word of it.   He never wrote to me without asking for money in his life, and all his letters are full of bad spelling, and dashes, and bad grammar. It is that little serpent of a governess who rules him.' They are all alike, Miss Crawley thought in her heart. They all want me dead, and are hankering for my money.

'I don't mind seeing Rawdon,' she added, after a pause, and in a tone of perfect indifference. 'I had just as soon shake hands with him as not. Provided there is no scene, why shouldn't we meet? I don't mind. But human patience has its limits; and mind, my dear, I respectfully decline to receive Mrs. Rawdon—I can't support *that* quite'—and Miss Briggs was fain to be content with this half-message of conciliation; and thought that the best method of bringing the old lady and her nephew together, was to warn Rawdon to be in waiting on the Cliff, when Miss Crawley went out for her air in her chair.

There they met. I don't know whether Miss Crawley had any private feeling of regard or emotion upon seeing her old favourite; but she held out a couple of fingers to him with as smiling and good-humoured an air as if they had met only the day before. And as for Rawdon, he turned as red as scarlet, and wrung off Briggs's hand, so great was his rapture and his confusion at the meeting. Perhaps it was interest that moved him: or perhaps affection: perhaps he was touched by the change which the illness of the last weeks had wrought in his aunt.

'The old girl has always acted like a trump to me,' he said to his wife, as he narrated the interview, 'and I felt, you know, rather queer, and that sort of thing. I walked by the side of the what-d'ye-call-'em, you know, and to her own door, where Bowls came to help her in. And I wanted to go in very much, only——'

'*You didn't go in*, Rawdon!' screamed his wife.

'No, my dear; I'm hanged if I wasn't afraid when it came to the point.'

'You fool! you ought to have gone in, and never come out again,' Rebecca said.

'Don't call me names,' said the big guardsman, sulkily. 'Perhaps I *was* a fool, Becky, but you shouldn't say so;' and he gave his wife a look, such as his countenance could wear when angered, and such as was not pleasant to face.

'Well, dearest, to-morrow you must be on the look-out. and go and see her, mind, whether she asks you or no,' Rebecca said, trying to soothe her angry yoke-mate. On which he replied, that he would do exactly as he liked, and would just thank her to keep a civil tongue in her head —and the wounded husband went away, and passed the forenoon at the billiard-room, sulky, silent, and suspicious.

But before the night was over he was compelled to give in, and own, as usual, to his wife's superior prudence and foresight, by the most melancholy confirmation of the presentiments which she had regarding the consequences of the mistake which he had made. Miss Crawley *must* have had some emotion upon seeing him and shaking hands with him after so long a rupture. She mused upon the meeting a considerable time. ' Rawdon is getting very fat and old, Briggs,' she said to her companion. ' His nose has become red, and he is exceedingly coarse in appearance. His marriage to that woman has hopelessly vulgarized him. Mrs. Bute always said they drank together ; and I have no doubt they do. Yes : he smelt of gin abominably. I remarked it. Didn't you ? '

In vain Briggs interposed that Mrs. Bute spoke ill of everybody : and, as far as a person in *her* humble position could judge, was an- - -

' An artful designing woman ? Yes, so she is, and she does speak ill of every one—but I am certain that woman has made Rawdon drink. All those low people do——'

' He was very much affected at seeing you, ma'am,' the companion said ; ' and I am sure, when you remember that he is going to the field of danger——'

' How much money has he promised you, Briggs ? ' the old spinster cried out, working herself into a nervous rage—' there now, of course you begin to cry. I hate scenes. Why am I always to be worried ? Go and cry up in your own room, and send Firkin to me,—no, stop, sit down and blow your nose, and leave off crying, and write a letter to Captain Crawley.' Poor Briggs went and placed herself obediently at the writing-book. Its leaves were blotted all over with the relics of the firm, strong, rapid handwriting of the spinster's late amanuensis, Mrs. Bute Crawley.

' Begin "My dear sir ", or " Dear sir ", that will be better, and say you are desired by Miss Crawley— no, by Miss Crawley's medical man, by Mr. Creamer, to state, that my health is such that all strong emotions would be dangerous in my present delicate condition—and that I must decline any family discussions or interviews whatever. And thank him for coming to Brighton, and so forth, and beg him not to stay any longer on my account. And, Miss Briggs, you may add that I wish him a *bon voyage*, and that if he will take the trouble to call upon my lawyer's in Gray's Inn Square, he will find there a communication for him. Yes, that will do ; and that will make him leave Brighton.' The benevolent Briggs penned this sentence with the utmost satisfaction.

' To seize upon me the very day after Mrs. Bute was gone,' the old lady prattled on ; ' it was too indecent. Briggs, my dear, write to Mrs. Crawley, and say *she* needn't come back. No—she needn't—and she shan't—and I won't be a slave in my own house—and I won't be starved and choked with poison. They all want to kill me—all—all——' and with this the lonely old woman burst into a scream of hysterical tears.

The last scene of her dismal Vanity Fair comedy was fast approaching ; the tawdry lamps were going out one by one ; and the dark curtain was almost ready to descend.

That final paragraph, which referred Rawdon to Miss Crawley's solicitor in London, and which Briggs had written so good-naturedly, consoled the dragoon and his wife somewhat, after their first blank disappointment on reading the spinster's refusal of a reconciliation. And it effected the purpose for which the old lady had caused it to be written, by making Rawdon very eager to get to London.

Out of Jos's losings and George Osborne's bank-notes, he paid his bill at the inn, the landlord whereof does not probably know to this day how doubtfully his account once stood. For, as a general sends his baggage to the rear before an action, Rebecca had wisely packed up all their chief valuables and sent them off under care of George's servant, who went in charge of the trunks on the coach back to London. Rawdon and his wife returned by the same conveyance next day.

' I should have liked to see the old girl before we went,' Rawdon said. ' She looks so cut up and altered that I'm sure she can't last long. I wonder what sort of a cheque I shall have at Waxy's. Two hundred—it can't be less than two hundred—hey, Becky ? '

In consequence of the repeated visits of the gentlemen whose portraits have been taken in a preceding page, Rawdon and his wife did not go back to their lodgings at Brompton, but put up at an inn.   Early the next morning, Rebecca had an opportunity of seeing them as she skirted that suburb on her road to old Mrs. Sedley's house at Fulham, whither she went to look for her dear Amelia and her Brighton friends.   They were all off to Chatham, thence to Harwich, to take shipping for Belgium with the regiment —kind old Mrs. Sedley very much depressed and tearful, solitary.   Returning from this visit, Rebecca found her husband, who had been off to Gray's Inn, and learnt his fate.   He came back furious.

' By Jove, Becky,' says he, ' she's only given me twenty pound ! '

Though it told against themselves, the joke was too good, and Becky burst out laughing at Rawdon's discomfiture.

CHAPTER XXVI

BETWEEN LONDON AND CHATHAM

N quitting Brighton, our friend George, as became a person of rank and fashion, travelling in a barouche with four horses, drove in state to a fine hotel in Cavendish Square,* where a suite of splendid rooms, and a table magnificently furnished with plate and surrounded by a half-dozen of black and silent waiters, was ready to receive the young gentleman and his bride.   George did the honours of the place with a princely air to Jos and Dobbin ;   and Amelia, for the first time, and with exceeding shyness and timidity, presided at what George called her own table.

George pooh-poohed the wine and bullied the waiters royally, and Jos gobbled the turtle with immense satisfaction.   Dobbin helped him to it ; for the lady of the house, before whom the tureen was placed, was so ignorant

of the contents, that she was going to help Mr. Sedley
without bestowing upon him either calipash or calipee.*

The splendour of the entertainment, and the apartments
in which it was given, alarmed Mr. Dobbin, who remonstrated after dinner, when Jos was asleep in the great chair.
But in vain he cried out against the enormity of turtle
and champagne that was fit for an archbishop. ' I've
always been accustomed to travel like a gentleman,'
George said, ' and, damme, my wife shall travel like a lady.
As long as there's a shot in the locker, *she* shall want for
nothing,' said the generous fellow, quite pleased with himself for his magnificence of spirit. Nor did Dobbin try and
convince him that Amelia's happiness was not centred
in turtle-soup.

A while after dinner, Amelia timidly expressed a wish
to go and see her mamma, at Fulham : which permission
George granted her with some grumbling. And she
tripped away to her enormous bedroom, in the centre
of which stood the enormous funereal bed, ' that the
Emperor Halixander's sister slep in when the allied sufferings was here,' and put on her little bonnet and shawl
with the utmost eagerness and pleasure. George was still
drinking claret when she returned to the dining-room,
and made no signs of moving. ' Aren't you coming with
me, dearest ? ' she asked him. No ; the ' dearest ' had
' business ' that night. His man should get her a coach,
and go with her. And the coach being at the door of the
hotel, Amelia made George a little disappointed curtsy
after looking vainly into his face once or twice, and went
sadly down the great staircase, Captain Dobbin after,
who handed her into the vehicle, and saw it drive away
to its destination. The very valet was ashamed of mentioning the address to the hackney-coachman before the
hotel-waiters, and promised to instruct him when they
got farther on.

Dobbin walked home to his old quarters at the Slaughter's,
thinking very likely that it would be delightful to be in
that hackney-coach, along with Mrs. Osborne. George
was evidently of quite a different taste ; for when he had
taken wine enough, he went off to half-price at the play,*
to see Mr. Kean perform in Shylock.* Captain Osborne
was a great lover of the drama, and had himself performed
high-comedy characters with great distinction in several

garrison theatrical entertainments. Jos slept on until long after dark, when he woke up with a start at the motions of his servant, who was removing and emptying the decanters on the table ; and the hackney-coach stand was again put into requisition for a carriage to convey this stout hero to his lodgings and bed.

Mrs. Sedley, you may be sure, clasped her daughter to her heart with all maternal eagerness and affection, running out of the door as the carriage drew up before the little garden-gate, to welcome the weeping, trembling, young bride. Old Mr. Clapp, who was in his shirt-sleeves, trimming the garden-plot, shrank back alarmed. The Irish servant-lass rushed up from the kitchen, and smiled a ' God bless you '. Amelia could hardly walk along the flags and up the steps into the parlour.

How the floodgates were opened and mother and daughter wept, when they were together embracing each other in this sanctuary, may readily be imagined by every reader who possesses the least sentimental turn. When don't ladies weep ? At what occasion of joy, sorrow, or other business of life ? and, after such an event as a marriage, mother and daughter were surely at liberty to give way to a sensibility which is as tender as it is refreshing. About a question of marriage I have seen women who hate each other kiss and cry together quite fondly. How much more do they feel when they love ! Good mothers are married over again at their daughters' weddings : and as for subsequent events, who does not know how ultra-maternal grandmothers are ?—in fact a woman, until she is a grandmother, does not often really know what to be a mother is. Let us respect Amelia and her mamma whispering and whimpering and laughing and crying in the parlour and the twilight. Old Mr. Sedley did. *He* had not divined who was in the carriage when it drove up. He had not flown out to meet his daughter, though he kissed her very warmly when she entered the room (where he was occupied, as usual, with his papers and tapes and statements of accounts), and after sitting with the mother and daughter for a short time, he very wisely left the little apartment in their possession.

George's valet was looking on in a very supercilious manner at Mr. Clapp in his shirt-sleeves, watering his

rose-bushes. He took off his hat, however, with much
condescension to Mr. Sedley, who asked news about his
son-in-law, and about Jos's carriage, and whether his
horses had been down to Brighton, and about that infernal
traitor Bonaparty, and the war; until the Irish maid-
servant came with a plate and a bottle of wine, from which
the old gentleman insisted upon helping the valet. He
gave him a half-guinea too, which the servant pocketed
with a mixture of wonder and contempt. 'To the health

of your master and mistress, Trotter,' Mr. Sedley said,
' and here's something to drink your health when you get
home, Trotter.'

There were but nine days past since Amelia had left that
little cottage and home—and yet how far off the time
seemed since she had bidden it farewell. What a gulf
lay between her and that past life. She could look back
to it from her present standing-place, and contemplate,
almost as another being, the young unmarried girl absorbed
in her love, having no eyes but for one special object,
receiving parental affection if not ungratefully, at least
indifferently, and as if it were her due—her whole heart
and thoughts bent on the accomplishment of one desire.
The review of those days, so lately gone yet so far away,
touched her with shame; and the aspect of the kind parents
filled her with tender remorse. Was the prize gained—the

heaven of life—and the winner still doubtful and unsatisfied ? As his hero and heroine pass the matrimonial barrier, the novelist generally drops the curtain, as if the drama were over then : the doubts and struggles of life ended : as if, once landed in the marriage country, all were green and pleasant there : and wife and husband had nothing but to link each other's arms together, and wander gently down-wards towards old age in happy and perfect fruition. But our little Amelia was just on the bank of her new country, and was already looking anxiously back towards the sad friendly figures waving farewell to her across the stream, from the other distant shore.

In honour of the young bride's arrival, her mother thought it necessary to prepare I don't know what festive entertainment, and after the first ebullition of talk, took leave of Mrs. George Osborne for a while, and dived down to the lower regions of the house to a sort of kitchen-parlour (occupied by Mr. and Mrs. Clapp, and in the evening, when her dishes were washed, and her curl-papers removed, by Miss Flannigan, the Irish servant), there to take measures for the preparing of a magnificent ornamented tea. All people have their ways of expressing kindness, and it seemed to Mrs. Sedley that a muffin and a quantity of orange marmalade spread out in a little cut-glass saucer would be peculiarly agreeable refreshments to Amelia in her most interesting situation.

While these delicacies were being transacted below, Amelia, leaving the drawing-room, walked upstairs and found herself, she scarce knew how, in the little room which she had occupied before her marriage, and in that very chair in which she had passed so many bitter hours. She sank back in its arms as if it were an old friend ; and fell to thinking over the past week, and the life beyond it. Already to be looking sadly and vaguely back : always to be pining for something which, when obtained, brought doubt and sadness rather than pleasure : here was the lot of our poor little creature, and harmless lost wanderer in the great struggling crowds of Vanity Fair.

Here she sat, and recalled to herself fondly that image of George to which she had knelt before marriage. Did she own to herself how different the real man was from that superb young hero whom she had worshipped ? It requires many, many years—and a man must be very

bad indeed—before a woman's pride and vanity will let
her own to such a confession. Then Rebecca's twinkling
green eyes and baleful smile lighted upon her, and filled
her with dismay. And so she sat for a while indulging
in her usual mood of selfish brooding, in that very listless
melancholy attitude in which the honest maidservant
had found her, on the day when she brought up the letter
in which George renewed his offer of marriage.

She looked at the little white bed, which had been hers
a few days before, and thought she would like to sleep in
it that night, and wake, as formerly, with her mother
smiling over her in the morning. Then she thought with
terror of the great funereal damask pavilion in the vast
and dingy state bedroom, which was awaiting her at the
grand hotel in Cavendish Square. Dear little white bed!
how many a long night had she wept on its pillow! How
she had despaired and hoped to die there; and now were
not all her wishes accomplished, and the lover of whom she
had despaired her own for ever? Kind mother! how
patiently and tenderly she had watched round that bed!
She went and knelt down by the bedside; and there this
wounded and timorous, but gentle and loving soul, sought

for consolation, where as yet, it must be owned, our little girl had but seldom looked for it. Love had been her faith hitherto; and the sad, bleeding, disappointed heart began to feel the want of another consoler.

Have we a right to repeat or to overhear her prayers? These, brother, are secrets, and out of the domain of Vanity Fair, in which our story lies.

But this may be said, that when the tea was finally announced, our young lady came downstairs a great deal more cheerful; that she did not despond, or deplore her fate, or think about George's coldness, or Rebecca's eyes, as she had been wont to do of late. She went downstairs and kissed her father and mother, and talked to the old gentleman, and made him more merry than he had been for many a day. She sat down at the piano which Dobbin had bought for her, and sang over all her father's favourite old songs. She pronounced the tea to be excellent, and praised the exquisite taste in which the marmalade was arranged in the saucers. And in determining to make everybody else happy, she found herself so; and was sound asleep in the great funereal pavilion, and only woke up with a smile when George arrived from the theatre.

For the next day, George had more important ' business ' to transact than that which took him to see Mr. Kean in Shylock. Immediately on his arrival in London he had written off to his father's solicitors, signifying his royal pleasure that an interview should take place between them on the morrow. His hotel losses at billiards and cards to Captain Crawley had almost drained the young man's purse, which wanted replenishing before he set out on his travels, and he had no resource but to infringe upon the two thousand pounds which the attorneys were commissioned to pay over to him. He had a perfect belief in his own mind that his father would relent before very long. How could any parent be obdurate for a length of time against such a paragon as he was? If his mere past and personal merits did not succeed in mollifying the father, George determined that he would distinguish himself so prodigiously in the ensuing campaign that the old gentleman must give in to him. And if not? Bah! the world was before him. His luck might change at

cards, and there was a deal of spending in two thousand
pounds.

So he sent off Amelia once more in a carriage to her
mamma, with strict orders and carte blanche to the two
ladies to purchase everything requisite for a lady of Mrs.
George Osborne's fashion, who was going on a foreign
tour. They had but one day to complete the outfit, and
it may be imagined that their business therefore occupied
them pretty fully. In a carriage once more, bustling about
from milliner to linen-draper, escorted back to the carriage
by obsequious shopmen or polite owners, Mrs. Sedley was
herself again almost, and sincerely happy for the first time
since their misfortunes. Nor was Mrs. Amelia at all above
the pleasure of shopping, and bargaining, and seeing and
buying pretty things. (Would any man, the most philosophic, give twopence for a woman who was ?) She gave
herself a little treat, obedient to her husband's orders, and
purchased a quantity of lady's gear, showing a great deal
of taste and elegant discernment, as all the shop-folks said.

And about the war that was ensuing, Mrs. Osborne was
not much alarmed ; Bonaparty was to be crushed almost
without a struggle. Margate packets were sailing every
day,* filled with men of fashion and ladies of note, on their
way to Brussels and Ghent. People were going not so
much to a war as to a fashionable tour. The newspapers
laughed the wretched upstart and swindler to scorn. Such
a Corsican wretch as that withstand the armies of Europe
and the genius of the immortal Wellington ! Amelia held
him in utter contempt ; for it needs not to be said that
this soft and gentle creature took her opinions from those
people who surrounded her, such fidelity being much too
humble-minded to think for itself. Well, in a word, she
and her mother performed a great day's shopping, and
she acquitted herself with considerable liveliness and
credit on this her first appearance in the genteel world
of London.

George meanwhile, with his hat on one side, his elbows
squared, and his swaggering martial air, made for Bedford
Row, and stalked into the attorney's offices as if he was
lord of every pale-faced clerk who was scribbling there.
He ordered somebody to inform Mr. Higgs that Captain
Osborne was waiting, in a fierce and patronizing way, as if
the *pékin** of an attorney, who had thrice his brains, fifty

times his money, and a thousand times his experience, was a wretched underling who should instantly leave all his business in life to attend on the captain's pleasure. He did not see the sneer of contempt which passed all round the room, from the first clerk to the articled gents, from the articled gents to the ragged writers and white-faced runners, in clothes too tight for them, as he sat there tapping his boot with his cane, and thinking what a parcel of miserable poor devils these were. The miserable poor devils knew all about his affairs. They talked about them over their pints of beer at their public-house clubs to other clerks of a night. Ye gods, what do not attorneys and attorneys' clerks know in London! Nothing is hidden from their inquisition, and their familiars mutely rule our city.

Perhaps George expected, when he entered Mr. Higgs's apartment, to find that gentleman commissioned to give him some message of compromise or conciliation from his father; perhaps his haughty and cold demeanour was adopted as a sign of his spirit and resolution : but if so, his fierceness was met by a chilling coolness and indifference on the attorney's part, that rendered swaggering absurd. He pretended to be writing at a paper, when the captain entered. ' Pray, sit down, sir,' said he, ' and I will attend to your little affair in a moment. Mr. Poe, get the release papers, if you please ; ' and then he fell to writing again.

Poe having produced those papers, his chief calculated the amount of two thousand pounds stock at the rate of the day ; and asked Captain Osborne whether he would take the sum in a cheque upon the bankers, or whether he should direct the latter to purchase stock to that amount. ' One of the late Mrs. Osborne's trustees is out of town,' he said indifferently, ' but my client wishes to meet your wishes, and have done with the business as quick as possible.'

' Give me a cheque, sir,' said the captain very surlily. ' Damn the shillings and halfpence, sir,' he added, as the lawyer was making out the amount of the draft ; and, flattering himself that by this stroke of magnanimity he had put the old quiz to the blush, he stalked out of his office with the paper in his pocket.

' That chap will be in gaol in two years,' Mr. Higgs said to Mr. Poe.

' Won't O. come round, sir, don't you think ? '

' Won't the Monument come round,' Mr. Higgs replied.

' He's going it pretty fast,' said the clerk. ' He's only married a week, and I saw him and some other military chaps handing Mrs. Highflyer to her carriage after the play.' And then another case was called, and Mr. George Osborne thenceforth dismissed from these worthy gentlemen's memory.

The draft was upon our friends Hulker and Bullock of Lombard Street, to whose house, still thinking he was doing business, George bent his way, and from whom he received his money. Frederick Bullock, Esq., whose yellow face was over a ledger, at which sat a demure clerk, happened to be in the banking-room when George entered. His yellow face turned to a more deadly colour when he saw the captain, and he slunk back guiltily into the inmost parlour. George was too busy gloating over the money (for he had never had such a sum before), to mark the countenance or flight of the cadaverous suitor of his sister.

Fred Bullock told old Osborne of his son's appearance and conduct, ' He came in as bold as brass,' said Frederick. ' He has drawn out every shilling. How long will a few hundred pounds last such a chap as that ? ' Osborne swore with a great oath that he little cared when or how soon he spent it. Fred dined every day in Russell Square now. But altogether, George was highly pleased with his day's business. All his own baggage and outfit was put into a state of speedy preparation, and he paid Amelia's purchases with cheques on his agents, and with the splendour of a lord.

CHAPTER XXVII

IN WHICH AMELIA JOINS HER REGIMENT

HEN Jos's fine carriage drove up to the inn door at Chatham, the first face which Amelia recognized was the friendly countenance of Captain Dobbin, who had been pacing the street for an hour past in expectation of his friends' arrival. The captain, with shells on his frock-coat,* and a crimson sash and sabre, presented a military appearance, which made Jos quite proud to be able to claim such an acquaintance, and the stout civilian hailed him with a cordiality very different from the reception which Jos vouchsafed to his friend in Brighton and Bond Street.

Along with the captain was Ensign Stubble ; who, as the barouche neared the inn, burst out with an exclamation of ' By Jove! what a pretty girl;' highly applauding Osborne's choice. Indeed, Amelia dressed in her wedding-pelisse and pink ribbons, with a flush in her face, occasioned by rapid travel through the open air, looked so fresh and pretty, as fully to justify the ensign's compliment. Dobbin liked him for making it. As he stepped forward to help the lady out of the carriage, Stubble saw what a pretty little hand she gave him, and what a sweet pretty little foot came tripping down the step. He blushed profusely, and made the very best bow of which he was capable ; to which Amelia, seeing the number of the —th regiment embroidered on the ensign's cap, replied with a blushing smile, and a curtsy on her part ; which finished the young ensign on the spot. Dobbin took most kindly to Mr. Stubble from that day, and encouraged him to talk about Amelia in their private walks, and at each other's quarters. It became the fashion, indeed, among all the honest young fellows of the —th to adore and admire Mrs. Osborne. Her simple artless behaviour, and modest kindness of demeanour, won all their unsophisticated

hearts; all which simplicity and sweetness are quite
impossible to describe in print. But who has not beheld
these among women, and recognized the presence of all
sorts of qualities in them, even though they say no more to
you than that they are engaged to dance the next quadrille,
or that it is very hot weather? George, always the champion
of his regiment, rose immensely in the opinion of the youth
of the corps, by his gallantry in marrying this portionless
young creature, and by his choice of such a pretty kind
partner.

In the sitting-room which was awaiting the travellers,
Amelia, to her surprise, found a letter addressed to Mrs.
Captain Osborne. It was a triangular billet, on pink
paper, and sealed with a dove and an olive branch, and
a profusion of light-blue sealing-wax, and it was written in
a very large, though undecided female hand.

'It's Peggy O'Dowd's fist,' said George, laughing. 'I know
it by the kisses on the seal.' And in fact, it was a note
from Mrs. Major O'Dowd, requesting the pleasure of Mrs.
Osborne's company that very evening to a small friendly
party. 'You must go,' George said. 'You will make
acquaintance with the regiment there. O'Dowd goes in
command of the regiment, and Peggy goes in command of
O'Dowd.'

But they had not been for many minutes in the enjoyment of Mrs. O'Dowd's letter, when the door was flung
open, and a stout jolly lady, in a riding-habit, followed by
a couple of officers of Ours, entered the room.

'Sure, I couldn't stop till tay-time. Present me, Garge,
my dear fellow, to your lady. Madam, I'm deloighted to
see ye; and to present to you me husband, Meejor O'Dowd;'
and with this, the jolly lady in the riding-habit grasped
Amelia's hand very warmly, and the latter knew at once that
the lady was before her whom her husband had so often
laughed at. 'You've often heard of me from that husband
of yours,' said the lady, with great vivacity.

'You've often heard of her,' echoed her husband, the
Major.

Amelia answered, smiling, 'that she had.'

'And small good he's told you of me,' Mrs. O'Dowd replied;
adding that 'George was a wicked divvle'.

'That I'll go bail for,' said the major, trying to look
knowing at which George laughed; and Mrs. O'Dowd,

with a tap of her whip, told the major to be quiet ; and then requested to be presented in form to Mrs. Captain Osborne.

' This, my dear,' said George with great gravity, ' is my very good, kind, and excellent friend, Auralia Margaretta, otherwise called Peggy.'

' Faith, you're right,' interposed the major.

' Otherwise called Peggy, lady of Major Michael O'Dowd, of our regiment, and daughter of Fitzjurld Ber'sford de Burgo Malony of Glenmalony, County Kildare.'

' And Muryan Squeer, Doblin,' said the lady, with calm superiority.

' And Muryan Square, sure enough,' the major whispered

' 'Twas there ye coorted me, meejor dear,' the lady said ; and the major assented to this as to every other proposition which was made generally in company.

Major O'Dowd, who had served his sovereign in every quarter of the world, and had paid for every step in his profession by some more than equivalent act of daring and gallantry, was the most modest, silent, sheep-faced, and

meek of little men, and as obedient to his wife as if he had
been her tay-boy. At the mess-table he sat silently, and
drank a great deal. When full of liquor, he reeled silently
home. When he spoke, it was to agree with everybody on
every conceivable point; and he passed through life in
perfect ease and good humour. The hottest suns of India
never heated his temper ; and the Walcheren ague* never
shook it. He walked up to a battery with just as much
indifference as to a dinner-table ; had dined on horseflesh
and turtle with equal relish and appetite ; and had an old
mother, Mrs. O'Dowd of O'Dowdstown indeed, whom he
had never disobeyed but when he ran away and enlisted, and
when he persisted in marrying that odious Peggy Malony.

Peggy was one of five sisters, and eleven children of the
noble house of Glenmalony ; but her husband, though her
own cousin, was of the mother's side, and so had not the
inestimable advantage of being allied to the Malonies, whom
she believed to be the most famous family in the world.
Having tried nine seasons at Dublin and two at Bath and
Cheltenham, and not finding a partner for life, Miss Malony
ordered her cousin Mick to marry her when she was about
thirty-three years of age ; and the honest fellow obeying,
carried her off to the West Indies, to preside over the ladies
of the ——th regiment, into which he had just exchanged.

Before Mrs. O'Dowd was half an hour in Amelia's (or
indeed in anybody else's) company, this amiable lady told
all her birth and pedigree to her new friend. ' My dear,'
said she, good-naturedly, ' it was my intention that Garge
should be a brother of my own, and my sister Glorvina would
have suited him entirely. But as bygones are bygones,
and he was engaged to yourself, why, I'm determined to
take you as a sister instead, and to look upon you as such,
and to love you as one of the family. Faith, you've got
such a nice good-natured face and way widg you, that I'm
sure we'll agree ; and that you'll be an addition to our
family anyway.'

'Deed and she will,' said O'Dowd, with an approving
air, and Amelia felt herself not a little amused and grateful
to be thus suddenly introduced to so large a party of
relations.

' We're all good fellows here,' the major's lady continued.
' There's not a regiment in the service where you'll find
a more united society nor a more agreeable mess-room.

There's no quarrelling, bickering, slandthering, nor small talk amongst *us*.   We all love each other.'

' Especially Mrs. Magenis,' said George, laughing.

' Mrs. Captain Magenis and me has made up, though her treatment of me would bring me grey hairs with sorrow to the grave.'

' And you with such a beautiful front of black, Peggy, my dear,' the major cried.

' Hould your tongue, Mick, you booby.   Them husbands are always in the way, Mrs. Osborne, my dear ; and as for my Mick, I often tell him he should never open his mouth but to give the word of command, or to put meat and drink into it.   I'll tell you about the regiment, and warn you when we're alone.   Introduce me to your brother now ; sure he's a mighty fine man, and reminds me of me cousin, Dan Malony (Malony of Ballymalony, my dear, you know, who mar'ied Ophalia Scully, of Oystherstown, own cousin to Lord Poldoody).   Mr. Sedley, sir, I'm deloighted to be made known te ye.   I suppose you'll dine at the mess to-day. (Mind that divvle of a docther, Mick, and whatever ye du, keep yourself sober for me party this evening.) '

' It's the 150th gives us a farewell dinner, my love,' interposed the major, ' but we'll easy get a card for Mr. Sedley.'

' Run, Simple (Ensign Simple, of Ours, my dear Amelia. I forgot to introjuice him to ye).   Run in a hurry, with Mrs. Major O'Dowd's compliments to Colonel Tavish, and Captain Osborne has brought his brothernlaw down, and will bring him to the 150th mess at five o'clock sharp—when you and I, my dear, will take a snack here, if you like.' Before Mrs. O'Dowd's speech was concluded, the young ensign was trotting downstairs on his commission.

' Obedience is the soul of the army.   We will go to our duty while Mrs. O'Dowd will stay and enlighten you, Emmy,' Captain Osborne said ; and the two captains, taking each a wing of the major, walked out with that officer, grinning at each other over his head.

And, now having her new friend to herself, the impetuous Mrs. O'Dowd proceeded to pour out such a quantity of information as no poor little woman's memory could ever tax itself to bear.   She told Amelia a thousand particulars relative to the very numerous family of which the amazed young lady found herself a member.   ' Mrs. Heavytop, the colonel's wife, died in Jamaica of the yellow faver and a broken heart comboined, for the horrud old colonel, with a head as bald as a cannon-ball, was making sheep's eyes at a half-caste girl there. Mrs. Magenis, though without education, was a good woman, but she had the divvle's tongue, and would cheat her own mother at whist. Mrs. Captain Kirk must turn up her lobster eyes forsooth at the idea of an honest round game (wherein me fawther, as pious a man as ever went to church, me uncle Dane Malony, and our cousin the bishop, took a hand at loo, or whist, every night of their lives). Nayther of 'em's goin' with the regiment this time,' Mrs. O'Dowd added. ' Fanny Magenis stops with her mother, who sells small coal and potatoes, most likely, in Islington-town, hard by London, though she's always bragging of her father's ships, and pointing them out to us as they go up the river : and Mrs. Kirk and her children will stop here in Bethesda Place, to be nigh to her favourite preacher, Dr. Ramshorn. Mrs. Bunny's in an interesting situation—faith, and she always is, then—and has given the lieutenant seven already. And Ensign Posky's wife, who joined two months before you, my dear, has quarl'd with Tom Posky a score of times, till you can hear 'em all over the bar'ck (they say they're come to broken pleets, and Tom never accounted for his black oi), and she'll go back to her mother, who keeps a ladies' siminary at Richmond,—bad luck to her for running away from it ! Where did ye get your finishing, my dear ? I had moin, and no expince speered, at Madame Flanahan's, at Ilyssus Grove, Booterstown, near Dublin, wid a marchioness to teach us the true Parisian pronunciation, and a retired mejor-general of the French service to put us through the exercise.'

Of this incongruous family our astonished Amelia found herself all of a sudden a member : with Mrs. O'Dowd as an elder sister. She was presented to her other female relations at tea-time, on whom, as she was quiet, good-natured, and not too handsome she made rather an agreeable impression until the arrival of the gentlemen from the mess of the 150th, who all admired her so, that her sisters began, of course, to find fault with her.

' I hope Osborne has sown his wild oats,' said Mrs. Magenis to Mrs. Bunny. ' If a reformed rake makes a good husband, sure it's she will have the fine chance with Garge,' Mrs.

O'Dowd remarked to Posky, who had lost her position as
bride in the regiment, and was quite angry with the usurper.
And as for Mrs. Kirk, the disciple of Dr. Ramshorn put
one or two leading professional questions to Amelia, to see
whether she was awakened, whether she was a professing
Christian and so forth, and finding from the simplicity of
Mrs. Osborne's replies that she was yet in utter darkness,
put into her hands three little penny books with pictures,
viz., the *Howling Wilderness*, the *Washerwoman of Wands-
worth Common*, and the *British Soldier's Best Bayonet*, which,
bent upon awakening her before she slept, Mrs. Kirk begged
Amelia to read that night ere she went to bed.

But all the men, like good fellows as they were, rallied
round their comrade's pretty wife, and paid her their court
with soldierly gallantry. She had a little triumph, which
flushed her spirits and made her eyes sparkle. George was
proud of her popularity, and pleased with the manner (which
was very gay and graceful, though naïve and a little timid)
with which she received the gentlemen's attentions, and
answered their compliments. And he in his uniform—how
much handsomer he was than any man in the room! She
felt that he was affectionately watching her, and glowed
with pleasure at his kindness. ' I will make all his friends
welcome,' she resolved in her heart. ' I will love all who
love him. I will always try and be gay and good-humoured
and make his home happy.'

The regiment indeed adopted her with acclamation. The
captains approved, the lieutenants applauded, the ensigns
admired. Old Cutler, the doctor, made one or two jokes,
which, being professional, need not be repeated; and
Cackle, the Assistant M.D. of Edinburgh, condescended to
examine her upon leeterature, and tried her with his three
best French quotations. Young Stubble went about from
man to man whispering, ' Jove, isn't she a pretty gal ? '
and never took his eyes off her except when the negus*
came in.

As for Captain Dobbin, he never so much as spoke to her
during the whole evening. But he and Captain Porter of
the 150th took home Jos to the hotel, who was in a very
maudlin state, and had told his tiger-hunt story with great
effect, both at the mess-table, and at the soirée to Mrs
O'Dowd in her turban and bird of paradise. Having put
the collector into the hands of his servant, Dobbin loitered

about, smoking his cigar before the inn door. George had
meanwhile very carefully shawled his wife, and brought her
away from Mrs. O'Dowd's after a general hand-shaking
from the young officers, who accompanied her to the fly,
and cheered that vehicle as it drove off. So Amelia gave
Dobbin her little hand as she got out of the carriage, and
rebuked him smilingly for not having taken any notice of
her all night.

The captain continued that deleterious amusement of
smoking, long after the inn and the street were gone to bed.
He watched the lights vanish from George's sitting-room
windows, and shine out in the bedroom close at hand. It
was almost morning when he returned to his own quarters.
He could hear the cheering from the ships in the river, where
the transports were already taking in their cargoes preparatory to dropping down the Thames.

CHAPTER XXVIII

IN WHICH AMELIA INVADES THE LOW COUNTRIES

HE regiment with its officers was
to be transported in ships provided by His Majesty's government for the occasion: and in two
days after the festive assembly
at Mrs. O'Dowd's apartments,
in the midst of cheering from all
the East India ships in the river,
and the military on shore, the
band playing ' God save the
King ', the officers waving their
hats, and the crews hurrahing
gallantly, the transports went
down the river and proceeded
under convoy to Ostend. Meanwhile the gallant Jos had agreed
to escort his sister and the
major's wife, the bulk of whose goods and chattels, including
the famous bird of paradise and turban, were with the
regimental baggage : so that our two heroines drove pretty

MRS. OSBORNE'S CARRIAGE STOPPING THE WAY

much unencumbered to Ramsgate, where there were plenty
of packets plying, in one of which they had a speedy
passage to Ostend.

That period of Jos's life which now ensued was so full of
incident, that it served him for conversation for many years
after, and even the tiger-hunt story was put aside for more
stirring narratives which he had to tell about the great campaign of Waterloo.   As soon as he had agreed to escort his
sister abroad, it was remarked that he ceased shaving his
upper lip.   At Chatham he followed the parades and drills
with great assiduity.   He listened with the utmost attention
to the conversation of his brother officers (as he called them
in afterdays sometimes), and learned as many military names
as he could.   In these studies the excellent Mrs. O'Dowd
was of great assistance to him ; and on the day finally when
they embarked on board the *Lovely Rose* which was to
carry them to their destination, he made his appearance in
a braided frock-coat and duck trousers, with a foraging cap
ornamented with a smart gold band.   Having his carriage
with him, and informing everybody on board confidentially
that he was going to join the Duke of Wellington's army,
folks mistook him for a great personage, a commissary-
general, or a government courier at the very least.

He suffered hugely on the voyage, during which the
ladies were likewise prostrate ; but Amelia was brought to
life again as the packet made Ostend, by the sight of the
transports conveying her regiment, which entered the
harbour almost at the same time with the *Lovely Rose*.
Jos went in a collapsed state to an inn, while Captain Dobbin
escorted the ladies, and then busied himself in freeing Jos's
carriage and luggage from the ship and the custom-house,
for Mr. Jos was at present without a servant, Osborne's man
and his own pampered menial having conspired together at
Chatham, and refused point-blank to cross the water.   This
revolt, which came very suddenly, and on the last day, so
alarmed Mr. Sedley, junior, that he was on the point of
giving up the expedition, but Captain Dobbin (who made
himself immensely officious in the business, Jos said), rated
him and laughed at him soundly : the moustachios were
grown in advance, and Jos finally was persuaded to embark.
In place of the well bred and well-fed London domestics,
who could only speak English, Dobbin procured for Jos's
party a swarthy little Belgian servant who could speak no

language at all; but who, by his bustling behaviour, and by invariably addressing Mr. Sedley as 'My lord', speedily acquired that gentleman's favour. Times are altered at Ostend now; of the Britons who go thither, very few look like lords, or act like those members of our hereditary aristocracy. They seem for the most part shabby in attire, dingy of linen, lovers of billiards and brandy, and cigars and greasy ordinaries.

But it may be said as a rule, that every Englishman in the Duke of Wellington's army paid his way. The remembrance of such a fact surely becomes a nation of shopkeepers. It was a blessing for a commerce-loving country to be over-run by such an army of customers*: and to have such creditable warriors to feed. And the country which they came to protect is not military. For a long period of history they have let other people fight there. When the present writer went to survey with eagle glance the field of Waterloo, we asked the conductor of the diligence, a portly warlike-looking veteran, whether he had been at the battle. ' *Pas si bête* '—such an answer and sentiment as no Frenchman would own to—was his reply. But on the other hand, the postilion who drove us was a *viscount*,* a son of some bank-rupt imperial general, who accepted a pennyworth of beer on the road. The moral is surely a good one.

This flat, flourishing, easy country never could have looked more rich and prosperous, than in that opening summer of 1815, when its green fields and quiet cities were enlivened by multiplied red-coats : when its wide *chaussées* swarmed with brilliant English equipages; when its great canal-boats, gliding by rich pastures and pleasant quaint old villages, by old châteaux lying amongst old trees, were all crowded with well-to-do English travellers : when the soldier who drank at the village inn, not only drank, but paid his score ; and Donald, the Highlander,* billeted in the Flemish farm-house, rocked the baby's cradle, while Jean and Jeannette were out getting in the hay. As our painters are bent on military subjects just now,* I throw out this as a good subject for the pencil, to illustrate the principle of an honest English war. All looked as brilliant and harmless as a Hyde Park review. Meanwhile, Napoleon, screened behind his curtain of frontier-fortresses, was preparing for the outbreak which was to drive

* This incident is mentioned in Mr. Gleig's *Story of the Battle of Waterloo.*

all these orderly people into fury and blood ; and lay so many of them low.

Everybody had such a perfect feeling of confidence in the leader (for the resolute faith which the Duke of Wellington had inspired in the whole English nation was as intense as that more frantic enthusiasm with which at one time the French regarded Napoleon), the country seemed in so perfect a state of orderly defence, and the help at hand in case of need so near and overwhelming, that alarm was unknown, and that our travellers, among whom two were naturally of a very timid sort, were, like all the other multiplied English tourists, entirely at ease. The famous regiment, with so many of whose officers we have made acquaintance, was drafted in canal-boats to Bruges and Ghent, thence to march to Brussels. Jos accompanied the ladies in the public boats ; the which all old travellers in Flanders must remember for the luxury and accommodation they afforded. So prodigiously good was the eating and drinking on board these sluggish but most comfortable vessels, that there are legends extant of an English traveller, who, coming to Belgium for a week, and travelling in one of these boats, was so delighted with the fare there that he went backwards

and forwards from Ghent to Bruges perpetually until the railroads were invented, when he drowned himself on the last trip of the passage-boat. Jos's death was not to be of this sort, but his comfort was exceeding, and Mrs. O'Dowd insisted that he only wanted her sister Glorvina to make his happiness complete. He sat on the roof of the cabin all day drinking Flemish beer, shouting for Isidor, his servant, and talking gallantly to the ladies.

His courage was prodigious. 'Boney attack *us !* ' he cried. 'My dear creature, my poor Emmy, don't be frightened. There's no danger. The allies will be in Paris in two months, I tell you ; when I'll take you to dine in the Palais Royal, by Jove ! There are three hundred thousand

Rooshians, I tell you, now entering France by Mayence
and the Rhine—three hundred thousand under Wittgenstein
and Barclay de Tolly, my poor love. You don't know
military affairs, my dear. I do, and I tell you there's no
infantry in France can stand against Rooshian infantry,
and no general of Boney's that's fit to hold a candle to
Wittgenstein. Then there are the Austrians, they are five
hundred thousand if a man, and they are within ten
marches of the frontier by this time, under Schwartzenberg
and Prince Charles. Then there are the Prooshians under
the gallant Prince Marshal. Show me a cavalry chief like
him now that Murat is gone.* Hey, Mrs. O'Dowd ? Do you
think our little girl here need be afraid ? Is there any cause
for fear, Isidor ? Hey, sir ? Get some more beer.'

Mrs. O'Dowd said that her ' Glorvina was not afraid of
any man alive, let alone a Frenchman,' and tossed off a glass
of beer with a wink which expressed her liking for the
beverage.

Having frequently been in presence of the enemy, or, in
other words, faced the ladies at Cheltenham and Bath, our
friend, the collector, had lost a great deal of his pristine
timidity, and was now, especially when fortified with liquor,
as talkative as might be. He was rather a favourite with
the regiment, treating the young officers with sumptuosity,
and amusing them by his military airs. And as there is one
well-known regiment of the army which travels with a goat
heading the column, whilst another is led by a deer, George
said with respect to his brother-in-law, that his regiment
marched with an elephant.

Since Amelia's introduction to the regiment, George
began to be rather ashamed of some of the company to which
he had been forced to present her ; and determined, as he
told Dobbin (with what satisfaction to the latter it need not
be said), to exchange into some better regiment soon, and
to get his wife away from those damned vulgar women. But
this vulgarity of being ashamed of one's society is much
more common among men than women (except very great
ladies of fashion, who, to be sure, indulge in it) ; and Mrs.
Amelia, a natural and unaffected person, had none of that
artificial shamefacedness which her husband mistook for
delicacy on his own part. Thus Mrs. O'Dowd had a
cock's plume in her hat, and a very large ' repayther ' on her
stomach, which she used to ring on all occasions, narrating

how it had been presented to her by her fawther, as she
stipt into the car'ge after her mar'ge ; and these ornaments,
with other outward peculiarities of the major's wife, gave
excruciating agonies to Captain Osborne, when his wife and
the major's came in contact ; whereas Amelia was only
amused by the honest lady's eccentricities, and not in the
least ashamed of her company.

As they made that well-known journey, which almost
every Englishman of middle rank has travelled since, there
might have been more instructive, but few more entertaining,
companions than Mrs. Major O'Dowd. ' Talk about kenal
boats, my dear ! Ye should see the kenal boats between
Dublin and Ballinasloe.* It's there the rapid travelling is ;
and the beautiful cattle. Sure my fawther got a goold
medal (and his Excellency himself eat a slice of it, and said
never was finer mate in his loif) for a four-year-old heifer, the
like of which ye never saw in *this* country any day.' And
Jos owned with a sigh, ' that for good streaky beef, really
mingled with fat and lean, there was no country like England.'

' Except Ireland, where all your best mate comes from,'
said the major's lady ; proceeding, as is not unusual with
patriots of her nation, to make comparisons greatly in favour
of her own country. The idea of comparing the market of
Bruges with those of Dublin, although she had suggested it
herself, caused immense scorn and derision on her part.
' I'll thank ye tell me what they mean by that old gazabo on
the top of the market-place,' said she, in a burst of ridicule
fit to have brought the old tower down. The place was full
of English soldiery as they passed. English bugles woke
them in the morning ; at nightfall they went to bed to the
note of the British fife and drum : all the country and
Europe was in arms, and the greatest event of history
pending : and honest Peggy O'Dowd, whom it concerned
as well as another, went on prattling about Ballinafad, and
the horses in the stables at Glenmalony, and the clar't
drunk there ; and Jos Sedley interposed about curry and
rice at Dumdum ; and Amelia thought about her husband,
and how best she should show her love for him ; as if these
were the great topics of the world.

Those who like to lay down the history-book, and to
speculate upon what *might* have happened in the world but
for the fatal occurrence of what actually did take place

(a most puzzling, amusing, ingenious, and profitable kind of meditation), have no doubt often thought to themselves what a specially bad time Napoleon took to come back from Elba, and to let loose his eagle from Gulf San Juan to Notre Dame. The historians on our side tell us that the armies of the allied powers were all providentially on a war-footing, and ready to bear down at a moment's notice upon the Elban Emperor. The august jobbers assembled at Vienna,* and carving out the kingdoms of Europe according to their wisdom, had such causes of quarrel among themselves as might have set the armies which had overcome Napoleon to fight against each other, but for the return of the object of unanimous hatred and fear. This monarch had an army in full force because he had jobbed to himself Poland, and was determined to keep it: another had robbed half Saxony, and was bent upon maintaining his acquisition : Italy was the object of a third's solicitude. Each was protesting against the rapacity of the other ; and could the Corsican but have waited in his prison until all these parties were by the ears, he might have returned and reigned unmolested. But what would have become of our story and all our friends, then ? If all the drops in it were dried up, what would become of the sea ?

In the meanwhile the business of life and living, and the pursuits of pleasure especially, went on as if no end were to be expected to them, and no enemy in front. When our travellers arrived at Brussels, in which their regiment was quartered, a great piece of good fortune, as all said, they found themselves in one of the gayest and most brilliant little capitals in Europe, and where all the Vanity Fair booths were laid out with the most tempting liveliness and splendour. Gambling was here in profusion, and dancing in plenty : feasting was there to fill with delight that great gourmand of a Jos: there was a theatre where a miraculous Catalani was delighting all hearers ;* beautiful rides, all enlivened with martial splendour ; a rare old city, with strange costumes and wonderful architecture, to delight the eyes of little Amelia, who had never before seen a foreign country, and fill her with charming surprises : so that now and for a few weeks' space, in a fine handsome lodging, whereof the expenses were borne by Jos and Osborne, who was flush of money and full of kind attentions to his wife— for about a fortnight, I say, during which her honeymoon

ended, Mrs. Amelia was as pleased and happy as any little
bride out of England.

Every day during this happy time there was novelty and
amusement for all parties. There was a church to see, or
a picture-gallery—there was a ride, or an opera. The bands
of the regiments were making music at all hours. The
greatest folks of England walked in the Park, there was
a perpetual military festival. George, taking out his wife
to a new jaunt or junket every night, was quite pleased with
himself as usual, and swore he was becoming quite a domestic
character. And a jaunt or a junket with *him!* Was it not
enough to set this little heart beating with joy ? Her letters
home to her mother were filled with delight and gratitude
at this season. Her husband bade her buy laces, millinery,
jewels, and gimcracks of all sorts. Oh, he was the kindest,
best, and most generous of men !

The sight of the very great company of lords and ladies
and fashionable persons who thronged the town, and
appeared in every public place, filled George's truly British
soul with intense delight. They flung off that happy
frigidity and insolence of demeanour which occasionally
characterizes the great at home, and appearing in numberless
public places, condescended to mingle with the rest of the
company whom they met there. One night at a party
given by the general of the division to which George's
regiment belonged, he had the honour of dancing with Lady
Blanche Thistlewood, Lord Bareacres's daughter; he bustled
for ices and refreshments for the two noble ladies ; he
pushed and squeezed for Lady Bareacres's carriage; he
bragged about the countess when he got home, in a way
which his own father could not have surpassed. He called
upon the ladies the next day ; he rode by their side in the
Park ; he asked their party to a great dinner at a restaurateur's, and was quite wild with exultation when they
agreed to come. Old Bareacres, who had not much pride
and a large appetite, would go for a dinner anywhere.

' I hope there will be no women besides our own party,'
Lady Bareacres said, after reflecting upon the invitation
which had been made, and accepted with too much pre-
cipitancy.

' Gracious Heaven, mamma—you don't suppose the man
would bring his wife,' shrieked Lady Blanche, who had been
languishing in George's arms in the newly-imported waltz

for hours the night before. 'The men are bearable, but
their women——'

'Wife, just married, dev'lish pretty woman, I hear,'
the old earl said.

'Well, my dear Blanche,' said the mother, 'I suppose,
as papa wants to go, we must go ; but we needn't know
them in England, you know.' And so, determined to cut
their new acquaintance in Bond Street, these great folks
went to eat his dinner at Brussels, and condescending to
make him pay for their pleasure, showed their dignity by
making his wife uncomfortable, and carefully excluding her
from the conversation. This is a species of dignity in which
the high-bred British female reigns supreme. To watch the
behaviour of a fine lady to other and humbler women
is a very good sport for a philosophical frequenter of Vanity
Fair.

This festival, on which honest George spent a great deal
of money, was the very dismallest of all the entertainments
which Amelia had in her honeymoon. She wrote the most
piteous accounts of the feast home to her mamma : how
the Countess of Bareacres would not answer when spoken
to ; how Lady Blanche stared at her with her eyeglass ;
and what a rage Captain Dobbin was in at their behaviour ;
and how my lord, as they came away from the feast, asked
to see the bill, and pronounced it a d—— bad dinner, and
d—— dear. But though Amelia told all these stories,
and wrote home regarding her guests' rudeness, and her
own discomfiture ; old Mrs. Sedley was mightily pleased
nevertheless, and talked about Emmy's friend, the Countess
of Bareacres, with such assiduity that the news how his son
was entertaining peers and peeresses actually came to
Osborne's ears in the City.

Those who know the present Lieutenant-General Sir
George Tufto,* K.C.B., and have seen him, as they may
on most days in the season, padded and in stays, strutting
down Pall Mall with a rickety swagger on his high-heeled
lacquered boots, leering under the bonnets of passers-by,
or riding a showy chestnut, and ogling broughams in tho
Parks—those who know the present Sir George Tufto
would hardly recognize the daring Peninsular and Waterloo
officer. He has thick curling brown hair and black eyebrows now, and his whiskers are of the deepest purple.
He was light-haired and bald in 1815, and stouter in the

person and in the limbs, which especially have shrunk very much of late. When he was about seventy years of age (he is now nearly eighty), his hair, which was very scarce and quite white, suddenly grew thick, and brown, and curly, and his whiskers and eyebrows took their present colour. Ill-natured people say that his chest is all wool, and that his hair, because it never grows, is a wig. Tom Tufto, with whose father he quarrelled ever so many years ago, declares that Mademoiselle de Jaisey, of the French theatre, pulled his grandpapa's hair off in the green-room ; but Tom is notoriously spiteful and jealous ; and the general's wig has nothing to do with our story.

One day, as some of our friends of the —th were saunter-ing in the flower-market of Brussels, having been to see the Hotel de Ville, which Mrs. Major O'Dowd declared was not near so large or handsome as her fawther's mansion of Glenmalony, an officer of rank, with an orderly behind him, rode up to the market, and descending from his horse, came amongst the flowers, and selected the very finest bouquet which money could buy. The beautiful bundle being tied up in a paper, the officer remounted, giving the nosegay into the charge of his military groom, who carried it with a grin, following his chief, who rode away in great state and self-satisfaction.

' You should see the flowers at Glenmalony,' Mrs. O'Dowd was remarking. ' Me fawther has three Scotch garners with nine helpers. We have an acre of hot-houses, and pines as common as pays in the sayson. Our greeps weighs six pounds every bunch of 'em, and upon me honour and conscience I think our magnolias is as big as taykettles.'

Dobbin, who never used to ' draw out ' Mrs. O'Dowd as that wicked Osborne delighted in doing (much to Amelia's terror, who implored him to spare her), fell back in the crowd, crowing and sputtering until he reached a safe distance, when he exploded amongst the astonished market-people with shrieks of yelling laughter.

' Hwhat's that gawky guggling about ? ' said Mrs. O'Dowd. ' Is it his nose bleedn ? He always used to say 'twas his nose bleedn, till he must have pomped all the blood out of um. An't the magnolias at Glenmalony as big as taykettles, O'Dowd ? '

' Deed then they are, and bigger, Peggy,' the major said. When the conversation was interrupted in the manner stated by the arrival of the officer who purchased the bouquet.

'Devlish fine horse—who is it ? ' George asked.

'You should see me brother Molloy Moloney's horse, Molasses, that won the cop at the Curragh,' the major's wife was exclaiming, and was continuing the family history, when her husband interrupted her by saying,

'It's General Tufto, who commands the —— cavalry division ; ' adding quietly, 'he and I were both shot in the same leg at Talavera.'*

'Where you got your step,' said George with a laugh. 'General Tufto ! Then, my dear, the Crawleys are come.'

Amelia's heart fell—she knew not why. The sun did not seem to shine so bright. The tall old roofs and gables looked less picturesque all of a sudden, though it was a brilliant sunset, and one of the brightest and most beautiful days at the end of May.

CHAPTER XXIX

BRUSSELS

R. Jos had hired a pair of horses for his open carriage, with which cattle, and the smart London vehicle, he made a very tolerable figure in the drives about Brussels. George purchased a horse for his private riding, and he and Captain Dobbin would often accompany the carriage in which Jos and his sister took daily excursions of pleasure. They went out that day in the park for their accustomed diversion, and there, sure enough, George's remark with regard to the arrival of Rawdon Crawley and his wife proved to be correct. In the midst of a little troop of horsemen, consisting of some of the very greatest persons in Brussels, Rebecca was seen in the prettiest and tightest of riding-habits, mounted on a beautiful little Arab, which she rode

MRS. O'DOWD AT THE FLOWER MARKET

to perfection (having acquired the art at Queen's Crawley, where the baronet, Mr. Pitt, and Rawdon himself had given her many lessons), and by the side of the gallant General Tufto.

'Sure it's the juke himself,' cried Mrs. Major O'Dowd to Jos, who began to blush violently; 'and that's Lord Uxbridge on the bay.* How elegant he looks! Me brother, Molloy Moloney, is as like him as two peas.'

Rebecca did not make for the carriage; but as soon as she perceived her old acquaintance, Amelia, seated in it, acknowledged her presence by a gracious word and smile, and by kissing and shaking her fingers playfully in the direction of the vehicle. Then she resumed her conversation with General Tufto, who asked 'who the fat officer was in the gold-laced cap?' on which Becky replied, 'that he was an officer in the East Indian service.' But Rawdon Crawley rode out of the ranks of his company, and came up and shook hands heartily with Amelia, and said to Jos, 'Well, old boy, how are you?' and stared in Mrs. O'Dowd's face and black cock's feathers until she began to think she had made a conquest of him.

George, who had been delayed behind, rode up almost immediately with Dobbin, and they touched their caps to the august personages, among whom Osborne at once perceived Mrs. Crawley. He was delighted to see Rawdon leaning over his carriage familiarly and talking to Amelia, and met the aide de camp's cordial greeting with more than corresponding warmth. The nods between Rawdon and Dobbin were of the very faintest specimens of politeness.

Crawley told George where they were stopping with General Tufto at the Hotel du Parc, and George made his friend promise to come speedily to Osborne's own residence. 'Sorry I hadn't seen you three days ago,' George said. 'Had a dinner at the restaurateur's—rather a nice thing. Lord Bareacres, and the countess, and Lady Blanche, were good enough to dine with us—wish we'd had you.' Having thus let his friend know his claims to be a man of fashion, Osborne parted from Rawdon, who followed the august squadron down an alley into which they cantered, while George and Dobbin resumed their places, one on each side of Amelia's carriage.

'How well the juke looked,' Mrs. O'Dowd remarked. 'The Wellesleys and Moloneys are related;* but, of course,

poor *I* would never dream of introjuicing myself unless
his Grace thought proper to remember our family-
tie.'

'He's a great soldier,' Jos said, much more at ease now
the great man was gone. 'Was there ever a battle won
like Salamanca ? Hey, Dobbin ? But where was it he
learnt his art ? In India, my boy !* The. jungle's the
school for a general, mark me that. I knew him myself,
too, Mrs. O'Dowd : we both of us danced the same evening
with Miss Cutler, daughter of Cutler of the Artillery, and
a devilish fine girl, at Dumdum.'

The apparition of the great personages held them all in
talk during the drive ; and at dinner ; and until the hour
came when they were all to go to the opera.

It was almost like Old England. The house was filled
with familiar British faces, and those toilettes for which
the British female has long been celebrated. Mrs. O'Dowd's
was not the least splendid amongst these ; and she had
a curl on her forehead, and a set of Irish diamonds and
Cairngorms, which outshone all the decorations in the
house, in her notion. Her presence used to excruciate
Osborne ; but go she would upon all parties of pleasure
on which she heard her young friends were bent. It never
entered into her thought but that they must be charmed
with her company.

'She's been useful to you, my dear,' George said to his
wife, whom he could leave alone with less scruple when
she had this society. 'But what a comfort it is that
Rebecca's come : you will have her for a friend, and we
may get rid now of this damn'd Irishwoman.' To this
Amelia did not answer, yes or no : and how do we know
what her thoughts were ?

The *coup d'œil* of the Brussels opera-house did not strike
Mrs. O'Dowd as being so fine as the theatre in Fishamble
Street, Dublin,* nor was French music at all equal, in her
opinion, to the melodies of her native country. She
favoured her friends with these and other opinions in
a very loud tone of voice, and tossed about a great clattering
fan she sported, with the most splendid complacency.

'Who is that wonderful woman with Amelia, Rawdon,
love ? ' said a lady in an opposite box (who, almost always
civil to her husband in private, was more fond than ever
of him in company). ' Don't you see that creature with

a yellow thing in her turban, and a red satin gown, and a great watch ? '

' Near the pretty little woman in white ? ' asked a middle-aged gentleman seated by the querist's side, with orders in his button, and several under-waistcoats, and a great, choky, white stock.

' That pretty woman in white is Amelia, general : you are remarking all the pretty women, you naughty man.'

' Only one, begad, in the warld ! ' said the general,

delighted, and the lady gave him a tap with a large bouquet which she had.

' Bedad it's him,' said Mrs. O'Dowd ; ' and that's the very bokay he bought in the Marshy aux Flures ! ' and when Rebecca, having caught her friend's eye, performed the little hand-kissing operation once more, Mrs. Major O'D., taking the compliment to herself, returned the salute with a gracious smile, which sent that unfortunate Dobbin shrieking out of the box again.

At the end of the act, George was out of the box in a moment, and he was even going to pay his respects to Rebecca in her *loge*. He met Crawley in the lobby, however,

where they exchanged a few sentences upon the occurrences
of the last fortnight.

'You found my cheque all right at the agent's ? ' George
said, with a knowing air.

'All right, my boy,' Rawdon answered. 'Happy to
give you your revenge. Governor come round ? '

'Not yet,' said George, 'but he will ; and you know
I've some private fortune through my mother. Has
aunty relented ? '

'Sent me twenty pound, damned old screw. When
shall we have a meet ? The general dines out on Tuesday.
Can't you come Tuesday ? I say, make Sedley cut off
his moustache. What the devil does a civilian mean with
a moustache and those infernal frogs to his coat ! By-bye.
Try and come on Tuesday ; ' and Rawdon was going off
with two brilliant young gentlemen of fashion, who were,
like himself, on the staff of a general officer.

George was only half pleased to be asked to dinner on
that particular day when the general was *not* to dine.
'I will go in and pay my respects to your wife,' said he ;
at which Rawdon said, 'Hm, as you please,' looking very
glum, and at which the two young officers exchanged
knowing glances. George parted from them, and strutted
down the lobby to the general's box, the number of which
he had carefully counted.

'*Entrez*,' said a clear little voice, and our friend found
himself in Rebecca's presence ; who jumped up, clapped
her hands together, and held out both of them to George,
so charmed was she to see him. The general, with the
orders in his button, stared at the newcomer with a sulky
scowl, as much as to say, who the devil are you ?

'My dear Captain George ! ' cried little Rebecca in an
ecstasy. 'How good of you to come. The general and
I were moping together *tête à tête*. General, this is my
Captain George of whom you heard me talk.'

'Indeed,' said the general, with a very small bow, 'of
what regiment is Captain George ? '

George mentioned the ——th : how he wished he could
have said it was a crack cavalry corps.

'Come home lately from the West Indies, I believe.
Not seen much service in the late war. Quartered here,
Captain George ? '—the general went on with killing
haughtiness.

'Not Captain George, you stupid man ; Captain Osborne,'
Rebecca said. The general all the while was looking
savagely from one to the other.

'Captain Osborne, indeed ! Any relation to the L——
Osbornes ? '*

'We bear the same arms,' George said, as indeed was the
fact ; Mr. Osborne having consulted with a herald in Long
Acre, and picked the L—— arms out of the *Peerage*, when
he set up his carriage fifteen years before. The general
made no reply to this announcement ; but took up his
opera-glass—the double-barrelled lorgnon was not invented
in those days—and pretended to examine the house ; but
Rebecca saw that his disengaged eye was working round
in her direction, and shooting out bloodshot glances at
her and George.

She redoubled in cordiality. 'How is dearest Amelia ?
But I needn't ask : how pretty she looks ! And who is
that nice good-natured looking creature with her—a flame
of yours ? Oh, you wicked men ! And there is Mr. Sedley
eating ices, I declare : how he seems to enjoy it ! General,
why have we not had any ices ? '

'Shall I go and fetch you some ? ' said the general,
bursting with wrath.

'Let *me* go, I entreat you,' George said.

'No, I will go to Amelia's box. Dear, sweet girl ! Give
me your arm, Captain George ; ' and so saying, and with
a nod to the general, she tripped into the lobby. She gave
George the queerest, knowingest look, when they were
together, a look which might have been interpreted, 'Don't
you see the state of affairs, and what a fool I'm making
of him ? ' But he did not perceive it. He was thinking
of his own plans, and lost in pompous admiration of his
own irresistible powers of pleasing.

The curses to which the general gave a low utterance,
as soon as Rebecca and her conqueror had quitted him,
were so deep, that I am sure no compositor in Messrs.
Bradbury and Evans's establishment would venture to
print them were they written down. They came from the
general's heart ; and a wonderful thing it is to think that
the human heart is capable of generating such produce,
and can throw out, as occasion demands, such a supply
of lust and fury, rage and hatred.

Amelia's gentle eyes, too, had been fixed anxiously on

the pair, whose conduct had so chafed the jealous general ;
but when Rebecca entered her box, she flew to her friend
with an affectionate rapture which showed itself, in spite
of the publicity of the place ; for she embraced her dearest
friend in the presence of the whole house, at least in full
view of the general's glass, now brought to bear upon the
Osborne party. Mrs. Rawdon saluted Jos, too, with the
kindliest greeting : she admired Mrs. O'Dowd's large
Cairngorm brooch and superb Irish diamonds, and wouldn't
believe that they were not from Golconda direct. She
bustled, she chattered, she turned and twisted, and smiled
upon one, and smirked on another, all in full view of the
jealous opera-glass opposite. And when the time for the
ballet came (in which there was no dancer that went through
her grimaces or performed her comedy of action better),
she skipped back to her own box, leaning on Captain
Dobbin's arm this time. No, she would not have George's :
he must stay and talk to his dearest, best, little Amelia.

   ' What a humbug that woman is,' honest old Dobbin
mumbled to George, when he came back from Rebecca's
box, whither he had conducted her in perfect silence, and
with a countenance as glum as an undertaker's. ' She
writhes and twists about like a snake. All the time she
was here, didn't you see, George, how she was acting at
the general over the way ? '

   ' Humbug—acting ? Hang it, she's the nicest little
woman in England,' George replied, showing his white
teeth, and giving his ambrosial whiskers a twirl. ' You
ain't a man of the world, Dobbin. Dammy, look at her
now, she's talked over Tufto in no time. Look how he's
laughing ! Gad, what a shoulder she has ! Emmy, why
didn't you have a bouquet ? Everybody has a bouquet.'

   ' Faith, then, why didn't you *boy* one ? ' Mrs. O'Dowd
said ; and both Amelia and William Dobbin thanked her
for this timely observation. But beyond this neither of
the ladies rallied. Amelia was overpowered by the flash
and the dazzle and the fashionable talk of her worldly rival.
Even the O'Dowd was silent and subdued after Becky's
brilliant apparition, and scarcely said a word more about
Glenmalony all the evening.

   ' When do you intend to give up play, George, as you
have promised me, any time these hundred years ? ' Dobbin

said to his friend a few days after the night at the opera. 'When do you intend to give up sermonizing?' was the other's reply. 'What the deuce, man, are you alarmed about? We play low; I won last night. You don't suppose Crawley cheats? With fair play it comes to pretty much the same thing at the year's end.'

'But I don't think he could pay if he lost,' Dobbin said; and his advice met with the success which advice usually commands. Osborne and Crawley were repeatedly together now. General Tufto dined abroad almost constantly. George was always welcome in the apartments (very close indeed to those of the general), which the aide de camp and his wife occupied in the hotel.

Amelia's manners were such when she and George visited Crawley and his wife at these quarters, that they had very nearly come to their first quarrel; that is, George scolded his wife violently for her evident unwillingness to go, and the high and mighty manner in which she comported herself towards Mrs. Crawley, her old friend; and Amelia did not say one single word in reply; but with her husband's eye upon her, and Rebecca scanning her as she felt, was, if possible, more bashful and awkward on the second visit which she paid to Mrs. Rawdon, than on her first call.

Rebecca was doubly affectionate, of course, and would not take notice, in the least, of her friend's coolness. I think Emmy has become prouder since her father's name was in the ——, since Mr. Sedley's *misfortunes*,' Rebecca said, softening the phrase charitably for George's ear. 'Upon my word, I thought when we were at Brighton she was doing me the honour to be jealous of me; and now I suppose she is scandalized because Rawdon, and I, and the general live together. Why, my dear creature, how could we, with our means, live at all, but for a friend to share expenses? And do you suppose that Rawdon is not big enough to take care of my honour? But I'm very much obliged to Emmy, very,' Mrs. Rawdon said.

'Pooh, jealousy!' answered George, 'all women are jealous.'

'And all men too. Weren't you jealous of General Tufto, and the general of you, on the night of the opera? Why, he was ready to eat me for going with you to visit that foolish little wife of yours; as if I care a pin for either of you,' Crawley's wife said, with a pert toss of her head.

'Will you dine here? The dragon dines with the commander-in-chief. Great news is stirring. They say the
French have crossed the frontier. We shall have a quiet
dinner.'

George accepted the invitation, although his wife was
a little ailing. They were now not quite six weeks married.
Another woman was laughing or sneering at her expense,
and he not angry. He was not even angry with himself,
this good-natured fellow. It is a shame, he owned to himself; but hang it, if a pretty woman *will* throw herself
into your way, why, what can a fellow do, you know?
I *am* rather free about women, he had often said, smiling
and nodding knowingly to Stubble and Spooney, and other
comrades of the mess-table; and they rather respected
him than otherwise for this prowess. Next to conquering
in war, conquering in love has been a source of pride, time
out of mind, amongst men in Vanity Fair, or how should
schoolboys brag of their amours, or Don Juan be popular?

So Mr. Osborne, having a firm conviction in his own
mind that he was a woman-killer and destined to conquer,
did not run counter to his fate, but yielded himself up to
it quite complacently. And as Emmy did not say much
or plague him with her jealousy, but merely became unhappy
and pined over it miserably in secret, he chose to fancy
that she was not suspicious of what all his acquaintance
were perfectly aware—namely, that he was carrying on
a desperate flirtation with Mrs. Crawley. He rode with
her whenever she was free. He pretended regimental
business to Amelia (by which falsehood she was not in the
least deceived), and consigning his wife to solitude or her
brother's society, passed his evenings in the Crawleys'
company; losing money to the husband and flattering
himself that the wife was dying in love for him. It is very
likely that this worthy couple never absolutely conspired
and agreed together in so many words: the one to cajole
the young gentleman, whilst the other won his money at
cards: but they understood each other perfectly well, and
Rawdon let Osborne come and go with entire good humour.

George was so occupied with his new acquaintances that
he and William Dobbin were by no means so much together
as formerly. George avoided him in public and in the
regiment, and, as we see, did not like those sermons which
his senior was disposed to inflict upon him. If some parts

of his conduct made Captain Dobbin exceedingly grave
and cool; of what use was it to tell George that though
his whiskers were large, and his own opinion of his knowing-
ness great, he was as green as a schoolboy? that Rawdon
was making a victim of him as he had done of many before,
and as soon as he had used him would fling him off with
scorn? He would not listen: and so, as Dobbin, upon
those days when he visited the Osborne house, seldom had
the advantage of meeting his old friend, much painful and
unavailing talk between them was spared. Our friend
George was in the full career of the pleasures of Vanity Fair.

There never was, since the days of Darius, such a brilliant
train of camp-followers as hung round the train of the
Duke of Wellington's army in the Low Countries, in 1815;
and led it dancing and feasting, as it were, up to the very
brink of battle. A certain ball* which a noble duchess
gave at Brussels, on the 15th of June in the above-named
year, is historical. All Brussels had been in a state of
excitement about it, and I have heard from ladies who
were in that town at the period, that the talk and interest
of persons of their own sex regarding the ball was much
greater even than in respect of the enemy in their front.
The struggles, intrigues, and prayers to get tickets were
such as only English ladies will employ, in order to gain
admission to the society of the great of their own nation.

Jos and Mrs. O'Dowd, who were panting to be asked,
strove in vain to procure tickets; but others of our friends
were more lucky. For instance, through the interest of
my Lord Bareacres, and as a set-off for the dinner at the
restaurateur's, George got a card for Captain and Mrs.
Osborne; which circumstance greatly elated him. Dobbin,
who was a friend of the general commanding the division
in which their regiment was, came laughing one day to
Mrs. Osborne, and displayed a similar invitation, which
made Jos envious, and George wonder how the deuce he
should be getting into society. Mr. and Mrs. Rawdon,
finally, were of course invited; as became the friends
of a general commanding a cavalry brigade.

On the appointed night, George, having commanded
new dresses and ornaments of all sorts for Amelia, drove
to the famous ball, where his wife did not know a single soul.
After looking about for Lady Bareacres, who cut him,

thinking the card was quite enough—and after placing
Amelia on a bench, he left her to her own cogitations there,
thinking, on his own part, that he had behaved very
handsomely in getting her new clothes, and bringing her
to the ball, where she was free to amuse herself as she liked.
Her thoughts were not of the pleasantest, and nobody
except honest Dobbin came to disturb them.

Whilst her appearance was an utter failure (as her husband
felt with a sort of rage), Mrs. Rawdon Crawley's début was,
on the contrary, very brilliant. She arrived very late.
Her face was radiant; her dress perfection, in the midst
of the great persons assembled, and the eyeglasses directed
to her. Rebecca seemed to be as cool and collected as
when she used to marshal Miss Pinkerton's little girls to
church. Numbers of the men she knew already, and the
dandies thronged round her. As for the ladies, it was
whispered among them that Rawdon had run away with
her from out of a convent, and that she was a relation of
the Montmorency family. She spoke French so perfectly
that there might be some truth in this report, and it was
agreed that her manners were fine, and her air *distingué*.
Fifty would-be partners thronged round her at once, and
pressed to have the honour to dance with her. But she
said she was engaged, and only going to dance very little;
and made her way at once to the place where Emmy sat
quite unnoticed, and dismally unhappy. And so, to finish
the poor child at once, Mrs. Rawdon ran and greeted affectionately her dearest Amelia, and began forthwith to
patronize her. She found fault with her friend's dress,
and her hairdresser, and wondered how she could be so
chaussée, and vowed that she must send her *corsetière*
the next morning. She vowed that it was a delightful
ball; that there was everybody that every one knew, and
only a *very* few nobodies in the whole room. It is a fact,
that in a fortnight, and after three dinners in general society,
this young woman had got up the genteel jargon so well,
that a native could not speak it better; and it was only
from her French being so good, that you could know she
was not a born woman of fashion.

George, who had left Emmy on her bench on entering
the ball-room, very soon found his way back when Rebecca
was by her dear friend's side. Becky was just lecturing
Mrs. Osborne upon the follies which her husband was

committing. 'For God's sake, stop him from gambling, my dear,' she said, ' or he will ruin himself. He and Rawdon are playing at cards every night, and you know he is very poor, and Rawdon will win every shilling from him if he does not take care. Why don't you prevent him, you little careless creature ? Why don't you come to us of an evening, instead of moping at home with that Captain Dobbin ? I dare say he is *très aimable ;* but how could one love a man with feet of such size ? Your husband's feet are darlings—Here he comes. Where have you been, wretch ? Here is Emmy crying her eyes out for you. Are you coming to fetch me for the quadrille ? ' And she left her bouquet and shawl by Amelia's side, and tripped off with George to dance. Women only know how to wound so. There is a poison on the tips of their little shafts, which stings a thousand times more than a man's blunter weapon. Our poor Emmy, who had never hated, never sneered all her life, was powerless in the hands of her remorseless little enemy.

George danced with Rebecca twice or thrice—how many times Amelia scarcely knew. She sat quite unnoticed in her corner, except when Rawdon came up with some words of clumsy conversation : and later in the evening, when Captain Dobbin made so bold as to bring her refreshments and sit beside her. He did not like to ask her why she was so sad ; but as a pretext for the tears which were filling in her eyes, she told him that Mrs. Crawley had alarmed her by telling her that George would go on playing.

' It is curious, when a man is bent upon play, by what clumsy rogues he will allow himself to be cheated,' Dobbin said ; and Emmy said, ' Indeed.' She was thinking of something else. It was not the loss of the money that grieved her.

At last George came back for Rebecca's shawl and flowers. She was going away. She did not even conde- scend to come back and say good-bye to Amelia. The poor girl let her husband come and go without saying a word, and her head fell on her breast. Dobbin had been called away, and was whispering deep in conversation with the general of the division, his friend, and had not seen this last parting. George went away then with the bouquet ; but when he gave it to the owner, there lay a note, coiled like a snake among the flowers. Rebecca's eye caught it at once. She had been used to deal with notes in early life. She put out her hand and took the nosegay. He saw by her eyes as they met, that she was aware what she should find there. Her husband hurried her away, still too intent upon his own thoughts, seemingly, to take note of any marks of recognition which might pass between his friend and his wife. These were, however, but trifling. Rebecca gave George her hand with one of her usual quick knowing glances, and made a curtsy and walked away. George bowed over the hand, said nothing in reply to a remark of Crawley's, did not hear it even, his brain was so throbbing with triumph and excitement, and allowed them to go away without a word.

His wife saw the one part at least of the bouquet-scene. It was quite natural that George should come at Rebecca's request to get her her scarf and flowers : it was no more than he had done twenty times before in the course of the last few days ; but now it was too much for her. ' William,' she said, suddenly clinging to Dobbin, who was near her, ' you've always been very kind to me—I'm—I'm not well. Take me home.' She did not know she called him by his Christian name, as George was accustomed to do. He went away with her quickly. Her lodgings were hard by ; and they threaded through the crowd without, where everything seemed to be more astir than even in the ballroom within.

George had been angry twice or thrice at finding his wife up on his return from the parties which he frequented : so she went straight to bed now ; but although she did not sleep, and although the din and clatter, and the galloping of horsemen was incessant, she never heard any of these noises, having quite other disturbances to keep her awake.

Osborne meanwhile, wild with elation, went off to a play-table, and began to bet frantically. He won repeatedly. ' Everything succeeds with me to-night,' he said. But his luck at play even did not cure him of his restlessness, and he started up after a while, pocketing his winnings, and went to a buffet, where he drank off many bumpers of wine.

Here, as he was rattling away to the people around, laughing loudly and wild with spirits, Dobbin found him. He had been to the card-tables to look there for his friend.

Dobbin looked as pale and grave as his comrade was flushed and jovial.

' Hullo, Dob! Come and drink, old Dob! The duke's wine is famous. Give me some more, you sir ; ' and he held out a trembling glass for the liquor.

' Come out, George,' said Dobbin, still gravely ; ' don't drink.'

' Drink! there's nothing like it. Drink yourself, and light up your lantern jaws, old boy. Here's to you.'

Dobbin went up and whispered something to him, at which George, giving a start and a wild hurray, tossed off his glass, clapped it on the table, and walked away speedily on his friend's arm. ' The enemy has passed the Sambre,' William said, ' and our left is already engaged. Come away. We are to march in three hours.'

Away went George, his nerves quivering with excitement at the news so long looked for, so sudden when it came. What were love and intrigue now ? He thought about a thousand things but these in his rapid walk to his quarters —his past life and future chances—the fate which might be before him—the wife, the child perhaps, from whom unseen he might be about to part. Oh, how he wished that night's work undone! and that with a clear conscience at least he might say farewell to the tender and guileless being by whose love he had set such little store!

He thought over his brief married life. In those few weeks he had frightfully dissipated his little capital. How wild and reckless he had been! Should any mischance befall him : what was then left for her ? How unworthy he was of her. Why had he married her ? He was not fit for marriage. Why had he disobeyed his father, who had been always so generous to him ? Hope, remorse, ambition, tenderness, and selfish regret filled his heart. He sat down and wrote to his father, remembering what he had said once before, when he was engaged to fight a duel. Dawn faintly streaked the sky as he closed this farewell letter. He sealed it, and kissed the superscription. He thought how he had deserted that generous father, and of the thousand kindnesses which the stern old man had done him.

He had looked into Amelia's bedroom when he entered ; she lay quiet, and her eyes seemed closed, and he was glad that she was asleep. On arriving at his quarters from the ball, he had found his regimental servant already making preparations for his departure : the man had understood his signal to be still, and these arrangements were very quickly and silently made. Should he go in and wake Amelia, he thought, or leave a note for her brother to break the news of departure to her ? He went in to look at her once again.

She had been awake when he first entered her room, but had kept her eyes closed, so that even her wakefulness should not seem to reproach him. But when he had returned, so soon after herself, too, this timid little heart had felt more at ease, and turning towards him as he stepped softly out of the room, she had fallen into a light sleep. George came in and looked at her again, entering still more softly. By the pale night-lamp he could see her sweet, pale face—the purple eyelids were fringed and closed, and one round arm, smooth and white, lay outside of the coverlet. Good God ! how pure she was ; how gentle, how tender, and how friendless ! and he, how selfish, brutal, and black with crime ! Heart-stained, and shame-stricken, he stood at the bed's foot, and looked at the sleeping girl. How dared he—who was he, to pray for one so spotless ! God bless her ! God bless her ! He came to the bedside, and looked at the hand, the little soft hand, lying asleep ; and he bent over the pillow noiselessly towards the gentle pale face.

Two fair arms closed tenderly round his neck as he stooped down. 'I am awake, George,' the poor child said, with a sob fit to break the little heart that nestled so closely by his own. She was awake, poor soul, and to what ? At that moment a bugle from the Place of Arms began sounding clearly, and was taken up through the town ; and amidst the drums of the infantry, and the shrill pipes of the Scotch, the whole city awoke.

CHAPTER XXX

W E do not claim to rank among the military novelists. Our place is with the non-combatants. When the decks are cleared for action we go below and wait meekly. We should only be in the way of the manœuvres that the gallant fellows are performing overhead. We shall go no farther with the —th than to the city gate : and, leaving Major O'Dowd to his duty, come back to the major's wife, and the ladies and the baggage.

Now, the major and his lady, who had not been invited to the ball at which in our last chapter other of our friends figured, had much more time to take their wholesome natural rest in bed, than was accorded to people who wished to enjoy pleasure as well as to do duty. 'It's my belief, Peggy, my dear,' said he, as he placidly pulled his nightcap over his ears, 'that there will be such a ball danced in a day or two as some of 'em has never heard the chune of ; ' and he was much more happy to retire to rest after partaking of a quiet tumbler, than to figure at any other sort of amusement. Peggy, for her part, would have liked to have shown her turban and bird of paradise at the ball, but for the information which her husband had given her, and which made her very grave.

'I'd like ye wake me about half an hour before the assembly beats,' the major said to his lady. 'Call me at half-past one, Peggy dear, and see me things is ready. Maybe I'll not come back to breakfast, Mrs. O'D.' With which words, which signified his opinion that the regiment would march the next morning, the major ceased talking, and fell asleep.

Mrs. O'Dowd, the good housewife, arrayed in curl-papers and a camisole, felt that her duty was to act, and not to sleep, at this juncture. 'Time enough for that,' she said, 'when Mick's gone ; ' and so she packed his

travelling-valise ready for the march, brushed his cloak,
his cap, and other warlike habiliments, set them out in
order for him ; and stowed away in the cloak-pockets
a light package of portable refreshments, and a wicker-
covered flask or pocket-pistol, containing near a pint of
a remarkably sound Cognac brandy, of which she and the
major approved very much ; and as soon as the hands
of the ' repayther ' pointed to half-past one, and its interior
arrangements (it had a tone quite aqual to a cathaydral,
its fair owner considered) knelled forth that fatal hour,
Mrs. O'Dowd woke up her major, and had as comfortable
a cup of coffee prepared for him as any made that morning
in Brussels. And who is there will deny that this worthy
lady's preparations betokened affection as much as the
fits of tears and hysterics by which more sensitive females
exhibited their love, and that their partaking of this
coffee, which they drank together while the bugles were
sounding the turn-out and the drums beating in the
various quarters of the town, was not more useful and to
the purpose than the outpouring of any mere sentiment
could be ? The consequence was, that the major appeared
on parade quite trim, fresh, and alert, his well-shaved rosy
countenance, as he sat on horseback, giving cheerfulness
and confidence to the whole corps. All the officers saluted
her when the regiment marched by the balcony on which
this brave woman stood and waved them a cheer as they
passed ; and I daresay it was not from want of courage,
but from a sense of female delicacy and propriety, that
she refrained from leading the gallant —th personally into
action.

On Sundays, and at periods of a solemn nature, Mrs.
O'Dowd used to read with great gravity out of a large
volume of her uncle the dean's sermons. It had been of
great comfort to her on board the transport as they were
coming home, and were very nearly wrecked, on their
return from the West Indies. After the regiment's departure she betook herself to this volume for meditation ;
perhaps she did not understand much of what she was
reading, and her thoughts were elsewhere : but the sleep project, with poor Mick's nightcap there on the pillow, was quite
a vain one. So it is in the world. Jack or Donald marches
away to glory with his knapsack on his shoulder, stepping
out briskly to the tune of *The Girl I left behind me.* It is

VENUS PREPARING THE ARMOUR OF MARS

she who remains and suffers,—and has the leisure to think, and brood, and remember.

Knowing how useless regrets are, and how the indulgence of sentiment only serves to make people more miserable, Mrs. Rebecca wisely determined to give way to no vain feelings of sorrow, and bore the parting from her husband with quite a Spartan equanimity. Indeed Captain Rawdon himself was much more affected at the leave-taking than the resolute little woman to whom he bade farewell. She had mastered this rude coarse nature; and he loved and worshipped her with all his faculties of regard and admiration. In all his life he had never been so happy, as, during the past few months, his wife had made him. All former delights of turf, mess, hunting-field, and gambling-table; all previous loves and courtships of milliners, opera-dancers, and the like easy triumphs of the clumsy military Adonis, were quite insipid when compared to the lawful matrimonial pleasures which of late he had enjoyed. She had known perpetually how to divert him; and he had found his house and her society a thousand times more pleasant than any place or company which he had ever frequented from his childhood until now. And he cursed his past follies and extravagances, and bemoaned his vast outlying debts above all, which must remain for ever as obstacles to prevent his wife's advancement in the world. He had often groaned over these in midnight conversations with Rebecca, although as a bachelor they had never given him any disquiet. He himself was struck with this phenomenon. ‘Hang it,’ he would say (or perhaps use a still stronger expression out of his simple vocabulary), ‘before I was married I didn't care what bills I put my name to, and so long as Moses would wait or Levy would renew for three months, I kept on never minding. But since I'm married, except renewing, of course, I give you my honour I've not touched a bit of stamped paper.’

Rebecca always knew how to conjure away these moods of melancholy. ‘Why, my stupid love,’ she would say, ‘we have not done with your aunt yet. If she fails us, isn't there what you call the *Gazette?* or, stop, when your uncle Bute's life drops, I have another scheme. The living has always belonged to the younger brother, and why shouldn't you sell out and go into the Church?’ The idea of this conversion set Rawdon into roars of laughter: you

might have heard the explosion through the hotel at
midnight, and the haw-haws of the great dragoon's voice.
General Tufto heard him from his quarters on the first
floor above them ; and Rebecca acted the scene with great
spirit, and preached Rawdon's first sermon, to the immense
delight of the general at breakfast.

But these were mere bygone days and talk. When the
final news arrived that the campaign was opened, and the
troops were to march, Rawdon's gravity became such that
Becky rallied him about it in a manner which rather hurt
the feelings of the Guardsman. ' You don't suppose I'm
afraid, Becky, I should think,' he said, with a tremor in
his voice. ' But I'm a pretty good mark for a shot, and
you see if it brings me down, why I leave one and perhaps
two behind me whom I should wish to provide for, as
I brought 'em into the scrape. It is no laughing matter
that, Mrs. C., anyways.'

Rebecca by a hundred caresses and kind words tried
to soothe the feelings of the wounded lover. It was only
when her vivacity and sense of humour got the better of
this sprightly creature (as they would do under most
circumstances of life indeed), that she would break out
with her satire, but she could soon put on a demure face.
' Dearest love,' she said, ' do you suppose I feel nothing ? '
and, hastily dashing something from her eyes, she looked
up in her husband's face with a smile.

' Look here,' said he. ' If I drop let us see what there
is for you. I have had a pretty good run of luck here,
and here's two hundred and thirty pounds. I have got
ten napoleons in my pocket. That is as much as I shall
want ; for the general pays everything like a prince ;
and if I'm hit, why you know I cost nothing. Don't cry,
little woman ; I may live to vex you yet. Well, I shan't
take either of my horses, but shall ride the general's grey
charger : it's cheaper, and I told him mine was lame.
If I'm done, those two ought to fetch you something.
Grigg offered ninety for the mare yesterday, before this
confounded news came, and like a fool I wouldn't let her
go under the two O's. Bulfinch will fetch his price any
day, only you'd better sell him in this country, because the
dealers have so many bills of mine, and so I'd rather he
shouldn't go back to England. Your little mare the
general gave you will fetch something, and there's no

d—d livery stable bills here as there are in London,'
Rawdon added, with a laugh. 'There's that dressing-
case cost me two hundred,—that is, I owe two for it ; and
the gold tops and bottles must be worth thirty or forty.
Please to put *that* up the spout, ma'am, with my pins,
and rings, and watch and chain, and things. They cost
a precious lot of money. Miss Crawley, I know, paid
a hundred down for the chain and ticker. Gold tops and
bottles, indeed ! dammy, I'm sorry I didn't take more
now. Edwards pressed on me a silver-gilt boot-jack,
and I might have had a dressing-case fitted up with a silver
warming-pan, and a service of plate. But we must make
the best of what we've got, Becky, you know.'

And so, making his last dispositions, Captain Crawley,
who had seldom thought about anything but himself, until
the last few months of his life, when Love had obtained
the mastery over the dragoon, went through the various
items of his little catalogue of effects, striving to see how
they might be turned into money for his wife's benefit,
in case any accident should befall him. He pleased himself
by noting down with a pencil, in his big schoolboy handwriting, the various items of his portable property which
might be sold for his widow's advantage—as, for example,
' My double-barril by Manton, say 40 guineas ; my driving-
cloak, lined with sable fur, 50*l.* ; my duelling pistols in
rosewood case (same which I shot Captain Marker), 20*l.*; my
regulation saddle-holsters and housings ; my Laurie*ditto,
and so forth, over all of which articles he made Rebecca
the mistress.

Faithful to his plan of economy, the captain dressed
himself in his oldest and shabbiest uniform and epaulets,
leaving the newest behind, under his wife's (or it might be
his widow's) guardianship. And this famous dandy of
Windsor and Hyde Park went off on his campaign with
a kit as modest as that of a sergeant, and with something
like a prayer on his lips for the woman he was leaving.
He took her up from the ground, and held her in his arms
for a minute, tight pressed against his strong beating
heart. His face was purple and his eyes dim, as he put her
down and left her. He rode by his general's side, and
smoked his cigar in silence as they hastened after the
troops of the general's brigade, which preceded them ;
and it was not until they were some miles on their way

that he left off twirling his moustache and broke
silence.

And Rebecca, as we have said, wisely determined not to
give way to unavailing sentimentality on her husband's
departure. She waved him an adieu from the window,
and stood there for a moment looking out after he was
gone. The cathedral towers and the full gables of the
quaint old houses were just beginning to blush in the
sunrise. There had been no rest for her that night. She
was still in her pretty ball-dress, her fair hair hanging
somewhat out of curl on her neck, and the circles round
her eyes dark with watching. 'What a fright I seem,'
she said, examining herself in the glass, 'and how pale
this pink makes one look!' So she divested herself of this
pink raiment; in doing which a note fell out from her

corsage, which she picked
up with a smile, and
locked into her dressing-
box. And then she put
her bouquet of the ball
into a glass of water, and
went to bed, and slept
very comfortably.

The town was quite
quiet when she woke up
at ten o'clock, and par-
took of coffee, very re-
quisite and comfortable
after the exhaustion and grief of the morning's occurrences.

This meal over, she resumed honest Rawdon's calculations of the night previous, and surveyed her position.
Should the worst befall, all things considered, she was
pretty well-to-do. There were her own trinkets and
trousseau, in addition to those which her husband had
left behind. Rawdon's generosity, when they were first
married, has already been described and lauded. Besides
these, and the little mare, the general, her slave and wor-
shipper, had made her many very handsome presents,
in the shape of cashmere shawls bought at the auction
of a bankrupt French general's lady, and numerous tributes
from the jewellers' shops, all of which betokened her
admirer's taste and wealth. As for 'tickers', as poor

Rawdon called watches, her apartments were alive with their clicking. For, happening to mention one night that hers, which Rawdon had given to her, was of English workmanship, and went ill, on the very next morning there came to her a little bijou marked Leroy, with a chain and cover charmingly set with turquoises, and another signed Breguet,* which was covered with pearls, and yet scarcely bigger than a half-crown. General Tufto had bought one, and Captain Osborne had gallantly presented the other. Mrs. Osborne had no watch; though, to do George justice, she might have had one for the asking, and the Honourable Mrs. Tufto in England had an old instrument of her mother's that might have served for the plate warming-pan which Rawdon talked about. If Messrs. Howell and James* were to publish a list of the purchasers of all the trinkets which they sell, how surprised would some families be : and if all these ornaments went to gentlemen's lawful wives and daughters, what a profusion of jewellery there would be exhibited in the genteelest homes of Vanity Fair !

Every calculation made of these valuables Mrs. Rebecca found, not without a pungent feeling of triumph and self-satisfaction, that should circumstances occur, she might reckon on six or seven hundred pounds at the very least, to begin the world with ; and she passed the morning disposing, ordering, looking out, and locking up her properties in the most agreeable manner. Among the notes in Rawdon's pocket-book, was a draft for twenty pounds on Osborne's banker. This made her think about Mrs. Osborne. ' I will go and get the draft cashed,' she said, ' and pay a visit afterwards to poor little Emmy.' If this is a novel without a hero, at least let us lay claim to a heroine. No man in the British army which has marched away, not the great duke himself, could be more cool or collected in the presence of doubts and difficulties, than the indomitable little aide de camp's wife.

And there was another of our acquaintances who was also to be left behind, a non-combatant, and whose emotions and behaviour we have therefore a right to know. This was our friend the ex-collector of Boggley Wollah, whose rest was broken, like other people's, by the sounding of the bugles in the early morning. Being a great sleeper, and fond of his bed, it is possible he would have snoozed on until his usual hour of rising in the forenoon, in spite of all the drums, bugles, and bagpipes in the British army, but for an interruption, which did not come from George Osborne, who shared Jos's quarters with him, and was as usual occupied too much with his own affairs, or with grief at parting with his wife, to think of taking leave of his slumbering brother-in-law—it was not George, we say, who interposed between Jos Sedley and sleep, but Captain Dobbin, who came and roused him up, insisting on shaking hands with him before his departure.

'Very kind of you,' said Jos, yawning, and wishing the captain at the deuce.

'I—I didn't like to go off without saying good-bye, you know,' Dobbin said, in a very incoherent manner ; ' because you know some of us mayn't come back again, and I like to see you all well, and—and that sort of thing, you know.'

'What do you mean ?' Jos asked, rubbing his eyes. The captain did not in the least hear him or look at the stout gentleman in the nightcap, about whom he professed to have such a tender interest. The hypocrite was looking and listening with all his might in the direction of George's apartments, striding about the room, upsetting the chairs, beating the tattoo, biting his nails, and showing other signs of great inward emotion.

Jos had always had rather a mean opinion of the captain, and now began to think his courage was somewhat equivocal. 'What is it I can do for you, Dobbin ? ' he said, in a sarcastic tone.

'I tell you what you can do,' the captain replied, coming up to the bed ; ' we march in a quarter of an hour, Sedley, and neither George nor I may ever come back. Mind you, you are not to stir from this town until you ascertain how things go. You are to stay here and watch over your sister, and comfort her, and see that no harm comes to her. If anything happens to George, remember she has no one but you in the world to look to. If it goes wrong with the army, you'll see her safe back to England ; and you will promise me on your word that you will never desert her. I know you won't : as far as money goes, you were always free enough with that. Do you want any ? I mean, have you enough gold to take you back to England in case of a misfortune ? '

'Sir,' said Jos majestically, 'when I want money, I know where to ask for it. And as for my sister, *you* needn't tell me how I ought to behave to her.'

'You speak like a man of spirit, Jos,' the other answered good-naturedly, 'and I am glad that George can leave her in such good hands. So I may give him your word of honour, may I, that in case of extremity you will stand by her?'

'Of course, of course,' answered Mr. Jos, whose generosity in money matters Dobbin estimated quite correctly.

'And you'll see her safe out of Brussels in the event of a defeat?'

'A defeat! D— it, sir, it's impossible. Don't try and frighten *me*,' the hero cried from his bed; and Dobbin's mind was thus perfectly set at ease now that Jos had spoken out so resolutely respecting his conduct to his sister. 'At least,' thought the captain, 'there will be a retreat secured for her in case the worst should ensue.'

If Captain Dobbin expected to get any personal comfort and satisfaction from having one more view of Amelia before the regiment marched away, his selfishness was punished just as such odious egotism deserved to be. The door of Jos's bedroom opened into the sitting-room which was common to the family party, and opposite this door was that of Amelia's chamber. The bugles had wakened everybody: there was no use in concealment now. George's servant was packing in this room: Osborne coming in and out of the contiguous bedroom, flinging to the man such articles as he thought fit to carry on the campaign. And presently Dobbin had the opportunity which his heart coveted, and he got sight of Amelia's face once more. But what a face it was! So white, so wild and despair-stricken, that the remembrance of it haunted him afterwards like a crime, and the sight smote him with inexpressible pangs of longing and pity.

She was wrapped in a white morning dress, her hair falling on her shoulders, and her large eyes fixed and without light. By way of helping on the preparations for the departure, and showing that she too could be useful at a moment so critical, this poor soul had taken up a sash of George's from the drawers whereon it lay, and followed him to and fro with the sash in her hand, looking on mutely as his packing proceeded. She came out and stood, leaning at the wall, holding this sash against her bosom, from which the heavy net of crimson dropped like a large stain of blood. Our gentle-hearted captain felt a guilty shock as he looked at her. ' Good God,' thought he, ' and is it grief like this I dared to pry into ? ' And there was no help : no means to soothe and comfort this helpless, speechless misery. He stood for a moment and looked at her, powerless and torn with pity, as a parent regards an infant in pain.

At last, George took Emmy's hand, and led her back into the bedroom, from whence he came out alone. The parting had taken place in that moment, and he was gone.

' Thank Heaven that is over,' George thought, bounding down the stair, his sword under his arm, and as he ran swiftly to the alarm-ground, where the regiment was mustered, and whither trooped men and officers hurrying from their billets, his pulse was throbbing and his cheeks flushed : the great game of war was going to be played, and he one of the players. What a fierce excitement of doubt, hope, and pleasure ! What tremendous hazards of loss or gain ! What were all the games of chance he had ever played compared to this one ? Into all contests requiring athletic skill and courage, the young man, from his boyhood upwards, had flung himself with all his might. The champion of his school and his regiment, the bravos of his companions had followed him everywhere ; from the boys' cricket-match to the garrison-races, he had won a hundred of triumphs ; and wherever he went, women and men had admired and envied him. What qualities are there for which a man gets so speedy a return of applause, as those of bodily superiority, activity, and valour ? Time out of mind strength and courage have been the theme of bards and romances ; and from the story of Troy down to to-day, poetry has always chosen a soldier for a hero. I wonder is it because men are cowards in heart that they admire bravery so much, and place military valour so far beyond every other quality for reward and worship ?

So, at the sound of that stirring call to battle, George jumped away from the gentle arms in which he had been dallying ; not without a feeling of shame (although his wife's hold on him had been but feeble), that he should have been detained there so long. The same feeling of eagerness and excitement was amongst all those friends of his of whom we have had occasional glimpses, from the

stout senior major, who led the regiment into action, to little
Stubble, the ensign, who was to bear its colours on that day.

The sun was just rising as the march began—it was a
gallant sight—the band led the column, playing the regimental march—then came the major in command, riding
upon Pyramus, his stout charger—then marched the grenadiers, their captain at their head ; in the centre were the
colours, borne by the senior and junior ensigns—then
George came marching at the head of his company. He
looked up, and smiled at Amelia, and passed on ; and even
the sound of the music died away.

CHAPTER XXXI

IN WHICH JOS SEDLEY TAKES CARE OF HIS SISTER

THUS all the superior officers being summoned on duty elsewhere, Jos Sedley
was left in command of the little
colony at Brussels, with Amelia
invalided, Isidor, his Belgian servant,
and the *bonne*, who was maid-of-all-
work for the establishment, as a
garrison under him.   Though he was
disturbed in spirit, and his rest
destroyed by Dobbin's interruption
and the occurrences of the morning, Jos nevertheless remained for many hours in bed, wakeful and rolling about
there until his usual hour of rising had arrived.   The sun
was high in the heavens, and our gallant friends of the —th
miles on their march, before the civilian appeared in his
flowered dressing-gown at breakfast.

About George's absence, his brother-in-law was very easy
in mind.   Perhaps Jos was rather pleased in his heart that
Osborne was gone, for during George's presence, the other
had played but a very secondary part in the household, and
Osborne did not scruple to show his contempt for the stout
civilian.   But Emmy had always been good and attentive
to him.   It was she who ministered to his comforts, who
superintended the dishes that he liked, who walked or rode
with him (as she had many, too many, opportunities of

doing, for where was George ?) and who interposed her
sweet face between his anger and her husband's scorn.
Many timid remonstrances had she uttered to George in
behalf of her brother, but the latter in his trenchant way cut
these entreaties short. ' I'm an honest man,' he said, ' and
if I have a feeling I show it, as an honest man will. How
the deuce, my dear, would you have me behave respectfully
to such a fool as your brother ? ' So Jos was pleased with
George's absence. His plain hat and gloves on a sideboard,
and the idea that the owner was away, caused Jos I don't
know what secret thrill of pleasure. ' *He* won't be troubling
me this morning,' Jos thought, ' with his dandified airs and
his impudence.'

' Put the captain's hat into the ante-room,' he said to
Isidor, the servant.

' Perhaps he won't want it again,' replied the lackey,
looking knowingly at his master. He hated George too,
whose insolence towards him was quite of the English sort.

' And ask if madam is coming to breakfast,' Mr. Sedley
said with great majesty, ashamed to enter with a servant
upon the subject of his dislike for George. The truth is,
he had abused his brother to the valet a score of times before.

Alas ! madam could not come to breakfast, and cut the
tartines that Mr. Jos liked. Madam was a great deal too
ill, and had been in a frightful state ever since her husband's
departure, so her *bonne* said. Jos showed his sympathy, by
pouring her out a large cup of tea. It was his way of
exhibiting kindness : and he improved on this ; he not only
sent her breakfast, but he bethought him what delicacies she
would most like for dinner.

Isidor, the valet, had looked on very sulkily, while
Osborne's servant was disposing of his master's baggage
previous to the captain's departure : for in the first place
he hated Mr. Osborne, whose conduct to him, and to all
inferiors, was generally overbearing (nor does the continental
domestic like to be treated with insolence as our own better-
tempered servants do) : and secondly, he was angry that so
many valuables should be removed from under his hands,
to fall into other people's possession when the English
discomfiture should arrive. Of this defeat he and a vast
number of other persons in Brussels and Belgium did not
make the slightest doubt. The almost universal belief was,
that the emperor would divide the Prussian and English

armies,* annihilate one after the other, and march into
Brussels before three days were over : when all the movables
of his present masters, who would be killed, or fugitives, or
prisoners, would lawfully become the property of Monsieur
Isidor.

As he helped Jos through his toilsome and complicated
daily toilette, this faithful servant would calculate what he
should do with the very articles with which he was decorating
his master's person.   He would make a present of the silver
essence-bottles and toilette knicknacks to a young lady of
whom he was fond ; and keep the English cutlery and the
large ruby pin for himself.   It would look very smart upon
one of the fine frilled shirts, which, with the gold-laced cap
and the frogged frock coat, that might easily be cut down
to suit his shape, and the captain's gold-headed cane, and the
great double ring with the rubies, which he would have made
into a pair of beautiful ear-rings, he calculated would make
a perfect Adonis of himself, and render Mademoiselle Reine
an easy prey.   ' How those sleeve-buttons will suit me,'
thought he, as he fixed a pair on the fat pudgy wrists of
Mr. Sedley.   ' I long for sleeve-buttons ; and the captain's
boots with brass spurs, in the next room, *corbleu*, what an
effect they will make in the Allée Verte ! ' So while Monsieur
Isidor with bodily fingers was holding on to his master's
nose, and shaving the lower part of Jos's face, his imagination was rambling along the Green Avenue, dressed out in
a frogged coat and lace, and in company with Mademoiselle
Reine; he was loitering in spirit on the banks, and examining
the barges sailing slowly under the cool shadows of the trees
by the canal, or refreshing himself with a mug of Faro* at
the bench of a beer-house on the road to Laeken.

But Mr. Joseph Sedley, luckily for his own peace, no more
knew what was passing in his domestic's mind than the
respected reader and I suspect what John or Mary, whose
wages we pay, think of ourselves.   What our servants
think of us !—Did we know what our intimates and dear
relations thought of us, we should live in a world that we
should be glad to quit, and in a frame of mind and a constant
terror, that would be perfectly unbearable.   So Jos's man
was marking his victim down, as you see one of Mr. Paynter's
assistants* in Leadenhall Street ornament an unconscious
turtle with a placard on which is written, ' Soup to-
morrow.'

Amelia's attendant was much less selfishly disposed. Few dependants could come near that kind and gentle creature without paying their usual tribute of loyalty and affection to her sweet and affectionate nature. And it is a fact that Pauline, the cook, consoled her mistress more than anybody whom she saw on this wretched morning ; for when she found how Amelia remained for hours, silent, motionless, and haggard, by the windows in which she had placed herself to watch the last bayonets of the column as it marched away, the honest girl took the lady's hand, and said, ' *Tenez, madame, est-ce qu'il n'est pas aussi à l'armée, mon homme à moi ?* ' with which she burst into tears, and Amelia falling into her arms, did likewise, and so each pitied and soothed the other.

Several times during the forenoon Mr. Jos's Isidor went from his lodgings into the town, and to the gates of the hotels and lodging-houses round about the Parc, where the English were congregated, and there mingling with other valets, couriers, and lackeys, gathered such news as was abroad, and brought back bulletins for his master's information. Almost all these gentlemen were in heart partisans of the emperor, and had their opinions about the speedy end of the campaign. The emperor's proclamation from Avesnes had been distributed everywhere plentifully in Brussels. ' Soldiers ! ' it said, ' this is the anniversary of Marengo and Friedland, by which the destinies of Europe were twice decided. Then, as after Austerlitz, as after Wagram, we were too generous. We believed in the oaths and promises of princes whom we suffered to remain upon their thrones. Let us march once more to meet them. We and they, are we not still the same men ? Soldiers ! these same Prussians who are so arrogant to-day, were three to one against you at Jena, and six to one at Montmirail. Those among you who were prisoners in England can tell their comrades what frightful torments they suffered on board the English hulks. Madmen ! a moment of prosperity has blinded them, and if they enter into France it will be to find a grave there ! '* But the partisans of the French prophesied a more speedy extermination of the Emperor's enemies than this ; and it was agreed on all hands that Prussians and British would never return except as prisoners in the rear of the conquering army.

These opinions in the course of the day were brought to

operate upon Mr. Sedley. He was told that the Duke of Wellington had gone to try and rally his army, the advance of which had been utterly crushed the night before.

' Crushed, psha ! ' said Jos, whose heart was pretty stout at breakfast-time. ' The duke has gone to beat the emperor as he has beaten all his generals before.'

' His papers are burned, his effects are removed, and his quarters are being got ready for the Duke of Dalmatia,'* Jos's informant replied. ' I had it from his own *maître d'hôtel*. Milor Duc de Richemont's people are packing up everything. His grace has fled already, and the duchess is only waiting to see the plate packed to join the King of France at Ostend.'

' The King of France is at Ghent, fellow,' replied Jos, affecting incredulity.

' He fled last night to Bruges, and embarks to-day from Ostend. The Duke de Berri is taken prisoner. Those who wish to be safe had better go soon, for the dykes will be open to-morrow, and who can fly when the whole country is under water ? '

' Nonsense, sir, we are three to one, sir, against any force Boney can bring in the field,' Mr. Sedley objected ; ' the Austrians and the Russians are on their march. He must, he shall be crushed,' Jos said, slapping his hand on the table.

' The Prussians were three to one at Jena, and he took their army and kingdom in a week. They were six to one at Montmirail, and he scattered them like sheep. The Austrian army *is* coming, but with the empress and the King of Rome at its head ; and the Russians, bah ! the Russians will withdraw. No quarter is to be given to the English, on account of their cruelty to our braves on board the infamous pontoons. Look here, here it is in black and white. Here's the proclamation of his majesty the emperor and king,' said the now declared partisan of Napoleon, and taking the document from his pocket, Isidor sternly thrust it into his master's face, and already looked upon the frogged coat and valuables as his own spoil.

Jos was, if not seriously alarmed as yet, at least considerably disturbed in mind. ' Give me my coat and cap, sir,' said he, ' and follow me. I will go myself and learn the truth of these reports.' Isidor was furious as Jos put on the braided frock. ' Milor had better not wear that

military coat,' said he; 'the Frenchmen have sworn not to
give quarter to a single British soldier.'

'Silence, sirrah!' said Jos, with a resolute countenance
still, and thrust his arm into the sleeve with indomitable
resolution, in the performance of which heroic act he was
found by Mrs. Rawdon Crawley, who at this juncture came
up to visit Amelia, and entered without ringing at the antechamber door.

Rebecca was dressed very neatly and smartly, as usual :
her quiet sleep after Rawdon's departure had refreshed her,

and her pink smiling cheeks were quite pleasant to look at,
in a town and on a day when everybody else's countenance
wore the appearance of the deepest anxiety and gloom.
She laughed at the attitude in which Jos was discovered,
and the struggles and convulsions with which the stout
gentleman thrust himself into the braided coat.

Are you preparing to join the army, Mr. Joseph?' she
said. 'Is there to be nobody left in Brussels to protect us
poor women?' Jos succeeded in plunging into the coat,
and came forward blushing and stuttering out excuses to
his fair visitor. 'How was she after the events of the

morning—after the fatigues of the ball the night before ? ' Monsieur Isidor disappeared into his master's adjacent bedroom, bearing off the flowered dressing-gown.

' How good of you to ask,' said she, pressing one of his hands in both her own. ' How cool and collected you look when everybody else is frightened ! How is our dear little Emmy ? It must have been an awful, awful parting.'

' Tremendous,' Jos said.

' You men can bear anything,' replied the lady. ' Parting or danger are nothing to you. Own now that you were going to join the army and leave us to our fate. I know you were—something tells me you were. I was so frightened, when the thought came into my head (for I do sometimes think of you when I'm alone, Mr. Joseph !), that I ran off immediately to beg and entreat you not to fly from us.'

This speech might be interpreted, ' My dear sir, should an accident befall the army, and a retreat be necessary, you have a very comfortable carriage, in which I propose to take a seat.' I don't know whether Jos understood the words in this sense. But he was profoundly mortified by the lady's inattention to him during their stay at Brussels. He had never been presented to any of Rawdon Crawley's great acquaintances : he had scarcely been invited to Rebecca's parties ; for he was too timid to play much, and his presence bored George and Rawdon equally, who neither of them, perhaps, liked to have a witness of the amusements in which the pair chose to indulge. ' Ah ! ' thought Jos, ' now she wants me she comes to me. When there is nobody else in the way she can think about old Joseph Sedley ! ' But besides these doubts he felt flattered at the idea Rebecca expressed of his courage.

He blushed a good deal, and put on an air of importance. ' I should like to see the action,' he said. ' Every man of any spirit would, you know. I've seen a little service in India, but nothing on this grand scale.'

' You men would sacrifice anything for a pleasure,' Rebecca answered. ' Captain Crawley left me this morning as gay as if he were going to a hunting-party. What does he care ? What do any of you care for the agonies and tortures of a poor forsaken woman ? (I wonder whether he *could* really have been going to the troops, this great lazy gourmand ?) Oh ! dear Mr. Sedley, I have come to you for comfort—for consolation. I have been on my knees all the

morning. I tremble at the frightful danger into which our
husbands, our friends, our brave troops and allies, are
rushing. And I come here for shelter, and find another of
my friends—the last remaining to me—bent upon plunging
into the dreadful scene ! '

'My dear madam,' Jos replied, now beginning to be quite
soothed. 'Don't be alarmed. I only said I should like to
go—what Briton would not ? But my duty keeps me here :
I can't leave that poor creature in the next room.' And he
pointed with his finger to the door of the chamber in which
Amelia was.

'Good noble brother!' Rebecca said, putting her handkerchief to her eyes, and smelling the eau-de-Cologne with which
it was scented. 'I have done you injustice : you have got
a heart. I thought you had not.'

'Oh, upon my honour ! ' Jos said, making a motion as if
he would lay his hand upon the spot in question. 'You do
me injustice, indeed you do—my dear Mrs. Crawley.'

'I do, now your heart is true to your sister. But I
remember two years ago—when it was false to me ! '
Rebecca said, fixing her eyes upon him for an instant, and
then turning away into the window.

Jos blushed violently. That organ which he was accused
by Rebecca of not possessing began to thump tumultuously.
He recalled the days when he had fled from her, and the
passion which had once inflamed him—the days when he
had driven her in his curricle : when she had knit the green
purse for him : when he had sat enraptured gazing at her
white arms and bright eyes.

'I know you think me ungrateful,' Rebecca continued,
coming out of the window, and once more looking at him
and addressing him in a low tremulous voice. 'Your coldness, your averted looks, your manner when we have met
of late—when I came in just now, all proved it to me. But
were there no reasons why I should avoid you ? Let your
own heart answer that question. Do you think my husband
was too much inclined to welcome you ? The only unkind
words I have ever had from him (I will do Captain Crawley
that justice) have been about you—and most cruel, cruel
words they were.'

'Good gracious ! what have I done ? ' asked Jos in a
flurry of pleasure and perplexity ; 'what have I done—to
—to——? '

'Is jealousy nothing?' said Rebecca. 'He makes me miserable about you. And whatever it might have been once—my heart is all his. I am innocent now. Am I not, Mr. Sedley?'

All Jos's blood tingled with delight, as he surveyed this victim to his attractions. A few adroit words, one or two knowing tender glances of the eyes, and his heart was inflamed again and his doubts and suspicions forgotten. From Solomon downwards, have not wiser men than he been cajoled and befooled by women? 'If the worst comes to the worst,' Becky thought, 'my retreat is secure; and I have a right-hand seat in the barouche.'

There is no knowing into what declarations of love and ardour the tumultuous passions of Mr. Joseph might have led him, if Isidor the valet had not made his reappearance at this minute, and begun to busy himself about the domestic affairs. Jos, who was just going to gasp out an avowal, choked almost with the emotion that he was obliged to restrain. Rebecca too bethought her that it was time she should go in and comfort her dearest Amelia. '*Au revoir*,' she said, kissing her hand to Mr. Joseph, and tapped gently at the door of his sister's apartment. As she entered and closed the door on herself, he sank down in a chair, and gazed and sighed and puffed portentously. 'That coat is very tight for Milor,' Isidor said, still having his eye on the frogs; but his master heard him not: his thoughts were elsewhere: now glowing, maddening, upon the contemplation of the enchanting Rebecca: anon shrinking guiltily before the vision of the jealous Rawdon Crawley, with his curling, fierce moustachios, and his terrible duelling pistols loaded and cocked.

Rebecca's appearance struck Amelia with terror, and made her shrink back. It recalled her to the world and the remembrance of yesterday. In the overpowering fears about to-morrow she had forgotten Rebecca,—jealousy—everything except that her husband was gone and was in danger. Until this dauntless worldling came in and broke the spell, and lifted the latch, we too have forborne to enter into that sad chamber. How long had that poor girl been on her knees! what hours of speechless prayer and bitter prostration had she passed there! The war-chroniclers who write brilliant stories of fight and triumph scarcely tell us of these. These are too mean parts of the pageant: and you

don't hear widows' cries or mothers' ,sobs in the midst of
the shouts and jubilation in the great Chorus of Victory.
And yet when was the time, that such have not cried out :
heart-broken, humble protestants, unheard in the uproar
of the triumph !

After the first movement of terror in Amelia's mind—
when Rebecca's green eyes lighted upon her, and rustling
in her fresh silks and brilliant ornaments, the latter tripped
up with extended arms to embrace her—a feeling of anger
succeeded, and from being deadly pale before, her face
flushed up red, and she returned Rebecca's look after a
moment with a steadiness which surprised and somewhat
abashed her rival.

'Dearest Amelia, you are very unwell,' the visitor said,
putting forth her hand to take Amelia's. 'What is it ?
I could not rest until I knew how you were.'

Amelia drew back her hand—never since her life began
had that gentle soul refused to believe or to answer any
demonstration of goodwill or affection. But she drew
back her hand, and trembled all over. 'Why are *you* here,
Rebecca ? ' she said, still looking at her solemnly with her
large eyes. These glances troubled her visitor.

'She must have seen him give me the letter at the ball,'
Rebecca thought. 'Don't be agitated, dear Amelia,' she
said, looking down. 'I came but to see if I could—if you
were well.'

'Are you well ? ' said Amelia. 'I dare say you are. You
don't love your husband. You would not be here if you
did. Tell me, Rebecca, did I ever do you anything but
kindness ? '

'Indeed, Amelia, no,' the other said, still hanging down
her head.

'When you were quite poor, who was it that befriended
you ? Was I not a sister to you ? You saw us all in happier
days before he married me. I was all in all then to him ; or
would he have given up his fortune, his family, as he nobly
did to make me happy ? Why did you come between my
love and me ? Who sent you to separate those whom God
joined, and take my darling's heart from me—my own husband ? Do you think you could love him as I did ? His love
was everything to me. You knew it, and wanted to rob
me of it. For shame, Rebecca ; bad and wicked woman—
false friend and false wife.'

'Amelia, I protest before God, I have done my husband no wrong,' Rebecca said, turning from her.

'Have you done *me* no wrong, Rebecca? You did not succeed, but you tried. Ask your heart if you did not?'

She knows nothing, Rebecca thought.

'He came back to me. I knew he would. I knew that no falsehood, no flattery, could keep him from me long. I knew he would come. I prayed so that he should.'

The poor girl spoke these words with a spirit and volubility which Rebecca had never before seen in her, and before which the latter was quite dumb. 'But what have I done to you,' she continued in a more pitiful tone, 'that you should try and take him from me? I had him but for six weeks. You might have spared me those, Rebecca. And yet, from the very first day of our wedding, you came and blighted it. Now he is gone, are you come to see how unhappy I am?' She continued, 'You made me wretched enough for the past fortnight: you might have spared me to-day.'

'I—I never came here,' interposed Rebecca, with unlucky truth.

'No. You didn't come. You took him away. Are you come to fetch him from me?' she continued in a wilder tone. 'He was here, but he is gone now. There on that very sofa he sat. Don't touch it. We sat and talked there. I was on his knee, and my arms were round his neck, and we said, "Our Father." Yes, he was here: and they came and took him away, but he promised me to come back.'

'He will come back, my dear,' said Rebecca, touched in spite of herself.

'Look,' said Amelia, 'this is his sash—isn't it a pretty colour?' and she took up the fringe and kissed it. She had tied it round her waist at some part of the day. She had forgotten her anger, her jealousy, the very presence of her rival seemingly. For she walked silently and almost with a smile on her face, towards the bed, and began to smooth down George's pillow.

Rebecca walked, too, silently away. 'How is Amelia?' asked Jos, who still held his position in the chair.

'There should be somebody with her,' said Rebecca. 'I think she is very unwell:' and she went away with a very grave face, refusing Mr. Sedley's entreaties that she

would stay and partake of the early dinner which he had
ordered.

Rebecca was of a good-natured and obliging disposition ;
and she liked Amelia rather than otherwise.   Even her hard
words, reproachful as they were, were complimentary—the
groans of a person stinging under defeat.   Meeting Mrs.
O'Dowd, whom the dean's sermons had by no means comforted, and who was walking very disconsolately in the Parc,
Rebecca accosted the latter, rather to the surprise of the
major's wife, who was not accustomed to such marks of
politeness from Mrs. Rawdon Crawley, and informing her that
poor little Mrs. Osborne was in a desperate condition, and
almost mad with grief, sent off the good-natured Irishwoman
straight to see if she could console her young favourite.

' I've cares of my own enough,' Mrs. O'Dowd said, gravely,
' and I thought poor Amelia would be little wanting for
company this day.   But if she's so bad as you say, and you
can't attend to her, who used to be so fond of her, faith I'll
see if I can be of service.   And so good marning to ye,
madam ; '   with which speech and a toss of her head, the
lady of the repayther took a farewell of Mrs. Crawley, whose
company she by no means courted.

Becky watched her marching off, with a smile on her lip.
She had the keenest sense of humour, and the Parthian look
which the retreating Mrs. O'Dowd flung over her shoulder
almost upset Mrs. Crawley's gravity.   ' My service to ye,
me fine madam, and I'm glad to see ye so cheerful,' thought
Peggy.   ' It's not *you* that will cry your eyes out with grief,
anyway.'   And with this she passed on, and speedily found
her way to Mrs. Osborne's lodgings.

The poor soul was still at the bedside, where Rebecca had
left her, and stood almost crazy with grief.   The major's
wife, a stronger-minded woman endeavoured her best to
comfort her young friend.   ' You must bear up, Amelia,
dear,' she said kindly, ' for he mustn't find you ill when he
sends for you after the victory.   It's not you are the only
woman that are in the hands of God this day.'

' I know that.   I am very wicked, very weak,' Amelia
said.   She knew her own weakness well enough.   The
presence of the more resolute friend checked it, however ;
and she was the better of this control and company.   They
went on till two o'clock ; their hearts were with the column

as it marched farther and farther away. Dreadful doubt and anguish—prayers and fears and griefs unspeakable—followed the regiment. It was the women's tribute to the war.. It taxes both alike, and takes the blood of the men, and the tears of the women.

At half-past two an event occurred of daily importance to Mr. Joseph : the dinner hour arrived. Warriors may fight and perish, but he must dine. He came into Amelia's room to see if he could coax her to share that meal. ' Try,' said he ; ' the soup is very good. Do try, Emmy,' and he kissed her hand. Except when she was married, he had not done so much for years before. ' You are very good and kind, Joseph,' she said. ' Everybody is, but, if you please, I will stay in my room to-day.'

The savour of the soup, however, was agreeable to Mrs. O'Dowd's nostrils : and she thought she would bear Mr. Jos company. So the two sat down to their meal. ' God bless the meat,' said the major's wife, solemnly : she was thinking of her honest Mick, riding at the head of his regiment : ' 'Tis but a bad dinner those poor boys will get to-day,' she said, with a sigh, and then, like a philosopher, fell to.

Jos's spirits rose with his meal. He would drink the regiment's health ; or, indeed, take any other excuse to indulge in a glass of champagne. ' We'll drink to O'Dowd and the brave —th,' said he, bowing gallantly to his guest. ' Hey, Mrs. O'Dowd. Fill Mrs. O'Dowd's glass, Isidor.'

But all of a sudden, Isidor started, and the major's wife laid down her knife and fork. The windows of the room were open, and looked southward, and a dull distant sound came over the sun-lighted roofs from that direction. ' What is it ? ' said Jos. ' Why don't you pour, you rascal ? '

' *C'est le feu !* ' said Isidor, running to the balcony.

' God defend us ; it's cannon ! ' Mrs. O'Dowd cried, starting up, and followed too to the window. A thousand pale and anxious faces might have been seen looking from other casements. And presently it seemed as if the whole population of the city rushed into the streets.*

CHAPTER XXXII

IN WHICH JOS TAKES FLIGHT, AND THE WAR IS BROUGHT TO A CLOSE

E of peaceful London City have never beheld—and please God never shall witness—such a scene of hurry and alarm, as that which Brussels presented. Crowds rushed to the Namur gate, from which direction the noise proceeded, and many rode along the level *chaussée*, to be in advance of any intelligence from the army. Each man asked his neighbour for news ; and even great English lords and ladies condescended to speak to persons whom they did not know. The friends of the French went abroad, wild with excitement, and prophesying the triumph of their emperor. The merchants closed their shops, and came out to swell the general chorus of alarm and clamour. Women rushed to the churches, and crowded the chapels, and knelt and prayed on the flags and steps. The dull sound of the cannon went on rolling, rolling. Presently carriages with travellers began to leave the town, galloping away by the Ghent barrier. The prophecies of the French partisans began to pass for facts. ' He has cut the armies in two,' it was said. ' He is marching straight on Brussels. He will overpower the English, and be here to-night.' ' He will overpower the English,' shrieked Isidor to his master, ' and will be here to-night.' The man bounded in and out from the lodgings to the street, always returning with some fresh particulars of disaster. Jos's face grew paler and paler. Alarm began to take entire possession of the stout civilian. All the champagne he drank brought no courage to him. Before sunset he was worked up to such a pitch of nervousness as gratified his friend Isidor to behold, who now counted surely upon the spoils of the owner of the laced coat.

The women were away all this time. After hearing the

firing for a moment, the stout major's wife bethought
her of her friend in the next chamber, and ran in to watch,
and if possible to console, Amelia. The idea that she had
that helpless and gentle creature to protect, gave additional
strength to the natural courage of the honest Irishwoman.
She passed five hours by her friend's side, sometimes in
remonstrance, sometimes talking cheerfully, oftener in
silence, and terrified mental supplication. ' I never let
go her hand once,' said the stout lady afterwards, ' until
after sunset, when the firing was over.' Pauline, the
bonne, was on her knees at church hard by, praying for
son homme à elle.

When the noise of the cannonading was over, Mrs. O'Dowd
issued out of Amelia's room into the parlour adjoining,
where Jos sat with two emptied flasks, and courage entirely
gone. Once or twice he had ventured into his sister's
bedroom, looking very much alarmed, and as if he would
say something. But the major's wife kept her place, and
he went away without disburthening himself of his speech.
He was ashamed to tell her that he wanted to fly.

But when she made her appearance in the dining-room,
where he sat in the twilight in the cheerless company of
his empty champagne-bottles, he began to open his mind to
her.

' Mrs. O'Dowd,' he said, ' hadn't you better get Amelia
ready ? '

' Are you going to take her out a walk ? ' said the major's
lady ; ' sure she's too weak to stir.'

' I—I've ordered the carriage,' he said, ' and—and post-
horses ; Isidor is gone for them,' Jos continued.

' What do you want with driving to-night ? ' answered
the lady. ' Isn't she better on her bed ? I've just got
her to lie down.'

' Get her up,' said Jos ; ' she must get up, I say : ' and
he stamped his foot energetically. ' I say the horses are
ordered—yes, the horses are ordered. It's all over, and——'*

' And what ? ' asked Mrs. O'Dowd.

' I'm off for Ghent,' Jos answered. ' Everybody is going ;
there's a place for you ! We shall start in half an hour.'

The major's wife looked at him with infinite scorn.
' I don't move till O'Dowd gives me the route,' said she.
' You may go if you like, Mr. Sedley ; but, faith, Amelia
and I stop here.'

' She *shall* go,' said Jos, with another stamp of his foot.
Mrs. O'Dowd put herself with arms akimbo before the
bedroom door.

' Is it her mother you're going to take her to ? ' she said ;
' or do you want to go to mamma yourself, Mr. Sedley ?
Good marning—a pleasant journey to ye, sir. *Bon voyage*,
as they say, and take my counsel, and shave off them moustachios, or they'll bring you into mischief.'

' D—n ! ' yelled out Jos, wild with fear, rage, and mortification ; and Isidor came in at this juncture, swearing
in his turn. ' *Pas de chevaux, sacrebleu !* ' hissed out the
furious domestic. All the horses were gone. Jos was not
the only man in Brussels seized with panic that day.

But Jos's fears, great and cruel as they were already,
were destined to increase to an almost frantic pitch before
the night was over. It has been mentioned how Pauline,
the *bonne*, had *son homme à elle*, also in the ranks of the
army that had gone out to meet the Emperor Napoleon,
This lover was a native of Brussels, and a Belgian hussar.
The troops of his nation signalized themselves in this war
for anything but courage, and young Van Cutsum, Pauline's
admirer, was too good a soldier to disobey his colonel's
orders to run away. Whilst in garrison at Brussels young
Regulus (he had been born in the revolutionary times)
found his great comfort, and passed almost all his leisure
moments in Pauline's kitchen ; and it was with pockets
and holsters crammed full of good things from her larder,
that he had taken leave of his weeping sweetheart, to
proceed upon the campaign a few days before.

As far as his regiment was concerned, this campaign was
over now. They had formed a part of the division under
the command of his sovereign apparent, the Prince of
Orange, and as respected length of swords and moustachios,
and the richness of uniform and equipments, Regulus and
his comrades looked to be as gallant a body of men as ever
trumpets sounded for.

When Ney dashed upon the advance of the allied troops,
carrying one position after the other, until the arrival of
the great body of the British army from Brussels changed
the aspect of the combat of Quatre Bras, the squadrons
among which Regulus rode showed the greatest activity
in retreating before the French, and were dislodged from
one post and another which they occupied with perfect

alacrity on their part.   Their movements were only checked
by the advance of the British in their rear.   Thus forced
to halt, the enemy's cavalry (whose bloodthirsty obstinacy
cannot be too severely reprehended) had at length an
opportunity of coming to close quarters with the brave
Belgians before them ;   who preferred to encounter the
British rather than the French, and at once turning tail,
rode through the English regiments that were behind them,
and scattered in all directions.   The regiment, in fact, did
not exist any more.   It was nowhere.   It had no headquarters.   Regulus found himself galloping many miles
from the field of action, entirely alone ;   and whither should
he fly for refuge so naturally as to that kitchen and those
faithful arms in which Pauline had so often welcomed
him ?

At some ten o'clock the clinking of a sabre might have
been heard up the stair of the house where the Osbornes
occupied a story in the Continental fashion.   A knock
might have been heard at the kitchen door ;   and poor
Pauline, come back from church, fainted almost with terror
as she opened it and saw before her her haggard hussar.
He looked as pale as the midnight dragoon who came to
disturb Leonora.*   Pauline would have screamed, but that
her cry would have called her masters, and discovered her
friend.   She stifled her scream, then, and leading her hero
into the kitchen, gave him beer, and the choice bits from
the dinner, which Jos had not had the heart to taste.   The
hussar showed he was no ghost by the prodigious quantity
of flesh and beer which he devoured—and during the
mouthfuls he told his tale of disaster.

His regiment had performed prodigies of courage, and
had withstood for a while the onset of the whole French
army.   But they were overwhelmed at last, as was the
whole British army by this time.   Ney destroyed each
regiment as it came up.   The Belgians in vain interposed
to prevent the butchery of the English.   The Bruns-
wickers were routed and had fled—their duke was killed.
It was a general *débâcle.**   He sought to drown his sorrow
for the defeat in floods of beer.

Isidor, who had come into the kitchen, heard the conversation and rushed out to inform his master.   ' It is all
over,' he shrieked to Jos.   ' Milor duke is a prisoner ;
the Duke of Brunswick is killed ;   the British army is in

full flight; there is only one man escaped, and he is in the kitchen now—come and hear him.' So Jos tottered into that apartment where Regulus still sat on the kitchen-table, and clung fast to his flagon of beer. In the best French which he could muster, and which was in sooth of a very ungrammatical sort, Jos besought the hussar to tell his tale. The disasters deepened as Regulus spoke. He was the only man of his regiment not slain on the field. He had seen the Duke of Brunswick fall, the black hussars fly, the Écossais pounded down by the cannon.

'And the —th?' gasped Jos.

'Cut in pieces,' said the hussar—upon which Pauline crying out, 'Oh, my mistress, *ma bonne petite dame*,' went

off fairly into hysterics, and filled the house with her screams.

Wild with terror, Mr. Sedley knew not how or where to seek for safety. He rushed from the kitchen back to the sitting-room, and cast an appealing look at Amelia's door, which Mrs. O'Dowd had closed and locked in his face; but he remembered how scornfully the latter had received him, and after pausing and listening for a brief space at the door, he left it, and resolved to go into the street, for the first time that day. So, seizing a candle, he looked about for his gold-laced cap, and found it lying in its usual place, on a console-table, in the ante-room, placed before

a mirror at which Jos used to coquet, always giving his
side-locks a twirl, and his cap the proper cock over his
eye, before he went forth to make appearance in public.
Such is the force of habit, that even in the midst of his
terror he began mechanically to twiddle with his hair, and
arrange the cock of his hat. Then he looked amazed at
the pale face in the glass before him, and especially at his
moustachios, which had attained a rich growth in the course
of near seven weeks, since they had come into the world.

They *will* mistake me for a military man, thought he,
remembering Isidor's warning, as to the massacre with
which all the defeated British army was threatened ; and
staggering back to his bedchamber, he began wildly pulling
the bell which summoned his valet.

Isidor answered that summons. Jos had sunk in a chair
—he had torn off his neck-cloths, and turned down his
collars, and was sitting with both his hands lifted to his
throat.

'*Coupez-moi*, Isidor,' shouted he ; '*vite! coupez-moi!*'

Isidor thought for a moment he had gone mad, and that he wished his valet to cut his throat.

'*Les moustaches*,' gasped Jos; '*les moustaches—coupy, rasy, vite!*'—his French was of this sort—voluble, as we have said, but not remarkable for grammar.

Isidor swept off the moustachios in no time with the razor, and heard with inexpressible delight his master's orders that he should fetch a hat and a plain coat. '*Ne porty ploo—habit militair—bonny—donny à voo, prenny dehors*'—were Jos's words,—the coat and cap were at last his property.

This gift being made, Jos selected a plain black coat and waistcoat from his stock, and put on a large white neck-cloth, and a plain beaver. If he could have got a shovel-hat he would have worn it. As it was, you would have fancied he was a flourishing, large parson of the Church of England.

'*Venny maintenong*,' he continued, '*sweevy—ally—party—dong la roo.*' And so having said, he plunged swiftly down the stairs of the house, and passed into the street.

Although Regulus had vowed that he was the only man of his regiment or of the allied army, almost, who had escaped being cut to pieces by Ney, it appeared that his statement was incorrect, and that a good number more of the supposed victims had survived the massacre. Many scores of Regulus's comrades had found their way back to Brussels, and—all agreeing that they had run away—filled the whole town with an idea of the defeat of the allies. The arrival of the French was expected hourly; the panic continued, and preparations for flight went on everywhere. No horses! thought Jos, in terror. He made Isidor inquire of scores of persons, whether they had any to lend or sell, and his heart sank within him, at the negative answers returned everywhere. Should he take the journey on foot? Even fear could not render that ponderous body so active.

Almost all the hotels occupied by the English in Brussels face the Parc, and Jos wandered irresolutely about in this quarter, with crowds of other people, oppressed as he was by fear and curiosity. Some families he saw more happy than himself, having discovered a team of horses, and rattling through the streets in retreat; others again there were whose case was like his own, and who could not for

any bribes or entreaties procure the necessary means of
flight. Amongst these would-be fugitives, Jos remarked
the Lady Bareacres and her daughter, who sat in their
carriage in the *porte-cochère* of their hotel, all their imperials
packed, and the only drawback to whose flight was the
same want of motive power which kept Jos stationary.

Rebecca Crawley occupied apartments in this hotel;
and had before this period had sundry hostile meetings
with the ladies of the Bareacres family. My Lady Bareacres cut Mrs. Crawley on the stairs when they met by
chance; and in all places where the latter's name was
mentioned, spoke perseveringly ill of her neighbour. The
countess was shocked at the familiarity of General Tufto
with the aide de camp's wife. The Lady Blanche avoided
her as if she had been an infectious disease. Only the
earl himself kept up a sly occasional acquaintance with
her, when out of the jurisdiction of his ladies.

Rebecca had her revenge now upon these insolent
enemies. It became known in the hotel that Captain
Crawley's horses had been left behind, and when the panic
began, Lady Bareacres condescended to send her maid
to the captain's wife with her ladyship's compliments,
and a desire to know the price of Mrs. Crawley's horses.
Mrs. Crawley returned a note with her compliments, and
an intimation that it was not her custom to transact
bargains with ladies' maids.

This curt reply brought the earl in person to Becky's
apartment; but he could get no more success than the
first ambassador. 'Send a lady's maid to *me!*' Mrs.
Crawley cried in great anger; 'why didn't my Lady
Bareacres tell me to go and saddle the horses! Is it her
ladyship that wants to escape, or her ladyship's *femme
de chambre?*' And this was all the answer that the earl
bore back to his countess.

What will not necessity do? The countess herself
actually came to wait upon Mrs. Crawley on the failure
of her second envoy. She entreated her to name her
own price; she even offered to invite Becky to Bareacres
House, if the latter would but give her the means of returning
to that residence. Mrs. Crawley sneered at her.

'I don't want to be waited on by bailiffs in livery,' she
said; 'you will never get back though most probably—at
least not you and your diamonds together. The French

will have those. They will be here in two hours, and I shall
be half-way to Ghent by that time. I would not sell you
my horses, no, not for the two largest diamonds that your
ladyship wore at the ball.' Lady Bareacres trembled with
rage and terror. The diamonds were sewed into her habit,
and secreted in my lord's padding and boots. 'Woman, the
diamonds are at the banker's, and I *will* have the horses,'
she said. Rebecca laughed in her face. The infuriate
countess went below, and sat in her carriage; her maid,
her courier, and her husband were sent once more through
the town, each to look for cattle; and woe betide those
who came last! Her ladyship was resolved on departing
the very instant the horses arrived from any quarter—with
her husband or without him.

Rebecca had the pleasure of seeing her ladyship in the
horseless carriage, and keeping her eyes fixed upon her,
and bewailing, in the loudest tone of voice, the countess's
perplexities. 'Not to be able to get horses!' she said,
'and to have all those diamonds sewed into the carriage
cushions! What a prize it will be for the French when
they come!—the carriage and the diamonds I mean;
not the lady!' She gave this information to the landlord,
to the servants, to the guests, and the innumerable stragglers
about the courtyard. Lady Bareacres could have shot
her from the carriage-window.

It was while enjoying the humiliation of her enemy
that Rebecca caught sight of Jos, who made towards her
directly he perceived her.

That altered, frightened, fat face, told his secret well
enough. He too wanted to fly, and was on the look-out
for the means of escape. '*He* shall buy my horses,' thought
Rebecca, 'and I'll ride the mare.'

Jos walked up to his friend, and put the question for the
hundredth time during the past hour, 'Did she know
where horses were to be had?'

'What, *you* fly?' said Rebecca, with a laugh. 'I thought
you were the champion of all the ladies, Mr. Sedley.'

'I—I'm not a military man,' gasped he.

'And Amelia?—Who is to protect that poor little sister
of yours?' asked Rebecca. 'You surely would not desert
her?'

'What good can I do her, suppose—suppose the enemy
arrive?' Jos answered. 'They'll spare the women; but

my man tells me that they have taken an oath to give
no quarter to the men—the dastardly cowards.'

'Horrid!' cried Rebecca, enjoying his perplexity.

'Besides, I don't want to desert her,' cried the brother.
'She *shan't* be deserted. There is a seat for her in my
carriage, and one for you, dear Mrs. Crawley, if you will
come ; and if we can get horses——' sighed he—

'I have two to sell,' the lady said. Jos could have flung
himself into her arms at the news. 'Get the carriage,
Isidor,' he cried ; 'we've found them—we have found
them.'

'My horses never were in harness,' added the lady.
'Bulfinch would kick the carriage to pieces, if you put him
in the traces.'

'But he is quiet to ride ? ' asked the civilian.

'As quiet as a lamb, and as fast as a hare,' answered
Rebecca.

'Do you think he is up to my weight ? ' Jos said. He
was already on his back, in imagination, without ever so
much as a thought for poor Amelia. What person who
loved a horse-speculation could resist such a temptation ?

In reply, Rebecca asked him to come into her room,
whither he followed her quite breathless to conclude the
bargain. Jos seldom spent a half-hour in his life which
cost him so much money. Rebecca, measuring the value
of the goods which she had for sale by Jos's eagerness to
purchase, as well as by the scarcity of the article, put
upon her horses a price so prodigious as to make even the
civilian draw back. 'She would sell both or neither,'
she said resolutely. Rawdon had ordered her not to part
with them for a price less than that which she specified.
Lord Bareacres below would give her the same money—
and with all her love and regard for the Sedley family,
her dear Mr. Joseph must conceive that poor people must
live—nobody, in a word, could be more affectionate, but
more firm about the matter of business.

Jos ended by agreeing, as might be supposed of him.
The sum he had to give her was so large that he was obliged
to ask for time ; so large as to be a little fortune to Rebecca,
who rapidly calculated that with this sum, and the sale
of the residue of Rawdon's effects, and her pension as a
widow should he fall, she would now be absolutely indepen-

dent of the world, and might look her weeds steadily in
the face.

Once or twice in the day she certainly had herself thought
about flying. But her reason gave her better counsel.
'Suppose the French do come,' thought Becky, 'what
can they do to a poor officer's widow ? Bah ! the times
of sacks and sieges are over. We shall be let to go home
quietly, or I may live pleasantly abroad with a snug little
income.'

Meanwhile Jos and Isidor went off to the stables to
inspect the newly-purchased cattle. Jos bade his man
saddle the horses at once. He would ride away that very
night, that very hour. And he left the valet busy in getting
the horses ready, and went homewards himself to prepare
for his departure. It must be secret. He would go to
his chamber by the back entrance. He did not care to
face Mrs. O'Dowd and Amelia, and own to them that he
was about to run.

By the time Jos's bargain with Rebecca was completed,
and his horses had been visited and examined, it was almost
morning once more. But though midnight was long passed,
there was no rest for the city ; the people were up, the
lights in the houses flamed, crowds were still about the
doors, and the streets were busy. Rumours of various
natures went still from mouth to mouth : one report
averred that the Prussians had been utterly defeated ;
another that it was the English who had been attacked
and conquered : a third that the latter had held their
ground. This last rumour gradually got strength. No
Frenchmen had made their appearance. Stragglers had
come in from the army bringing reports more and more
favourable : at last an aide de camp actually reached
Brussels* with dispatches for the commandant of the
place, who placarded presently through the town an
official announcement of the success of the allies at Quatre
Bras, and the entire repulse of the French under Ney after
a six hours' battle. The aide de camp must have arrived
some time while Jos and Rebecca were making their bargain
together, or the latter was inspecting his purchase. When
he reached his own hotel, he found a score of its numerous
inhabitants on the threshold discoursing of the news ;
there was no doubt as to its truth. And he went up to
communicate it to the ladies under his charge. He did

not think it was necessary to tell them how he had intended
to take leave of them, how he had bought horses, and what
a price he had paid for them.

But success or defeat was a minor matter to them, who
had only thought for the safety of those they loved. Amelia,
at the news of the victory, became still more agitated even
than before. She was for going that moment to the army.
She besought her brother with tears to conduct her thither.
Her doubts and terrors reached their paroxysm ; and the
poor girl, who for many hours had been plunged into
stupor, raved and ran hither and thither in hysteric insanity
—a piteous sight. No man writhing in pain on the hard-
fought field fifteen miles off, where lay, after their struggles,
so many of the brave—no man suffered more keenly than
this poor harmless victim of the war. Jos could not bear
the sight of her pain. He left his sister in the charge of
her stouter female companion, and descended once more
to the threshold of the hotel, where everybody still lingered,
and talked, and waited for more news.

It grew to be broad daylight as they stood here, and
fresh news began to arrive from the war, brought by men
who had been actors in the scene. Wagons and long
country carts laden with wounded came rolling into the
town ; ghastly groans came from within them, and haggard
faces looked up sadly from out of the straw. Jos Sedley
was looking at one of these carriages with a painful curiosity
—the moans of the people within were frightful—the
wearied horses could hardly pull the cart. 'Stop ! stop !'
a feeble voice cried from the straw, and the carriage stopped
opposite Mr. Sedley's hotel.

'It is George, I know it is !' cried Amelia, rushing in
a moment to the balcony, with a pallid face and loose
flowing hair. It was not George, however, but it was the
next best thing : it was news of him.

It was poor Tom Stubble,* who had marched out of
Brussels so gallantly twenty-four hours before, bearing
the colours of the regiment, which he had defended very
gallantly upon the field. A French lancer had speared
the young ensign in the leg, who fell, still bravely holding
to his flag. At the conclusion of the engagement, a place
had been found for the poor boy in a cart, and he had been
brought back to Brussels.

'Mr. Sedley, Mr. Sedley !' cried the boy, faintly, and

Jos came up almost frightened at the appeal. He had not at first distinguished who it was that called him.

Little Tom Stubble held out his hot and feeble hand. 'I'm to be taken in here,' he said. 'Osborne—and—and Dobbin said I was; and you are to give the man two napoleons: my mother will pay you.' This young fellow's thoughts, during the long feverish hours passed in the cart, had been wandering to his father's parsonage which he had quitted only a few months before, and he had sometimes forgotten his pain in that delirium.

The hotel was large, and the people kind, and all the inmates of the cart were taken in and placed on various couches. The young ensign was conveyed upstairs to Osborne's quarters. Amelia and the major's wife had rushed down to him, when the latter had recognized him from the balcony. You may fancy the feelings of these women when they were told that the day was over, and both their husbands were safe; in what mute rapture Amelia fell on her good friend's neck, and embraced her; in what a grateful passion of prayers she fell on her knees, and thanked the Power which had saved her husband.

Our young lady, in her fevered and nervous condition, could have had no more salutary medicine prescribed for her by any physician than that which chance put in her way. She and Mrs. O'Dowd watched incessantly by the wounded lad, whose pains were very severe, and in the duty thus forced upon her, Amelia had not time to brood over her personal anxieties, or to give herself up to her own fears and forebodings after her wont. The young patient told in his simple fashion the events of the day, and the actions of our friends of the gallant —th. They had suffered severely. They had lost very many officers and men. The major's horse had been shot under him as the regiment charged, and they all thought that O'Dowd was gone, and that Dobbin had got his majority, until on their return from the charge to their old ground, the major was discovered seated on Pyramus's carcass, refreshing himself from a case-bottle. It was Captain Osborne that cut down the French lancer who had speared the ensign. Amelia turned so pale at the notion that Mrs. O'Dowd stopped the young ensign in this story. And it was Captain Dobbin who at the end of the day, though wounded himself, took up the lad in his arms and carried

him to the surgeon, and thence to the cart which was to
bring him back to Brussels. And it was he who promised
the driver two louis if he would make his way to Mr. Sedley's hotel in the city ; and tell Mrs. Captain Osborne that
the action was over, and that her husband was unhurt
and well.

'Indeed, but he has a good heart that William Dobbin,'
Mrs. O'Dowd said, 'though he is always laughing at me.'

Young Stubble vowed there was not such another officer
in the army, and never ceased his praises of the senior
captain, his modesty, his kindness, and his admirable
coolness in the field. To these parts of the conversation,
Amelia lent a very distracted attention : it was only when
George was spoken of that she listened, and when he was
not mentioned, she thought about him.

In tending her patient, and in thinking of the wonderful
escapes of the day before, her second day passed away
not too slowly with Amelia. There was only one man in
the army for her : and as long as he was well, it must be
owned that its movements interested her little. All the
reports which Jos brought from the streets fell very vaguely
on her ears ; though they were sufficient to give that
timorous gentleman, and many other people then in
Brussels, every disquiet. The French had been repulsed
certainly, but it was after a severe and doubtful struggle,
and with only a division of the French army. The emperor,
with the main body, was away at Ligny, where he had
utterly annihilated the Prussians, and was now free to
bring his whole force to bear upon the allies. The Duke
of Wellington was retreating upon the capital, and a great
battle must be fought under its walls probably, of which
the chances were more than doubtful. The Duke of
Wellington had but twenty thousand British troops on
whom he could rely, for the Germans were raw militia, the
Belgians disaffected ; and with this handful his Grace
had to resist a hundred and fifty thousand men that had
broken into Belgium under Napoleon. Under Napoleon !
What warrior was there, however famous and skilful, that
could fight at odds with him ?

Jos thought of all these things, and trembled. So did
all the rest of Brussels—where people felt that the fight of
the day before was but the prelude to the greater combat
which was imminent. One of the armies opposed to the

emperor was scattered to the winds already. The few
English that could be brought to resist him would perish
at their posts, and the conqueror would pass over their
bodies into the city. Woe be to those whom he found
there! Addresses were prepared, public functionaries
assembled and debated secretly, apartments were got
ready, and tricoloured banners and triumphal emblems
manufactured, to welcome the arrival of his majesty the
emperor and king.

The emigration still continued, and wherever families
could find means of departure, they fled. When Jos, on
the afternoon of the 17th of June, went to Rebecca's hotel,
he found that the great Bareacres's carriage had at length
rolled away from the *porte-cochère*. The earl had procured
a pair of horses somehow, in spite of Mrs. Crawley, and
was rolling on the road to Ghent. Louis the Desired was
getting ready his portmanteau in that city, too. It seemed
as if Misfortune was never tired of worrying into motion
that unwieldy exile.

Jos felt that the delay of yesterday had been only a
respite, and that his dearly bought horses must of a surety
be put into requisition. His agonies were very severe all
this day. As long as there was an English army between
Brussels and Napoleon, there was no need of immediate
flight; but he had his horses brought from their distant
stables, to the stables in the courtyard of the hotel where
he lived; so that they might be under his own eyes, and
beyond the risk of violent abduction. Isidor watched
the stable-door constantly, and had the horses saddled, to
be ready for the start. He longed intensely for that event.

After the reception of the previous day, Rebecca did
not care to come near her dear Amelia. She clipped the
bouquet which George had brought her, and gave fresh
water to the flowers, and read over the letter which he
had sent her. ' Poor wretch,' she said, twirling round the
little bit of paper in her fingers, ' how I could crush her
with this!—and it is for a thing like this that she must
break her heart, forsooth—for a man who is stupid—
a coxcomb—and who does not care for her. My poor good
Rawdon is worth ten of this creature.' And then she fell
to thinking what she should do if—if anything happened
to poor good Rawdon, and what a great piece of luck it
was that he had left his horses behind.

In the course of this day, too, Mrs. Crawley, who saw
not without anger the Bareacres party drive off, bethought
her of the precaution which the countess had taken, and
did a little needlework for her own advantage ; she stitched
away the major part of her trinkets, bills, and bank-notes
about her person, and so prepared, was ready for any event
—to fly if she thought fit, or to stay and welcome the
conqueror, were he Englishman or Frenchman.   And I am
not sure that she did not dream that night of becoming
a duchess and madame la maréchale, while Rawdon wrapped
in his cloak, and making his bivouac under the rain at
Mount St. John,* was thinking, with all the force of his
heart, about the little wife whom he had left behind him.

The next day was a Sunday.   And Mrs. Major O'Dowd
had the satisfaction of seeing both her patients refreshed
in health and spirits by some rest which they had taken
during the night.   She herself had slept on a great chair
in Amelia's room, ready to wait upon her poor friend or
the ensign, should either need her nursing.   When morning
came, this robust woman went back to the house where
she and her major had their billet ;   and here performed
an elaborate and splendid toilette, befitting the day.   And
it is very possible that whilst alone in that chamber, which
her husband had inhabited, and where his cap still lay on
the pillow, and his cane stood in the corner, one prayer
at least was sent up to Heaven for the welfare of the brave
soldier Michael O'Dowd.

When she returned she brought her Prayer-book with
her, and her uncle the dean's famous book of sermons,
out of which she never failed to read every Sabbath ;   not
understanding all, haply, not pronouncing many of the
words aright, which were long and abstruse—for the dean
was a learned man, and loved long Latin words—but with
great gravity, vast emphasis, and with tolerable correctness
in the main.   How often has my Mick listened to these
sermons, she thought, and me reading in the cabin of a calm !
She proposed to resume this exercise on the present day,
with Amelia and the wounded ensign for a congregation.
The same service was read on that day in twenty thousand
churches at the same hour ;   and millions of British men
and women, on their knees, implored protection of the
Father of all.

They did not hear the noise which disturbed our little

congregation at Brussels. Much louder than that which
had interrupted them two days previously, as Mrs. O'Dowd
*was reading the service in her best voice, the cannon of
Waterloo began to roar.

When Jos heard that dreadful sound, he made up his
mind that he would bear this perpetual recurrence of
terrors no longer, and would fly at once. He rushed into
the sick man's room, where our three friends had paused
in their prayers, and further interrupted them by a passionate appeal to Amelia.

' I can't stand it any more, Emmy,' he said ; ' I won't
stand it ; and you must come with me. I have bought
a horse for you—never mind at what price—and you must
dress and come with me, and ride behind Isidor.'

' God forgive me, Mr. Sedley, but you are no better than
a coward,' Mrs. O'Dowd said, laying down the book.

' I say come, Amelia,' the civilian went on ; ' never mind
what she says ; why are we to stop here and be butchered
by the Frenchmen ? '

' You forget the —th, my boy,' said the little Stubble,
the wounded hero from his bed—' and—and you won't
leave me, will you, Mrs. O'Dowd ? '

' No, my dear fellow,' said she, going up and kissing the
boy. ' No harm shall come to you while I stand by.
I don't budge till I get the word from Mick. A pretty
figure I'd be, wouldn't I, stuck behind that chap on a
pillion ? '

This image caused the young patient to burst out laughing
in his bed, and even made Amelia smile. ' I don't ask
her,' Jos shouted out—' I don't ask that—that Irishwoman,
but you, Amelia ; once for all, will you come ? '

' Without my husband, Joseph ? ' Amelia said, with
a look of wonder, and gave her hand to the major's wife.
Jos's patience was exhausted.

' Good-bye, then,' he said, shaking his fist in a rage, and
slamming the door by which he retreated. And this time
he really gave his order for march : and mounted in the
courtyard. Mrs. O'Dowd heard the clattering hoofs of
the horses as they issued from the gate ; and looking on,
made many scornful remarks on poor Joseph as he rode
down the street with Isidor after him in the laced cap.
The horses, which had not been exercised for some days,
were lively, and sprang about the street. Jos, a clumsy

MR. JOS SHAVES OFF HIS MOUSTACHIOS

and timid horseman, did not look to advantage in the saddle. ' Look at him, Amelia dear, driving into the parlour window. Such a bull in a china-shop *I* never saw.' And presently the pair of riders disappeared at a canter down the street leading in the direction of the Ghent road, Mrs. O'Dowd pursuing them with a fire of sarcasm so long as they were in sight.

All that day from morning until past sunset, the cannon never ceased to roar. It was dark when the cannonading stopped all of a sudden.

All of us have read of what occurred during that interval. The tale is in every Englishman's mouth; and you and I, who were children when the great battle was won and lost, are never tired of hearing and recounting the history of that famous action. Its remembrance rankles still in the bosoms of millions of the countrymen of those brave men who lost the day. They pant for an opportunity of revenging that humiliation; and if a contest, ending in a victory on their part, should ensue, elating them in their turn, and leaving its cursed legacy of hatred and rage behind to us, there is no end to the so-called glory and shame, and to the alternations of successful and unsuccessful murder, in which two high-spirited nations might engage. Centuries hence, we Frenchmen and Englishmen might be boasting and killing each other still, carrying out bravely the Devil's code of honour.

All our friends took their share and fought like men in the great field. All day long, whilst the women were praying ten miles away, the lines of the dauntless English infantry were receiving and repelling the furious charges of the French horsemen. Guns which were heard at Brussels were ploughing up their ranks, and comrades falling, and the resolute survivors closing in. Towards evening, the attack of the French, repeated and resisted so bravely, slackened in its fury. They had other foes besides the British to engage, or were preparing for a final onset. It came at last : the columns of the Imperial Guard marched up the hill of St. Jean, at length and at once to sweep the English from the height which they had maintained all day, and spite of all : unscared by the thunder of the artillery, which hurled death from the English line—the dark rolling column pressed on and up the hill. It seemed almost to crest the eminence, when it began to wave and

falter. Then it stopped, still facing the shot. Then at
last the English troops rushed from the post from which
no enemy had been able to dislodge them, and the Guard
turned and fled.

No more firing was heard at Brussels—the pursuit rolled
miles away. Darkness came down on the field and city:*
and Amelia was praying for George, who was lying on his
face, dead, with a bullet through his heart.

CHAPTER XXXIII

IN WHICH MISS CRAWLEY'S RELATIONS ARE VERY ANXIOUS ABOUT HER

THE kind reader must please to
remember—while the army is
marching from Flanders, and,
after its heroic actions there,
is advancing to take the forti-
fications on the frontiers of
France, previous to an occupation of that country—that
there are a number of persons
living peaceably in England
who have to do with the history
at present in hand, and must
come in for their share of the
chronicle. During the time of these battles and dangers, old
Miss Crawley was living at Brighton, very moderately
moved by the great events that were going on. The great
events rendered the newspapers rather interesting, to be
sure, and Briggs read out the *Gazette*, in which Rawdon
Crawley's gallantry was mentioned with honour, and his
promotion was presently recorded.

'What a pity that young man has taken such an irretrievable step in the world!' his aunt said; 'with his rank
and distinction he might have married a brewer's daughter
with a quarter of a million—like Miss Grains; or have
looked to ally himself with the best families in England.
He would have had my money some day or other; or his
children would—for I'm not in a hurry to go, Miss Briggs,

although you may be in a hurry to be rid of me; and
instead of that, he is a doomed pauper, with a dancing-
girl for a wife.'

'Will my dear Miss Crawley not cast an eye of compassion upon the heroic soldier, whose name is inscribed
in the annals of his country's glory?' said Miss Briggs,
who was greatly excited by the Waterloo proceedings,
and loved speaking romantically when there was an occasion.
'Has not the captain—or the colonel as I may now style
him—done deeds which make the name of Crawley
illustrious?'

'Briggs, you are a fool,' said Miss Crawley: 'Colonel
Crawley has dragged the name of Crawley through the
mud, Miss Briggs. Marry a drawing-master's daughter
indeed!—marry a *dame de compagnie*—for she was no
better, Briggs; no, she was just what you are—only
younger, and a great deal prettier and cleverer. Were
you an accomplice of that abandoned wretch, I wonder,
of whose vile arts he became a victim, and of whom you
used to be such an admirer? Yes, I dare say you were
an accomplice. But you will find yourself disappointed in
my will, I can tell you: and you will have the goodness to
write to Mr. Waxy, and say that I desire to see him immediately.' Miss Crawley was now in the habit of writing
to Mr. Waxy her solicitor almost every day in the week,
for her arrangements respecting her property were all
revoked, and her perplexity was great as to the future
disposition of her money.

The spinster had, however, rallied considerably; as
was proved by the increased vigour and frequency of her
sarcasms upon Miss Briggs, all which attacks the poor
companion bore with meekness, with cowardice, with
a resignation that was half generous and half hypocritical
—with the slavish submission, in a word, that women of
her disposition and station are compelled to show. Who has
not seen how women bully women? What tortures have
men to endure, comparable to those daily-repeated shafts
of scorn and cruelty with which poor women are riddled
by the tyrants of their sex? Poor victims! But we are
starting from our proposition, which is, that Miss Crawley
was always particularly annoying and savage when she
was rallying from illness—as they say wounds tingle most
when they are about to heal.

While thus approaching, as all hoped, to convalescence, Miss Briggs was the only victim admitted into the presence of the invalid ; yet Miss Crawley's relatives afar off did not forget their beloved kinswoman, and by a number of tokens, presents, and kind affectionate messages, strove to keep themselves alive in her recollection.

In the first place, let us mention her nephew, Rawdon Crawley. A few weeks after the famous fight of Waterloo, and after the *Gazette* had made known to her the promotion and gallantry of that distinguished officer, the Dieppe packet brought over to Miss Crawley at Brighton, a box containing presents, and a dutiful letter, from the colonel, her nephew. In the box were a pair of French epaulets, a Cross of the Legion of Honour, and the hilt of a sword—relics from the field of battle : and the letter described with a good deal of humour how the latter belonged to a commanding-officer of the Guard, who having sworn that ' the Guard died but never surrendered ', was taken prisoner the next minute by a private soldier, who broke the Frenchman's sword with the butt of his musket, when Rawdon made himself master of the shattered weapon. As for the cross and epaulets they came from a colonel of French cavalry, who had fallen under the aide de camp's arm in the battle : and Rawdon Crawley did not know what better to do with the spoils than to send them to his kindest and most affectionate old friend. Should he continue to write to her from Paris, whither the army was marching ?* He might be able to give her interesting news from that capital, and of some of Miss Crawley's old friends of the emigration, to whom she had shown so much kindness during their distress.

The spinster caused Briggs to write back to the colonel a gracious and complimentary letter, encouraging him to continue his correspondence. His first letter was so excessively lively and amusing that she should look with pleasure for its successors. ' Of course, I know,' she explained to Miss Briggs, ' that Rawdon could not write such a good letter any more than you could, my poor Briggs, and that it is that clever little wretch of a Rebecca, who dictates every word to him ; but that is no reason why my nephew should not amuse me ; and so I wish to let him understand that I am in high good humour.'

I wonder whether she knew that it was not only Becky

who wrote the letters, but that Mrs. Rawdon actually took and sent home the trophies—which she bought for a few francs, from one of the innumerable pedlars who immediately began to deal in relics of the war. The novelist, who knows everything, knows this also. Be this, however, as it may, Miss Crawley's gracious reply greatly encouraged our young friends, Rawdon and his lady, who hoped for the best from their aunt's evidently pacified humour : and they took care to entertain her with many delightful letters from Paris, whither, as Rawdon said, they had the good luck to go in the track of the conquering army.

To the rector's lady, who went off to tend her husband's broken collar-bone at the Rectory at Queen's Crawley, the spinster's communications were by no means so gracious. Mrs. Bute, that brisk, managing, lively, imperious woman, had committed the most fatal of all errors with regard to her sister-in-law. She had not merely oppressed her and her household—she had bored Miss Crawley ; and if poor Miss Briggs had been a woman of any spirit, she might have been made happy by the commission which her principal gave her to write a letter to Mrs. Bute Crawley, saying that Miss Crawley's health was greatly improved since Mrs. Bute had left her, and begging the latter on no account to put herself to trouble, or quit her family for Miss Crawley's sake. This triumph over a lady who had been very haughty and cruel in her behaviour to Miss Briggs, would have rejoiced most women ; but the truth is, Briggs was a woman of no spirit at all, and the moment her enemy was discomfited, she began to feel compassion in her favour.

' How silly I was,' Mrs. Bute thought, and with reason, ' ever to hint that I was coming, as I did, in that foolish letter when we sent Miss Crawley the guinea-fowls. I ought to have gone without a word to the poor dear doting old creature, and taken her out of the hands of that ninny Briggs, and that harpy of a *femme de chambre*. Oh ! Bute, Bute, why did you break your collar-bone ? '

Why, indeed ? We have seen how Mrs. Bute, having the game in her hands, had really played her cards too well. She had ruled over Miss Crawley's household utterly and completely, to be utterly and completely routed when a favourable opportunity for rebellion came. She and her household, however, considered that she had been the

victim of horrible selfishness and treason, and that her
sacrifices in Miss Crawley's behalf had met with the most
savage ingratitude.   Rawdon's promotion, and the honour-
able.mention made of his name in the *Gazette*, filled this
good Christian lady also with alarm.   Would his aunt
relent towards him now that he was a lieutenant-colonel
and a C.B. ? and would that odious Rebecca once more
get into favour ?   The rector's wife wrote a sermon for her
husband about the vanity of military glory and the prosperity of the wicked, which the worthy parson read in his
best voice and without understanding one syllable of it.
He had Pitt Crawley for one of his auditors—Pitt, who
had come with his two half-sisters to church, which
the old baronet could now by no means be brought to
frequent.

Since the departure of Becky Sharp, that old wretch had
given himself up entirely to his bad courses, to the great
scandal of the county and the mute horror of his son.
The ribbons in Miss Horrocks's cap became more splendid
than ever.   The polite families fled the Hall and its owner
in terror.   Sir Pitt went about tippling at his tenants'
houses ; and drank rum-and-water with the farmers at
Mudbury and the neighbouring places on market-days.
He drove the family coach-and-four to Southampton with
Miss Horrocks inside : and the county people expected,
every week, as his son did in speechless agony, that his
marriage with her would be announced in the provincial
paper.   It was indeed a rude burden for Mr. Crawley to
bear.   His eloquence was palsied at the missionary meetings,
and other religious assemblies in the neighbourhood, where
he had been in the habit of presiding, and of speaking for
hours ; for he felt, when he rose, that the audience said,
' That is the son of the old reprobate Sir Pitt, who is very
likely drinking at the public-house at this very moment.'
And once, when he was speaking of the benighted condition
of the King of Timbuctoo, and the number of his wives who
were likewise in darkness, some tipsy miscreant from the
crowd asked, ' How many is there at Queen's Crawley, Young
Squaretoes ? ' to the surprise of the platform, and the
ruin of Mr. Pitt's speech.   And the two daughters of the
house of Queen's Crawley would have been allowed to run
utterly wild (for Sir Pitt swore that no governess should
ever enter into his doors again), had not Mr. Crawley, by

threatening the old gentleman, forced the latter to send them to school.

Meanwhile, as we have said, whatever individual differences there might be between them all, Miss Crawley's dear nephews and nieces were unanimous in loving her and sending her tokens of affection. Thus Mrs. Bute sent guinea-fowls, and some remarkably fine cauliflowers, and a pretty purse or pincushion worked by her darling girls, who begged to keep a *little* place in the recollection of their dear aunt, while Mr. Pitt sent peaches and grapes and venison from the Hall. The Southampton coach used to carry these tokens of affection to Miss Crawley at Brighton : it used sometimes to convey Mr. Pitt thither too : for his differences with Sir Pitt caused Mr. Crawley to absent himself a good deal from home now : and besides, he had an attraction at Brighton in the person of the Lady Jane Sheepshanks, whose engagement to Mr. Crawley has been formerly mentioned in this history. Her ladyship and her sisters lived at Brighton with their mamma, the Countess Southdown, that strong-minded woman so favourably known in the serious world.

A few words ought to be said regarding her ladyship and her noble family, who are bound by ties of present and future relationship to the house of Crawley. Respecting the chief of the Southdown family, Clement William, fourth Earl of Southdown, little need be told, except that his lordship came into Parliament (as Lord Wolsey) under the auspices of Mr. Wilberforce, and for a time was a credit to his political sponsor, and decidedly a serious young man. But words cannot describe the feelings of his admirable mother, when she learned, very shortly after her noble husband's demise, that her son was a member of several worldly clubs, had lost largely at play at Wattier's and the 'Cocoa-Tree' ; that he had raised money on post-obits, and encumbered the family estate ; that he drove four-in-hand, and patronized the ring ; and that he actually had an opera-box, where he entertained the most dangerous bachelor company. His name was only mentioned with groans in the dowager's circle.

The Lady Emily was her brother's senior by many years; and took considerable rank in the serious world as author of some of the delightful tracts before-mentioned, and of many hymns and spiritual pieces. A mature spinster,

and having but faint ideas*of marriage, her love for the
blacks occupied almost all her feelings. It is to her, I
believe, we owe that beautiful poem—

> Lead us to some sunny isle,
> Yonder in the western deep ;
> Where the skies for ever smile,
> And the blacks for ever weep, &c.*

She had correspondences with clerical gentlemen in most
of our East and West India possessions ; and was secretly
attached to the Reverend Silas Hornblower, who was
tattooed in the South Sea Islands.

As for the Lady Jane, on whom, as it has been said,
Mr. Pitt Crawley's affection had been placed, she was
gentle, blushing, silent, and timid. In spite of his falling
away, she wept for her brother, and was quite ashamed
of loving him still. Even yet she used to send him little
hurried smuggled notes, and pop them in the post in
private. The one dreadful secret which weighed upon her
life was, that she and the old housekeeper had been to pay
Southdown a furtive visit at his chambers in the Albany;*
and found him—Oh, the naughty dear abandoned wretch !
—smoking a cigar with a bottle of curaçao before him.
She admired her sister, she adored her mother, she thought
Mr. Crawley the most delightful and accomplished of
men, after Southdown, that fallen angel : and her mamma
and sister, who were ladies of the most superior sort, managed everything for her, and regarded her with that amiable
pity, of which your really superior woman always has such
a share to give away. Her mamma ordered her dresses,
her books, her bonnets, and her ideas for her. She was
made to take pony-riding, or piano-exercise, or any other
sort of bodily medicament, according as my Lady Southdown
saw meet ; and her ladyship would have kept her daughter
in pinafores up to her present age of six-and-twenty, but
that they were thrown off when Lady Jane was presented
to Queen Charlotte.*

When these ladies first came to their house at Brighton,
it was to them alone that Mr. Crawley paid his personal
visits, contenting himself by leaving a card at his aunt's
house, and making a modest inquiry of Mr. Bowls or his
assistant footman, with respect to the health of the invalid.
When he met Miss Briggs coming home from the library

with a cargo of novels under her arm, Mr. Crawley blushed
in a manner quite unusual to him, as he stepped forward
and shook Miss Crawley's companion by the hand. He
introduced Miss Briggs to the lady with whom he happened
to be walking, the Lady Jane Sheepshanks, saying, ' Lady
Jane, permit me to introduce to you my aunt's kindest
friend and most affectionate companion, Miss Briggs, whom
you know under another title, as authoress of the delightful

Lyrics of the Heart, of which you are so fond.' Lady Jane
blushed too as she held out a kind little hand to Miss
Briggs, and said something very civil and incoherent about
mamma, and proposing to call on Miss Crawley, and being
glad to be made known to the friends and relatives of
Mr. Crawley ; and with soft dove-like eyes saluted Miss
Briggs as they separated, while Pitt Crawley treated her
to a profound courtly bow, such as he had used to H.H. the
Duchess of Pumpernickel, when he was attaché at that
court.

The artful diplomatist and disciple of the Machiavellian Binkie ! It was he who had given Lady Jane that copy of poor Briggs's early poems, which he remembered to have seen at Queen's Crawley, with a dedication from the poetess to his father's late wife ; and he brought the volume with him to Brighton, reading it in the Southampton coach and marking it with his own pencil, before he presented it to the gentle Lady Jane.

It was he, too, who laid before Lady Southdown the great advantages which might occur from an intimacy between her family and Miss Crawley,—advantages both worldly and spiritual, he said : for Miss Crawley was now quite alone ; the monstrous dissipation and alliance of his brother Rawdon had estranged her affections from that reprobate young man ; the greedy tyranny and avarice of Mrs. Bute Crawley had caused the old lady to revolt against the exorbitant pretensions of that part of the family ; and though he himself had held off all his life from cultivating Miss Crawley's friendship, with perhaps an improper pride, he thought now that every becoming means should be taken, both to save her soul from perdition, and to secure her fortune to himself as the head of the house of Crawley.

The strong-minded Lady Southdown quite agreed in both proposals of her son-in-law, and was for converting Miss Crawley off-hand. At her own home, both at Southdown and at Trottermore Castle, this tall and awful missionary of the truth rode about the country in her barouche with outriders, launched packets of tracts among the cottagers and tenants, and would order Gaffer Jones to be converted, as she would order Goody Hicks to take a James's powder,* without appeal, resistance, or benefit of clergy. My Lord Southdown, her late husband, an epileptic and simple-minded nobleman, was in the habit of approving of everything which his Matilda did and thought. So that whatever changes her own belief might undergo (and it accommodated itself to a prodigious variety of opinion, taken from all sorts of doctors among the Dissenters) she had not the least scruple in ordering all her tenants and inferiors to follow and believe after her. Thus, whether she received the Reverend Saunders McNitre, the Scotch divine ; or the Reverend Luke Waters, the mild Wesleyan ; or the Reverend Giles Jowls, the illu-

minated cobbler, who dubbed himself reverend as Napoleon
crowned himself emperor—the household, children, tenantry of my Lady Southdown were expected to go down
on their knees with her ladyship, and say Amen to the
prayers of either doctor.   During these exercises old Southdown, on account of his invalid condition, was allowed
to sit in his own room, and have negus and the paper read
to him.   Lady Jane was the old earl's favourite daughter,
and tended him and loved him sincerely : as for Lady
Emily, the authoress of the *Washerwoman of Finchley
Common*, her denunciation of future punishments (at this
period, for her opinions modified afterwards) were so
awful that they used to frighten the timid old gentleman
her father, and the physicians declared his fits always
occurred after one of her ladyship's sermons.

' I will certainly call,' said Lady Southdown then, in
reply to the exhortation of her daughter's *prétendu*, Mr.
Pitt Crawley—' Who is Miss Crawley's medical man ? '

Mr. Crawley mentioned the name of Mr. Creamer.

' A most dangerous and ignorant practitioner, my dear
Pitt.   I have providentially been the means of removing
him from several houses ; though in one or two instances
I did not arrive in time.   I could not save poor dear General
Glanders, who was dying under the hands of that ignorant
man—dying.   He rallied a little under the Podgers pills
which I administered to him ; but alas ! it was too late.
His death was delightful, however ; and his change was
only for the better : Creamer, my dear Pitt, must leave
your aunt.'

Pitt expressed his perfect acquiescence.   He, too, had
been carried along by the energy of his noble kinswoman,
and future mother-in law.   He had been made to accept
Saunders McNitre, Luke Waters, Giles Jowls, Podgers's Pills,
Rodgers's Pills, Pokey's Elixir, every one of her ladyship's
remedies spiritual or temporal.   He never left her house
without carrying respectfully away with him piles of her
quack theology and medicine.   Oh, my dear brethren and
fellow-sojourners in Vanity Fair, which among you does not
know and suffer under such benevolent despots ?   It is in
vain you say to them, ' Dear madam, I took Podger's speci-
fic at your orders last year, and believe in it.   Why, why,
am I to recant and accept the Rodgers's articles now ? '
There is no help for it ; the faithful proselytizer, if she

cannot convince by argument, bursts into tears, and the recusant finds himself, at the end of the contest, taking down the bolus, and saying, ' Well, well, Rodger's be it.'

' And as for her spiritual state,' continued the lady, ' that of course must be looked to immediately ; with Creamer about her, she may go off any day : and in what a condition, my dear Pitt, in what a dreadful condition ! I will send the Reverend Mr. Irons to her instantly. Jane, write a line to the Reverend Bartholomew Irons, in the third person, and say that I desire the pleasure of his company this evening at tea at half-past six. He is an awakening man ; he ought to see Miss Crawley before she rests this night. And Emily, my love, get ready a packet of books for Miss Crawley. Put up *A Voice from the Flames, A Trumpet-warning to Jericho,* and the *Fleshpots Broken ; or, the Converted Cannibal.*'

' And the *Washerwoman of Finchley Common,* mamma,' said Lady Emily. ' It is as well to begin soothingly at first.'

' Stop, my dear ladies,' said Pitt the diplomatist. ' With every deference to the opinion of my beloved and respected Lady Southdown, I think it would be quite unadvisable to commence so early upon serious topics with Miss Crawley. Remember her delicate condition, and how little, how *very* little accustomed she has hitherto been to considerations connected with her immortal welfare.'

' Can we then begin too early, Pitt ? ' said Lady Emily, rising with six little books already in her hand.

' If you begin abruptly, you will frighten her altogether. I know my aunt's worldly nature so well as to be sure that any abrupt attempt at conversion will be the very worst means that can be employed for the welfare of that unfortunate lady. You will only frighten and annoy her. She will very likely fling the books away, and refuse all acquaintance with the givers.'

' You are as worldly as Miss Crawley, Pitt,' said Lady Emily, tossing out of the room, her books in her hand.

' And I need not tell you, my dear Lady Southdown,' Pitt continued, in a low voice, and without heeding the interruption, 'how fatal a little want of gentleness and caution may be to any hopes which we may entertain with regard to the worldly possessions of my aunt. Remember she has seventy thousand pounds ; think of her age, and her highly nervous and delicate condition ; I know that she has destroyed the

will which was made in my brother's (Colonel Crawley's)
favour : it is by soothing that wounded spirit that we must
lead it into the right path, and not by frightening it ; and
so I think you will agree with me that—that——'

' Of course, of course,' Lady Southdown remarked.
' Jane, my love, you need not send that note to Mr. Irons.
If her health is such that discussions fatigue her, we will
wait her amendment. I will call upon Miss Crawley to-
morrow.'

' And if I might suggest, my sweet lady,' Pitt said in a
bland tone, ' it would be as well not to take our precious
Emily, who is too enthusiastic ; but rather that you should
be accompanied by our sweet and dear Lady Jane.'

' Most certainly, Emily would ruin everything,' Lady
Southdown said ; and this time agreed to forgo her usual
practice, which was, as we have said, before she bore down
personally upon any individual whom she proposed to
subjugate, to fire in a quantity of tracts upon the menaced
party (as a charge of the French was always preceded by
a furious cannonade). Lady Southdown, we say, for the
sake of the invalid's health, or for the sake of her soul's
ultimate welfare, or for the sake of her money, agreed to
temporize.

The next day the great Southdown female family carriage,
with the earl's coronet and the lozenge (upon which the
three lambs trottant argent upon the field vert of the South-
downs, were quartered with sable on a bend or, three snuff-
mulls gules,* the cognizance of the house of Binkie), drove
up in state to Miss Crawley's door, and the tall serious footman handed in to Mr. Bowls her ladyship's cards for Miss
Crawley, and one likewise for Miss Briggs. By way of
compromise Lady Emily sent in a packet in the evening for
the latter lady, containing copies of the *Washerwoman*, and
other mild and favourite tracts for Miss B.'s own perusal ;
and a few for the servants' hall, viz. : *Crumbs from the
Pantry*, *The Frying-Pan and the Fire*, and *The Livery of Sin*,
of a much stronger kind.

CHAPTER XXXIV

JAMES CRAWLEY'S PIPE IS PUT OUT

THE amiable behaviour of Mr. Crawley, and Lady Jane's kind reception of her, highly flattered Miss Briggs, who was enabled to speak a good word for the latter, after the cards of the Southdown family had been presented to Miss Crawley. A countess's card left personally too for her, Briggs, was not a little pleasing to the poor friendless companion. 'What could Lady Southdown mean by leaving a card upon *you*, I wonder, Miss Briggs ? ' said the republican Miss Crawley ; upon which the companion meekly said ' that she hoped there could be no harm in a lady of rank taking notice of a poor gentlewoman ', and she put away this card in her work-box amongst her most cherished personal treasures. Furthermore, Miss Briggs explained how she had met Mr. Crawley walking with his cousin and long-affianced bride the day before : and she told how kind and gentle-looking the lady was, and what a plain, not to say common, dress she had, all the articles of which, from the bonnet down to the boots, she described and estimated with female accuracy.

Miss Crawley allowed Briggs to prattle on without interrupting her too much. As she got well, she was pining for society. Mr. Creamer, her medical man, would not hear of her returning to her old haunts and dissipation in London. The old spinster was too glad to find any companionship at Brighton, and not only were the cards acknowledged the very next day, but Pitt Crawley was graciously invited to come and see his aunt. He came, bringing with him Lady Southdown and her daughter. The dowager did not say a word about the state of Miss Crawley's soul ; but talked with much discretion about the weather : about the war and the downfall of the monster Bonaparte : and above all, about doctors, quacks, and the particular merits of Dr. Podgers, whom she then patronized.

During their interview Pitt Crawley made a great stroke, and one which showed that, had his diplomatic career not been blighted by early neglect, he might have risen to a high rank in his profession. When the Countess Dowager of Southdown fell foul of the Corsican upstart, as the fashion was in those days, and showed that he was a monster stained with every conceivable crime, a coward and a tyrant not fit to live, one whose fall was predicted, &c., Pitt Crawley suddenly took up the cudgels in favour of the man of Destiny. He described the First Consul as he saw him at Paris at the Peace of Amiens ; when he, Pitt Crawley, had the gratification of making the acquaintance of the great and good Mr. Fox, a statesman whom, however much he might differ with him, it was impossible not to admire fervently— a statesman who had always had the highest opinion of the Emperor Napoleon.* And he spoke in terms of the strongest indignation of the faithless conduct of the allies towards this dethroned monarch, who, after giving himself generously up to their mercy, was consigned to an ignoble and cruel banishment, while a bigoted Popish rabble was tyrannizing over France in his stead.

This orthodox horror of Romish superstition saved Pitt Crawley in Lady Southdown's opinion, whilst his admiration for Fox and Napoleon raised him immeasurably in Miss Crawley's eyes. Her friendship with that defunct British statesman was mentioned when we first introduced her in this history. A true Whig, Miss Crawley had been in opposition all through the war, and though, to be sure, the downfall of the emperor did not very much agitate the old lady, or his ill-treatment tend to shorten her life or natural rest, yet Pitt spoke to her heart when he lauded both her idols ; and by that single speech made immense progress in her favour.

' And what do you think, my dear ? ' Miss Crawley said to the young lady, for whom she had taken a liking at first sight, as she always did for pretty and modest young people ; though it must be owned her affections cooled as rapidly as they rose.

Lady Jane blushed very much, and said, ' that she did not understand politics, which she left to wiser heads than hers ; but though mamma was, no doubt, correct, Mr. Crawley had spoken beautifully.' And when the ladies were retiring at the conclusion of their visit, Miss Crawley hoped

Lady Southdown would be so kind as to send her Lady
Jane sometimes, if she could be spared to come down and
console a poor sick lonely old woman.' This promise was
graciously accorded, and they separated upon great terms
of amity.

'Don't let Lady Southdown come again, Pitt,' said the old
lady. ' She is stupid and pompous like all your mother's
family, whom I never could endure. But bring that nice
good-natured little Lady Jane as often as ever you please.'
Pitt promised that he would do so. He did not tell the
Countess of Southdown what opinion his aunt had formed
of her ladyship, who, on the contrary, thought that she had
made a most delightful and majestic impression on Miss
Crawley.

And so, nothing loath to comfort a sick lady, and perhaps
not sorry in her heart to be freed now and again from the
dreary spouting of the Reverend Bartholomew Irons, and
the serious toadies who gathered round the footstool of the
pompous countess, her mamma, Lady Jane became a
pretty constant visitor to Miss Crawley, accompanied her
in her drives, and solaced many of her evenings. She was
so naturally good and soft, that even Firkin was not jealous
of her ; and the gentle Briggs thought her friend was less
cruel to her, when kind Lady Jane was by. Towards her
ladyship Miss Crawley's manners were charming. The old
spinster told her a thousand anecdotes about her youth,
talking to her in a very different strain from that in which
she had been accustomed to converse with the godless little
Rebecca ; for there was that in Lady Jane's innocence
which rendered light talking impertinence before her, and
Miss Crawley was too much of a gentlewoman to offend such
purity. The young lady herself had never received kindness
except from this old spinster, and her brother and father :
and she repaid Miss Crawley's *engouement* by artless sweetness
and friendship.

In the autumn evenings (when Rebecca was flaunting at
Paris, the gayest among the gay conquerors there, and our
Amelia, our dear wounded Amelia, ah ! where was she ?)
Lady Jane would be sitting in Miss Crawley's drawing-
room singing sweetly to her, in the twilight, her little
simple songs and hymns, while the sun was setting and the
sea was roaring on the beach. The old spinster used to
wake up when these ditties ceased, and ask for more. As

for Briggs, and the quantity of tears of happiness which
she now shed as she pretended to knit, and looked out at
the splendid ocean darkling before the windows, and the
lamps of heaven beginning more brightly to shine—who, I
say, can measure the happiness and sensibility of Briggs ?

Pitt meanwhile in the dining-room, with a pamphlet of
the Corn Laws or a Missionary Register by his side, took
that kind of recreation which suits romantic and unromantic
men after dinner.   He sipped madeira :   built castles in the
air :   thought himself a fine fellow :   felt himself much more
in love with Jane than he had been any time these seven
years, during which their *liaison* had lasted without the
slightest impatience on Pitt's part—and slept a good deal.
When the time for coffee came, Mr. Bowls used to enter
in a noisy manner, and summon Squire Pitt, who would be
found in the dark very busy with his pamphlet.

' I wish, my love, I could get somebody to play piquet
with me,' Miss Crawley said, one night, when this functionary made his appearance with the candles and the coffee.
' Poor Briggs can no more play than an owl, she is so stupid '
(the spinster always took an opportunity of abusing Briggs
before the servants) ;   ' and I think I should sleep better if
I had my game.'

At this Lady Jane blushed to the tips of her little ears,
and down to the ends of her pretty fingers ;   and when
Mr. Bowls had quitted the room, and the door was quite
shut, she said :

' Miss Crawley, I can play a little.   I used to—to play
a little with poor dear papa.'

' Come and kiss me.   Come and kiss me this instant, you
dear good little soul,' cried Miss Crawley in an ecstasy :
and in this picturesque and friendly occupation Mr. Pitt
found the old lady and the young one, when he came upstairs with his pamphlet in his hand.   How she did blush
all the evening, that poor Lady Jane !

It must not be imagined that Mr. Pitt Crawley's artifices
escaped the attention of his dear relations at the Rectory
at Queen's Crawley.   Hampshire and Sussex lie very close
together, and Mrs. Bute had friends in the latter county who
took care to inform her of all, and a great deal more than all,
that passed at Miss Crawley's house at Brighton.   Pitt was
there more and more.   He did not come for months together

to the Hall, where his abominable old father abandoned himself completely to rum-and-water, and the odious society of the Horrocks family. Pitt's success rendered the rector's family furious, and Mrs. Bute regretted more (though she confessed less) than ever her monstrous fault in so insulting Miss Briggs, and in being so haughty and parsimonious to Bowls and Firkin, that she had not a single person left in Miss Crawley's household to give her information of what took place there. 'It was all Bute's collar-bone,' she persisted in saying ; 'if that had not broke, I never would have left her. I am a martyr to duty and to your odious unclerical habit of hunting, Bute.'

'Hunting ; nonsense ! It was you that frightened her, Barbara,' the divine interposed. 'You're a clever woman, but you've got a devil of a temper ; and you're a screw with your money, Barbara.'

'You'd have been screwed in gaol, Bute, if I had not kept your money.'

'I know I would, my dear,' said the rector, good-naturedly. 'You *are* a clever woman, but you manage too well, you know : ' and the pious man consoled himself with a big glass of port.

'What the deuce can she find in that spooney of a Pitt Crawley ?' he continued. 'The fellow has not pluck enough to say Bo to a goose. I remember when Rawdon, who *is* a man, and be hanged to him, used to flog him round the stables as if he was a whipping-top : and Pitt would go howling home to his ma—ha, ha ! Why, either of my boys would wap him with one hand. Jim says he's remembered at Oxford as Miss Crawley still—the spooney.

'I say, Barbara,' his reverence continued, after a pause.

'What !' said Barbara, who was biting her nails and drubbing the table.

'I say, why not send Jim over to Brighton to see if he can do anything with the old lady. He's very near getting his degree, you know. He's only been plucked twice—so was I—but he's had the advantages of Oxford and a university education. He knows some of the best chaps there. He pulls stroke in the Boniface boat. He's a handsome feller. D—it, ma'am, let's put him on the old woman, hey ; and tell him to thrash Pitt if he says anythink. Ha, ha, ha !'

'Jim might go down and see her, certainly,' the housewife

said, adding, with a sigh, ' If we could but get one of the
girls into the house ; but she could never endure them,
because they are not pretty ! ' Those unfortunate and well-
educated women made themselves heard from the neighbouring drawing-room, where they were thrumming away,
with hard fingers, an elaborate music-piece on the pianoforte, as their mother spoke ; and indeed they were at
music, or at backboard, or at geography, or at history, the
whole day long.   But what avail all these accomplishments,
in Vanity Fair, to girls who are short, poor, plain, and
have a bad complexion ? Mrs. Bute could think of nobody
but the curate to take one of them off her hands ; and Jim
coming in from the stable at this minute, through the
parlour window, with a short pipe stuck in his oilskin cap,
he and his father fell to talking about odds on the St. Leger,
and the colloquy between the rector and his wife ended.

Mrs. Bute did not augur much good to the cause from the
sending of her son James as an ambassador, and saw him
depart in rather a despairing mood.   Nor did the young
fellow himself, when told what his mission was to be,
expect much pleasure or benefit from it ; but he was consoled by the thought that possibly the old lady would give
him some handsome remembrance of her, which would pay
a few of his most pressing bills at the commencement of the
ensuing Oxford term, and so took his place by the coach
from Southampton, and was safely landed at Brighton on
the same evening, with his portmanteau, his favourite bulldog Towzer, and an immense basket of farm and garden
produce, from the dear Rectory folks to the dear Miss
Crawley.   Considering it was too late to disturb the invalid
lady on the first night of his arrival, he put up at an inn,
and did not wait upon Miss Crawley until a late hour in
the noon of next day.

James Crawley, when his aunt had last beheld him, was
a gawky lad, at that uncomfortable age when the voice
varies between an unearthly treble and a preternatural
bass ; when the face not uncommonly blooms out with
appearances for which Rowland's Kalydor is said to act as
a cure ; when boys are seen to shave furtively with their
sister's scissors, and the sight of other young women produces intolerable sensations of terror in them ; when the
great hands and ankles protrude a long way from garments
which have grown too tight for them ; when their presence

after dinner is at once frightful to the ladies, who are
whispering in the twilight in the drawing-room, and inexpressibly odious to the gentlemen over the mahogany, who
are restrained from freedom of intercourse and delightful
interchange of wit by the presence of that gawky innocence ;
when, at the conclusion of the second glass, papas say, 'Jack,
my boy, go out and see if the evening holds up,' and the
youth, willing to be free, yet hurt at not being yet a man,
quits the incomplete banquet.   James, then a hobbledehoy,
was now become a young man, having had the benefits of
a university education, and acquired the inestimable polish,
which is gained by living in a fast set at a small college, and
contracting debts, and being rusticated, and being plucked.

He was a handsome lad, however, when he came to
present himself to his aunt at Brighton, and good looks were
always a title to the fickle old lady's favour.   Nor did his
blushes and awkwardness take away from it : she was
pleased with these healthy tokens of the young gentleman's
ingenuousness.

He said ' he had come down for a couple of days to see
a man of his college, and—and to pay my respects to you,
ma'am, and my father's and mother's, who hope you are
well '.

Pitt was in the room with Miss Crawley when the lad was
announced, and looked very blank when his name was
mentioned.   The old lady had plenty of humour, and enjoyed
her correct nephew's perplexity.   She asked after all the
people at the Rectory with great interest ; and said she
was thinking of paying them a visit.   She praised the lad
to his face, and said he was well-grown and very much
improved, and that it was a pity his sisters had not some of
his good looks ; and finding, on inquiry, that he had taken
up his quarters at an hotel, would not hear of his stopping
there, but bade Mr. Bowls send for Mr. James Crawley's
things instantly ; ' and hark ye, Bowls,' she added, with
great graciousness, ' you will have the goodness to pay
Mr. James's bill.'

She flung Pitt a look of arch triumph, which caused that
diplomatist almost to choke with envy.   Much as he had
ingratiated himself with his aunt, she had never yet invited
him to stay under her roof, and here was a young whipper-
snapper, who at first sight was made welcome there.

' I beg your pardon, sir,' says Bowls, advancing with a

profound bow; ' what otel, sir, shall Thomas fetch the
luggage from ? '

' Oh, dam,' said young James, starting up, as if in some
alarm, ' I'll go.'

' What ! ' said Miss Crawley.

' The " Tom Cribb's Arms ",'*said James, blushing deeply.

Miss Crawley burst out laughing at this title. Mr. Bowls
gave one abrupt guffaw, as a confidential servant of the
family, but choked the rest of the volley ; the diplomatist
only smiled.

' I—I didn't know any better,' said James, looking down.
' I've never been here before ; it was the coachman told
me.' The young story-teller ! The fact is, that on the
Southampton coach, the day previous, James Crawley had
met the Tutbury Pet, who was coming to Brighton to make
a match with the Rottingdean Fibber ; and enchanted by
the Pet's conversation, had passed the evening in company
with that scientific man and his friends, at the inn in
question.

' I—I'd best go and settle the score,' James continued.
' Couldn't think of asking you, ma'am,' he added, generously.

This delicacy made his aunt laugh the more.

' Go and settle the bill, Bowls,' she said, with a wave of
her hand, ' and bring it to me.'

Poor lady, she did not know what she had done ! ' There
—there's a little *dawg*,' said James, looking frightfully
guilty. ' I'd best go for him. He bites footmen's calves.'

All the party cried out with laughing at this description ;
even Briggs and Lady Jane, who was sitting mute during
the interview between Miss Crawley and her nephew : ard
Bowls, without a word, quitted the room.

Still, by way of punishing her elder nephew, Miss Crawley
persisted in being gracious to the young Oxonian. There
were no limits to her kindness or her compliments when
they once began. She told Pitt he might come to dinner,
and insisted that James should accompany her in her
drive, and paraded him solemnly up and down the cliff, on
the back seat of the barouche. During all this excursion,
she condescended to say civil things to him : she quoted
Italian and French poetry to the poor bewildered lad, and
persisted that he was a fine scholar, and was perfectly sure
he would gain a gold medal, and be a Senior Wrangler.

' Haw, haw,' laughed James, encouraged by these compli-

ments ; ' Senior Wrangler, indeed ; that's at the other
shop.'

' What is the other shop, my dear child ? ' said the lady.

' Senior Wranglers at Cambridge, not Oxford,' said the
scholar, with a knowing air ; and would probably have been
more confidential, but that suddenly there appeared on the
cliff in a tax-cart,* drawn by a bang-up pony, dressed in
white flannel coats, with mother-of-pearl buttons, his friends
the Tutbury Pet and the Rottingdean Fibber, with three
other gentlemen of their acquaintance, who all saluted poor
James there in the carriage as he sat. This incident
damped the ingenuous youth's spirits, and no word of yea
or nay could he be induced to utter during the rest of the
drive.

On his return he found his room prepared, and his portmanteau ready, and might have remarked that Mr. Bowls's
countenance, when the latter conducted him to his apartment, wore a look of gravity, wonder, and compassion.
But the thought of Mr. Bowls did not enter his head. He
was deploring the dreadful predicament in which he found
himself, in a house full of old women, jabbering French and
Italian, and talking poetry to him. ' Reglarly up a tree,
by jingo ! ' exclaimed the modest boy, who could not face
the gentlest of her sex—not even Briggs—when she began
to talk to him ; whereas, put him at Iffley Lock, and he
could out-slang the boldest bargeman.

At dinner, James appeared choking in a white neckcloth,
and had the honour of handing my Lady Jane downstairs,
while Briggs and Mr. Crawley followed afterwards, conducting the old lady, with her apparatus of bundles, and shawls,
and cushions. Half of Briggs's time at dinner was spent in
superintending the invalid's comfort, and in cutting up
chicken for her fat spaniel. James did not talk much, but
he made a point of asking all the ladies to drink wine, and
accepted Mr. Crawley's challenge, and consumed the greater
part of a bottle of champagne which Mr. Bowls was ordered
to produce in his honour. The ladies having withdrawn,
and the two cousins being left together, Pitt, the ex-diplo-
matist, became very communicative and friendly. He
asked after James's career at college—what his prospects
in life were—hoped heartily he would get on ; and, in a
word, was frank and amiable. James's tongue unloosed
with the port, and he told his cousin his life, his prospects,

his debts, his troubles at the Little-go, and his rows with the proctors, filling rapidly from the bottles before him, and flying from port to madeira with joyous activity.

'The chief pleasure which my aunt has,' said Mr. Crawley, filling his glass, 'is that people should do as they like in her house. This is Liberty Hall, James, and you can't do Miss Crawley a greater kindness than to do as you please, and ask for what you will. I know you have all sneered at me in the country for being a Tory. Miss Crawley is liberal enough to suit any fancy. She is a Republican in principle, and despises everything like rank or title.'

'Why are you going to marry an earl's daughter ?' said James.

'My dear friend, remember it is not poor Lady Jane's fault that she is well born,' Pitt replied, with a courtly air. 'She cannot help being a lady. Besides, I am a Tory, you know.'

'Oh, as for that,' said Jim, 'there's nothing like old blood ; no, dammy, nothing like it. I'm none of your Radicals. I know what it is to be a gentleman, dammy. See the chaps in a boat-race ; look at the fellers in a fight ; aye, look at a dawg killing rats,—which is it wins ? the good blooded ones. Get some more port, Bowls, old boy, whilst I buzz this bottle* here. What was I a-saying ?'

'I think you were speaking of dogs killing rats,' Pitt remarked mildly, handing his cousin the decanter to 'buzz'.

'Killing rats was I ? Well, Pitt, are you a sporting man ? Do you want to see a dawg as *can* kill a rat ? If you do, come down with me to Tom Corduroy's, in Castle Street Mews, and I'll show you such a bull-terrier as——Pooh ! gammon,' cried James, bursting out laughing at his own absurdity,—'*you* don't care about a dawg or rat ; it's all nonsense. I'm blest if I think you know the difference between a dog and a duck.'

'No ; by the way,' Pitt continued with increased bland-ness, 'it was about blood you were talking, and the personal advantages which people derive from patrician birth. Here's the fresh bottle.'

'Blood's the word,' said James, gulping the ruby fluid down. 'Nothing like blood, sir, in hosses, dawgs, *and* men. Why, only last term, just before I was rusticated, that is, I mean just before I had the measles, ha, ha,—there was me and Ringwood of Christchurch, Bob Ringwood, Lord

Cinqbar's son, having our beer at the " Bell " at Blenheim,
when the Banbury bargeman offered to fight either of us
for a bowl of punch. I couldn't. My arm was in a sling ;
couldn't even take the drag down,—a brute of a mare of
mine had fell with me only two days before, out with the
Abingdon, and I thought my arm was broke. Well, sir,
I couldn't finish him, but Bob had his coat off at once—he
stood up to the Banbury man for three minutes, and polished
him off in four rounds easy. Gad, how he did drop, sir, and
what was it ? Blood, sir, all blood.'

' You don't drink, James,' the ex-attaché continued.
' In my time at Oxford, the men passed round the bottle
a little quicker than you young fellows seem to do.'

' Come, come,' said James, putting his hand to his nose
and winking at his cousin with a pair of vinous eyes, ' no
jokes, old boy ; no trying it on on me. You want to trot
me out, but it's no go. *In vino veritas*, old boy. Mars,
Bacchus, Apollo *virorum,** hey ? I wish my aunt would send
down some of this to the governor ; it's a precious good tap.'

' You had better ask her,' Machiavel continued, ' or make
the best of your time now. What says the bard, *Nunc
vino pellite curas Cras ingens iterabimus aequor,**and the
Bacchanalian, quoting the above with a House of Commons
air, tossed off nearly a thimbleful of wine with an immense
flourish of his glass.

At the Rectory, when the bottle of port wine was opened
after dinner, the young ladies had each a glass from a bottle
of currant wine. Mrs. Bute took one glass of port, honest
James had a couple commonly, but as his father grew very
sulky if he made further inroads on the bottle, the good lad
generally refrained from trying for more, and subsided
either into the currant wine, or to some private gin-and-
water in the stables, which he enjoyed in the company of
the coachman and his pipe. At Oxford, the quantity of
wine was unlimited, but the quality was inferior : but when
quantity and quality united, as at his aunt's house, James
showed that he could appreciate them indeed ; and hardly
needed any of his cousin's encouragement in draining off
the second bottle supplied by Mr. Bowls.

When the time for coffee came, however, and for a return
to the ladies, of whom he stood in awe, the young gentleman's agreeable frankness left him, and he relapsed into his
usual surly timidity : contenting himself by saying yes and

no, by scowling at Lady Jane, and by upsetting one cup of
coffee during the evening.

If he did not speak he yawned in a pitiable manner, and
his presence threw a damp upon the modest proceedings of
the evening, for Miss Crawley and Lady Jane at their piquet,
and Miss Briggs at her work, felt that his eyes were wildly
fixed on them, and were uneasy under that maudlin look.

' He seems a very silent, awkward, bashful lad,' said Miss
Crawley to Mr. Pitt.

' He is more communicative in men's society than with
ladies,' Machiavel drily replied : perhaps rather disappointed that the port wine had not made Jim speak more.

He had spent the early part of the next morning in writing
home to his mother a most flourishing account of his reception by Miss Crawley. But ah ! he little knew what evils
the day was bringing for him, and how short his reign of
favour was destined to be.   A circumstance which Jim had
forgotten—a trivial but fatal circumstance—had taken
place at the ' Cribb's Arms ' on the night before he had come
to his aunt's house. It was no other than this—Jim, who
was always of a generous disposition, and when in his cups
especially hospitable, had in the course of the night treated
the Tutbury champion and the Rottingdean man, and
their friends, twice or thrice to the refreshment of gin-and-
water—so that no less than eighteen glasses of that fluid at
eightpence per glass were charged in Mr. James Crawley's
bill.   It was not the amount of eightpences, but the
quantity of gin which told fatally against poor James's
character, when his aunt's butler, Mr. Bowls, went down
at his mistress's request to pay the young gentleman's bill.
The landlord, fearing lest the account should be refused
altogether, swore solemnly that the young gent had consumed personally every farthing's worth of the liquor : and
Bowls paid the bill finally, and showed it on his return home
to Mrs. Firkin, who was shocked at the frightful prodigality
of gin ; and took the bill to Miss Briggs as accountant-
general ; who thought it her duty to mention the circumstance to her principal, Miss Crawley.

Had he drunk a dozen bottles of claret the old spinster
could have pardoned him.   Mr. Fox and Mr. Sheridan
drank claret.* Gentlemen drank claret. But eighteen
glasses of gin consumed among boxers in an ignoble pot-
house—it was an odious crime and not to be pardoned

readily. Everything went against the lad : he came home
perfumed from the stables, whither he had been to pay his
dog Towzer a visit—and whence he was going to take his
friend out for an airing, when he met Miss Crawley and her
wheezy Blenheim spaniel, which Towzer would have eaten
up had not the Blenheim fled squealing to the protection of
Miss Briggs, while the atrocious master of the bulldog stood
laughing at the horrible persecution.

This day too the unlucky boy's modesty had likewise
forsaken him. He was lively and facetious at dinner.
During the repast he levelled one or two jokes against Pitt
Crawley : he drank as much wine as upon the previous day ;
and going quite unsuspiciously to the drawing-room, began
to entertain the ladies there with some choice Oxford stories.
He described the different pugilistic qualities of Molyneux
and Dutch Sam, offered playfully to give Lady Jane the
odds upon the Tutbury Pet against the Rottingdean man,
or take them, as her ladyship chose : and crowned the
pleasantry by proposing to back himself against his cousin
Pitt Crawley, either with or without the gloves. 'And
that's a fair offer, my buck,' he said with a loud laugh,
slapping Pitt on the shoulder, ' and my father told me to
make it too, and he'll go halves in the bet, ha, ha ! ' So
saying, the engaging youth nodded knowingly at poor Miss
Briggs, and pointed his thumb over his shoulder at Pitt
Crawley in a jocular and exulting manner.

Pitt was not pleased altogether perhaps, but still not
unhappy in the main. Poor Jim had his laugh out : and
staggered across the room with his aunt's candle, when the
old lady moved to retire, and offered to salute her with the
blandest tipsy smile : and he took his own leave and went
upstairs to his bedroom perfectly satisfied with himself, and
with a pleased notion that his aunt's money would be left
to him in preference to his father and all the rest of the
family.

Once up in the bedroom, one would have thought he could
not make matters worse ; and yet this unlucky boy did.
The moon was shining very pleasantly out on the sea, and
Jim, attracted to the window by the romantic appearance
of the ocean, and the heavens, thought he would farther
enjoy them while smoking. Nobody would smell the
tobacco, he thought, if he cunningly opened the window and
kept his head and pipe in the fresh air. This he did : but

being in an excited state, poor Jim had forgotten that his
door was open all this time, so that the breeze blowing
inwards and a fine thorough draught being established, the
clouds of tobacco were carried downstairs, and arrived
with quite undiminished fragrance to Miss Crawley and
Miss Briggs.

That pipe of tobacco finished the business : and the Bute-
Crawleys never knew how many thousand pounds it cost

them. Firkin rushed downstairs to Bowls, who was reading
out the *Fire and the Frying-Pan* to his aide de camp in a
loud and ghostly voice. The dreadful secret was told to him
by Firkin with so frightened a look, that for the first moment
Mr. Bowls and his young man thought that robbers were
in the house ; the legs of whom had probably been discovered by the woman under Miss Crawley's bed. When
made aware of the fact however—to rush upstairs at three
steps at a time—to enter the unconscious James's apartment, calling out, ' Mr. James,' in a voice stifled with alarm,

and to cry, 'For Gawd's sake, sir, stop that 'are pipe,' was the work of a minute with Mr. Bowls. 'Oh, Mr. James, what *'ave* you done,' he said in a voice of the deepest pathos, as he threw the implement out of the window. 'What 'ave you done, sir, missis can't abide 'em.'

'Missis needn't smoke,' said James with a frantic misplaced laugh, and thought the whole matter an excellent joke. But his feelings were very different in the morning, when Mr. Bowls's young man who operated upon Mr. James's boots, and brought him his hot water to shave that beard which he was so anxiously expecting, handed a note in to Mr. James in bed, in the handwriting of Miss Briggs.

'Dear sir,' it said, 'Miss Crawley has passed an exceedingly disturbed night, owing to the shocking manner in which the house has been polluted by tobacco; Miss Crawley bids me say she regrets that she is too unwell to see you before you go—and above all that she ever induced you to remove from the ale-house, where she is sure you will be much more comfortable during the rest of your stay at Brighton.'

And herewith honest James's career as a candidate for his aunt's favour ended. He *had* in fact, and without knowing it, done what he menaced to do. He had fought his cousin Pitt with the gloves.

Where meanwhile was he who had been once first favourite for this race for money? Becky and Rawdon, as we have seen, were come together after Waterloo, and were passing the winter of 1815 at Paris in great splendour and gaiety. Rebecca was a good economist, and the price poor Jos Sedley had paid for her two horses was in itself sufficient to keep their little establishment afloat for a year, at the least; there was no occasion to turn into money 'my pistols, the same which I shot Captain Marker,' or the gold dressing-case, or the cloak lined with sable. Becky had it made into a pelisse for herself, in which she rode in the Bois de Boulogne to the admiration of all: and you should have seen the scene between her and her delighted husband, whom she rejoined after the army had entered Cambray, and when she unsewed herself, and let out of her dress all those watches, knick-knacks, bank-notes, cheques, and valuables, which she had secreted in the wadding, previous to her meditated flight from Brussels! Tufto was charmed, and Rawdon

MR. JAMES'S PIPE IS PUT OUT

roared with delightful laughter, and swore that she was
better than any play he ever saw, by Jove. And the way
in which she jockeyed Jos, and which she described with
infinite fun, carried up his delight to a pitch of quite insane
enthusiasm. He believed in his wife as much as the French
soldiers in Napoleon.

Her success in Paris was remarkable. All the French
ladies voted her charming. She spoke their language admirably. She adopted at once their grace, their liveliness, their
manner. Her husband was stupid certainly—all English
are stupid—and, besides, a dull husband at Paris is always
a point in a lady's favour. He was the heir of the rich and
spirituelle Miss Crawley, whose house had been open to so
many of the French noblesse during the emigration. They
received the colonel's wife in their own hotels—' Why,'
wrote a great lady to Miss Crawley, who had bought her
lace and trinkets at the duchess's own price, and given her
many a dinner during the pinching times after the Revolution—' Why does not our dear miss come to her nephew and
niece, and her attached friends in Paris ? All the world
raffoles of the charming mistress and her *espiègle* beauty.
Yes, we see in her the grace, the charm, the wit of our dear
friend Miss Crawley ! The King took notice of her yesterday
at the Tuileries, and we are all jealous of the attention which
Monsieur pays her. If you could have seen the spite of
a certain stupid Miladi Bareacres (whose eagle-beak and
toque and feathers may be seen peering over the heads of
all assemblies), when Madame the Duchess of Angoulême,
the august daughter and companion of kings,* desired
especially to be presented to Mrs. Crawley, as your dear
daughter and protégée, and thanked her in the name of
France, for all your benevolence towards our unfortunates
during their exile ! She is of all the societies, of all the balls
—of the balls—yes—of the dances, no ; and yet how
interesting and pretty this fair creature looks surrounded
by the homage of the men, and so soon to be a mother ! To
hear her speak of you, her protectress, her mother, would
bring tears to the eyes of ogres. How she loves you ! how
we all love our admirable, our respectable Miss Crawley ! '

It is to be feared that this letter of the Parisian great lady
did not by any means advance Mrs. Becky's interest with
her admirable, her respectable, relative. On the contrary,
the fury of the old spinster was beyond bounds, when she

found what was Rebecca's situation, and how audaciously she had made use of Miss Crawley's name, to get an entrée into Parisian society.   Too much shaken in mind and body to compose a letter in the French language in reply to that of her correspondent, she dictated to Briggs a furious answer in her own native tongue, repudiating Mrs. Rawdon Crawley altogether, and warning the public to beware of her as a most artful and dangerous person.   But as Madame the Duchess of X—— had only been twenty years in England, she did not understand a single word of the language, and contented herself by informing Mrs. Rawdon Crawley at their next meeting, that she had received a charming letter from that *chère Mees*, and that it was full of benevolent things for Mrs. Crawley, who began seriously to have hopes that the spinster would relent.

Meanwhile, she was the gayest and most admired of Englishwomen : and had a little European congress on her reception night.   Prussians, and Cossacks, Spaniards and English—all the world was at Paris* during this famous winter : to have seen the stars and cordons in Rebecca's humble saloon would have made all Baker Street pale with envy.* Famous warriors rode by her carriage in the Bois, or crowded her modest little box at the Opera.   Rawdon was in the highest spirits.   There were no duns in Paris as yet : there were parties every day at Vérey's or Beauvilliers'*; play was plentiful and his luck good.   Tufto perhaps was sulky.   Mrs. Tufto had come over to Paris at her own invitation, and besides this *contretemps*, there were a score of generals now round Becky's chair, and she might take her choice of a dozen bouquets when she went to the play.   Lady Bareacres and the chiefs of the English society, stupid and irreproachable females, writhed with anguish at the success of the little upstart Becky, whose poisoned jokes quivered and rankled in their chaste breasts.   But she had all the men on her side.   She fought the women with indomitable courage, and they could not talk scandal in any tongue but their own.

So in *fêtes*, pleasures, and prosperity, the winter of 1815–16 passed away with Mrs. Rawdon Crawley, who accommodated herself to polite life as if her ancestors had been people of fashion for centuries past—and who from her wit, talent, and energy, indeed merited a place of honour in Vanity Fair. In the early spring of 1816, Galignani's journal* contained

the following announcement in an interesting corner of the
paper : ' On the 26th of March—the lady of Lieutenant-
Colonel Crawley, of the Life Guards Green—of a son and
heir.'

This event was copied into the London papers, out of
which Miss Briggs read the statement to Miss Crawley, at
breakfast, at Brighton. The intelligence, expected as it
might have been, caused a crisis in the affairs of the Crawley
family. The spinster's rage rose to its height, and sending
instantly for Pitt, her nephew, and for the Lady Southdown,
from Brunswick Square, she requested an immediate celebration of the marriage which had been so long pending between
the two families. And she announced that it was her intention to allow the young couple a thousand a year during her
lifetime, at the expiration of which the bulk of her property
would be settled upon her nephew and her dear niece, Lady
Jane Crawley. Waxy came down to ratify the deeds—Lord
Southdown gave away his sister—she was married by a
bishop, and not by the Rev. Bartholomew Irons—to the
disappointment of the irregular prelate.

When they were married—Pitt would have liked to take
a hymeneal tour with his bride, as became people of their
condition. But the affection of the old lady towards Lady
Jane had grown so strong, that she fairly owned she could
not part with her favourite. Pitt and his wife came therefore, and lived with Miss Crawley : and (greatly to the annoyance of poor Pitt, who conceived himself a most injured
character—being subject to the humours of his aunt on
one side, and of his mother-in-law on the other) Lady Southdown, from her neighbouring house, reigned over the whole
family—Pitt, Lady Jane, Miss Crawley, Briggs, Bowls,
Firkin, and all. She pitilessly dosed them with her tracts
and her medicine : she dismissed Creamer, she installed
Rodgers, and soon stripped Miss Crawley of even the semblance of authority. . The poor soul grew so timid that she
actually left off bullying Briggs any more, and clung to her
niece, more fond and more terrified every day. Peace to
thee, kind and selfish, vain and generous old heathen !—
We shall see thee no more. Let us hope that Lady Jane
supported her kindly, and led her with gentle hand out of
the busy struggle of Vanity Fair.

CHAPTER XXXV

WIDOW AND MOTHER

SACRED

T HE news of the great fights of Quatre Bras and Waterloo reached England at the same time. The *Gazette* first published the result of the two battles ; at which glorious intelligence all England thrilled with triumph and fear. Particulars then followed ; and after the announcement of the victories came the list of the wounded and the slain. Who can tell the dread with which that catalogue was opened and read ! Fancy, at every village and homestead almost through the three kingdoms, the great news coming of the battles of Flanders, and the feelings of exultation and gratitude, bereavement and sickening dismay, when the lists of the regimental losses were gone through, and it became known whether the dear friend and relative had escaped or had fallen. Anybody who will take the trouble of looking back to a file of the newspapers of the time, must, even now, feel at second-hand this breathless pause of expectation. The list of casualties are carried on from day to day : you stop in the midst as in a story which is to be continued in our next. Think what the feelings must have been as those papers followed each other fresh from the press ; and if such an interest could be felt in our country, and about a battle where but twenty thousand of our people were engaged, think of the condition of Europe for twenty years before, where people were fighting, not by thousands, but by millions ; each one of whom as he struck his enemy wounded horribly some other innocent heart far away.

The news which that famous *Gazette* brought to the Osbornes gave a dreadful shock to the family and its chief. The girls indulged unrestrained in their grief. The gloom-stricken old father was still more borne down by his fate and

sorrow. He strove to think that a judgement was on the
boy for his disobedience. He dared not own that the
severity of the sentence frightened him, and that its fulfil-
ment had come too soon upon his curses. Sometimes
a shuddering terror struck him, as if he had been the author
of the doom which he had called down on his son. There
was a chance before of reconciliation. The boy's wife might
have died ; or he might have come back and said, Father,
I have sinned. But there was no hope now. He stood on
the other side of the gulf impassable, haunting his parent
with sad eyes. He remembered them once before so in
a fever, when every one thought the lad was dying, and he
lay on his bed speechless, and gazing with a dreadful gloom.
Good God ! how the father clung to the doctor then ; and
with what a sickening anxiety he followed him : what a
weight of grief was off his mind when, after the crisis of the
fever, the lad recovered, and looked at his father once more
with eyes that recognized him. But now there was no help
or cure, or chance of reconcilement : above all, there were
no humble words to soothe vanity outraged and furious, or
bring to its natural flow the poisoned, angry blood. And
it is hard to say which pang it was that tore the proud
father's heart most keenly—that his son should have gone
out of the reach of his forgiveness, or that the apology which
his own pride expected should have escaped him.

Whatever his sensations might have been, however,
the stern old man would have no confidant. He never
mentioned his son's name to his daughters ; but ordered
the elder to place all the females of the establishment in
mourning ; and desired that the male servants should be
similarly attired in deep black. All parties and entertainments, of course, were to be put off. No communications
were made to his future son-in-law, whose marriage-day
had been fixed ; but there was enough in Mr. Osborne's
appearance to prevent Mr. Bullock from making any
inquiries, or in any way pressing forward that ceremony.
He and the ladies whispered about it under their voices
in the drawing-room sometimes, whither the father never
came. He remained constantly in his own study ; the
whole front part of the house being closed until some time
after the completion of the general mourning.

About three weeks after the 18th of June, Mr. Osborne's
acquaintance, Sir William Dobbin, called at Mr. Osborne's

house in Russell Square, with a very pale and agitated face,
and insisted upon seeing that gentleman. Ushered into
his room, and after a few words, which neither the speaker
nor the host understood, the former produced from an
enclosure a letter sealed with a large red seal. ' My son,
Major Dobbin,' the alderman said, with some hesitation,
' dispatched me a letter by an officer of the —th, who
arrived in town to-day. My son's letter contains one for
you, Osborne.' The alderman placed the letter on the
table, and Osborne stared at him for a moment or two in
silence. His looks frightened the ambassador, who after
looking guiltily for a little time at the grief-stricken man,
hurried away without a farther word.

The letter was in George's well-known bold handwriting.
It was that one which he had written before daybreak on
the 16th of June, and just before he took leave of Amelia.
The great red seal was emblazoned with the sham coat of
arms which Osborne had assumed from the *Peerage*, with
' *Pax in bello* ' for a motto ; that of the ducal house with
which the vain old man tried to fancy himself connected.
The hand that signed it would never hold pen or sword
more. The very seal that sealed it had been robbed from
George's dead body as it lay on the field of battle. The
father knew nothing of this, but sat and looked at the letter
in terrified vacancy. He almost fell when he went to open it.

Have you ever had a difference with a dear friend ?
How his letters, written in the period of love and confidence,
sicken and rebuke you ! What a dreary mourning it is
to dwell upon those vehement protests of dead affection !
What lying epitaphs they make over the corpse of love !
What dark, cruel comments upon Life and Vanities !
Most of us have got or written drawers full of them. They
are closet-skeletons which we keep and shun. Osborne
trembled long before the letter from his dead son.

The poor boy's letter did not say much. He had been
too proud to acknowledge the tenderness which his heart
felt. He only said, that on the eve of a great battle, he
wished to bid his father farewell, and solemnly to implore
his good offices for the wife—it might be for the child—
whom he left behind him. He owned with contrition that
his irregularities and extravagance had already wasted
a large part of his mother's little fortune. He thanked
his father for his former generous conduct ; and he pro-

mised him, that if he fell on the field or survived it, he would
act in a manner worthy of the name of George Osborne.

His English habit, pride, awkwardness perhaps, had
prevented him from saying more. His father could not
see the kiss George had placed on the superscription of
his letter. Mr. Osborne dropped it with the bitterest,
deadliest pang of balked affection and revenge. His son
was still beloved and unforgiven.

About two months afterwards, however, as the young
ladies of the family went to church with their father, they
remarked how he took a different seat from that which
he usually occupied when he chose to attend divine worship ;
and that from his cushion opposite, he looked up at the
wall over their heads. This caused the young women
likewise to gaze in the direction towards which the father's
gloomy eyes pointed : and they saw an elaborate monument upon the wall, where Britannia was represented
weeping over an urn, and a broken sword, and a couchant
lion, indicated that the piece of sculpture had been erected
in honour of a deceased warrior. The sculptors of those
days had stocks of such funereal emblems in hand ; as you
may see still on the walls of St. Paul's, which are covered
with hundreds of these braggart heathen allegories. There
was a constant demand for them during the first fifteen
years of the present century.

Under the memorial in question were emblazoned the
well-known and pompous Osborne arms ; and the inscription said, that the monument was ' Sacred to the
memory of George Osborne, Junior, Esq., late a Captain
in His Majesty's —th regiment of foot, who fell on the 18th
of June, 1815, aged 28 years, while fighting for his King
and country in the glorious victory of Waterloo. *Dulce
et decorum est pro patria mori.*'

The sight of that stone agitated the nerves of the sisters
so much that Miss Maria was compelled to leave the church.
The congregation made way respectfully for those sobbing
girls clothed in deep black, and pitied the stern old father
seated opposite the memorial of the dead soldier. ' Will
he forgive Mrs. George ? ' the girls said to themselves as
soon as their ebullition of grief was over. Much conversation passed too among the acquaintances of the
Osborne family, who knew of the rupture between the
son and father caused by the former's marriage, as to the

chance of a reconciliation with the young widow. There were bets among the gentlemen both about Russell Square and in the City.

If the sisters had any anxiety regarding the possible recognition of Amelia as a daughter of the family, it was increased presently, and towards the end of the autumn, by their father's announcement that he was going abroad. He did not say whither, but they knew at once that his steps would be turned towards Belgium, and were aware that George's widow was still in Brussels. They had pretty accurate news indeed of poor Amelia from Lady Dobbin and her daughters. Our honest captain had been promoted in consequence of the death of the second major of the regiment on the field ; and the brave O'Dowd, who had distinguished himself greatly here as upon all occasions where he had a chance to show his coolness and valour, was a colonel and Companion of the Bath.

Very many of the brave —th, who had suffered severely upon both days of action, were still at Brussels in the autumn, recovering of their wounds. The city was a vast military hospital for months after the great battles ;, and as men and officers began to rally from their hurts, the gardens and places of public resort swarmed with maimed warriors old and young, who, just rescued out of death, fell to gambling, and gaiety, and love-making, as people of Vanity Fair will do. Mr. Osborne found out some of the —th easily. He knew their uniform quite well, and had been used to follow all the promotions and exchanges in the regiment, and loved to talk about it and its officers as if he had been one of the number. On the day after his arrival at Brussels, and as he issued from his hotel, which faced the park, he saw a soldier in the well-known facings, reposing on a stone bench in the garden, and went and sat down trembling by the wounded convalescent man.

'Were you in Captain Osborne's company ?' he said, and added, after a pause, ' he was my son, sir.'

The man was not of the captain's company, but he lifted up his unwounded arm and touched his cap sadly and respectfully to the haggard broken-spirited gentleman who questioned him. 'The whole army didn't contain a finer or a better officer,' the soldier said. 'The sergeant of the captain's company (Captain Raymond had it now) was in town, though, and was just well of a shot in the shoulder

His honour might see him if he liked, who could tell him anything he wanted to know about—about the —th's actions. But his honour had seen Major Dobbin, no doubt, the brave captain's great friend ; and Mrs. Osborne, who was here too, and had been very bad, he heard everybody say. They say she was out of her mind like for six weeks or more. But your honour knows all about that—and asking your pardon '—the man added.

Osborne put a guinea into the soldier's hand, and told him he should have another if he would bring the sergeant to the Hotel du Parc ; a promise which very soon brought the desired officer to Mr. Osborne's presence. And the first soldier went away ; and after telling a comrade or two how Captain Osborne's father was arrived, and what a free-handed generous gentleman he was, they went and made good cheer with drink and feasting, as long as the guineas lasted which had come from the proud purse of the mourning old father.

In the sergeant's company, who was also just convalescent, Osborne made the journey of Waterloo and Quatre Bras, a journey which thousands of his countrymen were then taking. He took the sergeant with him in his carriage, and went through both fields under his guidance. He saw the point of the road where the regiment marched into action on the 16th, and the slope down which they drove the French cavalry who were pressing on the retreating Belgians. There was the spot where the noble captain cut down the French officer who was grappling with the young ensign for the colours, the colour-sergeants having been shot down. Along this road they retreated on the next day, and here was the bank at which the regiment bivouacked under the rain of the night of the 17th. Further on was the position which they took and held during the day, forming time after time to receive the charge of the enemy's horsemen, and lying down under shelter of the bank from the furious French cannonade. And it was at this declivity when at evening the whole English line received the order to advance, as the enemy fell back after his last charge, that the captain, hurraying and rushing down the hill waving his sword, received a shot and fell dead. ' It was Major Dobbin who took back the captain's body to Brussels,' the sergeant said, in a low voice, ' and had him buried as your honour knows.' The peasants and relic-hunters about the place were screaming round the pair, as the soldier told his story, offering for sale all sorts of mementoes of the fight, crosses, and epaulets, and shattered cuirasses, and eagles.

Osborne gave a sumptuous reward to the sergeant when he parted with him, after having visited the scenes of his son's last exploits. His burial-place he had already seen. Indeed, he had driven thither immediately after his arrival at Brussels. George's body lay in the pretty burial-ground of Laeken, near the city ; in which place, having once visited it on a party of pleasure, he had lightly expressed a wish to have his grave made. And there the young officer was laid by his friend, in the unconsecrated corner of the garden, separated by a little hedge from the temples and towns and plantations of flowers and shrubs, under which the Roman Catholic dead repose. It seemed a humiliation to old Osborne to think that his son, an English gentleman, a captain in the famous British army, should not be found worthy to lie in ground where mere foreigners were buried. Which of us is there can tell how much vanity lurks in our warmest regard for others, and how selfish our love is ? Old Osborne did not speculate much upon the mingled nature of his feelings, and how his instinct and selfishness were combating together. He firmly believed that every-thing he did was right, that he ought on all occasions to have his own way—and like the sting of a wasp or serpent his hatred rushed out armed and poisonous against any-thing like opposition. He was proud of his hatred as of everything else. Always to be right, always to trample forward, and never to doubt, are not these the great quali-ties with which dullness takes the lead in the world ?

As after the drive to Waterloo, Mr. Osborne's carriage was nearing the gates of the city at sunset, they met another open barouche, in which were a couple of ladies and a gen-tleman, and by the side of which an officer was riding. Osborne gave a start back, and the sergeant, seated with him, cast a look of surprise at his neighbour, as he touched his cap to the officer, who mechanically returned the salute. It was Amelia, with the lame young ensign by her side, and opposite to her her faithful friend Mrs. O'Dowd. It was Amelia, but how changed from the fresh and comely girl Osborne knew. Her face was white and thin. Her pretty brown hair was parted under a widow's cap—the

poor child. Her eyes were fixed, and looking nowhere.
They stared blank in the face of Osborne, as the carriages
crossed each other, but she did not know him ; nor did
he recognize her, until looking up, he saw Dobbin riding
by her ; and then he knew who it was. He hated her.
He did not know how much until he saw her there. When
her carriage had passed on, he turned and stared at the
sergeant, with a curse and defiance in his eye, cast at his
companion, who could not help looking at him—as much
as to say, ' How dare *you* look at me ? Damn you ! I *do*
hate her. It is she who has tumbled my hopes and all
my pride down.' ' Tell the scoundrel to drive on quick,'
he shouted with an oath, to the lackey on the box. A minute
afterwards, a horse came clattering over the pavement
behind Osborne's carriage, and Dobbin rode up. His
thoughts had been elsewhere as the carriages passed each
other, and it was not until he had ridden some paces forward, that he remembered it was Osborne who had just
passed him. Then he turned to examine if the sight of
her father-in-law had made any impression on Amelia,
but the poor girl did not know who had passed. Then
William, who daily used to accompany her in his drives,
taking out his watch, made some excuse about an engagement which he suddenly recollected, and so rode off. She
did not remark that either : but sat looking before her,
over the homely landscape towards the woods in the dis
tance, by which George marched away.

' Mr. Osborne, Mr. Osborne ! ' cried Dobbin, as he rode
up and held out his hand. Osborne made no motion to
take it, but shouted out once more and with another curse
to his servant to drive on.

Dobbin laid his hand on the carriage side. ' I will see
you, sir,' he said. ' I have a message for you.'

' From that woman ? ' said Osborne, fiercely.

'No,' replied the other, ' from your son ; ' at which Osborne
fell back into the corner of his carriage, and Dobbin allowing
it to pass on, rode close behind it, and so through the
town until they reached Mr. Osborne's hotel, and without
a word. There he followed Osborne up to his apartments.
George had often been in the rooms ; they were the lodgings
which the Crawleys had occupied during their stay in
Brussels.

' Pray, have you any commands for me, Captain Dobbin,

or, I beg your pardon, I should say, *Major* Dobbin, since
better men than you are dead, and you step into their
shoes,' said Mr. Osborne, in that sarcastic tone which he
sometimes was pleased to assume.

' Better men *are* dead,' Dobbin replied. ' I want to
speak to you about one.'

' Make it short, sir,' said the other with an oath, scowling
at his visitor.

' I am here as his closest friend,' the major resumed,
' and the executor of his will. He made it before we went
into action. Are you aware how small his means are,
and of the straitened circumstances of his widow ? '

' I don't know his widow, sir,' Osborne said. ' Let her
go back to her father.' But the gentleman whom he
addressed was determined to remain in good temper, and
went on without heeding the interruption.

' Do you know, sir, Mrs. Osborne's condition ? Her
life and her reason almost have been shaken by the blow
which has fallen on her. It is very doubtful whether she
will rally. There is a chance left for her, however, and it
is about this I came to speak to you. She will be a mother
soon. Will you visit the parent's offence upon the child's
head ? or will you forgive the child for poor George's sake ? '

Osborne broke out into a rhapsody of self-praise and
imprecations ; by the first, excusing himself to his own
conscience for his conduct ; by the second, exaggerating
the undutifulness of George. No father in all England
could have behaved more generously to a son, who had
rebelled against him wickedly. He had died without even
so much as confessing he was wrong. Let him take the
consequences of his undutifulness and folly. As for himself,
Mr. Osborne, he was a man of his word. He had sworn
never to speak to that woman, or to recognize her as his
son's wife. ' And that's what you may tell her,' he concluded with an oath ; ' and that's what I will stick to to
the last day of my life.'

There was no hope from that quarter then. The widow
must live on her slender pittance, or on such aid as Jos
could give her. ' I might tell her, and she would not heed
it,' thought Dobbin, sadly : for the poor girl's thoughts
were not here at all since her catastrophe, and, stupefied
under the pressure of her sorrow, good and evil were alike
indifferent to her. So, indeed, were even friendship and

kindness. She received them both uncomplainingly, and having accepted them, relapsed into her grief.

Suppose some twelve months after the above conversation took place to have passed in the life of our poor Amelia. She has spent the first portion of that time in a sorrow so profound and pitiable, that we who have been watching and describing some of the emotions of that weak and tender heart, must draw back in the presence of the cruel grief under which it is bleeding. Tread silently round the hapless couch of the poor prostrate soul. Shut gently the door of the dark chamber wherein she suffers, as those kind people did who nursed her through the first months of her pain, and never left her until heaven had sent her consolation. A day came—of almost terrified delight and wonder—when the poor widowed girl pressed a child upon her breast—a child, with the eyes of George who was gone —a little boy, as beautiful as a cherub. What a miracle it was to hear its first cry ! How she laughed and wept over it—how love, and hope, and prayer woke again in her bosom as the baby nestled there. She was safe. The doctors who attended her, and had feared for her life or for her brain, had waited anxiously for this crisis before they could pronounce that either was secure. It was worth the long months of doubt and dread which the persons who had constantly been with her had passed, to see her eyes once more beaming tenderly upon them.

Our friend Dobbin was one of them. It was he who brought her back to England and to her mother's house ; when Mrs. O'Dowd, receiving a peremptory summons from her colonel, had been forced to quit her patient. To see Dobbin holding the infant, and to hear Amelia's laugh of triumph as she watched him, would have done any man good who had a sense of humour. William was the god-father of the child, and exerted his ingenuity in the purchase of cups, spoons, pap-boats, and corals for this little Christian.

How his mother nursed him, and dressed him, and lived upon him ; how she drove away all nurses, and would scarce allow any hand but her own to touch him ; how she considered that the greatest favour she could confer upon his godfather, Major Dobbin, was to allow the major occasionally to dandle him, need not be told here. This child was her being. Her existence was a maternal caress.

She enveloped the feeble and unconscious creature with
love and worship.   It was her life which the baby drank
in from her bosom.   Of nights, and when alone, she had
stealthy and intense raptures of motherly love, such as
God's marvellous care has awarded to the female instinct—
joys how far higher and lower than reason—blind beautiful
devotions which only women's hearts know.   It was
William Dobbin's task to muse upon these movements of
Amelia's, and to watch her heart ; and if his love made
him divine almost all the feelings which agitated it, alas !
he could see with a fatal perspicuity that there was no
place there for him.   And so, gently, he bore his fate,
knowing it, and content to bear it.

I suppose Amelia's father and mother saw through the
intentions of the major, and were not ill-disposed to encourage him ; for Dobbin visited their house daily, and
stayed for hours with them, or with Amelia, or with the
honest landlord, Mr. Clapp, and his family.   He brought,
on one pretext or another, presents to everybody, and
almost every day ; and went, with the landlord's little
girl, who was rather a favourite with Amelia, by the name
of Major Sugarplums.   It was this little child who commonly acted as mistress of the ceremonies to introduce
him to Mrs. Osborne.   She laughed one day when Major
Sugarplums's cab drove up to Fulham, and he descended
from it, bringing out a wooden horse, a drum, a trumpet,
and other warlike toys, for little Georgy, who was scarcely
six months old, and for whom the articles in question
were entirely premature.

The child was asleep.   'Hush,' said Amelia, annoyed,
perhaps, at the creaking of the major's boots ; and she
held out her hand ; smiling because William could not
take it until he had rid himself of his cargo of toys.   'Go
downstairs, little Mary,' said he presently to the child,
'I want to speak to Mrs. Osborne.'   She looked up rather
astonished, and laid down the infant on its bed.

'I am come to say good-bye, Amelia,' said he, taking
her slender little white hand gently.

'Good-bye ? and where are you going ?' she said, with
a smile.

'Send the letters to the agents,' he said ; 'they will
forward them ; for you will write to me, won't you ?
I shall be away a long time.'

MAJOR SUGARPLUMS

'I'll write to you about Georgy,' she said. 'Dear William, how good you have been to him and to me! Look at him. Isn't he like an angel?'

The little pink hands of the child closed mechanically round the honest soldier's finger, and Amelia looked up in his face with bright maternal pleasure. The cruellest looks could not have wounded him more than that glance of hopeless kindness. He bent over the child and mother. He could not speak for a moment. And it was with all his strength that he could force himself to say a God bless you. 'God bless you,' said Amelia, and held up her face and kissed him.

'Hush! Don't wake Georgy!' she added, as William Dobbin went to the door with heavy steps. She did not hear the noise of his cab-wheels as he drove away: she was looking at the child, who was laughing in his sleep.

CHAPTER XXXVI

HOW TO LIVE WELL ON NOTHING A YEAR

SUPPOSE there is no man in this Vanity Fair of ours so little observant as not to think sometimes about the worldly affairs of his acquaintances, or so extremely charitable as not to wonder how his neighbour Jones, or his neighbour Smith, can make both ends meet at the end of the year. With the utmost regard for the family, for instance (for I dine with them twice or thrice in the season), I cannot but own that the appearance of the Jenkinses* in the Park, in the large barouche with the grenadier footmen, will surprise and mystify me to my dying day : for though I know the equipage is only jobbed, and all the Jenkins people are on board-wages, yet those three men and the carriage must represent an expense of six hundred a year at the very least—and then there are the splendid dinners, the two boys at Eton, the prize governess and masters for the girls, the trip abroad, or to Eastbourne or Worthing in the autumn, the annual ball with a supper from Gunter's* (who, by the way, supplies most of the *first-rate* dinners which J. gives, as I know very well, having been invited to one of them to fill a vacant place, when I saw at once that these repasts are very superior to the *common* run of entertainments for which the *humbler* sort of J.'s acquaintances get cards)—who, I say, with the most good-natured feelings in the world, can help wondering how the Jenkinses make out matters ?　What *is* Jenkins ?—we all know—Commissioner of the Tape and Sealing-Wax Office, with 1,200*l.* a year for a salary.　Had his wife a private fortune ?　Pooh !—Miss Flint—one of eleven children of a small squire in Buckinghamshire.　All she ever gets from her

family is a turkey at Christmas, in exchange for which she
has to board two or three of her sisters in the off season ;
and lodge and feed her brothers when they come to town.
How does Jenkins balance his income ? I say, as every
friend of his must say, How is it that he has not been out-
lawed long since ; and that he ever came back (as he did
to the surprise of everybody) last year from Boulogne ?

'I' is here introduced to personify the world in general—
the Mrs. Grundy of each respected reader's private circle—
every one of whom can point to some families of his acquaintance who live nobody knows how. Many a glass of wine
have we all of us drunk, I have very little doubt, hob-and-
nobbing with the hospitable giver, and wondering how
the deuce he paid for it.

Some three or four years after his stay in Paris, when
Rawdon Crawley and his wife were established in a very
small comfortable house in Curzon Street, Mayfair, there
was scarcely one of the numerous friends whom they
entertained at dinner, that did not ask the above question
regarding them. The novelist, it has been said before,
knows everything, and as I am in a situation to be able
to tell the public how Crawley and his wife lived without
any income, may I entreat the public newspapers*which
are in the habit of extracting portions of the various
periodical works now published, *not* to reprint the following
exact narrative and calculations—of which I ought, as the
discoverer (and at some expense, too), to have the benefit.
My son, I would say, were I blessed with a child—you may
by deep inquiry and constant intercourse with him, learn
how a man lives comfortably on nothing a year. But it is
best not to be intimate with gentlemen of this profession,
and to take the calculations at second-hand, as you do
logarithms, for to work them yourself, depend upon it,
will cost you something considerable.

On nothing per annum, then, and during a course of
some two or three years, of which we can afford to give
but a very brief history, Crawley and his wife lived very
happily and comfortably at Paris. It was in this period
that he quitted the Guards, and sold out of the army.
When we find him again, his moustachios and the title of
colonel on his card are the only relics of his military profession.

It has been mentioned that Rebecca, soon after her

arrival in Paris, took a very smart and leading position in the society of that capital, and was welcomed at some of the most distinguished houses of the restored French nobility. The English men of fashion in Paris courted her, too, to the disgust of the ladies their wives, who could not bear the parvenue. For some months the salons of the Faubourg St. Germain, in which her place was secured, and the splendours of the new Court, where she was received with much distinction, delighted, and perhaps a little intoxicated Mrs. Crawley, who may have been disposed during this period of elation to slight the people—honest young military men mostly—who formed her husband's chief society.

But the colonel yawned sadly among the duchesses and great ladies of the Court. The old women who played écarté made such a noise about a five-franc piece, that it was not worth Colonel Crawley's while to sit down at a card-table. The wit of their conversation he could not appreciate, being ignorant of their language. And what good could his wife get, he urged, by making curtsies every night to a whole circle of princesses? He left Rebecca presently to frequent these parties alone; resuming his own simple pursuits and amusements amongst the amiable friends of his own choice.

The truth is, when we say of a gentleman that he lives elegantly on nothing a year, we use the word 'nothing' to signify something unknown; meaning, simply, that we don't know how the gentleman in question defrays the expenses of his establishment. Now, our friend the colonel had a great aptitude for all games of chance: and exercising himself, as he continually did, with the cards, the dice-box, or the cue, it is natural to suppose that he attained a much greater skill in the use of these articles than men can possess who only occasionally handle them. To use a cue at billiards well is like using a pencil, or a German flute, or a small-sword—you cannot master any one of these implements at first, and it is only by repeated study and perseverance, joined to a natural taste, that a man can excel in the handling of either. Now, Crawley, from being only a brilliant amateur had grown to be a consummate master of billiards. Like a great general, his genius used to rise with the danger, and when the luck had been unfavourable to him for a whole game, and the bets were consequently against him, he would, with consummate skill and boldness, make some prodigious hits which would restore the battle, and come in a victor at the end, to the astonishment of everybody—of everybody, that is, who was a stranger to his play.   Those who were accustomed to see it were cautious how they staked their money against a man of such sudden resources, and brilliant and overpowering skill.

At games of cards he was equally skilful; for though he would constantly lose money at the commencement of an evening, playing so carelessly and making such blunders,

that new-comers were often inclined to think meanly of his talent ; yet when roused to action, and awakened to caution by repeated small losses, it was remarked that Crawley's play became quite different, and that he was pretty sure of beating his enemy thoroughly before the night was over. Indeed, very few men could say that they ever had the better of him.

His successes were so repeated that no wonder the envious and the vanquished spoke sometimes with bitterness regarding them.   And as the French say of the Duke of Wellington, who never suffered a defeat, that only an astonishing series of lucky accidents enabled him to be an invariable winner ; yet even they allow that he cheated at

Waterloo, and was enabled to win the last great trick :—
so it was hinted at head quarters in England, that some
foul play must have taken place in order to account for the
continuous successes of Colonel Crawley.

Though Frascati's* and the Salon were open at that
time in Paris, the mania for play was so widely spread, that
the public gambling-rooms did not suffice for the general
ardour, and gambling went on in private houses as much
as if there had been no public means for gratifying the
passion. At Crawley's charming little *réunions* of an
evening this fatal amusement commonly was practised—
much to good-natured little Mrs. Crawley's annoyance.
She spoke about her husband's passion for dice with the
deepest grief ; she bewailed it to everybody who came to
her house. She besought the young fellows never, never
to touch a box ; and when young Green, of the Rifles, lost
a very considerable sum of money, Rebecca passed a whole
night in tears, as the servant told the unfortunate young
gentleman, and actually went on her knees to her husband
to beseech him to remit the debt, and burn the acknowledgement. How could he ? He had lost just as much
himself to Blackstone of the Hussars, and Count Punter
of the Hanoverian Cavalry. Green might have any decent
time ; but pay ?—of course he must pay ;—to talk of
burning I O U's was child's play.

Other officers, chiefly young—for the young fellows
gathered round Mrs. Crawley—came from her parties with
long faces, having dropped more or less money at her fatal
card-tables. Her house began to have an unfortunate
reputation. The old hands warned the less experienced
of their danger. Colonel O'Dowd, of the —th regiment,
one of those occupying in Paris, warned Lieutenant Spooney
of that corps. A loud and violent fracas took place between
the infantry-colonel and his lady, who were dining at the
Café de Paris, and Colonel and Mrs. Crawley, who were
also taking their meal there. The ladies engaged on both
sides. Mrs. O'Dowd snapped her fingers in Mrs. Crawley's
face, and called her husband ' no betther than a blackleg '.
Colonel Crawley challenged Colonel O'Dowd, C.B. The
commander-in-chief hearing of the dispute sent for Colonel
Crawley, who was getting ready the same pistols, ' which
he shot Captain Marker,' and had such a conversation with
him that no duel took place. If Rebecca had not gone on

her knees to General Tufto, Crawley would have been sent
back to England; and he did not play. except with civilians,
for some weeks after.

But in spite of Rawdon's undoubted skill and constant
successes, it became evident to Rebecca, considering these
things. that their position was but a precarious one, and
that, even although they paid scarcely anybody, their
little capital would end one day by dwindling into zero.
'Gambling,' she would say. 'dear, is good to help your
income, but not as an income itself. Some day people may
be tired of play, and then where are we ? '   Rawdon acquiesced in the justice of her opinion ; and in truth he had
remarked that after a few nights of his little suppers, &c.,
gentlemen *were* tired of play with him, and, in spite of
Rebecca's charms, did not present themselves very eagerly.

Easy and pleasant as their life at Paris was, it was after
all only an idle dalliance and amiable trifling ; and Rebecca
saw that she must push Rawdon's fortune in their own
country. She must get him a place or appointment at
home or in the colonies : and she determined to make
a move upon England as soon as the way could be cleared
for her. As a first step she had made Crawley sell out of
the Guards, and go on half-pay. His function as aide de
camp to General Tufto had ceased previously. Rebecca
laughed in all companies at that officer, at his toupee
(which he mounted on coming to Paris), at his waistband,
at his false teeth, at his pretensions to be a lady-killer
above all, and his absurd vanity in fancying every woman
whom he came near was in love with him.   It was Mrs.
Brent, the beetle-browed wife of Mr. Commissary Brent,
to whom the general transferred his attentions now—his
bouquets, his dinners at the restaurateurs', his opera-
boxes, and his knick-knacks. Poor Mrs. Tufto was no
more happy than before, and had still to pass long evenings
alone with her daughters, knowing that her general was
gone off scented and curled to stand behind Mrs. Brent's
chair at the play. Becky had a dozen admirers in his
place to be sure ; and could cut her rival to pieces with
her wit.   But as we have said, she was growing tired of
this idle social life : opera-boxes and restaurateur dinners
palled upon her : nosegays could not be laid by as a provision for future years : and she could not live upon knick-
knacks, laced handkerchiefs, and kid gloves. She felt the

frivolity of pleasure, and longed for more substantial
benefits.

At this juncture news arrived which was spread among
the many creditors of the colonel at Paris, and which caused
them great satisfaction. Miss Crawley, the rich aunt from
whom he expected his immense inheritance, was dying;
the colonel must haste to her bedside. Mrs. Crawley and
her child would remain behind until he came to reclaim
them. He departed for Calais, and having reached that
place in safety, it might have been supposed that he went
to Dover; but instead he took the diligence to Dunkirk,
and thence travelled to Brussels, for which place he had
a former predilection. The fact is, he owed more money
at London than at Paris; and he preferred the quiet little
Belgian city to either of the more noisy capitals.

Her aunt was dead. Mrs. Crawley ordered the most
intense mourning for herself and little Rawdon. The
colonel was busy arranging the affairs of the inheritance.
They could take the premier now, instead of the little
entresol of the hotel which they occupied. Mrs. Crawley
and the landlord had a consultation about the new hangings,
an amicable wrangle about the carpets, and a final adjust-
ment of everything except the bill. She went off in one
of his carriages; her French *bonne* with her; the child
by her side; the admirable landlord and landlady smiling
farewell to her from the gate. General Tufto was furious
when he heard she was gone, and Mrs. Brent furious with
him for being furious; Lieutenant Spooney was cut to the
heart; and the landlord got ready his best apartments previous to the return of the fascinating little woman and her
husband. He *serré*'d the trunks which she left in his
charge with the greatest care. They had been especially
recommended to him by Madame Crawley. They were
not, however, found to be particularly valuable when opened
some time after.

But before she went to join her husband in the Belgic
capital, Mrs. Crawley made an expedition into England,
leaving behind her her little son upon the Continent, under
the care of her French maid.

The parting between Rebecca and the little Rawdon
did not cause either party much pain. She had not, to
say truth, seen much of the young gentleman since his
birth. After the amiable fashion of French mothers, she

MRS. RAWDON'S DEPARTURE FROM PARIS

had placed him out at nurse in a village in the neighbourhood of Paris, where little Rawdon passed the first months
of his life, not unhappily, with a numerous family of foster-
brothers, in wooden shoes. His father would ride over
many a time to see him here, and the elder Rawdon's
paternal heart glowed to see him rosy and dirty, shouting
lustily, and happy in the making of mud-pies under the
superintendence of the gardener's wife, his nurse.

Rebecca did not care much to go and see the son and
heir. Once he spoiled a new dove-coloured pelisse of hers.
He preferred his nurse's caresses to his mamma's, and
when finally he quitted that jolly nurse and almost parent,
he cried loudly for hours. He was only consoled by his
mother's promise that he should return to his nurse the
next day; indeed the nurse herself, who probably would
have been pained at the parting too, was told that the
child would immediately be restored to her, and for some
time awaited quite anxiously his return.

In fact, our friends may be said to have been among the
first of that brood of hardy English adventurers who have
subsequently invaded the Continent, and swindled in all
the capitals of Europe. The respect in those happy days

of 1817–18 was very great for the wealth and honour of
Britons.   They had not then learned, as I am told, to haggle
for bargains with the pertinacity which now distinguishes
them.   The great cities of Europe had not been as yet
open to the enterprise of our rascals.   And whereas, there
is now hardly a town of France or Italy in which you
shall not see some noble countryman of our own, with
that happy swagger and insolence of demeanour which
we carry everywhere, swindling inn-landlords, passing
fictitious cheques upon credulous bankers, robbing coach-
makers of their carriages, goldsmiths of their trinkets,
easy travellers of their money at cards,—even public
libraries of their books :—thirty years ago you needed but
to be a Milor Anglais, travelling in a private carriage, and
credit was at your hand wherever you chose to seek it, and
gentlemen, instead of cheating, were cheated.   It was not
for some weeks after the Crawleys' departure that the
landlord of the hotel which they occupied during their
residence at Paris, found out the losses which he had
sustained :   not until Madame Marabou, the milliner,
made repeated visits with her little bill for articles supplied
to Madame Crawley ;   not until Monsieur Didelot from the
Boule d'Or in the Palais Royal had asked half a dozen
times whether *cette charmante miladi* who had bought
watches and bracelets of him was *de retour*.   It is a fact
that even the poor gardener's wife, who had nursed madame's
child, was never paid after the first six months for that
supply of the milk of human kindness with which she had
furnished the lusty and healthy little Rawdon.   No, not
even the nurse was paid—the Crawleys were in too great
a hurry to remember their trifling debt to her.   As for the
landlord of the hotel, his curses against the English nation
were violent for the rest of his natural life.   He asked
all travellers whether they knew a certain Colonel Lor
Crawley—*avec sa femme—une petite dame, très spirituelle.*
' *Ah, monsieur !* ' he would add—' *ils m'ont affreusement
volé.*'   It was melancholy to hear his accents as he spoke
of that catastrophe.

Rebecca's object in her journey to London was to effect
a kind of compromise with her husband's numerous creditors,
and by offering them a dividend of ninepence or a shilling
in the pound, to secure a return for him into his own country.
It does not become us to trace the steps which she took in

the conduct of this most difficult negotiation ; but, having
shown them to their satisfaction, that the sum which she
was empowered to offer was all her husband's available
capital, and having convinced them that Colonel Crawley
would prefer a perpetual retirement on the Continent to
a residence in this country with his debts unsettled ; having
proved to them that there was no possibility of money
accruing to him from other quarters, and no earthly chance
of their getting a larger dividend than that which she
was empowered to offer, she brought the colonel's creditors
unanimously to accept her proposals, and purchased with
fifteen hundred pounds of ready money, more than ten
times that amount of debts.

Mrs. Crawley employed no lawyer in the transaction.
The matter was so simple, to have or to leave, as she justly
observed, that she made the lawyers of the creditors
themselves do the business. And Mr. Lewis representing
Mr. Davids, of Red Lion Square, and Mr. Moss acting
for Mr. Manasseh of Cursitor Street*(chief creditors of the
colonel's), complimented his lady upon the brilliant way
in which she did business, and declared that there was
no professional man who could beat her.

Rebecca received their congratulations with perfect
modesty ; ordered a bottle of sherry and a bread cake
to the little dingy lodgings where she dwelt, while conducting the business, to treat the enemy's lawyers : shook
hands with them at parting, in excellent good humour,
and returned straightway to the Continent, to rejoin her
husband and son, and acquaint the former with the glad
news of his entire liberation. As for the latter, he had
been considerably neglected during his mother's absence
by Mademoiselle Genevieve, her French maid ; for that
young woman, contracting an attachment for a soldier
in the garrison of Calais, forgot her charge in the society
of this *militaire*, and little Rawdon very narrowly escaped
drowning on Calais sands at this period, where the absent
Genevieve had left and lost him.*

And so, Colonel and Mrs. Crawley came to London : and
it is at their house in Curzon Street, Mayfair, that they
really showed the skill which must be possessed by those
who would live on the resources above-named.

CHAPTER XXXVII

THE SUBJECT CONTINUED

N the first place, and as a matter of the greatest necessity, we are bound to describe how a house may be got for nothing a year. These mansions are to be had either unfurnished, where, if you have credit with Messrs. Gillows or Bantings,* you can get them splendidly *montées** and decorated entirely according to your own fancy; or they are to be let furnished; a less troublesome and complicated arrangement to most parties. It was so that Crawley and his wife preferred to hire their house.

Before Mr. Bowls came to preside over Miss Crawley's house and cellar in Park Lane, that lady had had for a butler, a Mr. Raggles, who was born on the family estate of Queen's Crawley, and indeed was a younger son of a gardener there. By good conduct, a handsome person and calves, and a grave demeanour, Raggles rose from the knife-board to the foot-board of the carriage; from the foot-board to the butler's pantry. When he had been a certain number of years at the head of Miss Crawley's establishment, where he had had good wages, fat perquisites, and plenty of opportunities of saving, he announced that he was about to contract a matrimonial alliance with a late cook of Miss Crawley's, who had subsisted in an honourable manner by the exercise of a mangle, and the keeping of a small green shop in the neighbourhood. The truth is, that the ceremony had been clandestinely performed some years back; although the news of Mr. Raggles's marriage was first brought to Miss Crawley by a little boy and girl of seven and eight years of age, whose continual presence in the kitchen had attracted the attention of Miss Briggs.

Mr. Raggles then retired and personally undertook the superintendence of the small shop and the greens. He added milk and cream, eggs and country-fed pork to his

stores, contenting himself, whilst other retired butlers
were vending spirits in public-houses, by dealing in the
simplest country produce. And having a good connexion
amongst the butlers in the neighbourhood, and a snug
back parlour where he and Mrs. Raggles received them,
his milk, cream, and eggs got to be adopted by many of
the fraternity, and his profits increased every year. Year
after year he quietly and modestly amassed money, and
when at length that snug and complete bachelor's residence
at No. 201, Curzon Street,* May Fair, lately the residence
of the Honourable Frederick Deuceace, gone abroad,*
with its rich and appropriate furniture by the first makers,
was brought to the hammer, who should go in and purchase
the lease and furniture of the house but Charles Raggles ?
A part of the money he borrowed, it is true, and at rather
a high interest, from a brother butler, but the chief part
he paid down, and it was with no small pride that Mrs.
Raggles found herself sleeping in a bed of carved mahogany,
with silk curtains, with a prodigious cheval-glass opposite
to her, and a wardrobe which would contain her, and
Raggles, and all the family.

Of course, they did not intend to occupy permanently
an apartment so splendid. It was in order to let the house
again that Raggles purchased it. As soon as a tenant was
found, he subsided into the greengrocer's shop once more ;
but a happy thing it was for him to walk out of that tenement and into Curzon Street, and there survey his house—
his own house—with geraniums in the window and a carved
bronze knocker. The footman occasionally lounging at
the area railing treated him with respect ; the cook took
her green stuff at his house and called him Mr. Landlord ;
and there was not one thing the tenants did, or one dish
which they had for dinner, that Raggles might not know
of, if he liked.

He was a good man ; good and happy. The house
brought him in so handsome a yearly income, that he was
determined to send his children to good schools, and
accordingly, regardless of expense, Charles was sent to
boarding at Dr. Swishtail's, Sugarcane Lodge, and little
Matilda to Miss Peckover's, Laurentinum House,
Clapham.

Raggles loved and adored the Crawley family as the
author of all his prosperity in life. He had a silhouette

of his mistress in his back shop, and a drawing of the
porter's lodge at Queen's Crawley, done by that spinster
herself in India ink—and the only addition he made to the
decorations of the Curzon Street house was a print of
Queen's Crawley in Hampshire, the seat of Sir Walpole
Crawley, Baronet, who was represented in a gilded car
drawn by six white horses, and passing by a lake covered
with swans, and barges containing ladies in hoops, and
musicians with flags and periwigs. Indeed Raggles thought
there was no such palace in all the world, and no such
august family.

As luck would have it, Raggles's house in Curzon Street
was to let when Rawdon and his wife returned to London.
The colonel knew it and its owner quite well; the latter's
connexion with the Crawley family had been kept up
constantly, for Raggles helped Mr. Bowls whenever Miss
Crawley received friends. And the old man not only let
his house to the colonel, but officiated as his butler whenever
he had company; Mrs. Raggles operating in the kitchen
below, and sending up dinners of which old Miss Crawley
herself might have approved. This was the way, then,
Crawley got his house for nothing; for though Raggles
had to pay taxes and rates, and the interest of the mortgage
to the brother butler; and the insurance of his life; and
the charges for his children at school; and the value of
the meat and drink which his own family—and for a time
that of Colonel Crawley too—consumed; and though the
poor wretch was utterly ruined by the transaction, his
children being flung on the streets, and himself driven into
the Fleet Prison: yet somebody must pay even for
gentlemen who live for nothing a year—and so it was this
unlucky Raggles was made the representative of Colonel
Crawley's defective capital.

I wonder how many families are driven to roguery and
to ruin by great practitioners in Crawley's way?—how
many great noblemen rob their petty tradesmen, condescend to swindle their poor retainers out of wretched
little sums, and cheat for a few shillings? When we read
that a noble nobleman has left for the Continent, or that
another noble nobleman has an execution in his house—and
that one or other owe six or seven millions, the defeat seems
glorious even, and we respect the victim in the vastness
of his ruin. But who pities a poor barber who can't get

his money for powdering the footmen's heads ; or a poor
carpenter who has ruined himself by fixing up ornaments
and pavilions for my lady's *déjeuner ;* or the poor devil
of a tailor whom the steward patronizes, and who has
pledged all he is worth, and more, to get the liveries ready,
which my lord has done him the honour to bespeak ?—
When the great house tumbles down, these miserable
wretches fall under it unnoticed : as they say in the old
legends, before a man goes to the devil himself, he sends
plenty of other souls thither.

Rawdon and his wife generously gave their patronage
to all such of Miss Crawley's tradesmen and purveyors as
chose to serve them. Some were willing enough, especially
the poor ones. It was wonderful to see the pertinacity
with which the washerwoman from Tooting brought the
cart every Saturday, and her bills week after week. Mr.
Raggles himself had to supply the greengroceries. The
bill for servants' porter at the ' Fortune of War ' public-
house is a curiosity in the chronicles of beer. Every
servant also was owed the greater part of his wages, and
thus kept up perforce an interest in the house. Nobody in
fact was paid. Not the blacksmith who opened the lock ;
nor the glazier who mended the pane ; nor the jobber who
let the carriage ; nor the groom who drove it ; nor the
butcher who provided the leg of mutton ; nor the coals
which roasted it ; nor the cook who basted it ; nor the
servants who ate it : and this I am given to understand is
not unfrequently the way in which people live elegantly
on nothing a year.

In a little town such things cannot be done without
remark. We know there the quantity of milk our neighbour takes, and espy the joint or the fowls which are going
in for his dinner. So, probably, 200 and 202 in Curzon
Street might know what was going on in the house between
them, the servants communicating through the area-railings;
but Crawley and his wife and his friends did not know
200 and 202. When you came to 201 there was a hearty
welcome, a kind smile, a good dinner, and a jolly shake
of the hand from the host and hostess there, just for all
the world as if they had been undisputed masters of three
or four thousand a year—and so they were, not in money,
but in produce and labour—if they did not pay for the
mutton, they had it : if they did not give bullion in exchange

for their wine, how should we know ? Never was better
claret at any man's table than at honest Rawdon's ;
dinners more gay and neatly served. His drawing-rooms
were the prettiest little modest salons conceivable : they
were decorated with the greatest taste, and a thousand
knick-knacks from Paris, by Rebecca : and when she sat
at her piano trilling songs with a lightsome heart, the
stranger voted himself in a little paradise of domestic
comfort, and agreed that if the husband was rather stupid,
the wife was charming, and the dinners the pleasantest
in the world.

Rebecca's wit, cleverness, and flippancy made her
speedily the vogue in London among a certain class. You
saw demure chariots at her door, out of which stepped
very great people. You beheld her carriage in the Park,
surrounded by dandies of note. The little box in the third
tier of the Opera was crowded with heads constantly
changing ; but it must be confessed that the ladies held
aloof from her, and that their doors were shut to our little
adventurer.

With regard to the world of female fashion and its
customs, the present writer of course can only speak at
second-hand.   A man can no more penetrate or understand
those mysteries than he can know what the ladies talk
about when they go upstairs after dinner. It is only by
inquiry and perseverance, that one sometimes gets hints
of those secrets ; and by a similar diligence every person
who treads the Pall Mall pavement and frequents the
clubs of this metropolis, knows, either through his own
experience or through some acquaintance with whom he
plays at billiards or shares the joint, something about the
genteel world of London, and how, as there are men (such
as Rawdon Crawley, whose position we mentioned before),
who cut a good figure to the eyes of the ignorant world
and to the apprentices in the Park, who behold them consorting with the most notorious dandies there, so there are
ladies, who may be called men's women, being welcomed
entirely by all the gentlemen, and cut or slighted by all
their wives. Mrs. Firebrace is of this sort ; the lady with
the beautiful fair ringlets whom you see every day in
Hyde Park, surrounded by the greatest and most famous
dandies of this empire. Mrs. Rockwood is another, whose
parties are announced laboriously in the fashionable news-

papers, and with whom you see that all sorts of ambassadors and great noblemen dine ; and many more might be mentioned had they to do with the history at present in hand. But while simple folks who are out of the world, or country people with a taste for the genteel, behold these ladies in their seeming glory in public places, or envy them from afar off, persons who are better instructed could inform them that these envied ladies have no more chance of establishing themselves in 'society', than the benighted squire's wife in Somersetshire, who reads of their doings in the *Morning Post*. Men living about London are aware of these awful truths. You hear how pitilessly many ladies of seeming rank and wealth are excluded from this 'society'. The frantic efforts which they make to enter this circle, the meannesses to which they submit, the insults which they undergo, are matters of wonder to those who take human- or womankind for a study ; and the pursuit of fashion under difficulties would be a fine theme for any very great person who had the wit, the leisure, and the knowledge of the English language necessary for the compiling of such a history.

Now the few female acquaintances whom Mrs. Crawley had known abroad, not only declined to visit her when she came to this side of the Channel, but cut her severely when they met in public places. It was curious to see how the great ladies forgot her, and no doubt not altogether a pleasant study` to Rebecca. When Lady Bareacres met her in the waiting-room at the Opera, she gathered her daughters about her as if they would be contaminated by a touch of Becky, and retreating a step or two, placed herself in front of them, and stared at her little enemy. To stare Becky out of countenance required a severer glance than even the frigid old Bareacres could shoot out of her dismal eyes. When Lady de la Mole, who had ridden a score of times by Becky's side at Brussels, met Mrs. Crawley's open carriage in Hyde Park, her ladyship was quite blind, and could not in the least recognize her former friend. Even Mrs. Blenkinsop, the banker's wife, cut her at church. Becky went regularly to church now ; it was edifying to see her enter there with Rawdon by her side, carrying a couple of large gilt Prayer-books, and afterwards going through the ceremony with the gravest resignation.

Rawdon at first felt very acutely the slights which were
passed upon his wife, and was inclined to be gloomy and
savage. He talked of calling out the husbands or brothers
of every one of the insolent women who did not pay a proper
respect to his wife ; and it was only by the strongest commands and entreaties on her part, that he was brought
into keeping a decent behaviour. 'You can't shoot me
into society,' she said, good-naturedly. 'Remember,
my dear, that I was but a governess, and you, you poor
silly old man, have the worst reputation for debt, and dice,
and all sorts of wickedness. We shall get quite as many
friends as we want by and by, and in the meanwhile you
must be a good boy, and obey your schoolmistress in everything she tells you to do. When we heard that your aunt
had left almost everything to Pitt and his wife, do you
remember what a rage you were in ? You would have
told all Paris, if I had not made you keep your temper,
and where would you have been now ?—in prison at Sainte-
Pélagie for debt,* and not established in London in a handsome house, with every comfort about you—you were
in such a fury you were ready to murder your brother,
you wicked Cain you, and what good would have come
of remaining angry ? All the rage in the world won't
get us your aunt's money ; and it is much better that we
should be friends with your brother's family than enemies,
as those foolish Butes are. When your father dies, Queen's
Crawley will be a pleasant house for you and me to pass
the winter in. If we are ruined, you can carve and take
charge of the stable, and I can be a governess to Lady
Jane's children. Ruined ! fiddlededee ! I will get you
a good place before that ; or Pitt and his little boy will
die, and we will be Sir Rawdon and my lady. While there
is life, there is hope, my dear, and I intend to make a man
of you yet. Who sold your horses for you ? Who paid
your debts for you ? ' Rawdon was obliged to confess
that he owed all these benefits to his wife, and to trust
himself to her guidance for the future.

Indeed, when Miss Crawley quitted the world, and that
money for which all her relatives had been fighting so
eagerly was finally left to Pitt, Bute Crawley, who found
that only five thousand pounds had been left to him instead
of the twenty upon which he calculated, was in such a fury
at his disappointment, that he vented it in savage abuse

upon his nephew; and the quarrel always rankling between them ended in an utter breach of intercourse. Rawdon Crawley's conduct, on the other hand, who got but a hundred pounds, was such as to astonish his brother and delight his sister-in-law, who was disposed to look kindly upon all the members of her husband's family. He wrote to his brother a very frank, manly, good-humoured letter from Paris. He was aware, he said, that by his own marriage he had forfeited his aunt's favour; and though he did not disguise his disappointment that she should have been so entirely relentless towards him, he was glad that the money was still kept in their branch of the family, and heartily congratulated his brother on his good fortune. He sent his affectionate remembrances to his sister, and hoped to have her goodwill for Mrs. Rawdon; and the letter concluded with a postscript to Pitt in the latter lady's own handwriting. She, too, begged to join in her husband's congratulations. She should ever remember Mr. Crawley's kindness to her in early days when she was a friendless orphan, the instructress of his little sisters, in whose welfare she still took the tenderest interest. She wished him every happiness in his married life, and, asking his permission to offer her remembrances to Lady Jane (of whose goodness all the world informed her), she hoped that one day she might be allowed to present her little boy to his uncle and aunt, and begged to bespeak for him their goodwill and protection.

Pitt Crawley received this communication very graciously—more graciously than Miss Crawley had received some of Rebecca's previous compositions in Rawdon's handwriting; and as for Lady Jane, she was so charmed with the letter, that she expected her husband would instantly divide her aunt's legacy into two equal portions and send off one-half to his brother at Paris.

To her ladyship's surprise, however, Pitt declined to accommodate his brother with a cheque for thirty thousand pounds. But he made Rawdon a handsome offer of his hand whenever the latter should come to England and choose to take it; and, thanking Mrs. Crawley for her good opinion of himself and Lady Jane, he graciously pronounced his willingness to take any opportunity to serve her little boy.

Thus an almost reconciliation was brought about between

the brothers. When Rebecca came to town Pitt and his
wife were not in London. Many a time she drove by the
old door in Park Lane to see whether they had taken
possession of Miss Crawley's house there. But the new
family did not make its appearance; it was only through
Raggles that she heard of their movements—how Miss
Crawley's domestics had been dismissed with decent
gratuities, and how Mr. Pitt had only once made his appearance in London, when he stopped for a few days at the house,
did business with his lawyers there, and sold off all Miss
Crawley's French novels to a bookseller out of Bond Street.
Becky had reasons of her own which caused her to long
for the arrival of her new relation. 'When Lady Jane
comes,' thought she, 'she shall be my sponsor in London
society; and as for the women! bah! the women will
ask me when they find the men want to see me.'

An article as necessary to a lady in this position as her
brougham or her bouquet, is her companion. I have
always admired the way in which the tender creatures,
who cannot exist without sympathy, hire an exceedingly
plain friend of their own sex from whom they are almost
inseparable. The sight of that inevitable woman in her
faded gown seated behind her dear friend in the opera-box,
or occupying the back seat of the barouche, is always
a wholesome and moral one to me, as jolly a reminder as
that of the death's-head which figured in the repasts of
Egyptian *bon-vivants*, a strange sardonic memorial of
Vanity Fair. What?—even battered, brazen, beautiful,
conscienceless, heartless Mrs. Firebrace, whose father
died of her shame: even lovely, daring Mrs. Mantrap,
who will ride at any fence which any man in England will
take, and who drives her greys in the Park, while her
mother keeps a huxter's stall in Bath still;—even those
who are so bold, one might fancy they could face anything,
dare not face the world without a female friend. They
must have somebody to cling to, the affectionate creatures!
And you will hardly see them in any public place without
a shabby companion in a dyed silk, sitting somewhere in
the shade close behind them.

'Rawdon,' said Becky, very late one night, as a party
of gentlemen were seated round her crackling drawing-
room fire (for the men came to her house to finish the

night ; and she had ice and coffee for them, the best in
London) : ' I must have a sheep-dog.'

' A what ? ' said Rawdon, looking up from an écarté
table.

' A sheep-dog ! ' said young Lord Southdown. ' My dear
Mrs. Crawley, what a fancy ! Why not have a Danish dog ?
I know of one as big as a camelopard, by Jove.   It
would almost pull your brougham. Or a Persian greyhound, eh ? (I propose, if you please) ; or a little pug that
would go into one of Lord Steyne's snuff-boxes ?   There's
a man at Bayswater got one with such a nose that you
might,—I mark the king and play,—that you might hang
your hat on it.'

' I mark the trick,' Rawdon gravely said.   He attended
to his game commonly, and didn't much meddle with the
conversation except when it was about horses and betting.

' What *can* you want with a shepherd's dog ? ' the lively
little Southdown continued.

' I mean a *moral* shepherd's dog,' said Becky, laughing,
and looking up at Lord Steyne.

' What the devil's that ? ' said his lordship.

' A dog to keep the wolves off me,' Rebecca continued.
' A companion.'

' Dear little innocent lamb, you want one,' said the
marquis ; and his jaw thrust out, and he began to grin
hideously, his little eyes leering towards Rebecca.

The great Lord of Steyne was standing by the fire sipping
coffee. The fire crackled and blazed pleasantly. There
was a score of candles sparkling round the mantelpiece,
in all sorts of quaint sconces, of gilt and bronze and porcelain.
They lighted up Rebecca's figure to admiration, as she sat
on a sofa covered with a pattern of gaudy flowers. She
was in a pink dress, that looked as fresh as a rose ; her
dazzling white arms and shoulders were half covered with
a thin hazy scarf through which they sparkled ; her hair
hung in curls round her neck ; one of her little feet peeped
out from the fresh crisp folds of the silk : the prettiest
little foot in the prettiest little sandal in the finest silk
stocking in the world.

The candles lighted up Lord Steyne's shining bald head,
which was fringed with red hair. He had thick bushy
eyebrows, with little twinkling bloodshot eyes, surrounded
by a thousand wrinkles. His jaw was underhung, and

when he laughed, two white buck-teeth protruded themselves and glistened savagely in the midst of the grin.
He had been dining with royal personages, and wore his
garter and ribbon. A short man was his lordship, broad-
chested, and bow-legged, but proud of the fineness of his
foot and ankle, and always caressing his garter-knee.

'And so the Shepherd is not enough,' said he, 'to defend
his lambkin?'

'The Shepherd is too fond of playing at cards and going
to his clubs,' answered Becky, laughing.

'Gad, what a debauched Corydon!' said my lord—
'what a mouth for a pipe!'

'I take your three to two,' here said Rawdon, at the
card-table.

'Hark at Meliboeus,' snarled the noble marquis; 'he's
pastorally occupied too: he's shearing a Southdown-

What an innocent mutton, hey ? Damme, what a snowy fleece ! '

Rebecca's eyes shot out gleams of scornful humour. ' My lord,' she said, ' you are a knight of the Order.' He had the collar round his neck, indeed—a gift of the restored princes of Spain.

Lord Steyne in early life had been notorious for his daring and his success at play. He had sat up two days and two nights with Mr. Fox at hazard.* He had won money of the most august personages of the realm : he had won his marquisate, it was said, at the gaming-table ; but he did not like an allusion to those bygone *fredaines.** Rebecca saw the scowl gathering over his heavy brow.

She rose up from her sofa, and went and took his coffee-cup out of his hand with a little curtsy. ' Yes,' she said, ' I must get a watch-dog. But he won't bark at *you.*' And, going into the other drawing-room, she sat down to the piano, and began to sing little French songs in such a charming, thrilling voice, that the mollified nobleman speedily followed her into that chamber, and might be seen nodding his head and bowing time over her.

Rawdon and his friend meanwhile played écarté until they had enough. The colonel won ; but, say that he won ever so much and often, nights like these, which occurred many times in the week—his wife having all the talk and all the admiration, and he sitting silent without the circle, not comprehending a word of the jokes, the allusions, the mystical language within—must have been rather weari-some to the ex-dragoon.

' How is Mrs. Crawley's husband ? ' Lord Steyne used to say to him by way of a good day when they met : and indeed that was now his avocation in life. He was Colonel Crawley no more. He was Mrs. Crawley's husband.

About the little Rawdon, if nothing has been said all this while, it is because he is hidden upstairs in a garret some-where, or has crawled below into the kitchen for com-panionship. His mother scarcely ever took notice of him. He passed the days with his French *bonne* as long as that domestic remained in Mr. Crawley's family, and when the Frenchwoman went away, the little fellow, howl-ing in the loneliness of the night, had compassion taken

on him by a housemaid, who took him out of his solitary
nursery into her bed in the garret hard by, and comforted
him.

Rebecca, my Lord Steyne, and one or two more were
in the drawing-room taking tea after the Opera, when
this shouting was heard overhead. ' It's my cherub crying
for his nurse,' she said. She did not offer to move to go
and see the child. ' Don't agitate your feelings by going
to look for him,' said Lord Steyne, sardonically. ' Bah ! '
replied the other, with a sort of blush, ' he'll cry himself
to sleep ; ' and they fell to talking about the Opera.

Rawdon had stolen off though, to look after his son and
heir ; and came back to the company when he found that
honest Dolly was consoling the child. The colonel's
dressing-room was in those upper regions. He used to
see the boy there in private. They had interviews together
every morning when he shaved ; Rawdon minor sitting
on a box by his father's side and watching the operation
with never-ceasing pleasure. He and the sire were great
friends. The father would bring him sweetmeats from
the dessert, and hide them in a certain old epaulet box,
where the child went to seek them, and laughed with joy
on discovering the treasure : laughed, but not too loud :
for mamma was below asleep and must not be disturbed.
She did not go to rest till very late, and seldom rose till
after noon.

Rawdon bought the boy plenty of picture-books, and
crammed his nursery with toys. Its walls were covered
with pictures pasted up by the father's own hand, and
purchased by him for ready money. When he was off
duty with Mrs. Rawdon in the Park, he would sit up here,
passing hours with the boy ; who rode on his chest, who
pulled his great moustachios as if they were driving-reins,
and spent days with him in indefatigable gambols. The
room was a low room, and once, when the child was not
five years old his father, who was tossing him wildly up in his
arms, hit the poor little chap's skull so violently against the
ceiling, that he almost dropped the child, so terrified was he
at the disaster.

Rawdon minor had made up his face for a tremendous
howl—the severity of the blow indeed authorized that
indulgence : but just as he was going to begin, the father
interposed.

' For God's sake, Rawdy, don't wake mamma,' he cried.
And the child looking in a very hard and piteous way at his
father, bit his lips, clenched his hands, and didn't cry a bit.
Rawdon told that story at the clubs, at the mess, to everybody in town. ' By Gad, sir,' he explained to the public in
general, ' what a good plucked one that boy of mine is—
what a trump he is ! I half sent his head through the ceiling,
by Gad, and he wouldn't cry for fear of disturbing his
mother.'

Sometimes—once or twice in a week—that lady visited
the upper regions in which the child lived. She came in like
a vivified figure out of the *Magasin des Modes*—blandly
smiling in the most beautiful new clothes and little gloves
and boots. Wonderful scarfs, laces, and jewels glittered
about her. She had always a new bonnet on : and flowers
bloomed perpetually in it : or else magnificent curling
ostrich feathers, soft and snowy as camellias. She nodded
twice or thrice patronizingly to the little boy, who looked
up from his dinner or from the pictures of soldiers he was
painting. When she left the room an odour of rose, or
some other magical fragrance lingered about the nursery.
She was an unearthly being in his eyes, superior to his
father—to all the world : to be worshipped and admired at
a distance. To drive with that lady in the carriage was an
awful rite : he sat up in the back seat, and did not dare to
speak : he gazed with all his eyes at the beautifully-dressed
princess opposite to him. Gentlemen on splendid prancing
horses came up, and smiled and talked with her. How her
eyes beamed upon all of them ! Her hand used to quiver
and wave gracefully as they passed. When he went out
with her he had his new red dress on. His old brown holland
was good enough when he stayed at home. Sometimes, when
she was away, and Dolly his maid was making his bed, he
came into his mother's room. It was as the abode of a fairy
to him—a mystic chamber of splendour and delights.
There in the wardrobe hung those wonderful robes—pink
and blue, and many-tinted. There was the jewel-case,
silver-clasped : and the wondrous bronze hand on the
dressing-table, glistening all over with a hundred rings.
There was the cheval-glass, that miracle of art, in which he
could just see his own wondering head, and the reflection of
Dolly (queerly distorted, and as if up in the ceiling), plump-
ing and patting the pillows of the bed. O thou poor lonely

little benighted boy ! Mother is the name for God in the lips
and hearts of little children ; and here was one who was
worshipping a stone !

Now Rawdon Crawley, rascal as the colonel was, had certain manly tendencies of affection in his heart, and could
love a child and a woman still.   For Rawdon minor he had
a great secret tenderness then, which did not escape Rebecca,
though she did not talk about it to her husband.   It did
not annoy her : she was too good-natured.   It only increased
her scorn for him.   He felt somehow ashamed of this
paternal softness, and hid it from his wife—only indulging
in it when alone with the boy.

He used to take him out of mornings, when they would
go to the stables together and to the Park.   Little Lord
Southdown, the best-natured of men, who would make you
a present of the hat from his head, and whose main occupation in life was to buy knick-knacks that he might give them
away afterwards, bought the little chap a pony not much
bigger than a large rat, the donor said, and on this little
black Shetland pygmy young Rawdon's great father was
pleased to mount the boy, and to walk by his side in the
Park.   It pleased him to see his old quarters, and his old
fellow-guardsmen at Knightsbridge : he had begun to
think of his bachelorhood with something like regret.
The old troopers were glad to recognize their ancient officer,
and dandle the little colonel.   Colonel Crawley found
dining at mess and with his brother-officers very pleasant.
' Hang it, I ain't clever enough for her—I know it.   She
won't miss me,' he used to say : and he was right : his wife
did not miss him.

Rebecca was fond of her husband.   She was always
perfectly good-humoured and kind to him.   She did not
even show her scorn much for him ; perhaps she liked him
the better for being a fool.   He was her upper servant and
maître d'hôtel.   He went on her errands : obeyed her orders
without question : drove in the carriage in the ring* with
her without repining ; took her to the opera-box; solaced
himself at his club during the performance, and came punctually back to fetch her when due.   He would have liked
her to be a little fonder of the boy : but even to that he
reconciled himself.   ' Hang it, you know she's so clever,'
he said, ' and I'm not literary and that, you know.'   For,
as we have said before, it requires no great wisdom to be

GEORGY MAKES ACQUAINTANCE WITH A WATERLOO MAN

able to win at cards and billiards, and Rawdon made no
pretensions to any other sort of skill.

When the companion came, his domestic duties became
very light. His wife encouraged him to dine abroad : she
would let him off duty at the Opera. 'Don't stay and stupefy
yourself at home to-night, my dear,' she would say. ' Some
men are coming who will only bore you. I would not ask
them, but you know it's for your good, and now I have
a sheep-dog, I need not be afraid to be alone.'

' A sheep-dog—a companion ! Becky Sharp with a companion ! Isn't it good fun ? ' thought Mrs. Crawley to
herself. The notion tickled hugely her sense of humour.

One Sunday morning, as Rawdon Crawley, his little son,
and the pony, were taking their accustomed walk in the
Park, they passed by an old acquaintance of the colonel's,
Corporal Clink, of the regiment, who was in conversation
with a friend, an old gentleman, who held a boy in his arms
about the age of little Rawdon. This other youngster had
seized hold of the Waterloo medal which the corporal wore,
and was examining it with delight.

' Good morning, your honour,' said Clink, in reply to the
' How-do, Clink ? ' of the colonel. ' This 'ere young gentleman is about the little colonel's age, sir,' continued the
corporal.

' His father was a Waterloo man, too,' said the old gentleman who carried the boy. ' Wasn't he, Georgy ? '

' Yes,' said Georgy. He and the little chap on the pony
were looking at each other with all their might—solemnly
scanning each other as children do.

' In a line regiment,' Clink said, with a patronizing air.

' He was a captain in the —th Regiment,' said the old
gentleman, rather pompously. ' Captain George Osborne,
sir—perhaps you knew him. He died the death of a hero,
sir, fighting against the Corsican tyrant.'

Colonel Crawley blushed quite red. ' I knew him very
well, sir,' he said, ' and his wife, his dear little wife, sir—
how is she ? '

' She is my daughter, sir,' said the old gentleman,
pulling down the boy, and taking out a card with great
solemnity, which he handed to the colonel. On it was
written—

' Mr. Sedley, Sole Agent for the Black Diamond and

Anti-Cinder Coal Association, Bunker's Wharf, Thames Street, and Anna-Maria Cottages, Fulham Road West.'

Little Georgy went up and looked at the Shetland pony.

'Should you like to have a ride?' said Rawdon minor from the saddle.

'Yes,' said Georgy. The colonel, who had been looking at him with some interest, took up the child and put him on the pony behind Rawdon minor.

'Take hold of him, Georgy,' he said, 'take my little boy round the waist—his name is Rawdon.' And both the children began to laugh.

'You won't see a prettier pair, I think, *this* summer's day, sir,' said the good-natured corporal; and the colonel, the corporal, and old Mr. Sedley with his umbrella, walked by the side of the children.

CHAPTER XXXVIII

A FAMILY IN A VERY SMALL WAY

E must suppose little George Osborne has ridden from Knightsbridge towards Fulham, and will stop and make inquiries at that village regarding some friends whom we have left there. How is Mrs. Amelia after the storm of Waterloo? Is she living and thriving? What has come of Major Dobbin, whose cab was always hankering about her premises? and are there any news of the collector of Boggley Wollah? The facts concerning the latter are briefly these:—

Our worthy fat friend Joseph Sedley returned to India not long after his escape from Brussels. Either his furlough was up, or he dreaded to meet any witnesses of his Waterloo flight. However it might be, he went back to his duties in Bengal, very soon after Napoleon had taken up his residence at St. Helena, where Jos saw the ex-Emperor. To hear

Mr. Sedley talk on board ship you would have supposed that
it was not the first time he and the Corsican had met, and
that the civilian had bearded the French general at Mount
St. John. He had a thousand anecdotes about the famous
battles ; he knew the position of every regiment, and the
loss which each had incurred. He did not deny that he
had been concerned in those victories—that he had been
with the army, and carried dispatches for the Duke of
Wellington. And he described what the duke did and
said on every conceivable moment of the day of Waterloo,
with such an accurate knowledge of his grace's sentiments
and proceedings, that it was clear he must have been by
the conqueror's side throughout the day; though, as a non-
combatant, his name was not mentioned in the public
documents relative to the battle. Perhaps he actually
worked himself up to believe that he had been engaged with
the army ; certain it is that he made a prodigious sensation
for some time at Calcutta, and was called Waterloo Sedley
during the whole of his subsequent stay in Bengal.

The bills which Jos had given for the purchase of those
unlucky horses were paid without question by him and his
agents. He never was heard to allude to the bargain, and
nobody knows for a certainty what became of the horses, or
how he got rid of them, or of Isidor, his Belgian servant,
who sold a grey horse, very like the one which Jos rode, at
Valenciennes some time during the autumn of 1815.

Jos's London agents had orders to pay one hundred and
twenty pounds yearly to his parents at Fulham. It was
the chief support of the old couple ; for Mr. Sedley's speculations in life subsequent to his bankruptcy did not by any
means retrieve the broken old gentleman's fortune. He
tried to be a wine-merchant, a coal-merchant, a commission-
lottery agent, &c. &c. He sent round prospectuses to his
friends whenever he took a new trade, and ordered a new
brass plate for the door, and talked pompously about making
his fortune still. But Fortune never came back to the
feeble and stricken old man. One by one his friends dropped
off, and were weary of buying dear coals and bad wine from
him ; and there was only his wife in all the world who
fancied, when he tottered off to the City of a morning, that
he was still doing any business there. At evening he crawled
slowly back ; and he used to go of nights to a little club at
a tavern, where he disposed of the finances of the nation.

It was wonderful to hear him talk about millions, and agios,*
and discounts, and what Rothschild was doing, and Baring
Brothers. He talked of such vast sums that the gentlemen
of the club (the apothecary, the undertaker, the great
carpenter and builder, the parish clerk, who was allowed to
come stealthily, and Mr. Clapp, our old acquaintance)
respected the old gentleman. ' I was better off once, sir,'
he did not fail to tell everybody who ' used the room '.
' My son, sir, is at this minute chief magistrate of Ramgunge
in the Presidency of Bengal, and touching his four thousand
rupees *per mensem*. My daughter might be a colonel's lady
if she liked. I might draw upon my son, the first magistrate,
sir, for two thousand pound to-morrow, and Alexander*
would cash my bill, down sir, down on the counter, sir.
But the Sedleys were always a proud family.' You and
I, my dear reader, may drop into this condition one day :
for have not many of our friends attained it ? Our luck
may fail : our powers forsake us : our place on the boards
be taken by better and younger mimes—the chance of life
roll away and leave us shattered and stranded. Then men
will walk across the road when they meet you—or, worse
still, hold you out a couple of fingers and patronize you in
a pitying way—then you will know, as soon as your back is
turned, that your friend begins with a ' Poor devil, what
imprudences he has committed, what chances *that* chap has
thrown away ! ' Well, well—a carriage and three thousand
a year is not the summit of the reward nor the end of God's
judgement of men. If quacks prosper as often as they go
to the wall—if zanies succeed and knaves arrive at fortune,
and, vice versa, sharing ill luck and prosperity for all the
world like the ablest and most honest amongst us—I say,
brother, the gifts and pleasures of Vanity Fair cannot be
held of any great account, and that it is probable . . . but
we are wandering out of the domain of the story.

Had Mrs. Sedley been a woman of energy, she would have
exerted it after her husband's ruin, and, occupying a large
house, would have taken in boarders. The broken Sedley
would have acted well as the boarding-house landlady's
husband ; the Munoz of private life*; the titular lord and
master : the carver, house-steward, and humble husband
of the occupier of the dingy throne. I have seen men of
good brains and breeding, and of good hopes and vigour
once, who feasted squires and kept hunters in their youth,

meekly cutting up legs of mutton for rancorous old harri-
dans, and pretending to preside over their dreary tables—
but Mrs. Sedley, we say, had not spirit enough to bustle
about for ' a few select inmates to join a cheerful musical
family ', such as one reads of in the *Times*. She was content
to lie on the shore where fortune had stranded her—and you
could see that the career of this old couple was over.

I don't think they were unhappy. Perhaps they were
a little prouder in their downfall than in their prosperity.
Mrs. Sedley was always a great person for her landlady,
Mrs. Clapp, when she descended and passed many hours with
her in the basement or ornamented kitchen. The Irish
maid Betty Flanagan's bonnets and ribbons, her sauciness,
her idleness, her reckless prodigality of kitchen candles,
her consumption of tea and sugar, and so forth, occupied
and amused the old lady almost as much as the doings of
her former household, when she had Sambo and the coachman, and a groom, and a footboy, and a housekeeper with
a regiment of female domestics—her former household,
about which the good lady talked a hundred times a day.
And besides Betty Flanagan, Mrs. Sedley had all the maids-
of-all-work in the street to superintend. She knew how
each tenant of the cottages paid or owed his little rent.
She stepped aside when Mrs. Rougemont the actress passed
with her dubious family. She flung up her head when
Mrs. Pestler, the apothecary's lady, drove by in her husband's professional one-horse chaise. She had colloquies
with the greengrocer about the penn'orth of turnips which
Mr. Sedley loved : she kept an eye upon the milkman, and
the baker's boy ; and made visitations to the butcher,
who sold hundreds of oxen very likely with less ado than
was made about Mrs. Sedley's loin of mutton : and she
counted the potatoes under the joint on Sundays, on which
days, dressed in her best, she went to church twice and read
Blair's sermons*in the evening.

On that day, for ' business ' prevented him on week-days
from taking such a pleasure, it was old Sedley's delight to
take out his little grandson Georgy to the neighbouring
parks or Kensington Gardens, to see the soldiers or to feed
the ducks. Georgy loved the red-coats, and his grandpapa
told him how his father had been a famous soldier, and
introduced him to many sergeants and others with Waterloo
medals on their breasts, to whom the old grandfather

pompously presented the child as the son of Captain Osborne
of the —th, who died gloriously on the glorious 18th. He
has been known to treat some of these non-commissioned
gentlemen to a glass of porter, and, indeed, in their first
Sunday walks, was disposed to spoil little Georgy, sadly
gorging the boy with apples and parliament,* to the detri-
ment of his health—until Amelia declared that George
should never go out with his grandpapa, unless the latter
promised solemnly, and on his honour, not to give the child
any cakes, lollipops, or stall produce whatever.

Between Mrs. Sedley and her daughter there was a sort
of coolness about this boy, and a secret jealousy—for one
evening in George's very early days, Amelia, who had been
seated at work in their little parlour scarcely remarking that
the old lady had quitted the room, ran upstairs instinctively
to the nursery at the cries of the child, who had been asleep
until that moment—and there found Mrs. Sedley in the act
of surreptitiously administering Daffy's Elixir* to the infant.
Amelia, the gentlest and sweetest of every-day mortals,
when she found this meddling with her maternal authority,
thrilled and trembled all over with anger. Her cheeks,
ordinarily pale, now flushed up, until they were as red as
they used to be when she was a child of twelve years old.
She seized the baby out of her mother's arms, and then
grasped at the bottle, leaving the old lady gaping at her,
furious, and holding the guilty teaspoon.

Amelia flung the bottle crashing into the fireplace.
' I will *not* have baby poisoned, mamma,' cried Emmy,
rocking the infant about violently with both her arms
round him, and turning with flashing eyes at her mother.

' Poisoned, Amelia ! ' said the old lady ; ' this language
to me ? '

' He shall not have any medicine but that which Mr.
Pestler sends for him. He told me that Daffy's Elixir was
poison.'

' Very good : you think I'm a murderess then,' replied
Mrs. Sedley. ' This is the language you use to your mother.
I have met with misfortunes : I have sunk low in life : I
have kept my carriage, and now walk on foot : but I did
not know I was a murderess before, and thank you for the
news.'

' Mamma,' said the poor girl, who was always ready for
tears—' you shouldn't be hard upon me. I—I didn't mean

—I mean, I did not wish to say you would do any wrong
to this dear child : only——'

' Oh, no, my love—only that I was a murderess ; in which
case, I had better go to the Old Bailey. Though I didn't
poison *you*, when you were a child ; but gave you the best
of education, and the most expensive masters money could
procure. Yes ; I've nursed five children, and buried three :
and the one I loved the best of all, and tended through
croup, and teething, and measles, and whooping-cough, and
brought up with foreign masters, regardless of expense, and

with accomplishments at Minerva House—which I never
had when I was a girl—when I was too glad to honour my
father and mother, that I might live long in the land, and to
be useful, and not to mope all day in my room and act the
fine lady—says I'm a murderess. Ah, Mrs. Osborne ! may
you never nourish a viper in your bosom, that's *my* prayer.'

' Mamma, mamma ! ' cried the bewildered girl : and the
child in her arms set up a frantic chorus of shouts.

' A murderess, indeed ! Go down on your knees and pray
to God to cleanse your wicked ungrateful heart, Amelia,
and may He forgive you as I do ; ' and Mrs. Sedley tossed
out of the room, hissing out the word ' poison ' once more,
and so ending her charitable benediction.

Till the termination of her natural life, this breach between
Mrs. Sedley and her daughter was never thoroughly mended.
The quarrel gave the elder lady numberless advantages
which she did not fail to turn to account with female
ingenuity and perseverance. For instance, she scarcely
spoke to Amelia for many weeks afterwards. She warned
the domestics not to touch the child, as Mrs. Osborne might
be offended. She asked her daughter to see and satisfy
herself that there was no poison prepared in the little daily
messes that were concocted for Georgy. When neighbours
asked after the boy's health, she referred them pointedly
to Mrs. Osborne. *She* never ventured to ask whether the
baby was well or not. *She* would not touch the child
although he was her grandson, and own precious darling, for
she was not *used* to children, and might kill it. And whenever Mr. Pestler came upon his healing inquisition, she
received the doctor with such a sarcastic and scornful
demeanour, as made the surgeon declare that not Lady
Thistlewood herself, whom he had the honour of attending
professionally, could give herself greater airs than old
Mrs. Sedley, from whom he never took a fee. And very
likely Emmy was jealous too, upon her own part, as what
mother is not, of those who would manage her children for
her, or become candidates for the first place in their affections ? It is certain that when anybody nursed the child,
she was uneasy, and that she would no more allow Mrs. Clapp
or the domestic to dress or tend him, than she would have
let them wash her husband's miniature which hung up over
her little bed ;—the same little bed from which the poor
girl had gone to his ; and to which she retired now for many
long, silent, tearful, but happy years.

In this room was all Amelia's heart and treasure. Here
it was that she tended her boy, and watched him through
the many ills of childhood, with a constant passion of love.
The elder George returned in him somehow, only improved,
and as if come back from heaven. In a hundred little tones,
looks, and movements, the child was so like his father, that
the widow's heart thrilled as she held him to it ; and he
would often ask the cause of her tears. It was because of
his likeness to his father, she did not scruple to tell him.
She talked constantly to him about this dead father, and
spoke of her love for George to the innocent and wondering
child ; much more than she ever had done to George him-

self, or to any confidante of her youth.   To her parents she
never talked about this matter ; shrinking from baring her
heart to them.   Little George very likely could understand
no better than they ; but into his ears she poured her sentimental secrets unreservedly, and into his only.   The very
joy of this woman was a sort of grief, or so tender, at least,
that its expression was tears.   Her sensibilities were so weak
and tremulous, that perhaps they ought not to be talked
about in a book.   I was told by Dr. Pestler (now a most
flourishing lady's physician, with a sumptuous dark-green
carriage, a prospect of speedy knighthood, and a house in
Manchester Square), that her grief at weaning the child was
a sight that would have unmanned a Herod.   He was very
soft-hearted many years ago, and his wife was mortally
jealous of Mrs. Amelia, then and long afterwards.

Perhaps the doctor's lady had good reason for her
jealousy : most women shared it, of those who formed the
small circle of Amelia's acquaintance, and were quite angry
at the enthusiasm with which the other sex regarded her.
For almost all men who came near her loved her ; though
no doubt they would be at a loss to tell you why.   She was
not brilliant, nor witty, nor wise overmuch, nor extraordinarily handsome.   But wherever she went she touched and
charmed every one of the male sex, as invariably as she
awakened the scorn and incredulity of her own sisterhood.
I think it was her weakness which was her principal charm :
—a kind of sweet submission and softness, which seemed
to appeal to each man she met for his sympathy and protection.   We have seen how in the regiment, though she
spoke but to few of George's comrades there, all the swords
of the young fellows at the mess-table would have leapt from
their scabbards to fight round her ; and so it was in the little
narrow lodging-house and circle of Fulham, she interested
and pleased everybody.   If she had been Mrs. Mango herself, of the great house of Mango, Plantain, & Co , Crutched
Friars, and the magnificent proprietress of the Pineries,
Fulham, who gave summer *déjeuners* frequented by dukes
and earls, and drove about the parish with magnificent
yellow liveries and bay horses, such as the royal stables at
Kensington themselves could not turn out—I say had she
been Mrs. Mango herself, or her son's wife, Lady Mary
Mango (daughter of the Earl of Castlemouldy, who condescended to marry the head of the firm), the tradesmen

of the neighbourhood could not pay her more honour than they invariably showed to the gentle young widow, when she passed by their doors, or made her humble purchases at their shops.

Thus it was not only Mr. Pestler, the medical man, but Mr. Linton the young assistant, who doctored the servant-maids and small tradesmen, and might be seen any day reading the *Times* in the surgery, who openly declared himself the slave of Mrs. Osborne. He was a personable young gentleman, more welcome at Mrs. Sedley's lodgings than his principal ; and if anything went wrong with Georgy, he would drop in twice or thrice in the day, to see the little chap, and without so much as the thought of a fee. He would abstract lozenges, tamarinds, and other produce from the surgery drawers for little Georgy's benefit, and compounded draughts and mixtures for him of miraculous sweetness, so that it was quite a pleasure to the child to be ailing. He and Pestler, his chief, sat up two whole nights by the boy in that momentous and awful week when Georgy had the measles ; and when you would have thought, from the mother's terror, that there had never been measles in the world before. Would they have done as much for other people ? Did they sit up for the folks at the Pineries, when Ralph Plantagenet, and Gwendoline, and Guinever Mango had the same juvenile complaint ? Did they sit up for little Mary Clapp, the landlord's daughter, who actually caught the disease of little Georgy ? Truth compels one to say, no. They slept quite undisturbed, at least as far as she was concerned—pronounced hers to be a slight case, which would almost cure itself, sent her in a draught or two, and threw in bark*when the child rallied, with perfect indifference, and just for form's sake.

Again, there was the little French chevalier opposite, who gave lessons in his native tongue at various schools in the neighbourhood, and who might be heard in his apartment of nights playing tremulous old gavottes and minuets, on a wheezy old fiddle. Whenever this powdered and courteous old man, who never missed a Sunday at the convent chapel at Hammersmith, and who was in all respects, thoughts, conduct, and bearing, utterly unlike the bearded savages of his nation, who curse perfidious Albion, and scowl at you from over their cigars, in the Quadrant arcades at the present day—whenever the old Chevalier de Talonrouge

spoke of Mistress Osborne, he would first finish his pinch
of snuff, flick away the remaining particles of dust with
a graceful wave of his hand, gather up his fingers again into
a bunch, and, bringing them up to his mouth, blow them
open with a kiss, exclaiming, '*Ah! la divine créature!*'
He vowed and protested that when Amelia walked in the
Brompton Lanes flowers grew in profusion under her feet.
He called little Georgy Cupid, and asked him news of Venus,
his mamma; and told the astonished Betty Flanagan
that she was one of the Graces, and the favourite attendant
of the *Reine des Amours*.

Instances might be multiplied of this easily gained and
unconscious popularity. Did not Mr. Binney, the mild and
genteel curate of the district chapel, which the family
attended, call assiduously upon the widow, dandle the little
boy on his knee, and offer to teach him Latin, to the anger
of the elderly virgin, his sister, who kept house for him?
'There is nothing in her, Beilby,' the latter lady would say.
'When she comes to tea here she does not speak a word
during the whole evening. She is but a poor lackadaisical
creature, and it is my belief has no heart at all. It is only
her pretty face which all you gentlemen admire so. Miss
Grits, who has five thousand pounds, and expectations
besides, has twice as much character, and is a thousand
times more agreeable to *my* taste; and if she were good-
looking I know that you would think her perfection.'

Very likely Miss Binney was right to a great extent. It
is the pretty face which creates sympathy in the hearts of
men, those wicked rogues. A woman may possess the
wisdom and chastity of Minerva, and we give no heed to
her, if she has a plain face. What folly will not a pair of
bright eyes make pardonable? What dullness may not red
lips and sweet accents render pleasant? And so, with their
usual sense of justice, ladies argue that because a woman is
handsome, therefore she is a fool. O ladies, ladies! there
are some of you who are neither handsome nor wise.

These are but trivial incidents to recount in the life of our
heroine. Her tale does not deal in wonders, as the gentle
reader has already no doubt perceived; and if a journal
had been kept of her proceedings during the seven years
after the birth of her son, there would be found few incidents
more remarkable in it than that of the measles, recorded
in the foregoing page. Yes, one day, and greatly to her

wonder, the Reverend Mr. Binney, just mentioned, asked
her to change her name of Osborne for his own ; when, with
deep blushes, and tears in her eyes and voice, she thanked
him for his regard for her, expressed gratitude for his
attentions to her and to her poor little boy, but said that
she never, never could think of any but—but the husband
whom she had lost.

On the twenty-fifth of April, and the eighteenth of
June, the days of her marriage and widowhood, she kept

her room entirely, consecrating them (and we do not know
how many hours of solitary night-thought, her little boy
sleeping in his crib by her bedside) to the memory of that
departed friend. During the day she was more active.
She had to teach George to read and to write, and a little
to draw. She read books, in order that she might tell
him stories from them. As his eyes opened, and his mind
expanded, under the influence of the outward nature round
about him, she taught the child, to the best of her humble
power, to acknowledge the Maker of all ; and every night
and every morning he and she—(in that awful and touching
communion which I think must bring a thrill to the heart
of every man who witnesses or who remembers it)—the

mother and the little boy—prayed to Our Father together, the mother pleading with all her gentle heart, the child lisping after her as she spoke.   And each time they prayed to God to bless dear papa, as if he were alive and in the room with them.

To wash and dress this young gentleman—to take him for a run of the mornings, before breakfast, and the retreat of grandpapa for ' business '—to make for him the most wonderful and ingenious dresses, for which end the thrifty widow cut up and altered every available little bit of finery which she possessed out of her wardrobe during her marriage—for Mrs. Osborne herself (greatly to her mother's vexation, who preferred fine clothes, especially since her misfortunes) always wore a black gown, and a straw bonnet with a black ribbon—occupied her many hours of the day. Others she had to spare, at the service of her mother and her old father.   She had taken the pains to learn, and used to play cribbage with this gentleman on the nights when he did not go to his club.   She sang for him when he was so minded, and it was a good sign, for he invariably fell into a comfortable sleep during the music.   She wrote out his numerous memorials, letters, prospectuses, and projects.   It was in her handwriting that most of the old gentleman's former acquaintances were informed that he had become an agent for the Black Diamond and Anti-Cinder Coal Company, and could supply his friends and the public with the best coals at —s. per chaldron.   All he did was to sign the circulars with his flourish and signature, and direct them in a shaky, clerklike hand.   One of these papers was sent to Major Dobbin, — Regt., care of Messrs. Cox and Greenwood ; but the major being in Madras at the time, had no particular call for coals.   He knew, though, the hand which had written the prospectus.   Good God . what would he not have given to hold it in his own !   A second prospectus came out, informing the major that J. Sedley and Company, having established agencies at Oporto, Bordeaux, and St. Mary's, were enabled to offer to their friends and the public generally, the finest and most celebrated growths of ports, sherries, and claret wines at reasonable prices, and under extraordinary advantages.   Acting upon this hint, Dobbin furiously canvassed the governor, the commander-in-chief, the judges, the regiments, and everybody whom he knew in the Presidency,

and sent home to Sedley and Co. orders for wine which
perfectly astonished Mr. Sedley and Mr. Clapp, who was
the Co. in the business. But no more orders came after
that first burst of good fortune, on which poor old Sedley
was about to build a house in the City, a regiment of clerks,
a dock to himself, and correspondents all over the world.
The old gentleman's former taste in wine had gone : the
curses of the mess-room assailed Major Dobbin for the vile
drinks he had been the means of introducing there ; and
he bought back a great quantity of the wine, and sold it
at public outcry, at an enormous loss to himself. As
for Jos, who was by this time promoted to a seat at the
Revenue Board at Calcutta, he was wild with rage when
the post brought him out a bundle of these bacchanalian
prospectuses, with a private note from his father, telling
Jos that his senior counted upon him in this enterprise,
and had consigned a quantity of select wines to him, as
per invoice, drawing bills upon him for the amount of the
same. Jos, who would no more have it supposed that his
father, Jos Sedley's father, of the Board of Revenue, was
a wine merchant asking for orders, than that he was Jack
Ketch, refused the bills with scorn, wrote back contume-
liously to the old gentleman, bidding him to mind his
own affairs ; and the protested paper coming back, Sedley
and Co. had to take it up, with the profits which they had
made out of the Madras venture, and with a little portion
of Emmy's savings.

Besides her pension of fifty pounds a year, there had
been five hundred pounds, as her husband's executor stated,
left in the agent's hands at the time of Osborne's demise,
which sum, as George's guardian, Dobbin proposed to put
out at 8 per cent in an Indian house of agency. Mr. Sedley,
who thought the major had some roguish intentions of his
own about the money, was strongly against this plan ;
and he went to the agents to protest personally against
the employment of the money in question, when he learned,
to his surprise, that there had been no such sum in their
hands, that all the late captain's assets did not amount
to a hundred pounds, and that the five hundred pounds
in question must be a separate sum, of which Major Dobbin
knew the particulars. More than ever convinced that
there was some roguery, old Sedley pursued the major.
As his daughter's nearest friend, he demanded with a high

hand, a statement of the late captain's accounts. Dobbin's stammering, blushing, and awkwardness added to the other's convictions that he had a rogue to deal with ; and in a majestic tone he told that officer a piece of his mind, as he called it, simply stating his belief that the major was unlawfully detaining his late son-in-law's money.

Dobbin at this lost all patience, and if his accuser had not been so old and so broken, a quarrel might have ensued between them at the Slaughters' Coffee-house, in a box of which place of entertainment the gentlemen had their colloquy. 'Come upstairs, sir,' lisped out the major. 'I insist on your coming upstairs, and I will show which is the injured party, poor George or I ; ' and, dragging the old gentleman up to his bedroom, he produced from his desk Osborne's accounts, and a bundle of I O U's which the latter had given, who, to do him justice, was always ready to give an I O U. 'He paid his bills in England,' Dobbin added, ' but he had not a hundred pounds in the world when he fell. I and one or two of his brother-officers made up the little sum, which was all that we could spare, and you dare tell us that we are trying to cheat the widow and the orphan.' Sedley was very contrite and humbled, though the fact is, that William Dobbin had told a great falsehood to the old gentleman ; having himself given every shilling of the money, having buried his friend, and paid all the fees and charges incident upon the calamity and removal of poor Amelia.

About these expenses old Osborne had never given himself any trouble to think, nor any other relative of Amelia, nor Amelia herself, indeed. She trusted to Major Dobbin as an accountant, took his somewhat confused calculations for granted : and never once suspected how much she was in his debt.

Twice or thrice in the year, according to her promise, she wrote him letters to Madras, letters all about little Georgy. How he treasured these papers ! Whenever Amelia wrote he answered, and not until then. But he sent over endless remembrances of himself to his godson and to her. He ordered and sent a box of scarfs, and a grand ivory set of chess-men from China. The pawns were little green and white men, with real swords and shields ; the knights were on horseback, the castles were on the backs of elephants. ' Mrs. Mango's own set at the

Pineries was not so fine,' Mr. Pestler remarked. These chess-men were the delight of Georgy's life, who printed his first letter in acknowledgement of this gift of his godpapa. He sent over preserves and pickles, which latter the young gentleman tried surreptitiously in the sideboard, and half-killed himself with eating. He thought it was a judgement upon him for stealing, they were so hot. Emmy wrote a comical little account of this mishap to the major : it pleased him to think that her spirits were rallying, and that she could be merry sometimes now. He sent over a pair of shawls, a white one for her, and a black one with palm-leaves for her mother, and a pair of red scarfs, as winter wrappers, for old Mr. Sedley and George. The shawls were worth fifty guineas a piece at the very least, as Mrs. Sedley knew. She wore hers in state at church at Brompton, and was congratulated by her female friends upon, the splendid acquisition. Emmy's, too, became prettily her modest black gown. ' What a pity it is she won't think of him,' Mrs. Sedley remarked to Mrs. Clapp, and to all her friends of Brompton: ' Jos never sent us such presents, I am sure, and grudges us everything. It is evident that the major is over head and ears in love with her : and yet, whenever I so much as hint it, she turns red and begins to cry, and goes and sits upstairs with her miniature. I'm sick of that miniature. I wish we had never seen those odious purse-proud Osbornes.'

Amidst such humble scenes and associates George's early youth was passed, and the boy grew up delicate, sensitive, imperious, woman-bred—domineering the gentle mother whom he loved with passionate affection. He ruled all the rest of the little world round about him. As he grew, the elders were amazed at his haughty manner and his constant likeness to his father. He asked questions about everything, as inquiring youth will do. The profundity of his remarks and interrogatories astonished his old grandfather, who perfectly bored the club at the tavern with stories about the little lad's learning and genius. He suffered his grandmother with a good-humoured indifference. The small circle round about him believed that the equal of the boy did not exist upon the earth. Georgy inherited his father's pride, and perhaps thought they were not wrong.

When he grew to be about six years old, Dobbin began

to write to him very much. The major wanted to hear that Georgy was going to a school, and hoped he would acquit himself with credit there : or would he have a good tutor at home ? it was time that he should begin to learn ; and his godfather and guardian hinted that he hoped to be allowed to defray the charges of the boy's education, which would fall heavily upon his mother's straitened income. The major, in a word, was always thinking about Amelia and her little boy, and by orders to his agents kept the latter provided with picture-books, paint-boxes, desks, and all conceivable implements of amusement and instruction. Three days before George's sixth birthday, a gentleman in a gig, accompanied by a servant, drove up to Mr. Sedley's house, and asked to see Master George Osborne : it was Mr. Woolsey, military tailor, of Conduit Street,* who came at the major's order to measure the young gentleman for a suit of cloth clothes. He had had the honour of making for the captain, the young gentleman's father.

Sometimes, too, and by the major's desire no doubt, his sisters, the Misses Dobbin, would call in the family carriage to take Amelia and the little boy a drive if they were so inclined. The patronage and kindness of these ladies was very uncomfortable to Amelia, but she bore it meekly enough, for her nature was to yield ; and, besides, the carriage and its splendours gave little Georgy immense pleasure. The ladies begged occasionally that the child might pass a day with them, and he was always glad to go to that fine garden-house at Denmark Hill, where they lived, and where there were such fine grapes in the hothouses and peaches on the walls.

One day they kindly came over to Amelia with news which they were *sure* would delight her—something *very* interesting about their dear William.

' What was it : was he coming home ? ' she asked with pleasure beaming in her eyes.

' Oh, no—not the least—but they had very good reason to believe that dear William was about to be married —and to a relation of a very dear friend of Amelia's—to Miss Glorvina O'Dowd, Sir Michael O'Dowd's sister, who had gone out to join Lady O'Dowd at Madras—a very beautiful and accomplished girl, everybody said.'

Amelia said ' Oh ! ' Amelia was very, *very* happy indeed. But she supposed Glorvina could not be like her old

acquaintance, who was most kind—but—but she was very
happy indeed.   And by some impulse, of which I cannot
explain the meaning, she took George in her arms and
kissed him with an extraordinary tenderness. Her eyes
were quite moist when she put the child down ; and she
scarcely spoke a word during the whole of the drive—
though she was so very happy indeed.

CHAPTER XXXIX

A CYNICAL CHAPTER

UR duty now takes us back for a brief
space to some old Hampshire acquaintances of ours, whose hopes respecting
the disposal of their rich kinswoman's
property were so wofully disappointed.
After counting upon thirty thousand
pounds from his sister, it was a heavy
blow to Bute Crawley to receive but
five ; out of which sum, when he had paid his own debts
and those of Jim, his son at college, a very small fragment
remained to portion off his four plain daughters.   Mrs.
Bute never knew, or at least never acknowledged, how
far her own tyrannous behaviour had tended to ruin her
husband.   All that woman could do, she vowed and protested she had done.   Was it her fault if she did not possess
those sycophantic arts which her hypocritical nephew,
Pitt Crawley, practised ?   She wished him all the happiness
which he merited out of his ill-gotten gains.   ' At least
the money will remain in the family,' she said, charitably.
' Pitt will never spend it, my dear, that is quite certain ;
for a greater miser does not exist in England, and he is
as odious, though in a different way, as his spendthrift
brother, the abandoned Rawdon.'
   So Mrs. Bute, after the first shock of rage and disappointment, began to accommodate herself as best she could to
her altered fortunes, and to save and retrench with all
her might.   She instructed her daughters how to bear
poverty cheerfully, and invented a thousand notable
methods to conceal or evade it.   She took them about to

balls and public places in the neighbourhood, with praiseworthy energy : nay, she entertained her friends in a
hospitable comfortable manner at the Rectory, and much
more frequently than before dear Miss Crawley's legacy
had fallen in. From her outward bearing nobody would
have supposed that the family had been disappointed in
their expectations : or have guessed from her frequent
appearance in public how she pinched and starved at home.
Her girls had more milliner's furniture than they had ever
enjoyed before. They appeared perseveringly at the
Winchester and Southampton assemblies ; they penetrated
to Cowes for the race-balls and regatta-gaieties there ; and
their carriage, with the horses taken from the plough, was
at work perpetually, until it began almost to be believed
that the four sisters had had fortunes left them by their
aunt, whose name the family never mentioned in public
but with the most tender gratitude and regard. I know
no sort of lying which is more frequent in Vanity Fair
than this ; and it may be remarked how people who practise it take credit to themselves for their hypocrisy, and
fancy that they are exceedingly virtuous and praiseworthy,
because they are able to deceive the world with regard
to the extent of their means.

Mrs. Bute certainly thought herself one of the most
virtuous women in England, and the sight of her happy
family was an edifying one to strangers. They were so
cheerful, so loving, so well-educated, so simple ! Martha
painted flowers exquisitely, and furnished half the charity-
bazaars in the county. Emma was a regular County Bulbul,
and her verses in the *Hampshire Telegraph* were the glory
of its Poet's Corner. Fanny and Matilda sang duets
together, mamma playing the piano, and the other two
sisters sitting with their arms round each other's waists,
and listening affectionately. Nobody saw the poor girls
drumming at the duets in private. No one saw mamma
drilling them rigidly hour after hour. In a word, Mrs.
Bute put a good face against fortune, and kept up appearances in the most virtuous manner.

Everything that a good and respectable mother could do
Mrs. Bute did. She got over yachting men from Southampton, parsons from the Cathedral Close at Winchester,
and officers from the barracks there. She tried to inveigle
the young barristers at assizes, and encouraged Jim to

bring home friends with whom he went out hunting with
the H.H. What will not a mother do for the benefit of
her beloved ones ?

Between such a woman and her brother-in-law, the
odious baronet at the Hall, it is manifest that there could
be very little in common. The rupture between Bute
and his brother Sir Pitt was complete ; indeed, between
Sir Pitt and the whole county, to which the old man was
a scandal. His dislike for respectable society increased
with age, and the lodge-gates had not opened to a gentleman's carriage-wheels since Pitt and Lady Jane came to
pay their visit of duty after their marriage.

That was an awful and unfortunate visit, never to be
thought of by the family without horror. Pitt begged his
wife, with a ghastly countenance, never to speak of it ;
and it was only through Mrs. Bute herself, who still knew
everything which took place at the Hall, that the circumstances of Sir Pitt's reception of his son and daughter-in-
law were ever known at all.

As they drove up the avenue of the park in their neat and
well-appointed carriage, Pitt remarked with dismay and
wrath great gaps among the trees—his trees,—which the
old baronet was felling entirely without licence. The
park wore an aspect of utter dreariness and ruin. The
drives were ill kept, and the neat carriage splashed and
foundered in muddy pools along the road. The great sweep
in front of the terrace and entrance stair was black and
covered with mosses ; the once trim flower-beds rank
and weedy. Shutters were up along almost the whole
line of the house ; the great hall-door was unbarred after
much ringing of the bell ; an individual in ribbons was
seen flitting up the black oak stair, as Horrocks at length
admitted the heir of Queen's Crawley and his bride into
the halls of their fathers. He led the way into Sir Pitt's
' Library ', as it was called, the fumes of tobacco growing
stronger as Pitt and Lady Jane approached that apartment.
' Sir Pitt ain't very well,' Horrocks remarked apologetically,
and hinted that his master was afflicted with lumbago.

The library looked out on the front walk and park.
Sir Pitt had opened one of the windows, and was bawling
out thence to the postilion and Pitt's servant, who seemed
to be about to take the baggage down.

' Don't move none of them trunks,' he cried, pointing

with a pipe which he held in his hand. ' It's only a morning visit, Tucker, you fool. Lor, what cracks that off hoss has in his heels ! Ain't there no one at the ' King's Head ' to rub 'em a little ? How do, Pitt ? How do, my dear ? Come to see the old man, hey ? Gad—you've a pretty face, too. You ain't like that old horse-godmother, your mother. Come and give old Pitt a kiss, like a good little gal.'

The embrace disconcerted the daughter-in-law somewhat, as the caresses of the old gentleman, unshorn and perfumed with tobacco, might well do. But she remembered that her brother Southdown had moustachios, and smoked cigars, and submitted to the baronet with a tolerable grace.

' Pitt has got vat,' said the baronet, after this mark of affection. ' Does he read ee very long zermons, my dear ? Hundredth Psalm, Evening Hymn—hey, Pitt ? Go and get a glass of malmsey and a cake for my Lady Jane, Horrocks, you great big booby, and don't stand stearing there like a fat pig. I won't ask you to stop, my dear ; you'll find it too stoopid, and so should I too along a Pitt. I'm an old man now, and like my own ways, and my pipe and backgammon of a night.'

' I can play at backgammon, sir,' said Lady Jane, laughing. ' I used to play with papa and Miss Crawley, didn't I, Mr. Crawley ? '

' Lady Jane can play, sir, at the game to which you state that you are so partial,' Pitt said haughtily.

' But she wawn't stop for all that. Naw, naw, goo back to Mudbury and give Mrs. Rincer a benefit : or drive down to the Rectory, and ask Buty for a dinner. He'll be charmed to see you, you know ; he's so much obliged to you for gittin the old woman's money. Ha, ha ! Some of it will do to patch up the Hall when I'm gone.'

' I perceive, sir,' said Pitt, with a heightened voice, ' that your people will cut down the timber.'

' Yees, yees, very fine weather, and seasonable for the time of year,' Sir Pitt answered, who had suddenly grown deaf. ' But I'm gittin old, Pitt, now. Law bless you, you ain't far from fifty yourself. But he wears well, my pretty Lady Jane, don't he ? It's all godliness, sobriety, and a moral life. Look at me, I'm not very fur from fowr-score—he, he ; ' and he laughed, and took snuff, and leered at her and pinched her hand.

Pitt once more brought the conversation back to the timber; but the baronet was deaf again in an instant.

'I'm gittin very old, and have been cruel bad this year with the lumbago. I shan't be here now for long; but I'm glad ee've come, daughter-in-law. I like your face, Lady Jane: it's got none of the damned high-boned Binkie look in it; and I'll give ee something pretty, my dear, to go to Court in.' And he shuffled across the room to a cupboard, from which he took a little old case containing jewels of some value. 'Take that,' said he, 'my dear; it belonged to my mother, and afterwards to the first Lady Crawley. Pretty pearls—never gave 'em the ironmonger's daughter. No, no. Take 'em and put 'em up quick,' said he, thrusting the case into his daughter's hand, and clapping the door of the cabinet to, as Horrocks entered with a salver and refreshments.

'What have you a been and given Pitt's wife?' said the individual in ribbons, when Pitt and Lady Jane had taken leave of the old gentleman. It was Miss Horrocks, the butler's daughter—the cause of the scandal throughout the country—the lady who reigned now almost supreme at Queen's Crawley.

The rise and progress of those Ribbons had been marked with dismay by the county and family. The Ribbons opened an account at the Mudbury Branch Savings Bank; the Ribbons drove to church, monopolizing the pony-chaise, which was for the use of the servants at the Hall. The domestics were dismissed at her pleasure. The Scotch gardener, who still lingered on the premises, taking a pride in his walls and hothouses, and indeed making a pretty good livelihood by the garden, which he farmed, and of which he sold the produce at Southampton, found the Ribbons eating peaches in a sunshiny morning at the south wall, and had his ears boxed when he remonstrated about this attack on his property. He and his Scotch wife and his Scotch children, the only respectable inhabitants of Queen's Crawley, were forced to migrate, with their goods and their chattels, and left the stately comfortable gardens to go to waste, and the flower-beds to run to seed. Poor Lady Crawley's rose-garden became the dreariest wilderness. Only two or three domestics shuddered in the bleak old servants' hall. The stables and offices were vacant, and shut up, and half ruined. Sir Pitt lived in private, and boozed nightly with Horrocks, his butler or house-steward (as he now began to be called), and the abandoned Ribbons. The times were very much changed since the period when she drove to Mudbury in the spring-cart, and called the small tradesmen 'sir'. It may have been shame, or it may have been dislike of his neighbours, but the old Cynic of Queen's Crawley hardly issued from his park-gates at all now. He quarrelled with his agents, and screwed his tenants by letter. His days were passed in conducting his own correspondence; the lawyers and farm-bailiffs who had to do business with him, could not reach him but through the Ribbons, who received them at the door of the housekeeper's room, which commanded the back entrance by which they were admitted; and so the baronet's daily perplexities increased, and his embarrassments multiplied round him.

The horror of Pitt Crawley may be imagined, as these reports of his father's dotage reached the most exemplary and correct of gentlemen. He trembled daily lest he should hear that the Ribbons was proclaimed his second legal mother-in-law. After that first and last visit, his father's name was never mentioned in Pitt's polite and genteel establishment. It was the skeleton in his house, and all the family walked by it in terror and silence. The Countess Southdown kept on dropping per coach at the lodge-gate the most exciting tracts, tracts which ought to frighten the hair off your head. Mrs. Bute at the parsonage nightly looked out to see if the sky was red over the elms behind which the Hall stood, and the mansion was on fire. Sir G. Wapshot and Sir H. Fuddlestone, old friends of the house, wouldn't sit on the bench with Sir Pitt at Quarter Sessions, and cut him dead in the High Street of Southampton, where the reprobate stood offering his dirty old hands to them. Nothing had any effect upon him; he put his hands into his pockets, and burst out laughing, as he scrambled into his carriage-and-four; he used to burst out laughing at Lady Southdown's tracts; and he laughed at his sons, and at the world, and at the Ribbons when she was angry, which was not seldom.

Miss Horrocks was installed as housekeeper at Queen's Crawley, and ruled all the domestics there with great majesty and rigour. All the servants were instructed to address her as 'mum', or 'madam',—and there was one

little maid, on her promotion, who persisted in calling her
' my lady ', without any rebuke on the part of the housekeeper. ' There has been better ladies, and there has been
worser, Hester,' was Miss Horrocks's reply to this compliment of her inferior : so she ruled, having supreme power
over all except her father, whom, however, she treated with
considerable haughtiness, warning him not to be too
familiar in his behaviour to one ' as was to be a baronet's
lady '. Indeed, she rehearsed that exalted part in life with
great satisfaction to herself, and to the amusement of old
Sir Pitt, who chuckled at her airs and graces, and would
laugh by the hour together at her assumptions of dignity
and imitations of genteel life. He swore it was as good as
a play to see her in the character of a fine dame, and he
made her put on one of the first Lady Crawley's court-
dresses, swearing (entirely to Miss Horrocks's own concurrence) that the dress became her prodigiously, and threatening to drive her off that very instant to Court in a coach-
and-four. She had the ransacking of the wardrobes of the
two defunct ladies, and cut and hacked their posthumous
finery so as to suit her own tastes and figure. And she
would have liked to take possession of their jewels and
trinkets too ; but the old baronet had locked them away
in his private cabinet, nor could she coax or wheedle him
out of the keys. And it is a fact, that some time after she
left Queen's Crawley a copybook belonging to this lady
was discovered, which showed that she had taken great
pains in private to learn the art of writing in general, and
especially of writing her own name as Lady Crawley, Lady
Betsy Horrocks, Lady Elizabeth Crawley, &c.

Though the good people of the parsonage never went to
the Hall, and shunned the horrid old dotard its owner, yet
they kept a strict knowledge of all that happened there,
and were looking out every day for the catastrophe for
which Miss Horrocks was also eager. But Fate intervened
enviously, and prevented her from receiving the reward due
to such immaculate love and virtue.

One day the baronet surprised ' her ladyship ', as he
jocularly called her, seated at that old and tuneless piano in
the drawing-room, which had scarcely been touched since
Becky Sharp played quadrilles upon it. Seated at the
piano with the utmost gravity, and squalling to the best of
her power in imitation of the music which she had some-

times heard. The little kitchenmaid on her promotion was standing at her mistress's side, quite delighted during the operation, and wagging her head up and down, and crying, ' Lor, mum, 'tis bittiful,'—just like a genteel sycophant in a real drawing-room.

This incident made the old baronet roar with laughter, as usual. He narrated the circumstance a dozen times to Horrocks in the course of the evening, and greatly to the discomfiture of Miss Horrocks. He thrummed on the

table as if it had been a musical instrument and squalled in imitation of her manner of singing. He vowed that such a beautiful voice ought to be cultivated, and declared she ought to have singing-masters, in which proposals she saw nothing ridiculous. He was in great spirits that night; and drank with his friend and butler an extraordinary quantity of rum-and-water- -at a very late hour the faithful friend and domestic conducted his master to his bedroom.

Half an hour afterwards there was a great hurry and

bustle in the house. Lights went about from window to window in the lonely desolate old Hall, whereof but two or three rooms were ordinarily occupied by its owner. Presently a boy on a pony went galloping off to Mudbury, to the doctor's house there. And in another hour (by which fact we ascertain how carefully the excellent Mrs. Bute Crawley had always kept up an understanding with the great house), that lady in her clogs and calash,* the Reverend Bute Crawley, and James Crawley her son, had walked over from the Rectory through the park, and had entered the mansion by the open hall-door.

They passed through the hall and the small oak parlour, on the table of which stood the three tumblers and the empty rum-bottle which had served for Sir Pitt's carouse, and through that apartment into Sir Pitt's study, where they found Miss Horrocks, of the guilty ribbons, with a wild air, trying at the presses and escritoires with a bunch of keys. She dropped them with a scream of terror, as little Mrs. Bute's eyes flashed out at her from under her black calash.

'Look at that, James and Mr. Crawley,' cried Mrs. Bute, pointing at the scared figure of the black-eyed, guilty wench.

'He gave 'em me ; he gave 'em me ! ' she cried.

'Gave them you, you abandoned creature ! ' screamed Mrs. Bute. 'Bear witness, Mr. Crawley, we found this good-for-nothing woman in the act of stealing your brother's property ; and she will be hanged, as I always said she would.'

Betsy Horrocks quite daunted, flung herself down on her knees, bursting into tears. But those who know a really good woman are aware that she is not in a hurry to forgive, and that the humiliation of an enemy is a triumph to her soul.

'Ring the bell, James,' Mrs. Bute said. 'Go on ringing it till the people come.' The three or four domestics resident in the deserted old house came presently at that jangling and continued summons.

'Put that woman in the strong-room,' she said. 'We caught her in the act of robbing Sir Pitt. Mr. Crawley, you'll make out her committal—and, Beddoes, you'll drive her over in the spring-cart, in the morning, to Southampton Gaol.'

THE RIBBONS DISCOVERED IN THE FACT

'My dear,' interposed the magistrate and rector—'she's only——'

'Are there no handcuffs?' Mrs. Bute continued, stamping in her clogs. 'There used to be handcuffs. Where's the creature's abominable father?'

'He *did* give 'em me,' still cried poor Betsy; 'didn't he, Hester? You saw Sir Pitt—you know you did—give 'em me, ever so long ago—the day after Mudbury fair: not that I want 'em. Take 'em if you think they ain't mine.' And here the unhappy wretch pulled out from her pocket a large pair of paste shoe-buckles which had excited her admiration, and which she had just appropriated out of one of the bookcases in the study, where they had lain.

'Law, Betsy, how could you go for to tell such a wicked story!' said Hester, the little kitchenmaid late on her promotion—'and to Madam Crawley, so good and kind, and his rev'rince' (with a curtsy) 'and you may search all *my* boxes, mum, I'm sure, and here's my keys as I'm an honest girl though of pore parents and workhouse bred—and if you find so much as a beggarly bit of lace or a silk stocking out of all the gownds as *you've* had the picking of may I never go to church agin.'

'Give up your keys, you hardened hussy,' hissed out the virtuous little lady in the calash.

'And here's a candle, mum, and if you please, mum, I can show you her room, mum, and the press in the housekeeper's room, mum, where she keeps heaps and heaps of things, mum,' cried out the eager little Hester with a profusion of curtsies.

'Hold your tongue, if you please. I know the room which the creature occupies perfectly well. Mrs. Brown, have the goodness to come with me, and Beddoes, don't you lose sight of that woman,' said Mrs. Bute, seizing the candle.—'Mr. Crawley, you had better go upstairs, and see that they are not murdering your unfortunate brother'—and the calash, escorted by Mrs. Brown, walked away to the apartment, which, as she said truly, she knew perfectly well.

Bute went upstairs, and found the doctor from Mudbury, with the frightened Horrocks over his master in a chair. They were trying to bleed Sir Pitt Crawley.

With the early morning an express was sent off to Mr. Pitt Crawley by the rector's lady, who assumed the command

of everything, and had watched the old baronet through
the night.   He had been brought back to a sort of life ; he
could not speak, but seemed to recognize people.   Mrs.
Bute kept resolutely by his bedside.   She never seemed to
want to sleep, that little woman, and did not close her fiery
black eyes once, though the Doctor snored in the arm-chair.
Horrocks made some wild efforts to assert his authority
and assist his master : but Mrs. Bute called him a tipsy old
wretch, and bade him never show his face again in that house
or he should be transported like his abominable daughter.

Terrified by her manner he slunk down to the oak parlour
where Mr. James was, who, having tried the bottle standing
there and found no liquor in it, ordered Mr. Horrocks to
get another bottle of rum, which he fetched, with clean
glasses, and to which the rector and his son sat down :
ordering Horrocks to put down the keys at that instant and
never to show his face again.

Cowed by this behaviour Horrocks gave up the keys : and
he and his daughter slunk off silently through the night, and
gave up possession of the house of Queen's Crawley.

CHAPTER XL

IN WHICH BECKY IS RECOGNIZED BY THE FAMILY

THE heir of Crawley arrived at home,
in due time, after this catastrophe, and henceforth may be
said to have reigned in Queen's
Crawley.   For though the old
baronet survived many months,
he never recovered the use of
his intellect or his speech completely, and the government of
the estate devolved upon his
elder son.   In a strange condition Pitt found it.   Sir Pitt
was always buying and mort-
gaging : he had twenty men of
business,   and   quarrels   with
each ; quarrels with all his tenants, and lawsuits with them ;
lawsuits with the lawyers ; lawsuits with the Mining and

Dock Companies in which he was proprietor ; and with every person with whom he had business. To unravel these difficulties, and to set the estate clear was a task worthy of the orderly and persevering diplomatist of Pumpernickel : and he set himself to work with prodigious assiduity. His whole family, of course, was transported to Queen's Crawley, whither Lady Southdown, of course, came too ; and she set about converting the parish under the rector's nose, and brought down her irregular clergy to the dismay of the angry Mrs. Bute. Sir Pitt had concluded no bargain for the sale of the living of Queen's Crawley ; when it should drop, her ladyship proposed to take the patronage into her own hands, and present a young protégé to the Rectory ; on which subject the diplomatic Pitt said nothing.

Mrs. Bute's intentions with regard to Miss Betsy Horrocks were not carried into effect : and she paid no visit to Southampton Gaol. She and her father left the Hall, when the latter took possession of the ' Crawley Arms ' in the village, of which he had got a lease from Sir Pitt. The ex-butler had obtained a small freehold there likewise, which gave him a vote for the borough. The rector had another of these votes, and these and four others formed the representative body which returned the two members for Queen's Crawley.*

There was a show of courtesy kept up between the Rectory and the Hall ladies, between the younger ones at least, for Mrs. Bute and Lady Southdown never could meet without battles, and gradually ceased seeing each other. Her ladyship kept her room when the ladies from the Rectory visited their cousins at the Hall. Perhaps Mr. Pitt was not very much displeased at these occasional absences of his mamma-in-law. He believed the Binkie family to be the greatest and wisest, and most interesting in the world, and her ladyship and his aunt had long held ascendancy over him ; but sometimes he felt that she commanded him too much. To be considered young was complimentary doubtless ; but at six-and-forty to be treated as a boy was sometimes mortifying. Lady Jane yielded up everything, however, to her mother. She was only fond of her children in private ; and it was lucky for her that Lady Southdown's multifarious business, her conferences with ministers, and her correspondence with all the missionaries of Africa, Asia, and Australasia, &c., occupied the venerable countess a great deal, so that she had but little time to devote to her granddaughter, the little Matilda, and her grandson, Master Pitt Crawley. The latter was a feeble child : and it was only by prodigious quantities of calomel that Lady South-down was able to keep him in life at all.

As for Sir Pitt he retired into those very apartments where Lady Crawley had been previously extinguished, and here was tended by Miss Hester, the girl upon her promotion, with constant care and assiduity. What love, what fidelity, what constancy is there equal to that of a nurse with good wages ? They smooth pillows : and make arrowroot : they get up at nights : they bear complaints and querulousness : they see the sun shining out of doors and don't want to go abroad : they sleep on arm-chairs, and eat their meals in solitude : they pass long, long evenings doing nothing, watching the embers, and the patient's drink simmering in the jug : they read the weekly paper the whole week through ; and Law's *Serious Call* or the *Whole Duty of Man* suffices them for literature for the year—and we quarrel with them because, when their relations come to see them once a week, a little gin is smuggled in in their linen-basket. Ladies, what man's love is there that would stand a year's nursing of the object of his affection ? Whereas a nurse will stand by you for ten pounds a quarter, and we think her too highly paid. At least Mr. Crawley grumbled a good deal about paying half as much to Miss Hester for her constant attendance upon the baronet his father.

Of sunshiny days this old gentleman was taken out in a chair on the terrace—the very chair which Miss Crawley had had at Brighton, and which had been transported thence with a number of Lady Southdown's effects to Queen's Crawley. Lady Jane always walked by the old man ; and was an evident favourite with him. He used to nod many times to her and smile when she came in, and utter inarticu-late deprecatory moans when she was going away. When the door shut upon her he would cry and sob—whereupon Hester's face and manner, which was always exceedingly bland and gentle while her lady was present, would change at once and she would make faces at him, and clench her fist, and scream out, ' Hold your tongue, you stoopid old fool,' and twirl away his chair from the fire which he loved to look at—at which he would cry more. For this was all

SIR PITT'S LAST STAGE

that was left after more than seventy years of cunning and
struggling, and drinking, and scheming, and sin, and selfishness—a whimpering old idiot put in and out of bed and
cleaned and fed like a baby.

At last a day came when the nurse's occupation was over.
Early one morning as Pitt Crawley was at his steward's and
bailiff's books in the study, a knock came to the door, and
Hester presented herself dropping a curtsy, and said—

'If you please, Sir Pitt, Sir Pitt died this morning, Sir
Pitt. I was a-making of his toast, Sir Pitt, for his gruel,
Sir Pitt, which he took every morning reglar at six, Sir Pitt,
and—I thought I heard a moan like, Sir Pitt—and—and—
and——' She dropped another curtsy.

What was it that made Pitt's pale face flush quite red ?
Was it because he was Sir Pitt at last, with a seat in Parliament, and perhaps future honours in prospect ? ' I'll clear
the estate now with the ready money,' he thought, and
rapidly calculated its incumbrances and the improvements
which he would make. He would not use his aunt's money
previously lest Sir Pitt should recover and his outlay be
in vain.

All the blinds were pulled down at the Hall and Rectory :
the church bell was tolled, and the chancel hung in black ;
and Bute Crawley didn't go to a coursing meeting, but went
and dined quietly at Fuddlestone, where they talked about
his deceased brother and young Sir Pitt over their port.
Miss Betsy, who was by this time married to a saddler at
Mudbury, cried a good deal. The family surgeon rode
over and paid his respectful compliments, and inquiries for
the health of their ladyships. The death was talked about at
Mudbury and at the ' Crawley Arms' ; the landlord whereof
had become reconciled with the rector of late, who was
occasionally known to step into the parlour and taste Mr.
Horrocks's mild beer.

'Shall I write to your brother—or will you ? ' asked
Lady Jane of her husband, Sir Pitt.

' I will write, of course,' Sir Pitt said, ' and invite him to
the funeral : it will be but becoming.'

' And—and—Mrs. Rawdon,' said Lady Jane, timidly.

' Jane ! ' said Lady Southdown, ' how can you think of
such a thing ? '

' Mrs. Rawdon must of course be asked,' said Sir Pitt
resolutely.

' Not whilst *I* am in the house ! ' said Lady Southdown.

' Your ladyship will be pleased to recollect that I am
the head of this family,' Sir Pitt replied.   ' If you please,
Lady Jane, you will write a letter to Mrs. Rawdon Crawley,
requesting her presence upon this melancholy occasion.'

' Jane, I forbid you to put pen to paper ! ' cried the
countess.

' I believe I am the head of this family,' Sir Pitt repeated ;
' and however much I may regret any circumstance which
may lead to your ladyship quitting this house, must, if
you please, continue to govern it as I see fit.'

Lady Southdown rose up as magnificent as Mrs. Siddons
in Lady Macbeth,* and ordered that horses might be put to
her carriage.   If her son and daughter turned her out of
their house, she would hide her sorrows somewhere in loneliness, and pray for their conversion to better thoughts.

' We don't turn you out of our house, mamma,' said the
timid Lady Jane, imploringly.

' You invite such company to it as no Christian lady
should meet, and I will have my horses to-morrow morning.'

' Have the goodness to write, Jane, under my dictation,'
said Sir Pitt, rising, and throwing himself into an attitude
of command, like the Portrait of a Gentleman in the
Exhibition,* ' and begin.   " Queen's Crawley, September
14, 1822.—My dear brother——" '

Hearing these decisive and terrible words, Lady Macbeth,
who had been waiting for a sign of weakness or vacillation
on the part of her son-in-law, rose, and with a scared look,
left the library.   Lady Jane looked up to her husband, as
if she would fain follow and soothe her mamma ; but Pitt
forbade his wife to move.

' She won't go away,' he said.   ' She has let her house
at Brighton and has spent her last half-year's dividends.
A countess living at an inn is a ruined woman.   I have been
waiting long for an opportunity to take this—this decisive
step, my love ; for, as you must perceive, it is impossible
that there should be two chiefs in a family : and now, if you
please, we will resume the dictation.   " My dear brother,
the melancholy intelligence which it is my duty to convey
to my family must have long been anticipated by," ' &c.

In a word, Pitt having come to his kingdom, and having
by good luck, or desert rather, as he considered, assumed
almost all the fortune which his other relatives had expected.

was determined to treat his family kindly and respectably, and make a house of Queen's Crawley once more. It pleased him to think that he should be its chief. He proposed to use the vast influence that his commanding talents and position must speedily acquire for him in the county to get his brother placed and his cousins decently provided for, and perhaps had a little sting of repentance as he thought that he was the proprietor of all that they had hoped for. In the course of three or four days' reign his bearing was changed, and his plans quite fixed : he determined to rule justly and honestly, to depose Lady Southdown, and to be on the friendliest possible terms with all the relations of his blood.

So he dictated a letter to his brother Rawdon—a solemn and elaborate letter, containing the profoundest observations, couched in the longest words, and filling with wonder the simple little secretary, who wrote under her husband's order. 'What an orator this will be,' thought she, 'when he enters the House of Commons' (on which point, and on the tyranny of Lady Southdown, Pitt had sometimes dropped hints to his wife in bed) ; 'how wise and good, and what a genius my husband is! I fancied him a little cold ; but how good, and what a genius ! '

The fact is, Pitt Crawley had got every word of the letter by heart, and had studied it with diplomatic secrecy, deeply and perfectly, long before he thought fit to communicate it to his astonished wife.

This letter, with a huge black border and seal, was accordingly dispatched by Sir Pitt Crawley to his brother the colonel, in London. Rawdon Crawley was but half-pleased at the receipt of it. 'What's the use of going down to that stupid place?' thought he. 'I can't stand being alone with Pitt after dinner, and horses there and back will cost us twenty pound.'

He carried the letter, as he did all difficulties, to Becky, upstairs in her bedroom—with her chocolate, which he always made and took to her of a morning.

He put the tray with the breakfast and the letter on the dressing-table, before which Becky sat combing her yellow hair. She took up the black-edged missive, and having read it, she jumped up from the chair, crying 'Hurray! ' and waving the note round her head.

' Hurray ? ' said Rawdon, wondering at the little figure capering about in a streaming flannel dressing-gown, with tawny locks dishevelled. 'He's not left us anything, Becky. I had my share when I came of age.'

' You'll never be of age, you silly old man,' Becky replied. ' Run out now to Madam Bruncy's, for I must have some mourning : and get a crape on your hat, and a black waist-coat—I don't think you've got one ; order it to be brought

home to-morrow, so that we may be able to start on Thursday.'

' You don't mean to go ? ' Rawdon interposed.

' Of course I mean to go. I mean that Lady Jane shall present me at Court next year. I mean that your brother shall give you a seat in Parliament, you stupid old creature. I mean that Lord Steyne shall have your vote and his, my dear, old, silly man; and that you shall be an Irish Secretary, or a West Indian Governor : or a Treasurer, or a Consul, or some such thing.'

'Posting will cost a dooce of a lot of money,' grumbled Rawdon.

'We might take Southdown's carriage, which ought to be present at the funeral, as he is a relation of the family : but, no—I intend that we shall go by the coach. They'll like it better. It seems more humble——'

'Rawdy goes of course ? ' the colonel asked.

'No such thing ; why pay an extra place ? He's too big to travel bodkin between you and me. Let him stay here in the nursery, and Briggs can make him a black frock. Go you : and do as I bid you. And you had best tell Sparks, your man, that old Sir Pitt is dead, and that you will come in for something considerable when the affairs are arranged. He'll tell this to Raggles, who has been pressing for money, and it will console poor Raggles.' And so Becky began sipping her chocolate.

When the faithful Lord Steyne arrived in the evening, he found Becky and her companion, who was no other than our friend Briggs, busy cutting, ripping, snipping, and tearing all sorts of black stuffs available for the melancholy occasion.

'Miss Briggs and I are plunged in grief and despondency for the death of our papa,' Rebecca said. 'Sir Pitt Crawley is dead, my lord. We have been tearing our hair all the morning, and now we are tearing up our old clothes.'

'Oh, Rebecca, how can you——' was all that Briggs could say as she turned up her eyes.

'Oh, Rebecca, how can you——' echoed my lord. 'So that old scoundrel's dead, is he ? He might have been a peer if he had played his cards better. Mr. Pitt had very nearly made him ; but he ratted always at the wrong time. What an old Silenus it was.'

'I might have been Silenus's widow,' said Rebecca. 'Don't you remember, Miss Briggs, how you peeped in at the door, and saw old Sir Pitt on his knees to me ? ' Miss Briggs, our old friend, blushed very much at this reminiscence ; and was glad when Lord Steyne ordered her to go downstairs and make him a cup of tea.

Briggs was the house-dog whom Rebecca had provided as guardian of her innocence and reputation. Miss Crawley had left her a little annuity. She would have been content to remain in the Crawley family with Lady Jane, who was good to her and to everybody ; but Lady Southdown

dismissed poor Briggs as quickly as decency permitted ; and
Mr. Pitt (who thought himself much injured by the uncalled-
for generosity of his deceased relative towards a lady who
had only been Miss Crawley's faithful retainer a score of
years) made no objections to that exercise of the dowager's
authority.   Bowls and Firkin likewise received their legacies,
and their dismissals; and married and set up a lodging-house,
according to the custom of their kind.

Briggs tried to live with her relations in the country, but
found that attempt was vain after the better society to
which she had been accustomed.   Briggs's friends, small
tradesmen in a country town, quarrelled over Miss Briggs's
forty pounds a year, as eagerly and more openly than Miss
Crawley's kinsfolk had for that lady's inheritance.   Briggs's
brother, a Radical hatter and grocer, called his sister a purse-
proud aristocrat, because she would not advance a part
of her capital to stock his shop : and she would have done
so most likely, but that their sister, a Dissenting shoemaker's
lady, at variance with the hatter and grocer who went to
another chapel, showed how their brother was on the verge
of bankruptcy, and took possession of Briggs for a while.
The Dissenting shoemaker wanted Miss Briggs to send his
son to college, and make a gentleman of him.   Between
them the two families got a great portion of her private
savings out of her : and finally she fled to London followed
by the anathemas of both, and determined to seek for
servitude again as infinitely less onerous than liberty.   And
advertising in the papers that a ' Gentlewoman of agreeable
manners, and accustomed to the best society, was anxious
to,' &c., she took up her residence with Mr. Bowls in Half
Moon Street, and waited the result of the advertisement.

So it was that she fell in with Rebecca.   Mrs. Rawdon's
dashing little carriage and ponies was whirling down the
street one day, just as Miss Briggs, fatigued, had reached
Mr. Bowls's door, after a weary walk to the *Times* office in
the City, to insert her advertisement for the sixth time.
Rebecca was driving, and at once recognized the gentlewoman with agreeable manners, and being a perfectly good-
humoured woman, as we have seen, and having a regard for
Briggs, she pulled up the ponies at the doorsteps, gave
the reins to the groom, and jumping out had hold of both
Briggs's hands, before she of the agreeable manners had
recovered from the shock of seeing an old friend.

Briggs cried, and Becky laughed a great deal, and kissed the gentlewoman as soon as they got into the passage; and thence into Mrs. Bowls's front parlour, with the red moreen curtains, and the round looking-glass, with the chained eagle above, gazing upon the back of the ticket in the window which announced ' Apartments to Let '

Briggs told all her history amidst those perfectly uncalled-for sobs and ejaculations of wonder with which women of her soft nature salute an old acquaintance, or regard a rencontre in the street; for though people meet other people every day, yet some there are who insist upon discovering miracles; and women, even though they have disliked each other, begin to cry when they meet, deploring and remembering the time when they last quarrelled. So, in a word, Briggs told all her history, and Becky gave a narrative of her own life, with her usual artlessness and candour.

Mrs. Bowls, late Firkin, came and listened grimly in the passage to the hysterical sniffling and giggling which went on in the front parlour.   Becky had never been a favourite of hers.   Since the establishment of the married couple in London they had frequented their former friends of the house of Raggles, and did not like the latter's account of the colonel's *ménage*. ' *I* wouldn't trust him, Ragg, my boy,' Bowls remarked : and his wife, when Mrs. Rawdon issued from the parlour, only saluted the lady with a very sour curtsy; and her fingers were like so many sausages, cold and lifeless, when she held them out in deference to Mrs. Rawdon, who persisted in shaking hands with the retired lady's-maid.   She whirled away into Piccadilly, nodding, with the sweetest of smiles towards Miss Briggs, who hung nodding at the window close under the advertisement-card, and at the next moment was in the Park with a half-dozen of dandies cantering after her carriage.

When she found how her friend was situated, and how having a snug legacy from Miss Crawley, salary was no object to our gentlewoman, Becky instantly formed some benevolent little domestic plans concerning her.   This was just such a companion as would suit her establishment, and she invited Briggs to come to dinner with her that very evening, when she should see Becky's dear little darling Rawdon.

Mrs. Bowls cautioned her lodger against venturing into

the lion's den, ' wherein you will rue it, Miss B., mark my
words, and as sure as my name is Bowls.' And Briggs
promised to be very cautious. The upshot of which caution
was that she went to live with Mrs. Rawdon the next week,
and had lent Rawdon Crawley six hundred pounds upon
annuity before six more months were over.

CHAPTER XLI

IN WHICH BECKY REVISITS THE HALLS OF HER ANCESTORS

So the mourning being ready, and
Sir Pitt Crawley warned of their
arrival, Colonel Crawley and his
wife took a couple of places in the
same old ' Highflyer ' coach,* by
which Rebecca had travelled in
the defunct baronet's company,
on her first journey into the world
some nine years before. How
well she remembered the inn
yard, and the ostler to whom
she refused money, and the
insinuating Cambridge lad who
wrapped her in his coat on
the journey! Rawdon took
his place outside, and would have liked to drive, but his
grief forbade him. He sat by the coachman, and talked
about horses and the road the whole way; and who kept
the inns, and who horsed the coach by which he had travelled so many a time, when he and Pitt were boys going
to Eton. At Mudbury a carriage and a pair of horses
received them, with a coachman in black. ' It's the old
drag, Rawdon,' Rebecca said, as they got in. ' The worms
have eaten the cloth a good deal—there's the stain which
Sir Pitt—ha ! I see Dawson the ironmonger has his shutters
up*—which Sir Pitt made such a noise about. It was
a bottle of cherry brandy he broke which we went to fetch
for your aunt from Southampton. How time flies, to be
sure ! that can't be Polly Talboys, that bouncing girl
standing by her mother at the cottage there. I remember
her a mangy little urchin picking weeds in the garden.'

'Fine gal,' said Rawdon, returning the salute which the cottage gave him, by two fingers applied to his crape hatband. Becky bowed and saluted, and recognized people here and there graciously. These recognitions were inexpressibly pleasant to her. It seemed as if she was not an impostor any more, and was coming to the home of her ancestors. Rawdon was rather abashed, and cast down on the other hand. What recollections of boyhood and innocence might have been flitting across his brain ? What pangs of dim remorse and doubt and shame ?*

'Your sisters must be young women now,' Rebecca said, thinking of those girls for the first time perhaps since she had left them.

'Don't know, I'm shaw,' replied the colonel. 'Hullo! here's old Mother Lock. How-dy-do, Mrs. Lock ? Remember me, don't you ? Master Rawdon, hey ? Dammy, how those old women last ; she was a hundred when I was a boy.'

They were going through the lodge-gates kept by old Mrs. Lock, whose hand Rebecca insisted upon shaking, as she flung open the creaking old iron gate, and the carriage passed between the two moss-grown pillars surmounted by the dove and serpent.

'The governor has cut into the timber,' Rawdon said, looking about, and then was silent—so was Becky. Both of them were rather agitated, and thinking of old times. He about Eton, and his mother, whom he remembered, a frigid demure woman, and a sister who died, of whom he had been passionately fond ; and how he used to thrash Pitt ; and about little Rawdy at home. And Rebecca thought about her own youth, and the dark secrets of those early tainted days ; and of her entrance into life by yonder gates ; and of Miss Pinkerton, and Joe, and Amelia.

The gravel walk and terrace had been scraped quite clean. A grand painted hatchment was already over the great entrance, and two very solemn and tall personages in black flung open each a leaf of the door as the carriage pulled up at the familiar steps. Rawdon turned red, and Becky somewhat pale, as they passed through the old hall, arm in arm. She pinched her husband's arm as they entered the oak parlour, where Sir Pitt and his wife were ready to receive them. Sir Pitt in black, Lady Jane in black, and my Lady Southdown with a large black head-piece of bugles and feathers, which waved on her ladyship's head like an undertaker's tray.

Sir Pitt had judged correctly, that she would not quit the premises. She contented herself by preserving a solemn and stony silence, when in company of Pitt and his rebellious wife, and by frightening the children in the nursery by the ghastly gloom of her demeanour. Only a very faint bending of the head-dress and plumes welcomed Rawdon and his wife, as those prodigals returned to their family.

To say the truth, they were not affected very much one way or other by this coolness. Her ladyship was a person only of secondary consideration in their minds just then—they were intent upon the reception which the reigning brother and sister would afford them.

Pitt, with rather a heightened colour, went up and shook his brother by the hand ; and saluted Rebecca with a hand-shake and a very low bow. But Lady Jane took both the hands of her sister-in-law and kissed her affectionately. The embrace somehow brought tears into the eyes of the little adventuress—which ornaments, as we know, she wore very seldom. The artless mark of kindness and confidence touched and pleased her ; and Rawdon, encouraged by this demonstration on his sister's part, twirled up his moustachios, and took leave to salute Lady Jane with a kiss, which caused her ladyship to blush exceedingly.

' Dev'lish nice little woman, Lady Jane,' was his verdict, when he and his wife were together again. ' Pitt's got fat, too, and is doing the thing handsomely.' ' He can afford it,' said Rebecca, and agreed in her husband's farther opinion, ' that the mother-in-law was a tremendous old Guy—and that the sisters were rather well-looking young women.'

They, too, had been summoned from school to attend the funeral ceremonies. It seemed Sir Pitt Crawley, for the dignity of the house and family, had thought right to have about the place as many persons in black as could possibly be assembled. All the men and maids of the house, the old women of the almshouse, whom the elder Sir Pitt had cheated out of a great portion of their due, the parish clerk's family, and the special retainers of both Hall and Rectory were habited in sable ; added to these,

the undertaker's men, at least a score, with crapes and
hatbands, and who made a goodly show when the great
burying show took place—but these are mute personages
in our drama ; and, having nothing to do or say, need
occupy a very little space here.

With regard to her sisters-in-law Rebecca did not attempt
to forget her former position of governess towards them,
but recalled it frankly and kindly, and asked them about
their studies with great gravity, and told them that she
had thought of them many and many a day, and longed
to know of their welfare.   In fact you would have supposed
that ever since she had left them she had not ceased to
keep them uppermost in her thoughts, and to take the
tenderest interest in their welfare.   So supposed Lady
Crawley herself and her young sisters.

' She's hardly changed since eight years,' said Miss Rosalind to Miss Violet, as they were preparing for dinner.

' Those red-haired women look wonderfully well,' replied
the other.

' Hers is much darker than it was ; I think she must
dye it,' Miss Rosalind added. ' She is stouter, too, and
altogether improved,' continued Miss Rosalind, who was
disposed to be very fat.

' At least she gives herself no airs, and remembers that
she was our governess once,' Miss Violet said, intimating
that it befitted all governesses to keep their proper place,
and forgetting altogether that she was granddaughter not
only of Sir Walpole Crawley, but of Mr. Dawson of Mudbury,
and so had a coal-scuttle in her scutcheon.   There are
other very well-meaning people whom one meets every day
in Vanity Fair, who are surely equally oblivious.

' It can't be true what the girls at the Rectory said, that
her mother was an opera-dancer——'

' A person can't help their birth,' Rosalind replied with
great liberality. ' And I agree with our brother, that as
she is in the family, of course we are ,bound to notice her.
I am sure Aunt Bute need not talk : she wants to marry
Kate to young Hooper, the wine-merchant, and absolutely
asked him to come to the Rectory for orders.'

' I wonder whether Lady Southdown will go away ; she
looked very glum upon Mrs. Rawdon,' the other said.

' I wish she would. *I* won't read the *Washerwoman
of Finchley Common*,' vowed Violet ; and so saying, and

avoiding a passage at the end of which a certain coffin
was placed with a couple of watchers, and lights perpetually
burning in the closed room, these young women came down
to the family dinner, for which the bell rang as usual.

But before this, Lady Jane conducted Rebecca to the
apartments prepared for her, which, with the rest of the
house, had assumed a very much improved appearance of
order and comfort during Pitt's regency, and here beholding
that Mrs. Rawdon's modest little trunks had arrived, and
were placed in the bedroom and dressing-room adjoining,
helped her to take off her neat black bonnet and cloak,
and asked her sister-in-law in what more she could be useful.

' What I should like best,' said Rebecca, ' would be to
go to the nursery ; and see your dear little children ':
on which the two ladies looked very kindly at each other,
and went to that apartment hand in hand.

Becky admired little Matilda, who was not quite four
years old, as the most charming little love in the world ;
and the boy, a little fellow of two years—pale, heavy-eyed,
and large-headed, she pronounced to be a perfect prodigy
in point of size, intelligence, and beauty.

I wish mamma would not insist on giving him so much
medicine,' Lady Jane said, with a sigh. ' I often think
we should all be better without it.' And then Lady Jane
and her new-found friend had one of those confidential
medical conversations about the children, which all mothers,
and most women, as I am given to understand, delight in.
Fifty years ago, and when the present writer, being an
interesting little boy, was ordered out of the room with the
ladies after dinner, I remember quite well that their talk
was chiefly about their ailments ; and putting this question
directly to two or three since, I have always got from them
the acknowledgement that times are not changed. Let
my fair readers remark for themselves this very evening
when they quit the dessert-table, and assemble to celebrate
the drawing-room mysteries. Well—in half an hour Becky
and Lady Jane were close and intimate friends—and in
the course of the evening her ladyship informed Sir Pitt
that she thought her new sister-in-law was a kind, frank,
unaffected, and affectionate young woman.

And so having easily won the daughter's goodwill, the
indefatigable little woman bent herself to conciliate the
august Lady Southdown. As soon as she found her ladyship

alone, Rebecca attacked her on the nursery question at
once, and said that her own little boy was saved, actually
saved, by calomel, freely administered, when all the physicians in Paris had given the dear child up.   And then she
mentioned how often she had heard of Lady Southdown
from that excellent man the Reverend Lawrence Grills,
minister of the chapel in May Fair, which she frequented ;
and how her views were very much changed by circumstances and misfortunes ; and how she hoped that a past
life spent in worldliness and error might not incapacitate
her from *more serious*
thought for the future.
She described how in
former days she had
been indebted to Mr.
Crawley for religious
instruction,   touched
upon the *Washerwoman
of Finchley Common*,
which she had read
with the greatest profit,
and asked about Lady
Emily, its gifted author,
now Lady Emily Horn-
blower, at Cape Town,
where her husband had
strong hopes of be-
coming Bishop of Caf-
fraria.*

But she crowned all,
and confirmed herself
in Lady Southdown's
favour, by feeling very much agitated and unwell after
the funeral, and requesting her ladyship's medical advice,
which the dowager not only gave, but, wrapped up in
a bed-gown, and looking more like Lady Macbeth than
ever, came privately in the night to Becky's room, with a
parcel of favourite tracts, and a medicine of her own composition, which she insisted that Mrs. Rawdon should take.

Becky first accepted the tracts, and began to examine
them with great interest, engaging the dowager in a conversation concerning them and the welfare of her soul,
by which means she hoped that her body might escape

medication. But after the religious topics were exhausted,
Lady Macbeth would not quit Becky's chamber until her
cup of night-drink was emptied too; and poor Mrs. Rawdon
was compelled actually to assume a look of gratitude,
and to swallow the medicine under the unyielding old
dowager's nose, who left her victim finally with a benediction.

It did not much comfort Mrs. Rawdon; her countenance
was very queer when Rawdon came in and heard what
had happened; and his explosions of laughter were as
loud as usual, when Becky, with a fun which she could not
disguise, even though it was at her own expense, described
the occurrence, and how she had been victimized by Lady
Southdown. Lord Steyne, and her son in London, had
many a laugh over the story, when Rawdon and his wife
returned to their quarters in May Fair. Becky acted the
whole scene for them. She put on a nightcap and gown.
She preached a great sermon in the true serious manner:
she lectured on the virtue of the medicine which she pretended to administer, with a gravity of imitation so perfect,
that you would have thought it was the countess's
own Roman nose through which she snuffled. ' Give us
Lady Southdown and the black dose,' was a constant cry
amongst the folks in Becky's little drawing-room in
May Fair. And for the first time in her life the Dowager
Countess of Southdown was made amusing.

Sir Pitt remembered the testimonies of respect and
veneration which Rebecca had paid personally to himself
in early days, and was tolerably well disposed towards
her. The marriage, ill-advised as it was, had improved
Rawdon very much—that was clear from the colonel's
altered habits and demeanour—and had it not been a lucky
union as regarded Pitt himself? The cunning diplomatist
smiled inwardly as he owned that he owed his fortune to
it, and acknowledged that he at least ought not to cry out
against it. His satisfaction was not removed by Rebecca's
own statements, behaviour, and conversation.

She doubled the deference which before had charmed
him, calling out his conversational powers in such a manner
as quite to surprise Pitt himself, who, always inclined
to respect his own talents, admired them the more when
Rebecca pointed them out to him. With her sister-in-law,
Rebecca was satisfactorily able to prove, that it was Mrs.

Bute Crawley who brought about the marriage which she afterwards so calumniated : that it was Mrs. Bute's avarice —who hoped to gain all Miss Crawley's fortune, and deprive Rawdon of his aunt's favour—which caused and invented all the wicked reports against Rebecca. ' She succeeded in making us poor,' Rebecca said, with an air of angelical patience ; ' but how can I be angry with a woman who has given me one of the best husbands in the world ? And has not her own avarice been sufficiently punished by the ruin of her own hopes, and the loss of the property by which she set so much store ? Poor ! ' she cried. ' Dear Lady Jane, what care we for poverty ? I am used to it from childhood, and I am often thankful that Miss Crawley's money has gone to restore the splendour of the noble old family of which I am so proud to be a member. I am sure Sir Pitt will make a much better use of it than Rawdon would.'

All these speeches were reported to Sir Pitt by the most faithful of wives, and increased the favourable impression which Rebecca made ; so much so, that when on the third day after the funeral the family party were at dinner, Sir Pitt Crawley, carving fowls at the head of the table, actually said to Mrs. Rawdon, ' Ahem ! *Rebecca*, may I give you a wing ? '—a speech which made the little woman's eyes sparkle with pleasure.

While Rebecca was prosecuting the above schemes and hopes, and Pitt Crawley arranging the funeral ceremonial and other matters connected with his future progress and dignity, and Lady Jane busy with her nursery, as far as her mother would let her, and the sun rising and setting, and the clock-tower bell of the Hall ringing to dinner and to prayers as usual, the body of the late owner of Queen's Crawley lay in the apartment which he had occupied, watched unceasingly by the professional attendants who were engaged for that rite. A woman or two, and three or four undertaker's men, the best whom Southampton could furnish, dressed in black, and of a proper stealthy and tragical demeanour, had charge of the remains which they watched turn about, having the housekeeper's room for their place of rendezvous when off duty, where they played at cards in privacy and drank their beer.

The members of the family and servants of the house

kept away from the gloomy spot, where the bones of the
descendant of an ancient line of knights and gentlemen
lay, awaiting their final consignment to the family crypt.
No regrets attended them, save those of the poor woman
who had hoped to be Sir Pitt's wife and widow, and who
had fled in disgrace from the Hall over which she had so
nearly been a ruler. · Beyond her and a favourite old pointer
he had, and between whom and himself an attachment
subsisted during the period of his imbecility, the old man
had not a single friend to mourn him, having indeed, during
the whole course of his life, never taken the least pains to
secure one. Could the best and kindest of us who depart
from the earth, have an opportunity of revisiting it, I suppose he or she (assuming that any Vanity Fair feelings
subsist in the sphere whither we are bound) would have
a pang of mortification at finding how soon our survivors
were consoled. And so Sir Pitt was forgotten—like the
kindest and best of us—only a few weeks sooner.

Those who will may follow his remains to the grave,
whither they were borne on the appointed day, in the most
becoming manner, the family in black coaches, with their
handkerchiefs up to their noses, ready for the tears which
did not come: the undertaker and his gentlemen in deep
tribulation: the select tenantry mourning out of compliment
to the new landlord: the neighbouring gentry's carriages at
three miles an hour, empty, and in profound affliction: the
parson speaking out the formula about 'our dear brother
departed'. As long as we have a man's body, we play our
Vanities upon it, surrounding it with humbug and ceremonies, laying it in state, and packing it up in gilt nails
and velvet: and we finish our duty by placing over it
a stone, written all over with lies. Bute's curate, a smart
young fellow from Oxford, and Sir Pitt Crawley, composed
between them an appropriate Latin epitaph for the late
lamented baronet: and the former preached a classical
sermon, exhorting the survivors not to give way to grief,
and informing them in the most respectful terms that they
also would be one day called upon to pass that gloomy
and mysterious portal which had just closed upon the
remains of their lamented brother. Then the tenantry
mounted on horseback again, or stayed and refreshed
themselves at the 'Crawley Arms'. Then, after a lunch in
the servants' hall at Queen's Crawley, the gentry's carriages

wheeled off to their different destinations : then the undertaker's men, taking the ropes, palls, velvets, ostrich feathers, and other mortuary properties, clambered up on the roof of the hearse, and rode off to Southampton. Their faces relapsed into a natural expression as the horses, clearing the lodge gates, got into a brisker trot on the open road ; and squads of them might have been seen, speckling with black the public-house entrances, with pewter pots flashing in the sunshine. Sir Pitt's invalid-chair was wheeled away into a tool-house in the garden : the old pointer used to howl sometimes at first, but these were the only accents of grief which were heard in the Hall of which Sir Pitt Crawley, Baronet, had been master for some threescore years.

As the birds were pretty plentiful, and partridge-shooting is as it were the duty of an English gentleman of statesman-like propensities, Sir Pitt Crawley, the first shock of grief over, went out a little and partook of that diversion in a white hat with a crape round it. The sight of those fields of stubble and turnips, now his own, gave him many secret joys. Sometimes, and with an exquisite humility, he took no gun, but went out with a peaceful bamboo cane ; Rawdon, his big brother, and the keepers blazing away at his side. Pitt's money and acres had a great effect upon his brother. The penniless colonel became quite obsequious and respect-ful to the head of his house, and despised the milksop Pitt no longer. Rawdon listened with sympathy to his senior's prospects of planting and draining : gave his advice about the stables and cattle, rode over to Mudbury to look at a mare which he thought would carry Lady Jane, and offered to break her, &c. ; the rebellious dragoon was quite humbled and subdued, and became a most creditable younger brother. He had had constant bulletins from Miss Briggs in London respecting little Rawdon, who was left behind there : who sent messages of his own. ' I am very well,' he wrote. ' I hope you are very well. I hope mamma is very well. The pony is very well. Grey takes me to ride in the Park. I can canter. I met the little boy who rode before. He cried when he cantered. I do not cry.' Rawdon read these letters to his brother, and Lady Jane, who was delighted with them. The baronet promised to take charge of the lad at school ; and his kind-hearted wife gave Rebecca a bank-note, begging her to buy a present with it for her little nephew.

One day followed another, and the ladies of the house passed their life in those calm pursuits and amusements which satisfy country ladies. Bells rang to meals, and to prayers. The young ladies took exercise on the pianoforte every morning after breakfast, Rebecca giving them the benefit of her instruction. Then they put on thick shoes and walked in the park or shrubberies, or beyond the palings into the village, descending upon the cottages, with Lady Southdown's medicine, and tracts for the sick people there. Lady Southdown drove out in a pony-chaise, when Rebecca would take her place by the dowager's side, and listen to her solemn talk with the utmost interest. She sang Handel and Haydn to the family of evenings, and engaged in a large piece of worsted work, as if she had been born to the business, and as if this kind of life was to continue with her until she should sink to the grave in a polite old age, leaving regrets and a great quantity of Consols behind her—as if there were not cares and duns, schemes, shifts, and poverty, waiting outside the park gates, to pounce upon her when she issued into the world again.

'It isn't difficult to be a country gentleman's wife,' Rebecca thought. 'I think I could be a good woman if I had five thousand a year. I could dawdle about in the nursery, and count the apricots on the wall. I could water plants in a greenhouse, and pick off dead leaves from the geraniums. I could ask old women about their rheumatisms, and order half a crown's worth of soup for the poor. I shouldn't miss it much, out of five thousand a year. I could even drive out ten miles to dine at a neighbour's, and dress in the fashions of the year before last. I could go to church and keep awake in the great family pew : or go to sleep behind the curtains, with my veil down, if I only had practice. I could pay everybody, if I had but the money. This is what the conjurers* here pride themselves upon doing. They look down with pity upon us miserable sinners who have none. They think themselves generous if they give our children a five-pound note, and us contemptible if we are without one.' And who knows but Rebecca was right in her speculations—and that it was only a question of money and fortune which made the difference between her and an honest woman ? If you take tempta-

tions into account, who is to say that he is better than his
neighbour ?   A comfortable career of prosperity, if it does
not make people honest, at least keeps them so.   An
alderman coming from a turtle feast will not step out of
his carriage to steal a leg of mutton ; but put him to starve,
and see if he will not purloin a loaf.   Becky consoled herself
by so balancing the chances and equalizing the distribution
of good and evil in the world.

The old haunts, the old fields and woods, the copses,
ponds, and gardens, the rooms of the old house where
she had spent a couple of years seven years ago, were
all carefully revisited by her.   She had been young there,
or comparatively so, for she forgot the time when she
ever *was* young—but she remembered her thoughts and
feelings seven years back, and contrasted them with those
which she had at present, now that she had seen the
world and lived with great people, and raised herself far
beyond her original humble station.

' I have passed beyond it, because I have brains,' Becky
thought, ' and almost all the rest of the world are fools.
I could not go back, and consort with those people now,
whom I used to meet in my father's studio.   Lords come
up to my door with stars and garters instead of poor artists
with screws of tobacco in their pockets.   I have a gentleman
for my husband, and an earl's daughter for my sister in
the very house where I was little better than a servant
a few years ago.   But am I much better to do now in the
world than I was when I was the poor painter's daughter,
and wheedled the grocer round the corner for sugar and tea ?
Suppose I had married Francis who was so fond of me—
I couldn't have been much poorer than I am now.   Heigho !
I wish I could exchange my position in society, and all my
relations for a snug sum in the Three per Cent Consols;'*
for so it was that Becky felt the Vanity of human affairs,
and it was in those securities that she would have liked
to cast anchor.

It may perhaps have struck her that to have been honest
and humble, to have done her duty, and to have marched
straightforward on her way, would have brought her as
near happiness as that path by which she was striving to
attain it.   But,—just as the children at Queen's Crawley
went round the room, where the body of their father lay ;
—if ever Becky had these thoughts, she was accustomed

to walk round them, and not look in. She eluded them,
and despised them—or at least she was committed to the
other path from which retreat was now impossible. And
for my part I believe that remorse is the least active of all
a man's moral senses—the very easiest to be deadened
when wakened : and in some never wakened at all. We
grieve at being found out, and at the idea of shame or
punishment ; but the mere sense of wrong makes very
few people unhappy in Vanity Fair.

So Rebecca, during her stay at Queen's Crawley, made
as many friends of the Mammon of Unrighteousness as
she could possibly bring under control. Lady Jane and
her husband bade her farewell with the warmest demonstrations of goodwill. They looked forward with pleasure
to the time when the family-house in Gaunt Street being
repaired and beautified, they were to meet again in London.
Lady Southdown made her up a packet of medicine, and
sent a letter by her to the Rev. Lawrence Grills, exhorting
that gentleman to save the brand who ' honoured ' the
letter from the burning. Pitt accompanied them with
four horses in the carriage to Mudbury, having sent on their
baggage in a cart previously, accompanied with loads of
game.

' How happy you will be to see your darling little boy
again ! ' Lady Crawley said, taking leave of her kinswoman.

' Oh, so happy ! ' said Rebecca, throwing up the green
eyes. She was immensely happy to be free of the place,
and yet loath to go. Queen's Crawley was abominably
stupid ; and yet the air there was somehow purer than that
which she had been accustomed to breathe. Everybody
had been dull, but had been kind in their way. ' It is all
the influence of a long course of Three per Cents,' Becky
said to herself, and was right very likely.

However, the London lamps flashed joyfully as the stage
rolled into Piccadilly, and Briggs had made a beautiful
fire in Curzon Street, and little Rawdon was up to welcome
back his papa and mamma.

CHAPTER XLII

WHICH TREATS OF THE OSBORNE FAMILY

ONSIDERABLE time has elapsed since we have seen our respectable friend, old Mr. Osborne of Russell Square. He has not been the happiest of mortals since last we met him. Events have occurred which have not improved his temper, and in more instances than one he has not been allowed to have his own way. To be thwarted in this reasonable desire was always very injurious to the old gentleman ; and resistance became doubly exasperating when gout, age, loneliness, and the force of many disappointments combined to weigh him down. His stiff black hair began to grow quite white soon after his son's death ; his face grew redder ; his hands trembled more and more as he poured out his glass of port wine. He led his clerks a dire life in the City ; his family at home were not much happier. I doubt if Rebecca, whom we have seen piously praying for Consols, would have exchanged her poverty and the daredevil excitement and chances of her life, for Osborne's money and the humdrum gloom which enveloped him. He had proposed for Miss Swartz, but had been rejected scornfully by the partisans of that lady, who married her to a young sprig of Scotch nobility. He was a man to have married a woman out of low life, and bullied her dreadfully afterwards : but no person presented herself suitable to his taste ; and, instead, he tyrannized over his unmarried daughter, at home. She had a fine carriage and fine horses, and sat at the head of a table loaded with the grandest plate. She had a cheque-book, a prize footman to follow her when she walked, unlimited credit, and bows and compliments from all the tradesmen, and all the appurtenances of an heiress ; but she spent a woful time. The little charity-girls at the Foundling, the sweeperess at the crossing, the poorest under-kitchenmaid in the servants' hall, was happy compared to that unfortunate and now middle-aged young lady.

Frederick Bullock, Esq., of the house of Bullock, Hulker,
and Bullock, had married Maria Osborne, not without
a great deal of difficulty and grumbling on Mr. Bullock's
part. George being dead and cut out of his father's will,
Frederick insisted that the half of the old gentleman's
property should be settled upon his Maria, and indeed,
for a long time, refused ' to come to the scratch ' (it was
Mr. Frederick's own expression) on any other terms.
Osborne said Fred had agreed to take his daughter with
twenty thousand, and he should bind himself to no more.
' Fred might take it, and welcome, or leave it, and go and
be hanged.' Fred, whose hopes had been raised when
George had been disinherited, thought himself infamously
swindled by the old merchant, and for some time made
as if he would break off the match altogether. Osborne
withdrew his account from Bullock and Hulker's, went
on 'Change with a horsewhip which he swore he would
lay across the back of a certain scoundrel that should
be nameless, and demeaned himself in his usual violent
manner. Jane Osborne condoled with her sister Maria
during this family feud. ' I always told you, Maria, that
it was your money he loved, and not you,' she said, soothingly.

' He selected *me* and my money at any rate : he didn't
choose you and yours,' replied Maria, tossing up her head.

The rupture was, however, only temporary. Fred's
father and senior partners counselled him to take Maria,
even with the twenty thousand settled, half down, and
half at the death of Mr. Osborne, with the chances of the
further division of the property. So he 'knuckled down',
again to use his own phrase ; and sent old Hulker with
peaceable overtures to Osborne. It was his father, he
said, who would not hear of the match, and had made the
difficulties ; he was most anxious to keep the engagement.
The excuse was sulkily accepted by Mr. Osborne. Hulker
and Bullock were a high family of the City aristocracy, and
connected with the ' nobs ' at the West End. It was something for the old man to be able to say, ' My son, sir, of the
house of Hulker, Bullock and Co., sir ; my daughter's cousin,
Lady Mary Mango, sir, daughter of the Right Honourable
the Earl of Castlemouldy.' In his imagination he saw his
house peopled by the ' nobs '. So he forgave young Bullock
and consented that the marriage should take place.

It was a grand affair—the bridegroom's relatives giving the breakfast, their habitations being near St. George's, Hanover Square, where the business took place. The ' nobs of the West End ' were invited, and many of them signed the book. Mr. Mango and Lady Mary Mango were there, with the dear young Gwendoline and Gwinever Mango as bridesmaids ; Colonel Bludyer of the Dragoon Guards (eldest son of the house of Bludyer Brothers, Mincing Lane), another cousin of the bridegroom, and the Honourable Mrs. Bludyer ; the Honourable George Boulter, Lord Levant's son, and his lady, Miss Mango that was ; Lord Viscount Castletoddy ; Honourable James McMull and Mrs. McMull (formerly Miss Swartz), and a host of fashionables, who have all married into Lombard Street, and done a great deal to ennoble Cornhill.*

The young couple had a house near Berkeley Square, and a small villa at Roehampton, among the banking colony there. Fred was considered to have made rather a *mésalliance* by the ladies of his family, whose grandfather had been in a charity school, and who were allied through the husbands with some of the best blood in England. And Maria was bound, by superior pride and great care in the composition of her visiting-book, to make up for the defects of birth ; and felt it her duty to see her father and sister as little as possible.

That she should utterly break with the old man, who had still so many scores of thousand pounds to give away, is absurd to suppose. Fred Bullock would never allow her to do that. But she was still young and incapable of hiding her feelings : and by inviting her papa and sister to her third-rate parties, and behaving very coldly to them when they came, and by avoiding Russell Square, and indiscreetly begging her father to quit that odious vulgar place ; she did more harm than all Frederick's diplomacy could repair, and perilled her chance of her inheritance like a giddy heedless creature as she was.

' So Russell Square is not good enough for Mrs. Maria, hey ? ' said the old gentleman, rattling up the carriage-windows, as he and his daughter drove away one night from Mrs. Frederick Bullock's, after dinner. ' So she invites her father and sister to a second day's dinner (if those sides, or ontrys, as she calls 'em, weren't served yesterday, I'm d—d), and to meet City folks and littery men, and keeps the earls

and the ladies, and the honourables to herself. Honourables? Damn honourables! I am a plain British merchant,
I am : and could buy the beggarly hounds over and over.
Lords, indeed !—why, at one of her swarreys I saw one of
them speak to a dam fiddler—a fellar I despise. And they
won't come to Russell Square, won't they ? Why, I'll lay
my life I've got a better glass of wine, and pay a better
figure for it, and can show a handsomer service of silver,
and can lay a better dinner on my mahogany, than ever
they see on theirs—the cringing, sneaking, stuck-up fools.
Drive on quick, James : I want to get back to Russell
Square—ha, ha ! ' and he sank back into the corner with
a furious laugh. With such reflections on his own superior
merits it was the custom of the old gentleman not unfrequently to console himself.

Jane Osborne could not but concur in these opinions
respecting her sister's conduct ; and when Mrs. Frederick's
firstborn, Frederick Augustus Howard Stanley Devereux
Bullock,* was born, old Osborne, who was invited to the
christening and to be godfather, contented himself with
sending the child a gold cup, with twenty guineas inside it
for the nurse. ' That's more than any of your lords will
give, *I'll* warrant,' he said, and refused to attend at the
ceremony.

The splendour of the gift, however, caused great satisfaction to the house of Bullock. Maria thought that her
father was very much pleased with her, and Frederick
augured the best for his little son and heir.

One can fancy the pangs with which Miss Osborne in her
solitude in Russell Square read the *Morning Post*, where
her sister's name occurred every now and then, in the
articles headed ' Fashionable Réunions ', and where she had
an opportunity of reading a description of Mrs. F. Bullock's
costume, when presented at the Drawing-room by Lady
Frederica Bullock. Jane's own life, as we have said,
admitted of no such grandeur. It was an awful existence.
She had to get up of black winter's mornings to make breakfast for her scowling old father, who would have turned the
whole house out of doors if his tea had not been ready at half-
past eight. She remained silent opposite to him, listening
to the urn hissing, and sitting in tremor while the parent
read his paper, and consumed his accustomed portion of
muffins and tea. At half-past nine he rose and went to the

City, and she was almost free till dinner-time, to make
visitations in the kitchen and to scold the servants : to
drive abroad and descend upon the tradesmen, who were
prodigiously respectful : to leave her cards and her papa's
at the great glum respectable houses of their City friends ;
or to sit alone in the large drawing-room, expecting visitors ;
and working at a huge piece of worsted by the fire, on the
sofa, hard by the great Iphigenia clock, which ticked and
tolled with mournful loudness in the dreary room.   The
great glass over the mantelpiece, faced by the other great
console-glass at the opposite end of the room, increased and
multiplied between them the brown holland bag in which
the chandelier hung ; until you saw these brown holland
bags fading away in endless perspectives, and this apartment of Miss Osborne's seemed the centre of a system of
drawing-rooms.   When she removed the cordovan leather
from the grand piano, and ventured to play a few notes on
it, it sounded with a mournful sadness, startling the dismal
echoes of the house.   George's picture was gone, and laid
upstairs in a lumber-room in the garret ; and though there
was a consciousness of him, and father and daughter often
instinctively knew that they were thinking of him, no
mention was ever made of the brave and once darling son.

At five o'clock Mr. Osborne came back to his dinner,
which he and his daughter took in silence (seldom broken,
except when he swore and was savage, if the cooking was
not to his liking), or which they shared twice in a month
with a party of dismal friends of Osborne's rank and age.
Old Dr. Gulp and his lady from Bloomsbury Square : old
Mr. Frowser, the attorney, from Bedford Row, a very great
man, and from his business, hand-in-glove with the ' nobs
at the West End ' ;   old Colonel Livermore, of the Bombay
Army, and Mrs. Livermore from Upper Bedford Place :
old Serjeant Toffy and Mrs. Toffy ;   and sometimes old Sir
Thomas Coffin and Lady Coffin, from Bedford Square.   Sir
Thomas was celebrated as a hanging judge, and the particular
tawny port was produced when he dined with Mr. Osborne.

These people and their like gave the pompous Russell
Square merchant pompous dinners back again.   They had
solemn rubbers of whist, when they went upstairs after
drinking, and their carriages were called at half-past ten.
Many rich people, whom we poor devils are in the habit of
envying, lead contentedly an existence like that above

described. Jane Osborne scarcely ever met a man under
sixty, and almost the only bachelor who appeared in their
society was Mr. Smirk, the celebrated lady's doctor.

I can't say that nothing had occurred to disturb the
monotony of this awful existence : the fact is, there had
been a secret in poor Jane's life which had made her father
more savage and morose than even nature, pride, and over-
feeding had made him. This secret was connected with
Miss Wirt, who had a cousin an artist, Mr. Smee, very celebrated since as a portrait-painter and R.A.*, but who once
was glad enough to give drawing-lessons to ladies of
fashion. Mr. Smee has forgotten where Russell Square is
now, but he was glad enough to visit it in the year 1818,
when Miss Osborne had instruction from him.

Smee (formerly a pupil of Sharpe of Frith Street, a dissolute, irregular, and unsuccessful man, but a man with great
knowledge of his art) being the cousin of Miss Wirt, we say,
and introduced by her to Miss Osborne, whose hand and
heart were still free after various incomplete love affairs,
felt a great attachment for this lady, and it is believed
inspired one in her bosom. Miss Wirt was the confidante of
this intrigue. I know not whether she used to leave the
room where the master and his pupil were painting, in order
to give them an opportunity for exchanging those vows and
sentiments which cannot be uttered advantageously in the
presence of a third party : I know not whether she hoped
that should her cousin succeed in carrying off the rich
merchant's daughter, he would give Miss Wirt a portion of
the wealth which she had enabled him to win—all that is
certain is, that Mr. Osborne got some hint of the transaction,
came back from the City abruptly, and entered the drawing-
room with his bamboo-cane ; found the painter, the pupil,
and the companion all looking exceedingly pale there ;
turned the former out of doors with menaces that he would
break every bone in his skin, and half an hour afterwards
dismissed Miss Wirt likewise, kicking her trunks down the
stairs, trampling on her bandboxes, and shaking his fist
at her hackney-coach, as it bore her away.

Jane Osborne kept her bedroom for many days. She
was not allowed to have a companion afterwards. Her
father swore to her that she should not have a shilling of his
money if she made any match without his concurrence; and
as he wanted a woman to keep his house, he did not choose

that she should marry : so that she was obliged to give up
all projects with which Cupid had any share. During her
papa's life, then, she resigned herself to the manner of
existence here described, and was content to be an Old Maid.
Her sister, meanwhile, was having children with finer names
every year—and the intercourse between the two grew
fainter continually. 'Jane and I do not move in the
same sphere of life,' Mrs. Bullock said. 'I regard her as
a sister, of course'—which means—what does it mean when
a lady says that she regards Jane as a sister ?

It has been described how the Misses Dobbin lived with
their father at a fine villa at Denmark Hill, where there
were beautiful graperies and peach-trees which delighted
little Georgy Osborne. The Misses Dobbin, who drove
often to Brompton to see our dear Amelia, came sometimes
to Russell Square, too, to pay a visit to their old acquaint-
tance Miss Osborne. I believe it was in consequence of the
commands of their brother the major in India (for whom
their papa had a prodigious respect) that they paid attention to Mrs. George ; for the major, the godfather and
guardian of Amelia's little boy, still hoped that the child's
grandfather might be induced to relent towards him, and
acknowledge him for the sake of his son. The Miss Dobbins
kept Miss Osborne acquainted with the state of Amelia's
affairs ; how she was living with her father and mother ;
how poor they were ; how they wondered what men, and
such men as their brother and dear Captain Osborne, could
find in such an insignificant little chit ; how she was still,
as heretofore, a namby-pamby milk-and-water affected
creature—but how the boy was really the noblest little
boy ever seen—for the hearts of all women warm towards
young children, and the sourest spinster is kind to them.

One day, after great entreaties, on the part of the Misses
Dobbin, Amelia allowed little George to go and pass a day
with them at Denmark Hill—a part of which day she spent
herself in writing to the major in India. She congratulated
him on the happy news which his sisters had just conveyed
to her. She prayed for his prosperity, and that of the bride
he had chosen. She thanked him for a thousand, thousand
kind offices and proofs of steadfast friendship to her in her
affliction. She told him the last news about little Georgy,
and how he was gone to spend that very day with his sisters

in the country. She underlined the letter a great deal, and she signed herself affectionately his friend, Amelia Osborne. She forgot to send any message of kindness to Lady O'Dowd, as her wont was—and did not mention Glorvina by name, and only in italics, as the major's *bride*, for whom she begged *blessings*. But the news of the marriage removed the reserve which she had kept up towards him. She was glad to be able to own and feel how warmly and gratefully she regarded him—and as for the idea of being jealous of Glorvina (Glorvina, indeed!), Amelia would have scouted it, if an angel from heaven had hinted it to her.

That night, when Georgy came back in the pony-carriage in which he rejoiced, and in which he was driven by Sir William Dobbin's old coachman, he had round his neck a fine gold chain and watch. He said an old lady, not pretty, had given it him, who cried and kissed him a great deal. But he didn't like her. He liked grapes very much. And he only liked his mamma. Amelia shrunk and started: the timid soul felt a presentiment of terror when she heard that the relations of the child's father had seen him.

Miss Osborne came back to give her father his dinner. He had made a good speculation in the City, and was rather in a good humour that day, and chanced to remark the agitation under which she laboured. 'What's the matter, Miss Osborne?' he deigned to say.

The woman burst into tears. 'Oh, sir,' she said, 'I've seen little George. He is as beautiful as an angel—and so like him!' The old man opposite to her did not say a word, but flushed up, and began to tremble in every limb.

CHAPTER XLIII

IN WHICH THE READER HAS TO DOUBLE THE CAPE

THE astonished reader must be called upon to transport himself ten thousand miles to the military station of Bundlegunge, in the Madras division of our Indian empire, where our gallant old friends of the —th regiment are quartered under the command of the brave colonel, Sir Michael O'Dowd. Time has dealt kindly with that stout officer, as it does ordinarily with men who have good stomachs and good tempers, and are not perplexed over much by fatigue of the brain. The colonel plays a good knife and fork at tiffin, and resumes those weapons with great success at dinner. He smokes his hookah after both meals, and puffs as quietly while his wife scolds him, as he did under the fire of the French at Waterloo. Age and heat have not diminished the activity or the eloquence of the descendant of the Malonys and the Molloys. Her ladyship, our old acquaintance, is as much at home at Madras as at Brussels—in the cantonment as under the tents. On the march you saw her at the head of the regiment seated on a royal elephant, a noble sight. Mounted on that beast, she has been into action with tigers in the jungle : she has been received by native princes, who have welcomed her and Glorvina into the recesses of their zenanas*and offered her shawls and jewels which it went to her heart to refuse. The sentries of all arms salute her wherever she makes her appearance : and she touches her hat gravely to their salutation. Lady O'Dowd is one of the greatest ladies in the Presidency of Madras—her quarrel with Lady Smith, wife of Sir Minos Smith the puisne judge, is still remembered by some at Madras, when the colonel's lady snapped her fingers

in the judge's lady's face, and said *she'd* never walk behind
ever a beggarly civilian.   Even now, though it is five-and-
twenty years ago, people remember Lady O'Dowd performing a jig at Government House, where she danced down
two aides de camp, a major of Madras cavalry and two
gentlemen of the Civil Service ; and, persuaded by Major
Dobbin, C.B., second in command of the —th, to retire to
the supper-room, *lassata nondum satiata recessit.**

Peggy O'Dowd is indeed the same as ever : kind in act
and thought : impetuous in temper ; eager to command :
a tyrant over her Michael : a dragon amongst all the ladies
of the regiment : a mother to all the young men, whom
she tends in their sickness, defends in all their scrapes, and
with whom Lady Peggy is immensely popular.   But the
subalterns' and captains' ladies (the major is unmarried)
cabal against her a good deal. They say that Glorvina*
gives herself airs, and that Peggy herself is intolerably
domineering.   She interfered with a little congregation
which Mrs. Kirk had got up, and laughed the young men
away from her sermons, stating that a soldier's wife had
no business to be a parson : that Mrs. Kirk would be much
better mending her husband's clothes : and, if the regiment
wanted sermons, that she had the finest in the world, those
of her uncle, the dean.   She abruptly put a termination to
a flirtation which Lieutenant Stubble of the regiment had
commenced with the surgeon's wife, threatening to come
down upon Stubble for the money which he had borrowed
from her (for the young fellow was still of an extravagant
turn) unless he broke off at once and went to the Cape, on
sick leave.   On the other hand, she housed and sheltered
Mrs. Posky, who fled from her bungalow one night, pursued
by her infuriate husband, wielding his second brandy bottle,
and actually carried Posky through the delirium tremens,
and broke him of the habit of drinking, which had grown
upon that officer as all evil habits will grow upon men.   In
a word, in adversity she was the best of comforters, in good
fortune the most troublesome of friends ; having a perfectly
good opinion of herself always, and an indomitable resolution
to have her own way.

Among other points, she had made up her mind that
Glorvina should marry our old friend Dobbin. Mrs. O'Dowd
knew the major's expectations and appreciated his good
qualities, and the high character which he enjoyed in his

profession. Glorvina, a very handsome, fresh-coloured, black-haired, blue-eyed young lady, who could ride a horse, or play a sonata with any girl out of the County Cark, seemed to be the very person destined to ensure Dobbin's happiness—much more than that poor good little weak-spur'ted Amelia, about whom he used to take on so.— ' Look at Glorvina enter a room,' Mrs. O'Dowd would say, ' and compare her with that poor Mrs. Osborne, who couldn't say bo to a goose. She'd be worthy of you, major—you're a quiet man yourself, and want some one to talk for ye. And though she does not come of such good blood as the Malonys or Molloys, let me tell ye, she's of an ancient family that any nobleman might be proud to marry into.'

But before she had come to such a resolution, and determined to subjugate Major Dobbin by her endearments, it must be owned that Glorvina had practised them a good deal elsewhere. She had had a season in Dublin, and who knows how many in Cork, Killarney, and Mallow ? She had flirted with all the marriageable officers whom the dépôts of her country afforded, and all the bachelor squires who seemed eligible. She had been engaged to be married a half score times in Ireland, besides the clergyman at Bath who used her so ill. She had flirted all the way to Madras with the captain and chief mate of the *Ramchunder* East Indiaman, and had a season at the Presidency with her brother and Mrs. O'Dowd who was staying there, while the major of the regiment was in command at the station. Everybody admired her there : everybody danced with her : but no one proposed who was worth the marrying ; one or two exceedingly young subalterns sighed after her, and a beardless civilian or two ; but she rejected these as beneath her pretensions ; and other and younger virgins than Glorvina were married before her. There are women, and handsome women too, who have this fortune in life. They fall in love with the utmost generosity ; they ride and walk with half the Army List, though they draw near to forty, and yet the Miss O'Gradys are Miss O'Gradys still : Glorvina persisted that but for Lady O'Dowd's unlucky quarrel with the judge's lady, she would have made a good match at Madras, where old Mr. Chutney, who was at the head of the Civil Service (and who afterwards married Miss Dolby, a young lady, only thirteen years of age, who had

just arrived from school in Europe), was just at the point
of proposing to her.

Well, although Lady O'Dowd and Glorvina quarrelled
a great number of times every day, and upon almost every
conceivable subject—indeed, if Mick O'Dowd had not
possessed the temper of an angel, two such women constantly about his ears would have driven him out of his
senses—yet they agreed between themselves on this point,
that Glorvina should marry Major Dobbin, and were
determined that the major should have no rest until the
arrangement was brought about. Undismayed by forty or
fifty previous defeats, Glorvina laid siege to him. She sang
Irish Melodies*at him unceasingly. She asked him so
frequently and pathetically, will ye come to the bower ?
that it is a wonder how any man of feeling could have
resisted the invitation. She was never tired of inquiring,
if Sorrow had his young days faded ; and was ready to
listen and weep like Desdemona at the stories of his dangers
and his campaigns. It has been said that our honest and
dear old friend used to perform on the flute in private :
Glorvina insisted upon having duets with him, and Lady
O'Dowd would rise and artlessly quit the room, when the
young couple were so engaged. Glorvina forced the major
to ride with her of mornings. The whole cantonment saw
them set out and return. She was constantly writing
notes over to him at his house, borrowing his books, and
scoring with her great pencil-marks such passages of sentiment or humour as awakened her sympathy. She borrowed
his horses, his servants, his spoons, and palankeen ;—no
wonder that public rumour assigned her to him, and that
the major's sisters in England should fancy they were about
to have a sister-in-law.

Dobbin, who was thus vigorously besieged, was in the
meanwhile in a state of the most odious tranquillity. He
used to laugh when the young fellows of the regiment joked
him about Glorvina's manifest attentions to him. ' Bah ! '
said he, ' she is only keeping her hand in—she practises
upon me as she does upon Mrs. Tozer's piano, because it's
the most handy instrument in the station. I am much too
battered and old for such a fine young lady as Glorvina.'
And so he went on riding with her, and copying music and
verses into her albums, and playing at chess with her very
submissively ; for it is with these simple amusements that

GLORVINA TRIES HER FASCINATION ON THE MAJOR

some officers in India are accustomed to while away their
leisure moments ; while others of a less domestic turn hunt
hogs, and shoot snipes, or gamble and smoke cheroots, and
betake themselves to brandy-and-water. As for Sir Michael
O'Dowd, though his lady and her sister both urged him
to call upon the major to explain himself, and not keep on
torturing a poor innocent girl in that shameful way, the
old soldier refused point-blank to have anything to do with
the conspiracy. ' Faith, the major's big enough to choose
for himself,' Sir Michael said ; ' he'll ask ye when he wants
ye ; '—or else he would turn the matter off jocularly,
declaring that ' Dobbin was too young to keep house, and
had written home to ask lave of his mamma '. Nay, he
went farther, and in private communications with his
major, would caution and rally him—crying, ' Mind your
oi, Dob, my boy, them girls is bent on mischief—me lady
has just got a box of gowns from Europe, and there's a pink
satin for Glorvina, which will finish ye, Dob, if it's in the
power of woman or satin to move ye.'

But the truth is, neither beauty nor fashion could conquer
him. Our honest friend had but one idea of a woman in
his head, and that one did not in the least resemble Miss
Glorvina O'Dowd in pink satin. A gentle little woman in
black, with large eyes and brown hair, seldom speaking,
save when spoken to, and then in a voice not the least
resembling Miss Glorvina's—a soft young mother tending
an infant and beckoning the major up with a smile to look
at him—a rosy-cheeked lass coming singing into the room
in Russell Square or hanging on George Osborne's arm,
happy and loving—there was but this image that filled our
honest major's mind by day and by night, and reigned
over it always. Very likely Amelia was not like the portrait
the major had formed of her : there was a figure in a book
of fashions which his sisters had in England, and with which
William had made away privately, pasting it into the lid
of his desk, and fancying he saw some resemblance to Mrs.
Osborne in the print, whereas I have seen it, and can
vouch that it is but the picture of a high-waisted gown
with an impossible doll's face simpering over it—and,
perhaps, Mr. Dobbin's sentimental Amelia was no more
like the real one than this absurd little print which he
cherished. But what man in love, of us, is better informed ?
—or is he much happier when he sees and owns his delusion ?

Dobbin was under this spell. He did not bother his friends and the public much about his feelings, or indeed lose his natural zest or appetite on account of them. His head has grizzled since we saw him last ; and a line or two of silver may be seen in the soft brown hair likewise. But his feelings are not in the least changed or oldened ; and his love remains as fresh, as a man's recollections of boyhood are.

We have said how the two Miss Dobbins and Amelia, the major's correspondents in Europe, wrote him letters from

England ; Mrs. Osborne congratulating him with great candour and cordiality upon his approaching nuptials with Miss O'Dowd.

' Your sister has just kindly visited me,' Amelia wrote in her letter, ' and informed me of an *interesting event*, upon which I beg to offer my *most sincere congratulations.* I hope the young lady to whom I hear you are to be *united* will in every respect prove worthy of one who is himself all kindness and goodness. The poor widow has only her prayers to offer, and her cordial, cordial wishes for *your prosperity !* Georgy sends his love to *his dear godpapa*, and hopes that you will not forget him. I tell him that you are about to form *other ties*, with one who I am sure merits *all your affection*, but that although such ties must of course be the strongest and most sacred, and supersede *all others*, yet that I am sure the widow and the child whom you have ever protected and loved will always *have a corner in your heart.*' The letter, which has been before alluded to, went on in this strain, protesting throughout as to the extreme satisfaction of the writer.

This letter, which arrived by the very same ship which

brought out Lady O'Dowd's box of millinery from London
(and which you may be sure Dobbin opened before any one
of the other packets which the mail brought him), put the
receiver into such a state of mind that Glorvina, and her pink
satin, and everything belonging to her, became perfectly
odious to him. The major cursed the talk of women, and
the sex in general. Everything annoyed him that day—the
parade was insufferably hot and wearisome. Good heavens!
was a man of intellect to waste his life, day after day, inspecting cross-belts, and putting fools through their manœuvres?
The senseless chatter of the young men at mess was more
than ever jarring. What cared he, a man on the high road
to forty, to know how many snipes Lieutenant Smith had
shot, or what were the performances of Ensign Brown's
mare? The jokes about the table filled him with shame.
He was too old to listen to the banter of the assistant-
surgeon and the slang of the youngsters, at which old
O'Dowd, with his bald head and red face, laughed quite
easily. The old man had listened to those jokes any time
these thirty years—Dobbin himself had been fifteen years
hearing them. And after the boisterous dullness of the
mess-table, the quarrels and scandal of the ladies of the
regiment! It was unbearable, shameful. ' O Amelia,
Amelia,' he thought, ' you to whom I have been so faithful—
you reproach me! It is because you cannot feel for me,
that I drag on this wearisome life. And you reward me
after years of devotion by giving me your blessing upon my
marriage, forsooth, with this flaunting Irish girl!' Sick
and sorry felt poor William : more than ever wretched
and lonely. He would like to have done with life and its
vanity altogether—so bootless and unsatisfactory the
struggle, so cheerless and dreary the prospect seemed to
him. He lay all that night sleepless, and yearning to go
home. Amelia's letter had fallen as a blank upon him.
No fidelity, no constant truth and passion, could move
her into warmth. She would not see that he loved her.
Tossing in his bed, he spoke out to her. ' Good God,
Amelia!' he said, ' don't you know that I only love you
in the world—you, who are a stone to me—you, whom
I tended through months and months of illness and grief,
and who bade me farewell with a smile on your face, and
forgot me before the door shut between us!' The native
servants lying outside his verandahs beheld with wonder

the major, so cold and quiet ordinarily, at present so
passionately moved and cast down. Would she have
pitied him had she seen him ? He read over and over all
the letters which he ever had from her—letters of business
relative to the little property which he had made her
believe her husband had left to her—brief notes of invitation
—every scrap of writing that she had ever sent to him—
how cold, how kind, how hopeless, how selfish they were !

Had there been some kind gentle soul near at hand who
could read and appreciate this silent generous heart, who
knows but that the reign of Amelia might have been
over, and that friend William's love might have flowed
into a kinder channel ? But there was only Glorvina of
the jetty ringlets with whom his intercourse was familiar,
and this dashing young woman was not bent upon loving
the major, but rather on making the major admire her—
a most vain and hopeless task, too, at least considering the
means that the poor girl possessed to carry it out. She
curled her hair and showed her shoulders at him, as much
as to say, did ye ever see such jet ringlets and such a
complexion ? She grinned at him so that he might see
that every tooth in her head was sound—and he never
heeded all these charms. Very soon after the arrival of
the box of millinery, and perhaps indeed in honour of it,
Lady O'Dowd and the ladies of the King's Regiment gave
a ball to the Company's Regiments and the civilians at the
station. Glorvina sported the killing pink frock, and the
major, who attended the party and walked very ruefully
up and down the rooms, never so much as perceived the
pink garment. Glorvina danced past him in a fury with
all the young subalterns of the station, and the major was
not in the least jealous of her performance, or angry because
Captain Bangles of the Cavalry handed her to supper.
It was not jealousy, or frocks or shoulders, that could move
him, and Glorvina had nothing more.

So these two were each exemplifying the Vanity of this
life, and each longing for what he or she could not get.
Glorvina cried with rage at the failure. She had set her
mind on the major ' more than on any of the others,' she
owned, sobbing. ' He'll break my heart, he will, Peggy,'
she would whimper to her sister-in-law when they were
good friends ; ' sure every one of me frocks must be taken
in—it's such a skeleton I'm growing.' Fat or thin, laughing

or melancholy, on horseback or the music-stool, it was
all the same to the major. And the colonel, puffing his
pipe and listening to these complaints, would suggest that
Glory should have some black frocks out in the next box
from London, and told a mysterious story of a lady in
Ireland, who died of grief for the loss of her husband before
she got e'er a one.

While the major was going on in this tantalizing way,
not proposing, and declining to fall in love, there came
another ship from Europe bringing letters on board, and
amongst them some more for the heartless man. These
were home letters bearing an earlier postmark than that
of the former packets, and as Major Dobbin recognized
among his, the handwriting of his sister, who always crossed
and recrossed her letters to her brother—gathered together
all the possible bad news which she could collect, abused
him and read him lectures with sisterly frankness, and
always left him miserable for the day after ' dearest William'
had achieved the perusal of one of her epistles—the truth
must be told that, dearest William did not hurry himself
to break the seal of Miss Dobbin's letter, but waited for
a particularly favourable day and mood for doing so.
A fortnight before, moreover, he had written to scold her
for telling those absurd stories to Mrs. Osborne, and had
dispatched a letter in reply to that lady, undeceiving her
with respect to the reports concerning him, and assuring
her that ' he had no sort of present intention of altering
his condition '.

Two or three nights after the arrival of the second
package of letters, the major had passed the evening pretty
cheerfully at Lady O'Dowd's house, where Glorvina thought
that she listened with rather more attention than usual to
the ' Meeting of the Wathers', the ' Minsthrel Boy', and one
or two other specimens of song with which she favoured
him (the truth is, he was no more listening to Glorvina than
to the howling of the jackals in the moonlight outside,
and the delusion was hers as usual), and having played
his game at chess with her (cribbage with the surgeon was
Lady O'Dowd's favourite evening pastime), Major Dobbin
took leave of the colonel's family at his usual hour, and
retired to his own house.

There on his table, his sister's letter lay reproaching him.
He took it up, ashamed rather of his negligence regarding

it, and prepared himself for a disagreeable hour's communing with that crabbed-handed absent relative. : . . It
may have been an hour after the major's departure from
the colonel's house—Sir Michael was sleeping the sleep of
the just ; Glorvina had arranged her black ringlets in the
innumerable little bits of paper, in which it was her habit
to confine them ; Lady O'Dowd, too, had gone to her bed
in the nuptial chamber, on the ground-floor, and had
tucked her mosquito curtains round her fair form, when
the guard at the gates of the commanding-officer's compound beheld Major Dobbin, in the moonlight, rushing
towards the house with a swift step and a very agitated
countenance, and he passed the sentinel and went up to
the windows of the colonel's bedchamber.

'O'Dowd—colonel !' said Dobbin, and kept up a great
shouting.

'Heavens, meejor !' said Glorvina of the curl-papers,
putting out her head too, from her window.

'What is it, Dob, me boy ?' said the colonel, expecting
there was a fire in the station, or that the route had come
from head quarters.

'I—I must have leave of absence. I must go to England
—on the most urgent private affairs,' Dobbin said.

'Good heavens, what has happened !' thought Glorvina,
trembling with all the papillotes.*

'I want to be off—now—to-night,' Dobbin continued ;
and the colonel getting up, came out to parley with him.

In the postscript of Miss Dobbin's cross-letter—the
major had just come upon a paragraph, to the following
effect :—' I drove yesterday to see your old *acquaintance*,
Mrs. Osborne. The wretched place they live at, since they
were bankrupts, you know—Mr. S., to judge from a *brass
plate* on the door of his hut (it is little better) is a coal-
merchant. The little boy, your godson, is certainly a fine
child, though forward, and inclined to be saucy and self-
willed. But we have taken notice of him as you wish it,
and have introduced him to his aunt, Miss O., who was
rather pleased with him. Perhaps his grandpapa, not the
bankrupt one, who is almost doting, but Mr. Osborne, of
Russell Square, may be induced to relent towards the child
of your friend, *his erring and self-willed son*. And Amelia
will not be ill disposed to give him up. The widow is
consoled, and is about to marry a reverend gentleman, the

Rev. Mr. Binney, one of the curates of Brompton. . A poor match. But Mrs. O. is getting old, and I saw a great deal of grey in her hair—she was in very good spirits : and your little godson over-ate himself at our house. Mamma sends her love with that of your affectionate ANN DOBBIN.'

CHAPTER XLIV

A ROUNDABOUT CHAPTER BETWEEN LONDON AND HAMPSHIRE

 UR old friends the Crawleys' family house* in Great Gaunt Street, still bore over its front the hatchment which had been placed there as a token of mourning for Sir Pitt Crawley's demise, yet this heraldic emblem was in itself a very splendid and gaudy piece of furniture, and all the rest of the mansion became more brilliant than it had ever been during the late baronet's reign. The black outer-coating of the bricks was removed, and they appeared with a cheerful, blushing face streaked with white : the old bronze lions of the knocker were gilt handsomely, the railings painted, and the dismallest house in Great Gaunt Street became the smartest in the whole quarter, before the green leaves in Hampshire had replaced those yellowing ones which were on the trees in Queen's Crawley avenue when old Sir Pitt Crawley passed under them for the last time.

A little woman, with a carriage to correspond, was perpetually seen about this mansion ; an elderly spinster, accompanied by a little boy, also might be remarked coming thither daily. It was Miss Briggs and little Rawdon, whose business it was to see to the inward renovation of Sir Pitt's house, to superintend the female band engaged in stitching the blinds and hangings, to poke and rummage in the drawers and cupboards crammed with the dirty relics and congregated trumperies of a couple of generations of Lady Crawleys, and to take inventories of the china, the glass, and other properties in the closets and storerooms.

Mrs. Rawdon Crawley was general-in-chief over these

arrangements, with full orders from Sir Pitt to sell, barter,
confiscate, or purchase furniture : and she enjoyed herself
not a little in an occupation which gave full scope to her
taste and ingenuity. The renovation of the house was determined upon when Sir Pitt came to town in November to see
his lawyers, and when he passed nearly a week in Curzon
Street, under the roof of his affectionate brother and sister.

He had put up at an hotel at first ; but Becky, as soon
as she heard of the baronet's arrival, went off alone to greet
him, and returned in an hour to Curzon Street with Sir
Pitt in the carriage by her side. It was impossible sometimes to resist this artless little creature's hospitalities,
so kindly were they pressed, so frankly and amiably offered.
Becky seized Pitt's hand in a transport of gratitude when
he agreed to come. 'Thank you,' she said, squeezing it,
and looking into the baronet's eyes, who blushed a good
deal ; ' how happy this will make Rawdon.' She bustled
up to Pitt's bedroom, leading on the servants, who were
carrying his trunks thither. She came in herself laughing,
with a coal-scuttle out of her own room.

A fire was blazing already in Sir Pitt's apartment (it was
Miss Briggs's room, by the way. who was sent upstairs to

sleep with the maid). 'I knew I should bring you,' she
said, with pleasure beaming in her glance. Indeed, she
was really and sincerely happy at having him for a guest.

Becky made Rawdon dine out once or twice on business,
while Pitt stayed with them, and the baronet passed the
happy evening alone with her and Briggs. She went
downstairs to the kitchen and actually cooked little dishes
for him. 'Isn't it a good salmi?'*she said; 'I made it
for you. I can make you better dishes than that: and
will when you come to see me.'

'Everything you do, you do well,' said the baronet,
gallantly. 'The salmi is excellent indeed.'

'A poor man's wife,' Rebecca replied, gaily, 'must make
herself useful, you know:' on which her brother-in-law
vowed that 'she was fit to be the wife of an emperor, and
that to be skilful in domestic duties was surely one of the
most charming of woman's qualities'. And Sir Pitt thought,
with something like mortification, of Lady Jane at home,
and of a certain pie which she had insisted on making,
and serving to him at dinner—a most abominable pie.

Besides the salmi, which was made of Lord Steyne's
pheasants from his lordship's cottage of Stillbrook, Becky
gave her brother-in-law a bottle of white wine, some that
Rawdon had brought with him from France, and had picked
up for nothing, the little story-teller said; whereas the
liquor was, in truth, some White Hermitage from the
Marquis of Steyne's famous cellars, which brought fire into
the baronet's pallid cheeks and a glow into his feeble frame.

Then when he had drunk up the bottle of *petit vin blanc*
she gave him her hand and took him up to the drawing-
room, and made him snug on the sofa by the fire, and let
him talk as she listened with the tenderest kindly interest,
sitting by him, and hemming a shirt for her dear little
boy. Whenever Mrs. Rawdon wished to be particularly
humble and virtuous, this little shirt used to come out of
her work-box. It had got to be too small for Rawdon long
before it was finished, though.

Well, Rebecca listened to Pitt, she talked to him, she
sang to him, she coaxed him, and cuddled him, so that he
found himself more and more glad every day to get back
from the lawyer's at Gray's Inn, to the blazing fire in
Curzon Street—a gladness in which the men of law likewise
participated, for Pitt's harangues were of the longest—and

so that when he went away he felt quite a pang at departing.
How pretty she looked kissing her hand to him from the
carriage and waving her handkerchief when he had taken
his place in the mail! She put the handkerchief to her
eyes once. He pulled his sealskin cap over his, as the coach
drove away, and, sinking back, he thought to himself
how she respected him and how he deserved it, and how
Rawdon was a foolish dull fellow who didn't half appreciate
his wife: and how mum and stupid his own wife was compared to that brilliant little Becky. Becky had hinted
every one of these things herself, perhaps, but so delicately
and gently, that you hardly knew when or where. And,
before they parted, it was agreed that the house in London
should be redecorated for the next season, and that the
brothers' families should meet again in the country at
Christmas.

'I wish you could have got a little money out of him,'
Rawdon said to his wife moodily when the baronet was
gone. 'I should like to give something to old Raggles,
hanged if I shouldn't. It ain't right, you know, that the
old fellow should be kept out of all his money. It may be
inconvenient, and he might let to somebody else besides
us, you know.'

'Tell him,' said Becky, 'that as soon as Sir Pitt's affairs
are settled, everybody will be paid, and give him a little
something on account. Here's a cheque that Pitt left for
the boy,' and she took from her bag and gave her husband
a paper which his brother had handed over to her, on behalf
of the little son and heir of the younger branch of the
Crawleys.

The truth is, she had tried personally the ground on
which her husband expressed a wish that she should venture
—tried it ever so delicately, and found it unsafe. Even
at a hint about embarrassments, Sir Pitt Crawley was off
and alarmed. And he began a long speech, explaining how
straitened he himself was in money matters; how the
tenants would not pay; how his father's affairs, and the
expenses attendant upon the demise of the old gentleman,
had involved him; how he wanted to pay off incumbrances;
and how the bankers and agents were overdrawn; and
Pitt Crawley ended by making a compromise with his
sister-in-law, and giving her a very small sum for the
benefit of her little boy.

Pitt knew how poor his brother and his brother's family must be. It could not have escaped the notice of such a cool and experienced old diplomatist, that Rawdon's family had nothing to live upon, and that houses and carriages are not to be kept for nothing. He knew very well that he was the proprietor or appropriator of the money, which, according to all proper calculation, ought to have fallen to his younger brother, and he had, we may be sure, some secret pangs of remorse within him, which warned him that he ought to perform some act of justice, or, let us say, compensation, towards these disappointed relations. A just, decent man, not without brains, who said his prayers, and knew his Catechism, and did his duty outwardly through life, he could not be otherwise than aware that something was due to his brother at his hands, and that morally he was Rawdon's debtor.

But, as one reads in the columns of the *Times* newspaper every now and then, queer announcements from the Chancellor of the Exchequer, acknowledging the receipt of 50*l.* from A.B., or 10*l.* from W.T., as conscience-money, on account of taxes due by the said A.B. or W.T., which payments the penitents beg the right honourable gentleman to acknowledge through the medium of the public press ; so is the Chancellor, no doubt, and the reader likewise, always perfectly sure that the above-named A.B. and W.T. are only paying a very small instalment of what they really owe, and that the man who sends up a twenty pound-note has very likely hundreds or thousands more for which he ought to account. Such, at least, are my feelings, when I see A.B. or W.T.'s insufficient acts of repentance. And I have no doubt that Pitt Crawley's contrition, or kindness if you will, towards his younger brother, by whom he had so much profited, was only a very small dividend upon the capital sum in which he was indebted to Rawdon. Not everybody is willing to pay even so much. To part with money is a sacrifice beyond almost all men endowed with a sense of order. There is scarcely any man alive who does not think himself meritorious for giving his neighbour five pounds. Thriftless gives, not from a beneficent pleasure in giving, but from a lazy delight in spending. He would not deny himself one enjoyment ; not his opera-stall, not his horse, not his dinner, not even the pleasure of giving Lazarus the five pounds. Thrifty, who is good,

wise, just, and owes no man a penny, turns from a beggar,
haggles with a hackney-coachman, or denies a poor relation,
and I doubt which is the most selfish of the two. Money
has only a different value in the eyes of each.

So, in a word, Pitt Crawley thought he would do something for his brother, and then thought that he would think
about it some other time.

And with regard to Becky, she was not a woman who
expected too much from the generosity of her neighbours,
and so was quite content with all that Pitt Crawley had
done for her. She was acknowledged by the head of the
family. If Pitt would not give her anything, he would
get something for her some day. If she got no money
from her brother-in-law, she got what was as good as
money—credit. Raggles was made rather easy in his mind
by the spectacle of the union between the brothers, by
a small payment on the spot, and by the promise of a much
larger sum speedily to be assigned to him. And Rebecca
told Miss Briggs, whose Christmas dividend upon the
little sum lent by her, Becky paid with an air of candid joy,
and as if her exchequer was brimming over with gold—
Rebecca, we say, told Miss Briggs, in strict confidence,
that she had conferred with Sir Pitt, who was famous as
a financier, on Briggs's special behalf, as to the most
profitable investment of Miss B.'s remaining capital ; that
Sir Pitt, after much consideration, had thought of a most
safe and advantageous way in which Briggs could lay out
her money ; that, being especially interested in her as an
attached friend of the late Miss Crawley, and of the whole
family, and that long before he left town, he had recommended that she should be ready with the money at a
moment's notice, so as to purchase at the most favourable
opportunity the shares which Sir Pitt had in his eye. Poor
Miss Briggs was very grateful for this mark of Sir Pitt's
attention—it came so unsolicited, she said, for she never
should have thought of removing the money from the Funds
—and the delicacy enhanced the kindness of the office ;
and she promised to see her man of business immediately,
and be ready with her little cash at the proper hour.

And this worthy woman was so grateful for the kindness
of Rebecca in the matter, and for that of her generous
benefactor, the colonel, that she went out and spent
a great part of her half-year's dividend in the purchase

of a black velvet coat for little Rawdon, who, by the way, was grown almost too big for black velvet now, and was of a size and age befitting him for the assumption of the virile jacket and pantaloons.

He was a fine open-faced boy, with blue eyes and waving flaxen hair, sturdy in limb, but generous and soft in heart : fondly attaching himself to all who were good to him—to the pony—to Lord Southdown, who gave him the horse (he used to blush and glow all over when he saw that kind young nobleman)—to the groom who had charge of the pony—to Molly, the cook, who crammed him with ghost stories at night, and with good things from the dinner—to Briggs, whom he plagued and laughed at—and to his father especially, whose attachment towards the lad was curious too to witness. Here, as he grew to be about eight years old, his attachments may be said to have ended. The beautiful mother-vision had faded away after a while. During near two years she had scarcely spoken to the child. She disliked him. He had the measles and the whooping-cough. He bored her. One day when he was standing at the landing-place, having crept down from the upper regions, attracted by the sound of his mother's voice, who was singing to Lord Steyne, the drawing-room door opening suddenly, discovered the little spy, who but a moment before had been rapt in delight, and listening to the music.

His mother came out and struck him violently a couple of boxes on the ear. He heard a laugh from the marquis in the inner room (who was amused by this free and artless exhibition of Becky's temper), and fled down below to his friends of the kitchen, bursting in an agony of grief.

'It is not because it hurts me,' little Rawdon gasped out—'only—only'—sobs and tears wound up the sentence in a storm. It was the little boy's heart that was bleeding. 'Why mayn't I hear her singing ? Why don't she ever sing to me—as she does to that bald-headed man with the large teeth ? ' He gasped out at various intervals these exclamations of rage and grief. The cook looked at the housemaid : the housemaid looked knowingly at the footman—the awful kitchen inquisition which sits in judgement in every house, and knows everything—sat on Rebecca at that moment.

After this incident, the mother's dislike increased to

hatred; the consciousness that the child was in the house was a reproach and a pain to her. His very sight annoyed her. Fear, doubt, and resistance sprang up, too, in the boy's own bosom. They were separated from that day of the boxes on the ear.

Lord Steyne also heartily misliked the boy. When they met by mischance, he made sarcastic bows or remarks to the child, or glared at him with savage-looking eyes. Rawdon used to stare him in the face, and double his little fists in return. He knew his enemy; and this gentleman, of all who came to the house, was the one who angered him most. One day the footman found him squaring his fists at Lord Steyne's hat in the hall. The footman told the circumstance as a good joke to Lord Steyne's coachman; that officer imparted it to Lord Steyne's gentleman, and to the servants' hall in general. And very soon afterwards, when Mrs. Rawdon Crawley made her appearance at Gaunt House, the porter who unbarred the gates, the servants of all uniforms in the hall, the functionaries in white waistcoats, who bawled out from landing to landing the names of Colonel and Mrs. Rawdon Crawley, knew about her, or fancied they did. The man who brought her refreshment and stood behind her chair, had talked her character over with the large gentleman in motley-coloured clothes at his side. *Bon Dieu!* it is awful, that servants' inquisition! You see a woman in a great party in a splendid saloon, surrounded by faithful admirers, distributing sparkling glances, dressed to perfection, curled, rouged, smiling and happy:—Discovery walks respectfully up to her, in the shape of a huge powdered man with large calves and a tray of ices—with Calumny (which is as fatal as truth)—behind him, in the shape of the hulking fellow carrying the wafer-biscuits. Madam, your secret will be talked over by those men at their club at the public-house to-night. Jeames will tell Chawls his notions about you over their pipes and pewter beer-pots. Some people ought to have mutes for servants in Vanity Fair—mutes who could not write. If you are guilty, tremble. That fellow behind your chair may be a janissary with a bow-string in his plush breeches pocket. If you are not guilty, have a care of appearances: which are as ruinous as guilt.

'Was Rebecca guilty or not?' The *Vehmgericht* of the servants' hall had pronounced against her.

And, I shame to say, she would not have got credit had they not believed her to be guilty. It was the sight of the Marquis of Steyne's carriage-lamps at her door, contemplated by Raggles, burning in the blackness of midnight, ' that kep' him up,' as he afterwards said ; that even more than Rebecca's arts and coaxings.

And so—guiltless very likely—she was writhing and pushing onward towards what they call ' a position in society', and the servants were pointing at her as lost and ruined. So you see Molly, the housemaid, of a morning, watching a spider in the doorpost lay his thread and laboriously crawl up it, until, tired of the sport, she raises her broom and sweeps away the thread and the artificer.

A day or two before Christmas, Becky, her husband and her son made ready and went to pass the holidays at the seat of their ancestors at Queen's Crawley. Becky would have liked to leave the little brat behind, and would have done so but for Lady Jane's urgent invitations to the youngster ; and the symptoms of revolt and discontent which Rawdon manifested at her neglect of her son. ' He's the finest boy in England,' the father said, in a tone of reproach to her, ' and you don't seem to care for him, Becky, as much as you do for your spaniel. He shan't bother you much : at home he will be away from you in the nursery, and he shall go outside on the coach with me.'

' Where you go yourself because you want to smoke those filthy cigars,' replied Mrs. Rawdon.

' I remember when you liked 'em though,' answered the husband.

Becky laughed : she was almost always good-humoured. ' That was when I was on my promotion, Goosey,' she said. ' Take Rawdon outside with you, and give him a cigar too, if you like.'

Rawdon did not warm his little son for the winter's journey in this way, but he and Briggs wrapped up the child in shawls and comforters, and he was hoisted respectfully on to the roof of the coach in the dark morning, under the lamps of the ' White Horse Cellar ' : and with no small delight he watched the dawn rise, and made his first journey to the place which his father still called home. It was a journey of infinite pleasure to the boy, to whom the

incidents of the road afforded endless interest : his father
answering to him all questions connected with it, and
telling him who lived in the great white house to the right,
and whom the park belonged to. His mother, inside the
vehicle with her maid and her furs, her wrappers, and her
scent-bottles, made such a to-do that you would have
thought she never had been in a stage-coach before—much
less, that she had been turned out of this very one to make
room for a paying passenger on a certain journey performed
some half-score years ago.

It was dark again when little Rawdon was wakened up
to enter his uncle's carriage at Mudbury, and he sat and
looked out of it wondering as the great iron gates flew open,
and at the white trunks of the limes as they swept by, until
they stopped, at length, before the light windows of the
Hall, which were blazing and comfortable with Christmas
welcome. The hall-door was flung open—a big fire was
burning in the great old fireplace—a carpet was down
over the chequered black flags—' It's the old Turkey one
that used to be in the Ladies' Gallery,' thought Rebecca,
and the next instant was kissing Lady Jane.

She and Sir Pitt performed the same salute with great
gravity : but Rawdon having been smoking, hung back
rather from his sister-in-law, whose two children came up
to their cousin : and, while Matilda held out her hand
and kissed him, Pitt Binkie Southdown, the son and heir,
stood aloof rather, and examined him as a little dog does
a big dog.

Then the kind hostess conducted her guests to the snug
apartments blazing with cheerful fires. Then the young
ladies came and knocked at Mrs. Rawdon's door, under
the pretence that they were desirous to be useful, but in
reality to have the pleasure of inspecting the contents of
her band- and bonnet-boxes, and her dresses which, though
black, were of the newest London fashion. And they told
her how much the Hall was changed for the better, and
how old Lady Southdown was gone, and how Pitt was
taking his station in the county, as became a Crawley
in fact. Then the great dinner-bell having rung, the
family assembled at dinner, at which meal Rawdon Junior
was placed by his aunt, the good-natured lady of the house ;
Sir Pitt being uncommonly attentive to his sister-in-law
at his own right hand.

THE ARRIVAL AT QUEEN'S CRAWLEY

Little Rawdon exhibited a fine appetite, and showed
a gentlemanlike behaviour.

' I like to dine here,' he said to his aunt when he had
completed his meal, at the conclusion of which, and after
a decent grace by Sir Pitt, the young son and heir was
introduced, and was perched on a high chair by the baronet's
side, while the daughter took possession of the place and
the little wine-glass prepared for her near her mother.
' I like to dine here,' said Rawdon Minor, looking up at
his relation's kind face.

' Why ? ' said the good Lady Jane.

' I dine in the kitchen when I am at home,' replied
Rawdon Minor, ' or else with Briggs.'   But Becky was
so engaged with the baronet, her host, pouring out a flood
of compliments and delights and raptures, and admiring
young Pitt Binkie, whom she declared to be the most
beautiful, intelligent, noble-looking little creature, and so
like his father, that she did not hear the remarks of her own
flesh and blood at the other end of the broad shining table.

As a guest, and it being the first night of his arrival,
Rawdon the Second was allowed to sit up until the hour
when tea being over, and a great gilt book being laid
on the table before Sir Pitt, all the domestics of the family
streamed in, and Sir Pitt read prayers.   It was the first
time the poor little boy had ever witnessed or heard of
such a ceremonial.

The house had been much improved even since the
baronet's brief reign, and was pronounced by Becky to
be perfect, charming, delightful, when she surveyed it
in his company.   As for little Rawdon, who examined it
with the children for his guides, it seemed to him a perfect
palace of enchantment and wonder.   There were long
galleries, and ancient state-bedrooms, there were pictures,
and old china, and armour.   There were the rooms in
which grandpapa died, and by which the children walked
with terrified looks.   ' Who was grandpapa ? ' he asked ;
and they told him how he used to be very old, and used
to be wheeled about in a garden-chair, and they showed
him the garden-chair one day rotting in the outhouse in
which it had lain since the old gentleman had been wheeled
away yonder to the church, of which the spire was glittering
over the park elms.

The brothers had good occupation for several mornings in examining the improvements which had been effected by Sir Pitt's genius and economy. And as they walked or rode, and looked at them, they could talk without too much boring each other. And Pitt took care to tell Rawdon what a heavy outlay of money these improvements had occasioned ; and that a man of landed and funded* property was often very hard pressed for twenty pounds. ' There is that new lodge gate,' said Pitt, pointing to it humbly with the bamboo cane, ' I can no more pay for it before the dividends in January than I can fly.'

' I can lend you,* Pitt, till then,' Rawdon answered rather ruefully ; and they went in and looked at the restored lodge, where the family arms were just new scraped in stone ; and where old Mrs. Lock, for the first time these many long years, had tight doors, sound roofs, and whole windows.

CHAPTER XLV

BETWEEN HAMPSHIRE AND LONDON

 IR PITT CRAWLEY had done more than repair fences and restore dilapidated lodges on the Queen's Crawley estate. Like a wise man he had set to work to rebuild the injured popularity of his house, and stop up the gaps and ruins in which his name had been left by his disreputable and thriftless old predecessor. He was elected for the borough speedily after his father's demise ; a magistrate, a member of Parliament, a county magnate and representative of an ancient family, he made it his duty to show himself before the Hampshire public, subscribed handsomely to the county charities, called assiduously upon all the county folks, and laid himself out in a word to take that position in Hampshire, and in the Empire afterwards, to which he thought his prodigious talents

justly entitled him. Lady Jane was instructed to be
friendly with the Fuddlestones, and the Wapshots, and
the other famous baronets, their neighbours. Their carriages might frequently be seen in the Queen's Crawley
avenue now ; they dined pretty frequently at the Hall
(where the cookery was so good, that it was clear Lady
Jane very seldom had a hand in it), and in return Pitt and
his wife most energetically dined out in all sorts of weather,
and at all sorts of distances. For though Pitt did not care
for joviality, being a frigid man of poor health and appetite,
yet he considered that to be hospitable and condescending
was quite incumbent on his station, and every time that
he got a headache from too long an after-dinner sitting,
he felt that he was a martyr to duty. He talked about
crops, corn laws, politics, with the best country gentlemen.
He (who had been formerly inclined to be a sad freethinker
on these points) entered into poaching and game preserving
with ardour. He didn't hunt : he wasn't a hunting
man : he was a man of books and peaceful habits : but
he thought that the breed of horses must be kept up
in the country, and that the breed of foxes must therefore
be looked to, and for his part, if his friend, Sir Huddlestone
Fuddlestone, liked to draw his country, and meet as of
old the F. hounds used to do at Queen's Crawley, he should
be happy to see him there, and the gentlemen of the Fuddlestone Hunt. And to Lady Southdown's dismay too he
became orthodox in his tendencies every day : gave up
preaching in public and attending meeting-houses ; went
stoutly to church : called on the bishop, and all the clergy
at Winchester : and made no objection when the Venerable
Archdeacon Trumper asked for a game of whist. What
pangs must have been those of Lady Southdown, and
what an utter castaway she must have thought her son-in-
law for permitting such a godless diversion ! and when,
on the return of the family from an oratorio at Winchester,
the baronet announced to the young ladies that he should
next year very probably take them to the ' county balls ',
they worshipped him for his kindness. Lady Jane was
only too obedient, and perhaps glad herself to go. The
dowager wrote off the direst descriptions of her daughter's
worldly behaviour to the authoress of the *Washerwoman
of Finchley Common* at the Cape ; and her house in Brighton
being about this time unoccupied, returned to that watering-

place, her absence being not very much deplored by her
children. We may suppose, too, that Rebecca, on paying
a second visit to Queen's Crawley, did not feel particularly
grieved at the absence of the lady of the medicine-chest ;
though she wrote a Christmas letter to her ladyship, in
which she respectfully recalled herself to Lady Southdown's
recollection, spoke with gratitude of the delight which her
ladyship's conversation had given her on the former visit,
dilated on the kindness with which her ladyship had treated
her in sickness, and declared that everything at Queen's
Crawley reminded her of her absent friend.

A great part of the altered demeanour and popularity
of Sir Pitt Crawley might have been traced to the counsels
of that astute little lady of Curzon Street. ' *You* remain
a baronet—you consent to be a mere country gentleman,'
she said to him, while he had been her guest in London.
' No, Sir Pitt Crawley, I know you better. I know your
talents and your ambition. You fancy you hide them both :
but you can conceal neither from me. I showed Lord
Steyne your pamphlet on malt. He was familiar with it :
and said it was in the opinion of the whole Cabinet the most
masterly thing that had appeared on the subject. The
Ministry has its eye upon you, and I know what you want.
You want to distinguish yourself in Parliament ; every one
says you are the finest speaker in England (for your speeches
at Oxford are still remembered). You want to be member
for the county,* where with your own vote and your borough
at your back, you can command anything. And you want
to be Baron Crawley of Queen's Crawley, and will be before
you die. I saw it all. I could read your heart, Sir Pitt.
If I had a husband who possessed your intellect as he does
your name, I sometimes think I should not be unworthy
of him—but—but I am your kinswoman now,' she added
with a laugh. ' Poor little penniless I have got a little
interest—and who knows, perhaps the mouse may be able
to aid the lion.'

Pitt Crawley was amazed and enraptured with her
speech. ' How that woman comprehends me ! ' he said.
' I never could get Jane to read these pages of the malt
pamphlet. *She* has no idea that I have commanding
talents or secret ambition. So they remember my speaking
at Oxford, do they ? The rascals ! now that I represent
my borough and may sit for the county, they begin to

recollect me ! Why, Lord Steyne cut me at the Levée last year : they are beginning to find out that Pitt Crawley is some one at last. Yes, the man was always the same whom these people neglected : it was only the opportunity that was wanting, and I will show them now that I can speak and act as well as write. Achilles did not declare himself until they gave him the sword.* I hold it now, and the world shall yet hear of Pitt Crawley.'

Therefore it was that this roguish diplomatist had grown so hospitable; that he was so civil to oratorios and hospitals; so kind to deans and chapters ; so generous in giving and accepting dinners ; so uncommonly gracious to farmers on market-days ; and so much interested about county business ; and that the Christmas at the Hall was the gayest which had been known there for many a long day.

On Christmas Day a great family gathering took place. All the Crawleys from the Rectory came to dine. Rebecca was as frank and fond of Mrs. Bute, as if the other had never been her enemy : she was affectionately interested in the dear girls, and surprised at the progress which they had made in music since her time : and insisted upon encoring one of the duets out of the great song-books which Jim, grumbling, had been forced to bring under his arm from the Rectory. Mrs. Bute, perforce, was obliged to adopt a decent demeanour towards the little adventuress— of course being free to discourse with her daughters after- wards about the absurd respect with which Sir Pitt treated his sister-in-law. But Jim, who had sat next to her at dinner, declared she was a trump : and one and all of the rector's family agreed that the little Rawdon was a fine boy. They respected a possible baronet in the boy, between whom and the title there was only the little sickly pale Pitt Binkie.

The children were very good friends. Pitt Binkie was too little a dog for such a big dog as Rawdon to play with : and Matilda being only a girl, of course not fit companion for a young gentleman who was near eight years old, and going into jackets very soon. He took the command of this small party at once—the little girl and the little boy following him about with great reverence at such times as he condescended to sport with them. His happiness and pleasure in the country were extreme. The kitchen- garden pleased him hugely, the flowers moderately, but the

pigeons and the poultry, and the stables when he was
allowed to visit them, were delightful objects to him. He
resisted being kissed by the Miss Crawleys : but he allowed
Lady Jane sometimes to embrace him : and it was by her
side that he liked to sit when the signal to retire to the
drawing-room being given, the ladies left the gentlemen to
their claret—by her side rather than by his mother. For
Rebecca seeing that tenderness was the fashion, called
Rawdon to her one evening, and stooped down and kissed
him in the presence of all the ladies.

He looked her full in the face after the operation, trembling
and turning very red, as his wont was when moved. ' You
never kiss me at home, mamma,' he said ; at which there
was a general silence and consternation, and a by no means
pleasant look in Becky's eyes.

Rawdon was fond of his sister-in-law, for her regard for
his son. Lady Jane and Becky did not get on *quite* so well
at this visit as on occasion of the former one, when the
colonel's wife was bent upon pleasing. Those two speeches
of the child struck rather a chill. Perhaps Sir Pitt was
rather too attentive to her.

But Rawdon, as became his age and size, was fonder of
the society of the men than of the women ; and never
wearied of accompanying his sire to the stables, whither
the colonel retired to smoke his cigar—Jim, the rector's
son, sometimes joining his cousin in that and other amusements. He and the baronet's keeper were very close
friends, their mutual taste for ' dawgs ' bringing them
much together. On one day, Mr. James, the colonel, and
Horn, the keeper, went and shot pheasants, taking little
Rawdon with them. On another most blissful morning,
these four gentlemen partook of the amusement of rat-
hunting in a barn, than which sport Rawdon as yet had
never seen anything more noble. They stopped up the
ends of certain drains in the barn, into the other openings
of which ferrets were inserted ; and then stood silently
aloof with uplifted stakes in their hands, and an anxious
little terrier (Mr. James's celebrated ' dawg ' Forceps,
indeed) scarcely breathing from excitement, listening
motionless on three legs, to the faint squeaking of the rats
below. Desperately bold at last, the persecuted animals
bolted above-ground : the terrier accounted for one, the
keeper for another, Rawdon, from flurry and excitement,

missed his rat, but on the other hand he half-murdered a ferret.

But the greatest day of all was that on which Sir Huddlestone Fuddlestone's hounds met upon the lawn at Queen's Crawley.

That was a famous sight for little Rawdon. At half-past ten, Tom Moody, Sir Huddlestone Fuddlestone's huntsman, was seen trotting up the avenue, followed by the noble pack of hounds in a compact body—the rear being brought up by the two whips clad in stained scarlet frocks —light hard-featured lads on well-bred lean horses, possessing marvellous dexterity in casting the points of their long heavy whips at the thinnest part of any dog's skin who dares to straggle from the main body, or to take the slightest notice, or even so much as wink at the hares and rabbits starting under their noses.

Next comes boy Jack, Tom Moody's son, who weighs five stone, measures eight-and-forty inches, and will never be any bigger. He is perched on a large rawboned hunter, half covered by a capacious saddle. This animal is Sir Huddlestone Fuddlestone's favourite horse, The Nob. Other horses, ridden by other small boys, arrive from time to time, awaiting their masters, who will come cantering on anon.

Tom Moody rides up to the door of the Hall, where he is welcomed by the butler, who offers him drink, which he declines. He and his pack then draw off into a sheltered corner of the lawn, where the dogs roll on the grass, and play or growl angrily at one another, ever and anon breaking out into furious fight speedily to be quelled by Tom's voice, unmatched at rating, or the snaky thongs of the whips.

Many young gentlemen canter up on thoroughbred hacks, spatterdashed to the knee, and enter the house to drink cherry-brandy and pay their respects to the ladies, or more modest and sportsmanlike, divest themselves of their mud-boots, exchange their hacks for their hunters, and warm their blood by a preliminary gallop round the lawn. Then they collect round the pack in the corner, and talk with Tom Moody of past sport, and the merits of Sniveller and Diamond, and of the state of the country and of the wretched breed of foxes.

Sir Huddlestone presently appears mounted on a clever

cob, and rides up to the Hall, where he enters and does the
civil thing by the ladies, after which, being a man of few
words, he proceeds to business. The hounds are drawn
up to the Hall-door, and little Rawdon descends amongst
them, excited yet half alarmed by the caresses which they
bestow upon him, at the thumps he receives from their
waving tails, and at their canine bickerings, scarcely
restrained by Tom Moody's tongue and lash.

Meanwhile, Sir Huddlestone has hoisted himself un-
wieldily on The Nob : ' Let's try Sowster's Spinney, Tom,'
says the baronet : ' Farmer Mangle tells me there are two
foxes in it.' Tom blows his horn and trots off, followed by
the pack, by the whips, by the young gents from Winchester,
by the farmers of the neighbourhood, by the labourers of
the parish on foot, with whom the day is a great holiday ;
Sir Huddlestone bringing up the rear with Colonel Crawley,
and the whole *cortège* disappears down the avenue.

The Reverend Bute Crawley (who has been too modest
to appear at the public meet before his nephew's windows),
and whom Tom Moody remembers forty years back a
slender divine riding the wildest horses, jumping the widest
brooks, and larking over the newest gates in the country,—
his reverence, we say, happens to trot out from the Rectory
Lane on his powerful black horse, just as Sir Huddlestone
passes ; he joins the worthy baronet. Hounds and horsemen disappear, and little Rawdon remains on the doorsteps, wondering and happy.

During the progress of this memorable holiday, little
Rawdon, if he had got no special liking for his uncle, always
awful and cold, and locked up in his study, plunged in
justice-business and surrounded by bailiffs and farmers—
has gained the good graces of his married and maiden aunts,
of the two little folks of the Hall, and of Jim of the Rectory,
whom Sir Pitt is encouraging to pay his addresses to one
of the young ladies, with an understanding doubtless that
he shall be presented to the living*when it shall be vacated
by his fox-hunting old sire. Jim has given up that sport
himself, and confines himself to a little harmless duck or
snipe shooting, or a little quiet trifling with the rats during
the Christmas holidays, after which he will return to the
University and try and not be plucked, once more. He has
already eschewed green coats, red neckcloths, and other
worldly ornaments, and is preparing himself for a change

in his condition.   In this cheap and thrifty way Sir Pitt
tries to pay off his debt to his family.

Also before this merry Christmas was over, the baronet
had screwed up courage enough to give his brother another
draft on his bankers, and for no less a sum than a hundred
pounds, an act which caused Sir Pitt cruel pangs at first,
but which made him glow afterwards to think himself one
of the most generous of men.   Rawdon and his son went
away with the utmost heaviness of heart.   Becky and the
ladies parted with some alacrity, however : and our friend
returned to London to commence those avocations with
which we find her occupied when this chapter begins.
Under her care the Crawley House in Great Gaunt Street
was quite rejuvenescent, and ready for the reception of
Sir Pitt and his family, when the baronet came to London
to attend his duties in Parliament, and to assume that
position in the country for which his vast genius fitted him.
For the first session, this profound dissembler hid his
projects and never opened his lips but to present a petition
from Mudbury.   But he attended assiduously in his place,
and learned thoroughly the routine and business of the
House.   At home he gave himself up to the perusal of
Blue Books,* to the alarm and wonder of Lady Jane, who
thought he was killing himself by late hours and intense
application.   And he made acquaintance with the ministers,
and the chiefs of his party, determining to rank as one of
them before many years were over.
Lady Jane's sweetness and kindness had inspired Rebecca
with such a contempt for her ladyship as the little woman
found no small difficulty in concealing.   That sort of goodness and simplicity which Lady Jane possessed annoyed
our friend Becky, and it was impossible for her at times
not to show, or to let the other divine, her scorn.   Her
presence, too, rendered Lady Jane uneasy.   Her husband
talked constantly with Becky.   Signs of intelligence seemed
to pass between them : and Pitt spoke with her on subjects
on which he never thought of discoursing with Lady Jane.
The latter did not understand them to be sure, but it was
mortifying to remain silent ; still more mortifying to know
that you had nothing to say, and hear that little audacious
Mrs. Rawdon dashing on from subject to subject, with
a word for every man, and a joke always pat ; and to sit

in one's own house alone, by the fireside, and watching all
the men round your rival.

In the country, when Lady Jane was telling stories to
the children, who clustered about her knees (little Rawdon
into the bargain, who was very fond of her)—and Becky
came into the room, sneering, with green scornful eyes, poor
Lady Jane grew silent under those baleful glances. Her
simple little fancies shrank away tremulously, as fairies in
the story-books, before a superior bad angel. She could
not go on, although Rebecca, with the smallest inflection
of sarcasm in her voice, besought her to continue that
charming story. And on her side gentle thoughts and
simple pleasures were odious to Mrs. Becky, they discorded
with her; she hated people for liking them; she spurned
children and children-lovers. 'I have no taste for bread-
and-butter,' she would say, when caricaturing Lady Jane
and her ways to my Lord Steyne.

'No more has a certain person for holy water,' his lordship replied with a bow and a grin, and a great jarring
laugh afterwards.

So these two ladies did not see much of each other except
upon those occasions, when the younger brother's wife,
having an object to gain from the other, frequented her.
They my-loved and my-deared each other assiduously, but
kept apart generally : whereas Sir Pitt, in the midst of his
multiplied avocations, found daily time to see his sister-
in-law.

On the occasion of his first Speaker's dinner, Sir Pitt
took the opportunity of appearing before his sister-in-law
in his uniform—that old diplomatic suit which he had worn
when attaché to the Pumpernickel Legation.

Becky complimented him upon that dress, and admired
him almost as much as his own wife and children, to whom
he displayed himself before he set out. She said that it
was only the thoroughbred gentleman who could wear the
court suit with advantage : it was only your men of ancient
race whom the *culotte courte* became. Pitt looked down
with complacency at his legs, which had not, in truth, much
more symmetry or swell than the lean court sword which
dangled by his side : looked down at his legs, and thought
in his heart that he was killing.

When he was gone, Mrs. Becky made a caricature of his
figure, which she showed to Lord Steyne when he arrived.

His lordship carried off the sketch, delighted with the
accuracy of the resemblance.   He had done Sir Pitt Crawley
the honour to meet him at Mrs. Becky's house, and had
been most gracious to the new baronet and member.   Pitt

was struck too by the deference with which the great peer
treated his sister-in-law, by her ease and sprightliness in
the conversation, and by the delight with which the other
men of the party listened to her talk.   Lord Steyne made
no doubt but that the baronet had only commenced his
career in public life, and expected rather anxiously to hear

him as an orator; as they were neighbours (for Great Gaunt Street leads into Gaunt Square, whereof Gaunt House, as everybody knows, forms one side) my lord hoped that as soon as Lady Steyne arrived in London she would have the honour of making the acquaintance of Lady Crawley. He left a card upon his neighbour in the course of a day or two; having never thought fit to notice his predecessor, though they had lived near each other for near a century past.

In the midst of these intrigues and fine parties and wise and brilliant personages Rawdon felt himself more and more isolated every day. He was allowed to go to the club more: to dine abroad with bachelor friends: to come and go when he liked, without any questions being asked. And he and Rawdon the younger many a time would walk to Gaunt Street, and sit with the lady and the children there while Sir Pitt was closeted with Rebecca, on his way to the House, or on his return from it.

The ex-colonel would sit for hours in his brother's house very silent, and thinking and doing as little as possible. He was glad to be employed of an errand: to go and make inquiries about a horse or a servant: or to carve the roast mutton for the dinner of the children. He was beat and cowed into laziness and submission. Delilah had imprisoned him and cut his hair off, too. The bold and reckless young blood of ten years back was subjugated, and was turned into a torpid, submissive, middle-aged, stout gentleman.

And poor Lady Jane was aware that Rebecca had captivated her husband: although she and Mrs. Rawdon my-deared and my-loved each other every day they met.

CHAPTER XLVI

STRUGGLES AND TRIALS

UR friends at Brompton were meanwhile passing their Christmas after their fashion, and in a manner by no means too cheerful.

Out of the hundred pounds a year,* which was about the amount of her income, the widow Osborne had been in the habit of giving up nearly three-fourths to her father and mother, for the expenses of herself and her little boy. With 120*l.* more, supplied by Jos, this family of four people, attended by a single Irish servant who also did for Clapp and his wife, might manage to live in decent comfort through the year, and hold up their heads yet, and be able to give a friend a dish of tea still, after the storms and disappointments of their early life. Sedley still maintained his ascendancy over the family of Mr. Clapp, his ex-clerk. Clapp remembered the time when, sitting on the edge of the chair, he tossed off a bumper to the health of 'Mrs. S——, Miss Emmy, and Mr. Joseph in India', at the merchant's rich table in Russell Square. Time magnified the splendour of those recollections in the honest clerk's bosom. Whenever he came up from the kitchen-parlour to the drawing-room, and partook of tea or gin-and-water with Mr. Sedley, he would say, ' This was not what you was accustomed to once, sir,' and as gravely and reverentially drink the health of the ladies as he had done in the days of their utmost prosperity. He thought Miss 'Melia's playing the divinest music ever performed, and her the finest lady. He never would sit down before Sedley at the club even, nor would he hear that gentleman's character abused by any member of the society. He had seen the first men in London shaking hands with Mr. S—— ; he said. ' He'd known him in times when Rothschild might be seen on 'Change with him any day, and he owed him personally everythink.'

Clapp, with the best of characters and handwritings, had been able very soon after his master's disaster to find other employment for himself. 'Such a little fish as me can swim in any bucket,' he used to remark, and a member of the house from which old Sedley had seceded was very glad to make use of Mr. Clapp's services, and to reward them with a comfortable salary. In fine, all Sedley's wealthy friends had dropped off one by one, and this poor ex-dependent still remained faithfully attached to him.

Out of the small residue of her income, which Amelia kept back for herself, the widow had need of all the thrift and care possible in order to enable her to keep her darling boy dressed in such a manner as became George Osborne's son, and to defray the expenses of the little school to which, after much misgiving and reluctance, and many secret pangs and fears on her own part, she had been induced to send the lad. She had sat up of nights conning lessons and spelling over crabbed grammars and geography books in order to teach them to Georgy. She had worked even at the Latin accidence, fondly hoping that she might be capable of instructing him in that language. To part with him all day : to send him out to the mercy of a schoolmaster's cane and his schoolfellows' roughness, was almost like weaning him over again, to that weak mother, so tremulous and full of sensibility. He, for his part, rushed off to the school with the utmost happiness. He was longing for the change. That childish gladness wounded his mother, who was herself so grieved to part with him. She would rather have had him more sorry, she thought : and then was deeply repentant within herself, for daring to be so selfish as to wish her own son to be unhappy.

Georgy made great progress in the school, which was kept by a friend of his mother's constant admirer, the Rev. Mr. Binney. He brought home numberless prizes and testimonials of ability. He told his mother countless stories every night about his school companions : and what a fine fellow Lyons was, and what a sneak Sniffin was ; and how Steel's father actually supplied the meat for the establishment, whereas Golding's mother came in a carriage to fetch him every Saturday ; and how Neat had straps to his trousers—might he have straps ?—and how Bull

Major was so strong (though only in Eutropius)*that it was believed he could lick the usher, Mr. Ward, himself. So Amelia learned to know every one of the boys in that school as well as Georgy himself : and of nights she used to help him in his exercises and puzzle her little head over his lessons as eagerly as if she was herself going in the morning into the presence of the master. Once, after a certain combat with Master Smith, George came home to his mother with a black eye, and bragged prodigiously to his parent and his delighted old grandfather about his valour in the fight, in which, if the truth was known, he did not behave with particular heroism, and in which he decidedly had the worst. But Amelia has never forgiven that Smith to this day, though he is now a peaceful apothecary near Leicester Square.

In these quiet labours and harmless cares the gentle widow's life was passing away, a silver hair or two marking the progress of time on her head, and a line deepening ever so little on her fair forehead. She used to smile at these marks of time. ' What matters it,' she asked, ' for an old woman like me ? ' All she hoped for was to live to see her son great, famous, and glorious, as he deserved to be. She kept his copy-books, his drawings, and compositions, and showed them about in her little circle, as if they were miracles of genius. She confided some of these specimens to Miss Dobbin ; to show them to Miss Osborne, George's aunt, to show them to Mr. Osborne himself—to make that old man repent of his cruelty and ill-feeling towards him who was gone. All her husband's faults and foibles she had buried in the grave with him : she only remembered the lover, who had married her at all sacrifices ; the noble husband so brave and beautiful, in whose arms she had hung on the morning when he had gone away to fight, and die gloriously for his King. From heaven the hero must be smiling down upon that paragon of a boy whom he had left to comfort and console her.

We have seen how one of George's grandfathers (Mr. Osborne), in his easy chair in Russell Square, daily grew more violent and moody, and how his daughter, with her fine carriage, and her fine horses, and her name on half the public charity lists of the town, was a lonely, miserable, persecuted old maid. She thought again and again of the beautiful little boy, her brother's son whom she had seen.

She longed to be allowed to drive in the fine carriage to the house in which he lived ; and she used to look out day after day as she took her solitary drive in the Park, in hopes that she might see him. Her sister, the banker's lady, occasionally condescended to pay her old home and companion a visit in Russell Square. She brought a couple of sickly children attended by a prim nurse, and in a faint genteel giggling tone cackled to her sister about her fine acquaintance, and how her little Frederick was the image of Lord Claud Lollypop, and her sweet Maria had been noticed by the baroness as they were driving in their donkey-chaise at Roehampton. She urged her to make her papa do something for the darlings. Frederick she had determined should go into the Guards ; and if they made an elder son of him (and Mr. Bullock was positively ruining and pinching himself to death to buy land), how was the darling girl to be provided for ? ' I expect *you*, dear,' Mrs. Bullock would say, ' for of course my share of our papa's property must go to the head of the house, you know. Dear Rhoda Macmull will disengage the whole of the Castletoddy property as soon as poor dear Lord Castletoddy dies, who is quite epileptic ; and little Macduff Macmull will be Viscount Castletoddy. Both the Mr. Bludyers of Mincing Lane have settled their fortunes on Fanny Bludyer's little boy. My darling Frederick must positively be an eldest son ;* and—and do ask papa to bring us back his account in Lombard Street, will you, dear ? It doesn't look well, his going to Stumpy and Rowdy's.' After which kind of speeches, in which fashion and the main chance were blended together, and after a kiss, which was like the contact of an oyster—Mrs. Frederick Bullock would gather her starched nurslings, and simper back into her carriage.

Every visit which this leader of *ton* paid to her family was more unlucky for her. Her father paid more money into Stumpy and Rowdy's. Her patronage became more and more insufferable. The poor widow in the little cottage at Brompton, guarding her treasure there, little knew how eagerly some people coveted it.

On that night when Jane Osborne had told her father that she had seen his grandson, the old man had made her no reply : but he had shown no anger—and had bade her good night on going himself to his room in rather a kindly voice. And he must have meditated on what she said, and have made some inquiries of the Dobbin family regarding her visit ; for a fortnight after it took place, he asked her where was her little French watch and chain she used to wear ?

'I bought it with my money, sir,' she said in a great fright.

'Go and order another like it, or a better if you can get it,' said the old gentleman, and lapsed again into silence.

Of late, the Miss Dobbins more than once repeated their entreaties to Amelia, to allow George to visit them. His aunt had shown her inclination ; perhaps his grandfather himself, they hinted, might be disposed to be reconciled to him. Surely, Amelia could not refuse such advantageous chances for the boy. Nor could she : but she acceded to their overtures with a very heavy and suspicious heart, was always uneasy during the child's absence from her, and welcomed him back as if he was rescued out of some danger. He brought back money and toys, at which the widow looked with alarm and jealousy : she asked him always if he had seen any gentleman—'Only old Sir William, who drove him about in the four-wheeled chaise, and Mr. Dobbin, who arrived on the beautiful bay horse in the afternoon—in the green coat and pink neckcloth, with the gold-headed whip,* who promised to show him the Tower of London, and take him out with the Surrey Hounds.' At last, he said, 'There *was* an old gentleman, with thick eyebrows and a broad hat, and large chain and seals. He came one day as the coachman was lunging Georgy round the lawn on the grey pony. He looked at me very much. He shook very much. I said "My name is Norval "* after dinner. My aunt began to cry. She is always crying.' Such was George's report on that night.

Then Amelia knew that the boy had seen his grandfather : and looked out feverishly for a proposal which she was sure would follow, and which came, in fact, in a few days afterwards. Mr. Osborne formally offered to take the boy, and make him heir to the fortune which he had intended that his father should inherit. He would make Mrs. George Osborne an allowance, such as to assure her a decent competency. If Mrs. George Osborne proposed to marry again, as Mr. O. heard was her intention, he would not withdraw that allowance. But it must be understood,

that the child would live entirely with his grandfather in
Russell Square, or at whatever other place Mr. O. should
select ; and that he would be occasionally permitted to
see Mrs. George Osborne at her own residence. This
message was brought or read to her in a letter one day,
when her mother was from home, and her father absent as
usual, in the City.

She was never seen angry but twice or thrice in her life,
and it was in one of these moods that Mr. Osborne's attorney
had the fortune to behold her. She rose up trembling and
flushing very much as soon as, after reading the letter,
Mr. Poe handed it to her, and she tore the paper into a
hundred fragments, which she trod on. ' " I marry again !
—I take money to part from my child ! Who dares insult
me by proposing such a thing ? Tell Mr. Osborne it is a
cowardly letter, sir—a cowardly letter—I will not answer
it. I wish you good morning, sir "—and she bowed me out
of the room like a tragedy queen,' said the lawyer who told
the story.

Her parents never remarked her agitation on that day,
and she never told them of the interview. They had their
own affairs to interest them, affairs which deeply interested
this innocent and unconscious lady. The old gentleman,
her father, was always dabbling in speculation. We have
seen how the Wine Company and the Coal Company had
failed him. But, prowling about the City always eagerly
and restlessly still, he lighted upon some other scheme,
of which he thought so well that he embarked in it in spite
of the remonstrances of Mr. Clapp, to whom indeed he never
dared to tell how far he had engaged himself in it. And
as it was always Mr. Sedley's maxim not to talk about
money matters before women, they had no inkling of the
misfortunes that were in store for them until the unhappy
old gentleman was forced to make gradual confessions.

The bills of the little household, which had been settled
weekly, first fell into arrear. The remittances had not
arrived from India, Mr. Sedley told his wife with a disturbed
face. As she had paid her bills very regularly hitherto,
one or two of the tradesmen to whom the poor lady was
obliged to go round asking for time were very angry at
a delay, to which they were perfectly used from more
irregular customers. Emmy's contribution, paid over
cheerfully without any questions, kept the little company

in half rations however.   And the first six months passed
away pretty easily : old Sedley still keeping up with the
notion that his shares must rise, and that all would be well.

No sixty pounds, however, came to help the household
at the end of the half-year ; and it fell deeper and deeper
into trouble—Mrs. Sedley, who was growing infirm and
was much shaken, remained silent or wept a great deal
with Mrs. Clapp in the kitchen.   The butcher was particularly surly : the grocer insolent : once or twice little
Georgy had grumbled about the dinners : and Amelia,
who still would have been satisfied with a slice of bread
for her own dinner, could not but perceive that her son
was neglected, and purchased little things out of her private
purse to keep the boy in health.

At last they told her, or told her such a garbled story
as people in difficulties tell.   One day, her own money
having been received, and Amelia about to pay it over :
she who had kept an account of the moneys expended by
her, proposed to keep a certain portion back out of her
dividend, having contracted engagements for a new suit
for Georgy.

Then it came out that Jos's remittances were not paid ;
that the house was in difficulties which Amelia ought to
have seen before, her mother said, but she cared for nothing
or nobody except Georgy.   At this she passed all of her
money across the table, without a word, to her mother,
and returned to her room to cry her eyes out.   She had
a great access of sensibility too that day, when obliged to
go and countermand the clothes, the darling clothes on
which she had set her heart for Christmas Day, and the cut
and fashion of which she had arranged in many conversations
with a small milliner, her friend.

Hardest of all, she had to break the matter to Georgy,
who made a loud outcry.   Everybody had new clothes at
Christmas.   The others would laugh at him.   He *would* have
new clothes.   She had promised them to him.   The poor
widow had only kisses to give him.   She darned the old suit
in tears.   She cast about among her little ornaments to see
could she sell anything to procure the desired novelties ?
There was her India shawl that Dobbin had sent her.
She remembered in former days going with her mother to
a fine India shop on Ludgate Hill, where the ladies had
all sorts of dealings and bargains in these articles.   Her

cheeks flushed and her eyes shone with pleasure as she thought of this resource, and she kissed away George to school in the morning, smiling brightly after him. The boy felt that there was good news in her look.

Packing up her shawl in a handkerchief (another of the gifts of the good major), she hid them under her cloak, and walked flushed and eager all the way to Ludgate Hill, tripping along by the Park wall, and running over the crossings, so that many a man turned as she hurried by him, and looked after her rosy pretty face. She calculated how she should spend the proceeds of her shawl : how, besides the clothes, she would buy the books that he longed for, and pay his half-year's schooling ; and how she would buy a cloak for her father instead of that old greatcoat which he wore. She was not mistaken as to the value of the major's gift. It was a very fine and beautiful web : and the merchant made a very good bargain when he gave her twenty guineas for her shawl.

She ran on amazed and flurried with her riches to Darton's shop in St. Paul's Churchyard,* and there purchased the *Parent's Assistant,* and the *Sandford and Merton** Georgy longed for, and got into the coach there with her parcel, and went home exulting. And she pleased herself by writing in the fly-leaf in her neatest little hand, ' George Osborne, a Christmas gift from his affectionate mother.' The books are extant to this day, with the fair delicate superscription.

She was going from her own room with the books in her hand to place them on George's table, where he might find them on his return from school ; when in the passage, she and her mother met. The gilt bindings of the seven handsome little volumes caught the old lady's eye.

' What are those ? ' she said.

' Some books for Georgy,' Amelia replied ; 'I—I promised them to him at Christmas.'

' Books ! ' cried the elder lady, indignantly, ' books, when the whole house wants bread ! Books, when to keep you and your son in luxury, and your dear father out of gaol, I've sold every trinket I had, the India shawl from my back—even down to the very spoons, that our trades-men mightn't insult us, and that Mr. Clapp, which indeed he is justly entitled, being not a hard landlord, and a civil man, and a father, might have his rent. Oh, Amelia ! you break my heart with your books and that boy of yours, whom you are ruining, though part with him you will not. Oh, Amelia, may God send you a more dutiful child than I have had. There's Jos deserts his father in his old age : and there's George, who might be provided for, and who might be rich, going to school like a lord, with a gold watch and chain round his neck—while my dear, dear old man is without a sh—shilling.' Hysteric sobs and cries ended Mrs. Sedley's speech—it echoed through every room in the small house, whereof the other female inmates heard every word of the colloquy.

'Oh, mother, mother!' cried the poor Amelia in reply. 'You told me nothing—I—I promised him the books. I—I only sold my shawl this morning. Take the money—take everything'—and with quivering hands she took out her silver, and her sovereigns—her precious golden sovereigns,* which she thrust into the hands of her mother, whence they overflowed and tumbled, rolling down the stairs.

And then she went into her room, and sank down in despair and utter misery. She saw it all now. Her selfishness was sacrificing the boy. But for her he might have wealth, station, education, and his father's place, which the elder George had forfeited for her sake. She had but to speak the words, and her father was restored to competency : and the boy raised to fortune. Oh, what a conviction it was to that tender and stricken heart !

CHAPTER XLVII

GAUNT HOUSE

LL the world knows that Lord Steyne's town palace stands in Gaunt Square, out of which Great Gaunt Street leads,* whither we first conducted Rebecca, in the time of the departed Sir Pitt Crawley. Peering over the railings and through the black trees into the garden of the square, you see a few miserable governesses with wan-faced pupils wandering round and round it, and round the dreary grass-plot in the centre of which rises the statue of Lord Gaunt, who fought at Minden, in a three-tailed wig, and otherwise habited like a Roman Emperor. Gaunt House occupies nearly a side of the square. The remaining three sides are composed of mansions that have passed away into Dowagerism ;—tall, dark houses, with window-frames of stone, or picked out of a lighter red. Little light seems to be behind those lean, comfortless casements now : and hospitality to have passed away from those doors as much as the laced lackeys and link-boys of old times who used to put out their torches in the blank iron extinguishers that still flank the lamps over the steps. Brass plates have penetrated into the square—Doctors, the Diddlesex Bank Western Branch—the English and European Reunion, &c.—it has a dreary look—nor is my Lord Steyne's palace less dreary. All I have ever seen of it is the vast wall in front, with the rustic columns at the great gate, through which an old porter peers sometimes with a fat and gloomy red face—and over the wall the garret and bedroom windows, and the chimneys, out of which there seldom comes any smoke now. For the present Lord Steyne lives at Naples,* preferring the view of the bay and Capri and Vesuvius, to the dreary aspect of the wall in Gaunt Square.

A few score yards down New Gaunt Street, and leading into Gaunt Mews indeed, is a little modest back door, which you would not remark from that of any of the other stables. But many a little close carriage has stopped at that door, as my informant (little Tom Eaves, who knows everything, and who showed me the place) told me. 'The prince and Perdita have been in and out of that door, sir,' he has often told me; 'Marianne Clarke has entered it with the Duke of ——. It conducts to the famous *petits appartements* of Lord Steyne—one, sir, fitted up all in ivory and white satin, another in ebony and black velvet; there is a little banqueting-room taken from Sallust's house at Pompeii, and painted by Cosway*—a little private kitchen, in which every saucepan was silver, and all the spits were gold. It was there that Egalité Orleans roasted partridges on the night when he and the Marquis of Steyne won a hundred thousand from a great personage at Hombre. Half of the money went to the French Revolution, half to purchase Lord Gaunt's marquisate and garter—and the remainder——'* but it forms no part of our scheme to tell what became of the remainder, for every shilling of which, and a great deal more, little Tom Eaves, who knows everybody's affairs, is ready to account.

Besides his town palace, the marquis had castles and palaces in various quarters of the three kingdoms, whereof the descriptions may be found in the Road-books*—Castle Strongbow, with its woods, on the Shannon shore; Gaunt Castle, in Carmarthenshire, where Richard II was taken prisoner—Gauntly Hall in Yorkshire, where I have been informed there were two hundred silver teapots for the breakfasts of the guests of the house, with everything to correspond in splendour; and Stillbrook in Hampshire, which was my lord's farm, a humble place of residence, of which we all remember the wonderful furniture which was sold at my lord's demise by a late celebrated auctioneer.*

The Marchioness of Steyne* was of the renowned and ancient family of the Caerlyons, Marquises of Camelot, who have preserved the old faith ever since the conversion of the venerable Druid* their first ancestor, and whose pedigree goes far beyond the date of the arrival of King Brute in these islands. Pendragon is the title of the eldest son of the house. The sons have been called Arthurs, Uthers, and Caradocs, from immemorial time. Their heads have fallen in many a loyal conspiracy. Elizabeth chopped off the head of the Arthur of her day, who had been chamberlain to Philip and Mary, and carried letters between the

Queen of Scots and her uncles the Guises. A cadet of the house was an officer of the great duke, and distinguished in the famous St. Bartholomew conspiracy. During the whole of Mary's confinement, the house of Camelot conspired in her behalf. It was as much injured by its charges in fitting out an armament against the Spaniards, during the time of the Armada, as by the fines and confiscations levied on it by Elizabeth for harbouring of priests, obstinate recusancy, and Popish misdoings. A recreant of James's time was momentarily perverted from his religion by the arguments of that great theologian, and the fortunes of the family somewhat restored by his timely weakness. But the Earl of Camelot, of the reign of Charles, returned to the old creed of his family, and they continued to fight for it, and ruin themselves for it, as long as there was a Stuart left to head or to instigate a rebellion.

Lady Mary Caerlyon was brought up at a Parisian convent ; the Dauphiness Marie Antoinette was her god-mother. In the pride of her beauty she had been married—sold, it was said—to Lord Gaunt, then at Paris, who won vast sums from the lady's brother at some of Philip of Orleans's banquets. The Earl of Gaunt's famous duel with the Count de la Marche, of the Grey Musqueteers, was attributed by common report to the pretensions of that officer (who had been a page, and remained a favourite of the Queen) to the hand of the beautiful Lady Mary Caerlyon. She was married to Lord Gaunt while the count lay ill of his wound, and came to dwell at Gaunt House, and to figure for a short time in the splendid Court of the Prince of Wales. Fox had toasted her. Morris and Sheridan had written songs about her. Malmsbury had made her his best bow ; Walpole had pronounced her charming ; Devonshire had been almost jealous of her ; but she was scared by the wild pleasures and gaieties of the society into which she was flung, and after she had borne a couple of sons, shrank away into a life of devout seclusion. No wonder that my Lord Steyne, who liked pleasure and cheerfulness, was not often seen after their marriage, by the side of this trembling, silent, superstitious, unhappy lady.

The before-mentioned Tom Eaves (who has no part in this history, except that he knew all the great folks in London, and the stories and mysteries of each family)

had further information regarding my Lady Steyne, which
may or may not be true. ' The humiliations,' Tom used
to say, ' which that woman has been made to undergo, in
her own house, have been frightful ; Lord Steyne has
made her sit down to table with women with whom I would
rather die than allow Mrs. Eaves to associate—with Lady
Crackenbury,* with Mrs. Chippenham, with Madame de la
Cruchecassée, the French secretary's wife ' (from every
one of which ladies Tom Eaves—who would have sacrificed
his wife for knowing them—was too glad to get a bow or
a dinner), ' with the *reigning favourite*, in a word. And do
you suppose that that woman, of that family, who are as
proud as the Bourbons, and to whom the Steynes are but
lackeys, mushrooms of yesterday (for after all, they are
not of the old Gaunts, but of a minor and doubtful branch
of the house) ; do you suppose, I say ' (the reader must
bear in mind that it is always Tom Eaves who speaks),
' that the Marchioness of Steyne, the haughtiest woman
in England, would bend down to her husband so submissively, if there were not some cause ? Pooh ! I tell you
there are *secret reasons*. I tell you, that in the emigration,
the Abbé de la Marche who was here and was employed in
the Quiberoon business with Puisaye and Tinteniac, was
the same colonel of Mousquetaires Gris with whom Steyne
fought in the year '86—that he and the marchioness met
again : that it was after the reverend colonel was shot
in Brittany, that Lady Steyne took to those extreme
practices of devotion which she carries on now : for she
is closeted with her director every day—she is at service
at Spanish Place,* every morning, I've watched her there
—that is, I've happened to be passing there—and depend
on it there's a mystery in her case. People are not so
unhappy unless they have something to repent of,' added
Tom Eaves with a knowing wag of his head ; ' and depend
on it, that woman would not be so submissive as she is,
if the marquis had not some sword to hold over her.'

So, if Mr. Eaves's information be correct, it is very likely
that this lady, in her high station, had to submit to many
a private indignity, and to hide many secret griefs under
a calm face. And let us, my brethren who have not our
names in the Red Book,* console ourselves by thinking
comfortably how miserable our betters may be, and that
Damocles, who sits on satin cushions, and is served on gold

plate, has an awful sword hanging over his head in the
shape of a bailiff, or an hereditary disease, or a family
secret, which peeps out every now and then from the
embroidered arras in a ghastly manner, and will be sure
to drop one day or the other in the right place.

In comparing, too, the poor man's situation with that
of the great, there is (always according to Mr. Eaves)
another source of comfort for the former. You who have
little or no patrimony to bequeath or to inherit, may be
on good terms with your father or your son, whereas the
heir of a great prince, such as my Lord Steyne, must
naturally be angry at being kept out of his kingdom, and
eye the occupant of it with no very agreeable glances.
'Take it as a rule,' this sardonic old Eaves would say,
' the fathers and elder sons of all great families hate each
other. The crown prince is always in opposition to the
crown or hankering after it. Shakespeare knew the world,
my good sir, and when he describes Prince Hal (from whose
family the Gaunts pretend to be descended, though they
are no more related to John of Gaunt than you are) trying
on his father's coronet, he gives you a natural description
of all heirs-apparent. If you were heir to a dukedom and
a thousand pounds a day, do you mean to say you would
not wish for possession ? Pooh ! And it stands to reason
that every great man having experienced this feeling
towards his father, must be aware that his son entertains
it towards himself ; and so they can't but be suspicious
and hostile.

' Then again, as to the feeling of elder towards younger
sons. My dear sir, you ought to know that every elder
brother looks upon the cadets of the house as his natural
enemies, who deprive him of so much ready money which
ought to be his by right. I have often heard George Mac
Turk, Lord Bajazet's eldest son, say that if he had his will
when he came to the title, he would do what the sultans do,
and clear the estate by chopping off all his younger brothers'
heads at once ; and so the case is, more or less, with them
all. I tell you they are all Turks in their hearts. Pooh !
sir, they know the world.' And here, haply a great man
coming up, Tom Eaves's hat would drop off his head, and
he would rush forward with a bow and a grin, which showed
that he knew the world too—in the Tomeavesian way,
that is. And having laid out every shilling of his fòrtune

on an annuity, Tom could afford to bear no malice to his nephews and nieces, and to have no other feeling with regard to his betters, but a constant and generous desire to dine with them.

Between the marchioness and the natural and tender regard of mother for children, there was that cruel barrier placed of difference of faith. The very love which she might feel for her sons, only served to render the timid and

pious lady more fearful and unhappy. The gulf which separated them was fatal and impassable. She could not stretch her weak arms across it, or draw her children over to that side away from which her belief told her there was no safety. During the youth of his sons, Lord Steyne, who was a good scholar and amateur casuist, had no better sport in the evening after dinner in the country than in setting the boys' tutor, the Reverend Mr. Trail (now my Lord Bishop of Ealing), on her ladyship's director, Father Mole, over their wine, and in putting Oxford against St. Acheul. He cried, ' Bravo, Latimer ! Well said,

Loyola ! '*alternately ; he promised Mole a bishopric if
he would come over ; and vowed he would use all his
influence to get Trail a cardinal's hat if he would secede.
Neither divine allowed himself to be conquered ; and
though the fond mother hoped that her youngest and
favourite son would be reconciled to her Church—his mother
Church—a sad and awful disappointment awaited the
devout lady—a disappointment which seemed to be a
judgement upon her for the sin of her marriage.

My Lord Gaunt married, as every person who frequents
the *Peerage* knows, the Lady Blanche Thistlewood, a daughter
of the noble house of Bareacres, before mentioned in this
veracious history. A wing of Gaunt House was assigned
to this couple ; for the head of the family chose to govern
it, and while he reigned to reign supreme : his son and
heir, however, living little at home, disagreeing with his
wife, borrowing upon post-obits such moneys as he required
beyond the very moderate sums which his father was disposed to allow him. The marquis knew every shilling of
his son's debts. At his lamented demise, he was found
himself to be possessor of many of his heir's bonds, purchased for their benefit, and devised by his lordship to the
children of his younger son.

As, to my Lord Gaunt's dismay, and the chuckling delight
of his natural enemy and father, the Lady Gaunt had no
children—the Lord George Gaunt was desired to return
from Vienna, where he was engaged in waltzing and diplomacy, and to contract a matrimonial alliance with the
Honourable Joan, only daughter of John Johnes, First
Baron Helvellyn, and head of the firm of Jones, Brown,
and Robinson, of Threadneedle Street, Bankers ; from
which union sprang several sons and daughters, whose
doings do not appertain to this story.

The marriage at first was a happy and prosperous one.
My Lord George Gaunt could not only read, but write
pretty correctly. He spoke French with considerable
fluency ; and was one of the finest waltzers in Europe.
With these talents, and his interests at home, there was
little doubt that his lordship would rise to the highest
dignities in his profession. The lady, his wife, felt that
courts were her sphere ; and her wealth enabled her to
receive splendidly in those Continental towns whither her
husband's diplomatic duties led him. There was talk of

appointing him minister, and bets were laid at the Travellers'* that he would be ambassador ere long, when of a sudden, rumours arrived of the secretary's extraordinary behaviour. At a grand diplomatic dinner given by his chief, he had started up, and declared that a *pâté de foie gras* was poisoned. He went to a ball at the hotel of the Bavarian envoy, the Count de Springbock-Hohenlaufen, with his head shaved, and dressed as a Capuchin friar. It was not a masked ball, as some folks wanted to persuade you. It was something queer, people whispered. His grandfather was so. It was in the family.

His wife and family returned to this country, and took up their abode at Gaunt House. Lord George gave up his post on the European Continent, and was gazetted to Brazil. But people knew better; he never returned from that Brazil expedition—never died there—never lived there— never was there at all. He was nowhere : he was gone out altogether. ' Brazil,' said one gossip to another, with a grin—' Brazil is St. John's Wood. Rio Janeiro is a cottage surrounded by four walls ; and George Gaunt is accredited to a keeper, who has invested him with the order of the Strait Waistcoat.' These are the kinds of epitaphs which men pass over one another in Vanity Fair.

Twice or thrice in a week, in the earliest morning, the poor mother went for her sins and saw the poor invalid. Sometimes he laughed at her (and his laughter was more pitiful than to hear him cry) ; sometimes she found the brilliant dandy diplomatist of the Congress of Vienna dragging about a child's toy, or nursing the keeper's baby's doll. Sometimes he knew her and Father Mole, her director and companion : oftener he forgot her, as he had done wife, children, love, ambition, vanity. But he remembered his dinner-hour, and used to cry if his wine-and-water was not strong enough.

It was the mysterious taint of the blood : the poor mother had brought it from her own ancient race. The evil had broken out once or twice in the father's family, long before Lady Steyne's sins had begun, or her fasts and tears and penances had been offered in their expiation. The pride of the race was struck down as the firstborn of Pharaoh. The dark mark of fate and doom was on the threshold,—the tall old threshold surmounted by coronets and carved heraldry.

The absent lord's children meanwhile prattled and grew on quite unconscious that the doom was over them too. First they talked of their father, and devised plans against his return. Then the name of the living dead man was less frequently in their mouths—then not mentioned at all. But the stricken old grandmother trembled to think that these too were the inheritors of their father's shame as

well as of his honours : and watched sickening for the day when the awful ancestral curse should come down on them.

This dark presentiment also haunted Lord Steyne. He tried to lay the horrid bedside ghost in Red Seas of wine and jollity, and lost sight of it sometimes in the crowd and rout of his pleasures. But it always came back to him when alone, and seemed to grow more threatening with years. 'I have taken your son,' it said, 'why not you ? I may shut you up in a prison some day like your son George. I may tap you on the head to-morrow, and away go pleasure and honours, feasts and beauty, friends, flatterers, French cooks, fine horses and houses—in exchange

for a prison, a keeper, and a straw mattress like George
Gaunt's.' And then my lord would defy the ghost which
threatened him : for he knew of a remedy by which he
could balk his enemy.

So there was splendour and wealth, but no great happiness perchance behind the tall carved portals of Gaunt
House with its smoky coronets and ciphers. The feasts
there were of the grandest in London, but there was not
over-much content therewith, except among the guests
who sat at my lord's table. Had he not been so great a
prince very few possibly would have visited him : but in
Vanity Fair the sins of very great personages are looked at
indulgently. ' *Nous regardons à deux fois* ' (as the French
lady said) before we condemn a person of my lord's undoubted quality. Some notorious carpers and squeamish
moralists might be sulky with Lord Steyne, but they were
glad enough to come when he asked them.

' Lord Steyne is really too bad,' Lady Slingstone said,
' but everybody goes, and of course I shall see that my girls
come to no harm.' ' His lordship is a man to whom I owe
much, everything in life,' said the Right Reverend Doctor
Trail, thinking that the archbishop was rather shaky ;
and Mrs. Trail and the young ladies would as soon have
missed going to church as to one of his lordship's parties.
' His morals are bad,' said little Lord Southdown to his
sister, who meekly expostulated, having heard terrific
legends from her mamma with respect to the doings at
Gaunt House ; ' but hang it, he's got the best dry sillery
in Europe ! ' And as for Sir Pitt Crawley, Bart.—Sir
Pitt that pattern of decorum, Sir Pitt who had led off at
missionary meetings,—he never for one moment thought
of not going too. ' Where you see such persons as the
Bishop of Ealing and the Countess of Slingstone, you may
be pretty sure, Jane,' the baronet would say, ' that *we*
cannot be wrong. The great rank and station of Lord
Steyne put him in a position to command people in our
station in life. The lord lieutenant of a county, my
dear, is a respectable man. Besides George Gaunt and
I were intimate in early life : he was my junior when we
were attachés at Pumpernickel together.'

In a word everybody went to wait upon this great man—
everybody who was asked : as you the reader (do not say
nay) or I the writer hereof would go if we had an invitation.

CHAPTER XLVIII

IN WHICH THE READER IS INTRODUCED TO THE VERY BEST OF
COMPANY

A T last Becky's kindness and attention to the chief of her husband's family, were destined to meet with an exceeding great reward ; a reward which, though certainly somewhat unsubstantial, the little woman coveted with greater eagerness than more positive benefits. If she did not wish to lead a virtuous life, at least she desired to enjoy a character for virtue, and we know that no lady in the genteel world can possess this desideratum, until she has put on a train and feathers, and has been presented to her sovereign* at Court. From that august interview they come out stamped as honest women. The lord chamberlain gives them a certificate of virtue. And as dubious goods or letters are passed through an oven at quarantine, sprinkled with aromatic vinegar, and then pronounced clean—many a lady whose reputation would be doubtful otherwise and liable to give infection, passes through the wholesome ordeal of the royal presence, and issues from it free from all taint.

It might be very well for my Lady Bareacres, my Lady Tufto, Mrs. Bute Crawley in the country, and other ladies who had come into contact with Mrs. Rawdon Crawley, to cry fie at the idea of the odious little adventuress making her curtsy before the sovereign, and to declare, that if dear good Queen Charlotte had been alive, *she* never would have admitted such an extremely ill-regulated personage into Her chaste Drawing-room. But when we consider, that it was the First Gentleman in Europe in whose high presence Mrs. Rawdon passed her examination, and as it were, took her degree in reputation, it surely must be flat disloyalty to doubt any more about her virtue. I, for my part, look back with love and awe to that Great Character in history. Ah, what a high and noble appreciation of Gentlewomanhood there must have been in Vanity Fair, when that revered and august being was invested, by the universal acclaim of the refined and educated portion of this empire, with the title of Premier Gentilhomme of his Kingdom. Do you remember, dear M——,* O friend of my youth, how one blissful night five-and-twenty years since, *The Hypocrite* being acted, Elliston being manager, Dowton and Liston* performers, two boys had leave from their loyal masters to go out from Slaughter House School where they we e educated, and to appear on Drury Lane stage, amongst a crowd which assembled there to greet the King. THE KING? There he was. Beef-eaters were before the august box : the Marquis of Steyne (Lord of the Powder Closet) and other great officers of state were behind the chair on which he sat, *He* sat—florid of face, portly of person, covered with orders, and in a rich curling head of hair—How we sang God save him ! How the house rocked and shouted with that magnificent music. How they cheered, and cried, and waved handkerchiefs. Ladies wept : mothers clasped their children : some fainted with emotion. People were suffocated in the pit, shrieks and groans rising up amidst the writhing and shouting mass there of his people who were, and indeed showed themselves almost to be, ready to die for him. Yes, we saw him. Fate cannot deprive us of *that*. Others have seen Napoleon. Some few still exist who have beheld Frederick the Great, Doctor Johnson, Marie Antoinette, &c.—be it our reasonable boast to our children, that we saw George the Good, the Magnificent, the Great.

Well, there came a happy day in Mrs. Rawdon Crawley's existence when this angel was admitted into the paradise of a Court which she coveted ; her sister-in-law acting as her godmother. On the appointed day, Sir Pitt and his lady, in their great family carriage (just newly built, and ready for the baronet's assumption of the office of high sheriff of his county), drove up to the little house in Curzon Street, to the edification of Raggles who was watching from his greengrocer's shop, and saw fine plumes within,

and enormous bunches of flowers in the breasts of the new
livery-coats of the footmen.

Sir Pitt, in a glittering uniform, descended and went into
Curzon Street, his sword between his legs. Little Rawdon
stood with his face against the parlour window panes, smiling
and nodding with all his might to his aunt in the carriage
within ; and presently Sir Pitt issued forth from the house
again, leading forth a lady with grand feathers, covered in
a white shawl, and holding up daintily a train of magnificent
brocade. She stepped into the vehicle as if she were a
princess and accustomed all her life to go to Court, smiling
graciously on the footman at the door, and on Sir Pitt, who
followed her into the carriage.

Then Rawdon followed in his old Guards' uniform, which
had grown wofully shabby, and was much too tight. He
was to have followed the procession, and waited upon his
sovereign in a cab ; but that his good-natured sister-in-law
insisted that they should be a family party. The coach
was large, the ladies not very big, they would hold their
trains in their laps—finally, the four went fraternally
together ; and their carriage presently joined the line of
loyal equipages which was making its way down Piccadilly
and St. James's Street, towards the old brick palace where
the Star of Brunswick*was in waiting to receive his nobles
and gentlefolks.

Becky felt as if she could bless the people out of the
carriage windows, so elated was she in spirit, and so strong
a sense had she of the dignified position which she had at
last attained in life. Even our Becky had her weaknesses,
and as one often sees how men pride themselves upon
excellences which others are slow to perceive : how, for
instance, Comus firmly believes that he is the greatest
tragic actor in England ; how Brown, the famous novelist,
longs to be considered, not a man of genius, but a man of
fashion ; while Robinson, the great lawyer, does not in the
least care about his reputation in Westminster Hall, but
believes himself incomparable across country, and at a
five-barred gate—so to be, and to be thought, a respectable
woman, was Becky's aim in life, and she got up the genteel
with amazing assiduity, readiness, and success. We have
said, there were times when she believed herself to be a fine
lady, and forgot that there was no money in the chest at
home—duns round the gate, tradesmen to coax and wheedle

—no ground to walk upon, in a word. And as she went
to Court in the carriage, the family carriage, she adopted
a demeanour so grand, self-satisfied, deliberate, and im-
posing, that it made even Lady Jane laugh. She walked
into the royal apartments with a toss of the head which
would have befitted an empress, and I have no doubt had
she been one, she would have become the character perfectly.

We are authorized to state that Mrs. Rawdon Crawley's
costume de cour on the occasion of her presentation to the
sovereign was of the most elegant and brilliant description.
Some ladies we may have seen—we who wear stars and
cordons, and attend the St. James's assemblies, or we who,
in muddy boots, dawdle up and down Pall Mall, and peep
into the coaches as they drive up with the great folks in
their feathers—some ladies of fashion, I say, we may have
seen, about two o'clock of the forenoon of a Levée day, as
the laced-jacketed band of the Life Guards are blowing
triumphal marches seated on those prancing music-stools,
their cream-coloured chargers—who are by no means lovely
and enticing objects at that early period of noon. A stout
countess of sixty, *décolletée*, painted, wrinkled, with rouge
up to her drooping eyelids, and diamonds twinkling in her
wig, is a wholesome and edifying, but not a pleasant sight.
She has the faded look of a St. James's Street illumination,
as it may be seen of an early morning, when half the lamps
are out, and the others are blinking wanly, as if they were
about to vanish like ghosts before the dawn. Such charms
as those of which we catch glimpses while her ladyship's
carriage passes, should appear abroad at night alone. If
even Cynthia looks haggard of an afternoon, as we may see
her sometimes in the present winter season, with Phoebus
staring her out of countenance from the opposite side of the
heavens, how much more can old Lady Castlemouldy keep
her head up when the sun is shining full upon it through the
chariot windows, and showing all the chinks and crannies
with which time has marked her face ? No. Drawing-rooms
should be announced for November, or the first foggy day :
or the elderly sultanas of our Vanity Fair should drive up in
closed litters, descend in a covered way, and make their
curtsy to the sovereign under the protection of lamplight.

Our beloved Rebecca had no need, however, of any such
a friendly halo to set off her beauty. Her complexion could
bear any sunshine as yet ; and her dress, though if you were

to see it now, any present lady of Vanity Fair would pronounce it to be the most foolish and preposterous attire
ever worn, was as handsome in her eyes and those of the
public, some five-and-twenty years since, as the most
brilliant costume of the most famous beauty of the present
season. A score of years hence that, too, that milliner's
wonder, will have passed into the domain of the absurd,
along with all previous vanities. But we are wandering
too much. Mrs. Rawdon's dress was pronounced to be
charmante on the eventful day of her presentation. Even
good little Lady Jane was forced to acknowledge this effect,
as she looked at her kinswoman ; and owned sorrowfully
to herself that she was quite inferior in taste to Mrs. Becky.

She did not know how much care, thought, and genius
Mrs. Rawdon had bestowed upon that garment. Rebecca
had as good taste as any milliner in Europe, and such a
clever way of doing things as Lady Jane little understood.
The latter quickly spied out the magnificence of the brocade
of Becky's train, and the splendour of the lace on her dress.

The brocade was an old remnant, Becky said ; and as for
the lace, it was a great bargain. She had had it these
hundred years.

' My dear Mrs. Crawley, it must have cost a little fortune,'
Lady Jane said, looking down at her own lace, which was
not nearly so good ; and then, examining the quality of the
ancient brocade which formed the material of Mrs. Rawdon's
court dress, she felt inclined to say that she could not
afford such fine clothing, but checked that speech, with an
effort, as one uncharitable to her kinswoman.

And yet, if Lady Jane had known all, I think even her
kindly temper would have failed her. The fact is, when
she was putting Sir Pitt's house in order, Mrs. Rawdon had
found the lace and the brocade in old wardrobes, the property of the former ladies of the house, and had quietly
carried the goods home, and had suited them to her own
little person. Briggs saw her take them, asked no questions,
told no stories ; but I believe quite sympathized with her
on this matter, and so would many another honest woman.

And the diamonds—' Where the doose did you get the
diamonds, Becky ? ' said her husband, admiring some jewels
which he had never seen before, and which sparkled in her
ears and on her neck with brilliance and profusion.

Becky blushed a little, and looked at him hard for a

moment. Pitt Crawley blushed a little too, and looked out of window. The fact is, he had given her a very small portion of the brilliants ; a pretty diamond clasp, which confined a pearl necklace which she wore ; and the baronet had omitted to mention the circumstance to his lady.

Becky looked at her husband, and then at Sir Pitt, with an air of saucy triumph, as much as to say, ' Shall I betray you ? '

' Guess ! ' she said to her husband. ' Why, you silly man,' she continued, 'where do you suppose I got them—all except the little clasp, which a dear friend of mine gave me long ago. I hired them, to be sure. I hired them at Mr. Polonius's in Coventry Street. You don't suppose that all the diamonds which go to Court belong to the owners ; like those beautiful stones which Lady Jane has, and which are much handsomer than any which I have, I am certain.'

' They are family jewels,' said Sir Pitt, again looking uneasy. And in this family conversation the carriage rolled down the street, until its cargo was finally discharged at the gates of the palace where the sovereign was sitting in state.

The diamonds, which had created Rawdon's admiration, never went back to Mr. Polonius, of Coventry Street, and that gentleman never applied for their restoration ; but they retired into a little private repository, in an old desk, which Amelia Sedley had given her years and years ago, and in which Becky kept a number of useful and, perhaps, valuable things, about which her husband knew nothing. To know nothing, or little, is in the nature of some husbands. To hide, in the nature of how many women ? O ladies ! how many of you have surreptitious milliners' bills ? How many of you have gowns and bracelets, which you daren't show, or which you wear trembling ?—trembling, and coaxing with smiles the husband by your side, who does not know the new velvet gown from the old one, or the new bracelet from last year's, or has any notion that the ragged-looking yellow lace scarf cost forty guineas, and that Madame Bobinot is writing dunning letters every week for the money !

Thus Rawdon knew nothing about the brilliant diamond ear-rings, or the superb brilliant ornament which decorated the fair bosom of his lady ; but Lord Steyne, who was in his place at Court, as Lord of the Powder Closet, and one of the great dignitaries and illustrious defences of the throne of England, and came up with all his stars, garters, collars, and cordons, and paid particular attention to the little woman, knew whence the jewels came, and who paid for them.

As he bowed over her he smiled, and quoted the hackneyed and beautiful lines, from the *Rape of the Lock*,* about Belinda's diamonds, ' which Jews might kiss and infidels adore.'

' But I hope your lordship is orthodox,' said the little lady, with a toss of her head. And many ladies round about whispered and talked, and many gentlemen nodded and whispered, as they saw what marked attention the great nobleman was paying to the little adventuress.

What were the circumstances of the interview between Rebecca Crawley, *née* Sharp, and her Imperial Master, it does not become such a feeble and inexperienced pen as mine to attempt to relate. The dazzled eyes close before that Magnificent Idea. Loyal respect and decency tell even the imagination not to look too keenly and audaciously about the sacred audience-chamber, but to back away rapidly, silently, and respectfully, making profound bows out of the August Presence.

This may be said, that in all London there was no more loyal heart than Becky's after this interview. The name of her King was always on her lips, and he was proclaimed by her to be the most charming of men. She went to Colnaghi's* and ordered the finest portrait of him that art had produced, and credit could supply. She chose that famous one in which the best of monarchs is represented in a frock-coat with a fur collar, and breeches and silk stockings, simpering on a sofa from under his curly brown wig.* She had him painted in a brooch and wore it—indeed she amused and somewhat pestered her acquaintance with her perpetual talk about his urbanity and beauty. Who knows ? Perhaps the little woman thought she might play the part of a Maintenon or a Pompadour.*

But the finest sport of all after her presentation was to hear her talk virtuously. She had a few female acquaintances, not, it must be owned, of the very highest reputation in Vanity Fair. But being made an honest woman of, so to speak, Becky would not consort any longer with these dubious ones, and cut Lady Crackenbury when the latter nodded to her from her opera-box ; and gave Mrs. Washington White the go-by in the ring. 'One must, my dear, show one is somebody,' she said. 'One mustn't be seen with doubtful people. I pity Lady Crackenbury from my heart; and Mrs. Washington White may be a very good-natured person. *You* may go and dine with them, as you like your rubber. But *I* mustn't, and won't; and you will have the goodness to tell Smith to say I am not at home when either of them calls.'

The particulars of Becky's costume were in the news-papers—feathers, lappets, superb diamonds, and all the rest. Lady Crackenbury read the paragraph in bitterness of spirit, and discoursed to her followers about the airs which that woman was giving herself. Mrs. Bute Crawley and her young ladies in the country had a copy of the *Morning Post* from town; and gave a vent to their honest indigna-tion. 'If you had been sandy-haired, green-eyed, and a French rope-dancer's daughter,' Mrs. Bute said to her eldest girl (who, on the contrary, was a very swarthy, short, and snub-nosed young lady), 'you might have had superb diamonds forsooth, and have been presented at Court, by your cousin, the Lady Jane. But you're only a gentlewoman, my poor dear child. You have only some of the best blood in England in your veins, and good prin-ciples and piety for your portion. I, myself, the wife of a baronet's younger brother, too, never thought of such a thing as going to Court—nor would other people, if good Queen Charlotte had been alive.'* In this way the worthy rectoress consoled herself: and her daughters sighed, and sat over the *Peerage* all night.

A few days after the famous presentation, another great and exceeding honour was vouchsafed to the virtuous Becky. Lady Steyne's carriage drove up to Mr. Rawdon Crawley's door, and the footman, instead of driving down the front of the house, as by his tremendous knocking he appeared to be inclined to do, relented, and only delivered in a couple of cards, on which were engraven the names of the Marchioness of Steyne and the Countess of Gaunt. If these bits of pasteboard had been beautiful pictures, or had had a hundred yards of Malines lace rolled round them, worth twice the number of guineas, Becky could not have regarded them with more pleasure. You may be sure they occupied a conspicuous place in the china bowl on the drawing-room table, where Becky kept the cards of her visitors. Lord! lord! how poor Mrs. Washington White's card and Lady Crackenbury's card, which our little friend had been glad enough to get a few months back, and of which the silly little creature was rather proud once—Lord! lord! I say, how soon at the appearance of these grand court cards, did those poor little neglected deuces sink down to the bottom of the pack. Steyne! Bareacres, Johnes of Helvellyn! and Caerlyon of Camelot! we may be sure that Becky and Briggs looked out those august names in the *Peerage*, and followed the noble races up through all the ramifications of the family tree.

My Lord Steyne coming to call a couple of hours afterwards, and looking about him, and observing everything as was his wont, found his lady's cards already ranged as the trumps of Becky's hand, and grinned, as this old cynic always did at any naïve display of human weakness. Becky came down to him presently : whenever the dear girl expected his lordship, her toilette was prepared, her hair in perfect order, her *mouchoirs*, aprons, scarfs, little morocco slippers, and other female gimcracks arranged, and she seated in some artless and agreeable posture ready to receive him—whenever she was surprised, of course she had to fly to her apartment to take a rapid survey of matters in the glass, and to trip down again to wait upon the great peer.

She found him grinning over the bowl. She was discovered, and she blushed a little. 'Thank you, monseigneur,' she said. 'You see your ladies have been here. How good of you! I couldn't come before—I was in the kitchen making a pudding.'

'I know you were : I saw you through the area-railings as I drove up,' replied the old gentleman.

'You see everything,' she replied.

'A few things, but not that, my pretty lady,' he said, good-naturedly. 'You silly little fibster! I heard you in the room overhead, where I have no doubt you were putting a little rouge on ; you must give some of yours to my Lady Gaunt, whose complexion is quite preposterous ; and I heard the bedroom door open, and then you came downstairs.'

'Is it a crime to try and look my best when *you* come here?' answered Mrs. Rawdon, plaintively, and she rubbed

her cheek with her handkerchief as if to show there was no
rouge at all, only genuine blushes and modesty in her case.
About this who can tell ? I know there is some rouge that
won't come off on a pocket-handkerchief ; and some so
good that even tears will not disturb it.

'Well,' said the old gentleman, twiddling round his
wife's card, ' you are bent upon becoming a fine lady. You
pester my poor old life out to get you into the world. You
won't be able to hold your own there, you silly little fool.
You've got no money.'

' You will get us a place,' interposed Becky, as quick as
possible.

' You've got no money, and you want to compete with
those who have. You poor little earthenware pipkin, you
want to swim down the stream along with the great copper
kettles. All women are alike. Everybody is striving for
what is not worth the having ! Gad ! I dined with the King
yesterday and we had neck of mutton and turnips. A
dinner of herbs is better than a stalled ox very often. You
will go to Gaunt House. You give an old fellow no rest until
you get there. It's not half so nice as here. You'll be
bored there. I am. My wife is as gay as Lady Macbeth,
and my daughters as cheerful as Regan and Goneril. I
daren't sleep in what they call my bedroom. The bed is
like the baldaquin of St. Peter's, and the pictures frighten
me. I have a little brass bed in a dressing-room : and
a little hair mattress like an anchorite. I am an anchorite.
Ho ! ho ! You'll be asked to dinner next week. And *gare
aux femmes*, look out and hold your own ! How the women
will bully you ! ' This was a very long speech for a man
of few words like my Lord Steyne ; nor was it the first
which he uttered for Becky's benefit on that day.

Briggs looked up from the work-table at which she was
seated in the farther room, and gave a deep sigh as she heard
the great marquis speak so lightly of her sex.

' If you don't turn off that abominable sheep-dog,' said
Lord Steyne, with a savage look over his shoulder at her,
' I will have her poisoned.'

' I always give my dog dinner from my own plate,' said
Rebecca, laughing mischievously ; and having enjoyed for
some time the discomfiture of my lord, who hated poor
Briggs for interrupting his *tête-à-tête* with the fair colonel's
wife, Mrs. Rawdon at length had pity upon her admirer,

and calling to Briggs, praised the fineness of the weather to
her, and bade her to take out the child for a walk.

' I can't send her away,' Becky said presently, after a
pause, and in a very sad voice.   Her eyes filled with tears
as she spoke, and she turned away her head.

' You owe her her wages ? I suppose,' said the peer.

' Worse than that,' said Becky, still casting down her
eyes, ' I have ruined her.'

' Ruined her ?—then why don't you turn her out ? ' the
gentleman asked.

' Men do that,' Becky answered bitterly.   ' Women are
not so bad as you.   Last year when we were reduced to our
last guinea, she gave us everything.   She shall never leave
me, until we are ruined utterly ourselves, which does not
seem far off, or until I can pay her the uttermost
farthing.'

' —— it, how much is it ? ' said the peer with an oath.
And Becky, reflecting on the largeness of his means, men-
tioned not only the sum which she had borrowed from
Miss Briggs, but one of nearly double the amount.

This caused the Lord Steyne to break out in another
brief and energetic expression of anger, at which Rebecca
held down her head the more, and cried bitterly. ' I could
not help it.   It was my only chance.   I dare not tell my
husband.   He would kill me if I told him what I have done.
I have kept it a secret from everybody but you—and you
forced it from me.   Ah, what shall I do, Lord Steyne ? for
I am very, very unhappy ! '

Lord Steyne made no reply except by beating the devil's
tattoo, and biting his nails.   At last he clapped his hat on
his head, and flung out of the room.   Rebecca did not rise
from her attitude of misery until the door slammed upon
him, and his carriage whirled away.   Then she rose up
with the queerest expression of victorious mischief glittering
in her green eyes.   She burst out laughing once or twice
to herself, as she sat at work ; and sitting down to the piano,
she rattled away a triumphant voluntary on the keys, which
made the people pause under her window to listen to her
brilliant music.

That night, there came two notes from Gaunt House for
the little woman, the one containing a card of invitation
from Lord and Lady Steyne to a dinner at Gaunt House
next Friday : while the other enclosed a slip of grey paper

BECKY IN LOMBARD STREET

bearing Lord Steyne's signature and the address of Messrs.
Jones, Brown, and Robinson, Lombard Street.

Rawdon heard Becky laughing in the night once or
twice. It was only her delight at going to Gaunt House
and facing the ladies there, she said, which amused her so.
But the truth was, that she was occupied with a great number of other thoughts. Should she pay off old Briggs and
give her her *congé*? Should she astonish Raggles by settling
his account? She turned over all these thoughts on her
pillow, and on the next day, when Rawdon went out to
pay his morning visit to the club, Mrs. Crawley (in a modest
dress with a veil on) whipped off in a hackney-coach to the
City: and being landed at Messrs. Jones and Robinson's
bank, presented a document there to the authority at the
desk, who, in reply, asked her ' How she would take it ? '

She gently said ' she would take a hundred and fifty
pounds in small notes and the remainder in one note ': and
passing through St. Paul's Churchyard stopped there and
bought the handsomest black silk gown for Briggs which
money could buy ; and which, with a kiss and the kindest
speeches, she presented to the simple old spinster.

Then she walked to Mr. Raggles, inquired about his
children affectionately, and gave him fifty pounds on account.
Then she went to the livery-man from whom she jobbed
her carriages and gratified him with a similar sum. ' And
I hope this will be a lesson to you, Spavin,' she said, ' and
that on the next Drawing-room day my brother, Sir Pitt,
will not be inconvenienced by being obliged to take four of us
in his carriage to wait upon His Majesty, because my *own*
carriage is not forthcoming.' It appears there had been
a difference on the last Drawing-room day. Hence the
degradation which the colonel had almost suffered, of being
obliged to enter the presence of his sovereign in a hack cab.

These arrangements concluded, Becky paid a visit upstairs to the before-mentioned desk, which Amelia Sedley
had given her years and years ago, and which contained
a number of useful and valuable little things : in which
private museum she placed the one note which Messrs.
Jones and Robinson's cashier had given her.

CHAPTER XLIX

IN WHICH WE ENJOY THREE COURSES AND A DESSERT

WHEN the ladies of Gaunt House were at breakfast that morning Lord Steyne (who took his chocolate in private, and seldom disturbed the females of his household, or saw them except upon public days, or when they crossed each other in the hall, or when from his pit-box at the Opera he surveyed them in their box on the grand tier)—his lordship, we say, appeared among the ladies and the children who were assembled over the tea and toast, and a battle royal ensued à propos of Rebecca.

'My Lady Steyne,' he said, 'I want to see the list for your dinner on Friday; and I want you, if you please, to write a card for Colonel and Mrs. Crawley.'

'Blanche writes them,' Lady Steyne said, in a flutter. 'Lady Gaunt writes them.'

'I will not write to that person,' Lady Gaunt said, a tall and stately lady, who looked up for an instant and then down again after she had spoken. It was not good to meet Lord Steyne's eyes for those who had offended him.

'Send the children out of the room. Go!' said he, pulling at the bell-rope. The urchins, always frightened before him, retired: their mother would have followed too. 'Not you,' he said. 'You stop.'

'My Lady Steyne,' he said, 'once more will you have the goodness to go to the desk, and write that card for your dinner on Friday?'

'My lord, I will not be present at it,' Lady Gaunt said; 'I will go home.'

'I wish you would, and stay there. You will find the bailiffs at Bareacres very pleasant company, and I shall be freed from lending money to your relations, and from your own damned tragedy airs. Who are you to give orders here ? You have no money. You've got no brains. You were here to have children, and you have not had any. Gaunt's tired of you ; and George's wife is the only person in the family who doesn't wish you were dead. Gaunt would marry again if you were.'

'I wish I were,' her ladyship answered, with tears and rage in her eyes.

'You, forsooth, must give yourself airs of virtue ; while my wife, who is an immaculate saint, as everybody knows, and never did wrong in her life, has no objection to meet my young friend, Mrs. Crawley. My Lady Steyne knows that appearances are sometimes against the best of women ; that lies are often told about the most innocent of them. Pray, madame, shall I tell you some little anecdotes about my Lady Bareacres, your mamma ? '

'You may strike me if you like, sir, or hit any cruel blow,' Lady Gaunt said. To see his wife and daughter suffering always put his lordship into a good humour.

'My sweet Blanche,' he said, 'I am a gentleman, and never lay my hand upon a woman, save in the way of kindness. I only wish to correct little faults in your character. You women are too proud, and sadly lack humility, as Father Mole, I'm sure, would tell my Lady Steyne if he were here. You mustn't give yourselves airs : you must be meek and humble, my blessings. For all Lady Steyne knows, this calumniated, simple, good-humoured Mrs. Crawley is quite innocent—even more innocent than herself. Her husband's character is not good, but it is as good as Bareacres's, who has played a little and not paid a great deal, who cheated you out of the only legacy you ever had, and left you a pauper on my hands. And Mrs. Crawley is not very well born ; but she is not worse than Fanny's illustrious ancestor, the first de la Jones.'

'The money which I brought into the family, sir,' Lady George cried out——

'You purchased a contingent reversion* with it,' the marquis said, darkly. 'If Gaunt dies, your husband may come to his honours ; your little boys may inherit them, and who knows what besides ? In the meanwhile, ladies, be as proud and virtuous as you like abroad, but don't

give *me* any airs.   As for Mrs. Crawley's character, I shan't
demean myself or that most spotless and perfectly irreproachable lady, by even hinting that it requires a defence.
You will be pleased to receive her with the utmost cordiality,
as you will receive all persons whom I present in this house.
This house ? ' He broke out with a laugh. ' Who is the
master of it ? and what is it ? This Temple of Virtue
belongs to me.   And if I invite all Newgate or all Bedlam
here, by ——, they shall be welcome.'

After this vigorous allocution, to one of which sort Lord
Steyne treated his ' Hareem ', whenever symptoms of insubordination appeared in his household, the crestfallen
women had nothing for it but to obey.   Lady Gaunt wrote
the invitation which his lordship required, and she and
her mother-in-law drove in person, and with bitter and
humiliated hearts, to leave the cards on Mrs. Rawdon, the
reception of which caused that innocent woman so much
pleasure.

There were families in London who would have sacrificed
a year's income to receive such an honour at the hands
of those great ladies.   Mrs. Frederick Bullock, for instance,
would have gone on her knees from May Fair to Lombard
Street, if Lady Steyne and Lady Gaunt had been waiting
in the City to raise her up, and say, ' Come to us next
Friday,'—not to one of the great crushes, and grand balls
of Gaunt House, whither everybody went, but to the
sacred, unapproachable, mysterious, delicious entertainments, to be admitted to one of which was a privilege,
and an honour, and a blessing indeed.

Severe, spotless, and beautiful, Lady Gaunt held the
very highest rank in Vanity Fair.   The distinguished
courtesy with which Lord Steyne treated her, charmed
everybody who witnessed his behaviour, caused the severest
critics to admit how perfect a gentleman he was, and to
own that his lordship's heart at least was in the right place.

The ladies of Gaunt House called Lady Bareacres in to
their aid, in order to repulse the common enemy.   One of
Lady Gaunt's carriages went to Hill Street for her ladyship's mother, all whose equipages were in the hands of
the bailiffs, whose very jewels and wardrobe, it was said,
had been seized by those inexorable Israelites.   Bareacres
Castle was theirs, too, with all its costly pictures, furniture,

and articles of virtu—the magnificent Vandykes ; the noble
Reynolds pictures ; the Lawrence portraits, tawdry and
beautiful, and, thirty years ago, deemed as precious as
works of real genius ; the matchless Dancing Nymph of
Canova,* for which Lady Bareacres had sat in her youth—
Lady Bareacres splendid then, and radiant in wealth, rank,
and beauty—a toothless, bald, old woman now—a mere rag
of a former robe of state.   Her lord, painted at the same
time by Lawrence, as waving his sabre in front of Bareacres Castle, and clothed in his uniform as colonel of the
Thistlewood Yeomanry, was a withered, old, lean man in
a greatcoat and a Brutus wig :* slinking about Gray's Inn
of mornings chiefly, and dining alone at clubs.   He did
not like to dine with Steyne now.   They had run races
of pleasure together in youth when Bareacres was the
winner.   But Steyne had more bottom than he, and had
lasted him out.   The marquis was ten times a greater man
now than the young Lord Gaunt of '85 ; and Bareacres
nowhere in the race—old, beaten, bankrupt, and broken
down.   He had borrowed too much money of Steyne to
find it pleasant to meet his old comrade often.   The latter,
whenever he wished to be merry, used jeeringly to ask
Lady Gaunt, why her father had not come to see her ?
' He has not been here for four months,' Lord Steyne
would say.   ' I can always tell by my cheque-book afterwards, when I get a visit from Bareacres.   What a comfort
it is, my ladies, I bank with one of my sons' fathers-in-law,
and the other banks with me ! '

Of the other illustrious persons whom Becky had the
honour to encounter on this her first presentation to the
grand world, it does not become the present historian to
say much.   There was His Excellency the Prince of Peterwaradin, with his princess ; a nobleman tightly girthed,
with a large military chest, on which the *plaque* of his
order shone magnificently, and wearing the red collar of
the Golden Fleece round his neck.   He was the owner of
countless flocks.   ' Look at his face.   I think he must be
descended from a sheep,' Becky whispered to Lord Steyne.
Indeed, his excellency's countenance, long, solemn, and
white, with the ornament round his neck, bore some resemblance to that of a venerable bell-wether.

There was Mr. John Paul Jefferson Jones,* titularly
attached to the American Embassy, and correspondent of

the New York *Demagogue ;* who, by way of making himself agreeable to the company, asked Lady Steyne, during a pause in the conversation at dinner, how his dear friend, George Gaunt, liked the Brazils ?—He and George had been most intimate at Naples, and had gone up Vesuvius together. Mr. Jones wrote a full and particular account of the dinner, which appeared duly in the *Demagogue.* He mentioned the names and titles of all the guests, giving biographical sketches of the principal people. He described the persons of the ladies with great eloquence ; the service of the table ; the size and costume of the servants ; enumerated the dishes and wines served ; the ornaments of the sideboard, and the probable value of the plate. Such a dinner he calculated could not be dished up under fifteen or eighteen dollars per head. And he was in the habit, until very lately, of sending over protégés, with letters of recommendation, to the present Marquis of Steyne, encouraged to do so by the intimate terms on which he had lived with his dear friend, the late lord. He was most indignant that a young and insignificant aristocrat, the Earl of Southdown, should have taken the *pas* of him in their procession to the dining-room. ' Just as I was stepping up to offer my hand to a very pleasing and witty fashionable, the brilliant and exclusive Mrs. Rawdon Crawley,'—he wrote—' the young patrician interposed between me and the lady, and whisked my Helen off without a word of apology. I was fain to bring up the rear with the colonel, the lady's husband, a stout red-faced warrior who distinguished himself at Waterloo, where he had better luck than befell some of his brother red-coats at New Orleans.'

The colonel's countenance on coming into this polite society wore as many blushes as the face of a boy of sixteen assumes when he is confronted with his sister's schoolfellows. It has been told before that honest Rawdon had not been much used at any period of his life to ladies' company. With the men at the club or the mess-room, he was well enough ; and could ride, bet, smoke, or play at billiards with the boldest of them. He had had his time for female friendships too : but that was twenty years ago, and the ladies were of the rank of those with whom Young Marlow in the comedy* is represented as having been familiar before he became abashed in the presence of Miss Hardcastle. The times are such that one scarcely dares to allude to that kind of company which thousands of our young men in Vanity Fair are frequenting every day, which nightly fills casinos and dancing-rooms, which is known to exist as well as the ring in Hyde Park or the congregation at St. James's—but which the most squeamish if not the most moral of societies is determined to ignore. In a word, although Colonel Crawley was now five-and-forty years of age, it had not been his lot in life to meet with a half-dozen good women, besides his paragon of a wife. All except her and his kind sister Lady Jane, whose gentle nature had tamed and won him, scared the worthy colonel; and on occasion of his first dinner at Gaunt House he was not heard to make a single remark, except to state that the weather was very hot. Indeed Becky would have left him at home, but that virtue ordained that her husband should be by her side to protect the timid and fluttering little creature on her first appearance in polite society.

On her first appearance Lord Steyne stepped forward, taking her hand, and greeting her with great courtesy, and presenting her to Lady Steyne, and their ladyships, her daughters. Their ladyships made three stately curtsies, and the elder lady to be sure gave her hand to the newcomer, but it was as cold and lifeless as marble.

Becky took it, however, with grateful humility; and performing a reverence which would have done credit to the best dancing-master, put herself at Lady Steyne's feet, as it were, by saying that his lordship had been her father's earliest friend and patron, and that she, Becky, had learned to honour and respect the Steyne family from the days of her childhood. The fact is, that Lord Steyne had once purchased a couple of pictures of the late Sharp, and the affectionate orphan could never forget her gratitude for that favour.

The Lady Bareacres then came under Becky's cognizance—to whom the colonel's lady made also a most respectful obeisance: it was returned with severe dignity by the exalted person in question.

'I had the pleasure of making your ladyship's acquaintance at Brussels ten years ago,' Becky said, in the most winning manner. 'I had the good fortune to meet Lady

Bareacres, at the Duchess of Richmond's ball, the night
before the battle of Waterloo. And I recollect your ladyship, and my Lady Blanche, your daughter, sitting in the
carriage in the *porte-cochère* at the inn, waiting for horses.
I hope your ladyship's diamonds are safe.'

Everybody's eyes looked into their neighbours'. The
famous diamonds had undergone a famous seizure, it
appears, about which Becky, of course, knew nothing.
Rawdon Crawley retreated with Lord Southdown into a
window, where the latter was heard to laugh immoderately,
as Rawdon told him the story of Lady Bareacres wanting
horses, and ' knuckling down by Jove ', to Mrs. Crawley.
' I think I needn't be afraid of *that* woman,' Becky thought.
Indeed, Lady Bareacres exchanged terrified and angry looks
with her daughter, and retreated to a table, where she
began to look at pictures with great energy.

When the potentate from the Danube made his appearance, the conversation was carried on in the French language,
and the Lady Bareacres and the younger ladies found, to
their farther mortification, that Mrs. Crawley was much
better acquainted with that tongue, and spoke it with
a much better accent than they. Becky had met other
Hungarian magnates with the army in France, in 1816–17.
She asked after her friends with great interest. The
foreign personages thought that she was a lady of great
distinction ; and the prince and the princess asked severally
of Lord Steyne and the marchioness, whom they conducted
to dinner, who was that *petite dame* who spoke so well ?

Finally, the procession being formed in the order described
by the American diplomatist, they marched into the apartment where the banquet was served : and which, as I have
promised the reader he shall enjoy it, he shall have the
liberty of ordering himself so as to suit his fancy.

But it was when the ladies were alone that Becky knew
the tug of war would come. And then indeed the little
woman found herself in such a situation, as made her
acknowledge the correctness of Lord Steyne's caution to
her to beware of the society of ladies above her own sphere.
As they say the persons who hate Irishmen most are Irishmen ; so, assuredly, the greatest tyrants over women are
women. When poor little Becky, alone with the ladies,
went up to the fireplace whither the great ladies had
repaired, the great ladies marched away and took possession

of a table of drawings. When Becky followed them to
the table of drawings, they dropped off one by one to the
fire again. She tried to speak to one of the children (of
whom she was commonly fond in public places), but Master
George Gaunt was called away by his mamma ; and the
stranger was treated with such cruelty finally, that even
Lady Steyne herself pitied her, and went up to speak to
the friendless little woman.

' Lord Steyne,' said her ladyship, as her wan cheeks
glowed with a blush, ' says you sing and play very beautifully, Mrs. Crawley—I wish you would do me the kindness
to sing to me.'

' I will do anything that may give pleasure to my Lord
Steyne or to you,' said Rebecca, sincerely grateful, and
seating herself at the piano, began to sing.

She sang religious songs of Mozart, which had been early
favourites of Lady Steyne, and with such sweetness and
tenderness that the lady lingering round the piano, sat

VANITY FAIR

down by its side, and listened until the tears rolled down her eyes. It is true that the opposition ladies at the other end of the room kept up a loud and ceaseless buzzing and talking ; but the Lady Steyne did not hear those rumours. She was a child again—and had wandered back through a forty years' wilderness to her convent garden. The chapel organ had pealed the same tones, the organist, the sister whom she loved best of the community, had taught them to her in those early happy days. She was a girl once more, and the brief period of her happiness bloomed out again for an hour—she started when the jarring doors were flung open, and with a loud laugh from Lord Steyne, the men of the party entered full of gaiety.

He saw at a glance what had happened in his absence : and was grateful to his wife for once. He went and spoke to her, and called her by her Christian name, so as again to bring blushes to her pale face—' My wife says you have been singing like an angel,' he said to Becky. Now there are angels of two kinds, and both sorts, it is said, are charming in their way.

Whatever the previous portion of the evening had been, the rest of that night was a great triumph for Becky. She sang her very best, and it was so good that every one of the men came and crowded round the piano. The women, her enemies, were left quite alone. And Mr. Paul Jefferson Jones thought he had made a conquest of Lady Gaunt by going up to her ladyship, and praising her delightful friend's first-rate singing.

CHAPTER L

CONTAINS A VULGAR INCIDENT

THE Muse, whoever she be, who presides over this Comic History, must now descend from the genteel heights in which she has been soaring, and have the goodness to drop down upon the lowly roof of John Sedley at Brompton, and describe what events are taking place there. Here, too, in this humble tenement, live care, and distrust, and dismay. Mrs. Clapp in the kitchen is grumbling in secret to her husband about the rent, and urging the good fellow to rebel against his old friend and patron and his present lodger. Mrs. Sedley has ceased to visit her landlady in the lower regions now, and indeed is in a position to patronize Mrs. Clapp no longer. How can one be condescending to a lady to whom one owes a matter of forty pound, and who is perpetually throwing out hints for the money ? The Irish maidservant has not altered in the least in her kind and respectful behaviour ; but Mrs. Sedley fancies that she is growing insolent and ungrateful, and, as the guilty thief who fears each bush an officer, sees threatening innuendoes and hints of capture in all the girl's speeches and answers. Miss Clapp, grown quite a young woman now, is declared by the soured old lady to be an unbearable and impudent little minx. Why Amelia can be so fond of her, or have her in her room so much, or walk out with her so constantly, Mrs. Sedley cannot conceive. The bitterness of poverty has poisoned the life of the once cheerful and kindly woman. She is thankless for Amelia's constant and gentle bearing towards her ; carps at her for her efforts at kindness or service ; rails at her for her silly pride in her child, and her neglect of her parents. Georgy's house is not a very lively one since uncle Jos's annuity has been withdrawn, and the little family are almost upon famine diet.

Amelia thinks, and thinks, and racks her brain, to find some means of increasing the small pittance upon which the household is starving. Can she give lessons in any-thing ? paint card-racks ? do fine work ? She finds that women are working hard, and better than she can, for twopence a day. She buys a couple of begilt Bristol boards at the fancy stationer's, and paints her very best upon them—a shepherd with a red waistcoat on one, and a pink face smiling in the midst of a pencil landscape—a shep-herdess on the other, crossing a little bridge, with a little dog, nicely shaded. The man of the Fancy Repository and Brompton Emporium of Fine Arts (of whom she bought the screens, vainly hoping that he would re-purchase them when ornamented by her hand) can hardly hide the sneer with which he examines these feeble works of art. He looks askance at the lady who waits in the shop, and ties up the cards again in their envelope of whity-brown paper, and hands them to the poor widow and Miss Clapp, who had never seen such beautiful things in her life, and had been quite confident that the man must give at least two guineas for the screens. They try at other shops in the interior of London, with faint sickening hopes. ' Don't want 'em,' says one. ' Be off,' says another, fiercely. Three and sixpence have been spent in vain—the screens retire to Miss Clapp's bedroom, who persists in thinking them lovely.

She writes out a little card in her neatest hand, and after long thought and labour of composition ; in which the public is informed that ' A Lady who has some time at her disposal, wishes to undertake the education of some little girls, whom she would instruct in English, in French, in Geography, in History, and in Music—address A. O., at Mr. Brown's ' ; and she confides the card to the gentle-man of the Fine Art Repository, who consents to allow it to lie upon the counter, where it grows dingy and flyblown. Amelia passes the door wistfully many a time, in hopes that Mr. Brown will have some news to give her ; but he never beckons her in. When she goes to make little purchases, there is no news for her. Poor simple lady, tender and weak—how are you to battle with the struggling, violent world ?

She grows daily more careworn and sad : fixing upon her child alarmed eyes, whereof the little boy cannot interpret the expression. She starts up of a night and peeps into his room stealthily, to see that he is sleeping and not stolen away. She sleeps but little now. A constant thought and terror is haunting her. How she weeps and prays in the long silent nights—how she tries to hide from herself the thought which will return to her, that she ought to part with the boy,—that she is the only barrier between him and prosperity. She can't, she can't ! Not now, at least. Some other day. Oh ! it is too hard to think of and to bear.

A thought comes over her which makes her blush and turn from herself,—her parents might keep the annuity— the curate would marry her and give a home to her and the boy. But George's picture and dearest memory are there to rebuke her. Shame and love say no to the sacrifice. She shrinks from it as from something unholy ; and such thoughts never found a resting-place in that pure and gentle bosom.

The combat, which we describe in a sentence or two, lasted for many weeks in poor Amelia's heart : during which, she had no confidante : indeed, she could have none : as she would not allow to herself the possibility of yielding : though she was giving way daily before the enemy with whom she had to battle. One truth after another was marshalling itself silently against her, and keeping its ground. Poverty and misery for all, want and degradation for her parents, injustice to the boy—one by one the outworks of the little citadel were taken, in which the poor soul passionately guarded her only love and treasure.

At the beginning of the struggle, she had written off a letter of tender supplication to her brother at Calcutta, imploring him not to withdraw the support which he had granted to their parents, and painting in terms of artless pathos their lonely and hapless condition. She did not know the truth of the matter. The payment of Jos's annuity was still regular : but it was a money-lender in the City who was receiving it : old Sedley had sold it for a sum of money wherewith to prosecute his bootless schemes. Emmy was calculating eagerly the time that would elapse before the letter would arrive and be answered   She had

written down the date in her pocket-book of the day when
she dispatched it. To her son's guardian, the good major
at Madras, she had not communicated any of her griefs
and perplexities. She had not written to him since she
wrote to congratulate him on his approaching marriage.
She thought with sickening despondency, that that friend,—
the only one, the one who had felt such a regard for her,—
was fallen away.

One day, when things had come to a very bad pass—
when the creditors were pressing, the mother in hysteric
grief, the father in more than usual gloom, the inmates
of the family avoiding each other, each secretly oppressed
with his private unhappiness and notion of wrong—the
father and daughter happened to be left alone together ;
and Amelia thought to comfort her father, by telling him
what she had done. She had written to Joseph—an answer
must come in three or four months. He was always
generous, though careless. He could not refuse, when he
knew how straitened the circumstances of his parents.

Then the poor old gentleman revealed the whole truth
to her—that his son was still paying the annuity, which
his own imprudence had flung away. He had not dared
to tell it sooner. He thought Amelia's ghastly and terrified
look, when, with a trembling, miserable voice he made the
confession, conveyed reproaches to him for his concealment.

'Ah !' said he, with quivering lips and turning away,
' you despise your old father now.'

'Oh, papa ! it is not that,' Amelia cried out, falling on
his neck, and kissing him many times. ' You are always
good and kind. You did it for the best. It is not for the
money—it is—O my God ! my God ! have mercy upon
me, and give me strength to bear this trial ; ' and she
kissed him again wildly, and went away.

Still the father did not know what that explanation
meant, and the burst of anguish with which the poor girl
left him. It was that she was conquered. The sentence
was passed. The child must go from her—to others—to
forget her. Her heart and her treasure—her joy, hope,
love, worship—her God, almost ! She must give him up ;
and then—and then she would go to George ; and they
would watch over the child, and wait for him until he
came to them in heaven.

She put on her bonnet, scarcely knowing what she did,
and went out to walk in the lanes by which George used
to come back from school, and where she was in the habit
of going on his return to meet the boy. It was May,
a half-holiday. The leaves were all coming out, the weather
was brilliant : the boy came running to her, flushed with
health, singing, his bundle of school-books hanging by
a thong. There he was. Both her arms were round him.
No, it was impossible. They could not be going to part.
' What is the matter, mother ? ' said he ; ' you look very
pale.'

' Nothing, my child,' she said, and stooped down and
kissed him.

That night Amelia made the boy read the story of
Samuel to her, and how Hannah, his mother, having weaned
him, brought him to Eli the High Priest to minister before
the Lord. And he read the song of gratitude which Hannah
sang : and which says, Who it is who maketh poor and
maketh rich, and bringeth low and exalteth—how the poor
shall be raised up out of the dust, and how, in his own
might, no man shall be strong. Then he read how Samuel's
mother made him a little coat, and brought it to him from
year to year when she came up to offer the yearly sacrifice.
And then, in her sweet simple way, George's mother made
commentaries to the boy upon this affecting story. How
Hannah, though she loved her son so much, yet gave him
up because of her vow. And how she must always have
thought of him as she sat at home, far away, making the
little coat : and Samuel, she was sure, never forgot his
mother : and how happy she must have been as the time
came (and the years pass away very quick) when she
should see her boy, and how good and wise he had grown.
This little sermon she spoke with a gentle solemn voice,
and dry eyes, until she came to the account of their
meeting—then the discourse broke off suddenly, the tender
heart overflowed, and taking the boy to her breast, she
rocked him in her arms, and wept silently over him in
a sainted agony of tears.

Her mind being made up, the widow began to take such
measures as seemed right to her for advancing the end
which she proposed. One day, Miss Osborne, in Russell
Square (Amelia had not written the name or number of

the house for ten years—her youth, her early story came back to her as she wrote the superscription)—one day Miss Osborne got a letter from Amelia, which made her blush very much and look towards her father, sitting glooming in his place at the other end of the table.

In simple terms, Amelia told her the reasons which had induced her to change her mind respecting her boy. Her father had met with fresh misfortunes which had entirely ruined him. Her own pittance was so small that it would barely enable her to support her parents, and would not suffice to give George the advantages which were his due. Great as her sufferings would be at parting with him, she would, by God's help, endure them for the boy's sake. She knew that those to whom he was going, would do all in their power to make him happy. She described his disposition, such as she fancied it; quick and impatient of control or harshness; easily to be moved by love and kindness. In a postscript, she stipulated that she should have a written agreement, that she should see the child as often as she wished,—she could not part with him under any other terms.

'What? Mrs. Pride has come down, has she?' old Osborne said, when with a tremulous eager voice Miss Osborne read him the letter—'Reg'lar starved out, hey? ha, ha! I knew she would.' He tried to keep his dignity, and to read his paper as usual,—but he could not follow it. He chuckled and swore to himself behind the sheet.

At last he flung it down: and scowling at his daughter, as his wont was, went out of the room into his study adjoining, from whence he presently returned with a key. He flung it to Miss Osborne.

'Get the room over mine—his room that was—ready,' he said. 'Yes, sir,' his daughter replied in a tremble. It was George's room. It had not been opened for more than ten years. Some of his clothes, papers, handkerchiefs, whips and caps, fishing-rods and sporting gear, were still there. An Army List of 1814, with his name written on the cover; a little dictionary he was wont to use in writing; and the Bible his mother had given him, were on the mantelpiece; with a pair of spurs, and a dried inkstand covered with the dust of ten years. Ah, since that ink was wet, what days and people had passed away! The writing-book still on the table, was blotted with his hand.

Miss Osborne was much affected when she first entered this room with the servants under her. She sank quite pale on the little bed. 'This is blessed news, mam—indeed, mam,' the housekeeper said; 'and the good old times is returning, mam. The dear little feller, to be sure, mam; how happy he will be! But some folks in May Fair, mam, will owe him a grudge, mam;' and she clicked back the bolt which held the window-sash, and let the air into the chamber.

'You had better send that woman some money,' Mr. Osborne said, before he went out. 'She shan't want for nothing. Send her a hundred pound.'

'And I'll go and see her to-morrow?' Miss Osborne asked.

'That's your look out. She don't come in here, mind. No, by ——, not for all the money in London. But she mustn't want now. So look out, and get things right.' With which brief speeches Mr. Osborne took leave of his daughter, and went on his accustomed way into the City.

'Here, papa, is some money,' Amelia said that night, kissing the old man, her father, and putting a bill for a hundred pounds into his hands. 'And—and, mamma, don't be harsh with Georgy. He—he is not going to stop with us long.' She could say nothing more, and walked away silently to her room. Let us close it upon her prayers and her sorrow. I think we had best speak little about so much love and grief.

Miss Osborne came the next day, according to the promise contained in her note, and saw Amelia. The meeting between them was friendly. A look and a few words from Miss Osborne showed the poor widow that, with regard to this woman at least, there need be no fear lest she should take the first place in her son's affection. She was cold, sensible, not unkind. The mother had not been so well pleased, perhaps, had the rival been better-looking, younger, more affectionate, warmer-hearted. Miss Osborne, on the other hand, thought of old times and memories, and could not but be touched with the poor mother's pitiful situation. She was conquered, and laying down her arms, as it were, she humbly submitted. That day they arranged together, the preliminaries of the treaty of capitulation.

George was kept from school the next day, and saw his

aunt. Amelia left them alone together, and went to her room. She was trying the separation :—as that poor gentle Lady Jane Grey felt the edge of the axe that was to come down and sever her slender life. Days were passed in parleys, visits, preparations. The widow broke the matter to Georgy with great caution ; she looked to see him very much affected by the intelligence. He was rather elated than otherwise, and the poor woman turned sadly away. He bragged about the news that day to the boys at school ; told them how he was going to live with his grandpapa, his father's father, not the one who comes here sometimes : and that he would be very rich, and have a carriage, and a pony, and go to a much finer school, and when he was rich he would buy Leader's pencil-case, and pay the tart-woman. The boy was the image of his father, as his fond mother thought.

Indeed I have no heart, on account of our dear Amelia's sake, to go through the story of George's last days at home.

At last the day came, the carriage drove up, the little humble packets containing tokens of love and remembrance were ready and disposed in the hall long since—George was in his new suit, for which the tailor had come previously to measure him. He had sprung up with the sun and put on the new clothes ; his mother hearing him from the room close by, in which she had been lying, in speechless grief and watching. Days before she had been making preparations for the end ; purchasing little stores for the boy's use ; marking his books and linen ; talking with him and preparing him for the change—fondly fancying that he needed preparation.

So that he had change, what cared he ? He was longing for it. By a thousand eager declarations as to what he would do, when he went to live with his grandfather, he had shown the poor widow how little the idea of parting had cast him down. ' He would come and see his mamma often on the pony,' he said : ' he would come and fetch her in the carriage ; they would drive in the Park, and she should have everything she wanted.' The poor mother was fain to content herself with these selfish demonstrations of attachment, and tried to convince herself how sincerely her son loved her. He must love her. All children were so : a little anxious for novelty, and—no, not selfish, but self-willed. Her child must have his enjoyments and ambition in the world. She herself, by her own selfishness and imprudent love for him, had denied him his just rights and pleasures hitherto.

I know few things more affecting than that timorous debasement and self-humiliation of a woman. How she owns that it is she and not the man who is guilty : how she takes all the faults on her side : how she courts in a manner punishment for the wrongs which she has not committed, and persists in shielding the real culprit ! It is those who injure women who get the most kindness from them—they are born timid and tyrants, and maltreat those who are humblest before them.

So poor Amelia had been getting ready in silent misery for her son's departure, and had passed many and many a long solitary hour in making preparations for the end. George stood by his mother, watching her arrangements without the least concern. Tears had fallen into his boxes ; passages had been scored in his favourite books ; old toys, relics, treasures had been hoarded away for him, and packed with strange neatness and care,—and of all these things the boy took no note. The child goes away smiling as the mother breaks her heart. By heavens it is pitiful, the bootless love of women for children in Vanity Fair.

A few days are passed : and the great event of Amelia's life is consummated. No angel has intervened. The child is sacrificed and offered up to fate ; and the widow is quite alone.

The boy comes to see her often, to be sure. He rides on a pony with the coachman behind him, to the delight of his old grandfather, Sedley, who walks proudly down the lane by his side. She sees him, but he is not her boy any more. Why, he rides to see the boys at the little school, too, and to show off before them his new wealth and splendour. In two days he has adopted a slight imperious air and patronizing manner. He was born to command, his mother thinks, as his father was before him.

It is fine weather now. Of evenings on the days when he does not come, she takes a long walk into London— yes, as far as Russell Square, and rests on the stone by the railing of the garden opposite Mr. Osborne's house. It is so pleasant and cool. She can look up and see the drawing-room windows illuminated, and, at about nine o'clock the chamber in the upper story where Georgy sleeps. She knows—he has told her. She prays there as the light goes out, prays with a humble, humble heart, and walks home shrinking and silent. She is very tired when she comes home. Perhaps she will sleep the better for that long weary walk; and she may dream about Georgy.

One Sunday she happened to be walking in Russell

Square, at some distance from Mr. Osborne's house (she could see it from a distance though) when all the bells of Sabbath were ringing, and George and his aunt came out to go to church; a little sweep asked for charity, and the footman, who carried the books, tried to drive him away; but Georgy stopped and gave him money. May God's blessing be on the boy! Emmy ran round the square, and coming up to the sweep, gave him her mite too. All the bells of Sabbath were ringing, and she followed them until she came to the Foundling Church, into which she went.

GEORGY GOES TO CHURCH GENTEELLY

There she sat in a place whence she could see the head of the boy under his father's tombstone. Many hundred fresh children's voices rose up there and sang hymns to the Father Beneficent; and little George's soul thrilled with delight at the burst of glorious psalmody. His mother could not see him for awhile, through the mist that dimmed her eyes.

CHAPTER LI

IN WHICH A CHARADE IS ACTED WHICH MAY OR MAY NOT PUZZLE THE READER

FTER Becky's appearance at my Lord Steyne's private and select parties the claims of that estimable woman as regards fashion, were settled; and some of the very greatest and tallest doors in the metropolis were speedily opened to her—doors so great and tall that the beloved reader and writer hereof may hope in vain to enter at them. Dear brethren, let us tremble before those august portals. I fancy them guarded by grooms of the chamber with flaming silver forks with which they prong all those who have not the right of the entrée. They say the honest newspaper-fellow*who sits in the hall and takes down the names of the great ones who are admitted to the feasts, dies after a little time. He can't survive the glare of fashion long. It scorches him up, as the presence of Jupiter in full dress wasted that poor imprudent Semele—a giddy moth of a creature who ruined herself by venturing out of her natural atmosphere. Her myth ought to be taken to heart amongst the Tyburnians, the Belgravians,—her story, and perhaps Becky's too. Ah, ladies!—ask the Reverend Mr. Thurifer if Belgravia is not a sounding brass, and Tyburnia a tinkling cymbal.

These are vanities. Even these will pass away. And some day or other (but it will be after our time, thank goodness), Hyde Park Gardens will be no better known than the celebrated horticultural outskirts of Babylon; and Belgrave Square will be as desolate as Baker Street, or Tadmor in the wilderness.*

Ladies, are you aware that the Great Pitt lived in Baker Street? What would not your grandmothers have given to be asked to Lady Hester's parties in that now decayed mansion? I have dined in it—*moi qui vous parle.* I peopled the chamber with ghosts of the mighty dead. As we sat soberly drinking claret there with men of to-day, the spirits of the departed came in and took their places round the darksome board. The pilot who weathered the storm tossed off great bumpers of spiritual port : the shade of Dundas did not leave the ghost of a heeltap.—Addington sat bowing and smirking in a ghastly manner, and would not be behindhand when the noiseless bottle went round ; Scott, from under bushy eyebrows winked at the apparition of a beeswing ; Wilberforce's eyes went up to the ceiling, so that he did not seem to know how his glass went up full to his mouth and came down empty ;—up to the ceiling which was above us only yesterday, and which the great of the last days have all looked at. They let the house as a furnished lodging now. Yes, Lady Hester once lived in Baker Street, and lies asleep in the wilderness. Eöthen saw her there—not in Baker Street : but in the other solitude.*

It is all vanity to be sure : but who will not own to liking a little of it ? I should like to know what well-constituted mind, merely because it is transitory, dislikes roast-beef ? That is a vanity ; but may every man who reads this, have a wholesome portion of it through life, I beg : aye, though my readers were five hundred thousand. Sit down, gentlemen, and fall to, with a good hearty appetite ; the fat, the lean, the gravy, the horse-radish as you like it—don't spare it. Another glass of wine, Jones, my boy—a little bit of the Sunday side. Yes, let us eat our fill of the vain thing, and be thankful therefor. And let us make the best of Becky's aristocratic pleasures likewise—for these too, like all other mortal delights, were but transitory.

The upshot of her visit to Lord Steyne was, that His Highness the Prince of Peterwaradin took occasion to renew his acquaintance with Colonel Crawley, when they met on the next day at the club, and to compliment Mrs. Crawley in the ring of Hyde Park with a profound salute of the hat. She and her husband were invited immediately to one of the prince's small parties at Levant House, then occupied by his highness during the temporary absence from England of its noble proprietor. She sang after dinner to a very little *comité*. The Marquis of Steyne was present, paternally superintending the progress of his pupil.

At Levant House Becky met one of the finest gentlemen and greatest ministers that Europe has produced—the Duc de la Jabotière, then ambassador from the Most Christian King,* and subsequently minister to that monarch. I declare I swell with pride as these august names are transcribed by my pen ; and I think in what brilliant company my dear Becky is moving. She became a constant guest at the French embassy, where no party was considered to be complete without the presence of the charming Madame Ravdonn Cravley.

Messieurs de Truffigny (of the Périgord family) and Champignac, both attachés of the embassy, were straightway smitten by the charms of the fair colonel's wife : and both declared, according to the wont of their nation (for who ever yet met a Frenchman, come out of England, that has not left half a dozen families miserable, and brought away as many hearts in his pocket-book ?) both, I say, declared that they were *au mieux* with the charming Madame Ravdonn.

But I doubt the correctness of the assertion. Champignac was very fond of écarté, and made many *parties* with the colonel of evenings, while Becky was singing to Lord Steyne in the other room ; and as for Truffigny, it is a well-known fact that he dared not go to the Travellers', where he owed money to the waiters, and if he had not had the embassy as a dining-place, the worthy young gentleman must have starved. I doubt, I say, that Becky would have selected either of these young men as a person on whom she would bestow her special regard. They ran of her messages, purchased her gloves and flowers, went in debt for opera-boxes for her, and made themselves amiable in a thousand ways. And they talked English with adorable simplicity,

and to the constant amusement of Becky and my Lord
Steyne. She would mimic one or other to his face, and
compliment him on his advance in the English language
with a gravity which never failed to tickle the marquis, her
sardonic old patron. Truffigny gave Briggs a shawl by
way of winning over Becky's confidante, and asked her to
take charge of a letter which the simple spinster handed
over in public to the person to whom it was addressed;
and the composition of which amused everybody who read
it greatly. Lord Steyne read it: everybody, but honest
Rawdon; to whom it was not necessary to tell everything
that passed in the little house in May Fair.

Here, before long, Becky received not only 'the best'
foreigners (as the phrase is in our noble and admirable
society slang), but some of the best English people too.
I don't mean the most virtuous, or indeed the least virtuous,
or the cleverest, or the stupidest, or the richest, or the best
born, but 'the best',—in a word, people about whom there
is no question—such as the great Lady Fitz-Willis, that
Patron Saint of Almack's, the great Lady Slowbore, the
great Lady Grizzel Macbeth (she was Lady G. Glowry,
daughter of Lord Grey of Glowry), and the like. When
the Countess of Fitz-Willis (her ladyship is of the King-
street family, see Debrett and Burke) takes up a person,
he or she is safe. There is no question about them any
more. Not that my Lady Fitz-Willis is any better than
anybody else, being, on the contrary, a faded person, fifty-
seven years of age, and neither handsome, nor wealthy,
nor entertaining; but it is agreed on all sides that she is
of the 'best people'. Those who go to her are of the best:
and from an old grudge probably to Lady Steyne (for whose
coronet her ladyship, then the youthful Georgina Frederica,
daughter of the Prince of Wales's favourite, the Earl of
Portansherry, had once tried), this great and famous leader
of the fashion chose to acknowledge Mrs. Rawdon Crawley:
made her a most marked curtsy at the assembly over
which she presided: and not only encouraged her son,
St. Kitts (his lordship got his place through Lord Steyne's
interest), to frequent Mrs. Crawley's house, but asked her
to her own mansion, and spoke to her twice in the most
public and condescending manner during dinner. The
important fact was known all over London that night.
People who had been crying fie about Mrs. Crawley, were

silent. Wenham, the wit and lawyer,* Lord Steyne's right-
hand man, went about everywhere praising her : some
who had hesitated, came forward at once and welcomed
her ; little Tom Toady, who had warned Southdown about
visiting such an abandoned woman, now besought to be
introduced to her. In a word, she was admitted to be
among the 'best' people. Ah, my beloved readers and
brethren, do not envy poor Becky prematurely—glory like
this is said to be fugitive. It is currently reported that
even in the very inmost circles, they are no happier than
the poor wanderers outside the zone ; and Becky, who
penetrated into the very centre of fashion, and saw the
great George IV face to face, has owned since that there
too was Vanity.

We must be brief in descanting upon this part of her
career. As I cannot describe the mysteries of freemasonry,
although I have a shrewd idea that it is a humbug : so an
uninitiated man cannot take upon himself to portray the
great world accurately, and had best keep his opinions to
himself whatever they are.

Becky has often spoken in subsequent years of this
season of her life when she moved among the very greatest
circles of the London fashion. Her success excited, elated,
and then bored her. At first no occupation was more
pleasant than to invent and procure (the latter a work of
no small trouble and ingenuity, by the way, in a person
of Mrs. Rawdon Crawley's very narrow means)—to procure,
we say, the prettiest new dresses and ornaments ; to drive
to fine dinner parties, where she was welcomed by great
people ; and from the fine dinner parties to fine assemblies,
whither the same people came with whom she had been
dining, whom she had met the night before, and would see
on the morrow—the young men faultlessly appointed,
handsomely cravatted, with the neatest glossy boots and
white gloves—the elders portly, brass-buttoned, noble-
looking, polite, and prosy—the young ladies blonde, timid,
and in pink—the mothers grand, beautiful, sumptuous,
solemn, and in diamonds. They talked in English, not in
bad French, as they do in the novels. They talked about
each others' houses, and characters, and families : just as
the Joneses do about the Smiths. Becky's former acquaintances hated and envied her : the poor woman herself was
yawning in spirit. 'I wish I were out of it,' she said to

herself. ' I would rather be a parson's wife, and teach
a Sunday school than this ; or a sergeant's lady and ride
in the regimental wagon ; or, oh, how much gayer it
would be to wear spangles and trousers, and dance before
a booth at a fair.'

' You would do it very well,' said Lord Steyne, laughing.
She used to tell the great man her ennuis and perplexities
in her artless way—they amused him.

' Rawdon would make a very good Écuyer—Master of
the Ceremonies—what do you call him—the man in the
large boots and the uniform, who goes round the ring
cracking the whip ? He is large, heavy, and of a military
figure. I recollect,' Becky continued, pensively, ' my
father took me to see a show at Brookgreen Fair when
I was a child ; and when we came home I made myself
a pair of stilts, and danced in the studio to the wonder of
all the pupils.'

' I should have liked to see it,' said Lord Steyne.

' I should like to do it now,' Becky continued. ' How
Lady Blinkey would open her eyes, and Lady Grizzel
Macbeth would stare ! Hush ! silence ! there is Pasta
beginning to sing.' Becky always made a point of being
conspicuously polite to the professional ladies and gentlemen
who attended at these aristocratic parties—of following
them into the corners where they sat in silence, and shaking
hands with them, and smiling in the view of all persons.
She was an artist herself, as she said very truly : there
was a frankness and humility in the manner in which she
acknowledged her origin, which provoked, or disarmed, or
amused lookers-on, as the case might be. ' How cool that
woman is,' said one ; ' what airs of independence she
assumes, where she ought to sit still and be thankful if
anybody speaks to her.'   ' What an honest and good-
natured soul she is,' said another. ' What an artful little
minx,' said a third. They were all right very likely ; but
Becky went her own way, and so fascinated the professional
personages, that they would leave off their sore throats in
order to sing at her parties, and give her lessons for nothing.

Yes, she gave parties in the little house in Curzon Street.
Many scores of carriages, with blazing lamps, blocked up
the street, to the disgust of No. 100, who could not rest
for the thunder of the knocking, and of 102, who could
not sleep for envy. The gigantic footmen who accom-

panied the vehicles were too big to be contained in Becky's little hall, and were billeted off in the neighbouring public-houses, whence, when they were wanted, call-boys summoned them from their beer. Scores of the great dandies of London squeezed and trod on each other on the little stairs, laughing to find themselves there ; and many spotless and severe ladies of *ton* were seated in the little drawing-room, listening to the professional singers, who were singing according to their wont, and as if they wished to blow the windows down. And the day after, there appeared among the fashionable *réunions* in the *Morning Post*, a paragraph to the following effect :—

' Yesterday, Colonel and Mrs. Crawley entertained a select party at dinner, at their house in May Fair. Their Excellencies the Prince and Princess of Peterwaradin, H. E. Papoosh Pasha, the Turkish Ambassador (attended by Kibob Bey, dragoman of the mission), the Marquess of Steyne, Earl of Southdown, Mr. Pitt and Lady Jane Crawley, Mr. Wagg, &c. After dinner, Mrs. Crawley had an assembly, which was attended by the Duchess (Dowager) of Stilton, Duc de la Gruyère, Marchioness of Cheshire, Marchese Alessandro Strachino, Comte de Brie, Baron Schapzuger, Chevalier Tosti, Countess of Slingstone, and Lady F. Macadam, Major-General and Lady G. Macbeth, and (2) Miss Macbeths, Viscount Paddington, Sir Horace Fogey, Hon. Sands Bedwin, Bobbachy Bahawder,' and an &c. which the reader may fill at his pleasure through a dozen close lines of small type.

And in her commerce with the great our dear friend showed the same frankness which distinguished her transactions with the lowly in station. On one occasion, when out at a very fine house, Rebecca was (perhaps rather ostentatiously) holding a conversation in the French language with a celebrated tenor singer of that nation, while the Lady Grizzel Macbeth looked over her shoulder scowling at the pair.

' How very well you speak French,' Lady Grizzel said, who herself spoke the tongue in an Edinburgh accent most remarkable to hear.

' I ought to know it,' Becky modestly said, casting down her eyes. ' I taught it in a school, and my mother was a Frenchwoman.'

Lady Grizzel was won by her humility, and was mollified

towards the little woman. She deplored the fatal levelling
tendencies of the age, which admitted persons of all classes
into the society of their superiors ; but her ladyship owned,
that this one at least was well-behaved, and never forgot
her place in life. She was a very good woman : good to the
poor : stupid, blameless, unsuspicious.—It is not her ladyship's fault that she fancies herself better than you and me.
The skirts of her ancestors' garments have been kissed for
centuries : it is a thousand years, they say, since the tartans
of the head of the family were embraced by the defunct
Duncan's lords and councillors, when the great ancestor of
the house became King of Scotland.

Lady Steyne, after the music scene, succumbed before
Becky, and perhaps was not disinclined to her. The younger
ladies of the House of Gaunt were also compelled into submission. Once or twice they set people at her, but they
failed. The brilliant Lady Stunnington tried a passage
of arms with her, but was routed with great slaughter by
the intrepid little Becky. When attacked sometimes,
Becky had a knack of adopting a demure *ingénue* air, under
which she was most dangerous. She said the wickedest
things with the most simple unaffected air when in this
mood, and would take care artlessly to apologize for her
blunders, so that all the world should know that she had
made them.

Mr. Wagg, the celebrated wit,* and a led captain and
trencherman of my Lord Steyne, was caused by the
ladies to charge her ; and the worthy fellow, leering at his
patronesses, and giving them a wink, as much as to say,
' Now look out for sport,' one evening began an assault
upon Becky, who was unsuspiciously eating her dinner.
The little woman, attacked on a sudden, but never without
arms, lighted up in an instant, parried and riposted with
a home-thrust, which made Wagg's face tingle with shame ;
then she returned to her soup with the most perfect calm
and a quiet smile on her face. Wagg's great patron, who
gave him dinners and lent him a little money sometimes,
and whose election, newspaper, and other jobs Wagg did,
gave the luckless fellow such a savage glance with the eyes
as almost made him sink under the table, and burst into
tears. He looked piteously at my lord, who never spoke
to him during dinner, and at the ladies, who disowned him.
At last Becky herself took compassion upon him, and tried

to engage him in talk. He was not asked to dinner again for six weeks ; and Fiche, my lord's confidential man, to whom Wagg naturally paid a good deal of court, was instructed to tell him that if he ever dared to say a rude thing to Mrs. Crawley again, or make her the butt of his stupid jokes, Milor would put every one of his notes of hand into his lawyer's hands, and sell him up without mercy. Wagg wept before Fiche, and implored his dear friend to intercede for him. He wrote a poem in favour of Mrs. R. C., which appeared in the very next number of the *Harumscarum Magazine*, which he conducted. He implored her goodwill at parties where he met her. He cringed and coaxed Rawdon at the club. He was allowed to come back to Gaunt House after a while. Becky was always good to him, always amused, never angry.

His lordship's vizier and chief confidential servant (with a seat in Parliament and at the dinner-table), Mr. Wenham, was much more prudent in his behaviour and opinions than Mr. Wagg. However much he might be disposed to hate all parvenues (Mr. Wenham himself was a stanch old True Blue Tory, and his father a small coal-merchant in the North of England), this aide de camp of the marquis never showed any sort of hostility to the new favourite ; but pursued her with stealthy kindnesses, and a sly and deferential politeness, which somehow made Becky more uneasy than other people's overt hostilities.

How the Crawleys got the money which was spent upon the entertainments with which they treated the polite world, was a mystery which gave rise to some conversation at the time, and probably added zest to these little festivities. Some persons averred that Sir Pitt Crawley gave his brother a handsome allowance : if he did, Becky's power over the baronet must have been extraordinary indeed, and his character greatly changed in his advanced age. Other parties hinted that it was Becky's habit to levy contributions on all her husband's friends : going to this one in tears with an account that there was an execution in the house ; falling on her knees to that one, and declaring that the whole family must go to gaol or commit suicide unless such and such a bill could be paid. Lord Southdown, it was said, had been induced to give many hundreds through these pathetic representations. Young Feltham, of the —th Dragoons (and son of the firm of Tiler and Feltham,

hatters and army accoutrement-makers), and whom the
Crawleys introduced into fashionable life, was also cited
as one of Becky's victims in the pecuniary way. People
declared that she got money from various simply disposed
persons, under pretence of getting them confidential
appointments under Government. Who knows what stories
were or were not told of our dear and innocent friend?
Certain it is, that if she had had all the money which she
was said to have begged or borrowed or stolen, she might
have capitalized and been honest for life, whereas,—but
this is advancing matters.

The truth is that by economy and good management—
by a sparing use of ready money and by paying scarcely
anybody,—people can manage, for a time at least, to make
a great show with very little means : and it is our belief
that Becky's much-talked-of parties, which were not, after
all was said, very numerous, cost this lady very little more
than the wax candles which lighted the walls. Stillbrook
and Queen's Crawley supplied her with game and fruit
in abundance. Lord Steyne's cellars were at her disposal,
and that excellent nobleman's famous cooks presided over
her little kitchen, or sent by my lord's order the rarest
delicacies from their own. I protest it is quite shameful
in the world to abuse a simple creature, as people of her
time abused Becky, and I warn the public against believing
one-tenth of the stories against her. If every person is to
be banished from society who runs into debt and cannot
pay—if we are to be peering into everybody's private life,
speculating upon their income, and cutting them if we
don't approve of their expenditure—why, what a howling
wilderness and intolerable dwelling Vanity Fair would be!
Every man's hand would be against his neighbour in this
case, my dear sir, and the benefits of civilization would be
done away with. We should be quarrelling, abusing,
avoiding one another. Our houses would become caverns :
and we should go in rags because we cared for nobody.
Rents would go down. Parties wouldn't be given any
more. All the tradesmen of the town would be bankrupt.
Wine, wax-lights, comestibles, rouge, crinoline petticoats,
diamonds, wigs, Louis Quatorze gimcracks, and old china,
park hacks and splendid high-stepping carriage horses—
all the delights of life, I say,—would go to the deuce, if
people did but act upon their silly principles, and avoid

those whom they dislike and abuse. Whereas, by a little
charity and mutual forbearance, things are made to go on
pleasantly enough : we may abuse a man as much as we
like, and call him the greatest rascal unhung—but do we
wish to hang him therefore ? No. We shake hands when
we meet. If his cook is good we forgive him, and go and
dine with him ; and we expect he will do the same by us.
Thus trade flourishes—civilization advances : peace is kept ;
new dresses are wanted for new assemblies every week ;
and the last year's vintage of Lafite will remunerate the
honest proprietor who reared it.

At the time whereof we are writing, though the Great
George was on the throne and ladies wore *gigots* and large
combs like tortoise-shell shovels in their hair, instead of
the simple sleeves and lovely wreaths which are actually in
fashion, the manners of the very polite world were not, I take
it, essentially different from those of the present day : and
their amusements pretty similar. To us, from outside
gazing over the policemen's shoulders at the bewildering
beauties as they pass into Court or ball, they may seem
beings of unearthly splendour, and in the enjoyment of
an exquisite happiness by us unattainable. It is to console
some of these dissatisfied beings, that we are narrating our
dear Becky's struggles, and triumphs, and disappointments,
of all of which, indeed, as is the case with all persons of
merit, she had her share.

At this time the amiable amusement of acting charades
had come among us from France :* and was considerably
in vogue in this country, enabling the many ladies amongst
us who had beauty to display their charms, and the fewer
number who had cleverness, to exhibit their wit. My Lord
Steyne was incited by Becky, who perhaps believed herself
endowed with both the above qualifications, to give an
entertainment at Gaunt House, which should include some
of these little dramas—and we must take leave to introduce
the reader to this brilliant *réunion*, and with a melancholy
welcome too, for it will be among the very last of the
fashionable entertainments to which it will be our fortune
to conduct him.

A portion of that splendid room, the picture-gallery of
Gaunt House, was arranged as the charade theatre. It had
been so used when George III was king ; and a picture of
the Marquis of Gaunt is still extant, with his hair in powder

and a pink ribbon, in a Roman shape, as it was called,
enacting the part of Cato in Mr. Addison's tragedy of that
name, performed before Their Royal Highnesses the Prince
of Wales, the Bishop of Osnaburgh, and Prince William
Henry, then children like the actor. One or two of the
old properties were drawn out of the garrets, where they
had lain ever since, and furbished up anew for the present
festivities.

Young Bedwin Sands,* then an elegant dandy and Eastern
traveller, was manager of the revels. An Eastern traveller
was somebody in those days, and the adventurous Bedwin,
who had published his quarto, and passed some months
under the tents in the desert, was a personage of no small
importance.—In his volume there were several pictures of
Sands in various Oriental costumes; and he travelled about
with a black attendant of most unprepossessing appearance,
just like another Brian de Bois Guilbert. Bedwin, his
costumes, and black man, were hailed at Gaunt House as
very valuable acquisitions.

He led off the first charade. A Turkish officer with an
immense plume of feathers (the janissaries were supposed
to be still in existence, and the tarboosh had not as yet
displaced the ancient and majestic head-dress of the true
believers) was seen couched on a divan, and making believe
to puff at a *narghile*, in which, however, for the sake of the
ladies, only a fragrant pastille was allowed to smoke. The
Turkish dignitary yawns and expresses signs of weariness
and idleness. He claps his hands and Mesrour the Nubian
appears, with bare arms, bangles, and yataghans, every
Eastern ornament—gaunt, tall, and hideous. He makes
a salaam before my lord the Aga.

A thrill of terror and delight runs through the assembly.
The ladies whisper to one another. The black slave was
given to Sands Bedwin by an Egyptian pasha in exchange
for three dozen of maraschino. He has sewn up ever so
many *odalisques* in sacks and tilted them into the Nile.

'Bid the slave-merchant enter,' says the Turkish volup-
tuary, with a wave of his hand. Mesrour conducts the
slave-merchant into my lord's presence: he brings a veiled
female with him. He removes her veil. A thrill of
applause bursts through the house. It is Mrs. Winkworth
(she was a Miss Absolom), with the beautiful eyes and
hair. She is in a gorgeous Oriental costume; the black

braided locks are twined with innumerable jewels; her dress is covered over with gold piastres. The odious Mahometan expresses himself charmed by her beauty. She falls down on her knees, and entreats him to restore her to the mountains where she was born, and where her Circassian lover is still deploring the absence of his Zuleikah. No entreaties will move the obdurate Hassan. He laughs at the notion of the Circassian bridegroom. Zuleikah covers her face with her hands, and drops down in an attitude of the most beautiful despair. There seems to be no hope for her, when—when the Kislar Aga appears.

The Kislar Aga brings a letter from the Sultan. Hassan receives and places on his head the dread firman. A ghastly terror seizes him, while on the negro's face (it is Mesrour again in another costume) appears a ghastly joy. 'Mercy! mercy!' cries the pasha; while the Kislar Aga, grinning horribly, pulls out—a bowstring.*

The curtain draws just as he is going to use that awful weapon. Hassan from within bawls out, 'First two syllables'—and Mrs. Rawdon Crawley, who is going to act in the charade, comes forward and compliments Mrs. Winkworth on the admirable taste and beauty of her costume.

The second part of the charade takes place. It is still an Eastern scene. Hassan, in another dress, is in an attitude by Zuleikah, who is perfectly reconciled to him. The Kislar Aga has become a peaceful black slave. It is sunrise on the desert, and the Turks turn their heads eastward and bow to the sand. As there are no dromedaries at hand, the band facetiously plays 'The Camels are coming'. An enormous Egyptian head figures in the scene. It is a musical one,—and, to the surprise of the Oriental travellers, sings a comic song, composed by Mr. Wagg. The Eastern voyagers go off dancing, like Papageno and the Moorish king, in the *Magic Flute*. 'Last two syllables' roars the head.

The last act opens. It is a Grecian tent this time. A tall and stalwart man reposes on a couch there. Above him hang his helmet and shield. There is no need for them now. Ilium is down. Iphigenia is slain. Cassandra is a prisoner in his outer halls. The king of men (it is Colonel Crawley, who, indeed, has no notion about the sack of Ilium or the conquest of Cassandra), the *anax andrôn,** is asleep in his chamber at Argos. A lamp casts the broad shadow of the sleeping warrior flickering on the

wall—the sword and shield of Troy glitter in its light.
The band plays the awful music of *Don Juan*, before the
statue enters.

Aegisthus steals in pale and on tiptoe. What is that
ghastly face looking out balefully after him from behind
the arras ? He raises his dagger to strike the sleeper,
who turns in his bed, and opens his broad chest as if for
the blow. He cannot strike the noble slumbering chieftain.
Clytemnestra glides swiftly into the room like an apparition—her arms are bare and white,—her tawny hair floats
down her shoulders,—her face is deadly pale,—and her
eyes are lighted up with a smile so ghastly, that people
quake as they look at her.

A tremor ran through the room. 'Good God!' somebody said, 'it's Mrs. Rawdon Crawley.'

Scornfully she snatches the dagger out of Aegisthus's
hand, and advances to the bed. You see it shining over
her head in the glimmer of the lamp, and—and the lamp
goes out, with a groan, and all is dark.

The darkness and the scene frightened people. Rebecca
performed the part so well, and with such ghastly truth,
that the spectators were all dumb, until, with a burst, all
the lamps of the hall blazed out again, when everybody
began to shout applause. 'Brava! brava!' old Steyne's
strident voice was heard roaring over all the rest. 'By
——, she'd do it too,' he said between his teeth. The
performers were called by the whole house, which sounded
with cries of 'Manager! Clytemnestra!' AGAMEMNON
could not be got to show in his classical tunic, but stood
in the background with Aegisthus and others of the performers of the little play. Mr. Bedwin Sands led on Zuleikah and Clytemnestra. A great personage* insisted upon
being presented to the charming Clytemnestra. 'Heigh ha?
Run him through the body. Marry somebody else, hey ?'
was the apposite remark made by His Royal Highness.

'Mrs. Rawdon Crawley was quite killing in the part,'
said Lord Steyne. Becky laughed ; gay, and saucy looking,
and swept the prettiest little curtsy ever seen.

Servants brought in salvers covered with numerous cool
dainties, and the performers disappeared, to get ready for
the second charade-tableau.

The three syllables of this charade were to be depicted

THE TRIUMPH OF CLYTEMNESTRA

in pantomime, and the performance took place in the
following wise :—

First syllable. Colonel Rawdon Crawley, C.B., with
a slouched hat and a staff, a great coat, and a lantern
borrowed from the stables, passed across the stage bawling
out, as if warning the inhabitants of the hour. In the
lower window are seen two bagmen playing apparently at
the game of cribbage, over which they yawn much. To
them enters one looking like Boots (the Honourable G. Ringwood), which character the young gentleman performed
to perfection, and divests them of their lowering covering ; and presently Chambermaid (the Right Honourable
Lord Southdown) with two candlesticks, and a warming-
pan. She ascends to the upper apartment, and warms the
bed. She uses the warming-pan as a weapon wherewith
she wards off the attention of the bagmen. She exits.
They put on their nightcaps, and pull down the blinds.
Boots comes out and closes the shutters of the ground-
floor chamber. You hear him bolting and chaining the
door within. All the lights go out. The music plays
' *Dormez, dormez, chers Amours.*'* A voice from behind the
curtain says, ' First syllable.'

Second syllable. The lamps are lighted up all of a
sudden. The music plays the old air from *John of Paris*,
' *Ah, quel plaisir d'être en voyage !* ' It is the same scene.
Between the first and second floors of the house represented,
you behold a sign on which the Steyne arms are painted.
All the bells are ringing all over the house. In the lower
apartment you see a man with a long slip of paper presenting it to another, who shakes his fist, threatens and
vows that it is monstrous. ' Ostler, bring round my gig,'
cries another at the door. He chucks Chambermaid (the
Right Honourable Lord Southdown) under the chin ; she
seems to deplore his absence, as Calypso did that of that
other eminent traveller, Ulysses. Boots (the Honourable
G. Ringwood) passes with a wooden box, containing silver
flagons, and cries ' Pots ' with such exquisite humour and
naturalness, that the whole house rings with applause, and
a bouquet is thrown to him. Crack, crack, crack, go the
whips. Landlord, chambermaid, waiter rush to the door ;
but just as some distinguished guest is arriving, the curtains
close, and the invisible theatrical manager cries out, 'Second
syllable.'

'I think it must be "Hotel",' says Captain Grigg of
the Life Guards; there is a general laugh at the captain's
cleverness. He is not very far from the mark.

While the third syllable is in preparation, the band
begins a nautical medley—'All in the Downs,' 'Cease, Rude
Boreas,' 'Rule, Britannia,' 'In the Bay of Biscay O'—
some maritime event is about to take place. A bell is
heard ringing as the curtain draws aside. 'Now, gents,
for the shore!' a voice exclaims. People take leave of
each other. They point anxiously as if towards the clouds,
which are represented by a dark curtain, and they nod
their heads in fear. Lady Squeams (the Right Honourable
Lord Southdown), her lap-dog, her bags, reticules, and
husband sit down, and cling hold of some ropes. It is
evidently a ship.

The captain (Colonel Crawley, C.B.), with a cocked hat
and a telescope, comes in, holding his hat on his head,
and looks out; his coat-tails fly about as if in the wind.
When he leaves go of his hat to use his telescope, his hat
flies off, with immense applause. It is blowing fresh. The
music rises and whistles louder and louder; the mariners
go across the stage staggering, as if the ship was in severe
motion. The Steward (the Honourable G. Ringwood) passes
reeling by, holding six basins. He puts one rapidly by
Lord Squeams—Lady Squeams giving a pinch to her dog,
which begins to howl piteously, puts her pocket-handkerchief to her face, and rushes away as for the cabin. The
music rises up to the wildest pitch of stormy excitement,
and the third syllable is concluded.

There was a little ballet, *Le Rossignol*, in which Montessu
and Noblet*used to be famous in those days, and which
Mr. Wagg transferred to the English stage as an opera,
putting his verse, of which he was a skilful writer, to the
pretty airs of the ballet. It was dressed in old French
costume, and little Lord Southdown now appeared admirably attired in the disguise of an old woman hobbling
about the stage with a faultless crooked stick.

Trills of melody were heard behind the scenes, and
gurgling from a sweet pasteboard cottage covered with
roses and trellis-work. 'Philomèle, Philomèle,' cries the
old woman, and Philomèle comes out.

More applause—it is Mrs. Rawdon Crawley in powder
and patches, the most *ravissante* little marquise in the world.

She comes in laughing, humming, and frisks about the stage with all the innocence of theatrical youth—she makes

a curtsy. Mamma says, 'Why, child, you are always laughing and singing,' and away she goes with—

THE ROSE UPON MY BALCONY

The rose upon my balcony the morning air perfuming,
Was leafless all the winter-time and pining for the spring;
You ask me why her breath is sweet and why her cheek is blooming,
It is because the sun is out and birds begin to sing.

The nightingale, whose melody is through the greenwood ringing,
Was silent when the boughs were bare and winds were blowing keen;
And if, mamma, you ask of me the reason of his singing;
It is because the sun is out and all the leaves are green.

Thus each performs his part, mamma, the birds have found their voices,
The blowing rose a flush, mamma, her bonny cheek to dye;
And there's sunshine in my heart, mamma, which wakens and rejoices,
And so I sing and blush, mamma, and that's the reason why.

During the intervals of the stanzas of this ditty, the good-natured personage addressed as mamma by the singer, and

whose large whiskers appeared under her cap, seemed very
anxious to exhibit her maternal affection by embracing the
innocent creature who performed the daughter's part.
Every caress was received with loud acclamations of
laughter by the sympathizing audience.   At its conclusion
(while the music was performing a symphony as if ever
so many birds were warbling) the whole house was unanimous for an encore : and applause and bouquets without
end were showered upon the NIGHTINGALE of the evening.
Lord Steyne's voice of applause was loudest of all.   Becky,
the nightingale, took the flowers which he threw to her,
and pressed them to her heart with the air of a consummate comedian.   Lord Steyne was frantic with delight.
His guests' enthusiasm harmonized with his own.   Where
was the beautiful black-eyed houri whose appearance in
the first charade had caused such delight?   She was twice
as handsome as Becky, but the brilliancy of the latter had
quite eclipsed her.   All voices were for her.   Stephens,
Caradori, Ronzi de Begnis,* people compared her to one or
the other ; and agreed with good reason, very likely, that
had she been an actress none on the stage would have
surpassed her.   She had reached her culmination : her
voice rose trilling and bright over the storm of applause :
and soared as high and joyful as her triumph.   There was
a ball after the dramatic entertainments, and everybody
pressed round Becky as the great point of attraction of
the evening.   The royal personage declared with an oath,
that she was perfection, and engaged her again and again
in conversation.   Little Becky's soul swelled with pride
and delight at these honours ; she saw fortune, fame,
fashion before her.   Lord Steyne was her slave ; followed
her everywhere, and scarcely spoke to any one in the room
beside ; and paid her the most marked compliments and
attention.   She still appeared in her marquise costume,
and danced a minuet with Monsieur de Truffigny, Monsieur
le Duc de la Jabotière's attaché ; and the duke, who had
all the traditions of the ancient court, pronounced that
Madame Crawley was worthy to have been a pupil of
Vestris,* or to have figured at Versailles.   Only a feeling
of dignity, the gout, and the strongest sense of duty and
personal sacrifice, prevented his excellency from dancing
with her himself ; and he declared in public, that a lady
who could talk and dance like Mrs. Rawdon, was fit to be

ambassadress at any court in Europe. He was only consoled when he heard· that she was half a Frenchwoman
by birth. ' None but a compatriot,' his excellency declared,
' could have performed that majestic dance in such a way.'

Then she figured in a waltz with Monsieur de Klingen-
spohr, the Prince of Peterwaradin's cousin and attaché.
The delighted prince, having less *retenue* than his French
diplomatic colleague, insisted upon taking a turn with the
charming creature, and twirled round the ball-room with
her, scattering the diamond out of his boot-tassels and
hussar jacket until his highness was fairly out of breath.
Papoosh Pasha himself would have liked to dance with
her if that amusement had been the custom of his country.
The company made a circle round her, and applauded as
wildly as if she had been a Noblet or a Taglioni.* Everybody was in ecstasy ; and Becky too, you may be sure.
She passed by Lady Stunnington with a look of scorn.
She patronized Lady Gaunt and her astonished and mortified sister-in-law—she *écrasé*'d all rival charmers. As for
poor Mrs. Winkworth, and her long hair and great eyes,
which had made such an effect at the commencement of
the evening ; where was she now ? Nowhere in the race.
She might tear her long hair and cry her great eyes out ;
but there was not a person to heed or to deplore the
discomfiture.

The greatest triumph of all was at supper-time. She
was placed at the grand exclusive table with his royal
highness the exalted personage before mentioned, and the
rest of the great guests. She was served on gold plate.
She might have had pearls melted into her champagne if
she liked—another Cleopatra ; and the potentate of Peterwaradin would have given half the brilliants off his jacket
for a kind glance from those dazzling eyes. Jabotière wrote
home about her to his Government. The ladies at the
other tables, who supped off mere silver, and marked Lord
Steyne's constant attention to her, vowed it was a monstrous infatuation, a gross insult to ladies of rank. If
sarcasm could have killed, Lady Stunnington would have
slain her on the spot.

Rawdon Crawley was scared at these triumphs. They
seemed to separate his wife farther than ever from him
somehow. He thought with a feeling very like pain how
immeasurably she was his superior.

When the hour of departure came, a crowd of young men followed her to her carriage, for which the people without bawled, the cry being caught up by the link-men* who were stationed outside the tall gates of Gaunt House, congratulating each person who issued from the gate and hoping his lordship had enjoyed this noble party.

Mrs. Rawdon Crawley's carriage, coming up to the gate after due shouting, rattled into the illuminated courtyard, and drove up to the covered way. Rawdon put his wife into the carriage, which drove off. Mr. Wenham had proposed to him to walk home, and offered the colonel the refreshment of a cigar.

They lighted their cigars by the lamp of one of the many link-boys outside, and Rawdon walked on with his friend Wenham. Two persons separated from the crowd and followed the two gentlemen; and when they had walked down Gaunt Square a few score of paces, one of the men came up, and touching Rawdon on the shoulder, said, 'Beg your pardon, colonel, I vish to speak to you most particular.' The gentleman's acquaintance gave a loud whistle as the latter spoke, at which signal a cab came clattering up from those stationed at the gate of Gaunt House—and the aide de camp ran round and placed himself in front of Colonel Crawley.

That gallant officer at once knew what had befallen him. He was in the hands of the bailiffs. He started back, falling against the man who had first touched him.

'We're three on us—it's no use bolting,' the man behind said.

'It's you, Moss, is it?' said the colonel, who appeared to know his interlocutor. 'How much is it?'

'Only a small thing,' whispered Mr. Moss, of Cursitor Street,* Chancery Lane, and assistant officer to the Sheriff of Middlesex—'one hundred and sixty-six, six and eight-pence, at the suit of Mr. Nathan.'

'Lend me a hundred, Wenham, for God's sake,' poor Rawdon said—'I've got seventy at home.'

'I've not got ten pounds in the world,' said poor Mr. Wenham—'Good night, my dear fellow.'

'Good night,' said Rawdon ruefully. And Wenham walked away—and Rawdon Crawley finished his cigar as the cab drove under Temple Bar.

COLONEL CRAWLEY IS WANTED

CHAPTER LII

 HEN Lord Steyne was benevolently disposed, he did
nothing by halves, and
his kindness towards the
Crawley family did the
greatest honour to his
benevolent discrimina-
tion. His lordship ex-
tended his goodwill to
little Rawdon: he pointed
out to the boy's parents
the necessity of send-
ing him to a public
school; that he was of
an age now when emula-
tion, the first principles of the Latin language, pugilistic
exercises, and the society of his fellow boys would be of
the greatest benefit to the boy. His father objected that
he was not rich enough to send the child to a good public
school; his mother, that Briggs was a capital mistress for
him, and had brought him on (as indeed was the fact)
famously in English, the Latin rudiments, and in general
learning: but all these objections disappeared before the
generous perseverance of the Marquis of Steyne. His lordship was one of the governors of that famous old collegiate
institution called the Whitefriars.* It had been a Cistercian convent in old days, when the Smithfield, which is
contiguous to it, was a tournament ground. Obstinate
heretics used to be brought thither convenient for burning
hard by. Harry VIII, the Defender of the Faith, seized
upon the monastery and its possessions, and hanged and
tortured some of the monks who could not accommodate
themselves to the pace of his reform. Finally, a great
merchant bought the house and land adjoining, in which,
and with the help of other wealthy endowments of land
and money, he established a famous foundation hospital
for old men and children. An extern school grew round

the old almost monastic foundation, which subsists still
with its middle-age costume and usages : and all Cister-
cians pray that it may long flourish.

Of this famous house, some of the greatest noblemen,
prelates, and dignitaries in England are governors : and
as the boys are very comfortably lodged, fed, and educated,
and subsequently inducted to good scholarships at the
University and livings in the Church, many little gentlemen are devoted to the ecclesiastical profession from their
tenderest years, and there is considerable emulation to
procure nominations for the foundations.   It was originally
intended for the sons of poor and deserving clerics and
laics ; but many of the noble governors of the Institution,
with an enlarged and rather capricious benevolence, selected
all sorts of objects for their bounty.   To get an education
for nothing, and a future livelihood and profession assured,
was so excellent a scheme, that some of the richest people
did not disdain it ; and not only great men's relations,
but great men themselves, sent their sons to profit by the
chance—right reverend prelates sent their own kinsmen or
the sons of their clergy, while, on the other hand, some
great noblemen did not disdain to patronize the children
of their confidential servants,—so that a lad entering this
establishment had every variety of youthful society wherewith to mingle.

Rawdon Crawley, though the only book which he studied
was the *Racing Calendar*, and though his chief recollections
of polite learning were connected with the floggings which
he received at Eton in his early youth, had that decent
and honest reverence for classical learning which all English
gentlemen feel, and was glad to think that his son was
to have a provision for life, perhaps, and a certain opportunity of becoming a scholar.   And although his boy was
his chief solace and companion, and endeared to him by
a thousand small ties, about which he did not care to speak
to his wife, who had all along shown the utmost indifference
to their son, yet Rawdon agreed at once to part with him,
and to give up his own greatest comfort and benefit for
the sake of the welfare of the little lad.   He did not know
how fond he was of the child until it became necessary to
let him go away, When he was gone, he felt more sad
and downcast than he cared to own—far sadder than the
boy himself, who was happy enough to enter a new career,

and find companions of his own age. Becky burst out laughing once or twice, when the colonel, in his clumsy, incoherent way, tried to express his sentimental sorrows at the boy's departure. The poor fellow felt that his dearest pleasure and closest friend was taken from him. He looked often and wistfully at the little vacant bed in his dressing-room, where the child used to sleep. He missed him sadly of mornings, and tried in vain to walk in the Park without him. He did not know how solitary he was until little Rawdon was gone. He liked the people who were fond of him ; and would go and sit for long hours with his good-natured sister, Lady Jane, and talk to her about the virtues, and good looks, and hundred good qualities of the child.

Young Rawdon's aunt, we have said, was very fond of him, as was her little girl, who wept copiously when the time for her cousin's departure came. The elder Rawdon was thankful for the fondness of mother and daughter. The very best and honestest feelings of the man came out in these artless outpourings of paternal feeling in which he indulged in their presence, and encouraged by their sympathy. He secured not only Lady Jane's kindness, but her sincere regard, by the feelings which he manifested, and which he could not show to his own wife. The two kinswomen met as seldom as possible. Becky laughed bitterly at Jane's feelings and softness ; the other's kindly and gentle nature could not but revolt at her sister's callous behaviour.

It estranged Rawdon from his wife more than he knew or acknowledged to himself. She did not care for the estrangement. Indeed, she did not miss him or anybody. She looked upon him as her errand-man and humble slave. He might be ever so depressed or sulky, and she did not mark his demeanour, or only treated it with a sneer. She was busy thinking about her position or her pleasures or her advancement in society ; she ought to have held a great place in it, that is certain.

It was honest Briggs who made up the little kit for the boy which he was to take to school. Molly, the housemaid, blubbered in the passage when he went away—Molly kind and faithful in spite of a long arrear of unpaid wages. Mrs. Becky could not let her husband have the carriage to take the boy to school. Take the horses into the City !—such

a thing was never heard of.   Let a 'cab be brought.   She
did not offer to kiss him when he went : nor did the child propose to embrace her : but gave a kiss to old Briggs (whom,
in general, he was very shy of caressing), and consoled
her by pointing out that he was to come home on Saturdays,
when she would have the benefit of seeing him.   As the
cab rolled towards the City, Becky's carriage rattled off
to the Park.   She was chattering and laughing with a score
of young dandies by the Serpentine, as the father and son
entered at the old gates of the school—where Rawdon
left the child, and came away with a sadder, purer feeling
in his heart than perhaps that poor battered fellow had
ever known since he himself came out of the nursery.

He walked all the way home very dismally, and dined
alone with Briggs.   He was very kind to her, and grateful
for her love and watchfulness over the boy.   His conscience
smote him that he had borrowed Briggs's money and aided
in deceiving her.   They talked about little Rawdon a long
time, for Becky only came home to dress and go out to dinner—And then he went off uneasily to drink tea with Lady
Jane, and tell her of what had happened, and how little Rawdon went off like a trump, and how he was to wear a gown
and little knee-breeches, and how young Blackball, Jack
Blackball's son, of the old regiment, had taken him in
charge and promised to be kind to him.

In the course of a week, young Blackball had constituted
little Rawdon his fag, shoeblack, and breakfast toaster ;
initiated him into the mysteries of the Latin grammar,
and thrashed him three or four times ; but not severely.
The little chap's good-natured honest face won his way for
him.   He only got that degree of beating which was, no
doubt, good for him ; and as for blacking shoes, toasting
bread, and fagging in general, were these offices not deemed
to be necessary parts of every young English gentleman's
education ?

Our business does not lie with the second generation and
Master Rawdon's life at school, otherwise the present tale
might be carried to any indefinite length.   The colonel
went to see his son a short time afterwards, and found the
lad sufficiently well and happy, grinning and laughing in
his little black gown and little breeches.

His father sagaciously tipped Blackball, his master,
a sovereign, and secured that young gentleman's goodwill

towards his fag.   As a protégé of the great Lord Steyne, the
nephew of a county member,* and son of a colonel and
C.B., whose name appeared in some of the most fashionable
parties in the *Morning Post*, perhaps the school authorities
were disposed not to look unkindly on the child.   He had
plenty of pocket-money, which he spent in treating his
comrades royally to raspberry tarts, and he was often
allowed to come home on Saturdays to his father, who
always made a jubilee of that day.   When free, Rawdon

would take him to the play, or send him thither with the
footman ; and on Sundays he went to church with Briggs
and Lady Jane and his cousins.   Rawdon marvelled over
his stories about school, and fights, and fagging.   Before
long, he knew the names of all the masters and the principal
boys as well as little Rawdon himself.   He invited little
Rawdon's crony from school, and made both the children
sick with pastry, and oysters, and porter after the play.
He tried to look knowing over the Latin grammar when
little Rawdon showed him what part of that work he was

'in'. 'Stick to it, my boy,' he said to him with much
gravity, ' there's nothing like a good classical education !
nothing ! '

Becky's contempt for her husband grew greater every
day. ' Do what you like—dine where you please—go and
have ginger-beer and sawdust at Astley's,* or psalm-singing
with Lady Jane—only don't expect *me* to busy myself
with the boy. I have your interests to attend to, as you
can't attend to them yourself. I should like to know
where you would have been now, and in what sort of a
position in society, if I had not looked after you ? ' Indeed,
nobody wanted poor old Rawdon at the parties whither
Becky used to go. She was often asked without him now.
She talked about great people as if she had the fee-simple
of May Fair ; and when the Court went into mourning,
she always wore black.

Little Rawdon being disposed of, Lord Steyne, who took
such a parental interest in the affairs of this amiable poor
family, thought that their expenses might be very advantageously curtailed by the departure of Miss Briggs ; and
that Becky was quite clever enough to take the management of her own house. It has been narrated in a former
chapter, how the benevolent nobleman had given his
protégée money to pay off her little debt to Miss Briggs,
who however still remained behind with her friends ; whence
my lord came to the painful conclusion that Mrs. Crawley
had made some other use of the money confided to her
than that for which her generous patron had given the
loan. However, Lord Steyne was not so rude as to impart
his suspicions upon this head to Mrs. Becky, whose feelings
might be hurt by any controversy on the money question,
and who might have a thousand painful reasons for disposing otherwise of his lordship's generous loan. But he
determined to satisfy himself of the real state of the case,
and instituted the necessary inquiries in a most cautious
and delicate manner.

In the first place he took an early opportunity of pumping
Miss Briggs. That was not a difficult operation. A very
little encouragement would set that worthy woman to talk
volubly, and pour out all within her. And one day when
Mrs. Rawdon had gone out to drive (as Mr. Fiche, his
lordship's confidential servant, easily learned at the livery

stables where the Crawleys kept their carriage and horses,
or rather, where the livery-man kept a carriage and horses
for Mr. and Mrs. Crawley)—my lord dropped in upon the
Curzon Street house—asked Briggs for a cup of coffee—
told her that he had good accounts of the little boy at
school—and in five minutes found out from her that
Mrs. Rawdon had given her nothing except a black silk
gown, for which Miss Briggs was immensely grateful.

He laughed within himself at this artless story. For
the truth is our dear friend Rebecca had given him a most
circumstantial narration of Briggs's delight at receiving
her money—eleven hundred and twenty-five pounds—and
in what securities she had invested it ; and what a pang
Becky herself felt in being obliged to pay away such a
delightful sum of money. ' Who knows,' the dear woman
may have thought within herself, ' perhaps he may give
me a little more ? ' My lord, however, made no such
proposal to the little schemer—very likely thinking that
he had been sufficiently generous already.

He had the curiosity, then, to ask Miss Briggs about
the state of her private affairs—and she told his lordship
candidly what her position was—how Miss Crawley had
left her a legacy—how her relatives had had part of it—
how Colonel Crawley had put out another portion, for which
she had the best security and interest—and how Mr. and
Mrs. Rawdon had kindly busied themselves with Sir Pitt,
who was to dispose of the remainder most advantageously
for her, when he had time. My lord asked how much
the colonel had already invested for her, and Miss Briggs
at once and truly told him that the sum was six hundred
and odd pounds.

But as soon as she had told her story, the voluble Briggs
repented of her frankness, and besought my lord not to tell
Mr. Crawley of the confessions which she had made. ' The
colonel was so kind—Mr. Crawley might be offended and
pay back the money, for which she could get no such good
interest anywhere else.' Lord Steyne, laughing, promised
he never would divulge their conversation, and when he
and Miss Briggs parted he laughed still more.

' What an accomplished little devil it is ! ' thought he.
' What a splendid actress and manager ! She had almost
got a second supply out of me the other day, with her
coaxing ways. She beats all the women I have ever seen

in the course of all my well-spent life. They are babies
compared to her. I am a greenhorn myself, and a fool
in her hands—an old fool. She is unsurpassable in lies.'
His lordship's admiration for Becky rose immeasurably
at this proof of her cleverness. Getting the money was
nothing—but getting double the sum she wanted, and
paying nobody—it was a magnificent stroke. And Crawley,
my lord thought—Crawley is not such a fool as he looks
and seems. He has managed the matter cleverly enough
on his side. Nobody would ever have supposed from his
face and demeanour that he knew anything about this
money business ; and yet he put her up to it, and has spent
the money, no doubt. In this opinion my lord, we know,
was mistaken ; but it influenced a good deal his behaviour
towards Colonel Crawley, whom he began to treat with
even less than that semblance of respect which he had
formerly shown towards that gentleman. It never entered
into the head of Mrs. Crawley's patron that the little lady
might be making a purse for herself ; and, perhaps, if the
truth must be told, he judged of Colonel Crawley by his
experience of other husbands, whom he had known in
the course of the long and well-spent life, which had made
him acquainted with a great deal of the weakness of mankind. My lord had bought so many men during his life
that he was surely to be pardoned for supposing that he
had found the price of this one.

He taxed Becky upon the point on the very first occasion
when he met her alone, and he complimented her, good-
humouredly, on her cleverness in getting more than the
money which she required. Becky was only a little taken
aback. It was not the habit of this dear creature to tell
falsehoods, except when necessity compelled, but in these
great emergencies it was her practice to lie very freely ;
and in an instant she was ready with another neat, plausible,
circumstantial story which she administered to her patron.
The previous statement which she had made to him was
a falsehood—a wicked falsehood : she owned it ; but who
had made her tell it ?   ' Ah, my lord,' she said, ' you
don't know all I have to suffer and bear in silence : you
see me gay and happy before you—you little know what
I have to endure when there is no protector near me. It
was my husband, by threats and the most savage treatment, forced me to ask for that sum about which I deceived

you. It was he, who, foreseeing that questions might be
asked regarding the disposal of the money, forced me to
account for it as I did. He took the money. He told me
he had paid Miss Briggs ; I did not want, I did not dare
to doubt him. Pardon the wrong which a desperate man is
forced to commit, and pity a miserable, miserable woman.'
She burst into tears as she spoke. Persecuted virtue never
looked more bewitchingly wretched.

They had a long conversation, driving round and round
the Regent's Park in Mrs. Crawley's carriage together,
a conversation of which it is not necessary to repeat the
details ; but the upshot of it was, that, when Becky came
home, she flew to her dear Briggs with a smiling face,
and announced that she had some very good news for her.
Lord Steyne had acted in the noblest and most generous
manner. He was always thinking how and when he could
do good. Now that little Rawdon was gone to school,
a dear companion and friend was no longer necessary to
her. She was grieved beyond measure to part with Briggs ;
but her means required that she should practise every
retrenchment, and her sorrow was mitigated by the idea
that her dear Briggs would be far better provided for by
her generous patron than in her humble home. Mrs.
Pilkington, the housekeeper at Gauntly Hall, was growing
exceedingly old, feeble, and rheumatic : she was not equal
to the work of superintending that vast mansion, and must
be on the look out for a successor. It was a splendid
position. The family did not go to Gauntly once in two
years. At other times the housekeeper was the mistress
of the magnificent mansion—had four covers daily for her
table ; was visited by the clergy and the most respectable
people of the county—was the lady of Gauntly, in fact ;
and the two last housekeepers before Mrs. Pilkington had
married rectors of Gauntly ; but Mrs. P. could not, being
the aunt of the present rector. The place was not to be
hers yet ; but she might go down on a visit to Mrs. Pilkington and see whether she would like to succeed her.

What words can paint the ecstatic gratitude of Briggs !
All she stipulated for was that little Rawdon should be
allowed to come down and see her at the Hall. Becky
promised this—anything. She ran up to her husband when
he came home, and told him the joyful news. Rawdon
was glad, deuced glad ; the weight was off his conscience

about poor Briggs's money. She was provided for, at any
rate, but—but his mind was disquiet. He did not seem
to be all right somehow. He told little Southdown what
Lord Steyne had done, and the young man eyed Crawley
with an air which surprised the latter.

He told Lady Jane of this second proof of Steyne's bounty,
and she, too, looked odd and alarmed ; so did Sir Pitt.
' She is too clever and—and gay to be allowed to go from
party to party without a companion,' both said. ' You
must go with her, Rawdon, wherever she goes, and you
must have somebody with her—one of the girls from Queen's
Crawley, perhaps, though they were rather giddy guardians
for her.'

Somebody Becky should have. But in the meanwhile
it was clear that honest Briggs must not lose her chance of
settlement for life ; and so she and her bags were packed,
and she set off on her journey. And so two of Rawdon's
out-sentinels were in the hands of the enemy.

Sir Pitt went and expostulated with his sister-in-law upon
the subject of the dismissal of Briggs, and other matters
of delicate family interest. In vain she pointed out to
him how necessary was the protection of Lord Steyne for
her poor husband ; how cruel it would be on their part
to deprive Briggs of the position offered to her. Cajole-
ments, coaxings, smiles, tears could not satisfy Sir Pitt,
and he had something very like a quarrel with his once
admired Becky. He spoke of the honour of the family :
the unsullied reputation of the Crawleys ; expressed himself
in indignant tones about her receiving those young Frenchmen—those wild young men of fashion, my Lord Steyne
himself whose carriage was always at her door, who passed
hours daily in her company, and whose constant presence
made the world talk about her. As the head of the house
he implored her to be more prudent. Society was already
speaking lightly of her. Lord Steyne, though a nobleman
of the greatest station and talents, was a man whose
attentions would compromise any woman ; he besought,
he implored, he commanded his sister-in-law to be watchful
in her intercourse with that nobleman.

Becky promised anything and everything Pitt wanted ;
but Lord Steyne came to her house as often as ever, and
Sir Pitt's anger increased. I wonder was Lady Jane angry
or pleased that her husband at last found fault with his

favourite Rebecca ?   Lord Steyne's visits continuing, his
own ceased ; and his wife was for refusing all further intercourse with that nobleman, and declining the invitation
to the Charade-night which the marchioness sent to her ;
but Sir Pitt thought it was necessary to accept it, as his
royal highness would be there.

Although he went to the party in question, Sir Pitt
quitted it very early, and his wife, too, was very glad to
come away. Becky hardly so much as spoke to him or
noticed her sister-in-law. Pitt Crawley declared her
behaviour was monstrously indecorous, reprobated in
strong terms the habit of play-acting and fancy-dressing,
as highly unbecoming a British female ; and after the
charades were over, took his brother Rawdon severely to
task for appearing himself, and allowing his wife to join in
such improper exhibitions.

Rawdon said she should not join in any more such
amusements, but indeed, and perhaps from hints from his
elder brother and sister, he had already become a very
watchful and exemplary domestic character. He left off
his clubs and billiards. He never left home. He took
Becky out to drive : he went laboriously with her to all
her parties. Whenever my Lord Steyne called, he was
sure to find the colonel. And when Becky proposed to
go out without her husband, or received invitations for
herself, he peremptorily ordered her to refuse them ; and
there was that in the gentleman's manner which enforced
obedience. Little Becky, to do her justice, was charmed
with Rawdon's gallantry. If he was surly, she never was.
Whether friends were present or absent she had always
a kind smile for him, and was attentive to his pleasure
and comfort. It was the early days of their marriage over
again : the same good humour, *prévenances*, merriment,
and artless confidence and regard. ' How much pleasanter
it is,' she would say, ' to have you by my side in the carriage
than that foolish old Briggs ! Let us always go on so, dear
Rawdon. How nice it would be, and how happy we should
always be, if we had but the money ! ' He fell asleep after
dinner in his chair ; he did not see the face opposite to him,
haggard, weary, and terrible ; it lighted up with fresh
candid smiles when he woke. It kissed him gaily. He
wondered that he had ever had suspicions. No, he never
had suspicion ; all those dumb doubts and surly misgivings

which had been gathering on his mind were mere idle
jealousies. She was fond of him ; she always had been.
As for her shining in society it was no fault of hers ; she
was formed to shine there. Was there any woman who
could talk, or sing, or do anything like her ? If she would
but like the boy ! Rawdon thought. But the mother and
son never could be brought together.

And it was while Rawdon's mind was agitated with
these doubts and perplexities that the incident occurred
which was mentioned in the last chapter ; and the unfortunate colonel found himself a prisoner away from home.

CHAPTER LIII

A RESCUE AND A CATASTROPHE

FRIEND Rawdon drove
on then to Mr. Moss's
mansion in Cursitor
Street, and was duly
inducted into that dis-
mal place of hospi-
tality. Morning was
breaking over the
cheerful house-tops of
Chancery Lane as the
rattling cab woke up
the echoes there. A
little pink-eyed Jew-
boy, with a head as
ruddy as the rising morn, let the party into the house,
and Rawdon was welcomed to the ground-floor apartments
by Mr. Moss, his travelling companion and host, who cheerfully asked him if he would like a glass of something warm
after his drive.

The colonel was not so depressed as some mortals would
be, who, quitting a palace and a *placens uxor*, find themselves barred into a spunging-house, for, if the truth must
be told, he had been a lodger at Mr. Moss's establishment
once or twice before. We have not thought it necessary
in the previous course of this narrative to mention these

trivial little domestic incidents : but the reader may be
assured that they can't unfrequently occur in the life of
a man who lives on nothing a year.

Upon his first visit to Mr. Moss, the colonel, then a
bachelor, had been liberated by the generosity of his aunt ;
on the second mishap, little Becky, with the greatest spirit
and kindness, had borrowed a sum of money from Lord
Southdown, and had coaxed her husband's creditor (who
was her shawl, velvet gown, lace pocket-handkerchief,
trinket, and gimcrack purveyor, indeed) to take a portion
of the sum claimed, and Rawdon's promissory note for the
remainder : so on both these occasions the capture and
release had been conducted with the utmost gallantry on
all sides, and Moss and the colonel were therefore on the
very best of terms.

' You'll find your old bed, colonel, and everything
comfortable,' that gentleman said, ' as I may honestly say.
You may be pretty sure its kep aired, and by the best of
company, too. It was slep in the night afore last by the
Honourable Capting Famish, of the Fiftieth Dragoons,
whose mar took him out, after a fortnight, jest to punish
him, she said. But, Law bless you, I promise you, he
punished my champagne, and had a party ere every night—
reglar tip-top swells, down from the clubs and the West
End—Capting Ragg, the Honourable Deuceace, who lives
in the Temple, and some fellers as knows a good glass of
wine, I warrant you. I've got a Doctor of Diwinity upstairs, five gents in the coffee-room, and Mrs. Moss has
a tably-dy-hoty at half-past five, and a little cards or
music afterwards, when we shall be most happy to see you.'

' I'll ring, when I want anything,' said Rawdon, and
went quietly to his bedroom. He was an old soldier,
we have said, and not to be disturbed by any little shocks
of fate. A weaker man would have sent off a letter to
his wife on the instant of his capture. ' But what is the
use of disturbing her night's rest ? ' thought Rawdon.
' She won't know whether I am in my room or not. It will
be time enough to write to her when she has had her sleep
out, and I have had mine. It's only a hundred-and-seventy,
and the deuce is in it if we can't raise that.' And so,
thinking about little Rawdon (whom he would not have
know that he was in such a queer place), the colonel turned
into the bed lately occupied by Captain Famish, and fell

asleep. It was ten o'clock when he woke up, and the ruddy-headed youth brought him, with conscious pride, a fine silver dressing-case, wherewith he might perform the operation of shaving. Indeed Mr. Moss's house, though somewhat dirty, was splendid throughout. There were dirty trays, and wine-coolers *en permanence* on the sideboard, huge dirty gilt cornices, with dingy yellow satin hangings to the barred windows which looked into Cursitor Street— vast and dirty gilt picture-frames surrounding pieces sporting and sacred, all of which works were by the greatest masters ; and fetched the greatest prices, too, in the bill transactions, in the course of which they were sold and bought over and over again. The colonel's breakfast was served to him in the same dingy and gorgeous plated ware. Miss Moss, a dark-eyed maid in curl-papers appeared with the teapot, and, smiling, asked the colonel how he had slept? and she brought him in the *Morning Post*, with the names of all the great people who had figured at Lord Steyne's entertainment the night before. It contained a brilliant account of the festivities, and of the beautiful and accomplished Mrs. Rawdon Crawley's admirable personifications.

After a lively chat with this lady (who sat on the edge of the breakfast-table in an easy attitude displaying the drapery of her stocking and an ex-white satin shoe, which was down at heel), Colonel Crawley called for pens and ink, and paper ; and being asked how many sheets, chose one which was brought to him between Miss Moss's own finger and thumb. Many a sheet had that dark-eyed damsel brought in ; many a poor fellow had scrawled and blotted hurried lines of entreaty, and paced up and down that awful room until his messenger brought back the reply. Poor men always use messengers instead of the post. Who has not had their letters with the wafers wet, and the announcement that a person is waiting in the hall ?

Now on the score of his application, Rawdon had not many misgivings.

DEAR BECKY (Rawdon wrote), *I hope you slept well.* Don't be *frightened* if I don't bring you in your *coffy.* Last night as I was coming home smoking, I met with an *accadent.* I was *nabbed* by Moss of Cursitor Street—from whose *gilt and splendid parler* I write this—the same that had me this time two years. Miss Moss brought in my tea—she is grown very *fat*, and as usual, had *her stockens down at heal.*

It's Nathan's business—a hundred-and-fifty—with costs, hundred-and-seventy. Please send me my desk and some *cloths*—I'm in pumps and a white tye (something like Miss M.'s stockings)—I've seventy in it. And as soon as you get this, Drive to Nathan's— offer him seventy-five down, and ask *him to renew*—say I'll take wine* —we may as well have some dinner sherry ; but not *picturs*, they're too dear.

If he won't stand it. Take my ticker and such of your things as you can *spare*, and send them to Balls—we must, of coarse, have the sum to-night. It won't do to let it stand over, as to-morrow's Sunday ; the beds here are not very *clean*, and there may be other things out against me—I'm glad it an't Rawdon's Saturday for coming home. God bless you.

                                        Yours in haste, R. C.
   PS.—Make haste and come.

This letter, sealed with a wafer, was dispatched by one of the messengers who are always hanging about Mr. Moss's establishment ; and Rawdon, having seen him depart, went out in the courtyard, and smoked his cigar with a tolerably easy mind—in spite of the bars overhead ; for Mr. Moss's courtyard is railed in like a cage, lest the gentlemen who are boarding with him should take a fancy to escape from his hospitality.

Three hours, he calculated, would be the utmost time required, before Becky should arrive and open his prison doors : and he passed these pretty cheerfully in smoking, in reading the paper, and in the coffee-room with an acquaintance, Captain Walker, who happened to be there, and with whom he cut for sixpences for some hours, with pretty equal luck on either side.

But the day passed away and no messenger returned,— no Becky. Mr. Moss's tably-de-hoty was served at the appointed hour of half-past five, when such of the gentlemen lodging in the house as could afford to pay for the banquet, came and partook of it in the splendid front parlour before described, and with which Mr. Crawley's temporary lodging communicated, when Miss M. (Miss Hem, as her papa called her) appeared without the curl-papers of the morning, and Mrs. Hem did the honours of a prime boiled leg of mutton and turnips, of which the colonel ate with a very faint appetite. Asked whether he would ' stand ' a bottle of champagne for the company, he consented, and the ladies drank to his 'ealth, and Mr. Moss, in the most polite manner ' looked towards him '.

In the midst of this repast, however, the door-bell was heard,—young Moss of the ruddy hair, rose up with the keys and answered the summons, and coming back, told the colonel that the messenger had returned with a bag, a desk and a letter, which he gave him. 'No ceremony, colonel, I beg,' said Mrs. Moss, with a wave of her hand, and he opened the letter rather tremulously.—It was a beautiful letter, highly scented, on a pink paper, and with a light green seal.

MON PAUVRE CHER PETIT (Mrs. Crawley wrote), I could not sleep *one wink* for thinking of what had become of *my odious old monstre :* and only got to rest in the morning after sending for Mr. Blench (for I was in a fever), who gave me a composing draught and left orders with Finette that I should be disturbed *on no account.* So that my poor old man's messenger, who had *bien mauvaise mine,* Finette says, and *sentait le genièvre,* remained in the hall for some hours waiting my bell. You may fancy my state when I read your poor dear old ill-spelt letter.

Ill as I was, I instantly called for the carriage, and as soon as I was dressed (though I couldn't drink a drop of chocolate—I assure you I couldn't without my *monstre* to bring it to me), I drove *ventre à terre* to Nathan's. I saw him—I wept—I cried—I fell at his odious knees. Nothing would mollify the horrid man. He would have all the money, he said, or keep my poor *monstre* in prison. I drove home with the intention of paying that *triste visite chez mon oncle* (when every trinket I have should be at your disposal though they would not fetch a hundred pounds, for some, you know, are with *ce cher oncle* already), and found Milor there with the Bulgarian old sheep-faced monster, who had come to compliment me upon last night's performances. Paddington came in, too, drawling and lisping and twiddling his hair ; so did Champignac, and his chef—everybody with *foison* of compliments and pretty speeches—plaguing poor me, who longed to be rid of them, and was thinking *every moment of the time* of *mon pauvre prisonnier.*

When they were gone, I went down on my knees to Milor ; told him we were going to pawn everything, and begged and prayed him to give me two hundred pounds. He pish'd and psha'd in a fury— told me not to be such a fool as to pawn—and said he would see whether he could lend me the money. At last he went away, promising that he would send it me in the morning : when I will bring it to my poor old monster with a kiss from his affectionate

BECKY.

I am writing in bed. Oh, I have such a headache and such a heart-ache !

When Rawdon read over this letter, he turned so red and looked so savage that the company at the table d'hôte

easily perceived that bad news had reached him. All his
suspicions, which he had been trying to banish, returned
upon him. She could not even go out and sell her trinkets
to free him. She could laugh and talk about compliments
paid to her, whilst he was in prison. Who had put him
there ? Wenham had walked with him. Was there . . . .
He could hardly bear to think of what he suspected. Leaving the room hurriedly, he ran into his own—opened his
desk, wrote two hurried lines, which he directed to Sir Pitt
or Lady Crawley, and bade the messenger carry them at
once to Gaunt Street, bidding him to take a cab, and
promising him a guinea if he was back in an hour.

In the note he besought his dear brother and sister, for
the sake of God ; for the sake of his dear child and his
honour ; to come to him and relieve him from his difficulty.
He was in prison : he wanted a hundred pounds to set him
free—he entreated them to come to him.

He went back to the dining-room after dispatching his
messenger, and called for more wine. He laughed and
talked with a strange boisterousness, as the people thought.
Sometimes he laughed madly at his own fears, and went
on drinking for an hour ; listening all the while for the
carriage which was to bring his fate back.

At the expiration of that time, wheels were heard whirling
up to the gate—the young janitor went out with his gate-
keys. It was a lady whom he let in at the bailiff's door.

' Colonel Crawley,' she said, trembling very much. He
with a knowing look, locked the outer door upon her—
then unlocked and opened the inner one, and calling out,
' Colonel, you're wanted,' led her into the back parlour,
which he occupied.

Rawdon came in from the dining-parlour where all those
people were carousing, into his back-room ; a flare of
coarse light following him into the apartment where the
lady stood, still very nervous.

' It is I, Rawdon,' she said, in a timid voice, which she
strove to render cheerful. ' It is Jane.' Rawdon was
quite overcome by that kind voice and presence. He ran
up to her—caught her in his arms—gasped out some
inarticulate words of thanks, and fairly sobbed on her
shoulder. She did not know the cause of his emotion.

The bills of Mr. Moss were quickly settled, perhaps to the
disappointment of that gentleman, who had counted on

having the colonel as his guest over Sunday at least ; and
Jane, with beaming smiles and happiness in her eyes,
carried away Rawdon from the bailiff's house, and they
went homewards in the cab in which she had hastened to
his release. ' Pitt was gone to a Parliamentary dinner,'
she said, ' when Rawdon's note came, and so, dear Rawdon,
I—I came myself ; ' and she put her kind hand in his.
Perhaps it was well for Rawdon Crawley that Pitt was
away at that dinner.   Rawdon thanked his sister a hundred
times, and with an ardour of gratitude which touched and

almost alarmed that soft-hearted woman. ' Oh,' said he,
in his rude, artless way, ' you—you don't know how I'm
changed since I've known you, and—and little Rawdy.
I—I'd like to change somehow.   You see I want—I want—
to be——.'—He did not finish the sentence, but she could
interpret it.   And that night after he left her, and as she
sat by her own little boy's bed, she prayed humbly for
that poor wayworn sinner.

Rawdon left her and walked home rapidly.   It was
nine o'clock at night.   He ran across the streets, and the
great squares of Vanity Fair, and at length came up breath-

less opposite his own house. He started back and fell
against the railings, trembling as he looked up. The
drawing-room windows were blazing with light. She had
said that she was in bed and ill. He stood there for some
time, the light from the rooms on his pale face.

He took out his door-key and let himself into the house.
He could hear laughter in the upper rooms. He was in the
ball-dress in which he had been captured the night before.
He went silently up the stairs ; leaning against the banisters
at the stair-head.—Nobody was stirring in the house
besides—all the servants had been sent away. Rawdon
heard laughter within—laughter and singing. Becky was
singing a snatch of the song of the night before ; a hoarse
voice shouted, ' Brava ! Brava ! '—it was Lord Steyne's.

Rawdon opened the door and went in. A little table
with a dinner was laid out—and wine and plate. Steyne
was hanging over the sofa on which Becky sat. The
wretched woman was in a brilliant full toilette, her arms
and all her fingers sparkling with bracelets and rings ;
and the brilliants on her breast which Steyne had given
her. He had her hand in his, and was bowing over it to
kiss it, when Becky started up with a faint scream as she
caught sight of Rawdon's white face. At the next instant
she tried a smile, a horrid smile, as if to welcome her
husband : and Steyne rose up, grinding his teeth, pale, and
with fury in his looks.

He, too, attempted a laugh—and came forward holding
out his hand. ' What, come back ! How d'ye do, Crawley ? '
he said, the nerves of his mouth twitching as he tried to grin
at the intruder.

There was that in Rawdon's face which caused Becky
to fling herself before him. ' I am innocent, Rawdon,'
she said ; ' before God, I am innocent.' She clung hold of
his coat, of his hands ; her own were all covered with
serpents,* and rings, and baubles. ' I am innocent.—Say
I am innocent,' she said to Lord Steyne.

He thought a trap had been laid for him, and was as
furious with the wife as with the husband. ' You innocent !
Damn you,' he screamed out. ' You innocent ! Why,
every trinket you have on your body is paid for by me.
I have given you thousands of pounds which this fellow
has spent, and for which he has sold you. Innocent,
by —— ! You're as innocent as your mother, the ballet-

girl, and your husband the bully. Don't think to frighten
me as you have done others. Make way, sir, and let me
pass;' and Lord Steyne seized up his hat, and, with flame
in his eyes, and looking his enemy fiercely in the face,
marched upon him, never for a moment doubting that the
other would give way.

But Rawdon Crawley springing out, seized him by the
neckcloth, until Steyne, almost strangled, writhed, and
bent under his arm. 'You lie, you dog!' said Rawdon.
'You lie, you coward and villain!' And he struck the
peer twice over the face with his open hand, and flung
him bleeding to the ground. It was all done before Rebecca
could interpose. She stood there trembling before him.
She admired her husband, strong, brave, and victorious.

'Come here,' he said.—She came up at once.

'Take off those things.'—She began, trembling, pulling
the jewels from her arms, and the rings from her shaking
fingers, and held them all in a heap, quivering and looking
up at him. 'Throw them down,' he said, and she dropped
them. He tore the diamond ornament out of her breast,
and flung it at Lord Steyne. It cut him on his bald forehead. Steyne wore the scar to his dying day.

'Come upstairs,' Rawdon said to his wife. 'Don't kill
me, Rawdon,' she said. He laughed savagely.—'I want
to see if that man lies about the money as he has about
me. Has he given you any?'

'No,' said Rebecca, 'that is——'

'Give me your keys,' Rawdon answered, and they went
out together.

Rebecca gave him all the keys but one : and she was
in hopes that he would not have remarked the absence of
that. It belonged to the little desk which Amelia had
given her in early days, and which she kept in a secret
place. But Rawdon flung open boxes and wardrobes,
throwing the multifarious trumpery of their contents here
and there, and at last he found the desk. The woman
was forced to open it. It contained papers, love-letters
many years old—all sorts of small trinkets and woman's
memoranda. And it contained a pocket-book with bank-
notes. Some of these were dated ten years back, too, and
one was quite a fresh one—a note for a thousand pounds
which Lord Steyne had given her.

'Did he give you this?' Rawdon said.

'Yes,' Rebecca answered.

'I'll·send it to him to-day,' Rawdon said (for day had dawned again, and many hours had passed in this search), 'and I will pay Briggs, who was kind to the boy, and some of the debts. You will let me know where I shall send the rest to you. You might have spared me a hundred pounds, Becky, out of all this—I have always shared with you.'

'I am innocent,' said Becky. And he left her without another word.

What were her thoughts when he left her ? She remained for hours after he was gone, the sunshine pouring into the room, and Rebecca sitting alone on the bed's edge. The drawers were all opened and their contents scattered about, —dresses and feathers, scarfs and trinkets, a heap of tumbled vanities lying in a wreck. Her hair was falling over her shoulders ; her gown was torn where Rawdon had wrenched the brilliants out of it. She heard him go downstairs a few minutes after he left her, and the door slamming and closing on him. She knew he would never come back. He was gone for ever. Would he kill himself ?—she thought—not until after he had met Lord Steyne. She thought of her long past life, and all the dismal incidents of it. Ah, how dreary it seemed, how miserable, lonely and profitless ! Should she take laudanum, and end it, too— have done with all hopes, schemes, debts, and triumphs ? The French maid found her in this position—sitting in the midst of her miserable ruins with clasped hands and dry eyes. The woman was her accomplice and in Steyne's pay. '*Mon Dieu*, madame, what has happened ?' she asked.

What *had* happened ? Was she guilty or not ? She said not ; but who could tell what was truth which came from those lips ; or if that corrupt heart was in this case pure ? All her lies and her schemes, all her selfishness and her wiles, all her wit and genius had come to this bankruptcy. The woman closed the curtains, and with some entreaty and show of kindness, persuaded her mistress to lie down on the bed. Then she went below and gathered up the trinkets which had been lying on the floor, since Rebecca dropped them there at her husband's orders, and Lord Steyne went away.

CHAPTER LIV

SUNDAY AFTER THE BATTLE

HE mansion of Sir Pitt Crawley in Great Gaunt Street was just beginning to dress itself for the day, as Rawdon, in his evening costume, which he had now worn two days, passed by the scared female who was scouring the steps, and entered into his brother's study. Lady Jane, in her morning-gown, was up and above stairs in the nursery, superintending the toilettes of her children, and listening to the morning prayers which the little creatures performed at her knee. Every morning she and they performed this duty privately, and before the public ceremonial at which Sir Pitt presided, and at which all the people of the household were expected to assemble. Rawdon sat down in the study before the baronet's table, set out with the orderly Blue Books and the letters, the neatly docketed bills and symmetrical pamphlets; the locked account-books, desks, and dispatch boxes, the Bible, the *Quarterly Review*, and the *Court Guide*,* which all stood as if on parade awaiting the inspection of their chief.

A book of family sermons, one of which Sir Pitt was in the habit of administering to his family on Sunday mornings, lay ready on the study table, and awaiting his judicious selection. And by the sermon-book was the *Observer* newspaper, damp and neatly folded, and for Sir Pitt's own private use. His gentleman alone took the opportunity of perusing the newspaper before he laid it by his master's desk. Before he had brought it into the study that morning, he had read in the journal a flaming account of 'Festivities at Gaunt House', with the names of all the distinguished personages invited by the Marquis of Steyne to meet his royal highness. Having made comments upon this entertainment to the housekeeper and her niece as they were taking early tea and hot buttered toast in the former lady's apartment, and wondered how the Rawding Crawleys could git on, the valet had damped and folded the paper once more, so that it looked quite fresh and innocent against the arrival of the master of the house.

Poor Rawdon took up the paper and began to try and read it until his brother should arrive. But the print fell blank upon his eyes; and he did not know in the least what he was reading. The Government news and appointments (which Sir Pitt as a public man was bound to peruse, otherwise he would by no means permit the introduction of Sunday papers into his household), the theatrical criticisms, the fight for a hundred pounds a side between the Barking Butcher and the Tutbury Pet, the Gaunt House chronicle itself, which contained a most complimentary though guarded account of the famous charades of which Mrs. Becky had been the heroine—all these passed as in a haze before Rawdon, as he sat waiting the arrival of the chief of the family.

Punctually, as the shrill-toned bell of the black marble study clock began to chime nine, Sir Pitt made his appearance, fresh, neat, smugly shaved, with a waxy clean face, and stiff shirt collar, his scanty hair combed and oiled, trimming his nails as he descended the stairs majestically, in a starched cravat and a grey flannel dressing-gown— a real old English gentleman, in a word—a model of neatness and every propriety. He started when he saw poor Rawdon in his study in tumbled clothes, with bloodshot eyes, and his hair over his face. He thought his brother was not sober, and had been out all night on some orgy. 'Good gracious, Rawdon,' he said, with a blank face, 'what brings you here at this time of the morning? Why ain't you at home?'

'Home,' said Rawdon, with a wild laugh. 'Don't be frightened, Pitt. I'm not drunk. Shut the door; I want to speak to you.'

Pitt closed the door and came up to the table, where he sat down in the other arm-chair—that one placed for the reception of the steward, agent, or confidential visitor who came to transact business with the baronet—and trimmed his nails more vehemently than ever.

'Pitt, it's all over with me,' the colonel said, after a pause. 'I'm done.'

'I always said it would come to this,' the baronet cried peevishly, and beating a tune with his clean-trimmed nails. 'I warned you a thousand times. I can't help you any more. Every shilling of my money is tied up. Even the hundred pounds that Jane took you last night were promised to my lawyer to-morrow morning; and the want of it will put me to great inconvenience. I don't mean to say that I won't assist you ultimately. But as for paying your creditors in full, I might as well hope to pay the National Debt. It is madness, sheer madness, to think of such a thing. You must come to a compromise. It's a painful thing for the family; but everybody does it. There was George Kitely, Lord Ragland's son, went through the court last week, and was what they call whitewashed, I believe. Lord Ragland would not pay a shilling for him, and——'

'It's not money I want,' Rawdon broke in. 'I'm not come to you about myself. Never mind what happens to me——'

'What is the matter, then?' said Pitt, somewhat relieved.

'It's the boy,' said Rawdon, in a husky voice. 'I want you to promise me that you will take charge of him when I'm gone. That dear good wife of yours has always been good to him; and he's fonder of her than he is of his....—Damn it. Look here, Pitt—you know that I was to have had Miss Crawley's money. I wasn't brought up like a younger brother: but was always encouraged to be extravagant and kep idle. But for this I might have been quite a different man. I didn't do my duty with the regiment so bad. You know how I was thrown over about the money, and who got it.'

'After the sacrifices I have made, and the manner in which I have stood by you, I think this sort of reproach is useless,' Sir Pitt said. 'Your marriage was your own doing, not mine.'

'That's over now,' said Rawdon.—'That's over now.' And the words were wrenched from him with a groan, which made his brother start.

'Good God! is she dead?' Sir Pitt said, with a voice of genuine alarm and commiseration.

SIR PITT'S STUDY-CHAIR

'I wish *I* was,' Rawdon replied. 'If it wasn't for little Rawdon I'd have cut my throat this morning—and that damned villain's too.'

Sir Pitt instantly guessed the truth, and surmised that Lord Steyne was the person whose life Rawdon wished to take. The colonel told his senior briefly, and in broken accents, the circumstances of the case. 'It was a regular plan between that scoundrel and her,' he said. 'The bailiffs were put upon me: I was taken as I was going out of his house: when I wrote to her for money, she said she was ill in bed, and put me off to another day. And when I got home I found her in diamonds and sitting with that villain alone.' He then went on to describe hurriedly the personal conflict with Lord Steyne. To an affair of that nature, of course, he said, there was but one issue: and after his conference with his brother, he was going away to make the necessary arrangements for the meeting which must ensue. 'And as it may end fatally for me,' Rawdon said with a broken voice, 'and as the boy has no mother, I must leave him to you and Jane, Pitt—only it will be a comfort to me if you will promise me to be his friend.'

The elder brother was much affected, and shook Rawdon's hand with a cordiality seldom exhibited by him. Rawdon passed his hand over his shaggy eyebrows. 'Thank you, brother,' said he. 'I know I can trust your word.'

'I will, upon my honour,' the baronet said. And thus, and almost mutely, this bargain was struck between them.

Then Rawdon took out of his pocket the little pocket-book which he had discovered in Becky's desk; and from which he drew a bundle of the notes which it contained. 'Here's six hundred,' he said—'you didn't know I was so rich. I want you to give the money to Briggs, who lent it to us—and who was so kind to the boy—and I've always felt ashamed of having taken the poor old woman's money. And here's some more—I've only kept back a few pounds—which Becky may as well have, to get on with.' As he spoke he took hold of the other notes to give to his brother: but his hands shook, and he was so agitated that the pocket-book fell from him, and out of it the thousand-pound note which had been the last of the unlucky Becky's winnings.

Pitt stooped and picked them up, amazed at so much

wealth. 'Not that,' Rawdon said ; ' I hope to put a bullet
into the man whom that belongs to.' He had thought to
himself, it would be a fine revenge to wrap a ball in the
note, and kill Steyne with it.

After this colloquy the brothers once more shook hands
and parted. Lady Jane had heard of the colonel's arrival,
and was waiting for her husband in the adjoining dining-
room, with female instinct, auguring evil. The door of
the dining-room happened to be left open, and the lady
of course was issuing from it as the two brothers passed
out of the study. She held out her hand to Rawdon, and
said she was glad he was come to breakfast ; though she
could perceive, by his haggard unshorn face, and the dark
looks of her husband, that there was very little question
of breakfast between them. Rawdon muttered some
excuses about an engagement, squeezing hard the timid
little hand which his sister-in-law reached out to him.
Her imploring eyes could read nothing but calamity in
his face ; but he went away without another word. Nor
did Sir Pitt vouchsafe her any explanation. The children
came up to salute him, and he kissed them in his usual
frigid manner. The mother took both of them close to
herself, and held a hand of each of them as they knelt down
to prayers, which Sir Pitt read to them, and to the servants
in their Sunday suits or liveries, ranged upon chairs on the
other side of the hissing tea-urn. Breakfast was so late
that day, in consequence of the delays which had occurred,
that the church bells began to ring whilst they were sitting
over their meal : and Lady Jane was too ill, she said, to
go to church, though her thoughts had been entirely astray
during the period of family devotion.

Rawdon Crawley meanwhile hurried on from Great
Gaunt Street, and knocking at the great bronze Medusa's
head which stands on the portal of Gaunt House, brought
out the purple Silenus in a red and silver waistcoat, who
acts as porter of that palace. The man was scared also
by the colonel's dishevelled appearance, and barred the
way as if afraid that the other was going to force it. But
Colonel Crawley only took out a card and enjoined him
particularly to send it in to Lord Steyne, and to mark the
address written on it, and say that Colonel Crawley would
be all day after one o'clock at the Regent Club in St. James's
Street—not at home. The fat red-faced man looked after

him with astonishment as he strode away; so did the
people in their Sunday clothes who were out so early;
the charity boys with shining faces, the greengrocer lolling
at his door, and the publican shutting his shutters in the
sunshine, against service commenced. The people joked
at the cabstand about his appearance, as he took a carriage
there, and told the driver to drive him to Knightsbridge
Barracks.

All the bells were jangling and tolling as he reached that
place. He might have seen his old acquaintance Amelia
on her way from Brompton to Russell Square had he been
looking out. Troops of schools were on their march to
church, the shiny pavement and outsides of coaches in the
suburbs were thronged with people out upon their Sunday
pleasure; but the colonel was much too busy to take any
heed of these phenomena, and, arriving at Knightsbridge,
speedily made his way up to the room of his old friend and
comrade Captain Macmurdo, who Crawley found, to his
satisfaction, was in barracks.

Captain Macmurdo, a veteran officer and Waterloo man,
greatly liked by his regiment, in which want of money
alone prevented him from attaining the highest ranks,
was enjoying the forenoon calmly in bed. He had been
at a fast supper-party, given the night before by Captain
the Honourable George Cinqbars, at his house in Brompton
Square, to several young men of the regiment, and a number
of ladies of the *corps de ballet*, and old Mac, who was at
home with people of all ages and ranks, and consorted
with generals, dog-fanciers, opera-dancers, bruisers, and
every kind of person, in a word, was resting himself after
the night's labours, and, not being on duty, was in bed.

His room was hung round with boxing, sporting, and
dancing pictures, presented to him by comrades as they
retired from the regiment, and married and settled into
quiet life. And as he was now nearly fifty years of age,
twenty-four of which he had passed in the corps, he had
a singular museum. He was one of the best shots in England,
and, for a heavy man, one of the best riders; indeed, he
and Crawley had been rivals when the latter was in the
army. To be brief, Mr. Macmurdo was lying in bed,
reading in *Bell's Life* an account of that very fight between
the Tutbury Pet and the Barking Butcher, which has been
before mentioned—a venerable bristly warrior, with a little

close-shaved grey head, with a silk nightcap, a red face
and nose, and a great dyed moustache.

When Rawdon told the captain he wanted a friend, the
latter knew perfectly well on what duty of friendship he
was called to act, and indeed had conducted scores of
affairs for his acquaintances with the greatest prudence and
skill. His Royal Highness the late lamented Commander-
in-chief* had had the greatest regard for Macmurdo on

this account; and he was the common refuge of gentlemen
in trouble.

'What's the row about, Crawley, my boy?' said the
old warrior. 'No more gambling business, hey, like that
when we shot Captain Marker?'

'It's about—about my wife,' Crawley answered, casting
down his eyes and turning very red.

The other gave a whistle. 'I always said she'd throw
you over,' he began:—indeed there were bets in the regi-

ment and at the clubs regarding the probable fate of
Colonel Crawley, so lightly was his wife's character esteemed
by his comrades and the world ; but seeing the savage look
with which Rawdon answered the expression of this opinion,
Macmurdo did not think fit to enlarge upon it further.

'Is there no way out of it, old boy ?' the captain continued in a grave tone. 'Is it only suspicion, you know,
or—or what is it ? Any letters ? Can't you keep it quiet ?
Best not make any noise about a thing of that sort if you
can help it.' 'Think of his only finding her out now,' the
captain thought to himself, and remembered a hundred
particular conversations at the mess-table, in which Mrs.
Crawley's reputation had been torn to shreds.

'There's no way but one out of it,' Rawdon replied—
'and there's only a way out of it for one of us, Mac—do
you understand ? I was put out of the way : arrested :
I found 'em alone together. I told him he was a liar and
a coward, and knocked him down and thrashed him.'

'Serve him right,' Macmurdo said. 'Who is it ?'

Rawdon answered it was Lord Steyne.

'The deuce ! a marquis ! they said he—that is, they
said you ——'

'What the devil do you mean ?' roared out Rawdon ;
'do you mean that you ever heard a fellow doubt about my
wife, and didn't tell me, Mac ?'

'The world's very censorious, old boy,' the other replied.
'What the deuce was the good of my telling you what any
tom-fools talked about ?'

'It was damned unfriendly, Mac,' said Rawdon, quite
overcome ; and, covering his face with his hands, he gave
way to an emotion, the sight of which caused the tough
old campaigner opposite him to wince with sympathy.
'Hold up, old boy,' he said ; 'great man or not, we'll put
a bullet in him, damn him. As for women, they're all so.'

'You don't know how fond I was of that one,' Rawdon
said, half inarticulately. 'Damme, I followed her like
a footman. I gave up everything I had to her. I'm a
beggar because I would marry her. By Jove, sir, I've
pawned my own watch in order to get her anything she
fancied : and she—she's been making a purse for herself
all the time, and grudged me a hundred pound to get me
out of quod.' He then, fiercely and incoherently, and with
an agitation under which his counsellor had never before

seen him labour, told Macmurdo the circumstances of the story. His adviser caught at some stray hints in it.

'She may be innocent, after all,' he said. 'She says so. Steyne has been a hundred times alone with her in the house before.'

'It may be so,' Rawdon answered, sadly; 'but this don't look very innocent : ' and he showed the captain the thousand-pound note which he had found in Becky's pocket-book. 'This is what he gave her, Mac : and she kep it unknown to me : and with this money in the house, she refused to stand by me when I was locked up.' The captain could not but own that the secreting of the money had a very ugly look.

Whilst they were engaged in their conference, Rawdon dispatched Captain Macmurdo's servant to Curzon Street, with an order to the domestic there to give up a bag of clothes of which the colonel had great need. And during the man's absence, and with great labour and a Johnson's Dictionary, which stood them in much stead, Rawdon and his second composed a letter, which the latter was to send to Lord Steyne. Captain Macmurdo had the honour of waiting upon the Marquis of Steyne, on the part of Colonel Rawdon Crawley, and begged to intimate that he was empowered by the colonel to make any arrangements for the meeting which, he had no doubt, it was his lordship's intention to demand, and which the circumstances of the morning had rendered inevitable. Captain Macmurdo begged Lord Steyne, in the most polite manner, to appoint a friend, with whom he (Captain M'M.) might communicate, and desired that the meeting might take place with as little delay as possible.

In a postscript the captain stated that he had in his possession a bank-note for a large amount, which Colonel Crawley had reason to suppose was the property of the Marquis of Steyne. And he was anxious, on the colonel's behalf, to give up the note to its owner.

By the time this note was composed, the captain's servant returned from his mission to Colonel Crawley's house in Curzon Street, but without the carpet-bag and portmanteau, for which he had been sent ; and with a very puzzled and odd face.

'They won't give 'em up,' said the man ; 'there's a regular shinty in the house ; and everything at sixes and

sevens. The landlord's come in and took possession. The
servants was a-drinkin' up in the drawing-room. They
said—they said you had gone off with the plate, colonel,'—
the man added after a pause :—' One of the servants is
off already. And Simpson, the man as was very noisy and
drunk indeed, says nothing shall go out of the house until
his wages is paid up.'

The account of this little revolution in May Fair
astonished and gave a little gaiety to an otherwise very
triste conversation. The two officers laughed at Rawdon's
discomfiture.

' I'm glad the little 'un isn't at home,' Rawdon said,
biting his nails. ' You remember him, Mac, don't you,
in the Riding School ? How he sat the kicker to be sure !
didn't he ? '

' That he did, old boy,' said the good-natured captain.

Little Rawdon was then sitting, one of fifty gown-
boys, in the chapel of Whitefriars School : thinking, not
about the sermon, but about going home next Saturday,
when his father would certainly tip him, and perhaps
would take him to the play.

' He's a regular trump, that boy,' the father went on,
still musing about his son. ' I say, Mac, if anything goes
wrong—if I drop—I should like you to—to go and see him,
you know : and say that I was very fond of him, and that.
And—dash it—old chap, give him these gold sleeve-buttons :
it's all I've got.' He covered his face with his black hands ;
over which the tears rolled and made furrows of white.
Mr. Macmurdo had also occasion to take off his silk nightcap and rub it across his eyes.

' Go down and order some breakfast,' he said to his man
in a loud cheerful voice.—' What'll you have, Crawley ?
Some devilled kidneys and a herring—let's say—And, Clay,
lay out some dressing things for the colonel : we were
always pretty much of a size, Rawdon, my boy, and neither
of us ride so light as we did when we first entered the corps.'
With which, and leaving the colonel to dress himself,
Macmurdo turned round towards the wall, and resumed
the perusal of *Bell's Life*, until such time as his friend's
toilette was complete, and he was at liberty to commence
his own.

This, as he was about to meet a lord, Captain Macmurdo
performed with particular care. He waxed his moustachios

into a state of brilliant polish, and put on a tight cravat
and a trim buff waistcoat : so that all the young officers
in the mess-room, whither Crawley had preceded his friend,
complimented Mac on his appearance at breakfast, and
asked if he was going to be married that Sunday ?

CHAPTER LV

IN WHICH THE SAME SUBJECT IS PURSUED

ECKY did not rally from the
state of stupor and confusion
in which the events of the
previous night had plunged
her intrepid spirit, until the
bells of the Curzon Street
chapels*were ringing for afternoon service, and rising from
her bed she began to ply her
own bell, in order to summon
the French maid who had left
her some hours before.

Mrs. Rawdon Crawley rang
many times in vain ; and
though, on the last occasion,
she rang with such vehemence
as to pull down the bell-rope, Mademoiselle Fifine did not
make her appearance,—no, not though her mistress, in
a great pet, and with the bell-rope in her hand, came out
to the landing-place with her hair over her shoulders, and
screamed out repeatedly for her attendant.

The truth is, she had quitted the premises for many hours,
and upon that permission which is called French leave
among us. After picking up the trinkets in the drawing-
room, Mademoiselle had ascended to her own apartments,
packed and corded her own boxes there, tripped out and
called a cab for herself, brought down her trunks with her
own hand, and without ever so much as asking the aid of
any of the other servants, who would probably have refused
it, as they hated her cordially, and without wishing any one
of them good-bye, had made her exit from Curzon Street.

The game, in her opinion, was over in that little domestic establishment. Fifine went off in a cab, as we have known more exalted persons of her nation* to do under similar circumstances : but, more provident or lucky than these, she secured not only her own property, but some of her mistress's (if indeed that lady could be said to have any property at all)—and not only carried off the trinkets before alluded to, and some favourite dresses on which she had long kept her eye, but four richly gilt Louis Quatorze candlesticks, six gilt Albums, *Keepsakes*, and *Books of Beauty*, a gold enamelled snuff-box which had once belonged to Madame du Barri,* and the sweetest little inkstand and mother-of-pearl blotting-book, which Becky used when she composed her charming little pink notes, had vanished from the premises in Curzon Street together with Mademoiselle Fifine, and all the silver laid on the table for the little *festin* which Rawdon interrupted. The plated ware Mademoiselle left behind her was too cumbrous probably, for which reason, no doubt, she also left the fire-irons, the chimney-glasses, and the rosewood cottage piano.

A lady very like her subsequently kept a milliner's shop in the Rue du Helder at Paris, where she lived with great credit and enjoyed the patronage of my Lord Steyne. This person always spoke of England as of the most treacherous country in the world, and stated to her young pupils that she had been *affreusement volé* by natives of that island. It was no doubt compassion for her misfortunes which induced the Marquis of Steyne to be so very kind to Madame de Saint-Amaranthe. May she flourish as she deserves,—she appears no more in our quarter of Vanity Fair.

Hearing a buzz and a stir below, and indignant at the impudence of those servants who would not answer her summons, Mrs. Crawley flung her morning robe round her, and descended majestically to the drawing-room, whence the noise proceeded.

The cook was there with blackened face, seated on the beautiful chintz sofa by the side of Mrs. Raggles, to whom she was administering maraschino. The page with the sugar-loaf buttons, who carried about Becky's pink notes, and jumped about her little carriage with such alacrity, was now engaged putting his fingers into a cream dish ; the footman was talking to Raggles, who had a face full

of perplexity and woe—and yet, though the door was open,
and Becky had been screaming a half-dozen of times a few
feet off, not one of her attendants had obeyed her call.
' Have a little drop, do'ee now, Mrs. Raggles,' the cook was
saying as Becky entered, the white cashmere dressing-gown
flouncing around her.

' Simpson ! Trotter ! ' the mistress of the house cried
in great wrath. ' How dare you stay here when you heard
me call ? How dare you sit down in my presence ?
Where's my maid ? ' The page withdrew his fingers from
his mouth with a momentary terror : but the cook took
off a glass of maraschino, of which Mrs. Raggles had had
enough, staring at Becky over the little gilt glass as she
drained its contents. The liquor appeared to give the
odious rebel courage.

' *Your* sofy, indeed ! ' Mrs. Cook said. ' I'm a-settin'
on Mrs. Raggles's sofy. Don't you stir, Mrs. Raggles,
mum. I'm a-settin' on Mr. and Mrs. Raggles's sofy, which
they bought with honest money, and very dear it cost 'em,
too. And I'm thinkin' if I set here until I'm paid my wages,
I shall set a precious long time, Mrs. Raggles ; and set
I will, too—ha ! ha ! ' and with this she filled herself
another glass of the liquor, and drank it with a more
hideously satirical air.

' Trotter ! Simpson ! turn that drunken wretch out,'
screamed Mrs. Crawley.

' I shawn't,' said Trotter the footman ; ' turn out yourself. Pay our selleries, and turn me out too. *We'll* go
fast enough.'

' Are you all here to insult me ? ' cried Becky, in a fury ;
' when Colonel Crawley comes home I'll——'

At this the servants burst into a hoarse haw-haw, in
which, however, Raggles, who still kept a most melancholy
countenance, did not join. ' He ain't a-coming back,'
Mr. Trotter resumed. ' He sent for his things, and I
wouldn' let 'em go, although Mr. Raggles would : and I
don't b'lieve he's no more a colonel than I am. He's hoff :
and I suppose you're a-goin' after him. You're no better
than swindlers, both on you. Don't be a-bullyin' *me*.
I won't stand it. Pay us our selleries, I say. Pay us our
selleries.' It was evident, from Mr. Trotter's flushed
countenance and defective intonation, that he, too, had had
recourse to vinous stimulus.

'Mr. Raggles,' said Becky, in a passion of vexation, 'you will not surely let me be insulted by that drunken man?'
'Hold your noise. Trotter; do now,' said Simpson the page. He was affected by his mistress's deplorable situation, and succeeded in preventing an outrageous denial of the epithet 'drunken' on the footman's part.

'Oh, mam,' said Raggles, 'I never thought to live to see this year day. I've known the Crawley family ever since I was born. I lived butler with Miss Crawley for thirty years; and I little thought one of that family was a-goin' to ruing me—yes, ruing me'—said the poor fellow with tears in his eyes. 'Har you a-goin' to pay me? You've lived in this 'ouse four year.* You've 'ad my substance: my plate and linning. You ho me a milk and butter bill of two 'undred pound, you must 'ave noo laid heggs for your homlets, and cream for your spanil dog.'

'She didn't care what her own flesh and blood had,' interposed the cook. 'Many's the time, he'd have starved but for me.'

'He's a charaty boy now, cooky,' said Mr. Trotter, with a drunken 'ha! ha!'—and honest Raggles continued, in a lamentable tone, an enumeration of his griefs. All he said was true. Becky and her husband had ruined him. He had bills coming due next week and no means to meet them. He would be sold up and turned out of his shop and his house, because he had trusted to the Crawley family. His tears and lamentations made Becky more peevish than ever.

'You all seem to be against me,' she said, bitterly. 'What do you want? I can't pay you on Sunday. Come back to-morrow and I'll pay you everything. I thought Colonel Crawley had settled with you. He will to-morrow. I declare to you upon my honour that he left home this morning with fifteen hundred pounds in his pocket-book. He has left me nothing. Apply to him. Give me a bonnet and shawl and let me go out and find him. There was a difference between us this morning. You all seem to know it. I promise you upon my word that you shall all be paid. He has got a good appointment. Let me go out and find him.'

This audacious statement caused Raggles and the other personages present to look at one another with a wild surprise, and with it Rebecca left them. She went upstairs and dressed herself this time without the aid of her French maid. She went into Rawdon's room, and there saw that a trunk and bag were packed ready for removal, with a pencil direction that they should be given when called for ; then she went into the Frenchwoman's garret ; everything was clean, and all the drawers emptied there. She bethought herself of the trinkets which had been left on the ground, and felt certain that the woman had fled. ' Good Heavens ! was ever such ill luck as mine ? ' she said ; ' to be so near, and to lose all. Is it all too late ? No ; there was one chance more.'

She dressed herself, and went away unmolested this time, but alone. It was four o'clock. She went swiftly down the streets (she had no money to pay for a carriage), and never stopped until she came to Sir Pitt Crawley's door, in Great Gaunt Street. Where was Lady Jane Crawley ? She was at church. Becky was not sorry. Sir Pitt was in his study, and had given orders not to be disturbed—she must see him—she slipped by the sentinel in livery at once, and was in Sir Pitt's room before the astonished baronet had even laid down the paper.

He turned red and started back from her with a look of great alarm and horror.

' Do not look so,' she said. ' I am not guilty, Pitt, dear Pitt ; you were my friend once. Before God, I am not guilty. I seem so. Everything is against me. And oh ! at such a moment ! just when all my hopes were about to be realized : just when happiness was in store for us.'

' Is this true, what I see in the paper, then ? ' Sir Pitt said—a paragraph in which had greatly surprised him.

' It is true. Lord Steyne told me on Friday night, the night of that fatal ball. He has been promised an appoint- ment any time these six months. Mr. Martyr, the Colonial Secretary, told him yesterday that it was made out. That unlucky arrest ensued ; that horrible meeting. I was only guilty of too much devotedness to Rawdon's service. I have received Lord Steyne alone a hundred times before. I confess I had money of which Rawdon knew nothing. Don't you know how careless he is of it, and could I dare to confide it to him ? ' And so she went on with a perfectly connected story, which she poured into the ears of her perplexed kinsman.

It was to the following effect. Becky owned, and with

perfect frankness, but deep contrition, that having remarked
Lord Steyne's partiality for her (at the mention of which
Pitt blushed), and being secure of her own virtue, she had
determined to turn the great peer's attachment to the
advantage of herself and her family. ' I looked for a
peerage for you, Pitt,' she said (the brother-in-law again
turned red). ' We have talked about it. Your genius and
Lord Steyne's interest made it more than probable, had not
this dreadful calamity come to put an end to all our hopes.
But, first, I own that it was my object to rescue my dear
husband,—him whom I love in spite of all his ill usage and
suspicions of me,—to remove him from the poverty and
ruin which was impending over us. I saw Lord Steyne's
partiality for me,' she said, casting down her eyes. ' I own
that I did every thing in my power to make myself pleasing
to him, and as far as an honest woman may, to secure his—
his esteem. It was only on Friday morning that the news
arrived of the death of the governor of Coventry Island, and
my lord instantly secured the appointment for my dear
husband. It was intended as a surprise for him,—he was to
see it in the papers to-day. Even after that horrid arrest
took place (the expenses of which Lord Steyne generously
said he would settle, so that I was in a manner prevented from
coming to my husband's assistance), my lord was laughing
with me, and saying that my dearest Rawdon would be
consoled when he read of his appointment in the paper, in
that shocking spun—bailiff's house. And then—then he
came home. His suspicions were excited,—the dreadful
scene took place between my lord and my cruel, cruel
Rawdon,—and, oh, my God, what will happen next ? Pitt,
dear Pitt ! pity me, and reconcile us ! ' And as she spoke
she flung herself down on her knees, and bursting into tears,
seized hold of Pitt's hand, which she kissed passionately.

It was in this very attitude that Lady Jane, who, returning from church, ran to her husband's room directly she
heard Mrs. Rawdon Crawley was closeted there, found the
baronet and his sister-in-law.

' I am surprised that woman has the audacity to enter
this house,' Lady Jane said, trembling in every limb, and
turning quite pale. (Her ladyship had sent out her maid
directly after breakfast, who had communicated with
Raggles and Rawdon Crawley's household, who had told
her all, and a great deal more than they knew, of that

story, and many others besides). 'How dare Mrs. Crawley
to enter the house of—of an honest family?'

Sir Pitt started back, amazed at his wife's display of
vigour. Becky still kept her kneeling posture, and clung
to Sir Pitt's hand.

'Tell her that she does not know all. Tell her that I am
innocent, dear Pitt,' she whimpered out.

'Upon my word, my love, I think you do Mrs. Crawley

injustice,' Sir Pitt said; at which speech Rebecca was vastly
relieved. 'Indeed I believe her to be——'

'To be what?' cried out Lady Jane, her clear voice
thrilling, and her heart beating violently as she spoke.
'To be a wicked woman—a heartless mother, a false wife?
She never loved her dear little boy, who used to fly here
and tell me of her cruelty to him. She never came into
a family but she strove to bring misery with her, and to
weaken the most sacred affections with her wicked flattery
and falsehoods. She has deceived her husband, as she has
deceived everybody; her soul is black with vanity, worldliness, and all sorts of crime. I tremble when I touch her.
I keep my children out of her sight. I——'

'Lady Jane!' cried Sir Pitt, starting up, 'this is really
language——'

'I have been a true and faithful wife to you, Sir Pitt,' Lady Jane continued, intrepidly; 'I have kept my marriage vow as I made it to God, and have been obedient and gentle as a wife should. But righteous obedience has its limits, and I declare that I will not bear that—that woman again under my roof : if she enters it, I and my children will leave it. She is not worthy to sit down with Christian people. You—you must choose, sir, between her and me ; ' and with this my lady swept out of the room, fluttering with her own audacity, and leaving Rebecca and Sir Pitt not a little astonished at it.

As for Becky, she was not hurt ; nay, she was pleased. 'It was the diamond clasp you gave me,' she said to Sir Pitt, reaching him out her hand ; and before she left him (for which event you may be sure my Lady Jane was looking out from her dressing-room window in the upper story) the baronet had promised to go and seek out his brother, and endeavour to bring about a reconciliation.

Rawdon found some of the young fellows of the regiment seated in the mess-room at breakfast, and was induced without much difficulty to partake of that meal, and of the devilled legs of fowls and soda-water with which these young gentlemen fortified themselves. Then they had a conversation befitting the day and their time of life : about the next pigeon-match at Battersea, with relative bets upon Ross and Osbaldiston ;* about Mademoiselle Ariane of the French Opera, and who had left her, and how she was consoled by Panther Carr ; and about the fight between the Butcher and the Pet, and the probabilities that it was a cross. Young Tandyman, a hero of seventeen, laboriously endeavouring to get up a pair of moustachios, had seen the fight, and spoke in the most scientific manner about the battle, and the condition of the men. It was he who had driven the Butcher on to the ground in his drag, and passed the whole of the previous night with him. Had there not been foul play he must have won it. All the old files of the Ring*were in it : and Tandyman wouldn't pay; no, dammy, he wouldn't pay. It was but a year since the young cornet, now so knowing a hand in Cribb's parlour, had a still lingering liking for toffy, and used to be birched at Eton.

So they went on talking about dancers, fights, drinking,

demireps, until Macmurdo came down and joined the
boys and the conversation. He did not appear to think
that any especial reverence was due to their boyhood ; the
old fellow cut in with stories, to the full as choice as any
the youngest rake present had to tell ;—nor did his own
grey hairs, nor their smooth faces detain him. Old Mac
was famous for his good stories. He was not exactly a
lady's man ; that is, men asked him to dine rather at the
houses of their mistresses than of their mothers. There
can scarcely be a life lower, perhaps, than his ; but he was
quite contented with it, such as it was, and led it in perfect
good nature, simplicity, and modesty of demeanour.

By the time Mac had finished a copious breakfast, most
of the others had concluded their meal. Young Lord
Varinas was smoking an immense meerschaum pipe, while
Captain Hugues was employed with a cigar : that violent
little devil Tandyman, with his little bull-terrier between his
legs, was tossing for shillings with all his might (that fellow
was always at some game or other) against Captain Deuceace ; and Mac and Rawdon walked off to the club, neither,
of course, having given any hint of the business which was
occupying their minds. Both, on the other hand, had joined
pretty gaily in the conversation ; as, why should they
interrupt it ? Feasting, drinking, ribaldry, laughter, go on
alongside of all sorts of other occupations in Vanity Fair,—
the crowds were pouring out of church as Rawdon and his
friend passed down St. James's Street and entered into
their club.

The old bucks and *habitués*, who ordinarily stand gaping
and grinning out of the great front window of the club,
had not arrived at their posts as yet,—the newspaper-room
was almost empty. One man was present whom Rawdon
did not know ; another to whom he owed a little score for
whist, and whom, in consequence, he did not care to meet ;
a third was reading the *Royalist*(a periodical famous for
its scandal and its attachment to Church and King) Sunday
paper at the table, and, looking up at Crawley with some
interest, said, ' Crawley, I congratulate you.'

' What do you mean ? ' said the colonel.

' It's in the *Observer* and the *Royalist* too,' said Mr. Smith.

' What ? ' Rawdon cried, turning very red. He thought
that the affair with Lord Steyne was already in the public
prints. Smith looked up wondering and smiling at the

agitation which the colonel exhibited as he took up the
paper, and, trembling, began to read.

Mr. Smith and Mr. Brown (the gentleman with whom
Rawdon had the outstanding whist account) had been talking about the colonel just before he came in.

' It is come just in the nick of time,' said Smith.   ' I suppose Crawley had not a shilling in the world.'

' It's a wind that blows everybody good,' Mr. Brown said.
' He can't go away without paying me a pony*he owes me.'

' What's the salary ? ' asked Smith.

' Two or three thousand,' answered the other.   ' But the
climate's so infernal, they don't enjoy it long.   Liverseege
died after eighteen months of it : and the man before went
off in six weeks, I hear.'

' Some people say his brother is a very clever man.
I always found him a d—— bore,' Smith ejaculated.   ' He
must have good interest, though.   He must have got the
colonel the place.'

' He ! ' said Brown, with a sneer.—' Pooh.—It was Lord
Steyne got it.'

' How do you mean ? '

' A virtuous woman is a crown to her husband,' answered
the other, enigmatically, and went to read his papers.

Rawdon, for his part, read in the *Royalist* the following
astonishing paragraph :—

GOVERNORSHIP OF COVENTRY ISLAND.—H.M.S. *Yellowjack*, Commander Jaunders, has brought letters and papers from Coventry
Island.   H.E. Sir Thomas Liverseege had fallen a victim to the
prevailing fever at Swamptown.   His loss is deeply felt in the
flourishing colony.   We hear that the Governorship has been offered
to Colonel Rawdon Crawley, C.B., a distinguished Waterloo officer.
We need not only men of acknowledged bravery, but men of administrative talents to superintend the affairs of our colonies ;
and we have no doubt that the gentleman selected by the Colonial
Office to fill the lamented vacancy which has occurred at Coventry
Island is admirably calculated for the post which he is about to
occupy.

' Coventry Island ! where was it ? who had appointed
him to the government ? You must take me out as your
secretary, old boy,' Captain Macmurdo said, laughing ; and
as Crawley and his friend sat wondering and perplexed
over the announcement, the club waiter brought in to the

colonel a card, on which the name of Mr. Wenham was engraved, who begged to see Colonel Crawley.

The colonel and his aide de camp went out to meet the gentleman, rightly conjecturing that he was an emissary of Lord Steyne. 'How d'ye do, Crawley? I am glad to see you,' said Mr. Wenham, with a bland smile, and grasping Crawley's hand with great cordiality.

'You come, I suppose, from——'

'Exactly,' said Mr. Wenham.

'Then this is my friend Captain Macmurdo of the Life Guards Green.'

'Delighted to know Captain Macmurdo, I'm sure,' Mr. Wenham said, and tendered another smile and shake of the hand to the second, as he had done to the principal. Mac put out one finger, armed with a buckskin glove, and made a very frigid bow to Mr. Wenham over his tight cravat. He was, perhaps, discontented at being put in communication with a *pékin*, and thought that Lord Steyne should have sent him a colonel at the very least.

'As Macmurdo acts for me, and knows what I mean,' Crawley said, 'I had better retire and leave you together.'

'Of course,' said Macmurdo.

'By no means, my dear colonel,' Mr. Wenham said; 'the interview which I had the honour of requesting was with you personally, though the company of Captain Macmurdo cannot fail to be also most pleasing. In fact, captain, I hope that our conversation will lead to none but the most agreeable results, very different from those which my friend Colonel Crawley appears to anticipate.'

'Humph!' said Captain Macmurdo. Be hanged to these civilians, he thought to himself, they are always for arranging and speechifying. Mr. Wenham took a chair which was not offered to him—took a paper from his pocket, and resumed:—

'You have seen this gratifying announcement in the papers this morning, colonel? Government has secured a most valuable servant, and you, if you accept office, as I presume you will, an excellent appointment. Three thousand a year, delightful climate, excellent government-house, all your own way in the colony, and a certain promotion. I congratulate you with all my heart. I presume you know, gentlemen, to whom my friend is indebted for this piece of patronage?'

'Hanged if I know,' the captain said : his principal turned very red.

'To one of the most generous and kindest men in the world, as he is one of the greatest—to my excellent friend, the Marquis of Steyne.'

'I'll see him d—— before I take his place,' growled out Rawdon.

'You are irritated against my noble friend,' Mr. Wenham calmly resumed : 'and now, in the name of common sense and justice, tell me why ? '

'*Why ?* ' cried Rawdon, in surprise.

'Why ? Dammy ! ' said the captain, ringing his stick on the ground.

'Dammy, indeed,' said Mr. Wenham, with the most agreeable smile ; 'still look at the matter as a man of the world—as an honest man, and see if you have not been in the wrong. You come home from a journey, and find—what ?—my Lord Steyne supping at your house in Curzon Street with Mrs. Crawley. Is the circumstance strange or novel ? Has he not been a hundred times before in the same position ? Upon my honour and word as a gentleman ' (Mr. Wenham here put his hand on his waistcoat, with a parliamentary air), 'I declare I think that your suspicions are monstrous and utterly unfounded, and that they injure an honourable gentleman who has proved his goodwill towards you by a thousand benefactions—and a most spotless and innocent lady.'

'You don't mean to say that—that Crawley's mistaken ? ' said Mr. Macmurdo.

'I believe that Mrs. Crawley is as innocent as my wife, Mrs. Wenham,' Mr. Wenham said, with great energy. 'I believe that, misled by an infernal jealousy, my friend here strikes a blow against not only an infirm and old man of high station, his constant friend and benefactor, but against his wife, his own dearest honour, his son's future reputation, and his own prospects in life.

'I will tell you what happened,' Mr. Wenham continued, with great solemnity ; 'I was sent for this morning by my Lord Steyne, and found him in a pitiable state, as, I need hardly inform Colonel Crawley, any man of age and infirmity would be after a personal conflict with a man of your strength. I say to your face ; it was a cruel advantage you took of that strength, Colonel Crawley. It was not only

the body of my noble and excellent friend which was
wounded—his heart, sir, was bleeding. A man whom he
had loaded with benefits and regarded with affection, had
subjected him to the foulest indignity. What was this very
appointment, which appears in the journals of to-day, but
a proof of his kindness to you ? When I saw his lordship
this morning I found him in a state pitiable indeed to see :
and as anxious as you are to revenge the outrage committed
upon him, by blood. You know he has given his proofs,
I presume, Colonel Crawley ? '

' He has plenty of pluck,' said the colonel. ' Nobody
ever said he hadn't.'

' His first order to me was to write a letter of challenge,
and to carry it to Colonel Crawley. One or other of you,
he said, must not survive the outrage of last night.'

Crawley nodded. ' You're coming to the point, Wenham,'
he said.

' I tried my utmost to calm Lord Steyne. " Good God !
sir," I said, " how I regret that Mrs. Wenham and myself
had not accepted Mrs. Crawley's invitation to sup with
her ! " '

' She asked you to sup with her ? ' Captain Macmurdo
said.

' After the Opera. Here's the note of invitation—stop—
no, this is another paper—I thought I had it, but it's of no
consequence, and I pledge you my word to the fact. If we
had come, and it was only one of Mrs. Wenham's headaches
which prevented us—she suffers under them a good deal,
especially in the spring—if we had come, and you had
returned home, there would have been no quarrel, no insult,
no suspicion—and so it is positively because my poor wife
has a headache that you are to bring death down upon two
men of honour, and plunge two of the most excellent and
ancient families in the kingdom into disgrace and sorrow.'

Mr. Macmurdo looked at his principal with the air of a
man profoundly puzzled ; and Rawdon felt with a kind of
rage that his prey was escaping him. He did not believe
a word of the story, and yet, how discredit or disprove it ?

Mr. Wenham continued with the same fluent oratory,
which in his place in Parliament he had so often practised—
' I sat for an hour or more by Lord Steyne's bedside,
beseeching, imploring Lord Steyne to forgo his intention
of demanding a meeting. I pointed out to him that the

circumstances were after all suspicious—they were suspicious. I acknowledge it, any man in your position might
have been taken in—I said that a man furious with jealousy
is to all intents and purposes a madman, and should be as
such regarded—that a duel between you must lead to the
disgrace of all parties concerned—that a man of his lordship's exalted station had no right in these days, when the
most atrocious revolutionary principles, and the most
dangerous levelling doctrines are preached among the
vulgar, to create a public scandal ; and that, however
innocent, the common people would insist that he was
guilty. In fine, I implored him not to send the challenge.'

'I don't believe one word of the whole story,' said
Rawdon, grinding his teeth. 'I believe it a d—— lie, and
that you're in it, Mr. Wenham. If the challenge don't
come from him, by Jove it shall come from me.'

Mr. Wenham turned deadly pale at this savage interruption of the colonel, and looked towards the door.

But he found a champion in Captain Macmurdo. That
gentleman rose up with an oath, and rebuked Rawdon for
his language. 'You put the affair into my hands, and you
shall act as I think fit, by Jove, and not as you do. You
have no right to insult Mr. Wenham with this sort of language ; and dammy, Mr. Wenham, you deserve an apology.
And as for a challenge to Lord Steyne, you may get somebody else to carry it, I won't. If my lord, after being
thrashed, chooses to sit still, dammy let him. And as for
the affair with—with Mrs. Crawley, my belief is, there's
nothing proved at all : that your wife's innocent, as innocent
as Mr. Wenham says she is : and at any rate, that you
would be a d—— fool not to take the place and hold your
tongue.'

'Captain Macmurdo, you speak like a man of sense,'
Mr. Wenham cried out, immensely relieved—'I forget any
words that Colonel Crawley has used in the irritation of the
moment.'

'I thought you would,' Rawdon said, with a sneer.

'Shut your mouth, you old stoopid,' the captain said,
good-naturedly. 'Mr. Wenham ain't a fighting man ; and
quite right, too.'

'This matter, in my belief,' the Steyne emissary cried,
'ought to be buried in the most profound oblivion. A word
concerning it should never pass these doors. I speak in

the interest of my friend, as well as of Colonel Crawley, who
persists in considering me his enemy.'

' I suppose Lord Steyne won't talk about it very much,'
said Captain Macmurdo ; ' and I don't see why our side
should. The affair ain't a very pretty one, any way you
take it ; and the less said about it the better. It's you are
thrashed, and not us ; and if you are satisfied, why, I think,
we should be.'

Mr. Wenham took his hat, upon this, and Captain Macmurdo following him to the door, shut it upon himself and
Lord Steyne's agent, leaving Rawdon chafing within.
When the two were on the other side, Macmurdo looked
hard at the other ambassador, and with an expression of
anything but respect on his round jolly face.

' You don't stick at a trifle, Mr. Wenham,' he said.

' You flatter me, Captain Macmurdo,' answered the other,
with a smile. ' Upon my honour and conscience, now,
Mrs. Crawley did ask us to sup after the Opera.'

' Of course ; and Mrs. Wenham had one of her headaches.
I say, I've got a thousand-pound note here, which I will
give you if you will give me a receipt, please ; and I will
put the note up in an envelope for Lord Steyne. My man
shan't fight him. But we had rather not take his money.'

' It was all a mistake,—all a mistake, my dear sir,' the
other said, with the utmost innocence of manner ; and was
bowed down the club steps by Captain Macmurdo, just as
Sir Pitt Crawley ascended them. There was a slight
acquaintance between these two gentlemen ; and the
captain, going back with the baronet to the room where the
latter's brother was, told Sir Pitt, in confidence, that he had
made the affair all right between Lord Steyne and the
colonel.

Sir Pitt was well pleased, of course, at this intelligence ;
and congratulated his brother warmly upon the peaceful
issue of the affair, making appropriate moral remarks upon
the evils of duelling, and the unsatisfactory nature of that
sort of settlement of disputes.

And after this preface, he tried with all his eloquence to
effect a reconciliation between Rawdon and his wife. He
recapitulated the statements which Becky had made,
pointed out the probabilities of their truth, and asserted
his own firm belief in her innocence.

But Rawdon would not hear of it. ' She has kep money

concealed from me these ten years,' he said. ' She swore, last night only, she had none from Steyne. She knew it was all up, directly I found it. If she's not guilty, Pitt, she's as bad as guilty ; and I'll never see her again,—never.' His head sank down on his chest as he spoke the words ; and he looked quite broken and sad.

' Poor old boy,' Macmurdo said, shaking his head.

Rawdon Crawley resisted for some time the idea of taking the place which had been procured for him by so odious a patron : and was also for removing the boy from the school where Lord Steyne's interest had placed him. He was induced, however, to acquiesce in these benefits by the entreaties of his brother and Macmurdo : but mainly by the latter pointing out to him what a fury Steyne would be in, to think that his enemy's fortune was made through his means.

When the Marquis of Steyne came abroad after his accident, the Colonial Secretary bowed up to him and congratulated himself and the Service upon having made so excellent an appointment. These congratulations were received with a degree of gratitude which may be imagined on the part of Lord Steyne.

The secret of the rencontre between him and Colonel Crawley was buried in the profoundest oblivion, as Wenham said ; that is by the seconds and the principals. But before that evening was over it was talked of at fifty dinner-tables in Vanity Fair. Little Cackleby himself went to seven evening parties, and told the story with comments and emendations at each place. How Mrs. Washington White revelled in it ! The Bishopess of Ealing was shocked beyond expression : the bishop went and wrote his name down in the visiting-book at Gaunt House that very day. Little Southdown was sorry : so you may be sure was his sister Lady Jane, very sorry. Lady Southdown wrote it off to her other daughter at the Cape of Good Hope. It was town-talk for at least three days, and was only kept out of the newspapers by the exertions of Mr. Wagg, acting upon a hint from Mr. Wenham.

The bailiffs and brokers seized upon poor Raggles ·in Curzon Street, and the late fair tenant of that poor little mansion was in the meanwhile—where ? Who cared ? Who asked after a day or two ? Was she guilty or not ? We all

know how charitable the world is, and how the verdict of
Vanity Fair goes when there is a doubt. Some people said
she had gone to Naples in pursuit of Lord Steyne; whilst
others averred that his lordship quitted that city, and
fled to Palermo on hearing of Becky's arrival; some said
she was living in Bierstadt, and had become a *dame d'honneur* to the Queen of Bulgaria; some that she was at
Boulogne; and others, at a boarding-house at Cheltenham.

Rawdon made her a tolerable annuity; and we may be
sure that she was a woman who could make a little money
go a great way, as the saying is. He would have paid his
debts on leaving England, could he have got any Insurance
Office to take his life; but the climate of Coventry Island
was so bad that he could borrow no money on the strength
of his annuity. He remitted, however, to his brother
punctually, and wrote to his little boy regularly every mail.
He kept Macmurdo in cigars; and sent over quantities of
shells, cayenne pepper, hot pickles, guava jelly, and colonial
produce to Lady Jane. He sent his brother home the
Swamp Town Gazette, in which the new governor was
praised with immense enthusiasm; whereas the *Swamp
Town Sentinel*, whose wife was not asked to Government
House, declared that his excellency was a tyrant, compared
to whom Nero was an enlightened philanthropist. Little
Rawdon used to like to get the papers and read about his
excellency.

His mother never made any movement to see the child.
He went home to his aunt for Sundays and holidays; he
soon knew every bird's-nest about Queen's Crawley, and
rode out with Sir Huddlestone's hounds, which he admired
so on his first well-remembered visit to Hampshire.

CHAPTER LVI

GEORGY IS MADE A GENTLEMAN

EORGY OSBORNE was now fairly established in his grandfather's mansion in Russell Square : occupant of his father's room in the house, and heir-apparent of all the splendours there. The good looks, gallant bearing, and gentlemanlike appearance of the boy won the grandsire's heart for him. Mr. Osborne was as proud of him as ever he had been of the elder George.

The child had many more luxuries and indulgences than had been awarded to his father. Osborne's commerce had prospered greatly of late years. His wealth and importance in the City had very much increased. He had been glad enough in former days to put the elder George to a good private school ; and a commission in the army for his son had been a source of no small pride to him : for little George and his future prospects the old man looked much higher. He would make a gentleman of the little chap, was Mr. Osborne's constant saying regarding little Georgy. He saw him in his mind's eye, a collegian, a Parliament-man,— a baronet, perhaps. The old man thought he would die contented if he could see his grandson in a fair way to such honours. He would have none but a tip-top college man to educate him,—none of your quacks and pretenders,—no, no. A few years before, he used to be savage, and inveigh against all parsons, scholars, and the like,—declaring that they were a pack of humbugs, and quacks, that weren't fit to get their living but by grinding Latin and Greek, and a set of supercilious dogs, that pretended to look down upon British merchants and gentlemen, who could buy up half

a hundred of 'em. He would mourn now, in a very solemn
manner, that his own education had been neglected, and
repeatedly point out, in pompous orations to Georgy, the
necessity and excellence of classical acquirements.

When they met at dinner the grandsire used to ask the
lad what he had been reading during the day, and was greatly
interested at the report the boy gave of his own studies :
pretending to understand little George when he spoke
regarding them. He made a hundred blunders, and showed
his ignorance many a time. It did not increase the respect
which the child had for his senior. A quick brain and a
better education elsewhere showed the boy very soon that
his grandsire was a dullard : and he began accordingly to
command him and to look down upon him ; for his previous
education, humble and contracted as it had been, had made
a much better gentleman of Georgy than any plans of his
grandfather could make him. He had been brought up by
a kind, weak, and tender woman, who had no pride about
anything, but about him, and whose heart was so pure and
whose bearing was so meek and humble, that she could not
but needs be a true lady. She busied herself in gentle
offices and quiet duties ; if she never said brilliant
things, she never spoke or thought unkind ones : guileless
and artless, loving and pure, indeed how could our poor
little Amelia be other than a real gentlewoman ?

Young Georgy lorded over this soft and yielding nature :
and the contrast of its simplicity and delicacy with the
coarse pomposity of the dull old man with whom he next
came in contact, made him lord over the latter too. If he
had been a prince royal he could not have been better
brought up to think well of himself.

Whilst his mother was yearning after him at home, and
I do believe every hour of the day, and during most hours
of the sad lonely nights, thinking of him, this young gentleman had a number of pleasures and consolations administered to him, which made him for his part bear the separation from Amelia very easily. Little boys who cry when
they are going to school—cry because they are going to
a very uncomfortable place. It is only a very few who
weep from sheer affection. When you think that the eyes
of your childhood dried at the sight of a piece of gingerbread, and that a plum-cake was a compensation for the
agony of parting with your mamma and sisters ; oh, my

friend and brother, you need not be too confident of your own fine feelings.

Well, then, Master George Osborne had every comfort and luxury that a wealthy and lavish old grandfather thought fit to provide. The coachman was instructed to purchase for him the handsomest pony which could be bought for money; and on this George was taught to ride, first at a riding-school, whence, after he had performed satisfactorily without stirrups, and over the leaping-bar, he was conducted through the New Road to Regent's Park, and then to Hyde Park, where he rode in state with Martin the coachman behind him. Old Osborne, who took matters more easily in the City now, where he left his affairs to his junior partners, would often ride out with Miss O. in the same fashionable direction. As little Georgy came cantering up with his dandified air, and his heels down, his grandfather would nudge the lad's aunt, and say, ' Look, Miss O.' And he would laugh, and his face would grow red with pleasure, as he nodded out of the window to the boy, as the groom saluted the carriage, and the footman saluted Master George.

Here too his aunt, Mrs. Frederick Bullock (whose chariot might daily be seen in the Ring, with bullocks *or* emblazoned on the panels and harness, and three pasty-faced little Bullocks, covered with cockades and feathers, staring from the windows),—Mrs. Frederick Bullock, I say, flung glances of the bitterest hatred at the little upstart as he rode by with his hand on his side and his hat on one ear, as proud as a lord.

Though he was scarcely eleven years of age, Master George wore straps and the most beautiful little boots like a man. He had gilt spurs and a gold-headed whip, and a fine pin in his handkerchief; and the neatest little kid gloves which Lamb's Conduit Street could furnish. His

mother had givèn him a couple of neck-cloths, and carefully
hemmed and made some little shirts for him ; but when her
Samuel came to see the widow, they were replaced by much
finer linen. He had little jewelled buttons in the lawn shirt-
fronts. Her humble presents had been put aside—I believe
Miss Osborne had given them to the coachman's boy. Amelia
tried to think she was pleased at the change. Indeed, she
was happy and charmed to see the boy looking so beautiful.

She had had a little black profile of him done for a shilling ;
and this was hung up by the side of another portrait over
her bed. One day the boy came on his accustomed visit,
galloping down the little street at Brompton, and bringing,
as usual, all the inhabitants to the windows to admire his
splendour, and with great eagerness, and a look of triumph
in his face, he pulled a case out of his great-coat—(it was
a natty white great-coat, with a cape and a velvet collar)—
pulled out a red morocco case, which he gave her.

' I bought it with my own money, mamma,' he said.
' I thought you'd like it.'

Amelia opened the case, and giving a little cry of delighted
affection, seized the boy and embraced him a hundred
times. It was a miniature of himself, very prettily done
(though not half handsome enough, we may be sure, the
widow thought). His grandfather had wished to have
a picture of him by an artist whose works, exhibited in
a shop-window, in Southampton Row, had caught the old
gentleman's eyes ; and George, who had plenty of money,
bethought him of asking the painter how much a copy
of the little portrait would cost, saying that he would pay
for it out of his own money, and that he wanted to give
it to his mother. The pleased painter executed the copy
for a small price ; and old Osborne himself, when he
heard of the incident, growled out his satisfaction, and
gave the boy twice as many sovereigns as he paid for the
miniature.

But what was the grandfather's pleasure compared to
Amelia's ecstasy ? That proof of the boy's affection
charmed her so, that she thought no child in the world
was like hers for goodness. For long weeks after, the
thought of his love made her happy. She slept better with
the picture under her pillow ; and how many, many times
did she kiss it, and weep and pray over it ! A small kindness from those she loved made that timid heart grateful.

Since her parting with George she had had no such joy and consolation.

At his new home Master George ruled like a lord : at dinner he invited the ladies to drink wine with the utmost coolness, and took off his champagne in a way which charmed his old grandfather. 'Look at him,' the old man would say, nudging his neighbour with a delighted purple face, 'did you ever see such a chap ? Lord, Lord ! he'll be ordering a dressing-case next, and razors to shave with ; I'm blest if he won't.'

The antics of the lad did not, however, delight Mr. Osborne's friends so much as they pleased the old gentleman. It gave Mr. Justice Coffin no pleasure to hear Georgy cut into the conversation and spoil his stories. Colonel Fogey was not interested in seeing the little boy half tipsy. Mr. Serjeant Toffy's lady felt no particular gratitude when, with a twist of his elbow, he tilted a glass of port wine over her yellow satin, and laughed at the disaster : nor was she better pleased, although old Osborne was highly delighted, when Georgy 'whopped' her third boy (a young gentleman a year older than Georgy, and by chance home for the holidays from Dr. Tickleus's at Ealing School) in Russell Square. George's grandfather gave the boy a couple of sovereigns for that feat, and promised to reward him further for every boy above his own size and age whom he whopped in a similar manner. It is difficult to say what good the old man saw in these combats ; he had a vague notion that quarrelling made boys hardy, and that tyranny was a useful accomplishment for them to learn. English youth have been so educated time out of mind, and we have hundreds of thousands of apologists and admirers of injustice, misery, and brutality, as perpetrated among children.

Flushed with praise and victory over Master Toffy, George wished naturally to pursue his conquests further, and one day as he was strutting about in prodigiously dandified new clothes, near St. Pancras, and a young baker's boy made sarcastic comments upon his appearance, the youthful patrician pulled off his dandy jacket with great spirit, and giving it in charge to the friend who accompanied him (Master Todd, of Great Coram Street, Russell Square, son of the junior partner of the house of Osborne and Co.)—George tried to whop the little baker.

But the chances of war were unfavourable this time, and the little baker whopped Georgy; who came home with a rueful black eye and all his fine shirt frill dabbled with the claret drawn from his own little nose. He told his grandfather that he had been in combat with a giant; and frightened his poor mother at Brompton with long, and by no means authentic, accounts of the battle.

This young Todd, of Coram Street, Russell Square, was Master George's great friend and admirer. They both had

a taste for painting theatrical characters; for hard-bake and raspberry tarts; for sliding and skating in the Regent's Park and the Serpentine, when the weather permitted; for going to the play, whither they were often conducted, by Mr. Osborne's orders, by Rowson, Master George's appointed body-servant; with whom they sat in great comfort in the pit.

In the company of this gentleman they visited all the principal theatres of the metropolis—knew the names of all the actors from Drury Lane to Sadler's Wells: and performed, indeed, many of the plays to the Todd family

GEORGY A GENTLEMAN

and their youthful friends, with West's famous characters* on their pasteboard theatre. Rowson, the footman, who was of a generous disposition, would not unfrequently, when in cash, treat his young master to oysters after the play, and to a glass of rum-shrub for a nightcap. We may be pretty certain that Mr. Rowson profited in his turn, by his young master's liberality and gratitude for the pleasures to which the footman inducted him.

A famous tailor from the West End of the town,— Mr. Osborne would have none of your City or Holborn bunglers he said, for the boy (though a City tailor was good enough for *him*)—was summoned to ornament little George's person, and was told to spare no expense in so doing. So, Mr. Woolsey of Conduit Street, gave a loose to his imagination, and sent the child home fancy trousers, fancy waistcoats, and fancy jackets enough to furnish a school of little dandies. Georgy had little white waist-coats for evening parties, and little cut velvet waistcoats for dinners, and a dear little darling shawl dressing-gown, for all the world like a little man. He dressed for dinner every day, ' like a regular West End swell,' as his grand-father remarked ; one of the domestics was affected to his especial service, attended him at his toilette, answered his bell, and brought him his letters always on a silver tray.

Georgy, after breakfast, would sit in the arm-chair in the dining-room, and read the *Morning Post,* just like a grown-up man. ' How he *du* dam and swear,' the servants would cry, delighted at his precocity. Those who remem-bered the captain, his father, declared Master George was his pa every inch of him. He made the house lively by his activity, his imperiousness, his scolding, and his good nature.

George's education was confided to a neighbouring scholar and private pedagogue who ' prepared young noblemen and gentlemen for the Universities, the senate, and the learned professions : whose system did not embrace the degrading corporal severities, still practised at the ancient places of education, and in whose family the pupils would find the elegances of refined society and the confidence and affec-tion of a home '. It was in this way that the Reverend Lawrence Veal of Hart Street, Bloomsbury, and domestic chaplain to the Earl of Bareacres, strove, with Mrs. Veal, his wife, to entice pupils.

By thus advertising and pushing sedulously, the domestic chaplain and his lady generally succeeded in having one or two scholars by them : who paid a high figure : and were thought to be in uncommonly comfortable quarters. There was a large West Indian, whom nobody came to see, with a mahogany complexion, a woolly head, and an exceedingly dandified appearance ; there was another hulking boy, of three-and-twenty, whose education had been neglected, and whom Mr. and Mrs. Veal were to introduce into the polite world ; there were two sons of Colonel Bangles of the East India Company's Service. These four sat down to dinner at Mrs. Veal's genteel board, when Georgy was introduced to her establishment.

Georgy was, like some dozen other pupils, only a day boy ; he arrived in the morning under the guardianship of his friend Mr. Rowson, and if it was fine, would ride away in the afternoon on his pony, followed by the groom. The wealth of his grandfather was reported in the school to be prodigious. The Rev. Mr. Veal used to compliment Georgy upon it personally, warning him that he was destined for a high station ; that it became him to prepare, by sedulity and docility in youth, for the lofty duties to which he would be called in mature age ; that obedience in the child was the best preparation for command in the man ; and that he therefore begged George would not bring toffy into the school, and ruin the health of the Masters Bangles, who had everything they wanted at the elegant and abundant table of Mrs. Veal.

With respect to learning, ' the Curriculum,' as Mr. Veal loved to call it, was of prodigious extent : and the young gentlemen in Hart Street might learn a something of every known science. The Rev. Mr. Veal had an orrery, an electrifying machine, a turning lathe, a theatre (in the wash-house), a chemical apparatus, and what he called a select library of all the works of the best authors of ancient and modern times and languages. He took the boys to the British Museum, and descanted upon the antiquities and the specimens of natural history there, so that audiences would gather round him as he spoke, and all Bloomsbury highly admired him as a prodigiously well-informed man. And whenever he spoke (which he did almost always), he took care to produce the very finest and longest words of which the vocabulary gave him the use; rightly judging, that it was as cheap to employ a handsome, large, and sonorous epithet, as to use a little stingy one.

Thus he would say to George in school, ' I observed on my return home from taking the indulgence of an evening's scientific conversation with my excellent friend Dr. Bulders —a true archaeologian, gentlemen, a true archaeologian— that the windows of your venerated grandfather's almost princely mansion in Russell Square were illuminated as if for the purposes of festivity. Am I right in my conjecture, that Mr. Osborne entertained a society of chosen spirits round his sumptuous board last night ? '

Little Georgy, who had considerable humour, and used to mimic Mr. Veal to his face with great spirit and dexterity, would reply, that Mr. V. was quite correct in his surmise.

' Then those friends who had the honour of partaking of Mr. Osborne's hospitality, gentlemen, had no reason, I will lay any wager, to complain of their repast. I myself have been more than once so favoured. (By the way, Master Osborne, you came a little late this morning, and have been a defaulter in this respect more than once.) I myself, I say, gentlemen, humble as I am, have been found not unworthy to share Mr. Osborne's elegant hospitality. And though I have feasted with the great and noble of the world—for I presume that I may call my excellent friend and patron, the Right Honourable George Earl of Bareacres, as one of the number—yet I assure you that the board of the British merchant was to the full as richly served, and his reception as gratifying and noble. Mr. Bluck, sir, we will resume, if you please, that passage of Eutropius, which was interrupted by the late arrival of Master Osborne.'

To this great man George's education was for some time entrusted. Amelia was bewildered by his phrases, but thought him a prodigy of learning. That poor widow made friends of Mrs. Veal, for reasons of her own. She liked to be in the house, and see Georgy coming to school there. She liked to be asked to Mrs. Veal's *conversazioni*, which took place once a month (as you were informed on pink cards, with AΘHNH engraved on them), and where the professor welcomed his pupils and their friends to weak tea and scientific conversation. Poor little Amelia never missed one of these entertainments, and thought them

delicious so long as she might have Georgy sitting by her.
And she would walk from Brompton in any weather, and
embrace Mrs. Veal with tearful gratitude for the delightful
evening she had passed, when, the company having retired,
and Georgy gone off with Mr. Rowson, his attendant, poor
Mrs. Osborne put on her cloaks and her shawls preparatory
to walking home.

As for the learning which Georgy imbibed under this
voluble master of a hundred sciences, to judge from the
weekly reports which the lad took home to his grandfather,
his progress was remarkable. The names of a score or
more of desirable branches of knowledge were printed on
a table, and the pupil's progress in each was marked by
the professor. In Greek Georgy was pronounced *aristos*,
in Latin *optimus*, in French *très bien*, and so forth : and
everybody had prizes for everything at the end of the
year. Even Mr. Swartz, the woolly-headed young gentleman, and half-brother to the Honourable Mrs. McMull,
and Mr. Bluck, the neglected young pupil of three-and-
twenty from the agricultural districts, and that idle young
scapegrace of a Master Todd before mentioned, received
little eighteenpenny books, with ' Athene ' engraved in
them, and a pompous Latin inscription from the professor
to his young friends.

The family of this Master Todd were hangers-on of the
house of Osborne. The old gentleman had advanced Todd
from being a clerk to be a junior partner in his establishment.

Mr. Osborne was the godfather of young Master Todd
(who in subsequent life wrote Mr. Osborne Todd on his
cards, and became a man of decided fashion), while Miss
Osborne had accompanied Miss Maria Todd to the font,
and gave her protégée a Prayer-book, a collection of tracts,
a volume of very Low Church poetry, or some such memento
of her goodness every year. Miss O. drove the Todds out
in her carriage now and then : when they were ill her
footman, in large plush smalls and waistcoat, brought jellies
and delicacies from Russell Square to Coram Street. Coram
Street trembled and looked up to Russell Square indeed :
and Mrs. Todd, who had a pretty hand at cutting out
paper trimmings for haunches of mutton, and could make
flowers, ducks, &c., out of turnips and carrots in a very
creditable manner, would go to ' the Square ', as it was

called, and assist in the preparations incident to a great
dinner, without even so much as thinking of sitting down
to the banquet. If any guest failed at the eleventh hour,
Todd was asked to dine. Mrs. Todd and Maria came
across in the evening, slipped in with a muffled knock,
and were in the drawing-room by the time Miss Osborne
and the ladies under her convoy reached that apartment ;
and ready to fire off duets and sing until the gentlemen
came up. Poor Maria Todd ; poor young lady ! How she
had to work and thrum at these duets and sonatas in the
Street, before they appeared in public in the Square !

Thus it seemed to be decreed by fate, that Georgy was
to domineer over everybody with whom he came in contact,
and that friends, relatives, and domestics were all to bow
the knee before the little fellow. It must be owned that
he accommodated himself very willingly to this arrangement.
Most people do so. And Georgy liked to play the part of
master, and perhaps had a natural aptitude for it.

In Russell Square everybody was afraid of Mr. Osborne,
and Mr. Osborne was afraid of Georgy. The boy's dashing
manners, and off-hand rattle about books and learning, his
likeness to his father (dead unreconciled in Brussels yonder),
awed the old gentleman, and gave the young boy the
mastery. The old man would start at some hereditary
feature or tone unconsciously used by the little lad, and
fancy that George's father was again before him. He
tried by indulgence to the grandson to make up for harshness
to the elder George. People were surprised at his gentleness
to the boy. He growled and swore at Miss Osborne as
usual : and would smile when George came down late for
breakfast.

Miss Osborne, George's aunt, was a faded old spinster,
broken down by more than forty years of dullness and
coarse usage. It was easy for a lad of spirit to master *her*.
And whenever George wanted anything from her, from the
jam-pots in her cupboards, to the cracked and dry old
colours in her paint-box (the old paint-box which she had
had when she was a pupil of Mr. Smee, and was still almost
young and blooming), Georgy took possession of the object
of his desire, which obtained, he took no further notice of
his aunt.

For his friends and cronies, he had a pompous old schoolmaster, who flattered him, and a toady, his senior, whom

he could thrash. It was dear Mrs. Todd's delight to leave
him with her youngest daughter, Rosa Jemima, a darling
child of eight years old. The little pair looked so well
together, she would say (but not to the folks in 'the
Square', we may be sure),—' Who knows what might
happen? Don't they make a pretty little couple?' the
fond mother thought.

The broken-spirited, old, maternal grandfather was likewise subject to the little tyrant. He could not help
respecting a lad who had such fine clothes, and rode with
a groom behind him. Georgy, on his side, was in the
constant habit of hearing coarse abuse and vulgar satire
levied at John Sedley, by his pitiless old enemy, Mr. Osborne.
Osborne used to call the other the old pauper, the old coal-
man, the old bankrupt, and by many other such names
of brutal contumely. How was little George to respect
a man so prostrate? A few months after he was with his
paternal grandfather, Mrs. Sedley died. There had been
little love between her and the child. He did not care to
show much grief. He came down to visit his mother in
a fine new suit of mourning, and was very angry that he
could not go to a play upon which he had set his heart.

The illness of that old lady had been the occupation and
perhaps the safeguard of Amelia. What do men know
about women's martyrdoms? We should go mad had we
to endure the hundredth part of those daily pains which
are meekly borne by many women. Ceaseless slavery
meeting with no reward; constant gentleness and kindness
met by cruelty as constant; love, labour, patience, watchfulness, without even so much as the acknowledgement of
a good word; all this, how many of them have to bear in
quiet, and appear abroad with cheerful faces, as if they
felt nothing. Tender slaves that they are, they must needs
be hypocrites and weak.

From her chair Amelia's mother had taken to her bed,
which she had never left; and from which Mrs. Osborne
herself was never absent except when she ran to see George.
The old lady grudged her even those rare visits; she, who
had been a kind, smiling, good-natured mother once, in
the days of her prosperity, but whom poverty and infirmities
had broken down. Her illness or estrangement did not
affect Amelia. They rather enabled her to support the
other calamity under which she was suffering, and from

the thoughts of which she was kept by the ceaseless calls
of the invalid. Amelia bore her harshness quite gently;
smoothed the uneasy pillow; was always ready with a soft
answer to the watchful, querulous voice; soothed the
sufferer with words of hope, such as her pious simple heart
could best feel and utter, and closed the eyes that had once
looked so tenderly upon her.

Then all her time and tenderness were devoted to the
consolation and comfort of the bereaved old father, who
was stunned by the blow which had befallen him, and stood
utterly alone in the world. His wife, his honour, his
fortune, everything he loved best had fallen away from
him. There was only Amelia to stand by and support with
her gentle arms the tottering, heart-broken, old man.
We are not going to write the history; it would be too
dreary and stupid. I can see Vanity Fair yawning over
it *d'avance*.

One day as the young gentlemen were assembled in the
study at the Rev. Mr. Veal's, and the domestic chaplain
to the Right Honourable the Earl of Bareacres was spouting
away as usual—a smart carriage drove up to the door
decorated with the statue of Athene, and two gentlemen
stepped out. The young Masters Bangles rushed to the
window, with a vague notion that their father might have
arrived from Bombay. The great hulking scholar of three-
and-twenty, who was crying secretly over a passage of
Eutropius, flattened his neglected nose against the panes,
and looked at the drag, as the *laquais de place* sprang from
the box and let out the persons in the carriage.

'It's a fat one and a thin one,' Mr. Bluck said, as a thundering knock came to the door.

Everybody was interested, from the domestic chaplain
himself, who hoped he saw the fathers of some future
pupils, down to Master Georgy, glad of any pretext for
laying his book down.

The boy in the shabby livery, with the faded copper
buttons, who always thrust himself into the tight coat to
open the door, came into the study and said, 'Two gentlemen want to see Master Osborne.' The professor had had
a trifling altercation in the morning with that young gentleman, owing to a difference about the introduction of
crackers in school-time; but his face resumed its habitual

expression of bland courtesy, as he said, ' Master Osborne,
I give you full permission to go and see your carriage
friends—to whom I beg you to convey the respectful
compliments of myself and Mrs. Veal.'

Georgy went into the reception-room, and saw two
strangers, whom he looked at with his head up, in his usual
haughty manner. One was fat, with moustachios, and the
other was lean and long, in a blue frock-coat, with a brown
face, and a grizzled head.

' My God, how like he is ! ' said the long gentleman, with
a start. ' Can you guess who we are, George ? '

The boy's face flushed up, as it did usually when he was
moved, and his eyes brightened. ' I don't know the other,'
he said, ' but I should think you must be Major Dobbin.'

Indeed it was our old friend. His voice trembled with
pleasure as he greeted the boy, and taking both the other's
hands in his own, drew the lad to him.

' Your mother has talked to you about me—has she ? '
he said.

'That she has;' Georgy answered, ' hundreds and hundreds
of times.'

CHAPTER LVII

EOTHEN*

IT was one of the many causes for personal pride with which old Osborne chose to recreate himself, that Sedley, his ancient rival, enemy, and benefactor, was in his last days so utterly defeated and humiliated, as to be forced to accept pecuniary obligations at the hands of the man who had most injured and insulted him. The successful man of the world cursed the old pauper, and relieved him from time to time. As he furnished George with money for his mother, he gave the boy to understand by hints, delivered in his brutal, coarse way, that George's maternal grandfather was but a wretched old bankrupt and dependant, and that John Sedley might thank the man to whom he already owed ever so much money, for the aid which his generosity now chose to administer. George carried the pompous supplies to his mother and the shattered old widower whom it was now the main business of her life to tend and comfort. The little fellow patronized the feeble and disappointed old man.

It may have shown a want of 'proper pride' in Amelia that she chose to accept these money benefits at the hands of her father's enemy. But proper pride and this poor lady had never had much acquaintance together. A disposition naturally simple and demanding protection; a long course of poverty and humility, of daily privations, and hard words, of kind offices and no returns, had been her lot ever since womanhood almost, or since her luckless marriage with George Osborne. You who see your betters, bearing up under this shame every day, meekly suffering under the slights of fortune, gentle and unpitied, poor, and

rather despised for their poverty, do you ever step down
from your prosperity and wash the feet of these poor
wearied beggars ?   The very thought of them is odious and
low.   ' There must be classes—there must be rich and poor,'
Dives says, smacking his claret—(it is well if he even sends
the broken meat out to Lazarus sitting under the window).
Very true ; but think how mysterious and often unaccountable it is—that lottery of life which gives to this man the
purple and fine linen, and sends to the other rags for
garments and dogs for comforters.

So I must own, that without much repining, on the
contrary with something akin to gratitude, Amelia took
the crumbs that her father-in-law let drop now and then
and with them fed her own parent.   Directly she understood
it to be her duty, it was this young woman's nature (ladies,
she is but thirty still, and we choose to call her a young
woman even at that age)—it was, I say, her nature to
sacrifice herself and to fling all that she had at the feet of
the beloved object.   During what long thankless nights
had she worked out her fingers for little Georgy whilst at
home with her ; what buffets, scorns, privations, poverties
had she endured for father and mother !   And in the midst
of all these solitary resignations and unseen sacrifices, she
did not respect herself any more than the world respected
her ; but I believe thought in her heart that she was a poor-
spirited, despicable little creature, whose luck in life was
only too good for her merits.   O you poor women ! O you
poor secret martyrs and victims, whose life is a torture,
who are stretched on racks in your bedrooms, and who lay
your heads down on the block daily at the drawing-room
table ; every man who watches your pains, or peers into
those dark places where the torture is administered to you,
must pity you—and—and thank God that he has a beard.
I recollect seeing, years ago, at the prison for idiots and
madmen at Bicêtre, near Paris, a poor wretch bent down
under the bondage of his imprisonment and his personal
infirmity, to whom one of our party gave a halfpennyworth
of snuff in a *cornet* or ' screw ' of paper.   The kindness
was too much for the poor epileptic creature.   He cried
in an anguish of delight and gratitude : if anybody gave
you and me a thousand a year, or saved our lives, we could
not be so affected.   And so, if you properly tyrannize over
a woman, you will find a halfp'orth of kindness act upon

her, and bring tears into her eyes, as though you were an angel benefiting her.

Some such boons as these were the best which Fortune allotted to poor little Amelia. Her life, begun not unprosperously, had come down to this—to a mean prison and a long, ignoble bondage. Little George visited her captivity sometimes, and consoled it with feeble gleams of encouragement. Russell Square was the boundary of her prison : she might walk thither occasionally, but was always back to sleep in her cell at night ; to perform cheerless duties ; to watch by thankless sick-beds ; to suffer the harassment and tyranny of querulous disappointed old age. How many thousands of people are there, women for the most part, who are doomed to endure this long slavery ?—who are hospital nurses without wages,—sisters of Charity, if you like, without the romance and the sentiment of sacrifice, —who strive, fast, watch, and suffer, unpitied ; and fade away ignobly and unknown. The hidden and awful Wisdom which apportions the destinies of mankind is pleased so to humiliate and cast down the tender, good, and wise ; and to set up the selfish, the foolish, or the wicked. Oh, be humble, my brother, in your prosperity ! Be gentle with those who are less lucky, if not more deserving. Think, what right have you to be scornful, whose virtue is a deficiency of temptation, whose success may be a chance, whose rank may be an ancestor's accident, whose prosperity is very likely a satire.

They buried Amelia's mother at the churchyard at Brompton ; upon just such a rainy, dark day, as Amelia recollected when first she had been there to marry George. Her little boy sat by her side in pompous new sables. She remembered the old pew-woman and clerk. Her thoughts were away in other times as the parson read. But that she held George's hand in her own, perhaps she would have liked to change places with . . . Then, as usual, she felt ashamed of her selfish thoughts, and prayed inwardly to be strengthened to do her duty.

So she determined with all her might and strength to try and make her old father happy. She slaved, toiled, patched and mended, sang and played backgammon, read out the newspaper, cooked dishes for old Sedley, walked him out sedulously into Kensington Gardens or the Brompton

lanes, listened to his stories with untiring smiles and
affectionate hypocrisy, or sat musing by his side and communing with her own thoughts and reminiscences, as the
old man, feeble and querulous, sunned himself on the garden
benches and prattled about his wrongs or his sorrows.
What sad, unsatisfactory thoughts those of the widow were !
The children running up and down the slopes and broad
paths in the gardens, reminded her of George who was
taken from her : the first George was taken from her : her
selfish, guilty love, in both instances, had been rebuked and
bitterly chastised. She strove to think it was right that
she should be so punished. She was such a miserable
wicked sinner. She was quite alone in the world.

I know that the account of this kind of solitary imprisonment is insufferably tedious, unless there is some cheerful
or humorous incident to enliven it,—a tender gaoler, for
instance, or a waggish commandant of the fortress, or
a mouse to come out and play about Latude's beard and
whiskers, or a subterranean passage under the castle, dug
by Trenck*with his nails and a toothpick : the historian
has no such enlivening incident to relate in the narrative
of Amelia's captivity. Fancy her, if you please, during
this period, very sad, but always ready to smile when spoken
to ; in a very mean, poor, not to say vulgar position of
life ;   singing songs, making puddings, playing cards,
mending stockings, for her old father's benefit. So, never
mind, whether she be a heroine or no ; or you and I, however old, scolding, and bankrupt ;—may we have in our
last days a kind soft shoulder on which to lean, and a gentle
hand to soothe our gouty old pillows.

Old Sedley grew very fond of his daughter after his wife's
death ; and Amelia had her consolation in doing her duty
by the old man.

But we are not going to leave these two people long in
such a low and ungenteel station of life. Better days, as
far as worldly prosperity went, were in store for both.
Perhaps the ingenious reader has guessed who was the
stout gentleman who called upon Georgy at his school in
company with our old friend Major Dobbin. It was
another old acquaintance returned to England, and at a
time when his presence was likely to be of great comfort
to his relatives there.

Major Dobbin having easily succeeded in getting leave

from his good-natured commandant to proceed to Madras, and thence probably to Europe, on urgent private affairs, never ceased travelling night and day until he reached his journey's end, and had directed his march with such celerity, that he arrived at Madras in a high fever. His servants who accompanied him, brought him to the house of the friend, with whom he had resolved to stay until his departure for Europe, in a state of delirium ; and it was thought for many, many days that he would never travel farther than the burying-ground of the church of St. George's, where the troops should fire a salvo over his grave, and where many a gallant officer lies far away from his home.

Here as the poor fellow lay tossing in his fever, the people who watched him might have heard him raving about Amelia. The idea that he should never see her again depressed him in his lucid hours. He thought his last day was come ; and he made his solemn preparations for departure : setting his affairs in this world in order, and leaving the little property of which he was possessed to those whom he most desired to benefit. The friend in whose house he was located witnessed his testament. He desired to be buried with a little brown hair-chain which he wore round his neck, and which, if the truth must be known, he had got from Amelia's maid at Brussels, when the young widow's hair was cut off, during the fever which prostrated her after the death of George Osborne on the plateau of Mount St. John.

He recovered, rallied, relapsed again, having undergone such a process of blood-letting and calomel as showed the strength of his original constitution. He was almost a skeleton when they put him on board the *Ramchunder*, East Indiaman, Captain Bragg, from Calcutta touching at Madras ; and so weak and prostrate, that his friend who had tended him through his illness, prophesied that the honest major would never survive the voyage, and that he would pass some morning, shrouded in flag and hammock, over the ship's side, and carrying down to the sea with him, the relic that he wore at his heart. But whether it was the sea air, or the hope which sprang up in him afresh, from the day that the ship spread her canvas and stood out of the roads towards *home*, our friend began to amend, and he was quite well (though as gaunt as a greyhound) before they reached the Cape. 'Kirk will be disappointed of his

majority this time,' he said with a smile : ' he will expect
to find himself gazetted by the time the regiment reaches
home.' For it must be premised that while the major was
lying ill at Madras, having made such a prodigious haste to
go thither, the gallant —th which had passed many years
abroad, which after its return from the West Indies had
been balked of its stay at home by the Waterloo campaign,
and had been ordered from Flanders to India, had received
orders home ; and the major might have accompanied his
comrades, had he chosen to wait for their arrival at Madras.

Perhaps he was not inclined to put himself in his exhausted
state again under the guardianship of Glorvina. ' I think
Miss O'Dowd would have done for me,' he said, laughingly,
to a fellow-passenger, ' if we had had her on board, and when
she had sunk me, she would have fallen upon you, depend
upon it and carried you in as a prize to Southampton, Jos,
my boy.'

For indeed it was no other than our stout friend who
was also a passenger on board the *Ramchunder*. He had
passed ten years in Bengal.—Constant dinners, tiffins, pale
ale, and claret, the prodigious labours of cutcherry, and the
refreshment of brandy-pawnee*which he was forced to take
there, had their effect upon Waterloo Sedley. A voyage
to Europe was pronounced necessary for him—and having
served his full time in India, and had fine appointments
which had enabled him to lay by a considerable sum of money,
he was free to come home and stay with a good pension,
or to return and resume that rank in his service to which
his seniority and his vast talents entitled him.

He was rather thinner than when we last saw him, but
had gained in majesty and solemnity of demeanour. He
had resumed the moustachios to which his services at
Waterloo entitled him, and swaggered about on deck in
a magnificent velvet cap with a gold band, and a profuse
ornamentation of pins and jewellery about his person.
He took breakfast in his cabin, and dressed as solemnly
to appear on the quarter-deck, as if he was going to turn
out for Bond Street, or the Course at Calcutta. He brought
a native servant with him, who was his valet and pipe-
bearer ; and who wore the Sedley crest in silver on his
turban. That oriental menial had a wretched life under
the tyranny of Jos Sedley. Jos was as vain of his person
as a woman, and took as long a time at his toilette as any

fading beauty. The youngsters among the passengers, young Chaffers of the 150th, and poor little Ricketts, coming home after his third fever, used to draw out Sedley at the cuddy-table,* and make him tell prodigious stories about himself and his exploits against tigers and Napoleon. He was great when he visited the Emperor's tomb at Longwood,* when to these gentlemen and the young officers of the ship, Major Dobbin not being by, he described the whole battle of Waterloo, and all but announced that Napoleon never would have gone to St. Helena at all but for him, Jos Sedley.

After leaving St. Helena he became very generous, disposing of a great quantity of ship's stores, claret, preserved meats, and great casks packed with soda-water, brought out for his private delectation. There were no ladies on board : the major gave the *pas* of precedency to the civilian, so that he was the first dignitary at table ; and treated by Captain Bragg, and the officers of the *Ramchunder*, with the respect which his rank warranted. He disappeared rather in a panic during a two-days' gale, in which he had the port-holes of his cabin battened down ; and remained in his cot reading the *Washerwoman of Finchley Common*, left on board the *Ramchunder* by the Right Honourable the Lady Emily Hornblower, wife of the Rev. Silas Hornblower, then on their passage out to the Cape, where the reverend gentleman was a missionary : but, for common reading, he had brought a stock of novels and plays which he lent to the rest of the ship, and rendered himself agreeable to all by his kindness and condescension.

Many and many a night as the ship was cutting through the roaring dark sea, the moon and stars shining overhead, and the bell singing out the watch, Mr. Sedley and the major would sit on the quarter-deck of the vessel talking about home, as the major smoked his cheroot, and the civilian puffed at the hookah which his servant prepared for him.

In these conversations it was wonderful with what perseverance and ingenuity Major Dobbin would manage to bring the talk round to the subject of Amelia and her little boy. Jos, a little testy about his father's misfortunes and unceremonious applications to him, was soothed down by the major, who pointed out the elder's ill fortunes and old age. He would not perhaps like to live with the old

couple : whose ways and hours might not agree with those
of a younger man, accustomed to different society (Jos
bowed at this compliment) : but, the major pointed out,
how advantageous it would be for Jos Sedley to have a house
of his own in London, and not a mere bachelor's establishment as before : how his sister Amelia would be the very
person to preside over it ; how elegant, how gentle she was,
and of what refined good manners. He recounted stories

of the success which Mrs. George Osborne had had in former
days at Brussels, and in London, where she was much
admired by people of very great fashion : and he then
hinted how becoming it would be for Jos to send Georgy
to a good school and make a man of him ; for his mother
and her parents would be sure to spoil him. In a word
this artful major made the civilian promise to take charge
of Amelia and her unprotected child. He did not know
as yet what events had happened in the little Sedley family :

and how death had removed the mother, and riches had
carried off George from Amelia. But the fact is, that every
day and always, this love-smitten and middle-aged gentleman was thinking about Mrs. Osborne, and his whole heart
was bent upon doing her good. He coaxed, wheedled,
cajoled, and complimented Jos Sedley with a perseverance
and cordiality of which he was not aware himself, very
likely : but some men who have unmarried sisters or
daughters even, may remember how uncommonly agreeable
gentlemen are to the male relations when they are courting
the females ; and perhaps this rogue of a Dobbin was urged
by a similar hypocrisy.

The truth is, when Major Dobbin came on board the
Ramchunder, very sick, and for the three days she lay in
the Madras roads, he did not begin to rally, nor did even
the appearance and recognition of his old acquaintance,
Mr. Sedley, on board much cheer him, until after a conversation which they had one day, as the major was laid languidly
on the deck. He said then that he thought he was doomed ;
he had left a little something to his godson in his will ; and
he trusted Mrs. Osborne would remember him kindly, and
be happy in the marriage she was about to make. 'Married ?
not the least,' Jos answered ; ' he had heard from her : she
made no mention of the marriage, and by the way, it was
curious, she wrote to say that Major Dobbin was going to
be married, and hoped that *he* would be happy.' What
were the dates of Sedley's letters from Europe ? The
civilian fetched them. They were two months later than
the major's ; and the ship's surgeon congratulated himself
upon the treatment adopted by him towards his new
patient, who had been consigned to shipboard by the
Madras practitioner with very small hopes indeed ; for,
from that day, the very day that he changed the draught,
Major Dobbin began to mend. And thus it was that
deserving officer, Captain Kirk, was disappointed of his
majority.

After they passed St. Helena, Major Dobbin's gaiety and
strength was such as to astonish all his fellow-passengers.
He larked with the midshipmen, played singlestick with
the mates, ran up the shrouds like a boy, sang a comic song
one night to the amusement of the whole party assembled
over their grog after supper, and rendered himself so gay,
lively, and amiable, that even Captain Bragg, who thought

there was nothing in his passenger, and considered he was a poor-spirited feller at first, was constrained to own that the major was a reserved but well-informed and meritorious officer. ' He ain't got distangy manners, dammy,' Bragg observed to his first mate ; ' he wouldn't do at Government House, Roper, where his lordship and Lady William* was as kind to me, and shook hands with me before the whole company and asking me at dinner to take beer with him, before the commander-in-chief himself ; he ain't got manners, but there's something about him——.' And thus Captain Bragg showed that he possessed discrimination as a man, as well as ability as a commander.

But a calm taking place when the *Ramchunder* was within ten days' sail of England, Dobbin became so impatient and ill-humoured as to surprise those comrades who had before admired his vivacity and good temper. He did not recover until the breeze sprang up again, and was in a highly excited state when the pilot came on board. Good God, how his heart beat as the two friendly spires of Southampton came in sight !

CHAPTER LVIII

OUR FRIEND THE MAJOR

UR major had rendered himself so
popular on board the *Ramchunder*,
that when he and Mr. Sedley
descended into the welcome shore-
boat which was to take them from
the ship, the whole crew, men and
officers, the great Captain Bragg
himself leading off, gave three
cheers for Major Dobbin, who
blushed very much, and ducked
his head in token of thanks. Jos,
who very likely thought the cheers
were for himself, took off his gold-
laced cap and waved it majestically to his friends, and they were
pulled to shore and landed with
great dignity at the pier, whence
they proceeded to the 'Royal George' Hotel.

Although the sight of that magnificent round of beef,
and the silver tankard suggestive of real British home-
brewed ale and porter, which perennially greet the eyes
of the traveller returning from foreign parts, who enters
the coffee-room of the 'George', are so invigorating and
delightful, that a man entering such a comfortable snug
homely English inn, might well like to stop some days
there, yet Dobbin began to talk about a post-chaise instantly,
and was no sooner at Southampton than he wished to be
on the road to London. Jos, however, would not hear of
moving that evening. Why was he to pass the night in
a post-chaise, instead of a great large undulating downy
feather bed which was there ready to replace the horrid little
narrow crib in which the portly Bengal gentleman had been
confined during the voyage? He could not think of moving
till his baggage was cleared, or of travelling until he could
do so with his chillum.* So the major was forced to wait
over that night, and dispatched a letter to his family
announcing his arrival; entreating from Jos a promise to

write to his own friends. Jos promised, but didn't keep
his promise. The captain, the surgeon, and one or two
passengers came and dined with our two gentlemen at the
inn ; Jos exerting himself in a sumptuous way in ordering
the dinner : and promising to go to town the next day
with the major. The landlord said it did his eyes good
to see Mr. Sedley take off his first pint of porter. If I had
time and dared to enter into digressions, I would write
a chapter about that first pint of porter drunk upon English
ground. Ah, how good it is ! It is worth while to leave
home for a year, just to enjoy that one draught.

Major Dobbin made his appearance the next morning
very neatly shaved and dressed, according to his wont.
Indeed it was so early in the morning, that nobody was up
in the house except that wonderful boots of an inn who
never seems to want sleep ; and the major could hear the
snores of the various inmates of the house roaring through
the corridors as he creaked about in those dim passages.
Then the sleepless boots went shirking round from door
to door, gathering up at each the Bluchers, Wellingtons,
Oxonians, which stood outside.   Then Jos's native servant
arose and began to get ready his master's ponderous dressing
apparatus, and prepare his hookah : then the maidservants
got up, and meeting the dark man in the passages, shrieked,
and mistook him for the devil.   He and Dobbin stumbled
over their pails in the passages as they were scouring the
decks of the 'Royal George'. When the first unshorn waiter
appea ed and unbarred the door of the inn, the major
though, that the time for departure was arrived, and ordered
a post-chaise to be fetched instantly, that they might set off.

He then directed his steps to Mr. Sedley's room, and
opened the curtains of the great large family bed wherein
Mr. Jos was snoring. 'Come, up, Sedley,' the major said,
'it's time to be off ; the chaise will be at the door in half
an hour.'

Jos growled from under the counterpane to know what
the time was ; but when he at last extorted from the
blushing major (who never told fibs, however much they
might be to his advantage) what was the real hour of the
morning, he broke out into a volley of bad language, which we
will not repeat here, but by which he gave Dobbin to understand that he would jeopardy his soul if he got up at that
moment, that the major might go and be hanged, that he

MR. JOS'S HOOKAHBADAR

would not travel with Dobbin, and that it was most unkind
and ungentlemanlike to disturb a man out of his sleep in
that way ; on which the discomfited major was obliged to
retreat, leaving Jos to resume his interrupted slumbers.

The chaise came up presently, and the major would
wait no longer.

If he had been an English nobleman travelling on a
pleasure tour, or a newspaper courier bearing dispatches
(Government messages are generally carried much more
quietly), he could not have travelled more quickly. The
postboys wondered at the fees he flung amongst them.
How happy and green the country looked as the chaise
whirled rapidly from milestone to milestone, through neat
country towns where landlords came out to welcome him
with smiles and bows ; by pretty roadside inns, where the
signs hung on the elms, and horses and wagoners were
drinking under the chequered shadow of the trees ; by old
halls and parks ; rustic hamlets clustered round ancient
grey churches—and through the charming friendly English
landscape. Is there any in the world like it ? To a traveller
returning home it looks so kind—it seems to shake hands
with you as you pass through it. Well, Major Dobbin
passed over all this through from Southampton to London,
and without noting much beyond the milestones along
the road. You see he was so eager to see his parents at
Camberwell.

He grudged the time lost between Piccadilly and his old
haunt at the Slaughters', whither he drove faithfully. Long
years had passed since he saw it last, since he and George,
as young men, had enjoyed many a feast, and held
many a revel there. He had now passed into the stage
of old-fellow-hood. His hair was grizzled, and many a
passion and feeling of his youth had grown grey in that
interval. There, however, stood the old waiter at the
door in the same greasy black suit, with the same
double chin and flaccid face, with the same huge bunch
of seals at his fob, rattling his money in his pockets as
before, and receiving the major as if he had gone away only
a week ago. ' Put the major's things in twenty-three,
that's his room,' John said, exhibiting not the least
surprise. ' Roast fowl for your dinner, I suppose. You
ain't got married ? They said you was married—the Scotch
surgeon of yours was here. No, it was Captain Humby of

the Thirty-third, as was quartered with the —th in Injee. Like any warm water ? What do you come in a chay for— ain't the coach good enough ? ' And with this, the faithful waiter, who knew and remembered every officer who used the house, and with whom ten years were but as yesterday, led the way up to Dobbin's old room, where stood the great moreen bed, and the shabby carpet, a thought more dingy, and all the old black furniture covered with faded chintz, just as the major recollected them in his youth.

He remembered George pacing up and down the room, and biting his nails, and swearing that the governor must come round, and that if he didn't, he didn't care a straw, on the day before he was married. He could fancy him walking in, banging the door of Dobbin's room, and his own hard by—

' You ain't got young,' John said, calmly surveying his friend of former days.

Dobbin laughed. ' Ten years and a fever don't make a man young, John,' he said. ' It is you that are always young :—No, you are always old.'

' What became of Captain Osborne's widow ? ' John said. ' Fine young fellow that. Lord, how he used to spend his money. He never came back after that day he was married from here. He owes me three pound at this minute.' Look here, I have it in my book. " April 10, 1815, Captain Osborne : 3*l*." I wonder whether his father would pay me,' and so saying, John of the Slaughters' pulled out the very morocco pocketbook in which he had noted his loan to the captain, upon a greasy faded page still extant, with many other scrawled memoranda regarding the bygone frequenters of the house.

Having inducted his customer into the room, John retired with perfect calmness ; and Major Dobbin, not without a blush and a grin at his own absurdity, chose out of his kit the very smartest and most becoming civil costume he possessed, and laughed at his own tanned face and grey hair, as he surveyed them in the dreary little toilet-glass on the dressing-table.

' I'm glad old John didn't forget me,' he thought. ' She'll know me, too, I hope.' And he sallied out of the inn, bending his steps once more in the direction of Brompton.

Every minute incident of his last meeting with Amelia was present to the constant man's mind as he walked

towards her house. The arch and the Achilles statue
were up* since he had last been in Piccadilly ; a hundred
changes had occurred which his eye and mind vaguely noted.
He began to tremble as he walked up the lane from Brompton, that well-remembered lane leading to the street where
she lived. Was she going to be married or not ? If he
were to meet her with the little boy—Good God, what
should he do ? He saw a woman coming to him with
a child of five years old—was that she ? He began to
shake at the mere possibility. When he came up to the
row of houses, at last, where she lived, and to the gate,
he caught hold of it and paused. He might have heard the
thumping of his own heart. ' May God Almighty bless her,
whatever has happened,' he thought to himself. ' Psha !
she may be gone from here,' he said, and went in through
the gate.

The window of the parlour which she used to occupy
was open, and there were no inmates in the room. The
major thought he recognized the piano, though, with the
picture over it, as it used to be in former days, and his
perturbations were renewed. Mr. Clapp's brass plate was
still on the door, at the knocker of which Dobbin performed
a summons.

A buxom-looking lass of sixteen, with bright eyes and
purple cheeks, came to answer the knock, and looked hard
at the major as he leant back against the little porch.

He was as pale as a ghost, and could hardly falter out the
words—' Does Mrs. Osborne live here ? '

She looked him hard in the face for a moment—and then
turning white too—said, ' Lord bless me—it's Major
Dobbin.' She held out both her hands shaking—' Don't
you remember me ? ' she said, ' I used to call you Major
Sugarplums.' On which, and I believe it was for the first
time that he ever so conducted himself in his life, the major
took the girl in his arms and kissed her. She began to
laugh and cry hysterically, and calling out ' Ma, Pa ! '
with all her voice, brought up those worthy people, who
had already been surveying the major from the casement
of the ornamental kitchen, and were astonished to find
their daughter in the little passage in the embrace of a great
tall man in a blue frock-coat and white duck trousers.

' I'm an old friend,' he said—not without blushing though.
' Don't you remember me, Mrs. Clapp, and those good cakes

you used to make for tea ?—Don't you recollect me, Clapp ?
I'm George's godfather, and just come back from India ! '
A great shaking of hands ensued—Mrs. Clapp was greatly
affected and delighted; she called upon Heaven to interpose
a vast many times in that passage.

The landlord and landlady of the house led the worthy
major into the Sedleys' room (whereof he remembered every
single article of furniture, from the old brass ornamented
piano, once a natty little instrument, Stothard maker,* to
the screens and the alabaster miniature tombstone, in the
midst of which ticked Mr. Sedley's gold watch), and there
as he sat down in the lodger's vacant arm-chair, the father,
the mother, and the daughter, with a thousand ejaculatory
breaks in the narrative, informed Major Dobbin of what
we know already, but of particulars in Amelia's history of
which he was not aware—namely, of Mrs. Sedley's death,
of George's reconcilement with his grandfather Osborne,
of the way in which the widow took on at leaving him, and
of other particulars of her life. Twice or thrice he was
going to ask about the marriage question, but his heart
failed him. He did not care to lay it bare to these people.
Finally, he was informed that Mrs. O. was gone to walk
with her pa in Kensington Gardens, whither she always
went with the old gentleman (who was very weak and
peevish now, and led her a sad life, though she behaved to
him like an angel, to be sure), of a fine afternoon after dinner.

' I'm very much pressed for time,' the major said, ' and
have business to-night of importance. I should like to see
Mrs. Osborne though. Suppose Miss Polly would come with
me and show me the way.'

Miss Polly was charmed and astonished at this proposal.
' She knew the way. She would show Major Dobbin.
She had often been with Mr. Sedley when Mrs. O. was gone—
was gone Russell Square way : and knew the bench where
he liked to sit.' She bounced away to her apartment, and
appeared presently in her best bonnet and her mamma's
yellow shawl and large pebble brooch, of which she assumed
the loan in order to make herself a worthy companion for
the major.

That officer, then, in his blue frock-coat and buckskin
gloves, gave the young lady his arm, and they walked
away very gaily. He was glad to have a friend at hand
for the scene which he dreaded somehow. He asked a

thousand more questions from his companion about Amelia :
his kind heart grieved to think that she should have had
to part with her son.   How did she bear it ?   Did she see
him often ?   Was Mr. Sedley pretty comfortable now in
a worldly point of view ?   Polly answered all these questions
of Major Sugarplums to the very best of her power.

And in the midst of their walk an incident occurred which,
though very simple in its nature, was productive of the
greatest delight to Major Dobbin.   A pale young man with
feeble whiskers and a stiff white neckcloth came walking
down the lane, *en sandwich :*—having a lady, that is, on
each arm.   One was a tall and commanding middle-aged
female, with features and a complexion similar to those
of the clergyman of the Church of England by whose side
she marched, and the other a stunted little woman with
a dark face, ornamented by a fine new bonnet and white
ribbons, and in a smart pelisse with a rich gold watch in
the midst of her person.   The gentleman, pinioned as he
was by these two ladies, carried further a parasol, shawl,
and basket, so that his arms were entirely engaged, and of
course he was unable to touch his hat in acknowledgement
of the curtsy with which Miss Mary Clapp greeted him.

He meekly bowed his head in reply to her salutation,
which the two ladies returned in a patronizing air, and at
the same time looking severely at the individual in the blue
coat and bamboo cane, who accompanied Miss Polly.

'Who's that,' asked the major, amused by the group,
and after he had made way for the three to pass up the
lane.   Mary looked at him rather roguishly.

'That is our curate, the Reverend Mr. Binney' (a twitch
from Major Dobbin), 'and his sister Miss B.   Lord bless us,
how she did use to worret us at Sunday-school ; and the
other lady, the little one with a cast in her eye, and the
handsome watch, is Mrs. Binney—Miss Grits that was ;
her pa was a grocer, and kept the Little Original Gold Tea
Pot in Kensington Gravel Pits.   They were married last
month, and are just come back from Margate.   She's five
thousand pound to her fortune ; but her and Miss B., who
made the match, have quarrelled already.'

If the major had twitched before, he started now, and
slapped the bamboo on the ground with an emphasis which
made Miss Clapp cry, 'Law,' and laugh too.   He stood for
a moment silent with open mouth looking after the retreat-

ing young couple, while Miss Mary told their history ; but
he did not hear beyond the announcement of the reverend
gentleman's marriage ; his head was swimming with
felicity.   After this rencontre he began to walk double
quick towards the place of his destination ; and yet they
were too soon (for he was in a great tremor at the idea
of a meeting for which he had been longing any time these
ten years)—through the Brompton lanes, and entering at
the little old portal in Kensington Garden wall.

'There they are,' said Miss Polly, and she felt him again
start back on her arm.   She was a confidante at once of the
whole business.   She knew the story as well as if she had
read it in one of her favourite novel-books—*Fatherless
Fanny*, or the *Scottish Chiefs.**

'Suppose you were to run on and tell her,' the major said.
Polly ran forward, her yellow shawl streaming in the breeze.

Old Sedley was seated on a bench, his handkerchief
placed over his knees, prattling away according to his wont,
with some old story about old times, to which Amelia had
listened, and awarded a patient smile many a time before.
She could of late think of her own affairs, and smile or make
other marks of recognition of her father's stories, scarcely
hearing a word of the old man's tales.   As Mary came
bouncing along, and Amelia caught sight of her, she started
up from her bench.   Her first thought was, that something
had happened to Georgy ; but the sight of the messenger's
eager and happy face dissipated that fear in the timorous
mother's bosom.

'News !   News !' cried the emissary of Major Dobbin.
'He's come !   He's come !'

'Who is come ?' said Emmy, still thinking of her son.

'Look there,' answered Miss Clapp, turning round and
pointing ; in which direction Amelia looking, saw Dobbin's
lean figure and long shadow stalking across the grass.
Amelia started in her turn, blushed up, and, of course, began
to cry.   At all this simple little creature's fêtes, the *grandes
eaux* were accustomed to play.

He looked at her—oh, how fondly—as she came running
towards him, her hands before her, ready to give them to
him.   She wasn't changed.   She was a little pale : a little
stouter in figure.   Her eyes were the same, the kind trustful
eyes.   There were scarce three lines of silver in her soft
brown hair.   She gave him both her hands as she looked

A MEETING

up flushing and smiling through her tears into his honest
homely face. He took the two little hands between his
two, and held them there. He was speechless for a moment.
Why did he not take her in his arms, and swear that he
would never leave her? She must have yielded: she
could not but have obeyed him.

'I—I've another arrival to announce,' he said, after
a pause.

'Mrs. Dobbin?' Amelia said, making a movement back—
Why didn't he speak?

'No,' he said, letting her hands go: 'who has told you
those lies?—I mean, your brother Jos came in the same
ship with me, and is come home to make you all happy.'

'Papa, papa!' Emmy cried out, 'here are news! My
brother is in England. He is come to take care of you.—
Here is Major Dobbin.'

Mr. Sedley started up, shaking a great deal, and gathering
up his thoughts. Then he stepped forward and made an
old-fashioned bow to the major, whom he called Mr. Dobbin,
and hoped his worthy father, Sir William, was quite well.
He proposed to call upon Sir William, who had done him
the honour of a visit a short time ago. Sir William had
not called upon the old gentleman for eight years—it was
that visit he was thinking of returning.

'He is very much shaken,' Emmy whispered, as Dobbin
went up and cordially shook hands with the old man.

Although he had such particular business in London that
evening, the major consented to forgo it upon Mr. Sedley's
invitation to him to come home and partake of tea. Amelia
put her arm under that of her young friend with the yellow
shawl, and headed the party on their return homewards,
so that Mr. Sedley fell to Dobbin's share. The old man
walked very slowly, and told a number of ancient histories
about himself and his poor Bessy, his former prosperity,
and his bankruptcy. His thoughts, as is usual with failing
old men, were quite in former times. The present, with the
exception of the one catastrophe which he felt, he knew
little about. The major was glad to let him talk on. His
eyes were fixed upon the figure in front of him—the dear
little figure always present to his imagination and in his
prayers, and visiting his dreams wakeful or slumbering.

Amelia was very happy, smiling, and active all that
evening; performing her duties as hostess of the little

entertainment with the utmost grace and propriety, as
Dobbin thought. His eyes followed her about as they sat
in the twilight. How many a time had he longed for that
moment, and thought of her far away under hot winds
and in weary marches, gentle and happy, kindly ministering
to the wants of old age, and decorating poverty with sweet
submission—as he saw her now. I do not say that his
taste was the highest or that it is the duty of great intellects
to be content with a bread-and-butter paradise, such as
sufficed our simple old friend ; but his desires were of this
sort whether for good or bad ; and, with Amelia to help
him, he was as ready to drink as many cups of tea as Doctor
Johnson.

Amelia seeing this propensity, laughingly encouraged it ;
and looked exceedingly roguish as she administered to him
cup after cup. It is true she did not know that the major
had had no dinner, and that the cloth was laid for him at
the Slaughters', and a plate laid thereon to mark that the
table was retained, in that very box in which the major
and George had sat many a time carousing, when she
was a child just come home from Miss Pinkerton's school.

The first thing Mrs. Osborne showed the major was
Georgy's miniature, for which she ran upstairs on her
arrival at home. It was not half handsome enough of
course for the boy, but wasn't it noble of him to think of
bringing it to his mother ? Whilst her papa was awake
she did not talk much about Georgy. To hear about
Mr. Osborne and Russell Square was not agreeable to the
old man, who very likely was unconscious that he had been
living for some months past mainly on the bounty of his
richer rival ; and lost his temper if allusion was made to
the other.

Dobbin told him all, and a little more perhaps than all,
that had happened on board the *Ramchunder ;* and exagger-
ated Jos's benevolent dispositions towards his father, and
resolution to make him comfortable in his old days. The
truth is that during the voyage the major had impressed
this duty most strongly upon his fellow-passenger and
extorted promises from him that he would take charge of
his sister and her child. He soothed Jos's irritation with
regard to the bills which the old gentleman had drawn upon
him, gave a laughing account of his own sufferings on the same
score, and of the famous consignment of wine with which

the old man had favoured him : and brought Mr. Jos, who
was by no means an ill-natured person when well pleased
and moderately flattered, to a very good state of feeling
regarding his relatives in Europe.

And in fine I am ashamed to say that the major stretched
the truth so far as to tell old Mr. Sedley that it was mainly
a desire to see his parent which brought Jos once more to
Europe.

At his accustomed hour Mr. Sedley began to doze in his
chair, and then it was Amelia's opportunity to commence
her conversation, which she did with great eagerness ;—
it related exclusively to Georgy. She did not talk at all
about her own sufferings at breaking from him, for indeed
this worthy woman, though she was half-killed by the
separation from the child, yet thought it was very wicked
in her to repine at losing him ; but everything concerning
him, his virtues, talents, and prospects, she poured out.
She described his angelic beauty ; narrated a hundred
instances of his generosity and greatness of mind whilst
living with her : how a royal duchess had stopped and
admired him in Kensington Gardens ; how splendidly he
was cared for now, and how he had a groom and a pony ;
what quickness and cleverness he had, and what a prodigiously well-read and delightful person the Reverend Lawrence
Veal was, George's master. ' He knows *everything*,' Amelia
said. ' He has the most delightful parties. You who are
so learned yourself, and have read so much, and are so
clever and accomplished—don't shake your head and say
No—*he* always used to say you were—you will be charmed
with Mr. Veal's parties. The last Tuesday in every month.
He says there is no place in the bar or the senate that
Georgy may not aspire to. Look here,' and she went to
the piano-drawer and drew out a theme of Georgy's composition. This great effort of genius, which is still in the
possession of George's mother, is as follows :—

On Selfishness.—Of all the vices which degrade the human
character, Selfishness is the most odious and contemptible. An
undue love of Self leads to the most monstrous crimes ; and occasions the greatest misfortunes both in *States and Families*. As a
selfish man will impoverish his family and often bring them to
ruin : so a selfish king brings ruin on his people and often plunges
them into war.

Example : The selfishness of Achilles, as remarked by the poet

Homer, occasioned a thousand woes to the Greeks—μυρί 'Αχαιοῖς ἄλγε ἔθηκε—(Hom. *Il.* A. 2). The selfishness of the late Napoleon Bonaparte occasioned innumerable wars in Europe, and caused him to perish, himself, in a miserable island—that of St. Helena in the Atlantic Ocean.

We see by these examples that we are not to consult our own interest and ambition, but that we are to consider the interests of others as well as our own.

GEORGE S. OSBORNE.

ATHENÈ HOUSE, April 24, 1827.*

'Think of him writing such a hand, and quoting Greek too, at his age,' the delighted mother said. 'Oh, William,' she added, holding out her hand to the major—'what a treasure Heaven has given me in that boy! He is the comfort of my life—and he is the image of—of him that's gone!'

'Ought I to be angry with her for being faithful to him?' William thought. 'Ought I to be jealous of my friend in the grave, or hurt that such a heart as Amelia's can love only once and for ever? O George, George, how little you knew the prize you had, though.' This sentiment passed rapidly through William's mind, as he was holding Amelia's hand, whilst the handkerchief was veiling her eyes.

'Dear friend,' she said, pressing the hand which held hers, 'how good, how kind you always have been to me! See! papa is stirring. You will go and see Georgy to-morrow, won't you?'

'Not to-morrow,' said poor old Dobbin. 'I have business.' He did not like to own that he had not as yet been to his parents' and his dear sister Anne—a remissness for which I am sure every well-regulated person will blame the major. And presently he took his leave, leaving his address behind him for Jos, against the latter's arrival. And so the first day was over, and he had seen her.

When he got back to the Slaughters', the roast fowl was of course cold, in which condition he ate it for supper. And knowing what early hours his family kept, and that it would be needless to disturb their slumbers at so late an hour, it is on record, that Major Dobbin treated himself to half-price at the Haymarket Theatre that evening, where let us hope he enjoyed himself.

CHAPTER LIX

THE OLD PIANO

THE major's visit left old John
Sedley in a great state of agitation and excitement. His
daughter could not induce him
to settle down to his customary
occupations or amusements that
night. He passed the evening
fumbling amongst his boxes and
desks, untying his papers with
trembling hands, and sorting and
arranging them against Jos's
arrival. He had them in the
greatest order—his tapes and his
files, his receipts, and his letters
with lawyers and correspondents;
the documents relative to the
Wine Project (which failed from
a most unaccountable accident, after commencing with the
most splendid prospects), the Coal Project (which only a
want of capital prevented from becoming the most successful
scheme ever put before the public), the Patent Saw-mills
and Sawdust Consolidation Project, &c. &c.—All night,
until a very late hour, he passed in the preparation of these
documents, trembling about from one room to another,
with a quivering candle and shaky hands.—Here's the wine
papers, here's the sawdust, here's the coals; here's my
letters to Calcutta and Madras, and replies from Major
Dobbin, C.B., and Mr. Joseph Sedley to the same. ' He
shall find no irregularity about *me*, Emmy,' the old gentleman said.

Emmy smiled. ' I don't think Jos will care about seeing
those papers, papa,' she said.

' You don't know anything about business, my dear,'
answered the sire, shaking his head with an important air.
And it must be confessed that on this point Emmy was very
ignorant, and that is a pity, some people are so knowing.
All these twopenny documents arranged on a side table, old

Sedley covered them carefully over with a clean bandanna
handkerchief (one out of Major Dobbin's lot), and enjoined
the maid and landlady of the house, in the most solemn
way, not to disturb those papers, which were arranged
for the arrival of Mr. Joseph Sedley the next morning,
'Mr. Joseph Sedley of the Honourable East India Company's
Bengal Civil Service.'

Amelia found him up very early the next morning, more
eager, more hectic, and more shaky than ever. 'I didn't

sleep much, Emmy, my dear,' he said. 'I was thinking of
my poor Bessy. I wish she was alive, to ride in Jos's
carriage once again. She kept her own, and became it
very well.' And his eyes filled with tears, which trickled
down his furrowed old face. Amelia wiped them away,
and smilingly kissed him, and tied the old man's neckcloth
in a smart bow, and put his brooch into his best shirt frill,
in which, in his Sunday suit of mourning, he sat from six
o'clock in the morning awaiting the arrival of his son.

There are some splendid tailors' shops in the High Street

of Southampton, in the fine plate-glass windows of which
hang gorgeous waistcoats of all sorts, of silk and velvet,
and gold and crimson, and pictures of the last new fashions
in which those wonderful gentlemen with quizzing glasses,
and holding on to little boys with the exceeding large eyes
and curly hair, ogle ladies in riding habits prancing by the
Statue of Achilles at Apsley House. Jos, although provided
with some of the most splendid vests that Calcutta could
furnish, thought he could not go to town until he was
supplied with one or two of these garments, and selected
a crimson satin, embroidered with gold butterflies, and
a black and red velvet tartan with white stripes and a
rolling collar, with which, and a rich blue satin stock and
a gold pin, consisting of a five-barred gate with a horseman
in pink enamel jumping over it, he thought he might make
his entry into London with some dignity. For Jos's former
shyness and blundering blushing timidity had given way
to a more candid and courageous self-assertion of his worth.
' I don't care about owning it,' Waterloo Sedley would say
to his friends, ' I am a dressy man : ' and though rather
uneasy if the ladies looked at him at the Government House
balls, and though he blushed and turned away alarmed under
their glances, it was chiefly from a dread lest they should
make love to him, that he avoided them, being averse to
marriage altogether. But there was no such swell in Calcutta
as Waterloo Sedley, I have heard say : and he had the
handsomest turn-out, gave the best bachelor dinners, and
had the finest plate in the whole place.

To make these waistcoats for a man of his size and dignity
took at least a day, part of which he employed in hiring
a servant to wait upon him and his native ; and in instructing the agent who cleared his baggage, his boxes, his books,
which he never read ; his chests of mangoes, chutney, and
curry-powders ; his shawls for presents to people whom he
didn't know as yet ; and the rest of his *Persicos apparatus*.

At length, he drove leisurely to London on the third day,
and in the new waistcoat ; the native, with chattering
teeth, shuddering in a shawl on the box by the side of the
new European servant, Jos puffing his pipe at intervals
within, and looking so majestic, that the little boys cried
' Hooray,' and many people thought he must be a governor-
general. *He*, I promise, did not decline the obsequious
invitation of the landlords to alight and refresh himself in

the neat country towns. Having partaken of a copious
breakfast, with fish, and rice, and hard eggs, at Southampton, he had so far rallied at Winchester as to think a glass of
sherry necessary. At Alton he stepped out of the carriage,
at his servant's request, and imbibed some of the ale for
which the place is famous. At Farnham he stopped to
view the Bishop's Castle, and to partake of a light dinner
of stewed eels, veal cutlets, and French beans, with a bottle
of claret. He was cold over Bagshot Heath, where the
native chattered more and more, and Jos Sahib took some
brandy-and-water ; in fact, when he drove into town, he
was as full of wine, beer, meat, pickles, cherry-brandy, and
tobacco, as the steward's cabin of a steam-packet. It was
evening when his carriage thundered up to the little door
in Brompton, whither the affectionate fellow drove first,
and before hying to the apartments secured for him by
Mr. Dobbin at the Slaughters'.

All the faces in the street were in the windows ; the little
maidservant flew to the wicket-gate, the Mesdames Clapp
looked out from the casement of the ornamented kitchen ;
Emmy, in a great flutter, was in the passage among the hats
and coats, and old Sedley in the parlour inside, shaking all
over. Jos descended from the post-chaise and down the
creaking swaying steps in awful state, supported by the
new valet from Southampton and the shuddering native,
whose brown face was now livid with cold, and of the colour
of a turkey's gizzard. He created an immense sensation
in the passage presently, where Mrs. and Miss Clapp, coming
perhaps to listen at the parlour door, found Loll Jewab
shaking upon the hall bench under the coats, moaning in
a strange piteous way, and showing his yellow eyeballs and
white teeth.

For, you see, we have adroitly shut the door upon the
meeting between Jos and the old father, and the poor little
gentle sister inside. The old man was very much affected :
so, of course, was his daughter : nor was Jos without feeling.
In that long absence of ten years, the most selfish will
think about home and early ties. Distance sanctifies both.
Long brooding over those lost pleasures exaggerates their
charm and sweetness. Jos was unaffectedly glad to see and
shake the hand of his father, between whom and himself
there had been a coolness—glad to see his little sister, whom
he remembered so pretty and smiling, and pained at the

alteration which time, grief, and misfortune had made in
the shattered old man. Emmy had come out to the door
in her black clothes and whispered to him of her mother's
death, and not to speak of it to their father. There was no
need of this caution, for the elder Sedley himself began
immediately to speak of the event, and prattled about it,
and wept over it plenteously. It shocked the Indian not
a little, and made him think of himself less than the poor
fellow was accustomed to do.

The result of the interview must have been very satisfactory, for when Jos had reascended his post-chaise, and had
driven away to his hotel, Emmy embraced her father tenderly, appealing to him with an air of triumph, and asking
the old man whether she did not always say that her brother
had a good heart ?

Indeed, Joseph Sedley, affected by the humble position
in which he found his relations, and in the expansiveness and
overflowing of heart occasioned by the first meeting, declared
that they should never suffer want or discomfort any more,
that he was at home for some time at any rate, during
which his house and everything he had should be theirs :
and that Amelia would look very pretty at the head of his
table—until she would accept one of her own.

She shook her head sadly, and had, as usual, recourse
to the waterworks. She knew what he meant. She and
her young confidante, Miss Mary, had talked over the
matter most fully, the very night of the major's visit :
beyond which time the impetuous Polly could not refrain
from talking of the discovery which she had made, and
describing the start and tremor of joy by which Major
Dobbin betrayed himself when Mr. Binney passed with his
bride, and the major learned that he had no longer a rival
to fear. ' Didn't you see how he shook all over when you
asked if he was married, and he said, " Who told you those
lies ? " Oh, ma'am,' Polly said, ' he never kept his eyes off
you ; and I'm sure he's grown grey a-thinking of you.'

But Amelia, looking up at her bed, over which hung the
portraits of her husband and son, told her young protégée,
never, never, to speak on that subject again ; that Major
Dobbin had been her husband's dearest friend, and her own
and George's most kind and affectionate guardian ; that
she loved him as a brother—but that a woman who had been

married to such an angel as that, and she pointed to the
wall, could never think of any other union. Poor Polly
sighed : she thought what she should do if young Mr. Tom-
kins, at the surgery, who always looked at her so at church,
and who, by those mere aggressive glances had put her
timorous little heart into such a flutter that she was ready
to surrender at once,—what she should do if he were to die ?
She knew he was consumptive, his cheeks were so red, and
he was so uncommon thin in the waist.

Not that Emmy, being made aware of the honest major's
passion, rebuffed him in any way, or felt displeased with
him. Such an attachment from so true and loyal a gentleman could make no woman angry. Desdemona was not
angry with Cassio, though there is very little doubt she
saw the lieutenant's partiality for her (and I for my part
believe that many more things took place in that sad affair
than the worthy Moorish officer ever knew of) ; why,
Miranda was even very kind to Caliban, and we may be pretty
sure for the same reason. Not that she would encourage
him in the least,—the poor uncouth monster—of course
not. No more would Emmy by any means encourage her
admirer, the major. She would give him that friendly
regard, which so much excellence and fidelity merited ;
she would treat him with perfect cordiality and frankness
until he made his proposals : and *then* it would be time
enough for her to speak, and to put an end to hopes which
never could be realized.

She slept, therefore, very soundly that evening, after
the conversation with Miss Polly, and was more than
ordinarily happy, in spite of Jos's delaying. ' I am glad
he is not going to marry that Miss O'Dowd,' she thought.
' Colonel O'Dowd never could have a sister fit for such an
accomplished man as Major William.' Who was there
amongst her little circle, who would make him a good wife ?
Not Miss Binney, she was too old and ill-tempered ; Miss
Osborne ?—too old, too. Little Polly was too young.
Mrs. Osborne could not find anybody to suit the major
before she went to sleep.

However, when the postman made his appearance, the
little party were put out of suspense, by the receipt of a
letter from Jos to his sister, who announced, that he felt
a little fatigued after his voyage, and should not be able to
move on that day, but that he would leave Southampton

early the next morning, and be with his father and mother at evening. Amelia, as she read out the letter to her father, paused over the latter word ; her brother, it was clear, did not know what had happened in the family. Nor could he : for the fact is, that though the major rightly suspected that his travelling companion never would be got into motion in so short a space as twenty-four hours, and would find some excuse for delaying, yet Dobbin had not written to Jos to inform him of the calamity which had befallen the Sedley family ; being occupied in talking with Amelia until long after post-hour.

The same morning brought Major Dobbin a letter to the Slaughters' Coffee-house from his friend at Southampton ; begging dear Dob to excuse Jos for being in a rage when awakened the day before (he had a confounded headache, and was just in his first sleep), and entreating Dob to engage comfortable rooms at the Slaughters' for Mr. Sedley and his servants. The major had become necessary to Jos during the voyage. He was attached to him, and hung upon him. The other passengers were away to London. Young Ricketts and little Chaffers went away on the coach that day—Ricketts on the box, and taking the reins from Botley ; the doctor was off to his family at Portsea ; Bragg gone to town to his co-partners ; and the first mate busy in the unloading of the *Ramchunder*. Mr. Jos was very lonely at Southampton, and got the landlord of the ' George ' to take a glass of wine with him that day ; at the very hour at which Major Dobbin was seated at the table of his father, Sir William, where his sister found out (for it was impossible for the major to tell fibs) that he had been to see Mrs. George Osborne.*

Jos was so comfortably situated in St. Martin's Lane, he could enjoy his hookah there with such perfect ease, and could swagger down to the theatres, when minded, so agreeably, that, perhaps, he would have remained altogether at the Slaughters' had not his friend, the major, been at his elbow. That gentleman would not let the Bengalee rest until he had executed his promise of having a home for Amelia and his father. Jos was a soft fellow in anybody's hands ; Dobbin most active in anybody's concerns but his own ; the civilian was, therefore, an easy victim to the guileless arts of this good-natured diplomatist, and was

ready to do, to purchase, hire, or relinquish whatever his
friend thought fit. Loll Jewab, of whom the boys about
St. Martin's Lane used to make cruel fun whenever he
showed his dusky countenance in the street, was sent back
to Calcutta in the *Lady Kicklebury* East Indiaman, in which
Sir William Dobbin had a share ; having previously taught
Jos's European the art of preparing curries, pilaws, and
pipes. It was a matter of great delight and occupation to
Jos to superintend the building of a smart chariot, which
he and the major ordered in the neighbouring Long Acre :
and a pair of handsome horses were jobbed, with which
Jos drove about in state in the Park, or to call upon his
Indian friends. Amelia was not seldom by his side on these
excursions, when also Major Dobbin would be seen in the
back seat of the carriage. At other times old Sedley and
his daughter took advantage of it : and Miss Clapp, who
frequently accompanied her friend, had great pleasure in
being recognized as she sat in the carriage, dressed in the
famous yellow shawl, by the young gentleman at the
surgery, whose face might commonly be seen over the
window-blinds as she passed.

Shortly after Jos's first appearance at Brompton, a dismal
scene, indeed, took place at that humble cottage, at which
the Sedleys had passed the last ten years of their life. Jos's
carriage (the temporary one, not the chariot under con-
struction) arrived one day and carried off old Sedley and
his daughter—to return no more. The tears that were
shed by the landlady and the landlady's daughter at that
event were as genuine tears of sorrow as any that have been
outpoured in the course of this history. In their long
acquaintanceship and intimacy they could not recall a harsh
word that had been uttered by Amelia. She had been all
sweetness and kindness, always thankful, always gentle,
even when Mrs. Clapp lost her own temper, and pressed
for the rent. When the kind creature was going away for
good and all, the landlady reproached herself bitterly for
ever having used a rough expression to her—how she wept,
as they stuck up with wafers on the window, a paper notify-
ing that the little rooms so long occupied were to let !
They never would have such lodgers again, that was quite
clear. After-life proved the truth of this melancholy pro-
phecy : and Mrs. Clapp revenged herself for the deteriora-
tion of mankind by levying the most savage contributions

upon the tea-caddies and legs of mutton of her *locataires*.
Most of them scolded and grumbled ; some of them did not
pay : none of them stayed. The landlady might well
regret those old, old friends, who had left her.

As for Miss Mary, her sorrow at Amelia's departure was
such as I shall not attempt to depict. From childhood
upwards she had been with her daily, and had attached
herself so passionately to that dear good lady, that when
the grand barouche came to carry her off into splendour,
she fainted in the arms of her friend, who was indeed scarcely
less affected than the good-natured girl. Amelia loved her
like a daughter. During eleven years the girl had been her
constant friend and associate. The separation was a very
painful one indeed to her. But it was of course arranged
that Mary was to come and stay often at the grand new
house whither Mrs. Osborne was going ; and where Mary
was sure she would never be so happy as she had been in
their humble cot, as Miss Clapp called it in the language of
the novels which she loved.

Let us hope she was wrong in her judgement. Poor
Emmy's days of happiness had been very few in that humble
cot. A gloomy Fate had oppressed her there. She never
liked to come back to the house after she had left it, or to
face the landlady who had tyrannized over her when ill-
humoured and unpaid, or when pleased, had treated her
with a coarse familiarity scarcely less odious. Her servility
and fulsome compliments when Emmy was in prosperity
were not more to that lady's liking. She cast about notes
of admiration all over the new house, extolling every article
of furniture or ornament ; she fingered Mrs. Osborne's
dresses, and calculated their price. Nothing could be too
good for that sweet lady, she vowed and protested. But
in the vulgar sycophant who now paid court to her, Emmy
always remembered the coarse tyrant who had made her
miserable many a time, to whom she had been forced to
put up petitions for time, when the rent was overdue ; who
cried out at her extravagance if she bought delicacies for
her ailing mother or father ; who had seen her humble and
trampled upon her.

Nobody ever heard of these griefs, which had been part
of our poor little woman's lot in life. She kept them secret
from her father, whose improvidence was the cause of
much of her misery. She had to bear all the blame of his

misdoings, and indeed was so utterly gentle and humble as
to be made by nature for a victim.

I hope she is not to suffer much more of that hard usage.
And, as in all griefs, there is said to be some consolation,
I may mention that poor Mary, when left at her friend's
departure in a hysterical condition, was placed under the
medical treatment of the young fellow from the surgery,
under whose care she rallied after a short period. Emmy,
when she went away from Brompton, endowed Mary with
every article of furniture that the house contained : only
taking away her pictures (the two pictures over the bed)
and her piano—that little old piano which had now passed
into a plaintive jingling old age, but which she loved for
reasons of her own. She was a child when first she played
on it : and her parents gave it her. It had been given to
her again since, as the reader may remember, when her
father's house was gone to ruin, and the instrument was
recovered out of the wreck.

Major Dobbin was exceedingly pleased when, as he was
superintending the arrangements of Jos's new house, which
the major insisted should be very handsome and comfortable ; the cart arrived from Brompton, bringing the trunks
and bandboxes of the emigrants from that village, and with
them the old piano. Amelia would have it up in her sitting-
room, a neat little apartment on the second floor, adjoining
her father's chamber : and where the old gentleman sat
commonly of evenings.

When the men appeared then bearing this old music-box,
and Amelia gave orders that it should be placed in the
chamber aforesaid, Dobbin was quite elated. ' I'm glad
you've kept it,' he said in a very sentimental manner.
' I was afraid you didn't care about it.'

' I value it more than anything I have in the world,' said
Amelia.

' *Do* you, Amelia ? ' cried the major. The fact was, as
he had bought it himself, though he never said anything
about it, it never entered into his head to suppose that
Emmy should think anybody else was the purchaser, and
as a matter of course, he fancied that she knew the gift
came from him. ' Do you, Amelia ? ' he said ; and the
question, the great question of all, was trembling on his lips,
when Emmy replied—

' Can I do otherwise ?—did not *he* give it me ? '

' I did not know,' said poor old Dob, and his countenance fell.

Emmy did not note the circumstance at the time, nor take immediate heed of the very dismal expression which honest Dobbin's countenance assumed ; but she thought of it afterwards. And then it struck her, with inexpressible pain and mortification too, that it was William who was the giver of the piano ; and not George as she had fancied. It was not George's gift ; the only one which she had received from her lover, as she thought—the thing she had cherished beyond all others—her dearest relic and prize. She had spoken to it about George ; played his favourite airs upon it ; sat for long evening hours, touching, to the best of her simple art, melancholy harmonies on the keys, and weeping over them in silence. It was not George's relic. It was valueless now. The next time that old Sedley asked her to play, she said it was shockingly out of tune, that she had a headache, that she couldn't play.

Then, according to her custom, she rebuked herself for her pettishness and ingratitude, and determined to make a reparation to honest William for the slight she had not expressed to him, but had felt for his piano. A few days afterwards, as they were seated in the drawing-room, where Jos had fallen asleep with great comfort after dinner, Amelia said with rather a faltering voice to Major Dobbin,—

' I have to beg your pardon for something.'

' About what ? ' said he.

' About—about that little square piano. I never thanked you for it when you gave it me, many, many years ago, before I was married. I thought somebody else had given it. Thank you, William.' She held out her hand ; but the poor little woman's heart was bleeding ; and as for her eyes, of course they were at their work.

But William could hold no more. ' Amelia, Amelia,' he said, ' I did buy it for you. I loved you then as I do now. I must tell you. I think I loved you from the first minute that I saw you, when George brought me to your house,* to show me the Amelia whom he was engaged to. You were but a girl in white, with large ringlets ; you came down singing—do you remember ?—and we went to Vauxhall. Since then I have thought of but one woman in the world, and that was you. I think there is no hour of the day has passed for twelve years that I haven't thought

of you.　I came to tell you this before I went to India, but
you did not care, and I hadn't the heart to speak.　You
did not care whether I stayed or went.'

'I was very ungrateful,' Amelia said.

'No ; only indifferent,' Dobbin continued desperately.
'I have nothing to make a woman to be otherwise.　I know
what you are feeling now.　You are hurt in your heart at
that discovery about the piano ; and that it came from me
and not from George.　I forgot, or I should never have
spoken of it so.　It is for me to ask your pardon for being
a fool for a moment, and thinking that years of constancy
and devotion might have pleaded with you.'

'It is you who are cruel now,' Amelia said, with some
spirit.　'George is my husband, here and in heaven.　How
could I love any other but him ?　I am his now as when you
first saw me, dear William.　It was he who told me how
good and generous you were, and who taught me to love
you as a brother.　Have you not been everything to me
and my boy ?　Our dearest, truest, kindest friend and
protector ?　Had you come a few months sooner perhaps
you might have spared me that—that dreadful parting.
Oh, it nearly killed me, William—but you didn't come,
though I wished and prayed for you to come, and they
took him too away from me.　Isn't he a noble boy, William ?
Be his friend still and mine '—and here her voice broke, and
she hid her face on his shoulder.

The major folded his arms round her, holding her to him
as if she was a child, and kissed her head.　'I will not change,
dear Amelia,' he said.　'I ask for no more than your love.
I think I would not have it otherwise.　Only let me stay
near you, and see you often.'

'Yes, often,' Amelia said.　And so William was at liberty
to look and long : as the poor boy at school who has no
money may sigh after the contents of the tart-woman's tray.

CHAPTER LX

OOD fortune now begins to smile upon Amelia. We are glad to get her out of that low sphere in which she has been creeping hitherto, and introduce her into a polite circle, not so grand and refined as that in which our other female friend, Mrs. Becky, has appeared, but still having no small pretensions to gentility and fashion. Jos's friends were all from the three presidencies, and his new house was in the comfortable Anglo - Indian district of which Moira Place is the centre. Minto Square, Great Clive Street, Warren Street, Hastings Street, Ochterlony Place, Plassey Square, Assaye Terrace*(' Gardens' was a felicitous word not applied to stucco houses with asphalte terraces in front, so early as 1827)—who does not know these respectable abodes of the retired Indian aristocracy, and the quarter which Mr. Wenham calls the Black Hole, in a word ? Jos's position in life was not grand enough to entitle him to a house in Moira Place, where none can live but retired Members of Council, and partners of Indian firms (who break after having settled a hundred thousand pounds on their wives, and retire into comparative penury, to a country place and four thousand a year) : he engaged a comfortable house of a second- or third-rate order in Gillespie Street, purchasing the carpets, costly mirrors and handsome and appropriate planned furniture by Seddons, from the assignees of Mr. Scape, lately admitted partner into the great Calcutta house of Fogle, Fake, and Cracksman, in

which poor Scape had embarked seventy thousand pounds,
the earnings of a long and honourable life, taking Fake's
place, who retired to a princely park in Sussex (the Fogles
have been long out of the firm, and Sir Horace Fogle is about
to be raised to the peerage as Baron Bandanna)—admitted,
I say, partner into the great agency house of Fogle and
Fake two years before it failed for a million, and plunged
half the Indian public into misery and ruin.

Scape, ruined, honest, and broken-hearted at sixty-five
years of age, went out to Calcutta to wind up the affairs of
the house.   Walter Scape was withdrawn from Eton, and
put into a merchant's house.   Florence Scape, Fanny Scape,
and their mother, faded away to Boulogne, and will be heard
of no more.   To be brief, Jos stepped in and bought their
carpets and sideboards, and admired himself in the mirrors
which had reflected their kind handsome faces.   The Scape
tradesmen, all honourably paid, left their cards, and were
eager to supply the new household.   The large men in white
waistcoats, who waited at Scape's dinners, greengrocers,
bank-porters, and milkmen in their private capacity, left
their addresses, and ingratiated themselves with the butler.
Mr. Chummy, the chimney-purifier, who had swep the last
three families, tried to coax the butler and the boy under
him, whose duty it was to go out covered with buttons and
with stripes down his trousers, for the protection of Mrs.
Amelia whenever she chose to walk abroad.

It was a modest establishment.   The butler was Jos's
valet also, and never was more drunk than a butler in a small
family should be who has a proper regard for his master's
wine.   Emmy was supplied with a maid, grown on Sir
William Dobbin's suburban estate ; a good girl, whose kindness and humility disarmed Mrs. Osborne, who was at first
terrified at the idea of having a servant to wait upon herself,
who did not in the least know how to use one, and who
always spoke to domestics with the most reverential politeness.   But this maid was very useful in the family, in
dexterously tending old Mr. Sedley, who kept almost
entirely to his own quarter of the house, and never mixed
in any of the gay doings which took place there.

Numbers of people came to see Mrs. Osborne.   Lady
Dobbin and daughters were delighted at her change of
fortune, and waited upon her.   Miss Osborne from Russell
Square came in her grand chariot with the flaming hammer-

cloth*emblazoned with the Leeds arms. Jos was reported
to be immensely rich. Old Osborne had no objection that
Georgy should inherit his uncle's property as well as his
own. ' Damn it, we will make a man of the feller,' he said ;
' and I'll see him in Parliament before I die. *You* may go
and see his mother, Miss O., though I'll never set eyes on
her : ' and Miss Osborne came. Emmy, you may be sure,
was very glad to see her, and so be brought nearer to George.
That young fellow was allowed to come much more frequently than before to visit his mother. He dined once or
twice a week in Gillespie Street, and bullied the servants
and his relations there, just as he did in Russell Square.

He was always respectful to Major Dobbin, however, and
more modest in his demeanour when that gentleman was
present. He was a clever lad, and afraid of the major.
George could not help admiring his friend's simplicity, his
good humour, his various learning quietly imparted, his
general love of truth and justice. He had met no such
man as yet in the course of his experience, and he had an
instinctive liking for a gentleman. He hung fondly by his
godfather's side ; and it was his delight to walk in the Parks
and hear Dobbin talk. William told George about his
father, about India and Waterloo, about everything but
himself. When George was more than usually pert and
conceited, the major made jokes at him, which Mrs. Osborne
thought very cruel. One day, taking him to the play, and
the boy declining to go into the pit because it was vulgar,
the major took him to the boxes, left him there, and went
down himself to the pit. He had not been seated there
very long, before he felt an arm thrust under his, and a
dandy little hand in a kid-glove squeezing his arm. George
had seen the absurdity of his ways, and come down from
the upper region. A tender laugh of benevolence lighted
up old Dobbin's face and eyes as he looked at the repentant
little prodigal. He loved the boy, as he did everything
that belonged to Amelia. How charmed she was when she
heard of this instance of George's goodness ! Her eyes
looked more kindly on Dobbin than they ever had done.
She blushed, he thought, after looking at him so.

Georgy never tired of his praises of the major to his
mother. ' I like him, mamma, because he knows such lots
of things ; and he ain't like old Veal, who is always bragging
and using such long words, don't you know ? The chaps

call him " Longtail " at school. I gave him the name ;
ain't it capital ? But Dob reads Latin like English, and
French and that ; and when we go out together he tells
me stories about my papa, and never about himself ;
though I heard Colonel Buckler, at grandpapa's, say that
he was one of the bravest officers in the army, and had
distinguished himself ever so much. Grandpapa was quite
surprised, and said " *That* feller ! why, I didn't think he
could say Bo to a goose "—but *I* know he could, couldn't
he, mamma ? '

Emmy laughed : she thought it was very likely the major
could do thus much.

If there was a sincere liking between George and the
major, it must be confessed that between the boy and his
uncle no great love existed. George had got a way of blowing out his cheeks, and putting his hands in his waistcoat
pockets, and saying, ' God bless my soul, you don't say so,'
so exactly after the fashion of old Jos, that it was impossible
to restrain from laughter. The servants would explode at
dinner if the lad, asking for something which wasn't at
table, put on that countenance and used that favourite
phrase. Even Dobbin would shoot out a sudden peal at
the boy's mimicry. If George did not mimic his uncle to
his face, it was only by Dobbin's rebukes and Amelia's
terrified entreaties that the little scapegrace was induced to
desist. And the worthy civilian being haunted by a dim
consciousness that the lad thought him an ass, and was
inclined to turn him into ridicule, used to be extremely
timorous, and, of course, doubly pompous and dignified in
the presence of Master Georgy. When it was announced
that the young gentleman was expected in Gillespie Street
to dine with his mother, Mr. Jos commonly found that he
had an engagement at the club. Perhaps nobody was
much grieved at his absence. On those days Mr. Sedley
would commonly be induced to come out from his place of
refuge in the upper stories ; and there would be a small
family party, whereof Major Dobbin pretty generally formed
one. He was the *ami de la maison ;* old Sedley's friend,
Emmy's friend, Georgy's friend, Jos's counsel and adviser.
' He might almost as well be at Madras for anything *we* see
of him,' Miss Ann Dobbin remarked, at Camberwell. Ah !
Miss Ann, did it not strike you that it was not *you* whom
the major wanted to marry ?

Joseph Sedley then led a life of dignified otiosity such as became a person of his eminence. His very first point, of course, was to become a member of the Oriental Club : where he spent his mornings in the company of his brother Indians, where he dined, or whence he brought home men to dine.

Amelia had to receive and entertain these gentlemen and their ladies. From these she heard how soon Smith would be in Council ; how many lacs Jones had brought home with him ; how Thomson's House in London had refused the bills drawn by Thomson, Kibobjee and Co., the Bombay House, and how it was thought the Calcutta House must go too ; how very imprudent, to say the least of it, Mrs. Brown's conduct (wife of Brown of the Ahmednuggar Irregulars) had been with young Swankey of the Body Guard, sitting up with him on deck until all hours, and losing themselves as they were riding out at the Cape ; how Mrs. Hardyman had had out her thirteen sisters, daughters of a country curate, the Rev. Felix Rabbits, and married eleven of them, seven high up in the service ; how Hornby was wild because his wife would stay in Europe, and Trotter was appointed collector at Ummera-poora. This and similar talk took place, at the grand dinners all round. They had the same conversation ; the same silver dishes ; the same saddles of mutton, boiled turkeys, and entrées. Politics set in a short time after dessert, when the ladies retired upstairs and talked about their complaints and their children.

Mutato nomine, it is all the same. Don't the barristers' wives talk about Circuit ?—don't the soldiers' ladies gossip about the Regiment ?—don't the clergymen's ladies dis-course about Sunday-schools, and who takes whose duty ?—don't the very greatest ladies of all talk about that small clique of persons to whom they belong, and why shall our Indian friends not have their own conversation ?—only I admit it is slow for the laymen whose fate it sometimes is to sit by and listen.

Before long Emmy had a visiting-book, and was driving about regularly in a carriage, calling upon Lady Bludyer (wife of Major-General Sir Roger Bludyer, K.C.B., Bengal Army) ; Lady Huff, wife of Sir G. Huff, Bombay ditto ; Mrs. Pice, the lady of Pice the director, &c. We are not long in using ourselves to changes in life. That carriage

came round to Gillespie Street every day ; that buttony
boy sprang up and down from the box with Emmy's and
Jos's visiting cards ; at stated hours Emmy and the carriage
went for Jos to the club, and took him an airing ; or,
putting old Sedley into the vehicle, she drove the old man
round the Regent's Park.   The lady's maid and the chariot,
the visiting-book and the buttony page, became soon as
familiar to Amelia as the humble routine of Brompton.

She accommodated herself to one as to the other.   If Fate
had ordained that she should be a duchess, she would even
have done that duty too.   She was voted, in Jos's female
society, rather a pleasing young person—not much in her,
but pleasing, and that sort of thing.

The men, as usual, liked her artless kindness and simple
refined demeanour.   The gallant young Indian dandies at
home on furlough—immense dandies these—chained and
moustached—driving in tearing cabs, the pillars of the
theatres, living at West End hotels,—nevertheless admired

Mrs. Osborne, liked to bow to her carriage in the Park, and to be admitted to have the honour of paying her a morning visit. Swankey of the Body Guard himself, that dangerous youth, and the greatest buck of all the Indian army now on leave, was one day discovered by Major Dobbin *tête à tête* with Amelia, and describing the sport of pig-sticking to her with great humour and eloquence ; and he spoke afterwards of a d—d king's officer that's always hanging about the house—a long, thin, queer-looking oldish fellow—a dry fellow though, that took the shine out of a man in the talking line.

Had the major possessed a little more personal vanity he would have been jealous of so dangerous a young buck, as that fascinating Bengal captain. But Dobbin was of too simple and generous a nature to have any doubts about Amelia. He was glad that the young men should pay her respect ; and that others should admire her. Ever since her womanhood almost, had she not been persecuted and undervalued ? It pleased him to see how kindness brought out her good qualities, and how her spirits gently rose with her prosperity. Any person who appreciated her paid a compliment to the major's good judgement— that is, if a man may be said to have good judgement who is under the influence of Love's delusion.

After Jos went to Court, which we may be sure he did as a loyal subject of his sovereign (showing himself in his full Court suit at the club, whither Dobbin came to fetch him in a very shabby old uniform), he who had always been a stanch Loyalist and admirer of George IV, became such a tremendous Tory and pillar of the State, that he was for having Amelia to go to a Drawing-room too. He somehow had worked himself up to believe that he was implicated in the maintenance of the public welfare, and that the sovereign would not be happy unless Jos Sedley and his family appeared to rally round him at St. James's.

Emmy laughed. 'Shall I wear the family diamonds, Jos ? ' she said.

'I wish you would let me buy you some,' thought the major. 'I should like to see any that were too good for you.'

CHAPTER LXI

IN WHICH TWO LIGHTS ARE PUT OUT

HERE came a day when the round of decorous pleasures and solemn gaieties in which Mr. Jos Sedley's family indulged, was interrupted by an event which happens in most houses. As you ascend the staircase of your house from the drawing towards the bedroom floors, you may have remarked a little arch in the wall right before you, which at once gives light to the stair which leads from the second story to the third (where the nursery and servants' chambers commonly are), and serves for another purpose of utility, of which the undertaker's men can give you a notion. They rest the coffins upon that arch, or pass them through it so as not to disturb in any unseemly manner the cold tenant slumbering within the black ark.*

That second-floor arch in a London house, looking up and down the well of the staircase, and commanding the main thoroughfare by which the inhabitants are passing; by which cook lurks down before daylight to scour her pots and pans in the kitchen; by which young master stealthily ascends, having left his boots in the hall, and let himself in after dawn from a jolly night at the club; down which miss comes rustling in fresh ribbons and spreading muslins, brilliant and beautiful, and prepared for conquest and the ball; or Master Tommy slides, preferring the banisters for a mode of conveyance, and disdaining danger and the stair ; down which the mother is fondly carried smiling in her strong husband's arms, as he steps steadily step by step, and followed by the monthly nurse, on the day when the medical man has pronounced that the charming patient may go downstairs ; up which John lurks to bed, yawning with a sputtering tallow candle, and to gather up before sunrise the boots which are awaiting him in the passages :—that stair, up or down which babies are carried, old people are helped, guests are marshalled to the ball, the parson walks to the christening, the doctor to the sick-room, and the undertaker's men to the upper floor—what a memento of Life, Death, and Vanity it is— that arch and stair—if you choose to consider it, and sit on the landing, looking up and down the well ! The doctor will come up to us too for the last time there, my friend in motley. The nurse will look in at the curtains, and you take no notice—and then she will fling open the windows for a little, and let in the air. Then they will pull down all the front blinds of the house and live in the back rooms—then they will send for the lawyer and other men in black, &c.—Your comedy and mine will have been played then, and we shall be removed, oh how far, from the trumpets, and the shouting, and the posture-making. If we are gentlefolks they will put hatchments over our late domicile, with gilt cherubim, and mottoes stating that there is ' Quiet in Heaven '. Your son will new furnish the house, or perhaps let it, and go into a more modern quarter ; your name will be among the 'Members Deceased', in the lists of your clubs next year. However much you may be mourned, your widow will like to have her weeds neatly made—the cook will send or come up to ask about dinner—the survivors will soon bear to look at your picture over the mantelpiece, which will presently be deposed from the place of honour, to make way for the portrait of the son who reigns.

Which of the dead are most tenderly and passionately deplored ? Those who love the survivors the least, I believe. The death of a child occasions a passion of grief and frantic tears, such as your end, brother reader, will never inspire. The death of an infant which scarce knew you, which a week's absence from you would have caused to forget you, will strike you down more than the loss of your closest

friend, or your first-born son—a man grown like yourself,
with children of his own. We may be harsh and stern
with Judah and Simeon—our love and pity gushes out for
Benjamin, the little one. And if you are old, as some
reader of this may be or shall be—old and rich, or old
and poor—you may one day be thinking for yourself—
'These people are very good round about me; but they
won't grieve too much when I am gone. I am very rich,
and they want my inheritance—or very poor, and they
are tired of supporting me.'

The period of mourning for Mrs. Sedley's death was
only just concluded, and Jos scarcely had had time to
cast off his black and appear in the splendid waistcoats
which he loved, when it became evident to those about
Mr. Sedley, that another event was at hand, and that the
old man was about to go seek for his wife in the dark
land whither she had preceded him. 'The state of my
father's health,' Jos Sedley solemnly remarked at the club,
'prevents me from giving my *large* parties this season :
but if you will come in quietly at half-past six, Chutney,
my boy, and take a homely dinner with one or two of the
old set—I shall be always glad to see you.' So Jos and
his acquaintances dined and drank their claret among themselves in silence ; whilst the sands of life were running
out in the old man's glass upstairs. The velvet-footed
butler brought them their wine; and they composed themselves to a rubber after dinner ; at which Major Dobbin
would sometimes come and take a hand : and Mrs. Osborne
would occasionally descend, when her patient above was
settled for the night, and had commenced one of those
lightly troubled slumbers which visit the pillow of old age.

The old man clung to his daughter during this sickness.
He would take his broths and medicines from scarcely any
other hand. To tend him became almost the sole business
of her life. Her bed was placed close by the door which
opened into his chamber, and she was alive at the slightest
noise or disturbance from the couch of the querulous
invalid. Though, to do him justice, he lay awake many
an hour, silent and without stirring, unwilling to awaken
his kind and vigilant nurse.

He loved his daughter with more fondness now, perhaps,
than ever he had done since the days of her childhood.
In the discharge of gentle offices and kind filial duties,

this simple creature shone most especially. 'She walks into the room as silently as a sunbeam,' Mr. Dobbin thought, as he saw her passing in and out from her father's room : a cheerful sweetness lighting up her face as she moved to and fro, graceful and noiseless. When women are brooding over their children, or busied in a sick-room, who has not seen in their faces those sweet angelic beams of love and pity ?

A secret feud of some years standing was thus healed : and with a tacit reconciliation. In these last hours and touched by her love and goodness, the old man forgot all his grief against her, and wrongs which he and his wife had many a long night debated : how she had given up everything for her boy : how she was careless of her parents in their old age and misfortune, and only thought of the child : how absurdly and foolishly, impiously indeed she took on, when George was removed from her. Old Sedley forgot these charges as he was making up his last account, and did justice to the gentle and uncomplaining little martyr. One night when she stole into his room, she found him awake, when the broken old man made his confession. 'Oh, Emmy, I've been thinking we were very unkind and unjust to you,' he said, and put out his cold and feeble hand to her. She knelt down and prayed by his bedside, as he did too, having still hold of her hand. When our turn comes, friend, may we have such company in our prayers.

Perhaps as he was lying awake then, his life may have passed before him—his early hopeful struggles, his manly successes and prosperity, his downfall in his declining years, and his present helpless condition—no chance of revenge against Fortune, which had had the better of him—neither name nor money to bequeath—a spent-out, bootless life of defeat and disappointment, and the end here ! Which, I wonder, brother reader, is the better lot, to die prosperous and famous, or poor and disappointed ? To have, and to be forced to yield ; or to sink out of life, having played and lost the game ? That must be a strange feeling, when a day of our life comes and we say, '*To-morrow*, success or failure won't matter much : and the sun will rise, and all the myriads of mankind go to their work or their pleasure as usual, but I shall be out of the turmoil.'

So there came one morning and sunrise, when all the

world got up and set about its various works and pleasures,
with the exception of old John Sedley, who was not to
fight with fortune, or to hope or scheme any more : but
to go and take up a quiet and utterly unknown residence
in a churchyard at Brompton by the side of his old wife.

Major Dobbin, Jos, and Georgy followed his remains to
the grave, in a black cloth coach. Jos came on purpose from
the ' Star and Garter ' at Richmond, whither he retreated
after the deplorable event. He did not care to remain in
the house, with the—under the circumstances, you under-

stand. But Emmy stayed and did her duty as usual.
She was bowed down by no especial grief, and rather solemn
than sorrowful. She prayed that her own end might be
as calm and painless, and thought with trust and reverence
of the words which she had heard from her father during
his illness, indicative of his faith, his resignation, and his
future hope.

Yes, I think that will be the better ending of the two,
after all. Suppose you are particularly rich and well-to-
do, and say on that last day, ' I am very rich ; I am
tolerably well known ; I have lived all my life in the best
society, and, thank Heaven, come of a most respectable
family. I have served my King and country with honour.

I was in Parliament for several years, where, I may say,
my speeches were listened to, and pretty well received.
I don't owe any man a shilling : on the contrary, I lent
my old college friend, Jack Lazarus, fifty pounds, for which
my executors will not press him. I leave my daughters
with ten thousand pounds a piece—very good portions for
girls : I bequeath my plate and furniture, my house in
Baker Street, with a handsome jointure, to my widow for
her life ; and my landed property, besides money in the
Funds, and my cellar of well-selected wine in Baker Street,
to my son. I leave twenty pound a year to my valet ;
and I defy any man after I am gone to find anything
against my character.' Or suppose, on the other hand,
your swan sings quite a different sort of dirge, and you say,
' I am a poor, blighted, disappointed old fellow, and have
made an utter failure through life. I was not endowed
either with brains or with good fortune : and confess that
I have committed a hundred mistakes and blunders. I own
to having forgotten my duty many a time. I can't pay
what I owe. On my last bed I lie utterly helpless and
humble : and I pray forgiveness for my weakness, and
throw myself with a contrite heart at the feet of the Divine
Mercy.' Which of these two speeches, think you, would
be the best oration for your own funeral ? Old Sedley
made the last ; and in that humble frame of mind, and
holding by the hand of his daughter, life and disappointment and vanity sank away from under him.

' You see,' said old Osborne to George, ' what comes of
merit and industry, and judicious speculations, and that.
Look at me and my banker's account. Look at your poor
grandfather Sedley, and his failure. And yet he was a
better man than I was, this day twenty years—a better
man I should say by ten thousand pound.'

Beyond these people and Mr. Clapp's family, who came
over from Brompton to pay a visit of condolence, not
a single soul alive ever cared a penny piece about old John
Sedley, or remembered the existence of such a person.

When old Osborne first heard from his friend Colonel
Buckler (as little Georgy has already informed us) how
distinguished an officer Major Dobbin was, he exhibited
a great deal of scornful incredulity, and expressed his
surprise how ever such a feller as that should possess either

brains or reputation. But he heard of the major's fame
from various members of his society. Sir William Dobbin
had a great opinion of his son, and narrated many stories
illustrative of the major's learning, valour, and estimation
in the world's opinion. Finally, his name appeared in the
lists of one or two great parties of the nobility ; and this
circumstance had a prodigious effect upon the old aristocrat
of Russell Square.

The major's position, as guardian to Georgy, whose
possession had been ceded to his grandfather, rendered
some meetings between the two gentlemen inevitable ; and
it was in one of these that old Osborne, a keen man of
business, looking into the major's accounts with his ward
and the boy's mother, got a hint which staggered him very
much, and at once pained and pleased him, that it was
out of William Dobbin's own pocket that a part of the
fund had been supplied upon which the poor widow and
the child had subsisted.

When pressed upon the point, Dobbin, who could not
tell lies, blushed and stammered a good deal, and finally
confessed. 'The marriage,' he said (at which his interlocutor's face grew dark), 'was very much my doing.
I thought my poor friend had gone so far, that retreat
from his engagement would have been dishonour to him
and death to Mrs. Osborne ; and I could do no less, when
she was left without resources, than give what money
I could spare to maintain her.'

'Major D.,' Mr. Osborne said, looking hard at him, and
turning very red too—'You did me a great injury ; but
give me leave to tell you, sir, you are an honest feller.
There's my hand, sir, though I little thought that my flesh
and blood was living on you—' and the pair shook hands,
with great confusion on Major Dobbin's part, thus found
out in his act of charitable hypocrisy.

He strove to soften the old man, and reconcile him
towards his son's memory. 'He was such a noble fellow,'
he said, 'that all of us loved him, and would have done
anything for him. I, as a young man in those days, was
flattered beyond measure by his preference for me ; and
was more pleased to be seen in his company than in that
of the commander-in-chief. I never saw his equal for
pluck and daring, and all the qualities of a soldier ; ' and
Dobbin told the old father as many stories as he could

remember regarding the gallantry and achievements of his
son. 'And Georgy is so like him,' the major added.
  'He's so like him that he makes me tremble sometimes,'
the grandfather said.
  On one or two evenings the major came to dine with
Mr. Osborne (it was during the time of the sickness of
Mr. Sedley), and as the two sat together in the evening
after dinner all their talk was about the departed hero.
The father boasted about him according to his wont,
glorifying himself in recounting his son's feats and gallantry,
but his mood was at any rate better and more charitable
than that in which he had been disposed until now to regard
the poor fellow ; and the Christian heart of the kind major
was pleased at these symptoms of returning peace and
goodwill. On the second evening old Osborne called
Dobbin, William, just as he used to do at the time when
Dobbin and George were boys together ; and the honest
gentleman was pleased by that mark of reconciliation.
  On the next day at breakfast when Miss Osborne, with
the asperity of her age and character, ventured to make
some remark reflecting slightingly upon the major's appearance or behaviour—the master of the house interrupted
her. 'You'd have been glad enough to git him for yourself, Miss O. But them grapes are sour. Ha ! ha ! Major
William is a fine feller.'
  'That he is, grandpapa,' said Georgy, approvingly ; and
going up close to the old gentleman, he took a hold of his
large grey whiskers, and laughed in his face good-humouredly
and kissed him. And he told the story at night to his
mother : who fully agreed with the boy. 'Indeed he is,'
she said. 'Your dear father always said so. He is one
of the best and most upright of men.' Dobbin happened
to drop in very soon after this conversation, which made
Amelia blush perhaps ; and the young scapegrace increased
the confusion by telling Dobbin the other part of the story.
'I say, Dob,' he said, 'there's such an uncommon nice
girl wants to marry you. She's plenty of tin : she wears
a front : and she scolds the servants from morning till
night.'
  'Who is it ?' asked Dobbin.
  'It's Aunt O.,' the boy answered, 'grandpapa said so.
And I say, Dob, how prime it would be to have you for
my uncle.' Old Sedley's quavering voice from the next

room at this moment weakly called for Amelia, and the laughing ended.

That old Osborne's mind was changing was pretty clear. He asked George about his uncle sometimes, and laughed at the boy's imitation of the way in which Jos said ' God-bless-my-soul ', and gobbled his soup. Then he said, ' It's not respectful, sir, of you younkers to be imitating of your relations. Miss O., when you go out a-driving to-day, leave my card upon Mr. Sedley, do you hear ? There's no quarrel betwigst me and him, anyhow.'

The card was returned, and Jos and the major were asked to dinner,—to a dinner the most splendid and stupid that perhaps ever Mr. Osborne gave ; every inch of the family plate was exhibited, and the best company was asked. Mr. Sedley took down Miss O. to dinner, and she was very gracious to him ; whereas she hardly spoke to the major, who sat apart from her, and by the side of Mr. Osborne, very timid. Jos said, with great solemnity, it was the best clear turtle soup he had ever tasted in his life ; and asked Mr. Osborne where he got his madeira ?

' It is some of Sedley's wine,' whispered the butler to his master. ' I've had it a long time, and paid a good figure for it, too,' Mr. Osborne said aloud to his guest ; and then whispered to his right-hand neighbour how he had got it ' at the old chap's sale '.

More than once he asked the major about—about Mrs. George Osborne—a theme on which the major could be very eloquent when he chose. He told Mr. Osborne of her sufferings—of her passionate attachment to her husband, whose memory she worshipped still—of the tender and dutiful manner in which she had supported her parents and given up her boy, when it seemed to her her duty to do so. ' You don't know what she endured, sir,' said honest Dobbin, with a tremor in his voice ; ' and I hope and trust you will be reconciled to her. If she took your son away from you, she gave hers to you ; and however much you loved your George, depend on it, she loved hers ten times more.'

' By God, you are a good feller, sir,' was all Mr. Osborne said. It had never struck him that the widow would feel any pain at parting with the boy, or that his having a fine fortune could grieve her. A reconciliation was announced as speedy and inevitable ; and Amelia's heart already began to beat at the notion of the awful meeting with George's father.

It was never, however, destined to take place. Old Sedley's lingering illness and death supervened, after which a meeting was for some time impossible. That catastrophe and other events may have worked upon Mr. Osborne. He was much shaken of late, and aged, and his mind was working inwardly. He had sent for his lawyers, and probably changed something in his will. The medical man who looked in, pronounced him shaky, agitated, and talked of a little blood, and the sea-side; but he took neither of these remedies.

One day when he should have come down to breakfast, his servant, missing him, went into his dressing-room, and found him lying at the foot of the dressing-table, in a fit. Miss Osborne was apprised; the doctors were sent for; Georgy stopped away from school; the bleeders and cuppers came. Osborne partially regained cognizance; but never could speak again, though he tried dreadfully once or twice, and in four days he died. The doctors went down; the undertaker's men went up the stairs; and all the shutters were shut towards the garden in Russell Square. Bullock rushed from the City in a hurry. 'How much money had he left to that boy?—not half, surely? Surely share and share alike between the three?' It was an agitating moment.

What was it that poor old man had tried once or twice in vain to say? I hope it was that he wanted to see Amelia, and be reconciled before he left the world to the dear and faithful wife of his son: it was most likely that; for his will showed that the hatred which he had so long cherished had gone out of his heart.

They found in the pocket of his dressing-gown the letter with the great red seal, which George had written him from Waterloo. He had looked at the other papers, too, relative to his son, for the key of the box in which he kept them was also in his pocket, and it was found the seals and envelopes had been broken—very likely on the night before the seizure, when the butler had taken him tea into his study, and found him reading in the great red family Bible.

When the will was opened, it was found that half the property was left to George, and the remainder between the two sisters. Mr. Bullock to continue, for their joint benefit, the affairs of the commercial house, or to go out, as he thought fit. An annuity of five hundred pounds, chargeable on George's property, was left to his mother, ' the widow of my beloved son George Osborne,' who was to resume the guardianship of the boy.

'Major William Dobbin, my beloved son's friend,' was appointed executor; 'and as out of his kindness and bounty, and with his own private funds, he maintained my grandson, and my son's widow, when they were otherwise without means of support' (the testator went on to say), 'I hereby thank him heartily for his love and regard for them; and beseech him to accept such a sum as may be sufficient to purchase his commission as a lieutenant-colonel, or to be disposed of in any way he may think fit.'

When Amelia heard that her father-in-law was reconciled to her, her heart melted, and she was grateful for the fortune left to her. But when she heard how Georgy was restored to her, and knew how and by whom, and how it was William's bounty that supported her in poverty, how it was William who gave her her husband and her son— oh, then she sank on her knees, and prayed for blessings on that constant and kind heart : she bowed down and humbled herself, and kissed the feet, as it were, of that beautiful and generous affection.

And gratitude was all that she had to pay back for such admirable devotion and benefits—only gratitude! If she thought of any other return, the image of George stood up out of the grave, and said, ' You are mine, and mine only, now and for ever.'

William knew her feelings : had he not passed his whole life in divining them ?

When the nature of Mr. Osborne's will became known to the world, it was edifying to remark how Mrs. George Osborne rose in the estimation of the people forming her circle of acquaintance. The servants of Jos's establishment, who used to question her humble orders, and say they would ' ask master ', whether or not they could obey, never thought now of that sort of appeal. The cook forgot to sneer at her shabby old gowns (which, indeed, were quite eclipsed by that lady's finery when she was dressed to go to church of a Sunday evening) ; the others no longer grumbled at the sound of her bell, or delayed to answer that summons.

The coachman, who grumbled that his osses should be brought out, and his carriage made into an ospital for that old feller and Mrs. O., drove her with the utmost alacrity now, and trembling lest he should be superseded by Mr. Osborne's coachman, asked ' what them there Russell Square coachmen knew about town, and whether *they* was fit to sit on a box before a lady ? ' Jos's friends, male and female, suddenly became interested about Emmy, and cards of condolence multiplied on her hall-table. Jos himself, who had looked on her as a good-natured harmless pauper, to whom it was his duty to give victuals and shelter, paid her and the rich little boy, his nephew, the greatest respect—was anxious that she should have change and amusement after her troubles and trials, ' poor dear girl '— and began to appear at the breakfast-table, and most particularly to ask how she would like to dispose of the day.

In her capacity of guardian to Georgy, she, with the consent of the major, her fellow-trustee, begged Miss Osborne to live in the Russell Square house as long as ever she chose to dwell there ; but that lady, with thanks, declared that she never could think of remaining alone in that melancholy mansion, and departed in deep mourning, to Cheltenham, with a couple of her old domestics. The rest were liberally paid and dismissed ; the faithful old butler, whom Mrs. Osborne proposed to retain, resigning and preferring to invest his savings in a public-house, where, let us hope, he was not unprosperous. Miss Osborne not choosing to live in Russell Square, Mrs. Osborne also, after consultation, declined to occupy the gloomy old mansion there. The house was dismantled ; the rich furniture and effects, the awful chandeliers and dreary blank mirrors packed away and hidden, the rich rosewood drawing-room suite was muffled in straw, the carpets were rolled up and corded, the small select library of well-bound books were stowed into two wine chests, and the whole paraphernalia rolled away in several enormous vans to the Pantechnicon,* where they were to lie until Georgy's majority. And the great heavy dark plate-chests went off to Messrs. Stumpy and Rowdy, to lie in the cellars of those eminent bankers until the same period should arrive.

One day Emmy with George in her hand and clad in deep sables went to visit the deserted mansion which she had not entered since she was a girl. The place in front was littered with straw where the vans had been laden and rolled off. They went into the great blank rooms, the walls of which bore the marks where the pictures and mirrors had hung. Then they went up the great blank stone staircases into the upper rooms, into that where grandpapa died, as George said in a whisper, and then higher still into George's own room. The boy was still clinging by her side, but she thought of another besides him. She knew that it had been his father's room as well as his own.

She went up to one of the open windows (one of those at which she used to gaze with a sick heart when the child was first taken from her) and thence as she looked out she could see over the trees of Russell Square, the old house in which she herself was born, and where she had passed so many happy days of sacred youth. They all came back to her, the pleasant holidays, the kind faces, the careless, joyful past times ; and the long pains and trials that had since cast her down. She thought of these and of the man who had been her constant protector, her good genius, her sole benefactor, her tender and generous friend.

'Look here, mother,' said Georgy, 'here's a G. O. scratched on the glass with a diamond ; I never saw it before, *I* never did it.'

' It was your father's room long, long before you were born, George,' she said, and she blushed as she kissed the boy.

She was very silent as they drove back to Richmond where they had taken a temporary house : where the smiling lawyers used to come bustling over to see her (and we may be sure noted the visit in the bill) : and where of course there was a room for Major Dobbin too, who rode over frequently, having much business to transact in behalf of his little ward.

Georgy at this time was removed from Mr. Veal's on an unlimited holiday, and that gentleman was engaged to prepare an inscription for a fine marble slab, to be placed up in the Foundling under the monument of Captain George Osborne.

The female Bullock, aunt of Georgy, although despoiled by that little monster of one-half of the sum which she expected from her father, nevertheless showed her charitable-ness of spirit by being reconciled to the mother and the boy. Roehampton is not far from Richmond, and one day the chariot, with the golden Bullocks emblazoned on the panels, and the flaccid children within, drove to Amelia's house at Richmond ; and the Bullock family made an irruption into the garden, where Amelia was reading a book, Jos was in an arbour placidly dipping strawberries into wine, and the major in one of his Indian jackets was giving a back to Georgy, who chose to jump over him. He went over his head, and bounded into the little advance of Bullocks, with immense black bows in their hats, and huge black sashes, accompanying their mourning mamma.

'He is just of the age for Rosa,' the fond parent thought, and glanced towards that dear child, an unwholesome little miss of seven years of age.

'Rosa, go and kiss your dear cousin,' Mrs. Frederick said. 'Don't you know me, George ?—I am your aunt.'

'I know you well enough,' George said ; 'but I don't like kissing, please ; ' and he retreated from the obedient caresses of his cousin.

'Take me to your dear mamma, you droll child,' Mrs. Frederick said ; and those ladies accordingly met, after an absence of more than fifteen years. During Emmy's cares and poverty the other had never once thought about coming to see her ; but now that she was decently prosperous in the world, her sister-in-law came to her as a matter of course.

So did numbers more. Our old friend, Miss Swartz, and her husband came thundering over from Hampton Court, with flaming yellow liveries, and was as impetuously fond of Amelia as ever. Swartz would have liked her always if she could have seen her. One must do her that justice. But, *que voulez-vous ?*—in this vast town one has not the time to go and seek one's friends ; if they drop out of the rank they disappear, and we march on without them. Who is ever missed in Vanity Fair ?

But so, in a word, and before the period of grief for Mr. Osborne's death had subsided, Emmy found herself in the centre of a very genteel circle indeed ; the members of which could not conceive that anybody belonging to it was not very lucky. There was scarce one of the ladies that hadn't a relation a peer, though the husband might be a drysalter in the City. Some of the ladies were very

blue and well informed ; reading Mrs. Somerville, and
frequenting the Royal Institution ; others were severe and
Evangelical, and held by Exeter Hall.* Emmy, it must be
owned, found herself entirely at a loss in the midst of their
clavers, and suffered wofully on the one or two occasions
in which she was compelled to accept Mrs. Frederick
Bullock's hospitalities. That lady persisted in patronizing
her, and determined most graciously to form her. She
found Amelia's milliners for her, and regulated her household and her manners. She drove over constantly from
Roehampton, and entertained her friend with faint fashionable fiddlefaddle and feeble Court slipslop. Jos liked to
hear it, but the major used to go off growling at the appearance of this woman, with her twopenny gentility. He
went to sleep under Frederick Bullock's bald head, after
dinner, at one of the banker's best parties (Fred was still
anxious that the balance of the Osborne property should
be transferred from Stumpy and Rowdy's to them), and
whilst Amelia, who did not know Latin, or who wrote
the last crack article in the *Edinburgh*, and did not in the
least deplore, or otherwise, Mr. Peel's late extraordinary
tergiversation* in the fatal Catholic Relief Bill, sat dumb
amongst the ladies in the grand drawing-room, looking out
upon velvet lawns, trim gravel walks, and glistening hot-
houses.

  ' She seems good-natured but insipid,' said Mrs. Rowdy ;
' that major seems to be particularly *épris*.'

  ' She wants *ton* sadly,' said Mrs. Hollyock. ' My dear
creature, you never will be able to form her.'

  ' She is dreadfully ignorant or indifferent,' said Mrs.
Glowry, with a voice as if from the grave, and a sad shake
of the head and turban—' I asked her if she thought that
it was in 1836, according to Mr. Jowls, or in 1839, according
to Mr. Wapshot, that the Pope was to fall : and she said—
" Poor Pope ! I hope not—What has he done ? " '

  ' She is my brother's widow, my dear friends,' Mrs.
Frederick replied, ' and as such I think we're all bound
to give her every attention and instruction on entering
into the world. You may fancy there can be no *mercenary*
motive in those whose *disappointments* are well known.'

  ' That poor dear Mrs. Bullock,' said Rowdy to Hollyock,
as they drove away together—' she is always scheming and
managing. She wants Mrs. Osborne's account to be taken

from our house to hers—and the way in which she coaxes that boy, and makes him sit by that blear-eyed little Rosa, is perfectly ridiculous.'

'I wish Glowry was choked with her Man of Sin and her Battle of Armageddon,' cried the other ; and the carriage rolled away over Putney Bridge.

But this sort of society was too cruelly genteel for Emmy : and all jumped for joy when a foreign tour was proposed.

CHAPTER LXII

AM RHEIN

THE above every-day events had occurred, and a few weeks had passed, when, on one fine morning, Parliament being over, the summer advanced, and all the good company in London about to quit that city for their annual tour in search of pleasure or health, the *Batavier* steamboat left the Tower stairs laden with a goodly company of English fugitives. The quarter-deck awnings were up, and the benches and gangways crowded with scores of rosy children, bustling nursemaids, ladies in the prettiest pink bonnets and summer dresses, gentlemen in travelling caps and linen jackets, whose moustachios had just begun to sprout for the ensuing tour ; and stout trim old veterans with starched neckcloths and neat-brushed hats, such as have invaded Europe any time since the conclusion of the war, and carry the national Goddem into every city of the Continent. The congregation of hat-boxes, and Bramah desks,* and dressing-cases, was prodigious. There were jaunty young Cambridge men travelling with their tutor, and going for a reading excursion to Nonnenwerth or Königswinter : there were Irish gentlemen, with the most

dashing whiskers and jewellery, talking about horses incessantly, and prodigiously polite to the young ladies on board,
whom; on the contrary, the Cambridge lads and their pale-
faced tutor avoided with maiden coyness : there were old
Pall Mall loungers bound for Ems and Wiesbaden, and
a course of waters to clear off the dinners of the season, and
a little roulette and *trente-et-quarante* to keep the excitement
going : there was old Methuselah, who had married his
young wife, with Captain Papillon of the Guards holding
her parasol and guide-books : there was young May who was
carrying off his bride on a pleasure tour (Mrs. Winter that
was, and who had been at school with May's grandmother) ;
there was Sir John and my lady with a dozen children,
and corresponding nursemaids ; and the great grandee
Bareacres family that sat by themselves near the wheel,
stared at everybody, and spoke to no one. Their carriages,
emblazoned with coronets, and heaped with shining imperials, were on the fore-deck ; locked in with a dozen more
such vehicles : it was difficult to pass in and out amongst
them : and the poor inmates of the fore-cabin had scarcely
any space for locomotion. These consisted of a few magnificently attired gentlemen from Houndsditch, who brought
their own provisions, and could have bought half the gay
people in the grand saloon ; a few honest fellows with
moustachios and portfolios, who set to sketching before
they had been half an hour on board ; one or two French
femmes de chambre who began to be dreadfully ill by the
time the boat had passed Greenwich ; a groom or two who
lounged in the neighbourhood of the horse-boxes under their
charge, or leaned over the side by the paddle-wheels, and
talked about who was good for the Leger, and what they
stood to win or lose for the Goodwood Cup.

All the couriers, when they had done plunging about the
ship, and had settled their various masters in the cabins or
on the deck, congregated together and began to chatter and
smoke ; the Hebrew gentlemen joining them and looking
at the carriages. There was Sir John's great carriage that
would hold thirteen people ; my Lord Methuselah's carriage,
my Lord Bareacres's chariot, britzka, and fourgon, that
anybody might pay for who liked. It was a wonder how
my lord got the ready money to pay for the expenses of
the journey. The Hebrew gentlemen knew how he got it.
They knew what money his lordship had in his pocket at

that instant, and what interest he paid for it, and who gave
it him. Finally, there was a very neat, handsome travelling
carriage, about which the gentlemen speculated.

' *A qui cette voiture-là ?* ' said one gentleman-courier with
a large morocco money-bag and ear-rings, to another with
ear-rings and a large morocco money-bag.

' *C'est à Kirsch, je bense—je l'ai vu toute à l'heure—qui
brenait des sangviches dans la voiture,*' said the courier, in
a fine German French.

Kirsch emerging presently from the neighbourhood of
the hold where he had been bellowing instructions intermingled with polyglot oaths to the ship's men engaged in

secreting the passengers' luggage, came to give an account
of himself to his brother interpreters. He informed them
that the carriage belonged to a nabob from Calcutta and
Jamaica, enormously rich, and with whom he was engaged
to travel ; and at this moment a young gentleman who had

been warned off the bridge between the paddle-boxes, and
who had dropped thence on to the roof of Lord Methuselah's
carriage, from which he had made his way over other
carriages and imperials until he had clambered on to his
own, descended thence and through the window into the
body of the carriage to the applause of the couriers looking on.

'*Nous allons avoir une belle traversée*, Monsieur George,'
said the courier, with a grin, as he lifted his gold-laced cap.

'D— your French,' said the young gentleman, ' where's
the biscuits, eh ? ' Whereupon Kirsch answered him in the
English language or in such an imitation of it as he could
command,—for though he was familiar with all languages,
Mr. Kirsch was not acquainted with a single one and spoke
all with indifferent volubility and incorrectness.

The imperious young gentleman who gobbled the biscuits
(and indeed it was time to refresh himself, for he had
breakfasted at Richmond full three hours before) was our
young friend George Osborne. Uncle Jos and his mamma
were on the quarter-deck with a gentleman of whom they
used to see a good deal, and the four were about to make
a summer tour.

Jos was seated at that moment on deck under the awning,
and pretty nearly opposite to the Earl of Bareacres and his
family, whose proceedings absorbed the Bengalee almost
entirely. Both the noble couple looked rather younger
than in the eventful year '15, when Jos remembered to
have seen them at Brussels (indeed he always gave out in
India that he was intimately acquainted with them).   Lady
Bareacres's [1] hair which was then dark was now a beautiful
golden auburn, whereas Lord Bareacres's whiskers, formerly
red, were at present of a rich black with purple and green
reflections in the light. But changed as they were, the
movements of the noble pair occupied Jos's mind entirely.
The presence of a lord fascinated him, and he could look
at nothing else.

' Those people seem to interest you a good deal,' said
Dobbin, laughing and watching him.   Amelia too laughed.
She was in a straw bonnet with black ribbons, and otherwise
dressed in mourning : but the little bustle and holiday of
the journey pleased and excited her, and she looked particularly happy.

' What a heavenly day ! ' Emmy said, and added, with
great originality, ' I hope we shall have a calm passage.'

Jos waved his hand scornfully, glancing at the same time under his eyelids at the great folks opposite. 'If you had made the voyages *we* have,' he said, ' you wouldn't much care about the weather.' But nevertheless, traveller as he was, he passed the night direfully sick in his carriage, where his courier tended him with brandy-and-water and every luxury.

In due time this happy party landed at the quays of Rotterdam, whence they were transported by another steamer to the city of Cologne. Here the carriage and the family took to the shore, and Jos was not a little gratified to see his arrival announced in the Cologne newspapers as ' *Herr Graf Lord von Sedley, nebst Begleitung*,* *aus London.*' He had his Court dress with him : he had insisted that Dobbin should bring his regimental paraphernalia : he announced that it was his intention to be presented at some foreign Courts, and pay his respects to the sovereigns of the countries which he honoured with a visit.

Wherever the party stopped, and an opportunity was offered, Mr. Jos left his own card and the major's upon 'Our Minister'. It was with great difficulty that he could be restrained from putting on his cocked hat and tights to wait upon the English consul at the Free City of Juden-stadt,* when that hospitable functionary asked our travellers to dinner. He kept a journal of his voyage, and noted elaborately the defects or excellences of the various inns at which he put up, and of the wines and dishes of which he partook.

As for Emmy, she was very happy and pleased. Dobbin used to carry about for her her stool and sketch-book, and admired the drawings of the good-natured little artist, as they never had been admired before. She sat upon steamers' decks and drew crags and castles, or she mounted upon donkeys and ascended to ancient robber-towers, attended by her two aides de camp, Georgy and Dobbin. She laughed and the major did too, at his droll figure on donkey-back, with his long legs touching the ground. He was the interpreter for the party, having a good military knowledge of the German language ; and he and the delighted George fought the campaigns of the Rhine and the Palatinate. In the course of a few weeks, and by assiduously conversing with Herr Kirsch on the box of the carriage, Georgy made prodigious advance in the knowledge of High Dutch, and could talk to hotel waiters and postilions in a way that charmed his mother, and amused his guardian.

Mr. Jos did not much engage in the afternoon excursions of his fellow travellers. He slept a good deal after dinner, or basked in the arbours of the pleasant inn-gardens. Pleasant Rhine gardens ! Fair scenes of peace and sun-shine—noble purple mountains, whose crests are reflected in the magnificent stream—who has ever seen you, that has not a grateful memory of those scenes of friendly repose and beauty ? To lay down the pen, and even to think of that beautiful Rhineland makes one happy. At this time of summer evening, the cows are trooping down from the hills, lowing and with their bells tinkling, to the old town, with its old moats, and gates, and spires, and chestnut-trees, with long blue shadows stretching over the grass ; the sky and the river below flame in crimson and gold ; and the moon is already out, looking pale towards the sunset. The sun sinks behind the great castle-crested mountains, the night falls suddenly, the river grows darker and darker, lights quiver in it from the windows in the old ramparts, and twinkle peacefully in the villages under the hills on the opposite shore.

So Jos used to go to sleep a good deal with his bandanna over his face and be very comfortable, and read all the English news, and every word of Galignani's admirable newspaper (may the blessings of all Englishmen who have ever been abroad rest on the founders and proprietors of that piratical print !)* and whether he woke or slept his friends did not very much miss him. Yes, they were very happy. They went to the Opera often of evenings—to those snug, unassuming, dear old operas in the German towns, where the noblesse sits and cries, and knits stockings on the one side, over against the bourgeoisie on the other ; and his transparency the duke* and his transparent family, all very fat and good-natured, come and occupy the great box in the middle ; and the pit is full of the most elegant slim-waisted officers with straw-coloured moustaches, and twopence a day on full pay. Here it was that Emmy found her delight, and was introduced for the first time to the wonders of Mozart and Cimarosa. The major's musical taste has been before alluded to, and his performances on the flute commended. But perhaps the chief pleasure he

A FINE SUMMER EVENING

had in these operas was in watching Emmy's rapture while
listening to them. A new world of love and beauty broke
upon her when she was introduced to those divine compositions : this lady had the keenest and finest sensibility, and
how could she be indifferent when she heard Mozart ? The
tender parts of *Don Juan* awakened in her raptures so
exquisite that she would ask herself when she went to say
her prayers of a night, whether it was not wicked to feel
so much delight as that with which *Vedrai Carino* and
Batti, Batti filled her gentle little bosom ? But the
major, whom she consulted upon this head, as her theological adviser (and who himself had a pious and reverent soul),
said that for his part, every beauty of art or nature made
him thankful as well as happy ; and that the pleasure to
be had in listen'ng to fine music, as in looking at the stars in
the sky, or at a beautiful landscape or picture, was a benefit
for which we might thank Heaven as sincerely as for any other
worldly blessing. And in reply to some faint objections
of Mrs. Amelia's (taken from certain theological works like
the *Washerwoman of Finchley Common* and others of that
school, with which Mrs. Osborne had been furnished during
her life at Brompton) he told her an Eastern fable of the
Owl who thought that the sunshine was unbearable for the
eyes, and that the Nightingale was a most over-rated bird.
' It is one's nature to sing and the other's to hoot,' he said,
laughing, ' and with such a sweet voice as you have yourself,
you must belong to the Bulbul faction.'

I like to dwell upon this period of her life, and to think
that she was cheerful and happy. You see she has not had
too much of that sort of existence as yet, and has not fallen
in the way of means to educate her tastes or her intelligence.
She has been domineered over hitherto by vulgar intellects.
It is the lot of many a woman. And as every one of the
dear sex is the rival of the rest of her kind, timidity passes
for folly in their charitable judgements ; and gentleness for
dullness ; and silence—which is but timid denial of the
unwelcome assertion of ruling folks, and tacit protestantism
—above all, finds no mercy at the hands of the female
Inquisition. Thus, my dear and civilized reader, if you and
I were to find ourselves this evening in a society of greengrocers, let us say ; it is probable that our conversation
would not be brilliant ; if, on the other hand, a greengrocer
should find himself at your refined and polite tea-table,

where everybody was saying witty things, and everybody
of fashion and repute tearing her friends to pieces in the
most delightful manner, it is possible that the stranger
would not be very talkative, and by no means interesting
or interested.

And it must be remembered, that this poor lady had
never met a gentleman in her life until this present moment.
Perhaps these are rarer personages than some of us think
for. Which of us can point out many such in his circle—
men whose aims are generous, whose truth is constant, and
not only constant in its kind, but elevated in its degree ;
whose want of meanness makes them simple : who can look
the world honestly in the face with an equal manly sympathy
for the great and the small ? We all know a hundred whose
coats are very well made, and a score who have excellent
manners, and one or two happy beings who are what they
call, in the inner circles, and have shot into the very centre
and bull's-eye of the fashion ; but of gentlemen how many ?
Let us take a little scrap of paper and each make out his list.

My friend the major I write, without any doubt, in mine.
He had very long legs, a yellow face, and a slight lisp,
which at first was rather ridiculous. But his thoughts
were just, his brains were fairly good, his life was honest and
pure, and his heart warm and humble. He certainly had
very large hands and feet, which the two George Osbornes
used to caricature and laugh at ; and their jeers and laughter
perhaps led poor little Emmy astray as to his worth. But
have we not all been misled about our heroes, and changed
our opinions a hundred times ? Emmy, in this happy
time, found that hers underwent a very great change in
respect of the merits of the major.

Perhaps it was the happiest time of both their lives
indeed, if they did but know it—and who does ? Which
of us can point out and say that was the culmination—that
was the summit of human joy ? But at all events, this
couple were very decently contented and enjoyed as pleasant
a summer tour as any pair that left England that year.
Georgy was always present at the play, but it was the
major who put Emmy's shawl on after the entertainment ;
and in the walks and excursions the young lad would be
on ahead, and up a tower-stair or a tree, whilst the soberer
couple were below, the major smoking his cigar with great
placidity and constancy, whilst Emmy sketched the site or

the ruin. It was on this very tour that I, the present writer of a history of which every word is true, had the pleasure to see them first, and to make their acquaintance.

It was at the little comfortable ducal town of Pumpernickel (that very place where Sir Pitt Crawley had been so distinguished as an attaché ; but that was in early, early days, and before the news of the battle of Austerlitz*sent all the English diplomatists in Germany to the right-about) that I first saw Colonel Dobbin and his party. They had arrived with the carriage and courier at the 'Erbprinz' Hotel, the best of the town, and the whole party dined at the table d'hôte. Everybody remarked the majesty of Jos, and the knowing way in which he sipped, or rather sucked, the Johannisberger, which he ordered for dinner. The little boy, too, we observed, had a famous appetite, and consumed *Schinken* and *Braten*, and *Kartoffeln*, and cranberry jam, and salad, and pudding, and roast fowls, and sweetmeats, with a gallantry that did honour to his nation. After about fifteen dishes, he concluded the repast with dessert, some of which he even carried out of doors ; for some young gentlemen at table, amused with his coolness and gallant free and easy manner, induced him to pocket a handful of macaroons, which he discussed on his way to the theatre, whither everybody went in the cheery social little German place. The lady in black, the boy's mamma, laughed and blushed, and looked exceedingly pleased and shy as the dinner went on, and at the various feats and instances of *espièglerie* on the part of her son. The colonel—for so he became very soon afterwards—I remember joked the boy with a great deal of grave fun, pointing out dishes which he *hadn't* tried, and entreating him not to balk his appetite, but to have a second supply of this or that.

It was what they call a *Gast-rolle* night at the Royal Grand Ducal Pumpernickelisch Hof-*-or Court—Theatre : and Madame Schroeder Devrient, then in the bloom of her beauty and genius, performed the part of the heroine in the wonderful opera of *Fidelio*. From our places in the stalls we could see our four friends of the table d'hôte, in the loge which Schwendler of the 'Erbprinz' kept for his best guests : and I could not help remarking the effect which the magnificent actress and music produced upon Mrs. Osborne, for so we had heard the stout gentleman in the moustachios

call her. During the astonishing Chorus of the Prisoners
over which the delightful voice of the actress rose and soared
in the most ravishing harmony, the English lady's face wore
such an expression of wonder and delight that it struck
even little Fipps, the *blasé* attaché, who drawled out, as
he fixed his glass upon her, ' Gayd, it really does one good
to see a woman caypable of that stayt of excaytement.'
And in the Prison Scene where Fidelio, rushing to her
husband, cries ' *Nichts, nichts, mein Florestan* ', she fairly
lost herself and covered her face with her handkerchief.
Every woman in the house was snivelling at the time : but
I suppose it was because it was predestined that I was to
write this particular lady's memoirs, that I remarked her.

The next day they gave another piece of Beethoven :
Die Schlacht bei Vittoria. Malbrook is introduced at
the beginning of the performance, as indicative of the brisk
advance of the French Army. Then come drums, trumpets,
thunder of artillery, and groans of the dying, and at last
in a grand triumphal swell, ' God save the King ' is performed.

There may have been a score of Englishmen in the house,
but at the burst of that beloved and well-known music,
every one of them, we young fellows in the stalls, Sir John
and Lady Bullminster (who had taken a house at Pumpernickel for the education of their nine children), the fat
gentleman with the moustachios, the long major in white
duck trousers, and the lady with the little boy upon whom
he was so sweet : even Kirsch, the courier in the gallery,
stood bolt upright in their places, and proclaimed themselves
to be members of the dear old British nation. As for
Tapeworm, the chargé d'affaires, he rose up in his box and
bowed and simpered, as if he would represent the whole
empire. Tapeworm was nephew and heir of old Marshal
Tiptoff, who has been introduced in this story as General
Tiptoff, just before Waterloo, who was colonel of the —th
regiment, in which Major Dobbin served, and who died in
this year full of honours, and of an aspic of plovers' eggs ;
when the regiment was graciously given by his majesty to
Colonel Sir Michael O'Dowd, K.C.B., who had commanded
it in many glorious fields.

Tapeworm must have met with Colonel Dobbin at the
house of the colonel's colonel, the marshal, for he recognized
him on this night at the theatre ; and with the utmost

condescension, his majesty's minister came over from his own box, and publicly shook hands with his new-found friend.

'Look at that infernal sly-boots of a Tapeworm,' Fipps whispered, examining his chief from the stalls. 'Wherever there's a pretty woman he always twists himself in.' And I wonder what were diplomatists made for but for that?

'Have I the honour of addressing myself to Mrs. Dobbin?' asked the secretary, with a most insinuating grin.

Georgy burst out laughing, and said, 'By Jove, that *is* a good un.' — Emmy and the major blushed: we saw them from the stalls.

'This lady is Mrs. George Osborne,' said the major, 'and this is her brother, Mr. Sedley, a distinguished officer of the Bengal Civil Service: permit me to introduce him to your lordship.'

My lord nearly sent Jos off his legs, with the most fascinating smile. 'Are you going to stop in Pumpernickel?' he

said. ' It is a dull place : but we want some nice people,
and we would try and make it *so* agreeable to you. Mr.—
Ahum—Mrs.—Oho. I shall do myself the honour of calling
upon you to-morrow at your inn.'—And he went away with
a Parthian grin and glance, which he thought must finish
Mrs. Osborne completely.

The performance over, the young fellows lounged about
the lobbies, and we saw the society take its departure.
The duchess dowager went off in her jingling old coach,
attended by two faithful and withered old maids of honour,
and a little snuffy spindle-shanked gentleman in waiting,
in a brown jasey*and a green coat covered with orders—of
which the star and the grand yellow cordon of the order of
St. Michael of Pumpernickel was most conspicuous. The
drums rolled, the guards saluted, and the old carriage drove
away.

Then came his transparency the duke and transparent
family, with his great officers of state and household. He
bowed serenely to everybody. And amid the saluting of
the guards and the flaring of the torches of the running
footmen, clad in scarlet, the transparent carriages drove
away to the old Ducal Schloss, with its towers and pinnacles
standing on the Schlossberg. Everybody in Pumpernickel
knew everybody. No sooner was a foreigner seen there
than the Minister of Foreign Affairs, or some other great
or small officer of state, went round to the ' Erbprinz,' and
found out the name of the new arrival.

. We watched them too, out of the theatre. Tapeworm
had just walked off, enveloped in his cloak, with which
his gigantic chasseur was always in attendance, and looking
as much as possible like Don Juan. The Prime Minister's lady
had just squeezed herself into her sedan, and her daughter,
the charming Ida, had put on her calash and clogs ; when
the English party came out, the boy yawning drearily, the
major taking great pains in keeping the shawl over Mrs.
Osborne's head, and Mr. Sedley looking grand, with a crush
opera-hat on one side of his head, and his hand in the
stomach of a voluminous white waistcoat. We took off
our hats to our acquaintances of the table d'hôte, and the
lady, in return, presented us with a little smile and a curtsy,
for which everybody might be thankful.

The carriage from the inn, under the superintendence
of the bustling Mr. Kirsch, was in waiting to convey the

party ; but the fat man said he would walk, and smoke his cigar on his way homewards ; so the other three, with nods and smiles to us, went without Mr. Sedley, Kirsch, with the cigar-case, following in his master's wake.

We all walked together, and talked to the stout gentleman about the *agréments** of the place. It was very agreeable for the English. There were shooting parties and battues ; there was a plenty of balls and entertainments at the hospitable Court ; the society was generally good, the theatre excellent, and the living cheap.

'And our. minister seems a most delightful and affable person,' our new friend said. 'With such a representative, and—and a good medical man, I can fancy the place to be most eligible. Good night, gentlemen.' And Jos creaked up the stairs to bedward, followed by Kirsch, with a flambeau. We rather hoped that nice-looking woman would be induced to stay some time in the town.

CHAPTER LXIII

IN WHICH WE MEET AN OLD ACQUAINTANCE

Such polite behaviour as that of Lord Tapeworm did not fail to have the most favourable effect upon Mr. Sedley's mind, and the very next morning, at breakfast, he pronounced his opinion that Pumpernickel was the pleasantest little place of any which he had visited on their tour. Jos's motives and artifices were not very difficult of comprehension : and Dobbin laughed in his sleeve, like a hypocrite as he was, when he found by the knowing air of the civilian and the off-hand manner in which the latter talked about Tapeworm Castle, and the other members of the family, that Jos had been up already in the morning, consulting his travelling *Peerage*. Yes, he had seen the

Right Honourable the Earl of Bagwig, his lordship's father ;
he was sure he had, he had met him at—at the Levée—
didn't Dob remember ? and when the diplomatist called
on the party, faithful to his promise, Jos received him with
such a salute and honours as were seldom accorded to the
little envoy. He winked at Kirsch on his excellency's
arrival, and that emissary, instructed beforehand, went out
and superintended an entertainment of cold meats, jellies,
and other delicacies, brought in upon trays, and of which
Mr. Jos absolutely insisted that his noble guest should
partake.

Tapeworm, so long as he could have an opportunity of
admiring the bright eyes of Mrs. Osborne (whose freshness
of complexion bore daylight remarkably well) was not ill
pleased to accept any invitation to stay in Mr. Sedley's
lodgings ; he put one or two dexterous questions to him
about India and the dancing-girls there ; asked Amelia
about that beautiful boy who had been with her, and complimented the astonished little woman upon the prodigious
sensation which she had made in the house ; and tried to
fascinate Dobbin by talking of the late war, and the exploits
of the Pumpernickel contingent under the command of the
hereditary prince, now Duke of Pimpernickel.

Lord Tapeworm inherited no little portion of the family
gallantry, and it was his happy belief, that almost every
woman upon whom he himself cast friendly eyes, was in
love with him. He left Emmy under the persuasion that
she was slain by his wit and attractions, and went home to
his lodgings to write a pretty little note to her. She was
not fascinated ; only puzzled by his grinning, his simpering,
his scented cambric handkerchief, and his high-heeled
lacquered boots. She did not understand one-half the
compliments which he paid ; she had never, in her small
experience of mankind, met a professional lady's man as
yet, and looked upon my lord as something curious rather
than pleasant ; and if she did not admire, certainly wondered
at him. Jos, on the contrary, was delighted. ' How very
affable his lordship is,' he said ; ' how very kind of his lordship to say he would send his medical man ! Kirsch, you will
carry our cards to the Count de Schlüsselback directly :
the major and I will have the greatest pleasure in paying our
respects at Court as soon as possible. Put out my uniform,
Kirsch,—both our uniforms. It is a mark of politeness

which every English gentleman ought to show to the
countries which he visits to pay his respects to the sovereigns
of those countries, as to the representatives of his own.'

When Tapeworm's doctor came, Doctor von Glauber,
body physician to H.S.H. the Duke, he speedily convinced
Jos that the Pumpernickel mineral springs and the doctor's
particular treatment would infallibly restore the Bengalee
to youth and slimness.   ' Dere came here last year,' he said,
' Sheneral Bulkeley, an English sheneral, tvice so pic as
you, sir.   I sent him back qvite tin after tree months, and
he danced vid Baroness Glauber at the end of two.'

Jos's mind was made up : the springs, the doctor, the
Court, and the chargé d'affaires convinced him, and he
proposed to spend the autumn in these delightful quarters.
—And punctual to his word, on the next day the chargé
d'affaires presented Jos and the major to Victor Aurelius XVII, being conducted to their audience with that
sovereign by the Count de Schlüsselback, marshal of the
Court.

They were straightway invited to dinner at Court, and
their intention of staying in the town being announced,
the politest ladies of the whole town instantly called upon
Mrs. Osborne ; and as not one of these, however poor they
might be, was under the rank of a baroness, Jos's delight
was beyond expression.   He wrote off to Chutney at the
club to say that the Service was highly appreciated in
Germany, that he was going to show his friend, the Count
de Schlüsselback, how to stick a pig in the Indian fashion,
and that his august friends, the duke and duchess, were
everything that was kind and civil.

Emmy, too, was presented to the august family, and as
mourning is not admitted in Court on certain days, she
appeared in a pink crape dress, with a diamond ornament
in the corsage, presented to her by her brother, and she
looked so pretty in this costume that the duke and Court
(putting out of the question the major, who had scarcely
ever seen her before in an evening dress, and vowed that she
did not look five-and-twenty) all admired her excessively.

In this dress she walked a polonaise*with Major Dobbin
at a Court ball, in which easy dance Mr. Jos had the honour
of leading out the Countess of Schlüsselback, an old lady
with a humpback, but with sixteen good quarters of nobility,
and related to half the royal houses of Germany.

Pumpernickel stands in the midst of a happy valley, through which sparkles—to mingle with the Rhine somewhere, but I have not the map at hand to say exactly at what point—the fertilizing stream of the Pump. In some places the river is big enough to support a ferry-boat, in others to turn a mill ; in Pumpernickel itself, the last transparency but three, the great and renowned Victor Aurelius XIV, built a magnificent bridge, on which his own statue rises, surrounded by water-nymphs and emblems of victory, peace, and plenty ; he has his foot on the neck of a prostrate Turk (history says he engaged and ran a janissary through the body at the relief of Vienna by Sobieski);* but, quite undisturbed by the agonies of that prostrate Mahometan, who writhes at his feet in the most ghastly manner—the prince smiles blandly, and points with his truncheon in the direction of the Aurelius-platz, where he began to erect a new palace that would have been the wonder of his age, had the great-souled prince but funds to complete it. But the completion of Monplaisir (*Monblaisir* the honest German folks call it) was stopped for lack of ready money, and it and its park and garden are now in rather a faded condition, and not more than ten times big enough to accommodate the Court of the reigning sovereign.

The gardens were arranged to emulate those of Versailles, and amidst the terraces and groves there are some huge allegorical waterworks still, which spout and froth stupendously upon fête-days, and frighten one with their enormous aquatic insurrections. There is the Trophonius' cave in which, by some artifice, the leaden Tritons are made not only to spout water, but to play the most dreadful groans out of their lead conchs—there is the Nymph-bath and the Niagara cataract which the people of the neighbourhood admire beyond expression, when they come to the yearly fair at the opening of the Chamber, or to the fêtes with which the happy little nation still celebrates the birthdays and marriage-days of its princely governors.

Then from all the towns of the duchy which stretches for nearly ten miles,—from Bolkum, which lies on its western frontier bidding defiance to Prussia, from Grogwitz, where the prince has a hunting-lodge, and where his dominions are separated by the Pump river from those of the neighbouring Prince of Potzenthal : from all the little villages, which besides these three great cities, dot over the happy

JOS PERFORMS A POLONAISE

principality—from the farms and the mills along the Pump,
come troops of people in red petticoats and velvet head-
dresses, or with three-cornered hats and pipes in their
mouths, who flock to the Residenz and share in the pleasures
of the fair and the festivities there.   Then the theatre is
open for nothing, then the waters of Monblaisir begin to
play (it is lucky that there is company to behold them, for
one would be afraid to see them alone)—then there come
mountebanks and riding troupes (the way in which his
transparency was fascinated by one of the horse-riders, is
well known, and it is believed that *La Petite Vivandière*,* as
she was called, was a spy in the French interest), and the
delighted people are permitted to march through room after
room of the grand ducal palace, and admire the slippery
floor, the rich hangings, and the spittoons at the doors of
all the innumerable chambers.   There is one pavilion at
Monblaisir which Aurelius Victor XV had arranged—
a great prince but too fond of pleasure—and which I am told
is a perfect wonder of licentious elegance.   It is painted
with the story of Bacchus and Ariadne, and the table works
in and out of the room by means of a windlass, so that the
company was served without any intervention of domestics.
But the place was shut up by Barbara, Aurelius XV's widow,
a severe and devout princess of the house of Bolkum and
regent of the duchy during her son's glorious minority, and
after the death of her husband, cut off in the pride of his
pleasures.

The theatre of Pumpernickel is known and famous in that
quarter of Germany.   It languished a little when the
present duke in his youth insisted upon having his own
operas played there, and it is said one day, in a fury from
his place in the orchestra, when he attended a rehearsal,
broke a bassoon on the head of the chapel master, who was
conducting, and led too slow ; and during which time the
Duchess Sophia wrote domestic comedies which must have
been very dreary to witness.   But the prince executes his
music in private now, and the duchess only gives away her
plays to the foreigners of distinction who visit her kind
little Court.

It is conducted with no small comfort and splendour.
When there are balls, though there may be four hundred
people at supper, there is a servant in scarlet and lace to
attend upon every four, and every one is served on silver.

There are festivals and entertainments going continually
on ; and the duke has his chamberlains and equerries, and
the duchess her mistress of the wardrobe and ladies of honour
just like any other and more potent potentates.

The Constitution is or was a moderate despotism, tempered
by a Chamber that might or might not be elected.　I never
certainly could hear of its sitting in my time at Pumpernickel.
The Prime Minister had lodgings in a second floor ; and
the Foreign Secretary occupied the comfortable lodgings
over Zwieback's Conditorei.　The army consisted of a
magnificent band that also did duty on the stage, where it
was quite pleasant to see the worthy fellows marching in
Turkish dresses with rouge on and wooden scimitars, or as
Roman warriors with ophicleides and trombones,—to see
them again, I say, at night, after one had listened to them
all the morning in the Aurelius-platz, where they performed
opposite the café where we breakfasted.　Besides the band,
there was a rich and numerous staff of officers, and I believe
a few men.　Besides the regular sentries, three or four men,
habited as hussars, used to do duty at the palace, but
I never saw them on horseback, and *au fait*, what was the
use of cavalry in a time of profound peace ?—and whither
the deuce should the hussars ride ?

Everybody—everybody that was noble, of course, for as
for the bourgeois, we could not quite be expected to take
notice of *them*—visited his neighbour.　H.E. Madame de
Burst received once a week, H.E. Madame de Schnurrbart
had her night—the theatre was open twice a week, the
Court graciously received once, so that a man's life might
in fact be a perfect round of pleasure, in the unpretending
Pumpernickel way.

That there were feuds in the place, no one can deny.
Politics ran very high at Pumpernickel, and parties were
very bitter.　There was the Strumpff faction and the Lederlung party, the one supported by our envoy and the other
by the French chargé d'affaires, M. de Macabau.　Indeed
it sufficed for our minister to stand up for Madame Strumpff,
who was clearly the greatest singer of the two, and had three
more notes in her voice than Madame Lederlung her rival—
it sufficed, I say, for our minister to advance *any* opinion,
to have it instantly contradicted by the French diplomatist.

Everybody in the town was ranged in one or other of these
factions.　The Lederlung was a prettyish little creature

certainly, and her voice (what there was of it) was very
sweet, and there is no doubt that the Strumpff was not in
her first youth and beauty, and certainly too stout ; when
she came on in the last scene of the *Sonnambula* for instance,
in her night-chemise with a lamp in her hand, and had to
go out of the window and pass over the plank of the mill, it
was all she could do to squeeze out of the window, and the
plank used to bend and creak again under her weight—but
how she poured out the finale of the opera ! and with what
a burst of feeling she rushed into Elvino's arms—almost fit
to smother him ! Whereas the little Lederlung—but a truce
to this gossip—the fact is, that these two women were the
two flags of the French and the English party at Pumpernickel, and the society was divided in its allegiance to those
two great nations.

We had on our side the Home Minister, the Master of the
Horse, the duke's private secretary, and the prince's tutor :
whereas of the French party were the Foreign Minister, the
commander-in-chief's lady, who had served under Napoleon, and the Hofmarschall and his wife, who was glad
enough to get the fashions from Paris, and always had them
and her caps by M. de Macabau's courier. The secretary
of his chancery was little Grignac, a young fellow as malicious as Satan, and who made caricatures of Tapeworm in
all the albums of the place.

Their head quarters and table d'hôte were established at
the Pariser Hof, the other inn of the town ; and though, of
course, these gentlemen were obliged to be civil in public,
yet they cut at each other with epigrams that were as sharp
as razors, as I have seen a couple of wrestlers in Devonshire,
lashing at each other's shins, and never showing their agony
upon a muscle of their faces. Neither Tapeworm nor Macabau ever sent home a dispatch to his Government, without
a most savage series of attacks upon his rival. For instance,
on our side we would write : ' The interests of Great Britain
in this place, and throughout the whole of Germany, are
perilled by the continuance in office of the present French
envoy : this man is of a character so infamous that he will
stick at no falsehood, of hesitate at no crime, to attain his
ends. He poisons the mind of the Court against the English
minister, represents the conduct of Great Britain in the
most odious and atrocious light, and is unhappily backed
by a minister whose ignorance and necessities are as

notorious as his influence is fatal.' On their side they
would say : ' M. de Tapeworm continues his system of
stupid insular arrogance and vulgar falsehood against the
greatest nation in the world. Yesterday he was heard to
speak lightly of Her Royal Highness Madame the Duchess
of Berri ; on a former occasion he insulted the heroic Duke
of Angoulême, and dared to insinuate that H.R.H. the
Duke of Orleans*was conspiring against the august throne
of the lilies. His gold is prodigated in every direction which
his stupid menaces fail to frighten. By one and the other,
he has won over creatures of the Court here—and, in fine,
Pumpernickel will not be quiet, Germany tranquil, France
respected, or Europe content, until this poisonous viper be
crushed under heel ; ' and so on. When one side or the
other had written any particularly spicy dispatch, news of
it was sure to slip out.

Before the winter was far advanced it is actually on record
that Emmy took a night and received company with great
propriety and modesty. She had a French master who complimented her upon the purity of her accent and her facility
of learning ; the fact is she had learned long ago, and
grounded herself subsequently in the grammar, so as to be
able to teach it to George ; and Madame Strumpff came to
give her lessons in singing, which she performed so well and
with such a true voice that the major's windows, who had
lodgings opposite under the Prime Minister, were always
open to hear the lesson. Some of the German ladies, who
are very sentimental and simple in their tastes, fell in love
with her and began to call her *Du* at once. These are trivial
details, but they relate to happy times. The major made
himself George's tutor, and read Caesar and mathematics
with him, and they had a German master and rode out
of evenings by the side of Emmy's carriage—she was always
too timid, and made a dreadful outcry at the slightest
disturbance on horseback. So she drove about with one of
her dear German friends, and Jos asleep on the back seat
of the barouche.

He was becoming very sweet upon the Gräfin Fanny de
Butterbrod, a very gentle tender-hearted and unassuming
young creature, a canoness and countess in her own right,
but with scarcely ten pounds per year to her fortune, and
Fanny for her part declared that to be Amelia's sister was the
greatest delight that Heaven could bestow on her, and Jos

might have put a countess's shield and coronet by the
side of his own arms on his carriage and forks ; when—
when events occurred, and those grand fêtes given upon
the marriage of the Hereditary Prince of Pumpernickel
with the lovely Princess Amelia of Humbourg-Schlippen-
schloppen took place.

At this festival the magnificence displayed was such as
had not been known in the little German place since the
days of the prodigal Victor XIV. All the neighbouring
princes, princesses, and grandees were invited to the feast.
Beds rose to half a crown per night in Pumpernickel, and
the army was exhausted in providing guards of honour
for the highnesses, serenities, and excellencies, who arrived
from all quarters. The princess was married by proxy,
at her father's residence, by the Count de Schlüsselback.
Snuff-boxes were given away in profusion (as we learned
from the Court jeweller, who sold and afterwards bought
them again), and bushels of the Order of St. Michael of
Pumpernickel were sent to the nobles of the Court, while
hampers of the cordons and decorations of the Wheel of
St. Catherine of Schlippenschloppen were brought to ours.
The French envoy got both. ' He is covered with ribbons
like a prize cart-horse,' Tapeworm said, who was not
allowed by the rules of his service to take any decorations :
' Let him have the cordons ; but with whom is the victory ? '
The fact is, it was a triumph of British diplomacy : the
French party having proposed and tried their utmost to
carry a marriage with a princess of the house of Potz-
tausend-Donnerwetter, whom, as a matter of course, we
opposed.

Everybody was asked to the fêtes of the marriage. Gar-
lands and triumphal arches were hung across the road to
welcome the young bride. The great St. Michael's Fountain
ran with uncommonly sour wine, while that in the Artillery
Place frothed with beer. The great waters played ; and
poles were put up in the park and gardens for the happy
peasantry, which they might climb at their leisure, carrying
off watches, silver forks, prize sausages hung with pink
ribbon, &c., at the top. Georgy got one, wrenching it off,
having swarmed up the pole to the delight of the spectators,
and sliding down with the rapidity of a fall of water. But
it was for the glory's sake merely. The boy gave the
sausage to a peasant, who had very nearly seized it, and

stood at the foot of the mast, blubbering, because he was unsuccessful.

At the French chancellerie they had six more lampions* in their illumination than ours had ; but our transparency, which represented the young couple advancing, and Discord flying away, with the most ludicrous likeness to the French ambassador, beat the French picture hollow ; and I have no doubt got Tapeworm the advancement and the Cross of the Bath, which he subsequently attained.

Crowds of foreigners arrived for the fêtes : and of English of course. Besides the Court balls, public balls were given at the Town Hall and the Redoute, and in the former place there was a room for *trente-et-quarante* and roulette established, for the week of the festivities only, and by one of the great German companies from Ems or Aix-la-Chapelle. The officers or inhabitants of the town were not allowed to play at these games, but strangers, peasants, ladies were admitted, and any one who chose to lose or win money.

That little scapegrace Georgy Osborne amongst others, whose pockets were always full of dollars, and whose relations were away at the grand festival of the Court, came to the Stadthaus ball in company of his uncle's courier, Mr. Kirsch, and having only peeped into a play-room at Baden-Baden when he hung on Dobbin's arm, and where, of course, he was not permitted to gamble, came eagerly to this part of the entertainment, and hankered round the tables where the croupiers and the punters were at work. Women were playing ; they were masked, some of them ; this licence was allowed in these wild times of carnival.

A woman with light hair, in a low dress, by no means so fresh as it had been, and with a black mask on, through the eyelets of which her eyes twinkled strangely, was seated at one of the roulette-tables with a card and a pin, and a couple of florins before her. As the croupier called out the colour and number, she pricked on the card with great care and regularity, and only ventured her money on the colours after the red or black had come up a certain number of times. It was strange to look at her.

But in spite of her care and assiduity she guessed wrong, and the last two florins followed each other under the croupier's rake, as he cried out, with his inexorable voice, the winning colour and number. She gave a sigh, a shrug with her shoulders, which were already too much out of her gown, and dashing the pin through the card on to the table, sat thrumming it for a while. Then she looked round her, and saw Georgy's honest face staring at the scene. The little scamp! what business had he to be there?

When she saw the boy, at whose face she looked hard through her shining eyes and mask, she said, '*Monsieur n'est pas joueur.*'

'*Non, madame,*' said the boy: but she must have known, from his accent, of what country he was, for she answered him, with a slight foreign tone, 'You have nevare played— will you do me a littl' favour?'

'What is it?' said Georgy, blushing again. Mr. Kirsch was at work for his part at the *rouge et noir*, and did not see his young master.

'Play this for me, if you please, put it on any number, any number.' And she took from her bosom a purse, and out of it a gold piece, the only coin there, and she put it into George's hand. The boy laughed, and did as he was bid. The number came up sure enough. There is a power that arranges that, they say, for beginners.

'Thank you,' said she, pulling the money towards her; 'thank you. What is your name?'

'My name's Osborne,' said Georgy, and was fingering in his own pockets for dollars, and just about to make a trial, when the major, in his uniform, and Jos, *en marquis,* from the Court ball, made their appearance. Other people finding the entertainment stupid, and preferring the fun at the Stadthaus, had quitted the palace ball earlier; but it is probable the major and Jos had gone home and found the boy's absence, for the former instantly went up to him, and taking him by the shoulder, pulled him briskly back from the place of temptation. Then, looking round the room, he saw Kirsch employed as we have said, and going up to him, asked how he dared to bring Mr. George to such a place.

'*Laissez-moi tranquille,*' said Mr. Kirsch, very much excited by play and wine. '*Il faut s'amuser, parbleu. Je ne suis pas au service de monsieur.*'

Seeing his condition, the major did not choose to argue with the man; but contented himself with drawing away

George, and asking Jos if he would come away. He was standing close by the lady in the mask, who was playing with pretty good luck now ; and looking on much interested at the game.

'Hadn't you better come, Jos,' the major said, 'with George and me ? '

'I'll stop and go home with that rascal, Kirsch,' Jos said ; and for the same reason of modesty, which he thought ought to be preserved before the boy, Dobbin did not care to remonstrate with Jos, but left him and walked home with Georgy.

'Did you play ? ' asked the major, when they were out, and on their way home.

The boy said, 'No.'

'Give me your word of honour as a gentleman, that you never will.'

'Why ? ' said the boy : 'it seems very good fun.' And, in a very eloquent and impressive manner, the major showed him why he shouldn't, and would have enforced his precepts by the example of Georgy's own father, had he liked to say anything that should reflect on the other's memory. When he had housed him he went to bed, and saw his light, in the little room outside of Amelia's, presently disappear. Amelia's followed half an hour afterwards. I don't know what made the major note it so accurately.

Jos, however, remained behind over the play-table ; he was no gambler, but not averse to the little excitement of the sport now and then ; and he had some napoleons chinking in the embroidered pockets of his Court waistcoat. He put down one over the fair shoulder of the little gambler before him, and they won. She made a little movement to make room for him by her side, and just took the skirt of her gown from a vacant chair there.

'Come and give me good luck,' she said, still in a foreign accent, quite different from that frank and perfectly English 'Thank you,' with which she had saluted Georgy's *coup* in her favour. The portly gentleman, looking round to see that nobody of rank observed him, sat down ; he muttered, 'Ah, really, well now, God bless my soul. I'm very fortunate ; I'm sure to give you good fortune,'—and other words of compliment and confusion.

'Do you play much ? ' the foreign mask said.

'I put a nap or two down,' said Jos, with a superb air, flinging down a gold piece.

'Yes; ay nap after dinner,' said the mask, archly. But Jos looking frightened, she continued, in her pretty French accent, 'You do not play to win. No more do I. I play to forget, but I cannot. I cannot forget old times, monsieur. Your little nephew is the image of his father; and you— you are not changed—but yes, you are. Everybody changes, everybody forgets; nobody has ay heart.'

'Good Ged, who is it?' asked Jos, in a flutter.

'Can't you guess, Joseph Sedley?' said the little woman, in a sad voice, and undoing her mask, she looked at him. 'You have forgotten me.'

'Good Heavens! Mrs. Crawley!' gasped out Jos.

'Rebecca,' said the other, putting her hand on his; but she followed the game still, all the time she was looking at him.

'I am stopping at the "Elephant",' she continued. 'Ask for Madame de Raudon. I saw my dear Amelia to-day; how pretty she looked, and how happy! So do you! Everybody but me, who am wretched, Joseph Sedley.' And she put her money over from the red to the black, as if by a chance movement of her hand, and while she was wiping her eyes with a pocket-handkerchief fringed with torn lace.

The red came up again, and she lost the whole of that stake. 'Come away,' she said. 'Come with me a little— we are old friends, are we not, dear Mr. Sedley?'

And Mr. Kirsch having lost all his money by this time, followed his master out into the moonlight, where the illuminations were winking out, and the transparency over our mission was scarcely visible.

CHAPTER LXIV

A VAGABOND CHAPTER

W E must pass over a part of Mrs. Rebecca Crawley's biography with that lightness and delicacy which the world demands—the moral world, that has, perhaps, no particular objection to vice, but an insuperable repugnance to hearing vice called by its proper name. There are things we do and know perfectly well in Vanity Fair, though we never speak them: as the Ahrimanians worship the devil,* but don't mention him : and a polite public will no more bear to read an authentic description of vice than a truly-refined English or American female will permit the word 'breeches' to be pronounced in her chaste hearing. And yet, madam, both are walking the world before our faces every day, without much shocking us. If you were to blush every time they went by, what complexions you would have ! It is only when their naughty names are called out that your modesty has any occasion to show alarm or sense of outrage, and it has been the wish of the present writer, all through this story, deferentially to submit to the fashion at present prevailing, and only to hint at the existence of wickedness in a light, easy, and agreeable manner, so that nobody's fine feelings may be offended. I defy any one to say that our Becky, who has certainly some vices, has not been presented to the public in a perfectly genteel and inoffensive manner. In describing this siren, singing and smiling, coaxing and cajoling, the author, with modest pride, asks his readers all round, has he once forgotten the laws of politeness, and showed the monster's hideous tail above water ? No ! Those who like may peep down under waves that are pretty transparent, and see it writhing and twirling, diabolically hideous and slimy, flapping amongst bones, or curling round corpses ; but above the water line, I ask, has not everything been proper,

agreeable, and decorous, and has any the most squeamish
immoralist in Vanity Fair a right to cry fie ? When,
however, the siren disappears*and dives below, down among
the dead men, the water of course grows turbid over her,
and it is labour lost to look into it ever so curiously. They
look pretty enough when they sit upon a rock, twanging
their harps and combing their hair, and sing, and beckon
to you to come and hold the looking-glass ; but when
they sink into their native element, depend on it those
mermaids are about no good, and we had best not examine
the fiendish marine cannibals, revelling and feasting on
their wretched pickled victims. And so, when Becky is
out of the way, be sure that she is not particularly well
employed, and that the less that is said about her doings
is in fact the better.

If we were to give a full account of her proceedings
during a couple of years that followed after the Curzon
Street catastrophe, there might be some reason for people
to say this book was improper. The actions of very vain,
heartless, pleasure-seeking people are very often improper
(as are many of yours, my friend with the grave face and
spotless reputation ;—but that is merely by the way) ;
and what are those of a woman without faith—or love—
or character ? And I am inclined to think that there was
a period in Mrs. Becky's life, when she was seized, not by
remorse, but by a kind of despair, and absolutely neglected
her person, and did not even care for her reputation.

This *abattement* and degradation did not take place all
at once : it was brought about by degrees,after her calamity,
and after many struggles to keep up—as a man who goes
overboard hangs on to a spar whilst any hope is left, and
then flings it away and goes down, when he finds that
struggling is in vain.

She lingered about London whilst her husband was
making preparations for his departure to his seat of government ; and it is believed made more than one attempt to
see her brother-in-law, Sir Pitt Crawley, and to work upon
his feelings which she had almost enlisted in her favour.
As Sir Pitt and Mr. Wenham were walking down to the
House of Commons, the latter spied Mrs. Rawdon in a black
veil, and lurking near the palace of the legislature. She
sneaked away when her eyes met those of Wenham, and
indeed never succeeded in her designs upon the baronet.

Probably Lady Jane interposed. I have heard that she
quite astonished her husband by the spirit which she
exhibited in this quarrel, and her determination to disown
Mrs. Becky. Of her own movement, she invited Rawdon
to come and stop in Gaunt Street until his departure for
Coventry Island, knowing that with him for a guard
Mrs. Becky would not try to force her door : and she
looked curiously at the superscriptions of all the letters
which arrived for Sir Pitt, lest he and his sister-in-law
should be corresponding. Not but that Rebecca could
have written had she a mind : but she did not try to see
or to write to Pitt at his own house, and after one or two
attempts consented to his demand that the correspondence
regarding her conjugal differences should be carried on by
lawyers only.

The fact was, that Pitt's mind had been poisoned against
her. A short time after Lord Steyne's accident Wenham
had been with the baronet ; and given him such a biography
of Mrs. Becky as had astonished the member for Queen's
Crawley. He knew everything regarding her ; who her
father was ; in what year her mother danced at the Opera ;
what had been her previous history, and what her conduct
during her married life :—as I have no doubt that the
greater part of the story was false and dictated by interested
malevolence, it shall not be repeated here. But Becky was
left with a sad, sad reputation in the esteem of a country
gentleman and relative who had been once rather partial
to her.

The revenues of the governor of Coventry Island are
not large. A part of them were set aside by his excellency
for the payment of certain outstanding debts and liabilities,
the charges incident on his high situation required considerable expense ; finally, it was found that he could not
spare to his wife more than three hundred pounds a year,
which he proposed to pay to her on an undertaking that she
would never trouble him. Otherwise : scandal, separation,
Doctors' Commons would ensue. But it was Mr. Wenham's
business, Lord Steyne's business, Rawdon's, everybody's—
to get her out of the country, and hush up a most disagreeable affair.

She was probably so much occupied in arranging these
affairs of business with her husband's lawyers, that she
forgot to take any step whatever about her son, the little

Rawdon, and did not even once propose to go and see him.
That young gentleman was consigned to the entire guardianship of his aunt and uncle, the former of whom had always
possessed a great share of the child's affection. His mamma
wrote him a neat letter from Boulogne when she quitted
England, in which she requested him to mind his book,
and said she was going to take a Continental tour, during
which she would have the pleasure of writing to him again.
But she never did for a year afterwards, and not indeed,
until Sir Pitt's only boy, always sickly, died of whooping-
cough and measles :—then Rawdon's mamma wrote the
most affectionate composition to her darling son, who was
made heir of Queen's Crawley by this accident, and drawn
more closely than ever to the kind lady, whose tender
heart had already adopted him. Rawdon Crawley, then
grown a tall, fine lad, blushed when he got the letter.
' Oh, Aunt Jane, you are my mother ! ' he said ; ' and
not—and not that one.' But he wrote back a kind and
respectful letter to Mrs. Rebecca, then living at a boarding-
house at Florence.—But we are advancing matters.

Our darling Becky's first flight was not very far. She
perched upon the French coast at Boulogne, that refuge
of so much exiled English innocence ; and there lived in
rather a genteel, widowed manner, with a *femme de chambre*
and a couple of rooms, at an hotel. She dined at the
table d'hôte, where people thought her very pleasant, and
where she entertained her neighbours by stories of her
brother, Sir Pitt, and her great London acquaintance :
talking that easy, fashionable slipslop, which has so much
effect upon certain folks of small breeding. She passed
with many of them for a person of importance ; she gave
little tea-parties in her private room, and shared in the
innocent amusements of the place,—in sea-bathing, and in
jaunts in open carriages, in strolls on the sands, and in
visits to the play. Mrs. Burjoice, the printer's lady, who
was boarding with her family at the hotel for the summer,
and to whom her Burjoice came of a Saturday and Sunday,
voted her charming ; until that little rogue of a Burjoice
began to pay her too much attention. But there was
nothing in the story, only that Becky was always affable,
easy, and good-natured—and with men especially.

Numbers of people were going abroad as usual at the
end of the season, and Becky had plenty of opportunities

of finding out by the behaviour of her acquaintances of
the great London world the opinion of 'society' as regarded
her conduct.   One day it was Lady Partlet and her
daughters whom Becky confronted as she was walking
modestly on Boulogne pier, the cliffs of Albion shining in
the distance across the deep blue sea.   Lady Partlet
marshalled all her daughters round her with a sweep of
her parasol, and retreated from the pier darting savage
glances at poor little Becky who stood alone there.

On another day the packet came in.   It had been blowing
fresh, and it always suited Becky's humour to see the droll
woebegone faces of the people as they emerged from the
boat.   Lady Slingstone happened to be on board this day.
Her ladyship had been exceedingly ill in her carriage, and
was greatly exhausted and scarcely fit to walk up the
plank from the ship to the pier.   But all her energies
rallied the instant she saw Becky smiling roguishly under
a pink bonnet : and giving her a glance of scorn, such
as would have shrivelled up most women, she walked into
the Custom House quite unsupported. Becky only laughed :
but I don't think she liked it.   She felt she was alone,
quite alone : and the far-off shining cliffs of England were
impassable to her.

The behaviour of the men had undergone too I don't
know what change.   Grinstone showed his teeth and
laughed in her face with a familiarity that was not pleasant.
Little Bob Suckling, who was cap in hand to her three
months before, and would walk a mile in the rain to see
for her carriage in the line at Gaunt House, was talking
to Fitzoof of the Guards (Lord Heehaw's son) one day
upon the jetty, as Becky took her walk there.   Little
Bobby nodded to her over his shoulder without moving
his hat, and continued his conversation with the heir of
Heehaw.   Tom Raikes tried to walk into her sitting-room
at the inn with a cigar in his mouth : but she closed the
door upon him and would have locked it only that his
fingers were inside.   She began to feel that she was very
lonely indeed.   'If *he'd* been here,' she said, 'those cowards
would never have dared to insult me.'   She thought about
'him' with great sadness, and perhaps longing—about his
honest, stupid, constant kindness and fidelity : his never-
ceasing obedience ; his good humour ; his bravery and
courage.   Very likely she cried, for she was particularly

lively, and had put on a little extra rouge when she came down to dinner.

She rouged regularly now : and — and her maid got cognac for her besides that which was charged in the hotel bill.

Perhaps the insults of the men were not, however, so intolerable to her as the sympathy of certain women. Mrs. Crackenbury and Mrs. Washington White passed through Boulogne on their way to Switzerland. (The party were protected by Colonel Horner, young Beaumoris, and of course old Crackenbury, and Mrs. White's little girl.) *They* did not avoid her. They giggled, cackled, tattled, condoled, consoled, and patronized her until they drove her almost wild with rage. To be patronized by *them !* she thought, as they went away simpering after kissing her. And she heard Beaumoris's laugh ringing on the stair, and knew quite well how to interpret his hilarity.

It was after this visit that Becky, who had paid her weekly bills, Becky who had made herself agreeable to everybody in the house, who smiled at the landlady, called the waiters 'monsieur', and paid the chambermaids in politeness and apologies, what far more than compensated for a little niggardliness in point of money (of which Becky never was free), that Becky, we say, received a notice to quit from the landlord, who had been told by some one that she was quite an unfit person to have at his hotel, where English ladies would not sit down with her. And she was forced to fly into lodgings, of which the dullness and solitude were most wearisome to her.

Still she held up, in spite of these rebuffs, and tried to make a character for herself, and conquer scandal. She went to church very regularly, and sang louder than anybody there. She took up the cause of the widows of the shipwrecked fishermen, and gave work and drawings for the Quashyboo Mission ; she subscribed to the Assembly, and *wouldn't* waltz. In a word, she did everything that was respectable, and that is why we dwell upon this part of her career with more fondness than upon subsequent parts of her history, which are not so pleasant. She saw people avoiding her, and still laboriously smiled upon them ; you never could suppose from her countenance what pangs of humiliation she might be enduring inwardly.

Her history was, after all a mystery. Parties were

divided about her. Some people, who took the trouble
to busy themselves in the matter, said that she was the
criminal; whilst others vowed that she was as innocent
as a lamb, and that her odious husband was in fault. She
won over a good many by bursting into tears about her
boy, and exhibiting the most frantic grief when his name
was mentioned, or she saw anybody like him. She gained
good Mrs. Alderney's heart in that way, who was rather
the queen of British Boulogne, and gave the most dinners
and balls of all the residents there, by weeping when
Master Alderney came from Doctor Swishtail's academy
to pass his holidays with his mother. ' He and her Rawdon
were of the same age, and *so* like,' Becky said, in a voice
choking with agony; whereas there was five years' difference between the boys' ages, and no more likeness between
them than between my respected reader and his humble
servant. Wenham, when he was going abroad, on his way
to Kissingen to join Lord Steyne, enlightened Mrs. Alderney
on this point, and told her how he was much more able
to describe little Rawdon than his mamma, who notoriously
hated him, and never saw him; how he was thirteen
years old, while little Alderney was but nine; fair, while
the other darling was dark,—in a word, caused the lady
in question to repent of her good humour.

Whenever Becky made a little circle for herself with
incredible toils and labour, somebody came and swept it
down rudely, and she had all her work to begin over again.
It was very hard: very hard; lonely, and disheartening.

There was Mrs. Newbright, who took her up for some
time, attracted by the sweetness of her singing at church,
and by her proper views upon serious subjects, concerning
which in former days, at Queen's Crawley, Mrs. Becky had
had a good deal of instruction.—Well, she not only took
tracts, but she read them. She worked flannel petticoats
for the Quashyboos—cotton nightcaps for the Cocoanut
Indians—painted hand-screens for the conversion of the
Pope and the Jews—sat under Mr. Rowls on Wednesdays,
Mr. Huggleton on Thursdays, attended two Sunday services
at church, besides Mr. Bawler, the Darbyite, in the evening,
and all in vain. Mrs. Newbright had occasion to correspond
with the Countess of Southdown about the Warming-pan
Fund for the Feejee Islanders (for the management of which
admirable charity both these ladies formed part of a female

committee), and having mentioned her ' sweet friend ', Mrs. Rawdon Crawley, the dowager countess wrote back such a letter regarding Becky, with such particulars, hints, facts, falsehoods, and general comminations, that intimacy between Mrs. Newbright and Mrs. Crawley ceased forthwith : and all the serious world of Tours, where this misfortune took place, immediately parted company with the reprobate. Those who know the English colonies abroad know that we carry with us our pride, pills, prejudices, Harvey-sauces, cayenne-peppers, and other Lares, making a little Britain wherever we settle down.

From one colony to another Becky fled uneasily. From Boulogne to Dieppe, from Dieppe to Caen, from Caen to Tours—trying with all her might to be respectable, and alas ! always found out some day or other, and pecked out of the cage by the real daws.

Mrs. Hook Eagles took her up at one of these places :— a woman without a blemish in her character, and a house in Portman Square. She was staying at the hotel at Dieppe, whither Becky fled, and they made each other's acquaintance first at sea, where they were swimming together, and subsequently at the table d'hôte of the hotel. Mrs. Eagles had heard,—who indeed had not ?—some of the scandal of the Steyne affair ; but after a conversation with Becky, she pronounced that Mrs. Crawley was an angel, her husband a ruffian, Lord Steyne an unprincipled wretch, as everybody knew, and the whole case against Mrs. Crawley, an infamous and wicked conspiracy of that rascal Wenham. ' If you were a man of any spirit, Mr. Eagles, you would box the wretch's ears the next time you see him at the club,' she said to her husband. But Eagles was only a quiet old gentleman, husband to Mrs. Eagles, with a taste for geology, and not tall enough to reach anybody's ears.

The Eagles then patronized Mrs. Rawdon, took her to live with her at her own house at Paris, quarrelled with the ambassador's wife because she would not receive her protégée, and did all that lay in woman's power to keep Becky straight in the paths of virtue and good repute.

Becky was very respectable and orderly at first, but the life of humdrum virtue grew utterly tedious to her before long. It was the same routine every day, the same dullness and comfort, the same drive over the same stupid Bois de Boulogne, the same company of an evening, the same Blair's

Sermon of a Sunday night—the same opera always being
acted over and over again : Becky was dying of weariness,
when, luckily for her, young Mr. Eagles came from
Cambridge, and his mother, seeing the impression which
her little friend made upon him, straightway gave Becky
warning.

Then she tried keeping house with a female friend ; then
the double *ménage* began to quarrel and get into debt.
Then she determined upon a boarding-house existence, and
lived for some time at that famous mansion kept by Madame
de St. Amour, in the Rue Royale at Paris, where she began
exercising her graces and fascinations upon the shabby
dandies and fly-blown beauties who frequented her landlady's salons. Becky loved society, and, indeed, could no
more exist without it than an opium-eater without his dram,
and she was happy enough at the period of her boarding-
house life. ' The women here are as amusing as those in
May Fair,' she told an old London friend who met her—
' only, their dresses are not quite so fresh. The men wear
cleaned gloves, and are sad rogues, certainly, but they are
not worse than Jack This, and Tom That. The mistress
of the house is a little vulgar, but I don't think she is so
vulgar as Lady ——' and here she named the name of a
great leader of fashion that I would die rather than reveal.
In fact, when you saw Madame de St. Amour's rooms
lighted up of a night, men with *plaques* and *cordons* at the
écarté tables, and the women at a little distance, you might
fancy yourself for a while in good society, and that madame
was a real countess. Many people did so fancy : and Becky
was for a while one of the most dashing ladies of the
countess's salons.

But it is probable that her old creditors of 1815 found her
out and caused her to leave Paris, for the poor little woman
was forced to fly from the city rather suddenly ; and went
thence to Brussels.

How well she remembered the place ! She grinned as
she looked up at the little *entresol* which she had occupied,
and thought of the Bareacres family, bawling for horses
and flight, as their carriage stood in the *porte-cochère* of the
hotel. She went to Waterloo and to Laeken, where George
Osborne's monument much struck her. She made a little
sketch of it. ' That poor Cupid ! ' she said ; ' how dreadfully he was in love with me, and what a fool he was !

I wonder whether little Emmy is alive. It was a good little creature : and that fat brother of hers. I have his funny fat picture still among my papers. They were kind simple people.'

At Brussels Becky arrived, recommended by Madame de St. Amour to her friend, Madame la Comtesse de Borodino, widow of Napoleon's general, the famous Count de Borodino, who was left with no resource by the deceased hero but that of a table d'hôte and an écarté table. Second-rate dandies and *roués*, widow ladies who always have a law-suit, and very simple English folks, who fancy they see ' Continental society ' at these houses, put down their money, or ate their meals, at Madame de Borodino's tables. The gallant young fellows treated the company round to champagne at the table d'hôte, rode out with the women, or hired horses on country excursions, clubbed money to take boxes at the play or the Opera, betted over the fair shoulders of the ladies at the écarté tables, and wrote home to their parents in Devonshire about their felicitous introduction to foreign society.

Here, as at Paris, Becky was a boarding-house queen : and ruled in select *pensions*. She never refused the cham-pagne, or the bouquets, or the drives into the country, or the private boxes ; but what she preferred was the écarté at night,—and she played audaciously. First she played only for a little, then for five-franc pieces, then for napoleons, then for notes : then she would not be able to pay her month's *pension :* then she borrowed from the young gentlemen : then she got into cash again, and bullied Madame de Borodino, whom she had coaxed and wheedled before : then she was playing for ten sous at a time, and in a dire state of poverty : then her quarter's allowance would come in, and she would pay off Madame de Borodino's score : and would once more take the cards against Monsieur de Rossignol, or the Chevalier de Raff.

When Becky left Brussels, the sad truth is, that she owed three months' *pension* to Madame de Borodino, of which fact, and of the gambling, and of the drinking, and of the going down on her knees to the Reverend Mr. Muff, Ministre Anglican, and borrowing money of him, and of her coaxing and flirting with Milor Noodle, son of Sir Noodle, pupil of the Rev. Mr. Muff, whom she used to take into her private room, and of whom she won large sums at écarté—

of which fact, I say, and of a hundred of her other knaveries, the Countess de Borodino informs every English person who stops at her establishment, and announces that Madame Rawdon was no better than a *vipère*.

So our little wanderer went about setting up her tent in various cities of Europe, as restless as Ulysses or Bampfylde Moore Carew.* Her taste for disrespectability grew more and more remarkable. She became a perfect Bohemian

ere long, herding with people whom it would make your hair stand on end to meet.

There is no town of any mark in Europe but it has its little colony of English raffs—men whose names Mr. Hemp,* the officer, reads out periodically at the Sheriffs' Court— young gentlemen of very good family often, only that the latter disowns them; frequenters of billiard-rooms and estaminets, patrons of foreign races and gaming-tables. They people the debtors' prisons—they drink and swagger— they fight and brawl—they run away without paying— they have duels with French and German officers—they

cheat Mr. Spoony at écarté — they get the money, and
drive off to Baden in magnificent britzkas—they try their
infallible martingale, and lurk about the tables with empty
pockets, shabby bullies, penniless bucks, until they can
swindle a Jew banker with a sham bill of exchange, or find
another Mr. Spoony to rob. The alternations of splendour
and misery which these people undergo are very queer to
view. Their life must be one of great excitement. Becky
—must it be owned ?—took to this life, and took to it not
unkindly. She went about from town to town among these
Bohemians. The lucky Mrs. Rawdon was known at every
play-table in Germany. She and Madame de Cruchecassée
kept house at Florence together. It is said she was ordered
out of Munich ; and my friend Mr. Frederic Pigeon avers
that it was at her house at Lausanne that he was hocussed
at supper and lost eight hundred pounds to Major Loder
and the Honourable Mr. Deuceace. We are bound, you see,
to give some account of Becky's biography : but of this
part, the less, perhaps, that is said the better.

They say, that when Mrs. Crawley was particularly down
on her luck, she gave concerts and lessons in music here and
there. There was a Madame de Raudon who certainly had
a *matinée musicale* at Wildbad, accompanied by Herr Spoff,
premier pianist to the Hospodar of Wallachia, and my little
friend Mr. Eaves, who knew everybody, and had travelled
everywhere, always used to declare that he was at Strasburg
in the year 1830, when a certain Madame Rebecque made
her appearance in the opera of the *Dame Blanche*,* giving
occasion to a furious row in the theatre there. She was
hissed off the stage by the audience, partly from her own
incompetency, but chiefly from the ill-advised sympathy
of some persons in the *parquet* (where the officers of the
garrison had their admissions) ; and Eaves was certain that
the unfortunate *débutante* in question was no other than
Mrs. Rawdon Crawley.

She was, in fact, no better than a vagabond upon this
earth. When she got her money she gambled ; when she
had gambled it she was put to shifts to live ; who knows
how or by what means she succeeded ? It is said that she
once was seen at St. Petersburg, but was summarily dismissed from that capital by the police: so that there cannot be any possibility of truth in the report that she was a
Russian spy at Teplitz and Vienna afterwards. I have even

been informed, that at Paris she discovered a relation of her
own, no less a person than her maternal grandmother, who
was not by any means a Montmorenci, but a hideous old
box-opener at a theatre on the Boulevards. The meeting
between them, of which other persons, as it is hinted elsewhere, seem to have been acquainted, must have been a very
affecting interview. The present historian can give no
certain details regarding the event.

It happened at Rome once, that Mrs. de Rawdon's half-
year's salary had just been paid into the principal banker's
there, and, as everybody who had a balance of above five
hundred scudi was invited to the balls which this prince
of merchants gave during the winter, Becky had the honour
of a card, and appeared at one of the Prince and Princess
Polonia's splendid evening entertainments. The princess
was of the family of Pompili, lineally descended from the
second King of Rome, and Egeria of the house of Olympus,
while the prince's grandfather, Alessandro Polonia, sold
wash-balls, essences, tobacco, and pocket-handkerchiefs, ran
errands for gentlemen, and lent money in a small way. All
the great company in Rome thronged to his saloons—princes,
dukes, ambassadors, artists, fiddlers, monsignori, young
bears with their leaders—every rank and condition of man.
His halls blazed with light and magnificence ; were resplen-
dent with gilt frames (containing pictures) and dubious
antiques : and the enormous gilt crown and arms of the
princely owner, a gold mushroom on a crimson field (the
colour of the pocket-handkerchiefs which he sold), and the
silver fountain of the Pompili family shone all over the
roof, doors, and panels of the house, and over the grand
velvet baldaquins prepared to receive popes and emperors.

So Becky, who had arrived in the diligence from Florence,
and was lodged at an inn in a very modest way, got a card
for Prince Polonia's entertainment, and her maid dressed
her with unusual care, and she went to this fine ball leaning
on the arm of Major Loder, with whom she happened to
be travelling at the time (the same man who shot Prince
Ravioli at Naples the next year, and was caned by Sir John
Buckskin for carrying four kings in his hat besides those
which he used in playing at écarté)—and this pair went into
the rooms together, and Becky saw a number of old faces,
which she remembered in happier days, when she was not
innocent, but not found out. Major Loder knew a great

number of foreigners, keen-looking whiskered men with dirty
striped ribbons in their button-holes, and a very small
display of linen ; but his own countrymen, it might be
remarked, eschewed the major. Becky, too, knew some
ladies here and there—French widows, dubious Italian
countesses, whose husbands had treated them ill—faugh—
what shall we say, we who have moved among some of the
finest company of Vanity Fair, of this refuse and sediment
of rascals ? If we play, let it be with clean cards, and not

with this dirty pack. But every man who has formed one
of the innumerable army of travellers has seen these marauding irregulars hanging on, like Nym and Pistol, to the main
force ; wearing the king's colours, and boasting of his commission, but pillaging for themselves, and occasionally
gibbeted by the roadside.

Well, she was hanging on the arm of Major Loder, and
they went through the rooms together, and drank a great
quantity of champagne at the buffet, where the people, and
especially the major's irregular corps, struggled furiously
for refreshments, of which when the pair had had enough,
they pushed on until they reached the duchess's own pink
velvet saloon, at the end of the suite of apartments (where

the statue of the Venus is, and the great Venice looking-glasses, framed in silver), and where the princely family were entertaining their most distinguished guests at a round table at supper. It was just such a little select banquet as that of which Becky recollected that she had partaken at Lord Steyne's—and there he sat at Polonia's table, and she saw him.

The scar cut by the diamond on his white, bald, shining forehead, made a burning red mark ; his red whiskers were dyed of a purple hue, which made his pale face look still paler. He wore his collar and orders, his blue ribbon and garter. He was a greater prince than any there, though there was a reigning duke and a royal highness, with their princesses, and near his lordship was seated the beautiful Countess of Belladonna, *née* de Glandier, whose husband (the Count Paolo della Belladonna) so well known for his brilliant entomological collections, had been long absent on a mission to the Emperor of Morocco.

When Becky beheld that familiar and illustrious face, how vulgar all of a sudden did Major Loder appear to her, and how that odious Captain Rook did smell of tobacco ! In one instant she resumed her fine-ladyship, and tried to look and feel as if she was in May Fair once more. ' That woman looks stupid and ill-humoured,' she thought; ' I am sure she can't amuse him. No, he must be bored by her— he never was by me.' A hundred such touching hopes, fears, and memories palpitated in her little heart, as she looked with her brightest eyes (the rouge which she wore up to her eyelids made them twinkle) towards the great nobleman. Of a Star and Garter night Lord Steyne used also to put on his grandest manner, and to look and speak like a great prince, as he was. Becky admired him, smiling sumptuously, easy, lofty, and stately. Ah, *bon Dieu*, what a pleasant companion he was, what a brilliant wit, what a rich fund of talk, what a grand manner !—and she had exchanged this for Major Loder, reeking of cigars and brandy-and-water, and Captain Rook with his horse-jockey jokes and prize-ring slang, and their like. ' I wonder whether he will know me,' she thought. Lord Steyne was talking and laughing with a great and illustrious lady at his side, when he looked up and saw Becky.

She was all over in a flutter as their eyes met, and she put on the very best smile she could muster, and dropped

him a little, timid, imploring curtsy. He stared aghast
at her for a minute, as Macbeth might on beholding Banquo's
sudden appearance at his ball-supper; and remained looking
at her with open mouth, when that horrid Major Loder
pulled her away.

'Come away into the supper-room, Mrs. R.,' was that
gentleman's remark; 'seeing those nobs grubbing away
has made me peckish too. Let's go and try the old governor's
champagne.' Becky thought the major had had a great
deal too much already.

The day after she went to walk on the Pincian Hill—the
Hyde Park of the Roman idlers—possibly in hopes to have
another sight of Lord Steyne. But she met another acquaintance there: it was Mr. Fiche, his lordship's confidential
man, who came up nodding to her rather familiarly and
putting a finger to his hat. 'I knew that madame was
here,' he said; 'I followed her from her hotel. I have some
advice to give madame.'

'From the Marquis of Steyne?' Becky asked, resuming
as much of her dignity as she could muster, and not a little
agitated by hope and expectation.

'No,' said the valet; 'it is from me. Rome is very
unwholesome.'

'Not at this season, Monsieur Fiche—not till after Easter.'

'I tell madame it is unwholesome now. There is always
malaria for some people. That cursed marsh wind kills
many at all seasons. Look, Madame Crawley, you were
always *bon enfant*, and I have an interest in you, *parole
d'honneur*. Be warned. Go away from Rome, I tell you—
or you will be ill and die.'

Becky laughed, though in rage and fury. 'What! assas-
sinate poor little me?' she said. 'How romantic! Does
my lord carry bravos for couriers, and stilettos in the
fourgons?* Bah! I will stay, if but to plague him. I have
those who will defend me whilst I am here.'

It was Monsieur Fiche's turn to laugh now. 'Defend
you,' he said, 'and who? The major, the captain, any one
of those gambling men whom madame sees, would take her
life for a hundred louis. We know things about Major
Loder (he is no more a major than I am my lord the marquis)
which would send him to the galleys or worse. We know
everything, and have friends everywhere. We know whom
you saw at Paris, and what relations you found there. Yes,

madame may stare, but we do. And how was it that no
minister on the Continent would receive madame ? She has
offended somebody : who never forgives—whose rage
redoubled when he saw you. He was like a madman last
night when he came home. Madame de Belladonna made
him a scene about you, and fired off in one of her furies.'

'Oh, it was Madame de Belladonna, was it ?' Becky said,
relieved a little, for the information she had just got had
scared her.

'No—she does not matter—she is always jealous. I tell
you it was monseigneur. You did wrong to show yourself
to him. And if you stay here you will repent it. Mark my
words. Go. Here is my lord's carriage'—and seizing
Becky's arm, he rushed down an alley of the garden as Lord
Steyne's barouche, blazing with heraldic devices, came
whirling along the avenue, borne by the almost priceless
horses, and bearing Madame de Belladonna lolling on the
cushions, dark, sulky, and blooming, a King Charles in her
lap, a white parasol swaying over her head, and old Steyne
stretched at her side with a livid face and ghastly eyes.
Hate, or anger, or desire, caused them to brighten now and
then still ; but ordinarily, they gave no light, and seemed
tired of looking out on a world of which almost all the
pleasure and all the best beauty had palled upon the worn-
out wicked old man.

'Monseigneur has never recovered the shock of that night,
never,' Monsieur Fiche whispered to Mrs. Crawley as the
carriage flashed by, and she peeped out at it from behind
the shrubs that hid her. 'That was a consolation at any
rate,' Becky thought.

Whether my lord really had murderous intentions towards
Mrs. Becky, as Monsieur Fiche said—(since monseigneur's
death he has returned to his native country, where he lives
much respected, and has purchased from his prince the title
of Baron Ficci),—and the factotum objected to have to do
with assassination ; or whether he simply had a commission
to frighten Mrs. Crawley out of a city where his lordship
proposed to pass the winter, and the sight of her would be
eminently disagreeable to the great nobleman, is a point
which has never been ascertained : but the threat had its
effect upon the little woman, and she sought no more to
intrude herself upon the presence of her old patron.

Everybody knows the melancholy end of that nobleman,

which befell at Naples two months after the French Revolution of 1830 : when the Most Honourable George Gustavus, Marquis of Steyne, Earl of Gaunt and of Gaunt Castle, in the Peerage of Ireland, Viscount Hellborough, Baron Pitchley and Grillsby, a Knight of the Most Noble Order of the Garter, of the Golden Fleece of Spain, of the Russian Order of St. Nicholas of the First Class, of the Turkish Order of the Crescent, First Lord of the Powder Closet and Groom of the Back Stairs, Colonel of the Gaunt or Regent's Own Regiment of Militia, a Trustee of the British Museum, an Elder Brother of the Trinity House, a Governor of the White Friars, and D.C.L.,*—died, after a series of fits, brought on, as the papers said, by the shock occasioned to his lordship's sensibilities by the downfall of the ancient French monarchy.*

An eloquent catalogue appeared in a weekly print, describing his virtues, his magnificence, his talents, and his good actions. His sensibility, his attachment to the illustrious House of Bourbon, with which he claimed an alliance, were such that he could not survive the misfortunes of his august kinsmen. His body was buried at Naples, and his heart— that heart which always beat with every generous and noble emotion—was brought back to Castle Gaunt in a silver urn. ' In him,' Mr. Wagg said, ' the poor and the Fine Arts have lost a beneficent patron, society one of its most brilliant ornaments, and England one of her loftiest patriots and statesmen,' &c., &c.

His will was a good deal disputed, and an attempt was made to force from Madame de Belladonna the celebrated jewel called the ' Jew's-eye ' diamond, which his lordship always wore on his forefinger, and which it was said that she removed from it after his lamented demise. But his confidential friend and attendant, Monsieur Fiche, proved that the ring had been presented to the said Madame de Belladonna two days before the marquis's death ; as were the bank-notes, jewels, Neapolitan and French bonds, &c., found in his lordship's secretaire, and claimed by his heirs, from that injured woman.

CHAPTER LXV

FULL OF BUSINESS AND PLEASURE

THE day after the meeting at the play-table, Jos had himself arrayed with unusual care and splendour, and without thinking it necessary to say a word to any member of his family regarding the occurrences of the previous night, or asking for their company in his walk, he sallied forth at an early hour, and was presently seen making inquiries at the door of the 'Elephant' Hotel. In consequence of the fêtes the house was full of company, the tables in the street were already surrounded by persons smoking and drinking the national small beer, the public rooms were in a cloud of smoke, and Mr. Jos having, in his pompous way, and with his clumsy German, made inquiries for the person of whom he was in search, was directed to the very top of the house, above the first-floor rooms where some travelling pedlars had lived, and were exhibiting their jewellery and brocades ; above the second-floor apartments occupied by the *état-major* of the gambling firm ; above the third-floor rooms, tenanted by the band of renowned Bohemian vaulters and tumblers ; and so on to the little cabins of the roof, where, among students, bagmen, small tradesmen, and country-folks, come in for the festival, Becky had found a little nest ;—as dirty a little refuge as ever beauty lay hid in.

Becky liked the life. She was at home with everybody in the place, pedlars, punters, tumblers, students and all. She was of a wild, roving nature, inherited from father and mother, who were both Bohemians, by taste and circumstance : if a lord was not by, she would talk to his courier with the greatest pleasure ; the din, the stir, the drink, the smoke, the tattle of the Hebrew pedlars, the solemn, braggart ways of the poor tumblers, the *sournois**talk of the gambling-table officials, the songs and swagger of the students, and the general buzz and hum of the place had pleased and tickled the little woman, even when her luck was down, and she had not wherewithal to pay her bill. How pleasant was all the bustle to her now that her purse was full of the money which little Georgy had won for her the night before !

As Jos came creaking and puffing up the final stairs, and

was speechless when he got to the landing, and began to wipe his face and then to look for No. 92, the room where he was directed to seek for the person he wanted, the door of the opposite chamber, No. 90, was open, and a student, in jack-boots and a dirty *Schlafrock*, was lying on the bed smoking a long pipe ; whilst another student in long yellow hair and a braided coat, exceeding smart and dirty too, was actually on his knees at No. 92, bawling through the keyhole supplications to the person within.

'Go away,' said a well-known voice, which made Jos
thrill; 'I expect somebody; I expect my grandpapa.
He mustn't see you there.'

'Angel Engländerin!' bellowed the kneeling student
with the whity-brown ringlets and the large finger-ring,
'do take compassion upon us. Make an appointment.
Dine with me and Fritz at the inn in the park. We will
have roast pheasants and porter, plum-pudding and French
wine. We shall die if you don't.'

'That we will,' said the young nobleman on the bed; and
this colloquy Jos overheard, though he did not comprehend
it, for the reason that he had never studied the language in
which it was carried on.

'*Newmero kattervang dooze, si vous plait,*' Jos said in his
grandest manner, when he was able to speak.

'*Quater fang tooce!*' said the student, starting up, and
he bounced into his own room, where he locked the door,
and where Jos heard him laughing with his comrade on
the bed.

The gentleman from Bengal was standing disconcerted
by this incident, when the door of the 92 opened of itself,
and Becky's little head peeped out, full of archness and
mischief. She lighted on Jos. 'It's you,' she said, coming
out. 'How I have been waiting for you! Stop! not yet—
in one minute you shall come in.' In that instant she put
a rouge-pot, a brandy-bottle, and a plate of broken meat
into the bed, gave one smooth to her hair, and finally let
in her visitor.

She had, by way of morning robe, a pink domino, a trifle
faded and soiled, and marked here and there with pomatum;
but her arms shone out from the loose sleeves of the dress,
very white and fair, and it was tied round her little waist,
so as not ill to set off the trim little figure of the wearer.
She led Jos by the hand into her garret. 'Come in,' she
said. 'Come and talk to me. Sit yonder on the chair;'
and she gave the civilian's hand a little squeeze, and laughingly placed him upon it. As for herself, she placed herself
on the bed—not on the bottle and plate, you may be
sure—on which Jos might have reposed, had he chosen
that seat; and so there she sat, and talked with her old
admirer.

'How little years have changed you,' she said, with a look
of tender interest. 'I should have known you anywhere.

What a comfort it is amongst strangers to see once more
the frank honest face of an old friend ! '

The frank honest face, to tell the truth, at this moment
bore any expression but one of openness and honesty : it
was, on the contrary, much perturbed and puzzled in look.
Jos was surveying the queer little apartment in which he
found his old flame. One of her gowns hung over the bed,
another depending from a hook of the door : her bonnet
obscured half the looking-glass, on which, too, lay the
prettiest little pair of bronze boots ; a French novel was on
the table by the bedside, with a candle, not of wax. Becky
thought of popping that into the bed too, but she only put
in the little paper nightcap, with which she had put the
candle out on going to sleep.

'I should have known you anywhere,' she continued ;
'a woman never forgets some things.   And you were the
first man I ever—I ever saw.'

'Was I, really ? ' said Jos. 'God bless my soul, you—
you don't say so.'

'When I came with your sister from Chiswick, I was
scarcely more than a child,' Becky said. 'How is that
dear love ? Oh, her husband was a sad wicked man, and
of course it was of me that the poor dear was jealous. As
if I cared about him, heigho ! when there was somebody—
but no—don't let us talk of old times ; ' and she passed
her handkerchief with the tattered lace across her eyelids.

'Is not this a strange place,' she continued, 'for a
woman, who has lived in a very different world too, to be
found in ? I have had so many griefs and wrongs, Joseph
Sedley, I have been made to suffer so cruelly, that I am
almost made mad sometimes. I can't stay still in any place,
but wander about always restless and unhappy. All my
friends have been false to me—all. There is no such thing
as an honest man in the world. I was the truest wife
that ever lived, though I married my husband out of pique,
because somebody else—but never mind that. I was true,
and he trampled upon me, and deserted me. I was the
fondest mother. I had but one child, one darling, one
hope, one joy, which I held to my heart with a mother's
affection, which was my life, my prayer, my—my blessing ;
and they—they tore it from me—tore it from me ; ' and
she put her hand to her heart with a passionate gesture
of despair, burying her face for a moment on the bed.

The brandy-bottle inside clinked up against the plate which held the cold sausage. Both were moved, no doubt, by the exhibition of so much grief. Max and Fritz were at the door listening with wonder to Mrs. Becky's sobs and cries. Jos, too, was a good deal frightened and affected at seeing his old flame in this condition. And she began forthwith to tell her story—a tale so neat, simple, and artless, that it was quite evident, from hearing her, that if ever there was a white-robed angel escaped from heaven to be subject to the infernal machinations and villany of fiends here below, that spotless being—that miserable, un-sullied martyr—was present on the bed before Jos—on the bed, sitting on the brandy-bottle.

They had a very long, amicable, and confidential talk there; in the course of which, Jos Sedley was somehow made aware (but in a manner that did not in the least scare or offend him) that Becky's heart had first learned to beat at his enchanting presence : that George Osborne had certainly paid an unjustifiable court to *her*, which might account for Amelia's jealousy, and their little rup-ture ; but that Becky never gave the least encouragement to the unfortunate officer, and that she had never ceased to think about Jos from the very first day she had seen him, though, of course, her duties as a married woman were para-mount—duties which she had always preserved, and would, to her dying day, or until the proverbially bad climate in which Colonel Crawley was living, should release her from a yoke which his cruelty had rendered odious to her.

Jos went away, convinced that she was the most virtuous, as she was one of the most fascinating of women, and revolving in his mind all sorts of benevolent schemes for her welfare. Her persecutions ought to be ended : she ought to return to the society of which she was an orna-ment. He would see what ought to be done. She must quit that place and take a quiet lodging. Amelia must come and see her, and befriend her. He would go and settle about it, and consult with the major. She wept tears of heartfelt gratitude as she parted from him, and pressed his hand as the gallant stout gentleman stooped down to kiss hers.

So Becky bowed Jos out of her little garret with as much grace as if it was a palace of which she did the honours ; and that heavy gentleman having disappeared down the stairs, Hans and Fritz came out of their hole, pipe in mouth, and she amused herself by mimicking Jos to them as she munched her cold bread and sausage and took draughts of her favourite brandy-and-water.

Jos walked over to Dobbin's lodgings with great solemnity, and there imparted to him the affecting history with which he had just been made acquainted, without, however, mentioning the play business of the night before. And the two gentlemen were laying their heads together, and consulting as to the best means of being useful to Mrs. Becky, while she was finishing her interrupted *déjeuner à la four-chette.*

How was it that she had come to that little town ? How was it that she had no friends and was wandering about alone ? Little boys at school are taught in their earliest Latin book, that the path of Avernus is very easy of descent.* Let us skip over the interval in the history of her downward progress. She was not worse now than she had been in the days of her prosperity :—only a little down on her luck.

As for Mrs. Amelia, she was a woman of such a soft and foolish disposition, that when she heard of anybody unhappy, her heart straightway melted towards the sufferer ; and as she had never thought or done anything mortally guilty herself, she had not that abhorrence for wickedness which distinguishes moralists much more knowing. If she spoiled everybody who came near her with kindness and compliments,—if she begged pardon of all her servants for troubling them to answer the bell,—if she apologized to a shop-boy who showed her a piece of silk, or made a curtsy to a street-sweeper, with a complimentary remark upon the elegant state of his crossing—and she was almost capable of every one of these follies—the notion that an old acquaintance was miserable was sure to soften her heart ; nor would she hear of anybody's being deservedly unhappy. A world under such legislation as hers, would not be a very orderly place of abode ; but there are not many women, at least not of the rulers, who are of her sort. This lady, I believe, would have abolished all gaols, punishments, handcuffs, whippings, poverty, sickness, hunger, in the world ; and was such a mean-spirited creature, that—we are obliged to confess it—she could even forget a mortal injury.

When the major heard from Jos of the sentimental
adventure which had just befallen the latter, he was not,
it must be owned, nearly as much interested as the gentleman from Bengal. On the contrary, his excitement was
quite the reverse from a pleasurable one ; he made use
of a brief but improper expression regarding a poor woman
in distress, saying, in fact,—' The little minx, has she come
to light again ? ' He never had had the slightest liking
for her ; but had heartily mistrusted her from the very
first moment when her green eyes had looked at, and turned
away from, his own.

' That little devil brings mischief wherever she goes,'
the major said, disrespectfully. ' Who knows what sort
of life she has been leading ; and what business has she
here abroad and alone ? Don't tell me about persecutors
and enemies ; an honest woman always has friends, and
never is separated from her family. Why has she left her
husband ? He may have been disreputable and wicked,
as you say. He always was. I remember the confounded
blackleg, and the way in which he used to cheat and hood-
wink poor George. Wasn't there a scandal about their
separation ? I think I heard something,' cried out Major
Dobbin, who did not care much about gossip ; and whom
Jos tried in vain to convince that Mrs. Becky was in all
respects a most injured and virtuous female.

' Well, well ; let's ask Mrs. George,' said that arch-
diplomatist of a major. ' Only let us go and consult *her*.
I suppose you will allow that *she* is a good judge at any
rate, and knows what is right in such matters.'

' H'm ! Emmy is very well,' said Jos, who did not happen
to be in love with his sister.

' Very well ? by Gad, sir, she's the finest lady I ever
met in my life,' bounced out the major. ' I say at once,
let us go and ask her if this woman ought to be visited
or not—I will be content with her verdict.' Now . this
odious, artful rogue of a major was thinking in his own
mind that he was sure of his case. Emmy, he remembered,
was at one time cruelly and deservedly jealous of Rebecca,
never mentioned her name but with a shrinking and
terror—a jealous woman never forgives, thought Dobbin :
and so the pair went across the street to Mrs. George's
house, where she was contentedly warbling at a music-
lesson with Madame Strumpff.

When that lady took her leave, Jos opened the business
with his usual pomp of words. ' Amelia, my dear,' said
he, ' I have just had the most extraordinary—yes—God
bless my soul ! the most extraordinary adventure—an old
friend—yes, a most interesting old friend of yours, and
I may say in old times, has just arrived here, and I should
like you to see her.'

' Her ! ' said Amelia, ' who is it ? Major Dobbin, if you
please not to break my scissors.' The major was twirling
them round by the little chain from which they sometimes
hung to their lady's waist, and was thereby endangering
his own eye.

' It is a woman whom I dislike very much,' said the
major doggedly ; ' and whom you have no cause to love.'

' It is Rebecca, I'm sure it is. Rebecca,' Amelia said,
blushing, and being very much agitated.

' You are right ; you always are,' Dobbin answered.
Brussels, Waterloo, old, old times, griefs, pangs, remembrances, rushed back into Amelia's gentle heart, and caused
a cruel agitation there.

' Don't let me see her,' Emmy continued. ' I couldn't
see her.'

' I told you so,' Dobbin said to Jos.

' She is very unhappy, and—and that sort of thing,'
Jos urged. ' She is very poor and unprotected : and has
been ill—exceedingly ill—and that scoundrel of a husband
has deserted her.'

' Ah ! ' said Amelia.

' She hasn't a friend in the world,' Jos went on, not
undexterously ; ' and she said she thought she might trust
in you. She's so miserable, Emmy. She has been almost
mad with grief. Her story quite affected me :—'pon my
word and honour, it did—never was such a cruel persecution borne so angelically, I may say. Her family has
been most cruel to her.'

' Poor creature ! ' Amelia said.

' And if she can get no friend, she says she thinks she'll
die,' Jos proceeded, in a low tremulous voice.—' God bless
my soul ! do you know that she tried to kill herself ? She
carries laudanum with her—I saw the bottle in her room—
such a miserable little room—at a third-rate house, the
" Elephant," up in the roof at the top of all. I went there.'

This did not seem to affect Emmy. She even smiled

a little. Perhaps she figured Jos to herself panting up
the stair.

'She's beside herself with grief,' he resumed. 'The
agonies that woman has endured are quite frightful to
hear of. She had a little boy of the same age as Georgy.'

'Yes, yes, I think I remember,' Emmy remarked.
'Well?'

'The most beautiful child ever seen,' Jos said, who was
very fat, and easily moved, and had been touched by the
story Becky told; 'a perfect angel, who adored his mother.
The ruffians tore him shrieking out of her arms, and have
never allowed him to see her.'

'Dear Joseph,' Emmy cried out, starting up at once,
'let us go and see her this minute.' And she ran into
her adjoining bedchamber, tied on her bonnet in a flutter,
came out with her shawl on her arm, and ordered Dobbin
to follow.

He went and put her shawl—it was a white Cashmere,
consigned to her by the major himself from India—over
her shoulders. He saw there was nothing for it but to
obey; and she put her hand into his arm, and they went
away.

'It is number 92, up four pair of stairs,' Jos said, perhaps
not very willing to ascend the steps again; but he placed
himself in the window of his drawing-room, which commands the place on which the 'Elephant' stands, and saw
the pair marching through the market.

It was as well that Becky saw them too from her garret;
for she and the two students were chattering and laughing
there; they had been joking about the appearance of
Becky's grandpapa—whose arrival and departure they had
witnessed—but she had time to dismiss them, and have
her little room clear before the landlord of the 'Elephant',
who knew that Mrs. Osborne was a great favourite at the
Serene Court, and respected her accordingly, led the way
up the stairs to the roof-story, encouraging miladi and
Herr Major as they achieved the ascent.

'Gracious lady, gracious lady!' said the landlord, knocking at Becky's door; he had called her madame the day
before, and was by no means courteous to her.

'Who is it?' Becky said, putting out her head, and
she gave a little scream. There stood Emmy in a tremble,
and Dobbin, the tall major with his cane.

He stood still watching, and very much interested at the scene; but Emmy sprang forward with open arms towards Rebecca, and forgave her at that moment and embraced her and kissed her with all her heart. Ah, poor wretch, when was your lip pressed before by such pure kisses?

CHAPTER LXVI

AMANTIUM IRAE*

RANKNESS and kindness like Amelia's were likely to touch even such a hardened little reprobate as Becky. She returned Emmy's caresses and kind speeches with something very like gratitude, and an emotion which, if it was not lasting, for a moment was almost genuine. That was a lucky stroke of hers about the child 'torn from her arms shrieking'. It was by that harrowing misfortune that Becky had won her friend back, and it was one of the very first points, we may be certain, upon which our poor simple little Emmy began to talk to her new-found acquaintance.

'And so they took your darling child from you,' our simpleton cried out. 'Oh, Rebecca, my poor dear suffering friend, I know what it is to lose a boy, and to feel for those who have lost one. But please Heaven yours will be restored to you, as a merciful, merciful Providence has brought me back mine.'

'The child, my child? Oh, yes, my agonies were frightful,' Becky owned, not perhaps without a twinge of conscience. It jarred upon her, to be obliged to commence instantly to tell lies in reply to so much confidence and simplicity. But that is the misfortune of beginning with this kind of forgery. When one fib becomes due as it

were, you must forge another to take up the old accept-
ance ; and so the stock of your lies in circulation inevitably
multiplies, and the danger of detection increases every day.

'My agonies,' Becky continued, 'were terrible (I hope
she won't sit down on the bottle) when they took him
away from me ; I thought I should die ; but I fortunately
had a brain fever, during which my doctor gave me up,
and—and I recovered, and—and here I am, poor and
friendless.'

'How old is he ?' Emmy asked.

'Eleven,' said Becky.

'Eleven!' cried the other. 'Why, he was born the
same year with Georgy, who is——'

'I know, I know,' Becky cried out, who had in fact
quite forgotten all about little Rawdon's age. 'Grief has
made me forget so many things, dearest Amelia. I am
very much changed : half wild sometimes. He was eleven
when they took him away from me. Bless his sweet face ;
I have never seen it again.'

'Was he fair or dark ?' went on that absurd little
Emmy. 'Show me his hair.'

Becky almost laughed at her simplicity. 'Not to-day,
love,—some other time, when my trunks arrive from Leipsic,
whence I came to this place,—and a little drawing of him,
which I made in happy days.'

'Poor Becky, poor Becky !' said Emmy. 'How thankful, how thankful I ought to be !' (though I doubt whether
that practice of piety inculcated upon us by our womankind in early youth, namely, to be thankful because we are
better off than somebody else, be a very rational religious
exercise ;) and then she began to think as usual, how her
son was the handsomest, the best, and the cleverest boy
in the whole world.

'You will see my Georgy,' was the best thing Emmy
could think of to console Becky. If anything could make
her comfortable that would.

And so the two women continued talking for an hour
or more, during which Becky had the opportunity of giving
her new friend a full and complete version of her private
history. She showed how her marriage with Rawdon
Crawley had always been viewed by the family with feelings
of the utmost hostility ; how her sister-in-law (an artful
woman) had poisoned her husband's mind against her ;

how he had formed odious connexions, which had estranged his affections from her ; how she had borne everything— poverty, neglect, coldness from the being whom she most loved—and all for the sake of her child ; how, finally, and by the most flagrant outrage, she had been driven into demanding a separation from her husband, when the wretch did not scruple to ask that she should sacrifice her own fair fame so that he might procure advancement through the means of a very great and powerful but un-principled man—the Marquis of Steyne, indeed. The atrocious monster !

This part of her eventful history Becky gave with the utmost feminine delicacy, and the most indignant virtue. Forced to fly her husband's roof by this insult, the coward had pursued his revenge, by taking her child from her. And thus Becky said she was a wanderer, poor, unprotected, friendless, and wretched.

Emmy received this story, which was told at some length, as those persons who are acquainted with her character may imagine that she would. She quivered with indignation at the account of the conduct of the miserable Rawdon and the unprincipled Steyne. Her eyes made notes of admiration for every one of the sentences in which Becky described the persecutions of her aristocratic relatives, and the falling away of her husband. (Becky did not abuse him. She spoke rather in sorrow than in anger. She had loved him only too fondly : and was he not the father of her boy ?) And as for the separation scene from the child, while Becky was reciting it, Emmy retired altogether behind her pocket-handkerchief, so that the consummate little tragedian must have been charmed to see the effect which her performance produced on her audience.

Whilst the ladies were carrying on their conversation, Amelia's constant escort, the major (who, of course, did not wish to interrupt their conference, and found himself rather tired of creaking about the narrow stair passage of which the roof brushed the nap from his hat), descended to the ground-floor of the house and into the great room common to all the frequenters of the ' Elephant ', out of which the stair led. This apartment is always in a fume of smoke, and liberally sprinkled with beer. On a dirty table stand scores of corresponding brass candlesticks with tallow candles for the lodgers, whose keys hang up in rows over the candles. Emmy had passed blushing through the room anon, where all sorts of people were collected; Tyrolese glove-sellers and Danubian linen-merchants, with their packs; students recruiting themselves with *Butterbrods* and meat; idlers, playing cards or dominoes, on the sloppy, beery tables; tumblers refreshing during the cessation of their performances;—in a word, all the *fumum* and *strepitus** of a German inn in fair-time. The waiter brought the major a mug of beer, as a matter of course; and he took out a cigar, and amused himself with that pernicious vegetable and a newspaper until his charge should come down to claim him.

Max and Fritz came presently downstairs, their caps on one side, their spurs jingling, their pipes splendid with coats-of-arms and full-blown tassels, and they hung up the key of No. 90 on the board, and called for the ration of *Butterbrod* and beer. The pair sat down by the major, and fell into a conversation of which he could not help hearing somewhat. It was mainly about *Fuchs* and *Phili-ster,** and duels and drinking-bouts at the neighbouring University of Schoppenhausen, from which renowned seat of learning they had just come in the *Eilwagen,** with Becky, as it appeared, by their side, and in order to be present at the bridal fêtes at Pumpernickel.

'The little *Engländerin* seems to be *en bays de gon-naissance,*' said Max, who knew the French language, to Fritz, his comrade. 'After the fat grandfather went away, there came a pretty little compatriot. I heard them chattering and whimpering together in the little woman's chamber.'

'We must take the tickets for her concert,' Fritz said. 'Hast thou any money, Max?'

'Bah,' said the other, 'the concert is a concert *in nubibus.** Hans said that she advertised one at Leipzig: and the *Burschen** took many tickets. But she went off without singing. She said in the coach yesterday that her pianist had fallen ill at Dresden. She cannot sing, it is my belief: her voice is as cracked as thine, O thou beer-soaking Renowner!'

'It is cracked; *I* hear her trying out of her window a *schrecklich* English ballad, called "De Rose upon de Balgony".'

'*Saufen** and *Singen* go not together,' observed Fritz

with the red nose, who evidently preferred the former amusement. ' No, thou shalt take none of her tickets. She won money at the *trente-et-quarante* last night. I saw her : she made a little English boy play for her. We will spend thy money there or at the theatre, or we will treat her to French wine or cognac in the Aurelius-garden, but the tickets we will not buy. What sayest thou ? Yet another mug of beer ? ' and one and another successively having buried their blond whiskers in the

mawkish draught, curled them and swaggered off into the fair.

The major, who had seen the key of number 90 put up on its hook, and had heard the conversation of the two young university bloods, was not at a loss to understand that their talk related to Becky. ' The little devil is at her old tricks,' he thought, and he smiled as he recalled old days, when he had witnessed the desperate flirtation with Jos, and the ludicrous end of that adventure. He and George had often laughed over it subsequently, and until a few weeks after George's marriage, when he also was caught in the little Circe's toils, and had an under-standing with her which his comrade certainly suspected, but preferred to ignore. William was too much hurt or

ashamed to ask to fathom that disgraceful mystery, although
once, and evidently with remorse on his mind, George had
alluded to it. It was on the morning of Waterloo as the
young men stood together in front of their line, surveying
the black masses of Frenchmen who crowned the opposite
heights, and as the rain was coming down, ' I have been
mixing in a foolish intrigue with a woman,' George said.
' I am glad we were marched away. If I drop, I hope
Emmy will never know of that business. I wish to God
it had never been begun ! ' And William was pleased to
think, and had more than once soothed poor George's
widow with the narrative, that Osborne, after quitting his
wife, and after the action of Quatre Bras, on the first day,
spoke gravely and affectionately to his comrade of his
father and his wife. On these facts, too, William had
insisted very strongly in his conversations with the elder
Osborne : and had thus been the means of reconciling the
old gentleman to his son's memory, just at the close of
the elder man's life.

' And so this devil is still going on with her intrigues,'
thought William. ' I wish she were a hundred miles from
here. She brings mischief wherever she goes.' And he
was pursuing these forebodings and this uncomfortable
train of thought, with his head between his hands, and
the *Pumpernickel Gazette* of last week unread under his
nose, when somebody tapped his shoulder with a parasol,
and he looked up and saw Mrs. Amelia.

This woman had a way of tyrannizing over Major Dobbin
(for the weakest of all people will domineer over somebody),
and she ordered him about, and patted him, and made
him fetch and carry just as if he was a great Newfoundland dog. He liked, so to speak, to jump into the water
if she said ' High, Dobbin ! ' and to trot behind her with
her reticule in his mouth. This history has been written
to very little purpose if the reader has not perceived that
the major was a spoony.

' Why did you not wait for me, sir, to escort me downstairs ? ' she said, giving a little toss of her head, and
a most sarcastic curtsy.

' I couldn't stand up in the passage,' he answered, with
a comical deprecatory look ; and, delighted to give her
his arm, and to take her out of the horrid smoky place,
he would have walked off without even so much as remem-

bering the waiter, had not the young fellow run after him and stopped him on the threshold of the ' Elephant ', to make him pay for the beer which he had not consumed. Emmy laughed : she called him a naughty man, who wanted to run away in debt ; and, in fact, made some jokes suitable to the occasion and the small-beer. She was in high spirits and good humour, and tripped across the market-place very briskly. She wanted to see Jos that instant. The major laughed at the impetuous affection Mrs. Amelia exhibited ; for, in truth, it was not very often that she wanted her brother ' that instant '.

They found the civilian in his saloon on the first floor ; he had been pacing the room, and biting his nails, and looking over the market-place towards the ' Elephant ' a hundred times at least during the past hour, whilst Emmy was closeted with her friend in the garret, and the major was beating the tattoo on the sloppy tables of the public room below, and he was, on his side too, very anxious to see Mrs. Osborne.

' Well ? ' said he.

' The poor dear creature, how she has suffered ! ' Emmy said.

' God bless my soul, yes,' Jos said, wagging his head, so that his cheeks quivered like jellies.

' She may have Payne's room ; who can go upstairs,' Emmy continued. Payne was a staid English maid and personal attendant upon Mrs. Osborne, to whom the courier, as in duty bound, paid court, and whom Georgy used to ' lark ' dreadfully with accounts of German robbers and ghosts. She passed her time chiefly in grumbling, in ordering about her mistress, and in stating her intention to return the next morning to her native village of Clapham. ' She may have Payne's room,' Emmy said.

' Why, you don't mean to say you are going to have that woman into the *house ?* ' bounced out the major, jumping up.

' Of course we are,' said Amelia, in the most innocent way in the world. ' Don't be angry, and break the furniture, Major Dobbin. Of course we are going to have her here.'

' Of course, my dear,' Jos said.

' The poor creature, after all her sufferings,' Emmy continued : ' her horrid banker broken and run away : her

husband—wicked wretch—having deserted her and taken
her child away from her' (here she doubled her two little
fists and held them in a most menacing attitude before her,
so that the major was charmed to see such a dauntless
virago)—'the poor dear thing ! quite alone and absolutely
forced to give lessons in singing to get her bread—and not
have her here ! '

'Take lessons, my dear Mrs. George,' cried the major,
' but don't have her in the house. I implore you, don't.'

' Pooh,' said Jos.

' You who are always good and kind : always used to
be, at any rate : I'm astonished at you, Major William,'
Amelia cried. ' Why, what is the moment to help her but
when she is so miserable ? Now is the time to be of service
to her. The oldest friend I ever had, and not——'

' She was not always your friend, Amelia,' the major
said, for he was quite angry. This allusion was too much
for Emmy, who looking the major almost fiercely in the
face, said, ' For shame, Major Dobbin ! ' and, after having
fired this shot, she walked out of the room with a most
majestic air, and shut her own door briskly on herself and
her outraged dignity.

' To allude to *that !* ' she said, when the door was closed.
' Oh, it was cruel of him to remind me of it,' and she
looked up at George's picture, which hung there as usual,
with the portrait of the boy underneath. ' It was cruel
of him. If I had forgiven it, ought he to have spoken ?
No. And it is from his own lips that I know how wicked
and groundless my jealousy was ; and that you were pure—
Oh yes, you were pure, my saint in heaven ! '

She paced the room trembling and indignant. She went
and leaned on the chest of drawers over which the picture
hung, and gazed and gazed at it. Its eyes seemed to look
down on her with a reproach that deepened as she looked.
The early dear, dear memories of that brief prime of love
rushed back upon her. The wound which years had scarcely
cicatrized bled afresh, and oh, how bitterly ! She could
not bear the reproaches of the husband there before her.
It couldn't be. Never, never !

Poor Dobbin ; poor old William ! That unlucky word
had undone the work of many a year—the long laborious
edifice of a life of love and constancy—raised, too, upon
what secret and hidden foundations, wherein lay buried

passions, uncounted struggles, unknown sacrifices—a little word was spoken, and down fell the fair palace of hope—one word, and away flew the bird which he had been trying all his life to lure!

William, though he saw by Amelia's looks that a great crisis had come, nevertheless continued to implore Sedley, in the most energetic terms, to beware of Rebecca: and he eagerly, almost frantically, adjured Jos not to receive her. He besought Mr. Sedley to inquire at least regarding her: told him how he had heard that she was in the company of gamblers and people of ill repute: pointed out what evil she had done in former days: how she and Crawley had misled poor George into ruin: how she was now parted from her husband, by her own confession, and, perhaps, for good reason. What a dangerous companion she would be for his sister, who knew nothing of the affairs of the world! William implored Jos, with all the eloquence which he could bring to bear, and a great deal more energy than this quiet gentleman was ordinarily in the habit of showing, to keep Rebecca out of his household.

Had he been less violent, or more dexterous, he might have succeeded in his supplications to Jos; but the civilian was not a little jealous of the airs of superiority which the major constantly exhibited towards him, as he fancied (indeed, he had imparted his opinions to Mr. Kirsch, the courier, whose bills Major Dobbin checked on this journey, and who sided with his master), and he began a blustering speech about his competency to defend his own honour, his desire not to have his affairs meddled with, his intention, in fine, to rebel against the major, when the colloquy—rather a long and stormy one—was put an end to in the simplest way possible, namely, by the arrival of Mrs. Becky, with a porter from the 'Elephant' Hotel, in charge of her very meagre baggage.

She greeted her host with affectionate respect, and made a shrinking, but amicable, salutation to Major Dobbin, who, as her instinct assured her at once, was her enemy, and had been speaking against her; and the bustle and clatter consequent upon her arrival brought Amelia out of her room. Emmy went up and embraced her guest with the greatest warmth, and took no notice of the major, except to fling him an angry look—the most unjust and scornful glance that had perhaps ever appeared in that

poor little woman's face since she was born. But she had
private reasons of her own, and was bent upon being angry
with him.   And Dobbin, indignant at the injustice, not at
the defeat, went off, making her a bow quite as haughty
as the killing curtsy with which the little woman chose
to bid him farewell.

He being gone, Emmy was particularly lively and affectionate to Rebecca, and bustled about the apartments and
installed her guest in her room with an eagerness and
activity seldom exhibited by our placid little friend. But
when an act of injustice is to be done, especially by weak
people, it is best that it should be done quickly; and
Emmy thought she was displaying a great deal of firmness
and proper feeling and veneration for the 'late Captain
Osborne in her present behaviour.

Georgy came in from the fêtes for dinner-time, and
found four covers laid as usual; but one of the places
was occupied by a lady, instead of by Major Dobbin.
' Hullo ! where's Dob ? ' the young gentleman asked, with
his usual simplicity of language.   ' Major Dobbin is dining
out, I suppose,' his mother said ; and, drawing the boy
to her, kissed him a great deal, and put his hair off his
forehead, and introduced him to Mrs. Crawley. ' This is
my boy, Rebecca,' Mrs. Osborne said—as much as to say—
can the world produce anything like that ? Becky looked
at him with rapture, and pressed his hand fondly. ' Dear
boy !' she said—' he is just like my——' Emotion choked
her further utterance ; but Amelia understood, as well
as if she had spoken, that Becky was thinking of
her own blessed child. However, the company of her
friend consoled Mrs. Crawley, and she ate a very good
dinner.

During the repast, she had occasion to speak several
times, when Georgy eyed her and listened to her.   At the
dessert Emmy was gone out to superintend further domestic
arrangements : Jos was in his great chair dozing over
Galignani : Georgy and the new arrival sat close to each
other : he had continued to look at her knowingly more
than once, and at last, he laid down the nutcrackers.

' I say,' said Georgy.

' What do you say ? ' Becky said, laughing.

' You're the lady I saw in the mask at the *rouge et noir*.'

' Hush ! you little sly creature,' Becky said, taking up

his hand and kissing it. 'Your uncle was there too, and mamma mustn't know.'

'Oh, no—not by no means,' answered the little fellow.

'You see we are quite good friends already,' Becky said to Emmy, who now re-entered; and it must be owned that Mrs. Osborne had introduced a most judicious and amiable companion into her house.

William, in a state of great indignation, though still unaware of all the treason that was in store for him, walked about the town wildly until he fell upon the Secretary of Legation, Tapeworm, who invited him to dinner. As they were discussing that meal, he took occasion to ask the secretary whether he knew anything about a certain Mrs. Rawdon Crawley, who had, he believed, made some noise in London; and then Tapeworm, who of course knew all the London gossip, and was besides a relative of Lady Gaunt, poured out into the astonished major's ears such a history about Becky and her husband as astonished the querist, and supplied all the points of this narrative, for it was at that very table years ago that the present writer had the pleasure of hearing the tale. Tufto, Steyne, the Crawleys, and their history—everything connected with Becky and her previous life passed under the record of the bitter diplomatist. He knew everything and a great deal besides, about all the world :—in a word, he made the most astounding revelations to the simple-hearted major. When Dobbin said that Mrs. Osborne and Mr. Sedley had taken her into their house, Tapeworm burst into a peal of laughter which shocked the major, and asked if they had not better send into the prison, and take in one or two of the gentlemen in shaved heads and yellow jackets, who swept the streets of Pumpernickel, chained in pairs, to board and lodge, and act as tutor to that little scapegrace Georgy.

This information astonished and horrified the major not a little. It had been agreed in the morning (before meeting with Rebecca) that Amelia should go to the Court ball that night. That would be the place where he should tell her. The major went home and dressed himself in his uniform, and repaired to Court in hopes to see Mrs. Osborne. She never came. When he returned to his lodgings all the lights in the Sedley tenement were put out. He could not see her till the morning. I don't know what sort of a night's rest he had with this frightful secret in bed with him.

At the earliest convenient hour in the morning he sent his servant across the way with a note, saying, that he wished very particularly to speak with her. A message came back to say, that Mrs. Osborne was exceedingly unwell, and was keeping her room.

She, too, had been awake all that night. She had been thinking of a thing which had agitated her mind a hundred times before. A hundred times on the point of yielding, she had shrunk back from a sacrifice which she felt was too much for her. She couldn't, in spite of his love and constancy, and her own acknowledged regard, respect, and gratitude. What are benefits, what is constancy, or merit ? One curl of a girl's ringlet, one hair of a whisker, will turn the scale against them all in a minute. They did not weigh with Emmy more than with other women. She had tried them ; wanted to make them pass ; could not ; and the pitiless little woman had found a pretext, and determined to be free.

When at length, in the afternoon, the major gained admission to Amelia, instead of the cordial and affectionate greeting to which he had been accustomed now for many a long day, he received the salutation of a curtsy, and of a little gloved hand, retracted the moment after it was accorded to him.

Rebecca, too, was in the room, and advanced to meet him with a smile and an extended hand. Dobbin drew back rather confusedly. 'I—I beg your pardon, ma'am,' he said ; 'but I am bound to tell you that it is not as your friend that I am come here now.'

'Pooh ! damn ! don't let us have this sort of thing !' Jos cried out, alarmed, and anxious to get rid of a scene.

'I wonder what Major Dobbin has to say against Rebecca?' Amelia said in a low, clear voice with a slight quiver in it, and a very determined look about the eyes.

'I will *not* have this sort of thing in my house,' Jos again interposed. 'I say I will not have it : and Dobbin, I beg, sir, you'll stop it.' And he looked round trembling and turning very red, and gave a great puff, and made for his door.

'Dear friend !' Rebecca said with angelic sweetness, 'do hear what Major Dobbin has to say against me.'

'I will *not* hear it, I say,' squeaked out Jos at the top of his voice, and, gathering up his dressing-gown, he was gone.

'We are only two women,' Amelia said. 'You can speak now, sir.'

'This manner towards me is one which scarcely becomes you, Amelia,' the major answered haughtily ; 'nor I believe am I guilty of habitual harshness to women. It is not a pleasure to me to do the duty which I am come to do.'

'Pray, proceed with it quickly, if you please, Major Dobbin,' said Amelia, who was more and more in a pet. The expression of Dobbin's face, as she spoke in this imperious manner, was not pleasant.

'I came to say—and as you stay, Mrs. Crawley, I must say it in your presence—that I think you—you ought not to form a member of the family of my friends. A lady who is separated from her husband, who travels not under her own name, who frequents public gaming-tables——'

'It was to the ball I went,' cried out Becky.

'—is not a fit companion for Mrs. Osborne and her son,' Dobbin went on ; 'and I may add that there are people here who know you, and who profess to know that regarding your conduct, about which I don't even wish to speak before—before Mrs. Osborne.'

'Yours is a very modest and convenient sort of calumny, Major Dobbin,' Rebecca said. 'You leave me under the weight of an accusation which, after all, is unsaid. What is it ? Is it unfaithfulness to my husband ? I scorn it, and defy anybody to prove it—I defy you, I say. My honour is as untouched as that of the bitterest enemy who ever maligned me. Is it of being poor, forsaken, wretched, that you accuse me ? Yes, I am guilty of those faults, and punished for them every day. Let me go, Emmy. It is only to suppose that I have not met you, and I am no worse to-day than I was yesterday. It is only to suppose that the night is over and the poor wanderer is on her way. Don't you remember the song*we used to sing in old, dear old days ? I have been wandering ever since then—a poor castaway, scorned for being miserable, and insulted because I am alone. Let me go : my stay here interferes with the plans of this gentleman.'

'Indeed it does, madam,' said the major. 'If I have any authority in this house——'

'Authority, none !' broke out Amelia. 'Rebecca, you

stay with me. *I* won't desert you, because you have been
persecuted, or insult you, because—because Major Dobbin
chooses to do so. Come away, dear.' And the two women
made towards their door.

William opened it. As they were going out, however,
he took Amelia's hand, and said—' Will you stay a moment
and speak to me ? '

' He wishes to speak to you away from me,' said Becky,
looking like a martyr. Amelia gripped her hand in reply.

' Upon my honour it is not about you that I am going to
speak,' Dobbin said. ' Come back, Amelia,' and she came.
Dobbin bowed to Mrs. Crawley, as he shut the door upon
her. Amelia looked at him, leaning against the glass :
her face and her lips were quite white.

' I was confused when I spoke just now,' the major said,
after a pause ; ' and I misused the word " authority ".'

' You did,' said Amelia, with her teeth chattering.

' At least I have claims to be heard,' Dobbin continued.

' It is generous to remind me of our obligations to you,'
the woman answered.

' The claims I mean, are those left me by George's father,'
William said.

' Yes, and you insulted his memory. You did yesterday.
You know you did. And I will never forgive you. Never ! '
said Amelia. She shot out each little sentence in a tremor
of anger and emotion.

' You don't mean that, Amelia ? ' William said, sadly.
' You don't mean that these words, uttered in a hurried
moment, are to weigh against a whole life's devotion.
I think that George's memory has not been injured by the
way in which I have dealt with it, and if we are come to
bandying reproaches, I at least merit none from his widow
and the mother of his son. Reflect, afterwards when—when
you are at leisure, and your conscience will withdraw this
accusation. It does even now.' Amelia held down her head.

' It is not that speech of yesterday,' he continued, ' which
moves you. That is but the pretext, Amelia, or I have
loved you and watched you for fifteen years in vain. Have
I not learned in that time to read all your feelings, and look
into your thoughts ? I know what your heart is capable
of : it can cling faithfully to a recollection, and cherish
a fancy ; but it can't feel such an attachment as mine
deserves to mate with, and such as I would have won from

a woman more generous than you.   No, you are not worthy
of the love which I have devoted to you.   I knew all along
that the prize I had set my life on was not worth the
winning ; that I was a fool, with fond fancies, too, bartering
away my all of truth and ardour against your little feeble
remnant of love.   I will bargain no more : I withdraw.
I find no fault with you.   You are very good-natured, and
have done your best ; but you couldn't—you couldn't
reach up to the height of the attachment which I bore
you, and which a loftier soul than yours might have been
proud to share.   Good-bye, Amelia ! I have watched your
struggle.   Let it end.   We are both weary of it.'

Amelia stood scared and silent as William thus suddenly
broke the chain by which she held him, and declared his
independence and superiority.   He had placed himself at
her feet so long that the poor little woman had been accustomed to trample upon him.   She didn't wish to marry
him, but she wished to keep him.   She wished to give him
nothing, but that he should give her all.   It is a bargain
not unfrequently levied in love.

William's sally had quite broken and cast her down.   *Her*
assault was long since over and beaten back.

' Am I to understand then,—that you are going—away,—
William ? ' she said.

He gave a sad laugh.   ' I went once before,' he said,
' and came back after twelve years.   We were young then,
Amelia.   Good-bye.   I have spent enough of my life at
this play.'

Whilst they had been talking, the door into Mrs. Osborne's
room had opened ever so little ; indeed, Becky had kept
a hold of the handle, and had turned it on the instant when
Dobbin quitted it ; and she heard every word of the conversation that had passed between these two.   ' What
a noble heart that man has,' she thought, ' and how shamefully that woman plays with it.'   She admired Dobbin ;
she bore him no rancour for the part he had taken against
her.   It was an open move in the game, and played fairly.
' Ah ! ' she thought, ' if I could have had such a husband
as that—a man with a heart and brains too ! I would not
have minded his large feet ; ' and running into her room,
she absolutely bethought herself of something, and wrote
him a note, beseeching him to stop for a few days—not to
think of going—and that she could serve him with A.

The parting was over. Once more poor William walked
to the door and was gone ; and the little widow, the author
of all this work, had her will, and had won her victory, and
was left to enjoy it as she best might. Let the ladies envy
her triumph.

At the romantic hour of dinner Mr. Georgy made his
appearance, and again remarked the absence of ' Old Dob '.
The meal was eaten in silence by the party ; Jos's appetite
not being diminished, but Emmy taking nothing at all.

After the meal, Georgy was lolling in the cushions of the
old window, a large window, with three sides of glass
abutting from the gable, and commanding on one side the
market place, where the ' Elephant ' is,* his mother being
busy hard by, when he remarked symptoms of movement
at the major's house on the other side of the street.

' Hullo ! ' said he, ' there's Dobs's trap—they are bringing
it out of the courtyard.' The ' trap ' in question was a
carriage which the major had bought for six pounds sterling,
and about which they used to rally him a good deal.

Emmy gave a little start, but said nothing.

' Hullo ! ' Georgy continued, ' there's Francis coming out
with the portmanteaus, and Kunz, the one-eyed postilion,
coming down the market with three *Schimmels*.*   Look at
his boots and yellow jacket,—ain't he a rum one ?   Why—
they're putting the horses to Dobs's carriage. Is he going
anywhere ? '

' Yes,' said Emmy, ' he is going on a journey.'

' Going a journey ; and when is he coming back ? '

' He is—not coming back,' answered Emmy.

' Not coming back ! ' cried out Georgy, jumping up.
' Stay here, sir,' roared out Jos. ' Stay, Georgy,' said his
mother, with a very sad face. The boy stopped ; kicked
about the room, jumped up and down from the window-seat
with his knees, and showed every symptom of uneasiness
and curiosity.

The horses were put to. The baggage was strapped on.
Francis came out with his master's sword, cane, and umbrella tied up together, and laid them in the well, and his
desk and old tin cocked-hat case, which he placed under the
seat.   Francis brought out the stained old blue cloak lined
with red camlet, which had wrapped the owner up any
time these fifteen years, and had ' *manchen Sturm erlebt* '*,
as a favourite song of those days said. It had been new

for the campaign of Waterloo, and had covered George and
William after the night of Quatre Bras.

Old Burcke, the landlord of the lodgings, came out, then
Francis, with more packages—final packages—then Major
William,—Burcke wanted to kiss him. The major was
adored by all people with whom he had to do. It was
with difficulty he could escape from this demonstration of
attachment.

'By Jove, I *will* go!' screamed out George. 'Give him
this,' said Becky, quite interested, and put a paper into the
boy's hand. He had rushed down the stairs and flung
across the street in a minute—the yellow postilion was
cracking his whip gently.

William had got into the carriage, released from the
embraces of his landlord. George bounded in afterwards
and flung his arms round the major's neck (as they saw
from the window), and began asking him multiplied questions. Then he felt in his waistcoat-pocket and gave him
a note. William seized at it rather eagerly, he opened it
trembling, but instantly his countenance changed, and he
tore the paper in two, and dropped it out of the carriage.
He kissed Georgy on the head, and the boy got out, doubling
his fists into his eyes, and with the aid of Francis. He
lingered with his hand on the panel. *Fort, Schwager!**
The yellow postilion cracked his whip prodigiously, up
sprang Francis to the box, away went the *Schimmels*, and
Dobbin with his head on his breast. He never looked up
as they passed under Amelia's window: and Georgy, left
alone in the street, burst out crying in the face of all the
crowd.

Emmy's maid heard him howling again during the night,
and brought him some preserved apricots to console him.
She mingled her lamentations with his. All the poor, all
the humble, all honest folks, all good men who knew him,
loved that kind-hearted and simple gentleman.

As for Emmy, had she not done her duty? She had her
picture of George for a consolation.

CHAPTER LXVII

WHICH CONTAINS BIRTHS, MARRIAGES, AND DEATHS

WHATEVER Becky's private plan might be by which Dobbin's true love was to be crowned with success, the little woman thought that the secret might keep, and indeed, being by no means so much interested about anybody's welfare as about her own, she had a great number of things pertaining to herself to consider, and which concerned her a great deal more than Major Dobbin's happiness in this life.

She found herself suddenly and unexpectedly in snug comfortable quarters : surrounded by friends, kindness, and good-natured simple people, such as she had not met with for many a long day ; and, wanderer as she was by force and inclination, there were moments when rest was pleasant to her. As the most hardened Arab that ever careered across the Desert over the hump of a dromedary, likes to repose sometimes under the date-trees by the water ; or to come into the cities, walk in the bazaars, refresh himself in the baths, and say his prayers in the Mosques, before he goes out again marauding ; Jos's tents and pilau were pleasant to his little Ishmaelite. She picketed her steed, hung up her weapons, and warmed herself comfortably by his fire. The halt in that roving, restless life, was inexpressibly soothing and pleasant to her.

So, pleased herself, she tried with all her might to please everybody ; and we know that she was eminent and successful as a practitioner in the art of giving pleasure. As for Jos, even in that little interview in the garret at the ' Elephant ' Inn, she had found means to win back a great deal of his goodwill. In the course of a week, the civilian was her sworn slave and frantic admirer. He didn't go to sleep

after dinner, as his custom was, in the much less lively
society of Amelia. He drove out with Becky in his open
carriage. He asked little parties and invented festivities
to do her honour. Tapeworm, the chargé d'affaires, who
had abused her so cruelly, came to dine with Jos, and then
came every day to pay his respects to Becky. Poor Emmy,
who was never very talkative, and more glum and silent
than ever after Dobbin's departure, was quite forgotten
when this superior genius made her appearance. The French
minister was as much charmed with her as his English
rival. The German ladies, never particularly squeamish
as regards morals, especially in English people, were
delighted with the cleverness and wit of Mrs. Osborne's
charming friend ; and though she did not ask to go to
Court, yet the most august and transparent personages
there heard of her fascinations, and were quite curious to
know her. When it became known that she was noble, of
an ancient English family, that her husband was a colonel
of the Guard, excellenz and governor of an island, only
separated from his lady by one of those trifling differences
which are of little account in a country where *Werther* is
still read, and the *Wahlverwandschaften** of Goethe is considered an edifying moral book ; nobody thought of refusing
to receive her in the very highest society of the little duchy ;
and the ladies were even more ready to call her *Du*, and to
swear eternal friendship for her, than they had been to
bestow the same inestimable benefits upon Amelia. Love
and Liberty are interpreted by those simple Germans in
a way which honest folks in Yorkshire and Somersetshire
little understand ; and a lady might, in some philosophic
and civilized towns, be divorced ever so many times from
her respective husbands, and keep her character in society.
Jos's house never was so pleasant since he had a house of
his own, as Rebecca caused it to be. She sang, she played,
she laughed, she talked in two or three languages ; she
brought everybody to the house : and she made Jos believe
that it was his own great social talents and wit which
gathered the society of the place round about him.

As for Emmy, who found herself not in the least mistress
of her own house, except when the bills were to be paid,
Becky soon discovered the way to soothe and please her.
She talked to her perpetually about Major Dobbin sent
about his business, and made no scruple of declaring her

admiration for that excellent, high-minded gentleman, and
of telling Emmy that she had behaved most cruelly regarding
him. Emmy defended her conduct, and showed that it
was dictated only by the purest religious principles ; that
a woman once, &c., and to such an angel as him whom she
had had the good fortune to marry, was married for ever ;
but she had no objection to hear the major praised as much
as ever Becky chose to praise him ; and indeed brought
the conversation round to the Dobbin subject a score of
times every day.

Means were easily found to win the favour of Georgy and
the servants. Amelia's maid, it has been said, was heart
and soul in favour of the generous major. Having at first
disliked Becky for being the means of dismissing him from
the presence of her mistress, she was reconciled to Mrs.
Crawley subsequently, because the latter became William's
most ardent admirer and champion. And in these mighty
conclaves in which the two ladies indulged after their
parties, and while Miss Payne was ' brushing their 'airs',
as she called the yellow locks of the one, and the soft brown
tresses of the other, this girl always put in her word for that
dear good gentleman Major Dobbin. Her advocacy did not
make Amelia angry any more than Rebecca's admiration
of him. She made George write to him constantly, and
persisted in sending mamma's kind love in a postcript.
And as she looked at her husband's portrait of nights, it
no longer reproached her—perhaps she reproached it, now
William was gone.

Emmy was not very happy after her heroic sacrifice.
She was very *distraite*, nervous, silent, and ill to please.
The family had never known her so peevish. She grew pale
and ill. She used to try and sing certain songs (*Einsam
bin ich, nicht alleine*, was one of them ; that tender love-
song of Weber's,* which, in old-fashioned days, young ladies,
and when you were scarcely born, showed that those who
lived before you knew too how to love and to sing) ;—
certain songs, I say, to which the major was partial ; and
as she warbled them in the twilight in the drawing-room,
she would break off in the midst of the song, and walk into
her neighbouring apartment, and there, no doubt, take
refuge in the miniature of her husband.

Some books still subsisted, after Dobbin's departure, with
his name written in them ; a German Dictionary, for instance,

with ' William Dobbin, —th Reg.', in the fly-leaf ; a guide-
book with his initials, and one or two other volumes which
belonged to the major.   Emmy cleared these away, and
put them on the drawers, where she placed her workbox,
her desk, her Bible, and Prayer-book, under the pictures
of the two Georges.   And the major, on going away, having
left his gloves behind him, it is a fact that Georgy, rummag-
ing his mother's desk some time afterwards, found the gloves
neatly folded up, and put away in what they call the secret
drawers of the desk.

Not caring for society, and moping there a great deal,
Emmy's chief pleasure in the summer evenings was to take
long walks with Georgy (during which Rebecca was left to
the society of Mr. Joseph), and then the mother and son
used to talk about the major in a way which even made the
boy smile.   She told him that she thought Major William
was the best man in all the world ; the gentlest and the
kindest, the bravest, and the humblest.   Over and over
again, she told him how they owed everything which they
possessed in the world to that kind friend's benevolent care
of them ; how he had befriended them all through their
poverty and misfortunes ; watched over them when nobody
cared for them ; how all his comrades admired him, though
he never spoke of his own gallant actions ; how Georgy's
father trusted him beyond all other men, and had been
constantly befriended by the good William.   ' Why, when
your papa was a little boy,' she said, ' he often told me that
it was William who defended him against a tyrant at the
school where they were ;' and their friendship never ceased
from that day until the last, when your dear father fell.'

' Did Dobbin kill the man who killed papa ? ' Georgy
said.   ' I'm sure he did, or he would if he could have caught
him ; wouldn't he, mother ? When I'm in the army,
won't I hate the French ?—that's all.'

In such colloquies the mother and the child passed a great
deal of their time together.   The artless woman had made
a confidant of the boy.   He was as much William's friend
as was everybody else who knew him well.

By the way, Mrs. Becky, not to be behindhand in sentiment, had got a miniature*too hanging up in her room, to
the surprise and amusement of most people, and the delight
of the original, who was no other than our friend Jos.   On

her first coming to favour the Sedleys with a visit, the little
woman, who had arrived with a remarkably small shabby
kit, was perhaps ashamed of the meanness of her trunks and
bandboxes, and often spoke with great respect about her
baggage left behind at Leipzig, which she must have from
that city.   When a traveller talks to you perpetually about
the splendour of his luggage, which he does not happen to
have with him ; my son, beware of that traveller !   He is
ten to one, an impostor.

Neither Jos nor Emmy knew this important maxim.
It seemed to them of no consequence whether Becky had
a quantity of very fine clothes in invisible trunks ; but as
her present supply was exceedingly shabby, Emmy supplied
her out of her own stores, or took her to the best milliner
in the town, and there fitted her out.   It was no more torn
collars now, I promise you, and faded silks trailing off at
the shoulder.   Becky changed her habits with her situation
in life—the rouge-pot was suspended—another excitement
to which she had accustomed herself was also put aside,
or at least only indulged in in privacy ; as when she was
prevailed on by Jos of a summer evening, Emmy and the
boy being absent on their walks, to take a little spirit-and-
water.   But if she did not indulge—the courier did : that
rascal Kirsch could not be kept from the bottle ; nor could
he tell how much he took when he applied to it.   He was
sometimes surprised himself at the way in which Mr. Sedley's
cognac diminished.   Well, well ; this is a painful subject.
Becky did not very likely indulge so much as she used before
she entered a decorous family.

At last the much-bragged-about boxes arrived from
Leipzig;—three of them, not by any means large or splendid;
—nor did Becky appear to take out any sort of dresses or
ornaments from the boxes when they did arrive.   But out
of one, which contained a mass of her papers (it was that
very box which Rawdon Crawley had ransacked in his
furious hunt for Becky's concealed money), she took a
picture with great glee, which she pinned up in her room,
and to which she introduced Jos.   It was the portrait of
a gentleman in pencil, his face having the advantage of
being painted up in pink.   He was riding on an elephant,
away from some coco-nut trees, and a pagoda : it was an
Eastern scene.

'God bless my soul, it is my portrait,' Jos cried out.

It was he indeed, blooming in youth and beauty, in a nankeen jacket of the cut of 1804. It was the old picture that used to hang up in Russell Square.

'I bought it,' said Becky, in a voice trembling with emotion; 'I went to see if I could be of any use to my kind friends. I have never parted with that picture—I never will.'

'Won't you?' Jos cried, with a look of unutterable rapture and satisfaction. 'Did you really now value it for my sake?'

'You know I did, well enough,' said Becky; 'but why speak,—why think,—why look back? It is too late now!'

That evening's conversation was delicious for Jos. Emmy only came in to go to bed very tired and unwell. Jos and his fair guest had a charming *téte-à-téte*, and his sister could hear, as she lay awake in her adjoining chamber, Rebecca singing over to Jos the old songs of 1815. He did not sleep for a wonder, that night, any more than Amelia.

It was June, and, by consequence, high season in London; Jos, who read the incomparable *Galignani* (the exile's best friend) through every day, used to favour the ladies with extracts from his paper during their breakfast. Every week in this paper there is a full account of military movements, in which Jos, as a man who had seen service, was especially interested. On one occasion he read out:—

'ARRIVAL OF THE —th REGIMENT.—GRAVESEND, June 20.— The *Ramchunder*, East Indiaman, came into the river this morning, having on board 14 officers, and 132 rank and file of this gallant corps. They have been absent from England fourteen years, having been embarked the year after Waterloo, in which glorious conflict they took an active part, and having subsequently distinguished themselves in the Burmese war. The veteran colonel, Sir Michael O'Dowd, K.C.B., with his lady and sister, landed here yesterday with Captains Posky, Stubble, Macraw, Malony; Lieutenants Smith, Jones, Thompson, F. Thomson; Ensigns Hicks and Grady; the band on the pier playing the national anthem, and the crowd loudly cheering the gallant veterans as they went into Wayte's Hotel, where a sumptuous banquet was provided for the defenders of Old England. During the repast, which we need not say was served up in Wayte's best style, the cheering continued so enthusiastically, that Lady O'Dowd and the colonel came forward

to the balcony, and drank the healths of their fellow-country-
men in a bumper of Wayte's best claret.'

On a second occasion Jos read a brief announcement :—
Major Dobbin had joined the —th regiment at Chatham ;
and subsequently he promulgated accounts of the presentations at the Drawing-room, of Colonel Sir Michael O'Dowd,
K.C.B., Lady O'Dowd (by Mrs. Molloy Malony of Ballymalony), and Miss Glorvina O'Dowd (by Lady O'Dowd).
Almost directly after this, Dobbin's name appeared among
the lieutenant-colonels : for old Marshal Tiptoff had died
during the passage of the —th from Madras, and the
Sovereign was pleased to advance Colonel Sir Michael
O'Dowd to the rank of major-general on his return to
England, with an intimation that he should be colonel of
the distinguished regiment which he had so long commanded.

Amelia had been made aware of some of these movements.
The correspondence between George and his guardian had
not ceased by any means : William had even written once
or twice to her since his departure, but in a manner so un-
constrainedly cold, that the poor woman felt now in her
turn that she had lost her power over him, and that, as he
had said, he was free. He had left her, and she was
wretched. The memory of his almost countless services,
and lofty and affectionate regard, now presented itself to
her, and rebuked her day and night. She brooded over
those recollections according to her wont : saw the purity
and beauty of the affection with which she had trifled, and
reproached herself for having flung away such a treasure.
It was gone indeed. William had spent it all out. He
loved her no more, he thought, as he had loved her. He
never could again. That sort of regard, which he had
proffered to her for so many faithful years, can't be flung
down and shattered, and mended so as to show no scars.
The little heedless tyrant had so destroyed it. No, William
thought again and again, ' It was myself I deluded, and
persisted in cajoling ; had she been worthy of the love
I gave her, she would have returned it long ago. It was
a fond mistake. Isn't the whole course of life made up of
such ? and suppose I had won her, should I not have been
disenchanted the day after my victory ? Why pine, or be
ashamed of my defeat ? ' The more he thought of this long

passage of his life, the more clearly he saw his deception.
' I'll go into harness again,' he said, ' and do my duty in
that state of life in which it has pleased Heaven to place me.
I will see that the buttons of the recruits are properly bright,
and that the sergeants make no mistakes in their accounts.
I will dine at mess, and listen to the Scotch surgeon telling
his stories. When I am old and broke, I will go on half-pay,
and my old sisters shall scold me. I have *geliebt und gelebet**
as the girl in *Wallenstein* says. I am done.—Pay the bills
and get me a cigar : find out what there is at the play
to-night, Francis ; to-morrow we cross by the *Batavier*.'
He made the above speech, whereof Francis only heard
the last two lines, pacing up and down the Boompjes* at
Rotterdam. The *Batavier* was lying in the basin. He
could see the place on the quarter-deck, where he and Emmy
had sat on the happy voyage out. What had that little
Mrs. Crawley to say to him ? Psha ! to-morrow we will
put to sea, and return to England, home, and duty !

After June all the little Court society of Pumpernickel
used to separate, according to the German plan, and make
for a hundred watering-places, where they drank at the
wells ; rode upon donkeys ; gambled at the *redoutes*, if
they had money and a mind ; rushed with hundreds of
their kind, to gormandize at the tables d'hôte ; and idled
away the summer. The English diplomatists went off to
Toeplitz and Kissingen, their French rivals shut up their
chancellerie and whisked away to their darling Boulevard
de Gand. The transparent reigning family took, too, to
the waters, or retired to their hunting-lodges. Everybody
went away having any pretensions to politeness, and, of
course, with them, Doctor von Glauber, the Court doctor,
and his baroness. The seasons for the baths were the
most productive periods of the doctor's practice—he united
business with pleasure, and his chief place of resort was
Ostend, which is much frequented by Germans, and where
the doctor treated himself and his spouse to what he called
a ' dib ' in the sea.

His interesting patient, Jos, was a regular milch cow to
the doctor, and he easily persuaded the civilian, both for
his own health's sake and that of his charming sister, which
was really very much shattered, to pass the summer at
that hideous seaport town. Emmy did not care where she

went much. Georgy jumped at the idea of a move. As for
Becky, she came as a matter of course in the fourth place
inside of the fine barouche Mr. Jos had bought : the two
domestics being on the box in front. She might have some
misgivings about the friends whom she should meet at
Ostend, and who might be likely to tell ugly stories—but,
bah ! she was strong enough to hold her own. She had
cast such an anchor in Jos now as would require a strong
storm to shake. That incident of the picture had finished
him. Becky took down her elephant, and put it into the
little box which she had had from Amelia ever so many
years ago. Emmy also came off with her Lares,—her two
pictures,—and the party, finally, were lodged in an exceedingly dear and uncomfortable house at Ostend.

There Amelia began to take baths, and get what good she
could from them, and though scores of people of Becky's
acquaintance passed her and cut her, yet Mrs. Osborne,
who walked about with her, and who knew nobody, was
not aware of the treatment experienced by the friend whom
she had chosen so judiciously as a companion ; indeed,
Becky never thought fit to tell her what was passing under
her innocent eyes.

Some of Mrs. Rawdon Crawley's acquaintances, however,
acknowledged her readily enough,—perhaps more readily
than she would have desired. Among those were Major
Loder (unattached), and Captain Rook (late of the Rifles),
who might be seen any day on the Dyke, smoking and
staring at the women, and who speedily got an introduction
to the hospitable board and select circle of Mr. Joseph
Sedley. In fact, they would take no denial ; they burst
into the house whether Becky was at home or not, walked
into Mrs. Osborne's drawing-room, which they perfumed
with their coats and moustachios, called Jos ' old buck ',
and invaded his dinner-table, and laughed and drank for
long hours there.

' What can they mean ? ' asked Georgy, who did not like
these gentlemen. ' I heard the major say to Mrs. Crawley
yesterday, ' No, no, Becky, you shan't keep the old buck
to yourself. We must have the bones in, or dammy, I'll
split.' What could the major mean, mamma ? '

' Major ! don't call *him* major ! ' Emmy said. ' I'm sure
I can't tell what he meant.' His presence and that of his
friends inspired the little lady with intolerable terror and

aversion. They paid her tipsy compliments; they leered
at her over the dinner-table. And the captain made her
advances that filled her with sickening dismay, nor would
she ever see him unless she had George by her side.

Rebecca, to do her justice, never would let either of these
men remain alone with Amelia; the major was disengaged
too, and swore he would be the winner of her. A couple
of ruffians were fighting for this innocent creature, gambling
for her at her own table; and though she was not aware
of the rascals' designs upon her, yet she felt a horror and
uneasiness in their presence, and longed to fly.

She besought, she entreated Jos to go. Not he. He was
slow of movement, tied to his doctor, and perhaps to some
other leading-strings. At least Becky was not anxious to
go to England.

At last she took a great resolution—made the great plunge.
She wrote off a letter to a friend whom she had on the other
side of the water; a letter about which she did not speak
a word to anybody, which she carried herself to the post
under her shawl, nor was any remark made about it; only
that she looked very much flushed and agitated when
Georgy met her: and she kissed him and hung over him
a great deal that night. She did not come out of her room
after her return from her walk. Becky thought it was
Major Loder and the captain who frightened her.

'She mustn't stop here,' Becky reasoned with herself.
'She must go away, the silly little fool. She is still whimpering after that gaby of a husband—dead (and served
right!) these fifteen years. She shan't marry either of
these men. It's too bad of Loder. No; she shall marry
the bamboo-cane, I'll settle it this very night.'

So Becky took a cup of tea to Amelia in her private
apartment, and found that lady in the company of her
miniatures, and in a most melancholy and nervous condition.
She laid down the cup of tea.

'Thank you,' said Amelia.

'Listen to me, Amelia,' said Becky, marching up and
down the room before the other, and surveying her with
a sort of contemptuous kindness. 'I want to talk to you.
You must go away from here and from the impertinences
of these men. I won't have you harassed by them; and
they will insult you if you stay. I tell you they are rascals;
men fit to send to the hulks. Never mind how I know

them. I know everybody. Jos can't protect you, he is
too weak, and wants a protector himself. You are no
more fit to live in the world than a baby in arms. You
must marry, or you and your precious boy will go to ruin.
You must have a husband, you fool ; and one of the best
gentlemen I ever saw has offered you a hundred times, and
you have rejected him, you silly, heartless, ungrateful little
creature ! '

'I tried—I tried my best, indeed I did, Rebecca,' said
Amelia, deprecatingly, ' but I couldn't forget—— ; ' and
she finished the sentence by looking up at the portrait.

' Couldn't forget *him* ! ' cried out Becky, ' that selfish
humbug, that low-bred Cockney dandy, that padded booby,
who had neither wit, nor manners, nor heart, and was no
more to be compared to your friend with the bamboo-cane
than you are to Queen Elizabeth ! Why, the man was
weary of you, and would have jilted you, but that Dobbin
forced him to keep his word. He owned it to me. He
never cared for you. He used to sneer about you to me,
time after time ; and made love to me the week after he
married you.'

' It's false ! It's false ! Rebecca,' cried out Amelia,
starting up.

' Look there, you fool,' Becky said, still with provoking
good humour, and taking a little paper out of her belt, she
opened it and flung it into Emmy's lap. ' You know his
handwriting. He wrote that to me—wanted me to run
away with him—gave it me under your nose, the day before
he was shot—and served him right ! ' Becky repeated.

Emmy did not hear her ; she was looking at the letter.
It was that which George had put into the bouquet and
given to Becky on the night of the Duke of Richmond's
ball. It was as she said : the foolish young man had asked
her to fly.

Emmy's head sank down, and for almost the last time
in which she shall be called upon to weep in this history,
she commenced that work. Her head fell to her bosom,
and her hands went up to her eyes ; and there for awhile,
she gave way to her emotions, as Becky stood on and
regarded her. Who shall analyse those tears, and say
whether they were sweet or bitter ? Was she most grieved,
because the idol of her life was tumbled down and shivered
at her feet ; or indignant that her love had been so despised ;

THE LETTER BEFORE WATERLOO

or glad because the barrier was removed which modesty
had placed between her and a new, a real affection ? ' There
is nothing to forbid me now,' she thought. ' I may love
him with all my heart now. Oh, I will, I will, if he will
but let me, and forgive me.' I believe it was this feeling
rushed over all the others which agitated that gentle little
bosom.

Indeed, she did not cry so much as Becky expected—the
other soothed and kissed her—a rare mark of sympathy
with Mrs. Becky. She treated Emmy like a child, and
patted her head. ' And now let us get pen and ink, and
write to him to come this minute,' she said.

' I—I wrote to him this morning,' Emmy said, blushing
exceedingly.

Becky screamed with laughter—' *Un biglietto*,'* she sang
out with Rosina, ' *eccolo quà !* '—the whole house echoed
with her shrill singing.

Two mornings after this little scene, although the day
was rainy and gusty, and Amelia had had an exceedingly
wakeful night, listening to the wind roaring, and pitying
all travellers by land and by water, yet she got up early,
and insisted upon taking a walk on the Dyke with Georgy ;
and there she paced as the rain beat into her face, and she
looked out westward across the dark sea line, and over the
swollen billows which came tumbling and frothing to the
shore. Neither spoke much, except now and then, when
the boy said a few words to his timid companion, indicative
of sympathy and protection.

' I hope he won't cross in such weather,' Emmy said.

' I bet ten to one he does,' the boy answered. ' Look,
mother, there's the smoke of the steamer.' It was that
signal, sure enough.

But though the steamer was under weigh, he might not
be on board ; he might not have got the letter ; he might
not choose to come.—A hundred fears poured one over the
other into the little heart, as fast as the waves on to the
Dyke.

The boat followed the smoke into sight. Georgy had
a dandy telescope, and got the vessel under view in the
most skilful manner. And he made appropriate nautical
comments upon the manner of the approach of the steamer
as she came nearer and nearer, dipping and rising in the

water. The signal of an English steamer in sight went
fluttering up to the mast on the pier. I dare say Mrs.
Amelia's heart was in a similar flutter.

Emmy tried to look through the telescope over George's
shoulder, but she could make nothing of it. She only saw
a black eclipse*bobbing up and down before her eyes.

George took the glass again and raked the vessel. ' How
she does pitch ! ' he said. ' There goes a wave slap over
her bows. There's only two people on deck besides the
steersman. There's a man lying down, and a—chap in
a—cloak with a—Hooray !—It's Dob by Jingo ! ' He
clapped-to the telescope and flung his arms round his mother.
As for that lady : let us say what she did in the words of
a favourite poet—*Δακρυόεν γελασάσα. She was sure it was
William. It could be no other. What she had said about
hoping that he would not come was all hypocrisy. Of course
he would come : what could he do else but come ? She
knew he would come.

The ship came swiftly nearer and nearer. As they went
in to meet her at the landing-place at the Quay, Emmy's
knees trembled so that she scarcely could run. She would
have liked to kneel down and say her prayers of thanks
there. Oh, she thought, she would be all her life saying
them !

It was such a bad day that as the vessel came alongside
of the Quay there were no idlers abroad ; scarcely even
a commissioner on the look-out for the few passengers in
the steamer. That young scapegrace George had fled too :
and as the gentleman in the old cloak lined with red stuff
stepped on to the shore, there was scarcely any one present
to see what took place, which was briefly this :—

A lady in a dripping white bonnet and shawl, with her
two little hands out before her, went up to him, and in the
next minute she had altogether disappeared under the
folds of the old cloak, and was kissing one of his hands with
all her might ; whilst the other, I suppose, was engaged
in holding her to his heart (which her head just about
reached) and in preventing her from tumbling down. She
was murmuring something about—forgive—dear William—
dear, dear, dearest friend—kiss, kiss, kiss, and so forth—
and in fact went on under the cloak in an absurd manner.

When Emmy emerged from it, she still kept tight hold
of one of William's hands, and looked up in his face. It

was full of sadness and tender love and pity. She understood its reproach, and hung down her head.

'It was time you sent for me, dear Amelia,' he said.

'You will never go again, William.'

'No, never,' he answered : and pressed the dear little
soul once more to his heart.

As they issued out of the Custom-house precincts, Georgy
broke out on them, with his telescope up to his eye, and
a loud laugh of welcome ; he danced round the couple, and
performed many facetious antics as he led them up to the
house. Jos wasn't up yet ; Becky not visible (though she
looked at them through the blinds). Georgy ran off to see
about breakfast. Emmy, whose shawl and bonnet were off
in the passage in the hands of Mrs. Payne, now went to undo
the clasp of William's cloak, and—we will, if you please, go
with George and look after breakfast for the colonel. The
vessel is in port. He has got the prize he has been trying
for all his life. The bird has come in at last. There it is
with its head on his shoulder, billing and cooing close up
to his heart, with soft outstretched fluttering wings. This
is what he has asked for every day and hour for eighteen
years. This is what he pined after. Here it is—the summit,
the end—the last page of the third volume. Good-bye,
colonel—God bless you, honest William !—Farewell, dear
Amelia—Grow green again, tender little parasite, round the
rugged old oak to which you cling !

Perhaps it was compunction towards the kind and simple
creature who had been the first in life to defend her, perhaps
it was a dislike to all such sentimental scenes,—but Rebecca,
satisfied with her part in the transaction, never presented
herself before Colonel Dobbin and the lady whom he
married. 'Particular business,' she said, took her to
Bruges, whither she went ; and only Georgy and his uncle
were present at the marriage ceremony. When it was over,
and Georgy had rejoined his parents, Mrs. Becky returned
(just for a few days) to comfort the solitary bachelor Joseph
Sedley. He preferred a Continental life, he said, and
declined to join in housekeeping with his sister and her
husband.

Emmy was very glad in her heart to think that she had
written to her husband before she read or knew of that
letter of George's. 'I knew it all along,' William said ;

' but could I use that weapon against the poor fellow's
memory ? It was that which made me suffer so when
you——'

' Never speak of that day again,' Emmy cried out, so
contrite and humble, that William turned off the conversation, by his account of Glorvina and dear old Peggy O'Dowd,
with whom he was sitting when the letter of recall reached
him. ' If you hadn't sent for me,' he added with a laugh,
' who knows what Glorvina's name might be now ? '

At present it is Glorvina Posky (now Mrs. Major Posky),
she took him on the death of his first wife ; having resolved
never to marry out of the regiment. Lady O'Dowd is also
so attached to it that, she says, if anything were to happen
to Mick, bedad she'd come back and marry some of 'em.
But the major-general is quite well, and lives in great
splendour at O'Dowdstown, with a pack of beagles, and
(with the exception of perhaps their neighbour, Hoggarty
of Castle Hoggarty) he is the first man of his county. Her
ladyship still dances jigs, and insisted on standing up to
the master of the horse at the Lord Lieutenant's last ball.
Both she and Glorvina declared that Dobbin had used the
latter *sheamfully*, but Posky falling in, Glorvina was consoled, and a beautiful turban from Paris appeased the wrath
of Lady O'Dowd.

When Colonel Dobbin quitted the service, which he did
immediately after his marriage, he rented a pretty little
country place in Hampshire, not far from Queen's Crawley,
where, after the passing of the Reform Bill, Sir Pitt and his
family constantly resided now. All idea of a peerage was
out of the question, the baronet's two seats in Parliament
being lost. He was both out of pocket and out of spirits
by that catastrophe, failed in his health, and prophesied the
speedy ruin of the Empire.

Lady Jane and Mrs. Dobbin became great friends—there
was a perpetual crossing of pony-chaises between the Hall
and the Evergreens, the colonel's place (rented of his friend
Major Ponto, who was abroad with his family). Her ladyship was godmother to Mrs. Dobbin's child, which bore her
name, and was christened by the Rev. James Crawley, who
succeeded his father in the living ; and a pretty close
friendship subsisted between the two lads, George and
Rawdon, who hunted and shot together in the vacations,
were both entered of the same college at Cambridge, and

quarrelled with each other about Lady Jane's daughter, with whom they were both, of course, in love. A match between George and that young lady was long a favourite scheme of both the matrons, though I have heard that Miss Crawley herself inclined towards her cousin.

Mrs. Rawdon Crawley's name was never mentioned by either family. There were reasons why all should be silent regarding her. For wherever Mr. Joseph Sedley went, she travelled likewise ; and that infatuated man seemed to be entirely her slave. The colonel's lawyers informed him that his brother-in-law had effected a heavy insurance upon his life, whence it was probable that he had been raising money to discharge debts. He procured prolonged leave of absence from the East India House, and indeed his infirmities were daily increasing.

On hearing the news about the insurance, Amelia, in a good deal of alarm, entreated her husband to go to Brussels, where Jos then was, and inquire into the state of his affairs. The colonel quitted home with reluctance (for he was deeply immersed in his *History of the Punjaub*, which still occupies him, and much alarmed about his little daughter, whom he idolizes, and who was just recovering from the chicken-pox), and went to Brussels and found Jos living at one of the enormous hotels in that city. Mrs. Crawley, who had her carriage, gave entertainments, and lived in a very genteel manner, occupied another suite of apartments in the same hotel.

The colonel, of course, did not desire to see that lady, or even think proper to notify his arrival at Brussels, except privately to Jos by a message through his valet. Jos begged the colonel to come and see him that night, when Mrs. Crawley would be at a *soirée*, and when they could meet *alone*. He found his brother-in-law in a condition of pitiable infirmity ; and dreadfully afraid of Rebecca, though eager in his praises of her. She tended him through a series of unheard-of illnesses, with a fidelity most admirable. She had been a daughter to him. 'But—but—oh for God's sake, do come and live near me, and—and—see me sometimes,' whimpered out the unfortunate man.

The colonel's brow darkened at this. 'We can't, Jos,' he said. 'Considering the circumstances, Amelia can't visit you.'

'I swear to you—I swear to you on the Bible,' gasped out

Joseph, wanting to kiss the book, ' that she is as innocent
as a child, as spotless as your own wife.'

' It may be so,' said the colonel, gloomily ; ' but Emmy
can't come to you.   Be a man, Jos :   break off this disreputable connexion.   Come home to your family.   We hear
your affairs are involved.'

' Involved ! ' cried Jos.   ' Who has told such calumnies ?
All my money is placed out most advantageously.   Mrs.
Crawley—that is—I mean,—it is laid out to the best
interest.'

' You are not in debt, then ?   Why did you insure your
life ? '

' I thought—a little present to her—in case anything
happened ; and you know my health is so delicate—common
gratitude you know—and I intend to leave all my money
to you—and I can spare it out of my income, indeed I can,'
cried out William's weak brother-in-law.

The colonel besought Jos to fly at once—to go back to
India, whither Mrs. Crawley could not follow him ; to do
anything to break off a connexion which might have the
most fatal consequences to him.

Jos clasped his hands, and cried,—' He would go back
to India.   He would do anything ; only he must have
time : they mustn't say anything to Mrs. Crawley :—she'd—
she'd kill me if she knew it.   You don't know what a terrible
woman she is,' the poor wretch said.

' Then, why not come away with me ? ' said Dobbin in
reply ;   but Jos had not the courage.   ' He would see
Dobbin again in the morning : he must on no account
say that he had been there.   He must go now.   Becky
might come in.'   And Dobbin quitted him full of forebodings.

He never saw Jos more.   Three months afterwards Joseph
Sedley died at Aix-la-Chapelle.   It was found that all his
property had been muddled away in speculations, and was
represented by valueless shares in different bubble companies.   All his available assets were the two thousand
pounds for which his life was insured, and which were left
equally between his beloved ' sister Amelia, wife of, &c.,
and his friend and invaluable attendant during sickness,
Rebecca, wife of Lieutenant-Colonel Rawdon Crawley, C.B.,'
who was appointed administratrix.

The solicitor of the Insurance Company swore it was

BECKY'S SECOND APPEARANCE IN THE CHARACTER OF CLYTEMNESTRA

the blackest case that ever had come before him ; talked
of sending a commission to Aix to examine into the death,
and the company refused payment of the policy.   But Mrs.,
or Lady Crawley, as she styled herself, came to town at
once (attended with her solicitors, Messrs. Burke, Thurtell
& Hayes,* of Thavies Inn), and dared the company to refuse
the payment.   They invited examination, they declared
that she was the object of an infamous conspiracy, which
had been pursuing her all through life, and triumphed
finally.   The money was paid, and her character established,
but Colonel Dobbin sent back his share of the legacy to the
Insurance Office, and rigidly declined to hold any communication with Rebecca.

She never was Lady Crawley, though she continued so
to call herself.   His Excellency Colonel Rawdon Crawley
died of yellow fever at Coventry Island, most deeply
beloved and deplored, and six weeks before the demise of
his brother Sir Pitt.   The estate consequently devolved
upon the present Sir Rawdon Crawley, Bart.

He, too, has declined to see his mother, to whom he
makes a liberal allowance ; and who, besides, appears to
be very wealthy.   The baronet lives entirely at Queen's
Crawley, with Lady Jane and her daughter ; whilst Rebecca,
Lady Crawley, chiefly hangs about Bath and Cheltenham,
where a very strong party of excellent people consider her
to be a most injured woman.   She has her enemies.   Who
has not ?   Her life is her answer to them.   She busies
herself in works of piety.   She goes to church, and never
without a footman.   Her name is in all the Charity Lists.
The Destitute Orange-girl, the Neglected Washerwoman, the
Distressed Muffin-man, find in her a fast and generous friend.
She is always having stalls at Fancy Fairs for the benefit
of these hapless beings.   Emmy, her children, and the
colonel, coming to London some time back, found themselves suddenly before her at one of these fairs.   She cast
down her eyes demurely and smiled as they started away
from her : Emmy scurrying off on the arm of George (now
grown a dashing young gentleman), and the colonel seizing
up his little Janey, of whom he is fonder than of anything in the world—fonder even than of his *History of the
Punjaub.*

'Fonder than he is of me,' Emmy thinks, with a sigh.
But he never said a word to Amelia, that was not kind and

gentle; or thought of a want of hers that he did not try
to gratify.

Ah! *Vanitas Vanitatum!* Which of us is happy in this
world? Which of us has his desire? or, having it, is
satisfied?—Come, children, let us shut up the box and the
puppets, for our play is played out.

VIRTUE REWARDED: A BOOTH IN VANITY FAIR

EXPLANATORY NOTES

THE following notes are of several kinds. Where there is MS., textual or internal narrative evidence relating to Thackeray's conception and composition of the novel, I have commented on, and quoted, the more important changes (whose history is described in the introductory 'Composition and Publication of *Vanity Fair*'). The most numerous annotation has to do with the background to the Regency period, Waterloo, and England under George IV Thackeray's social-historical colouring is both authentic to the highest degree and—to use Sainstbury's word—brilliantly 'tangential'. By the deft insertion of some minor detail he awoke in his Victorian reader a complex sense of alienation from the present of 1848. Finally, I have explained some of his more difficult foreign and English usages.

As must every subsequent editor, I have found invaluable Geoffrey and Kathleen Tillotsons' annotations in their 1963 edition of the novel. Similarly invaluable for the understanding of the early composition of *Vanity Fair* is Edgar F. Harden's *The Emergence of Thackeray's Serial Fiction* (1979). Frequently cited is G. R. Gleig's *Story of the Battle of Waterloo* (see note to p. 336 below), first published in 1847; page references are to the edition of 1907, John Murray, London. The '*Works*' referred to is the collected Oxford edition, edited by George Saintsbury in 1908, of which the *Vanity Fair* text is reproduced in the present edition. A number of notes refer to Joseph Farington's *Diary* (ed. J. Y. T. Greig, 7 vols., 1922–7).

Page li. 'Facsimile of wrapper to one of the original monthly numbers': This design, unlike the frontispiece, was devised before publication. Its social and literary allusions are complex. Thackeray himself is, of course, 'the moralist, who is holding forth on the cover' (p. 95). He guys himself and his preaching by reference to Swift's *Tale of a Tub*. The moralist and his congregation are wearing donkey's ears. ('O you donkies!' exclaimed Thackeray of the readers—virtually every reader—who failed to notice the misplaced paragraphs in Chapter LIX (see note to p. 755).) The long-eared headwear slyly picks up a Carlylean diatribe against novelists in 'Biography' (*Fraser's Magazine*, April 1832):

Of no given Book, not even of a Fashionable Novel, can you

> predicate with certainty that its vacuity is absolute; that there
> are not other vacuities which shall partially replenish them-
> selves therefrom, and esteem it a *plenum*. How knowest thou,
> may the distressed Novelwright exclaim, that I, here where I sit,
> am the Foolishest of existing mortals; that this my Long-ear of a
> Fictitious Biography shall not find one and the other, into whose
> still longer ears it may be the means, under Providence, of
> instilling somewhat? We answer, None knows, none can
> certainly know: therefore write on, worthy Brother, even as thou
> canst, even as it has been given thee.

(For verbal echoes of this passage, see p. 95.)

Thackeray evidently took Carlyle's slighting comments against
the 'Novelwright' in fairly good part. But Trollope, in his
Autobiography, was more indignant. In order to appreciate the
importance they attach to a casual Carlylean aside, one has to
bear in mind the extraordinary authority his writings exercised in
the 1840s.

The background to Thackeray's allegorical design contains
topical detail which would have struck the contemporary reader.
To the right is the equestrian statue of the Duke of Wellington,
raised at the south-eastern entry to Hyde Park in mid-1846, and
which Thackeray and his *Punch* colleagues regarded as vulgar and
hideous. In the far left is either the Trafalgar Square Nelson statue
(put up in 1843, after considerable difficulties with finance),
or—more likely—the Duke of York's column (Carlton Gardens,
raised in 1833), with the elevated warrior standing on his head.
Although Thackeray does not use the subtitle here (preferring the
aboriginal 'Pen and Pencil Sketches of English Society'), these
allusions press home the 'without a Hero' motif. Military chiefs
can expect no respect in *Vanity Fair*.

The cover was coloured 'gaudy yellow', to distinguish it from
Dickens's gaudy green. And unlike Dickens (also published by
Bradbury and Evans), Thackeray's serial is issued from the *Punch*
office. Thackeray it may be noted took considerable pains with this
cover, which was to be the distinguishing uniform for his novel
over a year and a half. (See Edgar F. Harden, 'An Alternative
Design for the Title of *Vanity Fair*', *Thackeray Newsletter*, November
1979. For an exhaustive analysis of the iconography of this cover
illustration, see Joan Stevens, '*Vanity Fair* and the London
Skyline', *Costerus*, 1974, pp. 13–41.)

Page liii. '*Facsimile of title-page to the first edition*': The first book
edition was made up of over-printed monthly parts, gathered

together and issued collectively bound in one volume, costing 21s, in late 1848. This title-page was devised to embellish the edition: it shows Harlequin, off-stage, sadly regarding his own face in a cracked mirror. (The self-reflexive image was a favourite of Thackeray's; the concurrent *Book of Snobs* is advertised as written 'By One of Themselves'.) The church in the background, with the twin towers, has been identified as Ottery St. Mary, associated with Larkbeare in Devon where Thackeray passed his happiest childhood holidays. By the time he made this design, Thackeray had evidently written the last chapter of the novel with its 'puppet' motif (see note to p. 2). Compare, for instance, the box against which Harlequin is resting with the tailpiece illustration to the last paragraph of the book (p. 878).

For this title-page Thackeray still preferred the subtitle 'Novel without a Hero', the original name for his work.

The first one-volume edition of *Vanity Fair* was 'affectionately dedicated' to B. W. Procter, a professional attorney and amateur poet, whom Thackeray first met in 1837. He was particularly grateful to Mrs. Procter, for her energetic pushing of *Vanity Fair* with the critics.

Page 2. London, June 28, 1848: As Joan Stevens points out, we should mark the date carefully. 'Before the Curtain' was written after the novel, and is properly speaking an epilogue, designed to be attached to the collected numbers of the monthly issue. The point is important critically, since this 'preface' introduces the puppetry motif, which has been taken by hostile commentators to show Thackeray, condemned out of his own mouth, as an intrusive, manipulative narrator. In fact Thackeray did not happen on the idea until he had almost finished writing the novel. The anecdote is told by Eyre Crowe in *Thackeray's Haunts and Homes* (London, 1897, pp. 55–6):

> It occurred in June 1848, one day when Thackeray came at lunch-time to my father's Hampstead House. Torrens McCullough, happening to be one of the party, said across the table to Thackeray, 'Well, I see you are going to shut up your puppets in their box!' His immediate reply was, 'Yes; and with your permission, I'll work up that simile.' How skilfully that chance phrase was worked up in the prefatorial 'Before the Curtain' all his readers well know

Page 3. Miss Pinkerton's academy: There is a plausible original for this distinguished seminary (which Thackeray calls both 'Minerva House' and 'Johnson House'). When he was shipped back from

India as an unhappy little boy in 1817, Thackeray was sent to school with Dr. Turner. Turner's academy (where Thackeray stayed until 1822 when he proceeded to Slaughterhouse/Charterhouse) was located on Chiswick Mall, at the site subsequently well-known as Walpole House.

—*Mrs. Chapone herself*: Hester Chapone (1727–1801), essayist and author of *Letters on the Improvement of the Mind* (1774). Even more favoured by Johnson than Miss Pinkerton, Chapone had four billets published in the *Rambler*.

Page 5. the late revered Doctor Samuel Johnson: Very late. Johnson died in 1784.

Page 6. Billington . . . Hillisberg . . . Parisot: Elizabeth Billington (1768–1818) 'the greatest singer England has ever produced' according to the *DNB*. Hillisberg and Parisot were, as the Tillotsons note, 'two French dancers well-known at the King's Theatre Haymarket from the 1780s to the early 1800s'. None of these are comparisons which would suggest themselves to the hidebound mind of Miss Pinkerton, and it is possible that Thackeray's thoughts are ranging ahead to Becky, her dubious background and her criminal future.

Page 7. Miss Swartz: Commentators have noted Thackeray's animus against wealthy mulattoes. (See also 'Miss Pye' later in *Vanity Fair*, or—most odious—Captain Woolcomb in *Philip*.) George P. Davies ascribes the hostility to Thackeray's resentment at his half-sister, Sarah Blechynden, the illegitimate offspring of his father's Eurasian mistress, Charlotte Rudd. (See 'The Miscegenation Theme in the Works of Thackeray,' (*Modern Language Notes*), 1961, pp. 326–31.)

—*this little world of history*: Thackeray originally wrote and crossed out, 'this little three-volumed world of history', and earlier in the sentence, 'to the end of the third volume' rather than 'time'. The allusion to the three-decker form could be 'generic', as Edgar F. Harden suggests; see the extant reference to 'the last page of the third volume' on p. 871. Alternatively, it could indicate that when he wrote in early 1845, Thackeray was keeping his publication options open.

Page 8. Jones . . . at his Club: This picks up a satiric *Punch* campaign. Douglas Jerrold and Thackeray used the comic magazine's pages to attack James Silk Buckingham (founder of the British and Foreign Institute—the 'club' alluded to here) and his supporter George Jones (who was injudicious enough to write a letter to

Punch from the club). See *The Hitherto Unidentified Contributions of W. M. Thackeray to Punch* (London, 1899) by M. H. Spielmann, pp. 88, 161. (See also, *The Snobs of England*, Chapter I.)

Page 14. *Dr. Raine*: Matthew Raine (1760–1811), headmaster at Charterhouse from 1791. Thackeray arrived there in 1822, after his rule, but the legendary flogger's reputation evidently lived on.

Page 15. *misanthropist*: The MS. and first edition continue 'or misogynist, for of the world of men she can be pronounced [MS. presumed] as yet to have had but little experience'. This was probably removed because of the dalliance with the Reverend Mr. Crisp, revealed on pp. 16–17.

Page 16. *descent from them*: The MS. continues: 'ill natured persons however say that Rebecca was born before the lawful celebration of her excellent parents' union.' The following sentence 'And curious . . . splendour' is not in the MS., which suggests that Thackeray made the deletion in page proof, and added a substitute sentence to keep the length right.

—quarrelled over his corpse: That is, disputed who should have the right of denying its release to the next of kin for burying, until debts were settled; one of the more macabre of nineteenth-century debt collection practices.

—articled pupil: Bound over as an apprenticed pupil-cum-teacher.

Page 17. *Newman Street, Gerrard Street . . . Mr. Lawrence . . . President West*: Sharp is later said to live in Greek Street where until 1806 Lawrence resided, and in Frith Street. But given the popularity of Soho as an artists' quarter, and Becky's father's inability to keep up with the rent, there is nothing implausible in this flitting about. Sir Thomas Lawrence (1769–1830), knighted in 1815, and Benjamin West (1738–1820) were successive Presidents of the Royal Academy.

Page 18. *a seven-shilling piece*: Thackeray is very precise. These coins were issued from 1806 to 1813, in a rather chaotic period for British coinage. Later (p. 155) old Osborne refers to 'dollars'—another unusual coin. These during the period 1799–1804 were overstamped, confiscated Spanish coins which remained legal tender for some years after.

Page 21. *Kensington turnpike*: At this date, and until 1825, there was an actual toll barrier at the Hyde Park end of the Kensington Road.

Page 24. *this apparition*: on 6 May 1844 Thackeray reviewed

Captain Jesse's *Life of George Brummell, Esq.* for the *Morning Chronicle* and quoted from the book a description of Brummell's dress, which he evidently draws upon here.

> The collar, which was always fixed to his shirt, was so large that, before being folded down, it completely hid his head and face; and the white neckcloth was at least a foot in height . . . His morning dress was similar to that of every other gentleman—Hessians and pantaloons, or top boots [in the MS., incidentally, Thackeray wrote 'top boots' for 'hessian boots'] and buckskins, with a blue coat, and a light or buff coloured waistcoat.

Elsewhere in a review of Disraeli's *Coningsby* in the *Pictorial Times* (25 May 1844) Thackeray predicted that Jesse's book would be a valuable source for future historians of the early years of the century. (See also note to p. 75.)

Page 25. buggy: A light, one-horse vehicle. Amelia indicates its outlandishness since at this period the term had a distinctly Anglo-Indian connotation.

Page 26. Guthrie's Geography: William Guthrie's *New Geographical, Historical and Commercial Grammar* (1770). The author was admired by Johnson, which would explain the presence of his somewhat antique text book on the Pinkerton syllabus.

Page 27. Bluebeard . . . Alnaschar: Bluebeard is one of Thackeray's favourite sources of allusion (he may have found the central motif—that of a husband destroying and locking up wives—painfully applicable to himself). Here, as the Tillotsons observe, he refers to the opera with words by George Colman and music by Michael Kelly. Alnaschar is the day-dreaming beggar in the *Arabian Nights* and another favourite allusion.

—collector of Boggley Wollah: 'Collector' was (after 1772) the designation of an officer placed in charge of the revenues of an Indian district. Originally, he was also responsible for the administration of civil justice. But at this period (1813) the judicial responsibility was vested elsewhere in District Judges and Magistrates. Careful as to this detail, Thackeray makes the point about the magistrate at Ramgunge in the next paragraph. Later, as he rises in the world, Joseph is promoted to the Chief Magistracy at Ramgunge (see p. 484). Gordon Ray has very convincingly proposed an original for Jos Sedley in Thackeray's cousin, George Trant Shakespear (see *The Buried Life*, pp. 42–7).

—the Oriental Club was not as yet invented: It was invented in 1824, by Sir John Malcolm. Situated in Hanover Square, it was a

notoriously boring place, allegedly called the 'Horizontal Club' by satirical London cabbies. Its membership was largely returned Indian administrators, and in later life it is, indeed, patronized by Jos (see p. 765).

Page 28. *the paternal circle in Russell Square*: An appropriate residence for a newly rich merchant of the period. Russell Square was built in 1804 and was on completion the largest square in London, with the exception of Lincoln's Inn Fields. For businessmen like Osborne and Sedley, it was conveniently close to the City. The Osbornes are said to live at number 96; there is no such address (a natural enough precaution on Thackeray's part). But since it is opposite the Sedleys, 96 is probably on the south side of the square. That the Sedleys' house is on the north side at the eastern end seems evident from two references in the text. On p. 31 Jos gets a cab from 'a hackney-coach stand hard by in Southampton Row' and on p. 72 as George Osborne walks down Southampton Row from Holborn, he is amused to see Amelia and Becky looking out from two different storeys of the Sedley household.

Thackeray's fictional London is more confusing than Dickens's—something all commentators agree on. He makes it so deliberately. In parts of the narrative (as here, or Becky's later residence in Curzon Street) he uses geographically actual place names. In other parts (notoriously with Gaunt House and Square (see note to p. 588)) he invents names apparently to tantalise the reader. As with characters, Thackeray will on occasion devise a symbolically or morally apt name and the reader is left to judge for himself as to its authenticity. Thus in Chapter XVI Becky and Rawdon go to dine at the Star and Garter Coffee House (which is appropriate for its duelling connotations); in this chapter, Jos frequents the Piazza (appropriate for its fashionableness); and whenever he is in London, Dobbin stays at the Old Slaughter's Coffee House (appropriate since it was a favourite hostelry of military men). All these are actual. But in Chapter XX, John Sedley habituates the Tapioca Coffee House, Coffin Court. Here Thackeray has confected a name appropriate to the washed-up old merchant's condition in life.

—*the Piazza Coffee-house*: Presumably the Bedford Coffee House, Covent Garden (see p. 57: 'I met him at the Bedford'). The Bedford was under the Piazza and a resort of the fashionable young men of the day in the late eighteenth century; hence its attraction to the would-be buck, Jos.

Page 30. *Adamson's or Carbonnell's*: Robert Adamson, 14 John Street and Carbonnell and Son, 9 King Street; the leading London wine merchants of 1813.

Page 31. Miss Decamp's dance: The Tillotsons propose Adelaide De Camp (d. 1834, sister of Mrs. Kemble). It could also be the better known Marie Therese De Camp, who married Charles Kemble in 1806. Whichever, the point is that Jos can admire fast, fashionable women on stage (the demi-mondaine De Camp background was, incidentally, not unlike Becky's) but is terrified of them in the flesh.

Page 32. as the Drawing-room: This paragraph is not in the MS. Thackeray evidently added it in proof—either to make up length, or to point up Becky's cunning. Harden directs us to its thematic congruence with the capital vignette at the head of the page.

Page 35. Send to Exeter 'Change, Sambo: Cross's Menagerie was at Exeter 'Change in the Strand, where Burleigh Street now stands, and its main attraction was Chunee, the Indian elephant. With rebuilding, 'Change and elephant disappeared in 1829.

Page 36. in a curtain lecture: This is one of the principal pieces of evidence for dating the early composition of *Vanity Fair* as being done in spring 1845. Douglas Jerrold's *Mrs. Caudle's Curtain Lectures* began to be serialized in *Punch* in January 1845. They feature the bed-time nagging of a husband by his wife. The reference in this passage is fairly clearly to the illustration of Jerrold's serial in *Punch*, 22 March 1845. This shows two pillows on which are two round faces, one in an extravagantly laced night cap, the other in a simple wool or cotton one, ending in a tassel. (See Sutherland, 'A Date for the Early Composition of *Vanity Fair*', *English Studies*, 1972, pp. 47–52).

Page 38. the Medulla and the spelling-book: As the Tillotsons surmise, Thackeray may have some particular, allegorically illustrated editions of William Howell's *Medulla Historiae Anglicanae* and Dilworth's *Spelling Book* in mind. George is perhaps making a consciously jokey conjunction. The *Medulla* (a 'comprehensive history of the lives and reigns of the monarchs of England') was a dusty, venerable, antiquarian (1679) tome. It is hard to imagine the girls knowing it. On the other hand, they would have been quite familiar with the elementary spelling book.

Page 39. is a capital fellow: MS. and first edition have, 'is as good a fellow as ever breathed'. For a possible explanation of this change, and the slight derogation of George it implies, see note to p. 48.

Page 40. *Lord Minto, the Governor-General*: An exact historical reference Sir Gilbert Elliot (1751–1814) was appointed Governor-General of India in 1806. But he was not made first Earl of Minto until February 1813 (this is April of that year) and he died the year following. Elliot was born and brought up in Scotland; hence the Caledonian prejudice Jos alleges. He was better known for his enlightened administration and the huge fortune he made while Governor General.

Page 41 *Sehnsucht nach der Liebe   yearning after the Ideal*: The German means, 'yearning for love', and is drawn from the epigraph to the fourth chapter of the third volume of Mrs. Gore's *Cecil· A Peer* (1841). The sarcasm against the 'Ideal' and 'big words' is one of Thackeray's many hits at Bulwer Lytton. In 'George de Barnwell', the first of the *Novels by Eminent Hands*, the hero (burlesquing Eugene Aram) is a 'lover of the Ideal and the Beautiful' An apprentice, George kills his master ('who never had a feeling for the Truthful and the Beautiful') for his cashbox.

Page 42. *favoured nowadays*: In the years following Trafalgar, up to the 1830s, nautical ballads and tales were very popular. It will be obvious from this—and many other musical references (which the Tillotsons have annotated most valuably) that Thackeray had a cultivated and well-trained taste in music.

The MS. and first edition continue with the following paragraph and vignette:

Conversation of a sentimental sort, befitting the subject, was carried on between the songs, to which Sambo, after he had brought the tea, the delighted cook, and even Mrs. Blenkinsop, the housekeeper, condescended to listen on the landing-place. The reason for cutting this may be surmised. The 1853 edition dispensed with the charming little vignette, and without it, the text is very lame and simply clutters up the description.

—*the wind upon the hill!*: like 'The Rose on my Balcony' (see p. 651) this pathetic song is of Thackeray's own composition. It nicely balances on the edge of parodic absurdity. Thackeray remembers to bring it back again, later in the novel (see p. 851).

—*'deep-toned voice faltered'*: An allusion to Thomas Haynes Bayly's (1797–1839) 'We met—'twas in a crowd.' The melodramatic story in the extremely popular drawing-room ballad has to do with love, requited but unexpressed. Ray comments: 'For contemporary readers the quoted phrase was not merely laughably unexpected, it also emphasized the factitious aspect of Becky's appeal' (*The Uses of Adversity*, p. 403).

Page 43. after Cutcherry: The Cutcherry was an Indian public office, for administrative or judicial purposes; here, presumably, where Jos collects the Boggley Wollah revenues. Thackeray's Anglo-Indian background made him familiar with the jargon.

—*such an honour on Russell Square*: After this, the MS. concludes Chapter IV briefly with: 'When was the party fixed for Vauxhall that was the great question which brought him. The matter had not been fully arranged the night previous.' Thackeray's original 'tight' scheme for the novel then had an earlier version of Chapter VI ('Vauxhall') follow straight on. With the introduction of Dobbin, and having tried I–IV, VIA in page proof, Thackeray evidently decided that the Vauxhall expedition should be held back for the second number. From this point up to the end of Chapter IV (and the first number) he devises a witty and suspenseful climax and the 'curtain line':—'Gad, I'll pop the question at Vauxhall.' Jos's resolution is supported by the fine illustration of 'Mr. Joseph entangled' in the green silk of which Becky is 'netting' a purse (p. 45). This fine number ending was evidently written very late, since no record of it survives in manuscript.

Page 44. Mr. Lee's conservatories: James Lee (1715–95), the most famous nurseryman in English history. In 1760 he entered into partnership with Lewis Kennedy at the Vineyard, Hammersmith. He introduced many exotic species into England, including the fuchsia.

Page 48. Capital Vignette: Daily News: The little boy's paper hat is topical. The combative *Daily News* was started, with Dickens as editor, in 1846.

—DOBBIN OF OURS: The military flourish in this chapter's title is borrowed from Lever's novel, *Tom Burke of Ours* (1843: it contains, incidentally, a faithful servant called Darbie). Lever had a popular reputation for this and a string of other novels about the Napoleonic wars. The martial theme and elaborate reference to Waterloo (see p. 54) suggest that Thackeray now had the main business of his novel firmly in mind.

This chapter about Dobbin was, unlike its predecessors, conceived as a self-contained chapter for publication in a 32-page monthly number. (In the MS. we see that Thackeray initially intended to call it 'The Fight between Phipps [i.e. Cuff] and Dobbin', before hitting on the nice Leverian title.) The main event in this chapter—the fight in which the underdog beats the bullying cock of the school—is not original, since it follows closely Thackeray's earlier 'The Fight at Slaughterhouse', first published in *Fraser's Magazine*, March 1843. Nevertheless, Chapter V (which was probably written a year or more after Chapters I–IV) marks a distinct advance in the novel. George Osborne (originally given the less loaded Christian name 'John') would not appear to have been the vile snob whom we see in embryo in the following pages (see, for instance, his shame at having Dobbin as champion and his cutting out a coach in cardboard for Emmy). In the first version of Chapter VI, it is Tawney (Dobbin's morally neutral precursor) who taunts the hungover Jos. But Osborne, in the later version, is made to mortify his future brother-in-law from malicious and snobbish motives. Two significant changes in perspective would seem to have taken place. First, Thackeray's social criticism became sharper and more focused, influenced probably by the extended analysis of English ideology which he developed over 1846 in *The Snobs of England*. Secondly, he developed a sense of George Osborne and Dobbin as opposed types of false and true gentlemanliness. With the clear premonition of Waterloo, it is evident that Thackeray now saw the future of his narrative in some structural detail.

Page 49. *only a merchant*: The MS. has 'Your father [crossed out, 'grandfather' inserted] was in the same business.' At proof, Thackeray apparently had a more precise picture of old Osborne.

—*preferring Mr. Kean to Mr. Kemble*: A slight anachronism. Edmund Kean made his first appearance at Drury Lane some years later in 1814. Kemble's career came to an end in 1817.

Page 51. *as in praesenti*: One of the early sections in the Eton Latin grammar.

Page 52. *rum-shrub*: Fruit drink fortified with rum.

Page 54. *Napier   Bell's Life*: Sir William Napier (1785–1860), general and historian of the Peninsular War (published 1828–40). *Bell's Life in London* covered sporting events, such as boxing matches. The incongruous pairing is deliberate.

Page 56. *Télémaque*: Fénelon's epic. A popular school book; it deals, of course, with a son who eventually makes good.

—*Orson   Valentine   man Friday*: In the French romance Orson is abducted by a bear and raised as a wild man. Valentine, brought up a knight, captures and civilizes him. Friday is Robinson Crusoe's savage. Thackeray may originally have intended to stress Dobbin's uncouthness (his lisp and big feet, for instance) more than he eventually does later in the novel.

—*Little Warblers*: Children's song books.

Page 57. *your yellow face*: MS. and first issue continue: 'And what can Alderman Dobbin have [MS. leave] among fourteen.' See note to p. 583 on Dobbin's mysterious family. Osborne's yellow face perhaps calls for comment. In the second version of Chapter VI(B) Thackeray wrote the following 'short' ending to the chapter, which he later discarded:

> [Jos is suffering from the after-effects of the rack punch] He sent for his doctor, who prescribed unheard of doses. His ·friend Tawney [crossed out and replaced with 'Dobbin' crossed out and replaced with 'George Osborne'] came grinning with his lean yellow face, and asked him about his love—his love? Good Gad! had he revealed it. All his modesty came rushing back upon him with redoubled force,—he felt awkward, wretched, humiliated beyond measure. [he goes on to write the note which ends Becky's first campaign in life. For the printed version see pp. 70–4].

Tawney was the first choice, because Thackeray was cannibalizing fragments of VIA, where Tawney had the part Dobbin later assumes as odd-man-out at Vauxhall. When Tawney (whose name implies that he was a mulatto, like Miss Swartz) was replaced by Dobbin it was logical to give the teasing of Jos to him, and Thackeray at first did so. Then he saw in the minor episode certain possibilities for exposing the snobbish proclivities of George Osborne, so the name was changed yet again. It was at this stage, after he had written the revised draft. that I guess

Thackeray went back to write Chapter V, taking care to include
this quizzing of George by Mrs. Sedley over his yellow face.
Nothing earlier is said about Osborne's jaundiced complexion,
and it is never mentioned again. We may therefore suspect that it
was a temporary mask so that he could plausibly stand in for
Tawney with his 'lean yellow face'.

—*Nassau . . . St. Kitts*: Undesirable garrison stations. The —th. is
an unfashionable regiment (see, for instance, its later posting to
India). It is one of those 'second regiments' which saw no service
in the Peninsular War (1808–14) but which were scraped up to
fight at Waterloo.

Page 59. the Sovereign . . . the Duke of York: During the alarm about
French invasion in 1803, George III held a review of 27,000
volunteers in Hyde Park on 26 October. He declared that if the
French came, he would personally meet them at the head of his
troops.

Page 60. We might have treated this subject . . . in the facetious manner: In
the first edition, the introduction to this chapter was longer and
more elaborate. After 'panting' on p. 61, there followed:

THE NIGHT ATTACK

The night was dark and wild—the clouds black—black—
ink-black. The wild wind tore the chimney-pots from the roofs of
the old houses and sent the tiles whirling and crashing through the
desolate streets. No soul braved that tempest—the watchmen
shrank into their boxes, whither the searching rain followed
them—where the crashing thunderbolt fell and destroyed them—
one had so been slain opposite the Foundling. A scorched
gabardine, a shivered lantern, a staff rent in twain by the flash,
were all that remained of stout Will Steadfast. A hackney-
coachman had been blown off his coach-box in Southampton
Row—and whither? But the whirlwind tells no tidings of its
victim, save his parting scream as he is borne onwards! Horrible
night! It was dark, pitch dark; no moon, No, no. No moon. Not a
star. Not a little feeble, twinkling, solitary star. There had been
one at early evening, but he showed his face, shuddering, for a
moment in the black heaven, and then retreated back.

One, two, three! It is the signal that Black Vizard had agreed
on.

'Mofy! is that your snum?' said a voice from the area. 'I'll gully
the dag and bimbole the clicky in a snuffkin.'

'Nuffle your clod, and beladle your glumbanions,' said Vizard,
with a dreadful oath. 'This way, men; if they screak, out with your

snickers and slick! Look to the pewter-room, Blowser. You, Mark, to the old gaff's mopus box! and I,' added he, in a lower but more horrible voice, 'I will look to Amelia!'

There was a dead silence. 'Ha!' said Vizard, 'was that the click of a pistol?'

Or suppose we adopted the genteel rose-water style. The Marquis of Osborne has just dispatched his *petit tigre* with a *billet-doux* to the Lady Amelia.

The dear creature has received it from the hands of her *femme de chambre*, Mademoiselle Anastasie.

Dear Marquis! what amiable politeness! His lordship's note contains the wished-for invitation to Devonshire House!

'Who is that monstrous fine girl?' said the *sémillant* Prince G—rge of C-mbr-dge, at a mansion in Piccadilly the same evening (having just arrived from the omnibus at the opera). 'My dear Sedley, in the name of all the Cupids introduce me to her!'

'Her name, *Monseigneur*,' said Lord Joseph, bowing gravely, 'is Sedley.'

'*Vous avez alors un bien beau nom*,' said the young prince, turning on his heel rather disappointed, and treading on the foot of an old gentleman who stood behind, in deep admiration of the beautiful Lady Amelia.

'*Trente mille tonnerres!*' shouted the victim, writhing under the *agonie du moment*.

'I beg a thousand pardons of your grace,' said the young *étourdi*, blushing, and bending low his fair curls. He had trodden on the toe of the great captain of the age!

'Oh D——!' cried the young prince, to a tall and good-natured nobleman, whose features proclaimed him of the blood of the Cavendishes. 'A word with you! Have you still a mind to part with your diamond necklace?'

'I have sold it for two hundred and fifty thousand pounds, to Prince E[a]sterhazy here.'

'*Und das war gar nicht theuer, potztausend!*' exclaimed the princely Hungarian, &c. &c. &c. . . .

Thus you see, ladies, how this story *might* have been written, if the author had but a mind; for, to tell the truth, he is just as familiar with Newgate as with the palaces of our revered aristocracy, and has seen the outside of both. But as I don't understand the language or manners of the Rookery, nor that polyglot conversation which, according to the fashionable novelists, is spoken by the leaders of *ton*; we must, if you please, preserve our middle course modestly, amidst these scenes and personages with which we are most familiar. In a word, this chapter about Vauxhall would have been so exceeding short but for the above little disquisition, that it scarcely would have deserved to be called a chapter at all.

The web of parodic allusion is dense. The storm opening, or set-piece, was a commonplace in 'Newgate' historical fiction, and Thackeray probably was aiming closely at the famous Chapter VI

('The Storm') of Ainsworth's bestseller, *Jack Sheppard* (1839). As the Tillotsons point out, 'The Night Attack' bears some similarity to Eugène Sue's very popular crime novel, *The Mysteries of Paris* (1842–3), which Thackeray was translating in 1844, and which features the thieves' slang, or flash, pioneered in England by Ainsworth and parodied here by Thackeray. The paragraph's opening sentences also satirise, more glancingly, the beginning of G. P. R. James's *Agincourt* (1844). But Thackeray's main satirical venom is reserved, as always, for Bulwer Lytton, and the opening paragraphs of his *Paul Clifford* (1830).

Thackeray's motives for shortening the opening to Chapter VI in 1853 were various. The satire had dated quickly. He was probably strongly influenced by the opinion of John Forster, G. H. Lewes and Dickens that such exercises 'do no honour to literature or literary men, and should be left to very inferior hands.' He had clearly had pre-publication doubts as well, for the manuscript of VIA contains an even more extended version of 'The Night Attack' than appeared in the first edition.

Page 61. *so short . . . a chapter at all*: 'Vauxhall' evidently caused Thackeray trouble. Nor does he feel entirely happy with it, even after much rewriting. The brevity of the chapter which he alludes to is masked by the extraordinary number of woodcuts planted in the text (eight in the first edition—far more than any other chapter in the novel).

Page 62. *Westminster Bridge*: The second version of Chapter VI (B) has a briefer passage dealing with the entry of the party into the gardens:

> 'Keep clear of Jos and Amelia's little friend' Osborne whispered to Captain Dobbin—and I say Dobbin just look to the shawls and things theres a good fellow.
>
> Yes and of George and Amelia I suppose thought poor Dobbin to himself—and so he contented himself by paying at the door for the whole party while Jos squeezed through the gate.

I suspect that one reason for Thackeray's changing this was that it retains a trace of the 'benign' George Osborne, here apparently anxious to forward the blossoming romance between Becky and Jos. (In the chapter as it is finally rewritten, he will do all in his power to break the match.)

—*the Royal Gardens*: So-called, by permission of George IV, after 1822.

Page 63. *playing at the door for the whole party* The entrance price had been going up from the end of the eighteenth century (when Boswell complained at its outrageous increase to 2s). At this period, it was 3s–3s 6d, the highest, in fact, it was ever to reach. In the 1830's and '40s, when Vauxhall was in its decline, the price went as low as 6d.

—*He walked very modestly behind them*: In the second version of Chapter VI, it was necessary to accommodate Dobbin, and this fine paragraph was devised, reflecting the gaiety of Vauxhall through his melancholy eyes. In VIA's version (given by an impersonal Thackerayan narrator), there are, however, two passages substantially different in their description of Vauxhall. On p. 63, the Dobbin-less description of Vauxhall begins:

> Although the gardens of Vauxhall have passed away as much as the gardens of Babylon, yet there is no need to describe what our young people saw on their visit to the first mentioned of these two places of splendid entertainment. Fond memory has not forgotten as yet all the delights and wonders of the Royal Gardens—

And after 'invisible ham', in the same paragraph, VIA continues:

> All these things are present in the minds of every one of us, as is the gentle Simpson, that kind smiling idiot who aptly presided over the amusements of the place. Peace be with him. His Ghost may wander about now in the Ghost of a royal property where the spirit of Madame Sacqui is still dancing on the apparition of a tight rope, and the old departed ham-cutters are carving slices scarcely more visionary than those which in life they supplied.

In VIA, there are three references to Vauxhall's being a thing of the past. All were removed in the rewritten version, in which there remains no suggestion that Vauxhall Gardens have ceased to exist, and in fact Vauxhall, though feeble, did not 'pass away' until 1859. But during the winter of 1844–5 (the gardens were opened seasonally in spring and summer) there were strong rumours that the 'Royal Property' was closed for good; announcements in *The Times* (20 March 1845) and *Punch* (12 July 1845) allude to these rumours, which had clearly convinced Thackeray at the time.

—*the hundred thousand extra lamps*: Hyperbolic. 8,000 lamps were added at a gala in honour of the Prince Regent's birthday in 1811. Thereafter the number was increased at each subsequent gala. There were some 15,000 in 1815.

—*cocked-hats*: The fiddlers at Vauxhall, even in Thackeray's day, were famous for their eighteenth-century style cocked-hats. They were the last band in London to wear them.

—*Madame Saqui*: (1786–1866). The famous rope walker, who, as the Tillotsons point out, first appeared in Vauxhall in 1816.

—*slices of almost invisible ham*: Two items were traditional (if reviled) refreshment at Vauxhall: rack punch (i.e. punch fortified with 'arrack') and ultra-thin 'Vauxhall slices' of ham. As the *London Magazine* (September 1824) put it, Vauxhall catering offered:

Lilliput chickens boil'd
Bucelles warm, from Vauxhall ice
And hams that flit in airy slice
And salads scarcely soil'd.

—*Simpson . . . presided even then*: Beresford Chancellor notes that Simpson, the Master of Vauxhall Ceremonies, must indeed have been presiding in 1813.

—*Mrs. Salmon . . . the Battle of Borodino*: Eliza Salmon (1787–1849), the vocalist. She first appeared in oratorio at Covent Garden in 1803. In his reference to the battle of Borodino (September 1812) Thackeray seems to be thinking of the great festivity at Vauxhall in July 1813, when celebration was made (by song and illumination) of the recent triumph at Vittoria. On this occasion, 1,350 visitors were jammed into the rotunda.

Page 64. *an owl*: Thackeray's reconstruction of Vauxhall in its heyday is justly admired. He had probably the advantage of keen memory; as a schoolboy he must have visited the Royal Gardens during their most profitable era in the mid–1820s. The gardens had been famous in the eighteenth century, and had many previous literary associations. Evelyn and Pepys described them; Fanny Burney's *Evelina* and Addison's de Coverley papers feature visits there; they are the background to a scene in Fielding's *Amelia*; and Walpole in his letters recalls a memorably drunken evening at Vauxhall, when strangers invaded his box (as they are to do here). Dickens devotes one of his 'Boz' papers to the seedy appearance of the Gardens by daylight. The site, in Kennington, was later occupied by Tryers Street and St. Oswald Street.

Page 66. *Fair Rosamond . . . Alexander the Great . . . Dr. Lemprière*: Fair Rosamund, concubine to Henry II, was supposed in legend to have been poisoned by a jealous Queen Elianor. Alexander the Great was supposed to have died, after supping too deep of wine. John Lemprière's *Bibliotheca Classica* (1788) is a favourite source of classical allusion and information for Thackeray.

—*Daniel Lambert*: (1770–1809); 'the most corpulent man of whom authentic records exist' according to the *DNB*. He was on show from 1806 to his death and would still be memorable to Thackeray's contemporaries from numerous inn signs. He weighed something over fifty-two stone.

—*a gentleman in top-boots*: in VIA 'a hebrew gentleman'; see the illustration, 'Mr. Joseph in a state of excitement' where the fellow is shown with an exaggeratedly hooked nose.

Page 69. *the Archbishop of Canterbury at Lambeth*: The London residence of the Archbishop, Lambeth Palace, was handily nearby on the same side of the river.

Page 70. *like Molyneux*: In 1810 there was a great boxing match between Cribb, the champion of England, and 'Tom Molyneaux, an American black man'. Cribb won this encounter and the return bout in September 1811.

Page 71. *Osborne pursued his advantage pitilessly*: See note to p. 48.

Page 72. *Sister Anne is on the watch-tower*: Another allusion to the Bluebeard story. Anne climbs the tower to look out for her rescuing brothers.

Page 73. *Orphan of the Forest*: The Tillotsons surmise this may be William Dimond's *The Foundling of the Forest*. The title seems to have been devised with less thought to Jos's likely reading than for its appropriateness to Becky's forlorn condition.

Page 75. The first edition has the following footnote and illustration:

It was the author's intention, faithful to history, to depict all the characters of this tale in their proper costumes, as they wore them at the commencement of the century. But when I remember the appearance of people in those days, and that an officer and lady were actually habited like this—

I have not the heart to disfigure my heroes and heroines by costumes so hideous; and have, on the contrary, engaged a model of rank dressed according to the present fashion.

The illustration shows Vauxhall in the background. Thackeray's drawings are not, in fact, consistent in the historicity of the characters' dress (especially military dress) until later in the novel.

Page 77. forgot so completely: Sir Pitt, 'named after the great Commoner,' was presumably born in 1757, during the Newcastle and Pitt ministry. He is the son of Walpole Crawley, presumably born during that minister's era of power in the reign of George II. John Churchill Crawley was named after the great general Marlborough, and Charles Stuart after the monarchy whose chances Marlborough's victories effectively wrecked. The Reverend Bute Crawley was presumably born in 1762, during the Bute ministry. Grizzel (not a very patient wife, we gather) is cousin to Henry Dundas, the first Earl Melville, a political ally of Pitt's, impeached in 1805 and accused of financial maladministration of the navy. The young Pitt Crawley is named after the 'heaven-born minister' (the younger Pitt, so eulogized by the Duke of Chandos in 1789). Rawdon is named after Francis Rawdon-Hastings, first Marquis of Hastings and second Earl of Moira, Governor-General of India from 1812–21, who stood by the Prince of Wales in the Regency Crisis—but was later dropped.

The point Thackeray makes in this family genealogy is that 'the Crawleys always rat at the wrong time', as Steyne later puts it. Moreover their political affiliations go to all corners of the political field, as expediency dictates: the Stuarts and the Churchills are rivals; Pitt and Walpole are rivals; Pitt and Bute are rivals. The Crawleys are, we gather, sycophants, sucking up to whomever is in power.

Page 78. Mr. Wroughton at Covent Garden: (1748–1822). As the Tillotsons note, Richard Wroughton does not seem to have acted at Covent Garden after 1785. He retired in 1815.

—*Gaunt Square*: The first edition has the equally uncomfortable-sounding 'Shiverley Square' For the possible locations of Gaunt Square, see note to p. 588.

Page 81. cellaret: Small wine cabinet.

Page 85. Swallow Street: In Regency London, Swallow Street ran the length of what is now Regent Street. The Nash plans for this great thoroughfare were approved in 1813.

—*Jehu*: A coachman, humorously alluding to 2 Kgs. 9:20.

—*the 'Necks*: The Swan with Two Necks (i.e. 'nicks'—indicating the bird had been marked by royal swanmen) was in Lad Lane, where Gresham Street now stands. The 'Necks was a tavern and a booking office for points north of London. The Southampton coach (which would pass Queen's Crawley) left from this farestage.

—*Keep the box for me, Leader*: Sir Pitt is evidently one of the contractors hired by the Post Office to provide en route stabling and horses. Riding on the box, or driver's seat, was therefore a privilege he might claim. For passengers to take the reins was against the law, and punishable by a fine. But coachmen universally flouted the law in return for a bribe (here, of course, the coachman is frustrated). Mail coaches began carrying passengers outside around 1810.

—*Benjamins*: Overcoats—so called after the original tailor. The style was fashionable around 1815.

Page 86. *Fleet Market* 'White Bear' Fleet Market was the central market for meat and vegetables, on the west side of Farringdon Street. It was removed in 1829, the same year that the old Exeter 'Change in the Strand was knocked down. The White Bear (opened around 1685) and the Black Bear were inns standing at opposite ends of Piccadilly. The former was still standing at the period Thackeray wrote *Vanity Fair*.

—*Chelsea Greenwich old Weller*: Chelsea and Greenwich are places of honourable retirement for superannuated soldiers and sailors. In the *Pickwick Papers*, Mr. Pickwick's servant has a coach-driver father (Tony Weller).

Page 87. *Jack Sheppard*: Thackeray gets a dig in against Ainsworth's bestselling 1839 novel about the eighteenth-century cracksman.

Page 88. Chapter VII does not exist in MS. Since it is substantially an expansion of Becky's opening remarks in Chapter VIII, it is possible that Thackeray devised it at a fairly late stage of composition with the aim of filling out the second number.

—*Free*: Sir Pitt's mail goes free—either because he is an MP, or because he contracts horses for the mail coaches.

—*the Perkins's*: A Thackeray in-joke. His Christmas book, *Mrs. Perkins's Ball* was published in the New Year of 1847. It was very successful, and helped *Vanity Fair* to its eventual success.

Page 89. *Cecilia*: *Cecilia, or Memoirs of an Heiress* (1782) by Fanny Burney. Lord Orville, whom Becky mentions in the next sentence, is in fact the glamorous hero of *Evelina* (1778). Both novels deal with a beautiful, parentless girl who eventually marries into aristocracy. (The way Becky's mind is running is also suggested by the picture at the head of the chapter.)

—*of course I laughed too*: Thackeray originally wrote and crossed out 'of course I interceded for the poor beasts', which would seem more plausible for Becky (who is cunning, if no animal lover) to write. Harden, however, sees the change as in character (see pp. 46–7).

Page 91. *the dear castle of Udolpho*: Becky alludes to Mrs. Radcliffe's very famous gothic novel, *The Mysteries of Udolpho* (1794). It too features a beautiful orphan heroine.

—*dine upstairs*: There follow two deleted paragraphs in the MS.:

> Well, the great dinner bell rung—and we all assembled in the little green room where Lady Crawley always sits. She is a ⟨tall snuffy pompous old lady in grey silk—just like a school-mistress in a word⟩ poor pale sickly looking body—gentle and with weak eyes. With her was her ⟨son⟩ step son Mr. Crawley in full dress though his clothes look very old—He is a pale thin ugly silent young man with hay-coloured whiskers, and pink eyes and straw-coloured hair. ⟨Sir Pit⟩ Mr. Crawley said his mamma of whom he is the very picture—this is the governess of your sisters Miss Sharp.
>
> O said Mr. Crawley: and pushed out his head a little way by way of bowing. Miss Sharp continued my lady, you will be treated as one of the family of Queen's Crawley, and I hope that you will find everything conducive to your comfort and that we shall have every cause for mutual satisfaction My lady is a speech-maker like horrid old Miss Pinkerton I hate speech makers but of course I made a pretty speech in reply

[Angled brackets ⟨⟩ indicate legible crossings-out. This long deleted passage finishes on the end of a page, and may have been continued in a previous draft.]

It will be evident that Thackeray had two contrary conceptions of Lady Crawley here. His first intention seems to have been to have the haughty, pompous, aristocratic Griselda (also called 'Jemima'). Some crossings out later in the MS. identify her as 'My lady who is a great invalid'. While the rest of the company take their frugal meal she has 'a little private silver dish containing 3 mutton cutlets'. She speaks 'loftily' unlike the humble, proletarian Rose, the second Lady Crawley, who is remorselessly beaten down by all the family. In the above passage, it is evident that Thackeray tried to graft Rose into the scene, before deciding to reform it altogether. Thackeray's main motives for exchanging the grand with the timid Lady Crawley may be guessed at; the former would be less likely to condone Pitt's wayward attentions to Betsy Horrocks and Becky Sharp. Another reason is the implausibility of the haughty Lady Crawley (of an age with her husband, presumably) having offspring juvenile enough for Becky to be governess to.

Page 92. Rundell and Bridge's shop: Bridge and Rundell's, 'Jewellers and Goldsmiths to their Majesties,' 32 Ludgate Hill. In 1813, the most famous establishment of its kind in London.

Page 93. 'Mutton broth' . . . answered Lady Crawley: Deleted in the MS. is an earlier, rather simpler version of this comic dinner scene:

<your favourite meat she replied.> The black Hampshire Sir Pitt' said the butler 'and as fine a beast as ever I stuck a knife into.' There was a roast leg of pork on the silver dish before Sir Pitt, black puddings before me, another entree of pig's fry before the young ladies, a silver dish of cabbages and another of potatoes on the other side of the table. We had all silver tankards and the butler came round presently saying ale or water.

'Look you take some mock turtle soup Miss ah—Miss Blunt' says Mr. Crawley. My dear it was pig again!—a sort of pig's head broth, and so we made our first dinner at Queen's Crawley. (in a note) we have had pig for three days since; and yesterday we killed a sheep.

(Compare the joke about the omnipresent pig with Chapters XXIV–VII of *The Snobs of England*, written around the same time.)

Page 94. unsteady in his gait: There follows in the MS. the deleted passage:

and do you know the horrid man <poked> pinched me <once or twice in the ribs> at which the girls began to giggle

<Papa'th poking Mith Crawley in the wibth> Papas pinching Miss Sharp roared out Miss Rosa at which I blushed, and Mr. Crawley looked as black as thunder, and Lady Crawley blushed too as well as her tallowy face would let her. Sir Pitt was evidently tipsy, and was beginning to break out in some frightful oaths when the door opened and the servants came in.

—*we received*: In the MS. this sentence runs:

Mr. Crawley delivered an extempore prayer which lasted twenty minutes and then expounded a chapter of Habakkuk. Sir

Pitt hiccupped all the time in the drollest way. And then we received

The first intimation of Mr. Crawley's low-church tendencies, later to be enlarged on.

—*the tenants there*: There follows in the MS.:

That odious pert ogling creature with the red cheeks and the flaunting ribbons in her cap is Horrocks's daughter and I *very much fear* Sir Pitt is,—but hush! what would Miss Pinkerton say at such stories? My dear I will tell them to Mrs. George Osborne.

(See also other deleted material relating to Horrocks's daughter, note to p. 109.) Thackeray was keeping this turn of plot in store for later in the novel (see Chapter XXXIX).

—*everything considered*: The following fine passage was afterthought, and replaces a terse, sarcastic ending to the chapter, deleted in the MS.:

Miss Sharp's opinion with regard to the two young ladies whom she was to instruct was made with her usual intelligence and fine feeling. They had been educated by servants hitherto, the coachman imparted them instructions in the stable, the cook giving lectures ex cathedrâ in the kitchen, the housemaids and gardeners completing the rest of their education.

(As Harden notes, this seems to pick up the 'insignificant little chits' of p. 91.) For Thackeray's changes to the following six paragraphs of the printed text, and their general significance to the composition of the novel, see Gordon N. Ray, '*Vanity Fair*: One Version of the Novelist's Responsibility', *Essays by Divers Hands*, 1950, pp. 87–101; Sutherland, *Thackeray at Work*, pp. 17–22; Harden, op.cit. pp. 49–57).

Page 95. this history: The MS, and first edition have 'these histories in their gaudy yellow covers have'. This, together with the reference to the late conceived title 'Vanity Fair' suggest that these paragraphs were added only just before publication of the first number in January 1847.

—*my 'kyind friends'*: Thackeray mimics Alfred Bunn (1796–1860), the theatrical manager, who was in the habit of coming down to address his audiences over the footlights at Drury Lane. In the last number of *The Snobs of England* (*Punch*, 20 February 1847) Thackeray similarly pokes fun at how 'the poet BUNN comes forward at the end of the season, and with feelings too tumultuous to describe, blesses his *kyind* friends over the footlights'. Bunn's long autobiography, entitled *The Stage, Before and Behind the Curtain* (1840), may conceivably have suggested something of Thackeray's 'Before the Curtain' and prefatorial 'Manager of the Performance'.

Page 96. *a man and a brother*: Thackeray was very fond of the abolitionists' slogan (put in the mouth of a chained slave): 'am I not a man and a brother?'

Page 97. *ironmonger*: Thackeray originally in MS. has him a 'gardener'. Evidently he felt this might lead to confusion with the Queen's Crawley gardener, mentioned a few pages earlier and further identified later as a virtuous Scot. Rose, his daughter, inherits this ur-father's love of horticulture, however (see p. 98). In his initial mention of the second Lady Crawley in the first edition's printed text (Chapter VII, p. 77) Thackeray identified her as 'Rosa, daughter of Mr. G. Grafton of Mudbury'.

Page 100. *Strasburg pie*: Literally, pâté made with fatty goose livers. But Thackeray uses the term metaphorically for the vapidity of Pitt's dispatches. Deletions at the end of the previous paragraph and of this show Thackeray expatiating on Pitt's extreme stinginess ('[he] never could be got to owe more than a halfpenny') and his idiocy ('he was such a fool and so solemn that it is a wonder government did not see his merit and look to his rapid advancement'). At this stage in the narrative, Thackeray seems also to have developed a clear perception of Rawdon (as the deleted passage on Pitt's meanness puts it: '['Pitty' deleted] Rawdon Crawley's disposition was very different as we shall hear when we come to discuss that gentleman's character'). For the detailed evolution of this description of Pitt, see Harden, op.cit. p. 58.

—*a friend of Mr. Wilberforce's*: William Wilberforce (1759–1833), the great abolitionist. Pitt's adherence is presumably supposed to take place after 1792, when Wilberforce became associated with the so-called 'Clapham Sect'. From this point in the narrative there starts a running joke on evangelicalism (and tracts such as 'The Washerwoman [or 'Applewoman'] of Finchley Common'). Pitt's correspondence with Hornblower was presumably printed in the Clapham Sect organ, *The Christian Observer*, and had to do with the Church Missionary Society (with which Wilberforce was also associated). Possibly, however, Thackeray is making a more topical allusion in the 'Ashantee Mission' to the failed Niger mission of 1841 (elsewhere satirized by Dickens in *Bleak House* as the Borioboola Gha expedition).

—*Lord Southdown's*: The MS. and first edition have 'Mutton-

down's.' Thackeray probably made the change to add to the
Brighton, Sussex allusions with which the novel is redolent.

Page 101. *alieni . . . profusus*: 'greedy for others, wasteful of his own.'
Sallust, *Catiline*, 5. There is an allusion to the charges of bribery
and venality in office which hounded Sir Robert Walpole
throughout his political and diplomatic career.
—*Sir Pitt was a stickler*: The main part of this paragraph is written
in Thackeray's sloping (early) hand; this up to 'three footmen to
serve it' is added in the margin in Thackeray's upright (i.e.
presumably late) handwriting. It seems rather out of character
with the other description of Sir Pitt.

Page 102. *That blood-red hand*: All baronets are entitled to display in
their coats of arms, either on a canton or on an escutcheon, the red
hand of Ulster. This is in memory of the original intention in
creating the baronetage, which was to raise money for troops in
Ulster.
—*if you must pay your debts*: Nineteenth-century MPs were immune
from arrest for debt.
—*Vanity Fair—Vanity Fair!*: This paragraph is added in Thackeray's later hand. (The bulk of the third number is in Thackeray's
early 'sloping' writing.) Together with the similar apostrophe on
p. 98, and the last six paragraphs of Chapter VIII, it is cited by
Ray as evidence of Thackeray's 'change of heart'.

Page 104. *foolish dream!*: Deleted in the MS. is the following
continuation:

> Twice a year a big carriage drawn by fat horses driven by a fat
> coachman (the establishment of maiden ladies is always fat)
> used to drive up the avenue to Queen's Crawley and turn into
> the abode of the worthy rector of that parish.

Thackeray postponed this visit, and changed some details when he
finally got round to it again in Chapter XI. There, Miss Crawley
visits only once, and stays with Sir Pitt, and the senior branch of
the family.
—The cartoon which forms the chapter's tailpiece is a mocking
self-portrait of Thackeray.

Page 106. *Smollett . . . Voltaire . . . Hume . . . Humphry Clinker*: Gray's
notion of paradise was to read 'eternal new romances of Marivaux
and Crébillon'. Smollett wrote a continuation of Hume's history of
England; but it is the novel *Humphry Clinker* that the disingenuous
Becky is reading. Smollett's fiction, like Fielding's and the work of

the atheist Voltaire would strike Pitt as highly unsuitable for his half-sisters.

Page 109. *scour the plains like Camilla*: Pope, *An Essay on Criticism*, ll. 372–3: Not so, when swift Camilla scours the Plain,/Flies o'er th'unbending Corn, and skims along the Main.

—*and love her governess*: There follows in the MS. a long deleted passage dealing with Sir Pitt and Horrocks's daughter:

> A certain housemaid has been mentioned with red cheeks and a very fine ribbon to her cap the daughter of the butler Mr. Horrocks, who took a great dislike to Miss <Crawley> Sharp on her first arrival at Queen's Crawley and did not scruple (for she was a free-spoken wench to whom, somehow, any liberty of speech or action was permitted) to declare her animosity. Towards <Martha> Sarah Horrocks far from showing any sign of ill feeling Rebecca's conduct was on the other hand, extremely conciliatory. She bore her jealousy with infinite good humour, and though by no means of a lavish or what is called generous disposition tried to overcome her anger with presents as well as kind words. O <Martha> Sarah she would say how I wish I had that lovely black hair of yours and how these ribbons would become it! Also and at various intervals she gave <Martha> Sarah a worked collar, a satin slip, and a coral necklace all of which by the way were presents from Miss Sedley. Lady Crawley could not abide, as the phrase is, this <Martha> Sarah. Rebecca in her conversations with the young woman, did not give herself any trouble to disguise her contempt for her Ladyship; and many a laugh did they have together mimicking her ways. It was strange that some of Rebecca's jokes regarding Lady Crawley (jokes founded chiefly on the profession of the ironmonger her father) and only mentioned to Martha, found their way to Sir Pitt who loved a joke and took them very good naturedly. At last one evening walking in the Park alone, Miss Sharp found Miss Martha engaged in ernest conversationwith Mr. Stock the second keeper—and from that day the two ladies were perfect friends, or to all outward seeming appeared so to be.

Page 112. *leave the money to you?*: A deleted passage follows in the MS.:

> this was in fact the meaning of Mr. Crawley. No man for his own interest could accommodate himself to circumstances more. In London he would let a great man talk and laugh and

be as wicked as he liked but as he could get no good from Miss Crawley's money why compromise his conscience? This was another reason why he should hate Rawdon ⟨Pitty⟩ Crawley. He thought his brother robbed him. Elder brothers often do think so and curse the conspiracy of younger sons which temporally deprives them of their fortunes.

For Thackeray's motive for toning down his comments on Pitt, see Harden, p. 52.

—*St. Just*: Louis de St. Just (1767–94), ideologue of the French Revolution. He played a brutal and leading part in the reign of terror. His first book *Organt* (1789) was a satirical and licentious epic poem.

—*pictures of Mr. Fox . . . the great Whig statesman*: Charles James Fox (1749–1806), noted for his republican sympathies. Around 1792—when Miss Crawley had her day—he was largely away from parliament and out of office. He was associated with the watering-place Cheltenham (also favoured out of season by Miss Crawley, we are told). In 1798, Fox had his name erased from the Privy Council roll, for giving the republican toast: 'Our Sovereign—the People.' He was also legendary for his love of gambling and dissipation. Thackeray insinuates the malignant intra-familial rivalry of the Crawley family by their associations. They occupy, among them, all points of the moral-political-theological compass: Tory/Whig/Radical/Republican; Freethinking/High Church/Dissenting.

—*the Prince Regent*: George was made Regent in 1811. Thackeray is making the point that dandy regiments like Rawdon's let others do their fighting in the Peninsular War.

Page 113. *contempt for death*: This passage is a refinement of a previous portrait, deleted by Thackeray in the MS., in which Rawdon Crawley is nothing more than a bully. As rewritten, Rawdon is placed more securely as a corrupt social type, and the product of Regency profligacy. The emergence of Rawdon in Thackeray's mind can be partly reconstructed from examination of the MS. A crossing-out in Chapter IV (p. 33) shows him beginning as a humble colonial soldier. In reply to Amelia's demand that Jos persuade Mrs. Sedley to write to 'Sir Something Crawley', he was originally made to reply: 'Has he a son in the King's Light Dragoons in India? Sir Pitt Crawley?' This germinal question suggests that Thackeray envisaged only one Crawley son. When he decided on two, he confusingly named them at first 'Pitt' and 'Pitty'. As it later emerges, the soldier Crawley son ('Pitty') is

to serve in a crack Household Regiment, not with a line regiment
in India (like Dobbin's '—th.').

—*Bute Crawley and his wife*: The MS. continues, 'who had no little
influence in the end on Miss Rebecca Sharp's history'. The next
paragraph in the MS. begins: 'The Reverend Bute Crawley was of
a sort of ecclesiastics who are becoming daily more rare in the
country, but of whom most country districts contain a few jolly
specimens still. Bute was a tall . . . ' Thackeray was putting
together a patchwork of drafts in this chapter, which was
originally intended to begin with Becky's letter. (Harden gives a
lucid account, pp. 60–7.) The interest of the above comment about
the 'end of Miss Rebecca Sharp's history' is that it anticipates
Mrs. Bute Crawley's malevolent match-making between Becky
and Rawdon.

Page 114. *gig-lamps*: Safety lights for the one-horse gig carriage.
The *OED* suggests the reference here is slightly anachronistic.

—*a cloudy sky*: The Tillotsons identify this as a popular hunting
song known as 'The Fox Chase'.

—*Harrogate*: Fashionable in the middle and late eighteenth century
as a north country spa (see, for instance, *Humphry Clinker*). Miss
Crawley's favoured alternative to Cheltenham.

Page 118. *these many weeks*: The MS. has 'months' deleted. There is
some mystery about how long Becky is governess at Queen's
Crawley. The subsequent narrative (see Chapter XIV) makes it
seem that Rebecca wins over Miss Crawley on first acquaintance—which suggests an 'Arcadian' interlude of only a year. Yet
from the parallel narrative of Amelia's miseries, it is evident that
two years pass. Calculation would suggest that for Becky, 1814
does not happen: she goes straight from 1813 to 1815. (See
Sutherland, *Thackeray at Work*, Chapter 1.)

—*his spud*: This seems to mean that Sir Pitt is carrying a shovel.

—*a pretty pair they are*: These two sentences were inserted into the
margin of the MS. in Thackeray's upright (i.e. late) hand. The
Tillotsons (p. xxi) note that the 'single addition . . . sharpens our
picture and introduces Briggs'. Harden (p. 64) notes it as a pointer
to the full-page illustration opposite: 'Miss Crawley's affectionate
relatives.'

Page 121. *a very large young dandy*: How old is Rawdon? In his
old-boyhood, ten years after this (see p. 617) we are told he is
forty-five, which would make him thirty-five at this stage of the
narrative; hardly a 'young dandy'. At the same later date, old Sir

Pitt is given as 'not far off four score', which would make him seventy here.

—old put . . . old snob . . . old chaw-bacon: The sense of these derogatory terms is clear enough. But it is noteworthy that Thackeray is using 'snob' in its 'pre-Thackerayan' sense of 'low-bred vulgar fellow.' The modern usage—indicating someone socially on the make—was popularized by Thackeray himself in *The Snobs of England*.

Page 123. Adieu, adieu: This postscript was added in proof. The somewhat redundant illustration also added to the text here (supposedly by Becky) suggests to the Tillotsons that Thackeray had space to fill at the end of his third number.

Page 125. my own magistrate's room: deletions in MS. add some detail to Rawdon's delinquency. The Reverend Bute goes on 'Susan Rowdy and Betty Tufnell swore . . . ' At which his wife interjects: 'For Heaven's sake, Mr. Crawley . . . spare me the details of Susan Rowdy.' In the MS. and first edition, Rawdon's duelling victim is called 'Firebrace'. This was subsequently revised to fit in with later information about the history of Rawdon's pistols. (Thackeray made the same change on p. 228; in the revised edition 'Firebrace' becomes 'Marker'.)

Page 127. the H. H.: The Hampshire Hounds.

Page 128. swear by him: In the MS. and first edition, there is a footnote:

> If anybody considers this is an overdrawn picture of a noble and influential class of persons, I refer them to contemporaneous histories—such as Byron's Memoirs, for instance; in which popular illustration of Vanity Fair, you have the morals of Richelieu and the elegance of Dutch Sam.

'Dutch Sam the Jew' (as Thackeray calls him in *The Four Georges*) was the prizefighter, Samuel Elias (active in the ring 1801–14; see also p. 430). Like many of his contemporaries, Thackeray associated pugilism with the profligacy of the Regency, and wrongly conceived the sport to be in a final decline in the mid-Victorian era.

Page 129. walk back together: The MS. ends with a short conclusion to the chapter, which Thackeray subsequently worked up so as to create end-of-number suspense. Deleted after 'together' is:

> Take care of that scoundrel my son—whispered Sir Pitt, in his elegant way, to his governess—Take care on un—you little zilly thing.

I can take care against the son and the father Sir, said she with a toss of her head. And so she could, that's the truth.

Page 131. *Mangnall's Questions . . . Herz-manner:* The reference is to Richmal Mangnall's *Historical and Miscellaneous Questions for Young People* (1800) and to Henri Herz (1806–88), composer of piano exercises.

Page 132. *petit minois chiffonné:* sweet irregular features.

—*the oratorio . . . St. Paul's . . . the charity children . . . the Foundling:* Fashionable church-going. The Charity Schools' service was held at St. Paul's on the first Thursday in June. With up to 8,000 young choristers, it was invariably found very moving. Royalty were usually present. The Osborne ladies also make a point of attending the chapel of the Foundling Hospital. Founded by Captain Thomas Coram in 1739, the Hospital was nearby to Russell Square in Bloomsbury. During his lifetime, and after his death, Handel's oratorios were ceremonially performed at the chapel.

Page 134. *the prince's last ball at Carlton House:* Carlton House in Pall Mall was the Prince of Wales's (later Regent's) London residence from 1783. It had a magnificent circular room, 136 feet in diameter, suitable for balls.

Page 135. *in all games of skill:* On a separate MS. sheet, there is an earlier version of this paragraph which, as Harden puts it, indicates Thackeray's 'admirable inability merely to transcribe a passage without attempting to improve it':

> Poor little tender heart! and so it goes on hoping and throbbing and longing and trusting. You see—it's not much of a life to describe—There's not much of what you call incident in it—Only one feeling for all the day: and one thought to sleep and wake upon. When will he come? Why didn't he come? he promised

Underneath this passage is a sketchy cartoon of Punch looking at Prince Albert's famously ridiculous hat, on a William Tell pole. This would suggest composition during the period when Thackeray wrote the last of the 'Snob' papers in *Punch* in February 1847.

Page 137. *Courier . . . Vittoria . . . Leipsic:* Wellington won the battle of Vittoria on 21 June 1813. The French were decisively defeated at Leipsic 16–19 October and France was invaded in December. On 6 April 1814, Napoleon abdicated. For the period accuracy of Thackeray's description of the fevered mood of the time, see an entry in Joseph Farington's diary, 10 April, about the impact of the abdication in England: 'Westall sent the *Courier* newspaper to me . . . all the stamps of *Bell's Messenger* were exhausted and the scarcity of papers such that the newspaper horns were not heard about the streets as usual on less interesting occasions.' The allied victories were the occasion of huge celebrations in London, which Thackeray touches on in the next paragraph. In June 1814, Tsar Alexander and the King of Prussia visited London, and the night-time capital was illuminated for three nights. There was a service of gratitude ('*Te Deum*') in St. Paul's and a reception for the victorious visitors at Mansion House.

Page 138. *Had orange blossoms been invented then*: The Tillotsons note that the custom was introduced from France about 1820.

—*the prince's bow . . . Mr. Brummell*: The Prince Regent was very proud of his bow—as Thackeray sarcastically notes in *The Four Georges*. George ('Beau') Brummell was (until his bankruptcy and disgrace in 1815) the acknowledged leader of London fashion. (See note to p. 24.)

Page 144. *stupid*: The MS. and first edition give Dobbin a pronounced lisp in this passage.

Page 148. *Some cynical Frenchman*: La Rochefoucauld.

Page 149. *the Old Slaughters'*: Slaughter's coffee house. It stood at the upper end of St. Martin's Lane. It was named after Thomas Slaughter who founded it in 1692, and it took on the epithet 'Old' around 1760. At the period Thackeray is writing of, it seems to have been as much a resort of Soho artists as of soldiers.

—*a cheerful brass group of the sacrifice of Iphigenia*: Expediently sacrificed by her father at Aulis, to promote the success of the Trojan venture. In the MS. Thackeray originally made the clock recall the Old Testament patriarch Jephthah, who was also obliged to sacrifice his daughter. For Thackeray's wonderfully deft improvements to this sacrificial scene (which involved postponing the merciful arrival of George), see *Thackeray at Work*, pp. 11–17.

Page 153. *waltzes . . . newly imported*: The 'valse' was introduced into the English ballroom in 1812, when it created a storm. The dance was popularized (and made more respectable) when performed by the Emperor Alexander at Almack's in 1816.

—*the commander-in-chief*: Frederick Augustus, Duke of York; removed (because of scandal) from his post 1809–11.

Page 156. *the Yankee privateer Molasses*: There was armed hostility and mutual depredation of shipping between Britain and America from June 1812 until the Treaty of Ghent in 1814. Many British merchantmen were captured.

Page 157. at mess: The MS. finishes at this point.

Page 159. pawing among the straw: In the street alongside Hyde Park, there would be a constant parade of horses. To silence their hooves (and render droppings easier to clear away), straw is laid outside Mrs. Crawley's house.

Page 163. without a fee: Doctors were normally paid a guinea a visit; therefore there would be no extra charge for looking at more than one patient.

Page 169. a line-regiment: Infantry, therefore unfashionable.
—*the young flat*: Slang for 'simpleton'.

Page 175. a feminine hatchment: A square or lozenge-shaped tablet, affixed to the outside of a residence, indicating the armorial bearings of the deceased person.

Page 181. Pigault le Brun: (1753–1835), an author of novels suitably à la mode and improper for Miss Crawley. As the Tillotsons note, his *L'Enfant du Carnaval* was condemned in 1825.

Page 182. the Prince Regent's divorce: The Prince was notoriously at odds with his wife Caroline, whom he had married in 1795. A Bill promoting the divorce was abandoned in the Lords in 1820. She died in 1821.

Page 183. I'll doter Becky: Give her a dowry.

Page 188. Porteus's Sermons: Beilby Porteus (1731–1808), Bishop of London from 1787. was the author of many published sermons.

Page 189. Lord Eldon . . . runaway match: Thackeray read Horace Twiss's *Life of Lord Eldon* (1844) and was contemptuous of the romanticized poverty which followed the famous lawyer's early elopement. (See *The Snobs of England*, Chapter XLIII.) Another black mark was his attachment to George IV.

Page 190. some clippers: The *OED* records this as the first use of the slang expression meaning 'a fast one'—presumably derived from a horse which gallops at a good 'clip'.

Page 197. the 'Gloster': The Gloucester or Gloster Coffee House was in Piccadilly, and served the mails and coaches to and from the West of England. It later became the Berkeley Hotel. Even as a coffee house, it was fashionable and would have been expensive for the frugal Mrs. Bute Crawley.

Page 199. the 'Star and Garter': A coffee house in Pall Mall. It had appropriate associations with duelling. Nearby, there had taken place the Mohun-Hamilton affair (which Thackeray uses in *Henry*

Esmond) and one of the Lords Byron actually killed his man on the premises.

Page 200. George Robins: The famous auctioneer, proprietor of Robins's Rooms, the Piazza, Covent Garden. He died in February 1847. As the Tillotsons point out, Thackeray earlier mocked his manner of doing business in the *Fitz-Boodle Papers* (1842). Born in 1778, he would have been in business at this presumed period in the novel and 'An Elephant for Sale' may contain a picture of him as 'Mr. Hammerdown'.

Page 201. shampooing: i.e. rubbing vigorously.

Page 206. St. Adelaide Villas: As Beresford Chancellor observes, Brompton was practically in the country at this period. There was no Anna-Maria Road, but there was 'Amelia Place' described as 'a pleasant row of houses looking on a market garden' (now Pelham Crescent).

—polyandria polygynia: Belonging to little girls and little boys, all mixed up.

Page 208. Cornelia's husband . . . Potiphar: Cornelia was the famous Roman matron who declared that her sons were her 'jewels'. Potiphar's wife sexually tempted Joseph (see Gen. 39). The sense is that good and bad wife are both equally hypocritical.

Page 210. at Broadwood's: John Broadwood, the piano maker, had his business in Great Pulteney Street. In 1782 he patented his hugely successful design for a domestic pianoforte. Later in the novel (see p. 740) Thackeray identifies this instrument as by Broadwood's rival, Robert Stodart.

Page 211. Napoleon has landed . . . the present Marquis of Londonderry: Napoleon landed at Cannes on 1 March, inaugurating the 'hundred days' so important to the characters in *Vanity Fair*. He entered Paris on 20 March; on 22 March he was joined by all the French army. Prince Charles Maurice de Talleyrand had been a strong supporter of Napoleon's up to 1807; thereafter, he became involved with the allies and organized the Provisional Government in 1814. He argued for French interests at the Congress of Vienna, which was in progress as Napoleon landed. Prince Clemens Metternich of Austria was the dominant presence at the Congress. Prince Hardenberg was the Chancellor of Prussia. The 'present Marquis of Londonderry' (Charles William Stewart, 1778–1854) was British ambassador to Vienna. Thackeray seems here to refer to Stewart's declaration the year before that after the victory at Leipsic, Europe's peace was secure for a generation. In the 1840s,

Londonderry and his wife were favourite butts of Thackeray and *Punch* (see, for instance, *The Snobs of England*, Chapter III, 'The Influence of the Aristocracy on Snobs').

Page 215. *the irretrievable Gazette*: In which bankruptcies are listed, together with other official news.

Page 219. *the eagles in the Champ de Mai*: At the Champ de Mai on 1 June, loyalty was sworn to the new constitution. For the reference to 'eagles', see Scott's *Life of Napoleon* (1827): 'The Emperor seemed to view the scene as an empty pageant until he was summoned to the delivery of the eagles to the various new-raised regiments.' The four mighty hosts referred to later in the sentence are those of Russia, Austria, Prussia and England.

Page 224. *the immortal Alexis Soyer*: (1809–58), chef at the Reform Club to which Thackeray belonged. As the Tillotsons point out, the comment here probably alludes to his being in Ireland, lending his culinary expertise to the relief of famine, in April 1847. Thackeray was interested in Soyer, and often refers to him. (See, for instance: *The Snobs of England*, Chapter XXVII, the critical review of Soyer's *Gastronomic Regenerator* in the *Morning Chronicle*, 4 July 1846; the comic cook Mirabolant in *Pendennis* is usually taken to represent Soyer.)

Page 225. *Collingwood . . . an acorn*: Cuthbert Collingwood, the admiral who took command at Trafalgar on Nelson's death. Thackeray had a high regard for him (*vide* the last lecture of *The Four Georges*). The anecdote here is explained by William Davies in *A Fine Old English Gentleman* (London, 1875). 'Before everything,' Davies recalls, 'Collingwood's oaks claimed his special attention.' And he quotes a letter of Collingwood's to Lord Radstock: 'What I am most anxious about is the plantation of oaks in this country . . . I plant an oak wherever I have a place to put it in.'

Page 226. *the knocker put by with Mr. Bowls's plate*: Presumably the salver on which he receives visitors' cards.

Page 232. *Dr. Squills and myself*: By the Apothecaries Act of 1815 (this year in the novel), apothecaries were no longer allowed to attend the sick without the assistance of a qualified physician. Thackeray appropriately implies here and later that Clump has been treating (exploiting) Miss Crawley for much longer than the doctor.

Page 234. *the poodle*: Earlier (p. 118) and later (p. 430) the lap dog is a Blenheim spaniel.
—*his stanhope*: Light, open, four-wheeled carriage.

Page 237. *old tyrant of a Russia Merchant*: The main import from Russia at this period was animal skins. Osborne apparently extracts the grease from them for his tallow candle trade. In the historical circumstances, dealing with Russia would be commercially safer than dabbling in the French *bourse*, which is apparently the luckless John Sedley's line of business.

Page 242. *brought to a court martial, and shot*: Sedley bitterly recapitulates a turbulent and packed phase of European history. The victory and peace celebrations in London in summer 1814 included 'joybells' rung at churches throughout the country. In early June, the Emperor of Russia and the King of Prussia came to England, and stayed at the Pulteney Hotel (see note to p. 315). Crowds gathered outside their balconies, and they were much fêted (in the City as elsewhere, as Sedley angrily recalls). There were three nights of illuminations in the capital, and a 'Thanksgiving Day' at which the *Te Deum* was sung at St. Paul's on 7 July. The display in St. James's Park and nearby Green Park which Sedley refers to, was witnessed and recorded in Joseph Farington's diary for 28 July and 1 August.

Sedley, like most of England, was beguiled into believing in peace and investing in the newly buoyant French stock market (the 'funds' Sedley refers to is the 'Consols,' or Consolidated Fund. The 'French fives' are French five-per-cent shares). Colonel Neil Campbell was the British commissioner at Elba; his means were quite inadequate to keep Napoleon cooped up on the island.

Page 245. *a perfect Belle Sauvage*: Osborne alludes to the inn sign, about which Addison is witty in *Spectator* 28. It shows a savage by a bell. Addison ingeniously construes the likely etymology, 'belle sauvage', i.e. 'beautiful native woman'. The inn stood on Ludgate Hill and survived to Thackeray's day.

—*three stars to her name*: i.e., she had over £6,000 worth East India Company stock; much more—as the later narrative makes evident.

—*the Morning Post*: The newspaper loathed by Thackeray and *Punch* as the lickspittle, society worshipping, snob's journal. There are a number of sarcastic references to it in *The Snobs of England*, and elsewhere in *Vanity Fair* (see pp. 197, 452, 633).

Page 246. *the parlour boarder*: Parlour boarders were privileged by being allowed to live as one of the principal's own family.

Page 250. *five thousand pounds*: The first edition has 'ten thousand'.

Page 255. *the Battle of Prague . . . Fleuve du Tage*: The Tillotsons identify these musical references: the *Battle of Prague* (1788) is a piano sonata by F. Kotzvara; *Blue Eyed Mary* is a popular ballad (see p. 41); *The Cabinet* is T. J. Dibdin's comic opera (1802); 'O, Fleuve du Tage' are the opening words of B. Pollet's *Le Troubadour du Tage* (1806); as the Tillotsons point out, the ability to play this last does not argue any great musical skill.

Page 259. the black that sweeps opposite Fleet Market: i.e., the lowest of the low. Until 1829, the Fleet Market dealt in meat and vegetables and the way would be filthy with offal.

Page 261. the Hummums: The 'Old Hummums', Turkish baths in Covent Garden. The name is from the Arabic for bagnio. They were replaced in 1865.

Page 262. Apsley House . . . a certain chapel near the Fulham Road there: Aspley House, at Hyde Park Corner, later London residence of the Duke of Wellington. (See Introduction, pp. xvii–xviii.) For an extended and illustrated discussion of this passage, see Joan Stevens, '*Vanity Fair* and the London Skyline', *Costerus*, 1974, pp. 13–42.

—the gentleman . . . used to shave himself: The Tillotsons identify this as a reference to George Cruikshank's woodcut for the advertisement for Warren's blacking, current in the early 1830s. Thackeray was a connoisseur of Cruikshank's work, but he does not elsewhere, as far as I know, refer to this example.

Page 264. Master Omnium . . . Jacob . . . the Times: A reference to Matthew Higgins (1810–68) a friend of Thackeray's. He wrote numerous letters to *The Times*, under such pseudonyms as 'Paterfamilias', 'Mother of Six', etc. (On 22 April 1847, he wrote a particularly vivid account of Irish famine suffering for the paper.) The first 'Jacob Omnium' papers began to appear in the *New Monthly Magazine*, August 1845. Thackeray dedicated his last complete novel, *Philip*, to Higgins.

Page 265. Joinville . . . bombards it: The Prince de Joinville was the son of the French ruler Louis-Philippe. His proposals for the improvement of the French navy were attacked by Thackeray and an ultra chauvinistic *Punch* in mid-1844, who chose to see an 'amateur invasion' in prospect. Joinville's point was that French sea-power was inferior to the English, and the navy should invest in new steam-driven vessels.

—that five stroke: i.e. Jos potted the red for three points and got a simultaneous cannon for two.

Page 266. Dutton's: A favourite establishment of Thackeray's, who

liked to write at this period under the Jos-like character of 'Our
Fat Contributor'. See OFC's 'Brighton in 1847' (*Punch*, 23 and 30
October 1847) where the confectioner appears as 'Mutton's'.

—*the 'Lightning's' arrival*: I cannot find this name among the many
coaches plying between London and Brighton—which the Prince
had made fashionable—at the period. There were vehicles such as
the 'Meteor', the 'Comet' and the 'Dart', however, and the route
was a famously fast one. By June 1811, twenty-eight coaches were
running daily and the 'Eclipse' managed the journey in a
staggering six hours.

Page 267. the 'Ship' Inn: The Ship Tavern, later known as 'the Old
Ship'. Fanny Burney stayed there in 1779. The illustration on
p. 299 is nothing like the actual inn.

Page 269. Alexis . . . Dr. Elliotson: John Elliotson (1791–1868),
phrenologist and mesmerist. He published accounts of the
clairvoyance of his subject Alexis, while under mesmeric influence.
Elliotson's seances were attended by many of the fashionable and
the literary (including Dickens and Thackeray). Thackeray
credited Elliotson (in his capacity as a conventional physician)
with saving his life during the writing of *Pendennis*; hence the
dedication of that novel to him.

Page 270. chimney-glass: Chimney-glasses were presumably mirrors
placed over fireplaces. (But, if so, it is difficult to understand 'sit
down' in this sentence.)

Page 275. as he rode on the omnibus from Richmond: Thackeray plays off
contemporary transport against historical. Omnibus service was
introduced in July 1829. Only around 1847 were (male) passengers allowed on the top deck. For the depiction of an omnibus, see
the capital vignette to Chapter XLI.

Page 277. at the Horse Guards: HQ of the Commander-in-Chief,
Whitehall.

Page 281. Annual Register . . . Hume and Smollett: The standard
reference books and uplifting works for a gentleman's library. The
last reference is to Hume's *History of England*, as continued by
Smollett.

Page 284. presented to the Prince Regent at the levée: the *DNB*'s
description is appropriate to the kind of occasion which most
impresses the Osbornes: 'On 20 February [1811] the Prince
Regent held his first levée, and he celebrated his accession to
power by a costly entertainment of the most tasteless and
extravagant kind at Carlton House on 19 June.'

Page 287. *pen a poulet . . . Mademoiselle Aménaide of His Majesty's Theatre*: *poulet*: 'note'. His Majesty's, later Her Majesty's, Theatre stood in the Haymarket and at this stage of narrative was the building raised between the destructive fires of 1789 and 1867. The theatre was noted for performances of ballet and opera. I am not proud of my French, but 'Aménaide' seems to suggest one who is sexually amenable. (We should remember, perhaps, Becky's mother's profession, and her moral reputation.)

Page 288. *the Light Bobs . . . the Grenadier Company*: 'Light bobs' is military slang for light infantry. The Grenadier company were the unit's bombardiers, and carried heavier equipment.

Page 296. *We don't belong to the line*: Rawdon belongs to a crack regiment, not an infantry outfit. One of the historical points Thackeray makes in the subsequent narrative is that (as he put it in Chapter IX of *The Snobs of England*) 'The Duke's dandy regiments fought as well as any' at Waterloo.

Page 302. *'Wapping Old Stairs'*: Dibdin's(?) sentimental ballad, a favourite allusion of Thackeray's. It is a maudlin tribute to married fidelity in poverty:

Then be constant and kind nor your Dolly forsake
Still your trousers I'll wash and your grog too I'll make.

Page 303. *I must and will go*: As Gleig notes, one of the oddities of the Waterloo campaign was that numerous non-combatants travelled almost as far as the battlefield: 'Many officers brought their wives, and some their very children with them; under the impression that war, though inevitable, was distant; and that it would be aggressive on their part, not defensive.' (p. 48). (See also note to p. 322 below.)

Page 305. *a spunging-house in Chancery Lane . . . Mr. Moses, the sheriff's officer*: The spunging-house just off Chancery Lane, in Cursitor Street, run by Mr. Moss (actually 'Sloman' or 'Solomon') is to figure later in the novel (see Chapters LI–LII). The Sheriff for Middlesex (Mr. Hemp—the name is given in *The Snobs of England*) empowered Moss to apprehend victims and hold them in his premises. They would be given a few days (while residing at their own expense) to clear their obligations. If they could not do so, they would be hauled off to one of the four London debtors' prisons.

Page 315. *a fine hotel in Cavendish Square*: In the first week of June 1814, the Allied sovereigns (the Emperor of Russia and King of Prussia) came to London for victory celebrations (see note to

p. 242). They put up at the Pulteney Hotel in Piccadilly, which is
evidently what Thackeray intends here (see p. 316), although the
London geography doesn't quite fit. As asserted, a new bed was
indeed provided by the hotel for the visiting potentate.

Page 316. *calipash or calipee*: Choice morsels of turtle flesh.
—*half-price at the play:* Nineteenth-century theatres offered double
bills, with half-priced entrance for the second part of the
performance.
—*Mr. Kean perform in Shylock*: The irruption of Edmund Kean into
the London theatre world and his controversial portrayal of the
major Shakespearian roles was the sensation of the 1814–15
theatrical season. See, for instance, Farington in his diary, 2
March 1814: 'Thomson and Owen spoke to me of the extraordinary talents of Edmund Kean a new actor in tragedy, and of his
being perfectly *original* in his manner of representing characters.
They said that Wroughton, an old actor, spoke of him as having
much of what Garrick possessed.' In his first year, Kean was
credited with having single-handedly saved Drury Lane from
bankruptcy. He certainly played Shylock in 1814, but Thackeray
is more likely to be citing it here as appropriate to old Osborne's
ruthlessness with money (see p. 321).

Page 322. *Margate packets were sailing every day*: see Gleig, pp. 47–8:

During the spring and early summer of 1815 Brussels was
thronged with visitors. As fresh troops arrived, and they came in
as fast as the Governments which combined to form an army for
the Duke of Wellington could equip them, fresh families, some
of them wealthy and of good repute, arrived in their train. Many
officers brought their wives, and some their very children, along
with them; under the impression that war, though inevitable,
was distant; and that it would be aggressive on their parts, not
defensive. The same belief seemed to actuate noblemen and
gentlemen who had no official connection with the army. The
Duke and Duchess of Richmond, the Duke and Duchess of
Buccleugh, Lady Caroline Lamb, and many other persons of
distinction, hired houses or apartments according as one or the
other might be had; and, throwing open their saloons, rendered
the second capital of the Netherlands a scene of continual
hospitality and pleasant bustle. Meanwhile Louis XVIII, had
established his court at Ghent.

—*pékin*: Military slang, 'civvy'.

Page 323. *the old quiz*: Fool.

Page 325. shells on his frock-coat: Scales or plates worn instead of dress epaulettes; combat gear.

Page 328. the Walcheren ague: A reference to the unfortunate 1809 expedition aimed at destroying Napoleon's naval establishment at Antwerp. It failed. The amiable Hibernian warrior O'Dowd seems a friendly nod by Thackeray towards the Irish military novelists, W. H. Maxwell (who served in the Peninsular campaign and at Waterloo) and Charles Lever. Thackeray had, of course, offered a savagely satirical portrait of the Irish soldier of fortune in the immediately previous *Barry Lyndon*.

Page 331. negus: Wine sweetened with lemon and spice: topical.

Page 336. a blessing . . . to be overrun by such an army of customers: The Napoleonic wars had kept the British out of the continent for many years. In 1814–15, they flooded back, but (see Gleig, p. 47) mainly to the Low Countries.

—*'Pas si bête' . . . a viscount*: Thackeray slightly embellishes the journalistic account of this visit which he wrote up earlier in *Fraser's Magazine* ('Little Travels and Wayside Sketches', January 1845). There, the postilion is an 'actual baron' who 'as we changed horses, condescended to partake of half a pint of Louvain beer'. For Thackeray's mixed feelings on visiting Waterloo, see the Introduction (p. xvi).

—*Donald, the Highlander*: As Thackeray's footnote in the text observes, this fraternization is recorded in Gleig, p. 49:

> It is recorded of the Highland Regiments in particular, that so completely had they become domesticated with the people on whom they were billeted, that it was no unusual thing to find a kilted warrior rocking the cradle while the mother of the little Fleming, which slept under its mountain of feathers, was abroad on her household affairs.

The footnote is gratuitous at this point, but Thackeray probably introduced it to acknowledge, publicly and graciously, how extensively he was drawing on G. R. Gleig's *Story of the Battle of Waterloo* (1847) (currently a bestseller with *Vanity Fair*) for his own fictional account.

—*As our painters are bent on military subjects just now*: Thackeray complained about the militarism of the prize-winning pictures at the Royal Academy, in *Punch*, 10 July 1847. He selected for comment 'The Burial of Harold', 'The Battle of Meanee' and 'Mr. Cooper's Waterloo'.

Page 338. Wittgenstein and Barclay de Tolly . . . Prince Charles . . . now

that Murat is gone: Count Ludwig Wittgenstein was a Russian
General; Prince Michael Barclay de Tolly was the Russian
Commander in Chief; Marshal Schwartzenberg was Commander
in Chief of the Allied armies from August 1813. Joachim Murat
(1767–1815) was the King of Naples. Unskilfully, he attempted to
play the Allies off against Napoleon and on 2 May 1815 his forces
were routed by the Austrians at Tolentino. The victory restored
Ferdinand IV to the throne of Naples.

Page 339. between Dublin and Ballinasloe: See *The Irish Sketch Book*,
Chapter XXIII, for Thackeray's less glowing impression of the
arrangements for travel between Dublin and Ballinasloe.

Page 340. the august jobbers . . . at Vienna: Thackeray draws on
Gleig's second chapter, 'Proceedings at the Congress of Vienna'.
Between September 1814 and March 1815 the 'Allies' squabbled
over pickings from the war, only to be reunited again with the
news of Napoleon's landing at Cannes. Russia wanted Poland;
Prussia wanted Saxony; Austria meanwhile had seized the plain of
Lombardy and the Republic of Genoa.
—*Catalani was delighting all hearers*: Angelique Catalani
(1782–1849), the prima donna. (See Gleig, p. 50.)

Page 342. the present Lieutenant-General Sir George Tufto: See *The Snobs
of England*, Chapter IX, for the portrait of this veteran roué in later
life.

Page 344. at Talavera: O'Dowd must have been serving with a
different battalion of the —th. in the Peninsular wars.

Page 347. Lord Uxbridge on the bay: Uxbridge, later the first Marquis
of Anglesey, was second in command at Waterloo to the Duke of
Wellington. He lost a leg in the battle, almost with the last bullet
fired; so his elegant equestrian bearing will not last much longer.
—*The Wellesleys and Moloneys are related*: They might well have been.
The Duke of Wellington certainly had an Irish background. He
was born in County Meath and his mother was the eldest daughter
of Viscount Dungannon.

Page 348. Salamanca . . . In India, my boy!: Wellington won the
Peninsular War victory at Salamanca in July 1812. Earlier, in
1804, he received the thanks of Parliament and a sword of honour
from the inhabitants of Calcutta for his brilliant leadership in the
Indian wars. For once Jos knows what he is talking about.
—*the theatre in Fishamble Street, Dublin*: See *The Irish Sketch Book*,
Chapter XXXII: 'the theatre in Fishamble Street was given up to
the performances of the Reverend Mr. Gregg and his Protestant

Company, whose *soirées* I did not attend.' From which we may assume that Mrs. O'Dowd is Protestant.

Page 351. *Any relation to the L—— Osbornes?*: Tufto alludes to the Dukes of Leeds, who bore the surname Osborne. As the Tillotsons note, the sixth Duke was George Frederick Osborne (1775–1838). (See also p. 440, where Thackeray correctly identifies the Leeds–Osborne motto 'Pax in bello'; and p. 763.)

Page 355. *a certain ball*: The Duchess of Richmond's ball, famous for its literary treatment in Lever's *Charles O'Malley* and particularly in Canto 3 of Byron's *Childe Harold*. ('There was a sound of revelry by night . . . Arm, Arm! it is—it is—the cannon's opening roar'.)

Page 367. *Manton . . . Laurie*: Joseph Manton, 'Patentee for the Elevation and Breeching of Guns,' 27 Davies Street; P. Laurie, 'Army and Hunting Saddler and Harness Maker to the Prince Regent, His Majesty's Cavalry and the East India Company,' 296 Oxford Street.

Page 369. *Breguet*: Abraham-Louis Breguet, the watchmaker.
—*Messrs. Howell and James*: Warehousemen, 9 Regent Street. A contemporary reference; the firm was not trading in Becky's day.

Page 375. *would divide the Prussian and English armies*: According to Gleig, Napoleon's plan of campaign (assuming the ground was not too wet and heavy) was to use his cavalry to divide the allied army.
—*a mug of Faro*: Belgian beer.
—*Mr. Paynter's assistants*: A reference to the Ship and Turtle tavern, 129–30 Leadenhall Street, proprietor (in 1848), George Painter.

Page 376. *it will be to find a grave there!*: Gleig prints this proclamation in full, together with orders of the day (pp. 68–9).

Page 377. *the Duke of Dalmatia*: Marshal Nicolas Soult (1769–1851), Napoleon's Chief of Staff.

Page 385. *it's cannon . . . the whole population of the city rushed into the streets*: For the end of this, and the beginning of the next chapter, see Gleig, p. 157.

Page 387. *the horses are ordered. It's all over, and ——!*: See Gleig's description of the night of 16 June (p. 158), which evidently supplied Jos's 'all over' comment, and the comic business with the horses.

Page 389. *to disturb Leonora*: A reference to Gottfried Bürger's ballad, *Lenore*. The heroine is carried off on horseback by the spectre of her lover, and married at his graveside. It is a favourite allusion of Thackeray's (who may, perhaps, have also been thinking here of Maclise's picture of the story).

—their duke was killed ... It was a general débâcle: The Duke of Brunswick 'rushed into the field, and foremost fighting fell', as Byron famously lamented. Thackeray drew on historical sources for Regulus's poltroonery. As Scott drily noted, 'some apprehensions were entertained for the steadiness of the Belgian troops' (*Life of Napoleon*, 1827).

Page 396. *at last an aide de camp actually reached Brussels*: See Gleig, pp. 159–60, which also supplies Thackeray with details of the waggon loads of wounded arriving in Brussels, used a couple of paragraphs later.

Page 397. *It was poor Tom Stubble*: Thackeray made some plans for this stretch of the narrative, which suggest that he may originally have had Dobbin in mind for Stubble's part here. See Sutherland, *Thackeray at Work* (Chapter I).

Page 400. *Louis the Desired was getting ready his portmanteau*: The satirical association of Louis XVIII and hasty changes of residence was proverbial. Once finally restored to the throne of France in 1815, he never overcame the prejudice that he had ridden to power in the baggage train of the Allies.

Page 401. *under the rain at Mount St. John*: Mont St. Jean was at the crossroads of the Brussels and Paris main routes. It was where Wellington took up his main position.

Page 406. *Darkness came down on the field and city*: Thackeray seems to have the following passage from Gleig (p. 321) in mind:

Darkness now began to set in, and the confusion in the French ranks became so great as to involve, in some degree, the pursuers in similar disorder. The more advanced cavalry got so completely intermingled among crowds of fleeing men and horses, that they could neither extricate themselves nor deal their blows effectually. Moreover, as night set in, and the Prussians began to arrive at the scene of action, more than one awkward rencontre took place, which was with difficulty stayed. Nevertheless, the pursuit was not checked. Down their own slope, across the valley, up the face of the enemy's hill, and beyond the station of La Belle Alliance, the British line marched triumphant. They literally walked over the dead and dying, the numbers of which they were continually augmenting. Guns, tumbrils, ammunition wagons, drivers—the whole matériel, in short, of the dissolved army, remained in their possession. Once or twice some battalions endeavored to withstand them, and a particular corps of 'grenadiers à cheval' contrived, amid the wreck of all around, to retain their order. But the battalions were charged, rolled up, and dissolved in succession, while the horsemen effected no higher triumph that to quit the field like soldiers. Still the battle raged at Planchenoit and on the left of it, where Lobau and the Young Guard obstinately maintained themselves, till the tide of fugitives from the rear came rolling down upon them, and they too felt that all was lost. Then came the Prussians pouring in. Then, too, the Duke, feeling that the victory was won caused the order for a general halt to be passed: and regiment by regiment the weary but victorious English lay down upon the position which they had won.

Page 408. *whither the army was marching*: Paris was occupied by the Allies in early July.

Page 412. *having but faint ideas*: The first issue has 'having given up all ideas'. Thackeray changed it because Lady Emily eventually marries the Reverend Silas (see p. 527). This fringe romance is one of the incidental *amusettes* in *Vanity Fair*.
—*the blacks forever weep*: The verse echoes, as the Tillotsons note, an actual evangelical hymn. Thackeray had used the joke earlier in *The Irish Sketch Book*.
—*his chambers in the Albany*: The famous bachelor apartments, in Piccadilly.
—*presented to Queen Charlotte*: George III's queen (d. 1818) superintended over an extremely dull and decorous court, unlike that of George IV, to whom Becky is later presented.

Page 414. *James's powder*: Dr. Robert James patented his powder (effective against fevers) in 1746. Thackeray makes the point that Lady Southdown's medical ideas are prehistoric.

Page 417. *three snuff-mulls gules*: snuff-mulls are snuff boxes; gules, the heraldic term for red.

Page 419. *the Peace of Amiens . . . Mr. Fox . . . the highest opinion of the Emperor Napoleon*: Pitt is very diplomatic. The Peace of Amiens was ratified in 1802, and when Fox was in Paris, shortly after 1802, he had several interviews with the First Consul which did not, as the *DNB* puts it, 'raise his opinion of Napoleon'. Fox reported him 'a young man intoxicated with success'.

Page 425. *The 'Tom Cribb's Arms'*: After defeating Molyneaux in 1811 (see note to p. 70), Cribb retired. Many taverns were named after the folk hero.

Page 426. *a tax-cart*: A smart, two-wheel, one-horse vehicle ostensibly for agricultural use, and therefore subject to reduced sales tax.

Page 427. *buzz this bottle*: i.e. finish the dregs of.

Page 428. *Apollo virorum*: As the Tillotsons note, a misquotation from the Eton Latin Grammar.
—*iterabimus aequor*: Horace, *Odes*, i, 7: 'Now chase away care with wine, tomorrow we set out once more upon the boundless sea.'

Page 429. *Mr. Sheridan drank claret*: Richard Brinsley Sheridan, dramatist and parliamentary orator. A friend of Fox and of the Prince of Wales, he is recorded in the *DNB* as 'frequently drinking to excess'. He is, presumably, another of Miss Crawley's fashionable Cheltenham acquaintances.

Page 435. *Duchess of Angoulême . . . kings*: The King was restored, 9 July 1815. The Duchess of Angoulême was Marie-Thérèse, daughter of Marie-Antoinette.

Page 436. *all the world was at Paris*: Paris continued to be occupied by contingents of the victorious allied armies for some years after 1815. Hence Rawdon contrives to stay some while in the service and in the French capital (see p. 453).
—*all Baker Street pale with envy*: Thackeray hated Baker Street, as it had been recently gentrified. (See p. 634, and *The Snobs of England*, Chapter VI.)
—*Vérey's or Beauvilliers'*: Famous Parisian restaurants. The first was at the Tuileries, and was founded in 1805. Beauvilliers' was in the Palais Royal and older (it was closed during the Revolution). Thackeray was famously fond of his food; for his appreciation of these establishments, see 'On some Dinners at Paris', *Punch*, 3 March 1849.
—*Galignani's Journal*: See note to p. 788.

Page 452. *the Jenkinses*: For the reader of *Punch*, the name is comically resonant. 'Jenkins' was the generic name invented by Jerrold and employed by his colleagues (including Thackeray in a number of contributions) to personify the snobbish *Morning Post*. This is one of numerous incidental sarcasms against the newspaper in *Vanity Fair*; see, e.g., pp. 197, 469, 538, 605.
—*Gunter's*: James Gunter, confectioner, 7 Berkeley Square.

Page 453. *the public newspapers*: Newspapers tended not to review novels in numbers, but in an age when copyright was not closely enforced, they would 'notice' a work by printing long, choice extracts. A notable offender was Galignani's journal (see note to p. 788).

Page 456: *Frascati's*: Situated in the Rue de Richelieu, Les Salons de Frascati (originally a café) was the most fashionable of gambling halls until its closure in 1837.

Page 463. *Mr. Moss acting for Mr. Manasseh of Cursitor Street*: Rawdon's old adversary (see notes to pp. 305, 654). Moss (historically 'Sloman') had his spunging house at 2 Cursitor Street, just off Chancery Lane. Manasseh would seem to be a Jewish money lender (so, in one of his business roles, was Sloman).
—*and lost him*: The first issue continues:

> After a stay at Brussels, where they lived in good fashion, with carriages and horses, and giving pretty little dinners at their hotel, the Colonel and his lady again quitted that city. from which slander pursued them as it did from Paris, and where it is said they left a vast amount of debt behind them. Indeed, this is the way in which gentlemen who live upon nothing a-year, make both ends meet. From Brussels, Colonel and Mrs. Crawley . . .

Thackeray may have found the passage rather vague.

Page 464. *Messrs. Gillows or Bantings*: Gillows and Co.. merchants and upholders, 176–7 Oxford Street; William Banting and Son, upholsterers and cabinet-makers, 27 St. James's Street.
—*montées*: The first edition has 'arranged'. This correction has the Thackerayan touch; and it raises the question of how many of the often very inconsequential changes to the text in 1853 were his own and how many the intrusion of Bradbury and Evans sub-editors. It is hard, for instance. to credit that Thackeray would have bothered to make the change noted on p. 555.

Page 465. *No. 201, Curzon Street*: Later given as 101 (see p. 638). Neither number actually exists, but the style of house is quite authentic for Curzon Street; for instance, we later learn that it has a basement area, through which Steyne sees Becky 'making a pudding' in the kitchen (p. 606). Thackeray chose this address for the Crawleys with care. It was the site, until the mid-eighteenth century, of the old May Fair, which partly inspires the 'Before the Curtain' motif (see Introduction). In 1820 Curzon Street was right in the centre of fashionable Mayfair. Among others who lived there at the time of the Crawleys (supposedly) were Madame Vestris, the famous actress and singer, and, somewhat earlier, Beau Brummell. Hertford Street (named after Steyne's original) was nearby, as was Bute House (after whom Rawdon's uncle is named), Park Lane, Grosvenor House, and the Opera.

—*the Honourable Frederick Deuceace, gone abroad*: Thackeray makes an in-joke reference to one of his earlier works, 'Mr. Deuceace at Paris' (*Fraser's Magazine*, June 1838).

Page 470. *Sainte-Pélagie for debt*: The principal debtors' prison in Paris. It figures in the *Yellowplush Correspondence*.

Page 474. This is the famous 'suppressed woodcut', which disappeared between the first and second book editions of *Vanity Fair*, in 1848. At this distance in time, it is impossible to determine whether the woodcut was deliberately removed (because it too much resembled the Lawrence portrait of the Marquis of Hertford), or whether the block was accidentally damaged. But it may be noted that whereas Thackeray was often prepared to introduce characters of no social standing *in propria persona*, or only lightly disguised, he was increasingly cautious as the rank of his target increased. Hertford's valet Suisse is clearly hit off as Fiche in *Vanity Fair*. In *The Snobs of England* (Chapter XVII) there is a Centsuisse, valet to the 'Marquis of Borgia', and the implication that Hertford was a poisoner is echoed here in the name of Steyne's mistress, 'Belladonna' and in Fiche's warnings to Becky to leave Rome (in Chapter LXIV). Wagg and Wenham can confidently be identified as Theodore Hook and John Wilson Croker (see notes to pp. 637, 640). But Steyne is harder to pin down. It has plausibly been argued (by Lewis Melville and S. M. Ellis, for instance) that he is a compound of the second (1743–1822) and third (1777–1842) Marquis of Hertford. This woodcut resembles the third, but it was the second who was Lord Chamberlain of the King's Household (Steyne is 'Lord of the Powder Closet'), and who led the more dissolute career. The third Marquis married Maria Fagniani (who may have suggested the Countess of Belladonna, though in the novel Steyne has a puritanical Welsh wife). Fagniani was the putative daughter of an Italian Marchese, whose wife was a former ballet dancer (as was Becky's mother) (see note to p. 589).

Page 475. *a knight of the Order . . . two nights with Mr. Fox at hazard*: The third Marquis of Hertford was made a Knight of the Grand Cross of St. Anne, first class, by the Russian Tsar in 1821. But Thackeray seems to be thinking of some actual, but unrecorded scandal, to do with Hertford's ennoblement. (See the note to p. 589.)

—*fredaines*: pranks.

Page 477. the Magasin des Modes: The Tillotsons plausibly identify this as the *Journal des Modes*, which featured designs of fashionable clothes similar to those Becky is described as wearing.

Page 478. in the ring: i.e. in Hyde Park.

Page 484. agios: An agio is the premium payable for the exchange of one kind of money or currency into another. It seems carefully chosen by Thackeray, as does the accompanying reference to Rothschild. It was by speculating in French stock and currency that Sedley came by his ruin.

—*Alexander*: Henry Alexander, Broker, 18 Broker-Row, Moorfields.

—*the Munoz of private life*: Muñoz was the morganitic husband of the Queen of Spain. After eleven years, the marriage was made public in 1844.

Page 485. Blair's sermons: Hugh Blair (1718–1800), whose five volumes of sermons came out between 1777–1801.

Page 486. parliament: Gingerbread.

—*Daffy's Elixir*: The 'elixir salutis' invented by Thomas Daffy, who died in 1680. The medicine is sufficiently antique for Thackeray to imply that it might well be poisonous.

Page 490. threw in bark: Cinchona, Peruvian bark. It contained quinine.

Page 497. Mr. Woolsey ... of Conduit Street: Woolsey is a Thackeray joke name (also used in connection with the sheepish Southdown family). But as Thackeray noted in his review of Jesse's biography of Brummell, the Beau's tailors were in Conduit Street. Only the dandyish best is good enough for Georgy.

Page 506. in her clogs and calash: The calash was a hooped, silk hood, projecting over the head to shelter it from rain (as clogs protect the lady's feet from mud). Here it gives the overtone of the judge's black cap. Since the recent Peel reforms Horrocks was probably, by a year or two, safe from the hanging or transporting with which the vengeful Mrs. Bute threatens her.

Page 511. the two members for Queen's Crawley: Queen's Crawley is one of the rotten boroughs due for abolition in the soon forthcoming Reform Act (see p. 872).

Page 516. as magnificent as Mrs. Siddons in Lady Macbeth: Mrs. Siddons (1755–1831) gave her farewell performance as Lady Macbeth on 29 June 1812. It was a sensational theatrical event. After the sleepwalking scene, the audience clamorously insisted that the play be stopped. Lady Southdown is appropriately majestic in her nightgown appearance to Becky, p. 527.

—*like the Portrait of a Gentleman in the Exhibition*: Thackeray seems to have a contemporary picture in mind here; but I cannot identify it from the 1848 Royal Academy Catalogue.

Page 522. the same old 'Highflyer' coach: An actual coach, which at this period departed from the White Horse Cellars in Piccadilly (see p. 563). The Highflyer served northern England from 1790 to 1840; Thackeray may have taken it himself on childhood journeys to his family in Yorkshire. The White Horse Cellars was, as T. A. Trollope notes, a fashionable staging post (unlike the Swan with Two Necks, see note to p. 85).

—*has his shutters up*: The village snob is in mourning for the death of his daughter's noble husband.

Page 523. dim remorse and doubt and shame: Rawdon evidently has bastards around the estate (see note to p. 125).

Page 527. where her husband . . . Bishop of Caffraria: Emily has finally won the tattooed clergyman. He seems to have become rather higher church than previously.

Page 532. conjurers: It is not easy to see what this word means. It is, perhaps, a mistake for 'congregation'.

Page 533. the Three per Cent Consols: Consolidated annuities; the Government Securities of Great Britain.

Page 537. Lombard Street . . . Cornhill: Lombard Street was the headquarters of British banking, and Cornhill the business centre of the City of London.

Page 538. Frederick Augustus Howard Stanley Devereux Bullock: A compendium of snobbish forenames. Frederick Augustus pays homage to the Duke of York; Howard to the Duke of Norfolk; Stanley to the Earl of Derby. Devereux is also a noble English name, but Thackeray's satire is directed against Bulwer Lytton's novel (1829).

Page 540. Mr. Smee . . . R.A.: Thackeray uses this apparently sarcastic name here and in *The Newcomes*. It has been suggested that he bore a grudge against Sir Martin Archer Shee (1769–1850), portrait painter and President of the Royal Academy. (See Harold H. Scudder, 'Thackeray and Sir Martin Archer Shee,' PMLA (*Publications of the Modern Languages Association*), 1946, pp. 203–10.)

Page 543. zenanas: Indian harem quarters.

Page 544. lassata nondum satiata recessit: 'Wearied but not yet satiated, she withdrew;' Juvenal, *Satires*, vi. 130. Gordon Ray (*Adversity*, p. 403) comments:

> The words thus applied to honest, hearty Lady O'Dowd and her innocent pleasures . . . are drawn from the terrible passage in Juvenal's *Satires* which tells of the departure of the Empress Messalina from the brothels of Rome after a night spent there as a common prostitute. If wit derives from startling incongruity, it surely attains a kind of ultimate reach here.

—*Glorvina*: Lionel Stevenson (PMLA, 1933, pp. 547–51) finds a web of allusion around this name. Lady Sydney Morgan (1783–1859) was nicknamed Glorvina after the heroine of her most famous novel *The Wild Irish Girl* (1806). Between Lady Morgan's career and Becky's, Stevenson detects 'an amazing resemblance'. Moreover, another of Morgan's novels, (*Florence Macarthy*, 1818) features a family called 'Crawley'. All of which suggests that this well-known figure of London society in the period covered by *Vanity Fair* was vaguely present in Thackeray's mind.

Page 546. *She sang Irish Melodies*: The two songs subsequently alluded to are by Thomas Moore: 'Will you come to bower I have shaded for you' and 'Has sorrow thy young days shaded?' Later, on p. 553, there is an allusion to another song from Moore's *Irish Melodies* collection, 'The Minstrel boy who's gone to the war'.

Page 553. *crossed and recrossed her letters*: i.e. wrote down the page, then turned the sheet sideways to write across. This palimpsest style was for economy.

Page 554. *papillotes*: curl-papers.

Page 555. The revised edition of 1853 opens Chapter XLIV 'The family house of our friends the Crawleys'. This improvement in grammar was possible, since the revised version of the novel did not have the capital vignette, with its initial 'O'.

Page 557. *salmi*: A spiced dish of birds or game, stewed in wine.

Page 562. *the Vehmgericht of the servants' hall*: The *Vehmgericht* was a judicial institution peculiar to Germany, especially Westphalia. From the twelfth to the sixteenth century, it acted as an irregular court. Serious crimes (such as here, adultery) were tried by night in secret session.

Page 568. *funded*: The property has been invested (to its market value) in the 'funds'. It returns a dividend, which Sir Pitt is using as income for improvement.

—*I can lend you*: Rawdon's offer to lend his brother money until dividend day is odd, since he is living 'on nothing a year' and in imminent danger of seizure for debt.

Page 570. *You want to be a member for the county*: As one of two members for his rotten borough (the other paying him £1,500) Pitt has no electoral backing. Were he to stand successfully for a county seat, he would have an honest constituency behind him.

Page 571. *Achilles . . . until they gave him the sword*: Achilles was hidden among girls before Odysseus tempted him out.

Page 574. *he shall be presented to the living*: Old Sir Pitt earlier said (see p. 90) that the presentation had been sold off. It would seem to have been an idle boast.

Page 575. *Blue Books*: Parliamentary reports.

Page 579. *the hundred pounds a year*: We are told earlier, that thanks to Dobbin's generosity, Amelia has £500 capital. This could not yield £100 per annum. Possibly we are to assume here that Dobbin has been supplementing her income further from his own pocket.

Page 581. *Eutropius*: An elementary Latin history book. Georgy is easily impressed.

Page 582. *must positively be an eldest son*: i.e. must be given a fortune with which to hunt for an aristocratic wife.

Page 583. *Mr. Dobbin . . . with the gold-headed whip*: Dobbin's family circumstances are mysterious. His father is originally discovered (in Chapter V) as an itinerant grocer who in a very few years is promoted to alderman and knighted. In the first issue of the novel, this sire had fourteen children (Thackeray subsequently removed this detail; see note to p. 57). William would seem to have two sisters at this stage of the composition (one of whom, Ann, he is closer to). His mother was mentioned as a correspondent in Chapter V; but the lady is never heard of again in the narrative. This is the only appearance (and very striking it is) of Dobbin's dandy brother. It is possible that Thackeray held this younger Dobbin in reserve, with the option of using him later in the narrative.

—'*My name is Norval*': A speech from Home's *Douglas* (1756), a standard children's party-piece. Here it has a poignant significance, which Thackeray expected his readers to pick up:

My name is Norval; on the Grampian Hills
My father feeds his flocks; a frugal swain,
Whose constant cares were to increase his store
And keep his only son at home.

Page 586. *Darton's shop in St. Paul's Churchyard*: Darton's was a famous purveyor of children's books, but the premises were at 58 Holborn Hill. The slip is plausible, however. St. Paul's Churchyard was famous since the Elizabethan period for its book shops, and at the time of which Thackeray is writing there was at least one well-known children's book shop trading there, John Newberry's.

—the Parent's Assistant . . . Sandford and Merton: Maria Edgeworth published *The Parent's Assistant* (1796–1801); Thomas Day published *Sandford and Merton* (1783–9). Both were famous books about childhood, and the latter actually aimed at child readers.

Page 587. *her precious golden sovereigns*: The last guineas were minted in 1813.

Page 588. *Gaunt Square, out of which Great Gaunt Street leads*: There has been considerable controversy about the location and original of Gaunt Square and Steyne's 'town palace', which may be briefly summarized here. Beresford Chancellor holds that it must be Harcourt House (now demolished) in Cavendish Square (he provides a convincing period picture, with the prominent railings). The case for Cavendish Square is backed up by the fact of its having had prominently at its centre a statue of Butcher Cumberland (taken down in 1860); Thackeray refers to the statue of Lord Gaunt, who fought at Minden, 'habited like a Roman Emperor in the centre of the square'.

Lewis Melville, however, argues that Gaunt House is a composite: 'Lansdowne House, with a soupçon of Hertford House' (in Manchester Square). Cavendish Square, he observes, was not in the heart of fashionable London—as Steyne's residence clearly is. Earlier, in Chapter VII, it will be remembered that Tinker leaves Sir Pitt's house in Great Gaunt Street, and goes to Oxford Street for a cab 'in the neighbourhood of Swallow Street'. This suggests Berkeley Square, and the statue (illustrated on p. 655) clinches Lansdowne House and Berkeley Square for Melville, since in the centre of that square stood an equestrian statue of George III, in the character of Marcus Aurelius (taken down in 1872). This fits precisely the pompous, classicized monument which Thackeray describes. Melville concludes: 'Thackeray intended Gaunt Square to be Berkeley Square and Great Gaunt Street to be either Hill Street or Charles Street.'

But there is clearly no finality in this dispute, and in *Victorian Studies* (September 1969, pp. 53–7) Joan Stevens reopens the case. Her main new evidence is a paper which Thackeray wrote simultaneously with the Gaunt chapters of *Vanity Fair* ('A Roundabout Ride', *Punch*, 25 March 1848). From references to actual place names and his fictional Gaunt-Steyne locations, Stevens deduces that 'clearly Great Gaunt Street is Harley Street . . . Gaunt Square must be Cavendish Square'.

—*the present Lord Steyne lives at Naples*: This could allude to the fourth Marquis, who spent his life largely on the continent, forming the nucleus of what was later to become the Wallace Collection.

Page 589. *The prince and Perdita . . . Marianne Clarke has entered it*: Mrs. Mary Robinson (1758–1800) was the actress who captivated the Prince of Wales with her performance in *The Winter's Tale* at Drury Lane. A married woman, her career has its similarities to Becky's. Both began professional life as school teachers, for instance, and Becky, in performance, also catches the eye of George (see Chapter LI). Marianne Clarke (1776–1852), another married woman, was the Duke of York's mistress, who used her influence with the Commander-in-Chief to take bribes from ambitious army officers. She was finally disgraced, jailed, and retired to Paris in 1816. It may be taken as prophetic of what will happen to Becky.

—*painted by Cosway*: Richard Cosway (1740–1821), the Prince of Wales's favourite painter. In the description of Hertford's depraved love-nest, Thackeray may be recalling salacious descriptions given by Suisse, Hertford's valet, in a scurrilous little book published after the Marquis's death in 1842. (See *The Confessions of Nicholas Suisse*, London, 1843.)

—*Egalité Orleans . . . and the remainder*: The Duke of Orleans, a supporter of popular democracy, took on the name Philippe Egalité and renounced his title in 1792 (it did not save him from the guillotine in 1793). Thackeray correctly calls him by his aristocratic name on p. 590. One might think that Thackeray was inventing the business about Steyne winning his Marquisate—or at least winning huge sums—from a 'great personage' (i.e. the Prince of Wales) but that it is repeated as a historical fact in the otherwise veracious *The Four Georges* (*Works*, xiii, 798–89).

—*the Road-books*: These very intricate volumes gave the complete routes and timetables of English stage coaches in the 1820s. (The best known was *Cary*'s). They also indicated houses, estates and prospects worth observing on the journey.

—*a late celebrated auctioneer*: Another reference to George Robins (see note to p. 200), who died in February 1847.

—*The Marchioness of Steyne*: In fact, the wife of the third Marquis was rather more interesting than the one Thackeray offers here. Mme Fagniani was of dubious parentage and was made his inheritrix by a paternally inclined George Selwyn. She also inherited wealth from the Duke of Queensberry, and altogether she is estimated to have brought the young Yarmouth (i.e. Hertford/Steyne) some £200,000 at her marriage. The union was a failure, and led to a speedy separation.

—*the venerable Druid*: Thackeray satirizes *Burke's Peerage*, at this date published by Colburn. (See 'Fluke's Peerage' in Chapter VII of *The Snobs of England*.) In genealogical fact, the Hertford family was of twelfth-century foundation.

Page 590. *Morris . . . Sheridan . . . Malmsbury . . . Devonshire*: The leaders of fashion. Captain Charles Morris (1745–1838) was a song-writer and frequent guest at Carlton House. James, first Earl of Malmsbury (previously Sir James Harris, 1746–1820) was also an associate of the Prince of Wales. 'Devonshire' is Georgiana Cavendish (1752–1806), the 'beautiful Duchess'. The dates of these glittering social figures supports the Ellis/Melville contention that Thackeray was at least in part thinking of the second rather than the third Marquis of Hertford (see note to p. 474).

Page 591. *Lady Crackenbury*: As Gordon Ray points out, with this and the succeeding names Thackeray neatly implies ladies with chipped and scraped reputations. Lady Crackenbury might also shy at Lady Charlotte Bury (1775–1861), a beauty at court and lady-in-waiting to Caroline, Princess of Wales. She published an indiscreet and revealing *Diary Illustrative of the Times of George IV* in 1838, which Thackeray reviewed, finding it generally a sordid production.

—*at Spanish Place*: By Manchester Square and Hertford House (see note to p. 588).

—*the Red Book*: *Webster's Royal Red Book*, together with *Burke's Peerage*, a snob's bible. (See Chapter VII of *The Snobs of England*.)

Page 594. *St. Acheul . . . Oxford . . . Latimer . . . Loyola*: St. Acheul, the Jesuit seminary; Oxford, the centre of Anglican orthodoxy; Latimer is the Protestant martyr; Loyola founded the Jesuit order. As Ray points out, Thackeray hints a doubt about Mr. Trail (later Bishop of Ealing) and his firmness, in the name given him.

Page 595. *the Travellers'*: The club in London which members qualified for by having travelled at least five hundred miles from

London. As Thackeray wrote, the current Hertford was a well-known traveller and virtual exile from England.

Page 598. *presented to her sovereign*: The date must be after 1820, when George IV acceded to the throne.

Page 599. *dear M——*: The Tillotsons suggest this might be George Moody, Thackeray's contemporary at Charterhouse and Cambridge. Thackeray gives a slightly different recollection of this event, which he evidently attended, in a cancelled passage in *The Four Georges*:

> What were our own manners that we chose to forgive this profligate his? There were good people in our nation, virtuous, religious, of the highest honour and the purest life, who conscientiously had got to believe in George as the first gentleman of Europe, and looked on him with reverence and respect. I remember as yesterday standing with my parents in Drury Lane theatre and tears of enthusiasm almost of devotion in ladies' eyes; as, with trembling voices and waving handkerchiefs, all standing, the whole audience rang with the chorus of God save the King. Suppose in those days a stranger had said in Colonel Newcome's presence what is here written? I think the Colonel would have deemed him guilty of blasphemy almost— and yet what I have said is true. The man who ruled over us had neither courage nor taste nor public value nor private worth.

The passage would have come in *Works*, xiii, 792. It is reproduced and discussed in Ray's *Age of Wisdom*.
—*The Hypocrite . . . Elliston . . . Dowton . . . Liston*: Isaac Bickerstaffe's *The Hypocrite* was played before the King on 1 December 1823; after his splendid visit to the theatre, George withdrew almost entirely from public life. Robert Elliston (1774–1831) was manager of Drury Lane 1819–26; William Dowton (1764–1851) was a famous Drury Lane actor; as was also John Liston (1776–1846).

Page 600. *the Star of Brunswick*: This metonymy characterizes George in terms of the magnificent clasp he wore on his breast on state occasions. It is prominent in the famous Lawrence portrait, and Thackeray refers to it mockingly again in *The Four Georges*. (See also note to p. 604.)

Page 604. *the hackneyed and beautiful lines, from the Rape of the Lock*:

> On her white breast a sparkling cross she wore,
> Which Jews might kiss and infidels adore.
>   (Pope. Canto II, 11.7–8)

—*Colnaghi's*: The famous art dealers (although at this period their trade was more in prints), 14 Pall Mall Street.

—*his curly brown wig*: Which Thackeray never tired of mocking (see *The Four Georges* again). As the Tillotsons observe, Thackeray seems to have in his mind the portrait of George by Sir Thomas Lawrence, now in the Wallace Collection. Thackeray had no admiration for Lawrence, conceiving him a court lackey (see the comment on p. 615 about 'the Lawrence portraits, tawdry and beautiful').

—*a Maintenon or a Pompadour*: Famous royal mistresses of Louis XIV and Louis XV: see the earlier comments about Mrs. Robinson and Mrs. Clarke (note to p. 589). Now that the war is over, Becky can make more parade of her Frenchness.

Page 605: *if good Queen Charlotte had been alive*: See note to p. 412. She died in 1818.

Page 613. *a contingent reversion*: What Steyne means is: 'you gambled on the chance that the elder son would die childless, in which case your husband or children would inherit, and your dowry would be repaid with interest.'

Page 615. *the matchless Dancing Nymph of Canova*: Antonio Canova (1757–1822), who did several sculptures of dancing nymphs.

—*a Brutus wig*: A rough napped wig, popular with the Republican French, who revered Brutus the king-killer. It marks Bareacres as one of the old 'fast' set (like Fox) who admired the French Revolution.

—*Mr. John Paul Jefferson Jones*: A hit at N. P. Willis, one of *Punch*'s *bêtes noires*. He was an American author who wrote somewhat fantastic accounts of life among the great in London. In 1845 *Punch* reported: 'Mr. N. P. Willis gave great offence by publishing his private conversations with several English celebrities' (*Punch*, 1845, 2, Introduction). Thackeray reviewed Willis's *Dashes at Life* in the *Edinburgh Review*, October 1845.

Page 616. *Young Marlow in the comedy*: the comedy is Goldsmith's *She Stoops to Conquer*. Marlow's problem is that he can only make love to women whom he thinks to be of a lower rank than himself.

Page 633. *the honest newspaper-fellow*: Lionel Stevenson elaborates this reference. Rumsey Forster ('Jenkins' to *Punch*) of the *Morning Post* would be placed during great receptions at a little table outside the drawing-room. He would make up a list of the guests, to be published in strict hierarchy in the next day's paper. According to Stevenson, in April 1847, this lackey got his own back by *not* recording Thackeray's name when he visited the Marquis of Lansdowne's, which may possibly explain this sarcastic little jest. As Thackeray's friend Edward Fitzgerald observed, with the success of *Vanity Fair*, the novelist 'is become a great man, I am told; goes to Holland House and Devonshire House'. Thackeray maintained that his social promotion did not blunt his satire—as the Steyne sub-plot would seem to bear out.

Page 634. Tadmor in the wilderness: The fabulously rich trading metropolis, destroyed by the Romans, AD 273. The ruins near Palmyra were in Syria, which Thackeray passed through on the Eastern trip which inspired his *Journey from Cornhill to Grand Cairo* (1846).

—Eöthen saw her there . . . the other solitude: The train of thought in this paragraph seems to take off from the previous reference to Tadmor. William Pitt lived in the 'old' Baker Street (which Thackeray much preferred to its renovated successor) and from 1803–6 Lady Hester Stanhope (1776–1839), who was his niece, kept house for him. She left for the Levant in 1810. Famously, she camped with the Bedouin, near the ruins of Tadmor. Stanhope adopted Eastern habits, and was visited at Djoun ('the other solitude') by A. W. Kinglake (1809–1891) who records his encounter with her in *Eöthen* (1844). Kinglake's Eastern travel book was read carefully by Thackeray, in preparation for his own.

Page 635. Jabotière . . . the Most Christian King: 'Jabotière' means 'the frilled one'. The French king at this period was the notoriously lax Charles X. Thackeray proceeds to mock the arriviste new French aristocracy by investing them with the names of mushrooms.

Page 637. Wenham, the wit and laywer: Usually identified as John Wilson Croker (1780–1857), who managed Hertford's estate, and was left £20,000 in his will. In his review of *Coningsby*, Thackeray expressed great distaste for Disraeli's transparent representation of Croker as the odious Rigby. In *Vanity Fair*, the depiction is deliberately muzzy.

Page 640. Mr. Wagg, the celebrated wit: Taken here, and in *Pendennis*, to represent Theodore Hook (1788–1841). As the *DNB* puts it, he 'early entered the Prince of Wales's set and became known as an improviser and practical joker'. Patronage placed him as accountant-general in Mauritius, 1813 (see Steyne's later arranging for Rawdon to take over the Governorship of 'Coventry Island'); mismanagement led to his imprisonment on charges of embezzlement. In the 1820s, Wagg edited the Tory paper, *John Bull*, which brought him into contact with Hertford (see the reference on p. 641 to the *Harumscarum Magazine*).

Page 641. *Fiche, my lord's confidential man*: Nicholas Suisse, Hertford's valet (see note to p. 589).

—*a small coal-merchant*: Croker's father was, in fact, Surveyor General of Customs and Excise in Ireland.

Page 643. *At this time . . . from France*: In fact, charades were popular in the last decades of the eighteenth century. See, for instance, Boswell's surprise when Johnson invented rather a neat one.

Page 644. *Young Bedwin Sands*: The Tillotsons propose James Morier (1780–1849), diplomatist, traveller and novelist specializing in Eastern settings. He would hardly have been 'young' at this date.

Pages 644–5: *janissaries . . . tarboosh . . . narghile . . . yataghans . . . odalisques . . . Kislar Aga . . . firman . . . bowstring*: Thackeray was well up with Eastern jargon from his most recent travels. A glossary of the above may be helpful: guards . . . fez-like hat . . . hookah . . . swords . . . concubines . . . the chief of eunuchs . . . edict issued by the Sultan . . . garrotte.

—*anax andrôn*: The king of men, i.e. Agamemnon.

Page 646. *a great personage*: Recalling the Prince of Wales's becoming entranced with Mrs. Robinson in her performance as Perdita. Thackeray probably expects the reader to pick up the literary allusion as well: Clytemnestra and her lover Aegisthus murdered Agamemnon on his return from the Trojan War. Significantly, Rawdon plays the victim-husband's part.

Page 649. '*Dormez, dormez, chers Amours*': As the Tillotsons note, a popular musical romance of about 1830 by de Beauplan. *John of Paris*, in the next paragraph, is *Jean de Paris* by F. A. Boieldieu (1812).

Page 650. *Le Rossignol . . . Montessu . . . Noblet*: The Tillotsons guess that this refers to L. S. Lebrun's opera, *Le Rossignol*, often performed at the Paris Opera in the 1820s, when Lise Noblet and Pauline Montessu were in the company.

Page 652. *Stephens, Caradori, Ronzi de Begnis*: Famous vocalists and actresses: Catherine Stephens (later Countess of Essex, 1794–1882); Caradori (1800–65), Ronzi de Begnis (1800–53).

—*Vestris*: Auguste Vestris (1760–1842), the greatest dancer of his day, and a great ballet teacher. For thirty-six years he reigned over the Paris Opera.

Page 653. *a Noblet or a Taglioni*: for Noblet, see note to p. 650. Maria Taglioni (1804–1884) had just made her sensational debut as a ballet dancer in Paris in July 1827. Thackeray eulogises her grace in *The Newcomes*.

Page 654. *the link-men*: Torch bearers, who conducted paying customers through the dark London streets.
—*Mr. Moss, of Cursitor Street*: The famous spunging house in Cursitor Street, though 'Moss' is a pseudonym for Sloman (see note to p. 463).

Page 657. *the Whitefriars*: Thackeray frequently brings his old school Charterhouse into his fiction. In *Vanity Fair* it usually figures as 'Slaughterhouse'—a pseudonym alluding to its original site in the neighbourhood of Smithfields meat market, and to the brutal public school code of corporal discipline. Elsewhere it is 'Smiffle' and 'Greyfriars'. Philip goes there, and the school figures centrally in the history of the Newcome family. Charterhouse was founded by Thomas Sutton, a rich merchant, in 1611. The buildings were mostly sixteenth century and stood on the site of what was, until the Reformation, a monastery of Carthusian ('Cistercian') monks. Hence, Thackeray's pen names for the place.

Page 661. *the nephew of a county member*: Pitt has apparently bettered himself (see note to p. 570). Presumably he now gets two incomes from his rotten borough at Queen's Crawley (see note to p. 511).

Page 662. *sawdust at Astley's*: The Royal Saloon, or Astley's Amphitheatre. At this period, it was famous for equestrian performances; hence Becky's sarcasm about sawdust.

Page 671. *I'll take wine*: i.e. he will take part of the payment not in cash, but in overvalued stock—here wine. See *The Newcomes*, where the Reverend Honeyman's financial downfall is gauged by the increasing nastiness of the wine he serves.

Page 675. *covered with serpents*: Bracelets spiralling up the forearm.

Page 678. *the Bible . the Quarterly Review . . the Court Guide*: As a true blue Tory. Pitt does not have the *Edinburgh Review*. The *Observer* was founded as a Sunday paper in 1792.

Page 684. *the Regent Club in St. James's Street*: From a later reference to the great bay-window. this would seem to be White's.

Page 686. *the late lamented Commander-in-chief*: Frederick Augustus, Duke of York (1763–1827). Two scandals are evoked here. The first is the Duke's fighting a duel with Colonel Lennox in May

1789 (he manfully received the Colonel's shot and then fired his own pistol in the air). Secondly, in 1809, he was forced to retire for a time as Commander-in-Chief because of his involvement with the unscrupulous adventuress Marianne Clarke (see note to p. 589).

Page 690. the Curzon Street chapels: The association of Curzon Street and chapels is strong. In the eighteenth century, 'Mayfair marriages' were arranged without formality of banns or licence at a chapel in the street by the Reverend Alexander Keith (until he was put away). East Chapel Street and West Chapel Street lead into Curzon Street.

Page 691. more exalted persons of her nation: The Tillotsons point out that Louis-Philippe fled Paris in March 1848, the month in which Thackeray writes. See also the earlier sarcasms about Louis XVIII (note to p. 400).
—*Madame du Barri*: Mistress of Louis XV. The detail resonates.

Page 693. You've lived in this 'ouse four year: Have they? It is now after 1827 (the Duke of York is dead, see note to p. 686). Rawdon and Becky moved back to London in 1817–18, and apparently moved straightway into Raggles's house (see the opening to Chapter XXXVII). They have clearly been resident there for some time when Sir Pitt dies in 1822 (see p. 516). They should, therefore, have been living rent-free in the Curzon Street house for the better part of a decade—though it is inconceivable that even as soft a creditor as Raggles would have held off so long. A related question is how long Steyne waits before making his determined assault on Becky's virtue. Again, calculation suggests more years than seems likely, given his fearlessly lecherous nature.

Page 697. Ross and Osbaldiston: Thackeray names the two great sportsmen of the day: George Osbaldeston (1787–1866) and Horatio Ross (1801–86). The latter was just retired from the Dragoons. In 1831, Osbaldeston fought a duel with Bentinck, which may have put him in Thackeray's mind here.
—*All the old files of the Ring*: 'Old hands'; Partridge records the term as used by Dickens.

Page 698. the Royalist: As the Tillotsons point out, the description could fit Wagg Hook's paper, *John Bull*.

Page 699. a pony: £25; racing slang.

Page 707. The pictorial capital shows Georgy as George IV in his notoriously splendid coronation robes.

Page 715. *West's famous characters*: William West (1796–1888) the
famous comedian. He composed songs and before the age of ten
had appeared in various juvenile parts on stage.

Page 723. EÖTHEN: An allusion to Kinglake's book (see note to
p. 634). With its meaning 'at break of day' it is an odd chapter title
and suggestive of the conclusion of a narrative. It is possible that
Thackeray intended a rather earlier ending to his novel; advertise-
ments indicate that to a quite late stage, it was thought *Vanity Fair*
might finish in eighteen rather than twenty numbers. As far as we
know at this stage of the work, Becky is still at Cheltenham. The
prolonged conclusion to the narrative, which involves transporting
all the principal characters to Pumpernickel, seems to have been
decided on abruptly, without any preparation for the reader.

Page 726. *Latude's . . . Trenck*: J. H. Masers de Latude (1725–1805)
wrote an account of his thirty-five years in the state prisons of
France. Friedrich von der Trenck (1726–94) published various
accounts of his ten years' imprisonment at Magdeburg. Trenck's
book, particularly, was translated and widely read in England.

Page 728. *brandy-pawnee*: Brandy and water.

Page 729. *the cuddy-table*: Cabin table.
—*the Emperor's tomb at Longwood*: The house which imprisoned
Napoleon on St. Helena. His body was not returned to France
until 1840. This 'second funeral' was the occasion of Thackeray's
second published book.

Page 732. *his lordship and Lady William*: Lord William Bentinck,
Governor-General from 1828–35.

Page 733. *his chillum*: His hookah.

Page 739. *the arch and the Achilles statue were up*: The Pimlico arch
went up in 1828 and the Achilles statue in 1822. See Introduction,
pp. xvii–xviii.

Page 740. *Stothard maker*: See note to p. 210.

Page 742. *Fatherless Fanny, or the Scottish Chiefs*: *Fatherless Fanny: or a
young lady's first entrance into life being the memoirs of a little mendicant and
her benefactors* (1819); Jane Porter, *The Scottish Chiefs* (1810). The
first is appropriate to Amelia's forlorn condition in life; the second
to Major Dobbin's martial character.

Page 748. *April 24, 1827*: A resonant date. Thackeray evidently
intends us to recall the anniversary of George's marriage to Amelia
in 1815.

Page 751. *Persicos apparatus*: Persian luxury, Horace, *Odes*, i. 38. It hardly needs noting that Horace is Thackeray's favourite source of classical allusion. In the *Classical Journal* for 1919, Elizabeth Nitchie calculates that 'of about two hundred Latin quotations gathered from Thackeray's novels, essays and other writings, one hundred and forty are Horatian'.

Page 755. *Mrs. George Osborne*: Gordon Ray, following a cue in Thackeray's correspondence, makes the startling observation that this paragraph and the one preceding belong earlier in the chapter, and should follow ' . . . the arrival of his son' on p. 750. The misplacing (which persisted in all editions for over a hundred years) could have come about all too easily, since Thackeray habitually wrote on small, separate pieces of paper. There is also some excuse for the generations of unobservant Thackerayan readers. As John Lester has pointed out in an influential article (PMLA, 1954, pp. 392–409): 'Thackeray characteristically doubles backwards and forwards in the course of telling his story.' This 'doubling' relaxes the reader's attention.

Page 759. *when George brought me to your house*: This differs from the account given on p. 59, which implies that Dobbin first encountered Amelia much earlier, at a juvenile birthday party which his clumsiness marred.

Page 761. *Moira Place . . . Assaye Terrace*: By this barrage of names with Indian associations, Thackeray indicates the area around Fitzroy Square.

Page 762. *the great agency house of Fogle and Fake*: Thackeray lost the bulk of his inherited fortune in the Indian agency-house crashes of 1830–4. There is, as Gordon Ray points out, 'real bitterness' in this reference.

Page 763. *hammercloth*: The cloth covering the driver's seat or 'box' in a state or family coach.

Page 768. *the black ark*: Editions during Thackeray's lifetime have 'black arch', which is nonsensical. The Tillotsons plausibly conjecture that the sentence should conclude at 'within'.

Page 779. *the Pantechnicon*: Built in 1830 in Motcomb Street, Belgrave Square, the Pantechnicon was originally intended to be a bazaar, and then converted into a warehouse for stored furniture.

Page 782. *reading Mrs. Somerville . . . the Royal Institution . . . Exeter Hall*: Mrs. Somerville (1780–1872), was the famous woman scientist and writer; the Royal Institution was founded in 1799, and sponsored scientific lectures; Exeter Hall, erected in 1831, was the centre of evangelical Christianity in London: famous 'May meetings' were held there. The last is a slightly anachronistic reference.

—*the Edinburgh . . . Mr. Peel's late extraordinary tergiversation*: At this period, Brougham, Cockburn and Macaulay were writing 'crack articles' for the *Edinburgh Review*. Peel's tergiversation on the Catholic Relief Bill (later matched by his tergiversation in 1846 on the Corn Laws) occurred in March 1829, when he spoke successfully in favour of Catholic Emancipation. At an earlier period he had resigned rather than support the measure.

Page 783. Bramah desks: Travelling safes, patented by the English engineer and inventor, Joseph Bramah (1748–1814).

Page 787. nebst Begleitung: Accompanied.
—*the Free City of Judenstadt*: Frankfort am Main, so called, as the Tillotsons note, because of its Judengasse.

Page 788. Galignani's admirable newspaper . . . that piratical print: *Galignani's Messenger* was a newspaper catering for English readers on the continent. Thackeray calls it 'piratical' since its contents were principally extracts from the British press, lifted wholesale and unpaid for.
—*his transparency the duke*: A literal translation of the German honorific *Durchlaucht* ('serene').

Page 793. the battle of Austerlitz: Napoleon's great victory over the Austrians in 1805 made the conduct of English-Prussian diploma- cy too serious a matter to be left to the likes of Pitt.
—*the Royal Grand Ducal Pumpernickelisch Hof*: Between Cambridge and taking up the law (two rather inglorious phases of his early career) Thackeray spent a year travelling in Europe. Most of it was passed over 1830–31 at Weimar. He recalls the experience in this 'Pumpernickel' section. The Dobbin-Sedley-Osborne set are supposed to be visiting the Grand Duchy at precisely the period when, historically, the young novelist was there. (See the comment in the preceding paragraph about his 'first seeing Colonel Dobbin and his party'.) In 1831 Weimar was well past the glory it had enjoyed under Karl Augustus (the monarch who died in 1828 is called 'Victor Aurelius' here). Goethe survived, but only just; he died in 1832. Thackeray visited him; the bookish Dobbin does not. Nor is the great man mentioned in *Vanity Fair*, apart from a comment on his 'immoral' fiction (see note on p. 857). The shells and forms of Weimar's greatness remained, however, to tickle

Thackeray's sense of the absurd. There was the extravagant court ceremonial, and strict protocol; Dobbin and his party are 'courtworthy,' Becky is not—even though bankers may have her to their gala balls in Rome. There was rich comedy in the Lilliputian scale of Weimar (ten miles in one direction to Jena, ten miles in the other to Erfurt) and its having a 'capital' city of some 6,000 inhabitants and full diplomatic representation. (One of Thackeray's cronies, William Lettsom, was in the diplomatic service at Weimar, and possibly furnished the original of Tapeworm. Thackeray was tempted by the possibility of becoming a diplomat at Weimar himself.) In 1831, Weimar retained its magnificent *Hoftheater*, which was nothing to joke at. Here Thackeray was exposed to classical German drama, opera and acting styles. He was particularly taken with Ludwig Devrient, and his wife Wilhelmina Schroeder, whom he saw in *Fidelio*. If we credit the narrative here, it was also on that memorable evening that he met Dobbin and Amelia. Weimar was for Thackeray both ridiculous and charming; as Lionel Stevenson puts it: 'a kind of humanized puppet show.' He offers affectionate mockery of its nobility, its *Lustschloss* ('pleasure palace') Belvedere with its *Wasser Kunsten* ('water art'); its *Lustgarten* ('pleasure gardens') and the magnificent Park of which the inhabitants were so proud. It had been laid out some thirty years before by Goethe and the Grand Duke: see Thackeray's comments on 'Monplaisir'. Thackeray identifies the only two notable hostelries which Weimar possessed, the Erbprinz and the Elefant with their proper names (the association of Jos and elephants was too good to leave out).

Thackeray's early impressions and late recollections of Weimar are to be found in the first volume of the *Letters* and in a memorandum which he made up for G. H. Lewes for his biography of Goethe, dated 28 April 1855.

Page 796. a brown jasey: a worsted wig.

Page 797. agréments: Or 'agrémens'; pleasant features.

Page 799. walked a polonaise: The polonaise was a ponderously solemn dance, taken at a pace that would not incommode even Jos.

Page 800. by Sobieski: Vienna was relieved by Sobieski, the King of Poland, in 1683. Thackeray alludes to the Sternbrucke over the Ilm at Weimar.

Page 803. La Petite Vivandière: The little camp-follower. The exact significance of this reference is mysterious to me.

Page 805. *Sonnambula*: The Tillotsons note that Bellini's opera was not produced until 1831.

Page 806. *the Duchess of Berri ... Duke of Angoulême ... Duke of Orleans*: These references seem to place the dispatches as being made before the July Monarchy of 1830. The Duchesse de Berri was the mother of the so-called 'miracle child', whom Charles X wished to have installed on the throne when he abdicated. When the bourgeois monarch, Louis-Philippe, was preferred, the Duchess led an abortive uprising in favour of her child in 1832. The reference to HRH the Duke of Orleans (i.e. Louis-Philippe) is sly, in view of his later career. It was the less than heroic Angoulême, eldest son of Charles X, who was unable to prevent Napoleon's return to France, earlier in the century. He retired with Charles in 1830.

Page 808. *lampions*: Gala lights.

Page 812. The pictorial capital alludes to Haydon's 'Napoleon Musing at St. Helena'. That of the preceding chapter showed Becky as Circe. Chapter LXV shows her as Doll Tearsheet to Jos's Falstaff.
—*as Ahrimanians worship the devil*: According to the *Encyclopaedia of Religion and Ethics*, Ahriman is 'the later Persian designation by which the devil, or principle of evil is known in the religion of Zoroasther'.

Page 813. *the siren disappears*: Thackeray alludes, presumably, to Lorelei, the Rhine siren. Popularized by Brentano's novel *Godwi* (1800–2) the reference is apposite and ominous for Jos. Lorelei was a maiden who threw herself in the Rhine, after being jilted by her lover. She was transformed into a vengeful siren, who lured fishermen to their death.

Page 814. *outstanding debts and liabilities*: The first issue reads 'certain debts and the insurance of his life'. This was changed (not necessarily by Thackeray) because it contradicts what was said earlier about Rawdon being unable to insure himself before going to the fever-ridden Coventry Island.
—*Doctors' Commons*: i.e. divorce.

Page 818. *the Darbyite*: A Plymouth Brethren.

Page 822. *Bampfylde Moore Carew*: The so-called 'king of the English gipsies' (1693–1770).
—*Mr. Hemp*: Hemp was (as Thackeray wrote) Sheriffs'

Officer for Middlesex. Debtors were brought up before him (in person, or *in absentia*) at his office in Portugal Street.

Page 823. Dame Blanche: By F. A. Boieldieu, first put on in 1825.

Page 827. in the fourgons: In his baggage.

Page 829. the White Friars and D.C.L.: The Tillotsons note the burlesquing similarity of this to the obituary in the *Annual Register* when Hertford died in 1842.
—*the downfall of the ancient French monarchy*: The reference is to the French Revolution of 1830, which brought the bourgeois Louis-Philippe to the throne.

Page 831. sournois: Sly.

Page 835. the path of Avernus is very easy of descent: The Vergil reference ('Facilis descensus Averno ... ') is nicely relevant to Jos's labouring at the Elefant's stairs: 'Easy is the way down to the underworld; by night and by day Dis's door stands open; but to withdraw one's steps and make a way out to the upper air, that's the task, that's the labour.'

Page 839. AMANTIUM IRAE: The anger of lovers [is the renewal of love]. Terence, *Andria*, 1.555. Thackeray anticipates his later practice in chapter titling, which habitually features allusive Latin tags. It is an art he brought to perfection in *The Virginians*.

Page 842. fumum and strepitus: Smoke and din. Horace, *Odes*, iii. 29.
—*Fuchs and Philister . . . the neighbouring University*: A 'fox' is German slang for a freshman; a 'philistine' one of the townspeople. The neighbouring university is Jena or Erfurt.
—*Eilwagen*: Literally, fast coach.
—*in nubibus*: In the clouds—imaginary.
—*Burschen*: Students.
—*schrecklich . . . Saufen*: Terrible . . . boozing.

Page 851. Don't you remember the song: See p. 42.

Page 854. where the 'Elephant' is: The first edition has the addition: 'and in front the opposite side of "Goswell Street over the way," like the immortal casement of Mr. Pickwick—Georgy, I say, was lolling in this window'. The Tillotsons surmise that Thackeray may have removed this admiring allusion because of his deteriorated relations with Dickens in the early 1850s.
—*Schimmels*: Grey horses.
—*manchen Sturm erlebt*: Had lived through several storms; the allusion, as the Tillotsons note, is from the *Mantellied*, or coat song, in Karl von Holtei's drama *Lenore* (1828).

Page 855. *Fort, Schwager!*: 'Let's be off, postilion!'

Page 857. *Werther ... Wahlverwandtschaften*: Goethe's best-known novels. The second, *Elective Affinities*, traces the complex interactions and contradictions of 'chemical' attractions between man and woman, and the ways in which they defy marriage vows. Defenders of Goethe argue that objections to the morality of the book—such as Thackeray's here—are a misreading.

Page 858. *love-song of Weber's*: 'Solitary I am, not lonely'. From his opera, *Preciosa* (1821).

Page 859. *had got a miniature*: It has shrunk; see p. 203.

Page 863. *geliebt and gelebet as the girl in Wallenstein says*: 'Loved and lived'; the girl is Thekla and the play, *Wallenstein*, by Schiller—with Goethe, Weimar's most famous resident.
—*Boompjes*: waterfront.

Page 869. *Un biglietto*: From Rossini's *The Barber of Seville*; Becky alludes to the scene in which Rosina, prompted by Figaro, produces a letter she has already written.

Page 870. *eclipse*: Just possible—but the Tillotsons suggest the amendment 'ellipse'.
—*a favourite poet*: Homer, the *Iliad* (vi. 484); the Greek means, 'smiling through her tears'. (Like Andromache at Hektor's parting.)

Page 871. *tender little parasite*: A number of commentators have noted the finely double-edged quality of the word 'parasite' here. The allusion is, of course, traditional and commonplace (with some arboreal variations). Horace, *Odes* 2. xv. 4, takes the allegorical union of the elm and the vine as already conventional in literature. A version of the image is found in *Paradise Lost*, Bk. V, 215–9:

> or they led the vine
To wed her elm; she spoused about him twines
Her marriageable arms, and with her brings
Her dower the adopted clusters, to adorn
His barren leaves.

Thackeray fuses this fruitful emblem with the related one of the ivy and the oak, which was current in the nineteenth century (see the popular song, 'Just like the ivy . . . '). Ivy, of course, throttles the trees to which it clings. The image of the ivy, attachment and death is evoked again in *Esmond*, 'je meurs où je m'attache'. Given Thackeray's ambivalent comments on Amelia in his correspondence, there is no doubt that here the ironic contradiction of fertile union and strangulating clingingness is intentional.

Page 872. *the Reform Bill*: 1832. Once again, the Crawleys have backed the wrong political horse.

Page 877. *Burke, Thurtell & Hayes*:The names of murderers; see the Introduction, p. xx.